...g author o...
...ragonfly in Amber, Voyager,
...ery Cross, A Breath of Snow and Ashes
...an and the Private Matter, and one work of non-
...on, Through the Stones. She lives with her family and a lot of
...er assorted wildlife in Scottsdale, Arizona.

Praise for Diana Gabaldon

'Gabaldon is a born storyteller'
Los Angeles Daily News

'The writing is superb – lush, evocative, sensual, with a wealth of
historical detail'
Library Journal

'History comes deliciously alive on the page'
New York Daily News

'Triumphant . . . Her use of historical detail and a truly adult love
story confirm Diana Gabaldon as a superior writer'
Publishers Weekly

'A blockbuster hit'
Wall Street Journal

Also by Diana Gabaldon

Cross Stitch
Dragonfly in Amber
Voyager
Drums of Autumn
The Fiery Cross

Lord John and the Private Matter

Through the Stones (non-fiction)

A Breath of Snow and Ashes

DIANA GABALDON

arrow books

Published in the United Kingdom by Arrow Books in 2006

1 3 5 7 9 10 8 6 4 2

First published in the United Kingdom in 2005 by Century

Arrow Books
The Random House Group Limited
20 Vauxhall Bridge Road, London, SW1V 2SA

Random House Australia (Pty) Limited
20 Alfred Street, Milsons Point, Sydney
New South Wales 2061, Australia

Random House New Zealand Limited
18 Poland Road, Glenfield
Auckland 10, New Zealand

Random House (Pty) Limited
Isle of Houghton, Corner of Boundary Road & Carse O'Gowrie
Houghton 2198, South Africa

Random House Publishers India Private Limited
301 World Trade Tower, Hotel Intercontinental Grand Complex,
Barakhamba Lane, New Delhi 110 001, India

Random House Group Limited Reg. No. 954009

www.randomhouse.co.uk

A CIP catalogue record for this book
is available from the British Library

Papers used by Random House
are natural, recyclable products made from wood grown in
sustainable forests. The manufacturing processes conform to
the environmental regulations of the country of origin

ISBN 9780099278245 (from Jan 2007)
ISBN 0 09 927824 3

Typeset by Palimpsest Book Production Limited, Grangemouth, Stirlingshire

Printed and bound in Great Britain by Cox & Wyman Ltd, Reading, Berkshire

This book is dedicated to

Charles Dickens
Robert Louis Stevenson
Dorothy L. Sayers
John D. MacDonald
and
P. G. Wodehouse

Acknowledgments

My ENORMOUS thanks to . . .

My two marvelous editors, Jackie Cantor and Bill Massey, for insight, support, helpful suggestions (*"What about Marsali?!?!"*), enthusiastic responses, (*"Eeew!"*), and comparing me (favorably, I hasten to add) to Charles Dickens.

My excellent and admirable literary agents, Russell Galen and Danny Baror, who do so much to bring these books to the attention of the world—and put all of my children through college.

Bill McCrea, curator of the North Carolina Museum of History, and his staff, for maps, biographical sketches, general information, and a delightful breakfast in the museum. Love them cheese grits!

The staff of the Moore's Creek Bridge battlefield Visitors' Center, for their kind attention and for supplying me with forty-odd pounds of new and interesting books—particularly gripping works like *Roster of the Patriots in the Battle of Moore's Creek Bridge* and *Roster of the Loyalists in the Battle of Moore's Creek Bridge*—and for explaining to me what an ice-storm is, because they had just had one. We do not have ice-storms in Arizona.

Linda Grimes, for betting me that I couldn't write an appealing scene about nose-picking. That one is all her fault.

The awe-inspiring and superhuman Barbara Schnell, who translated the book into German as I wrote it, almost neck-and-neck with me, in order to complete it in time for the German premiere.

Acknowledgments

Silvia Kuttny-Walser and Petra Zimmerman, who have been moving heaven and earth to assist the German debut.

Dr. Amarilis Iscold, for a wealth of detail and advice—and periodic rolling on the floor with laughter—regarding the medical scenes. Any liberties taken or mistakes made are entirely mine.

Dr. Doug Hamilton, for expert testimony on dentistry, and what one could or could not do with a pair of forceps, a bottle of whisky, and an equine tooth-file.

Dr. David Blacklidge, for helpful advice on the manufacture, use, and dangers of ether.

Dr. William Reed and Dr. Amy Silverthorn, for keeping me breathing through the pollen season so I could finish this book.

Laura Bailey, for expert commentary—with drawings, no less—on period clothing, and in particular, for the useful suggestion of stabbing someone with a corset-busk.

Christiane Schreiter, to whose detective skills (and the goodwill of the librarians of the Braunschweig Library) we owe the German version of Paul Revere's ride.

The Reverend Jay McMillan, for a wealth of fascinating and useful information regarding the Presbyterian church in Colonial America—and to Becky Morgan, for introducing me to the Reverend Jay, and to Amy Jones, for information on Presbyterian doctrine.

Rafe Steinberg, for information on times, tides, and general seafaring issues—particularly the helpful information that the tide turns every twelve hours. Any mistakes in this regard are definitely mine. And if the tide did not turn at 5 A.M. on July 10th, 1776, I don't want to hear about it.

My assistant Susan Butler, for dealing with ten million sticky-notes, photo-copying three copies of a 2500-page manuscript, and FedExing it all over the landscape in a competent and timely fashion.

The untiring and diligent Kathy Lord, who copy-edited this entire manuscript in some impossible time frame, and did not either go blind or lose her sense of humor.

Virginia Norey, Goddess of Book Design, who has once again managed to cram The Whole Thing between two covers and make it not only readable but elegant.

Steven Lopata, for invaluable technical advice re explosions and burning things down.

Acknowledgments

Arnold Wagner, Lisa Harrison, Kateri van Huystee, Luz, Suzann Shepherd, and Jo Bourne, for technical advice on grinding pigments, storing paint, and other picturesque tidbits, such as the bit about "Egyptian Brown" being made of ground-up mummies. I couldn't figure out how to work that into the book, but it was too good not to share.

Karen Watson, for her former brother-in-law's notable quote regarding the sensations of a hemorrhoid sufferer.

Pamela Patchet, for her excellent and inspiring description of driving a two-inch splinter under her fingernail.

Margaret Campbell, for the wonderful copy of *Piedmont Plantation*.

Janet McConnaughey, for her vision of Jamie and Brianna playing Brag.

Marte Brengle, Julie Kentner, Joanne Cutting, Carol Spradling, Beth Shope, Cindy R., Kathy Burdette, Sherry, and Kathleen Eschenburg, for helpful advice and entertaining commentary on Dreary Hymns.

Lauri Klobas, Becky Morgan, Linda Allen, Nikki Rowe, and Lori Benton for technical advice on paper-making.

Kim Laird, Joel Altman, Cara Stockton, Carol Isler, Jo Murphey, Elise Skidmore, Ron Kenner, and many, many (many, many) other inhabitants of the Compuserve Literary Forum now renamed as the Books and Writers Community – (http://community.compuserve.com/books), but still the same gathering of eclectic eccentricity, trove of erudition, and source of Really Strange Facts, for their contributions of links, facts, and articles they thought I might find helpful. I always do.

Chris Stuart and Backcountry, for the gift of their marvelous CDs, *Saints and Strangers* and *Mohave River*, to which I wrote quite a bit of this book.

Ewan MacColl, whose rendition of "Eppie Morrie" inspired Chapter 85.

Gabi Eleby, for socks, cookies, and general moral support—and to the Ladies of Lallybroch, for their boundless goodwill, manifested in the form of food boxes, cards, and enormous quantities of soap, both commercial and handmade ("Jack Randall Lavender" is nice, and I quite like the one called "Breath of Snow." The one called "Lick Jamie All Over" was so sweet one of the dogs ate it, though).

Acknowledgments

Bev LaFrance, Carol Krenz, Gilbert Sureau, Laura Bradbury, Julianne, Julie, and several other nice people whose names I unfortunately forgot to write down, for help with the French bits.

Monika Berrisch, for allowing me to appropriate her persona.

And to my husband, Doug Watkins, who this time gave me the opening lines of the Prologue.

A BREATH OF
SNOW AND
ASHES

Prologue

Time is a lot of the things people say that God is. There's the always preexisting, and having no end. There's the notion of being all powerful—because nothing can stand against time, can it? Not mountains, not armies.

And time is, of course, all-healing. Give anything *enough* time, and everything is taken care of: all pain encompassed, all hardship erased, all loss subsumed.

Ashes to ashes, dust to dust. Remember, man, that thou art dust; and unto dust thou shalt return.

And if Time is anything akin to God, I suppose that Memory must be the Devil.

PART ONE

Rumors of War

An Interrupted Conversation

The dog sensed them first. Dark as it was, Ian Murray felt rather than saw Rollo's head lift suddenly near his thigh, ears pricking. He put a hand on the dog's neck, and felt the hair there ridged with warning.

So attuned as they were to each other, he did not even think consciously, "Men," but put his other hand to his knife and lay still, breathing. Listening.

The forest was quiet. It was hours 'til dawn and the air was still as that in a church, with a mist like incense rising slowly up from the ground. He had lain down to rest on the fallen trunk of a giant tulip tree, preferring the tickle of wood-lice to seeping damp. He kept his hand on the dog, waiting.

Rollo was growling, a low, constant rumble that Ian could barely hear but felt easily, the vibration of it traveling up his arm, arousing all the nerves of his body. He hadn't been asleep—he rarely slept at night anymore—but had been quiet, looking up into the vault of the sky, engrossed in his usual argument with God. Quietness had vanished with Rollo's movement. He sat up slowly, swinging his legs over the side of the half-rotted log, heart beating fast now.

Rollo's warning hadn't changed, but the great head swiveled, following something unseen. It was a moonless night; Ian could see the faint silhouettes of trees and the moving shadows of the night, but nothing more.

Then he heard them. Sounds of passage. A good distance away, but coming nearer by the moment. He stood and stepped softly into the pool of black under a balsam fir. A click of the tongue, and Rollo left off his growling and followed, silent as the wolf who had been his father.

Ian's resting-place overlooked a game trail. The men who followed it were not hunting.

White men. Now that was odd, and more than odd. He couldn't see them, but didn't need to; the noise they made was unmistakable. Indians traveling were not silent, and many of the Highlanders he lived among could move like ghosts in the wood—but he had no doubt whatever. Metal, that was it. He was hearing the jingle of harness, the clink of buttons and buckles—and gun barrels.

A lot of them. So close, he began to smell them. He leaned forward a little, eyes closed, the better to snuff up what clue he could.

They carried pelts; now he picked up the dried-blood cold-fur smell that had probably waked Rollo—but not trappers, surely; too many. Trappers moved in ones and twos.

Poor men, and dirty. Not trappers, and not hunters. Game was easy to come by at this season, but they smelled of hunger. And the sweat of bad drink.

Close by now, perhaps ten feet from the place where he stood. Rollo made a tiny snorting sound, and Ian closed his hand once more on the dog's ruff, but the men made too much noise to hear it. He counted the passing footsteps, the bumping of canteens and bullet boxes, foot-sore grunts and sighs of weariness.

Twenty-three men, he made it, and there was a mule—no, two mules with them; he could hear the creak of laden panniers and that querulous heavy breathing, the way a loaded mule did, always on the verge of complaint.

The men would never have detected them, but some freak of the air bore Rollo's scent to the mules. A deafening bray shattered the dark, and the forest erupted in front of him with a clishmaclaver of crashing and startled shouts. Ian was already running when pistol shots crashed behind him.

"A Dhia!" Something struck him in the head and he fell headlong. Was he killed?

No. Rollo was pushing a worried wet nose into his ear. His head buzzed like a hive and he saw bright flashes of light before his eyes.

"Run! Ruith!" he gasped, pushing at the dog. "Run out! Go!" The dog hesitated, whining deep in his throat. He couldn't see, but felt the big body lunge and turn, turn back, undecided.

"Ruith!" He got himself up onto hands and knees, urging, and the dog at last obeyed, running as he had been trained.

There was no time to run himself, even could he have gained his feet. He fell facedown, thrust hands and feet deep into the leaf mold, and wriggled madly, burrowing in.

A foot struck between his shoulder blades, but the breath it drove out of him was muffled in wet leaves. It didn't matter, they were making so much noise. Whoever had stepped on him didn't notice; it was a glancing blow as the man ran over him in panic, doubtless thinking him a rotted log.

The shooting ceased. The shouting didn't, but he made no sense of it. He knew he was lying flat on his face, cold damp on his cheeks and the tang of dead leaves in his nose—but felt as though very drunk, the world revolving slowly round him. His head didn't hurt much, past the first burst of pain, but he didn't seem able to lift it.

He had the dim thought that if he died here, no one would know. His mother would mind, he thought, not knowing what had become of him.

The noises grew fainter, more orderly. Someone was still bellowing, but it had the sound of command. They were leaving. It occurred to him dimly that he might call out. If they knew he was white, they might help him. And they might not.

He kept quiet. Either he was dying or he wasn't. If he was, no help was possible. If he wasn't, none was needed.

Well, I asked then, didn't I? he thought, resuming his conversation with God, calm as though he lay still on the trunk of the tulip tree, looking up into the depths of heaven above. *A sign, I said. I didna quite expect Ye to be so prompt about it, though.*

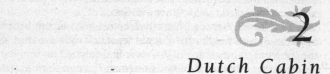

2

Dutch Cabin

March 1773

No one had known the cabin was there, until Kenny Lindsay had seen the flames, on his way up the creek.

"I wouldna ha' seen at all," he said, for perhaps the sixth time. "Save for the dark comin' on. Had it been daylight, I'd never ha' kent it, never." He wiped a trembling hand over his face, unable to take his eyes off the line of bodies that lay at the edge of the forest. "Was it savages, *Mac Dubh*? They're no scalped, but maybe—"

"No." Jamie laid the soot-smeared handkerchief gently back over the staring blue face of a small girl. "None of them is wounded. Surely ye saw as much when ye brought them out?"

Lindsay shook his head, eyes closed, and shivered convulsively. It was late afternoon, and a chilly spring day, but the men were all sweating.

"I didna look," he said simply.

My own hands were like ice; as numb and unfeeling as the rubbery flesh of the dead woman I was examining. They had been dead for more than a day; the rigor of death had passed off, leaving them limp and chilled, but the cold weather of the mountain spring had preserved them so far from the grosser indignities of putrefaction.

Still, I breathed shallowly; the air was bitter with the scent of burning. Wisps of steam rose now and then from the charred ruin of the tiny cabin. From the corner of my eye, I saw Roger kick at a nearby log, then bend and pick up something from the ground beneath.

Kenny had pounded on our door long before daylight, summoning us from warm beds. We had come in haste, even knowing that we were far too late to offer aid. Some of the tenants from the homesteads on Fraser's Ridge had come, too; Kenny's brother Evan stood with Fergus and Ronnie Sinclair in a small knot under the trees, talking together in low-voiced Gaelic.

"D'ye ken what did for them, Sassenach?" Jamie squatted beside me, face troubled. "The ones under the trees, that is." He nodded at the corpse in front of me. "I ken what killed this puir woman."

The woman's long skirt stirred in the wind, lifting to show long, slender feet shod in leather clogs. A pair of long hands to match lay still at her sides. She had been tall—though not so tall as Brianna, I thought, and looked automatically for my daughter's bright hair, bobbing among the branches on the far side of the clearing.

I had turned the woman's apron up to cover her head and upper body. Her hands were red, rough-knuckled with work, and with callused palms, but from the firmness of her thighs and the slenderness of her body, I thought she was no more than thirty—likely much younger. No one could say whether she had been pretty.

I shook my head at his remark.

"I don't think she died of the burning," I said. "See, her legs and feet aren't touched. She must have fallen into the hearth. Her hair caught fire, and it spread to the shoulders of her gown. She must have lain near enough to the wall or the chimney hood for the flames to touch; that caught, and then the whole bloody place went up."

Jamie nodded slowly, eyes on the dead woman.

"Aye, that makes sense. But what was it killed them, Sassenach? The others are singed a bit, though none are burned like this. But they must have been dead before the cabin caught alight, for none o' them ran out. Was it a deadly illness, perhaps?"

"I don't think so. Let me look at the others again."

I walked slowly down the row of still bodies with their cloth-covered faces, stooping over each one to peer again beneath the makeshift shrouds. There were any number of illnesses that could be quickly fatal in these days—with no antibiotics to hand, and no way of administering fluids save by mouth or rectum, a simple case of diarrhea could kill within twenty-four hours.

I saw such things often enough to recognize them easily; any doctor does, and I had been a doctor for more than twenty years. I saw things now and then in this century that I had never encountered in my own—particularly horrible parasitical diseases, brought with the slave trade from the tropics—but it was no parasite that had done for these poor souls, and no illness that I knew, to leave such traces on its victims.

All the bodies—the burned woman, a much older woman, and three children—had been found inside the walls of the flaming house. Kenny had pulled them out, just before the roof fell in, then ridden for help. All dead before the fire started; all dead virtually at the same time, then, for surely the fire had begun to smolder soon after the woman fell dead on her hearth?

The victims had been laid out neatly under the branches of a giant red spruce, while the men began to dig a grave nearby. Brianna stood by the smallest girl, her head bent. I came to kneel by the little body, and she knelt down across from me.

"What was it?" she asked quietly. "Poison?"

I glanced up at her in surprise.

"I think so. What gave you that idea?"

She nodded at the blue-tinged face below us. She had tried to close the eyes, but they bulged beneath the lids, giving the little girl a look of startled horror. The small, blunt features were twisted in a rictus of agony, and there were traces of vomit in the corners of the mouth.

"Girl Scout handbook," Brianna said. She glanced at the men, but no one was near enough to hear. Her mouth twitched, and she looked away from the body, holding out her open hand. *"Never eat any strange mushroom,"* she quoted. *"There are many poisonous varieties, and distinguishing one from another is a job for an expert.* Roger found these, growing in a ring by that log over there."

Moist, fleshy caps, a pale brown with white warty spots, the open gills and slender stems so pale as to look almost phosphorescent in the spruce shadows. They had a pleasant, earthy look to them that belied their deadliness.

"Panther toadstools," I said, half to myself, and picked one gingerly from her palm. *"Agaricus pantherinus*—or that's what they *will* be called, once somebody gets round to naming them properly. *Pantherinus,* because they kill so swiftly—like a striking cat."

I could see the gooseflesh ripple on Brianna's forearm, raising the soft, red-gold hairs. She tilted her hand and spilled the rest of the deadly fungus on the ground.

"Who in their right mind would eat toadstools?" she asked, wiping her hand on her skirt with a slight shudder.

"People who didn't know better. People who were hungry, perhaps," I answered softly. I picked up the little girl's hand, and traced the delicate bones of the forearm. The small belly showed signs of bloat, whether from malnutrition or postmortem changes I couldn't tell—but the collarbones were sharp as scythe blades. All of the bodies were thin, though not to the point of emaciation.

I looked up, into the deep blue shadows of the mountainside above the cabin. It was early in the year for foraging, but there was food in abundance in the forest—for those who could recognize it.

Jamie came and knelt down beside me, a big hand lightly on my back. Cold as it was, a trickle of sweat streaked his neck, and his thick auburn hair was dark at the temples.

"The grave is ready," he said, speaking low, as though he might alarm the child. "Is that what's killed the bairn?" He nodded at the scattered fungi.

"I think so—and the rest of them, too. Have you had a look around? Does anyone know who they were?"

He shook his head.

"Not English; the clothes are wrong. Germans would have gone to Salem, surely; they're clannish souls, and no inclined to settle on their own. These were maybe Dutchmen." He nodded toward the carved wooden clogs on the old woman's feet, cracked and stained with long use. "No books nor writing left, if there was any to begin with. Nothing that might tell their name. But—"

"They hadn't been here long." A low, cracked voice made me look up. Roger had come; he squatted next to Brianna, nodding toward the smoldering remains of the cabin. A small garden plot had been scratched into the earth nearby, but the few plants showing were no more than sprouts, the tender leaves limp and blackened with late frost. There were no sheds, no sign of livestock, no mule or pig.

"New emigrants," Roger said softly. "Not bond servants; this was a family. They weren't used to outdoor labor, either; the women's hands have blisters and fresh scars." His own broad hand rubbed unconsciously over a homespun knee; his palms were as smoothly callused as Jamie's now, but he had once been a tender-skinned scholar; he remembered the pain of his seasoning.

"I wonder if they left people behind—in Europe," Brianna murmured. She smoothed blond hair off the little girl's forehead, and laid the kerchief back over her face. I saw her throat move as she swallowed. "They'll never know what happened to them."

"No." Jamie stood abruptly. "They do say that God protects fools—but I think even the Almighty will lose patience now and then." He turned away, motioning to Lindsay and Sinclair.

"Look for the man," he said to Lindsay. Every head jerked up to look at him.

"Man?" Roger said, and then glanced sharply at the burned remnants of the cabin, realization dawning. "Aye—who built the cabin for them?"

"The women could have done it," Bree said, lifting her chin.

"*You* could, aye," he said, mouth twitching slightly as he cast a sidelong look at his wife. Brianna resembled Jamie in more than coloring; she stood six feet in her stockings and had her father's clean-limbed strength.

"Perhaps they could, but they didn't," Jamie said shortly. He nodded toward the shell of the cabin, where a few bits of furniture still held their fragile shapes. As I watched, the evening wind came down, scouring the ruin, and the shadow of a stool collapsed noiselessly into ash, flurries of soot and char moving ghostlike over the ground.

"What do you mean?" I stood and moved beside him, looking into the house. There was virtually nothing left inside, though the chimney stack still stood, and jagged bits of the walls remained, their logs fallen like jackstraws.

"There's no metal," he said, nodding at the blackened hearth, where the remnants of a cauldron lay, cracked in two from the heat, its contents vaporized. "No pots, save that—and that's too heavy to carry away. Nay tools. Not a knife, not an ax—and ye see whoever built it had that."

I did; the logs were unpeeled, but the notches and ends bore the clear marks of an ax.

Frowning, Roger picked up a long pine branch and began to poke through the piles of ash and rubble, looking to be sure. Kenny Lindsay and Sinclair didn't bother; Jamie had told them to look for a man, and they promptly went to do so, disappearing into the forest. Fergus went with them; Evan Lindsay, his brother

Murdo, and the McGillivrays began the chore of collecting stones for a cairn.

"If there *was* a man—did he leave them?" Brianna murmured to me, glancing from her father to the row of bodies. "Did this woman maybe think they wouldn't survive on their own?"

And thus take her own life, and those of her children, to avoid a long-drawn-out death from cold and starvation?

"Leave them and take all their tools? God, I hope not." I crossed myself at the thought, though even as I did so, I doubted it. "Wouldn't they have walked out, looking for help? Even with children . . . the snow's mostly gone." Only the highest mountain passes were still packed with snow, and while the trails and slopes were wet and muddy with runoff, they'd been passable for a month, at least.

"I've found the man," Roger said, interrupting my thoughts. He spoke very calmly, but paused to clear his throat. "Just—just here."

The daylight was beginning to fade, but I could see that he had gone pale. No wonder; the curled form he had unearthed beneath the charred timbers of a fallen wall was sufficiently gruesome as to give anyone pause. Charred to blackness, hands upraised in the boxer's pose so common to those dead by fire, it was difficult even to be sure that it *was* a man—though I thought it was, from what I could see.

Speculation about this new body was interrupted by a shout from the forest's edge.

"We've found them, milord!"

Everyone looked up from contemplation of this new corpse, to see Fergus waving from the edge of the wood.

"Them," indeed. Two men, this time. Sprawled on the ground within the shadow of the trees, found not together, but not far apart, only a short distance from the house. And both, so far as I could tell, probably dead of mushroom poisoning.

"*That's* no Dutchman," Sinclair said, for probably the fourth time, shaking his head over one body.

"He might be," said Fergus dubiously. He scratched his nose with the tip of the hook he wore in replacement of his left hand. "From the Indies, *non*?"

One of the unknown bodies was in fact that of a black man. The other was white, and both wore nondescript clothes of worn homespun—shirts and breeches; no jackets, despite the cold weather. And both were barefoot.

"No." Jamie shook his head, rubbing one hand unconsciously on his own breeches, as though to rid himself of the touch of the dead. "The Dutch keep slaves on Barbuda, aye—but these are better fed than the folk from the cabin." He lifted his chin toward the silent row of women and children. "They didna live here. Besides . . ." I saw his eyes fix on the dead men's feet.

The feet were grubby about the ankles and heavily callused, but basically clean. The soles of the black man's feet showed yellowish pink, with no smears of mud or random leaves stuck between the toes. These men hadn't been walking through the muddy forest barefoot, that much was sure.

"So there were perhaps more men? And when these died, their companions took their shoes—and anything else of value"— Fergus added practically, gesturing from the burned cabin to the stripped bodies—"and fled."

"Aye, maybe." Jamie pursed his lips, his gaze traveling slowly over the earth of the yard—but the ground was churned with footsteps, clumps of grass uprooted and the whole of the yard dusted with ash and bits of charred wood. It looked as though the place had been ravaged by rampaging hippopotami.

"I could wish that Young Ian was here. He's the best of the trackers; he could maybe tell what happened there, at least." He nodded into the wood, where the men had been found. "How many there were, maybe, and which way they've gone."

Jamie himself was no mean tracker. But the light was going fast now; even in the clearing where the burned cabin stood, the dark was rising, pooling under the trees, creeping like oil across the shattered earth.

His eyes went to the horizon, where streamers of cloud were beginning to blaze with gold and pink as the sun set behind them, and he shook his head.

"Bury them. Then we'll go."

One more grim discovery remained. Alone among the dead, the burned man had not died of fire or poison. When they lifted the charred corpse from the ashes to bear him to his grave, something fell free of the body, landing with a small, heavy thunk on the ground. Brianna picked it up, and rubbed at it with the corner of her apron.

"I guess they overlooked this," she said a little bleakly, holding it out. It was a knife, or the blade of one. The wooden hilt had burned entirely away, and the blade itself was warped with heat.

Steeling myself against the thick, acrid stench of burned fat and flesh, I bent over the corpse, poking gingerly at the mid-section. Fire destroys a great deal, but preserves the strangest things. The triangular wound was quite clear, seared in the hollow beneath his ribs.

"They stabbed him," I said, and wiped my sweating hands on my own apron.

"They killed him," Bree said, watching my face. "And then his wife—" She glanced at the young woman on the ground, the concealing apron over her head. "She made a stew with the mushrooms, and they all ate it. The children, too."

The clearing was silent, save for the distant calls of birds on the mountain. I could hear my own heart, beating painfully in my chest. Vengeance? Or simple despair?

"Aye, maybe," Jamie said quietly. He stooped to pick up an end of the sheet of canvas they had placed the dead man on. "We'll call it accident."

The Dutchman and his family were laid in one grave, the two strangers in another.

A cold wind had sprung up as the sun went down; the apron fluttered away from the woman's face as they lifted her. Sinclair gave a strangled cry of shock, and nearly dropped her.

She had neither face nor hair anymore; the slender waist narrowed abruptly into charred ruin. The flesh of her head had burned away completely, leaving an oddly tiny, blackened skull, from which her teeth grinned in disconcerting levity.

They lowered her hastily into the shallow grave, her children and mother beside her, and left Brianna and me to build a small cairn over them, in the ancient Scottish way, to mark the place and provide protection from wild beasts, while a more rudimentary resting place was dug for the two barefoot men.

The work finally done, everyone gathered, white-faced and silent, around the new-made mounds. I saw Roger stand close beside Brianna, his arm protectively about her waist. A small shudder went through her, which I thought had nothing to do with the cold. Their child, Jemmy, was a year or so younger than the smallest girl.

"Will ye speak a word, *Mac Dubh*?" Kenny Lindsay glanced inquiringly at Jamie, pulling his knitted bonnet down over his ears against the growing chill.

It was nearly nightfall, and no one wanted to linger. We would have to make camp, somewhere well away from the stink of burning, and that would be hard enough, in the dark. But Kenny was right; we couldn't leave without at least some token of ceremony, some farewell for the strangers.

Jamie shook his head.

"Nay, let Roger Mac speak. If these were Dutchmen, belike they were Protestant."

Dim as the light was, I saw the sharp glance Brianna shot at her father. It was true that Roger was a Presbyterian; so was Tom Christie, a much older man whose dour face reflected his opinion of the proceedings. The question of religion was no more than a pretext, though, and everyone knew it, including Roger.

Roger cleared his throat with a noise like tearing calico. It was always a painful sound; there was anger in it now as well. He didn't protest, though, and he met Jamie's eyes straight on, as he took his place at the head of the grave.

I had thought he would simply say the Lord's Prayer, or perhaps one of the gentler psalms. Other words came to him, though.

"Behold, I cry out of wrong, but I am not heard: I cry aloud, but there is no judgment. He hath fenced up my way that I cannot pass, and He hath set darkness in my paths."

His voice had once been powerful, and beautiful. It was choked now, no more than a rasping shadow of its former beauty—but there was sufficient power in the passion with which he spoke to make all those who heard him bow their heads, faces lost in shadow.

"He hath stripped me of my glory, and taken the crown from my head. He hath destroyed me on every side, and I am gone: and my hope hath He removed like a tree." His face was set, but his eyes rested for a bleak moment on the charred stump that had served the Dutch family for a chopping block.

"He hath put my brethren far from me, and mine acquaintance are verily estranged from me. My kinsfolk have failed, and my familiar friends have forgotten me." I saw the three Lindsay brothers exchange glances, and everyone drew a little closer together, against the rising wind.

"Have pity upon me, have pity upon me, O ye my friends," he said, and his voice softened, so that it was difficult to hear him, above the sighing of the trees. *"For the hand of God has touched me."*

Brianna made a slight movement beside him, and he cleared his throat once more, explosively, stretching his neck so that I caught a glimpse of the rope scar that marred it.

"Oh, that my words were now written! Oh, that they were printed in a book! That they were graven with an iron pen and lead in the rock forever!"

He looked slowly round from face to face, his own expressionless, then took a deep breath to continue, voice cracking on the words.

"For I know that my redeemer liveth, and that He shall stand at the latter day upon the earth: And though after my skin worms destroy this body"—Brianna shuddered convulsively, and looked away from the raw mound of dirt— *"yet in my flesh shall I see God. Whom I shall see for myself, and mine eyes shall behold."*

He stopped, and there was a brief collective sigh, as everyone let out the breath they had been holding. He wasn't quite finished, though. He had reached out, half-unconsciously, for Bree's hand, and held it tightly. He spoke the last words almost to himself, I thought, with little thought for his listeners.

"Be ye afraid of the sword: for wrath bringeth the punishments of the sword, that ye may know there is a judgment."

I shivered, and Jamie's hand curled round my own, cold but strong. He looked down at me, and I met his eyes. I knew what he was thinking.

He was thinking, as I was, not of the present, but the future. Of a small item that would appear three years hence, in the pages of the *Wilmington Gazette*, dated February 13, 1776.

It is with grief that the news is received of the deaths by fire of James MacKenzie Fraser and his wife, Claire Fraser, in a conflagration that destroyed their house in the settlement of Fraser's Ridge, on the night of January 21 last. Mr. Fraser, a nephew of the late Hector Cameron of River Run Plantation, was born at Broch Tuarach in Scotland. He was widely known in the Colony and deeply respected; he leaves no surviving children.

It had been easy, so far, not to think too much of it. So far in the future, and surely not an unchangeable future—after all, forewarned was forearmed . . . wasn't it?

I glanced at the shallow cairn, and a deeper chill passed through me. I stepped closer to Jamie, and put my other hand on his arm. He covered my hand with his, and squeezed tight in reassurance. No, he said to me silently. No, I will not let it happen.

As we left the desolate clearing, though, I could not free my mind of one vivid image. Not the burned cabin, the pitiful bodies, the pathetic dead garden. The image that haunted me was one I had seen some years before—a gravestone in the ruins of Beauly Priory, high in the Scottish Highlands.

It was the tomb of a noble lady, her name surmounted by the carving of a grinning skull—very like the one beneath the Dutchwoman's apron. Beneath the skull was her motto:

> *Hodie mihi cras tibi—sic transit gloria mundi.*
> *My turn today—yours tomorrow. Thus passes the glory*
> *of the world.*

3

Keep Your Friends Close

W e returned to Fraser's Ridge just before sunset the next day, to discover a visitor waiting. Major Donald MacDonald, late of His Majesty's army, and even more lately of Governor Tryon's personal light-horse guard, was sitting on the front stoop, my cat in his lap and a jug of beer beside him.

"Mrs. Fraser! Your servant, mum," he called genially, seeing me approach. He tried to stand up, but then let out a gasp as Adso, objecting to the loss of his cozy nest, dug his claws into the Major's thighs.

"Do sit, Major," I said, waving him hastily back. He subsided with a grimace, but nobly refrained from flinging Adso into the bushes. I came up onto the stoop beside him and sat down, sighing with relief.

"My husband is just seeing to the horses; he'll be down directly. I see that someone's made you welcome?" I nodded at the beer, which he promptly offered to me with a courtly gesture, wiping the neck of the jug on his sleeve.

"Oh, yes, mum," he assured me. "Mrs. Bug has been most assiduous of my welfare."

Not to seem uncordial, I accepted the beer, which in all truth went down very well. Jamie had been anxious to get back, and we'd been in the saddle since dawn, with only a brief break for refreshment at midday.

"It is a most excellent brew," the Major said, smiling as I exhaled after swallowing, my eyes half-closing. "Your own making, perhaps?"

I shook my head and took another swallow, before handing the jug back to him. "No, it's Lizzie's. Lizzie Wemyss."

"Oh, your bondmaid; yes, of course. Will you give her my compliments?"

"Isn't she here?" I glanced toward the open door behind him, rather surprised. At this time of day, I would have expected Lizzie to be in the kitchen, making supper, but she would surely have heard our arrival and come out. There was no smell of cooking, now that I noticed. She wouldn't have known when to expect us, of course, but . . .

"Mm, no. She is . . ." The Major knitted his brows in the effort of recall, and I wondered how full the jug had been before he got at it; there were no more than a couple of inches left now. "Ah, yes. She went to the McGillivrays' with her father, Mrs. Bug said. To visit her affianced, I believe?"

"Yes, she's engaged to Manfred McGillivray. But Mrs. Bug—"

"—is in the springhoose," he said, with a nod up the hill toward the small shed. "A matter of cheese, I believe she said. An omelette was most graciously proposed for my supper."

"Ah . . ." I relaxed a bit more, the dust of the ride settling with the beer. It was wonderful to come home, though my sense of peace was uneasy, tainted by the memory of the burned cabin.

I supposed that Mrs. Bug would have told him our errand, but he made no reference to it—nor to whatever had brought him up to the Ridge. Naturally not; all business would wait appropriately for Jamie. Being female, I would get impeccable courtesy and small bits of social gossip in the meantime.

I could do social gossip, but needed to be prepared for it; I hadn't a natural knack.

"Ah . . . Your relations with my cat seem somewhat improved," I hazarded. I glanced involuntarily at his head, but his wig had been expertly mended.

"It is an accepted principle of politics, I believe," he said, ruffling his fingers through the thick silver fur on Adso's belly. "Keep your friends close—but your enemies closer."

"Very sound," I said, smiling. "Er . . . I hope you haven't been waiting long?"

He shrugged, intimating that any wait was irrelevant— which it generally was. The mountains had their own time, and a wise man did not try to hurry them. MacDonald was a seasoned soldier, and well-traveled—but he had been born in Pitlochry, close enough to the Highland peaks to know their ways.

"I came this morning," he said. "From New Bern."

Small warning bells went off in the back of my mind. It would have taken him a good ten days to travel from New Bern, if he had come directly—and the state of his creased and mud-stained uniform suggested that he had.

New Bern was where the new royal governor of the colony, Josiah Martin, had taken up his residence. And for MacDonald to have said, "From New Bern," rather than mentioning some later stop on his journey, made it reasonably plain to me that whatever business had impelled this visit, it had originated *in* New Bern. I was wary of governors.

I glanced toward the path that led to the paddock, but Jamie wasn't visible yet. Mrs. Bug was, emerging from the springhouse; I waved to her and she gestured enthusiastically in welcome, though hampered by a pail of milk in one hand, a bucket of eggs in the other, a crock of butter under one arm, and a large chunk of cheese tucked neatly underneath her chin. She negotiated the steep descent with success, and disappeared round the back of the house, toward the kitchen.

"Omelettes all round, it looks like," I remarked, turning back to the Major. "Did you happen to come through Cross Creek, by chance?"

"I did indeed, mum. Your husband's aunt sends you her kind regards—and a quantity of books and newspapers, which I have brought with me."

I was wary of newspapers these days, too—though such events as they reported had undoubtedly taken place several weeks—or months—previously. I made appreciative noises, though, wishing Jamie would hurry up, so I could excuse myself. My hair smelled of burning and my hands still remembered the touch of cold flesh; I wanted a wash, badly.

"I beg your pardon?" I had missed something MacDonald was saying. He bent politely closer to repeat it, then jerked suddenly, eyes bulging.

"Frigging cat!"

Adso, who had been doing a splendid imitation of a limp dish-cloth, had sprung bolt upright in the Major's lap, eyes glowing and tail like a bottlebrush, hissing like a teakettle as he flexed his claws hard into the Major's legs. I hadn't time to react before he had leapt over MacDonald's shoulder and swarmed through the open surgery window behind him, ripping the Major's ruffle and knocking his wig askew in the process.

MacDonald was cursing freely, but I hadn't attention to spare for him. Rollo was coming up the path toward the house, wolflike and sinister in the gloaming, but acting so oddly that I was standing before conscious thought could bring me to my feet.

The dog would run a few steps toward the house, circle once or twice as though unable to decide what to do next, then run back into the wood, turn, and run again toward the house, all the while whining with agitation, tail low and wavering.

"Jesus H. Roosevelt Christ," I said. "Bloody Timmy's in the well!" I flew down the steps and ran for the path, barely registering the Major's startled oath behind me.

I found Ian a few hundred yards down the path, conscious, but groggy. He was sitting on the ground, eyes closed and both hands holding his head, as though to keep the bones of his skull from coming apart. He opened his eyes as I dropped to my knees beside him, and gave me an unfocused smile.

"Auntie," he said hoarsely. He seemed to want to say something else, but couldn't quite decide what; his mouth opened, but then simply hung that way, tongue moving thoughtfully to and fro.

"Look at me, Ian," I said, as calmly as possible. He did—that was good. It was too dark to see whether his pupils were unnaturally dilated, but even in the evening shadow of the pines that edged the trail, I could see the pallor of his face, and the dark trail of bloodstains down his shirt.

Hurried steps were coming after me down the trail; Jamie, followed closely by MacDonald.

"How is it, lad?"

Jamie gripped him by one arm, and Ian swayed very gently toward him, then dropped his hands, closed his eyes, and relaxed into Jamie's arms with a sigh.

"Is he bad?" Jamie spoke anxiously over Ian's shoulder, holding him up as I frisked him for damage. The back of his shirt was saturated with dried blood—but it *was* dried. The tail of his hair was stiff with it, too, and I found the head wound quickly.

"I don't think so. Something's hit him hard on the head and taken out a chunk of his scalp, but—"

"A tomahawk, do you think?"

MacDonald leaned over us, intent.

"No," said Ian drowsily, his face muffled in Jamie's shirt. "A ball."

"Go away, dog," Jamie said briefly to Rollo, who had stuck his nose in Ian's ear, eliciting a stifled squawk from the patient and an involuntary lifting of his shoulders.

"I'll have a look in the light, but it may not be too bad," I said, observing this. "He walked some way, after all. Let's get him up to the house."

The men made shift to get him up the trail, Ian's arms over their shoulders, and within minutes, had him laid facedown on the table in my surgery. Here, he told us the story of his adventures, in a disjoint fashion punctuated by small yelps as I cleaned the injury, clipped bits of clotted hair away, and put five or six stitches into his scalp.

"I thought I was dead," Ian said, and sucked air through his teeth as I drew the coarse thread through the edges of the ragged wound. "Christ, Auntie Claire! I woke in the morning, though, and I wasna dead after all—though I thought my head was split open, and my brains spilling down my neck."

"Very nearly was," I murmured, concentrating on my work. "I don't think it was a bullet, though."

That got everyone's attention.

"I'm not shot?" Ian sounded mildly indignant. One big hand lifted, straying toward the back of his head, and I slapped it lightly away.

"Keep still. No, you aren't shot, no credit to you. There was a deal of dirt in the wound, and shreds of wood and tree bark. If I had to guess, one of the shots knocked a dead branch loose from a tree, and it hit you in the head when it fell."

"You're quite sure as it wasn't a tomahawk, are ye?" The Major seemed disappointed, too.

I tied the final knot and clipped the thread, shaking my head.

"I don't believe I've ever seen a tomahawk wound, but I don't think so. See how jagged the edges are? And the scalp's torn badly, but I don't believe the bone is fractured."

"It was pitch-dark, the lad said," Jamie put in logically. "No sensible person would fling a tomahawk into a dark wood at something he couldna see." He was holding the spirit lamp for me to work by; he moved it closer, so we could see not only the ragged line of stitches, but the spreading bruise around it, revealed by the hair I had clipped off.

"Aye, see?" Jamie's finger spread the remaining bristles gently apart, tracing several deep scratches that scored the bruised area. "Your auntie's right, Ian; ye've been attacked by a tree."

Ian opened one eye a slit.

"Has anyone ever told ye what a comical fellow ye are, Uncle Jamie?"

"No."

Ian closed the eye.

"That's as well, because ye're not."

Jamie smiled, and squeezed Ian's shoulder.

"Feeling a bit better then, are ye?"

"No."

"Aye, well, the thing is," Major MacDonald interrupted, "that the lad did meet with some sort of banditti, no? Had ye reason to think they might be Indians?"

"No," said Ian again, but this time he opened the eye all the way. It was bloodshot. "They weren't."

MacDonald didn't appear pleased with this answer.

"How could ye be sure, lad?" he asked, rather sharply. "If it was dark, as ye say."

I saw Jamie glance quizzically at the Major, but he didn't interrupt. Ian moaned a little, then heaved a sigh and answered.

"I smelt them," he said, adding almost immediately, "I think I'm going to puke."

He raised himself on one elbow and promptly did so. This effectively put an end to any further questions, and Jamie took Major MacDonald off to the kitchen, leaving me to clean Ian up and settle him as comfortably as I could.

"Can you open both eyes?" I asked, having got him tidied and resting on his side, with a pillow under his head.

He did, blinking a little at the light. The small blue flame of the spirit lamp was reflected twice over in the darkness of his eyes, but the pupils shrank at once—and together.

"That's good," I said, and put down the lamp on the table. "Leave it, dog," I said to Rollo, who was nosing at the strange smell of the lamp—it was burning a mix of low-grade brandy and turpentine. "Take hold of my fingers, Ian."

I held out my index fingers and he slowly wrapped a large, bony hand round each of them. I put him through the drill for neurological damage, having him squeeze, pull, push, and then concluded by listening to his heart, which was thumping along reassuringly.

"Slight concussion," I announced, straightening up and smiling at him.

"Oh, aye?" he asked, squinting up at me.

"It means your head aches and you feel sick. You'll feel better in a few days."

"I could ha' told ye that," he muttered, settling back.

"So you could," I agreed. "But 'concussion' sounds so much more important than 'cracked heid,' doesn't it?"

He didn't laugh, but smiled faintly in response. "Will ye feed Rollo, Auntie? He wouldna leave me on the way; he'll be hungry."

Rollo pricked his ears at the sound of his name, and shoved his muzzle into Ian's groping hand, whining softly.

"He's fine," I said to the dog. "Don't worry. And yes," I added to Ian, "I'll bring something. Do you think you could manage a bit of bread and milk, yourself?"

"No," he said definitely. "A dram o' whisky, maybe?"

"No," I said, just as definitely, and blew out the spirit lamp.

"Auntie," he said, as I turned to the door.

"Yes?" I'd left a single candlestick to light him, and he looked very young and pale in the wavering yellow glow.

"Why d'ye suppose Major MacDonald wants it to be Indians I met in the wood?"

"I don't know. But I imagine Jamie does. Or will, by now."

4

Serpent in Eden

Brianna pushed open the door to her cabin, listening warily for the scamper of rodent feet or the dry whisper of scales across the floor. She'd once walked in in the dark and stepped within inches of a small rattlesnake; while the snake had been nearly as startled as she was, and slithered madly away between the hearthstones, she'd learned her lesson.

There was no scuttle of fleeing mice or voles this time, but something larger had been and gone, pushing its way through the oiled skin tacked over the window. The sun was just setting, and there was enough daylight left to show her the woven-grass basket in which she kept roasted peanuts, knocked from its shelf onto the floor and the contents cracked and eaten, a litter of shells scattered over the floor.

A loud rustling noise froze her momentarily, listening. It came again, followed by a loud clang as something fell to the ground, on the other side of the back wall.

"You little *bastard*!" she said. "You're in my pantry!"

Fired with righteous indignation, she seized the broom and

charged into the lean-to with a banshee yell. An enormous raccoon, tranquilly munching a smoked trout, dropped its prey at sight of her, dashed between her legs, and made off like a fat banker in flight from creditors, making loud *birring* noises of alarm.

Nerves pulsing with adrenaline, she put aside the broom and bent to salvage what she could of the mess, cursing under her breath. Raccoons were less destructive than squirrels, who would chew and shred with hapless abandon—but they had bigger appetites.

God knew how long he'd been in here, she thought. Long enough to lick all the butter out of its mold, pull down a cluster of smoked fish from the rafters—and how something so fat had managed the acrobatic feat required for *that* . . . Luckily, the honeycomb had been stored in three separate jars, and only one had been despoiled. But the root vegetables had been dumped on the floor, a fresh cheese mostly devoured, and the precious jug of maple syrup had been overturned, draining into a sticky puddle in the dirt. The sight of this loss enraged her afresh, and she squeezed the potato she had just picked up so hard that her nails sank through its skin.

"Bloody, bloody, beastly, horrible, bloody *beast*!"

"Who?" said a voice behind her. Startled, she whirled and fired the potato at the intruder, who proved to be Roger. It struck him squarely in the forehead and he staggered, clutching the door frame.

"Ow! Christ! Ow! What the hell's going on in here?"

"Raccoon," she said shortly, and stepped back, letting the waning light from the door illuminate the damage.

"He got the maple syrup? Bugger! Did you get the bastard?" Hand pressed to his forehead, Roger ducked inside the lean-to pantry, glancing about for furry bodies.

Seeing that her husband shared both her priorities and her sense of outrage soothed her somewhat.

"No," she said. "He ran. Are you bleeding? And where's Jem?"

"I don't think so," he said, taking the hand gingerly from his forehead and glancing at it. "Ow. You've a wicked arm, girl. Jem's at the McGillivrays'. Lizzie and Mr. Wemyss took him along to celebrate Senga's engagement."

"Really? Who did she pick?" Both outrage and remorse were immediately subsumed in interest. Ute McGillivray, with German thoroughness, had carefully selected partners for her son and three daughters according to her own criteria—land, money, and respectability ranking highest, with age, personal appearance, and charm coming well down the list. Not surprisingly, her children had other ideas—though such was the force of *Frau* Ute's personality that both Inga and Hilda had married men that she approved of.

Senga, though, was her mother's daughter—meaning that she possessed similarly strong opinions and a similar lack of inhibition in expressing them. For months, she had been hovering between two suitors: Heinrich Strasse, a dashing but poor young man—and a Lutheran!—from Bethania, and Ronnie Sinclair, the cooper. A well-off man, by the standards of the Ridge, and to Ute, the fact that Ronnie was thirty years Senga's senior was no bar.

The business of Senga McGillivray's marriage had been a topic of intense speculation on the Ridge for the last several months, and Brianna was aware of several substantial wagers riding on the outcome.

"So who's the lucky man?" she repeated.

"Mrs. Bug doesn't know, and it's driving her mad," Roger replied, breaking into a grin. "Manfred McGillivray came to fetch them yesterday morning, but Mrs. Bug hadn't come down to the Big House yet, so Lizzie left a note pinned to the back door to say where they'd gone—but she didn't think to say who the fortunate bridegroom is."

Brianna glanced at the setting sun; the orb itself had sunk out of sight, though the blazing light through the chestnut trees still lit the dooryard, making the spring grass look deep and soft as emerald velvet.

"I suppose we'll have to wait 'til tomorrow to find out," she said, with some regret. The McGillivrays' place was a good five miles; it would be full dark long before they reached it, and even past the thaw, one didn't wander the mountains at night without a good reason—or at least a better reason than mere curiosity.

"Aye. D'ye want to go up to the Big House for supper? Major MacDonald's come."

"Oh, him." She considered for a moment. She would like to hear any news the Major had brought—and there was something to be said for having Mrs. Bug make supper. On the other hand, she was really in no mood to be sociable, after a grim three days, a long ride, and the desecration of her pantry.

She became aware that Roger was carefully not contributing an opinion. One arm leaning on the shelf where the dwindling stock of winter apples was spread, he idly caressed one of the fruits, a forefinger slowly stroking the round yellow cheek of it. Faint, familiar vibrations were coming off him, suggesting silently that there might be advantages to an evening at home, sans parents, acquaintances—or baby.

She smiled at Roger.

"How's your poor head?"

He glanced at her briefly, the waning rays of the sun gilding the bridge of his nose and striking a flash of green from one eye. He cleared his throat.

"I suppose ye might kiss it," he suggested diffidently. "If ye liked."

She obligingly rose on her tiptoes and did so, gently, brushing back the thick black hair from his brow. There was a noticeable lump, though it hadn't begun to bruise yet.

"Is that better?"

"Not yet. Better try again. Maybe a bit lower?"

His hands settled on the swell of her hips, drawing her in. She was nearly as tall as he was; she'd noticed before what an advantage of fit this was, but the impression struck her forcibly anew. She wriggled slightly, enjoying it, and Roger drew a deep, rasping breath.

"Not quite that low," he said. "Not yet, anyway."

"Picky, picky," she said tolerantly, and kissed him on the mouth. His lips were warm, but the scent of bitter ash and damp earth clung to him—as it did to her—and she shivered a little, drawing back.

He kept a hand lightly on her back, but leaned past her, running a finger along the edge of the shelf where the jug of maple syrup had been overturned. He ran the finger lightly along her lower lip, then his own, and bent again to kiss her, sweetness rising up between them.

"I can't remember how long it's been since I've seen ye naked."

She closed one eye and looked at him skeptically.

"About three days. I guess it wasn't all that memorable." It had been a great relief to shed the clothes she'd been wearing for the last three days and nights. Even naked and hastily washed, though, she still smelled dust in her hair and felt the grime of the journey between her toes.

"Oh, well, aye. That's not what I mean, though—I mean, it's been a long while since we've made love in the daylight." He lay on his side, facing her, and smiled as he passed a light hand over the deep curve of her waist and the swell of buttock. "Ye've no idea how lovely ye look, stark naked, wi' the sun behind you. All gold, like ye were dipped in it."

He closed one eye, as though the sight dazzled him. She moved, and the sun shone in his face, making the open eye glow like an emerald in the split second before he blinked.

"Mmm." She put out a lazy hand and drew his head in close to kiss him.

She did know what he meant. It felt strange—almost wicked, in a pleasant sort of way. Most often, they made love at night, after Jem was asleep, whispering to each other in the hearth-lit shadows, finding each other among the rustling, secret layers of quilts and nightclothes. And while Jem normally slept as though he'd been poleaxed, they were always half-conscious of the small, heavy-breathing mound beneath the quilt of his trundle bed nearby.

She was oddly just as conscious of Jem now, in his absence. It felt strange to be apart from him; not constantly aware of where he was, not feeling his body as a small, very mobile extension of her own. The freedom was exhilarating, but left her feeling uneasy, as though she had misplaced something valuable.

They'd left the door open, the better to enjoy the flood of light and air on their skins. The sun was nearly down now, though, and while the air still glowed like honey, there was a shadow of chill in it.

A sudden gust of wind rattled the hide tacked over the window and blew across the room, slamming the door and leaving them abruptly in the dark.

Brianna gasped. Roger grunted in surprise and swung off the bed, going to open the door. He flung it wide, and she gulped in the freshet of air and sunshine, only then aware that she had held her breath when the door closed, feeling momentarily entombed.

Roger seemed to feel the same. He stood in the doorway, bracing himself against the frame, letting the wind stir the dark, curling hairs

of his body. His hair was still bound in a tail; he hadn't bothered undoing it, and she had a sudden desire to come behind him, untie the
leather thong and run her fingers through the soft, glossy black of it,
the legacy of some ancient Spaniard, shipwrecked among the Celts.

She was up and doing it before she had consciously decided to,
combing tiny yellow catkins and twigs from his locks with her
fingers. He shivered, from her touch or that of the wind, but his
body was warm.

"You have a farmer's tan," she said, lifting the hair off his neck
and kissing him on the bone at the base of his nape.

"Well, so. Am I not a farmer, then?" His skin twitched under
her lips, like a horse's hide. His face, neck, and forearms had
paled over the winter, but were still darker than the flesh of back
and shoulders—and a faint line still lingered round his waist, de-
marcating the soft buckskin color of his torso from the startling
paleness of his backside.

She cupped his buttocks, enjoying the high, round solidity of
them, and he breathed deeply, leaning back a little toward her, so
her breasts pressed against his back and her chin rested on his
shoulder, looking out.

It was still daylight, but barely. The last long shafts of the sinking sun burst through the chestnut trees, so the tender spring green
of their leaves burned with cool fire, brilliant above the lengthen-
ing shadows. It was near evening, but it was spring; the birds were
still at it, chattering and courting. A mockingbird sang from the
forest nearby, in a medley of trills, liquid runs, and odd yowls,
which she thought it must have learned from her mother's cat.

The air was growing nippy, and gooseflesh stippled her arms
and thighs—but Roger's body against her own was very warm.
She wrapped her arms around his waist, the fingers of one hand
playing idly with the thicket of his short and curlies.

"What are you looking at?" she asked softly, for his eyes were
fixed on the far side of the dooryard, where the trail emerged from
the forest. The trailhead was dim, shadowed by a growth of dark
pines—but empty.

"I'm watching out for a snake bearing apples," he said, and
laughed, then cleared his throat. "Are ye hungry, Eve?" His hand
came down to twine with hers.

"Getting there. Are you?" He must be starving; they had had
only a hasty snack at midday.

"Aye, I am, but—" He broke off, hesitating, and his fingers tightened in hers. "Ye'll think I'm mad, but—would ye mind if I went to fetch wee Jem tonight, instead of waiting for the morning? It's only, I'd feel a bit better to have him back."

She squeezed his hand in return, her heart lifting.

"We'll both go. It's a great idea."

"Maybe so, but it's five miles to McGillivrays', too. It'll be long dark before we're there." He was smiling, though, and his body brushed against her breasts as he turned to face her.

Something moved by her face, and she drew back sharply. A tiny caterpillar, green as the leaves on which it fed and vibrant against Roger's dark hair, reared itself into an S-shape, looking vainly for sanctuary.

"What?" Roger slid his eyes sideways, trying to see what she was looking at.

"Found your snake. I expect he's looking for an apple, too." She coaxed the tiny worm onto her finger, stepped outside, and squatted to let it crawl onto a grass blade that matched its vivid green. But the grass was in shadow. In only an instant, the sun had gone down, the forest no longer the color of life.

A thread of smoke reached her nose; chimney smoke from the Big House, but her throat closed at the smell of burning. Suddenly her uneasiness was stronger. The light was fading, night coming on. The mockingbird had fallen silent, and the forest seemed full of mystery and threat.

She rose to her feet, shoving a hand through her hair.

"Let's go, then."

"Do ye not want supper, first?" Roger looked quizzically at her, breeches in hand.

She shook her head, chill beginning to creep up her legs.

"No. Let's just go." Nothing seemed to matter, save to get Jem, and be together again, a family.

"All right," Roger said mildly, eyeing her. "I do think ye'd best put on your fig leaf first, though. Just in case we meet an angel with a flaming sword."

5

The Shadows Which
Fire Throws

I abandoned Ian and Rollo to the juggernaut of Mrs. Bug's benevolence—let Ian try telling *her* he didn't want bread and milk—and sat down to my own belated supper: a hot, fresh omelette, featuring not only cheese, but bits of salty bacon, asparagus, and wild mushroom, flavored with spring onions.

Jamie and the Major had finished their own meals already, and sat by the fire beneath a companionable fug of tobacco smoke from the Major's clay pipe. Evidently, Jamie had just finished telling Major MacDonald about the gruesome tragedy, for MacDonald was frowning and shaking his head in sympathy.

"Puir gomerels!" he said. "Ye'll be thinking that it was the same banditti, perhaps, who set upon your nephew?"

"I am," Jamie replied. "I shouldna like to think there were two such bands prowling the mountains." He glanced toward the window, cozily shuttered for the night, and I noticed suddenly that he had taken down his fowling piece from over the hearth and was absently wiping the spotless barrel with an oily rag. "Do I gather, *a charaid,* that ye've heard some report of similar doings?"

"Three others. At least." The Major's pipe threatened to go out, and he drew on it mightily, making the tobacco in the bowl glow and crackle sudden red.

A small qualm made me pause, a bite of mushroom warm in my mouth. The possibility that a mysterious gang of armed men might be roaming at large, attacking homesteads at random, had not occurred to me 'til this moment.

Obviously, it had occurred to Jamie; he rose, put the fowling piece back on its hooks, touched the rifle that hung above it for re-assurance, then went to the sideboard, where his dags and the case with its elegant pair of dueling pistols were kept.

MacDonald watched with approval, puffing clouds of soft blue smoke, as Jamie methodically laid out guns, shot pouches, bullet molds, patches, rods, and all the other impedimenta of his personal armory.

"Mmphm," MacDonald said. "A verra nice piece, that, Colonel." He nodded at one of the dags, a long-barreled, elegant thing with a scroll butt and silver-gilt fittings.

Jamie gave MacDonald a narrow glance, hearing the "Colonel," but answered calmly enough.

"Aye, it's a bonny thing. It doesna aim true at anything over two paces, though. Won it in a horse race," he added, with a small apologetic gesture at the gun, lest MacDonald think him fool enough to have paid good money for it.

He checked the flint nonetheless, replaced it, and set the gun aside.

"Where?" Jamie said casually, reaching for the bullet mold.

I had resumed chewing, but looked inquiringly at the Major myself.

"Mind, it's only what I've heard," MacDonald warned, taking the pipe from his mouth for a moment, then hastily putting it back for another puff. "A homestead some distance from Salem, burned to the ground. Folk called Zinzer—Germans." He sucked hard, cheeks hollowing.

"That was in February, late in the month. Then three weeks later, a ferry, on the Yadkin north of Woram's Landing—the house robbed, and the ferryman killed. The third—" Here he broke off, puffing furiously, and cut his eyes at me, then back at Jamie.

"Speak, o, friend," Jamie said in Gaelic, looking resigned. "She will have been seeing more dreadful things than you have, by far."

I nodded at this, forking up another bite of egg, and the Major coughed.

"Aye. Well, saving your presence, mum—I happened to find myself in a, er, establishment in Edenton. . . ."

"A brothel?" I put in. "Yes, quite. Do go on, Major."

He did, rather hurriedly, his face flushing dark beneath his wig.

"Ah . . . to be sure. Well, d'ye see, 'twas one of the, er, lasses in the place, told me as she'd been stolen from her home by outlaws who set upon the place one day without warning. She'd no but an auld grannie she lived with, and said they'd kilt the auld woman, and burned the house above her head."

"And who did she say had done it?" Jamie had turned his stool to face the hearth, and was melting lead scrap in a ladle for the bullet mold.

"Ah, mmphm." MacDonald's flush deepened, and the smoke fumed from his pipe with such ferocity that I could barely make out his features through the curling wreaths.

It transpired, with much coughing and circumlocution, that the Major had not really believed the girl at the time—or had been too interested in availing himself of her charms to pay much attention. Putting the story down simply as one of the tales whores often told to elicit sympathy and the odd extra glass of geneva, he had not bothered to ask for further detail.

"But when I heard by chance later of the other burnings . . . well, d'ye see, I've had the luck to be charged by the Governor with keeping an ear to the ground, as it were, in the backcountry, for signs of unrest. And I began to think that this particular instance of unrest was maybe not just sae much of a coincidence as might at first appear."

Jamie and I exchanged glances at that, Jamie's tinged with amusement, mine with resignation. He'd bet me that MacDonald—a half-pay cavalry officer who survived by freelancing—would not only survive Governor Tryon's resignation, but would succeed in worming his way promptly into some position with the new regime, now that Tryon had left to take up a superior position as governor of New York. *"He's a gentleman o' fortune, our Donald,"* he'd said.

The militant smell of hot lead began to permeate the room, competing with the Major's pipe smoke, and quite overpowering the pleasantly domestic atmosphere of rising bread, cooking, dried herbs, scouring rushes, and lye soap that normally filled the kitchen.

Lead melts suddenly; one instant, a deformed bullet or a bent button sits in the ladle, whole and distinct; the next, it's gone, a tiny puddle of metal shimmering dully in its place. Jamie poured the molten lead carefully into the mold, averting his face from the fumes.

"Why Indians?"

"Ah. Well, 'twas what the whore in Edenton said. She said some of those who burned her house and stole her away were Indians. But as I say, at the time I paid her story little mind."

Jamie made a Scottish noise indicating that he took the point, but with skepticism.

"And when did ye meet this lassie, Donald, and hear her story?"

"Near Christmas." The Major poked at the bowl of his pipe with a stained forefinger, not looking up. "Ye mean when was her house attacked? She didna say, but I think . . . perhaps not too long before. She was still . . . fairly, er, fresh." He coughed, caught my eye, caught his breath, and coughed again, hard, going red in the face.

Jamie's mouth pressed tight, and he looked down, flipping open the mold to drop a new-made ball onto the hearth.

I put down my fork, the remnants of appetite vanished.

"How?" I demanded. "How did this young woman come to be in the brothel?"

"Why, they sold her, mum." The flush still stained MacDonald's cheeks, but he had recovered his countenance enough to look at me. "The brigands. They sold her to a river trader, she said, a few days after they'd stolen her. He kept her for a bit, on his boat, but then a man came one night to do business, took a fancy to her, and bought her. He brought her as far as the coast, but I suppose he'd tired of her by then. . . ." His words trailed off, and he stuck the pipe back into his mouth, drawing hard.

"I see." I did, and the half of the omelette I'd eaten lay in a small hard ball in the bottom of my stomach.

"Still fairly fresh." How long did it take, I wondered? How long would a woman last, passed from hand to casual hand, from the splintered planks of a riverboat's deck to the tattered mattress of a hired room, given only what would keep her alive? It was more than possible that the brothel in Edenton had seemed a haven of sorts by the time she reached it. The thought didn't make me feel any more kindly toward MacDonald, though.

"Do you remember her name at least, Major?" I asked, with icy courtesy.

I thought I saw the edge of Jamie's mouth twitch, from the corner of my eye, but kept my stare focused on MacDonald.

He took the pipe from his mouth, exhaled a long stream of

smoke, then looked up into my face, his eyes pale blue and very direct.

"In truth, mum," he said, "I just call them all Polly. Saves trouble, ken?"

I was saved from reply—or from something worse—by the return of Mrs. Bug, bearing an empty bowl.

"The laddie's eaten, and now he'll sleep," she announced. Her sharp eyes flicked from my face to my half-empty plate. She opened her mouth, frowning, but then glanced at Jamie, and seeming to pick up some unspoken command from him, shut her mouth again, and picked up the plate with a brief "hmp!"

"Mrs. Bug," said Jamie quietly. "Will ye awa' just now, and ask Arch to come down to me? And, if it's no troubling ye too much, the same word to Roger Mac?"

Her small black eyes went round, then narrowed as she glanced at MacDonald, obviously suspecting that if there were mischief afoot, he was behind it.

"I will," she said, and shaking her head with admonishment at me for my lack of appetite, she put down the dishes and went out, leaving the door on the latch.

"Woram's Landing," Jamie said to MacDonald, resuming their conversation as though it had not been interrupted. "And Salem. And if it is the same men, Young Ian met them in the forest, a day's travel west of here. Near enough."

"Near enough to be the same? Aye, it is."

"It's early in the spring." Jamie glanced at the window as he spoke; it was dark now, and the shutters closed, but a cool breeze crept through and stirred the threads where I had strung mushrooms to dry, dark wizened shapes that swayed like tiny dancers, frozen against the pale wood.

I knew what he meant by that. The ground in the mountains was impassable during the winter; the high passes still held snow, and the lower slopes had only begun to green and blossom in the last few weeks. If there was an organized gang of marauders, they might only now be moving into the backcountry, after a winter spent lying low in the piedmont.

"It is," MacDonald agreed. "Early enough, perhaps, to have folk on their guard. But before your men come, sir—perhaps we should speak of what brought me?"

"Aye?" Jamie said, squinting carefully as he poured a glittering stream of lead. "Of course, Donald. I should have kent no small matter would bring ye so far. What is it?"

MacDonald smiled like a shark; now we'd come to it.

"Ye've done well wi' your place here, Colonel. How many families it is ye have on your land the noo?"

"Thirty-four," Jamie said. He didn't look up, but turned out another bullet into the ashes.

"Room for a few more, perhaps?" MacDonald was still smiling. We were surrounded by thousands of miles of wilderness; the handful of homesteads on Fraser's Ridge made scarcely a dent in it—and could vanish like smoke. I thought momentarily of the Dutch cabin, and shivered, despite the fire. I could still taste the bitter, cloying smell of burned flesh, thick in the back of my throat, lurking beneath the lighter flavors of the omelette.

"Perhaps," Jamie replied equably. "The new Scottish emigrants, is it? From up past Thurso?"

Major MacDonald and I both stared at him.

"How the devil d'ye ken that?" MacDonald demanded. "I heard it myself only ten days since!"

"Met a man at the mill yesterday," Jamie replied, picking up the ladle again. "A gentleman from Philadelphia, come into the mountains to collect plants. He'd come up from Cross Creek and seen them." A muscle near his mouth twitched. "Apparently, they made a bit of a stir at Brunswick, and didna feel themselves quite welcome, so they came up the river on flatboats."

"A bit of a stir? What did they do?" I asked.

"Well, d'ye see, mum," the Major explained, "there are a great many folk come flooding off ships these days, straight from the Highlands. Whole villages, packed into the bowels of a ship—and looking as though they've been shat out when they disembark, too. There's nothing for them on the coast, though, and the townsfolk are inclined to point and snigger, seein' them in their outlandish rig—so for the most part, they get straight onto a barge or a flatboat and head up the Cape Fear. Campbelton and Cross Creek at least have folk who can talk to them."

He grinned at me, brushing a smudge of dirt from the skirts of his uniform coat.

"The folk in Brunswick willna be quite accustomed to such rawboned Highlanders, they having seen only such civilized Scotch persons as your husband and his aunt."

He nodded toward Jamie, who gave him a small, ironic bow in return.

"Well, relatively civilized," I murmured. I was not ready to forgive MacDonald for the whore in Edenton. "But—"

"They've barely a word of English among them, from what I hear," MacDonald hurried on. "Farquard Campbell came down to speak wi' them, and brought them north to Campbelton, or I doubt not but they'd be milling about onshore yet, wi' no notion at all where to go or what to do next."

"What's Campbell done wi' them?" Jamie inquired.

"Ah, they're parceled out amongst his acquaintance in Campbelton, but 'twon't suit in the long run, ye can see that, of course." MacDonald shrugged. Campbelton was a small settlement near Cross Creek, centered around Farquard Campbell's successful trading store, and the land around it was entirely settled—mostly by Campbells. Farquard had eight children, many of whom were also married—and as fertile as their father.

"Of course," Jamie said, looking wary. "But they're from the northern coast. They'll be fishermen, Donald, not crofters."

"Aye, but they're willing to make a change, no?" MacDonald gestured toward the door, and the forest beyond. "There's nothing for them left in Scotland. They've come here, and now they must make the best of it. A man can learn to farm, surely?"

Jamie looked rather dubious, but MacDonald was in the full flush of his enthusiasm.

"I've seen many a fisher-lad and plowboy become a soldier, man, and so have you, I'll wager. Farming's no more difficult than soldiering, surely?"

Jamie smiled a little at that; he had left farming at nineteen and fought as a mercenary in France for several years before returning to Scotland.

"Aye, well, that's maybe true, Donald. But the thing about being a soldier is that someone's tellin' ye what to do, from the moment ye rise until ye fall down at night. Who's to tell these poor wee gomerels which end o' the cow to milk?"

"That would be you, I expect," I said to him. I stretched myself, easing my back, stiff from riding, and glanced across at MacDonald. "Or at least I suppose that's what you're getting at, Major?"

"Your charm is exceeded only by your quickness of wit, mum," said MacDonald, bowing gracefully in my direction. "Aye, that's the meat of it. All your folk are Highlanders, sir, and crofters; they can speak to these newcomers in their own tongue, show them what they'll need to know—help them to make their way."

"There are a good many other folk in the colony who have the *Gaidhlig*," Jamie objected. "And most of them a great deal more convenient to Campbelton."

"Aye, but you've vacant land that needs clearing, and they haven't." Obviously feeling that he had won the argument, MacDonald sat back and took up his neglected mug of beer.

Jamie looked at me, one eyebrow raised. It was perfectly true that we had vacant land: ten thousand acres, but barely twenty of them under cultivation. It was also true that lack of labor was acute in the entire colony, but even more so in the mountains, where the land didn't lend itself to tobacco or rice—the sorts of crops suited to slave labor.

At the same time, though—

"The difficulty is, Donald, how to settle them." Jamie bent to turn out another ball on the hearth, and straightened, brushing back a loose strand of auburn hair behind his ear. "I've land, aye, but little else. Ye canna be loosing folk straight from Scotland into the wilderness, and expect them to claw a living out of it. I couldna even give them the shoon and suit of clothes a bondsman would have, let alone tools. And to feed them and all their wives and weans through the winter? To offer them protection?" He lifted his ladle in illustration, then shook his head and dropped in another lump of lead.

"Ah, protection. Well, since ye've mentioned that, let me proceed to another wee matter of interest." MacDonald leaned forward, lowering his voice confidentially, though there was no one to hear.

"I've said I'm the Governor's man, aye? He's charged me to travel about, over the western part of the colony, and keep an ear to the ground. There are Regulators still unpardoned, and"—he glanced warily to and fro, as though expecting one of these persons to bound out of the fireplace—"ye'll have heard of the Committees of Safety?"

"A bit."

"Ye'll not have one established yet, here in the backcountry?"

"Not that I've heard of, no." Jamie had run out of lead to melt, and now stooped to scoop the new-made balls from the ashes at his feet, the warm light of the fire glowing red on the crown of his head. I sat down beside him on the settle, picking up the shot pouch from the table and holding it open for him.

"Ah," said MacDonald, looking pleased. "I see I've come in good time, then."

In the wake of the civil unrest that surrounded the War of the Regulation a year before, a number of such informal citizens' groups had sprung up, inspired by similar groups in the other colonies. If the Crown was no longer able to assure the safety of the colonists, they argued, then they must take the matter into their own hands.

The sheriffs could no longer be trusted to keep order; the scandals that had inspired the Regulator movement had assured that. The difficulty, of course, was that since the committees were self-appointed, there was no more reason to trust them than the sheriffs.

There were other committees, too. The Committees of Correspondence, loose associations of men who wrote letters to and fro, spreading news and rumor between the colonies. And it was out of these various committees that the seeds of rebellion would spring—were germinating even now, somewhere out in the cold spring night.

As I did now and then—and much more often, now—I reckoned up the time remaining. It was nearly April of 1773 And *on the eighteenth of April, in Seventy-five . . .* as Longfellow so quaintly put it . . .

Two years. But war has a long fuse, and a slow match. This one had been lit at Alamance, and the bright, hot lines of the creeping fire in North Carolina were already visible—for those who knew to look.

The lead balls in the shot pouch I held rolled and clicked together; my fingers had tightened on the leather. Jamie saw it and touched my knee, quick and light, in reassurance, then took the pouch and rolled it up, tucking it into the cartridge box.

"Good time," he repeated, looking at MacDonald. "What d'ye mean by that, Donald?"

"Why, who should lead such a committee other than yourself,

Colonel? I had suggested as much to the Governor." MacDonald tried to look modest, and failed.

"Verra obliging of ye, Major," Jamie said dryly. He raised an eyebrow at me. The state of the colony's government must be worse even than he had supposed, for Governor Martin to be not only tolerating the existence of the committees—but clandestinely sanctioning them.

The long-drawn whine of a dog's yawn reached me faintly from the hall, and I excused myself, to go and check on Ian.

I wondered whether Governor Martin had the slightest idea what he was loosing. I rather thought he did, and was making the best of a bad job, by trying to ensure that some, at least, of the Committees of Safety were run by men who had backed the Crown during the War of the Regulation. The fact remained that he could not control—or even know about—many such committees. But the colony was beginning to seethe and bump like a teakettle on the boil, and Martin had no official troops at his command, only such irregulars as MacDonald—and the militia.

Which was why MacDonald was calling Jamie "Colonel," of course. The previous governor, William Tryon, had appointed Jamie—quite against his will—colonel of militia for the backcountry above the Yadkin.

"Hmph," I said to myself. Neither MacDonald nor Martin was a fool. Inviting Jamie to set up a Committee of Safety meant that he would call upon those men who had served under him in the militia—but would commit the government to nothing, in terms of paying or equipping them—and the Governor would be clear of any responsibility for their actions, since a Committee of Safety was not an official body.

The danger to Jamie—and all of us—in accepting such a proposal, though—that was considerable.

It was dark in the hall, with no light but the spill from the kitchen behind me, and the faint glow of the single candle in the surgery. Ian was asleep, but restless, a faint frown of discomfort wrinkling the soft skin between his brows. Rollo raised his head, thick tail swishing to and fro across the floor in greeting.

Ian didn't respond when I spoke his name, or when I set a hand on his shoulder. I shook him gently, then harder. I could see him struggling, somewhere under the layers of unconsciousness, like a man drifting in the underwater currents, yielding to the beckoning depths, then snagged by an unexpected fishhook, a stab of pain in cold-numbed flesh.

His eyes opened suddenly, dark and lost, and he stared at me in incomprehension.

"Hallo there," I said softly, relieved to see him wake. "What's your name?"

I could see that the question made no sense to him at once, and repeated it, patiently. Awareness stirred somewhere in the depths of his dilated pupils.

"Who am I?" he said in Gaelic. He said something else, slurred, in Mohawk, and his eyelids fluttered, closing.

"Wake up, Ian," I said firmly, resuming the shaking. "Tell me who you are."

His eyes opened again, and he squinted at me in confusion.

"Try something easier," I suggested, holding up two fingers. "How many fingers do you see?"

A flicker of awareness sprang up in his eyes.

"Dinna let Arch Bug see ye do that, Auntie," he said drowsily, the hint of a smile touching his face. "That's verra rude, ken."

Well, at least he had recognized me, as well as the "V" sign; that was something. And he must know who he was, if he was calling me Auntie.

"What's your full name?" I asked again.

"Ian James FitzGibbons Fraser Murray," he said, rather crossly. "Why d'ye keep asking me my name?"

"FitzGibbons?" I said. "Where on earth did you get that one?"

He groaned and put two fingers against his eyelids, wincing as he pressed gently.

"Uncle Jamie gave it me—blame him," he said. "It's for his auld godfather, he said. Murtagh FitzGibbons Fraser, he was called, but my mother didna want me named Murtagh. I think I'm going to puke again," he added, taking his hand away.

In the event, he heaved and retched a bit over the basin, but didn't actually vomit, which was a good sign. I eased him back onto his side, white and clammy with sweat, and Rollo stood on his hind legs, front paws braced on the table, to lick his face, which made him giggle between groans and try feebly to push the dog away.

"Theirig dhachaigh, Okwaho," he said. *"Theirig dhachaigh"*

meant "go home," in Gaelic, and Okwaho was evidently Rollo's
Mohawk name. Ian seemed to be having some difficulty choosing
among the three languages in which he was fluent, but was obviously lucid, in spite of that. After I had made him answer a few
more annoyingly pointless questions, I wiped his face with a damp
cloth, let him rinse his mouth with well-watered wine, and tucked
him in again.

"Auntie?" he said drowsily, as I was turning for the door.
"D'ye think I'll ever see my Mam again?"

I stopped, having no idea how to answer that. In fact, there was
no need; he had dropped back into sleep with the suddenness that
concussion patients often showed, and was breathing deeply before I could find any words.

6

Ambush

I an woke abruptly, hand closing round his tomahawk. Or
what should have been his tomahawk, but was instead a
handful of breeches. For an instant, he had no notion at all
where he was, and sat up straight, trying to make out shapes in
the dark.

Pain shot through his head like heat lightning, making him
gasp soundlessly and clutch it. Somewhere in the dark below him,
Rollo gave a small, startled *wuff*?

Christ. The piercing smells of his aunt's surgery stabbed the
back of his nose, alcohol and burned wick and dried medicine
leaves and the foul brews she called penny-syllin. He closed his
eyes, put his forehead on his drawn-up knees, and breathed slowly
through his mouth.

What had he been dreaming? Some dream of danger, some-thing violent—but no clear image came to him, only the feel of being stalked, something following him through the wood.

He had to piss, badly. Fumbling for the edge of the table he lay on, he eased himself slowly upright, squinting against the flashes of pain in his head.

Mrs. Bug had left him a pot, he remembered her saying so, but the candle had gone out and he'd no mind to crawl round the floor looking for it. Faint light showed him where the door was; she had left it ajar, and a glow spread down the hall from the kitchen hearth. With that as bearing, he made his way to the window, got it open, fumbled free the shutter fastening, and stood in the flood of air from the cool spring night, eyes closed in relief as his bladder eased.

That was better, though with the relief came new awareness of the queasiness of his stomach and the throbbing in his head. He sat down, putting his arms on his knees and his head on his arms, waiting for everything to ease.

There were voices in the kitchen; he could hear them clearly, now that he paid attention.

It was Uncle Jamie and yon MacDonald, and old Arch Bug, as well, with Auntie Claire now and again putting in a word, her English voice sharp by contrast with the gruff mutter of Scots and Gaelic.

"Would ye care, perhaps, to be an Indian agent?" MacDonald was saying.

What was that? he wondered—then it came to him. Aye, of course; the Crown employed men to go out to the tribes, offer them gifts, tobacco, and knives and the like. Tell them silliness about German Geordie, as though the King was like to come and sit down by the council fires at the next Rabbit Moon and speak like a man.

He smiled grimly to think of it. The notion was plain enough; cozen the Indians to fight for the English, when fighting was needed. But why should they think it needed now? The French had yielded, retreated to their northern foothold in Canada.

Oh. He remembered belatedly what Brianna had told him about the new fighting to come. He'd not known whether to believe her—perhaps she was right, though, in which case . . . he didn't want to think about it. Or about anything.

Rollo padded over to him, sat and leaned heavily against him. He leaned back, resting his head in the thick fur.

An Indian agent had come once, while he lived in Snaketown. A fat wee fellow, shifty-eyed and with a tremble in his voice. He thought the man—Christ, what was his name? The Mohawk had called him Bad Sweat, and that fit; he stank as though with a mortal illness—he thought the man was not accustomed to the Kahnyen'kehaka; he'd not much of their speech, and plainly expected them to take his scalp at any moment, something they had thought hilarious—and one or two would likely have tried it, for a joke, save that Tewaktenyonh said to treat him with respect. Ian had been pressed to interpret for him, a job he'd done, though without much pleasure in it. He would much sooner think himself Mohawk than acknowledge any kinship with Bad Sweat.

Uncle Jamie, though . . . he'd make a better job of it, by far. Would he do it? Ian listened to the voices with a vague sense of interest, but it was clear that Uncle Jamie would not be pressed for a decision. MacDonald might as soon get a grip on a frog in a spring, he thought, hearing his uncle elude commitment.

He sighed, put his arm around Rollo, and eased more of his weight onto the dog. He felt awful. He would have supposed he was dying, save that Auntie Claire had said he'd feel poorly for several days. He was sure she would have stayed if he were dying, not gone and left him with only Rollo for company.

The shutters were still open, and cold air poured over him, chilly and soft at once, the way spring nights were. He felt Rollo raise his nose, sniffing, and utter a low, eager whine. Possum, maybe, or a raccoon.

"Go on, then," he said, straightening up and giving the dog a small push. "I'm fine."

The dog sniffed him suspiciously, and tried to lick the back of his head, where the stitches were, but left off when Ian yelped and covered them with his hands.

"Go, I said!" He cuffed the dog gently, and Rollo snorted, circled once, then sailed over his head and out through the window, hitting the ground outside with a solid thump. A frightful screech rent the air and there was the sound of scrabbling feet and heavy bodies tearing through shrubbery.

Startled voices came from the direction of the kitchen, and he heard Uncle Jamie's step in the hall, an instant before the surgery door pushed in.

"Ian?" called his uncle softly. "Where are ye, lad? What's amiss?"

He stood up, but a sheet of blinding white came down inside his eyes and he staggered. Uncle Jamie caught him by the arm, and set him down on a stool.

"What is it, lad?" His vision clearing, he could see his uncle in the light from the door, rifle in one hand, his face looking concerned but humorous as he glanced toward the open window. He sniffed deeply. "Not a skunk, I suppose."

"Aye, well, I suppose it's one thing or the other," Ian said, touching his head gingerly. "Either Rollo's gone after a painter, or he's treed Auntie's cat."

"Oh, aye. He'd fare better wi' the painter." His uncle set the rifle down and went to the window. "Shall I close the shutter, or d'ye need the air, lad? You're that bit peaked."

"I feel peaked," Ian admitted. "Aye, leave it, if ye will, Uncle."

"Shall ye rest, Ian?"

He hesitated. His stomach still lurched uneasily and he felt very much that he would like to lie down again—but the surgery made him uneasy, with its strong smells and the glints here and there of tiny blades and other mysterious and painful things. Uncle Jamie seemed to guess the trouble, for he bent and got a hand under Ian's elbow.

"Come along, lad. Ye can sleep upstairs in a proper bed, if ye dinna mind Major MacDonald in the other."

"I dinna mind," he said, "but I'll stay here, I think." He gestured toward the window, not wanting to nod and bother his head again. "Rollo will likely be back soon."

Uncle Jamie didn't argue with him, something he was grateful for. Women fussed. Men just got on with it.

His uncle boosted him unceremoniously back into his bed, covered him up, then began rootling about in the dark, in search of the rifle he had put down. Ian began to feel that perhaps he could do with just a wee bit of fuss, after all.

"Could ye get me a cup o' water, Uncle Jamie?"

"Eh? Oh, aye."

Auntie Claire had left a jug of water close to hand. There was the comfortable sound of glugging liquid, and then the rim of a pottery cup held to his mouth, his uncle's hand at his back to keep him upright. He didn't need it, but didn't object; the touch was warm and comforting. He hadn't realized how chilled he was from the night air, and shivered briefly.

"All right, laddie?" Uncle Jamie murmured, his hand tightening on Ian's shoulder.

"Aye, fine. Uncle Jamie?"

"Mphm?"

"Did Auntie Claire tell ye about—about a war? One coming, I mean. With England."

There was a moment's silence, his uncle's big form gone still against the light from the door.

"She has," he said, and took away his hand. "Did she tell you?"

"No, Cousin Brianna did." He lay down on his side, careful of his tender head. "D'ye believe them?"

There was no hesitation this time.

"Aye, I do." It was said with his uncle's usual dry matter-of-factness, but something in it prickled the hairs on the back of Ian's neck.

"Oh. Well, then."

The goose-down pillow was soft under his cheek, and smelled of lavender. His uncle's hand touched his head, smoothed the ruffled hair back from his face.

"Dinna fash yourself about it, Ian," he said softly. "There's time, yet."

He picked up the gun and left. From where he lay, Ian could see across the dooryard and above the trees where they dropped from the edge of the Ridge, past the slope of Black Mountain, and on into the black sky beyond, thick with stars.

He heard the back door open, and Mrs. Bug's voice, rising high above the others.

"They're no to hame, sir," she was saying, breathless. "And the hoose is dark, no fire in the hearth. Wherever might they go, this time o' night?"

He wondered dimly who was gone, but it didn't seem to matter much. If it was trouble, Uncle Jamie would deal with it. The thought was comforting; he felt like a small boy, safe in bed, hearing his father's voice outside, talking to a tenant in the cold dark of a Highland dawn.

Warmth spread slowly over him beneath the quilt, and he slept.

The moon was beginning to rise when they set out, and a good thing, too, Brianna thought. Even with the big, lopsided gold orb sailing up out of a cradle of stars and shedding its borrowed radiance over the sky, the trail beneath their feet was invisible. So were their feet, drowned in the absolute black of the forest at night.

Black, but not quiet. The giant trees rustled overhead, small things squealed and snuffled in the dark, and now and then the silent flutter of a bat passed close enough to startle her, as though part of the night had suddenly come loose and taken wing under her nose.

"The Minister's Cat is an apprehensive cat?" Roger suggested, as she gasped and clutched at him in the wake of one such leather-winged visitation.

"The Minister's Cat is an . . . appreciative cat," she replied, squeezing his hand. "Thank you." They'd likely end up sleeping on their cloaks in front of the McGillivrays' fire, instead of cozily tucked up in their own bed—but at least they'd have Jemmy.

He squeezed back, his hand bigger and stronger than hers, very reassuring in the dark.

"It's all right," he said. "I want him, too. It's a night to have your family all together, safe in one place."

She made a small sound in her throat, acknowledgment and appreciation, but wanted to keep up the conversation, as much to keep the sense of connection with him as because it would keep the dark at bay.

"The Minister's Cat was a very eloquent cat," she said delicately. "At the—the funeral, I mean. For those poor people."

Roger snorted; she saw the brief curl of his breath, white on the air.

"The Minister's Cat was a highly embarrassed cat," he said. "Your father!"

She smiled, since he couldn't see her.

"You did really well," she said mildly.

"Mmphm," he said, with another brief snort. "As for eloquence . . . if there was any, it was none of mine. All I did was quote bits of some psalm—I couldna even tell ye which it was."

"It didn't matter. Why did you pick—what you said, though?" she asked, curious. "I sort of thought you'd say the Lord's Prayer, or maybe the Twenty-Third Psalm—everybody knows that one."

"I thought I would, too," he admitted. "I meant to. But when I came to it . . ." He hesitated, and she saw in memory those raw, cold mounds, and shivered, smelling soot. He tightened his grasp on her hand, and drew her closer, tucking the hand into the crook of his elbow.

"I don't know," he said gruffly. "It just seemed—more suitable, somehow."

"It was," she said quietly, but didn't pursue the subject, choosing instead to steer the conversation into a discussion of her latest engineering project, a hand pump to raise water from the well.

"If I had something to use for pipe, I could get water into the house, easy as anything! I've already got most of the wood I need for a nice cistern, if I can get Ronnie to cooper it for me—so we can shower with rainwater, at least. But hollowing out tree limbs"—the method employed for the small amount of piping used for the pump—"it would take me months to manage enough just to get from the well to the house, let alone the stream. And there's not a chance of getting any rolled copper. Even if we could afford any, which we can't, bringing it up from Wilmington would be—" She threw her free hand up in frustration at the monumental nature of the undertaking.

He considered that for a bit, the chuff of their shoes on the rocky trail a comforting rhythm.

"Well, the ancient Romans did it with concrete; the recipe's in Pliny."

"I know. But it takes a particular kind of sand, which we don't happen to have. Likewise, quicklime, which we likewise don't have. And—"

"Aye, but what about clay?" he interrupted. "Did ye see that plate at Hilda's wedding? The big brown and red one, with the beautiful patterns?"

"Yes," she said. "Why?"

"Ute McGillivray said someone from Salem brought it. I dinna recall the name, but she said he was quite the big noise in potting—or whatever ye call making dishes."

"I'll bet you any amount of money she didn't say that!"

"Well, words to that effect." He went on, undeterred. "The point being that he made it *here;* it wasn't something he'd brought from Germany. So there's clay about that's suitable for firing, eh?"

"Oh, I *see.* Hmm. Well, now, that's an idea, isn't it?"

It was, and an attractive one whose discussion occupied them for most of the rest of the journey.

They had come down off the Ridge and were within a quarter-mile of the McGillivrays' place when she began to have an uneasy feeling down the back of her neck. It *could* be only imagination; after the sights they had seen in that deserted hollow, the dark air of the wood seemed thick with threat, and she had been imagining ambush at every blind bend, tensing with the anticipation of attack.

Then she heard something crack in the trees to her right—a small dry branch breaking, in a way that neither wind nor animal would break it. Real danger had its own taste, vivid as lemon juice, by contrast with the weak lemonade of imagination.

Her hand tightened on Roger's arm in warning, and he stopped at once.

"What?" he whispered, hand on his knife. "Where?" He hadn't heard it.

Damn, why hadn't she brought her gun, or at least her own dirk? All she had was her Swiss Army knife, carried always in her pocket—and what weapons the landscape offered.

She leaned into Roger, pointing, her hand close to his body to be sure he followed the direction of her gesture. Then she stooped, feeling about in the darkness for a rock, or a stick to use as a club.

"Keep talking," she whispered.

"The Minister's Cat is a fraidy cat, is she?" he said, his tone one of fairly convincing teasing.

"The Minister's Cat is a *ferocious* cat," she replied, trying to match his bantering tone, meanwhile fumbling one-handed in her pocket. Her other hand closed on a stone, and she pulled it free of the clinging dirt, cold and heavy in her palm. She rose, all her senses focused on the darkness to their right. "She'll freaking disembowel anything that—"

"Oh, it's you," said a voice in the woods behind her.

She shrieked, and Roger jerked in reflex, spun on his heel to face the threat, grabbed her and thrust her behind him, all in the same motion.

The push sent her staggering backward. She caught a heel in a hidden root in the dark, and fell, landing hard on her backside, from which position she had an excellent view of Roger in the moonlight, knife in hand, charging into the trees with an incoherent roar.

Belatedly, she registered what the voice had said, as well as the unmistakable tone of disappointment in it. A very similar voice, loud with alarm, spoke from the wood on the right.

"Jo?" it said. "What? Jo, what?"

There was a lot of thrashing and yelling going on in the woods to the left. Roger'd got his hands on someone.

"Roger!" she shouted. "Roger, stop! It's the Beardsleys!"

She'd dropped the rock when she fell, and now got to her feet, rubbing the dirt from her hand on the side of her skirt. Her heart was still pounding, her left buttock was bruised, and her urge to laugh was tinged with a strong desire to strangle one or both of the Beardsley twins.

"Kezzie Beardsley, come out of there!" she bellowed, then repeated it, even louder. Kezzie's hearing had improved after her mother had removed his chronically infected tonsils and adenoids, but he was still rather deaf.

A loud rustling in the brush yielded the slight form of Keziah Beardsley, dark-haired, white-faced, and armed with a large club, which he swung off his shoulder and tried abashedly to hide behind him when he saw her.

Meanwhile, much louder rustling and a certain amount of cursing behind her portended the emergence of Roger, gripping the scrawny neck of Josiah Beardsley, Kezzie's twin.

"What in the name of God d'ye wee bastards think ye're up to?" Roger said, shoving Jo across to stand by his brother in a patch of moonlight. "D'ye realize I nearly killed you?"

There was just enough light for Brianna to make out the rather cynical expression that crossed Jo's face at this, before it was erased and replaced with one of earnest apology.

"We're that sorry, Mr. Mac. We heard someone coming, and thought it might be brigands."

"Brigands," Brianna repeated, feeling the urge to laugh rising, but keeping it firmly in check. "Where on earth did you get that word?"

"Oh." Jo looked at his feet, hands clasped behind his back. "Miss Lizzie was a-readin' to us, from that book what Mr. Jamie brought. 'Twas in there. About brigands."

"I see." She glanced at Roger, who met her eye, his annoyance obviously waning into amusement, as well. *"The Pirate Gow,"* she explained. "Defoe."

"Oh, aye." Roger sheathed his dirk. "And why, exactly, did ye think there might be brigands coming?"

Kezzie, with the quirks of his erratic hearing, picked that up and answered, as earnestly as his brother, though his voice was louder and slightly flat, the result of his early deafness.

"We come across Mr. Lindsay, sir, on his way home, and he did tell us what passed, up by Dutchman's Creek. It's true, so, what he said? They was all burned to cinders?"

"They were all dead." Roger's voice had lost any tinge of amusement. "What's that to do with you lot lurking in the woods with clubs?"

"Well, you see, sir, McGillivrays' is a fine, big place, what with the cooper's shop and the new house and all, and being on a road, like—well, if *I* was a brigand, sir, 'tis just the sort of place I might choose," replied Jo.

"And Miss Lizzie's there, with her Pap. And your son, Mr. Mac," Kezzie added pointedly. "Shouldn't want no harm to come to 'em."

"I see." Roger smiled a little crookedly. "Well, thanks to ye, then, for the kind thought. I doubt the brigands will be anywhere near, though; Dutchman's Creek is a long way away."

"Aye, sir," Jo agreed. "But brigands might be anywhere, mightn't they?"

This was undeniable, and sufficiently true as to give Brianna a renewed feeling of chill in the pit of the stomach.

"They might be, but they aren't," Roger assured them. "Come along to the house with us, aye? We're just going to collect wee Jem. I'm sure *Frau* Ute would give ye a bed by the fire."

The Beardsleys exchanged inscrutable looks. They were nearly identical—small and lithe, with thick dark hair, distinguished only by Kezzie's deafness and the round scar on Jo's thumb—and to see the two fine-boned faces wearing precisely the same expression was a little unnerving.

Whatever information had been exchanged by that look, it had evidently included as much consultation as was required, for Kezzie nodded slightly, deferring to his brother.

"Ah, no, sir," Josiah said politely. "We'll bide, I think." And with no further talk, the two of them turned and crunched off into the dark, scuffling leaves and rocks as they went.

"Jo! Wait!" Brianna called after them, her hand having found something else in the bottom of her pocket.

"Aye, ma'am?" Josiah was back, appearing by her elbow with unsettling abruptness. His twin was no stalker, but Jo was.

"Oh! I mean, oh, there you are." She took a deep breath to slow her heart, and handed him the carved whistle she'd made for Germain. "Here. If you're going to stand guard, this might be helpful. To call for help, if someone *should* come."

Jo Beardsley had plainly never seen a whistle before, but didn't care to admit it. He turned the little object over in his hand, trying not to stare at it.

Roger reached out, took it from him, and blew a healthy blast that shattered the night. Several birds, startled from their rest, shot out of the nearby trees, shrieking, followed closely by Kezzie Beardsley, eyes huge with amazement.

"Blow in that end," Roger said, tapping the appropriate end of the whistle before handing it back. "Squeeze your lips a bit."

"Much obliged, sir," Jo murmured. His normal stoic facade had shattered with the silence, and he took the whistle with the wide-eyed look of a boy on Christmas morning, turning at once to show the prize to his twin. It struck her quite suddenly that neither boy likely ever *had* had a Christmas morning—or any other sort of gift.

"I'll make another one for you," she told Kezzie. "Then the two of you can signal back and forth. If you see any brigands," she added, smiling.

"Oh, yes, ma'am. We'll do that, we surely will!" he assured her, scarcely glancing at her in his eagerness to examine the whistle his brother had put in his hands.

"Blow it three times, if ye want help," Roger called after them, taking her arm.

"Aye, sir!" came back from the darkness, followed by a belated faint "Thank you, ma'am!"—this in turn followed at once by a fusillade of puffs, gasps, and breathless rattles, punctuated by briefly successful shrill toots.

"Lizzie's been teaching them manners, I see," Roger said. "As well as their letters. D'ye think they'll ever be truly civilized, though?"

"No," she said, with a trace of regret.

"Really?" She couldn't see his face in the dark, but heard the surprise in his voice. "I was only joking. Ye really think not?"

"I do—and no wonder, after the way they grew up. Did you see the way they were with that whistle? No one's ever given them a present, or a toy."

"I suppose not. D'ye think that's what makes boys civilized? If so, I imagine wee Jem will be a philosopher or an artist or something. Mrs. Bug spoils him rotten."

"Oh, as if you don't," she said tolerantly. "And Da, and Lizzie, and Mama, and everyone else in sight."

"Oh, well," Roger said, unembarrassed at the accusation. "Wait 'til he has a bit of competition. Germain's in no danger of spoiling, is he?" Germain, Fergus and Marsali's eldest son, was harried by two small sisters, known to one and all as the hell-kittens, who followed their brother constantly, teasing and pestering.

She laughed, but felt a slight sense of uneasiness. The thought of another baby always made her feel as though she were perched at the top of a roller coaster, short of breath and stomach clenched, poised somewhere between excitement and terror. Particularly now, with the memory of their lovemaking still softly heavy, shifting like mercury in her belly.

Roger seemed to sense her ambivalence, for he didn't pursue the subject, but reached for her hand and held it, his own large and warm. The air was cold, the last vestiges of a winter chill lingering in the hollows.

"What about Fergus, then?" he asked, taking up an earlier thread of the conversation. "From what I hear, he hadn't much of a childhood, either, but he seems fairly civilized."

"My aunt Jenny had the raising of him from the time he was ten," she objected. "You haven't met my aunt Jenny, but believe me, she could have civilized Adolf Hitler, if she put her mind to it. Besides, Fergus grew up in Paris, not the backwoods—even if it *was* in a brothel. And it sounds like it was a pretty high-class brothel, too, from what Marsali tells me."

"Oh, aye? What does she tell you?"

"Oh, just stories that he's told her, now and then. About the clients, and the wh—the girls."

"Can ye not say 'whore,' then?" he asked, amused. She felt the blood rise in her cheeks, and was pleased that it was dark; he teased her more when she blushed.

"I can't help it that I went to a Catholic school," she said, defensive. "Early conditioning." It was true; she couldn't say certain words, save when in the grip of fury or when mentally prepared.

"Why can you, though? You'd think a preacher's lad would have the same problem."

He laughed, a little wryly.

"Not precisely the same problem. It was more a matter of feeling obliged to curse and carry on in front of my friends, to prove I could."

"What kind of carrying on?" she asked, scenting a story. He didn't often talk about his early life in Inverness, adopted by his great-uncle, a Presbyterian minister, but she loved hearing the small tidbits he sometimes let fall.

"Och. Smoking, drinking beer, and writing filthy words on the walls in the boys' toilet," he said, the smile evident in his voice. "Tipping over dustbins. Letting air out of automobile tires. Stealing sweeties from the Post Office. Quite the wee criminal I was, for a time."

"The terror of Inverness, huh? Did you have a gang?" she teased.

"I did," he said, and laughed. "Gerry MacMillan, Bobby Cawdor, and Dougie Buchanan. I was odd man out, not only for being the preacher's lad, but for having an English father and an English name. So I was always out to show them I was a hard man. Meaning I was usually the one in most trouble."

"I had no idea you were a juvenile delinquent," she said, charmed at the thought.

"Well, not for long," he assured her wryly. "Come the summer I was fifteen, the Reverend signed me up on a fishing boat, and sent me to sea with the herring fleet. Couldna just say whether he did it to improve my character, keep me out of jail, or only because he couldn't stand me round the house any longer, but it did work. Ye want to meet hard men sometime, go to sea with a bunch of Gaelic fishermen."

"I'll remember that," she said, trying not to giggle and producing a series of small, wet snorts instead. "Did your friends end up in jail, then, or did they go straight, without you to mislead them?"

"Dougie joined the army," he said, a tinge of wistfulness in his voice. "Gerry took over his dad's shop—his dad was a tobacconist. Bobby . . . aye, well, Bobby's dead. Drowned, that same summer, out lobstering with his cousin off Oban."

She leaned closer to him and squeezed his hand, her shoulder brushing his in sympathy.

"I'm sorry," she said, then paused. "Only . . . he isn't dead, is he? Not yet. Not now."

Roger shook his head, and made a small sound of mingled humor and dismay.

"Is that a comfort?" she asked. "Or is it horrible to think about?"

She wanted to keep him talking; he hadn't talked so much in one go since the hanging that had taken his singing voice. Being forced to speak in public made him self-conscious, and his throat tightened. His voice was still rasping, but relaxed as he was now, he wasn't choking or coughing.

"Both," he said, and made the sound again. "I'll never see him again, either way." He shrugged slightly, pushing the thought away. "D'ye think of your old friends much?"

"No, not much," she said softly. The trail narrowed here, and she linked her arm in his, drawing close as they approached the last turn, which would bring them in sight of the McGillivrays'. "There's too much here." But she didn't want to talk about what *wasn't* here.

"Do you think Jo and Kezzie are just playing?" she asked. "Or are they up to something?"

"What should they be up to?" he asked, accepting her change of subject without comment. "I canna think they're lying in wait to commit highway robbery—not at this time of night."

"Oh, I believe them about standing guard," she said. "They'd do anything to protect Lizzie. Only—" She paused. They had come out of the forest onto the wagon road; the far verge fell away in a steep bank, looking at night like a bottomless pool of black velvet—by daylight, it would be a tangled mass of fallen snags, clumps of rhododendron, redbud, and dogwood, overgrown with the snarls of ancient grapevines and creepers. The road made a switchback further on and curved back on itself, arriving gently at the McGillivrays' place, a hundred feet below.

"The lights are still on," she said with some surprise. The small group of buildings—the Old Place, the New Place, Ronnie Sinclair's cooper's shop, Dai Jones's blacksmith's forge and cabin—were mostly dark, but the lower windows of the McGillivrays' New Place were striped with light, leaking through the cracks of the shutters, and a bonfire in front of the house made a brilliant blot of light against the dark.

"Kenny Lindsay," Roger said matter-of-factly. "The Beardsleys said they'd met him. He'll have stopped to share the news."

"Mm. We'd better be careful, then; if they're looking out for brigands, too, they might shoot at anything that moves."

"Not tonight; it's a party, remember? What were ye saying, though, about the Beardsley boys protecting Lizzie?"

"Oh." Her toe stubbed against some hidden obstacle, and she clutched his arm to keep from falling. "Oof! Only that I wasn't sure who they thought they were protecting her from."

Roger tightened his grip on her arm in reflex.

"Whatever d'ye mean by that?"

"Just that if I were Manfred McGillivray, I'd take good care to be nice to Lizzie. Mama says the Beardsleys follow her around like dogs, but they don't. They follow her like tame wolves."

"I thought Ian said it wasn't possible to tame wolves."

"It isn't," she said tersely. "Come on, let's hurry, before they smoor the fire."

The big log house was literally overflowing with people. Light spilled from the open door and glowed in the row of tiny arrow-slit windows that marched across the front of the house, and dark forms wove in and out of the bonfire's light. The sounds of a fiddle came to them, thin and sweet through the dark, borne on the wind with the scent of roasting meat.

"I suppose Senga's truly made her choice, then," Roger said, taking her arm for the final steep descent to the crossroad. "Who d'ye bet it is? Ronnie Sinclair or the German lad?"

"Oh, a bet? What are the stakes? Woops!" She stumbled, tripping on a half-buried rock in the path, but Roger tightened his grip, keeping her upright.

"Loser sets the pantry to rights," he suggested.

"Deal," she said promptly. "I think she chose Heinrich."

"Aye? Well, ye may be right," he said, sounding amused. "But I have to tell you, it was five to three in favor of Ronnie, last I heard. *Frau* Ute's a force to be reckoned with."

"She is," Brianna admitted. "And if it was Hilda or Inga, I'd say it was no contest. But Senga's got her mother's personality; nobody's telling *her* what to do—not even *Frau* Ute.

"Where did they get 'Senga,' anyway?" she added. "There are lots of Ingas and Hildas over toward Salem, but I've never heard of another Senga."

"Ah, well, ye wouldn't—not in Salem. It's not a German name, ken—it's Scots."

"Scots?" she said in astonishment.

"Oh, aye," he said, the grin evident in his voice. "It's Agnes, spelt backward. A girl named that is bound to be contrary, don't ye think?"

"You're kidding! Agnes, spelled backward?"

"I wouldna say it's common, exactly, but I've certainly met one or two Sengas in Scotland."

She laughed.

"Do the Scots do that with any other names?"

"Back-spelling?" He considered. "Well, I did go to school with a lass named Adnil, and there was a grocer's lad who got in the messages for old ladies in the neighborhood—his name's pronounced 'Kirry,' but it's spelt 'C-i-r-e.'"

She looked sharply at him, in case he was teasing, but he wasn't. She shook her head.

"I think Mama's right about Scots. So yours spelled backward would be—"

"Regor," he confirmed. "Sounds like something from a Godzilla film, doesn't it? A giant eel, maybe, or a beetle with death-ray eyes." He sounded pleased at the notion.

"You thought about it, didn't you?" she said, laughing. "Which would you rather be?"

"Well, when I was a kid, I thought the beetle with the death-ray eyes would be best," he admitted. "Then I went to sea and started hauling up the occasional Moray eel in my net. Those are not the kind of thing ye'd want to meet in a dark alley, believe me."

"More agile than Godzilla, at least," she said, shuddering slightly at the recollection of the one Moray eel she'd met personally. A four-foot length of spring steel and rubber, fast as lightning and equipped with a mouthful of razors, it had come up from the hold of a fishing boat she'd watched being unloaded in a little port town called MacDuff.

She and Roger had been leaning on a low rock wall, idly watching the gulls hover in the wind, when a shout of alarm from the fishing boat just below had made them look down in time to see fishermen scrambling back from something on deck.

A dark sine wave had flashed through the silver wash of fish on deck, shot under the rail, and landed on the wet stones of the quay, where it had caused similar panic among the fishermen hosing down their gear, writhing and lashing about like a crazed high-tension cable until one rubber-booted man, gathering his self-possession, had rushed up and kicked it back into the water.

"Well, they're no really bad sorts, eels," Roger said judiciously, evidently recalling the same memory. "Ye canna blame them, after all; being dragged up from the bottom of the sea without warning—anyone would thrash about a bit."

"So they would," she said, thinking of themselves. She took his hand, threading her fingers between his, and found his firm, cold grip a comfort.

They were close enough now to catch snatches of laughter and talk, billowing up into the cold night with the smoke of the fire. There were children running loose; she saw two small forms dart through the legs of the crowd around the fire, black and thin-limbed as Halloween goblins.

That wasn't Jem, surely? No, he was smaller, and surely Lizzie wouldn't—

"Mej," Roger said.

"What?"

"Jem, backward," he explained. "I was just thinking it would be a lot of fun to see Godzilla films with him. Maybe he'd like to be the beetle with death-ray eyes. Be fun, aye?"

He sounded so wistful that a lump came to her throat, and she squeezed his hand hard, then swallowed.

"Tell him Godzilla stories," she said firmly. "It's make-believe anyway. I'll draw him pictures."

He laughed at that.

"Christ, you do, and they'll be stoning ye for trafficking with the devil, Bree. Godzilla looks like something straight out of the Book of Revelation—or so I was told."

"Who told you that?"

"Eigger."

"Who . . . oh," she said, going into mental reverse. "Reggie? Who's Reggie?"

"The Reverend." His great-uncle, his adoptive father. There was still a smile in his voice, but one tinged with nostalgia. "When we went to the monster films together of a Saturday. Eigger and Regor—and ye should have seen the looks on the faces of the Ladies' Altar and Tea Society, when Mrs. Graham let them in without announcing them, and they came into the Reverend's study to find us stamping round and roaring, kicking hell out of a Tokyo built of blocks and soup tins."

She laughed, but felt tears prick at the backs of her eyes.

"I wish I'd known the Reverend," she said, squeezing his hand.

"I wish ye had, too," he said softly. "He would have liked ye so much, Bree."

For the space of a few moments, while he talked, the dark forest and the flaming fire below had faded away; they were in Inverness, cozy in the Reverend's study, with rain on the windows and the sound of traffic going by in the street. It happened so often when they talked like this, between themselves. Then some small thing would fracture the moment—now, it was a shout from the fire as people began to clap and sing—and the world of their own time vanished in an instant.

What if he were gone, she thought suddenly. Could I bring it back, all by myself?

A spasm of elemental panic gripped her, just for a moment, at the thought. Without Roger as her touchstone, with nothing but her own memories to serve as anchor to the future, that time would be lost. Would fade into hazy dreams, and be lost, leaving her no firm ground of reality to stand upon.

She took a deep breath of the cold night air, crisp with woodsmoke, and dug the balls of her feet hard into the ground as they walked, trying to feel solid.

"MamaMamaMAMA!" A small blob detached itself from the confusion round the fire and rocketed toward her, crashing into her knees with enough force to make her grab hold of Roger's arm.

"Jem! There you are!" She scooped him up and buried her face in his hair, which smelled pleasantly of goats, hay, and spicy sausage. He was heavy, and more than solid.

Then Ute McGillivray turned and saw them. Her broad face was creased in a frown, but broke into a beam of delight at seeing them. People turned at her call of greeting, and they were engulfed at once

by the crowd, everyone asking questions, expressing gratified surprise at their coming.

A few questions were asked about the Dutch family, but
Kenny Lindsay had brought the news of the burning earlier;
Brianna was glad of that. People clucked and shook their heads,
but by now they had exhausted most of their horrified speculations, and were turning to other matters. The cold of the graves
beneath the fir trees still lingered as a faint chill on her heart;
she had no wish to make *that* experience real again by talking
about it.

The newly engaged couple were seated together on a pair of
upturned buckets, holding hands, faces blissful in the glow of the
bonfire.

"I win," Brianna said, smiling at sight of them. "Don't they
look happy?"

"They do," Roger agreed. "I doubt Ronnie Sinclair is. Is he
here?" He glanced round, and so did she, but the cooper was
nowhere in sight.

"Wait—he's in his shop," she said, putting a hand on Roger's
wrist and nodding toward the small building on the opposite side
of the road. There were no windows on this side of the cooper's
shop, but a faint glow showed round the edge of the closed door.

Roger glanced from the darkened shop to the convivial crowd
round the fire; a good many of Ute's relations had ridden over
with the lucky bridegroom and his friends from Salem, bringing
with them an immense barrel of black beer, which was adding to
the festivities. The air was yeasty with the tang of hops.

By contrast, the cooper's shop had a desolate, glowering sort of
air about it. She wondered whether anyone around the fire had yet
missed Ronnie Sinclair.

"I'll go and have a bit of a blether with him, aye?" Roger
touched her back in brief affection. "He could maybe use a sympathetic ear."

"That and a stiff drink?" She nodded toward the house, where
Robin McGillivray was visible through the open door, pouring
what she assumed to be whisky for a select circle of friends.

"I imagine he will have managed that for himself," Roger
replied dryly. He left her, making his way around the convivial
group by the fire. He disappeared in the dark, but then she saw the
door of the cooper's shop open, and Roger silhouetted briefly

against the glow from within, his tall form blocking the light before vanishing inside.

"Wanna drink, Mama!" Jemmy was wriggling like a tadpole, trying to get down. She set him on the ground, and he was off like a shot, nearly upsetting a stout lady with a platter of corn fritters.

The aroma of the steaming fritters reminded her that she hadn't had any supper, and she made her way after Jemmy to the table of food, where Lizzie, in her role as almost-daughter-of-the-house, helped her importantly to sauerkraut, sausages, smoked eggs, and something involving corn and squash.

"Where's *your* sweetheart, Lizzie?" she asked, teasing. "Shouldn't you be spooning with him?"

"Oh, him?" Lizzie looked like someone recalling a thing of vague general interest, but no immediate importance. "Manfred, ye mean? He's . . . ower there." She squinted against the glow of the fire, then pointed with her serving spoon. Manfred McGillivray, her own betrothed, was with three or four other young men, all with arms linked, swaying to and fro as they sang something in German. They appeared to have trouble remembering the words, as each verse dissolved into giggles and shoving accusations.

"Here, *Schätzchen*—that's 'sweetheart,' ken, in German," Lizzie explained, leaning down to give Jemmy a bite of sausage. He snapped the tidbit up like a starving seal and chewed industriously, then mumbled, "Wagga gink," and wandered off into the night.

"Jem!" Brianna made to go after him, but was hampered by an oncoming crowd headed for the table.

"Ah, dinna fash yourself about him," Lizzie assured her. "Everyone kens who he is; he'll come to nay harm."

She might still have gone after him, save that she saw a small blond head pop up beside Jem's. Germain, Jem's bosom friend. Germain was two years older, and had a great deal more worldly knowledge than the average five-year-old, thanks in great part to his father's tutelage. She did hope he wasn't picking pockets in the crowd, and made a mental note to frisk him for contraband, later.

Germain had Jem firmly by the hand, so she allowed herself to be persuaded to sit down with Lizzie, Inga, and Hilda, on the bales of straw that had been placed a little way from the fire.

"Und where's *your* sweetheart, then?" teased Hilda. "Yon big bonny black devil?"

"Oh, him?" Brianna said, mimicking Lizzie, and they all broke into rather unladylike roars of laughter; evidently the beer had been making the rounds for some time.

"He's comforting Ronnie," she said, with a nod toward the darkened cooper's shop. "Is your mother upset about Senga's choice?"

"Och, aye," said Inga, rolling her eyes with great expressiveness. "Should ha' heard them at it, her and Senga. Hammer and tongs, hammer and tongs. Da went out to the fishing, and stayed awa' three days."

Brianna ducked her head to hide a grin. Robin McGillivray liked a peaceful life, something he was never likely to enjoy in the company of his wife and daughters.

"Ah, well," Hilda said philosophically, leaning back a little to ease the strain of her first pregnancy, which was well advanced. "She couldna really say so much, *meine Mutter.* Heinrich's her own cousin's son, after all. Even if he *is* poor."

"But young," Inga added practically. "Da says Heinrich will have time to get rich." Ronnie Sinclair wasn't precisely rich— and he *was* thirty years older than Senga. On the other hand, he did own both his cooper's shop and half of the house in which he and the McGillivrays lived. And Ute, having shepherded both her elder daughters to solid marriages with men of property, had obviously seen the advantages of a match between Senga and Ronnie.

"I can see that it might be a little awkward," Brianna said tactfully. "Ronnie going on living with your family, after—" She nodded at the betrothed couple, who were feeding each other bits of cake.

"Hoo!" Hilda exclaimed, rolling her eyes. "I'm that glad not to be living here!"

Inga nodded vigorous agreement, but added, "Well, but *Mutti* isna the one to be greetin' over spilt milk. She's got an eye out for a wife for Ronnie. Just watch her." She nodded toward the food table, where Ute was chatting and smiling with a group of German women.

"Who d'ye think it is she has picked out?" Inga asked her sister, eyes narrowed as she watched her mother operate. "That wee

Gretchen? Or your Archie's cousin, maybe? The walleyed one—Seona?"

Hilda, married to a Scot from Surry County, shook her head at this.

"She'll want a German girl," she objected. "For she'll be thinkin' of what will happen if Ronnie dies, and the wife marries again. If it's a German girl, chances are Mama can bully her into a new marriage with one of her nephews or cousins—keep the property in the family, aye?"

Brianna listened with fascination as the girls discussed the situation, with perfect matter-of-factness—and wondered whether Ronnie Sinclair had the slightest idea that his fate was being decided in this pragmatic fashion. But he'd been living with the McGillivrays for more than a year, she reasoned; he must have some idea of Ute's methods.

Thanking God silently that she was not herself compelled to live in the same house with the redoubtable *Frau* McGillivray, she looked round for Lizzie, feeling a pang of sympathy for her erstwhile bondmaid. Lizzie *would* be living with Ute, once her marriage to Manfred took place next year.

Hearing the name "Wemyss," she returned to the conversation at hand, only to discover that the girls were not discussing Lizzie, but rather her father.

"Auntie Gertrud," declared Hilda, and belched softly, fist to her mouth. "She's a widow-woman herself; she'd be the best for him."

"Auntie Gertrud would have poor wee Mr. Wemyss dead in a year," Inga objected, laughing. "She's twice his size. If she didna kill him from exhaustion, she'd roll over in her sleep and squash him flat."

Hilda clapped both hands to her mouth, but less in shock than to stifle her giggles. Brianna thought she'd had her share of beer, too; her cap was awry and her pale face looked flushed, even by firelight.

"Aye, weel, I think he's no much bothered at the thought. See him?" Hilda nodded past the beer-drinkers, and Brianna had no trouble picking out Mr. Wemyss's head, his hair pale and flyaway as his daughter's. He was in animated conversation with a stout woman in apron and cap, who nudged him intimately in the ribs, laughing.

As she watched, though, Ute McGillivray made her way toward them, followed by a tall blond woman, who hesitated a little, hands folded under her apron.

"Oh, who's that?" Inga craned her neck like a goose, and her sister elbowed her, scandalized.

"Lass das, du alte Ziege! Mutti's looking this way!"

Lizzie had half-risen to her knees, peering.

"Who—?" she said, sounding like an owl. Her attention was momentarily distracted by Manfred, who dropped beside her in the straw, grinning amiably.

"How is it, then, *Herzchen*?" he said, putting an arm round her waist and trying to kiss her.

"Who's that, Freddie?" she said, adroitly eluding his embrace and pointing discreetly toward the blond woman, who was smiling shyly as *Frau* Ute introduced her to Mr. Wemyss.

Manfred blinked, swaying a little on his knees, but answered readily enough.

"Oh. That's *Fraulein* Berrisch. Pastor Berrisch's sister."

Inga and Hilda made little cooing sounds of interest; Lizzie frowned a little, but then relaxed, seeing her father tilt back his head to address the newcomer; *Fraulein* Berrisch was nearly as tall as Brianna herself.

Well, that explains why she's still a Fraulein, Brianna thought with sympathy. The woman's hair was streaked with gray, where it showed beneath her cap, and she had a rather plain face, though her eyes held a calm sweetness.

"Oh, a Protestant, then," Lizzie said, in a dismissive tone that made it clear that the *Fraulein* could hardly be considered as a potential mate for her father.

"Aye, but she's a nice woman, for a' that. Come and dance, Elizabeth." Manfred had clearly lost any interest in Mr. Wemyss and the *Fraulein;* he pulled Lizzie, protesting, to her feet, and propelled her toward the circle of dancers. She went reluctantly, but Brianna saw that by the time they had reached the dance, Lizzie was laughing at something Manfred had said, and he was smiling down at her, the firelight glowing on the handsome planes of his face. They were a nice-looking couple, she thought, better-matched in appearance than Senga and her Heinrich—who was tall, but spindly and rather hatchet-faced.

Inga and Hilda had begun arguing with each other in German, allowing Brianna to devote herself to the wholehearted consumption of the excellent supper. Hungry as she was, she would have enjoyed almost anything, but the tart, crisp sauerkraut and the sausages, bursting with juice and spices, were a rare treat.

It was only as she wiped the last of the juice and grease from her wooden plate with a chunk of corn bread that she cast a glance at the cooper's shop, thinking guiltily that she ought perhaps to have saved some for Roger. He was so kind, taking thought for poor Ronnie's feelings. She felt a rush of pride and affection for him. Maybe she should go over there and rescue him.

She had put down her plate and was sorting out her skirts and petticoats, in preparation for putting this plan into action, when she was forestalled by a pair of small figures who came weaving out of the darkness.

"Jem?" she said, startled. "What's the matter?"

The flames gleamed on Jemmy's hair like freshly minted copper, but the face under it was white, and his eyes enormous dark pools, fixed and staring.

"Jemmy!"

He turned a blank face to her, said "Mama?" in a small, uncertain voice, then sat down suddenly, his legs collapsing under him like rubber bands.

She was dimly aware of Germain, swaying like a sapling in a high breeze, but had no attention to spare for him. She seized Jemmy, lifting his head and shaking him a little.

"Jemmy! Wake up! What's wrong?"

"The wee laddie's dead drunk, *a nighean*," said a voice above her, sounding amused. "Whatever have ye been givin' him?" Robin McGillivray, rather obviously a little the worse for wear himself, leaned over and prodded Jemmy gently, eliciting nothing more than a soft gurgle. He picked up one of Jemmy's arms, then let it go; it fell, boneless as a strand of boiled spaghetti.

"*I* didn't give him anything," she replied, panic giving way to a rising annoyance, as she saw that Jemmy was in fact merely asleep, his small chest rising and falling with a reassuring rhythm. "Germain!"

Germain had subsided into a small heap, and was singing "Alouette" to himself in a dreamy sort of way. Brianna had taught it to him; it was his favorite song.

"Germain! What did you give Jemmy to drink?"

"*. . . j'te plumerai la tete. . .*"

"*Germain!*" She grabbed him by the arm, and he ceased singing, looking surprised to see her.

"What did you give Jemmy, Germain?"

"He was thirsty, m'dame," Germain said, with a smile of surpassing sweetness. "He wanted a drink." Then his eyes rolled back in his head, and he keeled over backward, limp as a dead fish.

"Oh, Jesus Christ on a piece of *toast*!"

Inga and Hilda looked shocked, but she was in no mood to worry about their sensibilities.

"Where the bloody hell is Marsali?"

"She's no here," Inga said, bending forward to inspect Germain. "She stopped at hame wi' the wee *maedchen*. Fergus is . . ." She straightened up, looking vaguely round. "Well, I saw him a while ago."

"What's the trouble?" The hoarse voice at her shoulder surprised her, and she turned to find Roger looking quizzical, his face relaxed from its usual sternness.

"Your son is a drunkard," she informed him. Then she caught a whiff of Roger's breath. "Following in his father's footsteps, I see," she added coldly.

Disregarding this, Roger sat down beside her and gathered Jemmy up into his lap. Holding the little boy propped against his knees, he patted Jemmy's cheek, gently but insistently.

"Hallo there, Mej," he said softly. "Hallo, then. Ye're all right, are ye?"

Like magic, Jemmy's eyelids floated up. He smiled dreamily at Roger.

"Hallo, Daddy." Still smiling beatifically, his eyes closed and he relaxed into utter limpness, cheek flattened against his father's knee.

"He's all right," Roger told her.

"Well, good," she said, not particularly mollified. "What do you think they've been drinking? Beer?"

Roger leaned forward and sniffed at his offspring's red-stained lips.

"Cherry Bounce, at a guess. There's a vat of it, round by the barn."

"Holy God!" She'd never drunk Cherry Bounce, but Mrs. Bug had told her how to make it: *"Tak' the juice of a bushel o' cherries, dissolve twenty-four pound o' sugar ower it, then ye put it into a forty-gallon cask and fill it up wi' whisky."*

"He's all right." Roger patted her arm. "Is that Germain over there?"

"It is." She leaned over to check, but Germain was peacefully asleep, also smiling. "That Cherry Bounce must be good stuff."

Roger laughed.

"It's terrible. Like industrial-strength cough syrup. I will say it makes ye very cheerful, though."

"Have you been drinking it?" She eyed him narrowly, but his lips appeared to be their usual color.

"Of course not." He leaned over and kissed her, to prove it. "Surely ye dinna think a Scotsman like Ronnie would deal wi' disappointment by drinking Cherry Bounce? When there's decent whisky to hand?"

"True," she said. She glanced at the cooperage. The faint glow from the hearth fire had faded and the outline of the door had disappeared, leaving the building no more than a faint rectangle of black against the darker mass of the forest beyond. "How *is* Ronnie dealing with it?" She glanced round, but Inga and Hilda had taken themselves off to help *Frau* Ute; all of them were clustered round the food table, clearing things away.

"Oh, he's all right, Ronnie." Roger moved Jemmy off his lap, placing him gently on his side in the straw near Germain. "He wasna in love with Senga, after all. He's suffering from sexual frustration, not a broken heart."

"Oh, well, if that's all," she said dryly. "He won't have to suffer much longer; I'm informed that *Frau* Ute has the matter well in hand."

"Aye, she's told him she'll find him a wife. He's what ye might call philosophical about the matter. Though still reeking wi' lust," he added, wrinkling his nose.

"Ew. Do you want anything to eat?" She glanced at the little boys, getting her feet under her. "I'd better get you something before Ute and the girls clear it all away."

Roger yawned, suddenly and immensely.

"No, I'm all right." He blinked, smiling sleepily at her. "I'll go tell Fergus where Germain is, maybe snatch a bite on the way." He patted her shoulder, then stood up, swaying only a little, and moved off toward the fire.

She checked the boys again; both were breathing deeply and

regularly, dead to the world. With a sigh, she bundled them close together, piling up the straw around them, and covered them with her cloak. It was growing colder, but winter had gone; there was no feel of frost in the air.

The party was still going on, but it had shifted to a lower gear. The dancing had stopped and the crowd broken up into smaller groups, men gathered in a circle near the fire, lighting their pipes, the younger men disappeared somewhere. All around her, families were settling in for the night, making nests for themselves in the hay. Some were in the house, more in the barn; she could hear the sound of a guitar from somewhere behind the house, and a single voice, singing something slow and wistful. It made her yearn suddenly for the sound of Roger's voice as it had been, rich and tender.

Thinking of that, though, she realized something; his voice had been much better when he came back from consoling Ronnie. Still husky and with only a shadow of its former resonance—but it had come easily, without that choked note in it. Perhaps alcohol relaxed the vocal cords?

More likely, she thought, it simply relaxed Roger; removed some of his inhibitions about the way he sounded. That was worth knowing. Her mother had opined that his voice would improve, if he would stretch it, work with it, but he was shy of using it, wary of pain—whether from the actual sensation of speaking, or from the contrast with the way he had sounded before.

"So maybe I'll make a little Cherry Bounce," she said aloud. Then she looked at the two small forms slumbering in the hay, and contemplated the prospect of waking up alongside three hangovers, come morning. "Well, maybe not."

She bunched up enough hay for a pillow, spread her folded kerchief over it—they'd be picking hay out of their clothes most of tomorrow—and lay down, curling her body round Jem's. If either boy stirred or vomited in his sleep, she'd feel it and rouse.

The bonfire had burned down; only a ragged fringe of flames now flickered over the bed of glowing embers, and the lanterns set around the yard had all gone out or been thriftily extinguished. Guitar and singer had ceased. Without light and noise to keep it at bay, the night came in, spreading wings of cold silence over the mountain. The stars burned bright above, but they were pinpricks, millennia away. She closed her eyes against the immensity of the night, bowing to put her lips against Jem's head, cradling his warmth.

She tried to compose her mind for sleep, but without the distractions of company, and with the scent of burning timber strong in the air, memory stole back, and her normal prayers of blessing became pleas for mercy and protection.

"He hath put my brethren far from me, and mine acquaintance are verily estranged from me. My kinsfolk have failed, and my familiar friends have forgotten me."

I won't forget you, she said silently to the dead. It seemed so pitiful a thing to say—so small and futile. And yet the only thing in her power.

She shivered briefly, tightening her grip on Jemmy.

A sudden rustle of the hay, and Roger slid in behind her. He fumbled a bit, spreading his own cloak over her, then sighed with relief, his body relaxing heavily against hers as his arm came round her waist.

"Been a bloody long day, hasn't it?"

She groaned faintly in agreement. Now that everything was quiet, with no more need to talk, watch, pay attention, every fiber of her muscles seemed about to dissolve with fatigue. There was no more than a thin layer of hay between her and cold, hard ground, but she felt sleep lapping at her like the waves of the tide creeping up a sandy shore, soothing and inexorable.

"'Did you get something to eat?" She put a hand on his leg, and his arm tightened in reflex, holding her close.

"Aye, if ye think beer's food. Many folk do." He laughed, a warm fog of hops on his breath. "I'm fine." The warmth of his body was beginning to seep through the layers of cloth between them, dispelling the night's chill.

Jem always gave off heat when he slept; it was like holding a clay firepot, with him curled against her. Roger was putting out even more heat, though. Well, her mother did say that an alcohol lamp burned hotter than oil.

She sighed and snuggled back against him, feeling warm, protected. The cold immensity of the night had lifted, now that she had her family close, together again, and safe.

Roger was humming. She realized it quite suddenly. There was no tune to it, but she felt the vibration of his chest against her back. She didn't want to chance stopping him; surely that was good for his vocal cords. He stopped on his own, though, after a moment. Hoping to start him again, she reached back to stroke his leg, essaying a small questioning hum of her own.

"Hmmm-mmmm?"

His hands cupped her buttocks and fastened tight.

"Mmm-hmmm," he said, in what sounded like a combination of invitation and satisfaction.

She didn't reply, but made a slight dissentient motion of the behind. Under normal conditions, this would have caused him to let go. He *did* let go, but only with one hand, and this in order to slide it down her leg, evidently meaning to get hold of her skirt and ruckle it up.

She reached back hastily and grabbed the roving hand, bringing it round and placing it on her breast, as an indication that while she appreciated the notion and under other circumstances would be thrilled to oblige, just this moment she thought—

Roger was usually very good at reading her body language, but evidently this skill had dissolved in whisky. That, or—the thought came suddenly to her—he simply didn't *care* whether she wanted—

"Roger!" she hissed.

He *had* started humming again, the sound now interspersed with the low, bumping noises a teakettle makes, just before the boil. He'd got his hand down her leg and up her skirt, hot on the flesh of her thigh, groping swiftly upward—and inward. Jemmy coughed, jerking in her arms, and she made an attempt to kick Roger in the shin, as a signal of discouragement.

"God, you're beautiful," he murmured into the curve of her neck. "Oh, God, so beautiful. So beautiful . . . so . . . hmmm . . ." The next words were a mumble against her skin, but she *thought* he'd said "slippery." His fingers had reached their goal, and she arched her back, trying to squirm away.

"Roger," she said, keeping her voice low. "Roger, there are *people* around!" And a snoring toddler wedged like a doorstop in front of her.

He mumbled something in which the words "dark" and "nobody'll see" were distinguishable, and then the groping hand retreated—only to grab a handful of her skirts and start shoving them out of the way.

He had resumed the humming, pausing momentarily to murmur, "Love you, love you so much. . . ."

"I love you, too," she said, reaching back and trying to catch his hand. "Roger, *stop that!*"

He did, but immediately reached around her, and grasped her by the shoulder. A quick heave, and she was lying on her back staring up at the distant stars, which were at once blotted out by Roger's head and shoulders as he rolled on top of her in a tremendous rustling of hay and loosened clothing.

"Jem—" She flung out a hand toward Jemmy, who appeared not to have been disturbed by the sudden disappearance of his backstop, but was still curled up in the hay like a hibernating hedgehog.

Roger was, of all things, *singing* now, if one could call it that. Or chanting, at least, the words to a very bawdy Scottish song, about a miller who is pestered by a young woman wanting him to grind her corn. Whereupon he does.

"He flung her down upon the sacks, and there she got her corn ground, her corn ground. . . ." Roger was chanting hotly in her ear, his full weight pinning her to the ground and the stars spinning madly far above.

She'd thought his description of Ronnie as "reeking wi' lust" merely a figure of speech, but evidently not. Bare flesh met bare flesh, and then some. She gasped. So did Roger.

"Oh, God," he said. He paused, frozen for an instant against the sky above her, then sighed in an ecstasy of whisky fumes and began to move with her, humming. It *was* dark, thank God, though not nearly dark enough. The remnants of the fire cast an eerie glow over his face, and he looked for an instant the bonny big, black devil Inga had called him.

Lie back and enjoy it, she thought. The hay made a tremendous rustling—but there were other rustlings nearby, and the sound of the wind soughing through the trees in the cove was nearly enough to drown them all in sibilance.

She had managed to suppress her embarrassment and was indeed beginning to enjoy it, when Roger got his hands under her, lifting.

"Wrap your legs round me," he whispered, and nipped her earlobe with his teeth. "Wrap them round my back and hammer my arse wi' your heels."

Moved partly by an answering wantonness, and partly by a desire to squeeze the breath out of him like an accordion, she flung her legs apart and swung them high, scissoring them tight across his heaving back. He gave an ecstatic groan and redoubled his efforts. Wantonness was winning; she had nearly forgotten where they were.

Hanging on for dear life and thrilled by the ride, she arched her back and jerked, shuddering against the heat of him, the night wind's touch cool and electric on thighs and buttocks, bared to the dark. Trembling and moaning, she melted back against the hay, her legs still locked around his hips. Boneless and nerveless, she let her head roll to the side, and slowly, languidly, opened her eyes.

Someone was there; she saw movement in the dark, and froze. It was Fergus, come to fetch his son. She heard the murmur of his voice, speaking French to Germain, and the quiet rustle of his footsteps in the hay, moving off.

She lay still, heart pounding, legs still locked in place. Roger, meanwhile, had reached his own quietus. Head hanging so that his long hair brushed her face like cobwebs in the dark, he murmured, "Love you . . . God, I love you," and lowered himself, slowly and gently. Whereupon he breathed, "Thank you," in her ear and lapsed into warm half-consciousness on top of her, breathing heavily.

"Oh," she said, looking up to the peaceful stars. "Don't mention it." She unlocked her stiff legs, and with some difficulty, got herself and Roger disentangled, more or less covered, and restored to blessed anonymity in their hay-lined nest, Jemmy safely stowed between them.

"Hey," she said suddenly, and Roger stirred.

"Mm?"

"What sort of monster was Eigger?"

He laughed, and the sound was low and clear.

"Oh, Eigger was a giant sponge cake. With chocolate icing. He'd fall on the other monsters, and smother them wi' sweetness." He laughed again, hiccuped, and subsided in the hay.

"Roger?" she said softly, a moment later. There was no answer, and she stretched a hand across the slumbering body of her son, to rest light on Roger's arm.

"Sing to me," she whispered, though she knew that he already was asleep.

James Fraser, Indian Agent

"James Fraser, Indian Agent," I said, closing one eye as though reading it off a screen. "It sounds like a Wild West television show."

Jamie paused in the act of pulling off his stockings, and eyed me warily.

"It does? Is that good?"

"Insofar as the hero of a television show never dies, yes."

"In that case, I'm in favor of it," he said, examining the stocking he'd just pulled off. He sniffed it suspiciously, rubbed a thumb over a thin patch on the heel, shook his head, and tossed it into the laundry basket. "Must I sing?"

"Si—oh," I said, recollecting that the last time I had tried to explain television to him, my descriptions had focused largely on *The Ed Sullivan Show.* "No, I don't think so. Nor yet swing from a trapeze."

"Well, that's a comfort. I'm none sae young as I was, ken." He stood up and stretched himself, groaning. The house had been built with eight-foot ceilings, to accommodate him, but his fists brushed the pine beams, even so. "Christ, but it's been a long day!"

"Well, it's nearly over," I said, sniffing in turn at the bodice of the gown I'd just shed. It smelled strongly, though not disagreeably, of horse and woodsmoke. Air it a bit, I decided, and see whether it could go another little while without washing. "I couldn't have swung on a trapeze even when I *was* young."

"I'd pay money to see ye try," he said, grinning.

"What *is* an Indian agent?" I inquired. "MacDonald seemed to think he was doing you a signal favor by suggesting you for the job."

He shrugged, unbuckling his kilt.

"Nay doubt he thinks he is." He shook the garment experimentally, and a fine sifting of dust and horsehair bloomed on the floor beneath it. He went to the window, opened the shutters, and, thrusting the kilt outside, shook it harder.

"He would be"—his voice came faintly from the night outside, then more strongly, as he turned round again—"were it not for this war of yours."

"Of *mine*?" I said, indignant. "You sound as though you think I'm proposing to start it, single-handed."

He made a small gesture of dismissal.

"Ye ken what I mean. An Indian agent, Sassenach, is what it sounds like—a fellow who goes out and parleys wi' the local Indians, giving them gifts and talking them round, in hopes that they'll be inclined to ally themselves with the Crown's interests, whatever those might happen to be."

"Oh? And what's this Southern Department that MacDonald mentioned?" I glanced involuntarily toward the closed door of our room, but muffled snoring from across the hall indicated that our guest had already collapsed into the arms of Morpheus.

"Mmphm. There's a Southern Department and a Northern Department that deal wi' Indian affairs in the colonies. The Southern Department is under John Stuart, who's an Inverness man. Turn round, I'll do it."

I turned my back gratefully to him. With expertise born of long experience, he had the lacing of my stays undone in seconds. I sighed deeply as they loosened and fell. He plucked the shift away from my body, massaging my ribs where the boning had pressed the damp fabric into my skin.

"Thank you." I sighed in bliss and leaned back against him. "And being an Inverness man, MacDonald thinks this Stuart will have a natural predisposition to employ other Highlanders?"

"That might depend upon whether Stuart's ever met any of my kin," Jamie said dryly. "But MacDonald thinks so, aye." He kissed the top of my head in absent affection, then withdrew his hands and began untying the lace that bound his hair.

"Sit," I said, stepping out of my fallen stays. "I'll do it."

He sat on the stool in his shirt, closing his eyes in momentary relaxation as I unbraided his hair. He'd worn it clubbed in a tight queue for riding, bound up for the last three days; I ran my hands up into the warm fiery mass as it unraveled from its plait, and the loosened waves of it spilled cinnamon and gold and silver in the firelight as I rubbed the pads of my fingers gently into his scalp.

"Gifts, you said. Does the Crown supply these gifts?" The Crown, I had noticed, had a bad habit of "honoring" men of substance with offices that required them to come up with large amounts of their own money.

"Theoretically." He yawned hugely, broad shoulders slumping comfortably as I took up my hair brush and set about tidying him. "Oh, that's nice. That's why MacDonald thinks it a favor; there's the possibility of doing well in trade."

"Besides generally excellent opportunities for corruption. Yes, I see." I worked for a few minutes before asking, "Will you do it?"

"I dinna ken. I must think a bit. Ye were mentioning Wild West—Brianna's said such a thing, telling me about cowherds—"

"Cowboys."

He waved off the correction. "And the Indians. That's true, is it—what she says about the Indians?"

"If what she says is that they'll be largely exterminated over the next century or so—yes, she's right." I smoothed his hair, then sat down on the bed facing him and set about brushing my own. "Does that trouble you?"

His brows drew together a little as he considered it, and he scratched absently at his chest, where the curly red-gold hairs showed at the open neck of his shirt.

"No," he said slowly. "Not precisely. It's not as though I should be doing them to death wi' my own hands. But . . . we're coming to it, are we not? The time when I must tread wi' some care, if I'm to walk betwixt the fires."

"I'm afraid we are," I said, an uneasy tightness hovering between my shoulder blades. I saw what he meant, all too clearly. The battle lines were not clear yet—but they were being drawn. To become an Indian agent for the Crown was to appear to be a Loyalist—all very well for the moment, when the Rebel movement was no more than a radical fringe, with pockets of disaffection. But very, very dangerous, as we grew closer to the point where the disaffected seized power, and independence was declared.

Knowing the eventual outcome, Jamie dare not wait too long

to ally himself to the Rebel side—but to do so too early was to risk arrest for treason. Not a good prospect for a man who was already a pardoned traitor.

"Of course," I said diffidently, "if you *were* to be an Indian agent I suppose you might actually persuade some of the Indian tribes into supporting the American side—or staying neutral, at least."

"I might," he agreed, with a certain note of bleakness in his voice. "But putting aside any question as to the honor of such a course—that would help condemn them, no? Would the same thing happen to them in the end, d'ye think, if the English were to win?"

"They won't," I said, with a slight edge.

He glanced sharply at me.

"I do believe ye," he said, with a similar edge. "I've reason to, aye?"

I nodded, my lips pressed together. I didn't want to talk about the earlier Rising. I didn't want to talk about the oncoming Revolution, either, but there was little choice about that.

"I don't know," I said, and took a deep breath. "No one can say—since it didn't happen—but if I were to *guess* . . . then I think the Indians might quite possibly do better under British rule." I smiled at him, a little ruefully.

"Believe it or not, the British Empire did—or will, I should say—generally manage to run its colonies without *entirely* exterminating the native people in them."

"Bar the Hieland folk," he said, very dryly. "Aye, I'll take your word for it, Sassenach."

He stood up, running a hand back through his hair, and I caught a glimpse of the tiny streak of white that ran through it, legacy of a bullet wound.

"You should talk to Roger about it," I said. "He knows a great deal more than I do."

He nodded, but didn't reply, beyond a faint grimace.

"Where do you suppose Roger and Bree went, speaking of Roger?"

"To the MacGillivrays', I suppose," he replied, surprised. "To fetch wee Jem."

"How do you know that?" I asked, equally surprised.

"When there's mischief abroad, a man wants his family safe under his eye, ken?" He raised one brow at me, and reaching to the top of the wardrobe, took down his sword. He drew it halfway from its scabbard, then put it back and set the scabbard gently back in place, the sword loosened, hilt ready to hand.

He'd brought a loaded pistol upstairs with him; that was placed on the washstand by the window. The rifle and fowling piece too had been left loaded and primed, hanging from their hooks above the hearth downstairs. And, with a small ironic flourish, he drew the dirk from its belt sheath and slid it neatly under our pillow.

"Sometimes I forget," I said a little wistfully, watching this. There had been a dirk under the pillow of our wedding couch— and under many a one since then.

"Do ye?" He smiled at that; a little lopsidedly, but he smiled.

"Don't you? Ever?"

He shook his head, still smiling, though it had a rueful tinge.

"Sometimes I wish I did."

This colloquy was interrupted by a spluttering snort across the hall, followed at once by a thrashing of bedclothes, violent oaths, and a sharp *thump!* as something—likely a shoe—struck the wall.

"Fucking cat!" bellowed Major MacDonald. I sat, hand pressed across my mouth, as the stomp of bare feet vibrated through the floorboards, succeeded briefly by the crash of the Major's door, which flung open, then shut with a bang.

Jamie too had stood frozen for an instant. Now he moved, very delicately, and soundlessly eased our own door open. Adso, tail arrogantly S-shaped, strolled in. Magnificently ignoring us, he crossed the room, leapt lightly onto the washstand, and sat in the basin, where he stuck a back leg into the air and began calmly licking his testicles.

"I saw a man once in Paris who could do that," Jamie remarked, observing this performance with interest.

"Are there people willing to pay to watch such things?" I assumed that no one was likely to engage in a public exhibition of that sort merely for the fun of it. Not in Paris, anyway.

"Well, it wasna the man, so much. More his female companion, who was likewise flexible." He grinned at me, his eyes glinting blue in the candlelight. "Like watching worms mate, aye?"

"How fascinating," I murmured. I glanced at the washstand, where Adso was now doing something even more indelicate.

"You're lucky the Major doesn't sleep armed, cat. He might have potted you like a jugged hare."

"Oh, I doubt that. Our Donald likely sleeps with a blade—but he kens well enough which side of his bread's buttered. Ye wouldna be likely to give him breakfast, and he'd skewered your cat."

I glanced toward the door. The mattress-heaving and muttered curses across the hall had died down; the Major, with the practiced ease of a professional soldier, was already well on his way back to dreamland.

"I suppose not. You were right about his worming his way into a position with the new governor. Which is the real reason for his desire for your political advancement, I imagine?"

Jamie nodded, but had plainly lost interest in discussing MacDonald's machinations.

"I *was* right, no? That means ye owe me a forfeit, Sassenach."

He eyed me with an air of dawning speculation, which I hoped had not been too much inspired by his memories of the wormlike Parisians.

"Oh?" I regarded him warily. "And, um, *what* precisely . . . ?"

"Well, I havena quite worked out all the details as yet, but I think ye should maybe lie on the bed, to begin with."

That sounded like a reasonable start to the matter. I piled up the pillows at the head of the bed—pausing to remove the dirk—then began to climb onto it. I paused again, though, and instead bent to wind the bedkey, tightening the ropes that supported the mattress until the bedstead groaned and the ropes gave a creaking twang.

"Verra canny, Sassenach," Jamie said behind me, sounding amused.

"Experience," I informed him, clambering over the newly tautened bed on hands and knees. "I've waked up often enough after a night with you, with the mattress folded up round my ears and my arse no more than an inch off the ground."

"Oh, I expect your arse will end up somewhat higher than that," he assured me.

"Oh, you're going to let me be on top?" I had mixed feelings about that. I was desperately tired, and while I enjoyed riding Jamie, all right, I'd been riding a beastly horse for more than ten hours, and the thigh muscles required for both activities were trembling spasmodically.

"Perhaps later," he said, eyes narrowed in thought. "Lie back, Sassenach, and ruckle up your shift. Then open your legs for me, there's a good lass no, a bit wider, aye?" He began—with deliberate slowness—to remove his shirt.

I sighed and shifted my buttocks a little, looking for a position that wouldn't give me cramp if I had to hold it for long.

"If you have in mind what I think you have in mind, you'll regret it. I haven't even bathed properly," I said reproachfully. "I'm desperately filthy and I smell like a horse."

Naked, he raised one arm and sniffed appraisingly.

"Oh? Well, so do I. That's no matter; I'm fond of horses." He'd abandoned any pretense of delay, but paused to survey his arrangements, looking me over with approval.

"Aye, verra good. Now then, if ye'll just put your hands above your head and seize the bedstead—"

"You wouldn't!" I said, and then lowered my voice, with an involuntary glance toward the door. "Not with MacDonald just across the hall!"

"Oh, I would," he assured me, "and the devil wi' MacDonald and a dozen more like him." He paused, though, studying me thoughtfully, and after a moment, sighed and shook his head.

"No," he said quietly. "Not tonight. Ye're still thinking of that poor Dutch bastard and his family, no?"

"Yes. Aren't you?"

He sat down beside me on the bed with a sigh.

"I've been trying verra hard not to," he said frankly. "But the new dead dinna lie easy in their graves, do they?"

I laid a hand on his arm, relieved that he felt the same. The night air seemed restless with the passage of spirits, and I had felt the dragging melancholy of that desolate garden, that row of graves, all through the events and alarums of the evening.

It *was* a night to be securely locked inside, with a good fire on the hearth, and people nearby. The house stirred, shutters creaking in the wind.

"I do want ye, Claire," Jamie said softly. "I need . . . if ye will?"

And had they spent the night before their deaths like this, I wondered? Peaceful and snug betwixt their walls, husband and wife whispering together, lying close in their bed, having no notion what the future held. I saw in memory her long white thighs as the wind blew over her, and the glimpse I'd had of the small curly mat between them, the pudenda beneath its nimbus of brown hair pale as carved marble, the seam of it sealed like a virgin's statue.

"I need, too," I said, just as softly. "Come here."

He leaned close, and pulled the drawstring neatly from the neck of my shift, so the worn linen wilted off my shoulders. I made a grab for the fabric, but he caught my hand, and held it down by my side. One-fingered, he brushed the shift lower, then put out the candle, and in a dark that smelled of wax and honey and the sweat of horses, kissed my forehead, eyes, the corners of my cheeks, my lips and chin, and so continued, slow and soft-lipped, to the arches of my feet.

He raised himself then, and suckled my breasts for a long time, and I ran my hand up his back and cupped his buttocks, naked and vulnerable in the dark.

Afterward, we lay in a pleasantly vermiform tangle, the only light in the room a faint glow from the banked hearth. I was so tired that I could feel my body sinking into the mattress, and desired nothing more than to keep going down, down, into the welcoming dark of oblivion.

"Sassenach?"

"Um?"

A moment's hesitation, then his hand found mine, curling round it.

"Ye wouldna do what she did, would ye?"

"Who?"

"Her. The Dutchwoman."

Snatched back from the edge of sleep, I was muzzy and confused, sufficiently so that even the image of the dead woman, shrouded in her apron, seemed unreal, no more disturbing than the random fragments of reality my brain tossed overboard in a vain effort to keep afloat as I sank down into the depths of sleep.

"What? Fall into the fire? I'll try not," I assured him, yawning. "Good night."

"No. Wake up." He shook my arm gently. "Talk to me, Sassenach."

"Ng." It was a considerable effort, but I pushed away the enticing arms of Morpheus, and flounced over onto my side, facing him. "Mm. Talk to you. About . . . ?"

"The Dutchwoman," he repeated patiently. "If I were to be

killed, ye wouldna go and kill your whole family, would ye?"

"What?" I rubbed my free hand over my face, trying to make some sense of this, amid the drifting shreds of sleep. "Whose whole—oh. You think she did it on purpose? Poisoned them?"

"I think maybe so."

His words were no more than a whisper, but they brought me back to full consciousness. I lay silent for a moment, then reached out, wanting to be sure he was really there.

He was; a large, solid object, the smooth bone of his hip warm and live under my hand.

"It might as well have been an accident," I said, voice pitched low. "You can't know for sure."

"No," he admitted. "But I canna keep from seeing it." He turned restlessly onto his back.

"The men came," he said softly, to the beams overhead. "He fought them, and they killed him there, on his own threshold. And when she saw her man was gone I think she told the men she must feed the weans first, before . . . and then she put toadstools into the stew, and fed it to the bairns and her mother. She took the two men with them, but I think it was *that* that was the accident. She only meant to follow him. She wouldna leave him there, alone."

I wanted to tell him that this was a rather dramatic interpretation of what we had seen. But I couldn't very well tell him he was wrong. Hearing him describe what he saw in thought, I saw it, too, all too clearly.

"You don't know," I said at last, softly. "You can't know." *Unless you find the other men,* I thought suddenly, *and ask them.* I didn't say that, though.

Neither of us spoke for a bit. I could tell that he was still thinking, but the quicksand of sleep was once more pulling me down, clinging and seductive.

"What if I canna keep ye safe?" he whispered at last. His head moved suddenly on the pillow, turning toward me. "You and the rest of them? I shall try wi' all my strength, Sassenach, and I dinna mind if I die doing it, but what if I should die too soon—and fail?"

And what answer was there to that?

"You won't," I whispered back. He sighed, and bent his head, so his forehead rested against mine. I could smell eggs and whisky, warm on his breath.

"I'll try not," he said, and I put my mouth on his, soft against mine, acknowledgment and comfort in the dark.

I laid my head against the curve of his shoulder, wrapped a hand round his arm, and breathed in the smell of his skin, smoke and salt, as though he had been cured in the fire.

"You smell like a smoked ham," I murmured, and he made a low sound of amusement and wedged his hand into its accustomed spot, clasped between my thighs.

I let go then, at last, and let the heavy sands of sleep engulf me. Perhaps he said it, as I fell into darkness, or perhaps I only dreamed it.

"If I die," he whispered in the dark, "dinna follow me. The bairns will need ye. Stay for them. I can wait."

PART TWO

A Gathering of Shadows

8

Victim of a Massacre

From Lord John Grey
To Mr. James Fraser, Esq.

April 14, 1773

My dear friend—

 I write you in good Health, and trust that I find you and yours in similar condition.

 My Son has returned to England, there to complete his Education. He writes with Delight of his Experiences (I inclose a Copy of his most recent Letter), and assures me of his Well-being. More importantly, my Mother also writes to assure me that he flourishes, though I believe—more from what she does not say than from what she does—that he introduces an unaccustomed Element of Confusion and Upheaval in her Household.

 I confess to feeling the Lack of this Element in my own Household. So orderly and well-regulated a Life as mine is these Days, you would be astonished. Still, the Quiet seems oppressive to me, and while I am in Health in terms of Body, I find my Spirit somewhat flagging. I miss William sadly, I fear.

 For Distraction from my solitary State, I have of late undertaken a new Employment, that of making Wine. While I admit the Product lacks the Power of your own Distillations, I flatter myself that it is not undrinkable, and

*if allowed to stand for a Year or two, might eventually be
palatable. I shall send you a dozen Bottles later in the
Month, by the Hand of my new Servant, Mr. Higgins,
whose History you may find interesting.*

*You will perhaps have heard something of a
disreputable Brawl occurring in Boston in March of
three Years past, which I have often seen in Newspaper
and Broadside called a "Massacre," most irresponsibly—
and most inaccurately, to one who has been privy to the
actual Occurrence.*

*I was not present myself, but have spoken to numerous
of the Officers and Soldiers who were. If they speak truly,
and I believe they do, such a View as is given by the
Boston Press of the Matter has been monstrous.*

*Boston is by all Accounts a perfect Hellhole of
republican Sentiment, with so-called "Marching Societies"
at large in the Streets in every Weather, these being no more
than an Excuse for the Assembly of Mobs, whose chief
Sport is the tormenting of the Troops quartered there.*

*Higgins tells me that no Man would dare go out alone
in Uniform, for fear of these Mobs, and that even when in
greater Numbers, harassment from the public soon drove
them back to their Quarters, save when compelled by
Duty to persist.*

*A Patrol of five Soldiers was so beset one Evening,
pursued not only by insults of the grossest Nature, but by
hurled Stones, Clods of Earth and Dung, and other such
Rubbish. Such was the Press of the Mob around them that
the Men feared for their Safety, and thus presented their
Weapons, in hopes of discouraging the raucous Attentions
rained upon them. So far from accomplishing this Aim, the
Action provoked still greater Outrages from the Crowd,
and at some Point, a Gun was fired. No one can say for
sure whether the Shot was discharged from the Crowd, or
from one of the Soldier's Weapons, let alone whether it
were by Accident or in Deliberation, but the Effect of it . . .
well, you will have sufficient Knowledge of such Matters to
imagine the Confusion of subsequent Events.*

*In the End, five of the Mob were killed, and while the
Soldiers were buffeted and badly handled, they escaped*

*alive, only to be made Scapegoats by the malicious
Rantings of the mob's Leaders in the Press, these so styled
as to make it seem a wanton and unprovoked Slaughter of
Innocents, rather than a Matter of Self-defense against a
Mob inflamed by Drink and Sloganeering.*

*I confess that my Sympathies must lie altogether with
the Soldiers; I am sure so much is obvious to you. They
were brought to Trial, where the Judge discovered Three
to be Innocent, but no Doubt felt it would be Dangerous to
his own Situation to free them all.*

*Higgins, with one other, was convicted of
Manslaughter, but pled Clergy and was released after his
Branding. The Army of course discharged him, and
without means of making a Living and subject to the
Opprobrium of the Populace, he found himself in sad
Case. He tells me that he was beaten in a Tavern soon
after his Release, injuries inflicted therein depriving him
of the Sight in one Eye, and in fact, his very Life was
threatened on more than one Occasion. So seeking Safety,
he took Passage on a Sloop captained by my Friend,
Captain Gill, working as a Sailor, though I have seen him
sail and I assure you he is not one.*

*This state of Affairs became soon evident to Captain
Gill, who terminated his Employment upon arrival at their
first Port. I was in the Town on Business, and encountered
Captain Gill, who told me of Higgins's desperate
Situation.*

*I contrived to find the Man, feeling some Pity for a
Soldier who appeared to me to have performed his Duty
honorably, and thinking it hard that he should suffer by it.
Discovering him to be intelligent and of a generally
agreeable Character, I engaged him in Service, wherein he
has proved most faithful.*

*I send him with the Wine, in Hopes that your Wife
might be so kind as to examine him. The local Physician,
one Dr. Potts, has seen him, and declares the Injury to his
Eye irretrievable, as indeed it may be. Having some
personal Experience of your Wife's skill, however, I
wonder whether she might suggest Treatment for his other
Ills; Dr. Potts was unable to be of much Help. Tell her,*

*please, that I am her humble Servant, and remain in
perpetual Gratitude for her Kindness and Ability.*

*My warmest Regards to your Daughter, for whom I
have sent a small Present, to arrive with the Wine. I trust
her Husband will not take Offense at my Familiarity, by
Consideration of my long Acquaintance with your Family,
and will allow her to accept it.*

*As always, I remain your Ob't. Servant,
John Grey*

9

The Threshold of War

April 1773

Robert Higgins was a slight young man, so thin as to seem
that his bones were barely held together by his clothes,
and so pale that it was easy to imagine you could in fact
see through him. He was, however, graced with large, candid blue
eyes, a mass of wavy, light-brown hair, and a shy manner that
caused Mrs. Bug to take him at once under her wing and declare
a firm intent to "feed him up," before he should depart back to
Virginia.

I quite liked Mr. Higgins myself; he was a sweet-natured boy,
with the soft accent of his native Dorset. I did rather wonder,
though, whether Lord John Grey's generosity toward him was as
unselfish as it seemed.

I had come reluctantly to like John Grey, too, after our shared experience of the measles a few years earlier, and his friendship to Brianna while Roger was held captive by the Iroquois. Still, I remained acutely aware of the fact that Lord John did like men—specifically, Jamie, but certainly other men, as well.

"Beauchamp," I said to myself, laying out trillium roots to dry, "you have a very suspicious mind."

"Aye, ye have," said a voice behind me, sounding amused. "Whom do ye suspect of doing what?"

I jerked in startlement and sent trilliums flying in all directions.

"Oh, it's you," I said crossly. "Why must you sneak up on me like that?"

"Practice," Jamie said, kissing me on the forehead. "I shouldna like to lose my touch at stalking game. Why d'ye talk to yourself?"

"It assures me of a good listener," I said tartly, and he laughed, bending to help me pick up the roots from the floor.

"Who are ye suspecting, Sassenach?"

I hesitated, but was unable to come up with anything but the truth.

"I was wondering whether John Grey's buggering our Mr. Higgins," I said baldly. "Or intends to."

He blinked slightly, but didn't look shocked—which in itself suggested to me that he'd considered the same possibility.

"What makes ye think so?"

"He's a very pretty young man, for the one thing," I said, taking a handful of the roots from him and beginning to spread them out on a sheet of gauze. "And he's got the worst case of piles I've ever seen in a man of his age, for another."

"He let ye *look* at them?" Jamie had flushed up himself at the mention of buggery; he disliked me being indelicate, but he'd asked, after all.

"Well, it took no little persuasion," I said. "He told me about them readily enough, but he wasn't keen to have me examine them."

"I wouldna care for that prospect, either," Jamie assured me, "and I'm wed to ye. Why on earth would ye want to look at such a thing, beyond morbid curiosity?" He cast a wary glance at my big black casebook, open on the table. "Ye're no drawing pictures of poor Bobby Higgins's backside in there, are ye?"

"No need. I can't imagine a physician in any time who doesn't know what piles look like. The ancient Israelites and Egyptians had them, after all."

"They did?"

"It's in the Bible. Ask Mr. Christie," I advised.

He gave me a sidelong look.

"Ye've been discussing the Bible wi' Tom Christie? Ye're a braver man than I am, Sassenach." Christie was a most devout Presbyterian, and never happier than when hitting someone over the head with a fistful of Sacred Scripture.

"Not me. Germain asked me last week what 'emerods' are."

"What are they?"

"Piles. *Then said they, What shall be the trespass offering which we shall return to him? They answered, Five golden emerods, and five golden mice, according to the number of the lords of the Philistines,*" I quoted, "or something of the sort. That's as close as I can come from memory. Mr. Christie made Germain write out a verse from the Bible as punishment, and having an inquiring sort of mind, Germain wondered what it was he was writing."

"And he wouldna ask Mr. Christie, of course." Jamie frowned, rubbing a finger down the bridge of his nose. "Do I want to know what it was Germain did?"

"Almost certainly not." Tom Christie earned the quitrent on his land by serving as the local schoolmaster, and seemed capable of keeping discipline on his own terms. My opinion was that having Germain Fraser as a pupil was probably worth the entire amount, in terms of labor.

"Gold emerods," Jamie murmured. "Well, there's a thought." He had assumed the faintly dreamy air he often had just before coming up with some hair-raising notion involving the possibility of maiming, death, or life imprisonment. I found this expression mildly alarming, but whatever the train of thought triggered by golden hemorrhoids, he abandoned it for the moment, shaking his head.

"Well, so. We were speaking of Bobby's backside?"

"Oh, yes. As for why I wanted to look at Mr. Higgins's emerods," I said, returning to the previous point of conversation, "I wanted to see whether the best treatment was amelioration, or removal."

Jamie's eyebrows went up at that.

"Remove them? How? Wi' your wee knife?" He glanced at the

case where I kept my surgical tools, and hunched his shoulders in aversion.

"I could, yes, though I imagine it would be rather painful without anesthesia. There was a much simpler method just coming into widespread use, though, when I . . . left." Just for a moment, I felt a deep twinge of longing for my hospital. I could all but smell the disinfectant, hear the murmur and bustle of nurses and orderlies, touch the glossy covers of the research journals bulging with ideas and information.

Then it was gone, and I was estimating the desirability of leeches versus string, with reference to Mr. Higgins's achieving ideal anal health.

"Dr. Rawlings advises the use of leeches," I explained. "Twenty or thirty, he says, for a serious case."

Jamie nodded, showing no particular revulsion at the idea. Of course, he'd been leeched a few times himself, and assured me that it didn't hurt.

"Aye. Ye havena got that many on hand, do ye? Shall I collect the wee lads and set them to gathering?"

Jemmy and Germain would like nothing better than an excuse to go bogging through the creeks with their grandfather, coming back festooned with leeches and mud to the eyebrows, but I shook my head.

"No. Or I mean, yes," I corrected. "At your convenience—but I don't need them immediately. Using leeches would relieve the situation temporarily, but Bobby's hemorrhoids are badly thrombosed—have clots of dried blood in them—" I emended, "and I think he really would be better off if I remove them entirely. I believe I can ligate them—tie a thread very tightly round the base of each hemorrhoid, I mean. That starves them of blood, and eventually, they just dry up and fall off. Very neat."

"Verra neat," Jamie murmured, in echo. He looked mildly apprehensive. "Have ye done it before?"

"Yes, once or twice."

"Ah." He pursed his lips, apparently envisioning the process. "How . . . er, I mean . . . can he shit, d'ye think, while this is going on? It must take a bit of time, surely."

I frowned, tapping a finger on the countertop.

"His chief difficulty is that he *doesn't* shit," I said. "Not often enough, I mean, and not with the proper consistency. Horrible diet," I said, pointing an accusatory finger at him. "He told me. Bread, meat, and ale. No vegetables, no fruit. Constipation is absolutely *rife* in the British army, I don't doubt. I shouldn't be surprised if every man jack of them has piles hanging out of his arse like grape clusters!"

Jamie nodded, one eyebrow raised.

"There are a great many things I admire about ye, Sassenach—especially the delicate manner of your conversation." He coughed, glancing downward. "But if ye say it's costiveness that causes piles—"

"It is."

"Aye, well. It's only—what ye were saying about John Grey. I mean, ye don't think the state of Bobby's arse is to do with . . . mmphm."

"Oh. Well, no, not directly." I paused. "It was more that Lord John said in his letter that he wanted me to—how did he put it?—*I might suggest treatment for his other ills.* I mean, he might possibly know about Bobby's difficulty, without . . . er . . . personal inspection, shall we say? But as *I* say, piles are so commonplace an affliction, why ought he be concerned to the point of asking me to do something about them—unless he thought that they might hamper his own eventual . . . er . . . progress?"

Jamie's face had resumed its normal hue during the discussion of leeches and constipation, but at this point, went red again.

"His—"

"I mean," I said, folding my arms beneath my bosom, "I'm just a trifle put off . . . by the notion that he's sent Mr. Higgins down for repair, you might say." I had been suffering from a niggling feeling of unease regarding the matter of Bobby Higgins's backside, but hadn't put this notion into words before. Now that I had, I realized precisely what was bothering me.

"The thought that I'm meant to be fixing up poor little Bobby, and then sending him home to be—" I pressed my lips tight together, and turned abruptly back to my roots, needlessly turning them.

"I don't like the thought," I said, to the cupboard door. "I'll do what I can for Mr. Higgins, mind. Bobby Higgins hasn't many prospects; no doubt he'd do . . . whatever his Lordship required. But perhaps I'm wronging him. Lord John, I mean."

"Perhaps ye are."

I turned round, to find Jamie sitting on my stool, fiddling with a jar of goose grease that seemed to have his full attention.

"Well," I said uncertainly. "You know him better than I do. If you think he isn't . . ." My words trailed off. Outside, there was a sudden soft thump as a falling spruce cone struck the wooden stoop.

"I ken more about John Grey than I wish I did," Jamie said finally, and glanced at me, a rueful smile in the corner of his mouth. "And he kens a great deal more about me than I like to think on. But"—he leaned forward, setting down the jar, then put his hands on his knees and looked at me—"I ken the one thing beyond doubt. He's an honorable man. He wouldna take advantage of Higgins, nor any other man under his protection."

He sounded very definite about it, and I felt reassured. I did like John Grey. And still . . . the appearance of his letters, regular as clockwork, always gave me a faint sense of unease, like the hearing of distant thunder. There was nothing about the letters themselves to evoke such a response; they were like the man himself—erudite, humorous, and sincere. And he had reason to write, of course. More than one.

"He does still love you, you know," I said quietly.

He nodded, but didn't look at me, his gaze still fixed somewhere beyond the trees that edged the dooryard.

"Would you rather he didn't?"

He paused, then nodded again. This time, though, he did turn to look at me.

"I would, aye. For myself. For him, certainly. But for William?" He shook his head, uncertain.

"Oh, he may have taken William on for your sake," I said, leaning back against the counter. "But I've seen the two of them, remember. I've no doubt he loves Willie for his own sake now."

"No, I dinna doubt that, either." He got up, restless, and beat imaginary dust from the pleats of his kilt. His face was closed, looking inward at something he didn't wish to share with me.

"Do you—" I began, but stopped when he glanced up at me. "No. It doesn't matter."

"What?" He tilted his head to one side, eyes narrowing.

"Nothing."

He didn't move, merely intensified the stare.

"I can see from your face that it's not, Sassenach. What?"

I breathed deeply through my nose, fists wrapped in my apron.

"It's only—and I'm sure it isn't true, it's only a passing thought—"

He made a low Scottish noise, indicating that I had better stop blethering and cough it up. Having enough experience to realize that he wouldn't leave the matter 'til I did, I coughed.

"Did you ever wonder whether Lord John might have taken him because . . . well, William does look terribly like you, and evidently did from an early age. Since Lord John finds you physically . . . attractive . . ." The words died, and I could have cut my throat for speaking them, seeing the look on his face.

He closed his eyes for a moment, to stop me looking in. His fists were curled up so tightly that the veins stood out from knuckle to forearm. Very slowly, he relaxed his hands. He opened his eyes.

"No," he said, complete conviction in his voice. He gave me a straight, hard look. "And it's no that I canna bear the thought of it, either. I know."

"Of course," I said hastily, eager to leave the subject.

"I know," he repeated more sharply. His two stiff fingers tapped, once, against his leg, and then stilled. "I thought of it, too. When he first told me he meant to wed Isobel Dunsany."

He turned away, staring out through the window. Adso was in the dooryard, stalking something in the grass.

"I offered him my body," Jamie said abruptly, not looking round. The words were steady enough, but I could see from the knotted shoulders how much it cost him to speak them. "In thanks," I said. But it was—" He made an odd convulsive movement, as though trying to free himself from some constraint. "I meant to see, ken, what sort of man he might be, for sure. This man who would take my son for his own."

His voice shook, very slightly, when he said, "take my son," and I moved to him by instinct, wanting somehow to patch the open wound beneath those words.

He was stiff when I touched him, not wanting to be embraced—but he took my hand and squeezed it.

"Could you . . . really tell, do you think?" I was not shocked; John Grey had told me of that offer, years before, in Jamaica. I didn't think he had realized the true nature of it, though.

Jamie's hand tightened on mine, and his thumb traced the outline of mine, rubbing lightly over the nail. He looked down at me, and I felt his eyes search my face—not in question, but in the way one does when seeing anew some object grown familiar—seeing with the eyes what has been seen for a long time only with the heart.

His free hand rose and traced the line of my brows, two fingers resting for an instant on the bone of my cheek, then moved up, back, cool in the warmth of my hair.

"Ye canna be so close to another," he said finally. "To be within each other, to smell their sweat, and rub the hairs of your body with theirs and see nothing of their soul. Or if ye *can* do that . . ." He hesitated, and I wondered whether he thought of Black Jack Randall, or of Laoghaire, the woman he had married, thinking me dead. "Well . . . that is a dreadful thing in itself," he finished softly, and his hand dropped away.

There was silence between us. A sudden rustle came from the grass outside as Adso lunged and disappeared, and a mockingbird began to shriek alarm from the big red spruce. In the kitchen, something was dropped with a clang, and then the rhythmic *shoosh* of sweeping began. All the homely sounds of this life we had made.

Had I ever done that? Lain with a man, and seen nothing of his soul? Indeed I had, and he was right. A breath of coldness touched me, and the hairs rose, silent on my skin.

He heaved a sigh that seemed to come from his feet, and rubbed a hand over his bound hair.

"But he wouldna do it. John." He looked up then, and gave me a crooked smile. "He loved me, he said. And if I couldna give him that in return—and he kent I couldn't—then he'd not take counterfeit for true coin."

He shook himself, hard, like a dog coming out of the water.

"No. A man who would say such a thing is not one who'd bugger a child for the sake of his father's bonny blue eyes, I'll tell ye that for certain, Sassenach."

"No," I said. "Tell me . . ." I hesitated, and he looked at me, one eyebrow up. "If—if he *had* . . . er . . . taken you up on that offer—and you'd found him . . ." I fumbled for some reasonable wording. "Less, um, decent than you might hope—"

"I should have broken his neck there by the lake," he said. "It wouldna have mattered if they'd hanged me; I'd not have let him have the boy.

"But he didn't, and I did," he added with a half-shrug. "And if wee Bobby goes to his Lordship's bed, I think it will be of his own free will."

No man is really at his best with someone else's hand up his arse. I had noticed this before, and Robert Higgins was no exception to the general rule.

"Now, this won't hurt much at all," I said as soothingly as possible. "All you need to do is to keep quite still."

"Oh, I s'all do that, mum, indeed I will," he assured me fervently.

I had him on the surgery table, wearing only his shirt, and situated foursquare on hands and knees, which brought the area of operation conveniently to eye level. The forceps and ligatures I should need were placed on the small table to my right, with a bowl of fresh leeches alongside, in case of need.

He emitted a small shriek when I applied a wet cloth soaked in turpentine to the area, in order to cleanse it thoroughly, but was as good as his word and didn't move.

"Now, we are going to obtain a very good effect here," I assured him, taking up a pair of long-nosed forceps. "But if the relief is to be permanent, there will have to be a drastic change in your diet. Do you understand me?"

He gasped deeply, as I grasped one of the hemorrhoids and pulled it toward me. There were three, a classic presentation, at nine, two, and five o'clock. Bulbous as raspberries, and quite the same color.

"Oh! Y-yes, mum."

"Oatmeal," I said firmly, transferring the forceps to my other hand without lessening the grip, and taking up a needle threaded with silk thread in my right. "Porridge every morning, without fail. Have you noticed a change for the better in your bowel habits, since Mrs. Bug has been feeding you parritch for breakfast?"

I passed the thread loosely round the base of the hemorrhoid, then delicately pushed the needle up beneath the loop, making a small noose of it, and pulled tight.

"Ahhh . . . oh! Erm . . . tell 'ee truth, mum, it's like shitting house bricks covered with hedgehog skin, makes no matter what I eat."

"Well, it will," I assured him, securing the ligature with a knot. I released the hemorrhoid, and he breathed deeply. "Now, grapes. You like grapes, don't you?"

"No'm. Sets me teeth on edge to bite 'em."

"Really?" His teeth didn't look badly decayed; I should have a closer look at his mouth; he might be suffering from marginal scurvy. "Well, we'll have Mrs. Bug make a nice raisin pie for you; you can eat that with no difficulty. Does Lord John have a capable cook?" I took aim with my forceps and got hold of the next one. Now accustomed to the sensation, he only grunted a bit.

"Yessum. Be an Indian, he is, named Manoke."

"Hmm." Round, up, tighten, tie off. "I'll write out a receipt for the raisin pie, for you to carry back to him. Does he cook yams, or beans? Beans are quite good for the purpose."

"I b'lieve he does, mum, but his Lordship—"

I had the windows open for ventilation—Bobby was no filthier than the average, but he was certainly no cleaner—and at this point, I heard sounds from the trailhead; voices, and the jingle of harness.

Bobby heard them, too, and glanced wildly at the window, hindquarters tensing as though to spring off the table like a grasshopper. I grasped him by one leg, but then thought better of it. There was no way of covering the window, bar closing the shutters, and I needed the light.

"Go ahead and stand up," I told him, letting go and reaching for a towel. "I'll go and see who it is." He followed this direction with alacrity, scrambling down and reaching hastily for his breeches.

I stepped out onto the porch, in time to greet the two men who led their mules up over the last arduous slope and into the yard. Richard Brown, and his brother Lionel, from the eponymously named Brownsville.

I was surprised to see them; it was a good three-day ride to Brownsville from the Ridge, and there was little commerce between the two settlements. It was at least that far to Salem, in the opposite direction, but the inhabitants of the Ridge went there much more frequently; the Moravians were both industrious and great traders, taking honey, oil, salt fish, and hides in trade for cheese, pottery, chickens, and other small livestock. So far as I knew, the denizens of Brownsville dealt only in cheap trade goods for the Cherokee, and in the production of a very inferior type of beer, not worth the ride.

"Good day, mistress." Richard, the smaller and elder of the brothers, touched the brim of his hat, but didn't take it off. "Is your husband to home?"

"He's out by the hay barn, scraping hides." I wiped my hands carefully on the towel I was carrying. "Do come round to the kitchen; I'll bring up some cider."

"Don't trouble." Without further ado, he turned and set off purposefully round the house. Lionel Brown, a bit taller than his brother, though with the same spare, almost gangly build and the same tobacco-colored hair, nodded briefly to me as he followed.

They had left their mules, reins hanging, evidently for me to tend. The animals were beginning to amble slowly across the yard, pausing to crop the long grass that edged the path.

"Hmpf!" I said, glaring after the brothers Brown.

"Who are they?" said a low voice behind me. Bobby Higgins had come out and was peering off the corner of the porch with his good eye. Bobby tended to be wary of strangers—and no wonder, given his experiences in Boston.

"Neighbors, such as they are." I lunged off the porch and caught one of the mules by the bridle as he reached for the peach sapling I had planted near the porch. Disliking this interference in his affairs, he brayed ear-splittingly in my face, and attempted to bite me.

"Here, mum, let me." Bobby, already holding the other mule's reins, leaned past to take the halter from me. "Hark at 'ee!" he said to the obstreperous mule. "Hush tha noise, else I take a stick to 'ee, then!"

Bobby had been a foot soldier rather than cavalry, it was clear to see. The words were bold enough, but ill-matched with his tentative manner. He gave a perfunctory yank on the mule's reins. The mule promptly laid back its ears and bit him in the arm.

He screamed and let go both sets of reins. Clarence, my own mule, hearing the racket, set up a loud bray of greeting from his pen, and the two strange mules promptly trotted off in that direction, stirrup leathers bouncing.

Bobby wasn't badly hurt, though the mule's teeth had broken the skin; spots of blood seeped through the sleeve of his shirt. As I was turning back the cloth to have a look at it, I heard footsteps on the porch, and looked up to see Lizzie, a large wooden spoon in hand, looking alarmed.

"Bobby! What's happened?"

He straightened at once, seeing her, assuming nonchalance, and brushed a lock of curly brown hair off his brow.

"Ah, oh! Naught, miss. Bit o' trouble with tha sons o' Belial, like. No fear, it's fine."

Whereupon his eyes rolled up in his head and he fell over in a dead faint.

"Oh!" Lizzie flew down the steps and knelt beside him, urgently patting his cheek. "Is he all right, Mrs. Fraser?"

"God knows," I said frankly. "I think so, though." Bobby appeared to be breathing normally, and I found a reasonable pulse in his wrist.

"Shall we carry him inside? Or should I fetch a burnt feather, do you think? Or the spirits of ammonia from the surgery? Or some brandy?" Lizzie hovered like an anxious bumblebee, ready to fly off in any of several different directions.

"No, I think he's coming round." Most faints last only a few seconds, and I could see his chest lift as his breathing deepened.

"Bit o' brandy wouldn't come amiss," he murmured, eyelids beginning to flutter.

I nodded to Lizzie, who vanished back into the house, leaving her spoon behind on the grass.

"Feeling a bit peaky, are you?" I inquired sympathetically. The injury to his arm was no more than a scratch, and I certainly hadn't done anything of a shocking nature to him—well, not physically shocking. What was the trouble here?

"I dunno, mum." He was trying to sit up, and while he was white as a sheet, seemed otherwise all right, so I let him. "It's only, every now and again, I gets these spots, like, whirring round me head like a swarm o' bees, and then it all goes black."

"Now and again? It's happened before?" I asked sharply.

"Yessum." His head wobbled like a sunflower in the breeze, and I put a hand under his armpit, lest he fall over again. "His Lordship was in hopes you might know summat would stop it."

"His Lord—oh, he knew about the fainting?" Well, of course he would, if Bobby were in the habit of falling over in front of him.

He nodded, and took a deep, gasping breath.

"Doctor Potts bled me regular, twice a week, but it didn't seem to help."

"I daresay not. I hope he was of somewhat more help with your piles," I remarked dryly.

A faint tinge of pink—he had scarcely enough blood to provide a decent blush, poor boy—rose in his cheeks, and he glanced away, fixing his gaze on the spoon.

"Erm . . . I, um, didn't mention *that* to anybody."

"You didn't?" I was surprised at that. "But—"

"See, 'twas only the riding. From Virginia." The pink tinge grew. "I'd not have let on, save I was in such agony after a week on yon bloody horse—saving your presence, mum—I'd no chance of hiding it."

"So Lord John didn't know about that, either?"

He shook his head vigorously, making the disheveled brown curls flop back over his forehead. I felt rather annoyed—with myself for having evidently misjudged John Grey's motives, and with John Grey, for making me feel a fool.

"Well . . . are you feeling a bit better, now?" Lizzie was not appearing with the brandy, and I wondered momentarily where she was. Bobby was still very pale, but nodded gamely, and struggled to his feet, where he stood swaying and blinking, trying to keep his balance. The "M" branded on his cheek stood out, an angry red against the pallid skin.

Distracted by Bobby's faint, I had ignored the sounds coming from the other side of the house. Now, though, I became aware of voices, and approaching footsteps.

Jamie and the two Browns came into sight round the corner of the house, then stopped, seeing us. Jamie had been frowning slightly; the frown grew deeper. The Browns, by contrast, seemed oddly elated, though in a grim sort of way.

"So it's true, then." Richard Brown stared hard at Bobby Higgins, then turned to Jamie. "You've a murderer on your premises!"

"Have I?" Jamie was coldly polite. "I'd no idea." He bowed to Bobby Higgins with his best French-court manner, then straightened, gesturing to the Browns. "Mr. Higgins, may I present Mr. Richard Brown and Mr. Lionel Brown. Gentlemen, my guest, Mr. Higgins." The words "my guest" were spoken with a particular emphasis that made Richard Brown's thin mouth compress to near invisibility.

"Have a care, Fraser," he said, staring hard at Bobby, as though daring him to evaporate. "Keeping the wrong company can be dangerous, these days."

"I choose my company as I will, sir." Jamie spoke softly, biting off each word between his teeth. "And I do not choose yours. Joseph!"

Lizzie's father, Joseph Wemyss, appeared round the corner, leading the two renegade mules, who now seemed docile as kittens, though either of them dwarfed Mr. Wemyss.

Bobby Higgins, flabbergasted by the proceedings, looked wildly at me for explanation. I shrugged slightly, and kept silence as the two Browns mounted and rode out of the clearing, backs stiff with anger.

Jamie waited 'til they'd disappeared from view, then blew out his breath, rubbing a hand viciously through his hair and muttering something in Gaelic. I didn't follow the finer points, but I gathered that he was comparing the character of our recent visitors to that of Mr. Higgins's piles—to the detriment of the former.

"Beg pardon, sir?" Higgins looked bewildered, but anxious to please.

Jamie glanced at him.

"Let them awa' and bile their heids," he said, dismissing the Browns with a flip of the hand. He caught my eye and turned toward the house. "Come ben, Bobby; I've a thing or two to say to ye."

I followed them in, both from curiosity and in case Mr. Higgins should feel faint again; he seemed steady enough, but still very pale. By contrast with Bobby Higgins, Mr. Wemyss— fair-haired and slight as his daughter—looked the picture of ruddy health. Whatever was the matter with Bobby? I wondered. I stole a discreet look at the seat of his breeches as I followed him, but that was all right; no bleeding.

Jamie led the way into his study, gesturing at the motley collection of stools and boxes he used for visitors, but both Bobby and Mr. Wemyss chose to stand—Bobby for obvious reasons, Mr. Wemyss from respect; he was never comfortable sitting in Jamie's presence, save at meals.

Unhampered by either bodily or social reservations, I settled myself on the best stool and raised one eyebrow at Jamie, who had sat down himself at the table he used as a desk.

"This is the way of it," he said without preamble. "Brown and his brother have declared themselves head of a Committee of Safety, and came to enlist me and my tenants as members of it." He glanced at me, the corner of his mouth curling a little. "I declined, as ye doubtless noticed."

My stomach contracted slightly, thinking of what Major MacDonald had said—and of what I knew. It was beginning, then.

"Committee of Safety?" Mr. Wemyss looked bewildered, and glanced at Bobby Higgins—who was beginning to look substantially less so.

"Have they, so?" Bobby said softly. Strands of curly brown hair had escaped from their binding; he fingered one back behind his ear.

"Ye've heard of such committees before, Mr. Higgins?" Jamie inquired, raising one brow.

"Met one, zur. Close-like." Bobby touched a finger briefly below his blind eye. He was still pale, but beginning to recover his self-possession. "Mobs they be, zur. Like they mules, but more of them—and more wicious." He gave a lopsided smile, smoothing the shirt-sleeve over the bite on his arm.

The mention of mules reminded me abruptly, and I stood up, putting a sudden stop to the conversation.

"Lizzie! Where's Lizzie?"

Not waiting for an answer to this rhetorical question, I went to the study door and shouted her name—only to be met by silence. She'd gone in for brandy; there was plenty, in a jug in the kitchen, and she knew that—I'd seen her reach it down for Mrs. Bug only the night before. She must be in the house. Surely she wouldn't have gone—

"Elizabeth? Elizabeth, where are you?" Mr. Wemyss was right behind me, calling, as I strode down the hall to the kitchen.

Lizzie was lying in a dead faint on the hearth, a limp bundle of clothes, one frail hand flung out as though she had tried to save herself as she fell.

"Miss Wemyss!" Bobby Higgins shouldered his way past me, looking frantic, and scooped her up into his arms.

"Elizabeth!" Mr. Wemyss elbowed his way past me as well,

his face nearly as white as his daughter's.

"Do let me *look* at her, will you?" I said, elbowing firmly back. "Put her down on the settle, Bobby, do."

He rose carefully with her in his arms, then sat down on the settle, still holding her, wincing slightly as he did so. Well, if he wanted to be a hero, I hadn't time to argue with him. I knelt and seized her wrist in search of a pulse, smoothing the pale hair off her face with my other hand.

One look had been enough to tell me what was likely the matter. She was clammy to the touch, and the pallor of her face was tinged with gray. I could feel the tremor of oncoming chills that ran through her flesh, unconscious as she was.

"The ague's back, is it?" Jamie asked. He'd appeared by my side, and was gripping Mr. Wemyss by the shoulder, at once comforting and restraining.

"Yes," I said briefly. Lizzie had malaria, contracted on the coast a few years before, and was subject to occasional relapses— though she hadn't had one in more than a year.

Mr. Wemyss took a deep, audible breath, a little color coming back to his face. He was familiar with malaria, and had confidence that I could deal with it. I had, several times before.

I hoped that I could this time. Lizzie's pulse was fast and light under my fingers, but regular, and she was beginning to stir. Still, the speed and suddenness with which the attack had come on was frightening. Had she had any warning? I hoped the concern I felt didn't show on my face.

"Take her up to her bed, cover her, get a hot stone for her feet," I said, rising and addressing Bobby and Mr. Wemyss briskly in turn. "I'll start some medicine brewing."

Jamie followed me down to the surgery, glancing back over his shoulder to be sure that the others were out of earshot before speaking.

"I thought ye were out of the Jesuit bark?" he asked, low-voiced.

"I am. Damn it." Malaria was a chronic disease, but for the most part, I had been able to keep it under control with small, regular doses of cinchona bark. But I had run out of cinchona during the winter, and no one had yet been able to travel down to the coast for more.

"So, then?"

"I'm thinking."

I pulled open the door of the cupboard, and gazed at the neat ranks of glass bottles therein—many of them empty, or with no more than a few scattered crumbs of leaf or root inside. Everything was depleted, after a cold, wet winter of grippe, influenza, chilblains, and hunting accidents.

Febrifuges. I had a number of things that would help a normal fever; malaria was something else. There was plenty of dogwood root and bark, at least; I had collected immense quantities during the fall, foreseeing the need. I took that down, and after a moment's thought, added the jar containing a sort of gentian known locally as "agueweed."

"Put on the kettle, will you?" I asked Jamie, frowning to myself as I crumbled roots, bark, and weed into my mortar. All I could do was to treat the superficial symptoms of fever and chill. And shock, I thought, better treat for that, too.

"And bring me a little honey, too, please!" I called after him, as he had already reached the door. He nodded and went hurriedly toward the kitchen, his footsteps quick and solid on the oak floorboards.

I began to pound the mixture, still turning over additional possibilities. Some small part of my mind was half-glad of the emergency; I could put off for a little while the necessity of hearing about the Browns and their beastly committee.

I had a most uneasy feeling. Whatever they wanted, it didn't portend anything good, I was sure; they certainly hadn't left on friendly terms. As for what Jamie might feel obliged to do in response to them—

Horse chestnut. That was sometimes used for the tertian ague, as Dr. Rawlings called it. Did I have any left? Glancing quickly over the jars and bottles in the medicine chest, I stopped, seeing one with an inch or so of dried black globules left at the bottom. *Gallberries,* the label read. Not mine; it was one of Rawlings's jars. I'd never used them for anything. But something niggled at my memory. I'd heard or read something about gallberries; what was it?

Half-unconsciously, I picked up the jar and opened it, sniffing. A sharp, astringent smell rose from the berries, slightly bitter. And slightly familiar.

Still holding the jar, I went to the table where my big black casebook lay, and flipped hastily to the early pages, those notes left by the man who had first owned both book and medicine chest, Daniel Rawlings. Where had it been?

I was still flipping pages, scanning for the shape of a half-remembered note, when Jamie came back, a jug of hot water and a dish of honey in hand—and the Beardsley twins dogging his steps.

I glanced at them, but said nothing; they tended to pop up unexpectedly, like a pair of jack-in-the boxes.

"Is Miss Lizzie fearfully sick?" Jo asked anxiously, peering around Jamie to see what I was doing.

"Yes," I said briefly, only half paying attention to him. "Don't worry, though; I'm fixing her some medicine."

There it was. A brief notation, added as an obvious afterthought to the account of treatment of a patient whose symptoms seemed clearly malarial—and who had, I noticed with an unpleasant twinge, died.

I am told by the Trader from whom I procured Jesuit Bark that the Indians use a Plant called Gallberry, which rivals the Bark of Cinchona for bitterness and is thought capital for Use in tertian and quartan Fevers. I have collected some for Experiment and propose to try an Infusion so soon as the Opportunity presents itself.

I picked out one of the dried berries and bit into it. The pungent taste of quinine at once flooded my mouth—accompanied by a copious flood of saliva, as my mouth puckered at the eye-watering bitterness. Gallberry, indeed!

I dived for the open window, spat into the herb bed beneath and went on spitting, to the accompaniment of giggles and snorts from the Beardsleys, who were most diverted at the unexpected entertainment.

"Are ye all right, Sassenach?" Amusement was fighting with worry for dominance of Jamie's face. He poured a bit of water from the jug into a clay beaker, added a dollop of honey as an afterthought, and handed it to me.

"Fine," I croaked. "Don't drop that!" Kezzie Beardsley had picked up the jar of gallberries and was sniffing cautiously at it. He nodded at my admonition, but didn't put the jar down, instead handing it off to his brother.

I took a good mouthful of hot, honeyed water, and swallowed. "Those—they have something like quinine in them."

Jamie's face changed at once, the worry lessening.

"So they'll help the lass?"

"I hope so. There aren't many, though."

"D'ye mean you need more o' these things for Miss Lizzie, Mrs. Fraser?" Jo glanced up at me, dark eyes sharp over the little jar.

"Yes," I said, surprised. "You don't mean you know where to get any, surely?"

"Aye, ma'am," Kezzie said, his voice a little loud, as usual. "Indians got 'em."

"Which Indians?" Jamie asked, his gaze sharpening.

"Them Cherokee," Jo said, waving vaguely over one shoulder. "By the mountain."

This description might have suited half a dozen villages, but evidently it was a specific village that they had in mind, for the two of them turned as one, obviously intending to go directly and fetch back gallberries.

"Wait a bit, lads," Jamie said, snagging Kezzie by the collar. "I'll go along with ye. Ye'll be needing something to trade, after all."

"Oh, we got hides a-plenty, sir," Jo assured him. "'Twas a good season."

Jo was an expert hunter, and while Kezzie still hadn't sufficiently keen hearing to hunt well, his brother had taught him to run traplines. Ian had told me that the Beardsleys' shack was stacked nearly to the rooftree with the hides of beaver, marten, deer, and ermine. The smell of it always clung to them, a faint miasma of dried blood, musk, and cold hair.

"Aye? Well, that's generous of ye, Jo, to be sure. But I'll come, nonetheless." Jamie glanced at me, acknowledging the fact that he had made his decision—but asking for my approval, nonetheless. I swallowed, tasting bitterness.

"Yes," I said, and cleared my throat. "If—if you're going, let me send some things, and tell you what to ask for in trade. You won't leave until morning, surely?"

The Beardsleys were vibrating with impatience to be gone, but Jamie stood still, looking at me, and I felt him touch me, without words or movement.

"No," he said softly, "we'll bide for the night." He turned then to the Beardsleys. "Go up, will ye, Jo, and ask Bobby Higgins to come down. I'll need to speak with him."

"He's up with Miss Lizzie?" Jo Beardsley looked displeased at this, and his brother's face echoed his expression of slit-eyed suspicion.

"What's he a-doin' in her room, then? Don't he know she's betrothed?" Kezzie asked, righteously.

"Her father's with her, too," Jamie assured them. "Her reputation's safe, aye?"

Jo snorted briefly, but the brothers exchanged glances, then left together, slender shoulders set in determination to oust this threat to Lizzie's virtue.

"So you'll do it?" I set down the pestle. "Be an Indian agent?"

"I think I must. If I do not—Richard Brown surely will. I think I canna risk that." He hesitated, then drew close and touched me lightly, fingers on my elbow. "I'll send the lads back at once with the berries ye need. I may need to stay for a day, maybe two. For the talking, aye?" To tell the Cherokee that he was now an agent for the British Crown, he meant—and to make arrangements for word to be spread that the headmen of the mountain villages should come down later to a council for parley and gifts.

I nodded, feeling a small bubble of fear swell under my breastbone. It was starting. No matter how much one knows that something dreadful is going to happen in the future, one somehow never thinks it will be *today*.

"Not—don't stay away too long, will you?" I blurted, not wanting to burden him with my fears, but unable to keep quiet.

"No," he said softly, and his hand rested for an instant in the small of my back. "Dinna fash yourself; I'll not tarry."

The sound of feet descending the stairs echoed in the hall. I supposed Mr. Wemyss had shooed the Beardsleys out, along with Bobby. They didn't stop, but went off without speaking, casting looks of veiled dislike at Bobby, who seemed quite oblivious to them.

"Yon lad said you wanted to speak to me, zur?" He'd regained some color, I was glad to see, and seemed steady enough on his feet. He glanced uneasily at the table, still spread with the sheet I'd put him on, and then at me, but I merely shook my head. I'd finish dealing with his piles later.

"Aye, Bobby." Jamie made a brief gesture toward a stool, as though to invite Bobby to sit, but I cleared my throat in a meaningful manner, and he stopped, then leaned against the table, rather than sitting down himself.

"Those two who came—Brown, they're called. They've a settlement some way away. Ye said ye've heard of the Committees of Safety, aye? So ye'll have some notion what they're about."

"Aye, zur. Tha Browns, zur—did they want me?" He spoke calmly enough, but I saw him swallow briefly, Adam's apple bobbing in his slender throat.

Jamie sighed, and ran a hand through his hair. The sun was slanting through the window now, and struck him directly, making his red hair glow with flame—and picking out here and there a flicker of the silver that was beginning to show among the ruddy strands.

"They did. They kent ye were here; heard of ye, doubtless from someone ye met along the way. Ye'll have told folk where ye were headed, I suppose?"

Bobby nodded, wordless.

"What did they want with him?" I asked, tipping the ground root bark and berries into a bowl and pouring hot water over them to steep.

"They didna make that quite clear," Jamie said dryly. "But then, I didna give them the chance. I only told them they'd take a guest from my hearth over my dead body—and theirs."

"I thanks 'ee for that, zur." Bobby took a deep breath. "They—knew, I reckon? About Boston? I'd not told anyone *that,* surely."

Jamie's frown deepened slightly.

"Aye, they did. They pretended to think I didna ken; told me I was harboring a murderer unbeknownst, and a threat to the public welfare."

"Well, the first is true enough," Bobby said, touching his brand gingerly, as though it still burned him. He offered a wan smile. "But I dunno as I s'ould be a threat to anyone, these days."

Jamie dismissed that.

"The point is, Bobby, that they do ken ye're here. They'll not come and drag ye away, I think. But I'd ask ye to go canny about the place. I'll make provision to see ye safely back to Lord John, when the time comes, with an escort. I gather ye're no quite finished with him?" he asked, turning to me.

"Not quite," I replied equably. Bobby looked apprehensive.

"Well, then." Jamie reached into the waist of his breeches, and drew out a pistol, which had been hidden by the folds of his shirt. It was, I saw, the fancy gilt-edged one.

"Keep it by ye," Jamie said, handing it to Bobby. "There's powder and shot in the sideboard. Will ye look out for my wife and family, then, whilst I'm gone?"

"Oh!" Bobby looked startled, but then nodded, tucking the pistol away in his own breeches. "I will so, zur. Depend upon it!"

Jamie smiled at him, his eyes warming.

"That's a comfort to me, Bobby. Will ye maybe go and find my son-in-law? I'll need a word with him before I go."

"Aye, zur. Right away!" He squared his shoulders and set off, an expression of determination on his poet's face.

"What do you think they would have done with him?" I asked softly, as the outer door closed behind him. "The Browns."

Jamie shook his head.

"God knows. Hanged him at a crossroad, maybe—or maybe only beaten him and driven him out of the mountains. They want to make a show of being able to protect the folk, aye? From dangerous criminals and the like," he added, with a twist of the mouth.

"A government derives its powers from the just consent of the governed," I quoted, nodding. "For a Committee of Safety to have any legitimacy, there needs to be an obvious threat *to* the public safety. Clever of the Browns to have reasoned that out."

He gave me a look, one auburn brow raised.

"Who said that? *The consent of the governed.*"

"Thomas Jefferson," I replied, feeling smug. "Or rather, he will say it in another two years."

"He'll steal it from a gentleman named Locke in another two years," he corrected. "I suppose Richard Brown must ha' been decently educated."

"Unlike me, you mean?" I said, unruffled. "If you expect trouble from the Browns, though, should you have given Bobby *that* particular pistol?"

He shrugged.

"I'll need the good ones. And I doubt verra much that he'll fire that one."

"Counting on its deterrent effect?" I was skeptical, but he was likely right.

"Aye, that. But more on Bobby."

"How so?"

"I doubt he'd fire a gun again to save his own life—but he would, maybe, to save yours. And should it come to such a pass, they'll be too close to miss." He spoke with dispassion, but I felt the hairs prickle down my nape.

"Well, that's a comfort," I said. "And just how do you know what he'd do?"

"Talked to him," he said briefly. "The man he shot in Boston was the first he'd ever killed. He doesna want to do it again." He straightened, and moved restlessly toward the counter, where he busied himself in straightening a scatter of small instruments I had laid out for cleaning.

I moved to stand beside him, watching. There was a handful of small cautery irons and scalpels, soaking in a beaker of turpentine. He took them out, one by one, wiped them dry and laid them back in their box, neatly, side by side. The spade-shaped metal ends of the irons were blackened by use; the scalpel blades were weathered to a soft glow, but the sharp edges gleamed, a hairbreadth of bright silver.

"We'll be all right," I said quietly. I meant it to be a reassuring statement, but it came out with a tinge of question.

"Aye, I know," he said. He put the last iron in its box, but didn't replace the lid. Instead, he stood, hands spread flat on the counter, looking straight ahead.

"I dinna want to go," he said softly. "I dinna want to do this."

I wasn't sure whether he was speaking to me, or to himself—but I thought he wasn't referring only to his journey to the Cherokee village.

"Neither do I," I whispered, and moved a little closer, so I felt his breathing. He lifted his hands then and turned toward me, taking me into his arms, and we stood wrapped close, listening to each other's breathing, the bitter smell of the brewing tea seeping through the homely scents of linen, dust, and sun-warmed flesh.

There were still choices to be made, decisions to reach, actions to take. Many of them. But in one day, one hour, one single declaration of intent, we had stepped across the threshold of war.

10
Duty Calls

Jamie had sent Bobby after Roger Mac, but found himself too restless to wait, and set off himself, leaving Claire to her brewing.

Everything seemed peaceful and beautiful outside. A brown sheep with a pair of lambs stood indolently in her pen, jaws moving in a slow stupor of satisfaction, the lambs hopping awkwardly to and fro like fuzzy grasshoppers behind her. Claire's herb bed was full of leafing greens and sprouting flowers.

The well lid was ajar; he bent to draw it into place and found the boards had warped. He added fixing that to the constant list of chores and repairs that he carried in his head, wishing fervently that he could devote the next few days to digging, hauling manure, shingling, and the like, instead of what he was about to do.

He'd rather bury the old privy pit or castrate pigs than go and ask Roger Mac what he kent about Indians and revolutions. He found it mildly gruesome to discuss the future with his son-in-law, and tried never to do it.

The things Claire told him of her own time seemed often fantastic, with the enjoyable half-real sense of faery tales, and sometimes macabre, but always interesting, for what he learned of his wife from the telling. Brianna tended to share with him small, homely details of machinery, which were interesting, or wild stories of men walking on the moon, which were immensely entertaining, but no threat to his peace of mind.

Roger Mac, though, had a cold-blooded way of talking that reminded him to an uncomfortable degree of the works of the historians he'd read, and had therefore a sense of concrete doom about it. Talking to Roger Mac made it seem all too likely that this, that, or the other frightful happenstance was not only indeed *going* to happen—but would most likely have direct and personal consequences.

It was like talking to a particularly evil-minded fortune-teller, he thought, one you hadn't paid enough to hear something pleasant. The thought made a sudden memory pop up on the surface of his mind, bobbing like a fishing cork.

In Paris. He'd been with friends, other students, drinking in the piss-smelling taverns near the *université*. He'd been fairly drunk himself when someone took a fancy to have his palms read, and he had pushed with the others into the corner where the old woman who did it always sat, scarcely visible amid the gloom and clouds of pipe smoke.

He hadn't intended to do it himself; he had only a few pennies in his pocket, and didn't mean to waste them on unholy nonsense. He'd said so, loudly.

Whereupon a scraggy claw had shot out of the darkness and seized his hand, sinking long, filthy nails into his flesh. He'd yelped in surprise, and his friends all laughed. They laughed harder when she spat in his palm.

She rubbed the spittle into his skin in a businesslike way, bent close enough that he could smell the ancient sweat of her and see the lice crawling in the grizzled hair that keeked from the edge of her rusty-black shawl. She peered into his hand and a dirty nail traced the lines of it, tickling. He tried to pull his hand away, but she tightened her grip on his wrist, and he found to his surprise that he could not break it.

"T'es un chat, toi," the old woman had remarked, in tones of malicious interest. "You're a cat, you. A little red cat."

Dubois—that was his name, Dubois—had at once begun to miaou and yowl, to the amusement of the others. He himself refused to rise to the bait, and saying only, *"Merci, madame,"* tried again to pull away.

"Neuf," she said, tapping rapid random places on his palm, then seizing a finger and wiggling it by way of emphasis. "You have a nine in your hand. And death," she'd added offhandedly. "You'll die nine times before you rest in your grave."

She'd let go then, amidst a chorus of sarcastic *"aou-la-las!"* from the French students, and laughter from the rest.

He snorted, sending the memory back where it came from, and good riddance to it. The old woman refused to go so easily, though, and called to him through the years, as she'd called through the raucous, beer-filled air of the tavern.

"Sometimes dying doesn't hurt, *mon p'tit chat*," she'd called after him, mocking. "But more often it does."

"No it doesn't," he muttered, and stopped, appalled, hearing himself. Christ. It wasn't himself he was hearing, but his godfather. *"Don't be afraid, laddie. It doesna hurt a bit, to die."* He missed his footing and staggered, caught himself and stood still, a taste of metal on the back of his tongue.

His heart was thumping, suddenly, for no reason, as though he had run miles. He saw the cabin, certainly, and heard the calling of jays in the half-leafed chestnut trees. But he saw even more clearly Murtagh's face, the grim lines of it relaxing into peace and the deep-set black eyes fixed on his, shifting in and out of focus, as though his godfather looked at once at him and at something far beyond him. He felt the weight of Murtagh's body in his arms, growing suddenly heavy as he died.

The vision vanished, as abruptly as it had come, and he found himself standing next to a rain puddle, staring at a wooden duck half-mired in the mud.

He crossed himself, with a quick word for the repose of Murtagh's soul, then bent and retrieved the duck, washing the mud away in the puddle. His hands were trembling, and little wonder. His memories of Culloden were few and fragmentary— but they were beginning to come back.

So far, such things had come to him only in glimpses at the edge of sleep. He'd seen Murtagh there before, and in the dreams that followed.

He hadn't told Claire about them. Not yet.

He pushed open the door of the cabin, but it was empty, the hearth smoored, spinning wheel and loom standing idle. Brianna was likely at Fergus's place, visiting Marsali. Where would Roger Mac be now? He stepped back outside and stood listening.

The thump of an ax came faintly from somewhere in the forest beyond the cabin. It stopped, then, and he heard men's voices, raised in greeting. He turned and headed for the trail that led upslope, half grown over with spring grass, but showing the black smudges of fresh footmarks.

What might the old woman have told him if he'd paid her? he wondered. Had she lied to spite him for his miserliness—or told him the truth, for the same reason?

One of the more disagreeable things about talking to Roger Mac was that Jamie was sure he always told the truth.

He'd forgotten to leave the duck at the cabin. Wiping it on his breeches, he pushed grimly through the sprouting weeds, to hear what fate awaited him.

11

Bloodwork

I pushed the microscope toward Bobby Higgins, who had returned from his errand, his own discomforts forgotten in worry for Lizzie. "See the round pinkish things?" I said. "Those are Lizzie's blood cells. Everyone has blood cells," I added. "They're what make your blood red."

"'Strewth," he muttered, amazed. "I never knew!"

"Well, now you do," I said. "Do you see that some of the blood cells are broken? And that some have little spots in them?"

"I do, mum," he said, screwing up his face and peering intently. "What are 'ey, then?"

"Parasites. Little beasts that get into your blood if a certain kind of mosquito bites you," I explained. "They're called *Plasmodium.* Once you've got them, they go on living in your blood—but every so often, they begin to . . . er . . . breed. When there are too many of them, they burst out of the blood cells, and that's what causes a malarial attack—the ague. The sludge of the broken blood cells sort of silts up, you see, in the organs, and makes you feel terribly sick."

"Oh." He straightened up, making a face of deep aversion at the microscope. "That's . . . that's pure gashly, that is!"

"Yes, it is," I said, succeeding in keeping a straight face. "But quinine—Jesuit bark, you know?—will help stop it."

"Oh, that's good, mum, very good," he said, his face lightening. "However you do come to know such things," he said, shaking his head. "'Tis a wonder!"

"Oh, I know quite a lot of things about parasites," I said casually, taking the saucer off the bowl in which I had been brewing the mix of dogwood bark and gallberries. The liquid was a rich purplish black, and looked slightly viscous, now that it had cooled. It also smelled lethal, from which I deduced that it was about ready.

"Tell me, Bobby—have you ever heard of hookworms?"

He looked at me blankly.

"No, mum."

"Mm. Would you hold this for me, please?" I put a folded square of gauze over the neck of a flask and handed him the bottle to hold while I poured the purple mixture into it.

"These fainting fits of yours," I said, eyes on the stream. "How long have you had them?"

"Oh . . . six months, mebbe."

"I see. Did you by chance notice any sort of irritation—itching, say? Or a rash? Happening maybe seven months ago? Most likely on your feet."

He stared at me, soft blue eyes thunderstruck as though I had performed some feat of mind reading.

"Why, so I did have, mum. Last autumn, 'twas."

"Ah," I said. "Well, then. I think, Bobby, that you may just possibly have a case of hookworms."

He looked down at himself in horror.

"Where?"

"Inside." I took the bottle from him and corked it. "Hookworms are parasites that burrow through the skin—most often through the soles of the feet—and then migrate through the body until they reach your intestines—your, um, innards," I amended, seeing incomprehension cross his face. "The adult worms have nasty little hooked bills, like this"—I crooked my index finger in illustration—"and they pierce the intestinal lining and proceed to suck your blood. That's why, if you have them, you feel very weak, and faint frequently."

From the suddenly clammy look of him, I rather thought he was about to faint *now,* and guided him hastily to a stool, pushing his head down between his knees.

"I don't know for sure that that's the problem," I told him, bending down to address him. "I was just looking at the slides of Lizzie's blood, though, and thinking of parasites, and—well, it came to me suddenly that a diagnosis of hookworms would fit your symptoms rather well."

"Oh?" he said faintly. The thick tail of wavy hair had fallen forward, leaving the back of his neck exposed, fair-skinned and childlike.

"How old are you, Bobby?" I asked, suddenly realizing that I had no idea.

"Twenty-three, mum," he said. "Mum? I think I s'all have to puke."

I snatched a bucket from the corner and got it to him just in time.

"Have I got rid of them?" he asked weakly, sitting up and wiping his mouth on his sleeve as he peered into the bucket. "I could do it more."

"I'm afraid not," I said sympathetically. "Assuming that you have got hookworms, they're attached very firmly, and too far down for vomiting to dislodge them. The only way to be sure about it, though, is to look for the eggs they shed."

Bobby eyed me apprehensively.

"It's not exactly as I'm horrible shy, mum," he said, shifting gingerly. "You know that. But Dr. Potts did give me great huge clysters of mustard water. Surely that would ha' burnt they worms right out? If I was a worm, I s'ould let go and give up the ghost at once, did anyone souse me with mustard water."

"Well, you would think so, wouldn't you?" I said. "Unfortunately not. But I won't give you an enema," I assured him. "We need to see whether you truly do have the worms, to begin with, and if so, there's a medicine I can mix up for you that will poison them directly."

"Oh." He looked a little happier at that. "How d'ye mean to see, then, mum?" He glanced narrowly at the counter, where the assortment of clamps and suture jars were still laid out.

"Couldn't be simpler," I assured him. "I do a process called fecal sedimentation to concentrate the stool, then look for the eggs under the microscope."

He nodded, plainly not following. I smiled kindly at him.

"All you have to do, Bobby, is shit."

His face was a study in doubt and apprehension.

"If it's all the same to you, mum," he said, "I think I'll keep the worms."

Further Mysteries of Science

Late in the afternoon, Roger MacKenzie came back from the cooper's shop to discover his wife deep in contemplation of an object sitting on his dinner table.

"What *is* that? Some type of prehistoric Christmas tinned goods?" Roger extended a ginger forefinger toward a squat jar made of greenish glass and sealed with a cork, the latter covered with a stout layer of red wax. An amorphous chunk of something was visible inside, evidently submerged in liquid.

"Ho ho," said his wife tolerantly, moving the jar out of his reach. "You *think* you're being funny. It's white phosphorus—a present from Lord John."

He glanced at her; she was excited, the tip of her nose gone pink and bits of red hair pulled loose and waving in the breeze; like her father, she was inclined to run her hands through her hair when thinking.

"And you intend to do . . . *what* with it?" he asked, trying to keep any note of foreboding from his voice. He had the vaguest memories of hearing about the properties of phosphorus in his distant school days; he thought either it made you glow in the dark or it blew up. Neither prospect was reassuring.

"Wellll . . . make matches. Maybe." Her upper teeth fastened momentarily in the flesh of her lower lip as she considered the jar. "I know how—in theory. But it might be a little tricky in practice."

"Why is that?" he asked warily.

"Well, it bursts into flame if you expose it to air," she explained. "That's why it's packed in water. Don't touch, Jem! It's poisonous." Grabbing Jemmy round the middle, she pulled him down from the table, where he had been eyeing the jar with greedy curiosity.

"Oh, well, why worry about that? It will explode in his face before he has a chance to get it in his mouth." Roger picked up the jar for safekeeping, holding it as though it might go off in his hands. He wanted to ask whether she were insane, but had been married long enough to know the price of injudicious rhetorical questions.

"Where d'ye mean to keep it?" He cast an eloquent glance round the confines of the cabin, which in terms of storage boasted a blanket chest, a small shelf for books and papers, another for comb, toothbrushes, and Brianna's small cache of personal belongings, and a pie hutch. Jemmy had been able to open the pie hutch since the age of seven months or so.

"I'm thinking I'd better put it in Mama's surgery," she replied, keeping an absentminded grip on Jem, who was struggling with single-minded energy to get at the pretty thing. "Nobody touches anything in there."

That was true enough; the people who were not afraid of Claire Fraser personally were generally terrified of the contents of her surgery, these featuring fearsomely painful-looking implements, mysterious murky brews, and vile-smelling medicines. In addition, the surgery had cupboards too high for even a determined climber like Jem to reach.

"Good idea," Roger said, anxious to get the jar out of Jem's vicinity. "I'll take it up now, shall I?"

Before Brianna could answer, a knock came at the door, followed immediately by Jamie Fraser. Jem instantly ceased trying to get at the jar and instead flung himself on his grandfather with shrieks of joy.

"How is it, then, *a bhailach*?" Jamie inquired amiably, neatly turning Jem upside down and holding him by the ankles. "A word, Roger Mac?"

"Sure. Ye'll sit, maybe?" He'd told Jamie earlier what he knew—lamentably little—regarding the role of the Cherokee in the upcoming Revolution. Had he come to inquire further? Reluctantly setting down the jar, Roger pulled out a stool and pushed it in his father-in-law's direction. Jamie accepted it with a nod, dexterously transferring Jemmy to a position over one shoulder and sitting down.

Jemmy giggled madly, squirming until his grandfather slapped him lightly on the seat of his breeches, whereupon he subsided, hanging contentedly upside-down like a sloth, his bright hair spilling down the back of Jamie's shirt.

"It's this way, *a charaid*," Jamie said. "I must be going in the morning to the Cherokee villages, and there is a thing I'd ask ye to do in my place."

"Oh, aye. D'ye want me to see to the barley harvest, then?" The early grain was still ripening. Everyone had his fingers crossed that the weather would keep fair for another few weeks, but the prospects were good.

"No, Brianna can do that—if ye will, lass?" He smiled at his daughter, who raised thick ruddy eyebrows, the twins of his.

"I can," she agreed. "What are you planning to do with Ian, Roger, and Arch Bug, though?" Arch Bug was Jamie's factor, and the logical person to be overseeing the harvest in Jamie's absence.

"Well, I shall take Young Ian with me. The Cherokee ken him well, and he's comfortable wi' their speech. I'll take the Beardsley lads, too, so they can fetch back the berries and bits o' things your mother wants for Lizzie, straightaway."

"I go, too?" Jemmy inquired hopefully.

"Not this time, *a bhailach*. In the autumn, maybe." He patted Jemmy on the bottom, then returned his attention to Roger.

"That being so," he said, "I need ye to go to Cross Creek, if ye will, and collect the new tenants." Roger felt a small surge of excitement—and alarm—at the prospect, but merely cleared his throat and nodded.

"Aye. Of course. Will they—"

"Ye'll take Arch Bug along, and Tom Christie."

A moment of incredulous silence greeted this statement.

"Tom *Christie*?" Bree said, exchanging a glance of bafflement with Roger. "What on earth for?" The schoolmaster was a notably dour sort, and no one's idea of a congenial traveling companion.

Her father's mouth twisted wryly.

"Aye, well. There's the one small thing MacDonald neglected to tell me, when he asked if I'd take them. They're Protestants, the lot."

"Ah," said Roger. "I see." Jamie met his eye and nodded, relieved to be so immediately understood.

"*I* don't see." Brianna patted her hair, frowning, then pulled off the ribbon and began to comb her fingers slowly through it, undoing the tangles as a preliminary to brushing it. "What difference does it make?"

Roger and Jamie exchanged a brief but eloquent glance. Jamie shrugged, and pulled Jem down into his lap.

"Well." Roger rubbed his chin, trying to think how to explain two centuries of Scottish religious intolerance in any way that would make sense to an American of the twentieth century. "Ahh . . . ye recall the civil-rights thing in the States, integration in the South, all that?"

"Of course I do." She narrowed her eyes at him. "Okay. So, which side are the Negroes?"

"The what?" Jamie looked entirely baffled. "Where do Negroes come into the matter?"

"Not quite that simple," Roger assured her. "Just an indication of the depth of feeling involved. Let us say that the notion of having a Catholic landlord is likely to cause our new tenants severe qualms—and vice versa?" he asked, glancing at Jamie.

"What's Negroes?" Jemmy asked with interest.

"Er . . . .dark-skinned people," Roger replied, suddenly aware of the potential quagmire opened up by this question. It was true that the term "Negro" didn't invariably mean also "slave"—but near enough that there was little difference. "D'ye not remember them, from your great-auntie Jocasta's place?"

Jemmy frowned, adopting for an unsettling instant the precise expression his grandfather was wearing.

"No."

"Well, anyway," Bree said, calling the meeting to order with a sharp rap of her hairbrush on the table, "the point is that Mr. Christie is enough of a Protestant to make the new people feel comfortable?"

"Something of the sort," her father agreed, one side of his mouth curling up. "Between your man here and Tom Christie, at least they'll not think they're entering the Devil's realm entirely."

"I see," Roger said again, in a slightly different tone. So it wasn't only his position as son of the house and general right-hand man, was it—but the fact that he was a Presbyterian, at least in name. He raised a brow at Jamie, who shrugged in acknowledgment.

"Mmphm," Roger said, resigned.

"Mmphm," said Jamie, satisfied.

"Stop *doing* that," Brianna said crossly. "Fine. So you and Tom Christie are going to Cross Creek. Why is Arch Bug going?"

Roger became aware, in a subliminally marital way, that his wife was disgruntled at the thought of being left behind to organize the harvest—a filthy, exhausting job at the best of times—whilst he frolicked with a squad of his co-religionists in the romantically exciting metropolis of Cross Creek, population two hundred.

"It will be Arch, mostly, helping them to settle and build themselves shelter before the cold," Jamie said logically. "Ye dinna mean to suggest, I hope, that I send him alone to talk to them?"

Brianna smiled involuntarily at that; Arch Bug, married for decades to the voluble Mrs. Bug, was famous for his lack of speech. He *could* talk, but seldom did so, limiting his conversational contributions to the occasional genial "Mmp."

"Well, they'll likely never realize that Arch is Catholic," Roger said, rubbing his upper lip with a forefinger. "Or is he, come to that? I've never asked him."

"He is," Jamie said, very dryly. "But he's lived long enough to ken when to be silent."

"Well, I can see this is going to be a jolly expedition," Brianna said, raising one brow. "When do you think you'll be back?"

"Christ, I don't know," Roger said, feeling a stab of guilt at the casual blasphemy. He'd have to revise his habits, and quickly. "A month? Six weeks?"

"At least," his father-in-law said cheerfully. "They'll be on foot, mind."

Roger took a deep breath, contemplating a slow march, *en masse,* from Cross Creek to the mountains, with Arch Bug on one side of him and Tom Christie on the other, twin pillars of taciturnity. His eyes lingered wistfully on his wife, envisioning six weeks of sleeping by the roadside, alone.

"Yeah, fine," he said. "I'll . . . um . . . go speak to Tom and Arch tonight, then."

"Daddy go?" Catching the gist of the conversation, Jem scrambled off his grandfather's knee and scampered over to Roger, grabbing him round the leg. "Go with *you,* Daddy!"

"Oh. Well, I don't think—" He caught sight of Bree's face, resigned, and then the green and red jar on the table behind her. "Why not?" he said suddenly, and smiled at Jem. "Great-Auntie Jocasta would love to see you. And Mummy can blow things up to her heart's content without worrying where you are, aye?"

"She can do what?" Jamie looked startled.

"It doesn't *explode*," Brianna said, picking up the jar of phosphorus and cradling it possessively. "It just burns. Are you sure?" This last was addressed to Roger, and accompanied by a searching look.

"Yeah, sure," he said, affecting confidence. He glanced at Jemmy, who was chanting "Go! Go! Go!", meanwhile hopping up and down like a demented popcorn kernel. "At least I'll have someone to talk to on the way."

13

Safe Hands

It was nearly dark when Jamie came in to find me sitting at the kitchen table, head on my arms. I jerked upright at the sound of his footstep, blinking.

"Are ye all right, Sassenach?" He sat down on the opposite bench, eyeing me. "Ye look as though ye've been dragged through a hedge backward."

"Oh." I patted vaguely at my hair, which did seem to be sticking out a bit. "Um. Fine. Are you hungry?"

"Of course I am. Have ye eaten, yourself?"

I squinted and rubbed my face, trying to think.

"No," I decided at last. "I was waiting for you, but I seem to have fallen asleep. There's stew. Mrs. Bug left it."

He got up and peered into the small cauldron, then pushed the swinging hook back to bring it over the fire to warm.

"What have ye been doing, Sassenach?" he asked, coming back. "And how's the wee lass?"

"The wee lass is what I've been doing," I said, suppressing a yawn. "Mostly." I rose, slowly, feeling my joints protest, and staggered over to the sideboard to cut some bread.

"She couldn't keep it down," I said. "The gallberry medicine. Not that I blame her," I added, cautiously licking my lower lip. After she'd thrown it up the first time, I'd tasted it myself. My tastebuds were still in a state of revolt; I'd never met a more aptly named plant, and being boiled into syrup had merely concentrated the flavor.

Jamie sniffed deeply as I turned.

"Did she vomit on ye?"

"No, that was Bobby Higgins," I said. "He's got hookworms." He raised his brows.

"Do I want to hear about them whilst I'm eating?"

"Definitely not," I said, sitting down with the loaf, a knife, and a crock of soft butter. I tore off a piece, buttered it thickly, and gave it to him, then took one for myself. My tastebuds hesitated, but wavered on the edge of forgiving me for the gallberry syrup.

"What have *you* been doing?" I asked, beginning to wake up enough to take notice. He seemed tired, but more cheerful than he had been when he'd left the house.

"Talking to Roger Mac about Indians and Protestants." He frowned at the half-eaten chunk of bread in his hand. "Is there something amiss wi' the bread, Sassenach? It tastes odd."

I waved a hand apologetically.

"Sorry, that's me. I washed several times, but I couldn't get it off completely. Perhaps you'd better do the buttering." I pushed the loaf toward him with my elbow, gesturing at the crock.

"Couldna get *what* off?"

"Well, we tried and tried with the syrup, but no good; Lizzie simply couldn't hold it down, poor thing. But I remembered that quinine can be absorbed through the skin. So I mixed the syrup into some goose grease, and rubbed it all over her. Oh, yes, thanks." I leaned forward and took a delicate bite of the buttered bit of bread he held out for me. My tastebuds gave in gracefully, and I realized that I hadn't eaten all day.

"And it worked?" He glanced up at the ceiling. Mr. Wemyss and Lizzie shared the smaller room upstairs, but all was quiet above.

"I think so," I said, swallowing. "The fever finally broke, at least, and she's asleep. We'll keep using it; if the fever doesn't come back in two days, we'll know it works."

"That's good, then."

"Well, and then there was Bobby and his hookworms. Fortunately, I have some ipecacuanha and turpentine."

"Fortunately for the worms, or for Bobby?"

"Well, neither, really," I said, and yawned. "It will probably work, though."

He smiled faintly, and uncorked a bottle of beer, passing it automatically under his nose. Finding it all right, he poured some for me.

"Aye, well, it's a comfort to know I'm leaving things in your capable hands, Sassenach. Ill-smelling," he added, wrinkling his long nose in my direction, "but capable."

"Thanks so much." The beer was better than good; must be one of Mrs. Bug's batches. We sipped companionably for a bit, both too tired to get up and serve the stew. I watched him beneath my lashes; I always did, when he was about to leave on a journey, storing up small memories of him against his return.

He looked tired, and there were small twin lines between his heavy brows, betokening slight worry. The candlelight glowed on the broad bones of his face, though, and cast his shadow clear on the plastered wall behind him, strong and bold. I watched the shadow raise its spectral beer glass, the light making an amber glow in the shadow glass.

"Sassenach," he said suddenly, putting down the glass, "how many times, would ye say, have I come close to dying?"

I stared at him for a moment, but then shrugged and began to reckon, mustering my synapses into reluctant activity.

"Well . . . I don't know what horrible things happened to you before I met you, but after . . . well, you were dreadfully ill at the abbey." I glanced covertly at him, but he seemed not to be bothered at the thought of Wentworth prison, and what had been done to him there that had caused the illness. "Hmm. And after Culloden—you said you had a terrible fever then, from your wounds, and thought you might die, only Jenny forced you—I mean, nursed you through it."

"And then Laoghaire shot me," he said wryly. "And *you* forced me through it. Likewise, when the snake bit me." He considered for a moment.

"I had the smallpox when I was a wean, but I think I wasna in danger of dying then; they said it was a light case. So only four times, then."

"What about the day I first met you?" I objected. "You nearly bled to death."

"Oh, I did not," he protested. "That was no but a wee scratch."

I lifted one brow at him, and leaning over to the hearth, scooped a ladle of aromatic stew into a bowl. It was rich with the juices of rabbit and venison, swimming in a thick gravy spiced with rosemary, garlic, and onion. So far as my tastebuds were concerned, all was forgiven.

"Have it your way," I said. "But wait—what about your head? When Dougal tried to kill you with an ax. Surely that's five?"

He frowned, accepting the bowl.

"Aye, I suppose you're right," he said, seeming displeased. "Five, then."

I regarded him gently over my own bowl of stew. He was very large, solid, and beautifully formed. And if he was a bit battered by circumstance, that merely added to his charm.

"You're a very hard person to kill, I think," I said. "That's a great comfort to me."

He smiled, reluctant, but then reached out and lifted his glass in salute, touching it first to his own lips, then to mine.

"We'll drink to that, Sassenach, shall we?"

14

People of the Snowbird

"Guns," Bird-who-sings-in-the-morning said. "Tell your King we want guns."

Jamie suppressed the urge to reply, "Who doesn't?" for a moment, but then gave in to it, surprising the war chief into a blink of startlement, followed by a grin.

"Who, indeed?" Bird was a short man, shaped like a barrel, and young for his office—but shrewd, his affability no disguise to his intelligence. "They all tell you this, all the village war chiefs, eh? Of course they do. What do you tell them?"

"What I can." Jamie lifted one shoulder, let it fall. "Trade goods are certain, knives are likely—guns are possible, but I cannot yet promise them."

They were speaking a slightly unfamiliar dialect of Cherokee, and he hoped he had got right the manner of indicating probability. He did well enough with the usual tongue in casual matters of trade and hunting, but the matters he dealt in here would not be casual. He glanced briefly at Ian, who was listening closely, but evidently what he'd said was all right. Ian visited the villages near the Ridge frequently, and hunted with the young men; he shifted into the tongue of the Tsalagi as easily as he did into his native Gaelic.

"So, well enough." Bird settled himself more comfortably. The pewter badge Jamie had given him as a present glinted on his breast, firelight flickering over the broadly amiable planes of his face. "Tell your King about the guns—and tell him why we need them, eh?"

"You wish me to tell him that, do you? Do you think he will be

willing to send you guns with which to kill his own people?"
Jamie asked dryly. The incursion of white settlers across the
Treaty Line into the Cherokee lands was a sore point, and he
risked something by alluding to it directly, rather than addressing
Bird's other needs for guns: to defend his village from raiders—
or to go raiding himself.

Bird shrugged in reply.

"We can kill them without guns, if we vant to." One eyebrow
lifted a little, and Bird's lips pursed, waiting to see what Jamie
made of this statement.

He supposed Bird meant to shock him. He merely nodded.

"Of course you can. You are wise enough not to."

"Not yet." Bird's lips relaxed into a charming smile. "You tell
the King—not yet."

"His Majesty will be pleased to hear that you value his
friendship so much."

Bird burst into laughter at that, rocking back and forth, and his
brother Still Water, who sat beside him, grinned broadly.

"I like you, Bear-Killer," he said, recovering. "You're a funny
man."

"I may be," Jamie said in English, smiling. "Give it time."

Ian gave a small snort of amusement at that, causing Bird to
look sharply at him, then away, clearing his throat. Jamie raised
one brow at his nephew, who replied with a bland smile.

Still Water was watching Ian narrowly. The Cherokee welcomed them both with respect, but Jamie had noticed at once a
particular edge in their response to Ian. They perceived Ian to be
Mohawk—and he made them wary. In all honesty, he himself
sometimes thought there was some part of Ian that had not come
back from Snaketown, and perhaps never would.

Bird had given him an avenue to inquire about something,
though.

"You have been much troubled by persons who come into your
lands to settle," he said, nodding sympathetically. "You of course
do not kill these persons, being wise. But not everyone is wise, are
they?"

Bird's eyes narrowed briefly.

"What do you mean, Bear-Killer?"

"I hear of burning, Tsisqua." He held the other man's eyes with his own, careful to give no hint of accusation. "The King hears of houses burning, men killed and women taken. This does not please him."

"Hmp," Bird said, and pressed his lips together. He did not, however, say he had not heard of such things himself, which was interesting.

"Enough of such stories, and the King may send soldiers to protect his people. If he should do that, he will hardly wish to have them face guns that he himself has given," Jamie pointed out logically.

"And what should we do, then?" Still Water broke in hotly. "They come across the Treaty Line, build houses, plant fields, and take the game. If your King cannot keep his people where they belong, how can he protest if we defend our lands?"

Bird made a small flattening gesture with one hand, not looking at his brother, and Still Water subsided, though with bad grace.

"So, Bear-Killer. You will tell the King these things, will you?" Jamie inclined his head gravely.

"That is my office. I speak of the King to you, and I will take your words to the King."

Bird nodded thoughtfully, then waved a hand for food and beer, and the talk changed firmly to neutral matters. No more business would be done tonight.

It was late when they left Tsisqua's house for the small guest-house. He thought it was well past moonrise, but there was no moon to be seen; the sky glowed thick with cloud, and the scent of rain was live on the wind.

"Oh, God," Ian said, yawning and stumbling. "My bum's gone asleep."

Jamie yawned, too, finding it contagious, but then blinked and laughed. "Aye, well. Dinna bother waking it up; the rest of ye can join it."

Ian made a derisive noise with his lips.

"Just because Bird says ye're a funny man, Uncle Jamie, I wouldna go believing it. He's only being polite, ken?"

Jamie ignored this, murmuring thanks in Tsalagi to the young woman who had shown them the way to their quarters. She handed him a small basket—filled with corn bread and dried apples, from the smell—then wished them a soft "Good night, sleep well," before vanishing into the damp, restless night.

The small hut seemed stuffy after the cool freshness of the air, and he stood in the doorway for a moment, enjoying the movement of the wind through the trees, watching it snake through the pine boughs like a huge, invisible serpent. A spatter of moisture bloomed on his face, and he experienced the deep pleasure of a man who realizes that it's going to rain and he isn't going to have to spend the night out in it.

"Ask about, Ian, when ye're gossiping tomorrow," he said, ducking inside. "Let it be known—tactfully—that the King would be pleased to know exactly who in hell's been burning cabins—and might be pleased enough to cough up a few guns in reward. They'll not tell ye if it's them that's been doing it—but if it's another band, they might."

Ian nodded, yawning again. A small fire burned in a stone ring, the smoke of it wisping up toward a smoke hole in the roof overhead, and by its light, a fur-piled sleeping platform was visible across one side of the hut, with another stack of furs and blankets on the floor.

"Toss ye for the bed, Uncle Jamie," he said, digging in the pouch at his waist and coming out with a battered shilling. "Call it."

"Tails," Jamie said, setting down the basket and unbelting his plaid. It fell in a warm puddle of fabric round his legs and he shook out his shirt. The linen was creased and grimy against his skin, and he could smell himself; thank God this was the last of the villages. One more night, perhaps, two at the most, and they could go home.

Ian swore, picking up the coin.

"How d'ye do that? Every night ye've said 'tails,' and every night, tails it is!"

"Well, it's your shilling, Ian. Dinna blame me." He sat down on the bed platform and stretched himself pleasurably, then relented. "Look at Geordie's nose."

Ian flipped the shilling over in his fingers and held it to the light of the fire, squinting, then swore again. A tiny splotch of beeswax, so thin as to be invisible unless you were looking, ornamented the aristocratically prominent nose of George III, Rex Britannia.

"How did that get there?" Ian narrowed his eyes suspiciously at his uncle, but Jamie merely laughed and lay down.

"When ye were showing wee Jem how to spin a coin. Remember, he knocked the candlestick over; hot wax went everywhere."

"Oh." Ian sat looking at the coin in his hand for a moment, then shook his head, scraped the wax away with a thumbnail, and put the shilling away.

"Good night, Uncle Jamie," he said, sliding into the furs on the ground with a sigh.

"Good night, Ian."

He'd been ignoring his tiredness, holding it like Gideon, on a short rein. Now he dropped the reins and gave it leave to carry him off, his body relaxing into the comfort of the bed.

MacDonald, he reflected cynically, would be delighted. Jamie had planned on visits only to the two Cherokee villages closest to the Treaty Line, there to announce his new position, distribute modest gifts of whisky and tobacco—this last hastily borrowed from Tom Christie, who had fortunately purchased a hogshead of the weed on a seed-buying trip to Cross Creek— and inform the Cherokee that further largesse might be expected when he undertook ambassage to the more distant villages in the autumn.

He had been most cordially received in both villages—but in the second, Pigtown, several strangers had been visiting; young men in search of wives. They were from a separate band of Cherokee, called the Snowbird band, whose large village lay higher in the mountains.

One of the young men had been the nephew of Bird-who-sings-in-the-morning, headman of the Snowbird band, and had been exigent in pressing Jamie to return with him and his companions to their home village. Taking a hasty private inventory of his remaining whisky and tobacco, Jamie had agreed, and he and Ian had been most royally received there, as agents of His Majesty. The Snowbird had never been visited by an Indian agent before, and appeared most sensible of the honor—and prompt about seeing what advantages might accrue to themselves in consequence.

He thought Bird was the sort of man with whom he could do business, though—on various fronts.

That thought led him to belated recollection of Roger Mac and the new tenants. He'd had no time over the last few days to spare much worry there—but he doubted there was any cause for concern. Roger Mac was capable enough, though his shattered voice made him less certain than he should be. With Christie and Arch Bug, though. . .

He closed his eyes, the bliss of absolute fatigue stealing over him as his thoughts grew more disjointed.

A day more, maybe, then home in time to make the hay. Another malting, two maybe, before the cold weather. Slaughtering . . . could it be time at last to kill the damned white sow? No . . . the vicious creature was unbelievably fecund. What kind of boar had the balls to mate with her? he wondered dimly, and did she eat him, after? Wild boar . . . smoked hams, blood pudding . . .

He was just drifting down through the first layers of sleep when he felt a hand on his privates. Jerked out of drowsiness like a salmon out of a sea-loch, he clapped a hand to the intruder's, gripping tight. And elicited a faint giggle from his visitor.

Feminine fingers wiggled gently in his grasp, and the hand's fellow promptly took up operations in its stead. His first coherent thought was that the lassie would be an excellent baker, so good as she was at kneading.

Other thoughts followed rapidly on the heels of this absurdity, and he tried to grab the second hand. It playfully eluded him in the dark, poking and tweaking.

He groped for a polite protest in Cherokee, but came up with nothing but a handful of random phrases in English and Gaelic, none of them faintly suitable to the occasion.

The first hand was purposefully wriggling out of his grasp, eel-like. Reluctant to crush her fingers, he let go for an instant, and made a successful grab for her wrist.

"Ian!" he hissed, in desperation. "Ian, are ye there?" He couldn't see his nephew in the pool of darkness that filled the cabin, nor tell if he slept. There were no windows, and only the faintest light came from the dying coals.

"Ian!"

There was a stirring on the floor, bodies shifting, and he heard Rollo sneeze.

"What is it, Uncle?" He'd spoken in Gaelic, and Ian answered in the same language. The lad sounded calm, and not as though he'd just come awake.

"Ian, there is a woman in my bed," he said in Gaelic, trying to match his nephew's calm tone.

"There are two of them, Uncle Jamie." Ian sounded amused, damn him! "The other will be down by your feet. Waiting her turn."

That unnerved him, and he nearly lost his grip on the captive hand.

"Two of them! What do they think I am?"

The girl giggled again, leaned over, and bit him lightly on the chest.

"Christ!"

"Well, no, Uncle, they don't think you're Him," Ian said, obviously suppressing his own mirth. "They think you're the King. So to speak. You're his agent, so they're doing honor to His Majesty by sending you his women, aye?"

The second woman had uncovered his feet and was slowly stroking his soles with one finger. He was ticklish and would have found this bothersome, were he not so distracted by the first woman, with whom he was being compelled into a most undignified game of hide-the-sausage.

"Talk to them, Ian," he said between clenched teeth, fumbling madly with his free hand, meanwhile forcing back the questing fingers of the captive hand—which were languidly stroking his ear—and wiggling his feet in a frantic effort to discourage the second lady's attentions, which were growing bolder.

"Erm . . . what d'ye want me to say?" Ian inquired, switching back to English. His voice quivered slightly.

"Tell them I'm deeply sensible of the honor, but—gk!" Further diplomatic evasions were cut off by the sudden intrusion of someone's tongue into his mouth, tasting strongly of onions and beer.

In the midst of his subsequent struggles, he was dimly aware that Ian had lost any sense of self-control and was lying on the floor giggling helplessly. It was filicide if you killed a son, he thought grimly; what was the word for assassinating a nephew?

"Madam!" he said, disengaging his mouth with difficulty. He seized the lady by the shoulders and rolled her off his body with

enough force that she whooped with surprise, bare legs flying—
Jesus, was she naked?

She was. Both of them were; his eyes adapted to the faint glow
of the embers, he caught the shimmer of light from shoulders,
breasts, and rounded thighs.

He sat up, gathering furs and blankets round him in a sort of
hasty redoubt.

"Cease, the two of you!" he said severely in Cherokee. "You
are beautiful, but I cannot lie with you."

"No?" said one, sounding puzzled.

"Why not?" said the other.

"Ah . . . because there is an oath upon me," he said, necessity
producing inspiration. "I have sworn . . . sworn . . ." He groped for
the proper word, but didn't find it. Luckily, Ian leaped in at this
point, with a stream of fluent Tsalagi, too fast to follow.

"Ooo," breathed one girl, impressed. Jamie felt a distinct qualm.

"What in God's name did ye tell them, Ian?"

"I told them the Great Spirit came to ye in a dream, Uncle, and
told ye that ye mustn't go with a woman until ye'd brought guns to
all the Tsalagi."

"Until I *what*?!"

"Well, it was the best I could think of in a hurry, Uncle," Ian
said defensively.

Hair-raising as the notion was, he had to admit it was effective;
the two women were huddled together, whispering in awed tones,
and had quite left off pestering him.

"Aye, well," he said grudgingly. "I suppose it could be worse."
After all, even if the Crown were persuaded to provide guns, there
were a damn lot of Tsalagi.

"Ye're welcome, Uncle Jamie." The laughter was gurgling just
below the surface of his nephew's voice, and emerged in a stifled
snort.

"What?" he said testily.

"The one lady is saying it's a disappointment to her, Uncle, because you're verra nicely equipped. The other is more philosophical about it, though. She says they might have borne ye children,
and the bairns might have red hair." His nephew's voice quivered.

"What's wrong wi' red hair, for God's sake?"

"I dinna ken, quite, but I gather it's not something ye want your
bairn to be marked with, and ye can help it."

"Well, fine," he snapped. "No danger of it, is there? Can they not go home now?"

"It's raining, Uncle Jamie," Ian pointed out logically. It was; the wind had brought a patter of rain, and now the main shower arrived, beating on the roof with a steady thrum, drops hissing into the hot embers through the smoke hole. "Ye wouldna send them out in the wet, would ye? Besides, ye just said ye couldna lie wi' them, not that ye meant them to go."

He broke off to say something interrogative to the ladies, who replied with eager confidence. Jamie thought they'd said—they had. Rising with the grace of young cranes, the two of them clambered naked as jaybirds back into his bed, patting and stroking him with murmurs of admiration—though sedulously avoiding his private parts—pressed him down into the furs, and snuggled down on either side of him, warm bare flesh pressed cozily against him.

He opened his mouth, then shut it again, finding absolutely nothing to say in any of the languages he knew.

He lay on his back, rigid and breathing shallowly. His cock throbbed indignantly, clearly meaning to stay up and torment him all night in revenge for its abuse. Small chortling noises came from the pile of furs on the ground, interspersed with hiccuping snorts. He thought it was maybe the first time he'd heard Ian truly laugh since his return.

Praying for fortitude, he drew a long, slow breath, and closed his eyes, hands folded firmly across his ribs, elbows pressed to his sides.

15

Stakit to Droon

Roger walked out onto the terrace at River Run, feeling pleasantly exhausted. After three weeks of strenuous work, he'd gathered the new tenants from the highways and byways of Cross Creek and Campbelton, become acquainted with all the heads of households, managed to equip them at least minimally for the journey, in terms of food, blankets, and shoes—and got them all collected in one place, firmly overcoming their tendency to panic and stray. They'd start in the morning for Fraser's Ridge, and not a moment too soon.

He looked out over the terrace in satisfaction, toward the meadow that lay beyond Jocasta Cameron Innes's stables. They were all bedded down in a temporary camp there: twenty-two families, with seventy-six individual souls, four mules, two ponies, fourteen dogs, three pigs, and God only knew how many chickens, kittens, and pet birds, bundled into wicker cages for carrying. He had all the names on a list—animals excluded—dog-eared and crumpled in his pocket. He had several other lists there, as well, scribbled over, crossed out, and amended to the point of illegibility. He felt like a walking Book of Deuteronomy. He also felt like a very large drink.

This was luckily forthcoming; Duncan Innes, Jocasta's husband, had returned from his own day's labor and was sitting on the terrace, in company with a cut-glass decanter, from which the rays of the sinking sun struck a mellow amber glow.

"How is it, then, *a charaid*?" Duncan greeted him genially, gesturing toward one of the basketwork chairs. "Ye'll take a dram, perhaps?"

"I will, and thanks."

He sank gratefully into the chair, which creaked amiably beneath his weight. He accepted the glass Duncan handed him, and tossed it back with a brief *"Slàinte."*

The whisky burned through the strictures that bound his throat, making him cough, but seeming suddenly to open things, so that the constant faint sense of choking began to leave him. He sipped, grateful.

"Ready to go, are they?" Duncan nodded toward the meadow, where the smoke of campfires hung in a low golden haze.

"Ready as they'll ever be. Poor things," Roger added with some sympathy.

Duncan raised one shaggy brow.

"Fish out of water," Roger amplified, holding out his glass to accept the proffered refill. "The women are terrified, and so are the men, but they hide it better. Ye'd think I was taking them all to be slaves on a sugar plantation."

Duncan nodded. "Or sell them to Rome to clean the Pope's shoon," he said wryly. "I misdoubt most of them had ever smelt a Catholic before embarking. And from the wrinkled noses, they dinna care so much for the scent now, I think. Do they so much as tak' a dram now and then, d'ye ken?"

"Only medicinally, and only if in actual danger of death, I think." Roger took a slow, ambrosial swallow and closed his eyes, feeling the whisky warm his throat and curl in his chest like a purring cat. "Meet Hiram yet, did you? Hiram Crombie, the head man of this lot."

"The wee sour-drap wi' the stick up his arse? Aye, I met him." Duncan grinned, his drooping mustache lifting at the end. "He'll be at supper with us. Best have another."

"I will, thanks," said Roger, extending his glass. "Though they're none of them much for hedonistic pleasure, so far as I can tell. Ye'd think they were all still Covenanters to the bone. The Frozen Chosen, aye?"

Duncan laughed immoderately at that.

"Well, it's no like it was in my grandsire's day," he said, recovering and reaching across for the decanter. "And thank the Lord for that." He rolled his eyes, grimacing.

"Your grandsire was a Covenanter, then?"

"God, yes." Shaking his head, Duncan poured a goodly measure, first for Roger, then himself. "A fierce auld bastard, he was.

Not that he'd no cause, mind. His sister was stakit to droon, ken?"

"Was—Christ." He bit his tongue in penance, but was too interested to pay it much mind. "Ye mean—executed by drowning?"

Duncan nodded, eyes on his glass, then took a good gulp and held it for a moment in his mouth before swallowing.

"Margaret," he said. "Her name was Margaret. Eighteen she was, at the time. Her father and her brother—my grandfather, aye?—they'd fled, after the battle at Dunbar; hid in the hills. The troops came a-hunting them, but she wouldna say where they'd gone—and she had a Bible by her. They tried to make her recant then, but she wouldna do that, either—the women on that side o' the family, ye might as well talk to a stone," he said, shaking his head. "There's no moving them. But they dragged her doon to the shore, her and an auld Covenanter woman from the village, stripped them, and tied them both to stakes at the tide line. Waited there, the crowd o' them, for the water to come in."

He took another swallow, not waiting for the taste of it.

"The auld woman went under first; they'd tied her closer to the water—I suppose thinking Margaret would give in, if she saw the auld woman die." He grunted, shaking his head. "But nay, not a bit of it. The tide rose, and the waves came up ower her. She choked, and she coughed, and her hair loose, hanging over her face, plastered doon like kelp, when the water went out.

"My mither saw it," he explained, lifting his glass. "She was but seven at the time, but she never forgot. After the first wave, she said, there was the space of three breaths, and the wave came ower Margaret again. And then out . . . three breaths . . . and in again once more. And ye couldna see anything then but the swirl of her hair, floating on the tide."

He raised his glass an inch higher, and Roger lifted his own in involuntary toast. "Jesus," he said, and it was no blasphemy.

The whisky burned his throat as it went down and he breathed deep, giving thanks to God for the gift of air. Three breaths. It was the single malt of Islay, and the iodine taste of sea and kelp was strong and smoky in his lungs.

"May God give her peace," he said, his voice rasping.

Duncan nodded, and reached again for the decanter.

"I would suppose she earned it," he said. "Though they"—he pointed with his chin toward the meadow—"they'd say 'twas none of her doing at all; God chose her for salvation and chose the English to be damned; nay more to be said on the matter."

The light was fading and the campfires began to glow in the dimness of the meadow beyond the stables. The smoke of them reached Roger's nose, the scent warm and homelike, but nonetheless adding to the burn in his throat.

"I've no found sae much worth dyin' for, myself," Duncan said reflectively, then gave one of his quick, rare smiles. "But my grandsire, he'd say it only meant I was chosen to be damned. *'By the decree of God, for His everlasting glory, some men and angels are predestined unto everlasting life, and others fore-ordained to everlasting death.'* He'd say that, whenever anyone spoke of Margaret."

Roger nodded, recognizing the statement from the Westminster Confession. When was that—1646? 1647? A generation—or two—before Duncan's grandfather.

"I expect it was easier for him to think her death was God's will, and nothing to do with him," Roger said, not without sympathy. "Ye'll not believe it yourself, then? Predestination, I mean."

He asked with true curiosity. The Presbyterians of his own time did still espouse predestination as a doctrine—but, a bit more flexible in attitude, tended to soft-pedal the notion of pre-destined damnation, and not to think too much on the idea that every detail of life was so predestined. Himself? God knew.

Duncan lifted his shoulders, the right rising higher and making him seem momentarily twisted. "God knows," he said, and laughed. He shook his head, and drained his glass again.

"Nay, I think I don't. But I wouldna say as much before Hiram Crombie—nor yet yon Christie." Duncan lifted his chin toward the meadow, where he could see two dark figures, walking side by side toward the house. Arch Bug's tall, stooped frame was easy to recognize, as was Tom Christie's shorter, blocky build. He looked pugnacious even in silhouette, Roger thought, making short, sharp gestures as he walked, clearly arguing something with Arch.

"There'd be wicked fights ower it sometimes, in Ardsmuir," Duncan said, watching the progress of the two figures. "The Catholics took it amiss, to be told they were damned. And Christie and his wee band took the greatest pleasure in telling them so." His shoulders shook a little in suppressed laughter, and Roger wondered just how much whisky Duncan had had before he came out to the terrace. He'd never seen the older man so jovial.

"*Mac Dubh* put a stop to it, finally, when he made us all be Freemasons," he added, leaning forward to pour a fresh glass. "But a few men were nearly killed, before that." He lifted the decanter inquiringly in Roger's direction.

Looking forward to a supper including both Tom Christie and Hiram Crombie, Roger accepted.

As Duncan leaned toward him to pour, still smiling, the last of the sun shone across his weathered face. Roger caught a glimpse of a faint white line through Duncan's upper lip, half-visible beneath the hair, and realized quite suddenly why Duncan wore a long mustache—an unusual adornment, in a time when most men were clean-shaven.

He would not have spoken, likely, save for the whisky and the mood of strange alliance between them—two Protestants, amazingly bound to Catholics and bemused at the strange tides of fate that had washed over them; two men left quite alone by the misfortunes of life, and now surprised to find themselves the heads of households, holding the lives of strangers in their hands.

"Your lip, Duncan." He touched his own mouth briefly. "What did that?"

"Och, that?" Duncan touched his own lip, surprised. "Nay, I was born wi' a harelip, or so they said. I dinna recall it, myself; it was mended when I was nay more than a week old."

It was Roger's turn to be surprised.

"Who mended it?"

Duncan shrugged, one-shouldered this time.

"A traveling healer, my mither said. She'd quite resigned herself to losin' me, she said, because I couldna suck, of course. She and my aunties all took it in turn to drap milk into my mouth from a rag, but she said I'd wasted nearly to a wee skeleton, when this charmer came by the village."

He rubbed a knuckle self-consciously over his lip, smoothing the thick, grizzled hairs of his mustache.

"My faither gave him six herrings and a mull o' snuff, and he stitched it up, and gave my mither a bit o' some ointment to put on the wound. Well, and so . . ." He shrugged again, with a lopsided smile.

"Perhaps I was destined to live, after all. My grandsire said the

Lord had chosen me—though God only kens what for."

Roger was conscious of a faint ripple of unease, dulled though it was by whisky.

A Highland charmer who could repair a harelip? He took another drink, trying not to stare, but covertly examining Duncan's face. He supposed it was possible; the scar was just barely visible—if you knew to look—under Duncan's mustache, but didn't extend up into the nostril. It must have been a fairly simple harelip, then, not one of the hideous cases like that one he'd read about—unable to look away from the page for horror—in Claire's big black doctor's book, where Dr. Rawlings had described a child born not only with a split lip, but missing the roof of its mouth, and most of the center of its face, as well.

There had been no drawing, thank God, but the visual picture conjured up by Rawlings's spare description had been bad enough. He closed his eyes and breathed deep, inhaling the whisky's perfume through his pores.

Was it possible? Perhaps. People did *do* surgery now, blood-stained, crude, and agonizing as it was. He'd seen Murray MacLeod, the apothecary from Campbelton, expertly stitch up a man's cheek, laid open when the man was trampled by a sheep. Would it be any more difficult to stitch a child's mouth?

He thought of Jemmy's lip, tender as a blossom, pierced by needle and black thread, and shuddered.

"Are ye cold, then, *a charaid*? Shall we go in?" Duncan got his feet under him, as though to rise, but Roger waved the older man back.

"Ah, no. Goose walking on my grave." He smiled, and accepted another drop to keep the nonexistent evening chill away. And yet he felt the hairs on his arms rise, just a little. *Could there be another one—more—like us?*

There had been, he knew. His own multiple-times great-grandmother, Geillis, for one. The man whose skull Claire had found, complete with silver fillings in its teeth, for another. But had Duncan met another, in some remote Highland village half a century before?

Christ, he thought, freshly unnerved. *How often does it happen? And what happens to them?*

Before they had quite reached the bottom of the decanter, he heard footsteps behind him, and the rustle of silk.

"Mrs. Cameron." He rose at once, the world tilting just a little, and took his hostess's hand, bowing over it.

Her long hand touched his face, as was her habit, her sensitive fingertips confirming his identity.

"Och, there ye are, Jo. Had a good journey wi' the wee lad, did ye?" Duncan struggled to rise, handicapped by whisky and his single arm, but Ulysses, Jocasta's butler, had materialized silently out of the twilight behind his mistress in time to move her wicker chair into place. She sank into it without so much as putting a hand out to see that it was there, Roger noticed; she simply knew it would be.

Roger viewed the butler with interest, wondering who Jocasta had bribed to get him back. Accused—and very likely guilty of— the death of a British naval officer on Jocasta's property, Ulysses had been forced to flee the colony. But Lieutenant Wolff had not been considered a great loss to the navy—and Ulysses was indispensable to Jocasta Cameron. All things might not be possible with gold—but he was willing to bet that Jocasta Cameron hadn't yet met a circumstance she couldn't mend with money, political connections, or guile.

"Oh, aye," she replied to her husband, smiling and putting out a hand to him. "'Twas such fun to show him off, husband! We'd a wonderful luncheon with old Mrs. Forbes and her daughter, and the wee bairn sang a song and charmed them all. Mrs. Forbes had the Montgomery lasses in, as well, and Miss Ogilvie, and we had wee lamb cutlets wi' raspberry sauce and fried apples and— oh, is that you, Mr. Christie? Do come and join us!" She raised her voice a little, and her face, appearing to look expectantly into the gloom over Roger's shoulder.

"Mrs. Cameron. Your servant, madam." Christie stepped up onto the terrace, making a courtly bow that was no less punctilious for the fact that its recipient was blind. Arch Bug followed him, bowing in turn over Jocasta's hand, and making a genial noise in his throat by way of greeting.

Chairs were brought out, more whisky, a plate of savories appeared as by magic, candles were lit—and suddenly it was a party, echoing on a higher plane the sense of slightly nervous festivity taking place in the meadow below. There was music in the distance; the sound of a tin whistle, playing a jig.

Roger let it all wash over him, enjoying the brief sense of

relaxation and irresponsibility. Just for tonight, there was no need to worry; everyone was gathered, safe, fed, and prepared for the morrow's journey.

He needn't even trouble to keep up his end of the conversation; Tom Christie and Jocasta were enthusiastically discussing the literary scene in Edinburgh and a book he'd never heard of, with Duncan, looking so mellow that he might slide out of his chair any minute, putting in the occasional remark, and old Arch— where was Arch? Oh, there; gone back toward the meadow, having doubtless thought of some last minute thing he must tell someone.

He blessed Jamie Fraser for his forethought in sending Arch and Tom with him. Between the two of them, they'd saved him from any number of blunders, managed the ten thousand necessary details, and eased the fears of the new tenants regarding this latest leap into the unknown.

He took a deep, contented breath of air scented with the homely smells of campfires in the distance and roasting dinner near at hand—and belatedly recalled the one small detail whose welfare was still his exclusive concern.

Excusing himself, he made his way into the house, and discovered Jem down below in the main kitchen, cozily ensconced in the corner of a settle, eating bread pudding with melted butter and maple syrup on it.

"That's never your dinner, is it?" he asked, sitting down beside his son.

"Uh-huh. Want some, Daddy?" Jem extended a dripping spoon upward toward him, and he bent hastily to take the offered mouthful before it fell off. It was delicious, bursting-sweet and creamy on the tongue.

"Mmm," he said, swallowing. "Well, let's not tell Mummy or Grannie, shall we? They've this odd prejudice toward meat and vegetables."

Jem nodded, agreeable, and offered him another spoonful. They consumed the bowl together in a companionable silence, after which Jem crawled into his lap, and leaning a sticky face against his chest, fell sound asleep.

Servants bustled to and fro around them, smiling kindly now and then. He should, he thought vaguely, get up. Dinner would be being served in a moment—he saw the platters of roasted duck and mutton being skillfully laid out, bowls mounded with heaps of fluffy, steaming rice soaked with gravy, and a huge sallet of greens being tossed with vinegar.

Filled with whisky, bread pudding, and contentment, though, he lingered, putting off from moment to moment the necessity of parting from Jem and ending the sweet peace of holding his sleeping son.

"Mister Roger? I take him, shall I?" said a soft voice. He looked up from an examination of Jem's hair, which had bits of bread pudding stuck in it, to see Phaedre, Jocasta's body servant, stooping before him, hands held out to receive the boy.

"I wash him, put him to his bed, sir," she said, her oval face as soft as her voice as she looked at Jem.

"Oh. Yes, sure. Thanks." Roger sat up, Jem in his arms, and rose carefully, holding Jem's considerable weight. "Here—I'll carry him up for you."

He followed the slave up the narrow stairs from the kitchen, admiring—in a purely abstract and aesthetic sort of way—the grace of her carriage. How old was she? he wondered. Twenty, twenty-two? Would Jocasta allow her to marry? She must have admirers, surely. But he knew how valuable she was to Jocasta, too—seldom out of her mistress's presence. Not easy to reconcile that with a home and family of her own.

At the top of the stair, she stopped and turned to take Jem from him; he surrendered his limp burden with reluctance, but also with some relief. It was stifling-hot down below, and his shirt was damp with sweat where Jem had pressed against him.

"Mister Roger?" Phaedre's voice stopped him, as he was about to take his leave. She was looking at him over Jem's shoulder, eyes hesitant beneath the white curve of her head scarf.

"Aye?"

The thump of feet coming up the stairs made him move, narrowly avoiding Oscar, charging upstairs with an empty platter under his arm, evidently bound for the summer kitchen, where the fish were being fried. Oscar grinned at Roger as he passed, and blew a kiss toward Phaedre, whose lips tightened at the gesture.

She made a slight motion with her head, and Roger followed her down the hall, away from the bustle of the kitchen. She stopped near the door that led out to the stables, glancing round to be sure they were not overheard.

"I maybe shouldn't say nothin', sir—may be as it *is* nothin'. But I'm thinkin' I should tell you, anyway."

He nodded, shoving back the damp hair at his temple. The door stood open, and there was a little breeze here, thank God.

"We was in the town, sir, this morning, at Mr. Benjamin's warehouse, you know the one? Down by the river."

He nodded again, and she licked her lips.

"Master Jem, he got restless and went to pokin' round, whilst the mistress talked with Mr. Benjamin. I followed him, seein' as he falls into no trouble, and so I was right there when the man come in."

"Aye? Which man was this?"

She shook her head, dark eyes serious.

"I dunno, sir. Was a big man, tall as you. Light-haired; he wasn't wearin' no wig. Was a gentleman, though." By which, he assumed, she meant the man was well-dressed.

"And?"

"He looks round, sees Mr. Benjamin a-talkin' with Miss Jo, and he takes a step to the side, like as he don't want no one takin' notice he there. But then he sees Mr. Jem, and he get a sharp kind of look on his face."

She pulled Jem a little closer, recalling.

"I ain't likin' that look, sir, tell you truly. I see him start toward Jemmy and I go quick and pick the lad up, same as I got him now. The man look surprised, then like he think something's funny; he smile at Jem and ax him who his daddy be?"

She gave a quick smile, patting Jem's back.

"Folk ax him that all the time, sir, downtown, and he speak right up, say his daddy Roger MacKenzie, same as he always do. This man, he laugh and ruffle Jem's hair—they all do that, sir, he gots such pretty hair. Then he say, 'Is he, then, my wee maneen, is he indeed?'"

Phaedre was a natural mimic. She caught the Irish lilt of it perfectly, and the sweat turned cold on Roger's skin.

"And then what happened?" he demanded. "What did he do?" Unconsciously, he glanced over her shoulder through the open door, searching the night outside for danger.

Phaedre hunched her shoulders, shivering slightly.

"He ain't *do* nothin', sir. But he look at Jem real close, and then at me, and he smile, right in my eyes. I ain't likin' that smile, sir, not one bit." She shook her head. "But then I hear Mr. Benjamin lift his voice behind me, callin' out to say does the gentleman want him? And the man turn quick-like on his heel, and be gone out the door, just like *that*." She clutched Jem with one arm, and snapped the fingers of her free hand briefly.

"I see." The bread pudding had formed a solid mass that lay like iron in his stomach. "Did you say anything to your mistress about this man?"

She shook her head, solemn.

"No, sir. He ain't really done nothin', like I say. But he trouble me, sir, and so I study on it, comin' home, and think finally, well, I best tell you, sir, and I gets the chance."

"Ye did right," he said. "Thank you, Phaedre." He fought the urge to take Jem from her, hold him tight. "Would ye—when ye've got him to bed, will ye stay with him? Just until I come up. I'll tell your mistress I asked you to."

Her dark eyes met his with perfect understanding, and she nodded.

"Aye, sir. I keep him safe." She bobbed the shadow of a curtsy, and went up the stairs toward the room he shared with Jem, humming something soft and rhythmic to the boy.

He breathed slowly, trying to master the overwhelming urge to seize a horse from the stables, ride to Cross Creek, and search the place, going from house to house in the dark until he found Stephen Bonnet.

"Right," he said aloud. "And then what?" His fists curled up involuntarily, knowing quite well what to do, even as his mind acknowledged the futility of such a course.

He fought down rage and helplessness, the last of the whisky lighting his blood, throbbing in his temples. He stepped abruptly through the open door into the night, for it was full dark now. From this side of the house, the meadow was invisible, but he could still smell the smoke of their fires, and catch the faint trill of music on the air.

He'd known Bonnet would come again, one day. Down beside the lawn, the white bulk of Hector Cameron's mausoleum was a pale smear on the night. And safe inside it, hidden in the coffin that waited for Hector's wife, Jocasta, lay a fortune in Jacobite gold, the long-held secret of River Run.

Bonnet knew the gold existed, suspected it was on the plantation.

He had tried for it once before, and failed. He was not a careful man, Bonnet—but he *was* persistent.

Roger felt his bones strain in his flesh, urgent with desire to hunt and kill the man who had raped his wife, threatened his family. But there were seventy-six people depending on him—no, seventy-seven. Vengeance warred with responsibility—and, most reluctantly, gave way.

He breathed slow and deep, feeling the knot of the rope scar tighten in his throat. No. He had to go, see the new tenants safe. The thought of sending them with Arch and Tom, while he remained behind to search for Bonnet, was tempting—but the job was his; he couldn't abandon it for the sake of a time-consuming—and likely futile—personal quest.

Nor could he leave Jem unprotected.

He must tell Duncan, though; Duncan could be trusted to take steps for the protection of River Run, to send word to the authorities in Cross Creek, to make inquiries.

And Roger would make sure that Jem was safe away, too, come morning, held before him on his saddle, kept in his sight every inch of the way to the sanctuary of the mountains.

"Who's your daddy?" he muttered, and a fresh surge of rage pulsed through his veins. "God damn it, *I* am, you bastard!"

PARTTHREE

To Every Thing There Is a Season

16

Le mot juste

"Ye're smiling to yourself," Jamie said in my ear. "Nice, was it?"

I turned my head and opened my eyes, finding them on a level with his mouth—which was smiling, too.

"Nice," I said thoughtfully, tracing the line of his wide lower lip with the tip of one finger. "Are you being deliberately modest, or are you hoping to inspire me to raptures of praise by means of classic understatement?"

The mouth widened further, and his teeth closed gently on my questing finger for a moment before releasing it.

"Oh, modesty, to be sure," he said. "If I'd hopes of inspiring ye to raptures, it wouldna be with my words, now, would it?"

One hand ran lightly down my back in illustration.

"Well, the words *help*," I said.

"They do?"

"Yes. Just now, I was actually trying to rank 'I love you, I like you, I worship you, I have to have my cock inside you,' in terms of their relative sincerity."

"Did I say that?" he said, sounding slightly startled.

"Yes. Weren't you listening?"

"No," he admitted. "I meant every word of it, though." His hand cupped one buttock, weighing it appreciatively. "Still do, come to that."

"What, even the last one?" I laughed and rubbed my forehead gently against his chest, feeling his jaw rest snugly on top of my head.

"Oh, aye," he said, gathering me firmly against him with a sigh. "I will say the flesh requires a bit of supper and a wee rest before I think of doin' it again, but the spirit is always willing. God, ye have the sweetest fat wee bum. Only seeing it makes me want to give it ye again directly. It's lucky ye're wed to a decrepit auld man, Sassenach, or ye'd be on your knees with your arse in the air this minute."

He smelled delectably of road dust and dried sweat and the deep musk of a man who has just enjoyed himself thoroughly.

"Nice to be missed," I said contentedly into the small space beneath his arm. "I missed you, too."

My breath tickled him and his skin shivered suddenly, like a horse shedding flies. He shifted a bit, turning me so that my head fit into the hollow of his shoulder, and sighed in matching content.

"Well, so. I see the place is still standing."

It was. It was late afternoon, the windows open, and the sun came low through the trees to make shifting patterns on the walls and linen sheets, so that we floated in a bower of murmuring shadow leaves.

"The house is standing, the barley is mostly in, and nothing's died," I said, settling myself comfortably to report. Now that we'd taken care of the most important thing, he'd want to know how the Ridge had fared in his absence.

"Mostly?" he said, neatly catching the dicey bit. "What happened? It rained, aye, but the barley should all have been in a week before."

"Not rain. Grasshoppers." I shuddered in memory. A cloud of the nasty goggle-eyed things had come whirring through, just at the end of the barley harvest. I'd gone up to my garden to pick greens, only to discover said greens seething with wedge-shaped bodies and shuffling, clawed feet, my lettuces and cabbages gnawed to ragged nubbins and the morning-glory vine on the palisade hanging in shreds.

"I ran and got Mrs. Bug and Lizzie, and we drove them off with brooms—but then they all rose up in a big cloud and headed up through the wood to the field beyond the Green Spring. They settled in the barley; you could hear the chewing for miles. It sounded like giants walking through rice." Goosebumps of revulsion rose on my shoulders, and Jamie rubbed my skin absently, his hand large and warm.

"Mmphm. Was it only the one field they got, then?"

"Oh, yes." I took a deep breath, still smelling the smoke. "We torched the field, and burnt them alive."

His body jerked in surprise, and he looked down at me.

"What? Who thought of that?"

"I did," I said, not without pride. In cold-blooded retrospect, it was a sensible thing to have done; there were other fields at risk, not only of barley, but of ripening corn, wheat, potatoes, and hay—to say nothing of the garden patches most families depended on.

In actual fact, it had been a decision made in boiling rage— sheer, bloody-minded revenge for the destruction of my garden. I would happily have ripped the wings off each insect and stamped on the remains—burning them had been nearly as good, though.

It was Murdo Lindsay's field; slow in both thought and action, Murdo hadn't had time to react properly to my announcement that I meant to fire the barley, and was still standing on the stoop of his cabin, mouth hanging open, as Brianna, Lizzie, Marsali, Mrs. Bug, and I ran round the field with armsful of faggots, lighting them from torches and hurling the blazing sticks as far as we could out into the sea of ripe, dry grain.

The dry grass went up with a crackle, and then a roar, as the fire took hold. Confused by the heat and smoke of a dozen fires, the grasshoppers flew up like sparks, igniting as their wings caught fire and vanishing into the rising column of smoke and whirling ash.

"Of course, it *would* be just then that Roger chose to arrive with the new tenants," I said, repressing an urge to laugh inappropriately at the memory. "Poor things. It was getting dark, and here they all were, standing in the woods with their bundles and children, watching this—this bally conflagration going on, and all of us dancing round barefoot with our shifts kirtled up, hooting like gibbons and covered with soot."

Jamie covered his eyes with one hand, plainly visualizing the scene. His chest shook briefly, and a wide grin spread beneath the hand.

"Oh, God. They must ha' thought Roger Mac had brought them to hell. Or to a coven meeting, at least."

A bubble of guilty laughter was forcing itself up from under my ribs.

"They did. Oh, Jamie—the looks on their faces!" I lost my grip and buried my own face in his chest. We shook together for a moment, laughing almost soundlessly.

"I *did* try to make them welcome," I said, snorting a little. "We gave them supper, and found them all places to sleep—as many as we could fit in the house, the rest spread between Brianna's cabin, the stable, and the barn. I came down quite late at night, though— I couldn't sleep, for all the excitement—and found a dozen of them praying in the kitchen."

They had been standing in a circle near the hearth, hands linked and heads bowed reverently. All the heads had snapped up at my appearance, eyes showing white in thin, haggard faces. They'd stared at me in total silence, and one of the women had let go the hand of the man beside her to hide her own hand under her apron. In another time and place, I should have thought she was reaching for some weapon—and perhaps she was, at that; I was fairly sure she was making the sign of the horns beneath the shelter of the ragged cloth.

I'd already discovered that only a few of them spoke English. I asked in my halting Gaelic whether they needed anything? They stared at me as though I had two heads, then after a moment, one of the men, a wizened creature with a thin mouth, had shaken his head the barest inch.

"Then they went right back to their praying, leaving me to skulk off back to bed."

"Ye went down in your shift?"

"Well . . . yes. I didn't expect anyone to be awake at that hour."

"Mmphm." His knuckles grazed my breast, and I could tell exactly what he was thinking. My summer night rail was thin, worn linen, and yes, all right, dammit, I supposed one *could* see through it a bit in the light, but the kitchen had been lit only by the ruddy glow of a smoored hearth.

"I dinna suppose ye went down in a proper nightcap, Sassenach?" Jamie asked, running a thoughtful hand through my hair. I'd loosened it to go to bed with him, and it was writhing off merrily in all directions, à la Medusa.

"Of course not. I had it plaited, though," I protested. "Quite respectable!"

"Oh, quite," he agreed, grinning, and pushing his fingers up into the wild mass of my hair, cradled my head in his hands and kissed me. His lips were chapped from wind and sun, but agreeably soft.

He hadn't shaved since his departure and his beard was short and curly, springy to the touch.

"Well, so. They're sorted now, I expect? The tenants?" His lips brushed my cheek, and nibbled gently at my ear. I inhaled deeply.

"Ah. Oh. Yes. Arch Bug took them off in the morning; he's got them parceled out with families all over the Ridge, and already working on . . ." My train of thought temporarily derailed, and I closed my fingers by reflex in the muscle of his chest.

"And ye told Murdo I'd make it right with him, of course. About the barley?"

"Yes, of course." My drifting attention snagged momentarily and I laughed. "He just stared at me, and then nodded in a dazed sort of way, and said, oh, just as Himself liked, to be sure. I don't know if he realized even then why I'd burnt his field; perhaps he just thought I'd taken a sudden fancy to set fire to his barley."

Jamie laughed, too—a most unsettling sensation, as he had his teeth fixed in my earlobe.

"Um," I said faintly, feeling the tickle of red beard on my neck and the very warm, firm flesh beneath my palm. "The Indians. How did you manage with the Cherokee?"

"Fine."

He moved suddenly, rolling over on top of me. He was very big, and *very* warm, and he smelled of desire, strong and sharp. The leafy shadows moved across his face and shoulders, dappled the bed and the white skin of my thighs, opened wide.

"I like ye fine, Sassenach," he murmured in my ear. "I can see ye there, half-naked in your shift and your hair down, curling over your breest. . . . I love you. I wor—"

"What was that about a rest and supper?"

His hands were worming themselves under me, cupping my buttocks, squeezing, his breath soft and hot on my neck.

"I *have* to have my—"

"But—"

"Now, Sassenach." He rose up abruptly, kneeling on the bed before me. There was a faint smile on his face, but his eyes were dark blue and intent. He cupped his heavy balls in one hand, the thumb moving up and down his exigent member in a slow and thoughtful manner.

"On your knees, *a nighean*," he said softly. "Now."

17

The Limits of Power

From James Fraser, Esq., Fraser's Ridge
to Lord John Grey of Mount Josiah Plantation

August 14, 1773

My lord—

I write to inform you of my new Office, viz, that of
Indian Agent to the Crown, by Appointment to the
Southern Department under John Stuart.

I was originally of two Minds regarding Acceptance
of this Appointment, but found my Views made more
singular by Reason of a Visit by Mr. Richard Brown, a
distant Neighbor, and his Brother. I expect that Mr.
Higgins will already have given you an Account of their
so-called Committee of Safety, and its immediate
Object of arresting him.

Have you encountered such ad hoc Bodies in Virginia?
I think perhaps your Situation is not so unsettled as is our
own, or that in Boston, where Mr. Higgins also reports
their Presence. I hope it is not.

I think a Person of Sense must deplore these
committees in Principle. Their stated Purpose is to
provide Protection from Vagabonds and Banditti, and to
arrest Criminals in those Areas where no Sheriff or
Constable is available. With no Law to regulate their
Behavior save Self-interest, though, plainly there is

*Nothing to prevent an irregular Militia from becoming
more of a Threat to the Citizenry than the Dangers from
which it offers to preserve them.*

*The Appeal is plain, though, particularly in such Case
as we find ourselves here, so remotely situated. The
nearest Courthouse is—or was—three days' Ride, and in
the constant Unrest that has followed the Regulation,
Matters have decayed even from this unsatisfactory State.
The Governor and his Council are in constant Conflict
with the Assembly, the Circuit Court has effectually
ceased to exist, Judges are no longer appointed, and
there is no Sheriff of Surry County at present, the latest
Holder of that Office having resigned under Threat of
having his House fired.*

*The Sheriffs of Orange and Rowan Counties still boast
Office—but their Corruption is so well known that no one
may depend upon them, save those whose Interest is
invested in them.*

*We hear frequent reports these Days of House-
burnings, Assaults, and similar Alarums in the Wake of
the recent War of Regulation. Governor Tryon officially
pardoned some of those involved in the Conflict, but did
nothing to prevent local Retribution against them; his
Successor is still less able to deal with such Events—
which are in any Case occurring in the Backcountry, far
from his Palace in New Bern and thus the more easily
ignored. (In all Justice, the Man doubtless has Troubles
nearer at Hand to deal with.)*

*Still, while Settlers here are accustomed to defend
themselves from the normal Threats of the Wilderness, the
Occurrence of such random Attacks as these—and the
Possibility of Irruption of the Indians, so close to the
Treaty Line—is sufficient to unnerve them, and cause
them to greet with Relief the Appearance of any Body
willing to undertake the Role of public Protection. Hence
the Vigilantes of the Committees are welcomed—at least
to begin with.*

*I give you so much Detail by way of explaining my
Thoughts regarding the Appointment. My friend Major
MacDonald (late of the 32nd Cavalry) had told me that*

*should I ultimately decline to become an Indian Agent,
he would approach Mr. Richard Brown, Brown being in
the way of doing substantial Trade with the Cherokee,
and thus in a position of Acquaintance and presumed
Trust that would predispose his Acceptance by the
Indians.*

*My Acquaintance with Mr. Brown and his Brother
inclines me to regard this Prospect with Alarm. With such
Rise in Influence as such an Appointment would bring,
Brown's Stature in this unsettled Region might shortly
become so great that no man could easily oppose him in
any Venture—and that, I think, is dangerous.*

*My Son-in-law astutely observes that a Man's sense of
Morality tends to decrease as his Power increases, and I
suspect that the Brothers Brown possess relatively little
of the Former to begin with. It may be mere Hubris on my
part, to assume that I have more. I have seen the
corrosive Effects of Power upon a Man's Soul—and I
have felt its Burden, as you will understand, having
borne it so often yourself. Still, if it is a choice between
myself and Richard Brown, I suppose I must resort to the
old Scottish Adage that the Devil you ken is better than
the Devil you don't.*

*I am likewise made uneasy at the Thought of the long
Absences from Home which my new Duties must require.
And yet I cannot in Conscience allow the People under
my Dominion to be subject to the Vagaries and possible
Injuries of Brown's Committee.*

*I could of course convene my own such Committee—I
think you would urge such a Course—but will not.
Beyond the Inconvenience and Expense of such a Move, it
would be Tantamount to declaring open War with the
Browns, and I think that not prudent, not if I must be
frequently away from home, leaving my Family
unprotected. This new Appointment, though, will extend
my own Influence, and—I trust—put some Limit to the
Browns' Ambitions.*

*So having reached this Decision, I sent Word at once
to accept the Appointment, and essayed my first Visit to
the Cherokee in the Office of Indian Agent during the last*

Month. My initial Reception was most Cordial, and I hope my Relations with the Villages will remain so.

I shall visit the Cherokee again in the Autumn. If you should have any Matters of Business that my new Office might assist, send to me regarding them, and rest assured that I shall make every Effort on your Behalf.

To more domestic Matters. Our small Population has nearly doubled, as the Result of an Influx of Settlers newly arrived from Scotland. While most desirable, this Incursion has caused no little Turmoil, the Newcomers being Fisher-folk from the Coast. To these, the Mountain Wilderness is full of Threat and Mystery, such Threats and Mysteries being personified by Pigs and Plowshares.

(With regard to Pigs, I am not sure but that I share their Views. The white Sow has lately taken up Residence beneath the Foundation of my House and there engages in such debauches that our Dinner is disturbed daily by hellish Noises resembling the Sounds of Souls in Torment. These Souls apparently being torn Limb from Limb and devoured by Demons beneath our Feet.)

Since I speak of Matters hellish, I must observe that our Newcomers are also, alas, stern Sons of the Covenant, to whom a Papist such as myself presents himself as one fully furnished with Horns and Tail. You will recall one Thomas Christie, I think, from Ardsmuir? By comparison of these stiff-necked Gentlemen, Mr. Christie appears the Soul of compassionate Generosity.

I had not thought to thank Providence for the Fact that my Son-in-law is Presbyterian by inclination, but I see now how true it is that the Almighty does indeed have Designs beyond the Ken of us poor mortals. While even Roger MacKenzie is a sadly depraved Libertine by their Lights, the new Tenants are at least able to speak to him without the Necessity of small Gestures and Signs intended to repel Evil, which are the constant Accompaniment to their Conversations with myself.

As for their Behavior with Respect to my Wife, you would think her the Witch of Endor, if not the Great Whore of Babylon. This, because they consider the Furnishments of her Surgery to be "Enchantments," and *were appalled at witnessing the Entrance therein of a Number of Cherokee, gaily festooned for visiting, who had come to Trade in such Arcana as Snakes' Fangs and the Gallbladders of Bears.*

My wife begs me express her Pleasure at your kind Compliments regarding Mr. Higgins's improved Health—and still more, at your Offer to procure medicinal Substances for her from your Friend in Philadelphia. She bids me send you the enclosed List. As I cast an Eye upon this, I suspect that your supplying of her Desires will do nothing to allay the Suspicions of the Fisher-folk, but pray do not desist on that Account, as I think nothing save Time and Custom will decrease their Fears of her.

My Daughter likewise bids me express her Gratitude for your Present of the Phosphorus. I am not certain that I share this Sentiment, given that her Experiments with the Substance prove frighteningly incendiary to date. Fortunately, none of the Newcomers observed these Experiments, or they would be in no Doubt that Satan is indeed a particular Friend to me and mine.

In happier Vein, I congratulate you upon your latest Vintage, which is indeed drinkable. I send in return a Jug of Mrs. Bug's best Cider, and a Bottle of the barrel-aged Three-year-old, which I flatter myself you will find less corrosive to the Gullet than the last Batch.

Your ob't. servant,

J. Fraser

Postscriptum: I have had Report of a Gentleman who by Description resembles one Stephen Bonnet, this Man appearing briefly in Cross Creek last Month. If it was indeed the Gentleman, his Business is unknown, and he seems to have vanished without Trace; my Uncle-in-law, Duncan Innes, has made Inquiries in the Area, but writes to tell me that these have proved fruitless. Should you hear of anything in this Regard, I pray you will advise me at once.

18

Vroom!

From the Dreambook

Last night I dreamed of running water.
Generally, this means I drank too much before I
went to bed, but this was different. The water was
coming from the faucet in the sink at home. I was
helping Mama do the dishes; she was running hot
water from the hose-sprayer over the plates, then
handing them to me to dry; I could feel the hot china
through the dish towel, and feel the mist of water on
my face.

Mama's hair was curling up like mad because of
the humidity, and the pattern on the plates was the
lumpy pink roses of the good wedding china. Mama
didn't let me wash that until I was ten or so, for fear
I'd drop it, and when I got to wash it at last, I was
so proud!

I can still see every last thing in the china cabinet
in the living room: Mama's great-grandfather's
hand-painted cake stand (he was an artist, she said,
and won a competition with that cake stand, a
hundred years ago), the dozen crystal goblets that
Daddy's mother left him, along with the cut-glass
olive dish and the cup and saucer hand-painted with
violets and gilt rims.

I was standing in front of it, putting away the china—
but we didn't keep the china in that cabinet;
we kept it in the shelf over the oven—and the water
was overflowing from the sink in the kitchen, and

*running out across the floor, puddling round my
feet. Then it started to rise, and I was sloshing back
and forth to the kitchen, kicking up the water so it
sparkled like the cut-glass olive dish. The water got
deeper and deeper, but nobody seemed to be worried;
I wasn't.*

*The water was warm, hot, in fact, I could see steam
rising off it.*

*That's all there was to the dream—but when I got
up this morning, the water in the basin was so cold
I had to warm water in a pan on the fire before
I washed Jemmy. All the time I was checking the
water on the fire,
I kept remembering my dream, and all those gallons
and gallons of hot, running water.*

*What I wonder is, these dreams I have about then—
they seem so vivid and detailed; more than the dreams I
have about now. Why do I see things that don't exist
anywhere except inside my brain?*

*What I wonder about the dreams is—all the
new inventions people think up—how many of those
things are made by people like me—like us? How
many "inventions" are really memories, of the
things we once knew? And—how many of us are
there?*

"It isn't really that hard to have hot, running water. In theory."

"No? I suppose not." Roger only half-heard, concentrated as he was on the object taking shape beneath his knife.

"I mean, it would be a big, horrible job to *do*. But it's simple in concept. Dig ditches or build sluices—and around here, it would probably be sluices. . . ."

"It would?" Here was the tricky bit. He held his breath, chiseling delicate, tiny slivers of wood away, one shaving at a time.

"No metal," Bree said patiently. "If you had metal, you could make surface pipes. But I bet there isn't enough metal in the whole colony of North Carolina to make the piping you'd need to bring water from the creek to the Big House. Let alone a boiler! And if there was, it would cost a fortune."

"Mmm." Feeling that this was perhaps not an adequate response, Roger added hastily, "But there's some metal available. Jamie's still, for instance."

His wife snorted.

"Yeah. I asked him where he got it—he said he won it in a high-stakes game of loo against a ship's captain in Charleston. Think I could travel four hundred miles to bet my silver bracelet against a few hundred feet of rolled copper?"

One more sliver . . . two . . . the smallest scrape with the tip of the knife . . . ah. The tiny circle came free of the matrix. It turned!

"Er . . . sure," he said, belatedly realizing that she'd asked him a question. "Why not?"

She burst out laughing.

"You haven't heard one single word I've said, have you?"

"Oh, sure I have," he protested. "'Ditch,' ye said. And 'water.' I'm sure I remember that one."

She snorted again, though mildly.

"Well, you'd have to do it, anyway."

"Do what?" His thumb sought the little wheel, and set it spinning.

"Gamble. No one's going to let *me* into a high-stakes card game."

"Thank God," he said, in reflex.

"Bless your little Presbyterian heart," she said tolerantly, shaking her head. "You're not any kind of a gambler, Roger, are you?"

"Oh, and you are, I suppose." He said it jokingly, wondering even as he did so why he should feel vaguely reproached by her remark.

She merely smiled at that, wide mouth curving in a way that suggested untold volumes of wicked enterprise. He felt a slight sense of unease at that. She *was* a gambler, though so far . . . He glanced involuntarily at the large, charred spot in the middle of the table.

"That was an accident," she said defensively.

"Oh, aye. At least your eyebrows have grown back."

"Hmpf. I'm nearly there. One more batch—"

"That's what ye said last time." He was aware that he was treading on dangerous ground, but seemed unable to stop.

She took a slow, deep breath, gazing at him through slightly narrowed eyes, like one taking the range before firing off some major piece of artillery. Then she seemed to think better of whatever she had been going to say; her features relaxed and she stretched out her hand toward the object he was holding.

"What's that you've been making?"

"Just a wee bawbee for Jem." He let her take it, feeling the warmth of modest pride. "The wheels all turn."

"Mine, Daddy?" Jemmy had been wallowing on the floor with Adso the cat, who was tolerant of small children. Hearing his name, though, he abandoned the cat, who promptly escaped through the window, and popped up to see the new toy.

"Oh, look!" Brianna ran the little car over the palm of her hand and lifted it, letting all four tiny wheels spin free. Jem grabbed eagerly for it, pulling at the wheels.

"Careful, careful! You'll pull them off! Here, let me show you." Crouching, Roger took the car and rolled it along the hearthstones. "See? Vroom. Vroom-vroom!"

"Broom!" Jemmy echoed. "Lemme do it, Daddy, let me!"

Roger surrendered the toy to Jemmy, smiling.

"Broom! Broom-broom!" The little boy shoved the car enthusiastically, then, losing his grip on it, watched open-mouthed as it zoomed to the end of the hearthstone by itself, hit the edge, and flipped over. Squealing with delight, he scampered after the new toy.

Still smiling, Roger glanced up, to see Brianna looking after Jem, a rather odd expression on her face. She felt his eyes on her, and looked down at him.

"Vroom?" she said quietly, and he felt a small internal jolt, like a punch in the stomach.

"Whatsit, Daddy, what's it?" Jemmy had recaptured the toy and ran up to him, clutching it to his chest.

"It's a . . . a . . ." he began, helpless. It was in fact a crude replica of a Morris Minor, but even the word "car," let alone "automobile," had no meaning here. And the internal combustion engine, with its pleasantly evocative noises, was at least a century away.

"I guess it's a vroom, honey," said Bree, a distinct tone of sympathy in her voice. He felt the gentle weight of her hand, resting on his head.

"Er . . . yeah, that's right," he said, and cleared a thickening in his throat. "It's a vroom."

"Broom," said Jemmy happily, and knelt to roll it down the hearth again. "Broom-broom!"

Steam. *It would have to be steam- or wind-powered; a wind-mill would work, maybe, to pump water into the system, but if I want hot water, there would be steam anyway—why not use it?*

Containment is the problem; wood burns and leaks, clay won't hold against pressure. I need metal, that's all there is to it. What would Mrs. Bug do, I wonder, if I took the laundry caul-dron? Well, I know what she'd do, and a steam explosion is no comparison; besides, we do need to do *the laundry. I'll have to dream up something else.*

19

Making Hay

Major MacDonald returned on the final day of haymaking. I was just maneuvering my way along the side of the house with an immense basket of bread, when I saw him near the trailhead, tying up his horse to a tree. He lifted his hat to me and bowed, then came across the dooryard, looking curiously round at the preparations taking place.

We had set up trestles under the chestnut trees, with boards laid across them for tables, and a constant stream of women scurried to and fro like ants between the house and yard, fetching food. The sun was setting, and the men would be in soon for a celebratory feast; filthy, exhausted, starving—and exhilarated by the end of their labors.

I greeted the Major with a nod, and accepted with relief his offer to carry the bread to the tables for me.

"Haying, is it?" he said, in answer to my explanation. A nostalgic smile spread across his weathered face. "I remember the haymaking, from when I was a lad. But that was in Scotland, aye? We'd seldom such glorious weather as this for it." He looked up into the blazing deep blue bowl of the August sky above. It really was perfect haying weather, hot and dry.

"It's wonderful," I said, sniffing appreciatively. The scent of fresh hay was everywhere—and so was the hay; there were shimmering mounds of it in every shed, everyone carried bits of it on their clothes, and small trails of scattered straw lay everywhere. Now the smell of cut, dry hay was mingled with the delectable scent of the barbecue that had been simmering underground overnight, the fresh bread, and the heady tang of Mrs. Bug's cider. Marsali and Bree were bringing down jugs of it from the springhouse, where it had been cooling, along with buttermilk and beer.

"I see I've chosen my time well," the Major remarked, viewing all this effort with approval.

"If you came to eat, yes," I said, rather amused. "If you came to talk to Jamie, I rather think you'll have to wait until tomorrow."

He looked at me, puzzled, but had no opportunity to inquire further; I had caught another glimpse of movement at the trailhead. The Major turned, seeing the direction of my glance, and frowned slightly.

"Why, it's that fellow with the brand on his face," he said, wary disapproval in his voice. "I saw him down at Coopersville, but he saw me first, and steered well clear. Will ye have me drive him off, mum?" He set down the bread and was already settling his sword belt on his hip, when I gripped his forearm.

"You'll do no such thing, Major," I said sharply. "Mr. Higgins is a friend."

He gave me a flat look, then dropped his arm.

"As ye like, Mrs. Fraser, of course," he said coolly, and picking up the bread again, went off toward the tables.

Rolling my eyes in exasperation, I went to greet the newcomer. Plainly Bobby Higgins could have joined the Major on the path to the Ridge; just as plainly, he had chosen not to. He had become a little more familiar with mules, I saw; he was riding one and leading another, laden with a promising array of panniers and boxes.

"His Lordship's compliments, mum," he said, saluting me smartly as he slid off. From the corner of my eye, I saw MacDonald watching—and his small start of recognition at the military gesture. So, now he knew Bobby for a soldier, and doubtless would ferret out his background in short order. I repressed a sigh; I couldn't mend matters; they'd have to settle it between themselves—if there was anything to settle.

"You're looking well, Bobby," I said, smiling as I pushed aside my disquiet. "No difficulties with the riding, I hope?"

"Oh, no, mum!" He beamed. "And I's not fallen out once since I left you last!" "Fallen out" meant "fainted," and I congratulated him on the state of his health, looking him over as he unloaded the pack mule with deft efficiency. He did seem much better; pink and fresh-skinned as a child, bar the ugly brand on his cheek.

"Yonder lobsterback," he said, affecting insouciance as he set down a box. "He's known to ye, is he, mum?"

"That's Major MacDonald," I said, carefully not looking in the Major's direction; I could feel his stare boring into my back. "Yes. He . . . does things for the Governor, I believe. Not regular army, I mean; he's a half-pay officer."

That bit of information seemed to ease Bobby's mind a bit. He took a breath, as though to say something, but then thought better of it. Instead, he reached into his shirt and withdrew a sealed letter, which he handed over.

"That's for you," he explained. "From his Lordship. Is Miss Lizzie by any chance about?" His eyes were already searching the flock of girls and women readying the tables.

"Yes, she was in the kitchen last I saw," I replied, a small uneasy feeling skittering down my backbone. "She'll be out in a minute. But . . . you do know she's betrothed, don't you, Bobby? Her fiancé will be coming with the other men for supper."

He met my eyes and smiled with singular sweetness.

"Oh, aye, mum, I know that well enough. On'y thought as I s'ould thank her for her kindness when I last was here."

"Oh," I said, not trusting that smile in the slightest. Bobby was a very handsome lad, blind eye or not—and he had been a soldier. "Well . . . good."

Before I could say more, I caught the sound of male voices,

coming through the trees. It wasn't precisely singing; sort of a rhythmic chant. I wasn't sure what it was—there was a lot of Gaelic "Ho-ro!" and the like—but all of them seemed to be bellowing along in a cordial fashion.

Haymaking was a novel concept to the new tenants, who were much more accustomed to rake kelp than scythe grass. Jamie, Arch, and Roger had shepherded them through the process, though, and I had been asked to stitch no more than a handful of minor wounds, so I assumed it had been a success—no hands or feet lopped off, a few shouting matches, but no fistfights, and no more than the usual amount of hay trampled or ruined.

All of them seemed in good spirits as they poured into the dooryard, bedraggled, sweat-soaked, and thirsty as sponges. Jamie was in the thick of them, laughing and staggering as someone pushed him. He caught sight of me, and a huge grin split his sun-browned face. In a stride, he had reached me and swept me into an exuberant embrace, redolent of hay, horses, and sweat.

"Done, by God!" he said, and kissed me soundly. "Christ, I need a drink. And nay, that's no blasphemy, wee Roger," he added, with a glance behind him. "It's heartfelt gratitude and desperate need, aye?"

"Aye. First things first, though, hm?" Roger had appeared behind Jamie, his voice so hoarse that it was barely audible in the general uproar. He swallowed, grimacing.

"Oh, aye." Jamie shot a quick look at Roger, assessing, then shrugged and strode out into the center of the yard.

"Eìsd ris! Eìsd ris!" bellowed Kenny Lindsay, seeing him. Evan and Murdo joined him, clapping their hands and shouting "Hear him!" loudly enough that the crowd began to subside and pay attention.

> *"I say the prayer from my mouth,*
> *I say the prayer from my heart,*
> *I say the prayer to Thee Thyself,*
> *O, Healing Hand, O Son of the God of salvation."*

He didn't raise his voice much above its normal speaking level, but everyone quieted at once, so the words rang clear.

> *"Thou Lord God of the angels,*
> *Spread over me Thy linen robe;*
> *Shield me from every famine,*
> *Free me from every spectral shape.*
> *Strengthen me in every good,*
> *Encompass me in every strait,*
> *Safeguard me in every ill,*
> *And from every enmity restrain me."*

There was a stirring of faint approval in the crowd; I saw a few of the fisher-folk bow their heads, though their eyes stayed fixed on him.

> *"Be Thou between me and all things grisly,*
> *Be Thou between me and all things mean,*
> *Be Thou between me and all things gruesome*
> *Coming darkly toward me.*
>
> *"O God of the weak,*
> *O God of the lowly,*
> *O God of the righteous,*
> *O shield of homesteads:*
> *"Thou art calling upon us*
> *In the voice of glory,*
> *With the mouth of mercy*
> *Of Thy beloved Son."*

I glanced at Roger, who was nodding slightly with approval, as well. Evidently, they'd agreed on it together. Sensible; it would be a prayer familiar in form to the fisher-folk, and nothing specifically Catholic about it.

Jamie spread his arms, quite unconsciously, and the breeze caught the worn damp linen of his shirt as he tilted back his head and raised his face to the sky, open with joy.

> *"O may I find rest everlasting*
> *In the home of Thy Trinity,*
> *In the Paradise of the godly,*
> *In the Sun-garden of Thy love!"*

"Amen!" said Roger, as loudly as he could, and there were gratified murmurs of "amen" round the yard. Then Major MacDonald raised the tankard of cider he was holding, called *"Slàinte!"* and drained it.

Festivity became general after that. I found myself sitting on a cask, Jamie on the grass at my feet, with a platter of food and a constantly refilled mug of cider.

"Bobby Higgins is here," I told him, catching sight of Bobby in the midst of a small group of admiring young ladies. "Do you see Lizzie anywhere?"

"No," he said, stifling a yawn. "Why?"

"He asked for her particularly."

"Then I'm sure he'll find her. Will ye have a bit o' meat, Sassenach?" He held up a large rib bone, brow cocked inquiringly.

"I've had some," I assured him, and he at once tore into it, addressing himself to the vinegar-spiced barbecue as though he hadn't eaten for a week.

"Has Major MacDonald spoken to you?"

"No," he said, mouth full, and swallowed. "He'll keep. There's Lizzie—wi' the McGillivrays."

I felt reassured by that. The McGillivrays—particularly *Frau* Ute—would certainly discourage any inappropriate attentions to their new intended daughter-in-law. Lizzie was chatting and laughing with Robin McGillivray, who was smiling at her in fatherly fashion, while his son Manfred ate and drank with single-minded appetite. *Frau* Ute, I saw, was keeping a sharp and interested eye on Lizzie's father, who was sitting on the porch nearby, cozily side by side with a tall, rather plain-faced German lady.

"Who's that with Joseph Wemyss?" I asked, nudging Jamie with my knee to direct his attention.

He narrowed his eyes against the sun's glare, looking, then shrugged.

"I dinna ken. She's German; she must ha' come with Ute McGillivray. Matchmaking, aye?" He tilted up his mug and drank, sighing with bliss.

"Do you think so?" I looked at the strange woman with interest. She certainly seemed to be getting on well with Joseph—and he with her. His thin face was alight as he gestured, explaining something to her, and her neatly capped head was bent toward him, a smile on her lips.

I didn't always approve of Ute McGillivray's methods, which tended toward the juggernaut, but I had to admire the painstaking intricacy of her plans. Lizzie and Manfred would marry next spring, and I had wondered how Joseph would fare then; Lizzie was his whole life.

He might, of course, go with her when she married. She and Manfred would simply live in the McGillivrays' large house, and I imagined that they would find room for Joseph, too. Still, he would be torn, not wanting to leave us—and while any able-bodied man could always be of use on a homestead, he was by no means a natural farmer, let alone a gunsmith, like Manfred and his father. If he himself were to wed, though . . .

I gave Ute McGillivray a glance, and saw her watching Mr. Wemyss and his inamorata with the contented expression of a puppet master whose puppets are dancing precisely to her tune.

Someone had left a pitcher of cider beside us. I refilled Jamie's mug, then my own. It was wonderful, a dark, cloudy amber, sweet and pungent and with the bite of a particularly subtle serpent to it. I let the cool liquid trickle down my throat and bloom inside my head like a silent flower.

There was much talk and laughter, and I noticed that while the new tenants still kept to their own family groups, there was now a little more blending, as the men who had been working side-by-side for the last two weeks maintained their cordial relations, these social courtesies fueled by cider. The new tenants mostly regarded wine as a mocker, strong drink—whisky, rum, or brandy—as raging, but everyone drank beer and cider. Cider was wholesome, one of the women had told me, handing a mug to her small son. I gave it half an hour, I thought, sipping slowly, before they started dropping like flies.

Jamie made a small amused sound, and I looked down at him. He nodded at the far side of the dooryard, and I looked to see that Bobby Higgins had disentangled himself from his admirers, and by some alchemical legerdemain had managed to abstract Lizzie from the midst of the McGillivrays. They were standing in the shadow of the chestnut trees, talking.

I looked back at the McGillivrays. Manfred was leaning against the foundation of the house, head nodding over his plate. His father had curled up beside him on the ground and was snoring peacefully. The girls chatted around them, passing food to and fro over the drooping heads of their husbands, all in various stages of impending somnolence. Ute had moved to the porch, and was talking to Joseph and his companion.

I glanced back. Lizzie and Bobby were only talking, and there was a respectful distance between them. But there was something about the way he bent toward her, and the way she half-turned away from him, then back, swinging a fold of her skirt one-handed . . .

"Oh, dear," I said. I shifted a little, getting my feet under me, but unsure whether I ought really to go and interrupt them. After all, they were in plain sight, and—

"Three things astonish me, nay four, sayeth the prophet." Jamie's hand squeezed my thigh, and I looked down to see that he was also watching the couple under the chestnut trees, his eyes half-closed. "The way of an eagle in the air, the way of a serpent on the rock, the way of a ship in the midst of the sea—and the way of a man with a maid."

"Oh, so I'm not imagining it," I said dryly. "Do you think I'd best do something?"

"Mmphm." He took a deep breath and straightened up, shaking his head vigorously to wake himself. "Ah. No, Sassenach. If wee Manfred willna take the trouble to guard his woman, it's no your place to do it for him."

"Yes, I quite agree. I'm only thinking, if Ute should see them . . . or Joseph?" I wasn't sure what Mr. Wemyss would do; I thought Ute would probably make a major scene.

"Oh." He blinked, swaying a little. "Aye, I suppose ye're right." He turned his head, searching, then spotting Ian, lifted his chin in summons.

Ian had been sprawled dreamily on the grass a few feet away, next to a pile of greasy rib bones, but now rolled over and crawled obligingly to us.

"Mm?" he said. His thick brown hair had fallen half out of its binding, and several cowlicks were sticking straight up, the rest fallen disreputably over one eye.

Jamie nodded in the direction of the chestnut trees.

"Go and ask wee Lizzie to mend your hand, Ian."

Ian glanced blearily down at his hand; there was a fresh scratch across the back of it, though it was long since clotted. Then he looked in the direction Jamie indicated.

"Oh," he said. He remained on hands and knees, eyes narrowed thoughtfully, then slowly rose to his feet, and pulled the binding off his hair. Casually shoving it back with one hand, he strolled in the direction of the chestnut trees.

They were much too far away to hear anything, but we could see. Bobby and Lizzie parted like the waves of the Red Sea as Ian's tall, gangly form stepped purposefully between them. The three seemed to chat amiably for a moment, then Lizzie and Ian departed for the house, Lizzie giving Bobby a casual wave of the hand—and a brief, backward glance. Bobby stood for a moment looking after her, rocking thoughtfully on his heels, then shook his head and made for the cider.

The cider was taking its toll. I'd expected every man in the place to be laid out cold by nightfall; during haying, men commonly fell asleep in their plates from sheer exhaustion. As it was, there was still plenty of talk and laughter, but the soft twilight glow beginning to suffuse the dooryard showed an increasing number of bodies strewn in the grass.

Rollo was gnawing contentedly on Ian's discarded bones. Brianna sat a little way away; Roger lay with his head in her lap, sound asleep. The collar of his shirt was open, the ragged rope scar still vivid across his neck. Bree smiled at me, her hand gently stroking his glossy black hair, picking bits of hay out of it. Jemmy was nowhere to be seen—neither was Germain, as I ascertained with a quick look around. Luckily the phosphorus was under lock and key, in the top of my highest cupboard.

Jamie laid his own head against my thigh, warm and heavy, and I put my hand on his hair, smiling back at Bree. I heard him snort faintly, and looked in the direction of his gaze.

"For such a wee small lass, yon Lizzie does cause a good deal of trouble," he said.

Bobby Higgins was standing beside one of the tables, drinking cider, and quite evidently unaware that he was being stalked by the Beardsley twins. The two of them were slinking like foxes through the wood, not quite out of sight, converging on him from opposite directions.

One—Jo, probably—stepped out suddenly beside Bobby, startling him into spilling his drink. He frowned, wiping at the wet splotch on his shirt, while Jo leaned close, obviously muttering menaces and warnings. Looking offended, Bobby turned away from him, only to be confronted by Kezzie on the other side.

"I'm not sure it's Lizzie who's causing the trouble," I said defensively. "She only talked to him, after all." Bobby's face was growing noticeably flushed. He set down the mug he'd been drinking from and drew himself up a little, one hand folding into a fist.

The Beardsleys crowded closer, with the evident intention of forcing him into the wood. Glancing warily from one twin to the other, he took a step back, putting a solid tree trunk at his back.

I glanced down; Jamie was watching through half-closed lids, with an expression of dreamy detachment. He sighed deeply, his eyes closed altogether, and he went suddenly and completely limp, the weight of him heavy against me.

The reason for this sudden absquatulation loomed up a second later: MacDonald, ruddy with food and cider, his red coat glowing like a cinder in the sunset light. He looked down at Jamie, peacefully slumbering against my leg, and shook his head. He turned slowly round, surveying the scene.

"Strewth," he said mildly. "I'll tell ye, mum, I've seen battlefields with much less carnage."

"Oh, have you?" His appearance had distracted me, but at the mention of "carnage," I glanced back. Bobby and the Beardsley twins had disappeared, vanished like wisps of mist in the gloaming. Well, if they were beating each other to pulp in the wood, I was sure I'd hear about it before too long.

With a small shrug, MacDonald bent, took Jamie by the shoulders, and eased him off me, laying him down in the grass with surprising gentleness.

"May I?" he asked politely, and upon my nod of assent, sat down beside me on the other side, arms companionably hooked round his knees.

He was neatly dressed, as always, wig and all, but the collar of his shirt was grimy and the skirts of his coat frayed at the hem and spattered with mud.

"A great deal of travel these days, Major?" I asked, making conversation. "You look rather tired, if you'll pardon my mentioning it."

I had surprised him in the middle of a yawn; he swallowed it, blinking, then laughed.

"Aye, mum. I've been in the saddle for the last month, and seen a bed perhaps one night in three."

He did look tired, even in the soft sunset light; the lines of his face were cut deep with fatigue, the flesh beneath his eyes sagging and smudged. He was not a handsome man, but normally had a brash self-assurance that lent him an attractive air. Now he looked what he was: a half-pay soldier pushing fifty, lacking a regiment or regular duty, struggling for any small connections that might hold some hope of advancement.

I wouldn't normally have spoken to him of his business, but sympathy moved me to ask, "Are you working a lot on behalf of Governor Martin these days?"

He nodded, and took another gulp of cider, breathing deeply after it.

"Aye, mum. The Governor has been kind enough to charge me with bringing him news of conditions in the backcountry—and has done me the signal favor of accepting my advice, now and then." He glanced at Jamie, who had curled himself up like a hedgehog and commenced to snore, and smiled.

"With regard to my husband's appointment as Indian Agent, you mean? We do thank you, Major."

He waved a casual hand in dismissal of my thanks.

"Ah, no, mum; that had nothing to do wi' the Governor, save indirectly. Such appointments are the province of the Superintendent of the Southern Department. Though it is of course a matter of interest to the Governor," he added, taking another sip, "to hear news of the Indians."

"I'm sure he'll tell you all about it in the morning," I assured him, with a nod at Jamie.

"Indeed, mum." He hesitated for a moment. "Would ye ken . . . did Mr. Fraser perhaps mention, in his conversations in the villages—was there any mention of . . . burnings?"

I sat up straight, the cider buzz disappearing from my head.

"What's happened? Have there been more?"

He nodded, and rubbed a hand tiredly down his face, scrubbing at the sprout of whiskers.

"Aye, two—but the one was a barn-burning, down below Salem. One o' the Moravian brethren's. And from all I can learn of the matter, 'twas likely some of the Scotch-Irish Presbyterians who've settled in Surry County. There's a wee arsebite of a preacher who's got them riled about the Moravians—Godless heathen that they are—" He grinned suddenly at that, but then sobered again.

"There's been trouble brewing in Surry County for months. To the point that the brethren have been petitioning the Governor to redraw the boundary lines, so as to put them all in Rowan County. The line between Surry and Rowan goes right through their land, ken? And the sheriff in Surry is . . . " He twiddled a hand.

"Perhaps not so keen in the performance of his duty as he might be?" I suggested. "At least where the Moravians are concerned?"

"He's the arsebite's cousin," MacDonald said, and drained his cup. "Ye've had no trouble wi' your new tenants, by the way?" he added, lowering it. He smiled crookedly, looking round the dooryard at the small groups of women, chattering contentedly as their men slept by their feet. "It would appear ye've made them welcome."

"Well, they are Presbyterians, and fairly vehement about it—but they haven't tried to burn the house down yet, at least."

I took a quick glance at the porch, where Mr. Wemyss and his companion still sat, heads close in conversation. I thought Mr. Wemyss was probably the only man still conscious, bar the Major himself. The lady was plainly a German, but not, I thought, a Moravian; they very seldom married outside their community, nor did the women often travel far.

"Unless you think the Presbyterians have formed a gang for the purpose of purging the countryside of Papists and Lutherans—and you *don't* think that, do you?"

He smiled briefly at that, though without much humor.

"No. But then, I was raised Presbyterian myself, mum."

"Oh," I said. "Er . . . a drop more cider, Major?"

He held out his cup without demur.

"The other burning—that seems much like the others," he said, graciously choosing to overlook my remark. "An isolated homestead. A man living alone. But this one was just over the Treaty Line."

This last was said with a significant glance, and I looked involuntarily at Jamie. He'd told me that the Cherokee were upset about settlers intruding into their territory.

"I shall ask your husband in the morning, of course, mum," MacDonald said, correctly interpreting my glance. "But perhaps ye'd ken whether he's heard any references . . . ?"

"Veiled threats from a Snowbird chief," I confessed. "He wrote to John Stuart about them. But nothing specific. When did this latest burning happen?"

He shrugged.

"No telling. I heard of it three weeks ago, but the man who told me had heard of it a month before that—and he'd not seen it, only heard from someone else."

He scratched thoughtfully at his jaw.

"Someone should go and inspect the place, perhaps."

"Mm," I said, not bothering to hide the skepticism in my voice. "And you think it's Jamie's job, do you?"

"I shouldna be so presumptuous as to instruct Mr. Fraser in his duties, mum," he said, with the hint of a smile. "But I will suggest to him that the situation may be of interest, aye?"

"Yes, you do that," I muttered. Jamie had planned another quick trip to the Snowbird villages, squeezed in between harvesting and the onset of the cold weather. The notion of marching into the village and quizzing Bird-who-sings-in-the-morning about a burned homestead seemed more than slightly risky, viewed from my perspective.

A slight chill made me shiver, and I gulped the rest of my own cider, wishing suddenly that it was hot. The sun was fully set now, and the air had grown cool, but that wasn't what was cooling my blood.

What if MacDonald's suspicions were right? If the Cherokee had been burning homesteads? And if Jamie were to show up, asking inconvenient questions . . . .

I looked at the house, standing solid and serene, its windows glowing with candlelight, a pale bulwark against the darkening woods beyond.

It is with grief that the news is received of the deaths by fire of James MacKenzie Fraser and his wife, Claire Fraser, in a conflagration that destroyed their house. . . .

The fireflies were coming out, drifting like cool green sparks in the shadows, and I looked upward involuntarily, to see a spray of red and yellow ones from the chimney. Whenever I thought of that gruesome clipping—and I tried not to, nor to count the days between now and January 21 of 1776—I had thought of the fire as occurring by accident. Such accidents were more than common, ranging from hearth fires run amok and candlesticks tipped over, to blazes caused by the summer lightning storms. It hadn't consciously occurred to me before that it might be a deliberate act—an act of murder.

I moved my foot enough to nudge Jamie. He stirred in his sleep, reached out one hand, and clasped it warmly round my ankle, then subsided with a contented groan.

"Stand between me and all things grisly," I said, half-under my breath.

"Slàinte," said the Major, and drained his cup again.

20

Dangerous Gifts

Propelled by Major MacDonald's news, Jamie and Ian departed two days later for a quick visit to Bird-who-sings-in-the-morning, and the Major went off on his further mysterious errands, leaving me with Bobby Higgins for assistance.

I was dying to dig into the crates Bobby had brought, but what with one thing and another—the white pig's demented attempt to eat Adso, a goat with infected teats, a strange green mold that had got into the last batch of cheese, the completion of a much-needed summer kitchen, and a stern conversation with the Beardsleys regarding the treatment of guests, among other things—it was more than a week before I found leisure to unpack Lord John's present and read his letter.

September 4, 1773

From Lord John Grey, Mount Josiah Plantation
To Mrs. James Fraser

My dear Madam—

I trust that the Articles you requested will have arrived
intact. Mr. Higgins is somewhat nervous of carrying the
Oil of Vitriol, as I understand he has had some evil
Experience connected with it, but we have packed the
Bottle with some Care, leaving it sealed as it came from
England.

After examining the exquisite Drawings you sent—do I
detect your daughter's elegant Hand in them?—I rode to
Williamsburg, in order to consult with a famous
Glassmaker who abides there under the nomen (doubtless
fabulous) of Blogweather. Mr. Blogweather allowed that
the Pelican Retort would be simplicity itself, scarcely a
fair Test of his Skill, but was enchanted by the
Requirements of the distilling Apparatus, particularly the
detachable Coil. He apprehended immediately the
Desirability of such a Device in case of Breakage, and
has made three of them.

Pray consider these my Gift—a most insignificant
Demonstration of my abiding Gratitude for your many
Kindnesses, both toward myself and Mr. Higgins.

Your most humble and obedient servant,
John Grey

Postscriptum: I have thus far restrained my sense of vulgar
Curiosity, but I do venture to hope that on some future
Occasion, you may possibly gratify me by explaining the
Purpose to which you intend these Articles be put.

They *had* packed with some care. Pried open, the crates
proved to be filled with an immense quantity of straw, the bits of

glassware and sealed bottles gleaming within, cradled like roc's eggs.

"You *will* be careful with that, won't 'ee, mum?" Bobby inquired anxiously, as I lifted out a squat, heavy, brown-glass bottle, the cork heavily sealed with red wax. "It's turrible noxious, that stuff."

"Yes, I know." Standing on tiptoe, I boosted the bottle up onto a high shelf, safe from marauding children or cats. "Have you seen it used, then, Bobby?"

His lips drew in tight, and he shook his head.

"Not to say used, mum. But I've seen what it *does*. Was a . . . a lass, in London, what I come to know a bit, whilst we was a-waitin' the ship to carry us to America. Half her face pretty and smooth as a buttercup but t'other side was so scarred you could scarce look at it. Like as it was melted in a fire, but she said 'twas vitriol." He glanced up at the bottle, and swallowed visibly. "Another whore'd thrown it on her, she said, 'cause of jealousy."

He shook his head again, sighing, and reached for the broom to sweep up the scattered straw.

"Well, you needn't worry," I assured him. "I don't propose to throw it at anyone."

"Oh, no, mum!" He was quite shocked. "I s'ould never think that!"

I disregarded this reassurance, involved in delving for more treasure.

"Oh, *look*," I said, enchanted. I held in my hands the fruit of Mr. Blogweather's artistry: a globe of glass, the size of my head, blown to perfect symmetry and lacking even the hint of a bubble. There was a faint blue tinge to the glass, and I could see my own distorted reflection, wide-nosed and bug-eyed, like a mermaid peering out.

"Aye, mum," said Bobby, dutifully peering at the retort. "It's, er . . . big, in't it?"

"It's perfect. Just perfect!" Rather than being cut off cleanly from the blower's pipe, the neck of the globe had been drawn out into a thick-walled tube about two inches long and an inch in diameter. The edges and interior surface of this had been . . . sanded? Ground? I'd no idea what Mr. Blogweather had done, but the result was a silky, opaque surface that would form a lovely seal when a similarly finished piece was inserted into it.

My hands were damp with excitement and nervousness, lest I drop the precious thing. I clutched a fold of my apron round it, and turned to and fro, debating where best to put it. I hadn't expected one so large; I should need Bree or one of the men to make me a suitable support.

"It has to go over a small fire," I explained, frowning at the little brazier I used for brewing. "But the temperature is important; a charcoal bed may be too hard to keep at a steady heat." I placed the big ball in my cupboard, safely behind a row of bottles. "I think it will have to be an alcohol lamp—but it's bigger than I thought, I'll have to have a good-size lamp to heat it. . . ."

I became aware that Bobby was not listening to my babbling, his attention having been distracted by something outside. He was frowning at something, and I came up behind him, peering through the open window to see what it was.

I should have guessed; Lizzie Wemyss was out on the grass, churning butter under the chestnut trees, and Manfred McGillivray was with her.

I glanced at the pair, engaged in cheerful conversation, then at Bobby's somber countenance. I cleared my throat.

"Perhaps you'd open the other crate for me, Bobby?"

"Eh?" His attention was still fixed on the pair outside.

"Crate," I repeated patiently. "That one." I nudged it with my toe.

"Crate . . . oh! Oh, aye, mum, to be sure." Pulling his gaze from the window, he set about the task, looking glum.

I took the rest of the glassware from the open crate, shaking off the straw and putting globes, retorts, flasks, and coils carefully into a high cupboard—but I kept an eye on Bobby as I did so, pondering this newly revealed situation. I hadn't thought his feelings for Lizzie were more than a passing attraction.

And perhaps it was no more than that, I reminded myself. But if it was . . . Despite myself, I glanced through the window, only to discover that the pair had become a trio.

"Ian!" I exclaimed. Bobby glanced up, startled, but I was already heading for the door, hastily brushing straw from my clothes.

If Ian was back, Jamie was—

He came through the front door just as I barreled into the hallway, and grabbed me round the waist, kissing me with sun-dusty enthusiasm and sandpaper whiskers.

"You're back," I said, rather inanely.

"I am, and there are Indians just behind me," he said, clutching my bottom with both hands and rasping his whiskers fervently against my cheek. "God, what I'd give for a quarter of an hour alone wi' ye, Sassenach! My balls are burst—ah. Mr. Higgins. I, um, didna see ye there."

He let go and straightened abruptly, sweeping off his hat and smacking it against his thigh in an exaggerated pantomime of casualness.

"No, zur," Bobby said morosely. "Mr. Ian's back, as well, is he?" He didn't sound as though this was particularly good news; if Ian's arrival had distracted Lizzie from Manfred—and it had—it did nothing to redirect her attention to Bobby.

Lizzie had abandoned her churn to poor Manfred, who was turning the crank with an air of obvious resentment, as she went laughing off in the direction of the stable with Ian, presumably to show him the new calf that had arrived during his absence.

"Indians," I said, belatedly catching what Jamie had said. "What Indians?"

"A half-dozen of the Cherokee," he replied. "What's this?" He nodded at the trail of loose straw leading out of my surgery.

"Oh, that. That," I said happily, "is ether. Or going to be. We're feeding the Indians, I suppose?"

"Aye. I'll tell Mrs. Bug. But there's a young woman with them that they've fetched along for ye to tend."

"Oh?" He was already striding down the hall toward the kitchen, and I hurried to keep up. "What's the matter with her?"

"Toothache," he said briefly, and pushed open the kitchen door. "Mrs. Bug! *Cá bhfuil tú?* Ether, Sassenach? Ye dinna mean phlogiston, do you?"

"I don't *think* that I do," I said, trying to recall what on earth phlogiston was. "I've told you about anesthesia, though, I know—that's what ether is, a sort of anesthetic; puts people to sleep so you can do surgery without hurting them."

"Verra useful in case of the toothache," Jamie observed. "Where's the woman gone to? Mrs. Bug!"

"So it would be, but it will take some time to make. We'll have to make do with whisky for the moment. Mrs. Bug is in the summer kitchen, I expect; it's bread day. And speaking of alcohol—" He was already out the back door, and I scampered across the stoop after him. "I'll need quite a bit of high-quality alcohol, for the ether. Can you bring me a barrel of the new stuff tomorrow?"

"A barrel? Christ, Sassenach, what d'ye mean to do, bathe in it?"

"Well, as a matter of fact, yes. Or rather not me—the oil of vitriol. You pour it gently into a bath of hot alcohol, and it—"

"Oh, Mr. Fraser! I did think as how I heard someone a-callin'." Mrs. Bug appeared suddenly with a basket of eggs over one arm, beaming. "It's pleased I am to see ye home again safe!"

"And glad to be so, Mrs. Bug," he assured her. "Can we be feeding a half-dozen guests for supper?"

Her eyes went wide for a moment, then narrowed in calculation.

"Sausage," she declared. "And neeps. Here, wee Bobby, come and make yourself useful." Handing me the eggs, she seized Bobby, who had come out of the house after us, by the sleeve and towed him off toward the turnip patch.

I had the feeling of having been caught in some rapidly revolving apparatus like a merry-go-round, and took hold of Jamie's arm in order to steady myself.

"Did you know that Bobby Higgins is in love with Lizzie?" I asked.

"No, but it'll do him little good if he is," Jamie replied callously. Taking my hand on his arm as invitation, he took the eggs from me and set them on the ground, then pulled me in and kissed me again, more slowly, but no less thoroughly.

He let go with a deep sigh of content, and glanced at the new summer kitchen we had erected in his absence: a small framed structure consisting of coarse-woven canvas walls and a pine-branch roof, erected round a stone hearth and chimney—but with a large table inside. Enticing scents of rising dough, fresh-baked bread, oatcakes, and cinnamon rolls wafted through the air from it.

"Now, about that quarter of an hour, Sassenach . . . I believe I could manage wi' a bit less, if necessary. . . ."

"Well, *I* couldn't," I said firmly, though I did allow my hand to fondle him for a thoughtful instant. My face was burning from contact with his whiskers. "And when we do have time, you can tell me *what* on earth you've been doing to bring this on."

"Dreaming," he said.

"What?"

"I kept havin' terrible lewd dreams about ye, all the night long," he explained, twitching his breeks into better adjustment. "Every time I rolled over, I'd lie on my cock and wake up. It was awful."

I burst out laughing, and he affected to look injured, though I could see reluctant amusement behind it.

"Well, *you* can laugh, Sassenach," he said. "Ye havena got one to trouble ye."

"Yes, and a great relief it is, too," I assured him. "Er . . . what sort of lewd dreams?"

I could see a deep blue gleam of speculation at the back of his eyes as he looked at me. He extended one finger, and very delicately ran it down the side of my neck, the slope of my breast where it disappeared into my bodice, and over the thin cloth covering my nipple—which promptly popped up like a puffball mushroom in response to this attention.

"The sort that make me want to take ye straight into the forest, far enough that no one will hear when I lay ye on the ground, lift your skirts, and split ye like a ripe peach," he said softly. "Aye?"

I swallowed, audibly.

At this delicate moment, whoops of greeting came from the trailhead on the other side of the house.

"Duty calls," I said, a trifle breathless.

Jamie drew a deep breath of his own, squared his shoulders, and nodded.

"Well, I havena died of unrequited lust yet; I suppose I shallna do it now."

"Don't suppose you will," I said. "Besides, didn't you tell me once that abstinence makes . . . er . . . things . . . grow firmer?"

He gave me a bleak look.

"If it gets any firmer, I'll faint from a lack of blood to the heid. Dinna forget the eggs, Sassenach."

It was late afternoon, but plenty of light left for the job, thank goodness. My surgery was positioned to take advantage of morning light for operations, though, and was dim in the afternoons, so I set up an impromptu theater of operation in the dooryard.

This was an advantage, insofar as everyone wished to watch; Indians always regarded medical treatment—and almost anything else—as a community affair. They were particularly enthusiastic about operations, as these held a high degree of entertainment value. Everyone crowded eagerly around, commenting on my preparations, arguing with each other and talking to the patient, whom I had the greatest difficulty in discouraging from talking back.

Her name was Mouse, and I could only assume that she had been given it for some metaphysical reason, as it certainly wasn't suited either to appearance or personality. She was round-faced, unusually snub-nosed for a Cherokee, and if she wasn't precisely pretty, she had a force of character that is often more attractive than simple beauty.

It was certainly working on the males present; she was the only woman in the Indian party, the others consisting of her brother, Red Clay Wilson, and four friends who had come along, either to keep the Wilsons company, offer protection on the journey—or to vie for Miss Mousie's attention, which seemed to me the most likely explanation of their presence.

Despite the Wilsons' Scottish name, none of the Cherokee spoke any English beyond a few basic words—these including "no," "yes," "good," "bad," and "whisky!" Since the Cherokee equivalent of these terms was the extent of my own vocabulary, I was taking little part in the conversation.

We were at the moment waiting for whisky, in fact, as well as translators. A settler named Wolverhampton, from some nameless hollow to the east, had inadvertently amputated one and a half toes a week before, while splitting logs. Finding this state of things inconvenient, he had proceeded to try to remove the remaining half-digit himself with a froe.

Say what you will regarding general utility; a froe is not a precision instrument. It is, however, sharp.

Mr. Wolverhampton, a burly sort with an irascible temper, lived on his own, some seven miles from his nearest neighbor. By the time he had reached this neighbor—on foot, or what remained of it—and the neighbor had bundled him onto a mule for transport to Fraser's Ridge, nearly twenty-four hours had passed, and the partial foot had assumed the dimensions and appearance of a mangled raccoon.

The requirements of the cleanup surgery, the multiple subsequent debridements to control the infection, and the fact that Mr. Wolverhampton refused to surrender the bottle, had quite exhausted my usual surgical supply. As I needed a keg of the raw spirit for my ether-making in any case, Jamie and Ian had gone to fetch more from the whisky spring, which was a good mile from the house. I hoped they would return while there was still enough light to see what I was doing.

I interrupted Miss Mousie's loud remonstrance with one of the gentlemen, who was evidently teasing her, and indicated by means of sign language that she should open her mouth for me. She did, but went on expostulating by means of rather explicit hand signals, which seemed to be indicating various acts she expected the gentleman in question to perform upon himself, judging from his flushed countenance, and the way his companions were falling about with hilarity.

The side of her face was puffed and obviously tender. She didn't wince or shy away, though, even when I turned her face farther toward the light for a better view.

"Toothache, forsooth!" I said, involuntarily.

"Ooth?" Miss Mouse said, cocking an eyebrow at me.

"Bad," I explained, pointing at her cheek. *"Uyoi."*

"Bad," she agreed. There followed a voluble exposition—interrupted only by my inserting my fingers into her mouth periodically—which I took to be an explanation of what had happened to her.

Blunt trauma, by the look of it. One tooth, a lower canine, had been knocked completely out, and the neighboring bicuspid was so badly broken I would have to extract it. The next to that could be saved, I thought. The inside of her mouth was badly lacerated by the sharp edges, but the gum was not infected. That was heartening.

Bobby Higgins came down from the stable, drawn by the chatter, and was promptly sent back to bring me a file. Miss Mousie grinned lopsidedly at him when he brought it, and he bowed extravagantly to her, making all of them laugh.

"These folk are Cherokee, are they, mum?" He smiled at Red Clay, and made a hand sign, which seemed to amuse the Indians, though they returned it. "I've not met any Cherokee before. It's mostly other tribes near his Lordship's place in Virginia."

I was pleased to see that he was familiar with Indians, and easy in his manner toward them. Hiram Crombie, who appeared at this point, was not.

He stopped dead at the edge of the clearing, seeing the assemblage. I waved cheerily at him, and—with evident reluctance—he advanced.

Roger had told me Duncan's description of Hiram as "that wee sour-drap." It was apt. He was small and stringy, with thin grizzled hair that he wore strained back in a plait so tight that I thought he must find it difficult to blink. His face deeply lined by the rigors of a fisherman's life, he looked about sixty, but was likely much younger—and his mouth was habitually downturned, in the expression of one who has sucked not merely a lemon, but a rotten lemon.

"I was looking for Mr. Fraser," he said, with a wary eye on the Indians. "I had heard he was back." He had a hatchet in his belt, and kept a tight grip on it with one hand.

"He'll be back directly. You've met Mr. Higgins, haven't you?" Evidently he had, and had been unfavorably impressed by the experience. His eyes fixed on Bobby's brand, he made the smallest possible nod of acknowledgment. Nothing daunted, I waved a hand round at the Indians, who were all examining Hiram with much more interest than he showed in them. "May I introduce Miss Wilson, her brother Mr. Wilson, and . . . er . . . their friends?"

Hiram stiffened further, if such a thing was possible.

"Wilson?" he said, in an unfriendly voice.

"Wilson," agreed Miss Mouse cheerily.

"That is my wife's family name," he said, in a tone that made it clear he considered the use of it by Indians to be grossly outrageous.

"Oh," I said. "How nice. Do you think they might be your wife's relatives, perhaps?"

His eyes bulged slightly at that, and I heard a strangled gurgle from Bobby.

"Well, they plainly got the name from a Scottish father or grandfather," I pointed out. "Perhaps . . ."

Hiram's face was working like a nutcracker, emotions from fury to dismay passing in swift succession over it. His right hand curled up, forefinger and little finger protruding in the horns, the sign against evil.

"Great-Uncle Ephraim," he whispered. "Jesus save us." And

without further word, he turned on his heel and tottered off.

"Goodbye!" called Miss Mousie in English, waving. He cast a single, haunted glance over his shoulder at her, then fled as though pursued by demons.

The whisky finally arrived, and, a fair amount of it passed out to patient and spectators alike, the operation at last commenced.

The file was normally used on horses' teeth, and thus a little larger than I would have liked, but worked reasonably well. Miss Mouse was inclined to be loud about the discomfort involved, but her complaints grew less with her increasing intake of whisky. By the time I had to draw her broken tooth, I thought, she wouldn't feel a thing.

Bobby, meanwhile, was entertaining Jamie and Ian with imitations of Hiram Crombie's response to the discovery that he might possibly share some family connection with the Wilsons. Ian, between bursts of laughter, translated the matter for the Indians, who all rolled on the grass in paroxysms of mirth.

"*Do* they have an Ephraim Wilson in their family tree?" I asked, taking a firm grip of Miss Mousie's chin.

"Well, they're not sure of the 'Ephraim,' but aye, they do." Jamie grinned broadly. "Their grandsire was a Scottish wanderer. Stayed long enough to get their grandmother wi' child, then fell off a cliff and was buried by a rockslide. She marrit again, of course, but liked the name."

"I wonder what it was made Great-Uncle Ephraim leave Scotland?" Ian sat up, wiping tears of laughter from his eyes.

"The proximity of people like Hiram, I expect," I said, squinting to see what I was doing. "Do you think—" I realized suddenly that everyone had quit talking and laughing, their attention focused on something across the clearing.

This something was the arrival of another Indian, carrying something in a bundle over his shoulder.

The Indian was a gentleman named Sequoyah, somewhat older than the young Wilsons and their friends. He nodded soberly to Jamie, and swinging the bundle off his shoulder, laid it on the ground at Jamie's feet, saying something in Cherokee.

Jamie's face changed, the lingering traces of amusement vanishing, replaced by interest—and wariness. He knelt, and carefully turning back the ragged canvas, revealed a jumble of weathered bones, a hollow-eyed skull staring up from the midst of them.

"Who in bloody hell is *that*?" I had stopped work, and with everyone else, including Miss Mouse, stood staring down at this latest arrival.

"He says it's the auld man who owned the homestead MacDonald told of—the one that burned inside the Treaty Line." Jamie reached down and picked up the skull, turning it gently in his hands.

He heard my small intake of breath, for he glanced at me, then turned the skull over, holding it for me to see. Most of the teeth were missing, and had been missing long enough that the jawbone had closed over the empty sockets. But the two molars remaining showed nothing but cracks and stains—no gleam of silver filling, no empty space where such fillings might have been.

I let my breath out slowly, not sure whether to be relieved or disappointed.

"What happened to him? And why is he *here*?"

Jamie knelt and laid the skull gently back in the canvas, then turned some of the bones over, examining them. He looked up, and with a small motion of the head, invited me to join him.

The bones showed no sign of having been burned, but several of them *did* show signs of having been gnawed by animals. One or two of the long bones had been cracked and split, no doubt to get at the marrow, and many of the smaller bones of hands and feet were missing. All of them had the gray, fragile look of bones that had lain outside for some time.

Ian had relayed my question to Sequoyah, who squatted down next to Jamie, explaining as he jabbed a finger here and there amongst the bones.

"He says," Ian translated, frowning, "that he knew the man a long time. They werena friends, exactly, but now and again, when he was near the man's cabin, he would stop, and the man would share his food. So he would bring things, too, when he came—a hare for the pot, a bit o' salt."

One day, a few months back, he had found the old man's body in the wood, lying under a tree, some distance from his house.

"No one kilt him, he says," Ian said, frowning in concentration at the rapid stream of words. "He just . . . died. He thinks the man was hunting—he had a knife on him, and his gun beside him—when the spirit left him, and he just fell down." He echoed Sequoyah's shrug.

Seeing no reason to do anything with the body, Sequoyah had left it there, and left the knife with it, in case the spirit should require it, wherever it had gone; he did not know where the spirits of white men went, or whether they hunted there. He pointed—there was an old knife, the blade almost rusted away, under the bones.

He had taken the gun, which seemed too good to leave, and as it was on his way, had stopped at the cabin. The old man had owned very little, and what he had was mostly worthless. Sequoyah had taken an iron pot, a kettle, and a jar of cornmeal, which he had carried back to his village.

"He's no from Anidonau Nuya, is he?" Jamie asked, then repeated the question in Cherokee. Sequoyah shook his head, the small ornaments braided into his hair making a tiny chiming sound.

He was from a village some miles west of Anidonau Nuya—Standing Stone. Bird-who-sings had sent word to the nearby towns, in the wake of Jamie's visit, asking if there was anyone who knew of the old man and his fate. Hearing Sequoyah's account, Bird had sent him to collect what was left of the old man, and to bring the remains to Jamie, in proof that no one had killed him.

Ian asked a question, in which I caught the Cherokee word for "fire." Sequoyah shook his head again, and replied with a stream of words.

He had not burned the cabin—why should he do such a thing? He thought no one had done so. After collecting the old man's bones—his face showed his distaste for the procedure—he had gone to look at the cabin again. True, it was burned—but it was clear to him that a tree nearby had been struck by lightning, and had set fire to a good bit of the forest near it. The cabin was only half-burned.

He rose to his feet with an air of finality.

"Will he stay for supper?" I asked, seeing that he seemed about to depart.

Jamie conveyed the invitation, but Sequoyah shook his head. He had done what was required of him; now he had other business. He nodded to the other Indians, then turned to go.

Something struck him, though, and he stopped, turning back.

"Tsisqua says," he said, in the careful way of one who has memorized a speech in an unfamiliar tongue, "you re-mem-ber de guns." He nodded then decisively, and went.

The grave was marked with a small cairn of stones and a small wooden cross made of pine twigs. Sequoyah hadn't known his acquaintance's name, and we had no idea of his age, nor yet the dates of birth and death. We hadn't known if he was Christian, either, but the cross seemed a good idea.

It was a very small burial service, consisting of myself, Jamie, Ian, Bree and Roger, Lizzie and her father, the Bugs, and Bobby Higgins—who I was fairly sure was in attendance only because Lizzie was. Her father seemed to think so, too, judging from the occasional suspicious glances he cast at Bobby.

Roger read a brief psalm over the grave, then paused. He cleared his throat and said simply, "Lord, we commend to Thy care the soul of this our brother . . ."

"Ephraim," murmured Brianna, eyes cast modestly down.

A subterranean sense of laughter moved through the crowd, though no one actually laughed. Roger gave Bree a dirty look, but I saw the corner of his mouth twitching, as well.

". . . of our brother, whose name Thou knowest," Roger concluded with dignity, and closed the Book of Psalms he had borrowed from Hiram Crombie—who had declined an invitation to attend the funeral.

The light had gone by the time Sequoyah had finished his revelations the night before, and I was obliged to put off Miss Mouse's dental work to the morning. Stewed to the gills, she made no objection, and was helpfully supported off to a bed on the kitchen floor by Bobby Higgins—who might or might not be in love with Lizzie, but who seemed nonetheless most appreciative of Miss Mouse's charms.

Once finished with the tooth-drawing, I had suggested that she and her friends stay for a bit, but they, like Sequoyah, had business elsewhere, and with many thanks and small gifts, had departed by mid-afternoon, smelling strongly of whisky, and leaving us to dispose of the mortal remains of the late Ephraim.

Everyone went back down the hill after the service, but Jamie and I loitered behind, seeking an opportunity to be alone for a few minutes. The house had been full of Indians the night before, with much talk and storytelling by the fire, and by the time we had finally gone to bed, we had simply curled up in each other's arms and fallen asleep, barely exchanging the brief civility of a "good night."

The graveyard was sited on a small rise, some distance from the house, and was a pretty, peaceful place. Surrounded by pines whose golden needles blanketed the earth, and whose murmuring branches provided a constant soft susurrus, it seemed a comforting spot.

"Poor old creature," I said, putting a final pebble on Ephraim's cairn. "How do you suppose he ended up in such a place?"

"God knows." Jamie shook his head. "There are always hermits, men who mislike the society of their fellows. Perhaps he was one o' those. Or perhaps some misfortune drove him into the wilderness, and he . . . stayed." He shrugged a little, and gave me a half-smile.

"I sometimes wonder how any of us came to be where we are, Sassenach. Don't you?"

"I used to," I said. "But after a time, there didn't seem to be any possibility of an answer, so I stopped."

He looked down at me, diverted.

"Have ye, then?" He put out a hand and tucked back a lock of windblown hair. "Perhaps I shouldna ask it, then, but I will. Do ye mind, Sassenach? That ye *are* here, I mean. Do ye ever wish ye were—back?"

I shook my head.

"No, not ever."

And that was true. But I woke sometimes in the dead of night, thinking, *Is now the dream?* Would I wake again to the thick warm smell of central heating and Frank's Old Spice? And when I fell asleep again to the scent of woodsmoke and the musk of Jamie's skin, would feel a faint, surprised regret.

If he saw the thought on my face, he gave no sign of it, but bent and kissed me gently on the forehead. He took my arm, and we walked a little way into the wood, away from the house and its clearing below.

"Sometimes I smell the pines," he said, taking a deep, slow breath of the pungent air. "And I think for an instant I am in Scotland. But then I come to myself and see; there is no kindly bracken here, nor great barren mountains—not the wildness that I kent, but only wilderness that I do not."

I thought I heard nostalgia in his voice, but not sorrow. He'd asked, though; so would I.

"And do you ever wish to be . . . back?"

"Oh, aye," he said, surprising me—and then laughed at the look on my face. "But not enough not to wish more to be here, Sassenach."

He glanced over his shoulder at the tiny graveyard, with its small collection of cairns and crosses, with here and there a larger boulder marking a particular grave.

"Did ye ken, Sassenach, that some folk believe the last person to lie in a graveyard becomes its guardian? He must stand on guard until the next person dies and comes to take his place—only then can he rest."

"I suppose our mysterious Ephraim might be rather surprised. to find himself in such a position, when here he'd lain down under a tree all alone," I said, smiling a little. "But I do wonder: what is the guardian of a graveyard guarding—and from whom?"

He laughed at that.

"Oh . . . vandals, maybe; desecraters. Or charmers."

"Charmers?" I was surprised at that; I'd thought the word "charmer" synonymous with "healer."

"There are charms that call for bones, Sassenach," he said. "Or the ashes of a burnt body. Or soil from a grave." He spoke lightly enough, but with no sense of jesting. "Aye, even the dead may need defending."

"And who better to do it than a resident ghost?" I said. "Quite."

We climbed up through a stand of quivering aspen, whose light dappled us with green and silver, and I paused to scrape a blob of the crimson sap from a paper-white trunk. How odd, I thought, wondering why the sight of it gave me pause—and then remembered, and turned sharply to look again at the graveyard.

Not a memory, but a dream—or a vision. A man, battered and broken, rising to his feet amid a stand of aspen, rising for what he knew was the last time, his last fight, baring shattered teeth stained with blood that was the color of the aspens' sap. His face was painted black for death—and I knew that there were silver fillings in his teeth.

But the granite boulder stood silent and peaceful, drifted all about with yellow pine needles, marking the rest of the man who had once called himself Otter-Tooth.

The moment passed, and vanished. We walked out of the aspens, and into another clearing, this one higher than the rise the graveyard stood on.

I was surprised to see that someone had been cutting timber here, and clearing the ground. A sizable stack of felled logs lay to one side, and nearby lay a tangle of uprooted stumps, though several more, still rooted in the ground, poked through the heavy growth of wood sorrel and bluet.

"Look, Sassenach." Jamie turned me with a hand on my elbow.

"Oh. Oh, my."

The ground rose high enough here that we could look out over a stunning vista. The trees fell away below us, and we could see beyond our mountain, and beyond the next, and the next, into a blue distance, hazed with the breath of the mountains, clouds rising from their hollows.

"D'ye like it?" The note of proprietorial pride in his voice was palpable.

"Of course I like it. What—?" I turned, gesturing at the logs, the stumps.

"The next house will stand here, Sassenach," he said simply.

"The *next* house? What, are we building another?"

"Well, I dinna ken will it be us, or maybe our children—or grandchildren," he added, mouth curling a little. "But I thought, should anything happen—and I dinna think anything *will*, mind, but if it should—well, I should be happier to have made a start. Just in case."

I stared at him for a moment, trying to make sense of this. "Should anything happen," I said slowly, and turned to look to the east, where the shape of our house was just visible among the trees, its chimney smoke a white plume among the soft green of the chestnuts and firs. "Should it really . . . burn down, you mean." Just putting the idea into words made my stomach curl up into a ball.

Then I looked at him again, and saw that the notion scared him, too. But Jamie-like, he had simply set about to take what action he could, against the day of disaster.

"D'ye like it?" he repeated, blue eyes intent. "The site, I mean. If not, I can choose another."

"It's beautiful," I said, feeling tears prickle at the backs of my eyes. "Just beautiful, Jamie."

Hot after the climb, we sat down in the shade of a giant hemlock, to admire our future view. And, with the silence broken concerning the dire possibility of the future, found we could discuss it.

"It's not so much the idea of us dying," I said. "Or not entirely. It's that 'no surviving children' that gives me the whim-whams."

"Well, I take your point, Sassenach. Though I'm no in favor of us dying, either, and I mean to see we don't," he assured me. "Think, though. It might not mean they're dead. They might only . . . go."

I took a deep breath, trying to accept that supposition without panic.

"Go. Go back, you mean. Roger and Bree—and Jemmy, I suppose. We're assuming he can—can travel through the stones."

He nodded soberly, arms clasped about his knees.

"After what he did to that opal? Aye, I think we must assume he can." I nodded, recalling what he'd done to the opal: held it, complaining of it growing hot in his hand—until it exploded, shattering into hundreds of needle-sharp fragments. Yes, I thought we must assume he could time-travel, too. But what if Brianna had another child? It was plain to me that she and Roger wanted another—or at least that Roger did, and she was willing.

The thought of losing them was acutely painful, but I supposed the possibility had to be faced.

"Which leaves a choice, I suppose," I said, trying to be brave and objective. "If we're dead, they'd go, because without us, they've no real reason to be here. But if we're *not* dead—will they go anyway? Will we send them away, I mean? Because of the war. It won't be safe."

"No," he said softly. His head was bent, stray auburn hairs lifting from his crown, from the cowlicks he had bequeathed both to Bree and to Jemmy.

"I dinna ken," he said at last, and lifted his head, looking out into the distance of land and sky. "No one does, Sassenach. We must just meet what comes as we can."

He turned and laid his hand over mine, with a smile that had as much of pain in it as joy.

"We've ghosts enough between us, Sassenach. If the evils of the past canna hinder us—neither then shall any fears of the future. We must just put things behind us and get on. Aye?"

I laid a light hand on his chest, not in invitation, but only because I wanted the feel of him. His skin was cool from sweating, but he had helped dig the grave; the heat of his labor glowed in the muscle beneath.

"You were one of my ghosts," I said. "For a long time. And for a long time, I tried to put *you* behind me."

"Did ye, then?" His own hand came to rest lightly on my back, moving unconsciously. I knew that touch—the need of touching only to reassure oneself that the other was actually there, present in flesh.

"I thought I couldn't live, looking back—couldn't bear it." My throat was thick with the memory of it.

"I know," he said softly, his hand rising to touch my hair. "But ye had the bairn—ye had a husband. It wasna right to turn your back on them."

"It wasn't right to turn my back on *you*." I blinked, but tears were leaking from the corners of my eyes. He drew my head close, put out his tongue, and delicately licked my face, which surprised me so much that I laughed in the midst of a sob, and nearly choked.

"I do love thee, as meat loves salt," he quoted, and laughed, too, very softly. "Dinna weep, Sassenach. Ye're here; so am I. There's naught that matters, aside from that."

I leaned my forehead against his cheek, and put my arms around him. My hands rested flat on the planes of his back, and I stroked him from the blade of his shoulder to the tapering small of his back, lightly, always lightly, tracing the whole of him, the shape of him, and not the scars that reamed his skin.

He held me close, and sighed deeply.

"D'ye ken we've been wed this time nearly twice as long as the last?"

I drew back and frowned dubiously at him, accepting the distraction.

"Were we not married in between?"

That took him by surprise; he frowned, too, and ran a finger slowly down the sunburnt bridge of his nose in thought.

"Well, there's a question for a priest, to be sure," he said. "I should think we were—but if so, are we not both bigamists?"

"Were, not are," I corrected, feeling slightly uneasy. "But we weren't, really. Father Anselme said so."

"Anselme?"

"Father Anselme—a Franciscan priest at the Abbey of St. Anne. But perhaps you wouldn't recall him; you were very ill at the time."

"Oh, I recall him," he said. "He would come and sit wi' me at night, when I couldna sleep." He smiled, a little lopsided; that time wasn't something he wished to remember. "He liked ye a great deal, Sassenach."

"Oh? And what about you?" I asked, wanting to distract him from the memory of St. Anne. "Didn't you like me?"

"Oh, I liked ye fine then," he assured me. "I maybe like ye even more now, though."

"Oh, do you, indeed." I sat up a little straighter, preening. "What's different?"

He tilted his head to one side, eyes narrowing a bit in appraisal.

"Well, ye fart less in your sleep," he began judiciously, then ducked, laughing, as a pinecone whizzed past his left ear. I seized a chunk of wood, but before I could bat him over the head with it, he lunged and caught me by the arms. He shoved me flat in the grass and collapsed on top of me, pinning me effortlessly.

"Get off, you oaf! I do *not* fart in my sleep!"

"Now, how would ye ken that, Sassenach? Ye sleep so sound, ye wouldna wake, even to the sound of your own snoring."

"Oh, you want to talk about snoring, do you? You—"

"Ye're proud as Lucifer," he said, interrupting. He was still smiling, but the words were more serious. "And ye're brave. Ye were always bolder than was safe; now ye're fierce as a wee badger."

"So I'm arrogant and ferocious. This does not sound like

much of a catalog of womanly virtues," I said, puffing a bit as I strained to wriggle out from under him.

"Well, ye're kind, too," he said, considering. "Verra kind. Though ye are inclined to do it on your own terms. Not that that's bad, mind," he added, neatly recapturing the arm I had extricated. He pinned my wrist over my head.

"Womanly," he murmured, brows knotted in concentration. "Womanly virtues . . ." His free hand crept between us and fastened on my breast.

"Besides that!"

"You're verra clean," he said approvingly. He let go my wrist and ruffled a hand through my hair—which was indeed clean, smelling of sunflower and marigolds.

"I've never seen any woman wash herself sae much as you do—save Brianna, perhaps.

"Ye're no much of a cook," he went on, squinting thoughtfully. "Though ye've never poisoned anyone, save on purpose. And I will say ye sew a neat seam—though ye like it much better if it's through someone's flesh."

"Thanks so much!"

"Tell me some more virtues," he suggested. "Perhaps I've missed one."

"Hmph! Gentleness, patience . . ." I floundered.

"Gentle? Christ." He shook his head. "Ye're the most ruthless, bloodthirsty—"

I darted my head upward, and nearly succeeded in biting him in the throat. He jerked back, laughing.

"No, ye're no verra patient, either."

I gave up struggling for the moment and collapsed flat on my back, tousled hair spread out on the grass.

"So what *is* my most endearing trait?" I demanded.

"Ye think I'm funny," he said, grinning.

"I . . . do . . . not . . ." I grunted, struggling madly. He merely lay on top of me, tranquilly oblivious to my pokings and thumpings, until I exhausted myself and lay gasping underneath him.

"And," he said thoughtfully, "ye like it verra much when I take ye to bed. No?"

"Er . . ." I wanted to contradict him, but honesty forbade. Besides, he bloody well knew I did.

"You are squashing me," I said with dignity. "Kindly get off."

"No?" he repeated, not moving.

"Yes! All right! Yes! Will you bloody get *off*?!"

He didn't get off, but bent his head and kissed me. I was close-lipped, determined not to give in, but he was determined, too, and if one came right down to it . . . the skin of his face was warm, the plush of his beard stubble softly scratchy, and his wide sweet mouth . . . My legs were open in abandon and he was solid between them, bare chest smelling of musk and sweat and sawdust caught in the wiry auburn hair. . . . I was still hot with struggling, but the grass was damp and cool around us. . . . Well, all right; another minute, and he could have me right there, if he cared to.

He felt me yield, and sighed, letting his own body slacken; he no longer held me prisoner, but simply held me. He lifted his head then, and cupped my face with one hand.

"D'ye want to know what it is, really?" he asked, and I could see from the dark blue of his eyes that he meant it. I nodded, mute.

"Above all creatures on this earth," he whispered, "you are faithful."

I thought of saying something about St. Bernard dogs, but there was such tenderness in his face that I said nothing, instead merely staring up at him, blinking against the green light that filtered through the needles overhead.

"Well," I said at last, with a deep sigh of my own, "so are you. Quite a good thing, really. Isn't it?"

21

We Have Ignition

Mrs. Bug had made chicken fricassee for supper, but that wasn't sufficient to account for the air of suppressed excitement that Bree and Roger brought with them when they came in. They were both smiling, her cheeks were flushed, and his eyes as bright as hers.

So when Roger announced that they had great news, it was perhaps only reasonable that Mrs. Bug should leap directly to the obvious conclusion.

"You're wi' child again!" she cried, dropping a spoon in her excitement. She clapped her hands together, inflating like a birthday balloon. "Oh, the joy of it! And about time, too," she added, letting go her hands to wag a finger at Roger. "And here was me thinkin' as I should add a bit o' ginger and brimstone to your parritch, young man, so as to bring ye up to scratch! But ye kent your business weel enough in the end, I see. And you, *a bhailach*, what d'ye think? A bonny wee brother for ye!"

Jemmy, thus addressed, stared up at her, mouth open.

"Er . . ." said Roger, flushing up.

"Or, of course, it might be a wee sister, I suppose," Mrs. Bug admitted. "But good news, good news, either way. Here, *a luaidh,* have a sweetie on the strength of it, and the rest of us will drink to it!"

Obviously bewildered, but strongly in favor of sweeties, Jem took the proffered molasses drop and stuck it promptly in his mouth.

"But he isn't—" Bree began.

"Nank you, Missus Bug," Jem said hastily, putting a hand over his mouth lest his mother try to repossess this distinctly forbidden predinner treat on grounds of impoliteness.

"Oh, a wee sweetie will do him nay harm," Mrs. Bug assured her, picking up the fallen spoon and wiping it on her apron. "Call Arch in, *a muirninn,* and we'll tell him your news. Blessed Bride save ye, lass, I thought ye'd never get round to it! Here was all the ladies sayin' as they didna ken whether ye'd turned cold to your husband, or was it him maybe, lackin' the vital spark, but as it is—"

"Well, *as* it is," said Roger, raising his voice in order to be heard.

"I'm *not pregnant!*" said Bree, very loudly.

The succeeding silence echoed like a thunderclap.

"Oh," said Jamie mildly. He picked up a serviette and sat down, tucking it into the neck of his shirt. "Well, then. Shall we eat?" He held out a hand to Jem, who scrambled up onto the bench beside him, still sucking fiercely on his molasses drop.

Mrs. Bug, momentarily turned to stone, revived with a marked "Hmpf!" Massively affronted, she turned to the sideboard and slapped down a stack of pewter plates with a clatter.

Roger, still rather flushed, appeared to find the situation funny, judging from the twitching of his mouth. Brianna was incandescent, and breathing like a grampus.

"Sit down, darling," I said, in the tentative manner of one addressing a large explosive device. "You . . . um . . . had some news, you said?"

"Never mind!" She stood still, glaring. "Nobody cares, since I'm not pregnant. After all, what *else* could I possibly do that anybody would think was worthwhile?" She shoved a violent hand through her hair, and encountering the ribbon tying it back, yanked this loose and flung it on the ground.

"Now, sweetheart . . ." Roger began. I could have told him this was a mistake; Frasers in a fury tended to pay no attention to honeyed words, being instead inclined to go for the throat of the nearest party unwary enough to speak to them.

"Don't you 'sweetheart' me!" she snapped, turning on him. "You think so, too! You think everything I do is a waste of time if it isn't washing clothes or cooking dinner or mending your effing socks! And you blame me for not getting pregnant, too, you think it's my fault! Well, it's NOT, and you know it!"

"No! I don't think that, I don't at all. Brianna, please. . . ." He stretched out a hand to her, then thought better of the gesture and withdrew it, clearly feeling that she might take his hand off at the wrist.

"Less EAT, Mummy!" Jemmy piped up helpfully. A long string of molasses-tinged saliva flowed from the corner of his mouth and dripped down the front of his shirt. Seeing this, his mother turned on Mrs. Bug like a tiger.

"Now see what you've done, you interfering old busybody! That was his last clean shirt! And how dare you talk about our private lives with everybody in sight, what possible earthly business of yours is it, you beastly old gossiping—"

Seeing the futility of protest, Roger put his arms round her from behind, picked her up bodily off the floor, and carried her out the back door, this departure accented by incoherent protests from Bree and grunts of pain from Roger, as she kicked him repeatedly in the shins, with considerable force and accuracy.

I went to the door and closed it delicately, shutting off the sounds of further altercation in the yard.

"She gets that from *you,* you know," I said reproachfully, sitting down opposite Jamie. "Mrs. Bug, that smells wonderful. *Do* let's eat!"

Mrs. Bug dished the fricassee in huffy silence, but declined to join us at table, instead putting on her cloak and stamping out the front door, leaving us to deal with the clearing-up. An excellent bargain, if you asked me.

We ate in blissful peace, the quiet broken only by the clink of spoons on pewter and the occasional question from Jemmy as to why molasses was sticky, how did milk get *into* the cow, and when would he get his little brother?

"*What* am I going to say to Mrs. Bug?" I asked, in the brief hiatus between queries.

"Why ought ye to say anything, Sassenach? It wasna you calling her names."

"Well, no. But I'd be willing to bet that Brianna isn't going to apologize—"

"Why should she?" He shrugged. "She was provoked, after all. And I canna think Mrs. Bug has lived sae long without being called a gossiping busybody before. She'll wear herself out, telling Arch all about it, and tomorrow it will be fine again."

"Well," I said uncertainly. "Perhaps so. But Bree and Roger—"

He smiled at me, dark blue eyes crinkling into triangles.

"Dinna feel as though every disaster is yours to fash yourself about, *mo chridhe,*" he said. He reached across and patted my hand. "Roger Mac and the lass must work it out between them—and the lad did appear to have a decent grip on the situation."

He laughed, and I joined him, reluctantly.

"Well, it will be mine to fash about, if she's broken his leg," I remarked, getting up to fetch cream for the coffee. "Likely he'll come crawling back to have it mended."

At this apropos moment, a knock sounded on the back door. Wondering why Roger would knock, I opened it, and stared in astonishment at the pale face of Thomas Christie.

He was not only pale, but sweating, and had a bloodstained cloth wrapped round one hand.

"I wouldna discommode ye, mistress," he said, holding himself stiffly. "I'll just . . . wait upon your convenience."

"Nonsense," I said, rather shortly. "Come into the surgery while there's still some light."

I took care not to catch Jamie's eye directly, but I glanced at him as I bent to push in the bench. He was leaning forward to put a saucer over my coffee, his eyes on Tom Christie with an air of thoughtful speculation that I had last seen in a bobcat watching a flight of ducks overhead. Not urgent, but definitely taking notice.

Christie was taking no notice of anything beyond his injured hand, reasonably enough. My surgery's windows were oriented to east and south, to take best advantage of morning light, but even near sunset, the room held a soft radiance—the setting sun's reflection from the shimmering leaves of the chestnut grove. Everything in the room was suffused with golden light, save Tom Christie's face, which was noticeably green.

"Sit down," I said, shoving a stool hastily behind him. His knees buckled as he lowered himself; he landed harder than he had intended, jarring his hand, and let out a small exclamation of pain.

I put a thumb on the big vein at the wrist, to help slow the bleeding, and unwound the cloth. Given his aspect, I was expecting a severed finger or two, and was surprised to find a simple gash in the meat at the base of the thumb, angled down and running onto the wrist. It was deep enough to gape, and still bleeding freely, but no major vessels had been cut, and he had by great good fortune only nicked the thumb tendon; I could mend that with a stitch or two.

I looked up to tell him this, only to see his eyes roll back in his head.

"Help!" I shouted, dropping the hand and grabbing for his shoulders as he toppled backward.

A crash of overturned bench and the thump of running feet answered my call, and Jamie burst into the room in a heartbeat. Seeing me dragged off my feet by Christie's weight, he seized the man by the scruff of the neck and shoved him forward like a rag doll, pushing Christie's head down between his legs.

"Is he desperate bad?" Jamie asked, squinting at Christie's injured hand, which was resting on the floor, oozing blood. "Shall I lay him on the table?"

"I don't think so." I had a hand under Christie's jaw, feeling for his pulse. "He's not hurt badly; he's only fainted. Yes, see, he's coming round. Keep your head down for a bit, now, you'll be quite all right in a moment." I addressed this latter remark to Christie, who was breathing like a steam engine, but had steadied a little.

Jamie removed his hand from Christie's neck, and wiped it on his kilt with an expression of mild distaste. Christie had broken out in a profuse cold sweat; I could feel my own hand slimy with it, but picked up the fallen cloth and wiped my hand more tactfully with that.

"Would you like to lie down?" I asked, bending to look at Christie's face. He was still a ghastly color, but shook his head.

"No, mistress. I'm quite all right. Only taken queer for a moment." He spoke hoarsely, but firmly enough, so I contented myself with pressing the cloth hard against the wound to stanch the dripping blood.

Jemmy was loitering in the doorway, wide-eyed, but showing no particular alarm; blood was nothing new to him.

"Shall I fetch ye a dram, Tom?" Jamie said, eyeing the patient warily. "I ken ye dinna hold wi' strong drink, but there's a time for it, surely?"

Christie's mouth worked a little, but he shook his head.

"I . . . no. Perhaps . . . a little wine?"

"*Take a little wine for thy stomach's sake,* eh? Aye, fine. Take heart, man, I'll fetch it." Jamie clapped him encouragingly on the shoulder, and went briskly off, taking Jemmy by the hand as he went out.

Christie's mouth tightened in a grimace. I had noticed before that like some Protestants, Tom Christie regarded the Bible as being a document addressed specifically to himself and confided to his personal care for prudent distribution to the masses. Thus, he quite disliked hearing Catholics—i.e., Jamie—quoting casually from it. I had also noticed that Jamie was aware of this, and took every opportunity to make such quotes.

"What happened?" I asked, as much to distract Christie as because I wished to know.

Christie broke off his glower at the empty doorway and glanced at his left hand—then hastily away, going pale again.

"An accident," he said gruffly. "I was cutting rushes; the knife slipped." His right hand flexed slightly as he said this, and I glanced at it.

"No bloody wonder!" I said. "Here, keep that up in the air." I lifted the injured left hand, tightly wrapped, above his head, let go of it, and reached for the other.

He had been suffering from a condition in the right hand called Dupuytren's contracture—or at least it *would* be called that, once Baron Dupuytren got round to describing it in another sixty or seventy years. Caused by a thickening and shortening of the fibrous sheet that kept the hand's tendons in place when the fingers flexed, the result of it was to draw the ring finger in toward the palm of the hand. In advanced cases, the little finger and sometimes the middle finger as well were involved. Tom Christie's case had advanced quite a bit since I had last had the chance of a good look at his hand.

"Did I tell you?" I demanded rhetorically, pulling gently on the clawed fingers. The middle finger could still be halfway unfolded; the ring and little fingers could barely be lifted away from the palm. "I said it would get worse. No wonder the knife slipped—I'm surprised you could even hold it."

A slight flush appeared under the clipped salt-and-pepper beard, and he glanced away.

"I could have taken care of it easily months ago," I said,

turning the hand to look critically at the angle of contracture. "It would have been a very simple matter. Now it will be rather more complicated—but I can still correct it, I think."

Had he been a less stolid man, I should have described him as wriggling with embarrassment. As it was, he merely twitched slightly, the flush deepening over his face.

"I—I do not desire—"

"I don't bloody care what you desire," I told him, putting the clawed hand back in his lap. "If you don't allow me to operate on that hand, it will be all but useless inside six months. You can barely write with it now, am I right?"

His eyes met mine, deep gray and startled.

"I can write," he said, but I could tell that the belligerence in his voice hid a deep uneasiness. Tom Christie was an educated man, a scholar, and the Ridge's schoolteacher. It was to him that many of the Ridge people went for help in the composition of letters or legal documents. He took great pride in this; I knew the threat of loss of this ability was the best lever I had—and it was no idle threat.

"Not for long," I said, and widened my eyes at him to make my meaning clear. He swallowed uneasily, but before he could reply, Jamie reappeared, holding a jug of wine.

"Best listen to her," he advised Christie, setting it on the counter. "I ken what it's like to try to write wi' a stiff finger, aye?" He held up his own right hand and flexed it, looking rueful. "If she could mend *that* wi' her wee knife, I'd lay my hand on the block this instant."

Jamie's problem was almost the reverse of Christie's, though the effect was quite similar. The ring finger had been smashed so badly that the joints had frozen; it could not be bent. Consequently, the two fingers on either side had limited motion, as well, though the joint capsules were intact.

"The difference being that your hand isn't getting any worse," I told Jamie. "His is."

Christie made a small movement, pushing his right hand down between his thighs, as though to hide it.

"Aye, well," he said uncomfortably. "It can bide awhile, surely."

"At least long enough to let my wife mend the other," Jamie observed, pouring out a cup of wine. "Here—can ye hold it, Tom, or shall I—?" He made a questioning gesture, holding the cup as though to feed it to Christie, who snatched his right hand out of the sheltering folds of his clothes.

"I'll manage," he snapped, and took the wine—holding the cup between thumb and forefinger with an awkwardness that made him flush even more deeply. His left hand still hung in the air above his shoulder. He looked foolish, and obviously felt it.

Jamie poured another cup and handed it to me, ignoring Christie. I would have thought it natural tact on his part, were I not aware of the complicated history between the two men. There was always a small barbed edge in any dealings between Jamie and Tom Christie, though they managed to keep an outwardly cordial face on things.

With any other man, Jamie's display of his own injured hand would have been just what it seemed—reassurance, and the offering of fellowship in infirmity. With Tom Christie, it might have been consciously *meant* as reassurance, but there was a threat implied, as well, though perhaps Jamie couldn't help that.

The simple fact was that people came to Jamie for help more often than they did to Christie. Jamie had widespread respect and admiration, despite his crippled hand. Christie was not a personally popular man; he might well lose what social position he had, if he lost his ability to write. And—as I had bluntly noted— Jamie's hand would not get worse.

Christie's eyes had narrowed a little over his cup. He hadn't missed the threat, whether intended or not. He wouldn't; Tom Christie was a suspicious man by nature, and inclined to see threat where it *wasn't* intended.

"I think that's settled a bit by now; let me take care of it." I took hold of his left hand, gently, and unwrapped it. The bleeding had stopped. I set the hand to soak in a bowl of water boiled with garlic, added a few drops of pure ethanol for additional disinfection, and set about gathering my kit.

It was beginning to grow dark, and I lit the alcohol lamp Brianna had made for me. By its bright, steady flame, I could see that Christie's face had lost its momentary flush of anger. He wasn't as pale as he had been, but looked uneasy as a vole at a convention of badgers, his eyes following my hands as I laid out my sutures, needles, and scissors, all clean and gleaming-sharp in the light.

Jamie didn't leave, but stayed leaning against the counter,

sipping his own cup of wine—presumably, in case Christie passed out again.

A fine trembling ran through Christie's hand and arm, braced as they were on the table. He was sweating again; I could smell it, acrid and bitter. It was the scent of that, half-forgotten, but immediately familiar, that finally made me realize the difficulty: it was fear. He was afraid of blood, perhaps; afraid of pain, certainly.

I kept my eyes fixed on my work, bending my head lower to keep him from seeing anything in my face. I should have seen it sooner; I would have, I thought, had he not been a man. His paleness, the fainting . . . not due to loss of blood, but to shock at seeing blood lost.

I stitched up men and boys routinely; mountain farming was rough work, and it was a rare week when I wasn't presented with ax wounds, hoe gouges, spud slashes, hog bites, scalp lacerations sustained while falling over something, or some other minor calamity requiring stitches. By and large, all my patients behaved with complete matter-of-factness, accepting my ministrations stoically, and going right back to work. But nearly all of the men were Highlanders, I realized, and many not only Highlanders but erstwhile soldiers.

Tom Christie was a townsman, from Edinburgh—he had been imprisoned in Ardsmuir as a Jacobite supporter, but had never been a fighting man. He had been a commissary officer. In fact, I realized with surprise, he had likely never even *seen* a real military battle, let alone engaged in the daily physical conflict with nature that Highland farming entailed.

I became aware of Jamie, still standing in the shadows, sipping wine and watching with a faintly ironic dispassion. I glanced up quickly at him; his expression didn't alter, though he met my eyes and nodded, very slightly.

Tom Christie's lip was fixed between his teeth; I could hear the faint whistle of his breath. He couldn't see Jamie, but knew he was there; the stiffness of his back said as much. He might be afraid, Tom Christie, but he had some courage to him.

It would have hurt him less, could he have relaxed the clenched muscles of arm and hand. Under the circumstances, though, I could hardly suggest as much. I could have insisted that Jamie leave, but I was nearly finished. With a sigh of mingled exasperation and puzzlement, I clipped the final knot and laid down the scissors.

"All right, then," I said, swiping the last of the coneflower ointment across the wound and reaching for a clean linen bandage. "Keep it clean. I'll make up some fresh ointment for you; send Malva for it. Then come back in a week and I'll take the stitches out." I hesitated, glancing at Jamie. I felt some reluctance to use his presence as blackmail, but it was for Christie's own good.

"I'll take care of your right hand, then, too, shall I?" I said firmly.

He was still sweating, though the color in his face had begun to come back. He glanced at me, and then, involuntarily, at Jamie.

Jamie smiled faintly.

"Go on, then, Tom," he said. "It's naught to trouble ye. No but a wee nick. I've had worse."

The words were spoken casually, but they might as well have been written in flaming letters a foot high. *I've had worse.*

Jamie's face was still in shadow, but his eyes were clearly visible, slanted with his smile.

Tom Christie had not relaxed his rigid posture. He matched Jamie's stare, closing his gnarled right hand over the bandaged left.

"Aye," he said. "Well." He was breathing deeply. "I will, then." He rose abruptly, knocking the stool aside, and headed for the door, a little off-balance, like a man the worse for strong drink.

At the door, he paused, fumbling for the knob. Finding it, he drew himself up and turned back, looking for Jamie.

"At least," he said, breathing so hard that he stumbled over the words, "at least it will be an honorable scar. Won't it, *Mac Dubh*?"

Jamie straightened up abruptly, but Christie was already out, stamping down the corridor with a step heavy enough to rattle the pewter plates on the kitchen shelf.

"Why, ye wee pissant!" he said, in a tone somewhere between anger and astonishment. His left hand clenched involuntarily into a fist, and I thought it a good thing that Christie had made such a rapid exit.

I was rather unsure as to exactly *what* had happened—or been happening—but relieved that Christie was gone. I'd felt like a handful of grain, trapped between two grindstones, both of them trying to grind each other's faces, with no heed for the hapless corn in between.

"I've never heard Tom Christie call you *Mac Dubh,*" I observed cautiously, turning to tidy away my surgical leavings. Christie was not, of course, a Gaelic-speaker, but I had never heard him use even the Gaelic nickname that the other Ardsmuir men still called Jamie by. Christie always called Jamie "Mr. Fraser," or simply "Fraser," in moments of what passed for cordiality.

Jamie made a derisive Scottish noise, then picked up Christie's half-full cup and thriftily drained it.

"No, he wouldna—frigging Sassenach." Then he caught a glimpse of my face, and gave me a lopsided smile. "I didna mean you, Sassenach."

I knew he didn't mean me; the word was spoken with a completely different—and quite shocking—intonation; a bitterness that reminded me that "Sassenach" was by no means a friendly term in normal usage.

"Why do you call him that?" I asked curiously. "And just what did he mean by that 'honorable scar' crack?"

He looked down, and didn't answer for a moment, though the stiffened fingers of his right hand drummed soundlessly against his thigh.

"Tom Christie's a solid man," he said at last. "But by God, he is a stiff-necked wee son of a bitch!" He looked up then, and smiled at me, a little ruefully.

"Eight years he lived in a cell wi' forty men who had the Gaelic—and he wouldna lower himself to let a word of such a barbarous tongue pass his lips! Christ, no. He'd speak in English, no matter who it was he spoke to, and if it was a man who had no English, why, then, he'd just stand there, dumb as a stone, 'til someone came along to interpret for him."

"Someone like you?"

"Now and then." He glanced toward the window, as though to catch a glimpse of Christie, but the night had come down altogether, and the panes gave back only a dim reflection of the surgery, our own forms ghostlike in the glass.

"Roger did say that Kenny Lindsay mentioned something about Mr. Christie's . . . pretensions," I said delicately.

Jamie shot me a sharp glance at that.

"Oh, he did, did he? So, Roger Mac had second thoughts about his wisdom in taking on Christie as a tenant, I suppose. Kenny wouldna have said, unless he was asked."

I had more or less got used to the speed of his deductions and the accuracy of his insights, and didn't question this one.

"You never told me about that," I said, coming to stand in front of him. I put my hands on his chest, looking up into his face.

He put his own hands over mine, and sighed, deep enough for me to feel the movement of his chest. Then he wrapped his arms around me, and drew me close, so my face rested against the warm fabric of his shirt.

"Aye, well. It wasna really important, ken."

"And you didn't want to think about Ardsmuir, perhaps?"

"No," he said softly. "I have had enough of the past."

My hands were on his back now, and I realized suddenly what Christie had likely meant. I could feel the lines of the scars through the linen, clear to my fingertips as the lines of a fishnet, laid across his skin.

"Honorable scars!" I said, lifting my head. "Why, that little *bastard*! Is that what he meant?"

Jamie smiled a little at my indignation.

"Aye, he did," he said dryly. "That's why he called me *Mac Dubh*—to remind me of Ardsmuir, so I'd ken for sure what he meant by it. He saw me flogged there."

"That—that—" I was so angry, I could barely speak. "I wish I'd stitched his fucking hand to his balls!"

"And you a physician, sworn to do nay harm? I'm verra much shocked, Sassenach."

He was laughing now, but I wasn't amused at all.

"Beastly little coward! He's afraid of blood, did you know that?"

"Well, aye, I did. Ye canna live in a man's oxter for three years without learning a great many things ye dinna want to know about him, let alone something like that." He sobered a bit, though a hint of wryness still lurked at the corner of his mouth. "When they brought me back from being whipped, he went white as suet, went and puked in the corner, then lay down with his face to the wall. I wasna really taking notice, but I remember thinking that was a bit raw; I was the one was a bloody mess, why was he takin' on like a lass wi' the vapors?"

I snorted. "Don't you go making jokes about it! How dare he? And what does he mean, anyway—I know what happened at Ardsmuir, and those bloody well . . . I mean, those certainly *are* honorable scars, and everyone there knew it!"

"Aye, maybe," he said, all hint of laughter disappearing. "That time. But everyone could see when they stood me up that I'd been flogged before, aye? And no man there has ever said a word to me about those scars. Not 'til now."

That brought me up short.

Flogging wasn't merely brutal; it was shameful—meant to permanently disfigure, as well as to hurt, advertising a criminal's past as clearly as a branded cheek or cropped ear. And Jamie would, of course, prefer to have his tongue torn out by the roots, sooner than reveal to anyone the reasons for his scars, even if that meant leaving everyone with the assumption that he had been flogged for some disgraceful act.

I was so used to Jamie's always keeping his shirt on in anyone else's presence that it had never occurred to me that of course the Ardsmuir men would know about the scars on his back. And yet he hid them, and everyone pretended they did not exist—save Tom Christie.

"Hmph," I said. "Well . . . God damn the man, anyway. Why would he say such a thing?"

Jamie uttered a short laugh.

"Because he didna like me watching him sweat. He wanted a bit of his own back, I expect."

"Hmph," I said again, and folded my arms beneath my bosom. "Since you mention it—why *did* you do that? If you knew he couldn't stand blood and the like, I mean, why stay and watch him like that?"

"Because I kent he wouldna whimper or faint if I did," he replied. "He'd let ye thrust red-hot needles through his eyeballs before he'd squeal in front of me."

"Oh, so you noticed that?"

"Well, of course I did, Sassenach. What d'ye think I was there for? Not that I dinna appreciate your skill, but watching ye stitch up wounds isna really good for the digestion." He cast a brief glance at the discarded cloth, splotched with blood, and grimaced. "D'ye think the coffee's gone cold by now?"

"I'll heat it up." I slid the clean scissors back into their sheath, then sterilized the needle I'd used, ran a fresh silk suture through it, and coiled it up in its jar of alcohol—still trying to make sense of things.

I put everything back into the cupboard, then turned to Jamie.

"You aren't afraid of Tom Christie, are you?" I demanded.

He blinked, astonished, then laughed.

"Christ, no. What makes ye think that, Sassenach?"

"Well . . . the way the two of you act sometimes. It's like wild sheep, butting heads to see who's stronger."

"Oh, that." He waved a hand, dismissive. "I've a harder head by far than Tom, and he kens it well enough. But he's no going to give in and follow me round like a yearling lamb, either."

"Oh? But what do you think you're doing, then? You weren't just torturing him to prove you could, were you?"

"No," he said, and smiled faintly at me. "A man stubborn enough to speak English to Hieland men in prison for eight years is a man stubborn enough to fight beside me for the next eight years; that's what I think. It would be good if he were sure of it, himself, though."

I drew a deep breath and sighed, shaking my head.

"I do *not* understand men."

That made him chuckle, deep in his chest.

"Yes, ye do, Sassenach. Ye only wish ye didn't."

The surgery lay neat again, ready for whatever emergencies the morrow might bring. Jamie reached for the lamp, but I laid a hand on his arm, stopping him.

"You promised *me* honesty," I said. "But are you quite sure you're being honest with yourself? You weren't baiting Tom Christie just because he challenges you?"

He stopped, his eyes clear and unguarded, a few inches from mine. He lifted a hand and cupped the side of my face, his palm warm on my skin.

"There are only two people in this world to whom I would never lie, Sassenach," he said softly. "Ye're one of them. And I'm the other."

He kissed me gently on the forehead, then leaned past me and blew out the lamp.

"Mind," his voice came from the darkness, and I saw his tall form silhouetted against the faint oblong of light from the doorway as he straightened up, "I can be fooled. But I wouldna be doing it on purpose."

Roger moved a little, and groaned.

"I think ye broke my leg."

"Did not," said his wife, calmer now, but still disposed to argument. "But I'll kiss it for you, if you want."

"That'd be nice."

Tremendous rustlings of the corn-shuck mattress ensued as she clambered into position to execute this treatment, ending with a naked Brianna straddling his chest, and leaving him with a view that caused him to wish they'd taken time to light the candle.

She was in fact kissing his shins, which tickled. Given the circumstances, though, he was inclined to put up with it. He reached up with both hands. Lacking light, Braille would do.

"When I was fourteen or so," he said dreamily, "one of the shops in Inverness had a most daring window display—daring for the times, that is—a lady mannequin wearing nothing but underwear."

"Mm?"

"Aye, a full-length pink girdle, garters, the lot—with matching brassiere. Everyone was shocked. Committees were got up to protest, and calls were made to all the ministers in town. Next day, they took it down, but meanwhile, the entire male population of Inverness had been past that window, taking pains to look casual about it. 'Til this minute, I'd always thought that was the most erotic thing I'd ever seen."

She suspended her operations for a moment, and he thought from the sense of movement that she was looking back over her shoulder at him.

"Roger," she said thoughtfully. "I do believe you're a pervert."

"Yes, but one with really good night vision."

That made her laugh—the thing he'd been striving for since he'd finally got her to stop frothing at the mouth—and he raised himself briefly, planting a light kiss on either side of the looming object of his affections before sinking contentedly back onto the pillow.

She kissed his knee, then put her head down, cheek against his thigh, so the mass of her hair spilled over his legs, cool and soft as a cloud of silk threads.

"I'm sorry," she said softly, after a moment.

He made a dismissive noise, and ran a soothing hand over the round of her hip.

"Och, it's no matter. Too bad, though; I wanted to see their faces when they saw what ye'd done."

She snorted briefly, and his leg twitched at the warmth of her breath.

"Their faces were something to see, anyway." She sounded a little bleak. "And it would have been a real anticlimax, after *that*."

"Well, you're right about that," he admitted. "But ye'll show them tomorrow, when they're in a frame of mind to appreciate it properly."

She sighed, and kissed his knee again.

"I didn't mean it," she said, after a moment. "Implying it was your fault."

"Aye, ye did," he said softly, still caressing. "It's all right. Ye're probably right." Likely she was. He wasn't going to pretend it hadn't hurt to hear it, but he wouldn't let himself be angry; that would help neither of them.

"You don't know that." She raised up suddenly, looming like an obelisk in silhouette against the pale rectangle of the window. Swinging one leg neatly over his supine body, she slithered down beside him. "It could be me. Or neither of us. Maybe it just isn't the right time, yet."

He put an arm around her and hugged her close in answer.

"Whatever the cause, we'll not blame each other, aye?" She made a small sound of assent and nestled closer. Well enough; there was no way to keep from blaming himself, though.

The facts were clear enough; she'd got pregnant with Jemmy after one night—whether with himself, or Stephen Bonnet, no one knew, but once was all it took. Whereas they'd been trying for the last several months, and Jem was looking more and more like being an only child. Possibly he *did* lack the vital spark, as Mrs. Bug and her chums speculated.

Who's your Daddy? echoed mockingly in the back of his mind—in an Irish accent.

He coughed explosively, and settled back, determined not to dwell on *that* little matter.

"Well, I'm sorry, too," he said, changing the subject. "Ye're maybe right about me acting like I'd rather ye cook and clean than mess about with your wee chemistry set."

"Only because you *would*," she said without rancor.

"It's not so much the not cooking as it is the setting things on fire I mind."

"Well, you'll love the next project, then," she said, nuzzling his shoulder. "It's mostly water."

"Oh . . . good," he said, though even he could hear the dubious note in his voice. "Mostly?"

"There's some dirt involved, too."

"Nothing that burns?"

"Just wood. A little. Nothing special."

She was running her fingers slowly down his chest. He caught her hand and kissed her fingertips; they were smooth, but hard, callused from the constant spinning she did to help keep them clothed.

"Who can find a virtuous woman?" he quoted, *"for her price is far above rubies. She seeketh wool and flax and worketh willingly with her hands. She maketh herself coverings of tapestry; her clothing is silk and purple."*

"I would *love* to find some dye plant that gives a true purple," she said wistfully. "I miss the bright colors. Remember the dress I wore to the man-on-the-moon party? The black one, with the bands of Day-Glo pink and lime green?"

"That was pretty memorable, aye." Privately, he thought the muted colors of homespun suited her much better; in skirts of rust and brown, jackets of gray and green, she looked like some exotic, lovely lichen.

Seized by the sudden desire to see her, he reached out, fumbling on the table by the bed. The little box was where she'd thrown it when they came back. She'd designed it to be used in the dark, after all; a turn of the lid dispensed one of the small, waxy sticks, and the tiny strip of roughened metal glued to the side was cool to his hand.

A *skritch!* that made his heart leap with its simple familiarity, and the tiny flame appeared with a whiff of sulfur—magic.

"Don't waste them," she said, but smiled in spite of the protest, delighted at the sight as she'd been when she first showed him what she'd done.

Her hair was loose and clean, just washed; shimmering over the pale round of her shoulder, clouds of it lying soft over his chest, cinnamon and amber and roan and gold, sparked by the flame.

"She does not fear the snow for her household, for all her household are clothed in scarlet," he said softly, his free hand round her, twining a lock near her face round his finger, twisting the tiny strand as he'd seen her spin yarn.

The long lids of her eyes closed halfway, like a basking cat's, but the smile remained on that wide, soft mouth—those lips that hurt, then healed. The light glowed in her skin, bronzed the tiny brown mole beneath her right ear. He could have watched her forever, but the match was burning low. Just before the flame touched his fingers, she leaned forward and blew it out.

And in the smoke-wisped dark, whispered in his ear, *"The heart of her husband doth safely trust in her. She will do him good and not evil all the days of her life.* So there."

22

Ensorcellment

Tom Christie didn't come back to the surgery, but he did send his daughter, Malva, to get the ointment. The girl was dark-haired, slender, and quiet, but seemed intelligent. She paid close attention as I quizzed her on the look of the wound—so far, so good, a bit of redness, but no suppuration, no reddish streaks up the arm—and gave her instructions on how to apply the ointment and change the dressing.

"Good, then," I said, giving her the jar. "If he should begin a fever, come and fetch me. Otherwise, make him come in a week, to have the stitches taken out."

"Yes, ma'am, I'll do that." She didn't turn and go, though, but lingered, her gaze flickering over the mounds of drying herbs on the gauze racks and the implements of my surgery.

"Do you need something else, dear? Or did you have a question?" She'd seemed to understand my instructions perfectly well—but perhaps she wanted to ask something more personal. After all, she had no mother . . .

"Well, aye," she said, and nodded at the table. "I only wondered—what is it that ye write in yon black book, ma'am?"

"This? Oh. It's my surgical notes, and recipes . . . er . . . receipts, I mean, for medicines. See?" I turned the book round and opened it so that she could see the page where I had drawn a sketch of the damage to Miss Mouse's teeth.

Malva's gray eyes were bright with curiosity, and she leaned forward to read, hands carefully folded behind her back as though afraid she might touch the book by accident.

"It's all right," I said, a little amused by her caution. "You can look through it, if you like." I pushed it toward her, and she stepped back, startled. She glanced up at me, a look of doubt wrinkling her brow, but when I smiled at her, she took a tiny, excited breath, and reached out to turn a page.

"Oh, look!" The page she'd turned to wasn't one of mine, but one of Daniel Rawlings's—it showed the removal of a dead child from the uterus, via the use of assorted tools of dilatation and curettage. I glanced at the page, and hastily away. Rawlings hadn't been an artist, but he had had a brutal knack for rendering the reality of a situation.

Malva didn't seem to be distressed by the drawings, though; she was bug-eyed with interest.

I began to be interested, too, watching covertly as she turned pages at random. She naturally paid most attention to the drawings—but she paused to read the descriptions and recipes, as well.

"Why d'ye write things down that ye've done?" she asked, glancing up with raised eyebrows. "The receipts, aye, I see ye might forget things—but why d'ye draw these pictures and write down the bits about how ye took off a toe wi' the frost-rot? Would ye do it differently, another time?"

"Well, sometimes you might," I said, laying aside the stalk of dried rosemary I'd been stripping of its needles. "Surgery isn't the same each time. All bodies are a bit different, and even though you may do the same basic procedure a dozen times, there will be a dozen things that happen differently—sometimes only tiny things, sometimes big ones.

"But I keep a record of what I've done for several reasons," I added, pushing back my stool and coming round the table to stand beside her. I turned another few pages, stopping at the record I kept of old Grannie MacBeth's complaints—a list so extensive that I had alphabetized it for my own convenience, beginning with *Arthritis—all joints,* running through *Dyspepsia, Earache,* and *Fainting,* and then onward for most of two pages, terminating with *Womb, prolapsed.*

"Partly, it's so that I'll know what's been done for a particular person, and what happened—so that if they need treatment later, I can look back and have an accurate description of their earlier state. To compare, you see?"

She nodded eagerly.

"Aye, I see. So ye'd know were they getting better or worse. What else, then?"

"Well, the most important reason," I said slowly, seeking the right words, "is so that another doctor—someone who might come later—so that person could read the record, and see how I'd done this or that. It might show them a way to do something they hadn't done themselves—or a better way."

Her mouth pursed up in interest.

"Ooh! Ye mean someone might learn from this"—she touched a finger to the page, delicately—"how to do what it is ye do? Without 'prenticing himself to a doctor?"

"Well, it's best if you have someone to teach you," I said, amused at her eagerness. "And there are things you can't really learn from a book. But if there's no one to learn from—" I glanced out the window, at the vista of green wilderness swarming over the mountains. "It's better than nothing," I concluded.

"Where did you learn?" she asked, curious. "From this book? I see there's another hand, besides yours. Whose was it?"

I ought to have seen that one coming. I hadn't quite bargained on Malva Christie's quickness, though.

"Ah . . . I learned from a *lot* of books," I said. "And from other doctors."

"Other doctors," she echoed, looking at me in fascination. "D'ye call yourself a doctor, then? I didna ken women ever could be."

For the rather good reason that no women *did* call themselves physicians or surgeons now—nor were accepted as such.

I coughed.

"Well . . . it's a name, that's all. A good many people just say wisewoman, or conjure woman. Or *ban-lichtne*," I added. "But it's all the same, really. It only matters whether I know something that might help them."

"Ban—" She mouthed the unfamiliar word. "I haven't heard that before."

"It's the Gaelic. The Highland tongue, you know? It means 'female healer' or something like."

"Oh, the Gaelic." An expression of mild derision crossed her face; I expected she had absorbed her father's attitude toward the Highlanders' ancient language. She evidently saw something in *my* face, though, for she instantly erased the disdain from her own features and bent over the book again. "Who was it wrote these other bits, then?"

"A man named Daniel Rawlings." I smoothed a creased page, with the usual sense of affection for my predecessor. "He was a doctor from Virginia."

"Him?" She looked up, surprised. "The same who's buried in the boneyard up the mountain?"

"Ah . . . yes, that's him." And the story of how he came to be there was not something to be shared with Miss Christie. I glanced out of the window, estimating the light. "Will your father be wanting his dinner?"

"Oh!" She stood up straight at that, glancing out the window, too, with a faint look of alarm. "Aye, he will." She cast a last look of longing toward the book, but then brushed down her skirt and set her cap straight, ready to go. "I thank ye, Mrs. Fraser, for showing me your wee book."

"Happy to," I assured her sincerely. "You're welcome to come again and look at it. In fact . . . would you—" I hesitated, but plunged on, encouraged by her look of bright interest. "I'm going to take a growth from Grannie Macbeth's ear tomorrow. Would you like to come along with me, to see how? It would be a help to me, to have another pair of hands," I added, seeing sudden doubt war with the interest in her eyes.

"Oh, aye, Mrs. Fraser—I'd dearly like it!" she said. "It's only my father—" She looked uneasy as she said it, but then seemed to make up her mind. "Well . . . I'll come. I'm sure I can talk him round."

"Would it help if I were to send a note? Or come and speak with him?" I was suddenly quite desirous that she should come with me.

She gave a small shake of the head.

"Nay, ma'am, it'll be all right, I'm sure." She dimpled at me suddenly, gray eyes sparkling. "I'll tell him I've had a keek at your black book, and it's no by way of being spells in it, at all, but only receipts for teas and purges. I'll maybe not say about the drawings, though," she added.

"Spells?" I asked incredulously. "Is that what he thought?"

"Oh, aye," she assured me. "He warned me not to touch it, for fear of ensorcellment."

"Ensorcellment," I murmured, bemused. Well, Thomas Christie *was* a schoolmaster, after all. In fact, he might have been right, I thought; Malva glanced back at the book as I went with her to the door, obvious fascination on her face.

23

Anesthesia

I closed my eyes and, holding my hand a foot or so in front of my face, wafted it gently toward my nose, like one of the *parfumeurs* I'd seen in Paris, testing a fragrance.

The smell hit me in the face like an ocean wave, and with approximately the same effect. My knees buckled, black lines writhed through my vision, and I ceased to make any distinction between up and down.

In what seemed an instant later, I came to, lying on the floor of the surgery with Mrs. Bug staring down at me in horror.

"Mrs. Claire! Are ye all right, *mo gaolach*? I saw ye fall—"

"Yes," I croaked, shaking my head gingerly as I got up on one elbow. "Put—put the cork in." I gestured clumsily at the large open flask on the table, its cork lying alongside. "Don't get your face near it!"

Face averted and screwed into a grimace of caution, she got the cork and inserted it, at arm's length.

"Phew, what *is* yon stuff?" she said, stepping back and making faces. She sneezed explosively into her apron. "I've never smelt anything like that—and Bride kens I've smelt a good many nasty things in this room!"

"That, my dear Mrs. Bug, is ether." The swimming sensation in my head had almost disappeared, replaced by euphoria.

"Ether?" She looked at the distilling apparatus on my counter in fascination, the alcohol bath bubbling gently away in its great glass bubble over a low flame and the oil of vitriol—later to be known as sulfuric acid—slicking its slow way down the slanted tubing, its malign hot scent lurking below the usual surgery smells of roots and herbs. "Fancy! And what's ether, then?"

"It puts people asleep, so they won't feel pain when you cut them," I explained, thrilled by my success. "And I know exactly who I'm going to use it on first!"

"Tom Christie?" Jamie repeated. "Have ye told him?"

"I told Malva. She's going to work on him; soften him up a bit."

Jamie snorted briefly at the thought.

"Ye could boil Tom Christie in milk for a fortnight, and he'd still be hard as a grindstone. And if ye think he'll listen to his wee lass prattle about a magic liquid that will put him to sleep—"

"No, she isn't to tell him about the ether. I'll do that," I assured him. "She's just to pester him about his hand; convince him he needs it mended."

"Mm." Jamie still appeared dubious, though not, it seemed, entirely on Thomas Christie's account.

"This ether ye've made, Sassenach. Might ye not kill him with it?"

I had, in fact, worried considerably about that very possibility.

I'd done operations frequently where ether was used, and it was on the whole a fairly safe anesthetic. But homemade ether, administered by hand . . . and people *did* die of anesthetic accidents, even in the most careful settings, with trained anesthetists and all sorts of resuscitating equipment to hand. And I remembered Rosamund Lindsay, whose accidental death still haunted my dreams now and then. But the possibility of having a reliable anesthetic, of being able to do surgery without pain—

"I might," I admitted. "I don't think so, but there's always some risk. Worth it, though."

Jamie gave me a slightly jaundiced look.

"Oh, aye? Does Tom think so?"

"Well, we'll find out. I'll explain it all carefully to him, and if he won't—well, he won't. But I do hope he does!"

The edge of Jamie's mouth curled up and he shook his head tolerantly.

"Ye're like wee Jem wi' a new toy, Sassenach. Take care the wheels dinna come off."

I might have made some indignant reply to this, but we had come in sight of the Bugs' cabin, and Arch Bug was sitting on his stoop, peacefully smoking a clay pipe. He took this from his mouth and made to stand up when he saw us, but Jamie motioned him back.

"Ciamar a tha thu, a charaid?"

Arch replied with his customary "Mmp," infused with a tone of cordiality and welcome. A raised white brow in my direction, and a twiddle of the pipe stem toward the trail indicated that his wife was at our house, if that's who I was looking for.

"No, I'm just going into the woods to forage a bit," I said, lifting my empty basket by way of evidence. "Mrs. Bug forgot her needlework, though—may I fetch it for her?"

He nodded, eyes creasing as he smiled round his pipe. He shifted his lean buttocks courteously to allow me to go past him into the cabin. Behind me, I heard a "Mmp?" of invitation, and felt the boards of the stoop shift as Jamie sat down beside Mr. Bug.

There were no windows, and I was obliged to stand still for a moment to let my eyes adjust to the dimness. It was a small cabin, though, and it took no more than half a minute before I could make out the contents: little more than the bed frame, a blanket chest, and a table with two stools. Mrs. Bug's workbag hung from a hook on the far wall, and I crossed to get it.

On the porch behind me, I heard the murmur of male conversation, featuring the quite unusual sound of Mr. Bug's voice. He could and did talk, of course, but Mrs. Bug talked so volubly that when she was present, her spouse's contribution was generally not much more than a smile and an occasional "mmp" of accord or disagreement.

"Yon Christie," Mr. Bug was saying now, in a meditative tone of voice. "D'ye find him strange, *a Sheaumais*?"

"Aye, well, he's a Lowlander," Jamie said, with an audible shrug.

A humorous "mmp" from Mr. Bug indicated that this was a perfectly sufficient explanation, and was succeeded by the sucking noises of a pipe being encouraged to draw.

I opened the bag, to be sure that the knitting was inside; in fact, it was not, and I was obliged to poke round the cabin, squinting in the dimness. Oh—there it was; a dark puddle of something soft in the corner, fallen from the table and knocked aside by someone's foot.

"Is he stranger than he might be, Christie?" I heard Jamie ask, his own tone casual.

I glanced through the door in time to see Arch Bug nod toward Jamie, though he didn't speak, being engaged in a fierce battle with his pipe. However, he raised his right hand and waggled it, displaying the stumps of his two missing fingers.

"Aye," he said finally, releasing a triumphant puff of white smoke with the word. "He wished to ask me whether it hurt a good deal, when this was done."

His face wrinkled up like a paper bag, and he wheezed a little—high hilarity for Arch Bug.

"Oh, aye? And what did ye tell him, then, Arch?" Jamie asked, smiling a little.

Arch sucked meditatively on his pipe, now fully cooperative, then pursed his lips and blew a small, perfect ring of smoke.

"Weeel, I said it didna hurt a bit—at the time." He paused, blue eyes twinkling. "Of course, that may have been because I was laid out cold as a mackerel from the shock of it. When I came round, it stung a bit." He lifted the hand, looking it over dispassionately, then glanced through the door at me. "Ye didna mean to use an ax on poor old Tom, did ye, ma'am? He says ye're set to mend his hand next week."

"Probably not. May I see?" I stepped out on the porch, bending to him, and he let me take the hand, obligingly switching his pipe to the left.

The index and middle finger had been severed cleanly, right at the knuckle. It was a very old injury; so old that it had lost that shocking look common to recent mutilations, where the mind still sees what *should* be there, and tries vainly for an instant to reconcile reality with expectation. The human body is amazingly plastic, though, and will compensate for missing bits as well as it can; in the case of a maimed hand, the remnant often undergoes a subtle sort of useful deformation, to maximize what function remains.

I felt along the hand carefully, fascinated. The metacarpals of the severed digits were intact, but the surrounding tissues had shrunk and twisted, withdrawing that part of the hand slightly, so that the remaining two fingers and the thumb could make a better opposition; I'd seen old Arch use that hand with perfect grace, holding a cup to drink, or wielding the handle of a spade.

The scars over the finger stumps had flattened and paled, forming a smooth, calloused surface. The remaining finger joints were knobbed with arthritis, and the hand as a whole was so twisted that it really didn't resemble a hand anymore—and yet it was not at all repulsive. It felt strong and warm in mine, and in fact, was oddly attractive, in the same way that a piece of weathered driftwood is.

"It was done with an ax, you said?" I asked, wondering exactly how he had managed to inflict such an injury on himself, given that he was right-handed. A slippage might have gashed an arm or leg, but to take two fingers of the same hand right off like that . . . Realization dawned and my grasp tightened involuntarily. Oh, no.

"Oh, aye," he said, and exhaled a plume of smoke. I looked up, straight into his bright blue eyes.

"Who did it?" I asked.

"The Frasers," he said. He squeezed my hand gently, then withdrew his own and turned it to and fro. He glanced at Jamie.

"Not the Frasers of Lovat," he assured him. "Bobby Fraser of Glenhelm, and his nephew. Leslie, his name was."

"Oh? Well, that's good," Jamie replied, one eyebrow lifted. "I shouldna like to hear it was close kin of mine."

Arch chuckled, almost soundlessly. His eyes still gleamed bright in their webs of wrinkled skin, but there was something in that laugh that made me want suddenly to step back a little.

"No, ye wouldna," he agreed. "Nor me. But this was maybe the year ye would have been born, *a Sheaumais,* or a bit before. And there are no Frasers at Glenhelm now."

The hand itself had not troubled me at all, but the imagined vision of how it had got that way was making me a trifle faint. I sat down beside Jamie, not waiting for invitation.

"Why?" I said bluntly. "How?"

He drew on his pipe, and blew another ring. It struck the remnants of the first and both disintegrated in a haze of fragrant smoke. He frowned a little, and glanced down at the hand, now resting on his knee.

"Ah, well. It was my choice. We were bowmen, see," he explained to me. "All the men of my sept, we were brought up to it, early. I'd my first bow at three, and could strike a grouse through the heart at forty feet by the time I was six."

He spoke with an air of simple pride, squinting a little at a small flock of doves that were foraging under the trees nearby, as though estimating how easily he could have bagged one.

"I did hear my father tell of the archers," Jamie said. "At Glenshiels. Many of them Grants, he said—and some Campbells." He leaned forward, elbows on his knees, interested in the story, but wary.

"Aye, that was us." Arch puffed industriously, smoke wreathing up round his head. "We'd crept down through the bracken in the night," he explained to me, "and hid among the rocks above the river at Glenshiels, under the bracken and the rowans. Ye could have stood a foot away and not seen one of us, so thick as it was.

"A bit cramped," he added confidentially to Jamie. "Ye couldna stand up to take a piss, and we'd had our suppers—with a bit o' beer—before we came up the other side o' the mountain. All squatting like women, we were. Trying like the devil to keep our bowstrings dry in our shirts, too, what wi' the rain coming down and dripping down our necks through the fern.

"But come the dawn," he went on cheerfully, "and we stood on the signal and let fly. I will say 'twas a bonny sight, our arrows hailing down from the hills on the poor sods camped there by the river. Aye, your faither fought there, too, *a Sheaumais*," he added, pointing the stem of his pipe at Jamie. "He was one o' those by the river." A spasm of silent laughter shook him.

"No love lost, then," Jamie replied, very dryly. "Between you and the Frasers."

Old Arch shook his head, not at all discomposed.

"None," he said. He turned his attention back to me, his manner sobering a little.

"So when the Frasers would capture a Grant alone on their land, it was their habit to give him a choice. He could lose his right eye, or the twa fingers of his right hand. Either way, he wouldna draw a bow again against them."

He rubbed the maimed hand slowly to and fro against his thigh, stretching it out, as though his phantom fingers reached and yearned for the touch of singing sinew. Then he shook his head, as though dismissing the vision, and curled his hand into a fist. He turned to me.

"Ye werena intending to take Christie's fingers straight off, were ye, Mrs. Fraser?"

"No," I said, startled. "Of course not. He doesn't think . . . ?"

Arch shrugged, bushy white brows raised toward his receding hairline.

"I couldna say for sure, but he seemed verra much disturbed at the thought of being cut."

"Hmm," I said. I'd have to speak to Tom Christie.

Jamie had stood up to take his leave, and I followed suit automatically, shaking out my skirts and trying to shake out of my head the mental image of a young man's hand, pinned to the ground, and an ax chunking down.

"No Frasers at Glenhelm, ye said?" Jamie asked thoughtfully, looking down at Mr. Bug. "Leslie, the nephew—he would have been Bobby Fraser's heir, would he?"

"Aye, he would." Mr. Bug's pipe had gone out. He turned it over and knocked the dottle neatly out against the edge of the porch.

"Both killed together, were they? I mind my father telling of it, once. Found in a stream, their heads caved in, he said."

Arch Bug blinked up at him, eyelids lowered, lizardlike, against the sun's glare.

"Weel, ye see, *a Sheaumais,*" he said, "a bow's like a good-wife, aye? Knows her master, and answers his touch. An ax, though—" He shook his head. "An ax is a whore. Any man can use one—and it works as well in either hand."

He blew through the stem of the pipe to clear it of ash, wiped the bowl with his handkerchief, and tucked it carefully away—left-handed. He grinned at us, the remnants of his teeth sharp-edged and yellowed with tobacco.

"Go with God, *Seaumais mac Brian.*"

Later in the week, I went to the Christies' cabin, to take the stitches out of Tom's left hand and explain to him about the ether. His son, Allan, was in the yard, sharpening a knife on a foot-treadled grindstone. He smiled and nodded to me, but didn't speak, unable to be heard above the rasping whine of the grindstone.

Perhaps it was that sound, I thought, a moment later, that had aroused Tom Christie's apprehensions.

"I have decided that I shall leave my other hand as it is," he said stiffly, as I clipped the last stitch and pulled it free.

I set down my tweezers and stared at him.

"Why?"

A dull red rose in his cheeks, and he stood up, lifting his chin and looking over my shoulder, so as not to meet my eye.

"I have prayed about it, and I have come to the conclusion that if this infirmity be God's will, then it would be wrong to seek to change it."

I suppressed the strong urge to say "Stuff and nonsense!", but with great difficulty.

"Sit down," I said, taking a deep breath. "And tell me, if you would, just why you think God wants you to go about with a twisted hand?"

He did glance at me then, surprised and flustered.

"Why . . . it is not my place to question the Lord's ways!"

"Oh, isn't it?" I said mildly. "I rather thought that's what you were doing last Sunday. Or wasn't it you I heard, inquiring as to what the Lord thought He was about, letting all these Catholics flourish like the green bay tree?"

The dull red color darkened substantially.

"I am sure you have misunderstood me, Mistress Fraser." He straightened himself still further, so that he was nearly leaning over backward. "The fact remains that I shall not require your assistance."

"Is it because I'm a Catholic?" I asked, settling back on the stool and folding my hands on my knee. "You think perhaps I'll take advantage of you, and baptize you into the church of Rome when you're off your guard?"

"I have been suitably christened!" he snapped. "And I will thank you to keep your Popish notions to yourself."

"I have an arrangement with the Pope," I said, giving him stare for stare. "I issue no bulls on points of doctrine, and he doesn't do surgery. Now, about your hand—"

"The Lord's will—" he began stubbornly.

"Was it the Lord's will that your cow should fall into the gorge and break her leg last month?" I interrupted him. "Because if it was, then you presumably ought to have left her there to die, rather than fetching my husband to help pull her out, and then allowing me to set her leg. How is she, by the way?"

I could see the cow in question through the window, peacefully grazing at the edge of the yard, and evidently untroubled either by her nursing calf, or by the binding I had applied to support her cracked cannon bone.

"She is well, I thank you." He was beginning to sound a little strangled, though his shirt was loose at the collar. "That is—"

"Well, then," I said. "Do you think the Lord regards you as less deserving of medical help than your cow? It seems unlikely to me, what with Him regarding sparrows and all that."

He'd gone a sort of dusky purple round the jowls by this point, and clutched the defective hand with the sound one, as though to keep it safe from me.

"I see that you have heard something of the Bible," he began, very pompous.

"Actually, I've read it for myself," I said. "I read quite well, you know."

He brushed this remark aside, a dim light of triumph gleaming in his eye.

"Indeed. Then I am sure you will have read the Letter of St. Paul to Timothy, in which he says, *Let a woman be silent*—"

I had, in fact, encountered St. Paul and his opinions before, and had a few of my own.

"I expect St. Paul ran into a woman who could outargue him, too," I said, not without sympathy. "Easier to try to put a stopper on the entire sex than to win his point fairly. I should have expected better of *you,* though, Mr. Christie."

"But that's blasphemy!" he gasped, clearly shocked.

"It is not," I countered, "unless you're saying that St. Paul is actually God—and if you are, then I rather think *that's* blasphemy. But let's not quibble," I said, seeing his eyes begin to bulge. "Let me . . ." I rose from my stool and took a step forward, bringing me within touching distance of him. He backed up so hastily that he bumped into the table and knocked it askew, sending Malva's workbasket, a pottery jug of milk, and a pewter plate cascading to the floor with a crash.

I bent swiftly and grabbed the workbasket, in time to prevent it being soaked by the flood of milk. Mr. Christie had as swiftly seized a rag from the hearth, and bent to mop up the milk. We narrowly missed bumping heads, but did collide, and I lost my balance, falling heavily against him. He caught hold of my arms by reflex, dropping the rag, then hastily let go and recoiled, leaving me swaying on my knees.

He was on his knees, as well, breathing heavily, but now a safe distance away.

"The truth of it is," I said severely, pointing a finger at him, "you're afraid."

"I am not!"

"Yes, you are." I got to my feet, replaced the workbasket on the table, and shoved the rag delicately over the puddle of milk with my foot. "You're afraid that I'll hurt you—but I won't," I assured him. "I have a medicine called ether; it will make you go to sleep, and you won't feel anything."

He blinked at that.

"And perhaps you're afraid that you'll lose a few fingers, or what use of your hand you have."

He was still kneeling on the hearth, staring up at me.

"I can't absolutely guarantee that you won't," I said. "I don't *think* that will happen—but man proposes, and God disposes, doesn't He?"

He nodded, very slowly, but didn't say anything. I took a deep breath, for the moment out of argument.

"I *think* I can mend your hand," I said. "I can't guarantee it. Sometimes things happen. Infections, accidents—something unexpected. But . . ."

I reached out a hand to him, motioning toward the crippled member. Moving like a hypnotized bird trapped in a serpent's gaze, he extended his arm and let me take it. I grasped his wrist and pulled him to his feet; he rose easily and stood before me, letting me hold his hand.

I took it in both of mine and pressed the gnarled fingers back, rubbing my thumb gently over the thickened palmar aponeurosis that was trapping the tendons. I could feel it clearly, could see in my mind exactly how to approach the problem, where to press with the scalpel, how the calloused skin would part. The length and depth of the Z-shaped incision that would free his hand and make it useful once more.

"I've done it before," I said softly, pressing to feel the submerged bones. "I can do it again, God willing. If you'll let me?"

He was only a couple of inches taller than I; I held his eyes, as well as his hand. They were a clear, sharp gray, and searched my face with something between fear and suspicion—but with something else at the back of them. I became quite suddenly aware of his breathing, slow and steady, and felt the warmth of his breath on my cheek.

"All right," he said at last, hoarsely. He pulled his hand away from mine, not abruptly, but almost with reluctance, and stood cradling it in his sound one. "When?"

"Tomorrow," I said, "if the weather is good. I'll need good light," I explained, seeing the startled look in his eyes. "Come in the morning, but don't eat breakfast."

I picked up my kit, bobbed an awkward curtsy to him, and left, feeling rather queer.

Allan Christie waved cheerfully to me as I left, and went on with his grinding.

"Do you think he'll come?" Breakfast had been eaten, and no sign yet of Thomas Christie. After a night of broken sleep, in which I dreamed repeatedly of ether masks and surgical disasters, I wasn't sure whether I wanted him to come or not.

"Aye, he'll come." Jamie was reading the *North Carolina Gazette*, four months out of date, while munching the last of Mrs. Bug's cinnamon toast. "Look, they've printed a letter from the Governor to Lord Dartmouth, saying what an unruly lot of seditious, conniving, thieving bastards we all are, and asking General Gage to send him cannon to threaten us back into good behavior. I wonder if MacDonald knows that's public knowledge?"

"Did they really?" I said absently. I rose, and picked up the ether mask I had been staring at all through breakfast. "Well, if he does come, I suppose I'd best be ready."

I had the ether mask Bree had made for me and the dropping bottle laid out ready in my surgery, next to the array of instruments I would need for the surgery itself. Unsure, I picked up the bottle, uncorked it, and waved a hand across the neck, wafting fumes toward my nose. The result was a reassuring wave of dizziness that blurred my vision for a moment. When it cleared, I recorked the bottle and set it down, feeling somewhat more confident.

Just in time. I heard voices at the back of the house, and footsteps in the hall.

I turned expectantly, to see Mr. Christie glowering at me from the doorway, his hand curled protectively into his chest.

"I have changed my mind." Christie lowered his brows still further, to emphasize his position. "I have considered the matter, and prayed upon it, and I shall not allow ye to employ your foul potions upon me."

"You stupid man," I said, thoroughly put out. I stood up and glowered back. "What *is* the matter with you?"

He looked taken aback, as though a snake in the grass at his feet had dared to address him.

"There is nothing whatever the matter with me," he said, quite gruff. He lifted his chin aggressively, bristling his short beard at me. "What is the matter with *you*, madam?"

"And I thought it was only Highlanders who were stubborn as rocks!"

He looked quite insulted at this comparison, but before he

could take further issue with me, Jamie poked his head into the surgery, drawn by the sounds of altercation.

"Is there some difficulty?" he inquired politely.

"Yes! He refuses—"

"There is. She insists—"

The words collided, and we both broke off, glaring at each other. Jamie glanced from me to Mr. Christie, then at the apparatus on the table. He cast his eyes up to heaven, as though imploring guidance, then rubbed a finger thoughtfully beneath his nose.

"Aye," he said. "Well. D'ye want your hand mended, Tom?"

Christie went on looking mulish, cradling the crippled hand protectively against his chest. After a moment, though, he nodded slowly.

"Aye," he said. He gave me a deeply suspicious look. "But I shall not be having any of this Popish nonsense about it!"

"Popish?" Jamie and I spoke at the same time, Jamie sounding merely puzzled, myself deeply exasperated.

"Aye, and ye need not be thinking ye can cod me into it, either, Fraser!"

Jamie shot me an "I told ye so, Sassenach" sort of look, but squared himself to give it a try.

"Well, ye always were an awkward wee bugger, Tom," he said mildly. "Ye must please yourself about it, to be sure—but I can tell ye from experience that it does hurt a great deal."

I thought Christie paled a little.

"Tom. Look." Jamie nodded at the tray of instruments: two scalpels, a probe, scissors, forceps, and two suture needles, already threaded with gut and floating in a jar of alcohol. They gleamed dully in the sunlight. "She means to cut into your hand, aye?"

"I know that," Christie snapped, though his eyes slid away from the sinister assemblage of sharp edges.

"Aye, ye do. But ye've not the slightest notion what it's like. I have. See here?" He held up his right hand, the back of it toward Christie, and waggled it. In that position, with the morning sun full on it, the thin white scars that laced his fingers were stark against the deep bronze skin.

"That bloody *hurt*," he assured Christie. "Ye dinna want to do something like that, and there's a choice about it—which there is."

Christie barely glanced at the hand. Of course, I thought, he would be familiar with the look of it; he'd lived with Jamie for three years.

"I have made my choice," Christie said with dignity. He sat down in the chair and laid his hand palm-up on the napkin. All the color had leached out of his face, and his free hand was clenched so hard that it trembled.

Jamie looked at him under heavy brows for a moment, then sighed.

"Aye. Wait a moment, then."

Obviously, there was no further point in argument, and I didn't bother trying. I took down the bottle of medicinal whisky I kept on the shelf and poured a healthy tot into a cup.

"Take a little wine for thy stomach's sake," I said, thrusting it firmly into his upturned hand. "Our mutual acquaintance, St. Paul. If it's all right to drink for the sake of a stomach, surely to goodness you can take a drop for the sake of a hand."

His mouth, grimly compressed in anticipation, opened in surprise. He glanced from the cup to me, then back. He swallowed, nodded, and raised the cup to his lips.

Before he had finished, though, Jamie came back, holding a small, battered green book, which he thrust unceremoniously into Christie's hand.

Christie looked surprised, but held the book out, squinting to see what it was. *HOLY BIBLE* was printed on the warped cover, *King James Version.*

"Ye'll take help where ye can, I suppose?" Jamie said a little gruffly.

Christie looked at him sharply, then nodded, a very faint smile passing through his beard like a shadow.

"I thank you, sir," he said. He took his spectacles out of his coat and put them on, then opened the little book with great care and began to thumb through it, evidently looking for a suitable inspiration for undergoing surgery without anesthetic.

I gave Jamie a long look, to which he responded with the faintest of shrugs. It wasn't merely a Bible. It was the Bible that had once belonged to Alexander MacGregor.

Jamie had come by it as a very young man, when he was imprisoned in Fort William by Captain Jonathan Randall. Flogged once, and awaiting another, frightened and in pain, he had been left in solitary confinement with no company save his thoughts—and this Bible, given to him by the garrison's surgeon for what comfort it might offer.

Alex MacGregor had been another young Scottish prisoner—one who had died by his own hand, rather than suffer the further attentions of Captain Randall. His name was written inside the book, in a tidy, rather sprawling hand. The little Bible was no stranger to fear and suffering, and if it wasn't ether, I hoped it might still possess its own power of anodyne.

Christie had found something that suited him. He cleared his throat, straightened himself in the chair, and laid his hand on the towel, palm up, in such a forthright manner that I wondered whether he had settled on the passage in which the Maccabees willingly present their hands and tongues for amputation at the hands of the heathen king.

A peek over his shoulder indicated that he was somewhere in the Psalms, though.

"At your convenience, then, Mistress Fraser," Christie said politely.

If he wasn't to be unconscious, I needed a bit of extra preparation. Manly fortitude was all very well, and so was Biblical inspiration—but there are relatively few people capable of sitting motionless while having their hand sliced into, and I didn't think Thomas Christie was one of them.

I had a plentiful supply of linen strips for bandaging. I rolled back his sleeve, then used a few of the strips to bind his forearm tightly to the little table, with an additional band holding back the clawed fingers from the site of operation.

Though Christie seemed rather shocked at the notion of drinking liquor while reading the Bible, Jamie—and, just possibly, the sight of the waiting scalpels—had convinced him that circumstances justified it. He had consumed a couple of ounces by the time I had him properly secured and his palm thoroughly swabbed with raw alcohol, and was looking significantly more relaxed than he had upon entering the room.

This sense of relaxation disappeared abruptly when I made the first incision.

His breath rushed out in a high-pitched gasp and he arched upward out of the chair, jerking the table across the floor with a screech. I grabbed his wrist in time to prevent his ripping the bandages away, and Jamie seized him by both shoulders, pressing him back into the chair.

"Now then, now then," Jamie said, squeezing firmly. "You'll do, Tom. Aye, you'll do."

Sweat had popped out all over Christie's face, and his eyes were huge behind the lenses of his spectacles. He gulped, swallowed, took a quick look at his hand, which was welling blood, then looked away fast, white as a sheet.

"If you're going to vomit, Mr. Christie, do it there, will you?" I said, shoving an empty bucket toward him with one foot. I still had one hand on his wrist, the other pressing a wad of sterilized lint hard onto the incision.

Jamie was still talking to him like one settling a panicked horse. Christie was rigid, but breathing hard, and trembling in every limb, including the one I meant to be working on.

"Shall I stop?" I asked Jamie, giving Christie a quick appraisal. I could feel his pulse hammering in the wrist I grasped. He wasn't in shock—quite—but plainly wasn't feeling at all well.

Jamie shook his head, eyes on Christie's face.

"No. Shame to waste that much whisky, aye? And he'll not want to go through the waiting again. Here, Tom, have another dram; it will do ye good." He pressed the cup to Christie's lips, and Christie gulped it without hesitation.

Jamie had let go of Christie's shoulders as he settled; now he took hold of Christie's forearm with one hand, gripping firmly. With the other, he picked up the Bible, which had fallen to the floor, and thumbed it open.

"The right hand of the Lord is exalted," he read, squinting over Christie's shoulder at the book. *"The right hand of the Lord doeth valiantly.* Well, that's appropriate, no?" He glanced down at Christie, who had subsided, his free hand clenched in a fist against his belly.

"Go on," Christie said, voice hoarse.

"I shall not die, but live, and declare the works of the Lord," Jamie went on, his voice low but firm. *"The Lord hath chastened me sore, but he hath not given me over unto death."*

Christie seemed to find this heartening; his breathing slowed a little.

I couldn't spare time to look at him, and his arm under Jamie's grasp was hard as wood. Still, he was beginning to murmur along with Jamie, catching every few words.

"Open to me the gates of righteousness. . . . I will praise thee, for thou hast heard me. . . ."

I had the aponeurosis laid bare, and could clearly see the thickening. A flick of the scalpel freed the edge of it; then a ruthless slice, cutting hard down through the fibrous band of tissue . . . the scalpel struck bone, and Christie gasped.

"God is the Lord which has showed us light; bind the sacrifice with cords, even unto the horns of the altar. . . ." I could hear a tinge of amusement in Jamie's voice as he read that bit, and felt the shift of his body as he glanced toward me.

It did look rather as though I had been sacrificing something; hands don't bleed as profusely as head wounds, but there are plenty of small vessels in the palm, and I was hastily blotting away the blood with one hand as I worked with the other; discarded wads of bloodstained lint littered the table and the floor around me.

Jamie was flipping to and fro, picking out random bits of Scripture, but Christie was with him now, speaking the words along with him. I stole a hasty glance at him; his color was still bad, and his pulse thundering, but the breathing was better. He was clearly speaking from memory; the lenses of his spectacles were fogged.

I had the hindering tissue fully exposed now, and was trimming away the tiny fibers from the surface of the tendon. The clawed fingers twitched, and the exposed tendons moved suddenly, silver as darting fish. I grabbed the feebly wiggling fingers and squeezed them fiercely.

"You mustn't move," I said. "I need both hands; I can't hold yours."

I couldn't look up, but felt him nod, and released his fingers. With the tendons gleaming softly in their beds, I removed the last bits of the aponeurosis, sprayed the wound with a mixture of alcohol and distilled water for disinfection, and set about closing the incisions.

The men's voices were no more than whispers, a low susurrus to which I had paid no attention, engrossed as I was. As I relaxed my attention and began to suture the wound, though, I became aware of them again.

"The Lord is my shepherd, I shall not want. . . ."

I looked up, wiping perspiration from my forehead with my sleeve, and saw that Thomas Christie now held the small Bible, closed and pressed against his body with his free arm. His chin

jammed hard into his chest, his eyes tight closed and face contorted with pain.

Jamie still held the bound arm tight, but had his other hand on
Christie's shoulder, his own head bent near Christie's; his eyes,
too, were closed, as he whispered the words.

*"Yea, though I walk through the valley of the shadow of
death, I will fear no evil. . . ."*

I knotted the last suture, clipped the thread, and in the same
movement, cut through the linen bindings with my scissors, and let
go the breath I'd been holding. The men's voices stopped abruptly.

I lifted the hand, wrapped a fresh dressing tightly around it,
and pressed the clawed fingers gently back, straightening them.

Christie's eyes opened, slowly. His pupils were huge and dark
behind his lenses, as he blinked at his hand. I smiled at him, and
patted it.

*"Surely goodness and mercy shall follow me all the days of
my life,"* I said softly. *"And I shall dwell in the house of the Lord
forever."*

24

Touch Me Not

C hristie's pulse was a little rapid, but strong. I set down the
wrist I had been holding, and put the back of my hand
against his forehead.

"You're a bit feverish," I said. "Here, swallow this." I put a
hand behind his back to help him sit up in bed, which alarmed
him. He sat up in a flurry of bedclothes, drawing in his breath
sharply as he jostled the injured hand.

I tactfully affected not to notice his discomposure, which I put down to the fact that he was clad in his shirt and I in my nightclothes. These were modest enough, to be sure, with a light shawl covering my linen night rail, but I was reasonably sure that he hadn't been anywhere near a woman in *dishabille* since his wife died—if then.

I murmured something meaningless, holding the cup of comfrey tea for him as he drank, and then settled his pillows in comfortable but impersonal fashion.

Rather than send him back to his own cabin, I had insisted that he stay the night, so I could keep an eye on him in case of postoperative infection. Intransigent as he was by nature, I didn't by any means trust him to follow instructions and not to be slopping hogs, cutting wood, or wiping his backside with the wounded hand. I wasn't letting him out of sight until the incision had begun to granulate—which it should do by the next day, if all went well.

Still shaky from the shock of surgery, he had made no demur, and Mrs. Bug and I had put him to bed in the Wemysses' room, Mr. Wemyss and Lizzie having gone to the McGillivrays'.

I had no laudanum, but had slipped Christie a strong infusion of valerian and St. John's wort, and he had slept most of the afternoon. He had declined any supper, but Mrs. Bug, who approved of Mr. Christie, had been plying him through the evening with toddies, syllabubs, and other nourishing elixirs—all containing a high percentage of alcohol. Consequently, he seemed rather dazed, as well as flushed, and made no protest as I picked up the bandaged hand and brought the candle close to examine it.

The hand was swollen, which was to be expected, but not excessively so. Still, the bandage was tight, and cutting uncomfortably into the flesh. I snipped it, and holding the honeyed dressing that covered the wound carefully in place, lifted the hand and sniffed at it.

I could smell honey, blood, herbs, and the faintly metallic scent of fresh-severed flesh—but no sweet whiff of pus. Good. I pressed carefully near the dressing, watching for signs of sharp pain or streaks of vivid red in the skin, but bar a reasonable tenderness, I saw only a small degree of inflammation.

Still, he *was* feverish; it would bear watching. I took a fresh length of bandage and wound it carefully over the dressing, finishing with a neat bow at the back of the hand.

"Why do you never wear a proper kerch or cap?" he blurted.

"What?" I looked up in surprise, having temporarily forgotten the man attached to the hand. I put my free hand to my head. "Why should I?"

I sometimes plaited my hair before bed, but hadn't tonight. I had brushed it, though, and it floated loose around my shoulders, smelling pleasantly of the hyssop and nettle-flower infusion I combed through it to keep lice at bay.

"Why?" His voice rose a little. *"Every woman that prayeth or prophesieth with her head uncovered dishonoureth her head: for that is even all one as if she were shaven."*

"Oh, are we back to Paul again?" I murmured, returning my attention to his hand. "Does it not occur to you that that man had rather a bee in his bonnet when it came to women? Besides, I'm not praying at the moment, and I want to see how this does overnight, before I risk any prophesying about it. So far, though, it seems—"

"Your hair." I looked up to see him staring at me, mouth curved downward in disapproval. "It's . . ." He made a vague movement round his own clipped poll. "It's . . ."

I raised my brows at him.

"There's a great deal of it," he ended, rather feebly.

I eyed him for a moment, then put down his hand and reached for the little green Bible, which was sitting on the table.

"Corinthians, was it? Hmm, oh, yes, here we are." I straightened my back and read the verse: *"Doth not even nature itself teach you, that, if a man have long hair, it is a shame unto him? But if a woman have long hair, it is a glory to her: for her hair is given her for a covering."* I closed the book with a snap and set it down.

"Would you care to step across the landing and explain to my husband how shameful *his* hair is?" I asked politely. Jamie had gone to bed; a faint, rhythmic snoring was audible from our room. "Or do you expect he knows that already?"

Christie was already flushed from drink and fever; at this, an ugly dark red washed him from chest to hairline. His mouth moved, opening and closing soundlessly. I didn't wait for him to decide on something to say, but merely turned my attention back to his hand.

"Now," I said firmly, "you must do exercise regularly, to make sure that the muscles don't contract as they heal. It will be painful at first, but you must do it. Let me show you."

I took hold of his ring finger, just below the first joint, and keeping the finger itself straight, bent the top joint a little inward. "Do you see? Here, you do it. Take hold with your other hand, and then try to bend just that one joint. Yes, that's it. Do you feel the pull, down through the palm of your hand? That's just what's wanted. Now, do it with the little finger . . . yes. Yes, that's very good!"

I looked up and smiled at him. The flush had faded a little, but he still looked thoroughly nonplussed. He didn't smile back at me, but glanced hastily away, down at his hand.

"Right. Now, put your hand flat on the table—yes, that's the way—and try to raise your fourth finger and little finger by themselves. Yes, I know it isn't easy. Keep trying, though. Are you hungry, Mr. Christie?"

His stomach had given a loud growl, startling him as much as me.

"I suppose I might eat," he mumbled ungraciously, scowling at his uncooperative hand.

"I'll fetch you something. Keep trying those exercises for a bit, why don't you?"

The house was quiet, settled for the night. Warm as it was, the shutters had been left open, and enough moonlight streamed through the windows that I didn't need to light a candle. A shadow detached itself from the darkness in my surgery, and followed me down the hallway to the kitchen—Adso, leaving off his nocturnal hunt for mice, in hopes of easier prey.

"Hallo, cat," I said, as he slithered past my ankles into the pantry. "If you think you're having any of the ham, think again. I might go as far as a saucer of milk, though." The milk jug was white earthenware with a blue band round it, a squat, pale shape floating in the darkness. I poured out a saucer and put it down on the floor for Adso, then set about assembling a light supper—aware that Scottish expectations of a light meal involved sufficient food to founder a horse.

"Ham, cold fried potatoes, cold fried mush, bread and butter," I chanted under my breath, shoveling it all onto a large wooden tray. "Rabbit dumpling, tomato pickle, a bit of raisin pie for pudding . . . what else?" I glanced down toward the soft lapping noises coming from the shadows at my feet. "I'd give him milk, too, but he wouldn't drink it. Well, we might as well keep on as we've started, I suppose; it will help him to sleep." I reached for the whisky decanter and put that on the tray, as well.

A faint scent of ether floated in the dark air of the hallway as I made my way back toward the stairs. I sniffed suspiciously—had Adso tipped over the bottle? No, it wasn't strong enough for that, I decided, just a few wayward molecules seeping around the cork.

I was simultaneously relieved and regretful that Mr. Christie had refused to let me use the ether. Relieved, because there was no telling how it might have worked—or not. Regretful, because I would have liked very much to add the gift of unconsciousness to my arsenal of skills—a precious gift to bestow on future patients, and one I should very much have liked to give Mr. Christie.

Beyond the fact that the surgery had hurt him badly, it was very much more difficult to operate on a conscious person. The muscles were tensed, adrenaline was flooding through the system, heart rate was vastly speeded up, causing blood to spurt rather than flow. . . . For the dozenth time since the morning, I envisioned exactly what I had done, asking myself whether I might have done better.

To my surprise, Christie was still doing the exercises; his face was sheened with sweat and his mouth set grimly, but he was still doggedly bending the joints.

"That's very good," I said. "Do stop now, though. I don't want you to start bleeding again." I picked up the napkin automatically and blotted the sweat from his temples.

"Is there someone else in the house?" he asked, irritably jerking his head away from my ministrations. "I heard you speaking to someone downstairs."

"Oh," I said, rather embarrassed. "No, just the cat." Prompted by this introduction, Adso, who had followed me upstairs, leapt onto the bed and stood kneading the covers with his paws, big green eyes fixed on the plate of ham.

Christie turned a gaze of deep suspicion from the cat to me.

"No, he is not my familiar," I said tartly, scooping up Adso and dumping him unceremoniously on the floor. "He's a cat. Talking to him is slightly less ridiculous than talking to myself, that's all."

An expression of surprise flitted across Christie's face—perhaps surprise that I had read his mind, or simple surprise at my idiocy—but the creases of suspicion round his eyes relaxed.

I cut up his food with brisk efficiency, but he insisted upon feeding himself. He ate clumsily with his left hand, eyes on his plate and brows knotted in concentration.

When he had finished, he drank off a cup of whisky as though it were water, set down the empty cup, and looked at me.

"Mistress Fraser," he said, speaking very precisely, "I am an educated man. I do not think ye are a witch."

"Oh, you don't?" I said, rather amused. "So you don't believe in witches? But there are witches mentioned in the Bible, you know."

He stifled a belch with his fist and regarded me fishily.

"I did not say I do not believe in witches. I do. I said ye aren't one. Aye?"

"I'm very much obliged to hear it," I said, trying not to smile. He was quite drunk; though his speech was even more precise than usual, his accent had begun to slip. Normally, he suppressed the inflections of his native Edinburgh as much as possible, but it was growing broader by the moment.

"A bit more?" I didn't wait for an answer, but poured a solid tot of whisky into his empty cup. The shutters were open and the room was cool, but sweat still gleamed in the creases of his neck. He was clearly in pain, and wasn't likely to sleep again without help.

He sipped it this time, watching me over the rim of the cup as I tidied up the supper leavings. In spite of whisky and a full stomach, he was increasingly restive, shifting his legs beneath the quilt and twitching his shoulders. I thought he needed the chamber pot, and was debating whether I ought to offer to help him with it, or simply leave promptly so he could manage by himself. The latter, I thought.

I was mistaken, though. Before I could excuse myself, he set down his cup on the table and sat up straight in bed.

"Mistress Fraser," he said, fixing me with a beady eye. "I wish to apologize to ye."

"What for?" I said, startled.

His lips pressed tight.

"For . . . my behavior this morning."

"Oh. Well . . . that's quite all right. I can see how the idea of being put to sleep must seem . . . quite peculiar to you."

"I dinna mean that." He glanced up sharply, then down again. "I meant . . . that I . . . could not keep myself still."

I saw the deepening flush rise up his cheeks again, and had a sudden pang of surprised sympathy. He was truly embarrassed.

I set down the tray and sat down slowly on the stool beside him, wondering what I could say that might assuage his feelings—and not make matters worse.

"But, Mr. Christie," I said. "I wouldn't expect *anyone* to hold still while having their hand taken apart. It's—it's simply not human nature!"

He shot me a quick, fierce glance.

"Not even your husband?"

I blinked, taken aback. Not so much by the words, as by the tone of bitterness. Roger had told me a bit of what Kenny Lindsay had said about Ardsmuir. It had been no secret that Christie had been envious of Jamie's leadership then—but what had that to do with this?

"What makes you say that?" I asked quietly. I took his injured hand, ostensibly to check the bindings—in fact, merely to give me somewhere to look other than into his eyes.

"It's true, aye? Your husband's hand." His beard jutted pugnaciously at me. "He said ye'd mended it for him. *He* didna wriggle and squirm when ye did it, now, did he?"

Well, no, he hadn't. Jamie had prayed, cursed, sweated, cried—and screamed, once or twice. But he hadn't moved.

Jamie's hand wasn't a matter I wanted to discuss with Thomas Christie, though.

"Everyone's different," I said, giving him as straight a look as I could. "I wouldn't expect—"

"Ye wouldna expect any man to do as well as him. Aye, I ken that." The dull red color was burning in his cheeks again, and he looked down at his bandaged hand. The fingers of his good hand were clenched in a fist.

"That's not what I meant," I protested. "Not at all! I've stitched wounds and set bones for a good many men—almost all the Highlanders were terribly brave about—" It occurred to me, that fraction of a second too late, that Christie was *not* a Highlander.

He made a deep growling noise in his throat.

"Highlanders," he said, "hmp!" in a tone that made it clear he would have liked to spit on the floor, had he not been in the presence of a lady.

"Barbarians?" I said, responding to the tone. He glanced at me, and I saw his mouth twist, as he had his own moment of belated realization. He looked away, and took a deep breath—I smelled the gust of whisky as he let it out.

"Your husband . . . is . . . certainly a gentleman. He comes of a noble family, if one tainted by treason." The "r"s of "treason" rolled like thunder—he really was quite drunk. "But he is also . . . also . . ." He frowned, groping for a better word, then gave it up. "One of them. Surely ye ken that, and you an Englishwoman?"

"One of them," I repeated, mildly amused. "You mean a Highlander, or a barbarian?"

He gave me a look somewhere between triumph and puzzlement. "The same thing, is it not?"

I rather thought he had a point. While I had met Highlanders of wealth and education, like Colum and Dougal MacKenzie—to say nothing of Jamie's grandfather, the treasonous Lord Lovat to whom Christie was referring—the fact was that every single one of them had the instincts of a Viking freebooter. And to be perfectly honest, so did Jamie.

"Ah . . . well, they, um, do tend to be rather . . ." I began feebly. I rubbed a finger under my nose. "Well, they are raised to be fighting men, I suppose. Or is that what you mean?"

He sighed deeply, and shook his head a little, though I thought it was not in disagreement, but simply in dismay at the contemplation of Highland customs and manners.

Mr. Christie was himself well-educated, the son of a self-made Edinburgh merchant. As such, he had pretensions—painful ones—to being a gentleman—but would obviously never make a proper barbarian. I could see why Highlanders both puzzled and annoyed him. What must it have been like, I wondered, for him to find himself imprisoned alongside a horde of uncouth—by his standards—violent, flamboyant, Catholic barbarians, treated—or mistreated—as one of them?

He had leaned back a little on his pillow, eyes closed and mouth compressed. Without opening his eyes, he asked suddenly, "D'ye ken that your husband bears the stripes of flogging?"

I opened my mouth to reply tartly that I *had* been married to Jamie for nearly thirty years—when I realized that the question implied something about the nature of Mr. Christie's own concept of marriage that I didn't want to consider too closely.

"I know," I said instead, briefly, with a quick glance toward the open door. "Why?"

Christie opened his eyes, which were a little unfocused. With some effort, he brought his gaze to bear on me.

"Ye know why?" he asked, slurring a little. "Wha' he did?"

I felt heat rise in my cheeks, on Jamie's behalf.

"At Ardsmuir," Christie said before I could answer, leveling a finger at me. He poked it at the air, almost in accusation. "He claimed a bit of tartan, aye? Forbidden."

"Aye?" I said, in baffled reflex. "I mean—did he?"

Christie shook his head slowly back and forth, looking like a large, intoxicated owl, eyes fixed now and glaring.

"Not his," he said. "A young lad's."

He opened his mouth to speak further, but only a soft belch emerged from it, surprising him. He closed his mouth and blinked, then tried again.

"It was an act of extra . . . extraordinary . . . nobility and—and courage." He looked at me, and shook his head slightly. "Im—incompre . . . hensible."

"Incomprehensible? How he did it, you mean?" I knew how, all right; Jamie was so bloody-mindedly stubborn that he would see out any action he intended, no matter whether hell itself barred the way or what happened to him in the process. But surely Christie knew *that* about him.

"Not how." Christie's head lolled a little, and he pulled it upright with an effort. "Why?"

"Why?" I wanted to say, *Because he's an effing hero, that's why; he can't help it*—but that wouldn't really have been right. Besides, I didn't know why Jamie had done it; he hadn't told me, and I did wonder why not.

"He'd do anything to protect one of his men," I said instead.

Christie's gaze was rather glassy, but still intelligent; he looked at me for a long moment, unspeaking, thoughts passing slowly behind his eyes. A floorboard in the hall creaked, and I strained my ears for Jamie's breathing. Yes, I could hear it, soft and regular; he was still asleep.

"Does he think that I am one of 'his men'?" Christie asked at last. His voice was low, but full of both incredulity and outrage. "Because I am not, I ass—ashure you!"

I began to think that last glass of whisky had been a grave mistake.

"No," I said with a sigh, repressing the urge to close my eyes and rub my forehead. "I'm sure he doesn't. If you mean that"—I nodded at the little Bible—"I'm sure it was simple kindness. He'd do as much for any stranger—you would yourself, wouldn't you?"

He breathed heavily for a bit, glaring, but then nodded once and lay back, as though exhausted—as well he might be. All the belligerence had gone out of him as suddenly as air from a balloon, and he looked somehow smaller, and rather forlorn.

"I am sorry," he said softly. He lifted his bandaged hand a little, and let it fall.

I wasn't sure whether he was apologizing for his remarks about Jamie, or for what he saw as his lack of bravery in the morning. I thought it wiser not to inquire, though, and stood up, smoothing down the linen night rail over my thighs.

I pulled the quilt up a bit and tugged it straight, then blew out the candle. He was no more than a dark shape against the pillows, his breathing slow and hoarse.

"You did very well," I whispered, and patted his shoulder. "Good night, Mr. Christie."

My personal barbarian was asleep, but woke, catlike, when I crawled into bed. He stretched out an arm and gathered me into himself with a sleepily interrogative "mmmm?"

I nestled against him, tight muscles beginning to relax automatically into his warmth.

"Mmmm."

"Ah. And how's our wee Tom, then?" He leaned back a little and his big hands came down on my trapezius, kneading the knots from my neck and shoulders.

"Oh. Oh. Obnoxious, prickly, censorious, and very drunk. Otherwise, fine. Oh, yes. More, please—up a bit, oh, yes. Oooh."

"Aye, well, that sounds like Tom at his best—bar the drunkenness. If ye groan like that, Sassenach, he'll think I'm rubbing something other than your neck."

"I do *not* care," I said, eyes closed, the better to appreciate the exquisite sensations vibrating through my spinal column. "I've had quite enough of Tom Christie for the moment. Besides, he's likely passed out by now, with as much as he's had to drink."

Still, I tempered my vocal response, in the interests of my patient's rest.

"Where did that Bible come from?" I asked, though the answer was obvious. Jenny must have sent it from Lallybroch; her last parcel had arrived a few days before, while I was visiting Salem.

Jamie answered the question I'd really asked, sighing so his breath stirred my hair.

"It gave me a queer turn to see it, when I came to it among the books my sister sent. I couldna quite decide what to do with it, aye?"

Little wonder if it had given him a turn.

"Why did she send it, did she say?" My shoulders were beginning to relax, the ache between them dulling. I felt him shrug behind me.

"She sent it with some other books; said she was turning out the attic and found a box of them, so decided to send them to me. But she did mention hearing that the village of Kildennie had decided to emigrate to North Carolina; they're all MacGregors up near there, ken?"

"Oh, I see." Jamie had once told me that his intention was one day to find the mother of Alex MacGregor, and give her his Bible, with the information that her son had been avenged. He had made inquiries after Culloden, but discovered that both of the MacGregor parents were dead. Only a sister remained alive, and she had married and left her home; no one knew quite where she was, or even whether she was still in Scotland.

"Do you think Jenny—or Ian, rather—found the sister at last? And she lived in that village?"

He shrugged again, and with a final squeeze of my shoulders, left off.

"It may be. Ye ken Jenny; she'd leave it to me whether to search for the woman."

"And will you?" I rolled over to face him. Alex MacGregor had hanged himself, rather than live as prey to Black Jack Randall. Jack Randall was dead, had died at Culloden. But Jamie's memories of Culloden were no more than fragments, driven from him by the trauma of the battle and the fever he had suffered afterward. He had waked, wounded, with Jack Randall's body lying on top of him—but had no recollection of what had happened.

And yet, I supposed, Alex MacGregor *had* been avenged—whether or not by Jamie's hand.

He thought about that for a moment, and I felt the small stirring as he tapped the two stiff fingers of his right hand against his thigh.

"I'll ask," he said finally. "Her name was Mairi."

"I see," I said. "Well, there can't be more than, oh . . . three or four hundred women named Mairi in North Carolina."

That made him laugh, and we drifted off to sleep, to the accompaniment of Tom Christie's stertorous snores across the hall.

It might have been minutes or hours later that I woke suddenly, listening. The room was dark, the fire cold on the hearth, and the shutters rattling faintly. I tensed a little, trying to wake enough to rise and go to my patient—but then heard him, a long wheezing inspiration, followed by a rumbling snore.

It wasn't that that had wakened me, I realized. It was the sudden silence beside me. Jamie was lying stiff beside me, scarcely breathing.

I put out a hand slowly, so he would not be shocked at the touch, and rested it on his leg. He hadn't had nightmares for some months, but I recognized the signs.

"What is it?" I whispered.

He drew breath a little deeper than usual, and his body seemed momentarily to draw in upon itself. I didn't move, but left my hand on his leg, feeling the muscle flex microscopically beneath my fingers, a tiny intimation of flight.

He didn't flee, though. He moved his shoulders in a brief, violent twitch, then let out his breath and settled into the mattress. He didn't speak for a bit, but his weight drew me closer, like a moon pulled near to its planet. I lay quiet, my hand on him, my hip against his—flesh of his flesh.

He stared upward, into the shadows between the beams. I could see the line of his profile, and the shine of his eyes as he blinked now and then.

"In the dark . . ." he whispered at last, "there at Ardsmuir, we lay in the dark. Sometimes there was a moon, or starlight, but even then, ye couldna see anything on the floor where we lay. It was naught but black—but ye could hear."

Hear the breathing of the forty men in the cell, and the shuffles and shifts of their movement. Snores, coughing, the sounds of restless sleep—and the small furtive sounds from those who lay awake.

"It would be weeks, and we wouldna think of it." His voice was coming easier now. "We were always starved, cold. Worn to the bone. Ye dinna think much, then; only of how to put one foot in front of another, lift another stone. . . . Ye dinna really *want* to think, ken? And it's easy enough not to. For a time."

But every now and then, something would change. The fog of exhaustion would lift, suddenly, without warning.

"Sometimes ye kent what it was—a story someone told, maybe, or a letter that came from someone's wife or sister. Sometimes it came out of nowhere; no one said a thing, but ye'd wake to it, in the night, like the smell of a woman lying next to ye."

Memory, longing . . . need. They became men touched by fire—roused from dull acceptance by the sudden searing recollection of loss.

"Everyone would go a bit mad, for a time. There would be fights, all the time. And at night, in the dark . . ."

At night, you would hear the sounds of desperation, stifled sobs or stealthy rustlings. Some men would, in the end, reach out to another—sometimes to be rebuffed with shouts and blows. Sometimes not.

I wasn't sure what he was trying to tell me, nor what it had to do with Thomas Christie. Or, perhaps, Lord John Grey.

"Did any of them ever . . . touch you?" I asked tentatively.

"No. None of them would ever think to touch me," he said very softly. "I was their chief. They loved me—but they wouldna think, ever, to touch me."

He took a deep, ragged breath.

"And did you want them to?" I whispered. I could feel my own pulse begin to throb in my fingertips, against his skin.

"I hungered for it," he said so softly I could barely hear him, close as I was. "More than food. More than sleep—though I wished most desperately for sleep, and not only for the sake of tiredness. For when I slept, sometimes I saw ye.

"But it wasna the longing for a woman—though Christ knows, that was bad enough. It was only—I wanted the touch of a hand. Only that."

His skin had ached with need, 'til he felt it must grow transparent, and the raw soreness of his heart be seen in his chest.

He made a small rueful sound, not quite a laugh.

"Ye ken those pictures of the Sacred Heart—the same as we saw in Paris?"

I knew them—Renaissance paintings, and the vividness of stained glass glowing in the aisles of Notre Dame. The Man of Sorrows, his heart exposed and pierced, radiant with love.

"I remembered that. And I thought to myself that whoever saw that vision of Our Lord was likely a verra lonely man himself, to have understood so well."

I lifted my hand and laid it on the small hollow in the center of his chest, very lightly. The sheet was thrown back, and his skin was cool.

He closed his eyes, sighing, and clasped my hand, hard.

"The thought of that would come to me sometimes, and I would think I kent what Jesus must feel like there—so wanting, and no one to touch Him."

25

Ashes to Ashes

Jamie checked his saddlebags once more, though he had done it so often of late that the exercise was little more than custom. Each time he opened the left-hand one, he still smiled, though. Brianna had remade it for him, stitching in loops of leather that presented his pistols, hilt up, ready to be seized in an emergency, and a clever arrangement of compartments that held handy his shot pouch, powder horn, a spare knife, a coil of fishing line, a roll of twine for a snare, a hussif with pins, needles, and thread, a packet of food, a bottle of beer, and a neatly rolled clean shirt.

On the outside of the bag was a small pouch that held what Bree was pleased to call a "first-aid kit," though he was unsure what it was meant to be in aid of. It contained several gauze packets of a bitter-smelling tea, a tin of salve, and several strips of her adhesive plaster, none of which seemed likely to be of use in any imaginable misadventure, but did no harm.

He removed a cake of soap she had added, along with a few more unnecessary fripperies, and carefully hid them under a bucket, lest she be offended.

Just in time, too; he heard her voice, exhorting wee Roger about the inclusion of sufficient clean stockings in his bags. By the time they came round the corner of the hay barn, he had everything securely buckled up.

"Ready, then, *a charaid*?"

"Oh, aye." Roger nodded, and slung the saddlebags he was carrying on his shoulder off onto the ground. He turned to Bree, who was carrying Jemmy, and kissed her briefly.

"I go with *you*, Daddy!" Jem exclaimed hopefully.

"Not this time, sport."

"Wanna see Indians!"

"Later, perhaps, when ye're bigger."

"I can talk Indian! Uncle Ian tellt me! Wanna go!"

"Not this time," Bree told him firmly, but he wasn't inclined to listen, and began struggling to get down. Jamie made a small rumble in his throat, and fixed him with a quelling eye.

"Ye've heard your parents," he said. Jem glowered, and stuck out his lower lip like a shelf, but ceased his fuss.

"Someday ye must tell me how ye do that," Roger said, eyeing his offspring.

Jamie laughed, and leaned down to Jemmy. "Kiss Grandda goodbye, eh?"

Disappointment generously abandoned, Jemmy reached up and seized him round the neck. He picked the little boy up out of Brianna's arms, hugged him, and kissed him. Jem smelled of parritch, toast, and honey, a homely warm and heavy weight in his arms.

"Be good and mind your mother, aye? And when ye're a wee bit bigger, ye'll come, too. Come and say farewell to Clarence; ye can tell him the words Uncle Ian taught ye." And God willing, they'd be words suitable for a three-year-old child. Ian had a most irresponsible sense of humor.

Or perhaps, he thought, grinning to himself, *I'm only recalling some o' the things I taught Jenny's bairns—including Ian—to say in French.*

He'd already saddled and bridled Roger's horse, and Clarence the pack mule was fully loaded. Brianna was checking the girth and stirrup leathers while Roger slung his saddlebags—more to keep herself busy than because of any need. Her lower lip was caught in her teeth; she was being careful not to seem worried, but was fooling no one.

Jamie took Jem up to pat the mule's nose, in order to give the lass and her man a moment's privacy. Clarence was a good sort, and suffered Jem's enthusiastic patting and mispronounced Cherokee phrases with long-suffering tolerance, but when Jem turned in his arms toward Gideon, Jamie leaned back sharply.

"Nay, lad, ye dinna want to touch yon wicked bugger. He'll take your hand right off."

Gideon twitched his ears and stamped once, impatient. The big stallion was dying to get under way and have another chance at killing him.

"Why do you keep that vicious thing?" Brianna asked, seeing Gideon's long lip wrinkle back to show his yellow teeth in anticipation. She took Jemmy from him, stepping well away from Gideon.

"What, wee Gideon? Oh, we get on. Besides, he's half my trade goods, lass."

"Really?" She gave the big chestnut a suspicious glance. "Are you sure you won't start a war, giving the Indians something like him?"

"Oh, I dinna mean to give him to them," he assured her. "Not directly, at least."

Gideon was a bad-tempered, thrawn-headed reester of a horse, with a mouth like iron and a will to match. However, these unsociable qualities seemed most appealing to the Indians, as did the stallion's massive chest, long wind, and stoutly muscled frame. When Quiet Air, the sachem in one of the villages, had offered him three deerskins for the chance to breed his spotted mare to Gideon, Jamie had realized suddenly that he had something here.

"'Twas the greatest good fortune that I never found the time to castrate him," he said, slapping Gideon familiarly on the withers and dodging by reflex as the stallion whipped his head round to snap. "He earns his keep, and more, standing at stud to the Indian ponies. It's the only thing I've ever asked him to do that he's not balked at."

The lass was pink as a Christmas rose from the morning cold; she laughed at that, though, going an even deeper color.

"What's castrate?" Jemmy inquired.

"Your mother will tell ye." He grinned at her, ruffled Jemmy's hair, and turned to Roger. "Ready, lad?"

Roger Mac nodded and stepped up into his stirrup, swinging aboard. He had a steady old bay gelding named Agrippa, who tended to grunt and wheeze, but was sound enough for all that, and good for a rider like Roger—competent enough, but with an abiding sense of inner reservation about horses.

Roger leaned down from the saddle for a last kiss from Brianna, and they were under way. Jamie'd taken a private—and thorough—leave of Claire earlier.

She was in the window of their bedroom, watching out to wave to them as they rode past, her hairbrush in her hand. Her hair was standing out in a great curly swash round her head, and the early-morning sun caught in it like flames in a thornbush. It gave him a sudden queer feeling to see her thus so disordered, half-naked in her shift. A sense of strong desire, despite what he'd done to her not an hour past. And something almost fear, as though he might never see her again.

Quite without thought, he glanced at his left hand, and saw the ghost of the scar at the base of his thumb, the "C" so faded that it was scarcely visible. He had not noticed it or thought of it in years, and felt suddenly as though there was not air enough to breathe.

He waved, though, and she threw him a mocking kiss, laughing. Christ, he'd marked *her*; he could see the dark patch of the love bite he'd left on her neck, and a hot flush of embarrassment rose in his face. He dug his heels into Gideon's side, causing the stallion to give a squeal of displeasure and turn round to try to bite him in the leg.

With this distraction, they were safe away. He looked back only once, at the trailhead, to see her still there, framed by light. She lifted one hand, as though in benediction, and then the trees hid her from sight.

The weather was fair, though cold for as early in the autumn as it was; the horses' breath steamed as they made their way down from the Ridge through the tiny settlement folk now called Cooperville, and along the Great Buffalo Trail to the north. He kept an eye on the sky; it was much too early for snow, but heavy rains were not uncommon. What clouds there were were mare's tails, though; no cause for worry.

They didn't speak much, each man alone with his thoughts. Roger Mac was easy company, for the most part. Jamie did miss Ian, though; he would have liked to talk over the situation as it stood now with Tsisqua. Ian understood the minds of Indians better than most white men, and while Jamie understood Bird's gesture of sending the hermit's bones well enough—it was meant as a proof of his continuing goodwill toward settlers, if the King should send them guns—he would have valued Ian's opinion.

And while it was necessary that he introduce Roger Mac in the villages, for the sake of future relations . . . Well, he blushed at the thought of having to explain to the man about . . .

Damn Ian. The lad had simply gone in the night, a few days past, him and his dog. He'd done it before, and would doubtless be back as suddenly as he'd gone. Whatever darkness he'd brought back from the north would now and then become too much for him, and he would vanish into the wood, coming back silent and withdrawn, but somewhat more at peace with himself.

Jamie understood it well enough; solitude was in its own way a balm for loneliness. And whatever memory the lad was fleeing—or seeking—in the wood . . .

"Has he ever spoken to you about them?" Claire had asked him, troubled. *"His wife? His child?"*

He had not. Ian did not speak of anything about his time among the Mohawk, and the only token he had brought back from the north was an armlet, made of blue-and-white wampum shells. Jamie had caught a glimpse of it in Ian's sporran once, but not enough to tell the pattern of it.

Blessed Michael defend you, lad, he thought silently toward Ian. *And may the angels mend you.*

With one thing and another, he had no real conversation with Roger Mac until they'd stopped for their noon meal. They ate the fresh stuff the women had sent, enjoying it. Enough for supper left; next day, it would be corn dodgers and anything that came across their path that could be easily caught and cooked. And one day more, and the Snowbird women would have them royally fed, as representatives of the King of England.

"Last time, it was ducks, stuffed wi' yams and corn," he told Roger. "It's manners to eat as much as ye can, mind, no matter what's served, and ye're the guest."

"Got it." Roger smiled faintly, then looked down at the half-eaten sausage roll in his hand. "About that. Guests, I mean. There's a wee problem, I think—with Hiram Crombie."

"Hiram?" Jamie was surprised. "What's to do wi' Hiram?"

Roger's mouth twitched, unsure whether to laugh or not.

"Well, it's only—ye ken everybody's calling the bones we buried Ephraim, aye? It's all Bree's fault, but there it is."

Jamie nodded, curious.

"Well, so. Yesterday Hiram came along to me, and said he'd been studying upon the matter—praying and the like—and had come to the conclusion that if it were true that some of the Indians were his wife's kin, then it stood to reason that some of them must be saved, as well."

"Oh, aye?" Amusement began to kindle in his own breast.

"Yes. And so, he says, he feels called upon to bring these hapless savages the word of Christ. For how else are they to hear it?"

Jamie rubbed a knuckle over his upper lip, torn now between amusement and dismay at the thought of Hiram Crombie invading the Cherokee villages, psalmbook in hand.

"Mmphm. Well, but . . . do ye not believe—Presbyterians, I mean—that it's all predestined? That some are saved, I mean, and some damned, and not a thing to be done about it? Which is why the Papists are all bound for hell in a handbasket?"

"Ah . . . well . . ." Roger hesitated, clearly not quite willing to put the matter so baldly himself. "Mmphm. There may be some difference of opinion among Presbyterians, I imagine. But yes, that's more or less what Hiram and his cohorts think."

"Aye. Well, then, if he thinks some o' the Indians must be saved already, why must they be preached to?"

Roger rubbed a finger between his brows.

"Well, d'ye see, it's the same reason Presbyterians pray and go to kirk and all. Even if they're saved, they feel they want to praise God for it, and—and learn to do better, so as to live as God wishes them to. In gratitude for their salvation, see?"

"I rather think Hiram Crombie's God might take a dim view of the Indian way of living," Jamie said, with vivid memories of naked bodies in the dimness of ember glow, and the smell of furs.

"Quite," Roger said, catching Claire's dry tone so exactly that Jamie laughed.

"Aye, I see the difficulty," he said, and he did, though he still found it funny. "So Hiram means to go to the Cherokee villages and preach? Is that it?"

Roger nodded, swallowing a bit of sausage.

"To be more exact, he wants you to take him there. And make introduction for him. He wouldna expect ye to interpret the preaching, he says."

"Holy God." He took a moment to contemplate this prospect, then shook his head decidedly. "No."

"Of course not." Roger pulled the cork from a bottle of beer, and offered it to him. "I just thought I should tell ye, so ye can decide best what to say to him when he asks."

"Verra thoughtful of ye," Jamie said, and taking the bottle, drank deeply.

He lowered it, took breath—and froze. He saw Roger Mac's head turn sharply and knew he had caught it, too, borne on the chilly breeze.

Roger Mac turned back to him, black brows furrowed.

"Do ye smell something burning?" he said.

Roger heard them first: a raucous caucus of cries and cackles, shrill as witches. Then a clappering of wings as they came in sight, and the birds flew up, mostly crows, but here and there a huge black raven.

"Oh, God," he said softly.

Two bodies hung from a tree beside the house. What was left of them. He could tell that it was a man and a woman, but only by their clothes. A piece of paper was pinned to the man's leg, so crumpled and stained that he saw it only because one edge lifted in the breeze.

Jamie ripped it off, unfolded it enough to read, and threw it on the ground. *Death to Regulators*, it read; he saw the scrawl for an instant, before the wind blew it away.

"Where are the bairns?" Jamie asked, turning sharply to him. "These folk have children. Where are they?"

The ashes were cold, already scattering in the wind, but the smell of burning filled him, clogged his breathing, seared his throat so that words rasped like gravel, meaningless as the scrape of pebbles underfoot. Roger tried to speak, cleared his throat, and spat.

"Hiding, maybe," he rasped, and flung out an arm toward the wood.

"Aye, maybe." Jamie stood abruptly, called into the wood, and, not waiting for an answer, set off into the trees, calling again.

Roger followed, sheering off as they reached the forest's edge, going upslope behind the house, both of them shouting words of reassurance that were swallowed up at once by the forest's silence.

Roger stumbled through the trees, sweating, panting, heedless of the pain in his throat as he shouted, barely stopping long enough to hear if anyone answered. Several times he saw movement from the corner of his eye and swung toward it, only to see nothing but the ripple of wind through a patch of drying sedges, or a dangling creeper, swaying as though someone had passed that way.

He half-imagined he was seeing Jem, playing at hide-and-seek, and the vision of a darting foot, sun gleaming off a small head, lent him strength to shout again, and yet again. At last, though, he was forced to admit that children would not have run so far, and he circled back toward the cabin, still calling intermittently, in hoarse, strangled croaks.

He came back into the dooryard to find Jamie stooping for a rock, which he threw with great force at a pair of ravens that had settled in the hanging tree, edging bright-eyed back toward its burden. The ravens squawked and flapped away—but only so far as the next tree, where they sat watching.

The day was cold, but both of them were soaked with sweat, hair straggling wet on their necks. Jamie wiped his face with his sleeve, still breathing hard.

"H-how many . . . children?" Roger's own breath was short, his throat so raw that the words were barely a whisper.

"Three, at least." Jamie coughed, hawked, and spat. "The eldest is twelve, maybe." He stood for a moment, looking at the bodies. Then he crossed himself and drew his dirk to cut them down.

They had nothing to dig with; the best that could be managed was a wide scrape in the leaf mold of the forest, and a thin cairn of rocks, as much to spite the ravens as for the sake of decency.

"Were they Regulators?" Roger asked, pausing in the midst of it to wipe his face on his sleeve.

"Aye, but . . ." Jamie's voice trailed away. "It's naught to do wi' that business." He shook his head and turned away to gather more rocks.

Roger thought it *was* a rock at first, half-hidden in the leaves that had drifted against the scorched cabin wall. He touched it, and it moved, bringing him to his feet with a cry that would have done credit to any of the corbies.

Jamie reached him in seconds, in time to help dig the little girl out of the leaves and cinders.

"Hush, *a muirninn*, hush," Jamie said urgently, though in fact the child was not crying. She was maybe eight, her clothes and hair burned away and her skin so blackened and cracked that she might have been made of stone indeed, save for her eyes.

"Oh, God, oh, God." Roger kept saying it, under his breath, long after it became clear that if it was a prayer, it was long past answering.

He was cradling her against his chest, and her eyes opened halfway, regarding him with nothing like relief or curiosity—only a calm fatality.

Jamie had poured water from his canteen onto a handkerchief; he fed the tip of it between her lips to wet them, and Roger saw her throat move in reflex as she sucked.

"Ye'll be all right," Roger whispered to her. "It's all right, *a leannan*."

"Who has done this, *a nighean*?" Jamie asked, just as gently. Roger saw that she understood; the question stirred the surface of her eyes like wind on a pond—but then passed over, leaving them calm again. She did not speak, no matter what questions they asked, only looked at them with incurious eyes, and went on sucking dreamily at the wet cloth.

"Are ye baptized, *a leannan*?" Jamie asked her at last, and Roger felt a deep jolt at the question. In the shock of finding her, he had not truly taken in her condition.

"Elle ne peut pas vivre," Jamie said softly, his eyes meeting Roger's. She cannot live.

His first instinct was a visceral denial. Of course she could live, she must. But huge patches of her skin were gone, the raw flesh crusted but still oozing. He could see the white edge of a knee bone, and literally see her heart beating, a reddish, translucent bulge that pulsed at the notch of her rib cage. She was light as a corn-dolly, and he became painfully aware that she seemed to float in his arms, like a slick of oil on water.

"Does it hurt, sweetheart?" he asked her.

"Mama?" she whispered. Then she closed her eyes and would say no more, only muttering "Mama?" now and then.

He had thought at first they would take her back to the Ridge, to Claire. But it was more than a day's ride; she wouldn't make it. Not possibly.

He swallowed, realization closing on his throat like a noose. He looked at Jamie, seeing the same sick acknowledgment in his eyes. Jamie swallowed, too.

"Do ye . . . know her name?" Roger could scarcely breathe, and forced the words. Jamie shook his head, then gathered himself, hunching his shoulders.

She had stopped sucking, but still murmured "Mama?" now and then. Jamie took the handkerchief from her lips and squeezed a few drops from it onto her blackened forehead, whispering the words of baptism.

Then they looked at each other, acknowledging necessity. Jamie was pale, sweat beading on his upper lip among the bristles of red beard. He took a deep breath, steeling himself, and lifted his hands, offering.

"No," Roger said softly. "I'll do it." She was his; he could no more surrender her to another than he could have torn off an arm.

He reached for the handkerchief, and Jamie put it into his hand, soot-stained, still damp.

He'd never thought of such a thing, and couldn't think now. He didn't need to; without hesitation, he cradled her close and put the handkerchief over her nose and mouth, then clamped his hand tight over the cloth, feeling the small bump of her nose caught snug between his thumb and index finger.

Wind stirred in the leaves above, and a rain of gold fell on them, whispering on his skin, brushing cool past his face. She would be cold, he thought, and wished to cover her, but had no hand to spare.

His other arm was round her, hand resting on her chest; he could feel the tiny heart beneath his fingers. It jumped, beat rapidly, skipped, beat twice more . . . and stopped. It quivered for a moment; he could feel it trying to find enough strength to beat one last time, and suffered the momentary illusion that it would not only do so, but would force its way through the fragile wall of her chest and into his hand in its urge to live.

But the moment passed, as did the illusion, and a great stillness came. Near at hand, a raven called.

They had almost finished the burying, when the sound of hooves and jingling harness announced visitors—a lot of visitors.

Roger, ready to decamp into the woods, glanced at his father-in-law, but Jamie shook his head, answering his unasked question.

"Nay, they'd no come back. What for?" His bleak gaze took in the smoking ruin of the homestead, the trampled dooryard, and the low mounds of the graves. The little girl still lay nearby, covered with Roger's cloak. He hadn't been able to bear putting her into the ground just yet; the knowledge of her alive was still too recent.

Jamie straightened, stretching his back. Roger saw him glance to see that his rifle was to hand, leaning against a tree trunk. Then he settled himself, leaning on the scorched board he had been using as a shovel, waiting.

The first of the riders came out of the woods, his horse snorting and tossing its head at the smell of burning. The rider pulled it

skillfully round and urged it closer, leaning forward to see who
they were.

"So it's you, is it, Fraser?" Richard Brown's lined face looked
grimly jovial. He glanced at the charred and steaming timbers,
then round at his comrades. "Didn't think you made your money
just by selling whisky."

The men—Roger counted six of them—shifted in their sad-
dles, snorting with amusement.

"Have a bit o' respect for the dead, Brown." Jamie nodded at
the graves, and Brown's face hardened. He glanced sharply at
Jamie, then at Roger.

"Just the two of you, is it? What are you doing here?"

"Digging graves," Roger said. His palms were blistered; he
rubbed a hand slowly on the side of his breeches. "What are *you*
doing here?"

Brown straightened abruptly in his saddle, but it was his
brother Lionel who answered.

"Coming down from Owenawisgu," he said, jerking his head at
the horses. Looking, Roger saw that there were four packhorses,
laden with skins, and that several of the other horses carried
bulging saddlebags. "Smelled the fire and come to see." He
glanced down at the graves. "Tige O'Brian, was it?"

Jamie nodded.

"Ye kent them?"

Richard Brown shrugged.

"Aye. It's on the way to Owenawisgu. I've stopped a time or
two; taken supper with them." Belatedly, he removed his hat, plastering down wisps of hair over his balding crown with the flat of
his hand. "God rest 'em."

"Who's burnt 'em out, if it wasn't you?" one of the younger
men in the party called. The man, a Brown by his narrow shoulders and lantern jaw, grinned inappropriately, evidently thinking this a jest.

The singed bit of paper had flown with the wind; it fluttered
against a rock near Roger's foot. He picked it up and with a step
forward, slapped it against Lionel Brown's saddle.

"Know anything about that, do you?" he asked. "It was
pinned to O'Brian's body." He sounded angry, knew it, and
didn't care. His throat ached and his voice came out as a strangled rasp.

Lionel Brown glanced at the paper, brows raised, then handed it to his brother.

"No. Write it yourself, did you?"

"What?" He stared up at the man, blinking against the wind.

"Indians," Lionel Brown said, nodding at the house. "Indians done this."

"Oh, aye?" Roger could hear the undercurrents in Jamie's voice—skepticism, wariness, and anger. "Which Indians? The ones from whom ye bought the hides? Told ye about it, did they?"

"Don't be a fool, Nelly." Richard Brown kept his voice pitched low, but his brother flinched a little, hearing it. Brown edged his horse nearer. Jamie stood his ground, though Roger saw his hands tighten on the board.

"Got the whole family, did they?" he asked, glancing at the small body under its cloak.

"No," Jamie said. "We've not found the two elder children. Only the wee lassie."

"Indians," Lionel Brown repeated stubbornly, from behind his brother. "They took 'em."

Jamie took a deep breath, and coughed from the smoke.

"Aye," he said. "I'll ask in the villages, then."

"Won't find 'em," Richard Brown said. He crumpled the note, tightening his fist suddenly. "If Indians took them, they won't keep them near. They'll sell them on, into Kentucky."

There was a general mutter of agreement among the men, and Roger felt the ember that had simmered in his chest all afternoon burst into fire.

"Indians didn't write that," he snapped, jerking a thumb at the note in Brown's hand. "And if it was revenge against O'Brian for being a Regulator, they wouldn't have taken the children."

Brown gave him a long look, eyes narrowed. Roger felt Jamie shift his weight slightly, preparing.

"No," said Brown softly. "They wouldn't. That's why Nelly figured you wrote it yourself. Say the Indians came and stole the little 'uns, but then *you* come along and decide to take what's left. So you fired the cabin, hung O'Brian and his wife, pinned that note, and here you are. How say you to that bit of reasoning, Mr. MacKenzie?"

"I'd ask how ye kent they were hanged, Mr. Brown."

Brown's face tightened, and Roger felt Jamie's hand on his arm in warning, realizing only then that his fists were clenched.

"The ropes, *a charaid*," Jamie said, his voice very calm. The words penetrated dimly, and he looked. True, the ropes they had cut from the bodies lay by the tree where they had fallen. Jamie was still talking, his voice still calm, but Roger couldn't hear the words. The wind deafened him, and just below the whine of it he heard the intermittent soft thump of a beating heart. It might have been his own—or hers.

"Get off that horse," he said, or thought he had. The wind swept into his face, heavy with soot, and the words caught in his throat. The taste of ash was thick and sour in his mouth; he coughed and spat, eyes watering.

Vaguely, he became aware of a pain in his arm, and the world swam back into view. The younger men were staring at him, with expressions ranging from smirks to wariness. Richard Brown and his brother were both sedulously avoiding looking at him, focused instead on Jamie—who was still gripping his arm.

With an effort, he shook off Jamie's hand, giving his father-in-law the slightest nod by way of reassurance that he wasn't about to go berserk—though his heart still pounded, and the feel of the noose was so tight about his throat that he couldn't have spoken, even had he been able to form words.

"We'll help." Brown nodded at the little body on the ground, and began to swing one leg over his saddle, but Jamie stopped him with a small gesture.

"Nay, we'll manage."

Brown stopped, awkwardly half-on, half-off. His lips thinned and he pulled himself back on, reined around and rode off with no word of farewell. The others followed, looking curiously back as they went.

"It wasna them." Jamie had taken up his rifle and held it, gazing at the wood where the last of the men had disappeared. "They ken something more about it than they'll say, though."

Roger nodded, wordless. He walked deliberately to the hanging tree, kicked aside the ropes, and drove his fist into the trunk, twice, three times. Stood panting, his forehead pressed against the rough bark. The pain of raw knuckles helped, a bit.

A trail of tiny ants was scurrying upward between the plates of bark, bound on some momentous business, all-absorbing. He watched them for a little, until he could swallow again. Then straightened up and went to bury her, rubbing at the bone-deep bruise on his arm.

PART FOUR

Abduction

26

An Eye to the Future

October 9, 1773

R oger dropped his saddlebags on the ground beside the pit
and peered in.

"Where's Jem?" he said.

His mud-smeared wife looked up at him and brushed a sweat-
matted lock of hair out of her face.

"Hello to you, too," she said. "Have a good trip?"

"No," he said. "Where's Jem?"

Her brows rose at that, and she stabbed her shovel into the bottom of the pit, extending a hand for him to help her scramble out.

"He's at Marsali's. He and Germain are playing Vroom with
the little cars you made them—or they were when I left him
there."

The knot of anxiety he had carried under his ribs for the last
two weeks began slowly to relax. He nodded, a sudden spasm of
the throat preventing him from speaking, then reached out and
pulled her to him, crushing her against him in spite of her startled
yelp and mud-stained clothes.

He held her hard, his own heart hammering loud in his ears,
and wouldn't—couldn't—let go, until she wriggled out of his
embrace. She kept her hands on his shoulders, but cocked her
head to one side, one brow raised.

"Yeah, I missed you, too," she said. "What's wrong? What happened?"

"Terrible things." The burning, the little girl's death—these had
become dreamlike during their travel, their horror muted to the
surreal by the monotonous labor of riding, walking, the constant

whine of wind and crunch of boots on gravel, sand, pine needles, mud, the engulfing blur of greens and yellows in which they lost themselves beneath an endless sky.

But now he was home, no longer adrift in the wilderness. And the memory of the girl who had left her heart in his hand was suddenly as real as she had been in the moment she died.

"You come inside." Brianna was peering closely at him, concerned. "You need something hot, Roger."

"I'm all right," he said, but followed her without protest.

He sat at the table while she put the kettle on for tea, and told her everything that had happened, head in his hands, staring down at the battered tabletop, with its homely spills and burn scars.

"I kept thinking there must be something . . . some way. But there wasn't. Even while I—I put my hand over her face—I was sure it wasna really happening. But at the same time—" He sat up, then, looking into the palms of his hands. At the same time, it had been the most vivid experience of his life. He could not bear to think of it, save in the most fleeting way, but knew he could never forget the slightest thing about it. His throat closed suddenly again.

Brianna looked searchingly into his face, saw his hand touch the ragged rope scar on his throat.

"Can you breathe?" she said anxiously. He shook his head, but it wasn't true, he *was* breathing, somehow, though it felt as though his throat had been crushed in some huge hand, larynx and windpipe mangled into a bloody mass.

He flapped a hand to indicate that he would be all right, much as he doubted it himself. She came round behind him, pulled his hand from his throat, and laid her own fingers lightly over the scar.

"It'll be all right," she said quietly. "Just breathe. Don't think. Just breathe."

Her fingers were cold and her hands smelled of dirt. There was water in his eyes. He blinked, wanting to see the room, the hearth and candle and dishes and loom, to convince himself of where he was. A drop of warm moisture rolled down his cheek.

He tried to tell her that it was all right, he wasn't crying, but she merely pressed closer, holding him across the chest with one arm, the other hand still cool on the painful lump in his throat. Her breasts were soft against his back, and he could feel, rather than hear, her humming, the small tuneless noise she made when she was anxious, or concentrating very hard.

Finally, the spasm began to ease, and the feel of choking left him. His chest swelled with the unbelievable relief of a free breath, and she let go.

"What . . . is it . . . that ye're digging?" he asked, with only a little effort. He looked round at her and smiled, with a lot more. "A bar . . . becue pit for . . . a hippopot . . . amus?"

The ghost of a smile touched her face, though her eyes were still dark with concern.

"No," she said. "It's a groundhog kiln."

He tried for a moment to compose some witty remark about it being a really large hole for killing something as small as a groundhog, but he wasn't up to it.

"Oh," he said instead.

He took the hot mug of catnip tea she placed in his hand and held it near his face, letting the fragrant steam warm his nose and mist on the cold skin of his cheeks.

Brianna poured out a mug for herself, as well, and sat down across from him.

"I'm glad you're home," she said softly.

"Yeah. Me, too." He essayed a sip; it was still scalding. "A kiln?" He'd told her about the O'Brians; he had to, but he didn't want to talk about it. Not now. She seemed to sense this, and didn't press him.

"Uh-huh. For the water." He must have looked confused, for her smile grew more genuine. "I told you there was dirt involved, didn't I? Besides, it was your idea."

"It was?" At this point, almost nothing would surprise him, but he had no memory of having bright ideas about water.

The problem of bringing water to the houses was one of transport. God knew there was plenty of water; it ran in creeks, fell in waterfalls, dripped from ledges, sprang from springs, seeped in boggy patches under the cliffs . . . but making it go where you wanted required some method of containment.

"Mr. Wemyss told *Fraulein* Berrisch—that's his girlfriend; *Frau* Ute fixed them up—what I was doing, and she told him that the men's choir over in Salem was working on the same problem, so—"

"The choir?" He tried another cautious sip and found it drinkable. "Why would the choir—"

"That's just what they call them. There's the single men's choir, the single women's choir, the married choir . . . they don't just sing together, though, it's more like a social group, and each choir has particular jobs they do for the community. But anyway"—she flapped a hand—"they're trying to bring water into the town, and having the same problem—no metal for pipes.

"You remember, though—you reminded me about the pottery they do in Salem. Well, they tried making water pipes out of logs, but that's really hard and time-consuming, because you have to bore the middle of the log out with an augur, and you still need metal collars to bind the logs together. And they rot, after a while. But then they had the same idea you had—why not make pipes out of fired clay?"

She was becoming animated, talking about it. Her nose was no longer red from cold, but her cheeks were flushed pink and her eyes bright with interest. She waved her hands when she talked— she got that from her mother, he thought to himself, amused.

". . . so we parked the kids with Mama and Mrs. Bug, and Marsali and I went to Salem—"

"Marsali? But she couldn't be riding, surely?" Marsali was enormously pregnant, to the point that merely being around her made him slightly nervous, for fear she might go into labor at any moment.

"She isn't due for a month. Besides, we didn't ride; we took the wagon, and traded honey and cider and venison for cheese and quilts and—see my new teapot?" Proud, she waved at the pot, a homely squat thing with a red-brown glaze and yellow squiggly shapes painted round the middle. It was one of the uglier objects he'd ever seen, and the sight of it made tears come to his eyes from the sheer joy of being home.

"You don't like it?" she said, a small frown forming between her brows.

"No, it's great," he said hoarsely. He fumbled for a handkerchief and blew his nose to hide his emotion. "Love it. You were saying . . . Marsali?"

"I was saying about the water pipes. But—there's something about Marsali, too." The frown deepened. "I'm afraid Fergus isn't behaving very well."

"No? What's he doing? Having a mad affair with Mrs. Crombie?"

This suggestion was greeted with a withering look, but it didn't last.

"He's gone a lot, for one thing, leaving poor Marsali to mind the children *and* do all the work."

"Totally normal, for the time," he observed. "Most men do that. Your father does that. *I* do that; had ye not noticed?"

"I noticed," she said, giving him a faintly evil look. "But what I mean is, most men do the heavy work, like plowing and planting, and let their wives manage the inside stuff, the cooking and the spinning and the weaving, *and* the laundry, *and* the preserving, *and*—well, anyway, all that stuff. But Marsali's doing it all, plus the kids and the outdoor work, *and* working at the malting floor. And when Fergus *is* home, he's grumpy and he drinks too much."

This also sounded like normal behavior for the father of three small, wild children and the husband of a very pregnant wife, Roger thought, but didn't say so.

"I'd not have thought Fergus a layabout," he observed mildly. Bree shook her head, still frowning, and poured more tea into his mug.

"No, he's not lazy, really. It's hard for him, with only one hand; he really can't handle some of the heavy chores—but he won't help with the kids, or cook and clean while Marsali does them. Da and Ian help with the plowing, but . . . And he leaves for days on end—sometimes he's picking up little jobs here and there, translating for a traveler—but mostly, he's just gone. And . . ." She hesitated, darting a look at him as though wondering whether to go on.

"And?" he said obligingly. The tea was working; the pain in his throat was almost gone.

She looked down at the table, drawing invisible patterns on the oak with a forefinger.

"She didn't say so . . . but I think he hits her."

Roger felt a sudden weight on his heart. His first reaction was to dismiss the notion out of hand—but he had seen too much, living with the Reverend. Too many families, outwardly content and respectable, where the wives poked fun at their own "clumsiness," brushing away concern at black eyes, broken noses, dislocated wrists. Too many men who dealt with the pressures of providing for a family by resorting to the bottle.

"Damn," he said, feeling suddenly exhausted. He rubbed at his forehead, where a headache was starting.

"Why do you think so?" he asked bluntly. "Has she got marks?"

Bree nodded unhappily, still not looking up, though her finger had stilled.

"On her arm." She wrapped a hand around her forearm, in illustration. "Little round bruises, like fingermarks. I saw when she reached up to get a bucket of honeycomb from the wagon and her sleeve fell back."

He nodded, wishing there was something stronger than tea in his mug.

"Shall I talk to him, then, d'ye think?"

She did look up at him then, her eyes softening, though the look of worry remained.

"You know, most men wouldn't offer to do that."

"Well, it's no my idea of fun," he admitted. "But ye canna let that sort of thing go on, hoping it will cure itself. Someone has to say *something*."

God knew what, though—or how. He was already regretting the offer, trying to think what the hell he *could* say. *"So, Fergus, old man. Hear you're beating your wife. Be a good fellow and stop that, okay?"*

He drained the rest of his mug, and got up to look for the whisky.

"We're out," Brianna said, seeing his intent. "Mr. Wemyss had a cold."

He put down the empty bottle with a sigh. She touched his arm delicately.

"We're invited up to the Big House for supper. We could go early." That was a cheering suggestion. Jamie invariably had a bottle of excellent single-malt, secreted somewhere on the premises.

"Aye, all right." He took her cloak from the peg and swung it round her shoulders. "Hey. D'ye think I should mention the business about Fergus to your Da? Or best handle it myself?" He had a sudden, unworthy hope that Jamie would consider it his business and take care of the matter.

That seemed to be what Brianna was afraid of; she was shaking her head, simultaneously fluffing out her half-dried hair.

"No! I think Da would break his neck. And Fergus won't be any good to Marsali if he's dead."

"Mmphm." He accepted the inevitable, and opened the door for her. The big white house glowed on the hill above them, tranquil in the afternoon light, the big red spruce behind it a looming but benign presence; not for the first time, he felt that the tree was somehow guarding the house—and in his present fragile mental state, found that notion a comfort.

They made a short detour, so that he could properly admire the new pit and be told all about the internal workings of a groundhog kiln. He failed to follow these in any detail, only grasping the notion that the point was to make the inside very hot, but he found the flow of Brianna's explanation soothing.

". . . bricks for the chimney," she was saying, pointing at the far end of the eight-foot pit, which at present resembled nothing so much as the resting place for an extremely large coffin. She'd made a nice, neat job of it so far, though; the corners were squared as though done with a instrument of some sort, and the walls painstakingly smoothed. He said as much, and she beamed at him, thumbing a lock of red hair behind her ear.

"It needs to be a lot deeper," she said, "maybe another three feet. But the dirt here is really good for digging; it's soft, but it doesn't crumble too much. I hope I can finish the hole before it starts to snow, but I don't know." She rubbed a knuckle under her nose, squinting dubiously at the hole. "I really need to card and spin enough more wool to weave the fabric for winter shirts for you and Jem, but I'll have to pick and preserve for the next week or so, and—"

"I'll dig it for you."

She stood on tiptoe and kissed him, just under the ear, and he laughed, suddenly feeling better.

"Not for this winter," she said, taking him contentedly by the arm, "but eventually—I'm wondering if I can vent some of the heat from the kiln, and run it under the floor of the cabin. You know what a Roman hypocaust is?"

"I do." He turned to eye the foundation of his domicile, a simple hollow base of fieldstone on which the log walls were built. The notion of central heating in a crude mountain cabin made him want to laugh, but there was really nothing impossible about it, he supposed. "You'd what? Run pipes of warm air through the foundation stones?"

"Yes. Always assuming I can actually make good pipes, which remains to be seen. What do you think?"

He glanced from the proposed project up the hill to the Big House. Even at this distance, a mound of dirt by the foundation was visible, evidence of the white sow's burrowing capabilities.

"I think ye run a great danger of having that big white buggeress transfer her affections to us, if ye make a cozy warm den under our house."

"Buggeress?" she said, diverted. "Is that physically possible?"

"It's a metaphysical description," he informed her. "And ye saw what she tried to do to Major MacDonald."

"That pig really doesn't like Major MacDonald," Bree said reflectively. "I wonder why not?"

"Ask your mother; she's none so fond of him, either."

"Oh, well, that—" She stopped suddenly, lips pursed, and looked thoughtfully at the Big House. A shadow passed the window of the surgery, someone moving inside. "Tell you what. You find Da and have a drink with him, and while you're doing that, I'll tell Mama about Marsali and Fergus. She might have a good idea."

"I don't know that it's a medical problem, exactly," he said. "But anesthetizing Germain would certainly be a start."

27

The Malting-Floor

I could smell the sweet, musty scent of damp grain on the wind as I made my way up the trail. It was nothing like the heady pungency of the barm mash, the faintly coffeelike toasted smell of malting, nor yet the reek of distilling—but still spoke as strongly of whisky. It was a very fragrant business, making *uisge-baugh,* and the reason why the whisky clearing was located nearly a mile from the Big House. As it was, I often caught a wild faint scent of spirit through my open surgery windows when the wind was right and the mash was making.

The whisky-making had its own cycle, and one that everyone on the Ridge was subconsciously attuned to, whether directly involved in it or not. Which was how I knew without asking that the barley in the malting shed had just begun its germination, and therefore, Marsali would be there, turning and spreading the grain evenly before the malting fire was lit.

The grain must be allowed to germinate, to assure a maximal sweetness—but must not sprout, or the mash would have a bitter taste and be ruined. No more than twenty-four hours must pass after germination began, and I had smelled the fecund damp scent of the grain begin to rise as I foraged in the woods the afternoon before. The time was here.

It was by far the best place to have a private conversation with Marsali; the whisky clearing was the only place she was ever without a cacophonous assortment of children. I often thought that she valued the solitude of the work much more than the share of whisky Jamie gave her for minding the grain—valuable though *that* was.

Brianna told me that Roger had gallantly offered to have a

word with Fergus, but I thought that I should talk to Marsali first, just to find out what was really going on.

What ought I to say? I wondered. A straightforward *"Is Fergus beating you?"* I couldn't quite believe that, despite—or perhaps because of—an intimate knowledge of emergency rooms filled with the debris of domestic disputes.

It wasn't that I thought Fergus incapable of violence; he'd seen—and experienced—any amount of it from an early age, and growing up among Highlanders in the middle of the Rising and its aftermath probably did not inculcate a young man with any deep regard for the virtues of peace. On the other hand, Jenny Murray had had a hand in his upbringing.

I tried and failed to imagine any man who had lived with Jamie's sister for more than a week *ever* lifting his hand to a woman. Besides, I knew by my own observations that Fergus was a very gentle father, and there was usually an easiness between him and Marsali that seemed—

There was a sudden commotion overhead. Before I could so much as glance up, something huge crashed down through the branches in a shower of dust and dead pine needles. I leapt backward and swung my basket up in instinctive defense—but even as I did so, I realized that I was not in fact being attacked. Germain lay flat on the path in front of me, eyes bulging as he struggled for the breath that had been knocked out of him.

"What on *earth*—?" I began, rather crossly. Then I saw that he was clutching something to his chest; a late nest, filled with a clutch of four greenish eggs, which he had miraculously contrived not to break in his fall.

"For . . . *Maman*," he gasped, grinning up at me.

"*Very* nice," I said. I had had enough to do with young males—well, any age, really; they all did it—to realize the complete futility of reproach in such situations, and since he had broken neither the eggs nor his legs, I merely took the nest and held it while he gulped for air and my heart resumed beating at its normal speed.

Recovered, he scrambled to his feet, disregarding the dirt, pitch, and broken pine needles that covered him from head to toe.

"*Maman*'s in the shed," he said, reaching for his treasure. "You come too, *Grandmère*?"

"Yes. Where are your sisters?" I asked suspiciously. "Are you meant to be watching them?"

"Non," he said airily. "They are at home; that's where women belong."

"Oh, really? And who told you that?"

"I forget." Thoroughly recovered, he hopped ahead of me, singing a song, the refrain of which seemed to be *"Na tuit, na tuit, na tuit, Germain!"*

Marsali was indeed at the whisky clearing; her cap, cloak, and gown hung from a branch of the yellow-leaved persimmon, and a clay firepot full of coals sat nearby, smoking in readiness.

The malting floor had been enclosed now by proper walls, making a shed in which the damp grain could be heaped, first to germinate and then to be gently toasted by a low-burning fire under the floor. The ash and charcoal had been scraped out and oak wood for a new fire laid in the space beneath the stilted floor, but it wasn't yet lit. Even without a fire, the shed was warm; I felt it from several feet away. As the grain germinated, it gave off such heat that the shed fairly glowed with it.

A rhythmic shush and scrape came from within; Marsali was turning the grain with a wooden shovel, making sure it was evenly spread before lighting the malting fire. The door of the shed was open, but there were of course no windows; from a distance, I could see only a dim shadow moving within.

The shushing of the grain had masked our footsteps; Marsali looked up, startled, when my body blocked the light from the doorway.

"Mother Claire!"

"Hallo," I said cheerfully. "Germain said you were here. I thought I'd just—"

"Maman! Look, look, see what I have!" Germain pushed past me with single-minded eagerness, thrusting out his prize. Marsali smiled at him, and pushed a damp strand of fair hair back behind her ear.

"Oh, aye? Well, that's grand, no? Let's take it out to the light, shall we, so I can have a proper look."

She stepped out of the shed, sighing in pleasure at the touch of the cool air. She was stripped to her shift, the muslin so wet with sweat that I could see not only the dark rounds of her areolae, but even the tiny bulge of her popped-out navel, where the cloth clung to the massive curves of her belly.

Marsali sat down with another huge sigh of relief, stretching her legs out, bare toes pointed. Her feet were somewhat swollen, and blue veins showed, distended, beneath the transparent skin of her legs.

"Ah, it's good to sit! So then, *a chuisle,* show me what ye've got."

I took the opportunity to circle round behind her, as Germain displayed his prize, and covertly check for bruises or other sinister signs.

She was thin—but Marsali simply *was* thin, bar the bulge of her pregnancy, and always had been. Her arms were slender, but hard with muscle, as were her legs. There were smudges of tiredness beneath her eyes—but she had three small children, after all, besides the discomforts of pregnancy to keep her awake. Her face was rosy and damp, thoroughly healthy-looking.

There were a couple of small bruises on her lower legs, but I dismissed those; pregnant women did bruise easily, and with all the obstructions presented by living in a log cabin and traversing wild mountains, there were few people on the Ridge—male *or* female—not sporting the odd contusion.

Or was I only seeking excuses, not wanting to admit the possibility of what Brianna had suggested?

"One for me," Germain was explaining, touching the eggs, "and one for Joan, and one for Félicité, and one for *Monsieur L'Oeuf.*" He pointed at the melonlike swell of her stomach.

"Ah, now, what a sweet lad," Marsali said, pulling him close and kissing his smudged forehead. "Ye're my wee nestling, to be sure."

Germain's beam of pleasure faded into a look of speculation as he came in contact with his mother's protruding belly. He patted it cautiously.

"When the egg hatches inside, what do you do with the shell?" he inquired. "Can I have it?"

Marsali went pink with suppressed laughter.

"People dinna come in shells," she said. "Thank God."

"You are sure, *Maman*?" He eyed her belly dubiously, then poked it gently. "It *feels* like an egg."

"Well, so it does, but it's not. That's only what Papa and I call a wee one before it's born. *You* were '*Monsieur L'Oeuf*' once, aye?"

"I was?" Germain looked thunderstruck at this revelation.

"Ye were. So were your sisters."

Germain frowned, shaggy blond fringe almost touching his nose.

"No, they weren't. They are *Mademoiselles L'Oeufs.*"

"*Oui, certainement,*" Marsali said, laughing at him. "And perhaps this one is, too—but *Monsieur* is easier to say. Here, look." She leaned back a little and pushed a hand firmly into the side of her mound. Then she seized Germain's hand and put it on the spot. Even from where I stood, I could see the surge of flesh as the baby kicked vigorously in response to being poked.

Germain jerked his hand away, startled, then put it back, looking fascinated, and pushed.

"Hello!" he said loudly, putting his face close to his mother's belly. "*Comment ça va* in there, *Monsieur L'Oeuf*?"

"He's fine," his mother assured him. "Or she. But babies dinna talk right at first. Ye ken that much. Félicité doesna say anything but 'Mama' yet."

"Oh, aye." Losing interest in his impending sibling, he stooped to pick up an interesting-looking stone.

Marsali lifted her head, squinting at the sun.

"Ye should go home, Germain. Mirabel will be wanting milked, and I've a bit to do here yet. Go and help Papa, aye?" Mirabel was a goat, and a sufficiently new addition to the household as still to be interesting, for Germain brightened at the suggestion.

"*Oui, Maman. Au'voir, Grandmère!*" He took aim and flipped his rock at the shed, missing it, then turned and scampered toward the path.

"Germain!" Marsali called after him. "*Na tuit!*"

"What does that mean?" I asked curiously. "It's Gaelic, is it—or French?"

"It's the Gaelic," she said, smiling. "It means 'Don't fall!'" She shook her head in mock dismay. "That laddie canna stay out of trees to save his life." Germain had left the nest with its eggs; she set it gently on the ground, and I saw then the faint yellowed ovals on the underside of her forearm—faded, but just as Brianna had described them.

"And how *is* Fergus?" I asked, as though it had anything to do with the conversation.

"He's well enough," she replied, a look of wariness closing over her features.

"Really?" I glanced deliberately at her arm, then into her eyes. She flushed, and turned her arm quickly, hiding the marks.

"Aye, he's fine!" she said. "He's no verra good at the milking just yet, but he'll have the way of it soon enough. It's awkward wi' the one hand, to be sure, but he's—"

I sat down on the log beside her, and took hold of her wrist, turning it over.

"Brianna told me," I said. "Did Fergus do this?"

"Oh." She seemed embarrassed, and pulled her wrist away, pressing the forearm against her belly to hide the marks. "Well, aye. Aye, he did."

"Do you want me to speak to Jamie about it?"

A rich tide of color surged into her face, and she sat up in alarm.

"Christ, no! Da would break Fergus's neck! And it wasna his fault, really."

"Certainly it was his fault," I said firmly. I had seen all too many beaten women in Boston emergency rooms, all of whom claimed that it wasn't really their husband's or boyfriend's fault. Granted, the women often *did* have something to do with it, but still—

"But it wasn't!" Marsali insisted. The color had not gone from her face; if anything, it intensified. "I—he—I mean, he grabbed my arm, aye, but 'twas only because I . . . er . . . well, I was tryin' to brain him wi' a stick of wood at the time." She glanced away, blushing fiercely.

"Oh." I rubbed my nose, a little taken aback. "I see. And why were you trying to do that? Was he . . . attacking you?"

She sighed, shoulders slumping a little.

"Oh. No. Weel, it was because Joanie spilled the milk, and he shouted at her, and she cried, and . . ." She shrugged a little, looking uncomfortable. "I just had a wee de'il sittin' on my shoulder, I suppose."

"It's not like Fergus to shout at the children, is it?"

"Oh, no, it's not!" she said quickly. "He hardly ever . . . well, he didna used to, but with so many . . . well, I couldna blame him, this time. It took him a terrible time to milk the goat, and then to have it all spilt and wasted—I would ha' shouted, too, I expect."

Her eyes were fixed on the ground, avoiding mine, and she was fingering the seam of her shift, running a thumb over and over the stitching.

"Small children can certainly be trying," I agreed, with vivid memories of an incident involving a two-year-old Brianna, a phone call that had distracted me, a large bowl of spaghetti with meatballs, and Frank's open briefcase. Frank normally exhibited a saintly degree of patience with Bree—if somewhat less with me—but on that particular occasion his bellows of outrage had rattled the windows.

And now that I recalled the occasion, I actually *had* thrown a meatball at him in a fury verging on hysteria. So had Bree, though she had done it out of glee, rather than vindictiveness. Had I been standing by the stove at the time, it might easily have been the pot I threw. I rubbed a finger under my nose, not sure whether to regret the memory or to laugh at it. I never did get the stains out of the rug.

It was a shame that I couldn't share the memory with Marsali, as she was in ignorance not only of spaghetti and briefcases, but also of Frank. She was still looking down, scuffing at the dead oak leaves with a pointed toe.

"'Twas all my fault, really," she said, and bit her lip.

"No, it wasn't." I squeezed her arm in reassurance. "Things like that are no one's fault; accidents happen, people get upset . . . but it all comes right in the end." So it did, I thought—though often not in any expected way.

She nodded, but the shadow still lay on her face, her lower lip tucked in.

"Aye, it's only . . ." she began, then trailed off.

I sat patiently, careful not to push her. She wanted—needed—to talk. And I needed to hear it, before deciding what—or if—to tell Jamie. There was something going on between her and Fergus, that was sure.

"I . . . was just thinking of it now, whilst I was shoveling. I wouldna have done it, I don't think, only it minded me so much . . . it was only I felt as though it was the same again. . . ."

"The same as what?" I asked, when it became clear that she had trailed off.

"I spilt the milk," she said, all in a rush. "When I was a wean. I was hungry, and I reached to pull the jug, and it spilled."

"Oh?"

"Aye. And he shouted." Her shoulders hunched a little, as though in memory of a blow.

"Who shouted?"

"I dinna ken, for sure. It might ha' been my father, Hugh—but it might have been Simon—Mam's second husband. I dinna really remember—only bein' so scairt that I wet myself, and that made him angrier." Color flamed in her face, and her toes curled with shame.

"My mother cried, for it was all the food there was, a bit o' bread and milk, and now the milk was gone—but *he* shouted that he couldna bear the noise, for Joan and I were both howling, too . . . and then he slapped my face, and Mam went for him bald-heided, and he pushed her so she fell against the hearth and smacked her face on the chimney—I could see the blood running from her nose."

She sniffed and brushed a knuckle under her own nose, blinking, her eyes still fixed on the leaves.

"He stamped out, then, slammin' the door, and Joanie and I rushed up to Mam, both shriekin' our heids off, for we thought she was deid . . . but she got up onto her hands and knees and told us it was all right, it would be all right—and her swayin' to and fro, with her cap fallen off and strings of bloody snot dripping from her face onto the floor . . . I'd forgot that. But when Fergus started shouting at poor wee Joanie . . . 'twas like he was Simon. Or maybe Hugh. *Him,* whoever he was." She closed her eyes and heaved a deep sigh, leaning forward so her arms cradled the burden of her pregnancy.

I reached out and smoothed the damp strings of hair out of her face, brushing them back from her rounded brow.

"You miss your mother, don't you?" I said softly. For the first time, I felt some sympathy for her mother, Laoghaire, as well as for Marsali.

"Oh, aye," Marsali said simply. "Something terrible." She sighed again, closing her eyes as she leaned her cheek against my hand. I drew her head against me, holding her, and stroked her hair in silence.

It was late afternoon, and the shadows lay long, cold in the oak wood. The heat had left her now, and she shivered briefly in the cooling air, a stipple of gooseflesh coming up on her fine-boned arms.

"Here," I said, standing up and swinging the cloak off my shoulders. "Put this on. You don't want to take a chill."

"Ah, no, it's all right." She straightened up, shaking back her hair, and wiped her face with the back of a hand. "There's no but a bit more to do here, and then I've got to be going home and making up the supper—"

"I'll do it," I said firmly, and tucked the cloak around her shoulders. "You rest a bit."

The air inside the tiny shed was ripe enough to make one light-headed, all by itself, thick with the fecund musk of sprouting grain and the fine sharp dust of barley hulls. The warmth was welcoming after the chill of the air outside, but within moments, my skin was damp beneath dress and shift, and I pulled the gown off over my head and hung it on a nail by the door.

No matter; she was right, there wasn't much to be done. The work would keep me warm, and then I would walk home with Marsali straightaway. I would make supper for the family, letting her rest—and while I was about it, I'd perhaps have a word with Fergus and discover more about what was going on.

Fergus could have been making the supper, I thought, frowning as I dug into the dim heaps of sticky grain. Not that he would think of such a thing, the little French layabout. Milking the goat was as far as he was likely to go in the direction of "women's work."

Then I thought of Joan and Félicité, and felt more charitable toward Fergus. Joan was three, Félicité one and a half—and anyone alone in a house with those two had my complete sympathy, no matter *what* kind of work they were doing.

Joan was outwardly a sweet brown wren of a child, and by herself was even-tempered and biddable—to a point. Félicité was the spitting image of her father, dark, fine-boned, and given to alternate bouts of languishing charm and intemperate passion. Together . . . Jamie referred to them casually as the hell-kits, and if they were at home, it was no wonder that Germain was out wandering in the woods—nor that Marsali found it a relief to be out here by herself, doing heavy labor.

"Heavy" was the operative term, I thought, thrusting the

shovel in again and heaving. Sprouting grain was damp grain, and each shovelful weighed pounds. The turned grain was patchy, splotched dark with moisture from the underlying layers. The unturned grain was paler in color, even in the failing light. Only a few mounds of pale grain remained, in the far corner.

I attacked them with a will, realizing as I did so that I was trying very hard not to think of the story Marsali had told me. I didn't want to like Laoghaire—and I didn't. But I didn't want to feel sympathy for her, either, and that was proving harder to avoid.

It hadn't been an easy life for her, apparently. Well, nor had it been for anyone else living in the Highlands then, I thought, grunting as I flung a shovelful of grain to the side. Being a mother was not that easy anywhere—but it seemed she had made a good job of it.

I sneezed from the grain dust, paused to wipe my nose on my sleeve, then went back to shoveling.

It wasn't as though she had tried to steal Jamie from me, after all, I told myself, striving for compassion and high-minded objectivity. Rather the reverse, in fact—or at least she might well see it that way.

The edge of the shovel gritted hard against the floor as I scraped up the last of the grain. I sent the grain flying to the side, then used the flat of the blade to shove some of the new-turned grain into the empty corner and smooth down the highest hillocks.

I knew all the reasons why he said he'd married her—and I believed him. However, the fact remained that the mention of her name conjured up assorted visions—starting with Jamie kissing her ardently in an alcove at Castle Leoch, and ending with him fumbling up her nightgown in the darkness of their marriage bed, hands warm and eager on her thighs—that made me snort like a grampus and feel the blood throb hotly in my temples.

Perhaps, I reflected, I was not really a very high-minded sort of person. Occasionally quite low-minded and grudge-bearing, in fact.

This bout of self-criticism was cut short by the sound of voices and movement outside. I stepped to the door of the shed, squinting against the dazzle of the late afternoon sun.

I couldn't see their faces, nor even tell for sure how many there

might be. Some were on horseback, some on foot, black silhouettes with the sinking sun behind them. I caught a movement in
the corner of my eye; Marsali was on her feet, backing toward the
shed.

"Who are ye, sirs?" she said, chin high.

"Thirsty travelers, mistress," said one of the black forms, edging his horse ahead of the others. "In search of hospitality."

The words were courteous enough; the voice wasn't. I stepped
out of the shed, still gripping the shovel.

"Welcome," I said, making no effort to sound welcoming.
"Stay where you are, gentlemen; we'll be pleased to bring you a
drink. Marsali, will you fetch the keg?"

There was a small keg of raw whisky kept nearby for just such
occasions. My heartbeat was loud in my ears, and I was clutching
the wooden handle of the shovel so tightly that I could feel the
grain of the wood.

It was more than unusual to see so many strangers in the
mountains at one time. Now and then, we would see a hunting
party of Cherokee—but these men were not Indians.

"No bother, mistress," said another of the men, swinging down
off his horse. "I'll help her fetch it. I do think we shall be needing
more than one keg, though."

The voice was English, and oddly familiar. Not a cultivated
accent, but with a careful diction.

"We have only one keg ready," I said, slowly moving sideways
and keeping my eyes on the man who had spoken. He was short
and very slender, and moved with a stiff, jerky gait, like a marionette.

He was moving toward me; so were the others. Marsali had
reached the woodpile, and was fumbling behind the chunks of oak
and hickory. I could hear her breath, harsh in her throat. The keg
was hidden in the woodpile. There was an ax lying next to the
wood, too, I knew.

"Marsali," I said. "Stay there. I'll come and help you."

An ax was a better weapon than a shovel—but two women
against . . . how many men? Ten . . . a dozen . . . more? I blinked,
eyes watering against the sun, and saw several more walk out of
the wood. I could see these clearly; one grinned at me and I had to
steel myself not to look away. His grin broadened.

The short man was coming closer, too. I glanced at him, and a

brief itch of recognition tickled me. Who the hell was he? I knew
him; I'd seen him before—and yet I hadn't any name to attach to
the lantern jaws and narrow brow.

He stank of long-dried sweat, dirt ground into the skin, and the
tang of dribbled urine; they all did, and the odor of them floated
on the wind, feral as the stink of weasels.

He saw me recognize him; thin lips pulled in for a moment,
then relaxed.

"Mrs. Fraser," he said, and the feeling of apprehension deepened sharply as I saw the look in his small, clever eyes.

"I think you have the advantage of me, sir," I said, putting as
bold a face on it as I might. "Have we met?"

He didn't answer that. One side of his mouth turned up a little,
but his attention was distracted by the two men who had lunged
forward to take the keg as Marsali rolled it out of its hiding place.
One had already seized the ax I had my eye on, and was about to
stave in the top of the cask, when the thin man shouted at him.

"Leave it!"

The man looked up at him, mouth open in heavy incomprehension.

"I said leave it!" the thin man snapped, as the other glanced
from the cask to the ax and back in confusion. "We'll take it with
us; I'll not have you all befuddled with drink now!"

Turning to me, as though continuing a conversation, he said,
"Where's the rest of it?"

"That's all there is," Marsali said, before I could answer. She
was frowning at him, wary of him, but also angry. "Take it, then,
and ye must."

The thin man's attention shifted to her for the first time, but he
gave her no more than a casual glance before turning back to me.

"Don't trouble lying to me, Mrs. Fraser. I know well enough
there's more, and I'll have it."

"There is not. Give me that, ye great oaf!" Marsali snatched
the ax neatly from the man holding it, and scowled at the thin
man. "This is how ye repay proper welcome, is it—by thieving?
Well, take what ye came for and leave, then!"

I had no choice but to follow her lead, though alarm bells were
ringing in my brain every time I looked at the thin little man.

"She's right," I said. "See for yourselves." I pointed at the shed,
the mash tubs and the pot still that stood nearby, unsealed and

patently empty. "We're only beginning the malting. It will be weeks yet before there's a new batch of whisky."

Without the slightest change of expression, he took a quick step forward and slapped me hard across the face.

The blow wasn't hard enough to knock me down, but it snapped my head back and left my eyes watering. I was more shocked than hurt, though there was a sharp taste of blood in my mouth, and I could already feel my lip beginning to puff.

Marsali uttered a sharp cry of shock and outrage, and I heard some of the men murmur in interested surprise. They had drawn in, surrounding us.

I put the back of my hand to my bleeding mouth, noticing in a detached sort of way that it was trembling. My brain, though, had withdrawn to a safe distance and was making and discarding suppositions so quickly that they fluttered past, fast as shuffling cards.

Who were these men? How dangerous were they? What were they prepared to do? The sun was setting—how long before Marsali or I was missed and someone came looking for us? Would it be Fergus, or Jamie? Even Jamie, if he came alone . . .

I had no doubt that these men were the same who had burned Tige O'Brian's house, and were likely responsible for the attacks inside the Treaty Line, as well. Vicious, then—but with theft as their major purpose.

There was a copper taste in my mouth; the metal tang of blood and fear. No more than a second had passed in these calculations, but as I lowered my hand, I had concluded that it would be best to give them what they wanted, and hope that they left with the whisky at once.

I had no chance to say so, though. The thin man seized my wrist and twisted viciously. I felt the bones shift and crack with a tearing pain, and sank to my knees in the leaves, unable to make more than a small, breathless sound.

Marsali made a louder sound and moved like a striking snake. She swung the ax from the shoulder with all the power of her bulk behind it, and the blade sank deep in the shoulder of the man beside her. She wrenched it free and blood sprayed warm across my face, pattering like rain upon the leaves.

She screamed, high and thin, and the man screamed, too, and then the whole clearing was in motion, men surging inward with a roar like collapsing surf. I lunged forward and seized the thin man's knees, butted my head hard upward into his crotch. He made a choking wheeze and fell on top of me, flattening me to the ground.

I squirmed out from under his knotted body, knowing only that I had to get to Marsali, get between her and the men—but they were upon her. A scream cut in half by the sound of fists on flesh, and a dull boom as bodies fell hard against the wall of the malting shed.

The clay firepot was in reach. I seized it, heedless of its searing heat, and flung it straight into the group of men. It struck one hard in the back and shattered, hot coals spraying. Men yelled and jumped back, and I saw Marsali slumped against the shed, neck canted over on one shoulder and her eyes rolled back white in her head, legs splayed wide and the shift torn down from her neck, leaving her heavy breasts bare on the bulge of her belly.

Then someone struck me in the side of the head and I flew sideways, skidding through the leaves and ending boneless, flat on the ground, unable to rise or move or think or speak.

A great calm came over me and my vision narrowed—it seemed very slowly—the closing of some great iris, spiraling shut. Before me, I saw the nest on the ground, inches from my nose, its interwoven sticks slender, clever, the four greenish eggs round and fragile, perfect in its cup. Then a heel smashed down on the eggs and the iris closed.

The smell of burning roused me. I could have been unconscious for no more than moments; the clump of dry grass near my face was barely beginning to smoke. A hot coal glowed in a nest of char, shot with sparks. Threads of incandescence shot up the withered grass blades and the clump burst into flame, just as hands seized me by arm and shoulder, dragging me up.

Still dazed, I flailed at my captor as he lifted me, but was hustled unceremoniously to one of the horses, heaved up, and flung across the saddle with a force that knocked the wind out of me. I had barely the presence of mind to grab at the stirrup leather, as someone smacked the horse's rump and we set off at a bruising trot.

Between dizziness and jostling, everything I saw was frac-

tured, crazed like broken glass—but I caught one last glimpse of
Marsali, now lying limp as a rag doll among a dozen tiny fires, as
the scattered coals began to catch and burn.

I made some strangled noise, trying to call to her, but it was
lost in the clatter of harness and men's voices, speaking urgently,
near at hand.

"You crazed, Hodge? You don't want that woman. Put her
back!"

"I shan't." The small man's voice sounded cross, but controlled, somewhere near at hand. "She'll show us to the whisky."

"Whisky'll do us no good if we're dead, Hodge! That's Jamie
Fraser's *wife*, for Christ's sake!"

"I know who she is. Get on with you!"

"But he—you don't know the man, Hodge! I see him one
time—"

"Spare me your memories. Get *on*, I said!"

This last was punctuated by a sudden vicious *thunk*, and a startled sound of pain. A pistol butt, I thought. Square across the face,
I added mentally, swallowing as I heard the wet, wheezing gasps
of a man with a broken nose.

A hand seized me by the hair and jerked my head round
painfully. The thin man's face stared down at me, eyes narrowed
in calculation. He seemed only to want to assure himself that I
was indeed alive, for he said nothing, and dropped my head again,
indifferent as though it were a pinecone he had picked up along
the way.

Someone was leading the horse I was on; there were several
men on foot, as well. I heard them, calling to one another, half-
running to keep up as the horses lurched up a rise, crashing and
grunting like pigs through the undergrowth.

I couldn't breathe, save in shallow gasps, and was being jolted
unmercifully with each step—but I had no attention to spare for
physical discomfort. Was Marsali dead? She had looked it, surely,
but I'd seen no blood, and I clung to that small fact for the slim—
and temporary—comfort that it was.

Even if she wasn't dead yet, she soon might be. Whether from
injury, shock, a sudden miscarriage—oh, God, oh, God, poor little
Monsieur L'Oeuf—

My hands clenched helpless on the stirrup leathers, desperate.
Who might find her—and when?

It had lacked little more than an hour to suppertime when I had arrived at the malting shed. How late was it now? I caught glimpses of the ground juddering past below, but my hair had come loose and streamed across my face whenever I tried to raise my head. There was a growing chill to the air, though, and a still look to the light that told me the sun was near the horizon. Within a few minutes, the light would start to fade.

And then what? How long before a search began? Fergus would notice Marsali's absence when she didn't appear to cook supper—but would he go to look for her, with the little girls in his care? No, he'd send Germain. That caused my heart to lurch and catch in my throat. For a five-year-old boy to find his mother . . .

I could still smell burning. I sniffed, once, twice, again, hoping that I was imagining it. But above the dust and sweat of horse, the tang of stirrup leather, and the whiff of crushed plants, I could distinctly smell the reek of smoke. The clearing, the shed—or both—were well and truly alight now. Someone would see the smoke, and come. But in time?

I shut my eyes tight, trying to stop thinking, seeking any distraction to keep from seeing in my mind's eye the scene that must be taking place behind me.

There were still voices near. The man they called Hodge again. It must be his horse I rode; he was walking near its head, on the far side of the animal. Someone else was expostulating with him, but to no more effect than the first man.

"Spread them out," he was saying tersely. "Divide the men in two groups—you'll 'ave one, the rest go with me. Join again in three days' time at Brownsville."

Bloody hell. He expected pursuit, and meant to frustrate it by splitting his group and confusing the trail. Frantically, I tried to think of something to drop; surely I had *something* to leave as a means of telling Jamie which way I had been taken.

But I wore nothing save shift, stays, and stockings—my shoes had been lost when they dragged me to the horse. The stockings seemed the only possibility; though the garters, with extreme perversity, were for once snugly tied, and quite out of my reach at the moment.

All around me I could hear the noise of men and horses moving, calling and shoving as the main body split. Hodge chirruped to the horse, and we began to move faster.

My floating hair snagged on a twig as we brushed past a bush, held for a second, then broke free with a painful *ping!* as the twig snapped, ricocheting off my cheekbone and narrowly missing my eye. I said something very rude, and someone—Hodge, for a guess—dealt me a censorious smack across the bottom.

I said something much, much ruder, but under my breath and through clenched teeth. My sole comfort was the thought that it would be no great trick to follow a band such as this, leaving as they were a wide trail of broken branches, hoofprints, and overturned stones.

I'd seen Jamie track things small and sly, as well as large and lumbering—and had seen him check the bark of trees and the twigs of bushes as he went, for scratched bark and betraying tufts of . . . hair.

No one was walking on the side of the horse where my head hung down. Hastily, I began to pluck hairs from my head. Three, four, five—was that enough? I stretched out my hand and dragged it through a yaupon bush; the long, curly hairs drifted on the breeze of the horse's passing, but stayed safely tangled in the jagged foliage.

I did the same thing four times more. Surely he would see at least one of the signs, and would know which trail to follow—if he didn't waste time following the other first. There was nothing I could do about that save pray—and I set in to do that in good earnest, beginning first with a plea for Marsali and *Monsieur L'Oeuf*, whose need was plainly much greater than mine.

We continued upward for quite some time; it was full dark before we reached what seemed to be the summit of a ridge, and I was nearly unconscious, my head throbbing with blood and my stays pushed so hard into my body that I felt each strip of whalebone like a brand against my skin.

I had just enough energy left to push myself backward when the horse stopped. I hit the ground and crumpled at once into a heap, where I sat light-headed and gasping, rubbing my hands, which had swollen from hanging down for so long.

The men were gathered in a small knot, occupied in low-voiced conversation, but too near for me to think of trying to creep away into the shrubbery. One man stood only a few feet away, keeping a steady eye on me.

I looked back the way we had come, half-fearing, half-hoping to see the glow of fire far below. The fire would have drawn attention from someone—someone would know by now what had happened, be even now spreading the alarm, organizing pursuit. And yet . . . Marsali.

Was she already dead, and the baby with her?

I swallowed hard, straining my eyes at the dark, as much to prevent tears as in hopes of seeing anything. As it was, though, the trees grew thick around us, and I could see nothing at all, save variations on inky blackness.

There was no light; the moon had not yet risen, and the stars were still faint—but my eyes had had more than enough time to adapt, and while I was no cat to see in the dark, I could distinguish enough to make a rough count. They were arguing, glancing at me now and then. Perhaps a dozen men . . . How many had there been, originally? Twenty? Thirty?

I flexed my fingers, trembling. My wrist was badly bruised, but that wasn't what was troubling me at present.

It was clear to me—and therefore presumably to them, as well—that they couldn't head directly for the whisky cache, even were I able to find it at night. Whether Marsali survived to talk or not—I felt my throat close at the thought—Jamie would likely realize that the whisky was the intruders' goal, and have it guarded.

Had things not fallen out as they did, the men would ideally have forced me to lead them to the cache, taken the whisky, and fled, hoping to escape before the theft was discovered. Leaving me and Marsali alive to raise the alarm and describe them? I wondered. Perhaps; perhaps not.

In the panic following Marsali's attack, though, the original plan had fallen apart. Now what?

The knot of men was breaking up, though the argument continued. Footsteps approached.

"I tell you, it won't do," one man was saying heatedly. From the thickened voice, I assumed it was the gentleman with the broken nose, undeterred by his injury. "Kill her now. Leave her here; no one'll find her before the beasts have scattered her bones."

"Aye? And if no one finds her, they'll think she's still with us, won't they?"

"But if Fraser catches up to us, and she's not, who shall he blame . . ."

They stopped, four or five of them surrounding me. I scrambled to my feet, my hand closing by reflex around the nearest thing approaching a weapon—an unfortunately small rock.

"How far are we from the whisky?" Hodge demanded. He had taken off his hat, and his eyes gleamed, ratlike in the shadow.

"I don't know," I said, keeping a firm grip on my nerves—and the rock. My lip was still tender, puffed from the blow he had dealt me, and I had to form the words carefully. "I don't know where we *are*."

This was true, though I could have made a reasonable guess. We had traveled for a few hours, mostly upward, and the trees nearby were fir and balsam; I could smell their resin, sharp and clean. We were on the upper slopes, and probably near a small pass that crossed the shoulder of the mountain.

"Kill her," urged one of the others. "She's no good to us, and if Fraser finds her with us—"

"Shut your face!" Hodge rounded on the speaker with such violence that the man, much larger, stepped back involuntarily. That threat disposed of, Hodge ignored him and seized me by the arm.

"Don't play coy with me, woman. You'll tell me what I want to know." He didn't bother with the "or else"—something cold passed across the top of my breast, and the hot sting of the cut followed a second later, as blood began to bloom from it.

"Jesus H. Roosevelt Christ!" I said, more from surprise than pain. I jerked my arm out of his grasp. "I told you, I don't even know where we *are,* you idiot! How do you expect me to tell you where anything else is?"

He blinked, startled, and brought the knife up by reflex, wary, as though he thought I might attack him. Realizing that I wasn't about to, he scowled at me.

"I'll tell you what I *do* know," I said, and was distantly pleased to hear that my voice was sharp and steady. "The whisky cache is about half a mile from the malting shed, roughly northwest. It's in a cave, well-hidden. I could take you there—if we began from the spring where you took me—but that's all I can tell you in the way of direction."

This was true, too. I could find it easily enough—but to give directions? *"Go through a gap in the brush a little way, until you see the cluster of oak where Brianna shot a possum, bear left to a squarish rock with a bunch of adder's-tongue growing over it. . . ."* The fact that the need for my services as a guide was probably all that kept them from killing me on the spot was, of course, a secondary consideration.

It was a very shallow cut; I wasn't bleeding badly at all. My face and hands were ice-cold, though, and small flashing lights came and went at the edges of my vision. Nothing was keeping me upright save a vague conviction that if it came to that, I preferred to die on my feet.

"I tell you, Hodge, you don't want nothing to do with that one—nothing." A larger man had joined the small group round me. He leaned over Hodge's shoulder, looking at me, and nodded. They were all black in the shadow, but this man had a voice tinged with the lilt of Africa—an ex-slave, or perhaps a slave-trader. "That woman—I hear about her. She is a conjure woman. I know them. They are like serpents, conjure wives. You don't touch that one, hear me? She will curse you!"

I managed to give a rather nasty-sounding laugh in answer to this, and the man closest to me took a half-step back. I was vaguely surprised; where had *that* come from?

But I was breathing better now, and the flashing lights were gone.

The tall man stretched his neck, seeing the dark line of blood on my shift.

"You draw her blood? Damn you, Hodge, you done it now." There was a distinct note of alarm in his voice, and he drew back a little, making some sort of sign toward me with one hand.

Without the slightest notion as to what moved me to do it, I dropped the rock, ran the fingers of my right hand across the cut, and in one swift motion, reached out and drew them down the thin man's cheek. I repeated the nasty laugh.

"Curse, is it?" I said. "How's this? Touch me again, and you'll die within twenty-four hours."

The streaks of blood showed dark on the white of his face. He was close enough that I could smell the sourness of his breath, and see the fury gather on his face.

What on earth do you think you are doing, Beauchamp? I thought, utterly surprised at myself. Hodge drew back his fist to strike me, but the large man caught him by the wrist with a cry of fear.

"Don't you do that! You will kill us all!"

"I'll friggin' kill *you* right now, arsebite!"

Hodge was still holding the knife in his other hand; he stabbed awkwardly at the larger man, grunting with rage. The big man gasped at the impact, but wasn't badly stricken—he wrenched at the wrist he held and Hodge gave a high, squealing cry, like a rabbit seized by a fox.

Then the others were all in it, pushing and shouting, grappling for weapons. I turned and ran, but got no more than a few steps before one of them grabbed me, flinging his arms round me and jerking me hard against himself.

"You're not going anywhere, lady," he said, panting in my ear.

I wasn't. He was no taller than I, but a good deal stronger. I lunged against his grip, but he had both arms wrapped tight around me, and squeezed tighter. I stood stiff then, heart pounding with anger and fear, not wanting to give him an excuse to maul me. He was excited; I could feel his heart pounding, too, and smell the reek of fresh sweat over the fetor of stale clothes and body.

I couldn't see what was going on, but I didn't think they were fighting so much as merely shouting at each other now. My captor shifted his weight and cleared his throat.

"Ahh . . . where do you come from, ma'am?" he asked, quite politely.

"What?" I said, no end startled. "Come from? Er . . . ah . . . England. Oxfordshire, originally. Then Boston."

"Oh? I'm from the north myself."

I repressed the automatic urge to reply, "Pleased to meet you," since I wasn't, and the conversation languished.

The fight had stopped, abruptly as it had started. With a lot of token snarling and growling, the rest of them backed down in the face of Hodge's bellowed assertions that he was in command here, and they'd bleedin' well do as he said or take the consequences.

"He means it, too," muttered my captor, still pressing me firmly to his filthy bosom. "You don't want to cross him, lady, believe me."

"Hmph," I said, though I assumed the advice was well-meant. I had been hoping the conflict would be noisy and prolonged, thus increasing the chances of Jamie catching up to us.

"And where is this Hodge from, speaking of origins?" I asked. He still seemed remarkably familiar to me; I was sure I had seen him *somewhere*—but where?

"Hodgepile? Ahhh . . . England, I reckon," said the young man gripping me. He sounded surprised. "Don't he sound like it?"

Hodge? Hodgepile? That rang a bell, certainly, but . . .

There was a good deal of muttering and milling round, but in much too little time, we were off again. This time, thank God, I was allowed to ride astride, though my hands were tied and bound to the saddle.

We moved very slowly; there was a trail of sorts, but even with the faint light shed by a rising moon, the going was difficult. Hodgepile no longer led the horse I rode; the young man who had recaptured me held the bridle, tugging and coaxing the increasingly reluctant horse through the thickets of brush. I could glimpse him now and then, slender, with thick, wild hair that hung past his shoulders and rendered him lion-maned in silhouette.

The threat of immediate death had receded a little, but my stomach was still knotted and the muscles of my back stiff with apprehension. Hodgepile had his way for the moment, but there had been no real agreement among the men; one of those in favor of killing me and leaving my corpse for the skunks and weasels might easily decide to put a quick end to the controversy with a lunge out of the dark.

I could hear Hodgepile's voice, sharp and hectoring, somewhere up ahead. He seemed to be passing up and down the column, bullying, nagging, nipping like a sheepdog, trying to keep his flock on the move.

They *were* moving, though it was clear even to me that the horses were tired. The one I rode was shambling, jerking her head with irritation. God knew where the marauders had come from, or how long they had traveled before reaching the whisky clearing. The men were slowing, too, a gradual fog of fatigue settling on them as the adrenaline of flight and conflict receded. I could feel lassitude stealing upon me, too, and fought against it, struggling to stay alert.

It was still early autumn, but I was wearing only my shift and stays, and we were high enough that the air chilled rapidly after dark. I shivered constantly, and the cut on my chest burned as the tiny muscles flexed beneath the skin. It wasn't at all serious, but what if it became infected? I could only hope that I would live long enough for that to be a problem.

Hard as I tried, I could *not* keep from thinking of Marsali, nor keep my mind from making medical speculations, envisioning everything from concussion with intracranial swelling to burns with smoke inhalation. I could do something—perhaps even an emergency C-section—if I were there. No one else could.

I clenched my hands hard on the edge of the saddle, straining against the rope that bound them. I needed to be there!

But I was not, and might never be.

The quarreling and muttering had all but ceased as the darkness of the forest closed in upon us, but a lingering sense of unease lay heavy on the group. In part, I thought it was apprehension and fear of pursuit, but in much greater part, a sense of internal discord. The fight had not been settled, merely postponed to a more convenient season. A sense of simmering conflict was sharp in the air.

A conflict focused squarely on *me*. Unable to see clearly during the argument, I couldn't be sure which men held which opinions, but the division was clear: one party, headed by Hodgepile, was in favor of keeping me alive, at least long enough to lead them to the whisky. A second group was for cutting their losses, and my throat. And a minority opinion, voiced by the gentleman with the African speech, was for turning me loose, the sooner the better.

Obviously, it would behoove me to cultivate this gentleman, and try to turn his beliefs to my advantage. How? I'd made a start by cursing Hodgepile—and I was still quite startled that I'd done that. I didn't think it would be advisable to start cursing them wholesale, though—ruin the effect.

I shifted in the saddle, which was beginning to chafe me badly. This wasn't the first time I'd had men recoil from me in fear of what they thought I was. Superstitious fear could be an effective weapon—but it was a very dangerous one to use. If I truly frightened them, they'd kill me without a moment's hesitation.

We had crossed into the pass. There were few trees among the boulders here, and as we emerged onto the far side of the mountain, the sky opened out before me, vast and glowing, fiery with a multitude of stars.

I must have let out a gasp at the sight, for the young man leading my horse paused, lifting his own head skyward.

"Oh," he said softly. He stared for a moment, then was pulled back to earth by the passage of another horse that brushed past us, its rider turning to peer closely at me as it did so.

"Did you have stars like this—where you came from?" my escort asked.

"No," I said, still slightly under the spell of the silent grandeur overhead. "Not so bright."

"No, they weren't," he said, shaking his head, and pulled at the rein. That seemed an odd remark, but I could make nothing of it. I might have engaged him in further conversation—God knew I needed all the allies I could get—but there was a shout from up ahead; evidently, we were making camp.

I was untied and pulled off the horse. Hodgepile pushed his way through the scrum and grasped me by the shoulder.

"You try to run, woman, and you'll wish you 'adn't." He squeezed viciously, fingers digging into my flesh. "I need you alive—I don't need you 'ole."

Still gripping my shoulder, he lifted his knife and pressed the flat of the blade against my lips, jammed the tip of it up my nose, then leaned close enough that I felt the moist warmth of his very repugnant breath on my face.

"The one thing I *won't* cut off is your tongue," he whispered. The knife blade drew slowly out of my nose, down my chin, along the line of my neck, and circled round the curve of my breast. "You take my meaning, do you?"

He waited until I managed a nod, then released me and disappeared into the darkness.

If he meant to unnerve me, he'd managed nicely. I was sweating despite the chill, and still shaking when a tall shadow loomed up beside me, took one of my hands, and pressed something into it.

"My name is Tebbe," he murmured. "You remember that—Tebbe. Remember I was good to you. Tell your spirits they don't hurt Tebbe, he was good to you."

I nodded once more, astonished, and was left again, this time with a lump of bread in my hand. I ate it hastily, observing that while very stale, it had originally been good dark rye bread, of the sort the German women of Salem made. Had the men attacked some house near there, or merely bought the bread?

A horse's saddle had been flung down on the ground near me; a canteen hung from the pommel, and I sank down on my knees to drink from it. The bread and the water—tasting of canvas and wood—tasted better than anything I'd eaten in a long while. I'd noticed before that standing very close to death improves the appetite remarkably. Still, I did hope for something more elaborate as a last meal.

Hodgepile returned a few minutes later, with rope. He didn't bother with further threats, evidently feeling that he'd made his point. He merely tied me hand and foot, and pushed me down on the ground. No one spoke to me, but someone, with a kindly impulse, threw a blanket over me.

The camp settled quickly. No fire was lit, and so no supper was cooked; the men presumably refreshed themselves in the same makeshift way I had, then scattered into the wood to seek their rest, leaving the horses tethered a little way off.

I waited until the comings and goings died down, then took the blanket in my teeth and wriggled carefully away from the spot where I had been placed, making my way inchworm fashion to another tree, a dozen yards away.

I had no thought of escape in doing this; but if one of the bandits in favor of disposing of me should think to take advantage of the darkness in order to achieve their aims, I didn't mean to be lying there like a staked goat. With luck, if anyone came skulking round the spot where I'd been, I would have enough warning to scream for help.

I knew beyond the shadow of a doubt that Jamie would come. My job was to survive until he did.

Panting, sweating, covered with crumbled leaves and with my stockings in rags, I curled up under a big hornbeam, and burrowed back under the blanket. Thus concealed, I had a try at undoing the knots in the rope around my wrists with my teeth. Hodgepile had tied them, though, and had done so with military thoroughness. Short of gnawing gopherlike through the ropes themselves, I was going nowhere.

Military. It was that thought that recalled suddenly to me who he was, and where I had seen him before. Arvin Hodgepile! He had been the clerk at the Crown's warehouse in Cross Creek. I had met him briefly, three years before, when Jamie and I brought the body of a murdered girl to the sergeant of the garrison there.

Sergeant Murchison was dead—and I'd thought Hodgepile

was, as well, killed in the conflagration that had destroyed the warehouse and its contents. So, a deserter, then. Either he had had time to escape the warehouse before it went up in flames, or had simply not been there at the time. In either case, he'd been clever enough to realize that he could take this opportunity to disappear from His Majesty's army, leaving his death to be assumed.

What he had been doing since then was clear, too. Wandering the countryside, stealing, robbing, and killing—and collecting a number of like-minded companions along the way.

Not that they appeared to be of one mind just at present. While Hodgepile might be the self-proclaimed leader of this gang at the moment, it was plain to see that he hadn't held the position for long. He wasn't accustomed to command, didn't know how to manage men, save by threat. I'd seen many military commanders in my time, good and bad, and recognized the difference.

I could hear Hodgepile even now, voice raised in distant argument with someone. I'd seen his sort before, vicious men who could temporarily cow those near them by outbursts of unpredictable violence. They seldom lasted long—and I doubted that Hodgepile was going to last much longer.

He wasn't going to last any longer than it took for Jamie to find us. That thought calmed me like a slug of good whisky. Jamie would surely be looking for me by now.

I curled tighter under my blanket, shivering a little. Jamie would need light to track at night—torches. That would make him and his party visible—and vulnerable—if they came within sight of the camp. The camp itself wouldn't be visible; there was no fire lit, and the horses and men were scattered through the wood. I knew sentries had been posted; I could hear them moving in the wood now and then, talking low-voiced.

But Jamie was no fool, I told myself, trying to drive away visions of ambush and massacre. He would know, from the freshness of the horses' dung, if he were drawing close, and certainly wouldn't be marching right up to the camp, torches blazing. If he had tracked the party this far, he would—

The sound of quiet footsteps froze me. They were coming from the direction of my original resting place, and I cowered under my blanket like a field mouse with a weasel in sight.

The steps shuffled slowly to and fro, as though someone was

poking his way through the dried leaves and pine needles, looking for me. I held my breath, though surely no one could hear that, with the night wind sighing through the branches overhead.

I strained my eyes at the darkness, but could make out nothing more than a faint blur moving among the tree trunks, a dozen yards away. A sudden thought struck me—could it be Jamie? If he had come close enough to locate the camp, he would very likely steal in on foot, looking for me.

I drew breath at the thought, straining against my bonds. I wanted urgently to call out, but didn't dare. If it *should* be Jamie, calling to him would expose his presence to the bandits. If I could hear the sentries, they could certainly hear me.

But if it were *not* Jamie, but one of the bandits, seeking to kill me quietly . . .

I let my breath out very slowly, every muscle in my body clenched and trembling. It was cool enough, but I was bathed in sweat; I could smell my own body, the reek of fear mingling with the colder smells of earth and vegetation.

The blur had vanished, the footsteps gone, and my heart was pounding like a kettledrum. The tears I had held back for hours seeped out, hot on my face, and I wept, shaking silently.

The night was immense around me, the darkness filled with threat. Overhead, the stars hung bright and watchful in the sky, and at some point, I slept.

28

Curses

I woke just before dawn, in a muck sweat and with a throbbing headache. The men were already moving, grumbling about the lack of coffee or breakfast.

Hodgepile stopped beside me, looking down with narrowed eyes. He glanced toward the tree beneath which he had left me the night before and the deep furrow of disturbed leaf mold I had created in worm-crawling toward my present spot. He had very little in the way of lips, but his lower jaw compressed in displeasure.

He pulled the knife from his belt, and I felt the blood drain from my face. However, he merely knelt and cut my bonds, rather than slicing off a finger by way of expressing his emotions.

"We leave in five minutes," he said, and stalked off. I was quivering and faintly nauseated with fear, and so stiff that I could barely stand. I managed to get to my feet, though, and staggered the short distance to a small stream.

The air was damp and I was now chilly in my sweat-soaked shift, but cold water splashed on my hands and face seemed to help a little, soothing the throb behind my right eye. I had just time to make a hasty toilet, removing the rags of my stockings and running wet fingers through my hair, before Hodgepile reappeared to march me off again.

This time, I was put on a horse, but not tied, thank God. I wasn't allowed to hold the reins, though; my mount was on a leading rein, held by one of the bandits.

It was my first chance to get a good look at my captors, as they came out of the wood and shook themselves into rough order, coughing, spitting, and urinating on trees without reference to my presence. Beyond Hodgepile, I counted twelve more men—a baker's dozen of villains.

It was easy to pick out the man called Tebbe; his height aside, he was a mulatto. There was another man of mixed blood—black and Indian, I thought—but he was short and squat. Tebbe didn't glance in my direction, but went about his business with head lowered, scowling.

That was a disappointment; I didn't know what had passed among the men during the night, but evidently Tebbe's insistence that I be released was no longer so insistent. A rust-spotted kerchief bound his wrist; that might have something to do with it.

The young man who had guided my horse the night before was also easy to pick out, by way of his long, bushy hair, but he didn't come near, and avoided looking at me, too. Rather to my surprise, he was an Indian—not Cherokee; perhaps a Tuscarora? I hadn't expected that from his speech, nor his curly hair. Clearly he was mixed-blood, too.

The rest of the gang were more or less white, but a motley crew, nonetheless. Three of them were no more than half-bearded boys in their mid-teens, scruffy and gangling. They *did* look at me, goggling drop-jawed, and nudging one another. I stared at one of them until he met my eye; he went bright scarlet beneath his sparse whiskers, and looked away.

Fortunately, the shift I was wearing was one with sleeves; the thing covered me decently enough from drawstring neck to the hem at mid-calf, but there was no denying that I felt uncomfortably exposed. The shift was damp and clung limply to the curve of my breasts—a sensation I was uncomfortably aware of. I wished I had kept hold of the blanket.

The men swirled slowly round me, loading the horses, and I had the distinct and unpleasant sense of being the center of the mass—in much the same way a bull's-eye lies at the center of a target. I could only hope that I looked aged and cronelike enough for my state of untidiness to be repellent, rather than interesting; my hair was loose, wild, and tangled as witch's moss around my shoulders, and I certainly *felt* as though I had been crumpled up like an old paper bag.

I held myself bolt upright in the saddle, giving an unfriendly glare to anyone who so much as glanced in my direction. One

man blinked blearily at my bare leg with a faint look of speculation—only to recoil noticeably when he met my eye.

That gave me a momentary feeling of grim satisfaction—
superseded almost immediately by shock. The horses had begun
to move, and as mine obediently followed the man in front of me,
two more men came into view, standing under a big oak. I knew
them both.

Harley Boble was tying the strings on a packsaddle, scowling as he said something to another, larger man. Harley Boble
was an erstwhile thieftaker, now evidently turned thief. A thoroughly nasty little man, he was unlikely to be well-disposed
toward me, owing to an occurrence at a Gathering some time
before.

I wasn't at all pleased to see him here, though I was by no
means surprised to find him in such company. But it was the sight
of his companion that caused my empty stomach to contract, and
my skin to twitch like a horse with flies.

Mr. Lionel Brown, of Brownsville.

He looked up, caught sight of me, and turned hastily away
again, shoulders hunching. He must have realized that I had seen
him, though, for he turned back to face me, thin features set in a
sort of weary defiance. His nose was swollen and discolored,
a dark red bulb visible even in the grayish light. He stared at me
for a moment, then nodded as though making some reluctant
acknowledgment, and turned away again.

I risked a glance back over my shoulder as we entered the
trees, but couldn't see him anymore. What was *he* doing here? I
hadn't recognized his voice at the time, but clearly it had been he
who had argued with Hodgepile about the wisdom of taking me.
Little wonder! He wasn't the only one disturbed by our mutual
recognition.

Lionel Brown and his brother, Richard, were traders; the
founders and patriarchs of Brownsville, a tiny settlement in the
hills some forty miles from the Ridge. It was one thing for free-
booters like Boble or Hodgepile to roam the countryside, robbing
and burning; quite another for the Browns of Brownsville to be
providing a base for their depredations. The very last thing in the
world Mr. Lionel Brown could wish would be for me to reach
Jamie with word of what he had been up to.

And I rather thought he would take steps to prevent me doing so. The sun was coming up, beginning to warm the air, but I felt suddenly cold, as though I had been dropped in a well.

Rays of light shone through the branches, gilding the remnants of the night mist that veiled the trees and silvering the dripping edges of their leaves. The trees were alive with birdsong, and a towhee hopped and scratched in a patch of sun, oblivious of the passing men and horses. It was too early yet for flies and mosquitoes, and the soft morning breeze caressed my face. Definitely one of those prospects where only man was vile.

The morning passed quietly enough, but I was aware of the constant state of tension among the men—though no more tense than I was.

Jamie Fraser, where are *you?* I thought, concentrating fiercely on the forest around us. Every distant rustle or snap of twig might presage rescue, and my nerves began to be distinctly frayed in anticipation.

Where? When? How? I had neither reins nor weapons; if—when—an attack was made on the group, my best—well, the only possible—strategy was to fling myself off the horse and run. As we rode I constantly evaluated each patch of witch-hazel and stand of spruce, spotting footholds, plotting a zigzag path through saplings and boulders.

It wasn't only an attack by Jamie and his men that I was preparing for; I couldn't see Lionel Brown, but I knew he was somewhere nearby. A spot between my shoulder blades clenched in a knot, anticipating a knife.

I kept an eye out for potential weapons: rocks of a useful size, branches that might be seized from the ground. If and when I ran, I meant to let no one stop me. But we pushed on, moving as quickly as the horses' footing allowed, men glancing back constantly over their shoulders, hands on their guns. As for me, I was obliged to relinquish my imaginary grasp on each possible weapon in turn as it slid past, out of sight.

To my intense disappointment, we reached the gorge near midday, without incident.

I had visited the gorge once with Jamie. The cataract fell sixty feet down a granite cliff face, sparkling with rainbows and roaring with a voice like the archangel Michael. Fronds of red chokeberry and wild indigo fringed the falls, and yellow poplars overhung the river below the cataract's pool, so thick that no more than a fugitive gleam from the water's surface showed between the banks of lush vegetation. Hodgepile, of course, had not been drawn by the scenic beauty of the spot.

"Get off." A gruff voice spoke near my elbow, and I looked down to see Tebbe. "We will swim the horses across. You come with me."

"I'll take her." My heart sprang up into my throat at the sound of a thickly nasal voice. It was Lionel Brown, pushing his way past an overhanging rope of creeper, dark eyes intent on me.

"Not you." Tebbe rounded on Brown, fist closed.

"Not you," I repeated firmly. "I'm going with him." I slid off the horse and promptly took shelter behind the big mulatto's menacing frame, peering out at Brown from beneath the bigger man's arm.

I wasn't under the slightest illusion about Brown's intent. He wouldn't risk assassinating me under Hodgepile's eye, but he could—and would—drown me easily, and claim it was an accident. The river was shallow here, but still fast; I could hear it whooshing past the rocks near shore.

Brown's eyes darted right, then left, thinking whether to try it on—but Tebbe hunched his massive shoulders, and Brown gave it up as a bad job. He snorted, spat to one side, and stamped away, snapping branches.

I might never have a better chance. Not waiting for the sounds of Brown's huffy exit to subside, I slipped a hand over the big man's elbow and squeezed his arm.

"Thank you," I said, low-voiced. "For what you did last night. Are you badly hurt?"

He glanced down at me, apprehension clear in his face. My touching him plainly disconcerted him; I could feel the tension in his arm as he tried to decide whether to pull away from me or not.

"No," he said at last. "I am all right." He hesitated a moment, but then smiled uncertainly.

It was obvious what Hodgepile intended; the horses were being led, one at a time, down a narrow deer trail that edged the escarpment. We were more than a mile from the cataract, but the air was still loud with its noise. The sides of the gorge plunged steeply down to the water, more than fifty feet below, and the opposite bank was equally steep and overgrown.

A thick fringe of bushes hid the edge of the bank, but I could see that the river spread out here, becoming slower as it shallowed. With no dangerous currents, the horses could be taken downstream, to come out at some random point on the opposite shore. Anyone who had succeeded in tracking us to the gorge would lose the trail here, and have no little difficulty in picking it up on the opposite side.

With an effort, I stopped myself looking back over my shoulder for signs of imminent pursuit. My heart was beating fast. If Jamie was nearby, he would wait and attack the group when they entered the water, when they were most vulnerable. Even if he were not yet near, it would be a confusing business, crossing the river. If there were ever a time to attempt an escape . . .

"You shouldn't go with them," I said conversationally to Tebbe. "You'll die, too."

The arm under my hand jerked convulsively. He glanced down at me, wide-eyed. The sclera of his eyes were yellow with jaundice, and the irises broken, giving him an odd, smudgy stare.

"I told him the truth, you know." I lifted my chin toward Hodgepile, visible in the distance. "He'll die. So will all those with him. There's no need for you to die, though."

He muttered something under his breath, and pressed a fist against his chest. He had something on a string there, hanging beneath his shirt. I didn't know whether it might be a cross or some more pagan amulet, but he seemed to be responding well to suggestion so far.

So close to the river, the air was thick with moisture, live with the smell of green things and water.

"The water is my friend," I said, trying for an air of mystery suitable to a conjure woman. I was not a good liar, but I was lying for my life. "When we go into the river, let go your hold. A water horse will rise up to carry me away."

His eyes couldn't get any wider. Evidently, he'd heard of kelpies, or something like them. Even this far from the cataract, the roar of the water had voices in it—if one chose to listen.

"I am not going away with a water horse," he said with conviction. "I know about them. They take you down, drown you, and eat you."

"It won't eat me," I assured him. "You needn't go near it. Just stand clear, once we're in the water. Keep well away."

And if he did, I'd be under the water and swimming for my life before he could say Jack Robinson. I would be willing to bet that most of Hodgepile's bandits couldn't swim; few people in the mountains could. I flexed my leg muscles, readying myself, aches and stiffness dissolved in a flood of adrenaline.

Half the men were over the edge with the horses already—I could delay Tebbe, I thought, until the rest were safely in the water. Even if he wouldn't deliberately connive at my escape, if I slipped his grasp, I thought he wouldn't try to catch me.

He pulled halfheartedly at my arm, and I stopped abruptly.

"Ouch! Wait, I've stepped on a bur."

I lifted one foot, peering at the sole. Given the dirt and resin stains adhering to it, no one could possibly have told whether I had picked up cockleburs, bramble thorns, or even a horseshoe nail.

"We need to go, woman." I didn't know whether it was my proximity, the roar of the water, or the thought of water horses that was disturbing Tebbe, but he was sweating with nerves; his odor had changed from simple musk to something sharp and pungent.

"Just a moment," I said, pretending to pick at my foot. "Nearly got it."

"Leave it. I will carry you."

Tebbe was breathing heavily, looking back and forth from me to the edge of the gorge, where the deer trail disappeared into the growth, as though fearing the reappearance of Hodgepile.

It wasn't Hodgepile who popped out of the bushes, though. It was Lionel Brown, his face set with purpose, two younger men behind him, looking equally determined.

"I'll take her," he said without preamble, grabbing my arm.

"No!" By reflex, Tebbe clutched my other arm and pulled.

An undignified tug-of-war ensued, with Tebbe and Mr. Brown each jerking one of my arms. Before I could be split like a wishbone, Tebbe fortunately changed tactics. Releasing my arm, he seized me instead about the body and clutched me to himself, kicking out with one foot at Mr. Brown.

The result of this maneuver was to cause Tebbe and myself to fall backward into an untidy pile of arms and legs, while Brown also lost his balance, though I didn't realize at first that he had. All I was aware of was a loud yell and stumbling noises, followed by a crash and the rattle of dislodged stones bounding down a rocky slope.

Disengaging myself from Tebbe; I crawled out, to discover the rest of the men grouped round an ominously flattened spot in the bushes fringing the gorge. One or two were hurriedly fetching ropes and yelling contradictory orders, from which I deduced that Mr. Brown had indeed fallen into the gorge, but was not yet certifiably dead.

I rapidly reversed directions, meaning to dive headfirst into the vegetation, but came up instead against a pair of cracked boots, belonging to Hodgepile. He seized me by the hair and yanked, causing me to shriek and lash out at him in reflex. I caught him across the midriff. He oomphed and went open-mouthed, gasping for air, but didn't let go his iron grip on my hair.

Making furious faces in my direction, he let go then, and boosted me toward the edge of the gorge with a knee. One of the younger men was clinging to the bushes, feeling gingerly for footholds on the slope below, one rope tied round his waist and another slung in a coil over his shoulder.

"Frigging mort!" Hodgepile yelled, digging his fingers into my arm as he leaned through the broken bushes. "What d'ye mean by this, you bitch?"

He capered on the edge of the gorge like Rumpelstiltskin, shaking his fist and hurling abuse impartially at his damaged business partner and at me, while the rescue operations commenced. Tebbe had withdrawn to a safe distance, where he stood looking offended.

At length, Brown was hauled up, groaning loudly, and laid out on the grass. Those men not already in the river gathered round, looking hot and flustered.

"You mean to mend him, conjure woman?" Tebbe asked, glancing skeptically at me. I didn't know whether he meant to cast doubt upon my abilities, or only on the wisdom of my helping Brown, but I nodded, a little uncertainly, and came forward.

"I suppose so." An oath was an oath, though I rather wondered if Hippocrates ever ran into this sort of situation himself. Possibly he did; the ancient Greeks were a violent lot, too.

The men gave way to me easily enough; once having got Brown out of the gorge, it was obvious that they had no notion what to do about him.

I did a hasty triage. Aside from multiple cuts, contusions, and a thick coating of dust and mud, Mr. Lionel Brown had fractured his left leg in at least two places, broken his left wrist, and probably crushed a couple of ribs. Only one of the leg fractures was compound, but it was nasty, the jagged end of the broken thighbone poking through skin and breeches, surrounded by a steadily widening patch of red.

He had unfortunately not severed his femoral artery, since if he had, he would have been dead already. Still, Mr. Brown had probably ceased to be a personal threat to me for the moment, which was all to the good.

Lacking any equipment or medication, bar several filthy neckcloths, a pine branch, and some whisky from a canteen, my ministrations were necessarily limited. I managed—with no little difficulty and quite a lot of whisky—to get the femur roughly straightened and splinted without having Brown die of shock, which I thought no small accomplishment under the circumstances.

It was a difficult job, though, and I was muttering to myself under my breath—something I hadn't realized I was doing, until I glanced up to find Tebbe crouched on his heels on the other side of Brown's body, regarding me with interest.

"Oh, you curse him," he said approvingly. "Yes, that is a good idea."

Mr. Brown's eyes sprang open and bugged out. He was half off his head with pain, and thoroughly drunk by now, but not quite so drunk as to overlook this.

"Make her stop," he said hoarsely. "Here, Hodgepile—make her stop! Make her take it back!"

"'Ere, what's this? What did you say, woman?" Hodgepile had simmered down a bit, but his animus was instantly rekindled by this. He reached down and grabbed my wrist just as I was feeling my way over Brown's injured torso. It was the wrist he had twisted so viciously the day before, and a stab of pain shot up my forearm.

"If you must know, I expect I said 'Jesus H. Roosevelt Christ'!" I snapped. "Let go of me!"

"That's what she said when she cursed you! Get her away from me! Don't let her touch me!" Panicked, Brown made to squirm away from me, a very bad idea for a man with freshly broken bones. He went dead-white under the smears of mud, and his eyes rolled back in his head.

"Look at that! He's dead!" one of the onlookers exclaimed. "She's done it! She witched him!"

This caused no little uproar, between the vocal approbation of Tebbe and his supporters, my own protests, and outcries of concern from Mr. Brown's friends and relations, one of whom squatted down by the body, putting an ear to the chest.

"He's alive!" this man exclaimed. "Uncle Lionel! You all right?"

Lionel Brown groaned loudly and opened his eyes, causing further commotion. The young man who had called him Uncle drew a large knife from his belt and pointed it at me. His eyes were open so wide that the whites showed all around.

"You get back!" he said. "Don't you touch him!"

I raised my hands, palms out, in gesture of abnegation.

"Fine!" I snapped. "I won't!" There was, in fact, little more I could do for Brown. He should be kept warm, dry, and well-hydrated, but something told me that Hodgepile would not be open to any such suggestions.

He wasn't. By means of furious and repeated bellows, he quelled the incipient riot, then declared that we were crossing the gorge, and right quickly, too.

"Put 'im on a stretcher, then," he said impatiently, in reply to protests from Brown's nephew. "And as for you—" He rounded on me, glaring. "Did I tell you? No tricks, I said!"

"Kill her," Brown said hoarsely from the ground. "Kill her now."

"Kill her? Not bloody likely, oul' son." Hodgepile's eyes gleamed with malice. "She's no more risk to *me* alive than dead—and a good bit more profit alive. But I'll keep her in line."

The knife was never far from his grasp. He had it out in an instant, and had seized my hand. Before I could so much as draw breath, I felt the blade press down, cutting partway into the base of my forefinger.

"Remember what I told you, do you?" He breathed it, his face was soft with anticipation. "I don't need you whole."

I did remember, and my belly hollowed, my throat dried to silence. My skin burned where he cut, and pain spread in a flash through my nerves; the need to jerk away from the blade was so strong that the muscles of my arm cramped with it.

I could imagine vividly the spurting stump, the shock of broken bone, ripped flesh, the horror of irrevocable loss.

But behind Hodgepile, Tebbe had risen to his feet. His odd, smudgy stare was fixed on me, with an expression of fascinated dread. I saw his hand close in a fist, his throat move as he swallowed, and felt the saliva return to my own. If I was to keep his protection, I must keep his belief.

I fixed my eyes on Hodgepile's, and made myself lean toward him. My skin quivered and jumped, and the blood roared louder in my ears than the voice of the cataract—but I opened my eyes wide. A witch's eyes—or so some said.

Very, very slowly, I lifted my free hand, still wet with Brown's blood. I reached the bloody fingers toward Hodgepile's face.

"I remember," I said, my voice a hoarse whisper. "Do you remember what *I* said?"

He would have done it. I saw the decision flash in his eyes, but before he could press the knife blade down, the bushy-haired young Indian leaped forward, grabbing at his arm with a cry of horror. Distracted, Hodgepile let go his grip, and I pulled free.

In an instant, Tebbe and two more men surged forward, hands on knives and pistol grips.

Hodgepile's thin face was pinched with fury, but the moment of incipient violence had passed. He lowered his own knife, the menace receding.

I opened my mouth to say something that might help defuse the situation further, but was forestalled by a panicked cry from Brown's nephew.

"Don't let her talk! She'll curse us all!"

"Oh, bleedin' 'ell," said Hodgepile, fury transmuted to mere crossness.

I had used several neckcloths to bind Brown's splint. Hodgepile stooped and snatched one from the ground, wadded it into a ball, and stepped forward.

"Open your mouth," he said tersely, and seizing my jaw with one hand, he forced open my mouth and crammed the wadded fabric into it. He glared at Tebbe, who had made a jerky move forward.

"I shan't kill her. But she says not a word more. Not to 'im"— he nodded at Brown, then Tebbe—"not to you. Nor me." He glanced back at me, and to my surprise, I saw a lurking uneasiness in his eyes. "Not to anyone."

Tebbe looked uncertain, but Hodgepile was already tying his own neckcloth round my head, effectively gagging me.

"Not a word," Hodgepile repeated, glaring round at the company. "Now, let's go!"

We crossed the river. To my surprise, Lionel Brown survived, but it was a lengthy business, and the sun was low by the time we made camp, two miles past the gorge on the farther side.

Everyone was wet, and a fire was kindled without discussion. The currents of dissension and distrust were still there, but had been damped by the river and exhaustion. Everyone was simply too tired for further strife.

They had tied my hands loosely, but left my feet unbound; I made my way to a fallen log near the fire and sank down, utterly drained. I was damp and chilled, my muscles trembling with exhaustion—I had been forced to walk from the river—and for the first time, I began to wonder whether Jamie would in fact find me. Ever.

Perhaps he had followed the wrong group of bandits. Perhaps he had found and attacked them—and been wounded or killed in the fight. I had closed my eyes, but opened them again, seeking to avoid the visions this thought had conjured up. I still worried about Marsali—but either they had found her in time or they hadn't; either way, her fate had been decided.

The fire was burning well, at least; cold, wet, and eager for hot food, the men had brought an immense pile of wood. A short, silent black man was stoking the fire, while a couple of the teenagers rifled the packs for food. A pot of water was set on the fire with a chunk of salt beef, and the lion-haired young Indian poured cornmeal into a bowl with a lump of lard.

Another bit of lard sizzled on an iron girdle, melting into grease. It smelled wonderful.

Saliva flooded my mouth, absorbed at once into the wad of fabric, and despite discomfort, the smell of food bolstered my spirits a little. My stays, loosened by the travel of the last twenty-four hours, had tightened again as the wet laces dried and shrank. My skin itched beneath the fabric, but the thin ribs of the boning did give me a sense of support, more than welcome at the moment.

Mr. Brown's two nephews—Aaron and Moses, I had learned—limped slowly into camp, a makeshift stretcher sagging between them. They set it gratefully down beside the fire, evoking a loud yell from the contents.

Mr. Brown had survived the river crossing, but it hadn't done him any good. Of course, I *had* told them he should be kept well-hydrated. The thought undid me, tired as I was, and I made a muffled snorting sound behind my gag.

One of the young lads nearby heard me, and reached tentatively for the knot of my gag, but dropped his hand at once when Hodgepile barked at him.

"Leave her!"

"But—don't she need to eat, Hodge?" The boy glanced uneasily at me.

"Not just yet she doesn't." Hodgepile squatted down in front of me, looking me over. "Learned your lesson yet, 'ave you?"

I didn't move. Just sat and looked at him, infusing my gaze with as much scorn as possible. The cut on my finger burned; my palms had begun to sweat—but I stared. He tried to stare back, but couldn't do it—his eyes kept slipping away.

That made him even angrier; a flush burned high on his bony cheeks.

"Stop looking at me!"

I blinked slowly, once, and kept looking, with what I hoped appeared to be interested dispassion. He was looking rather strained, our Mr. Hodgepile was. Dark circles under the eyes, muscle fibers bracketing his mouth like lines carved in wood. Sweat stains wet and hot beneath the armpits. Constant browbeating must take it out of one.

All at once, he stood up, grabbed me by the arm, and yanked me to my feet.

"I'll put you where you can't stare, bitch," he muttered, and marched me past the fire, shoving me ahead of him. A little way outside the camp, he found a tree to his liking. He untied my hands and rebound my wrists, with a loop of line wrapped round my waist and my hands fastened to it. Then he pushed me down into a seated position, fashioned a crude noose with a slipknot, and put it round my neck, tying the free end to the tree.

"So as you won't wander away," he said, pulling the rough hemp snug around my neck. "Shouldn't want you to get lost.

Might be eaten by a bear, and then what, eh?" This had quite restored his humor; he laughed immoderately, and was still chuckling when he left. He turned, though, to glance back at me. I sat upright, staring, and the humor abruptly left his face. He turned and strode off, shoulders stiff as wood.

In spite of hunger, thirst, and general discomfort, I actually felt a sense of profound, if momentary, relief. If I was not strictly speaking alone, I was at least unobserved, and even this modicum of privacy was balm.

I was a good twenty yards from the fire ring, out of sight of all the men. I sagged against the tree trunk, the muscles of face and body giving way all at once, and a shiver seized me, though it wasn't cold.

Soon. Surely Jamie would find me soon. Unless—I pushed the dubious thought aside as though it were a venomous scorpion. Likewise any thought of what had happened to Marsali, or might happen if and when—no, *when*—he did find us. I didn't know how he'd manage, but he would. He just *would*.

The sun was nearly down; shadows were pooling under the trees and the light faded slowly from the air, making colors fugitive and solid objects lose their depth. There was rushing water somewhere nearby, and the calling of the occasional bird in the distant trees. These began to fall silent as the evening cooled, replaced by the rising chirp of crickets near at hand. My eye caught the flicker of movement, and I saw a rabbit, gray as the dusk, sitting up on its hind legs under a bush a few feet distant, nose twitching.

The sheer normalcy of it all made my eyes sting. I blinked away the tears, and the rabbit was gone.

The sight of it had restored my nerve a little; I essayed a few experiments, to see the limits of my present bondage. My legs were free—that was good. I could rise up into a sort of ungainly squat, and duck-waddle round the tree. Even better; I would be able to relieve myself in privacy on the far side.

I could not, however, rise entirely to my feet, nor could I reach the knot of the line that circled the tree trunk; the rope either slid or caught on the bark, but in either case, the knot remained frustratingly on the opposite side of the trunk—which had to measure nearly three feet in diameter.

I had about two feet of line between the trunk and the noose about my neck; enough to allow me to lie down, or to turn from side to side. Hodgepile was rather obviously well-acquainted with convenient methods of restraining captives; I thought of the O'Brians' homestead, and the two bodies there. The two elder children missing. A small shudder passed over me again.

Where were they? Sold to one of the Indian tribes as slaves? Taken to a sailors' brothel in one of the coastal towns? Or onto a ship, to be pressed into use on the sugar plantations of the Indies?

I was under no illusions that any of these picturesquely unpleasant fates lay in store for me. I was much too old, much too obstreperous—and much too notorious. No, the only value I held for Hodgepile was my knowledge of the whisky cache. Once he had got within sniffing distance of that, he would slit my throat without a moment's compunction.

The smell of roasting meat floated through the air, flooding my mouth with fresh saliva—a welcome relief, in spite of the growling of my stomach, since the gag dried my mouth unpleasantly.

A tiny jolt of panic tensed my muscles. I didn't want to think about the gag. Or the ropes around my wrists and neck. It would be too easy to succumb to the panic of confinement, and exhaust myself in futile struggle. I had to preserve my strength; I didn't know when or how I would need it, but need it I surely would. *Soon,* I prayed. *Let it be soon.*

The men had settled to their supper, the contentions of the day sunk in appetite. They were far enough away that I couldn't hear the particulars of their conversation, but only the stray word or phrase borne on the evening breeze. I turned my head to let the breeze smooth the hair from my face, and found that I could see a long, narrow swath of sky above the distant gorge, gone a deep, unearthly blue, as though the fragile layer of atmosphere that covered the earth grew thinner still, and the darkness of space beyond shone through.

The stars began to prick out, one by one, and I managed to lose myself in watching, counting them as they appeared, one by one by one . . . touching them as I might the beads of a rosary, and saying to myself such astronomical names as I knew, comforting in their sound, even though I had no idea whether such names bore any relation to the celestial bodies I saw. Alpha Centauri, Deneb, Sirius, Betelgeuse, the Pleiades, Orion . . .

I succeeded in soothing myself to the extent that I dozed off, only to rouse some time later to find it now full dark. The light of the fire sent a flickering glow through the underbrush, painting my feet, which lay in an open spot, with rosy shadows. I stirred and stretched myself as well as I could, trying to relieve the stiffness in my back, and wondered whether Hodgepile thought himself safe now, to be allowing such a large fire?

A loud groan came to me on the wind—Lionel Brown. I grimaced, but there was nothing I could do for him in my present condition.

I heard shuffling and a murmur of voices; someone was attending to him.

". . . hot as a pistol . . ." one voice said, sounding only mildly concerned.

". . . fetch the woman? . . ."

"No," said a definite voice. Hodgepile. I sighed.

". . . water. No help for *that* . . ."

I was listening so intently, in hopes of hearing what was happening by the fire, that it was some time before I became aware of noises in the brush nearby. Not animals; only bears would make that much noise, and bears didn't giggle. The giggling was subdued, not only muffled but repeatedly interrupted.

There was whispering, too, though I couldn't make out most of the words. The overall atmosphere was so much one of excited juvenile conspiracy, though, that I knew it must be some of the younger members of the gang.

". . . go *on,* then!" I caught, spoken in a vehement tone, and accompanied by a crashing noise, indicating that someone had been pushed into a tree. Another crash, indicating retaliation.

More rustling. Whisper, whisper, snigger, snort. I sat up straight, wondering what in God's name they were up to.

Then I heard, "Her legs aren't tied . . ." and my heart gave a small jump.

"But what if she . . ." mumble, mumble.

"Won't matter. She can't scream."

That came through very clearly, and I jerked my feet back to scramble up—only to be brought up short by the noose around my neck. It felt like an iron bar across my windpipe, and I fell back, seeing blood-red blotches at the corners of my eyes.

I shook my head and gulped air, trying to shake off the

dizziness, adrenaline racing through my blood. I felt a hand on my ankle, and kicked out sharply.

"Hey!" he said out loud, sounding surprised. He took his hand off my ankle and sat back a little. My vision was clearing; I could see him now, but the firelight was behind him; it was one of the young lads, but no more than a faceless, hunched silhouette in front of me.

"Shh," he said, and giggled nervously, reaching out a hand toward me. I made a deep growling noise behind my gag, and he stopped, frozen in mid-reach. There was a rustling in the brush behind him.

This seemed to remind him that his friend—or friends—were watching, and he reached out with renewed resolution, patting me on the thigh.

"Don't you worry, ma'am," he whispered, duck-walking closer on his heels, "I don't mean you no harm."

I snorted, and he hesitated again—but then another rustle from the bush seemed to stiffen his resolve, and he grasped me by the shoulders, trying to make me lie down. I struggled hard, kicking and kneeing at him, and he lost his grip, lost his balance, and fell on his backside.

A muffled explosion of sniggering from the bush brought him up on his feet like a jack-in-the-box. He reached down with decision, seized my ankles, and yanked, jerking me flat. Then he flung himself on top of me, pinning me with his weight.

"Hush!" he said urgently into my ear. His hands were grappling for my throat, and I squirmed and thrashed under his weight, trying to buck him off. His hands closed tight on my neck, though, and I stopped, my vision going black and bloody once again.

"Hush, now," he said more quietly. "You just hush, ma'am, all right?" I was making small choking noises, which he must have taken for assent, for his grip slackened.

"I ain't gonna hurt you, ma'am, I really ain't," he whispered, trying to hold me down with one hand while fumbling about between us with the other. "Would you just be *still*, please?"

I wouldn't, and he finally put a forearm across my throat and leaned on it. Not hard enough to make me black out again, but hard enough to take some of the fight out of me. He was thin and wiry, but very strong, and by dint of simple determination, succeeded in pushing up my shift and wedging his knee between my thighs.

He was breathing nearly as hard as I was, and I could smell the goaty reek of his excitement. His hands had left my throat, and were feverishly grasping at my breasts, in a manner that made it reasonably clear that the only other breast he'd ever touched was likely his mother's.

"Hush, now, don't you be scared, ma'am, it's all right, I ain't . . . oh. Oh, my. I . . . uh . . . oh." His hand was poking about between my thighs, then left off momentarily as he raised himself briefly and wriggled down his breeches.

He collapsed heavily on top of me, hips pumping frantically as he thrust madly away—making no contact save that of friction, as he very obviously had no idea of the way in which female anatomy was constructed. I lay still, astonished into immobility, then felt a warm pulse of liquid under my thighs as he lost himself in panting ecstasy.

All the wiry tension went out of him in a rush, and he subsided on my chest like a limp balloon. I could feel his young heart pounding like a steam hammer, and his temple was pressed against my cheek, damp with sweat.

I found the intimacy of this contact quite as objectionable as the softening presence wedged between my thighs, and rolled abruptly to the side, dumping him off. He came to life suddenly, and scrambled to his knees, yanking at his drooping breeches.

He swayed to and fro for a moment, then dropped to his hands and knees and crawled up close beside me.

"I'm really sorry, ma'am," he whispered.

I made no move, and after a moment, he reached out a tentative hand and patted me gently on the shoulder.

"I'm real sorry," he repeated, still whispering, and then was gone, leaving me lying on my back in a puddle, wondering whether such an incompetent assault could legitimately be termed rape.

Distant rustling in the bushes, accompanied by muffled whoops of young male delight, decided me firmly that it could. Christ, the rest of the obnoxious little beasts would be at me in no time. Panicked, I sat up, mindful of the noose.

The glow from the fire was irregular and flickering, barely enough to make out the trunks of trees and the pale layer of needles and leaf mold on the ground. Enough to see the protrusions of granite boulders through the leaf layer, and the occasional hump of a fallen twig. Not that the lack of potential weapons mattered, given that my hands were still firmly tied.

The weight of the young assailant had made things worse; the knots had pulled tighter during my struggles, and my hands throbbed with lack of circulation. My fingers were beginning to go numb at the tips. Bloody hell. Was I about to lose several fingers to gangrene, as a result of this absurdity?

For an instant, I contemplated the wisdom of behaving compliantly with the next horrible little boy, in hopes that he would remove the gag. If he would, I could at least beg him to loosen the ropes—and then scream for help, in hopes that Tebbe would come and stop further assault, out of fear of my eventual supernatural revenge.

Here he came, a stealthy rustling in the bushes. I gritted my teeth on the gag and looked up, but the shadowy form in front of me wasn't one of the young boys.

The only thought that came to mind when I realized who the new visitor was was, *Jamie Fraser, you bastard, where* are *you?*

I froze, as though not moving might somehow render me invisible. The man moved in front of me, squatting down so as to look into my face.

"Not laughin' so much now, are you?" he said conversationally. It was Boble, the erstwhile thieftaker. "You and your husband thought it was damn funny, didn't you, what them German women did to me? And then Mr. Fraser tellin' me as they meant to make sausage meat of me, and him with a face like a Christian readin' the Bible. Thought that was funny, too, didn't you?"

To be perfectly honest, it had been funny. He was quite correct, though; I wasn't laughing now. He drew back his arm and slapped me.

The blow made my eyes water, but the fire lit him from the side; I could still see the smile on his pudgy face. A cold qualm ran through me, making me shudder. He saw that, and the smile broadened. His canine teeth were short and blunt, so the incisors stood out by contrast, long and yellowed, rodentlike.

"Reckon you'll think this is even funnier," he said, rising to his feet and reaching for his flies. "Hope Hodge don't kill you right away, so you get to tell your husband about it. Bet you he'll enjoy the joke, man with a sense of humor like he's got."

The boy's semen was still damp and sticky on my thighs. I jerked back by reflex, trying to scramble to my feet, but was brought up short by the noose round my neck. My vision went dark for an instant as the rope tightened on my carotids, then cleared, and I found Boble's face inches from mine, his breath hot on my skin.

He seized my chin in his hand and rubbed his face over mine, biting at my lips and rasping the stubble of his beard hard across my cheeks. Then he drew back, leaving my face wet with his saliva, pushed me flat, and climbed on top of me.

I could feel the violence in him, pulsing like an exposed heart, thin-walled and ready to burst. I knew I couldn't escape or prevent him—knew he would hurt me, given the slightest excuse. The only thing to do was be still and endure him.

I couldn't. I heaved under him and rolled to the side, bringing up my knee as he pushed my shift aside. It hit him a glancing blow in the thigh, and he drew back his fist by reflex and punched me in the face, sharp and quick.

Red-black pain bloomed sudden from the center of my face, filled my head, and I went blind, shocked into momentary immobility. *You utter fool*, I thought, with total clarity. *Now he'll kill you.* The second blow struck my cheek and snapped my head to the side. Perhaps I moved again in blind resistance, perhaps I didn't.

Suddenly he was kneeling astride me, punching and slapping, blows dull and heavy as the thump of ocean waves on sand, too remote as yet for pain. I twisted, curling, bringing up my shoulder and trying to shield my face against the ground, and then his weight was gone.

He was standing. He was kicking me and cursing, panting and half-sobbing as his boot thudded into sides and back and thighs and buttocks. I panted in short gasps, trying to breathe. My body jerked and quivered with each blow, skidding on the leaf-strewn ground, and I clung to the sense of the ground below me, trying so hard to sink down, be swallowed by the earth.

Then it stopped. I could hear him panting, trying to speak. "Goddamn . . . goddamn . . . oh, goddamn . . . frig . . . friggin' . . . bitch. . ."

I lay inert, trying to disappear into the darkness that enveloped me, knowing that he was going to kick me in the head. I could feel my teeth shatter, the fragile bones of my skull splinter and collapse into the wet soft pulp of my brain, and I trembled, clenching my teeth in futile resistance against the impact. It would sound like a melon being smashed, dull, sticky-hollow. Would I hear it?

It didn't come. There was another sound, a fast, hard rustling that made no sense. A faintly meaty sound, flesh on flesh in a soft smacking rhythm, and then he gave a groan and warm gouts of fluid fell wet on my face and shoulders, splattering on bare skin where the cloth of my shift had torn away.

I was frozen. Somewhere in the back of my mind, the detached observer wondered aloud whether this was in fact the single most disgusting thing I had ever encountered. Well, no, it wasn't. Some of the things I had seen at L'Hôpital des Anges, to say nothing of Father Alexandre's death, or the Beardsleys' attic . . . the field hospital at Amiens . . . heavens, no, this wasn't even close.

I lay rigid, eyes shut, recalling various nasty experiences of my past and wishing I were in fact in attendance at one of those events, instead of here.

He leaned over, seized my hair, and banged my head several times against the tree, wheezing as he did so.

"Show you . . ." he muttered, then dropped his hand and I heard shuffling noises as he staggered away.

When I finally opened my eyes again, I was alone.

I remained alone, a small mercy. Boble's violent attack seemed to have frightened away the boys.

I rolled onto my side and lay still, breathing. I felt very tired, and utterly forlorn.

Jamie, I thought, *where are you?*

I wasn't afraid of what might happen next; I couldn't see any further than the moment I was in, a single breath, a single heartbeat. I didn't think, and wouldn't feel. Not yet. I just lay still, and breathed.

Very slowly I began to notice small things. A fragment of bark caught in my hair, scratchy on my cheek. The give of the thick dead leaves beneath me, cradling my body. The sense of effort as my chest lifted. Increasing effort.

A tiny nerve began to twitch near one eye.

I realized quite suddenly that with the gag in my mouth and my nasal tissues being rapidly congested by blood and swelling, I was in some actual danger of suffocation. I twisted as far onto my side as I could get without strangling, and rubbed my face first against the ground, then—with increasing desperation—dug my heels into the ground and wriggled upward, scraping my face hard against the bark of the tree, trying without success to loosen or dislodge the gag.

The bark rasped lip and cheek, but the kerchief tied round my head was so tight that it cut hard into the corners of my mouth, forcing it open so that saliva leaked constantly into the wad of fabric in my mouth. I gagged at the tickle of sodden cloth in my throat, and felt vomit burn the back of my nose.

You aren't, you aren't, you aren'tyouaren'tyou aren't *going to vomit!* I dragged air bubbling through my bloody nose, tasted thick copper as it slimed down my throat, gagged harder, doubled up—and saw white light at the edge of vision, as the noose went tight around my throat.

I fell back, my head hitting hard against the tree. I hardly noticed; the noose loosened again, thank God, and I managed one, two, three precious breaths of blood-clogged air.

My nose was puffed from cheekbone to cheekbone, and swelling fast. I clenched my teeth on the gag and blew outward through my nose, trying to clear it, if only for a moment. Blood tinged with bile sprayed warm across my chin and splattered on my chest—and I sucked air fast, getting a bit.

Blow, inhale. Blow, inhale. Blow . . . but my nasal passages were almost swollen shut by now, and I nearly sobbed in panic and frustration, as no air came.

Christ, don't cry! You're dead if you cry, for God's sake don't cry!

Blow . . . blow . . . I snorted with the last reserve of stale air in my lungs, and got a hair of clearance, enough to fill them once more.

I held my breath, trying to stay conscious long enough to discover a way to breathe—there *had* to be a way to breathe.

I would *not* let a wretch like Harley Boble kill me by simple inadvertence. That wasn't right; it couldn't be.

I pressed myself, half-sitting, up against the tree to ease the strain on the noose around my neck as much as possible, and let my head fall forward, so that the blood from my nose ran down, dripping. That helped, a little. Not for long, though.

My eyelids began to feel tight; my nose was definitely broken, and the flesh all round the upper part of my face was puffing now, swelling with the blood and lymph of capillary trauma, squeezing my eyes shut, further constricting my thread of air.

I bit the gag in an agony of frustration, then, seized by desperation, began to chew at it, grinding the fabric between my teeth, trying to smash it down, compress it, shift it somehow inside my mouth. . . . I bit the inside of my cheek and felt the pain but didn't mind, it wasn't important, nothing mattered but breath, oh, God, I couldn't *breathe,* please help me breathe, please. . . .

I bit my tongue, gasped in pain—and realized that I had succeeded in thrusting my tongue past the gag, reaching the tip of it to the corner of my mouth. By poking as hard as I could with my tongue tip, I had made a tiny channel of air. No more than a wisp of oxygen could ooze through it—but it was air, and that was all that mattered.

I had my head canted painfully to one side, forehead pressed against the tree, but was afraid to move at all, for fear of losing my slender lifeline of air, if the gag should shift when I moved my head. I sat still, hands clenched, drawing long, gurgling, horribly shallow breaths, and wondering how long I could stay this way; the muscles of my neck were already quivering from strain.

My hands were throbbing again—they hadn't ever stopped, I supposed, but I hadn't had attention to spare for them. Now I did, and momentarily welcomed the shooting pains that outlined each nail with liquid fire, for distraction from the deadly stiffness spreading down my neck and through my shoulder.

The muscles of my neck jumped and spasmed; I gasped, lost my air, and arched my body bowlike, fingers dug into the binding ropes as I fought to get it back.

A hand came down on my arm. I hadn't heard him approach. I turned blindly, butting at him with my head. I didn't care who he was or what he wanted, provided he would remove the gag. Rape seemed a perfectly reasonable exchange for survival, at least at the moment.

I made desperate noises, whimpering, snorting, and spewing gouts of blood and snot as I shook my head violently, trying to indicate that I was choking—given the level of sexual incompetence so far demonstrated, he might not even realize that I couldn't breathe, and simply proceed about his business, unaware that simple rape was becoming necrophilia.

He was fumbling round my head. Thank God, thank God! I held myself still with superhuman effort, head swimming as little bursts of fire went off inside my eyeballs. Then the strip of fabric came away and I thrust the wad of cloth out of my mouth by reflex, instantly gagged, and threw up, whooping air and retching simultaneously.

I hadn't eaten; no more than a thread of bile seared my throat and ran down my chin. I choked and swallowed and *breathed,* sucking air in huge, greedy, lung-bursting gulps.

He was saying something, whispering urgently. I didn't care, couldn't listen. All I heard was the grateful wheeze of my own breathing, and the thump of my heart. Finally slowing from its frantic race to keep oxygen moving round my starved tissues, it pounded hard enough to shake my body.

Then a word or two got through to me, and I lifted my head, staring at him.

"Whad?" I said thickly. I coughed, shaking my head to try to clear it. It hurt very much. "*What* did you say?"

He was visible only as a ragged, lion-haired silhouette, bony-shouldered in the faint glow from the fire.

"I said," he whispered, leaning close, "does the name 'Ringo Starr' mean anything to you?"

I was by this time well beyond shock. I merely wiped my split lip gingerly on my shoulder, and said, very calmly, "Yes."

He had been holding his breath; I realized it only when I heard the sigh as he released it, and saw his shoulders slump.

"Oh, God," he said, half under his breath. "Oh, God."

He lunged forward suddenly and caught me against him in a hard embrace. I recoiled, choking as the noose round my neck tightened once again, but he didn't notice, absorbed in his own emotion.

"Oh, God," he said, and buried his face in my shoulder, nearly sobbing. "Oh, God. I knew, I knew you hadda be, I knew it, but I couldn't believe it, oh, God, oh, God, oh, God! I didn't think I'd ever find another one, not ever—"

"Kk," I said. I arched my back, urgently.

"Wha—oh, shit!" He let go and grabbed for the rope around my neck. He scrabbled hold of it and yanked the noose over my head, nearly tearing my ear off in the process, but I didn't mind. "Shit, you okay?"

"Yes," I croaked. "Un . . . tie me."

He sniffed, wiping his nose on his sleeve, and glanced back over his shoulder.

"I can't," he whispered. "The next guy who comes along'll see."

"The *next* guy?" I screamed, as well as I could scream in a strangled whisper. "What do you mean, the next—"

"Well, you know. . . ." It seemed suddenly to dawn on him that I might have objections to waiting tamely like a trussed turkey for the next would-be rapist in the lineup. "Er . . . I mean . . . well, never mind. Who are you?"

"You know damn well who I am," I croaked furiously, shoving him with my bound hands. "I'm Claire Fraser. Who in *bloody* hell are you, what are you doing here, and if you want one more word out of me, you'll bloody well untie me this minute!"

He turned again to glance apprehensively over his shoulder, and it occurred to me vaguely that he was afraid of his so-called comrades. So was I. I could see his profile in silhouette; it was indeed the bushy-haired young Indian, the one I had thought might be a Tuscaroran. Indian . . . some connection clicked into place, deep in the tangled synapses.

"Bloody hell," I said, and dabbed at a trickle of blood that ran from the raw corner of my mouth. "Otter-Toof. Tooth. You're one of his."

"What?!" His head swung back to face me, eyes so wide the whites showed briefly. "Who?"

"Oh, what in hell was his real name? Robert . . . Robert th-something . . ." I was trembling with fury, terror, shock, and exhaustion, groping through the muddled remnants of what used to be my mind. Wreck though I might be, I remembered Otter-Tooth, all right. I had a sudden vivid memory of being alone in the dark, on a night like this, wet with rain and all alone, a long-buried skull cupped in my hands.

"Springer," he said, and gripped my arm eagerly. "Springer—was that it? Robert Springer?"

I had just enough presence of mind to clamp my jaw, thrust out my chin, and hold up my bound hands in front of him. Not another word until he cut me loose.

"Shit," he muttered again, and with another hasty glance behind him, fumbled for his knife. He wasn't skillful with it. If I had needed any evidence that he wasn't a real Indian of the time . . . but he got my hands free without cutting me, and I doubled up with a groan, hands tucked under my armpits as the blood surged into them. They felt like balloons filled and stretched to the point of bursting.

"When?" he demanded, paying no attention to my distress. "When did you come? Where did you find Bob? Where is he?"

"1946," I said, squeezing my arms down tight on my throbbing hands. "The first time. 1968, the second. As for Mr. Springer—"

"The second—did you say the *second* time?" His voice rose in astonishment. He choked it off, looking guiltily back, but the sounds of the men dicing and arguing round the fire were more than loud enough to drown out a simple exclamation.

"Second time," he repeated more softly. "So you did it? You went back?"

I nodded, pressing my lips together and rocking back and forth a little. I thought my fingernails would pop off with each heartbeat.

"What about you?" I asked, though I was fairly sure that I already knew.

"1968," he said, confirming it.

"What year did you turn up in?" I asked. "I mean—how long have you been here? Er . . . now, I mean."

"Oh, God." He sat back on his heels, running a hand back through his long, tangled hair. "I been here six years, as near as I can tell. But you said—second time. If you made it home, why in hell'd you come *back*? Oh—wait. You didn't make it home, you went to another time, but not the one you came from? Where'd you start from?"

"Scotland, 1946. And no, I made it home," I said, not wanting to go into details. "My husband was here, though. I came back on purpose, to be with him." A decision whose wisdom seemed presently in severe doubt.

"And speaking of my husband," I added, beginning to feel as though I might possess a few shreds of sanity after all, "I was *not* joking. He's coming. You don't want him to find you keeping me captive, I assure you. But if you—"

He disregarded this, leaning eagerly toward me.

"But that means you know how it works! You can steer!"

"Something like that," I said, impatient. "I take it that you and your companions *didn't* know how to steer, as you put it?" I massaged one hand with the other, gritting my teeth against the throb of blood. I could feel the furrows the rope had left in my flesh.

"We thought we did." Bitterness tinged his voice. "Singing stones. Gemstones. That's what we used. Raymond said . . . It didn't work, though. Or maybe . . . maybe it did." He was making deductions; I could hear the excitement rising again in his tone.

"You met Bob Springer—Otter-Tooth, I mean. So he *did* make it! And if he made it, maybe the others did, too. See, I thought they were all dead. I thought—thought I was alone." There was a catch in his voice, and despite the urgency of the situation and my annoyance at him, I felt a pang of sympathy. I knew very well what it felt like to be alone in that way, marooned in time.

In a way, I hated to disillusion him, but there was no point in keeping the truth from him.

"Otter-Tooth is dead, I'm afraid."

He suddenly stopped moving and sat very still. The faint glow of firelight through the trees outlined him; I could see his face. A few long hairs lifted in the breeze. They were the only thing that moved.

"How?" he said at last, in a small, choked voice.

"Killed by the Iroquois," I said. "The Mohawk." My mind was beginning, very slowly, to work again. Six years ago, this man— whoever he was—had come. 1767, that would be. And yet Otter-Tooth, the man who had once been Robert Springer, had died more than a generation earlier. They'd started out together, but ended in different times.

"Shit," he said, though the obvious distress in his voice was mingled with something like awe. "That would have been a real bummer, especially for Bob. He, like, idolized those guys."

"Yes, I expect he was most put out about it," I replied, rather dryly. My eyelids felt thick and heavy. It was an effort to force them open, but I could still see. I glanced at the fire glow, but couldn't see anything beyond the faint movement of shadows in the distance. If there actually was a lineup of men waiting for my services, at least they were tactfully keeping out of sight. I doubted it, and gave silent thanks that I wasn't twenty years younger—there might have been.

"I met some Iroquois—Christ, I went *looking* for 'em, if you can believe that! That was the whole point, see, to find the Iroquois tribes and get them to—"

"Yes, I know what you had in mind," I interrupted. "Look, this is not really the time or place for a long discussion. I think that—"

"Those Iroquois are some nasty tumblers, I tell *you,* man," he said, jabbing me in the chest with a finger for emphasis. "You wouldn't *believe* what they do to—"

"I know. So is my husband." I gave him a glare, which—judging from the way he flinched—was probably rendered highly effective by the state of my face. I hoped so; it hurt a lot to do it.

"Now, what *you* want to do," I said, mustering as much authority into my voice as I could, "is to go back to the fire, wait for a bit, then leave casually, sneak round, and get two horses. I hear a stream down there—" I waved briefly to the right. "I'll meet you there. Once we're safely away, I'll tell you everything I know."

In fact, I probably couldn't tell him anything very helpful, but he didn't know that. I heard him swallow.

"I don't know . . ." he said uncertainly, glancing round again. "Hodge, he's kind of gnarly. He shot one guy, a few days ago. Didn't even say anything, just walked up to him, pulled his gun, and *boom!*"

"What for?"

He shrugged, shaking his head.

"I don't even know, man. Just . . . *boom,* you know?"

"I know," I assured him, holding on to temper and sanity by a thread. "Look, let's not trouble with the horses, then. Let's just go." I lurched awkwardly onto one knee, hoping that I would be able to rise in a few moments, let alone walk. The big muscles in my thighs were knotted hard in the spots where Boble had kicked me; trying to stand made the muscles jump and quiver in spasms that effectively hamstrung me.

"Shit, not now!" In his agitation, the young man seized my arm and jerked me down beside him. I hit the ground hard on one hip and let out a cry of pain.

"You all right there, Donner?" The voice came out of the darkness somewhere behind me. It was casual—obviously one of the men had merely stepped out of camp to relieve himself—but the effect on the young Indian was galvanizing. He flung himself full-length upon me, banging my head on the ground and knocking all the breath out of me.

"Fine . . . really . . . great," he called to his companion, gasping in an exaggerated manner, evidently trying to sound like a man in the throes of half-completed lust. He sounded like someone dying of asthma, but I wasn't complaining. I couldn't.

I'd been knocked on the head a few times, and generally saw nothing but blackness as a result. This time I honestly did see colored stars, and lay limp and bemused, feeling as though I sat tranquilly some distance above my battered body. Then Donner laid a hand on my breast and I came instantly back to earth.

"Let go of me this instant!" I hissed. "What do you think you're doing?"

"Hey, hey, nothing, nothing, sorry," he assured me hastily. He removed the hand, but didn't get off me. He squirmed a bit, and I realized that he was aroused by the contact, whether intended or not.

"Get *off*!" I said, in a furious whisper.

"Hey, I don't mean anything, I mean I wouldn't hurt you or nothing. It's just I haven't had a woman in—"

I grabbed a handful of his hair, lifted my head, and bit his ear, hard. He shrieked and rolled off me.

The other man had gone back toward the fire. At this, though, he turned and called back, "Christ, Donner, is she *that* good? I'll have to give her a try!" This got a laugh from the men by the fire, but luckily it died away and they returned to their own concerns. I returned to mine, which was escape.

"You didn't have to do that," Donner whined in an undertone, holding his ear. "I wasn't going to *do* anything! Christ, you got nice tits, but you're like old enough to be my mother!"

"Shut up!" I said, pushing myself to a sitting position. The effort made my head spin; tiny colored lights flickered like Christmas-tree bulbs at the edge of my vision. In spite of this, some part of my mind was actively working again.

He was at least partly right. We couldn't leave immediately. After drawing so much attention to himself, the others would be expecting him to come back within a few minutes; if he didn't, they'd start looking for him—and we needed more than a few minutes' start.

"We can't go now," he whispered, rubbing his ear reproachfully. "They'll notice. Wait 'til they go to sleep. I'll come get you then."

I hesitated. I was in mortal danger every moment that I spent within reach of Hodgepile and his feral gang. If I had needed any convincing, the encounters of the last two hours had demonstrated that. This Donner needed to go back to the fire and show himself—but I could steal away. Was it worth the risk that someone would come and find me gone, before I had got beyond pursuit? It would be more certain to wait until they slept. But did I dare wait that long?

And then there was Donner himself. If he wanted to talk to me, I certainly wanted to talk to him. The chance of stumbling on another time-traveler . . .

Donner read my hesitation, but misunderstood it.

"You're not going without me!" He grabbed my wrist in sudden alarm, and before I could jerk away, had whipped a bit of the cut line around it. I fought and pulled away, hissing to try to make him understand, but he was panicked at the thought that I might slip away without him, and wouldn't listen. Hampered by my injuries, and unwilling to make enough noise to draw attention, I could only delay but not prevent his determined efforts to tie me up again.

"Okay." He was sweating; a drop fell warm on my face as he leaned over me to check the bindings. At least he hadn't put the noose round my neck again, instead tethering me to the tree with a rope around my waist.

"I shoulda known what you are," he murmured, intent on his job. "Even before you said 'Jesus H. Roosevelt Christ.'"

"What the hell do you mean by that?" I snapped, squirming away from his hand. "Don't bloody do that—I'll suffocate!" He was trying to put the cloth strip back in my mouth, but seemed to pick up the note of panic in my voice, because he hesitated.

"Oh," he said uncertainly. "Well. I guess—" Once again, he looked back over his shoulder, but then made up his mind and dropped the gag on the ground. "Okay. But you be quiet, all right? What I meant—you don't act afraid of men. Most of the women from now do. You oughta act more afraid."

And with that parting shot, he rose and brushed dead leaves from his clothes before heading back to the fire.

There comes a point when the body has simply had enough. It snatches at sleep, no matter what menace the future may hold. I'd seen that happen: the Jacobite soldiers who slept in the ditches where they fell, the British pilots who slept in their planes while mechanics fueled them, only to leap to full alert again in time to take off. For that matter, women in long labor routinely sleep between contractions.

In the same manner, I slept.

That kind of sleep is neither deep nor peaceful, though. I came out of it with a hand across my mouth.

The fourth man was neither incompetent nor brutal. He was large and soft-bodied, and he had loved his dead wife. I knew that, because he wept into my hair, and called me by her name at the end. It was Martha.

I came out of sleep again sometime later. Instantly, fully conscious, heart pounding. But it wasn't my heart—it was a drum.

Sounds of startlement came from the direction of the fire, men rousing in alarm from sleep.

"Indians!" someone shouted, and the light broke and flared, as someone kicked at the fire to scatter it.

It wasn't an Indian drum. I sat up, listening hard. It was a drum with a sound like a beating heart, slow and rhythmic, then triphammer fast, like the frantic surge of a hunted beast.

I could have told them that Indians never used drums as weapons; Celts did. It was the sound of a bodhran.

What next? I thought, a trifle hysterically, *bagpipes*?

It was Roger, certainly; only he could make a drum talk like that. It was Roger, and Jamie was nearby. I scrambled to my feet, wanting, needing urgently to *move*. I jerked at the rope around my waist in a frenzy of impatience, but I was going nowhere.

Another drum began, slower, less skilled, but equally menacing. The sound seemed to move—it *was* moving. Fading, coming back full force. A third drum began, and now the thumping seemed to come from everywhere, fast, slow, mocking.

Someone fired a gun into the forest, panicked.

"Hold, there!" Hodgepile's voice came, loud and furious, but to no avail; there was a popcorn rattle of gunfire, nearly drowned by the sound of the drums. I heard a *snick* near my head, and a cluster of needles brushed past me as it fell. It dawned on me that standing upright while guns were blindly fired all round me was a dangerous strategy, and I promptly fell flat, burrowing into the dead needles, trying to keep the trunk of the tree betwixt me and the main body of men.

The drums were weaving, now closer, now farther, the sound unnerving even to one who knew what it was. They were circling the camp, or so it seemed. Should I call out, if they came near enough?

I was saved from the agony of decision; the men were making so much noise round the campfire that I couldn't have been heard if I'd screamed myself hoarse. They were calling out in alarm, shouting questions, bellowing orders—which apparently went ignored, judging from the ongoing sounds of confusion.

Someone blundered through the brush nearby, running from the drums. One, two more—the sound of gasping breath and crunching footsteps. *Donner?* The thought came to me suddenly and I sat up, then fell flat again as another shot whistled past overhead.

The drums stopped abruptly. Chaos reigned around the fire, though I could hear Hodgepile trying to get his men in order, yelling and threatening, nasal voice raised above the rest. Then the drums began again—much closer.

They were drawing in, drawing together, somewhere out in the forest on my left, and the mocking *tip-tap-tip-tap* beating had changed. They were thundering now. No skill, just menace. Coming closer.

Guns fired wildly, close enough for me to see the muzzle flash and smell the smoke, thick and hot on the air. The faggots of the fire had been scattered, but still burned, making a muted glow through the trees.

"There they are! I see 'em!" someone yelled from the fire, and there was another burst of musket-fire, toward the drums.

Then the most unearthly howl rose out of the dark to my right.

I'd heard Scots scream going into battle before, but that particular Highland shriek made the hairs on my body prickle from tailbone to nape. *Jamie.* Despite my fears, I sat bolt upright and peered round my sheltering tree, in time to see demons boil out of the wood.

I knew them—knew I knew them—but cowered back at sight of them, blackened with soot and shrieking with the madness of hell, firelight red on the blades of knives and axes.

The drums had stopped abruptly, with the first scream, and now another set of howls broke out to the left, the drummers racing in to the kill. I pressed myself flat back against the tree, heart chokingly huge in my throat, petrified for fear the blades would strike at any random movement in the shadows.

Someone crashed toward me, blundering in the dark— Donner? I croaked his name, hoping to attract his attention, and the slight form turned toward me, hesitated, then spotted me and lunged.

It wasn't Donner, but Hodgepile. He seized my arm, dragging me up, even as he slashed at the rope that bound me to the tree. He was panting hard with exertion, or fear.

I realized at once what he was about; he knew his chances of escape were slight—having me to hostage was his only hope. But I was *damned* if I'd be his hostage. No more.

I kicked at him, hard, and caught him on the side of the knee. It didn't knock him over, but distracted him for a second. I charged him, head down, butted him square in the chest, and sent him flying.

The impact hurt badly, and I staggered, eyes watering from the pain. He was up, and at me again. I kicked, missed, fell heavily on my backside.

"Come *on*, damn you!" he hissed, jerking hard at my bound hands. I ducked my head, pulled back, and yanked him down with me. I rolled and scrabbled in the leaf mold, trying as hard as I could to wrap my legs around him, meaning to get a grip on his ribs and crush the life out of the filthy little worm, but he squirmed free and rolled atop me, punching at my head, trying to subdue me.

He struck me in one ear and I flinched, eyes shutting in reflex. Then the weight of him was suddenly gone, and I opened my eyes to see Jamie holding Hodgepile several inches off the ground. Hodgepile's spindly legs churned madly in a futile effort at escape, and I felt an insane desire to laugh.

In fact, I must actually have laughed, for Jamie's head jerked round to look at me; I caught a glimpse of the whites of his eyes before he turned his attention to Hodgepile again. He was silhouetted against a faint glow from the embers; I saw him in profile for a second, then his body flexed with effort as he bent his head.

He held Hodgepile close against his chest, one arm bent. I blinked; my eyes were swollen half-shut, and I wasn't sure what he was doing. Then I heard a small grunt of effort, and a strangled shriek from Hodgepile, and saw Jamie's bent elbow go sharply down.

The dark curve of Hodgepile's head moved back—and back. I glimpsed the marionette-sharp nose and angled jaw—angled impossibly high, the heel of Jamie's hand wedged hard beneath it. There was a muffled *pop!* that I felt in the pit of my stomach as Hodgepile's neckbones parted, and the marionette went limp.

Jamie flung the puppet body down, reached for me, and pulled me to my feet.

"You are alive, you are whole, *mo nighean donn*?" he said urgently in Gaelic. He was groping, hands flying over me, trying at the same time to hold me upright—my knees seemed suddenly to have turned to water—and to locate the rope that bound my hands.

I was crying and laughing, snuffing tears and blood, bumping at him with my bound hands, trying awkwardly to thrust them at him so that he could cut the rope.

He quit grappling, and clutched me so hard against him that I yelped in pain as my face was pressed against his plaid.

He was saying something else, urgently, but I couldn't manage to translate it. Energy pulsed through him, hot and violent, like the current in a live wire, and I vaguely realized that he was still almost berserk; he had no English.

"I'm all right," I gasped, and he let me go. The light flared up in the clearing beyond the trees; someone had collected the scattered embers, and thrown more kindling on them. His face was black, his eyes picked out blue in a sudden blaze as he turned his head and the light struck his face.

There was still some struggle going on; no screaming now, but I could hear the grunt and thud of bodies locked in combat. Jamie raised my hands, drew his dirk, and sawed through the rope; my hands dropped like lead weights. He stared at me for an instant, as though trying to find words, then shook his head, cupped a hand for an instant to my face, and disappeared, back in the direction of the fight.

I sank down on the ground, dazed. Hodgepile's body lay nearby, limbs askew. I glanced at it, the picture clear in my mind of a necklace Bree had had as a child, made of linked plastic beads that came apart when you pulled them. Pop-It pearls, they were called. I wished vaguely that I didn't remember that.

The face was lantern-jawed and hollow-cheeked; he looked surprised, eyes wide open to the flickering light. Something seemed oddly wrong, though, and I squinted, trying to make it out. Then I realized that his head was on backward.

It may have been seconds or minutes that I sat there staring at him, arms round my knees and my mind a total blank. Then the sound of soft footsteps made me look up.

Arch Bug came out of the dark, tall and thin and black against the flicker of a growing fire. I saw that he had an ax gripped hard in his left hand; it too was black, and the smell of blood came strong and rich as he leaned near.

"There are some left still alive," he said, and I felt something cold and hard touch my hand. "Will ye have your vengeance now upon them, *a bana-mhaighistear*?"

I looked down and found that he was offering me a dirk, hilt-first. I had stood up, but couldn't remember rising.

I couldn't speak, and couldn't move—and yet my fingers curled without my willing them to, my hand rising up to take the knife as I watched it, faintly curious. Then Jamie's hand came down upon the dirk, snatching it away, and I saw as from a great distance that the light fell on his hand, gleaming wet with blood smeared past the wrist. Random drops shone red, dark jewels glowing, caught in the curly hairs of his arm.

"There is an oath upon her," he said to Arch, and I realized dimly that he was still speaking in Gaelic, though I understood him clearly. "She may not kill, save it is for mercy or her life. It is myself who kills for her."

"And I," said a tall figure behind him, softly. Ian.

Arch nodded understanding, though his face was still in darkness. Someone else was there beside him—Fergus. I knew him at once, but it took a moment's struggle for me to put a name to the streaked pale face and wiry figure.

"Madame," he said, and his voice was thin with shock. "Milady."

Then Jamie looked at me, and his own face changed, awareness coming back into his eyes. I saw his nostrils flare, as he caught the scent of sweat and semen on my clothes.

"Which of them?" he said. "How many?" He spoke in English now, and his voice was remarkably matter-of-fact, as it might be if he were inquiring as to the number of guests expected for dinner, and I found the simple tone of it steadying.

"I don't know," I said. "They—it was dark."

He nodded, squeezed my arm hard, and turned.

"Kill them all," he said to Fergus, his voice still calm. Fergus's eyes were huge and dark, sunk into his head, burning. He merely nodded, and took hold of the hatchet in his belt. The front of his shirt was splashed, and the end of his hook looked dark and sticky.

In a distant sort of way, I thought I should say something. But I didn't. I stood up straight with the tree against my back and said nothing at all.

Jamie glanced at the dirk he held as though to ensure that it was in good order—it was not; he wiped the blade on his thigh, ignoring the drying blood that gummed the wooden hilt—and went back to the clearing.

I stood quite still. There were more sounds, but I paid no more heed to them than to the rush of wind through the needles overhead; it was a balsam tree, and the breath of it was clean and fresh, falling over me in a wash of fragrant resins, powerful enough to taste on my palate, though little penetrated the clotted membranes of my nose. Beneath the gentle veil of the tree's perfume, I tasted blood, and sodden rags, and the stink of my own weary skin.

Dawn had broken. Birds sang in the distant wood, and light lay soft as wood ash on the ground.

I stood quite still, and thought of nothing but how pleasant it would be to stand neck-deep in hot water, to scrub the skin quite away from my flesh, and let the blood run red and clean down my legs, billowing out in soft clouds that would hide me.

29

Perfectly Fine

T hey'd ridden away then. Left them, without burial or word
of consecration. In a way, that was more shocking than the
killing. Roger had gone with the Reverend to more than
one deathbed or scene of accident, helped comfort the bereaved,
stood by as the spirit fled and the old man said the words of grace.
It was what you did when someone died; turned toward God and
at least acknowledged the fact.

And yet . . . how could you stand over the body of a man you'd
killed, and look God in the face?

He couldn't sit. The tiredness filled him like wet sand, but he
couldn't sit.

He stood, picked up the poker, but stood with it in hand, staring at the banked fire on his hearth. It was perfect, satin-black
embers crusted with ash, the red heat smothered just beneath. To
touch it would break the embers, make the flame leap up—only
to die at once, without fuel. A waste of wood, to throw more on,
so late at night.

He put the poker down, wandered from one wall to another, an
exhausted bee in a bottle, still-buzzing, though his wings hung tattered and forlorn.

It hadn't troubled Fraser. But then, Fraser had ceased even to
think of the bandits, directly they were dead; all his thought had
been for Claire, and that was surely understandable.

He'd led her through the morning light in that clearing, a
blood-soaked Adam, a battered Eve, looking upon the knowledge
of good and evil. And then he had wrapped her in his plaid, picked
her up, and walked away to his horse.

The men had followed, silent, leading the bandits' horses behind their own. An hour later, with the sun warm on their backs, Fraser had turned his horse's head downhill, and led them to a stream. He had dismounted, helped Claire down, then vanished with her through the trees.

The men had exchanged puzzled looks, though no one spoke. Then old Arch Bug had swung down from his mule, saying matter-of-factly, "Well, she'll want to wash then, no?"

A sigh of comprehension went over the group, and the tension lessened at once, dissolving into the small homely businesses of dismounting, hobbling, girth-checking, spitting, having a piss. Slowly, they sought each other, looking for something to say, searching for relief in commonplace.

He caught Ian's eye, but they were yet too stiff with each other for this; Ian turned, clapped a hand round Fergus's shoulder, and hugged him, then pushed him away with a small rude joke about his stink. The Frenchman gave him a tiny smile and lifted the darkened hook in salute.

Kenny Lindsay and old Arch Bug were sharing out tobacco, stuffing their pipes in apparent tranquillity. Tom Christie wandered over to them, pale as a ghost, but pipe in hand. Not for the first time, Roger realized the valuable social aspects of smoking.

Arch had seen him, though, standing aimless near his horse, and come to talk to him, the old man's voice calm and steadying. He had no real idea what Arch said, let alone what he replied; the simple act of conversation seemed to let him breathe again and still the tremors that ran over him like breaking waves.

Suddenly, the old man broke off what he was saying, and nodded over Roger's shoulder.

"Go on, lad. He needs ye."

Roger had turned to see Jamie standing at the far side of the clearing, half-turned away and leaning on a tree, his head bowed in thought. Had he made some sign to Arch? Then Jamie glanced round, and met Roger's eye. Yes, he wanted him, and Roger found himself standing beside Fraser, with no clear memory of having crossed the ground between them.

Jamie reached out and squeezed his hand, hard, and he held on, squeezing back.

"A word, *a cliamhuinn*," Jamie said, and let go. "I wouldna speak so now, but there may be no good time later, and there's little time to bide." He sounded calm, too, but not like Arch. There were broken things in his voice; Roger felt the hairy bite of the rope, hearing it, and cleared his own throat.

"Say, then."

Jamie took a deep breath, and shrugged a bit, as though his shirt were too tight.

"The bairn. It's no right to ask ye, but I must. Would ye feel the same for him, and ye kent for sure he wasna your own?"

"What?" Roger simply blinked, making no sense whatever of this. "Bai—ye mean Jem?"

Jamie nodded, eyes intent on Roger's.

"Well, I . . . I dinna ken, quite," Roger said, baffled as to what this was about. Why? And why *now*, of all times?

"Think."

He *was* thinking, wondering what the hell? Evidently this thought showed, for Fraser ducked his head in acknowledgment of the need to explain himself further.

"I ken . . . it's no likely, aye? But it's possible. She might be wi' child by the night's work, d'ye see?"

He did see, with a blow like a fist under the breastbone. Before he could get breath to speak, Fraser went on.

"There's a day or two, perhaps, when I might—" He glanced away, and a dull flush showed through the streaks of soot with which he had painted his face. "There could be doubt, aye? As there is for you. But . . ." He swallowed, that "but" hanging eloquent.

Jamie glanced away, involuntarily, and Roger's eyes followed the direction of his gaze. Beyond a screen of bush and red-tinged creeper, there was an eddy pool, and Claire knelt on the far side, naked, studying her reflection. The blood thundered in Roger's ears, and he jerked his eyes away, but the image was seared on his mind.

She did not look human, was the first thing he thought. Her body mottled black with bruises, her face unrecognizable, she looked like something strange and primal, an exotic creature of the forest pool. Beyond appearance, though, it was her attitude that struck him. She was remote, somehow, and still, in the way that a tree is still, even as the air stirs its leaves.

He glanced back, unable not to. She bent over the water, studying her face. Her hair hung wet and tangled down her back, and she skimmed it back with the palm of a hand, holding it out of the way as she surveyed her battered features with dispassionate intentness.

She prodded gently here and there, opening and closing her jaw as her fingertips explored the contours of her face. Testing, he supposed, for loose teeth and broken bones. She closed her eyes and traced the lines of brow and nose, jaw and lip, hand as sure and delicate as a painter's. Then she seized the end of her nose with determination and pulled hard.

Roger cringed in reflex, as blood and tears poured down her face, but she made no sound. His stomach was already knotted into a small, painful ball; it rose up into his throat, pressing against the rope scar.

She sat back on her heels, breathing deeply, eyes closed, hands cupped over the center of her face.

He became suddenly aware that she *was* naked, and he was still staring. He jerked away, blood hot in his face, and glanced surreptitiously toward Jamie in hopes that Fraser had not noticed. He hadn't—he was no longer there.

Roger looked wildly round, but spotted him almost at once. His relief at not being caught staring was superseded at once by a jolt of adrenaline, when he saw what Fraser was doing.

He was standing beside a body on the ground.

Fraser's gaze flicked briefly round, taking note of his men, and Roger could almost feel the effort with which Jamie suppressed his own feelings. Then Fraser's bright blue eyes fastened on the man at his feet, and Roger saw him breathe in, very slowly.

Lionel Brown.

Quite without meaning to, Roger had found himself striding across the clearing. He took up his place at Jamie's right without conscious thought, his attention similarly fixed on the man on the ground.

Brown's eyes were shut, but he wasn't asleep. His face was bruised and swollen, as well as patched with fever, but the expression of barely suppressed panic was plain on his battered features. Fully justified, too, so far as Roger could see.

The sole survivor of the night's work, Brown was still alive only because Arch Bug had stopped young Ian Murray inches away from smashing his skull with a tomahawk. Not from any hesitation about killing an injured man, from cold pragmatism.

"Your uncle will have questions," Arch had said, narrowed eyes on Brown. "Let this one live long enough to answer them."

Ian had said nothing, but pulled his arm from Arch Bug's grasp and turned on his heel, disappearing into the shadows of the forest like smoke.

Jamie's face was much less expressive than his captive's, Roger thought. He himself could tell nothing of Fraser's thoughts from his expression—but scarcely needed to. The man was still as stone, but seemed nonetheless to throb with something slow and inexorable. Merely to stand near him was terrifying.

"How say you, O, friend?" Fraser said at last, turning to Arch, who stood on the far side of the pallet, white-haired and blood-streaked. "Can he be traveling further, or will the journey kill him?"

Bug leaned forward, peering dispassionately at the supine Brown.

"I say he will live. His face is red, not white, and he is awake. You wish to take him with us, or ask your questions now?"

For a brief instant the mask lifted, and Roger, who had been watching Jamie's face, saw in his eyes precisely what he wished to do. Had Lionel Brown seen it, too, he would have leaped off his pallet and run, broken leg or no. But his eyes stayed stubbornly shut, and as Jamie and old Arch were speaking in Gaelic, Brown remained in ignorance.

Without answering Arch's question, Jamie knelt and put his hand on Brown's chest. Roger could see the pulse hammering in Brown's neck and the man's breathing, quick and shallow. Still, he kept his lids squeezed tight shut, though the eyeballs rolled to and fro, frantic beneath them.

Jamie stayed motionless for what seemed a long time—and must have been an eternity to Brown. Then he made a small sound that might have been either a contemptuous laugh or a snort of disgust, and rose.

"We take him. See that he lives, then," he said in English. "For now."

Brown had continued to play possum through the journey to the Ridge, in spite of the bloodthirsty speculations various of the party had made within his hearing on the way. Roger had helped to unstrap him from the travois at journey's end. His garments and wrappings were soaked with sweat, the smell of fear a palpable miasma round him.

Claire had made a movement toward the injured man, frowning, but Jamie had stopped her with a hand on her arm. Roger hadn't heard what he murmured to her, but she nodded and went with him into the Big House. A moment later, Mrs. Bug had appeared, uncharacteristically silent, and taken charge of Lionel Brown.

Murdina Bug was not like Jamie, nor old Arch; her thoughts were plain to see in the bloodless seam of her mouth and the thunderous brow. But Lionel Brown took water from her hand and, open-eyed, watched her as though she were the light of his salvation. She would, Roger thought, have been pleased to kill Brown like one of the cockroaches she ruthlessly exterminated from her kitchen. But Jamie wished him kept alive, so alive he would stay.

For now.

A sound at the door jerked Roger's attention back to the present. Brianna!

It wasn't, though, when he opened the door; only the rattle of wind-tossed twigs and acorn caps. He looked down the dark path, hoping to see her, but there was no sign of her yet. Of course, he told himself, Claire would likely need her.

So do I.

He squashed the thought, but stayed at the door, looking out, wind whining in his ears. She'd gone up to the Big House at once, the moment he came to tell her that her mother was safe. He hadn't said much more, but she had seen something of how matters stood—there was blood on his clothes—and had barely paused to assure herself that none of it was his before rushing out.

He closed the door carefully, looking to see that the draft hadn't wakened Jemmy. He had an immense urge to pick the boy up, and in spite of long-ingrained parental wariness about disturbing a sleeping child, scooped Jem out of his trundle; he had to.

Jem was heavy in his arms, and groggy. He stirred, lifted his head, and blinked, blue eyes glassy with sleep.

"It's okay," Roger whispered, patting his back. "Daddy's here."

Jem sighed like a punctured tire and dropped his head on Roger's shoulder with the force of a spent cannonball. He seemed to inflate again for a moment, but then put his thumb in his mouth and subsided into that peculiarly boneless state common to sleeping children. His flesh seemed to melt comfortably into Roger's own, his trust so complete that it was not necessary even to maintain the boundaries of his body—Daddy would do that.

Roger closed his eyes against starting tears, and pressed his mouth against the soft warmth of Jemmy's hair.

The firelight made black and red shadows on the insides of his lids; by looking at them, he could keep the tears at bay. It didn't matter what he saw there. He had a small collection of grisly moments, vivid from the dawn, but he could look at those un-moved—for now. It was the sleeping trust in his arms that moved him, and the echo of his own whispered words.

Was it even a memory? Perhaps it was no more than a wish—that he had once been roused from sleep, only to sleep again in strong arms, hearing, "Daddy's here."

He took deep breaths, slowing to the rhythm of Jem's breathing, calming himself. It seemed important not to weep, even though there was no one to see or care.

Jamie had looked at him, as they moved from Brown's pallet, the question clear in his eyes.

"Ye dinna think I mind only for myself, I hope?" he had said, low-voiced. His eyes had turned toward the gap in the brush where Claire had gone, half-squinting as though he could not bear to look, but couldn't keep his eyes away.

"For her," he said, so low that Roger scarcely heard. "Would she rather . . . have the doubt, d'ye think? If it came to that."

Roger took a deep breath of his son's hair, and hoped to God he'd said the right thing, there among the trees.

"I don't know," he'd said. "But for you—if there's room for doubt—I say, take it."

If Jamie were disposed to follow that advice, Bree should be home soon.

"I'm fine," I said firmly. "Perfectly fine."

Bree narrowed her eyes at me.

"Sure you are," she said. "You look like you've been run over by a locomotive. *Two* locomotives."

"Yes," I said, and touched my split lip gingerly. "Well. Yes. Other than that, though . . ."

"Are you hungry? Sit down, Mama, I'll make you some tea, then maybe a little supper."

I wasn't hungry, didn't want tea, and particularly didn't want to sit down—not after a long day on horseback. Brianna was already taking down the teapot from its shelf above the sideboard, though, and I couldn't find the proper words to stop her. All of a sudden, I seemed to have no words at all. I turned toward Jamie, helpless.

He somehow divined my feeling, though he couldn't have read much of anything on my face, given its current state. He stepped forward, though, and took the teapot from her, murmuring something too low for me to catch. She frowned at him, glanced at me, then back, still frowning. Then her face changed a little, and she came toward me, looking searchingly into my face.

"A bath?" she asked quietly. "Shampoo?"

"Oh, yes," I said, and my shoulders sagged in grateful relief. "Please."

I did sit down then, after all, and let her sponge my hands and feet, and wash my hair in a basin of warm water drawn from the cauldron in the hearth. She did it quietly, humming under her breath, and I began to relax under the soothing scrub of her long, strong fingers.

I'd slept—from sheer exhaustion—part of the way, leaning on Jamie's chest. There's no way of achieving real rest on horseback, though, and I found myself now close to nodding off, noticing only in a dreamy, detached sort of way that the water in the basin had turned a grubby, cloudy red, full of grit and leaf fragments.

I'd changed to a clean shift; the feel of the worn linen on my skin was sheer luxury, cool and smooth.

Bree was humming softly, under her breath. What was it . . . "Mr. Tambourine Man," I thought. One of those sweetly silly songs of the sixt—

1968.

I gasped, and Bree's hands gripped my head, steadying me.

"Mama? Are you all right? Did I touch something—"

"No! No, I'm fine," I said, looking down into the swirls of dirt and blood. I took a deep breath, heart pounding. "Perfectly fine. Just—began to doze off, that's all."

She snorted, but took her hands away and went to fetch a pitcher of water for rinsing, leaving me gripping the edge of the table and trying not to shudder.

You don't act afraid of men. You oughta act more afraid. That particularly ironic echo came to me clearly, along with the outline of the young man's head, leonine hair seen silhouetted by the firelight. I couldn't recall his face clearly—but surely I would have noticed that hair?

Jamie had taken my arm, afterward, and led me out from under my sheltering tree, into the clearing. The fire had been scattered during the fight; there were blackened rocks and patches of singed and flattened grass here and there—among the bodies. He had led me slowly from one to another. At the last, he had paused, and said quietly, "Ye see that they are dead?"

I did, and knew why he had shown me—so I need not fear their return, or their vengeance. But I had not thought to count them. Or to look closely at their faces. Even had I been sure how many there were . . . another shiver struck me, and Bree wrapped a warm towel around my shoulders, murmuring words I didn't hear for the questions clamoring in my head.

Was Donner among the dead? Or had he heeded me, when I'd told him that if he were wise, he'd run? He hadn't struck me as a wise young man.

He *had* struck me as a coward, though.

Warm water sluiced around my ears, drowning out the sound of Jamie's and Brianna's voices overhead; I caught only a word or two, but when I sat back up, with water dripping down my neck, clutching a towel to my hair, Bree was reluctantly moving toward her cloak, hung on the peg by the door.

"Are you *sure* you're all right, Mama?" The worried frown was back between her brows, but this time I could muster a few words of reassurance.

"Thank you, darling; that was wonderful," I said, with complete sincerity. "All I want just now is sleep," I added with somewhat less.

I was still terribly tired, but now completely wakeful. What I did want was . . . well, I didn't know quite what I *did* want, but a general absence of solicitous company was on the list. Besides, I'd caught a glimpse of Roger earlier, bloodstained, white, and swaying with weariness; I wasn't the only victim of the recent unpleasantness.

"Go home, lass," Jamie said softly. He swung the cloak from its peg and over her shoulders, patting her gently. "Feed your man. Take him to bed, and say a prayer for him. I'll mind your mother, aye?"

Bree's gaze swung between us, blue and troubled, but I put on what I hoped was a reassuring expression—it hurt to do it, rather—and after a moment's hesitation, she hugged me tight, kissed my forehead very gently, and left.

Jamie shut the door and stood with his back against it, hands behind him. I was used to the impassive facade he normally used to shield his thoughts when troubled or angry; he wasn't using it, and the expression on his face troubled *me* no end.

"You mustn't worry about me," I said, as reassuringly as I could. "I'm not traumatized, or anything of that sort."

"I mustn't?" he asked guardedly. "Well . . . perhaps I wouldna, if I kent what ye meant by it."

"Oh." I blotted my damp face gingerly, and patted at my neck with the towel. "Well. It means . . . very much injured—or dreadfully shocked. It's Greek, I think—the root word, I mean, 'trauma.'"

"Oh, aye? And you're not . . . shocked. Ye say."

His eyes narrowed, as he examined me with the sort of critical attention usually employed when contemplating the purchase of expensive bloodstock.

"I'm fine," I said, backing away a little. "Just—I'm all right. Only a bit . . . shaken."

He took a step toward me, and I backed up abruptly, aware belatedly that I was clutching the towel to my bosom as though it were a shield. I forced myself to lower it, and felt blood prickle unpleasantly in patches over face and neck.

He stood very still, regarding me with that same narrow look. Then his gaze dropped to the floor between us. He stood as though deep in thought, and then his big hands flexed. Once, twice. Very slowly. And I heard—heard clearly—the sound of Arvin Hodgepile's vertebrae parting one from another.

Jamie's head jerked up, startled, and I realized that I was standing on the other side of the chair from him, the towel wadded and pressed against my mouth. My elbows moved like rusty hinges, stiff and slow, but I got the towel down. My lips were nearly as stiff, but I spoke, too.

"I am a little shaken, yes," I said very clearly. "I'll be all right. Don't worry. I don't want you to worry."

The troubled scrutiny in his eyes wavered suddenly, like the glass of a window struck by a stone, in the split second before it shatters, and he shut his eyes. He swallowed once, and opened them again.

"Claire," he said very softly, and the smashed and splintered fragments showed clear, sharp and jagged in his eyes. "I have *been* raped. And ye say I must not worry for ye?"

"Oh, God damn it!" I flung the towel on the floor, and immediately wished I had it back again. I felt naked, standing in my shift, and hated the crawling of my skin with a sudden passion that made me slap my thigh to kill it.

"Damn, damn, damn it! I *don't* want you to have to think of that again. I don't!" And yet I had known from the first that this would happen.

I took hold of the chairback with both hands and held tight, and tried to force my own gaze into his, wanting so badly to throw myself upon those glittering shards, to shield him from them.

"Look," I said, steadying my voice. "I don't want—I don't want to make you recall things better left forgotten."

The corner of his mouth actually twitched at that.

"God," he said, in something like wonder. "Ye think I'd forgot any of it?"

"Maybe not," I said, surrendering. I looked at him through swimming eyes. "But—oh, Jamie, I so wanted you to forget!"

He put out a hand, very delicately, and touched the tip of his index finger to the tip of mine, where I clutched the chair.

"Dinna mind it," he said softly, and withdrew the finger. "It's no matter now. Will ye rest a bit, Sassenach? Or eat, maybe?"

"No. I don't want . . . no." In fact, I couldn't decide *what* I wanted to do. I didn't want to do anything at all. Other than unzip my skin, climb out, and run—and that didn't seem feasible. I took a few deep breaths, hoping to settle myself and go back to that nice sense of utter exhaustion.

Should I ask him about Donner? But what was there to ask? *"Did you happen to kill a man with long, tangled hair?"* They'd all looked like that, to some extent. Donner had been—or possibly still was—an Indian, but no one would have noticed that in the dark, in the heat of fighting.

"How—how is Roger?" I asked, for lack of anything better to say. "And Ian? Fergus?"

He looked a little startled, as though he had forgotten their existence.

"Them? The lads are well enough. No one took any hurt in the fight. We had luck."

He hesitated, then took a careful step toward me, watching my face. I didn't scream or bolt, and he took another, coming close enough that I could feel the warmth of his body. Not startled this time, and chilly in my damp shift, I relaxed a little, swaying toward him, and saw the tension in his own shoulders let go slightly, seeing it.

He touched my face, very gently. The blood throbbed just below the surface, tender, and I had to brace myself not to flinch away from his touch. He saw it, and drew back his hand a little, so that it hovered just above my skin—I could feel the heat of his palm.

"Will it heal?" he asked, fingertips moving over the split in my left brow, then down the minefield of my cheek to the scrape on my jaw where Harley Boble's boot had just missed making a solid connection that would have broken my neck.

"Of course it will. You know that; you've seen worse on battlefields." I would have smiled in reassurance, but didn't want to open the deep split in my lip again, and so made a sort of pouting goldfish mouth, which took him by surprise and made *him* smile.

"Aye, I know." He ducked his head a little, shy. "It's only . . ." His hand still hovered near my face, an expression of troubled anxiety on his own. "Oh, God, *mo nighean donn,*" he said softly. "Oh, Christ, your lovely face."

"Can you not bear to look at it?" I asked, turning my own eyes away and feeling a sharp little pang at the thought, but trying to convince myself that it didn't matter. It *would* heal, after all.

His fingers touched my chin, gently but firmly, and drew it up, so that I faced him again. His mouth tightened a little as his gaze moved slowly over my battered face, taking inventory. His eyes were soft and dark in the candlelight, the corners tight with pain.

"No," he said quietly, "I cannot bear it. The sight of ye tears my heart. And it fills me with such rage I think I must kill someone or burst. But by the God who made ye, Sassenach, I'll not lie with ye and be unable to look ye in the face."

"Lie with me?" I said blankly. "What . . . you mean *now*?"

His hand dropped from my chin, but he looked steadily at me, not blinking.

"Well . . . aye. I do."

Had my jaw not been so swollen, my mouth would have dropped open in pure astonishment.

"Ah . . . why?"

"Why?" he repeated. He dropped his gaze then, and made the odd shrugging motion that he made when embarrassed or discomposed. "I—well—it seems . . . necessary."

I had a thoroughly unsuitable urge to laugh.

"Necessary? Do you think it's like being thrown by a horse? I ought to get straight back on?"

His head jerked up and he shot me an angry glance.

"No," he said, between clenched teeth. He swallowed hard and visibly, obviously reining in strong feelings. "Are ye—are ye badly damaged, then?"

I stared at him as best I could, through my swollen lids.

"Is that a joke of some—oh," I said, it finally dawning on me what he meant. I felt heat rise in my face, and my bruises throbbed.

I took a deep breath, to be sure of being able to speak steadily.

"I have been beaten to a bloody pulp, Jamie, and abused in several nasty ways. But only one . . . there was only the one who actually . . . He—he wasn't . . . rough." I swallowed, but the hard knot in my throat didn't budge perceptibly. Tears made the candlelight blur so that I couldn't see his face, and I looked away, blinking.

"No!" I said, my voice sounding rather louder than I intended. "I'm not . . . damaged."

He said something in Gaelic under his breath, short and explosive, and shoved himself away from the table. His stool fell over with a loud crash, and he kicked it. Then he kicked it again, and again, and stamped on it with such violence that bits of wood flew across the kitchen and struck the pie safe with little pinging sounds.

I sat completely still, too shocked and numb to feel distress. Should I not have told him? I wondered vaguely. But he knew, surely. He had asked, when he found me. *"How many?"* he had demanded. And then had said, *"Kill them all."*

But then . . . to know something was one thing, and to be told the details another. I did know that, and watched with a dim sense of guilty sorrow as he kicked away the splinters of the stool and flung himself at the window. It was shuttered, but he stood, hands braced on the sill and his back turned to me, shoulders heaving. I couldn't tell if he was crying.

The wind was rising; there was a squall coming in from the west. The shutters rattled, and the night-smoored fire spouted puffs of soot as the wind came down the chimney. Then the gust passed, and there was no sound but the small sudden *crack!* of an ember in the hearth.

"I'm sorry," I said at last, in a small voice.

Jamie swiveled on his heel at once and glared at me. He wasn't crying, but he had been; his cheeks were wet.

"Don't you dare be sorry!" he roared. "I willna have it, d'ye hear?" He took a giant step toward the table and crashed his fist down on it, hard enough to make the saltcellar jump and fall over. "Don't be sorry!"

I had closed my eyes in reflex, but forced myself to open them again.

"All right," I said. I felt terribly, terribly tired again, and very much like crying myself. "I won't."

There was a charged silence. I could hear chestnuts falling in the grove behind the house, dislodged by the wind. One, and then another, and another, a rain of muffled tiny thumps. Then Jamie drew a deep, shuddering breath, and wiped a sleeve across his face.

I put my elbows on the table and leaned my head on my hands; it seemed much too heavy to hold up anymore.

"Necessary," I said, more or less calmly to the tabletop. "What did you mean, necessary?"

"Does it not occur to you that ye might be with child?" He'd got himself back under control, and said this as calmly as he might have asked whether I planned to serve bacon with the breakfast porridge.

Startled, I looked up at him.

"I'm not." But my hands had gone by reflex to my belly.

"I'm not," I repeated more strongly. "I can't be." I could, though—just possibly. The chance was a remote one, but it existed. I normally used some form of contraception, just to be certain—but obviously . . .

"I am *not*," I said. "I'd know."

He merely stared at me, eyebrows raised. I wouldn't; not so soon. So soon—soon enough that if it *were* so, and if there were more than one man . . . there would be doubt. The benefit of the doubt; that's what he offered me—and himself.

A deep shudder started in the depths of my womb and spread instantly through my body, making goose bumps break out on my skin, despite the warmth of the room.

"Martha," the man had whispered, the weight of him pressing me into the leaves.

"Bloody, bloody hell," I said very quietly. I spread my hands out flat on the table, trying to think.

"Martha." And the stale smell of him, the meaty press of damp bare thighs, rasping with hair—

"No!" My legs and buttocks pressed together so tightly in revulsion that I rose an inch or two on the bench.

"You might—" Jamie began stubbornly.

"I'm not," I repeated, just as stubbornly. "But even if—you can't, Jamie."

He looked at me, and I caught the flicker of fear in his eyes. That, I realized with a jolt, was exactly what he was afraid of. Or one of the things.

"I mean we can't," I said quickly. "I'm almost sure that I'm not pregnant—but I'm not at all sure that I haven't been exposed to some disgusting disease." That was something else I hadn't thought of until now, and the goose bumps were back in full force. Pregnancy was unlikely; gonorrhea or syphilis weren't. "We—we can't. Not until I've had a course of penicillin."

I was rising from the bench even as I spoke.

"Where are ye going?" he asked, startled.

"The surgery!"

The hallway was dark, and the fire out in my surgery, but that didn't stop me. I flung open the door of the cupboard, and began groping hastily about. A light fell over my shoulder, illuminating the shimmering row of bottles. Jamie had lit a taper and come after me.

"What in the name of God are ye doing, Sassenach?"

"Penicillin," I said, seizing one of the bottles and the leather pouch in which I kept my snake-fang syringes.

"Now?"

"Yes, bloody now! Light the candle, will you?"

He did, and the light wavered and grew into a globe of warm yellow, gleaming off the leather tubes of my homemade syringes. I had a good bit of penicillin mixture to hand, luckily. The liquid in the bottle was pink; many of the *Penicillium* colonies from this batch had been grown in stale wine.

"Are ye sure it will work?" Jamie asked quietly, from the shadows.

"No," I said, tight-lipped. "But it's what I have." The thought of spirochetes, multiplying silently in my bloodstream, second by second, was making my hand shake. I choked down the fear that the penicillin might be defective. It had worked miracles on gross superficial infections. There was no reason why—

"Let me do it, Sassenach." Jamie took the syringe from my hand; my fingers were slippery and fumbling. His were steady, his face calm in candlelight as he filled the syringe.

"Do me first, then," he said, handing it back.

"What—you? But you don't need to—I mean—you hate injections," I ended feebly.

He snorted briefly and lowered his brows at me.

"Listen, Sassenach. If I mean to fight my own fears, and yours—and I do—then I shallna boggle at pinpricks, aye? Do it!" He turned his side to me and bent over, one elbow braced on the counter, and hitched up the side of his kilt, baring one muscular buttock.

I wasn't sure whether to laugh or cry. I might have argued further with him, but a glance at him, standing there bare-arsed and stubborn as Black Mountain, decided me of the futility of that. He'd made up his mind, and we were both going to live with the consequences.

Feeling suddenly and oddly calm, I lifted the syringe, squeezing gently to remove any air bubbles.

"Shift your weight, then," I said, nudging him rudely. "Relax this side; I don't want to break the needle."

He drew in his breath with a hiss; the needle was thick, and there was enough alcohol from the wine to make it sting badly, as I discovered when I took my own injection a minute later.

"Ouch! Ow! Oh, Jesus H. Roosevelt Christ!" I exclaimed, gritting my teeth as I withdrew the needle from my thigh. "Christ, that hurts!"

Jamie gave me a lopsided smile, still rubbing his backside.

"Aye, well. The rest of it won't be worse than this, I expect."

The rest of it. I felt suddenly hollow, and light-headed with it, as though I hadn't eaten for a week.

"You—you're sure?" I asked, putting down the syringe.

"No," he said. "I'm not." He took a deep breath then, and looked at me, his face uncertain in the wavering candlelight. "But I mean to try. I must."

I smoothed the linen night rail down over my punctured thigh, looking at him as I did it. He'd dropped all his masks long since; the doubt, the anger, and the fear were all there, etched plain in the desperate lines of his face. For once, I thought, my own countenance was less easy to read, masked behind its bruises.

Something soft brushed past my leg with a small *mirp!* and I looked down to see that Adso had brought me a dead vole, no doubt by way of sympathy. I started to smile, felt my lip tingle, and then looked up at Jamie and let it split as I did smile, the taste of blood warm silver on my tongue.

"Well . . . you've come whenever I've needed you; I rather think you'll do it this time, too."

He looked completely blank for an instant, not grasping the feeble joke. Then it struck him, and blood rushed to his face. His lip twitched, and twitched again, unable to decide between shock and laughter.

I thought he turned his back then to hide his face, but in fact, he had only turned to search the cupboard. He found what he was looking for, and turned round again with a bottle of my best muscat wine in his hand, shining dark. He held it to his body with his elbow, and took down another.

"Aye, I will," he said, reaching out his free hand to me. "But if ye think either one of us is going to do this sober, Sassenach, ye're verra much mistaken."

A gust of wind from the open door roused Roger from uneasy sleep. He had fallen asleep on the settle, his legs trailing on the floor, Jemmy snuggled warmly heavy on his chest.

He looked up, blinking and disoriented, as Brianna stooped to take the little boy from his arms.

"Is it raining out?" he said, catching a whiff of damp and ozone from her cloak. He sat up and rubbed a hand over his face to rouse himself, feeling the scruff of a four-day beard.

"No, but it's going to." She laid Jemmy back in his trundle, covered him, and hung up the cloak before coming to Roger. She smelled of the night, and her hand was cold on his flushed cheek. He put his arms round her waist and leaned his head against her, sighing.

He would have been happy to stay that way forever—or at least the next hour or two. She stroked his head gently for a moment, though, then moved away, stooping to light the candle from the hearth.

"You must be starved. Shall I fix you something?"

"No. I mean . . . yes. Please." As the last remnants of grogginess fell away, he realized that he was, in fact, starving. After their stop at the stream in the morning, they hadn't stopped again, Jamie anxious to get home. He couldn't recall when he'd last eaten, but hadn't felt any sense of hunger at all until this minute.

He fell on the bread and butter and jam she brought him, ravenous. He ate single-mindedly, and it was several minutes before he thought to ask, swallowing a final thick, buttery, sweet bite, "How's your mother?"

"Fine," she said, with an excellent imitation of Claire with her stiffest English upper lip. "*Perfectly* fine." She grimaced at him, and he laughed, though quietly, with an automatic glance at the trundle.

"Is she, then?"

Bree raised an eyebrow at him.

"Do *you* think so?"

"No," he admitted, sobering. "But I don't think she's going to tell you if she's not. She'll not want ye worrying."

She made a rather rude glottal noise in response to this notion, and turned her back on him, lifting the long veil of hair off her neck.

"Will you do my laces?"

"You sound just like your father when ye make that noise— only higher-pitched. Have ye been practicing?" He stood up and pulled the laces loose. Undid her stays as well, then on impulse, slid his hands inside the opened gown, resting them on the warm swell of her hips.

"Every day. Have you?" She leaned back against him, and his hands came up, cupping her breasts by reflex.

"No," he admitted. "It hurts." It was Claire's suggestion—that he try to sing, pitching his voice both higher and lower than normal, in hopes of loosening his vocal cords, perhaps restoring a bit of his original resonance.

"Coward," she said, but her voice was nearly as soft as the hair that brushed his cheek.

"Aye, I am," he said as softly. It did hurt, but it wasn't the physical pain that he minded. It was feeling the echo of his old voice in his bones—the ease and power of it—and then hearing the uncouth noises that emerged with such difficulty now from his throat—croaks and grunts and squeals. Like a pig choking to death on a crow, he thought disparagingly.

"It's them that are cowards," Bree said, still speaking softly, but with steel in her voice. She tensed a little in his arms. "Her face—her poor face! How could they? How could anybody do something like that?"

He had a sudden vision of Claire, naked by the pool, silent as the rocks, her breasts streaked with the blood from her newly set nose. He drew back, nearly jerking his hands away.

"What?" Brianna said, startled. "What's the matter?"

"Nothing." He pulled his hands out of her gown and stepped back. "I—er, is there maybe a bit of milk?"

She looked at him oddly, but went out to the lean-to at the back and brought in a jug of milk. He drank it thirstily, aware of her eyes on him, watchful as a cat's, as she undressed and changed into her night rail.

She sat down on the bed and began to brush out her hair, preparing to plait it for sleep. On impulse, he reached out and took the brush from her. Without speaking, he ran one hand through the thickness of her hair, lifting it, smoothing it back from her face.

"You're beautiful," he whispered, and felt tears come to his eyes again.

"So are you." She lifted her hands to his shoulders and brought him slowly down to his knees before her. She looked searchingly into his eyes—he did his best to look back. She smiled a little, then, and reached to untie the thong that held his own hair back.

It fell around his shoulders in a dusty black tangle, smelling of burned things, stale sweat, and horses. He protested when she took up her hairbrush, but she ignored him, and made him bend his head over her lap, while she picked pine straw and sandburs from his head, slowly working out the snarls. His head bent lower, and lower still, and he found himself at last with his forehead pressed into her lap, breathing in the close scent of her.

He was reminded of medieval paintings, sinners kneeling, heads bowed in confession and remorse. Presbyterians did not confess on their knees—Catholics still did, he thought. In darkness, like this—in anonymity.

"Ye've not asked me what happened," he whispered at last, to the shadows of her thighs. "Did your father tell ye?"

He heard her draw breath, but her voice was calm when she replied.

"No."

She said no more, and the room was quiet, save for the sound of the brush through his hair, and the rising rush of the wind outside.

How would it be for Jamie? Roger wondered suddenly. Would he really do it? Try to . . . He shied away from the thought, unable to contemplate it. Seeing instead a picture of Claire, coming out of the dawn, her face a swollen mask. Still herself, but remote as a distant planet on an orbit departing for the outer reaches of deep space—when might it come in sight again? Stooping to touch the dead, at Jamie's urging, to see for herself the price of her honor.

It wasn't the possibility of a child, he thought suddenly. It was fear—but not of that. It was Jamie's fear that he would lose her— that she would go, swing out into a dark and solitary space without him, unless he could somehow bind her to him, keep her with him. But, Christ, what a risk to take—with a woman so shocked and brutalized, how could he risk it?

How could he not?

Brianna laid down the brush, though she kept a hand gently on his head, stroking it. He knew that fear too well himself—remembered the gulf that once had lain between them, and the courage it had taken to leap over it. For both of them.

He was some kind of a coward, maybe—but not that kind.

"Brianna," he said, and felt the lump in his throat, the scar of the rope. She heard the need in his voice and looked at him as he raised his head, hand lifting toward his face, and he seized it hard, pressing the palm of it against his cheek, rubbing against it.

"Brianna," he said again.

"What? What is it?" Her voice was soft, not to wake the bairn, but full of urgency.

"Brianna, will ye hear me?"

"You know I will. What is it?" Her body was against him, wanting to tend him, and he desired the comfort of her so badly that he would have lain down there on the rug before the fire and buried his head between her breasts—but not yet.

"Only—listen to what I must say. And then—please God—tell me I have done right." *Tell me that you love me, still,* he meant, but could not say it.

"You don't have to tell me anything," she whispered. Her eyes were dark and soft, bottomless with forgiveness not yet earned. And somewhere beyond them, he saw another pair of eyes, staring up at him in drunken bewilderment, changing abruptly into fear as he raised his arm for the killing blow.

"Yes, I do," he said softly. "Put out the candle, aye?"

Not the kitchen, still strewn with emotional wreckage. Not the surgery, with all its sharp-edged memories. Jamie hesitated, but then nodded toward the stair, raising one eyebrow. I nodded, and followed him up to our bedroom.

It seemed both familiar and strange, as places do when one is away for a time. Perhaps it was only my injured nose that made it smell strange, too; perhaps I only imagined that I could smell it—cold and somehow stale, though everything was swept and dusted. Jamie poked up the fire and light sprang up, wavering in bright swaths over the wooden walls, the scents of smoke and hot resin helping to fill the sense of emptiness in the room.

Neither of us glanced toward the bed. He lit the candlestick on the washstand, then set our two stools near the window, and opened the shutters to the restless night. He'd brought two pewter cups; he filled these and set them on the broad sill, along with the bottles.

I stood just inside the doorway, watching his preparations, feeling thoroughly peculiar.

I was suffering the oddest contradiction of feelings. On the one hand, I felt as though he were a complete stranger. I could not even imagine, let alone recall, a sense of ease in touching him. His body was no longer the comfortable extension of my own, but something foreign, unapproachable.

At the same time, alarming surges of lust ripped through me without warning. It had been happening all day. This was nothing like the slow burn of accustomed desire, nor yet the instant spark of passion. Not even that cyclic and mindless womb-yearning sense of a need to mate that belonged entirely to the body. This was frightening.

He stooped to put another stick on the fire, and I nearly staggered, as all the blood left my head. The light shone on the hair of his arms, the dark hollows of his face—

It was the sheer impersonal sense of a voracious *appetite*—something that possessed me, but was not part of me—that terrified me. It was fear of it that made me avoid his touch, more than the feeling of estrangement.

"Are ye all right, Sassenach?" He had caught sight of my face, and stepped toward me, frowning. I held up a hand to stop him.

"Fine," I said, feeling breathless. I sat down hastily, my knees weak, and picked up one of the cups he had just filled. "Um . . . cheers."

Both his brows went up, but he moved to take his own seat opposite me.

"Cheers," he said quietly, and touched his cup to mine, the wine heavy and sweet-smelling in my hand.

My fingers were cold; so were my toes, and the tip of my nose. That changed, too, without warning. Another minute, and I might be suffused with heat, sweating and flushed. But for the moment, I was cold, and shivered in the rainy breeze from the window.

The wine's aroma was strong enough to make an impact, even on my damaged membranes, and the sweetness was a comfort to nerves and stomach alike. I drank the first cup quickly, and poured another, urgently wanting a small layer of oblivion between reality and myself.

Jamie drank more slowly, but refilled his own cup when I did. The cedar blanket chest, warmed by the fire, was beginning to spread its own familiar fragrance through the room. He glanced at me now and then, but said nothing. The silence between us was not awkward, precisely, but it *was* charged.

I should say something, I thought. But what? I sipped the second cup, racking my brain.

At last, I reached out slowly and touched his nose, where the thin line of the long-healed break pressed white against the skin.

"Do you know," I said, "you've never told me how you came to break your nose. Who set it for you?"

"Och, that? No one." He smiled, touching his nose a little self-consciously. "'Twas only luck that the break was a clean one, for I didna pay it the slightest heed at the time."

"I suppose not. You said—" I broke off, suddenly recalling what he *had* said. When I had found him again, in his printer's shop in Edinburgh, I'd asked him when he'd broken it. He'd answered, *"About three minutes after I last saw ye, Sassenach."* On the eve of Culloden, then—on that rocky Scottish hill, below the ring of standing stones.

"I'm sorry," I said a little weakly. "You probably don't want to think about that, do you?"

He seized my free hand, hard, and looked down at me.

"You may have it," he said. His voice was very low, but he met my eyes straight on. "All of it. Anything that was ever done to me. If ye wish it, if it helps ye, I will live it through again."

"Oh, God, Jamie," I said softly. "No. I don't need to know; all I need is to know that you *did* live through it. That you're all right. But . . ." I hesitated. "Will I tell *you*?" What was done to me, I meant, and he knew it. He did glance away then, though he held my hand in both of his, cradling it and rubbing his palm gently over my bruised knuckles.

"Must you?"

"I think so. Sometime. But not now—not unless you . . . you need to hear." I swallowed. "First."

He shook his head, very slightly, but still didn't look at me.

"Not now," he whispered. "Not now."

I took my hand away, and swallowed the rest of the wine in my cup, rough and warm and musky with the tang of grape skins. I had stopped going hot and cold by turns; now I was only warm throughout, and grateful for it.

"Your nose," I said, and poured another cup. "Tell me, then. Please."

He shrugged slightly.

"Aye, well. There were two English soldiers, come scouting up the hill. I think they didna expect to find anyone—neither had his musket loaded, or I should ha' died there."

He spoke quite casually. A small shiver went over me, but not from cold.

"They saw me, ken, and then one of them saw you, up above. He shouted, and made to go after ye, so I threw myself on him. I didna care at all what happened, so long as ye were safe away, so I went for him bald-heided; plunged my dirk into his side. But his bullet box swung into my way and the knife stuck in it, and—" He smiled, lopsided. "And while I was trying to get it free and keep from bein' killed, his friend came up and swung the stock of his musket into my face."

His free hand had curled up as he spoke, grasping the hilt of a remembered dirk.

I flinched, knowing now exactly what that had felt like. Just hearing about it made my own nose throb. I sniffed, dabbed cautiously at it with the back of my hand, and poured more wine.

"How did you get away?"

"I took the musket from him and clubbed them both to death with it."

He spoke quietly, almost colorlessly, but there was an odd resonance to his voice that made my stomach shift uneasily. It was too fresh, that sight of the blood drops gleaming by dawn light in the hairs of his arm. Too fresh, that undertone of—what was it? satisfaction?—in his voice.

I was suddenly too restless to sit still. A moment before I had been so exhausted that my bones were melting; now I had to move. I stood up, leaning out over the sill. The storm was coming; the wind was freshening, blowing back my new-washed hair, and lightning flickered in the distance.

"I'm sorry, Sassenach," Jamie said, sounding worried. "I shouldna have told ye. Are ye bothered by it?"

"Bothered? No, not by that."

I spoke a little tersely. Why had I asked him about his nose, of all things? Why now, when I had been content to live in ignorance for the last several years?

"What bothers ye, then?" he asked quietly.

What was bothering me was that the wine had been doing its job of anesthetizing me nicely; now I had ruined it. All the images of the night before were back inside my head, thrown into vivid Technicolor by that simple statement, that oh-so-matter-of-fact, *"I took the musket from him and clubbed them both to death with it."* And its unspoken echo, *It is myself who kills for her.*

I wanted to throw up. Instead, I gulped more wine, not even

tasting it, swallowing it down as fast as I could. I dimly heard Jamie ask again what bothered me, and swung round to glare at him.

"What bothers me—bothers! What a stupid word! What drives me absolutely *mad* is that I might have been anyone, anything—a convenient warm spot with spongy bits to squeeze—God, I was no more than a *hole* to them!"

I struck the sill with my fist, then, angered by the impotent little thump of it, picked up my cup, turned round, and hurled it against the wall.

"It wasn't that way with Black Jack Randall, was it?" I demanded. "He knew you, didn't he? He saw *you* when he used you; it wouldn't have been the same if you were anyone—he wanted *you.*"

"My God, ye think that was better?" he blurted, and stared at me, eyes wide.

I stopped, panting for breath and feeling dizzy.

"No." I dropped onto the stool and closed my eyes, feeling the room go round and round me, colored lights like a carousel behind my eyes. "No. I don't. I think Jack Randall was a bloody sociopathic, grade-A pervert, and these—these"—I flipped a hand, unable to think of a suitable word—"they were just . . . men."

I spoke the last word with a sense of loathing evident even to me.

"Men," Jamie said, his voice sounding odd.

"Men," I said. I opened my eyes and looked at him. My eyes felt hot, and I thought they must glow red, like a possum's in torchlight.

"I have lived through a fucking world war," I said, my voice low and venomous. "I have lost a child. I have lost two husbands. I have starved with an army, been beaten and wounded, been patronized, betrayed, imprisoned, and attacked. And I have fucking survived!" My voice was rising, but I was helpless to stop it. "And now should I be shattered because some wretched, pathetic excuses for men stuck their nasty little appendages between my legs and *wiggled* them?!" I stood up, seized the edge of the washstand and heaved it over, sending everything flying with a crash—basin, ewer, and lighted candlestick, which promptly went out.

"Well, I won't," I said quite calmly.

"Nasty little appendages?" he said, looking rather stunned.

"Not yours," I said. "I didn't mean yours. I'm rather fond of yours." Then I sat down and burst into tears.

His arms came round me, slowly and gently. I didn't startle or jerk away, and he pressed my head against him, smoothing my damp, tangled hair, his fingers catching in the mass of it.

"Christ, ye are a brave wee thing," he murmured.

"Not," I said, eyes closed. "I'm not." I grabbed his hand and brought it to my lips, closing my eyes as I did so.

I brushed my battered mouth across his knuckles, blind. They were swollen, as bruised as mine; I touched my tongue to his flesh, tasted soap and dust and the silver taste of scrapes and gashes—marks left by bones and broken teeth. Pressed my fingers to the veins beneath the skin of wrist and arm, softly resilient, and the solid lines of the bones beneath. I felt the tributaries of his veins, wished to enter into his bloodstream, travel there, dissolved and bodiless, to take refuge in the thick-walled chambers of his heart. But I couldn't.

I ran my hand up his sleeve, exploring, clinging, relearning his body. I touched the hair in his oxter and stroked it, surprised at the soft, silky feel of it.

"Do you know," I said, "I don't believe I've ever touched you there before?"

"I dinna believe ye have," he said, with a hint of nervous laughter in his voice. "I would ha' remembered. Oh!" A stipple of gooseflesh burst out over the soft skin there, and I pressed my forehead to his chest.

"The worst of it is," I said, into his shirt, "that I knew *them*. Each one of them. And I'll remember them. And feel guilty that they're dead, because of me."

"No," he said softly, but very firmly. "They are dead because of *me*, Sassenach. And because of their own wickedness. If there is guilt, let it rest upon them. Or on me."

"Not on you alone," I said, my eyes still closed. It was dark in there, and soothing. I could hear my voice, distant but clear, and wondered dimly where the words were coming from. "You're blood of my blood, bone of my bone. You said so. What you do rests on me, as well."

"Then may your vow redeem me," he whispered.

He lifted me to my feet and gathered me to him, like a tailor gathering up a length of fragile, heavy silk—slowly, long-fingered, fold upon fold. He carried me then across the room, and laid me gently on the bed, in the light from the flickering fire.

He'd meant to be gentle. Very gentle. Had planned it with care, worrying each step of the long way home. She was broken; he must go canny, take his time. Be careful in gluing back her shattered bits.

And then he came to her and discovered that she wished no part of gentleness, of courting. She wished directness. Brevity and violence. If she was broken, she would slash him with her jagged edges, reckless as a drunkard with a shattered bottle.

For a moment, two moments, he struggled, trying to hold her close and kiss her tenderly. She squirmed like an eel in his arms, then rolled over him, wriggling and biting.

He'd thought to ease her—both of them—with the wine. He'd known she lost all sense of restraint when in drink; he simply hadn't realized what she was restraining, he thought grimly, trying to seize her without hurting.

He, of all people, should have known. Not fear or grief or pain—but rage.

She raked his back; he felt the scrape of broken nails, and thought dimly that was good—she'd fought. That was the last of his thought; his own fury took him then, rage and a lust that came on him like black thunder on a mountain, a cloud that hid all from him and him from all, so that kind familiarity was lost and he was alone, strange in darkness.

It might be her neck he grasped, or anyone's. The feel of small bones came to him, knobbled in the dark, and the screams of rabbits, killed in his hand. He rose up in a whirlwind, choked with dirt and the scourings of blood.

Wrath boiled and curdled in his balls, and he rode to her spurs. Let his lightning blaze and sear all trace of the intruder from her womb, and if it burnt them both to bone and ash—then let it be.

When sense came back to him, he lay with his weight full on her, crushing her into the bed. Breath sobbed in his lungs; his hands clenched her arms so hard he felt the bones like sticks about to snap within his grasp.

He had lost himself. Was not sure where his body ended. His mind flailed for a moment, panicked lest it have been unseated altogether—no. He felt a drop of cold, sudden on his shoulder, and the scattered parts of him drew at once together like shattered bits of quicksilver, to leave him quaking and appalled.

He was still joined to her. He wanted to bolt like a startled quail, but managed to move slowly, loosening his fingers one by one from their death grip on her arms, lifting his body gently away, though the effort of it seemed immense, as though his weight were that of moons and planets. He half-expected to see her crushed and flattened, lifeless on the sheet. But the springy arch of her ribs rose and fell and rose again, roundly reassuring.

Another drop struck him in the back of his neck, and he hunched his shoulders in surprise. Caught by his movement, she looked up, and he met her eyes with shock. She shared it; the shock of strangers meeting one another naked. Her eyes flicked away from his, up toward the ceiling.

"The roof's leaking," she whispered. "There's a wet patch."

"Oh." He had not even realized that it was raining. The room was dark with rainlight, though, and the roof thrummed overhead. The sound of it seemed inside his blood, like the beat of the bodhrana inside the night, like the beat of his heart in the forest.

He shuddered, and for lack of any other notion, kissed her forehead. Her arms came up sudden as a snare and held him fiercely, pulling him down onto her again and he seized her, too, crushing her to him hard enough to feel the breath go out of her, unable to let go. He thought vaguely of Brianna's talk of giant orbs that whirled through space, the thing called gravity—and what was grave about it? He saw that well enough just now: a force so great as to balance some body unthinkably immense in thin air, unsupported—or send two such bodies crashing into each other, in an explosion of destruction and the smoke of stars.

He'd bruised her; there were dark red marks on her arms where his fingers had been. They would be black within the day. The marks of other men bloomed black and purple, blue and yellow, clouded petals trapped beneath the whiteness of her skin.

His thighs and buttocks were strained with effort, and a cramp took him hard, making him groan and twist to ease it. His skin was wet; so was hers, and they slid apart with slow reluctance.

Eyes puffed and bruised, clouded like wild honey, inches from his own.

"How do you feel?" she asked softly.

"Terrible," he replied with complete honesty. He was hoarse, as though he had been screaming—God, perhaps he had been. Her mouth had bled again; there was a red smear on her chin, and the taste of metal from it in his own mouth.

He cleared his throat, wanting to look away from her eyes, but unable to do it. He rubbed a thumb over the smear of blood, clumsily erasing it.

"You?" he asked, and the words were like a rasp in his throat. "How do ye feel?"

She had drawn back a little at his touch, but her eyes were still fixed on his. He had the feeling that she was looking far beyond him, through him—but then the focus of her gaze came back, and she looked directly at him, for the first time since he had brought her home.

"Safe," she whispered, and closed her eyes. She took one huge breath and her body relaxed all at once, going limp and heavy like a dying hare.

He held her, both arms wrapped around her as though to save her from drowning, but felt her sink away all the same. He wished to call out to her not to go, not to leave him alone. She vanished into the depths of sleep, and he yearned after her, wishing her healed, fearing her flight, and bent his head, burying his face in her hair and her scent.

The wind banged the open shutters as it passed, and in the dark outside, one owl hooted and another answered, hiding from the rain.

Then he cried, soundless, muscles strained to aching that he might not shake with it, that she might not wake to know it. He wept to emptiness and ragged breath, the pillow wet beneath his face. Then lay exhausted beyond the thought of tiredness, too far from sleep even to recall what it was like. His only comfort was the small, so fragile weight that lay warm upon his heart, breathing.

Then her hands rose and rested on him, the tears cool on his face, congealing, the white of her clean as the silent snow that covers char and blood and breathes peace upon the world.

30

The Captive

I t was a still, warm morning; the last of the Indian summer. A woodpecker hammered in the wood nearby, and some insect was making a noise like rasping metal in the tall grass beyond the house. I came downstairs slowly, feeling mildly disembodied—and wishing I were, since the body I had hurt almost everywhere.

Mrs. Bug hadn't come this morning; perhaps she wasn't feeling well. Or perhaps she wasn't sure yet how to deal with seeing me, or what to say to me when she did. My mouth tightened a little, something I realized only because the partially healed split in my lip stung when I did it.

I very consciously relaxed my face and went about getting down the coffee things from the kitchen shelf. There was a trail of tiny black ants running along the edge of the shelf, and a swarm of them over the small tin box in which I kept lump sugar. I flicked them off with a few stern swipes of my apron, and made a mental note to see about finding some avens root for repellant.

That resolve, small as it was, made me feel better and steadier at once. Ever since Hodgepile and his men had turned up at the malting shed, I had been completely at the mercy of someone else, prevented from any sort of independent action. For the first time in days—it seemed much longer—I was able to decide what I was going to do. It seemed a precious liberty.

Very well, I thought. What would I do, then? I would . . . drink some coffee. Eat a bit of toast? No. I felt gingerly with my tongue; several teeth on one side were loose, and my jaw muscles so sore that serious chewing was out of the question. Just coffee, then, and while I drank it, I would decide upon the shape of my day.

Feeling pleased with this plan, I put back the plain wooden cup, and instead ceremoniously set out my sole china cup and saucer, a delicate bit of porcelain Jocasta had given me, hand-painted with violets.

Jamie had poked up the fire earlier and the kettle was boiling; I dipped out enough water to warm the pot, swished it round, and opened the back door in order to toss it out. Fortunately, I looked first.

Ian was sitting cross-legged on the back porch, a small whet-stone in one hand, knife in the other.

"Good morn to ye, Auntie," he said cheerfully, and drew the knife across the stone, making the thin, monotonous rasping noise I had heard earlier. "Feeling better, then?"

"Yes, fine," I assured him. He raised one eyebrow dubiously, looking me over.

"Well, better than ye look, I hope."

"Not *that* good," I said tartly, and he laughed. He put down the knife and stone and got to his feet. He was much taller than I; nearly Jamie's height, though thinner. He'd inherited his father's whipcord leanness, as well as the elder Ian's sense of humor—and his toughness.

He took me by the shoulders and turned me into the sunlight, pursing his lips a little as he inspected me at close range. I blinked up at him, imagining what I must look like. I hadn't had the nerve to look into a mirror yet, but I knew the bruising must be going from blacks and reds to a colorful assortment of blues, greens, and yellows. Add in assorted knobbly swellings, flecks of crusty black for the split lip and the scabby bits, and I was undoubtedly quite the picture of health.

Ian's soft hazel eyes peered intently into my face with no ap-parent surprise or distress, though. At last he let go, and patted my shoulder gently.

"Ye'll do, Auntie," he said. "It's still you, isn't it?"

"Yes," I said. And with no warning at all, tears welled up and overflowed. I knew exactly what he'd meant, and why he'd said it—and it was true.

I felt as though my center had turned unexpectedly to liquid and was gushing out, not from grief, but from relief. I *was* still me. Fragile, battered, sore, and wary—but myself. Only when I recognized that, did I realize how much I had feared that I might not be—that I might emerge from shock and find myself irrevocably altered, some vital part forever missing.

"I'm all right," I assured Ian, hastily wiping my eyes with the edge of my apron. "Just a bit—"

"Aye, I know," he said, and took the pot from me, tossing the water into the grass by the path. "It's a bit strange, aye? Coming back."

I took the coffeepot from him, squeezing his hand hard as I did so. He had come back twice from captivity: rescued from Geillis Duncan's strange compound on Jamaica, only to choose later exile with the Mohawk. He had come to manhood on that journey, and I did wonder what parts of himself might have been left behind on the way.

"Do you want breakfast, Ian?" I asked, sniffing and dabbing gingerly at my swollen nose.

"Of course I do," he said, grinning. "Come and sit yourself down, Auntie—I'll fetch it."

I followed him inside, filled the coffeepot and set it to brew, then sat at the table, the sun on my back through the open door, and watched as Ian rummaged the pantry. My mind felt soggy and incapable of thought, but a sense of peace crept over me, gentle as the wavering light through the chestnut trees. Even the small throbbings here and there seemed pleasant, a sense of healing being quietly accomplished.

Ian spread an armload of random foodstuffs on the table and sat down across from me.

"All right, Auntie?" he asked again, raising one of his father's feathery eyebrows.

"Yes. It's rather like sitting on a soap bubble, though. Isn't it?" I glanced at him as I poured the coffee, but he looked down at the chunk of bread he was buttering. I thought a slight smile touched his lips, but couldn't tell for sure.

"Something like," he said quietly.

The heat of the coffee warmed my hands through the china, and soothed the raw membranes of my nose and palate. I felt as though I had been screaming for hours, but didn't recall actually doing any such thing. Had I, with Jamie the night before?

I didn't quite want to think about the night before; it was part of the soap-bubble feeling. Jamie had been gone when I woke, and I wasn't sure whether I was glad or sorry about that.

Ian didn't talk, but ate his way in a businesslike manner through half a loaf with butter and honey, three raisin muffins, two thick slices of ham, and a jug of milk. Jamie had done the milking, I saw; he always used the blue jug, while Mr. Wemyss used the white one. I wondered vaguely where Mr. Wemyss was—I hadn't seen him, and the house felt empty—but didn't really care. It occurred to me that perhaps Jamie had told both Mr. Wemyss and Mrs. Bug to stay away for a bit, feeling that I might need a little time alone.

"More coffee, Auntie?"

At my nod, Ian rose from the table, reached down the decanter from the shelf, and poured a large slug of whisky into my cup before refilling it.

"Mam always said it's good for what ails ye," he said.

"Your mother is right. Do you want some?"

He sniffed at the aromatic fumes, but shook his head.

"No, I think not, Auntie. I must have a clear head this morning."

"Really? Why?" The porridge in the pot wasn't nine days old—quite—but it had been there for three or four. Of course; no one had been here to eat it. I eyed the cementlike glob adhering to my spoon critically, then decided that it was still soft enough to eat, and doused it with honey.

Ian was dealing with a mouthful of the same substance, and took a moment to clear it from his palate before replying.

"Uncle Jamie means to ask his questions," he answered, giving me a cautious glance as he reached for the bread.

"Does he?" I said, rather blankly, but before I could inquire what he meant by that, the sound of footsteps on the path announced the arrival of Fergus.

He looked as though he had been sleeping in the woods—well, of course, I thought, he had been. Or rather, not sleeping; the men had barely stopped to rest in their pursuit of Hodgepile's gang. Fergus had shaved, but his normally fastidious grooming was sadly lacking, and his handsome face was gaunt, the deep eyes shadowed.

"Milady," he murmured, and unexpectedly bent to kiss my cheek, hand on my shoulder. *"Comment ça va?"*

"Tres bien, merci," I replied, smiling gingerly. "How are

Marsali and the children? And our hero, Germain?" I had asked Jamie about Marsali on the way back, and had been assured that she was all right. Germain, monkey that he was, had gone straight up a tree when he heard Hodgepile's men approaching. He had seen everything from his perch, and as soon as the men departed, had scrambled down, dragged his semiconscious mother away from the fire, and run for help.

"Ah, Germain," Fergus said, a faint smile momentarily lifting the shadows of fatigue. "*Nous p'tit guerrier.* He says *Grandpère* has promised him a pistol of his own, to shoot bad people with."

Grandpère undoubtedly meant it, I reflected. Germain couldn't manage a musket, being somewhat shorter than the gun itself—but a pistol would do. In my present state of mind, the fact that Germain was only six didn't seem particularly important.

"Have you had breakfast, Fergus?" I pushed the pot toward him.

"Non. Merci." He helped himself to cold biscuit, ham, and coffee, though I noticed that he ate without much appetite.

We all sat quietly, sipping coffee and listening to the birds. Carolina wrens had built a late nest under the eaves of the house and the parent birds swooped in and out, just above our heads. I could hear the high-pitched cheeping of the nestlings begging, and saw a scatter of twigs and a bit of empty eggshell on the floorboards of the porch. They were nearly ready to fledge; just in time, before the real cold weather came.

The sight of the brown-speckled eggshell reminded me of *Monsieur L'Oeuf.* Yes, that's what I would do, I decided, with a small sense of relief at having something firm in mind. I would go and see Marsali later. And perhaps Mrs. Bug, as well.

"Did you see Mrs. Bug this morning?" I asked, turning to Ian. His cabin—little more than a brush-roofed lean-to—lay just beyond the Bugs'; he would have passed them on his way to the house.

"Oh, aye," he said, looking a little surprised. "She was sweeping out as I went by. Offered me breakfast, but I said I'd eat here. I kent Uncle Jamie had a ham, aye?" He grinned, lifting his fourth ham biscuit in illustration.

"So she's all right? I thought she might be ill; she usually comes quite early."

Ian nodded, and took an enormous bite of the biscuit.

"Aye, I expect she's busy, minding the *ciomach*."

My fragile sense of well-being cracked like the wrens' eggs. A *ciomach* was a captive. In my soggy-minded euphoria, I had somehow managed to forget Lionel Brown's existence.

Ian's remark that Jamie meant to ask questions this morning dropped suddenly into context—as did Fergus's presence. And the knife Ian had been sharpening.

"Where is Jamie?" I asked, rather faintly. "Have you seen him?"

"Oh, aye," Ian said, looking surprised. He swallowed, and gestured toward the door with his chin. "He's just out in the woodshed, makin' new shingles. He says the roof's sprung a leak."

No sooner had he said this than the sound of hammering came from the roof, far above. Of course, I thought. First things first. But then, I supposed Lionel Brown wasn't going anywhere, after all.

"Perhaps . . . I should go and see Mr. Brown," I said, swallowing.

Ian and Fergus exchanged glances.

"No, Auntie, ye shouldn't," Ian said quite calmly, but with an air of authority I wasn't accustomed to seeing in him.

"Whatever do you mean?" I stared at him, but he merely went on eating, though a trifle more slowly.

"Milord says you should not," Fergus amplified, drizzling a spoonful of honey into his coffee.

"He says what?" I asked incredulously.

Neither of them would look at me, but they seemed to draw together, emanating a reluctant sort of stubborn resistance. Either one would do anything I asked, I knew—except defy Jamie. If Jamie thought I ought not to see Mr. Brown, I wasn't going to do it with the assistance of either Ian or Fergus.

I dropped the spoon back into my bowl of porridge, uneaten lumps still adhering to it.

"Did he happen to mention *why* he thinks I ought not to visit Mr. Brown?" I asked calmly, under the circumstances.

Both men looked surprised, then exchanged another look, this one longer.

"No, milady," Fergus said, his voice carefully neutral.

There was a brief silence, during which both of them seemed to be considering. Then Fergus glanced at Ian, deferring to him with a shrug.

"Well, d'ye see, Auntie," Ian said carefully, "we do mean to question the fellow."

"And we will have answers," Fergus said, eyes on the spoon with which he was stirring his coffee.

"And when Uncle Jamie is satisfied that he has told us what he can . . ."

Ian had laid his newly sharpened knife on the table beside his plate. He picked it up, and thoughtfully drew it down the length of a cold sausage, which promptly split open, with an aromatic burst of sage and garlic. He looked up then, and met my eyes directly. And I realized that while I might still be me—Ian was no longer the boy he used to be. Not at all.

"You'll kill him, then?" I said, my lips feeling numb in spite of the hot coffee.

"Oh, yes," Fergus said very softly. "I expect that we shall." He met my eyes now, too. There was a bleak, grim look about him, and his deep-set eyes were hard as stone.

"He—it—I mean . . . it wasn't him," I said. "It couldn't have been. He'd already broken his leg when—" I didn't seem to have enough air to finish my sentences. "And Marsali. It wasn't—I don't think he . . ."

Something behind Ian's eyes changed, as he grasped my meaning. His lips pressed tight for a moment, and he nodded.

"As well for him, then," he said shortly.

"As well," Fergus echoed, "but I think it will not matter in the end. We killed the others—why should he live?" He pushed back from the table, leaving his coffee undrunk. "I think I will go, cousin."

"Aye? I'll come too, then." Ian shoved his plate away, nodding to me. "Will ye tell Uncle Jamie we've gone ahead, Auntie?"

I nodded numbly, and watched them go, vanishing one after the other under the big chestnut tree that overhung the trail leading to the Bugs' cabin. Mechanically, I got up and began slowly to clear away the remains of the makeshift breakfast.

I really wasn't sure whether I minded a lot about Mr. Brown or not. On the one hand, I did disapprove on principle of torture and cold-blooded murder. On the other . . . while it was true enough that Brown had not personally violated or injured me, and he *had* tried to make Hodgepile release me—he'd been all in favor of killing me, later. And I hadn't the slightest doubt that he would have drowned me in the gorge, had Tebbe not intervened.

No, I thought, carefully rinsing my cup and drying it on my apron, perhaps I didn't really mind terribly about Mr. Brown.

Still, I felt uneasy and upset. What I *did* mind about, I realized, were Ian and Fergus. And Jamie. The fact was, killing someone in the heat of battle is a quite different thing from executing a man, and I knew that. Did they?

Well, Jamie did.

"And may your vow redeem me." He had whispered that to me, the night before. It was just about the last thing I recalled him saying, in fact. Well, all right; but I would greatly prefer that he didn't feel in need of redemption to start with. And as for Ian and Fergus . . .

Fergus had fought in the Battle of Prestonpans, at the age of ten. I still remembered the face of the small French orphan, soot-smeared and dazed with shock and exhaustion, looking down at me from his perch atop a captured cannon. *"I killed an English soldier, madame,"* he'd said to me. *"He fell down and I stuck him with my knife."*

And Ian, a fifteen-year-old, weeping in remorse because he thought he had accidentally killed an intruder to Jamie's Edinburgh print shop. God knew what he had done, since; he wasn't talking. I had a sudden vision of Fergus's hook, dark with blood, and Ian, silhouetted in the dark. *"And I,"* he'd said, echoing Jamie. *"It is myself who kills for her."*

It was 1773. And *on the eighteenth of April, in Seventy-five* . . . the shot heard round the world was already being loaded. The room was warm, but I shuddered convulsively. What in the name of God did I think I could shield them from? Any of them.

A sudden roar from the roof above startled me out of my thoughts.

I walked out into the dooryard and looked up, shading my eyes against the morning sun. Jamie was sitting astride the rooftree, rocking to and fro over one hand, which he held curled into his belly.

"What's going on up there?" I called.

"I've got a splinter," came the terse answer, obviously spoken through clenched teeth.

I wanted to laugh, if only as small escape from tension, but didn't.

"Well, come down, then. I'll pull it out."

"I'm no finished!"

"I don't care!" I said, suddenly impatient with him. "Come down this minute. I want to talk to you."

A bag of nails hit the grass with a sudden clank, followed instantly by the hammer.

First things first, then.

Technically, I supposed, it was a splinter. It was a two-inch sliver of cedarwood, and he'd driven it completely under the nail of his middle finger, nearly to the first joint.

"Jesus H. Roosevelt Christ!"

"Aye," he agreed, looking a little pale. "Ye might say that."

The protruding stub was too short to grip with my fingers. I hauled him into the surgery and jerked the sliver out with forceps, before one could say Jack Robinson. Jamie was saying a good deal more than Jack Robinson—mostly in French, which is an excellent language for swearing.

"You're going to lose that nail," I observed, submerging the offended digit in a small bowl of alcohol and water. Blood bloomed from it like ink from a squid.

"To hell wi' the nail," he said, gritting his teeth. "Cut the whole bloody finger off and ha' done with it! *Merde d'chevre!*"

"The Chinese used to—well, no, I suppose they still do, come to think of it—shove splinters of bamboo under people's fingernails to make them talk."

"Christ! *Tu me casses les couilles!*"

"Obviously a very effective technique," I said, lifting his hand out of the bowl and wrapping the finger tightly in a strip of linen. "Were you trying it out, before using it on Lionel Brown?" I tried to speak lightly, keeping my eyes on his hand. I felt his own gaze fix on me, and he snorted.

"What in the name of saints and archangels was wee Ian telling ye, Sassenach?"

"That you meant to question the man—and get answers."

"I do, and I shall," he said shortly. "So?"

"Fergus and Ian seemed to think that—you might be moved to use any means necessary," I said with some delicacy. "They're more than willing to help."

"I imagine they are." The first agony had abated somewhat. He breathed more deeply, and color was beginning to come back into his face. "Fergus has a right. It was his wife attacked."

"Ian seemed . . ." I hesitated, searching for the right word. Ian had seemed so calm as to be terrifying. "You didn't call Roger to help with the—the questioning?"

"No. Not yet." One corner of his mouth tucked in. "Roger Mac's a good fighter, but no the sort to scare a man, save he's truly roused. He's no deceit in him at all."

"Whereas you, Ian, and Fergus . . ."

"Oh, aye," he said dryly. "Wily as snakes, the lot of us. Ye've only to look at Roger Mac to see how safe their time must be, him and the lass. A bit of a comfort, that," he added, the tuck growing deeper. "To ken things will get better, I mean."

I could see that he was trying to change the subject, which was not a good sign. I made a small snorting noise, but it hurt my nose.

"And *you're* not truly roused, is that what you're telling me?"

He made a much more successful snorting noise, but didn't reply. He tilted his head to one side, watching as I laid out a square of gauze and began to rub dried leaves of comfrey into it. I didn't know how to say what was troubling me, but he plainly saw that something was.

"Will you kill him?" I asked baldly, keeping my eyes on the jar of honey. It was made of brown glass, and the light glowed through it as though it were a huge ball of clear amber.

Jamie sat still, watching me. I could feel his speculative gaze, though I didn't look up.

"I think so," he said.

My hands had started to tremble, and I pressed them on the surface of the table to still them.

"Not today," he added. "If I kill him, I shall do it properly."

I wasn't sure I wanted to know what constituted a proper killing, in his opinion, but he told me anyway.

"If he dies at my hand, it will be in the open, before witnesses who ken the truth of the matter, and him standing upright. I willna have it said that I killed a helpless man, whatever his crime."

"Oh." I swallowed, feeling mildly ill, and took a pinch of powdered bloodroot to add to the salve I was making. It had a faint, astringent smell, which seemed to help. "But—you might let him live?"

"Perhaps. I suppose I might ransom him to his brother—depending."

"Do you know, you sound quite like your uncle Colum. He would have thought it through like that."

"Do I?" The corner of his mouth turned up slightly. "Shall I take that as compliment, Sassenach?"

"I suppose you might as well."

"Aye, well," he said thoughtfully. The stiff fingers tapped on the tabletop, and he winced slightly as the movement jarred the injured one. "Colum had a castle. And armed clansmen at his beck. I should have some difficulty in defending this house against a raid, perhaps."

"That's what you mean by 'depending'?" I felt quite uneasy at this; the thought of armed raiders attacking the house had not occurred to me—and I saw that Jamie's forethought in storing Mr. Brown off our premises had perhaps not been entirely for the purpose of sparing my sensibilities.

"One of the things."

I mixed a bit of honey with my powdered herbs, then scooped a small dollop of purified bear grease into the mortar.

"I suppose," I said, eyes on my mixing, "that there's no point in turning Lionel Brown over to the—the authorities?"

"Which authorities did ye have in mind, Sassenach?" he asked dryly.

A good question. This part of the backcountry had not yet formed nor joined a county, though a movement was afoot to that purpose. Were Jamie to deliver Mr. Brown to the sheriff of the nearest county for trial . . . well, no, perhaps not a good idea. Brownsville lay just within the borders of the nearest county, and the current sheriff was in fact named Brown.

I bit my lip, considering. In times of stress, I tended still to respond as what I was—a civilized Englishwoman, accustomed to rely on the sureties of government and law. Well, all right, Jamie had a point; the twentieth century had its own dangers, but some things had improved. *This* was nearly 1774, though, and the colonial government was already showing cracks and fault lines, signs of the collapse to come.

"I suppose we could take him to Cross Creek." Farquard Campbell was a justice of the peace there—and a friend to Jamie's aunt, Jocasta Cameron. "Or to New Bern." Governor Martin and the bulk of the Royal Council were in New Bern—three hundred miles away. "Maybe Hillsborough?" That was the center of the Circuit Court.

"Mmphm."

This noise denoted a marked disinclination to lose several weeks' work in order to haul Mr. Brown before any of these seats of justice, let alone entrust a matter of importance to the highly unreliable—and frequently corrupt—judicial system. I looked up and met his eye, humorous but bleak. If I responded as what I was, so did Jamie.

And Jamie was a Highland laird, accustomed to follow his own laws, and fight his own battles.

"But—" I began.

"Sassenach," he said quite gently. "What of the others?"

The others. I stopped moving, paralyzed by the sudden memory: a large band of black figures, coming out of the wood with the sun behind them. But that group had split in two, intending to meet again in Brownsville, in three days' time—today, in fact.

For the moment, presumably no one from Brownsville yet knew what had happened—that Hodgepile and his men were dead, or that Lionel Brown was now a captive on the Ridge. Given the speed with which news spread in the mountains, though, it would be public knowledge within a week.

In the aftermath of shock, I had somehow overlooked the fact that there were still a number of bandits at large—and while I didn't know who they were, they knew both who I was and where I was. Would they realize that I could not identify them? Or be willing to take that risk?

Obviously, Jamie was not willing to take the risk of leaving the Ridge to escort Lionel Brown anywhere, whether or not he decided to let the man live.

The thought of the others had brought something important back to me, though. It might not be the best time to mention it, but then again, there wasn't going to be a good one.

I took a deep breath, squaring myself for it.

"Jamie."

The tone of my voice jerked him immediately from whatever he'd been thinking; he looked sharply at me, one eyebrow raised.

"I—I have to tell you something."

He paled a little, but reached out at once, grasping my hand. He took a deep breath of his own, and nodded.

"Aye."

"Oh," I said, realizing that he thought I meant that I had suddenly arrived at a point where I needed to tell him the grisly details of my experiences. "Not—not that. Not exactly." I squeezed his hand, though, and held on, while I told him about Donner.

"Another," he said. He sounded slightly stunned. "Another one?"

"Another," I confirmed. "The thing is . . . I, um, I don't remember seeing him . . . seeing him dead." The eerie sense of that dawn returned to me. I had very sharp, distinct memories—but they were disjointed, so fractured as to bear no relation to the whole. An ear. I remembered an ear, thick and cup-shaped as a woodland fungus. It was shaded in the most exquisite tones of purple, brown, and indigo, shadowed in the carved whorls of the inner parts, nearly translucent at the rim; perfect in the light of a sunbeam that cut through the fronds of a hemlock to touch it.

I recalled that ear so perfectly that I could almost reach into my memory and touch it myself—but I had no idea whose ear it had been. Was the hair that lay behind it brown, black, reddish, straight, wavy, gray? And the face . . . I didn't know. If I had looked, I hadn't seen.

He shot me a sharp look.

"And ye think he's maybe not."

"Maybe not." I swallowed the taste of dust, pine needles, and blood, and breathed the comforting fresh scent of buttermilk. "I warned him, you see. I told him you were coming, and that he didn't want you to find him with me. When you attacked the camp—he might have run. He struck me as a coward, certainly. But I don't know."

He nodded, and sighed heavily.

"Can you . . . recall, do you think?" I asked hesitantly. "When you showed me the dead. Did you look at them?"

"No," he said softly. "I wasna looking at anything save you."

His eyes had been on our linked hands. He raised them now, and looked at my face, troubled and searching. I lifted his hand and laid my cheek against his knuckles, closing my eyes for an instant.

"I'll be all right," I said. "The thing is—" I said, and stopped.

"Aye?"

"If he *did* run—where do you suppose he'd go?"

He closed his own eyes and drew a deep breath.

"To Brownsville," he said, in resignation. "And if he did, Richard Brown kens already what's become of Hodgepile and his men—and likely thinks his brother is dead, as well."

"Oh." I swallowed, and changed the subject slightly.

"Why did you tell Ian I wasn't to be allowed to see Mr. Brown?"

"I didna say that. But I think it best if ye dinna see him, that much is true."

"Because?"

"Because ye've an oath upon you," he said, sounding mildly surprised that I didn't understand immediately. "Can ye see a man injured, and leave him to suffer?"

The ointment was ready. I unwrapped his finger, which had stopped bleeding, and tamped as much of the salve under the damaged nail as I could manage.

"Probably not," I said, eyes on my work. "But why—"

"If ye mend him, care for him—and then I decide he must die?" His eyes rested on me, questioning. "How would that be for ye?"

"Well, that *would* be a bit awkward," I said, taking a deep breath to steady myself. I wrapped a thin strip of linen around the nail and tied it neatly. "Still, though . . ."

"Ye wish to care for him? Why?" He sounded curious, but not angry. "Is your oath so strong, then?"

"No." I put both hands on the table to brace myself; my knees seemed suddenly weak.

"Because I'm glad they're dead," I whispered, looking down. My hands were raw, and I fumbled while I worked because my fingers were still swollen; there were deep purple marks still sunk in the skin of my wrists. "And I am very much—" What? Afraid; afraid of the men, afraid of myself. Thrilled, in a horrible sort of way. "Ashamed," I said. "Terribly ashamed." I glanced up at him. "I hate it."

He held out his hand to me, waiting. He knew better than to touch me; I couldn't have borne being touched just then. I didn't take it, not at once, though I longed to. I looked away, speaking rapidly to Adso, who had materialized on the countertop and was regarding me with a bottomless green gaze.

"If I—I keep thinking . . . if I were to see him, help him—Christ, I *don't* want to, I don't at all! But if I could—perhaps that would . . . help somehow." I looked up then, feeling haunted. "Make . . . amends."

"For being glad they are dead—and for wanting him dead, too?" Jamie suggested gently.

I nodded, feeling as though a small, heavy weight had lifted with the speaking of the words. I didn't remember taking his hand, but it was tight on mine. Blood from his finger was seeping through the fresh bandage, but he paid no attention.

"Do you *want* to kill him?" I asked.

He looked at me for a long moment before replying.

"Oh, aye," he said very softly. "But for now, his life is surety for yours. For all of us, perhaps. And so he lives. For now. But I will ask questions—and I shall have answers."

I sat in my surgery for some time after he left. Emerging slowly from shock, I had felt safe, surrounded by home and friends, by Jamie. Now I must come to grips with the fact that nothing was safe—not I, not home nor friends—and certainly not Jamie.

"But then, you never are, are you, you bloody Scot?" I said aloud, and laughed, weakly.

Feeble as it was, it made me feel better. I rose with sudden decision and began to tidy my cupboards, lining up bottles in order of size, sweeping out bits of scattered herbs, throwing away solutions gone stale or suspect.

I had meant to go and visit Marsali, but Fergus had told me during breakfast that Jamie had sent her with the children and Lizzie to stay with the McGillivrays, where she would be cared for, and safe. If there was safety in numbers, the McGillivrays' house was certainly the place for it.

Located near Woolam's Creek, the McGillivrays' home place adjoined Ronnie Sinclair's cooper's shop, and enclosed a seething mass of cordial humanity, including not only Robin and Ute McGillivray, their son, Manfred, and their daughter Senga, but also Ronnie, who boarded with them. The usual mob scene was augmented intermittently by Senga McGillivray's fiancé,

Heinrich Strasse, and his German relatives from Salem, and by Inga and Hilda, their husbands and children, and their husbands' relatives.

Add in the men who congregated daily in Ronnie's shop, a convenient stopping place on the road to and from Woolam's Mill, and likely no one would even notice Marsali and her family, in the midst of that mob. Surely no one would seek to harm her there. But for me to go and see her . . .

Highland tact and delicacy were one thing. Highland hospitality and curiosity were another. If I stayed peacefully at home, I would likely be left in peace—at least for a while. If I were to set foot near the McGillivrays' . . . I blenched at the thought, and hastily decided that perhaps I would visit Marsali tomorrow. Or the next day. Jamie had assured me she was all right, only shocked and bruised.

The house stood around me in peace. No modern background of furnace, fans, plumbing, refrigerators. No whoosh of pilot lights or hum of compressors. Just the occasional creak of beam or floorboard, and the odd muffled scrape of a wood wasp building its nest up under the eaves.

I looked round the ordered world of my surgery—ranks of shining jars and bottles, linen screens laden with drying arrowroot and masses of lavender, bunches of nettle and yarrow and rosemary hanging overhead. The bottle of ether, sunlight glowing on it. Adso curled on the countertop, tail neatly tucked around his feet, eyes half-closed in purring contemplation.

Home. A small shiver ran down my spine. I wanted nothing more than to be alone, safe and alone, in my own home.

Safe. I had a day, perhaps two, in which home would still be safe. And then . . .

I realized that I had been standing still for some moments, staring blankly into a box of yellow nightshade berries, round and shiny as marbles. Very poisonous, and a slow and painful death. My eyes rose to the ether—quick and merciful. If Jamie did decide to kill Lionel Brown . . . But no. In the open, he'd said, standing on his feet before witnesses. Slowly, I closed the box and put it back on the shelf.

What then?

There were always chores that could be done—but nothing pressing, with no one clamoring to be fed, clothed, or cared for. Feeling quite odd, I wandered round the house for a bit, and finally went into Jamie's study, where I poked among the books on the shelf there, settling at last on Henry Fielding's *Tom Jones*.

I couldn't think how long it had been since I had read a novel. And in the daytime! Feeling pleasantly wicked, I sat by the open window in my surgery and resolutely entered a world far from my own.

I lost track of time, moving only to brush away roving insects that came through the window, or to absently scratch Adso's head when he nudged against me. Occasional thoughts of Jamie and Lionel Brown drifted through the back of my mind, but I shooed them away like the leafhoppers and midges who landed on my page, drifting in through the window. Whatever was happening in the Bugs' cabin had happened, or would happen—I simply couldn't think about it. As I read, the soap bubble formed around me once more, filled with perfect stillness.

The sun was halfway down the sky before faint pangs of hunger began to stir. It was as I looked up, rubbing my forehead and wondering vaguely whether there was any ham left, that I saw a man standing in the doorway to the surgery.

I shrieked, and leaped to my feet, sending Henry Fielding flying.

"Your pardon, mistress!" Thomas Christie blurted, looking nearly as startled as I felt. "I didna realize that you'd not heard me."

"No. I—I—was reading." I gestured foolishly toward the book on the floor. My heart was pounding, and blood surged to and fro in my body, seemingly at random, so that my face flushed, my ears throbbed, and my hands tingled, all out of control.

He stooped and picked the book up, smoothing its cover with the careful attitude of one who values books, though the volume itself was battered, its cover scarred with rings where wet glasses or bottles had been set down upon it. Jamie had got it from the owner of an ordinary in Cross Creek, in partial trade for a load of firewood; some customer had left it, months before.

"Is there no one here to care for you?" he asked, frowning as he looked around. "Shall I go and fetch my daughter to you?"

"No. I mean—I don't need anyone. I'm quite all right. What

about you?" I asked quickly, forestalling any further expressions of concern on his part. He glanced at my face, then hastily away. Eyes fixed carefully in the vicinity of my collarbone, he laid the book on the table and held out his right hand, wrapped in a cloth.

"I beg your pardon, mistress. I wouldna intrude, save . . ."

I was already unwrapping the hand. He'd ripped the incision in his right hand—probably, I realized with a small tightening of the belly, in the course of the fight with the bandits. The wound was no great matter, but there were bits of dirt and debris in the wound, and the edges were red and gaping, raw surfaces clouded with a film of pus.

"You should have come at once," I said, though with no tone of rebuke. I knew perfectly well why he hadn't—and in fact, I should have been in no state to deal with him, if he had.

He shrugged slightly, but didn't bother replying. I sat him down and went to fetch things. Luckily, there was some of the antiseptic salve left that I'd made for Jamie's splinter. That, a quick alcohol wash, clean bandage . . .

He was turning the pages of *Tom Jones* slowly, lips pursed in concentration. Evidently Henry Fielding would do as anesthetic for the job at hand; I shouldn't need to fetch a Bible.

"Do you read novels?" I asked, meaning no rudeness, but merely surprised that he might countenance anything so frivolous.

He hesitated. "Yes. I—yes." He took a very deep breath as I submerged his hand in the bowl, but it contained only water, soap-root, and a very small amount of alcohol, and he let the breath go with a sigh.

"Have you read *Tom Jones* before?" I asked, making conversation to relax him.

"Not precisely, though I know the story. My wife—"

He stopped abruptly. He'd never mentioned his wife before; I supposed that it was sheer relief at not experiencing agony yet that had made him talkative. He seemed to realize that he must complete the sentence, though, and went on, reluctantly. "My wife . . . read novels."

"Did she?" I murmured, setting about the job of debridement. "Did she like them?"

"I suppose that she must have."

There was something odd in his voice that made me glance up

from the job at hand. He caught the glance and looked away, flushing.

"I—did not approve of reading novels. Then."

He was quiet for a moment, holding his hand steady. Then he blurted, "I burnt her books."

That sounded rather more like the response I would have expected of him.

"She couldn't have been pleased about that," I said mildly, and he shot me a startled glance, as though the question of his wife's reaction was so irrelevant as to be unworthy of remark.

"Ah . . . what caused you to alter your opinion?" I asked, concentrating on the bits of debris I was picking out of the wound with my forceps. Splinters and shreds of bark. What had he been doing? Wielding a club of some kind, I thought—a tree branch? I breathed deeply, concentrating on the job to avoid thinking of the bodies in the clearing.

He moved his legs restively; I was hurting him a bit now.

"I—it—in Ardsmuir."

"What? You read it in prison?"

"No. We had no books there." He took a long breath, glanced at me, then away, and fixed his eyes on the corner of the room, where an enterprising spider had taken advantage of Mrs. Bug's temporary absence to set up web-keeping.

"In fact, I have never actually read it. Mr. Fraser, though, was accustomed to recount the story to the other prisoners. He has a fine memory," he added, rather grudgingly.

"Yes, he does," I murmured. "I'm not going to stitch it; it will be better if the wound's left to heal by itself. I'm afraid the scar won't be as neat," I added regretfully, "but I think it will heal up all right."

I spread salve thickly over the injury, and pulled the edges of the wound together as tightly as I could, without cutting off the circulation. Bree had been experimenting with adhesive bandages, and had produced something quite useful in the way of small butterfly shapes, made of starched linen and pine tar.

"So you liked Tom Jones, did you?" I said, returning to the subject. "I shouldn't have thought you'd find him an admirable character. Not much of a moral example, I mean."

"I don't," he said bluntly. "But I saw that fiction"—he pronounced the word gingerly, as though it were something dangerous—"is perhaps not, as I had thought, merely an inducement to idleness and wicked fancy."

"Oh, isn't it?" I said, amused, but trying not to smile because of my lip. "What are its redeeming characteristics, do you think?"

"Aye, well." His brows drew together in thought "I found it most remarkable. That what is essentially nothing save a confection of lies should somewise still contrive to exert a beneficial effect. For it did," he concluded, sounding still rather surprised.

"Really? How was that?"

He tilted his head, considering.

"It was distraction, to be sure. In such conditions, distraction is not evil," he assured me. "While it is of course more desirable to escape into prayer . . ."

"Oh, of course," I murmured.

"But beyond that consideration . . . it drew the men together. You would not think that such men—Highlanders, crofters—that they would find themselves in particular sympathy with . . . such situations, such persons." He waved his free hand at the book, indicating such persons as Squire Allworthy and Lady Bellaston, I supposed.

"But they would talk it over for hours—whilst we labored the next day, they would wonder why Ensign Northerton had done as he had with regard to Miss Western, and argue whether they themselves would or would not have behaved so." His face lightened a little, recalling something. "And invariably, a man would shake his head and say, 'At least I've never been treated in *that* manner!' He might be starved, cold, covered in sores, permanently separated from his family and customary circumstances—and yet he could take comfort in never having suffered such vicissitudes as had befallen these imaginary beings!"

He actually smiled, shaking his head at the thought, and I thought the smile much improved him.

I'd finished the job, and laid his hand on the table.

"Thank you," I said quietly.

He looked startled.

"What? Why?"

"I'm assuming that that injury was perhaps the result of b-battle done on my behalf," I said. I touched his hand lightly. "I, er . . . well." I took a deep breath. "Thank you."

"Oh." He looked thoroughly taken aback at this, and quite embarrassed.

"I . . . erm . . . hmm!" He pushed back the stool and rose, looking flustered.

I rose, as well.

"You'll need to have fresh salve put on every day," I said, resuming a businesslike tone. "I'll make up some more; you can come, or send Malva to fetch it."

He nodded, but said nothing, having evidently exhausted his supply of sociability for the day. I saw his eye linger on the cover of the book, though, and on impulse offered it to him.

"Would you like to borrow it? You should really read it for yourself; I'm sure Jamie can't have recalled all the details." •

"Oh!" He looked startled, and pursed his lips, frowning, as though suspecting it was a trap of some sort. When I insisted, though, he took the book, picking it up with an expression of guarded avidity that made me wonder how long it had been since he had had any book other than the Bible to read.

He nodded thanks to me, and donned his hat, turning to go. Upon a moment's impulse, I asked, "Did you ever have the chance to apologize to your wife?"

That was a mistake. His face tightened into coldness and his eyes went flat as a snake's.

"No," he said shortly. I thought for a moment that he would put the book down and refuse to take it. But instead, he tightened his lips, tucked the volume more securely under his arm, and left, without further farewell.

31

And So To Bed

No one else came. By the time night fell, I was beginning to feel rather edgy, starting at noises, searching the deepening shadows under the chestnut trees for lurking men—or worse. I thought I should cook something; surely Jamie and Ian intended coming home for supper? Or perhaps I should go down to the cabin, join Roger and Bree.

But I flinched from the notion of being exposed to any kind of solicitude, no matter how well meant, and while I hadn't yet got up the nerve to look in a mirror, was reasonably sure that the sight of me would frighten Jemmy—or at least lead to a lot of questions. I didn't want to have to try to explain to him what had happened to me. I was fairly sure that Jamie had told Brianna to stay away for a bit, and that was good. I really was in no shape to pretend to be all right. Not quite yet.

Dithering round the kitchen, I picked things up and put them down pointlessly. I opened the drawers of the sideboard and closed them—then opened the second one again, the one where Jamie kept his pistols.

Most of the pistols were gone. Only the gilt-trimmed one that didn't shoot straight was left, with a few loads and a tiny powder horn, the sort made for fancy dueling pistols.

Hands shaking only a little, I loaded it, and poured a bit of powder into the firing pan.

When the back door opened, quite some time later, I was sitting at the table, a copy of *Don Quixote* lying in front of me, pointing the pistol with both hands at the door.

Ian froze momentarily.

"Ye'd never hit anyone wi' that gun at this distance, Auntie," he said mildly, coming in.

"They wouldn't know that, would they?" I set the pistol down, gingerly. My palms were damp, and my fingers ached.

He nodded, taking the point, and sat down.

"Where's Jamie?" I asked.

"Washing. Are ye well, Auntie?" His soft hazel eyes took a casual but careful estimation of my state.

"No, but I'll do." I hesitated. "And . . . Mr. Brown? Did he— tell you anything?"

Ian made a derogatory noise.

"Pissed himself when Uncle Jamie took the dirk from his belt to clean his fingernails. We didna touch him, Auntie, dinna fash yourself."

Jamie came in then, clean-shaven, his skin cold and fresh from the well water, hair damp at his temples. Despite that, he looked tired to death, the lines of his face cut deep and his eyes shadowed. The shadows lifted a bit, though, when he saw me and the pistol.

"It's all right, *a nighean*," he said softly, touching my shoulder as he sat down beside me. "I've men set to watch the house—just in case. Though I dinna expect any trouble for some days yet."

My breath went out in a long sigh.

"You could have told me that."

He glanced at me, surprised.

"I thought ye'd know. Surely ye wouldna think I'd leave ye un-protected, Sassenach?"

I shook my head, momentarily unable to speak. Had I been in any condition to think logically, of course I wouldn't. As it was, I had spent most of the afternoon in a state of quiet—and unnecessary—terror, imagining, remembering. . . .

"I'm sorry, lass," he said softly, and put a large, cold hand on mine. "I shouldna have left ye alone. I thought—"

I shook my head, but put my other hand over his, pressing tight.

"No, you were right. I couldn't have borne any company, be-yond Sancho Panza."

He glanced at *Don Quixote*, then at me, brows raised. The book was in Spanish, which I didn't happen to speak.

"Well, some of it was close to French, and I did know the

story," I said. I took a deep breath, taking what comfort I could in the warmth of the fire, the flicker of the candle, and the proximity of the two of them, large, solid, pragmatic, and—outwardly, at least—imperturbable.

"Is there any food, Auntie?" Ian inquired, getting up to look. Lacking any appetite myself, and too jittery to focus on anything, I hadn't eaten dinner nor made anything for supper—but there was always food in that house, and without any particular fuss, Jamie and Ian had equipped themselves in short order with the remains of a cold partridge pie, several hard-cooked eggs, a dish of piccalilli, and half a loaf of bread, which they sliced up and toasted over the fire on a fork, buttering the slices and cramming them into me in a manner brooking no argument.

Hot, buttered toast is immensely comforting, even nibbled tentatively with a sore jaw. With food in my stomach, I began to feel much calmer, and capable of inquiring what they had learned from Lionel Brown.

"He put it all on Hodgepile," Jamie told me, loading piccalilli onto a slice of pie. "He would, of course."

"You didn't meet Arvin Hodgepile," I said, with a small shiver. "Er . . . to talk to, I mean."

He shot me a sharp look, but didn't address that matter any further, instead leaving it to Ian to explain Lionel Brown's version of events.

It had started with him and his brother, Richard, establishing their Committee of Safety. This, he had insisted, was intended as public service, pure and simple. Jamie snorted at that, but didn't interrupt.

Most of the male inhabitants of Brownsville had joined the committee—most of the homesteaders and small farmers nearby had not. Still, so far, so good. The committee had dealt with a number of small matters, meting out justice in cases of assault, theft, and the like, and if they had appropriated the odd hog or deer carcass by way of payment for their trouble, there hadn't been too much complaint.

"There's a great deal of feeling still, about the Regulation," Ian explained, frowning as he sliced another piece of bread. "The Browns didna join the Regulation; they'd no need to, as their cousin was sheriff, and half the courthouse ring are Browns, or marrit to Browns." Corruption, in other words, had been on their side.

Regulator sentiment still ran high in the backcountry, even though the main leaders of the movement, such as Hermon Husband and James Hunter, had left the colony. In the aftermath of Alamance, most Regulators had grown more cautious of expressing themselves—but several Regulator families who lived near Brownsville had become vocal in their criticism of the Browns' influence on local politics and business.

"Tige O'Brian was one of those?" I asked, feeling the buttered toast coalesce into a small, hard lump in my stomach. Jamie had told me what had happened to the O'Brians—and I'd seen Roger's face when he'd come back.

Jamie nodded, not looking up from his pie.

"Enter Arvin Hodgepile," he said, and took a ferocious bite. Hodgepile, having neatly escaped the constraints of the British army by pretending to die in the warehouse fire at Cross Creek, had set about making a living in various unsavory ways. And, water having a strong tendency to seek its own level, had ended up with a small gang of like-minded thugs.

This gang had begun simply enough, by robbing anyone they came across, holding up taverns, and the like. This sort of behavior tends to attract attention, though, and with various constables, sheriffs, Committees of Safety, and the like on their trail, the gang had retired from the piedmont where they began, and moved up into the mountains, where they could find isolated settlements and homesteads. They had also begun killing their victims, to avoid the nuisance of identification and pursuit.

"Or most of them," Ian murmured. He regarded the half-eaten egg in his hand for a moment, then put it down.

In his career with the army in Cross Creek, Hodgepile had made various contacts with a number of river traders and coastal smugglers. Some dealt in furs, others in anything that would bring a profit.

"And it occurred to them," Jamie said, drawing a deep breath, "that girls and women and young boys are more profitable than almost anything—save whisky, maybe." The corner of his mouth twitched, but it wasn't a smile.

"Our Mr. Brown insists he'd nothing to do wi' this," Ian added, a cynical note in his voice. "Nor had his brother or their committee."

"But how did the Browns get involved with Hodgepile's

gang?" I asked. "And what did they do with the people they kidnapped?"

The answer to the first question was that it had been the happy outcome of a botched robbery.

"Ye recall Aaron Beardsley's auld place, aye?"

"I do," I said, wrinkling my nose in reflex at the memory of that wretched sty, then emitting a small cry and clapping both hands over my abused appendage.

Jamie glanced at me, and put another bit of bread on his toasting fork.

"Well, so," he went on, ignoring my protest that I was full, "the Browns took it over, of course, when they adopted the wee lass. They cleaned it out, stocked it fresh, and went on using it as a trading post."

The Cherokee and Catawba had been accustomed to come to the place—horrid as it was—when Aaron Beardsley had operated as an Indian trader, and had continued to do business with the new management—a very beneficial and profitable arrangement all round.

"Which is what Hodgepile saw," Ian put in. The Hodgepile gang, with their usual straightforward methods of doing business, had walked in, shot the couple in charge, and begun systematically looting the place. The couple's eleven-year-old daughter, who had fortunately been in the barn when the gang arrived, had slipped out, mounted a mule, and ridden hell-for-leather for Brownsville and help. By good fortune, she had encountered the Committee of Safety, returning from some errand, and brought them back in time to confront the robbers.

There then ensued what in later years would be called a Mexican standoff. The Browns had the house surrounded. Hodgepile, however, had Alicia Beardsley Brown—the two-year-old girl who legally owned the trading post, and who had been adopted by the Browns upon the death of her putative father.

Hodgepile had enough food and ammunition inside the trading post to withstand a siege of weeks; the Browns were disinclined to set fire to their valuable property in order to drive him out, or to risk the girl's life by storming the place. After a day or two during which desultory shots were exchanged, and the members of the committee became increasingly edgy at having to camp in the woods surrounding the trading post, a flag of truce had been waved from the upper window, and Richard Brown had gone inside to parley with Hodgepile.

The result being a wary sort of merger. Hodgepile's gang would continue their operations, steering clear of any settlement under the Browns' protection, but would bring the proceeds of their robberies to the trading post, where they could be disposed of inconspicuously at a good profit, with Hodgepile's gang taking a generous cut.

"The proceeds," I said, accepting a fresh slice of buttered toast from Jamie. "That—you do mean captives?"

"Sometimes." His lips pressed tight as he poured a mug of cider and handed it to me. "And depending upon where they were. When they took captives in the mountains, some of them were sold to the Indians, through the trading post. Those they took from the piedmont, they sold to river pirates, or took to the coast to sell on to the Indies—that would be the best price, aye? A fourteen-year-old lad would bring a hundred pound, at least."

My lips felt numb, and not only from the cider.

"How long?" I said, appalled. "How many?" Children, young men, young women, wrenched from their homes and sold cold-bloodedly into slavery. No one to follow. Even if they were somehow to escape eventually, there would be no place—no one—to return to.

Jamie sighed. He looked unutterably tired.

"Brown doesna ken," Ian said quietly. "He says . . . He says he'd nothing to do with it."

"Like bloody hell he hadn't," I said, a flash of fury momentarily eclipsing horror. "He was *with* Hodgepile when they came here. He knew they meant to take the whisky. And he must have been with them before, when they—did other things."

Jamie nodded.

"He claims he tried to stop them from taking you."

"He did," I said shortly. "And then he tried to make them kill me, to stop me telling you he'd been there. And then he bloody meant to drown me himself! I don't suppose he told you that."

"No, he didn't." Ian exchanged a brief look with Jamie, and I saw some unspoken agreement pass between them. It occurred to me that I might possibly just have sealed Lionel Brown's fate. If so, I was not sure I felt guilty about it.

"What—what do you mean to do with him?" I asked.

"I think perhaps I will hang him," Jamie replied, after a moment's pause. "But I've more questions I want answered. And I must think about how best to manage the matter. Dinna bother about it, Sassenach; ye'll not see him again."

With that, he stood and stretched, muscles cracking, then shifted his shoulders, settling himself with a sigh. He gave me a hand and helped me to my feet.

"Go up to bed, Sassenach, and I'll be up directly. I must just have a wee word with Ian first."

Hot buttered toast, cider, and conversation had made me feel momentarily better. I found myself so tired, though, that I could barely drag myself up the stairs, and was obliged to sit on the bed, swaying blearily, in hopes of getting up the strength to take off my clothes. It was a few moments before I noticed that Jamie was hovering in the doorway.

"Erm . . . ?" I said vaguely.

"I didna ken, did ye want me to stay with ye tonight?" he asked diffidently. "If ye'd rest better alone, I could take Joseph's bed. Or if ye'd like, I could sleep beside ye, on the floor."

"Oh," I said blankly, trying to weigh these alternatives. "No. Stay. Sleep with me, I mean." From the bottom of a well of fatigue, I summoned something like a smile. "You can warm the bed, at least."

A most peculiar expression flitted across his face at that, and I blinked, not sure I'd seen it. I had, though; his face was caught between embarrassment and dismayed amusement—with somewhere behind all that the sort of look he might have worn if going to the stake: heroically resigned.

"What on *earth* have you been doing?" I asked, sufficiently surprised as to be shaken out of my torpor.

Embarrassment was getting the upper hand; the tips of his ears were going red, and a flush was visible in his cheeks, even by the dim light of the taper I'd set on the table.

"I wasna going to tell ye," he muttered, avoiding my gaze. "I swore wee Ian and Roger Mac to silence."

"Oh, they've been silent as the grave," I assured him. Though this statement did perhaps explain the occasional odd look on Roger's face, of late. "What's been going on?"

He sighed, scraping the edge of his boot across the floor.

"Aye, well. It's Tsisqua, d'ye see? He meant it as hospitality, the first time, but then when Ian told him . . . well, it wasna the best thing to have said, under the circumstances, only . . . And then the next time we came, and there they were again, only a different pair, and when I tried to make them leave, they said Bird said to say that it was honor to my vow, for what good was a vow that cost nothing to keep? And I will be damned if I ken does he mean that, or is he only thinking that either I'll crack and he'll have the upper hand of me for good, or that I'll get him the guns he wants to put an end to it one way or the other—or is he only having a joke at my expense? Even Ian says he canna tell which it is, and if he—"

"Jamie," I said. "What are you talking about?"

He stole a quick glance at me, then looked away again.

"Ah . . . naked women," he blurted, and went red as a piece of new flannel.

I stared at him for a moment. My ears still buzzed slightly, but there wasn't anything wrong with my hearing. I pointed a finger at him—carefully, because all my fingers were swollen and bruised.

"You," I said, in measured tones, "come here right now. Sit down right there"—I pointed at the bed beside me—"and tell me in words of one syllable *exactly* what you've been doing."

He did, with the result that five minutes later I was lying flat on the bed, wheezing with laughter, moaning with the pain to my cracked ribs, and with helpless tears running down my temples and into my ears.

"Oh, God, oh, God, oh, God," I gasped. "I can't stand it, I really can't. Help me sit up." I extended a hand, yelped with pain as his fingers closed on my lacerated wrist, but got upright at last, bent over with a pillow clutched to my middle, and clutched it tighter each time a gust of recurrent laughter struck me.

"I'm glad ye think it's sae funny, Sassenach," Jamie said very dryly. He'd recovered himself to some extent, though his face was still flushed. "Ye're sure ye're no hysterical?"

"No, not at all." I sniffed, dabbing at my eyes with a damp linen hankie, then snorted with uncontainable mirth. "Oh! Ow, God, that hurts."

Sighing, he poured a cup of water from the flask on the bed-side table, and held it for me to drink. It was cool, but flat and rather stale; I thought perhaps it had been standing since before . . .

"All right," I said, waving the cup away and dabbing moisture very carefully from my lips. "I'm fine." I breathed shallowly, feeling my heart begin to slow down. "Well. So. At least now I know why you've been coming back from the Cherokee villages in such a state of—of—" I felt an unhinged giggle rising, and bent over, moaning as I stifled it. "Oh, Jesus H. Roosevelt Christ. And here I thought it was thoughts of me, driving you mad with lust."

He snorted then himself, though mildly. He put down the cup, rose, and turned back the coverlet. Then he looked at me, and his eyes were clear, unguarded.

"Claire," he said, quite gently, "it *was* you. It's always been you, and it always will be. Get into bed, and put the candle out. As soon as I've fastened the shutters, smoored the hearth, and barred the door, I'll come and keep ye warm."

"Kill me." *Randall's eyes were fever-bright. "Kill me," he said. "My heart's desire."*

He jerked awake, hearing the words echo in his head, seeing the eyes, seeing the rain-matted hair, Randall's face, wet as that of a drowned man.

He rubbed a hand hard over his own face, surprised to feel his skin dry, his beard no more than a shadow. The sense of wet, the itching scurf of a month's whiskers, was still so strong that he got up, moving quietly by instinct, and went to the window, where moonlight shone through the cracks in the shutter. He poured a little water into the basin, moved the bowl into a shaft of light, and looked in, to rid himself of that lingering sense of being someone else, somewhere else.

The face in the water was no more than a featureless oval, but smooth-shaven, and the hair lay loose on his shoulders, not bound up for battle. And yet it seemed the face of a stranger.

Unsettled, he left the water in the bowl, and after a moment, padded softly back to the bed.

She was asleep. He had not even thought of her when he woke, but now the sight of her steadied him. That face he knew, even battered and swollen as it was.

He set his hand on the bedstead, comforted by the solid wood. Sometimes when he woke, the dream stayed with him, and he felt the real world ghostly, faint around him. Sometimes he feared he was a ghost.

But the sheets were cool on his skin, and Claire's warmth a re-assurance. He reached for her, and she rolled over, curled herself backward into his arms with a small moan of content, her bum roundly solid against him.

She fell asleep again at once; she hadn't really waked. He had an urge to rouse her, make her talk to him—only to be quite sure she could see him, hear him. He only held her tight, though, and over her curly head he watched the door, as though it might open and Jack Randall stand there, soaked and streaming.

Kill me, he'd said. My heart's desire.

His heart beat slow, echoing in the ear he pressed against the pillow. Some nights, he would fall asleep listening to it, comforted by the fleshy, monotonous thump. Other times, like now, he would hear instead the mortal silence in between the beats—that silence that patiently awaits all men.

He had drawn the quilts up, but now put them back, so that Claire was covered but his own back lay bare, open to the chill of the room, that he might not slip warmly into sleep and risk returning to the dream. Let sleep struggle for him in the cold, and at last pull him off the precipice of consciousness, down to the deeps of black oblivion.

For he did not wish to know what Randall had meant by what he said.

32

Hanging's Too Good

In the morning, Mrs. Bug was back in the kitchen, and the air was warm and fragrant with the smells of cooking. She seemed quite as usual, and beyond a brief glance at my face and a "tsk!", not inclined to fuss. Either she had more sensitivity than I'd thought, or Jamie had had a word.

"Here, *a muirninn*, have it while it's hot." Mrs. Bug slid a heap of turkey hash from the platter onto my plate, and deftly topped it with a fried egg.

I nodded thanks and picked up my fork, with a certain lack of enthusiasm. My jaw was still so sore that eating was a slow and painful business.

The egg went down all right, but the smell of burned onion seemed very strong, oily in my nostrils. I separated a small bite of potato and mashed it against the roof of my mouth, squashing it with my tongue in lieu of chewing it, then washing it down with a sip of coffee.

More in hopes of distracting myself than because I truly wanted to know, I asked, "And how is Mr. Brown this morning?"

Her lips tightened, and she smacked down a spatula of fried potatoes as though they were Brown's brains.

"Nowhere near sae badly off as he ought to be," she said. "Hanging's too good for him, and him nay more than a wretched dungheap, crawling wi' maggots."

I spit out the bit of potato I'd been mangling, and took another hasty gulp of coffee. It hit bottom and started back up. I pushed back the bench and ran for the door, reaching it just in time to throw up into the blackberry bush, retching coffee, bile, and fried egg.

I was dimly aware of Mrs. Bug, hovering anxiously in the

doorway, and waved her away with one hand. She hesitated for a moment, but then went in again, as I stood up and started toward the well.

The entire inside of my head tasted of coffee and bile, and the back of my nose stung terribly. I felt as though my nose were bleeding again, but when I touched it gingerly, discovered that it wasn't. Careful swilling with water cleansed my mouth, and did a bit to remedy the nasty taste—but nothing to drown the panic that had come in the wake of the nausea.

I had the sudden, distinct, and thoroughly bizarre impression that my skin was missing. My legs felt shaky, and I sat down on the stump where we split kindling, heedless of splinters.

I can't, I thought. *I simply can't.*

I sat on the chopping block, lacking the will to rise. I could feel my womb, very distinctly. A small, round weight at the base of my abdomen, feeling slightly swollen, very tender.

Nothing, I thought, with what determination I could muster. Entirely normal. It always feels that way, at a particular point of my cycle. And after what we had done, Jamie and I . . . well, no bloody wonder if I were still conscious of my interior workings. Granted, we hadn't, the night before; I'd wanted nothing but to be held. On the other hand, I'd nearly ruptured myself, laughing. A small laugh escaped me now, remembering Jamie's confession. It hurt, and I clutched my ribs, but felt a little better.

"Well, bloody hell anyway," I said aloud, and got up. "I've things to do."

Propelled by this bold statement, I fetched my basket and foraging knife, told Mrs. Bug I was off, and set out toward the Christies'.

I'd check Tom's hand, then invite Malva to come out with me in search of ginseng root, and any other useful things we might come across. She was an apt pupil, observant and quick, with a good memory for plants. And I'd meant to teach her how to prepare penicillin colonies. Picking through a collection of damp, moldy garbage would be soothing. I ignored a slight tendency of my gorge to rise at the thought, and lifted my battered face to the morning sun.

And I wasn't going to worry about what Jamie meant to do with Lionel Brown, either.

33

In Which Mrs. Bug
Takes a Hand

By the next morning, I had recovered quite a bit. My stomach had settled, and I felt much more resilient, emotionally; a good thing, as whatever warnings Jamie had given Mrs. Bug about fussing over me had plainly worn off.

Everything hurt less, and my hands had nearly returned to normal, but I was still desperately tired, and it was in fact rather comforting to put my feet up on the settle and be brought cups of coffee—the tea was running very low, and no chance of more likely for several years—and dishes of rice pudding with raisins in.

"And ye're quite sure as your face will go back to lookin' like a face, are ye?" Mrs. Bug handed me a fresh muffin, dripping with butter and honey, and peered dubiously at me, lips pursed.

I was tempted to ask her what the thing on the front of my head looked like now, but was fairly sure I didn't want to hear the answer. Instead, I contented myself with a brief "Yes" and a request for more coffee.

"I kent a wumman up in Kirkcaldy once, as was kicked in the face by a cow," she said, still eyeing me critically as she dished up the coffee. "Lost her front teeth, puir creature, and ever after, her nose pointed off to the side, like *that*." She pushed her own small round nose sharply to the side with an index finger in illustration, simultaneously tucking her upper lip under the lower one to simulate toothlessness.

I touched the bridge of my own nose carefully, but it was reassuringly straight, if still puffy.

"And then there was William McCrea of Balgownie, him who fought at Sheriffsmuir with my Arch. Got in the way of an English pike, and cleaved off half his jaw, *and* the best part of his nose! Arch said ye could see straight into his gullet and his brain-box both—but he lived. On parritch, mostly," she added. "And whisky."

"What a very good idea," I said, putting down the nibbled muffin. "I believe I'll go and get some."

Carrying my cup, I escaped as quickly as I could down the hall to my surgery, followed by shouted reminiscences of Dominic Mulroney, an Irishman who'd walked face-first into a church door in Edinburgh and him sober as a sheep at the time. . . .

I shut the door of the surgery behind me, opened the window, and tossed the remains of the coffee out, then took down the bottle from the shelf and filled my cup to the brim.

I had intended to ask Mrs. Bug about Lionel Brown's state of health, but . . . perhaps that could wait. I found that my hands were trembling again, and had to press them flat on the table for a moment to steady them before I could pick up the cup.

I took a deep breath, and a swallow of whisky. Another. Yes, that was better.

Small waves of pointless panic tended still to seize me unawares. I hadn't had one this morning, and had rather hoped they'd gone away. Not quite yet, apparently.

I sipped whisky, dabbed cold sweat from my temples, and looked round for something useful to do. Malva and I had started some fresh penicillin the day before, and had made up fresh tinctures of boneset and troutlilly, and some fresh gentian salve, as well. I ended up thumbing slowly through my big black casebook, sipping whisky and dwelling on pages recounting various horrible complications of childbirth.

I realized what I was doing, but didn't seem able to stop doing it. I was *not* pregnant. I was sure of it. And yet my womb felt tender, inflamed, and my whole being disturbed.

Oh, there was a jolly one; one of Daniel Rawlings's entries, describing a slave woman of middle age, suffering from a recto-vaginal fistula that caused her to leak a constant small stream of fecal matter through the vagina.

Such fistulas were caused by battering during childbirth, and were more common in very young girls, where the strain of prolonged labor often caused such tears—or in older women, where the tissues had grown less elastic. Of course, in older women, the damage was quite likely to be accompanied by complete perineal collapse, allowing uterus, urethra—and possibly the anus for good measure—to sag through the pelvic floor.

"How extremely fortunate that I am not pregnant," I said aloud, closing the book firmly. Perhaps I'd have another go at *Don Quixote.*

On the whole, it was a considerable relief when Malva Christie came and tapped on the door, just before noon.

She gave my face a quick glance, but as she had the day before, merely accepted my appearance without comment.

"How's your father's hand?" I asked.

"Oh, it's fine, ma'am," she replied quickly. "I looked just as ye said, but no red streaks, no pus, and just that tiny bit of redness near where the skin is cut. I made him wiggle his fingers like ye said," she added, a dimple showing briefly in her cheek. "He didna want to, and carried on like I was poking thorns into him—but he did it."

"Oh, well done!" I said, and patted her on the shoulder, which made her pinken with pleasure.

"I think that deserves a biscuit with honey," I added, having noted the delectable aroma of baking that had been wafting down the hall from the kitchen for the last hour. "Come along."

As we entered the hallway and turned toward the kitchen, though, I heard an odd sort of noise from behind us. A peculiar kind of thumping or dragging outside, as though some large animal was lumbering across the hollow boards of the front stoop.

"What's that?" Malva said, looking over her shoulder in alarm.

A loud groan answered her, and a *thud!* that shook the front door as something fell against it.

"Mary, Joseph, and Bride!" Mrs. Bug had popped out of the kitchen, crossing herself. "What's that?"

My heart had begun to race at the noises, and my mouth went dry. Something large and dark blocked the line of light beneath the door, and stertorous breathing was clearly audible, interspersed with groans.

"Well, whatever it is, it's sick or injured," I said. "Stand back." I wiped my hands on my apron, swallowed, walked forward, and pulled open the door.

For a moment, I didn't recognize him; he was no more than a heap of flesh, wild hair, and disheveled garments smeared with dirt. But then he struggled up onto one knee and raised his head, panting, showing me a dead-white face, marked with bruises and glossy with sweat.

"Mr. Brown?" I said, incredulous.

His eyes were glazed; I wasn't sure that he saw me at all, but clearly he recognized my voice, for he lunged forward, nearly knocking me over. I stepped smartly back, but he caught me by the foot and held on, crying, "Mercy! Mistress, have mercy on me, I pray you!"

"What in the name of—let go. Let go, I say!" I shook my foot, trying to dislodge him, but he clung like a limpet, and went on shouting, "Mercy!" in a sort of hoarse, desperate chant.

"Oh, shut your noise, man," Mrs. Bug said crossly. Recovered from the shock of his entrance, she appeared not at all discomposed by his appearance, though substantially annoyed by it.

Lionel Brown did not shut up, but went on imploring me for mercy, despite my attempts to placate him. These were interrupted by Mrs. Bug leaning past me, a large meat-mallet in her hand, and dotting Mr. Brown smartly on the head with it. His eyes rolled back in his head and he dropped on his face without another word.

"I'm that sorry, Mrs. Fraser," Mrs. Bug said, apologetic. "I canna think how he got out, let alone came all this way!"

I didn't know how he'd got out, either, but it was quite clear how he'd come—he'd crawled, dragging his broken leg. His hands and legs were scratched and bloody, his breeches in tatters, and the whole of him covered with smears of mud, stuck full of grass and leaves.

I leaned down and plucked an elm leaf from his hair, trying to think what on earth to do with him. The obvious, I supposed.

"Help me get him into the surgery," I said, sighing as I bent to get him under the arms.

"Ye canna be doing that, Mrs. Fraser!" Mrs. Bug was scandalized. "Himself was verra fierce about it; ye mustna be troubled by this scoundrel, he said, nor even catch sight of the man!"

"Well, I'm afraid it's a bit late not to catch sight of him," I said, tugging at the inert body. "We can't just let him lie on the porch, can we? Help me!"

Mrs. Bug appeared to see no good reason why Mr. Brown ought *not* to continue lying on the porch, but when Malva—who had been pressed flat against the wall, wide-eyed, during the up-roar—came to help, Mrs. Bug gave in with a sigh, laying down her weapon and lending a hand.

He had recovered consciousness by the time we got him man-handled onto the surgery table, and was moaning, "Don't let him kill me . . . please don't let him kill me!"

"Would you be quiet?" I said, thoroughly irritated. "Let me look at your leg."

No one had improved on my original rough splinting job, and his journey from the Bugs' cabin hadn't done it any good; blood was seeping through the bandages. I was frankly amazed that he had made it, considering his other injuries. His flesh was clammy and his breath shallow, but he wasn't badly fevered.

"Will you bring me some hot water, please, Mrs. Bug?" I asked, gingerly prodding the fractured limb. "And perhaps a little whisky? He'll need something for shock."

"I will not," Mrs. Bug said, giving the patient a look of intense dislike, "We should just be saving Mr. Fraser the trouble of dealing wi' the gobshite, if he hasna got the courtesy to die by himself." She was still holding her mallet, and raised it in a threatening man-ner, causing Mr. Brown to cower and cry out, as the movement hurt his broken wrist.

"I'll fetch the water," Malva said, and disappeared.

Ignoring my attempts to deal with his injuries, Mr. Brown seized my wrist with his one good hand, his grip surprisingly strong.

"Don't let him kill me," he said hoarsely, fixing me with bloodshot eyes. "Please, I beg you!"

I hesitated. I hadn't exactly forgotten Mr. Brown's existence, but I had more or less suppressed the knowledge of it over the last day or so. I had been only too glad not to think of him.

He saw my hesitation, and licked his lips, trying again.

"Save me, Mrs. Fraser—I implore you! You are the only one he will listen to!"

With some difficulty, I detached his hand from my wrist.

"Why, exactly, do you think anyone wants to kill you?" I asked carefully.

Brown didn't laugh, but his mouth twisted bitterly at that.

"He says that he will. I don't doubt him." He seemed a little calmer now, and took a deep, shuddering breath. "Please, Mrs. Fraser," he said more softly. "I beg you—save me."

I glanced up at Mrs. Bug, and read the truth in her folded arms and tight lips. She knew.

At this point, Malva hurried in, a beaker of hot water in one hand, the whisky jug in the other.

"What shall I do?" she asked breathlessly.

"Er . . . in the cupboard," I said, trying to focus my mind. "Do you know what comfrey looks like—boneset?" I had hold of Brown's wrist, automatically checking his pulse. It was galloping.

"Aye, ma'am. Shall I put some to steep, then?" She had set down the jug and beaker and was already hunting through the cupboard.

I met Brown's eyes, trying for dispassion.

"You would have killed me, if you could," I said very quietly. My own pulse was going nearly as fast as his.

"No," he said, but his eyes slid away from mine. Only a fraction, but away. "No, I never would!"

"You told H-Hodgepile to kill me." My voice shook on the name and a flush of anger burgeoned suddenly inside me. "You know you did!"

His left wrist was likely broken, and no one had set it; the flesh was puffy, dark with bruising. Even so, he pressed his free hand over mine, urgent with the need to convince me. The smell of him was rank, hot, and feral, like—

I ripped my hand free, revulsion crawling over my skin like a swarm of centipedes. I rubbed my palm hard on my apron, trying not to throw up.

It hadn't been him. I knew that much. Of all the men, it couldn't have been him; he had broken his leg in the afternoon. There was no way in which he could have been that heavy, inexorable presence in the night, shoving, stinking. And yet I felt he was, and swallowed bile, my head going suddenly light.

"Mrs. Fraser? Mrs. Fraser!" Malva and Mrs. Bug both spoke together, and before I knew quite what was happening, Mrs. Bug had eased me onto a stool, holding me upright, and Malva was pressing a cup of whisky urgently against my mouth.

I drank, eyes closed, trying to lose myself momentarily in the clean, pungent scent and the searing taste of it.

I remembered Jamie's fury, the night he had brought me home. Had Brown been in the room with us then, there was no doubt he would have killed the man. Would he do so now, in colder blood? I didn't know. Brown clearly thought so.

I could hear Brown crying, a low, hopeless sound. I swallowed the last of the whisky, pushed the cup away, and sat up, opening my eyes. To my vague surprise, I was crying, too.

I stood up, and wiped my face on my apron. It smelled comfortingly of butter and cinnamon and fresh applesauce, and the scent of it calmed my nausea.

"The tea's ready, Mrs. Fraser," Malva whispered, touching my sleeve. Her eyes were fixed on Brown, huddled miserably on the table. "Will ye drink it?"

"No," I said. "Give it to him. Then fetch me some bandages— and go home."

I had no idea what Jamie meant to do; I had no idea what I might do, when I discovered his intent. I didn't know what to think, or how to feel. The only thing I did know for certain was that I had an injured man before me. For the moment, that would have to be enough.

For a little while, I managed to forget who he was. Forbidding him to speak, I gritted my teeth and became absorbed in the tasks before me. He sniveled, but kept still. I cleaned, bandaged, tidied, administering impersonal comfort. But as the tasks ended, I was still left with the man, and was conscious of increasing distaste each time I touched him.

At last, I was finished, and went to wash, meticulously wiping my hands with a cloth soaked in turpentine and alcohol, cleaning under each fingernail despite the soreness. I was, I realized, behaving as though he harbored some vile contagion. But I couldn't stop myself.

Lionel Brown watched me apprehensively.

"What d'ye mean to do?"

"I haven't decided yet." This was more or less true. It hadn't been a process of conscious decision, though my course of action—or lack of it—had been determined. Jamie—damn him—had been right. I saw no reason to tell Lionel Brown that, though. Not yet.

He was opening his mouth, no doubt to plead with me further, but I stopped him with a sharp gesture.

"There was a man with you named Donner. What do you know about him?"

Whatever he'd expected, it wasn't that. His mouth hung open a little.

"Donner?" he repeated, looking uncertain.

"Don't dare to tell me you don't remember him," I said, my agitation making me sound fierce.

"Oh, no, ma'am," he assured me hastily. "I recall him fine—just fine! What"—his tongue touched the raw corner of his mouth—"what d'ye want to know about him?"

The main thing I wanted to know was whether he was dead or not, but Brown almost certainly didn't know that.

"Let's start with his full name," I proposed, sitting down gingerly beside him, "and go from there."

In the event, Brown knew little more for sure about Donner *than* his name—which, he said, was Wendigo.

"What?" I said incredulously, but Brown appeared to find nothing odd in it.

"That's what he said it was," he said, sounding hurt that I should doubt him. "Indian, in't it?"

It was. It was, to be precise, the name of a monster from the mythology of some northern tribe—I couldn't recall which. Brianna's high-school class had once done a unit of Native American myths, with each child undertaking to explain and illustrate a particular story. Bree had done the Wendigo.

I recalled it only because of the accompanying picture she had drawn, which had stuck with me for some time. Done in a reverse technique, the basic drawing done in white crayon, showing through an overlay of charcoal. Trees, lashing to and fro in a swirl of snow and wind, leaf-stripped and needle-flying, the spaces between them part of the night. The picture had a sense of urgency about it, wildness and movement. It took several moments of looking at it before one glimpsed the face amid the branches. I had actually yelped and dropped the paper when I saw it—much to Bree's gratification.

"I daresay," I said, firmly suppressing the memory of the Wendigo's face. "Where did he come from? Did he live in Brownsville?"

He had stayed in Brownsville, but only for a few weeks. Hodgepile had brought him from somewhere, along with his other men. Brown had taken no notice of him; he caused no trouble.

"He stayed with the widow Baudry," Brown said, sounding suddenly hopeful. "Might be he told her something of himself. I could find out for you. When I go home." He gave me a look of what I assumed he meant to be doglike trust, but which looked more like a dying newt.

"Hmm," I said, giving him a look of extreme skepticism. "We'll see about that."

He licked his lips, trying to look pitiful.

"Could I maybe have some water, ma'am?"

I didn't suppose I could let him die of thirst, but I had had quite enough of ministering to the man personally. I wanted him out of my surgery and out of my sight, as soon as possible. I nodded brusquely and stepped into the hall, calling for Mrs. Bug to bring some water

The afternoon was warm, and I was feeling unpleasantly prickly after working on Lionel Brown. Without warning, a flush of heat rose suddenly upward through my chest and neck and flowed like hot wax over my face, so that sweat popped out behind my ears. Murmuring an excuse, I left the patient to Mrs. Bug, and hurried out into the welcome air.

There was a well outside; no more than a shallow pit, neatly edged with stones. A big gourd dipper was wedged between two of the stones; I pulled it out and, kneeling, scooped up enough water to drink and to splash over my steaming face.

Hot flushes in themselves were not really unpleasant—rather interesting, in fact, in the same way that pregnancy was; that odd feeling as one's body did something quite unexpected, and not within one's conscious control. I wondered briefly whether men felt that way about erections.

At the moment, a hot flush seemed quite welcome. Surely, I told myself, I couldn't be experiencing hot flushes if I were pregnant. Or could I? I had the uneasy knowledge that the hormonal surges of early pregnancy were quite as capable of causing all kinds of peculiar thermal phenomena as were those of the menopause. I was certainly having the sorts of emotional connip- tions that went with being pregnant—or menopausal—or from be- ing raped—

"Don't be ridiculous, Beauchamp," I said out loud. "You know quite well you're not pregnant."

Hearing it gave me an odd feeling—nine parts relief, one part regret. Well, perhaps nine thousand, nine hundred, and ninety- nine parts relief, to one of regret—but it was still there.

The flood of sweat that sometimes followed in the wake of a hot flush, though, was something I could do without. The roots of my hair were soaked, and while the cool water on my face was lovely, waves of heat were still blooming over me, spreading like a cling- ing veil over chest and face and neck and scalp. Seized by impulse, I tipped half a dipperful of water down the inside of my bodice, ex- haling in relief as the wetness soaked the cloth, trickling between my breasts and down over my belly, tickling cool between my legs and dripping to the ground.

I looked a mess, but Mrs. Bug wouldn't mind—and the devil with what bloody Lionel Brown thought. Dabbing at my temples with the end of my apron, I made my way back to the house.

The door stood ajar, as I'd left it. I pushed it open, and the strong pure light of the afternoon shone past me, illuminating Mrs. Bug in the act of pressing a pillow over Lionel Brown's face with all her strength.

I stood blinking for a moment, so surprised that I simply couldn't translate the sight into realization. Then I darted forward with an incoherent cry and grabbed her arm.

She was terribly strong, and so focused on what she was doing that she didn't budge, veins standing out in her forehead and her face nearly purple with effort. I jerked hard on her arm, failed to dislodge her grip, and in desperation shoved her as hard as I could.

She staggered, off-balance, and I snatched the edge of the pil- low, yanking it sideways, off Brown's face. She lunged back, intent on completing the job, blunt hands shoving down into the mass of the pillow and disappearing to the wrists.

I drew back a step and flung myself at her bodily. We went over with a crash, hitting the table, upsetting the bench, and end- ing in a tangle on the floor amid a litter of broken earthenware and the scents of mint tea and a spilled chamber pot.

I rolled, gasped for breath, pain from my cracked ribs paralyz-ing me for a moment. Then I gritted my teeth, pushing her away and trying to extricate myself from a snarl of skirts—and stum-bled to my feet.

His hand hung limp, trailing from the table, and I grabbed his jaw, pulling back his head, and pressed my mouth fervently to his. I blew what little breath I had into him, gasped, and blew again, all the time feeling frantically for some trace of a pulse in his neck.

He was warm, the bones of his jaw, his shoulder felt normal—but his flesh had a terrible slackness, the lips under mine flattening obscenely as I pressed and blew, blood from my split lip splatter-ing everywhere, falling somehow away, so that I was forced to suck frantically to keep them sealed, breathing in hard through the corners of my mouth, fighting my ribs for enough air to blow again.

I felt someone behind me—Mrs. Bug—and kicked out at her. She made an effort to seize my shoulder, but I wrenched aside and her fingers slipped off. I turned round fast and hit her, as hard as I could, in the stomach, and she fell down on the floor with a loud *whoof!* No time to spare for her; I whirled and flung myself once more on Brown.

The chest under my hand rose reassuringly as I blew—but fell abruptly as I stopped. I drew back and pounded hard with both fists, smacking the hard springiness of the sternum with enough force to bruise my own hands further—and Brown's flesh, had he been capable of bruising any longer.

He wasn't. I blew and thumped and blew, until bloody sweat ran down my body in streams and my thighs were slick with it and my ears rang and black spots swam before my eyes with hyper-ventilating. Finally, I stopped. I stood panting in deep, wheezing gasps, wet hair hanging in my face, my hands throbbing in time to my pounding heart.

The bloody man was dead.

I rubbed my hands on my apron, then used it to wipe my face. My mouth was swollen and tasted of blood; I spat on the floor. I felt quite calm; the air had that peculiar sense of stillness that often accompanies a quiet death. A Carolina wren called in the wood nearby, "Teakettle, teakettle, teakettle!"

I heard a small rustling noise and turned round. Mrs. Bug had righted the bench and sat down on it. She sat hunched forward, hands folded together in her lap, a small frown on her wrinkled round face as she stared intently at the body on the table. Brown's hand hung limp, fingers slightly cupped, holding shadows.

The sheet was stained over his body; that was the source of the chamber pot smell. So, he'd been dead before I began my resuscitation efforts.

Another wave of heat bloomed upward, coating my skin like hot wax. I could smell my own sweat. I closed my eyes briefly, then opened them, and turned back to Mrs. Bug.

"Why on *earth*," I asked conversationally, "did you do that?"

"She's done what?" Jamie stared at me uncomprehendingly, then at Mrs. Bug, who sat at the kitchen table, head bowed, her hands clasped together in front of her.

Not waiting for me to repeat what I'd said, he strode down the hall to the surgery. I heard his footsteps come to a sudden stop. There was an instant's silence, and then a heartfelt Gaelic oath. Mrs. Bug's plump shoulders rose around her ears.

The footsteps came back, more slowly. He came in, and walked to the table where she sat.

"O, woman, how have you dared to lay hands upon a man who was mine?" he asked very softly, in Gaelic.

"Oh, sir," she whispered. She was afraid to look up; she cowered under her cap, her face almost invisible. "I—I didna mean to. Truly, sir!"

Jamie glanced at me.

"She smothered him," I repeated. "With a pillow."

"I think ye do not do such a thing without meaning it," he said, with an edge in his voice that could have sharpened knives. "What were ye about, *a boireannach*, to do it?"

The round shoulders began to quiver with fright.

"Oh, sir, oh, sir! I ken 'twas wrong—only . . . only it was the wicked tongue of him. All the time I had care of him, he'd cower and tremble, aye, when you or the young one came to speak to him, even Arch—but me—" She swallowed, the flesh of her face seeming suddenly loose. "I'm no but a woman, he could speak his mind to me, and he did. Threatening, sir, and cursing most awfully. He said—he said as how his brother would come, him and his men, to free him, and would slaughter us all in our blood and burn the houses over our heids." Her jowls trembled as she spoke, but she found the courage to look up and meet Jamie's eyes.

"I kent ye'd never let that happen, sir, and did my best to pay him no mind. And when he did get under my skin enough, I told him he'd be deid long before his brother heard where he was. But then the wicked wee cur escaped—and I'm sure I've no idea how 'twas done, for I'd have sworn he was in no condition even to rise from the bed, let alone come so far, but he did, and threw himself upon your wife's mercy, and she took him up—I would have dragged his evil carcass away myself, but she wouldna have it—" Here she darted a briefly resentful glance at me, but returned an imploring gaze to Jamie almost at once.

"And she took him to mend, sweet gracious lady that she is, sir—and I could see it in her face, that having tended him so, it was coming to her that she couldna bear to see him killed. And he saw it, too, the gobshite, and when she went out, he jeered at me, saying now he was safe, he'd fooled her into tending him and she'd never let him be killed, and directly he was free of the place, he'd have a score of men down upon us like vengeance itself, and then . . ." She closed her eyes, swaying briefly, and pressed a hand to her chest.

"I couldn't help it, sir," she said very simply. "I really couldn't."

Jamie had been attending to her, a look like thunder on his brow. At this point, he glanced sharply at me—and evidently saw corroborative evidence upon my own battered features. His lips pressed tight together.

"Go home," he said to Mrs. Bug. "Tell your husband what you have done, and send him to me."

He turned on his heel then, and headed for his study. Not looking at me, Mrs. Bug rose awkwardly to her feet and went out, walking like a blind woman.

"You were right. I'm sorry." I stood stiffly in the door of the study, hand on the jamb.

Jamie was sitting with his elbows on his desk, head resting on his hands, but looked up at this, blinking.

"Did I not forbid ye to be sorry, Sassenach?" he said, and gave me a lopsided smile. Then his eyes traveled over me, and a look of concern came over his face.

"Christ, ye look like ye're going to fall down, Claire," he said, getting up hastily. "Come and sit."

He put me in his chair, and hovered over me.

"I'd call Mrs. Bug to bring ye something," he said, "but as I've sent her away . . . shall I bring ye a cup of tea, Sassenach?"

I'd been feeling like crying, but laughed instead, blinking back tears.

"We haven't got any. We haven't had for months. I'm all right. Just rather—rather shocked."

"Aye, I suppose so. Ye're bleeding a bit." He pulled a crumpled handkerchief from his pocket and, bending over, dabbed my mouth, his brows drawn together in an anxious frown.

I sat still and let him, fighting a sudden wave of exhaustion. All at once, I wanted nothing save to lie down, go to sleep, and never wake up again. And if I did wake up, I wanted the dead man in my surgery to be gone. I also wanted the house not to be burned over our heads.

But it isn't time, I thought suddenly, and found that thought—idiotic as it was—obscurely comforting.

"Will it make things harder for you?" I asked, struggling to fight off the weariness and think sensibly. "With Richard Brown?"

"I dinna ken," he admitted. "I've been trying to think. I could wish we were in Scotland," he said a little ruefully. "I'd ken better what Brown might do, were he a Scotsman."

"Oh, really? Say you were dealing with your uncle Colum, for instance," I suggested. "What would he do, do you think?"

"Try to kill me and get his brother back," he replied promptly. "If he kent I had him. And if your Donner *did* go back to Brownsville—Richard knows by now."

He was entirely right, and the knowledge made small fingers of apprehension creep briskly up my back.

The worry evidently showed on my face, for he smiled a little.

"Dinna fash yourself, Sassenach," he said. "The Lindsay brothers left for Brownsville the morning after we came back. Kenny's keeping an eye on the town, and Evan and Murdo are waiting at points along the road, with fresh horses. If Richard

Brown and his bloody Committee of Safety should come this way, we'll hear of it in good time."

That was reassuring, and I sat up a little straighter.

"That's good. But—even if Donner did go back, he wouldn't know that you had Lionel Brown captive; you might have killed him d-during the fight."

He flicked a narrow blue glance at me, but merely nodded.

"I could wish I had," he said with a slight grimace. "It would have saved trouble. But then—I'd not have found out what they were doing, and I did need to know that. If Donner's gone back, though, he'll ha' told Richard Brown what happened, and led them back to claim the bodies. He'll see his brother's no among them."

"Whereupon he'll draw the logical conclusion and come here looking for him."

The sound of the back door opening at this point made me jump, heart pounding, but it was succeeded by the soft shuffle of moccasined feet in the hall, announcing Young Ian, who peered inquiringly into the study.

"I've just met Mrs. Bug, hurrying off to her house," he said, frowning. "She wouldna stop and speak to me, and she looked verra queer indeed. What's amiss?"

"What isn't?" I said, and laughed, causing him to glance sharply at me.

Jamie sighed.

"Sit," he said, pushing a stool toward Ian with one foot. "And I'll tell ye."

Ian listened with great attention, though his mouth fell open a little when Jamie reached the point about Mrs. Bug putting the pillow over Brown's face.

"Is he still there?" he asked, at the end of the tale. He hunched a little, looking suspiciously back over his shoulder, as though expecting Brown to come through the surgery door at any moment.

"Well, I hardly think he's going anywhere under his own steam," I observed tartly.

Ian nodded, but got up to look anyway. He came back in a moment, looking thoughtful.

"He's no marks on him," he said to Jamie, sitting down.

Jamie nodded. "Aye, and he's freshly bandaged. Your auntie had just tended him."

They exchanged nods, both obviously thinking the same thing.

"Ye canna tell by looking that he's been killed, Auntie," Ian explained, seeing that I was not yet on their wavelength. "He might have died of himself."

"I suppose you could say that he *did*. If he hadn't tried to terrorize Mrs. Bug . . ." I rubbed a hand—gently—over my forehead, where a headache was beginning to throb.

"How do ye feel—" Ian began, in a worried tone, but I had quite suddenly had more than enough of people asking me how I felt.

"I scarcely know," I said abruptly, dropping my hand. I looked down at my fists, curled in my lap.

"He—he wasn't a *wicked* man, I don't think," I said. There was a splotch of blood on my apron. I didn't know whether it was his or mine. "Just . . . terribly weak."

"Better off dead then," said Jamie matter-of-factly, and without any particular malice. Ian nodded in agreement.

"Well, so." Jamie returned to the point of the discussion. "I was just saying to your auntie, if Brown were a Scot, I should better know how to deal with him—but then it struck me, that while he isna Scottish, he *is* by way of doing business in a Scottish manner. Him and his committee. They're like a Watch."

Ian nodded, sketchy brows raised.

"So they are." He looked interested. "I've never seen one, but Mam told me—about the one that arrested you, Uncle Jamie, and how she and Auntie Claire went after them." He grinned at me, his gaunt face suddenly transforming to show a hint of the boy he'd been.

"Well, I was younger then," I said. "And braver."

Jamie made a small noise in his throat that might have been amusement.

"They're no verra thrifty about it," he said. "Killing and burning, I mean—"

"As opposed to ongoing extortion." I was beginning to see where he was going with this. Ian had been born after Culloden; he'd never seen a Watch, one of those organized bands of armed men that rode the country, charging fees from the Highland chiefs to protect tenants, land, and cattle—and if the black rent they charged was not paid, promptly seizing goods and cattle themselves. I had. And in all truth, I'd heard of them burning and killing now and then, too—though generally only to create an example and improve cooperation.

Jamie nodded. "Well, Brown's no Scot, as I said. But business is business, isn't it?" A contemplative look had come over his face, and he leaned back a little, hands linked over one knee. "How fast can ye get to Anidonau Nuya, Ian?"

After Ian left, we stayed in the study. The situation in my surgery would have to be dealt with, but I was not quite ready yet to go and face it. Beyond a minor remark to the effect that it was a pity he had not yet had time to build an icehouse, Jamie made no reference to it, either.

"Poor old Mrs. Bug," I said, beginning to get a grip. "I'd no idea he'd been playing on her that way. He must have thought she was a soft touch." I laughed weakly. "*That* was a mistake. She's terribly strong. I was amazed."

I shouldn't have been; I'd seen Mrs. Bug walk for a mile with a full-grown goat across her shoulders—but somehow one never translates the strength required for daily farm life into a capacity for homicidal fury.

"So was I," Jamie said dryly. "Not that she was strong enough to do it, but that she dared take matters into her own hands. Why did she no tell Arch, if not myself?"

"I suppose it's what she said—she thought it wasn't her place to say anything; you'd given her the job of looking after him, and she'd move heaven and earth to do anything you asked. I daresay she thought she was coping well enough, but when he showed up that way, she . . . just snapped. It does happen; I've seen it."

"So have I," he muttered. A small frown had formed, deepening the crease between his brows, and I wondered what violent incidents he might be recalling. "But I shouldna have thought . . ."

Arch Bug came in so quietly that I didn't hear him; I only realized that he was there when I saw Jamie look up, stiffening. I whirled about, and saw the ax in Arch's hand. I opened my mouth to speak, but he strode toward Jamie, taking no notice of his surroundings. Clearly, for him, there was no one in the room save Jamie.

He reached the desk and laid the ax upon it, almost gently.

"My life for hers, O, chieftain," he said quietly in Gaelic. He stepped back then, and knelt, head bowed. He had braided his soft white hair in a narrow plait and bound it up, so that the back of his neck was left bare. It was walnut-brown and deeply seamed from weather, but still thick and muscular above the white band of his collar.

- A tiny noise from the door made me turn from the scene, riveting as it was. Mrs. Bug was there, clinging to the jamb for support, and in obvious need of it. Her cap was askew, and sweaty strands of iron-gray hair stuck to a face the color of cream gone bad.

Her eyes flickered to me when I moved, but then shot back to fix again upon her kneeling husband—and on Jamie, who was now standing, looking from Arch to his wife, then back again. He rubbed a finger slowly up and down the bridge of his nose, eyeing Arch.

"Oh, aye," he said mildly. "I'm to take your head, am I? Here in my own room and have your wife mop up the blood, or shall I do it in the dooryard, and nail ye up by the hair over my lintel as a warning to Richard Brown? Get up, ye auld fraudster."

Everything in the room was frozen for an instant—long enough for me to notice the tiny black mole in the exact middle of Arch's neck—and then the old man rose, very slowly.

"It is your right," he said, in Gaelic. "I am your tacksman, *a ceann-cinnidh*, I swear by my iron; it is your right." He stood very straight, but his eyes were hooded, fixed on the desk where his ax lay, the sharpened edge a silver line against the dull gray metal of the head.

Jamie drew breath to reply, but then stopped, eyeing the old man narrowly. Something changed in him, some awareness taking hold.

"A ceann-cinnidh?" he said, and Arch Bug nodded, silent.

The air of the room had thickened in a heartbeat, and the hairs prickled on the back of my own neck.

"A ceann-cinnidh," Arch had said. O, chieftain. One word, and we stood in Scotland. It was easy to see the difference in attitude between Jamie's new tenants and his Ardsmuir men— the difference of a loyalty of agreement and one of acknowledgment. This was different still: an older allegiance, which had

ruled the Highlands for a thousand years. The oath of blood and iron.

I saw Jamie weigh the present and the past and realize where Arch Bug stood between them. I saw it in his face, exasperation changing to realization—and saw his shoulders drop a little, in acceptance.

"By your word, then, it is my right," he said softly, also in Gaelic. He drew himself up, picked up the ax, and held it out, handle first. "And by that right, I give you back your woman's life—and your own."

Mrs. Bug let out a small sobbing breath. Arch didn't look round at her, but reached out and took the ax, with a grave inclination of the head. He turned then, and walked out without a further word—though I saw the fingers of his maimed hand brush his wife's sleeve, very softly, in passing.

Mrs. Bug straightened herself, hastily tucking up the straggling bits of hair with trembling fingers. Jamie didn't look at her, but sat down again, and took up his quill and a sheet of paper, though I thought he had no intention of writing anything. Not wanting to embarrass her, I affected great interest in the bookshelf, picking up Jamie's little cherrywood snake as though to examine it more closely.

Cap on straight now, she came into the room, and bobbed a curtsy in front of him.

"Will I fetch ye a bit to eat, sir? There's bannocks made fresh." She spoke with great dignity, head upright. He raised his own head from his paper, and smiled at her.

"I should like that," he said. *"Gun robh math agaibh, a nighean."*

She nodded smartly and turned on her heel. At the door, though, she paused, looking back. Jamie raised his brows.

"I was there, ken," she said, fixing him with a direct look. "When the Sassenachs killed your grandsire, there on Tower Hill. There was a lot of blood." She pursed her lips, examining him through narrowed, reddened eyes, then relaxed.

"Ye're a credit to him," she said, and was gone in a whisk of petticoats and apron strings.

Jamie looked at me in surprise, and I shrugged.

"It wasn't necessarily a compliment, you know," I said, and his shoulders began to shake in silent laughter.

"I know," he said at last, and swiped a knuckle beneath his nose. "D'ye ken, Sassenach—sometimes I mourn the auld bastard?" He shook his head. "Sometime I must ask Mrs. Bug if it's true what he said, at the last. What they say he said, I mean."

"What's that?"

"He gave the headsman his fee, and told him to do a good job—'For I shall be very angry indeed if ye don't.'"

"Well, it certainly sounds like something he *would* say," I said, smiling a little. "What do you suppose the Bugs were doing in London?"

He shook his head again, and turned his face to me, lifting his chin so the sun from the window glimmered like water along his jaw and cheekbone.

"God knows. D'ye think she's right, Sassenach? About me being like him?"

"Not to look at," I said, smiling a little. The late Simon, Lord Lovat, had been short and squat, though powerfully built despite his age. He had also borne a strong resemblance to a malevolent—but very clever—toad.

"No," Jamie agreed. "Thank God. But otherwise?" The light of humor was still in his eyes, but he was serious; he truly wanted to know.

I studied him thoughtfully. There was no trace of the Old Fox in his bold, clean-cut features—those had come mostly from his mother's MacKenzie side—nor yet in the broad-shouldered height of him, but somewhere behind those slanted dark blue eyes, I now and then sensed a faint echo of Lord Lovat's deep-set gaze, glittering with interest and sardonic humor.

"You have something of him," I admitted. "More than a little, sometimes. You haven't the overweening ambition, but . . ." I squinted a bit, considering. "I was going to say that you aren't as ruthless as him," I went on slowly, "but you are, really."

"Am I, then?" He didn't seem either surprised or put out to hear this.

"You can be," I said, and felt somewhere in the marrow of my bones the popping sound of Arvin Hodgepile's neck breaking. It was a warm afternoon, but gooseflesh rippled suddenly up my arms, and then was gone.

"Have I the devious nature, d'ye think?" he asked seriously.

"I don't know, quite," I said with some dubiousness. "You're not a proper twister like he was—but that may be only because you've a sense of honor that he lacked. You don't use people like he did."

He smiled at that, but with less real humor than he'd shown before.

"Oh, but I do, Sassenach," he said. "It's only I try not to let it show."

He sat for a moment, his gaze fixed on the little cherrywood snake that I held, but I didn't think he was looking at it. At last, he shook his head and looked up at me, the corner of his mouth tucking wryly in.

"If there is a heaven, and my grandsire's in it—and I take leave to doubt that last—he's laughing his wicked auld head off now. Or he would be, if it weren't tucked underneath his arm."

34

The Exhibits in the Case

And so it was that several days later, we rode into Brownsville. Jamie, in full Highland regalia, with Hector Cameron's gold-knurled dirk at his waist and a hawk's feather in his bonnet. On Gideon, who had his ears laid back and blood in his eye, as usual.

By his side, Bird-who-sings-in-the-morning, peace chief of the Snowbird Cherokee. Bird, Ian told me, was from the Long Hair clan, and looked it. His hair was not only long and glossily anointed with bear fat, but most resplendently dressed, with a high tail twisted up from the crown of his head and dropping down his back, ending in a dozen tiny braids decorated—like the rest of his costume—with wampum shell beads, glass beads, small brass bells, parakeet feathers, and a Chinese yen; God knew where he'd got that. Slung by his saddle, his newest and most prized possession—Jamie's rifle.

By Jamie's other side, me—Exhibit A. On my mule Clarence, dressed and cloaked in indigo wool—which played up the paleness of my skin and beautifully highlighted the yellow and green of the healing bruises on my face—with my necklace of freshwater pearls about my neck for moral support.

Ian rode behind us with the two braves Bird had brought as retinue, looking more like an Indian than a Scot, with the semicircles of tattooed dots that swooped across his tanned cheekbones, and his own long brown hair greased back from his face and tied in a knot, a single turkey quill thrust through it. At least he hadn't plucked his scalp in the Mohawk fashion; he looked sufficiently menacing without that.

And on a travois behind Ian's horse rode Exhibit B—the corpse of Lionel Brown. We'd put him in the springhouse to keep cool with the butter and eggs, and Bree and Malva had done their best, packing the body with moss to absorb liquids, adding as many strongly aromatic herbs as they could find, then wrapping the unsavory package in a deer's hide, bound with rawhide strips in the Indian fashion. Despite this attention, none of the horses was enthusiastic about being anywhere near it, but Ian's mount was grimly acquiescent, merely snorting loudly every few minutes and shaking his head so his harness rattled, a lugubrious counterpoint to the soft thump of hooves.

We didn't talk much.

Visitors to any mountain settlement were cause for public notice and comment. Our little entourage brought folk popping out of their houses like winkles on pins, mouths agape. By the time we reached Richard Brown's house, which doubled as the local tavern, we had a small band of followers, mostly men and boys.

The sound of our arrival brought a woman—Mrs. Brown, I recognized her—out onto the crudely built stoop. Her hand flew to her mouth, and she rushed back into the house.

We waited in silence. It was a cool, bright autumn day, and the breeze stirred the hair on my neck; I'd worn it pulled back, at Jamie's request, and wore no cap. My face was exposed, the truth written on it.

Did they know? Feeling strangely remote, as though I watched from somewhere outside my own body, I looked from face to face among the crowd.

They couldn't know. Jamie had assured me of it; I knew it, myself. Unless Donner had escaped, and come to tell them all that had happened during that final night. But he hadn't. If he had, Richard Brown would have come to us.

All they knew was what showed on my face. And that was too much.

Clarence felt the hysteria that quivered under my skin like a pool of mercury; he stamped, once, and shook his head as though wanting to dislodge flies in his ears.

The door opened, and Richard Brown came out. There were several men behind him, all armed.

Brown was pale, unkempt, with a sprouting beard and greasy hair. His eyes were red and bleared, and a miasma of beer seemed to surround him. He'd been drinking heavily, and was plainly trying to pull himself together enough to deal with whatever threat we represented.

"Fraser," he said, and stopped, blinking.

"Mr. Brown." Jamie nudged Gideon closer, so he was at eye level with the men on the porch, no more than six feet from Richard Brown.

"Ten days past," Jamie said levelly, "a band of men came upon my land. They stole my property, assaulted my daughter who is with child, burnt my malting shed, destroyed my grain, and abducted and abused my wife."

Half the men had been staring at me already; now all of them were. I heard the small, metallic click of a pistol being cocked. I kept my face immobile, my hands steady on the reins, my eyes fixed on Richard Brown's face.

Brown's mouth began to work, but before he could speak, Jamie raised a hand, commanding silence.

"I followed them, with my men, and killed them," he said, in the same level tone. "I found your brother with them. I took him captive, but did not slay him."

There was a general intake of breath, and uneasy murmurs from the crowd behind us. Richard Brown's eyes darted to the bundle on the travois, and his face went white under the scabby beard.

"You—" he croaked. "Nelly?"

This was my cue. I took a deep breath and nudged Clarence forward.

"Your brother suffered an accident before my husband found us," I said. My voice was hoarse, but clear enough. I forced more air into it, to be heard by everyone. "He was badly injured in a fall. We tended his injuries. But he died."

Jamie let a moment of stunned silence pass, before continuing.

"We have brought him to you, so that you may bury him." He made a small gesture, and Ian, who had dismounted, cut the ropes that held the travois. He and the two Cherokee pulled it to the porch and left it lying in the rutted road, returning silently to their horses.

Jamie inclined his head sharply, and swung Gideon's head around. Bird followed him, pleasantly impassive as the Buddha. I didn't know whether he understood enough English to have followed Jamie's speech, but it didn't matter. He understood his role, and had carried it out perfectly.

The Browns might have had a profitable sideline in murder, theft, and slavery, but their chief income lay in trade with the Indians. By his presence at Jamie's side, Bird gave clear warning that the Cherokee regarded their relationship with the King of England and his agent as more important than trade with the Browns. Harm Jamie or his property again, and that profitable connection would be broken.

I didn't know everything Ian had said to Bird, when asking him to come—but I thought it quite likely that there was also an unspoken agreement that no formal inquiry would be made on behalf of the Crown into the fate of any captives who might have passed into Indian hands.

This was, after all, a matter of business.

I kicked Clarence in the ribs and wheeled into place behind Bird, keeping my eyes firmly fixed on the Chinese yen that glinted in the middle of his back, dangling from his hair on a scarlet thread. I had an almost uncontrollable urge to look back, and clenched my hands on the reins, digging my fingernails into my palms.

Was Donner dead, after all? He wasn't among the men with Richard Brown; I'd looked.

I didn't know whether I *wanted* him to be dead. The desire to find out more about him was strong—but the desire to be done with the matter, to leave that night on the mountainside behind once and for all, all witnesses safely consigned to the silence of the grave—that was stronger.

I heard Ian and the two Cherokee come into line behind us, and within moments, we were out of sight of Brownsville, though the scent of beer and chimney smoke lingered in my nostrils. I pushed Clarence up beside Jamie; Bird had fallen back to ride with his men and Ian; they were laughing at something.

"Will this be the end of it?" I asked. My voice felt thin in the cold air, and I wasn't sure he'd heard me. But he did. He shook his head slightly.

"There is never an end to such things," he said quietly. "But we are alive. And that is good."

PART FIVE

Great
Unexpectations

35

Laminaria

S afely returned from Brownsville, I took firm steps to resume normal life. And among these was a visit to Marsali,
who had returned from her refuge with the McGillivrays.
I'd seen Fergus, who had assured me that she was well recovered
from her injuries and feeling well—but I needed to see for myself.

The homestead was in good order, I saw, but showing certain
signs of dilapidation; a few shingles had blown off the roof, one
corner of the stoop was sagging, and the oiled parchment over
the single window had split partway up, the flaw hastily
mended with rag stuffed through the hole. Small things, but
things that should be dealt with before the snow came—and it
was coming; I could feel the touch of it in the air, the brilliant
blue sky of late autumn fading into the hazy gray of oncoming
winter.

No one rushed out to meet me, but I knew they were home;
there was a cloud of smoke and sparks from the chimney, and I
thought tartly that at least Fergus seemed able to provide enough
wood for the hearth. I called out a cheery "hallooo!" and pushed
open the door.

I had the feeling at once. I didn't trust most of my feelings at
the moment, but that one went bone-deep. It's the feeling you
have, as a doctor, when you walk into an examination room and
know that something's very wrong. Before you ask the first question, before you've taken the first vital sign. It doesn't happen
often, and you'd rather it never did—but there it is. You know, and
there's no way round it.

It was the children that told me, as much as anything else.

Marsali sat by the window, sewing, the two girls playing quietly close by her feet. Germain—uncharacteristically indoors—sat swinging his legs at the table, frowning at a ragged but treasured picture book Jamie had brought him from Cross Creek. They knew, too.

Marsali looked up when I came in, and I saw her face tighten in shock at sight of mine—though it was much better than it had been.

"I'm fine," I said briskly, stopping her exclamation. "Only bruises. How are you, though?"

I set down my bag and cupped my hands round her face, turning it gently to the light. One cheek and ear were badly bruised, and there was a fading knot on her forehead—but she wasn't cut, and her eyes looked back at me, clear and healthy. A good color to her skin, no jaundice, no faint scent of kidney dysfunction.

She's all right. It's the baby, I thought, and dropped my hands to her middle without asking. My heart felt cold as I cupped the bulge and lifted gently. I nearly bit my tongue in surprise when a small knee shifted in answer to my touch.

I was terribly heartened at that; I had thought the child might be dead. A quick glance at Marsali's face muted my relief. She was strained between hope and fear, hoping that I would tell her that what she knew to be true wasn't.

"Has the baby moved very much, these last few days?" I asked, keeping my voice calm as I went about fetching out my stethoscope. I'd had it made by a pewtersmith in Wilmington—a small bell with a flat end piece; primitive, but effective.

"Not so much as he did," Marsali answered, leaning back to let me listen to her stomach. "But they don't, do they, when they're nearly ready to come? Joanie lay like the de—like a millstone, all the night before the waters broke."

"Well, yes, often they do do that," I agreed, ignoring what she'd nearly said. "Resting up, I suppose." She smiled in response, but the smile vanished like a snowflake on a griddle as I leaned close and put my ear to the flattened end of the flared metal tube, the wide, bell-shaped opening over her stomach.

It took some time to pick up the heartbeat, and when I did, it was unusually slow. It was also skipping beats; the hair on my arms rippled with gooseflesh when I heard it.

I went on with the examination, asking questions, making small jokes, pausing to answer questions from the other children, who were crowding round, stepping on each other's feet and getting in the way—and all the time, my mind was racing, envisioning possibilities, all bad.

The child *was* moving—but wrong. Heartbeat was there—but wrong. Everything about that belly felt *wrong* to me. What was it, though? Umbilical cord around the neck was thoroughly possible, and quite dangerous.

I pushed the smock further back, trying for a better listen, and saw the heavy bruising—ugly splotches of healing green and yellow, a few still with deep red-black centers that bloomed like deadly roses over the curve of her belly. My teeth sank into my lip at sight of them; they'd kicked her, the bastards. A wonder she hadn't miscarried on the spot.

Anger swelled suddenly under my breastbone, a huge, solid thing, pushing hard enough to burst it.

Was she bleeding at all? No. No pain, bar tenderness from the bruises. No cramping. No contractions. Her blood pressure seemed normal, so far as I could tell.

A cord accident was still possible—likely, even. But it could be a partially detached placenta, bleeding into the uterus. A ruptured uterus? Or something rarer—a dead twin, an abnormal growth . . . The only thing I knew for sure was that the child needed to be delivered into the air-breathing world, and as soon as possible.

"Where's Fergus?" I said, still speaking calmly.

"I dinna ken," she said, matching my tone of absolute calm. "He's no been home since the day before yesterday. Dinna put that in your mouth, *a chuisle.*" She lifted a hand toward Félicité, who was gnawing a candle stub, but couldn't reach her.

"Hasn't he? Well, we'll find him." I removed the candle stub; Félicité made no protest, aware that something was going on, but not knowing what. In search of reassurance, she seized her mother's leg and began determinedly trying to climb up into Marsali's nonexistent lap.

"No, *bébé,*" Germain said, and clasped his sister round the waist, dragging her backward. "You come with me, *a piuthar.* Want milkie?" he added, coaxing. "We'll go to the springhoose, aye?"

"Want Mama!" Félicité windmilled arms and legs, trying to escape, but Germain hoisted her fat little body into his arms.

"You wee lassies come with me," he said firmly, and trundled awkwardly out the door, Félicité grunting and squirming in his grasp, Joanie scampering at his heels—pausing at the door to look back at Marsali, her big brown eyes wide and scared.

"Go on then, *a muirninn*," Marsali called, smiling. "Take them to see Mrs. Bug. It will be all right.

"He's a sweet lad, Germain," Marsali murmured, folding her hands across her belly as the smile faded.

"Very sweet," I agreed. "Marsali—"

"I know," she said simply. "Might this one live, d'ye think?" She passed a hand gently over her belly, looking down.

I wasn't at all sure, but the child *was* alive for the moment. I hesitated, turning over possibilities in my mind. Anything I did would entail hideous risk—to her, the child, or both.

Why had I not come sooner? I berated myself for taking Jamie's and then Fergus's word that she was all right, but there was no time for self-reproach—and it might not have mattered, either.

"Can you walk?" I asked. "We'll need to go to the Big House."

"Aye, of course." She rose carefully, holding to my arm. She looked around the cabin, as though memorizing all its homely details, then gave me a sharp, clear glance. "We'll talk on the way."

There were options, most of them horrifying to contemplate. If there was danger of a placental abruption, I *could* do an emergency cesarean and possibly save the child—but Marsali would die. To deliver the child slowly, via induction of labor, was to risk the child, but was much safer for Marsali. Of course—and I kept this thought to myself—induction of labor raised the risk of hemorrhage. If that happened . . .

I could perhaps stop the bleeding and save Marsali—but would be unable to help the infant, who would likely also be in distress. There *was* the ether . . . a tempting thought, but I reluctantly put it aside. It *was* ether—but I'd not used it, had no clear idea of its concentration or effectiveness, nor did I have anything like an anesthetist's training that would allow me to calculate its effects in such a dicey situation as dangerous childbirth. For a minor operation, I could go slowly, judge the patient's respiration, and simply back off if things seemed to be going wrong. If I were in the middle of a cesarean section and things went pearshaped, there was no way out.

Marsali seemed preternaturally calm, as though she were listening to what was going on inside rather than to my explanations and speculations. As we came near the Big House, though, we met Young Ian, coming down the hillside with a clutch of dead rabbits, dangling by their ears, and she sharpened to attention.

"Ho, cousin! How is it, then?" he asked cheerfully.

"I need Fergus, Ian," she said without preliminary. "Can ye find him?"

The smile faded from his face as he took in Marsali's paleness, and my support of her.

"Christ, the bairn's coming? But why—" He glanced up the pathway behind us, clearly wondering why we had left Marsali's cabin.

"Go and find Fergus, Ian," I cut in. *"Now."*

"Oh." He swallowed, suddenly looking quite young. "Oh. Aye. I will. Directly!" He began to bound off, then whirled back and thrust the rabbits into my hand. Then he leapt off the path and tore down the hillside, rocketing between trees and vaulting fallen logs. Rollo, not wishing to be left out of anything, flashed past in a gray blur and hurtled down the hillside after his master like a falling rock.

"Don't worry," I said, patting Marsali's arm. "They'll find him."

"Oh, aye," she said, looking after them. "If they shouldna find him in time, though . . ."

"They will," I said firmly. "Come on."

I sent Lizzie to find Brianna and Malva Christie—I thought I might well need more hands—and sent Marsali to the kitchen to rest with Mrs. Bug, while I readied the surgery. Fresh bedding and pillows, spread on my examination table. A bed would be better, but I needed to have my equipment to hand.

And the equipment itself: the surgical instruments, carefully hidden beneath a clean towel; the ether mask, lined with fresh thick gauze; the dropping bottle—could I trust Malva to administer the ether, if I had to perform emergency surgery? I thought perhaps I could; the girl was very young, and quite untrained, but she had a remarkable coolness about her, and I knew she wasn't squeamish. I filled the dropping bottle, averting my face from the sweet, thick scent that drifted from the liquid, and put a small twist of cotton in the spout, to keep the ether from evaporating and gassing us all—or catching fire. I glanced hastily at the hearth, but the fire was out.

What if labor was prolonged and then things went wrong—if I had to do this at night, by candlelight? I couldn't; ether was hideously inflammable. I shoved away the mental picture of myself performing an emergency cesarean section in the pitch-dark, by feel.

"If you have a moment to spare, this would be a bloody good time to have a look-in," I muttered, addressing this remark collectively to Saints Bride, Raymond, and Margaret of Antioch, all presumably patrons of childbirth and expectant mothers, plus any guardian angels—mine, Marsali's, or the child's—who might be hovering about in the offing.

Evidently, someone was listening. When I got Marsali boosted up onto the table, I was terribly relieved to find that the cervix had begun to dilate—but there was no sign of bleeding. It didn't remove the risk of hemorrhage, by any means, but it did mean the probability was much lower.

Her blood pressure seemed all right, so far as I could tell by looking at her, and the baby's heartbeat had steadied, though the baby had stopped moving, refusing to respond to pokes and shoves.

"Sound asleep, I expect," I said, smiling at Marsali. "Resting up."

She gave me a tiny smile in return, and turned onto her side, grunting like a hog.

"I could use a bit of a rest, myself, after that walk." She sighed, settling her head into the pillow. Adso, seconding this motion, leapt up onto the table, and curled himself into her breasts, rubbing his face affectionately against her.

I would have slung him out, but Marsali seemed to find some comfort in his presence, scratching his ears until he curled up under her chin, purring madly. Well, I'd delivered children in much less sanitary surroundings, cat notwithstanding, and this was likely to be a slow process; Adso would have decamped long before his presence became a hindrance.

I was feeling a bit more reassured, but not to the point of confidence. That subtle feeling of wrongness was still there. On the way, I'd considered the various options available to me; given the slight dilatation of the cervix and the now-steady heartbeat, I thought we might try the most conservative method of inducing labor, so as not to put undue stress upon mother or child. If emergency intervened . . . well, we'd deal with that when and if we had to.

I only hoped the contents of the jar were usable; I'd never had occasion to open it before. *Laminaria,* said the label, written in Daniel Rawlings's flowing script. It was a small jar of dark green glass, corked tight, and very light. When I opened it, a faint whiff of iodine floated out, but no scent of decay, thank goodness.

Laminaria is seaweed. Dried, it's no more than paper-thin slips of brownish-green. Unlike many dried seaweeds, though, *Laminaria* doesn't crumble easily. And it has a most astonishing capacity to absorb water.

Inserted into the opening of the cervix, it absorbs moisture from the mucous membranes—and swells, slowly forcing the cervix further open as it does so, thus eventually causing labor to start. I'd seen *Laminaria* used, even in my own time, though in modern times it was most frequently employed to assist in expelling a dead child from the uterus. I shoved *that* thought well to the back of my mind, and selected a good piece.

It was a simple thing to do, and once done, nothing to do but wait. And hope. The surgery was very peaceful, full of light and the sounds of barn swallows rustling under the eaves.

"I hope Ian finds Fergus," Marsali said after a period of silence.

"I'm sure he will," I replied, distracted by an attempt to light my small brazier using flint and steel. I should have told Lizzie to have Brianna bring matches. "You said Fergus hadn't been home?"

"No." Her voice sounded muffled, and I looked up to see her head bent over Adso, face hidden in his fur. "I've scarce seen him at all, since . . . since the men came to the malting floor."

"Ah."

I didn't know what to say to this. I hadn't realized that Fergus had made himself scarce—though knowing what I did of eighteenth-century men, I supposed I could see why.

"He's ashamed, the wee French gomerel," Marsali said matter-of-factly, confirming my supposition. She turned her face, one blue eye visible above the curve of Adso's head. "Thinks it was his fault, aye? That I was there, I mean. Thinks if he was better able to provide, I shouldna have had to go and tend the malting."

"Men," I said, shaking my head, and she laughed.

"Aye, men. Not that he'd *say* what the trouble is, o' course. Much better go off and brood about it, and leave me to hame wi' three wild bairns!" She rolled her eyes.

"Aye, well, they do that, men," said Mrs. Bug tolerantly, coming in with a lighted taper. "No sense at all to them, but they mean weel. I heard ye clickin' away with that steel like a deathwatch, Mrs. Claire; why would ye no just come and fetch a bit o' fire like a sensible person?" She touched the taper to the kindling in my brazier, which promptly popped into flame.

"Practice," I said mildly, adding sticks to the infant flame. "I have hopes of eventually learning to light a fire in less than a quarter of an hour."

Marsali and Mrs. Bug snorted in simultaneous derision.

"Bless ye, lamb, a quarter-hour's no time at all! Why, often I've spent an hour and more, trying to catch a spark in damp tinder—in Scotland, 'specially, since nothing's ever dry in the winter there. Whyever d'ye think folk go to such trouble, a-smooring the fire?"

This caused a spirited discussion of the best way in which to smoor a fire for the night, including an argument over the proper blessing to be said while doing so, and this lasted long enough for me to have coaxed the brazier into a decent glow and set a small kettle in it for tea-making. Raspberry-leaf tea would encourage contractions.

Mention of Scotland seemed to have reminded Marsali of something, for she raised herself on one elbow.

"Mother Claire—d'ye think Da would mind, if I was to borrow a sheet of paper and some ink? I'm thinkin' it would be as well if I wrote to my mother."

"I think that would be an excellent idea." I went to fetch paper and ink, heart beating a little faster. Marsali was entirely calm; I wasn't. I'd seen it before, though; I wasn't sure whether it was fatalism, religious faith, or something purely physical—but women giving birth seemed very often to lose any sense of fear or misgiving, turning inward upon themselves and exhibiting an absorption that amounted to indifference—simply because they had no attention to spare for anything beyond the universe bounded by their bellies.

As it was, my lingering sense of dread was muted, and two or three hours passed in quiet peace. Marsali wrote to Laoghaire, but also brief notes to each of her children. "Just in case," she said laconically, handing the folded notes to me to put away. I noticed that she didn't write to Fergus—but her eyes darted toward the door every time there was a sound.

Lizzie returned to report that Brianna was nowhere to be found, but Malva Christie turned up, looking excited, and was promptly put to work, reading aloud from Tobias Smollett's *The Adventures of Peregrine Pickle*.

Jamie came in, covered with road dust, and kissed me on the lips and Marsali on the forehead. He took in the unorthodox situation, and gave me the ghost of a raisèd eyebrow.

"How is it, then, *a muirninn*?" he asked Marsali.

She made a small face and put her tongue out, and he laughed.

"You haven't seen Fergus anywhere, have you?" I asked.

"Aye, I have," he said, looking slightly surprised. "D'ye want him?" This question was addressed to both Marsali and myself.

"We do," I said firmly. "Where is he?"

"Woolam's Mill. He's been interpreting for a French traveler, an artist come in search of birds."

"Birds, is it?" The notion seemed to affront Mrs. Bug, who put down her knitting and sat up straight. "Our Fergus speaks bird-tongue, does he? Well, ye just go and fetch the mannie this minute. Yon Frenchman can mind his own birds!"

Looking rather taken aback at this vehemence, Jamie allowed me to usher him out into the hallway and as far as the front door. Safely out of earshot, he stopped.

"What's to do wi' the lass?" he demanded, low-voiced, and darted a glance back toward the surgery, where Malva's clear, high voice had taken up her reading again.

I told him, as well as I could.

"It may be nothing; I hope so. But—she wants Fergus. She

says he's been keeping away, feeling guilty for what happened at the malting floor."

Jamie nodded.

"Well, aye, he would."

"He would? Why, for heaven's sake?" I demanded in exasperation. "It wasn't *his* fault!"

He gave me a look suggesting that I had missed something patently obvious to the meanest intelligence.

"Ye think that makes a difference? And if the lass should die—or mischief come to the child? Ye think he'd not blame himself?"

"He *shouldn't*," I said. "But rather obviously he does. You don't—" I stopped short, because in fact he *did*. He'd told me so, very clearly, the night he brought me back.

He saw the memory cross my face, and the hint of a smile, wry and painful, showed in his eyes. He reached out and traced the line of my eyebrow, where a healing gash had split through it.

"Ye think I dinna feel that?" he asked quietly.

I shook my head, not in negation, but in helplessness.

"A man's wife is his to protect," he said simply, and turned away. "I'll go fetch Fergus."

The *Laminaria* had been accomplishing its slow, patient work, and Marsali was beginning to have occasional contractions, though we had not really got down to it, yet. The light was beginning to fade when Jamie arrived with Fergus—and Ian, met on the way.

Fergus was unshaven, covered with dust, and plainly hadn't bathed in days, but Marsali's face lighted like the sun when she saw him. I didn't know what Jamie had told him; he looked grim and worried—but at sight of Marsali, he went to her like an arrow to its target, gathering her to him with such fervor that Malva dropped her book on the floor, staring in astonishment.

I relaxed a little, for the first time since I had entered Marsali's house that morning.

"Well," I said, and took a deep breath. "Perhaps we'll have a little food, shall we?"

I left Fergus and Marsali alone, while the rest of us ate, and returned to the surgery to find them with heads close together, talking quietly. I hated to disturb them, but it was necessary.

On the one hand, the cervix had dilated very appreciably, and there was no sign of abnormal bleeding, which was a tremendous relief. On the other . . . the baby's heartbeat was skipping again. Almost certainly a cord problem, I thought.

I was very conscious of Marsali's eyes, fixed on my face as I listened through my stethoscope, and I exerted every ounce of will in order to let nothing show.

"You're doing very well," I assured her, smoothing tumbled hair off her forehead and smiling into her eyes. "I think perhaps it's time to help things along a little."

There were assorted herbs that could assist labor, but most of them were not things I'd use, were there any danger of hemorrhage. At this point, though, I was uneasy enough to want to get things moving as quickly as possible. Raspberry-leaf tea might be a help without being so strong as to induce major or abrupt contractions. Ought I add blue cohosh? I wondered.

"The babe needs to come quickly," Marsali told Fergus, with every appearance of calm. Obviously, I hadn't been as successful in hiding my concern as I'd thought.

She had her rosary with her, and now wound it round her hand, the cross dangling. "Help me, *mon cher.*"

He lifted the hand with the rosary, and kissed it.

"Oui, cherie." He crossed himself then, and set to work.

Fergus had spent the first ten years of his life in the brothel where he'd been born. Consequently, he knew a great deal more about women—in some ways—than any other man I'd ever met. Even so, I was astonished to see him reach for the strings at the neck of Marsali's shift, and draw it down, exposing her breasts.

Marsali didn't seem at all surprised, merely lying back and turning slightly toward him, the hump of her belly nudging him as she did so.

He knelt on a stool beside the bed, and placing a hand tenderly but absently on the bulge, bent his head toward Marsali's breast, lips slightly pursed. Then he appeared to notice me gaping at him, and glanced up over her belly.

"Oh." He smiled at me. "You have not—well, I suppose you would perhaps not have seen this, milady?"

"I can't say that I have." I was torn between fascination and a feeling that I should avert my eyes. "What . . . ?"

"When the birth pangs are slow to start, suckling the woman's breasts encourages the womb to move, thus to hasten the child," he explained, and brushed a thumb unconsciously over one dark-brown nipple, so that it rose, round and hard as a spring cherry. "In the brothel, if one of *les filles* had a difficulty, sometimes another would do such service for her. I have done it for *ma douce* before—when Félicité came. It helps; you will see."

And without more ado, he cupped the breast in both hands and took the nipple into his mouth, sucking gently, but with great concentration, his eyes closed.

Marsali sighed, and her body seemed to relax in the flowing way that a pregnant woman's does, as though she were suddenly boneless as a stranded jellyfish.

I was more than disconcerted, but I couldn't leave, in case anything drastic should happen.

I hesitated for a moment, then pulled out a stool and sat down on it, trying to be inconspicuous. In fact, though, neither of them appeared to be at all concerned with my presence—if they were even aware of me anymore. I did, however, turn away a little, so as not to stare.

I was both astonished and interested by Fergus's technique. He was entirely right; suckling by an infant does cause the uterus to contract. The midwives I had known at L'Hôpital des Anges in Paris had told me that, too; a newly delivered woman should be handed the child at once to nurse, so that the bleeding would slow. None of them had happened to mention use of the technique as a means of inducing labor, though.

"*In the brothel, if one of* les filles *had a difficulty, sometimes another would do such service for her,*" he'd said.

His mother had been one of *les filles,* though he had never known her. I could imagine a Parisian prostitute, dark-haired, likely young, groaning in labor—and a friend kneeling to suckle her tenderly, cupping tender, swollen breasts and whispering encouragement, as the boisterous noises of satisfied customers echoed through the floors and walls.

Had she died, his mother? In childbirth with him or a subsequent child? Throttled by a drunken client, beaten by the madame's enforcer? Or was it only that she hadn't wanted him, hadn't wished to be responsible for a bastard child, and thus she had left him to the pity of the other women, one of the nameless sons of the street, a child of no one?

Marsali shifted on the bed, and I glanced to see that she was all right. She was. She had only moved in order to put her arms about Fergus's shoulders, bending her head to his. She had left off her cap; her yellow hair was loose, bright against the sleek darkness of his.

"Fergus . . . I think I'm maybe going to die," she whispered, her voice barely audible above the wind in the trees.

He released her nipple, but moved his lips delicately over the surface of her breast, murmuring. "You always think you will die, *p'tite puce*, all women think it."

"Aye, that's because a good many of them *do*, too," she said a little sharply, and opened her eyes. He smiled, eyes still closed, the tip of his tongue flicking gently against her nipple.

"Not you," he said softly, but with great assurance. He passed his hand over her stomach, first gently, then with more strength. I could see the mound firm itself, suddenly drawing up round and solid. Marsali drew a deep, sudden breath, and Fergus pressed the heel of his hand against the base of the mound, hard against her pubic bone, holding it there until the contraction relaxed.

"Oh," she said, sounding breathless.

"Tu . . . non," he whispered, still more softly. "Not you. I will not let you go."

I curled my hands in the stuff of my skirt. That looked like a nice, solid contraction. Nothing horrible seemed to be happening as a result.

Fergus resumed his work, pausing now and then to murmur something ridiculous to Marsali in French. I got up and sidled cautiously round toward the foot of the bed table. No, nothing untoward. I cast a quick look at the counter, to be sure all was in readiness, and it was.

Perhaps it would be all right. There was a streak of blood on the sheet—but it was only a bit of bloody show, quite normal. There was still the child's worrying heartbeat, the possibility of a cord accident—but I could do nothing about that now. Marsali had made her decision, and it was the right one.

Fergus had resumed his suckling. I stepped quietly out into the hall, and swung the door half-closed, to give them privacy. If she did hemorrhage, I could be with her in a second.

I still had the jar of raspberry leaves in my hand. I supposed I might as well go ahead and make the tea—if only to make myself feel useful!

Not finding his wife at home, old Arch Bug had come up to the house with the children. Félicité and Joan were sound asleep on the settle, and Arch was smoking his pipe by the hearth, blowing smoke rings for a rapt Germain. Meanwhile Jamie, Ian, and Malva Christie seemed to be engaged in an amiable literary argument regarding the merits of Henry Fielding, Tobias Smollett, and . . .

"Ovid?" I said, catching the tail end of one remark. "Really?"

"So long as you are secure you will count many friends," Jamie quoted. *"If your life becomes clouded you will be alone.* D'ye not think that's the case for poor Tom Jones and wee Perry Pickle?"

"But surely true friends wouldnae abandon a man, only because he's in some difficulty!" Malva objected. "What sort of friend is that?"

"Rather the common sort, I'm afraid," I said. "Luckily, there *are* a few of the other kind."

"Aye, there are," Jamie agreed. He smiled at Malva. "Highlanders make the truest friends—if only because they make the worst enemies."

She was slightly pink in the face, but realized that she was being teased.

"Hmp," she said, and lifted her nose in order to look down it. "My faither says Highlanders are such fierce fighters because there's sae little of any value *in* the Highlands, and the worst battles are always fought for the lowest stakes."

Everyone dissolved in laughter at that, and Jamie rose to come to me, leaving Ian and Malva to resume their wrangle.

"How is it wi' the lass?" he asked quietly, dipping up hot water from the kettle for me.

"I'm not sure," I said. "Fergus is . . . er . . . helping her."

Jamie's eyebrows went up.

"How?" he asked. "I didna ken there was much a man had to do wi' that business, once he's got it properly begun."

"Oh, you'd be surprised," I assured him. "*I* certainly was!"

He looked intrigued by this, but was prevented from asking further questions by Mrs. Bug's demand that everyone leave off talking about wretched folk who get up to no good in the pages of books, and come sit down to eat.

I sat down to supper, too, but couldn't really eat, distracted as I was by concern for Marsali. The raspberry-leaf tea had finished steeping as we ate; I poured it out and took it to the surgery—rapping cautiously on the door before entering.

Fergus was flushed and breathless, but bright-eyed. He could not be persuaded to come and eat, insisting that he would stay with Marsali. His efforts were showing fruit; she was having regular contractions now, though still fairly far apart.

"It will be fast, once the waters break," Marsali told me. She was a little flushed, too, with a look of inward listening. "It always is."

I checked the heartbeat again—no great change; still bumpy, but not weakening—and excused myself. Jamie was in his study, across the hall. I went in and sat with him, so as to be handy when needed.

He was writing his usual evening note to his sister, pausing now and then to rub the cramp from his right hand before resuming. Upstairs, Mrs. Bug was putting the children to bed. I could hear Félicité whining, and Germain attempting to sing to her.

Across the hall, small shufflings and murmurings, the shifting of weight and the creak of the table. And in the depths of my inner ear, echoing my own pulse, the soft, rapid beat of a baby's heart.

It could so easily end badly.

"What are ye doing, Sassenach?"

I looked up, startled.

"I'm not doing anything."

"Ye're staring fit to see through the wall, and it doesna seem that ye like what ye're looking at."

"Oh." I dropped my gaze, and realized that I had been pleating and repleating the fabric of my skirt between my fingers; there was a large wrinkled patch in the fawn-colored homespun. "Reliving my failures, I suppose."

He looked at me for a moment, then rose and came behind me, putting his hands on the base of my neck, kneading my shoulders with a strong, warm touch.

"What failures?" he asked.

I closed my eyes and let my head nod forward, trying not to groan with the sensations of pain from knotted muscles and the simultaneous exquisite relief.

"Oh," I said, and sighed. "Patients I couldn't save. Mistakes. Disasters. Accidents. Stillbirths."

That last word hung in the air, and his hands paused in their work for a moment, then resumed more strongly.

"There are times, surely, when there's nothing ye could do? You or anyone. Some things are beyond the power of anyone to make right, aye?"

"*You* never believe that, when it's you," I said. "Why should I?"

He paused in his kneading, and I looked up over my shoulder at him. He opened his mouth to contradict me, then realized that he couldn't. He shook his head, sighed, and resumed.

"Aye, well. I suppose it's true enough," he said, with extreme wryness.

"That what the Greeks called *hubris*, do you think?"

He gave a small snort, which might have been amusement.

"I do. And ye ken where *that* leads."

"To a lonely rock under a burning sun, with a vulture gnawing on your liver," I said, and laughed.

So did Jamie.

"Aye, well, a lonely rock under a burning sun is a verra good place to have company, I should think. And I dinna mean the vulture, either."

His hands gave a final squeeze to my shoulders, but he didn't take them away. I leaned my head back against him, eyes closed, taking comfort in his company.

In the momentary silence, we could hear small sounds across the hall, from the surgery. A muffled grunt from Marsali as a contraction came on, a soft French question from Fergus.

I felt that we really ought not to be listening—but neither of us could think of anything to say, to cover the sounds of their private conversation.

A murmur from Marsali, a pause, then Fergus said something hesitant.

"Aye, like we did before Félicité," came Marsali's voice, muffled, but quite clear.

"*Oui*, but—"

"Put something against the door, then," she said, sounding impatient.

We heard footsteps, and the door to the surgery swung open. Fergus stood there, dark hair disheveled, shirt half-buttoned, and his handsome face deeply flushed under the shadow of beard stubble. He saw us, and the most extraordinary look flitted across his face. Pride, embarrassment, and something indefinably . . . French. He gave Jamie a lopsided smile and a one-shouldered shrug of supreme Gallic insouciance—then firmly shut the door. We heard the grating sounds of a small table being moved, and a small thump as it was shoved against the door.

Jamie and I exchanged looks of bafflement.

Giggles came from behind the closed door, accompanied by a massive creaking and rustling.

"He's no going to—" Jamie began, and stopped abruptly, looking incredulous. "Is he?"

Evidently so, judging from the faint rhythmic creaks that began to be heard from the surgery.

I felt a slight warmth wash through me, along with a mild sense of shock—and a slightly stronger urge to laugh.

"Well . . . er . . . I *have* heard that . . . um . . . it does sometimes seem to bring on labor. If a child was overdue, the *maîtresses sage femme* in Paris would sometimes tell women to get their husbands drunk and . . . er-hmm."

Jamie gave the surgery door a look of disbelief, mingled with grudging respect.

"And him with not even a dram taken. Well, if that's what he's up to, the wee bugger's got balls, I'll say that for him."

Ian, coming down the hall in time to hear this exchange, stopped dead. He listened for a moment to the noises proceeding from the surgery, looked from Jamie and me to the surgery door, back, then shook his head and turned around, going back to the kitchen.

Jamie reached out and gently closed the study door.

Without comment, he sat down again, picked up his pen, and began scratching doggedly away. I went over to the small bookshelf, and stood there staring at the collection of battered spines, taking nothing in.

Old wives' tales were sometimes nothing more than old wives' tales. Sometimes they weren't.

I was seldom troubled by personal recollections while dealing with patients; I had neither time nor attention to spare. At the moment, though, I had much too much of both. And a very vivid memory indeed of the night before Bree's birth.

People often say that women forget what childbirth is like, because if they remembered, no one would ever do it more than once. Personally, I had no trouble at all remembering.

The sense of massive inertia, particularly. That endless time toward the end, when it seems that it never *will* end, that one is mired in some prehistoric tar pit, every small move a struggle doomed to futility. Every square centimeter of skin stretched as thin as one's temper.

You don't forget. You simply get to the point where you don't care what birth will feel like; anything is better than being pregnant for an instant longer.

I'd reached that point roughly two weeks before my due date. The date came—and passed. A week later, I was in a state of chronic hysteria, if one could be simultaneously hysterical and torpid.

Frank was physically more comfortable than I was, but in terms of nerves, there wasn't much to choose between us. Both of us were terrified—not merely of the birth, but of what might come after. Frank being Frank, he reacted to terror by becoming very quiet, withdrawing into himself, to a place where he could control what was happening, by refusing to let anything in.

But I was in no mood to respect anyone's barriers, and broke down in tears of sheer despair, after being informed by a cheerful obstetrician that I was not dilated at all, and "it might be several days—maybe another week."

Trying to calm me, Frank had resorted to rubbing my feet. Then my back, my neck, my shoulders—anything I would let him touch. And gradually, I had exhausted myself and lain quiet, letting him touch me. And . . . and we were both terrified, and terribly in need of reassurance, and neither of us had any words with which to give it.

And he made love to me, slowly and gently, and we fell asleep in each other's arms—and woke up in a state of panic several hours later when my water broke.

"Claire!" I suppose Jamie had called my name more than once; I had been so lost in memory that I had forgotten entirely where I was.

"What?" I swung round, heart pounding. "Has something happened?"

"No, not yet." He studied me for a moment, brow creased, then got up and came to stand by me.

"Are ye all right, Sassenach?"

"Yes. I—I was just thinking."

"Aye, I saw that," he said dryly. He hesitated, then—as a particularly loud moan came through the door—touched my elbow.

"Are ye afraid?" he said softly. "That ye might be wi' child yourself, I mean?"

"No," I said, and heard the note of desolation in my voice as clearly as he did. "I know I'm not." I looked up at him; his face was blurred by a haze of unshed tears. "I'm sad that I'm not—that I never will be again."

I blinked hard, and saw the same emotions on his face that I felt—relief and regret, mingled in such proportion that it was impossible to say which was foremost. He put his arms round me and I rested my forehead on his chest, thinking what comfort it was to know that I had company on this rock, as well.

We stood quietly for some time, just breathing. Then there came a sudden change in the surreptitious noises in the surgery. There was a small cry of surprise, a louder exclamation in French, and then the sound of feet landing heavily on the floor, together with the unmistakable splash of amniotic fluid.

Things did move quickly. Within an hour, I saw the crowning of a black-fuzzed skull.

"He's got lots of hair," I reported, easing the perineum with oil. "Be careful, don't push too hard! Not yet." I spanned the curve of the emerging skull with my hand. "He's got a really big head."

"I wouldna ever have guessed that," said Marsali, red-faced and panting. "Thank ye for telling me."

I barely had time to laugh, before the head eased neatly out into my hands, facedown. The cord *was* round the neck, but not tightly, thank God! I got a finger under it and eased it free, and didn't have to say, "Push!" before Marsali took a breath that went to China and shot the infant into my middle like a cannonball.

It was like being suddenly handed a greased pig, and I fumbled madly, trying to get the little creature turned upright and see whether he—or she—was breathing.

Meanwhile, there were shrieks of excitement from Malva and Mrs. Bug, and heavy footsteps hastening down the hall from the kitchen.

I found the baby's face, hastily cleared the nostrils and mouth, blew a short puff of air into the mouth, snapped a finger against the sole of one foot. The foot jerked back in reflex, and the mouth opened wide in a lusty howl.

"Bon soir, Monsieur L'Oeuf," I said, checking hastily to be sure that it was indeed *Monsieur.*

"Monsieur?" Fergus's face split in an ears-wide grin.

"Monsieur," I confirmed, and hastily wrapping the baby in a flannel, thrust him into his father's arms while I turned my attention to tying and cutting the cord, then tending to his mother.

His mother, thank God, was doing well. Exhausted and sweat-drenched, but likewise grinning. So was everyone else in the room. The floor was puddled, the bedding soaked, and the atmosphere thick with the fecund scents of birth, but no one seemed to notice in the general excitement.

I kneaded Marsali's belly to encourage the uterus to contract, while Mrs. Bug brought her an enormous mug of beer to drink.

"He's all right?" she said, emerging after thirstily engulfing this. "Truly all right?"

"Well, he's got two arms, two legs, and a head," I said. "I hadn't time to count the fingers and toes."

Fergus laid the baby on the table beside Marsali.

"See for yourself, *ma cher,*" he said. He folded back the blanket. And blinked, then leaned closer, frowning.

Ian and Jamie stopped talking, seeing him.

"Is there something amiss, then?" Ian asked, coming over.

Sudden silence struck the room. Malva glanced from one face to another, bewildered.

"Maman?"

Germain stood in the doorway, swaying sleepily.

"Is he here? *C'est Monsieur?"*

Without waiting for answer or permission, he staggered forward and leaned on the bloodstained bedding, mouth a little open as he stared at his newborn brother.

"He looks funny," he said, and frowned a little. "What's wrong with him?"

Fergus had been standing stock-still, as had we all. At this, he looked down at Germain, then glanced back at the baby, then again to his firstborn son.

"Il est un nain," he said, almost casually. He squeezed Germain's shoulder, hard enough to elicit a yelp of startlement from the boy, then turned suddenly on his heel and went out. I heard the opening of the front door, and a cold draft swept down the hall and through the room.

Il est un nain. He is a dwarf.

Fergus hadn't closed the door, and the wind blew out the candles, leaving us in semidarkness, lit only by the glow of the brazier.

36

Winter Wolves

L ittle Henri-Christian appeared to be perfectly healthy; he was simply a dwarf. He was slightly jaundiced, though, with a faint gold cast to his skin that gave his round cheeks a delicate glow, like the petals of a daffodil. With a slick of black hair across the top of his head, he might have been a Chinese baby—bar the huge, round blue eyes.

In a way, I supposed I should feel grateful to him. Nothing less than the birth of a dwarf could have deflected the attention of the Ridge from me and the events of the past month. As it was, people no longer stared at my healing face or stumbled awkwardly to find something to say to me. They had quite a lot to say—to me, to each other, and not infrequently, to Marsali, if neither Bree nor I was in time to stop them.

I supposed they must be saying the same things to Fergus—if they saw him. He had come back, three days following the baby's birth, silent and dark-faced. He had stayed long enough to assent to Marsali's choice of name, and to have a brief, private conversation with her. Then he had left again.

If she knew where he was, she wasn't saying. For the time being, she and the children remained at the Big House with us. She smiled and paid attention to the other children, as mothers must, though she seemed always to be listening for something that wasn't there. Fergus's footsteps? I wondered.

One good thing: she kept Henri-Christian always close to her, carrying him in a sling, or sitting by her feet in his basket of woven rushes. I'd seen parents who had given birth to children with defects; often, their response was to withdraw, unable to deal with the situation. Marsali dealt with it in the other way, becoming fiercely protective of him.

Visitors came, ostensibly to speak to Jamie about something or to get a bit of a tonic or a salve from me—but really in hopes of catching a glimpse of Henri-Christian. It was no surprise, therefore, that Marsali tensed, clutching Henri-Christian to her bosom, when the back door opened and a shadow fell across the threshold.

She relaxed a little, though, seeing that the visitor was Young Ian.

"Hello, coz," he said, smiling at her. "Are ye well, then, and the bairn, too?"

"Verra well," she said firmly. "Come to visit your new cousin, have ye?" I could see that she eyed him narrowly.

"I have, aye, and brought him a wee present, too." He lifted one big hand, and touched his shirt, which bulged a little with whatever was inside it. "Ye're well, too, I hope, Auntie Claire?"

"Hallo, Ian," I said, getting to my feet and putting aside the shirt I'd been hemming. "Yes, I'm fine. Do you want some beer?" I was grateful to see him; I'd been keeping Marsali company while she sewed—or rather, standing guard over her to repel the less-welcome sort of visitor, while Mrs. Bug was tending to the chickens. But I had a decoction of stinging-nettle brewing in the surgery, and needed to check on it. Ian could be trusted to take care of her.

Leaving them with refreshment, I escaped to my surgery and

spent a pleasant quarter of an hour alone with the herbs, decanting infusions and separating a heap of rosemary to dry, surrounded by pungent scent and the peacefulness of plants. Such solitude was hard to come by these days, with children popping up underfoot like mushrooms. Marsali was anxious to go back to her own home, I knew—but I was loath to let her go without Fergus there to provide *some* help.

"Bloody man," I muttered under my breath. "Selfish little beast."

Evidently, I wasn't the only one who thought so. As I came back down the hall, reeking of rosemary and ginseng root, I overheard Marsali expressing a similar opinion to Ian.

"Aye, I ken he's taken back, who wouldna be?" she was saying, her voice full of hurt. "But why must he run awa, and leave us alone? Did ye speak to him, Ian? Did he *say* anything?"

So that was it. Ian had been gone on one of his mysterious journeys; he must have encountered Fergus somewhere, and told Marsali about it.

"Aye," he said, after a moment's hesitation. "Just a bit." I hung back, not wanting to interrupt them, but I could see his face, the ferocity of his tattoos at odds with the sympathy that clouded his eyes. He leaned across the table, holding out his arms. "Can I hold him, coz? Please?"

Marsali's back stiffened with surprise, but she handed over the baby, who squirmed and kicked a little in his wrappings, but quickly settled against Ian's shoulder, making little smacking noises. Ian bent his head, smiling, and brushed his lips across Henri-Christian's big round head.

He said something soft to the baby, in what I thought was Mohawk.

"What's that ye said?" Marsali asked, curious.

"A sort of blessing, ye'd call it." He patted Henri-Christian's back, very softly. "Ye call upon the wind to welcome him, the sky to give him shelter, and the water and the earth to yield him food."

"Oh." Marsali's voice was soft. "That's so nice, Ian." But then she squared her shoulders, unwilling to be distracted. "Ye spoke wi' Fergus, ye said."

Ian nodded, eyes closed. His cheek rested lightly on the baby's head. He didn't speak for a moment, but I saw his throat move, the big Adam's apple bobbing as he swallowed.

"I had a child, cousin," he whispered, so softly that I barely heard him.

Marsali heard him. She froze, the needle she had picked up glinting in her hand. Then, moving very slowly, put it down again.

"Did ye, then?" she said just as softly. And rising, went round the table in a quiet rustle of skirts to sit beside him on the bench, close enough that he could feel her there, and laid a small hand against his elbow.

He didn't open his eyes, but drew breath, and with the baby nestled against his heart, began to talk, in a voice hardly louder than the crackle of the fire.

He woke out of sleep, knowing that something was deeply wrong. He rolled toward the back of the bed platform, where his weapons lay at hand, but before he could seize knife or spear, he heard again the sound that must have wakened him. It came from behind him; no more than a slight catch of breath, but he heard both pain and fear in it.

The fire burned very low; he saw no more than the dark top of Wako'teqehsnonhsa's head, a red glow outlining it, and the double mound of shoulder and hip beneath the furs. She didn't move or make the sound again, but something in those still dark curves cleft through his heart like a tomahawk striking home.

He gripped her shoulder fiercely, willing her to be all right. Her bones were small and hard through her flesh. He could find no proper words; all the Kahnyen'kehaka had fled out of his head, and so he spoke in the first words that came to him.

"Lass—love—are ye all right, then? Blessed Michael defend us, are ye well?"

She knew he was there, but didn't turn to him. Something— a strange ripple, like a stone thrown in water—went through her, and the breath caught in her throat again, a small dry sound.

He didn't wait, but scrambled naked from the furs, calling for help. People came tumbling out into the dim light of the longhouse, bulky shapes hurrying toward him in a fog of questions. He couldn't speak; didn't need to. Within moments, Tewaktenyonh was there, her strong old face set in grim calm, and the women of the longhouse rushed past him, pushing him aside as they carried Emily away, wrapped in a deer's hide.

He followed them outside, but they ignored him, disappearing into the women's house at the end of the village. Two or three men came out, looked after them, then shrugged, turned, and went back inside. It was cold, and very late, and plainly women's business.

He went inside himself, after a few moments, but only long enough to pull on a few clothes. He couldn't stay in the longhouse, not with the bed empty of her and smelling of blood. There was blood on his skin as well, but he didn't pause to wash.

Outside, the stars had faded, but the sky was still black. It was bone-cold, and very still.

The hide that hung over the door of his longhouse moved, and Rollo slipped through, gray as a ghost. The big dog extended his paws and stretched, groaning with the stiffness of the hour and the cold. Then he shook his heavy ruff, snorted out a puff of white breath, and ambled slowly to his master's side. He sat down heavily, with a resigned sigh, and leaned against Ian's leg.

Ian stood a moment longer, looking toward the house where his Emily was. His face was hot, fevered with urgency. He burned harsh and bright, like a coal, but he could feel the heat seeping out of him into the cold sky, and his heart turning slowly black. Finally, he slapped his palm against his thigh and turned away into the forest, walking fast, the dog padding big and soundless by his side.

"Hail Mary, full of grace . . ." He paid no attention to where he was going, praying under his breath, but aloud, for the comfort of his own voice in the silent dark.

Ought he to be praying to one of the Mohawk spirits, he wondered? Would they be angry that he spoke to his old God, to God's mother? Might they take revenge for such a slight, on his wife and child?

The child is dead already. He had no notion where that knowledge came from, but he knew it was so, as surely as if someone had spoken the words to him aloud. The knowledge was dispassionate, not yet food for grief; only a fact he knew to be true—and was appalled to know it.

On he went into the woods, walking, then running, slowing only when he must, to draw breath. The air was knife-cold and still, smelling of rot and turpentine, but the trees whispered just a little as he passed. Emily could hear them talk; she knew their secret voices.

"Aye, and what good is that?" he muttered, face turned up to the starless void between the branches. "Ye dinna say anything worth knowing. Ye dinna ken how it is with her now, do ye?"

He could hear the dog's feet now and then, rustling among the dead leaves just behind him, thudding softly on patches of bare ground. He stumbled now and then, feet lost in the darkness, fell once bruisingly, stumbled to his feet, and ran clumsily on. He had stopped praying; his mind wouldn't form words any longer, couldn't choose among the fractured syllables of his different tongues, and his breath burned thick in his throat as he ran.

He felt her body against him in the cold, her full breasts in his hands, her small round buttocks thrusting back, heavy and eager as he rammed her, oh, God, he knew he ought not, he knew! And yet he'd done it, night after night, mad for the slippery tight clutch of her, long past the day when he knew he should stop, selfish, mindless, mad and wicked with lust. . . .

He ran, and her trees murmured condemnation above him as he went.

He had to stop, sobbing for breath. The sky had turned from black to the color that comes before the light. The dog nosed at him, whining softly in his throat, amber eyes gone blank and dark in the no-light of the hour.

Sweat poured down his body under the leather shirt, soaked the draggled breechclout between his legs. His privates were chilled, shriveled against his body, and he could smell himself, a rank, bitter scent of fear and loss.

Rollo's ears pricked, and the dog whined again, moving a step away, back, away again, tail twitching nervously. *Come*, he was saying, as clearly as words. *Come now!*

For himself, Ian could have lain down on the frozen leaves, buried his face in the earth, and stayed. But habit pulled at him; he was accustomed to heed the dog.

"What?" he muttered, dragging a sleeve across his wet face. "What is it, then?"

Rollo growled, deep in his throat. He was standing rigid, the hackles slowly rising on his neck. Ian saw it, and some distant tremor of alarm made itself felt through the fog of exhausted despair. His hand went to his belt, found emptiness there, and slapped at it, unbelieving. Christ, he had not so much as a skinning knife!

Rollo growled again, louder. A warning, meant to be heard. Ian turned, looking, but saw only the dark trunks of cedar and pine, the ground beneath them a mass of shadows, the air between them filled with mist.

A French trader who had come to their fire had called such a time, such a light, *l'heure du loup*—the hour of the wolf. And for good reason: it was a hunting time, when the night grows dim, and the faint breeze that comes before the light begins to rise, carrying the scent of prey.

His hand went to the other side of his belt, where the pouch of *taseng* should hang: bear grease steeped with mint leaves, to hide a man's scent while hunting—or hunted. But that side too was empty, and he felt his heart beat quick and hard, as the cold wind dried the sweat from his body.

Rollo's teeth were bared, the growl a continuous rolling thunder. Ian stooped and seized a fallen pine branch from the ground. It was a good length, though flimsier than he would have liked, and unwieldy, clawed with long twigs.

"Home," he whispered to the dog. He had no notion where he was, or where the village lay, but Rollo did. The dog backed slowly, eyes still fixed on the gray shadows—did they move, those shadows?

He was walking faster now, still backward, feeling the slope of the ground through the soles of his moccasins, sensing Rollo's presence from the rustle of the dog's feet, the faint whine that came now and then behind him. There. Yes, a shadow *had* moved! A gray shape, far away and seen too briefly to recognize, but there all the same—and recognizable by its presence alone.

If there was one, there were more. They did not hunt alone. They weren't near yet, though; he turned, beginning almost to run. Not in panic now, despite the fear in the pit of his stomach. A quick, steady lope, the hill-walker's gait that his uncle had shown him, that would devour the steep, endless miles of the Scottish mountains, steady effort without exhaustion. He must save strength to fight.

He observed that thought with a wry twist of the mouth, snapping off the brittle pine twigs from his club as he went. A moment

ago, he had wanted to die, and perhaps he would again, if Emily—
But not now. If Emily . . . and besides, there was the dog. Rollo
wouldn't leave him; they must defend each other.

There was water near; he heard it gurgling under the wind. But
carried on the wind came another sound, a long, unearthly howl
that brought the sweat out cold on his face again. Another answered it, to the west. Still far away, but they were hunting now,
calling to one another. Her blood was on him.

He turned, seeking the water. It was a small creek, no more
than a few feet across. He splashed into it without hesitation,
splintering the skin of ice that clung to the banks, feeling the cold
bite into his legs and feet as it soaked his leggings and filled his
moccasins. He stopped for a split second, pulling off the moccasins, lest they be carried away in the current; Emily had made
them for him, of moose hide.

Rollo had crossed the stream in two gigantic bounds, and
paused on the opposite bank to shake a freezing spray of water
from his coat before going on. He held to the bank, though; Ian
stayed in the water, splashing shin-deep, staying as long as might
be managed. Wolves hunted by wind as much as by ground scent,
but no need to make it easy for them.

He had thrust the wet moccasins down the neck of his shirt,
and icy trickles ran down chest and belly, soaking his breechclout.
His feet were numb; he couldn't feel the rounded stones of the
streambed, but now and then his foot slid on one, slippery with algae, and he lurched and stumbled to keep his balance.

He could hear the wolves more clearly; that was good,
though—the wind had changed, was toward him now, carrying
their voices. Or was it only that they were closer now?

Closer. Rollo was wild, darting to and fro on the far bank,
whining and growling, urging him on with brief yips. A deer's
path came down to the stream on that side; he stumbled out of the
water onto it, panting and shaking. It took several tries to get the
moccasins on again. The soaked leather was stiff, and his hands
and feet refused to work. He had to put down his club and use both
hands.

He had just managed the second one when Rollo suddenly
charged down the bank, roaring a challenge. He whirled on the
frozen mud, catching up his club, in time to see a gray shape, nearly
Rollo's size, on the far side of the water, its pale eyes startlingly near.

He screeched and flung the club in reflex. It sailed across the stream and struck the ground near the wolf's feet, and the thing vanished as though by magic. He stood stock-still for an instant, staring. He had not imagined it, surely?

No, Rollo was raving, bellowing and teeth bared, flecks of foam flying from his muzzle. There were stones at the stream's edge; Ian seized one, another, scraped up a handful, another, stubbing his fingers in haste on the rocks and frozen soil, holding up the front of his shirt to make a bag.

The more-distant wolf howled again; the near one answered, so close that the hairs rose up straight on the back of his neck. He heaved a rock in the direction of the call, turned, and ran, the bundle of rocks clutched hard against his belly.

The sky had lightened into dawn. Heart and lungs strained for blood and air, and yet it seemed as though he ran so slowly that he floated over the forest floor, passing like a drifting cloud, unable to go faster. He could see each tree, each separate needle of a spruce he passed, short and thick, soft silver-green in the light.

His breath came hard, his vision blurred and cleared, as tears of effort clouded his eyes, were blinked away, welled back again. A tree branch lashed his face and blinded him, the scent of it sharp in his nose.

"Red Cedar, help me!" he gasped, the Kahnyen'kehaka coming to his lips as though he had never spoken English or called upon Christ and His mother.

Behind you. It was a small voice, quiet, perhaps no more than the voice of his own instinct, but he whirled at once, stone in hand, and slung it with all his force. Another, and another, and another, as fast as he could fling. There was a crack, a thump, and a yelp, and Rollo slewed and skidded, eager to turn and attack.

"Come-come-come!" He seized the big dog's ruff as he ran, dragging him round, forcing him along.

He could hear them now, or thought he could. The wind that comes at dawn rustled through the trees, and they whispered overhead, calling him this way, then that, guiding him as he ran. He saw nothing but color, half-blind with effort, but felt their embrace, cool in his mind; a prickling touch of spruce and fir, the skin of white aspen, smooth as a woman's, sticky with blood.

Go here, come this way, he thought he heard, and followed the sound of the wind.

A howl came from behind them, followed by short yips, and another of acknowledgment. Close, too close! He flung stones behind him as he ran, not looking, no time to turn and aim.

Then there were no more stones and he dropped the empty flap of shirt, arms pumping as he ran, a harsh panting in his ears that might have been his own breath, or the dog's—or the sound of the beasts behind him.

How many of them? How far to go? He was beginning to stagger, streaks of black and red shooting through his vision. If the village was not nearby, he had no chance.

He lurched sideways, hit the yielding branch of a tree that bent under his weight, then pushed him upright, setting him roughly back on his feet. He had lost his impetus, though, and his sense of direction.

"Where?" he gasped to the trees. "Which way?"

If there was an answer, he didn't hear it. There was a roar and a thud behind him, a mad scuffle punctuated with the growls and yelps of dogs fighting.

"Rollo!" He turned and flung himself through a growth of dead vines, to find dog and wolf squirming and biting in a writhing ball of fur and flashing teeth.

He dashed forward, kicking and shouting, punching wildly, glad at last to have something to hit, to be fighting back, even if it was the last fight. Something ripped across his leg, but he felt only the jar of impact as he rammed his knee hard into the wolf's side. It squealed and rolled away, rounding on him at once.

It leaped, and its paws struck him in the chest. He fell back, struck his head glancingly on something, lost breath for an instant, and came to himself to find his hand braced beneath the slavering jaws, straining to keep them from his throat.

Rollo sprang onto the wolf's back, and Ian lost his grip, collapsing under the weight of reeking fur and squirming flesh. He flung out a hand, seeking anything—a weapon, a tool, a grip to pull himself free—and gripped something hard.

He wrenched it from its bed in the moss and smashed it against the wolf's head. Fragments of bloody teeth flew through the air and struck his face. He struck again, sobbing, and again.

Rollo was whining, a high keening noise—no, it was him. He bashed the rock down once more on the battered skull, but the wolf had stopped fighting; it lay across his thighs, legs twitching, eyes glazing as it died. He pushed it off in a frenzy of revulsion. Rollo's teeth sank into the wolf's outstretched throat, and ripped it out, in a final spray of blood and warm flesh.

Ian closed his eyes and sat still. It didn't seem possible to move, or to think.

After a time, it seemed possible to open his eyes, and to breathe, at least. There was a large tree at his back; he had fallen against the trunk when the wolf struck him; it supported him now. Among the twisted roots was a muddy hole, from which he had wrenched the stone.

He was still holding the stone; it felt as though it had grown to his skin; he couldn't open his hand. When he looked he saw that this was because the stone had shattered; sharp fragments had cut his hand, and the pieces of the stone were glued to his hand by drying blood. Using the fingers of his other hand, he bent back the clenched fingers, and pushed the broken pieces of the stone off his palm. He scraped moss from the tree roots, made a wad of it in his hand, then let the curled fingers close over it again.

A wolf howled, in the middle distance. Rollo, who had lain down by Ian, lifted his head with a soft *wuff!* The howl came again, and seemed to hold a question, a worried tone.

For the first time, he looked at the body of the wolf. For an instant, he thought it moved, and shook his head to clear his vision. Then he looked again.

It was moving. The distended belly rose gently, subsided. It was full light now, and he could see the tiny nubs of pink nipples, showing through the belly fur. Not a pack. A pair. But a pair no more. The wolf in the distance howled again, and Ian leaned to one side and vomited.

Eats Turtles came upon him a little later, sitting with his back against the red-cedar tree by the dead wolf, Rollo's bulk pressed close against him. Turtle squatted down, a short distance away, balanced on his heels, and watched.

"Good hunting, Wolf's Brother," he said finally, in greeting. Ian felt the knot between his shoulder blades relax just a little. Turtle's voice held a quiet tone, but no sorrow. She lived, then.

"She whose hearth I share," he said, careful to avoid speaking her name. To speak it aloud might expose her to evil spirits nearby. "She is well?"

Turtle closed his eyes and raised both brows and shoulders.

She was alive, and not in danger. Still, it was not for a man to say what might happen. Ian didn't mention the child. Neither did Turtle.

Turtle had brought a gun, a bow, and his knife, of course. He took the knife from his belt and handed it to Ian, matter-of-factly.

"You will want the skins," he said. "To wrap your son, when he shall be born."

A shock went through Ian, like the shock of sudden rain on bare skin. Eats Turtles saw his face, and turned his head aside, avoiding his eyes.

"This child was a daughter," Turtle said matter-of-factly. "Tewaktenyonh told my wife, when she came for a rabbit skin to wrap the body."

The muscles in his belly tightened and quivered; he thought that perhaps his own skin would burst, but it didn't. His throat was dry, and he swallowed once, painfully, then shook the moss away and held out his wounded hand for the knife. He bent slowly to skin the wolf.

Eats Turtles was poking with interest at the bloodstained remnants of the shattered stone, when the howl of a wolf brought him upright, staring.

It echoed through the forest, that howl, and the trees moved above them, murmuring uneasily at the sound of loss and desolation. The knife drew swiftly down the pale fur of the belly, dividing the two rows of pink nipples.

"Her husband will be nearby," Wolf's Brother said, not looking up. "Go and kill him."

Marsali stared at him, scarcely breathing. The sadness in her eyes was still there, but had somehow diminished, overwhelmed with compassion. The anger had left her; she had taken back Henri-Christian, and held the fat bundle of her baby with both arms against her breast, her cheek against the bold round curve of his head.

"Ah, Ian," she said softly. *"Mo charaid, mo chridhe."*

He sat looking down at his hands, clasped loosely in his lap, and seemed not to have heard her. Finally, though, he stirred, like a statue waking. Without looking up, he reached into his shirt and drew out a small, rolled bundle, bound with hair twine, and decorated with a wampum bead.

He undid this, and leaning over, spread the cured skin of an unborn wolf over the baby's shoulders. His big, bony hand smoothed the pale fur, cupping for a moment over Marsali's hand where it held the child.

"Believe me, cousin," he said, very softly, "your husband grieves. But he will come back." Then he rose and left, silent as an Indian.

37

Le Maître des Champignons

The small limestone cave we used for a stable was home at the moment only to a nanny goat with two brand-new kids. All the animals born in the spring were now large enough to be turned out to forage in the wood with their mothers. The goat was still getting room service, though, in the form of kitchen scraps and a little cracked corn.

It had been raining for several days, and the morning broke cloudy and damp, every leaf dripping and the air thick with the scents of resin and soggy leaf mulch. Luckily, the cloudiness kept the birds subdued; the jays and mockingbirds were quick to learn, and kept a beady eye on the comings and goings of people with food—they dive-bombed me regularly as I made my way up the hill with my basin.

I was on my guard, but even so, a bold jay dropped from a branch in a flash of blue and landed *in* the basin, startling me.

Before I could react, it had seized a fragment of corn muffin and darted off, so quickly that I could scarcely believe I'd seen it, save for the racing of my heart. Luckily I hadn't dropped the basin; I heard a triumphant screech from the trees, and hurried to get inside the stable before the jay's friends should try the same tactic.

I was surprised to find that the Dutch door was unbolted at the top and stood an inch or two ajar. There was no danger of the goats escaping, of course, but foxes and raccoons were more than capable of climbing over the lower door, and so both doors were normally bolted at night. Perhaps Mr. Wemyss had forgotten; it was his job to muck out the used straw and settle the stock for the night.

As soon as I pushed open the door, though, I saw that Mr. Wemyss was not to blame. There was a tremendous rustle of straw at my feet, and something big moved in the darkness.

I uttered a sharp yelp of alarm, and this time *did* drop the basin, which fell with a clang, scattering food across the floor and rousing the nanny goat, who started blatting her head off.

"*Pardon*, milady!"

Hand to my thumping heart, I stepped out of the doorway, so the light fell on Fergus, crouched on the floor, with straws sticking out of his hair like the Madwoman of Chaillot.

"Oh, so there you are," I said quite coldly.

He blinked and swallowed, rubbing his hand over a face dark with sprouting whiskers.

"I—yes," he said. He seemed to have nothing further to add to this. I stood glaring down at him for a moment, then shook my head and stooped to retrieve the potato peelings and other fragments that had fallen from the basin. He moved as though to help me, but I stopped him with a shooing gesture.

He sat still, watching me, hands around his knees. It was dim inside the stable, and water dripped steadily from the plants growing out of the cliffside above, making a curtain of falling drops across the open door.

The goat had stopped making noise, having recognized me, but was now stretching her neck through the railing of her pen, blueberry-colored tongue extended like an anteater's, in an effort to reach an apple core that had rolled near the pen. I picked it up and handed it to her, trying to think where to start, and what to say when I did.

"Henri-Christian's doing well," I said, for lack of anything else. "Putting on weight."

I let the remark trail off, bending over the rail to pour corn and scraps into the wooden feed trough.

Dead silence. I waited a moment, then turned round, one hand on my hip.

"He's a very sweet little baby," I said.

I could hear him breathing, but he said nothing. With an audible snort, I went and pushed the bottom half of the door open wide, so that the cloudy light outside streamed in, exposing Fergus. He sat with his face turned stubbornly away. I could smell him at a goodly distance; he reeked of bitter sweat and hunger.

I sighed.

"Dwarves of this sort have got quite normal intelligence. I've checked him thoroughly, and he has all the usual reflexes and responses that he should have. There's no reason why he can't be educated, be able to work—at something."

"Something," Fergus echoed, the word holding both despair and derision. "Something." At last, he turned his face toward me, and I saw the hollowness of his eyes. "With respect, milady—you have never seen the life of a dwarf."

"And you have?" I asked, not so much in challenge as curiosity.

He closed his eyes against the morning light, nodding.

"Yes," he whispered, and swallowed. "In Paris."

The brothel where he had grown up in Paris was a large one, with a varied clientele, famous for being able to offer something for almost any taste.

"The house itself had *les filles*, *naturellement*, and *les enfants*. They are of course the bread and butter of the establishment. But there are always those who desire . . . the exotic, and will pay. And so now and then the madame would send for those who dealt in such things. *La Maîtresse des Scorpions—avec les flagellantes, tu comprends? Ou Le Maître des Champignons.*"

"The Master of Mushrooms?" I blurted.

"*Oui.* The Dwarf Master."

His eyes had sunk into his head, his gaze turned inward and his face haggard. He was seeing in memory sights and people who had been absent from his thoughts for many years—and was not enjoying the recollection.

"*Les chanterelles*, we called them," he said softly. "The females. The males, they were *les morels*." Exotic fungi, valued for the rarity of their twisted shapes, the strange savor of their flesh.

"They were not badly treated, *les champignons*," he said, abstracted. "They were of value, you see. *Le Maître* would buy such infants from their parents—there was one born in the brothel, once, and the madame was delighted at her good fortune—or collect them from the streets."

He looked down at his hand, the long, delicate fingers moving restlessly, pleating the cloth of his breeches.

"The streets," he repeated. "Those who escaped the brothels—they were beggars. I knew one of them quite well—Luc, he was called. We would sometimes assist each other—" The shadow of a smile touched his mouth, and he waved his intact hand in the deft gesture of one picking pockets.

"But he was alone, Luc," he continued matter-of-factly. "He had no protector. I found him one day in the alley, with his throat cut. I told the madame, and she sent the doorkeep out at once to seize the body, and sold it to a doctor in the next *arondissement*."

I didn't ask what the doctor had wanted with Luc's body. I'd seen the broad, dried hands of dwarves, sold for divination and protection. And other parts.

"I begin to see why a brothel might seem safe," I said, swallowing heavily. "But still . . ."

Fergus had been sitting with his head braced on his hand, staring at the straw. At this, he looked up at me.

"I have parted my buttocks for money, milady," he said simply. "And thought nothing of it, save when it hurt. But then I met milord, and found a world beyond the brothel and the streets. That my son might return to such places . . ." He stopped abruptly, unable to speak. He closed his eyes again, and shook his head, slowly.

"Fergus. Fergus, dear. You can't think that Jamie—that we—would ever let such a thing happen," I said, distressed beyond measure.

He drew a deep, trembling breath, and thumbed away the tears that hung on his lashes. He opened his eyes and gave me a smile of infinite sadness.

"No, you would not, milady. But you will not live forever, nor will milord. Nor I. But the child will be a dwarf forever. And *les petits,* they cannot well defend themselves. They will be plucked up by those who seek them, taken and consumed." He wiped his nose on his sleeve and sat up a little.

"If, that is, they should be so fortunate," he added, his voice hardening. "They are not valued, outside the cities. Peasants, they believe the birth of such a child is at best a judgment on the sins of his parents." A deeper shadow crossed his face, his lips drawing tight. "It may be so. My sins—" But he broke off abruptly, turning away.

"At worst—" His voice was soft, head turned away, as though he whispered secrets to the shadows of the cave. "At worst, they are seen as monstrous, children born of some demon who has lain with the woman. People stone them, burn them—sometimes the woman, too. In the mountain villages of France, a dwarf child would be left for the wolves. But do you not know these things, milady?" he asked, suddenly turning back to face me.

"I—I suppose so," I said, and put out a hand to the wall, suddenly feeling the need of some support. I *had* known such things, in the abstract way one thinks of the customs of aborigines and savages—people whom one will never meet, safely distant in the pages of geography books, of ancient histories.

He was right; I knew it. Mrs. Bug had crossed herself, seeing the child, and then made the sign of the horns as protection from evil, pale horror on her face.

Shocked as we had all been, and then concerned with Marsali, and with Fergus's absence, I hadn't been away from the house for a week or more. I had no idea what people might be saying, on the Ridge. Fergus plainly did.

"They'll . . . get used to him," I said as bravely as I could. "People will see that he isn't a monster. It may take some time, but I promise you, they'll see."

"Will they? And if they let him live, what then will he do?" He rose to his feet quite suddenly. He stretched out his left arm, and with a jerk, freed the leather strip that held his hook. It fell with a soft thump into the straw, and left the narrow stump of his wrist bare, the pale skin creased with red from the tightness of the wrappings.

"Me, I cannot hunt, cannot do a proper man's work. I am fit for nothing but to pull the plow, like a mule!" His voice shook with anger and self-loathing. "If I cannot work as a man does, how shall a dwarf?"

"Fergus, it isn't—"

"I cannot keep my family! My wife must labor day and night to feed the children, must put herself in the way of scum and filth who misuse her, who— Even if I was in Paris, I am too old and crippled to whore!" He shook the stump at me, face convulsed, then whirled and swung his maimed arm, smashing it against the wall, over and over.

"Fergus!" I seized his other arm, but he jerked away.

"What work will he do?" he cried, tears streaming down his face. "How shall he live? *Mon Dieu! Il est aussi inutile que moi!*"

He bent and seized the hook from the ground, and hurled it as hard as he could at the limestone wall. It made a small chiming sound as it struck, and fell into the straw, startling the nanny and her kids.

Fergus was gone, the Dutch door left swinging. The goat called after him, a long *maaaah!* of disapproval.

I held on to the railing of the pen, feeling as though it was the only solid thing in a slowly tilting world. When I could, I bent and felt carefully in the straw until I touched the metal of the hook, still warm from Fergus's body. I drew it out and wiped bits of straw and manure carefully off it with my apron, still hearing Fergus's last words.

"My God! He is as useless as I am!"

38

A De'il in the Milk

Henri-Christian's eyes nearly crossed with the effort of focusing on the yarn bobble Brianna dangled over his face.

"I think his eyes might stay blue," she said, peering thoughtfully at him. "What do you think he's looking at?" He lay in her lap, knees drawn up nearly to his chin, the soft blue eyes in question fixed somewhere far beyond her.

"Oh, the wee ones still see heaven, my Mam said." Marsali was spinning, trying out Brianna's new treadle wheel, but spared a quick glance at her newest son, smiling a little. "Maybe there's an angel sitting on your shoulder, aye? Or a saint who stands behind ye."

That gave her an odd feeling, as though someone *did* stand behind her. Not creepy, though—more a mild, warm sense of reassurance. She opened her mouth to say, "Maybe it's my father," but caught herself in time.

"Who's the patron saint of laundry?" she said instead. "That's who we need." It was raining; it had been raining for days, and small mounds of clothing lay scattered about the room or draped over the furniture: damp things in various states of drying, filthy things destined for the wash cauldron as soon as the weather broke, less-filthy things that might be brushed, shaken, or beaten into another few days' wearing, and an ever-growing pile of things needing mending.

Marsali laughed, deftly feeding thread to the bobbin.

"Ye'd have to ask Da about that. He kens more saints than anybody. This is wonderful, this wheel! I've not seen this kind before. However did ye come to think of such a thing?"

"Oh—saw one somewhere." Bree flicked a hand, dismissing it.

She had—in a folk-art museum. Building it had been time-consuming—she'd first had to make a crude lathe, as well as soak and bend the wood for the wheel itself—but not terribly difficult. "Ronnie Sinclair helped a lot; he knows what wood will do and what it won't. I can't believe how good you are at that, and this your first time using one like it."

Marsali snorted, likewise dismissing the compliment.

"I've spun since I was five, *a piuthar*. All that's different here is I can sit while I do it, instead of walking to and fro 'til I fall over wi' tiredness."

Her stockinged feet flickered back and forth under the hem of her dress, working the treadle. It made a pleasant *whish-whir* sound—though this was barely audible over the babble at the other side of the room, where Roger was carving yet another car for the children.

Vrooms were a big hit with the small-fry, and the demand for them unceasing. Brianna watched with amusement as Roger fended off Jem's inquisitiveness with a deft elbow, frowning in concentration. The tip of his tongue showed between his teeth, and wood shavings littered the hearth and his clothes, and—of course—one was stuck in his hair, a pale curl against its darkness.

"What's that one?" she asked, raising her voice to reach him. He looked up, his eyes a mossy green in the dim rainlight from the window behind him.

"I think it's a '57 Chevrolet pickup truck," he said, grinning. "Here, then, *a nighean*. This one's yours." He brushed a last shaving from his creation and handed the blocky thing to Félicité, whose mouth and eyes were round with awe.

"Issa vroom?" she said, clutching it to her bosom. "*My* vroom?"

"It's a druck," Jemmy informed her with kindly condescension. "Daddy says."

"A truck is a vroom," Roger assured Félicité, seeing doubt begin to pucker her forehead. "It's just a bigger kind."

"Issa *big* vroom, see!" Félicité kicked Jem in the shin. He yelped and grabbed for her hair, only to be butted in the stomach by Joan, always there to defend her sister.

Brianna tensed, ready to intervene, but Roger broke up the incipient riot by holding Jem and Félicité each at arm's length, glaring Joan into retreat.

"Right, you lot. No fighting, or we put the vrooms away 'til to-morrow."

That quelled them instantly, and Brianna felt Marsali relax, re-suming the rhythm of her spinning. The rain hummed on the roof, solid and steady; it was a good day to be inside, despite the diffi-culty of entertaining bored children.

"Why don't you play something nice and quiet?" she said, grinning at Roger. "Like . . . oh . . . Indianapolis 500?"

"Oh, you're a great help," he said, giving her a dirty look, but he obligingly set the children to work laying out a racetrack in chalk on the big hearthstone.

"Too bad Germain's not here," he said casually. "Where's he gone in the rain and all, Marsali?" Germain's vroom—according to Roger, it was a Jaguar X-KE, though so far as Brianna could tell, it looked exactly like the others: a block of wood with a rudi-mentary cab and wheels—was sitting on the mantelpiece, await-ing its master's return.

"He's with Fergus," Marsali answered calmly, not faltering in her rhythm. Her lips pressed together, though, and it was easy to hear the note of strain in her voice.

"And how's Fergus, then?" Roger looked up at her, kindly, but intent.

The thread skipped, bounced in Marsali's hand, and wound itself up with a visible slub in it. She grimaced, and didn't reply until the thread was running once more smoothly through her fingers.

"Well, I will say, for a man wi' one hand, he's a bonny wee fighter," she said at last, eyes on the thread and a wry note in her voice.

Brianna glanced at Roger, who raised an eyebrow back at her.

"Who's he been fighting?" she asked, trying to sound casual.

"He doesna often tell me," Marsali said evenly. "Though yes-terday it was the husband of a woman who asked him why he didna just strangle Henri-Christian at birth. He took offense," she added, offhand, leaving it unclear as to whether it was Fergus, the husband, or both who had taken offense. Lifting the thread, she bit it sharply off.

"I should think so," Roger murmured. His head was bent, mark-ing off the starting line, so his hair fell over his forehead, obscuring his face. "Not the only one, though, I take it."

"No." Marsali began winding the thread onto the niddy-noddy, a small, seemingly permanent frown showing between her fair brows. "I suppose it's better than the ones who point and whisper. Those are the ones who think Henri-Christian's the—the devil's seed," she finished bravely, though her voice quivered a little. "I think they'd burn the wee man—and me and the other weans along with him, if they thought they could."

Brianna felt the bottom of her stomach drop, and cuddled the object of discussion in her lap.

"What sort of idiots could *possibly* think such a thing?" she demanded. "Let alone say it out loud!"

"Let alone do it, ye mean." Marsali put aside the yarn and rose, leaning over to take Henri-Christian and put him to her breast. With his knees still curled up, his body was scarcely half the size of a normal baby's—and with his large, round head with its sprout of dark hair, Brianna had to admit that he did look . . . odd.

"Da had a word here and there," Marsali said. Her eyes were closed, and she was rocking slowly back and forth, cradling Henri-Christian close. "If it weren't for that . . ." Her slender throat moved as she swallowed.

"Daddy, Daddy, let's *go!*" Jem, impatient with incomprehensible adult conversation, plucked at Roger's sleeve.

Roger had been looking at Marsali, his lean face troubled. At this reminder, he blinked and glanced down at his thoroughly normal son, clearing his throat.

"Aye," he said, and took down Germain's car. "Well, then, look. Here's the starting line. . . ."

Brianna laid a hand on Marsali's arm. It was thin, but strongly muscled, the fair skin gold from sun, spattered with tiny freckles. The sight of it, so small and brave-looking, clutched at her throat.

"They'll stop," she whispered. "They'll see. . . ."

"Aye, maybe." Marsali cupped Henri-Christian's small round bottom, holding him closer. Her eyes were still closed. "Maybe not. But if Germain's wi' Fergus, he'll maybe be more careful who he fights. I'd rather they didna kill him, aye?"

She bowed her head over the baby, settling into the nursing and plainly disinclined to talk any further. Brianna patted her arm, a little awkwardly, then moved to take the seat by the spinning wheel.

She'd heard the talk, of course. Or some of it. Particularly right after Henri-Christian's birth, which had sent shock waves through the Ridge. Beyond the first overt expressions of sympathy, there had been a lot of muttering, about recent events and what malign influence might have caused them—from the assault on Marsali and the burning of the malting shed, to the kidnapping of her mother, the slaughter in the woods, and the birth of a dwarf. She'd heard one injudicious girl murmur within her hearing something about ". . . witchcraft, what would ye expect?"—but had rounded fiercely to glare at the girl, who had paled and slunk off with her two friends. The girl had glanced back once, though, then turned away, the three of them spitefully sniggering.

But no one had ever treated her or her mother with any lack of respect. It was clear that a number of the tenants were rather afraid of Claire—but they were much more afraid of her father. Time and habituation had seemed to be working, though—until the birth of Henri-Christian.

Working the treadle was soothing; the whir of the spinning wheel faded into the sound of the rain and the bickering of the children.

At least Fergus had come back. When Henri-Christian was born, he had left the house and not come back for several days. *Poor Marsali*, she thought, with a mental scowl at Fergus. Left alone to deal with the shock. And everyone had *been* shocked, her included. Perhaps she couldn't really blame Fergus.

She swallowed, imagining, as she did whenever she saw Henri-Christian, what it would be like to have a child born with some terrible defect. She saw them now and then—children with cleft lips, the misshapen features of what her mother said was congenital syphilis, retarded children—and every time, crossed herself and thanked God that Jemmy was normal.

But then, so were Germain and his sisters. Something like this could come out of the blue, at any time. Despite herself, she glanced at the small shelf where she kept her personal things, and the dark brown jar of *dauco* seeds. She'd been taking them again, ever since Henri-Christian's birth, though she hadn't mentioned it to Roger. She wondered whether he knew; he hadn't said anything.

Marsali was singing softly under her breath. *Did* Marsali blame Fergus? she wondered. Or he her? She hadn't seen Fergus to talk to in some time. Marsali didn't seem critical of him—and she had said she didn't want him killed. Brianna smiled involuntarily at the memory. Yet there was an undeniable sense of distance when she mentioned him.

The thread thickened suddenly, and she trod faster, trying to compensate, only to have it catch and snap. Muttering to herself, she stopped and let the wheel run itself down—only then realizing that someone had been pounding on the door of the cabin for some time, the sound of it lost in the racket inside.

She opened the door to find one of the fisher-folks' children dripping on the stoop, small, bony, and feral as a wild cat. There were several of them among the tenant families, so alike that she had trouble telling them apart.

"Aidan?" she guessed. "Aidan McCallum?"

"Good day, mistress," the little boy said, bobbing his head in nervous acknowledgment of identity. "Is meenister to hame?"

"Mee—oh. Yes, I suppose so. Come in, won't you?" Suppressing a smile, she swung the door wide, beckoning him in. The boy looked quite shocked to see Roger, crouched on the floor, playing Vroom with Jemmy and Joan and Félicité, all industriously screeching and roaring to such effect that they hadn't noticed the newcomer.

"You have a visitor," she said, raising her voice to interrupt the bedlam. "He wants the minister." Roger broke off in mid-vroom, glancing up in inquiry.

"The what?" he said, sitting up, cross-legged, his own car in hand. Then he spotted the boy, and smiled. "Oh. Aidan, *a charaid*! What is it, then?"

Aidan screwed up his face in concentration. Obviously, he had been given a specific message, committed to memory.

"Mither says will ye come, please," he recited, "for to drive out a de'il what's got intae the milk."

The rain was falling more lightly now, but they were still soaked nearly through by the time they reached the McCallum residence. If it could be dignified by such a term, Roger thought, slapping rain from his hat as he followed Aidan up the narrow, slippery path to the cabin, which was perched in a high and inconvenient notch in the side of the mountain.

Orem McCallum had managed to erect the walls of his shakily built cabin, and then had missed his footing and plunged into a rock-strewn ravine, breaking his neck within a month of arrival on the Ridge, and leaving his pregnant wife and young son to its dubious shelter.

The other men had come and hastily put a roof on, but the cabin as a whole reminded Roger of nothing so much as a pile of giant jackstraws, poised precariously on the side of the mountain and obviously only awaiting the next spring flood to slide down the mountain after its builder.

Mrs. McCallum was young and pale, and so thin that her dress flapped round her like an empty flour sack. *Christ*, he thought, *what did they have to eat?*

"Oh, sir, I do thank ye for coming." She bobbed an anxious curtsy to him. "I'm that sorry to bring ye out in the rain and all— but I just didna ken what else I might do!"

"Not a problem," he assured her. "Er . . . Aidan said, though, that ye wanted a minister. I'm not that, ye know."

She looked disconcerted at that.

"Oh. Well, maybe not exactly, sir. But they do say as how your faither was a minister, and that ye do ken a great deal about the Bible and all."

"Some, yes," he replied guardedly, wondering what sort of emergency might require Bible knowledge. "A . . . um . . . devil in your milk, was it?"

He glanced discreetly from the baby in its cradle to the front of her dress, unsure at first whether she might mean her own breast milk, which would be a problem he was definitely not equipped to deal with. Fortunately, the difficulty seemed to lie with a large wooden pail sitting on the ramshackle table, a muslin cloth draped across it to keep flies out, small stones knotted into the corners as weights.

"Aye, sir." Mrs. McCallum nodded at it, obviously afraid to go nearer. "Lizzie Wemyss, her from the Big House, she brought that to me last night. She said Herself said as I must give it to Aidan, and drink of it myself." She looked helplessly at Roger. He understood her reservations; even in his own time, milk was regarded as a beverage only for infants and invalids; coming from a fishing village on the Scottish coast, she had quite possibly never seen a cow before coming to America. He was sure she knew what milk was, and that it technically was edible, but she had likely never tasted any.

"Aye, that's quite all right," he assured her. "My family all drink milk; it makes the weans grow tall and strong." And wouldn't come amiss to a nursing mother on lean rations, which was undoubtedly what Claire had thought.

She nodded, uncertain.

"Well . . . aye, sir. I wasna quite sure . . . but the lad was hungry, and said he'd drink it. So I went to dip him out a bit, but it—" She glanced at the bucket with an expression of fearful suspicion. "Weel, if it's no a de'il's got into it, it's something else. It's haunted, sir, I'm sure of it!"

He didn't know what made him look at Aidan at that moment, but he surprised a fleeting look of deep interest that vanished immediately, leaving the boy with a preternaturally solemn expression.

So it was with a certain sense of forewarning that he leaned forward and gingerly lifted the cloth. Even so, he let out a yelp and jerked back, the weighted cloth flying sideways to clack against the wall.

The malevolent green eyes that glared at him from the middle of the bucket disappeared and the milk went *gollup!*, a spray of creamy drops erupting from the bucket like a miniature volcano.

"Shit!" he said. Mrs. McCallum had backed away as far as she could get and was staring at the bucket in terror, both hands clapped across her mouth. Aidan had one hand pressed over his own mouth, and was similarly wide-eyed—but a faint fizzing sound was audible from his direction.

Roger's heart was pounding from adrenaline—and a strong desire to wring Aidan McCallum's scrawny neck. He wiped the splattered cream deliberately from his face, then, gritting his teeth, reached gingerly into the bucket of milk.

It took several tries to grab the thing, which felt like nothing so much as a very muscular and animated glob of mucus, but the fourth try succeeded, and he triumphantly pulled a very large and indignant bullfrog out of the bucket, showering milk in every direction.

The frog dug its back legs ferociously into his slippery palm and broke his grip, launching itself in a soaring leap that covered half the distance to the door and made Mrs. McCallum scream out loud. The startled baby woke and added to the uproar, while the cream-covered frog plopped its way rapidly out of the door and into the rain, leaving yellow splotches in its wake.

Aidan prudently followed it out at a high rate of speed.

Mrs. McCallum had sat down on the floor, thrown her apron over her head, and was having hysterics under it. The baby was shrieking, and milk dripped slowly from the edge of the table, punctuating the patter of rain outside. The roof was leaking, he saw; long wet streaks darkened the unbarked logs behind Mrs. McCallum, and she was sitting in a puddle.

With a deep sigh, he plucked the baby out of its cradle, surprising it sufficiently that it gulped and quit screaming. It blinked at him, and stuck its fist in its mouth. He had no idea of its sex; it was an anonymous bundle of rags, with a pinched wee face and a wary look.

Holding it in one arm, he crouched and put the other round Mrs. McCallum's shoulders, patting her gingerly in hopes of getting her to stop.

"It's all right," he said. "It was just a frog, ye know."

She'd been moaning like a banshee and uttering small intermittent screams, and she kept doing that, though the screams became less frequent, and the moaning disintegrated at last into more or less normal crying, though she refused to come out from under the apron.

His thigh muscles were cramped from squatting, and he was wet, anyway. With a sigh, he lowered himself into the puddle beside her and sat, patting her shoulder every now and then so she'd know he was still there.

The baby seemed happy enough, at least; it was sucking its fist, undisturbed by its mother's fit.

"How old's the wean?" he said conversationally, during a brief pause for breath. He knew its age approximately, because it had been born a week after Orem McCallum's death—but it was something to say. And for as old as it was, it seemed terribly small and light, at least by contrast to his memories of Jemmy at that age.

She mumbled something inaudible, but the crying eased off into hiccups and sighs. Then she said something else.

"What's that, Mrs. McCallum?"

"Why?" she whispered from under the faded calico. "Why has God brought me here?"

Well, that was a bloody good question; he'd asked that one fairly often himself, but hadn't got back any really good answers yet.

"Well . . . we trust He's got a plan of some sort," he said a little awkwardly. "We just don't know what it is."

"A fine plan," she said, and sobbed once. "To bring us all this way, to this terrible place, and then take my man from me and leave me here to starve!"

"Oh . . . it's no such a terrible place," he said, unable to refute anything else in her statement. "The woods and all . . . the streams, the mountains . . . it's . . . um . . . very pretty. When it's not raining." The inanity of this actually made her laugh, though it quickly devolved into more weeping.

"What?" He put an arm round her and pulled her a little closer, both to offer comfort, and in order to make out what she was saying, under her makeshift refuge.

"I miss the sea," she said very softly, and leaned her calico-swathed head against his shoulder, as though she was very tired. "I never shall see it again."

She was very likely right, and he could find nothing to say in reply. They sat for some time in a silence broken only by the baby's slobbering over its fist.

"I won't let ye starve," he said at last, softly. "That's all I can promise, but I do. Ye won't starve." Muscles cramped, he got stiffly to his feet, and reached down to one of the small rough hands that lay limply in her lap. "Come on, then. Get up. Ye can feed the wean, while I tidy up a bit."

The rain had ceased by the time he left, and the clouds had begun to drift apart, leaving patches of pale blue sky. He paused at a turn in the steep, muddy path to admire a rainbow—a complete one, that arched from one side of the sky to the other, its misty colors sinking down into the dark wet green of the dripping mountainside across from him.

It was quiet, save for the splat and drip of water from the leaves and the gurgle of water running down a rocky channel near the trail.

"A covenant," he said softly, out loud. "What's the promise, then? Not a pot of gold at the end." He shook his head and went on, grabbing at branches and bushes to keep from sliding down the mountainside; he didn't want to end up like Orem McCallum, in a tangle of bones at the bottom.

He'd talk to Jamie, and also to Tom Christie and Hiram Crombie. Among them, they could put out the word, and ensure the widow McCallum and her children got enough food. Folk were generous to share—but someone had to ask.

He glanced back over his shoulder; the crooked chimney was just visible above the trees, but no smoke came from it. They could gather enough firewood, she said—but wet as it was, it would be days before they had anything that would burn. They needed a shed for the wood, and logs cut, big enough to burn for a day, not the twigs and fallen branches Aidan could carry.

As though the thought had summoned him, Aidan came into view then. The boy was fishing, squatting on a rock beside a pool some thirty feet below, back turned to the trail. His shoulder blades stuck out through the worn fabric of his shirt, distinct as tiny angel wings.

The noise of the water covered Roger's footsteps as he made his way down the rocks. Very gently, he fitted his hand around the skinny, pale neck, and the bony shoulders hunched in surprise.

"Aidan," he said. "A word wi' you, *if* ye please."

The dark came down on All Hallows' Eve. We went to sleep to the sound of howling wind and pelting rain, and woke on the Feast of All Saints to whiteness and large soft flakes falling down and down in absolute silence. There is no more perfect stillness than the solitude in the heart of a snowstorm.

This is the thin time, when the beloved dead draw near. The world turns inward, and the chilling air grows thick with dreams and mystery. The sky goes from a sharp clear cold where a million stars burn bright and close, to the gray-pink cloud that enfolds the earth with the promise of snow.

I took one of Bree's matches from its box and lit it, thrilling to the tiny leap of instant flame, and bent to put it to the kindling. Snow was falling, and winter had come; the season of fire. Candles and hearth fire, that lovely, leaping paradox, that destruction contained but never tamed, held at a safe distance to warm and enchant, but always, still, with that small sense of danger.

The smell of roasting pumpkins was thick and sweet in the air. Having ruled the night with fire, the jack-o'-lanterns went now to a more peaceful fate as pies and compost, to join the gentle rest of the earth before renewal. I had turned the earth in my garden the day before, planting the winter seeds to sleep and swell, to dream their buried birth.

Now is the time when we reenter the womb of the world, dreaming the dreams of snow and silence. Waking to the shock of frozen lakes under waning moonlight and the cold sun burning low and blue in the branches of the ice-cased trees, returning from our brief and necessary labors to food and story, to the warmth of firelight in the dark.

Around a fire, in the dark, all truths can be told, and heard, in safety.

I pulled on my woolen stockings, thick petticoats, my warmest shawl, and went down to poke up the kitchen fire. I stood watching wisps of steam rise from the fragrant cauldron, and felt myself turn inward. The world could go away, and we would heal.

39

I Am the Resurrection

November 1773

A hammering on the door roused Roger just before dawn. Next to him, Brianna made an inarticulate noise that experience interpreted as a statement that if he didn't get up and answer the door, she would—but he'd regret it, and so would the unfortunate person on the other side.

Resigned, he flung back the quilt and ran a hand through his tangled hair. The air struck cold on his bare legs, and there was an icy breath of snow in the air.

"Next time I marry someone, I'll pick a lass who wakes up cheerful in the morning," he said to the hunched form beneath the bedclothes.

"You do that," said a muffled voice from under the pillow—whose indistinct nature did nothing to disguise its hostile intonation.

The hammering was repeated, and Jemmy—who *did* wake up cheerful in the mornings—popped up in his trundle, looking like a redheaded dandelion gone to seed.

"Somebody's knocking," he informed Roger.

"Oh, are they? Mmphm." Repressing an urge to groan, he rose and went to unbolt the door.

Hiram Crombie stood outside, looking more dour than usual in the milky half-light. Evidently not a happy riser, either, Roger reflected.

"My wife's auld mither's passed i' the night," he informed Roger without preamble.

"Passed what?" asked Jemmy with interest, poking his disheveled head out from behind Roger's leg. He rubbed one eye with a fist, and yawned widely. "Mr. Stornaway passed a stone—he showed it to me and Germain."

"Mr. Crombie's mother-in-law has died," Roger said, putting a quelling hand on Jem's head, with an apologetic cough toward Crombie. "I'm sorry to hear that, Mr. Crombie."

"Aye." Mr. Crombie appeared indifferent to condolence. "Murdo Lindsay says as ye ken a bit of Scripture for the burying. The wife's wonderin' would ye maybe come and say a word at the grave?"

"Murdo said . . . oh!" The Dutch family, that was it. Jamie had forced him to speak at the graves. "Aye, of course." He cleared his throat by reflex; his voice was desperately hoarse—as usual in the mornings, until he'd had a cup of something hot. No wonder Crombie was looking dubious.

"Of course," he repeated more strongly. "Is there . . . er . . . anything we can do to help?"

Crombie made a small negative gesture.

"The women will have her laid out by now, I expect," he said, with the briefest of glances at the mound Brianna made in the bed. "We'll start the diggin' after breakfast. With luck, we'll have her under before snow falls." He lifted a sharp chin toward an opaque sky the soft gray of Adso's belly fur, then nodded, turned on his heel, and left without further congenialities.

"Daddy—look!" Roger looked down to see Jem, fingers hooked in the corners of his mouth, pulled down to simulate the inverted "U" of Hiram Crombie's customary expression. Small red brows wrinkled in a ferocious scowl, making the resemblance startling. Surprised into laughter, Roger gasped and choked, then coughed until he doubled over, wheezing.

"Are you all right?" Brianna had unearthed herself and was sitting up in bed, squint-eyed with sleep, but looking concerned.

"Aye, fine." The words came out in a thready wheeze, nearly soundless. He took a breath and hawked deeply, expectorating a repellent glob into his hand, for lack of a handkerchief.

"Eew!" said the tender wife of his bosom, recoiling.

"Lemme see, Daddy!" said his son and heir, jostling for a look. "Eeew!"

Roger stepped outside and wiped his hand in the wet grass by the door. It was cold out, so early, but Crombie was undoubtedly right; snow was on the way again. The air had that soft, muffled feel to it.

"So old Mrs. Wilson is dead?" Brianna had come out after him, a shawl wrapped round her shoulders. "That's too bad. Imagine coming so far, and then dying in a strange place, before you've even had time to settle."

"Well, she had her family with her, at least. I expect she wouldna have wanted to be left alone to die in Scotland."

"Mm." Bree brushed strands of hair off her cheeks; she'd put her hair into a thick plait for sleeping, but a good bit of it had escaped from captivity and was waving up round her face in the cold, humid air. "Should I go up there, do you think?"

"Pay our respects? He said they've laid the old lady out already."

She snorted, white wisps of breath from her nostrils momentarily making him think of dragons.

"It can't be later than seven A.M.; it's still bloody dark out! And I don't believe for a minute that his wife and sister have been laying out the old lady by candlelight. Hiram would balk at the expense of the extra candle, for one thing. No, he felt itchy about asking a favor, so he was trying to get under your skin about your wife being a lazy slattern."

That was perceptive, Roger thought, amused—particularly as she hadn't seen Crombie's eloquent glance at her recumbent form.

"What's a slattern?" Jemmy inquired, picking up instantly on anything vaguely improper-sounding.

"That's a lady who's no lady," Roger informed him. "And a bad housekeeper, to boot."

"That's one of the words that Mrs. Bug will wash out your mouth with soap if she hears you say it," amended his wife with ungrammatical acuity.

Roger was still attired in nothing but a nightshirt, and his legs and feet were freezing. Jem was hopping around barefoot, too, but without the slightest sign of being cold.

"Mummy is not one," Roger said firmly, taking Jem's hand. "Come on, chum, let's nip up to the privy while Mummy makes breakfast."

"Thanks for the vote of confidence," Brianna said, yawning. "I'll take up a jar of honey or something to the Crombies later."

"I go, too," Jemmy announced promptly.

Brianna hesitated for a moment, then looked at Roger and raised her brows. Jem had never seen a dead person.

Roger lifted one shoulder. It would have been a peaceful death, and it was, God knew, a fact of life on the mountain. He didn't suppose that seeing Mrs. Wilson's body would give the child nightmares—though knowing Jem, it *was* quite likely to lead to a number of loud and embarrassing public questions. A bit of preparatory explanation might not be out of place, he reflected.

"Sure," he told Jem. "But first we have to go up to the Big House after breakfast, and borrow a Bible from Grandda."

He found Jamie at breakfast, the warm oatmeal smell of fresh parritch wrapping him like a blanket as he stepped into the kitchen. Before he could explain his errand, Mrs. Bug had sat him down with a bowl of his own, a jug of honey, a plate of savory fried bacon, hot toast dripping butter, and a fresh cup of something dark and fragrant that looked like coffee. Jem was next to him, already smeared with honey and buttered to the ears. For a traitorous instant, he wondered whether Brianna was perhaps a bit of a sluggard, though certainly never a slattern.

Then he glanced across the table at Claire, uncombed hair standing on end as she blinked sleepily at him over the toast, and generously concluded that it probably wasn't a conscious choice on Bree's part, but rather the influence of genetics.

Claire roused at once, though, when he explained his errand, between bites of bacon and toast.

"Old Mrs. Wilson?" she asked with interest. "What did she die of, did Mr. Crombie say?"

Roger shook his head, swallowing oatmeal.

"Only that she'd passed in the night. I suppose they found her dead. Her heart, maybe—she must have been at least eighty."

"She was about five years older than I am," Claire said dryly. "She told me."

"Oh. Mmphm." Clearing his throat hurt, and he took a sip of the hot, dark stuff in his cup. It was a brew of roasted chicory and acorns, but not that bad.

"I hope ye didna tell her how old *you* are, Sassenach." Jamie reached across and snared the last piece of toast. Mrs. Bug, ever-vigilant, whisked the plate away to refill it.

"I'm not that careless," Claire said, dabbing a forefinger delicately into a smear of honey and licking it. "They already think I've made some sort of pact with the devil; if I told them my age, they'd be sure of it."

Roger chuckled, but thought privately that she was right. The marks of her ordeal had nearly vanished, bruises faded and the bridge of her nose healed straight and clean. Even unkempt and puffy-eyed from sleep, she was more than handsome, with lovely skin, lushly thick curly hair, and an elegance of feature undreamt of among the Highland fisher-folk. To say nothing of the eyes, sherry-gold and startling.

Add to these natural gifts the twentieth-century practices of nutrition and hygiene—she had all of her teeth, white and straight—and she easily appeared a good twenty years younger than other women of her own age. He found that a comforting thought; perhaps Bree had inherited the art of aging beautifully from her mother, as well. He could always make his own breakfast, after all.

Jamie had finished his own meal and gone to fetch the Bible. He came back, laying it beside Roger's plate.

"We'll go up with ye to the burying," he said, nodding at the book. "Mrs. Bug—can ye maybe put up a wee basket for the Crombies?"

"Done it already," she informed him, and plunked a large basket on the table before him, covered with a napkin and bulging with goodies. "Ye'll take it, then? I must go tell Arch and fetch my good shawl, and we'll see ye at the graveside, aye?"

Brianna came in then, yawning but well-groomed, and set about making Jem presentable while Claire vanished to find cap and shawl. Roger picked up the Bible, intending to thumb through the Psalms for something suitably somber but uplifting.

"Maybe the Twenty-third?" he said, half to himself. "Nice and short. Always a classic. And it does mention death, at least."

"Are you going to give a eulogy?" Brianna asked, interested. "Or a sermon?"

"Oh, Christ, I hadn't thought of that," he said in dismay. He cleared his throat experimentally. "Is there more coffee?"

He'd been to a great many funerals in Inverness presided over by the Reverend, and was well aware that the paying customers considered such an event a dismal failure unless the preaching went on for at least half an hour. Granted, beggars couldn't be choosers, and the Crombies couldn't expect—

"Why do you have a Protestant Bible, Da?" Bree paused in the act of disentangling a piece of toast from Jemmy's hair, peering over Roger's shoulder.

Surprised, he shut the cover, but she was right; *King James Version,* it said, the letters of the inscription nearly worn away.

"It was given to me," Jamie said. The reply was casual, but Roger glanced up; there was something odd in Jamie's voice. Brianna heard it, too; she shot her father a brief, sharp look, but his face was tranquil as he took a final bite of bacon and wiped his lips.

"D'ye want a dram in your coffee, Roger Mac?" he said, nodding at Roger's cup, as though it were the most natural thing in the world to offer whisky with breakfast.

In fact, the notion sounded really appealing, given the immediate prospects, but Roger shook his head.

"No, thanks; I'll do."

"Are you sure?" Brianna transferred the sharp look to him. "Maybe you should. For your throat."

"It'll be fine," he said shortly. He was worried about his voice himself; he didn't need solicitude from the redheaded contingent, all three of whom were giving him thoughtful looks that he interpreted as casting extreme doubt upon his speaking abilities. Whisky might help his throat, but he doubted it would do much for his preaching—and the last thing he wanted was to show up at a funeral reeking of strong drink in front of a lot of strict teetotalers.

"Vinegar," advised Mrs. Bug, bending to take away his plate. "Hot vinegar's the thing. Cuts the phlegm, aye?"

"I'll bet it would," Roger said, smiling despite his misgivings. "But I think I won't, Mrs. Bug, thanks." He'd awakened with a slight sore throat, and hoped the consumption of breakfast would cure it. It hadn't, and the thought of drinking hot vinegar made his tonsils seize up.

He held out his cup for more chicory coffee, instead, and set his mind to the task ahead.

"Now—does anyone know anything about old Mrs. Wilson?"

"She's dead," Jemmy piped up confidently. Everybody laughed, and Jem looked confused, but then joined the laughter, though plainly having not the slightest idea what was funny.

"Good start, sport." Roger reached out and brushed crumbs from Jemmy's shirtfront. "Might be a point, at that. The Reverend had a decent sermon on something in the Epistles—the wages of sin is death, but the gift of God is eternal life. I heard him give it more than once. What d'ye think?" He raised a brow at Brianna, who frowned in thought and picked up the Bible.

"That would probably work. Does this thing have a concordance?"

"No." Jamie put down his coffee cup. "It's in Romans, chapter six, though." Seeing the looks of surprise turned upon him, he flushed slightly, and jerked his head toward the Bible.

"I had that book in prison," he said. "I read it. Come along, *a bhailach*, are ye ready now?"

The weather was louring, clouds threatening anything from freezing rain to the first snow of the season, and occasional cold gusts of wind catching cloaks and skirts, bellying them out like sails. The men held tight to their hats, and the women huddled deep in their hoods, all walking with their heads down, like sheep pushing stubbornly into the wind.

"Great weather for a funeral," Brianna murmured, pulling her cloak tight around her after one such gust.

"Mmphm." Roger responded automatically, obviously unaware of what she'd said, but registering that she'd spoken. His brow was furrowed, and he seemed tight-lipped and pale. She put a hand on his arm, squeezing in reassurance, and he glanced at her with a faint smile, his face easing.

An unearthly wail cut through the air, and Brianna froze, clutching Roger's arm. It rose to a shriek, then broke in a series of short, jerky gulps, coming down a scale of sobs like a dead body rolling down a staircase.

Gooseflesh prickled down her spine and her stomach clenched. She glanced at Roger; he looked nearly as pale as she felt, though he pressed her hand reassuringly.

"That will be the *ban-treim*," her father remarked calmly. "I didna ken there was one."

"Neither did I," said her mother. "Who do you suppose it is?" She had startled, too, at the sound of it, but now looked merely interested.

Roger had been holding his breath, too; he let it out now, with a small rattling sound, and cleared his throat.

"A mourning woman," he said. The words emerged thickly, and he cleared his throat again, much harder. "They, um, keen. After the coffin."

The voice rose again out of the wood, this time with a more deliberate sound. Brianna thought there were words in the wailing, but couldn't make them out. *Wendigo.* The word came unbidden into her mind, and she shivered convulsively. Jemmy whimpered, trying to burrow inside his grandfather's coat.

"It's nothing to fear, *a bhailach*." He patted Jemmy on the back. Jem appeared unconvinced, and put his thumb in his mouth, huddling round-eyed into Jamie's chest as the wailing faded into moans.

"Well, come, then, we'll meet her, shall we?" Jamie turned

aside and began making his way into the forest, toward the voice.

There was nothing to do but follow. Brianna squeezed Roger's arm, but left him, walking close to her father so Jemmy could see her and be reassured.

"It's okay, pal," she said softly. The weather was growing colder; her breath puffed out in wisps of white. The end of Jemmy's nose was red and his eyes seemed a little pink around the edges—was he catching a cold, too?

She put out a hand to touch his forehead, but just then the voice broke out afresh. This time, though, something seemed to have happened to it. It was a high, thready sound, not the robust keening they'd heard before. And uncertain—like an apprentice ghost, she thought in uneasy jest.

An apprentice it proved to be, though not a ghost. Her father ducked under a low pine and she followed him, emerging in a clearing facing two surprised women. Or rather, a woman and a teenaged girl, with shawls wrapped over their heads. She knew them, but what were their names?

"Maduinn mhath, maighistear," the older woman said, recovering from her surprise and dropping into a low curtsy to Jamie. Good morn to you, sir

"And to you, my mistresses," he replied, also in Gaelic.

"Good morn, Mrs. Gwilty," Roger said in his soft, hoarse voice. "And to you, *a nighean,*" he added, bowing courteously to the girl. Olanna, that was it; Brianna recalled the round face, just like the "O" that began her name. She was Mrs. Gwilty's . . . daughter? Or her niece?

"Ach, bonny boy," the girl crooned, reaching out a finger to touch Jem's rounded cheek. He pulled back a little and sucked harder on his thumb, watching her suspiciously under the edge of his blue woolly bonnet.

The women spoke no English, but Brianna's Gaelic was sufficient by now to allow her to follow the conversation, if not to join fluently in it. Mrs. Gwilty was, she explained, showing her niece the way of a proper *coronach.*

"And a fine job of work you will make of it between you, I'm sure," Jamie said politely.

Mrs. Gwilty sniffed, and gave her niece a disparaging look.

"Mmphm," she said. "A voice like a bat farting, but she is the only woman left of my family, and I shall not live forever."

Roger made a small choking noise, which he hastily developed into a convincing cough. Olanna's pleasant round face, already flushed from the cold, went a blotchy red, but she said nothing, merely cast her eyes down and huddled deeper into her shawl. It was a dark brown homespun, Brianna saw; Mrs. Gwilty's was a fine wool, dyed black—and if it was a trifle frayed around the edges, she wore it still with the dignity of her profession.

"It is sorrowful we are for you," Jamie said, in formal condolence. "She who is gone . . . ?" He paused in delicate inquiry.

"My father's sister," answered Mrs. Gwilty promptly. "Woe, woe, that she should be buried among strangers." She had a lean, underfed face, the spare flesh deeply hollowed and bruised-looking round dark eyes. She turned these deep-set eyes on Jemmy, who promptly grabbed the edge of his bonnet and pulled it down over his face. Seeing the dark, bottomless eyes swivel in her direction, Brianna was hard-pressed not to do the same.

"I hope—that her shade will find comfort. With—with your family being here," Claire said, in her halting Gaelic. It sounded most peculiar in her mother's English accent, and Brianna saw her father bite his lower lip in order not to smile.

"She will not lack company for long." Olanna blurted it out, then, catching Jamie's eye, went beet-red and buried her nose in her shawl.

This odd statement seemed to make sense to her father, who nodded.

"Och, so? Who is it ails?" He looked at her mother in question, but she shook her head slightly. If anyone was sick, they hadn't sought her help.

Mrs. Gwilty's long, seamed upper lip pressed down over dreadful teeth.

"Seaumais Buchan," she remarked with grim satisfaction. "He lies fevered and his chest will kill him before the week is out, but we've beaten him. A fortunate thing."

"What?" said Claire, frowning in bewilderment.

Mrs. Gwilty's eyes narrowed at her.

"The last person buried in a graveyard must stand watch over it, Sassenach," Jamie explained in English. "Until another comes to take his place."

Switching smoothly back to Gaelic, he said, "Fortunate is she, and the more fortunate, in having such *bean-treim* to follow her."

He put a hand into his pocket and handed over a coin, which Mrs. Gwilty glanced at, then blinked and looked again.

"Ah," she said, gratified. "Well, we will do our best, the girl and I. Come then, *a nighean,* let me hear you."

Olanna, thus pressed to perform before company, looked terrified. Under her aunt's monitory eye, though, there was no escape. Closing her eyes, she inflated her chest, thrust back her shoulders, and emitted a piercing, "EEEEEEEEEEEEEEeeeeeeeeeeeEEEEEEEeeeEEE-uh-Ee-uh-Ee-uh," before breaking off, gasping for breath.

Roger flinched as though the sound were bamboo splinters being shoved under his fingernails and Claire's mouth dropped open. Jemmy's shoulders were hunched up round his ears, and he clung to his grandfather's coat like a small blue bur. Even Jamie looked a little startled.

"Not bad," said Mrs. Gwilty judiciously. "Perhaps it will not be a complete disgrace. I am hearing that Hiram asked you to speak a word?" she added with a disparaging glance at Roger.

"He has," Roger replied, still hoarse, but as firmly as possible. "I am honored."

Mrs. Gwilty did not reply to this, but merely looked him up and down, then, shaking her head, turned her back and raised her arms.

"AaaaaaaaAAAAAAAAaaaaAAAAAAAAaaaIIIeeeeeeee," she wailed, in a voice that made Brianna feel ice crystals in her blood. "Woe, woe, wooooooooooooe! AAaayaaaAAaayaaaAAhaaaaahaaa! Woe is come to the house of Crombie—Woe!"

Dutifully turning her back on them, as well, Olanna joined in with a descant wail of her own. Claire rather untactfully but practically put her fingers in her ears.

"*How* much did you give them?" she asked Jamie in English.

Jamie's shoulders shook briefly, and he hastily ushered her away, a firm hand on her elbow.

Beside Brianna, Roger swallowed, the sound just audible under the noise.

"You should have had that drink," she said to him.

"I know," he said hoarsely, and sneezed.

"Have you even heard of Seaumais Buchan?" I asked Jamie, as we picked our way across the sodden earth of the Crombie's dooryard. "Who is he?"

"Oh, I've heard of him, aye," he replied, putting an arm round me to help swing me across a fetid puddle of what looked like goat urine. "Oof. God, you're a solid wee thing, Sassenach."

"That's the basket," I replied absently. "I believe Mrs. Bug's put lead shot in it. Or maybe only fruitcake. Who is he, then? One of the fisher-folk?"

"Aye. He's great-uncle to Maisie MacArdle, her who's marrit to him that was a boatbuilder. Ye recall her? Red hair and a verra long nose, six bairns."

"Vaguely. However do you remember these things?" I demanded, but he merely smiled, and offered me his arm. I took it, and we strode gravely through the mud and the scattered straw laid down across it, the laird and his lady come to the funeral.

The door of the cabin was open despite the cold, to let the spirit of the dead go out. Fortunately, it also let a little light come in, as the cabin was crudely built and had no windows. It was also completely packed with people, most of whom had not bathed any time in the preceding four months.

I was no stranger to claustrophobic cabins or unwashed bodies, though, and since I knew that one of the bodies present was probably clean but certainly dead, I had already begun breathing through my mouth by the time one of the Crombie daughters, shawled and red-eyed, invited us in.

Grannie Wilson was laid out on the table with a candle at her head, wrapped in the shroud she had no doubt woven as a new bride; the linen cloth was yellowed and creased with age, but clean and soft in the candlelight, embroidered on the edges with a simple pattern of vine leaves. It had been carefully kept, brought from Scotland at the cost of who knew what pains.

Jamie paused at the door, removing his hat, and murmured formal condolences, which the Crombies, male and female, accepted with nods and grunts, respectively. I handed over the basket of food and nodded back, with what I hoped was a suitable expression of dignified sympathy, keeping an eye on Jemmy.

Brianna had done her best to explain to him, but I had no idea what he might make of the situation—or the corpse. He had been persuaded with some difficulty to emerge from his bonnet, and was looking round now with interest, his cowlick standing on end.

"Is that the dead lady, Grandma?" he whispered loudly to me, pointing at the body.

"Yes, dear," I said, with an uneasy glance at old Mrs. Wilson. She looked perfectly all right, though, done up properly in her best cap with a bandage under her jaw to keep her mouth closed, dry eyelids sealed against the glimmer of the candle. I didn't think Jemmy had ever met the old lady in life; there was no real reason for him to be upset at seeing her dead—and he'd been taken hunting regularly since he could walk; he certainly understood the concept of death. Besides, a corpse was definitely anticlimactic, after our encounter with the *bean-treim*. Still . . .

"We'll pay our respects now, lad," Jamie said quietly to him, and set him on the floor. I caught Jamie's glance at the door, where Roger and Bree were murmuring condolences in their turn, and realized he had been waiting for them to catch up, so that they could watch him, and know what to do next.

He led Jemmy through the press of people, who gave way respectfully, and up to the table, where he laid his hand on the corpse's chest. Oh, so it was that sort of funeral.

At some Highland funerals, it was the custom for everyone to touch the body, so that the dead person should not haunt them. I doubted that Grannie Wilson would have any interest in haunting me, but care never hurt—and I did have an uneasy memory of a skull with silver fillings in its teeth, and my encounter with what might have been its possessor, seen by corpse-light on a black mountain night. Despite myself, I glanced at the candle, but it seemed a perfectly normal thing of brown beeswax, pleasantly fragrant and leaning a little crooked in its pottery candlestick.

Steeling myself, I leaned over and laid my own hand gently on the shroud. An earthenware saucer, holding a piece of bread and a heap of salt, sat on the dead woman's chest, and a small wooden bowl filled with dark liquid—wine?—sat beside her on the table. What with the good beeswax candle, the salt, and the *bean-treim*, it looked as though Hiram Crombie was trying to do right by his late mother-in-law—though I wouldn't put it past him to thriftily reuse the salt after the funeral.

Something seemed wrong, though; an air of uneasiness curled among the cracked boots and rag-wrapped feet of the crowd like the cold draft from the door. At first I had thought it might be due to our presence, but that wasn't it; there had been a brief exhalation of approval when Jamie approached the body.

Jamie whispered to Jemmy, then boosted him up, legs dangling, to touch the corpse. He showed no reluctance, and peered into the dead woman's waxen face with interest.

"What's that for?" he asked loudly, reaching for the bread. "Is she going to eat it?"

Jamie grabbed his wrist, and planted his hand firmly on the shroud instead.

"That's for the sin-eater, *a bhailach.* Leave it, aye?"

"What's a—"

"Later." No one argued with Jamie when he used that tone of voice, and Jemmy subsided, putting his thumb back in his mouth as Jamie set him down. Bree came up and scooped him into her arms, belatedly remembering to touch the corpse herself, and murmur, "God rest you."

Then Roger stepped forward, and there was a stir of interest among the crowd.

He looked pale, but composed. His face was lean and rather ascetic, usually saved from sternness by the gentleness of his eyes and a mobile mouth, ready to laugh. This was no time for laughter, though, and his eyes were bleak in the dim light.

He laid a hand on the dead woman's chest, and bowed his head. I wasn't sure whether he was praying for the repose of her soul, or for inspiration, but he stayed that way for more than minute. The crowd watched respectfully, with no sound save coughs and the clearing of throats. Roger wasn't the only one catching a cold, I thought—and thought suddenly again of Seaumais Buchan.

"He lies fevered and his chest will kill him before the week is out." So Mrs. Gwilty had said. Pneumonia, perhaps—or bronchitis, or even consumption. And no one had told me.

I felt a slight pang at that, equal parts annoyance, guilt, and unease. I knew the new tenants didn't yet trust me; I had thought that I should allow them to get used to me before I started dropping in on them at random. Many of them would never have seen an English person, before coming to the colonies—and I was well aware of their attitude toward both Sassenachs and Catholics.

But evidently there was now a man dying virtually on my doorstep—and I hadn't even known of his existence, let alone his illness.

Should I go to see him, as soon as the funeral was over? But where in bloody hell did the man live? It couldn't be very close; I *did* know all the fisher-folk who had settled down the mountain; the MacArdles must be up across the ridge. I stole a look at the door, trying to judge how soon the threatening clouds would cut loose their burden of snow.

There were shufflings and the murmurs of low speech outside; more people had arrived, coming up from the nearby hollows, crowding round the door. I caught the words, *"dèan caithris,"* in a questioning tone, and suddenly realized what was odd about the present occasion.

There was no wake. Customarily, the body would have been washed and laid out, but then kept on display for a day or two, to allow everyone in the area time to come and pay their regards. Listening intently, I caught a distinct tone of disgruntlement and surprise—the neighbors thought this haste unseemly.

"Why isn't there a wake?" I whispered to Jamie. He lifted one shoulder a fraction of an inch, but nodded toward the door, and the muffled sky beyond.

"There's going to be a great deal of snow by nightfall, *a Sorcha,*" he said. "And likely to go on for days, by the looks of it. I wouldna want to be having to dig a grave and bury a coffin in the midst of that, myself. And should it snow for days, where are they to put the body in the meantime?"

"That's true, *Mac Dubh,*" said Kenny Lindsay, overhearing. He glanced round at the people near us, and edged closer, lowering his voice. "But it's true, too, as Hiram Crombie's no owerfond of the auld bes—er, his good-mother." He raised his chin a fraction, indicating the corpse. "Some say as he canna get the auld woman underground fast enough—before she changes her mind, aye?" He grinned briefly, and Jamie hid his own smile, looking down.

"Saves a bit on the food, too, I suppose." Hiram's reputation as a cheapskate was well-known—which was saying something, among the thrifty but hospitable Highlanders.

A fresh bustle was taking place outside, as new arrivals came. There was a sort of congestion at the door, as someone sought to press inside, though the house was filled shoulder to shoulder, with the only bit of open floor space left under the table on which Mrs. Wilson reposed.

The people near the door gave way reluctantly, and Mrs. Bug

surged into the cabin, arrayed in her best cap and shawl, Arch at her shoulder.

"Ye forgot the whisky, sir," she informed Jamie, handing him a corked bottle. Looking round, she at once spotted the Crombies and bowed to them ceremoniously, murmuring sympathy. Bobbing upright, she set her cap straight and looked expectantly round. Clearly, the festivities could now commence.

Hiram Crombie glanced round, then nodded to Roger.

Roger drew himself up slightly, nodded back, and began. He spoke simply for a few minutes, generalities about the preciousness of life, the enormity of death, and the importance of kin and neighbors in facing such things. This all seemed to be going over well with the punters, who were nodding slightly in approval and seemed to be settling down in expectation of decent entertainment.

Roger paused to cough and blow his nose, then shifted into what appeared to be some version of the Presbyterian funeral service—or what he recalled of it, from his life with the Reverend Wakefield.

This too seemed to be acceptable. Bree seemed to relax a little, and put Jemmy down.

It was going well . . . and yet I was still conscious of a faint sense of uneasiness. Part of that, of course, was that I could see Roger. The growing warmth of the cabin was making his nose run; he kept his handkerchief in his hand, dabbing furtively and now and then stopping to blow his nose as discreetly as possible.

Phlegm, though, runs downhill. And as the congestion got worse, it began to affect his vulnerable throat. The choked note in his voice, always present, was getting noticeably worse. He was having to clear his throat repeatedly, in order to speak.

Beside me, Jemmy stirred restively, and from the corner of my eye, I saw Bree put a hand on his head to quiet him. He looked up at her, but her attention was fixed anxiously on Roger.

"We give thanks to God for the life of this woman," he said, and paused to clear his throat—again. I found myself doing it with him in sheer nervous sympathy.

"She is a servant of God, faithful and true, and now praises Him before His throne, with the sa—" I saw sudden doubt flicker across his face as to whether his present congregation countenanced the concept of saints, or would consider such a mention to be Romish heresy. He coughed, and resumed, "With the angels."

Evidently angels were innocuous; the faces around me looked somber, but unoffended. Exhaling visibly, Roger picked up the little green Bible and opened it at a marked page.

"Let us speak together a psalm in praise of Him who—" He glanced at the page and, too late, realized the difficulty of translating an English psalm into Gaelic on the wing.

He cleared his throat explosively, and half a dozen throats among the crowd echoed him in reflex. On my other side, Jamie murmured, "Oh, God," in heartfelt prayer.

Jemmy tugged at his mother's skirt, whispering something, but was peremptorily shushed. I could see Bree yearning toward Roger, body tensed in the urgent desire to help somehow, if only by mental telepathy.

With no alternative in sight, Roger began to read the psalm, haltingly. Half the crowd had taken him at his word when he invited them to "speak together," and were reciting the psalm from memory—several times faster than he could read.

I closed my eyes, unable to watch, but there was no way to avoid hearing, as the congregation ripped through the psalm and fell silent, waiting in dour patience for Roger to stumble his way to the end. Which he did, doggedly.

"Amen," said Jamie loudly. And alone. I opened my eyes to find everyone staring at us, with looks ranging from mild surprise to glowering hostility. Jamie took a deep breath and let it out, very slowly.

"Jesus Christ," he said very softly.

A bead of sweat ran down Roger's cheek, and he wiped it away with the sleeve of his coat.

"Would anyone wish to say a few words regarding the deceased?" he asked, glancing from face to face. Silence and the whine of the wind answered him.

He cleared his throat, and someone snickered.

"Grannie—" whispered Jemmy, tugging on my skirt.

"Shh."

"But *Grandma*—" The sense of urgency in his voice made me turn and look down at him.

"Do you need to go to the privy?" I whispered, bending down to him. He shook his head, violently enough to make the heavy mop of red-gold hair flop to and fro on his forehead.

"O, God, our Heavenly Father, who art leading us through the changes of time to the rest and blessedness of eternity, be Thou near to us now, to comfort and to uphold."

I glanced up, to see that Roger had laid his hand once more on the corpse, evidently deciding to bring the proceedings to a close. From the relief evident in his face and voice, I thought he must be falling back on some accustomed prayer from the Book of Common Worship, familiar enough to him that he could manage it with fair fluency in Gaelic.

"Make us to know that Thy children are precious in Thy sight. . . ." He stopped, visibly struggling; the muscles of his throat worked, trying vainly to clear the obstruction in silence, but it was no good.

"Err . . . HRRM!" A sound, not quite laughter, ran through the room, and Bree made a small rumbling noise in her own throat, like a volcano getting ready to spew lava.

"Grannie!"

"Shh!"

". . . thy sight. That they . . . live evermore with Thee and that Thy mercy—"

"Grannie!"

Jemmy was wiggling as though a colony of ants had taken up residence in his breeches, an expression of agonized urgency on his face.

"I am the Resurrection and the Life, saith the Lord; he that believeth in Me, though he were dead . . . rr-hm . . . yet shall he live—" With the end in sight, Roger was making a gallant finish, forcing his voice past its limits, hoarser than ever and cracking on every other word, but firm and loud.

"Just a *minute*," I hissed. "I'll take you out in a—"

"No, Grannie! *Look!*"

I followed his outthrust finger, and for a moment, thought he was pointing at his father. But he wasn't.

Old Mrs. Wilson had opened her eyes.

There was an instant's silence, as everyone's eyes fastened at once on Mrs. Wilson. Then there was a collective gasp, and an instinctive stepping back, with shrieks of dismay and cries of pain as toes were trodden on and people squashed against the unyielding rough logs of the walls.

Jamie grabbed Jemmy up off the floor in time to save his being crushed, inflated his lungs, and bellowed, *"Sheas!"* at the top of his voice. Such was his volume that the crowd did indeed freeze momentarily—long enough for him to thrust Jemmy into Brianna's arms and elbow his way toward the table.

Roger had got hold of the erstwhile corpse, and was lifting her into a sitting position, her hand feebly flapping at the bandage round her jaws. I pushed after Jamie, ruthlessly shoving people out of the way.

"Give her a bit of air, please," I said, raising my voice. The stunned silence was giving way to a rising murmur of excitement, but this quelled as I fumbled to untie the bandage. The room waited in quivering expectation as the corpse worked stiff jaws.

"Where am I?" she said in a quavering voice. Her gaze passed disbelievingly round the room, settling at last on her daughter's face.

"Mairi?" she said dubiously, and Mrs. Crombie rushed forward and fell on her knees, bursting into tears as she gripped her mother's hands.

"A Màthair! A Màthair!" she cried. The old woman set a trembling hand on her daughter's hair, looking as though she were not quite sure she was real.

I, meanwhile, had been doing my best to check the old lady's vital signs, which were not all that vital, but nonetheless fairly good for someone who had been dead a moment before. Respiration very shallow, labored, a color like week-old oatmeal, cold, clammy skin despite the heat in the room, and I couldn't find a pulse at all—though plainly she must have one. Mustn't she?

"How do you feel?" I asked.

She put a trembling hand to her belly.

"I do feel that wee bit poorly," she whispered.

I put my own hand on her abdomen, and felt it instantly. A pulse, where no pulse should be. It was irregular, stumbling, and bumping—but most assuredly there.

"Jesus H. Roosevelt Christ," I said. I didn't say it loudly, but Mrs. Crombie gasped, and I saw her apron twitch, as she doubtless made the horns beneath it.

I hadn't time to bother with apology, but stood and grabbed Roger by the sleeve, pulling him aside.

"She has an aortic aneurysm," I said to him very softly. "She must have been bleeding internally for some time, enough to make her lose consciousness and seem cold. It's going to rupture *very* soon, and then she'll die for real."

He swallowed audibly, his face very pale, but said only, "Do you know how long?"

I glanced at Mrs. Wilson; her face was the same gray as the snow-laden sky, and her eyes were going in and out of focus like the flickering of a candle in a wind.

"I see," Roger said, though I hadn't spoken. He took a deep breath and cleared his throat.

The crowd, which had been hissing amongst themselves like a flock of agitated geese, ceased at once. Every eye in the place was riveted on the tableau before them.

"This our sister has been restored to life, as we all shall be one day by the grace of God," Roger said softly. "It is a sign to us, of hope and faith. She will go soon again to the arms of the angels, but has come back to us for a moment, to bring us assurance of God's love." He paused a moment, obviously groping for something further to say. He cleared his throat and bent his head toward Mrs. Wilson's.

"Did you . . . wish to say anything, O, mother?" he whispered in Gaelic.

"Aye, I do." Mrs. Wilson seemed to be gaining strength—and with it, indignation. A faint pinkness showed in her waxy cheeks as she glared round at the crowd.

"What sort of wake is *this*, Hiram Crombie?" she demanded, fixing her son-in-law with a gimlet eye. "I see nay food laid out, nay drink—and what is this?" Her voice rose in a furious squeak, her eye having fallen on the plate of bread and salt, which Roger had hastily set aside when he lifted her.

"Why—" She looked wildly round at the assembled crowd, and the truth of it dawned upon her. Her sunken eyes bulged. "Why . . . ye shameless skinflint! This is nay wake at all! Ye've meant to bury me wi' nothing but a crust o' bread and a drap o' wine for the sin-eater, and a wonder ye spared *that*! Nay doot ye'll thieve the winding claes from my corpse to make cloots for your snotty-nosed bairns, and where's my good brooch I said I wanted

to be buried with?" One scrawny hand closed on her shrunken
bosom, catching a fistful of wilted linen.

"Mairi! My brooch!"

"Here it is, Mother, here it is!" Poor Mrs. Crombie, altogether
undone, was fumbling in her pocket, sobbing and gasping. "I put
it away to be safe—I meant to put it on ye before—before . . ." She
came out with an ugly lump of garnets, which her mother
snatched from her, cradling it against her breast, and glaring
round with jealous suspicion. Clearly she suspected her neighbors
of waiting the chance to steal it from her body; I heard an
offended inhalation from the woman standing behind me, but had
no time to turn and see who it was.

"Now, now," I said, using my best soothing bedside manner.
"I'm sure everything will be all right." *Aside from the fact that
you're going to die in the next few minutes, that is,* I thought, suppressing a hysterical urge to laugh inappropriately. Actually, it
might be in the next few seconds, if her blood pressure rose any
higher.

I had my fingers on the thumping big pulse in her abdomen
that betrayed the fatal weakening of her abdominal aorta. It had to
have begun to leak already, to make her lose consciousness to
such a degree as to seem dead. Eventually, she would simply blow
a gasket, and that would be it.

Roger and Jamie were both doing their best to soothe her, muttering in English and Gaelic and patting her comfortingly. She
seemed to be responding to this treatment, though still breathing
like a steam engine.

Jamie's production of the bottle of whisky from his pocket
helped still further.

"Well, that's more like it!" Mrs. Wilson said, somewhat mollified, as he hastily pulled the cork and waved the bottle under
her nose so she could appreciate the quality of it. "And ye've
brought food, too?" Mrs. Bug had bustled her way to the front,
basket held before her like a battering ram. "Hmph! I never
thought I should live to see Papists kinder than my ain kin!" This
last was directed at Hiram Crombie, who had so far been opening and closing his mouth, without finding anything whatever to
say in reply to his mother-in-law's tirade.

"Why . . . why . . ." he stammered in outrage, torn between

shock, obvious fury, and a need to justify himself before his neighbors. "Kinder than your ain kin! Why, have I not given ye a hame, these twenty years past? Fed and clothed ye as ye were my ain mither? B-borne your wicked tongue and foul t-tempers for *years,* and never—"

Jamie and Roger both leapt in to try to stifle him, but instead interrupted each other, and in the confusion, Hiram was allowed to go on speaking his mind, which he did. So did Mrs. Wilson, who was no slouch at invective, either.

The pulse in her belly was throbbing under my hand, and I was hard put to it to keep her from leaping off the table and dotting Hiram with the bottle of whisky. The neighbors were agog.

Roger took matters—and Mrs. Wilson—firmly into his own hands, seizing her by her scrawny shoulders.

"Mrs. Wilson," he said hoarsely, but loudly enough to drown Hiram's indignant rebuttal of Mrs. Wilson's most recent depiction of his character. "Mrs. Wilson!"

"Eh?" She paused for breath, blinking up at him in momentary confusion.

"Cease. And you, too!" He glared at Hiram, who was opening his mouth again. Hiram shut it.

"I'll no have this," Roger said, and thumped the Bible down on the table. "It's not fitting, and I'll not have it, d'ye hear me?" He glowered from one to the other of the combatants, black brows low and fierce.

The room was silent, bar Hiram's heavy breathing, Mrs. Crombie's small sobs, and Mrs. Wilson's faint, asthmatic wheeze.

"Now, then," Roger said, still glaring round to prevent any further interruptions. He put a hand over Mrs. Wilson's thin, age-spotted one.

"Mrs. Wilson—d'ye not ken that you stand before God this minute?" He darted a look at me, and I nodded; yes, she was definitely going to die. Her head was wobbling on her neck and the glow of anger fading from her eyes, even as he spoke.

"God is near to us," he said, lifting his head to address the congregation at large. He repeated this in Gaelic, and there was a sort of collective sigh. He narrowed his eyes at them.

"We will not profane this holy occasion with anger nor

bitterness. Now—sister." He squeezed her hand gently. "Compose your soul. God will—"

But Mrs. Wilson was no longer listening. Her withered mouth dropped open in horror.

"The sin-eater!" she cried, looking wildly round. She grabbed the dish from the table next to her, showering salt down the front of her winding-sheet. "Where is the sin-eater?"

Hiram stiffened as though goosed with a red-hot poker, then whirled and fought his way toward the door, the crowd giving way before him. Murmurs of speculation rose in his wake, only to stop abruptly as a piercing wail rose from outside, another rising behind it as the first one fell.

An awed "oooh!" rose from the crowd, and Mrs. Wilson looked gratified, as the *bean-treim* started in to earn their money in earnest.

Then there was a stirring near the door, and the crowd parted like the Red Sea, leaving a narrow path to the table. Mrs. Wilson sat bolt upright, dead-white and barely breathing. The pulse in her abdomen skittered and jumped under my fingers. Roger and Jamie had hold of her arms, supporting her.

A complete hush had fallen over the room; the only sounds were the howling of the *bean-treim*—and slow, shuffling footsteps, soft on the ground outside, then suddenly louder on the boards of the floor. The sin-eater had arrived.

He was a tall man, or had been, once. It was impossible to tell his age; either years or illness had eaten away his flesh, so that his wide shoulders bowed and his spine had hunched, a gaunt head poking forward, crowned with a balding straggle of graying strands.

I glanced up at Jamie, eyebrows raised. I had never seen the man before. He shrugged slightly; he didn't know him, either. As the sin-eater came closer, I saw that his body was crooked; he seemed caved in on one side, ribs perhaps crushed by some accident.

Every eye was fixed on the man, but he met none of them, keeping his gaze focused on the floor. The path to the table was narrow, but the people shrank back as he passed, careful that he should not touch them. Only when he reached the table did he lift his head, and I saw that one eye was missing, evidently clawed away by a bear, judging from the welted mass of scar tissue.

The other one was working; he halted in surprise, seeing Mrs.

Wilson, and glanced round, obviously unsure what to do next.

She wiggled one arm free of Roger's grip and pushed the dish containing the bread and salt toward him.

"Get on, then," she said, her voice high and a little frightened.

"But you're not dead." It was a soft, educated voice, betraying only puzzlement, but the crowd reacted as though it had been the hissing of a serpent, and recoiled further, if such a thing were possible.

"Well, what of it?" Agitation was making Mrs. Wilson tremble even more; I could feel a small constant vibration through the table. "Ye've been paid to eat my sins—be after doing it, then!" A thought occurred to her and she jerked upright, squinting at her son-in-law. "Ye *did* pay him, Hiram?"

Hiram was still flushed from the previous exchanges, but went a sort of puce at this, and clutched his side—clutching at his purse, I thought, rather than his heart.

"Well, I'm no going to pay him *before* he's done the job," he snapped. "What sort of way is that to be carrying on?"

Seeing renewed riot about to break out, Jamie let go his hold on Mrs. Wilson and fumbled hastily in his sporran, emerging with a silver shilling, which he thrust across the table toward the sin-eater—though careful, I saw, not to touch the man.

"Now ye've been paid," he said gruffly, nodding to him. "Best be about your business, sir."

The man looked slowly round the room, and the intake of breath from the crowd was audible, even over the wails of "WOOOOOOOOOOOOEEEE to the house of CROMMMMMBII-IEEEEEE" going on outside.

He was standing no more than a foot away from me, close enough that I could smell the sweet-sour odor of him: ancient sweat and dirt in his rags, and something else, some faint aroma that spoke of pustulant sores and unhealed wounds. He turned his head and looked straight at me. It was a soft brown eye, amber in color, and startlingly like my own. Meeting his gaze gave me a queer feeling in the pit of the stomach, as though I looked for a moment into a distorting mirror, and saw that cruelly misshapen face replace my own.

He did not change expression, and yet I felt something nameless pass between us. Then he turned his head away, and reached out a long, weathered, very dirty hand to pick up the piece of bread.

A sort of sigh went through the room as he ate—slowly gumming the bread, for he had few teeth. I could feel Mrs. Wilson's pulse, much lighter now, and fast, like a hummingbird's. She hung nearly limp in the men's grasp, the withered lids of her eyes drooping as she watched.

He wrapped both hands around the cup of wine, as though it were a chalice, and drank it down, eyes closed. He set the empty cup down and looked at Mrs. Wilson, curiously. I supposed he never had met one of his clients alive before, and wondered how long he had fulfilled this strange office.

Mrs. Wilson stared into his eyes, face blank as a child's. Her abdominal pulse was skipping like a stone, a few light beats, a pause, then a thump that struck my palm like a blow, and back to its erratic jumps.

The sin-eater bowed to her, very slowly. Then he turned round, and scampered for the door, with amazing speed for such an infirm specimen.

Several of the boys and younger men near the door rushed out after him, yelling; one or two seized sticks of wood from the fire basket by the hearth. Others were torn; they glanced toward the open door, where shouts and the thumps of thrown stones mingled with the wailing of the *bean-treim*—but their eyes were drawn back ineluctably to Mrs. Wilson.

She looked . . . peaceful, was the only word. It was no surprise whatever to feel the pulse beneath my hand simply stop. Somewhere deeper, in my own depths, I felt the dizzying rush of the hemorrhage begin, a flooding warmth that pulled me into it, made black spots whirl before my eyes, and caused a ringing in my ears. I knew to all intents and purposes she had now died for good. I felt her go. And yet I heard her voice above the racket, very small but calm and clear.

"I forgive ye, Hiram," she said. "Ye've been a good lad."

My vision had gone dark, but I could still hear and sense things dimly. Something grasped me, pulled me away, and a moment later I came to myself, leaning against Jamie in a corner, his arms supporting me.

"Are ye all right, Sassenach?" he was saying urgently, shaking me a little and patting my cheek.

The black-clad *bean-treim* had come as far as the door. I could see them outside, standing like twin pillars of darkness, falling snow beginning to whirl round them as the cold wind came inside, small hard dry flakes skittering and bouncing in its wake across the floor. The women's voices rose and fell, blending with the wind. By the table, Hiram Crombie was trying to fix his mother-in-law's garnet brooch to her shroud, though his hands shook and his narrow face was wet with tears.

"Yes," I said faintly, then "yes" a little stronger. "Everything is all right now."

PART SIX

On the Mountain

40

Bird-Spring

I t was spring, and the long months of desolation melted into running water, with streamlets pouring from every hill and miniature waterfalls leaping from stone to stone to stone.

The air was filled with the racket of birds, a cacophony of melody that replaced the lonely calling of geese passing by far overhead.

Birds go one by one in the winter, a single raven hunched brooding in a barren tree, an owl fluffed against the cold in the high, dark shadows of a barn. Or they go in flocks, a massed thunder of wings to bear them up and away, wheeling through the sky like handsful of pepper grains thrown aloft, calling their way in Vs of mournful courage toward the promise of a distant and problematic survival.

In winter, the raptors draw apart unto themselves; the songbirds flee away, all the color of the feathered world reduced to the brutal simplification of predator and prey, gray shadows passing overhead, with no more than a small bright drop of blood fallen back to earth here and there to mark the passing of life, leaving a drift of scattered feathers, borne on the wind.

But as spring blooms, the birds grow drunk with love and the bushes riot with their songs. Far, far into the night, darkness mutes but does not silence them, and small melodious conversations break out at all hours, invisible and strangely intimate in the dead of night, as though one overheard the lovemaking of strangers in the room next door.

I moved closer to Jamie, hearing the clear, sweet song of a

thrush in the great red spruce that stood behind the house. It was still cold at night, but not with the bitter chill of winter; rather with the sweet fresh cold of thawing earth and springing leaves, a cold that sent the blood tingling and made warm bodies seek one another, nesting.

A rumbling snore echoed across the landing—another harbinger of spring. Major MacDonald, who had arrived mud-caked and wind-bitten the night before, bringing unwelcome news of the outside world.

Jamie stirred briefly at the sound, groaned, farted briefly, and lay still. He'd stayed up late, entertaining the Major—if entertainment was the word for it.

I could hear Lizzie and Mrs. Bug in the kitchen below, talking as they banged pots and slammed doors in hopes of rousing us. Breakfast smells began to rise up the stairs, enticing, the bitter smell of roasting chicory spicing the thick warmth of buttered porridge.

The sound of Jamie's breathing had changed, and I knew he was awake, though he still lay with his eyes closed. I didn't know whether this denoted an urge to continue the physical pleasure of sleep—or a marked disinclination to get up and deal with Major MacDonald.

He resolved this doubt at once by rolling over, enveloping me in his arms, and moving his lower body against mine in a manner that made it obvious that, while physical pleasure was what was on his mind, he was quite through sleeping.

He hadn't reached the point of coherent speech yet, though, and nuzzled my ear, making small interrogatory hums in his throat. Well, the Major was still asleep, and the coffee—such as it was— wouldn't be ready for a bit. I hummed back, reached to the bedside table for a bit of almond cream, and commenced a slow and pleasurable rummage through the layers of bedclothes and nightshirt to apply it.

Some small while later, snorts and thumps across the hall denoted the resurrection of Major MacDonald, and the delectable scents of frying ham and potatoes with onions had joined the throng of olfactory stimuli. The sweet smell of almond cream was stronger, though.

"Greased lightning," Jamie said with a drowsy air of satisfaction. He was still in bed, lying on his side to watch me dress.

"What?" I turned from my looking glass to eye him. "Who?"

"Me, I suppose. Or were ye not thunderstruck, there at the end?" He laughed, almost silently, rustling the bedclothes.

"Oh, you've been talking to Bree again," I said tolerantly. I turned back to the glass. "That particular figure of speech is a metaphor for extreme speed, not lubricated brilliance."

I smiled at him in the glass as I brushed knots out of my hair. He had unplaited it while I was anointing him, and subsequent exertions had caused it to explode. Come to think, it did faintly resemble the effects of electrocution.

"Well, I can be fast, too," he said judiciously, sitting up and rubbing a hand through his own hair. "But not first thing in the morning. There are worse ways to wake up, aye?"

"Yes, much worse." Sounds of hawking and spitting came from across the landing, followed by the distinctive sound of someone with very vigorous bladder function employing a chamber pot. "Is he staying long, did he say?"

Jamie shook his head. Rising slowly, he stretched himself like a cat and then came across in his shirt to put his arms around me. I hadn't yet poked up the fire, and the room was chilly; his body was pleasantly warm.

He rested his chin on top of my head, regarding our stacked reflections in the mirror.

"I'll have to go," he said softly. "Tomorrow, perhaps."

I stiffened a little, brush in hand.

"Where? To the Indians?"

He nodded, eyes on mine.

"MacDonald brought newspapers, wi' the text of letters from Governor Martin to various people—Tryon in New York, General Gage—asking help. He's losing his grip upon the colony—insofar as he ever had one—and is seriously thinking of arming the Indians. Though *that* bit of information hasna made it into the newspapers, and a good thing, too."

He released me, and reached for the drawer where his clean shirts and stockings stayed.

"That *is* a good thing," I said, bundling back my hair and hunting for a ribbon to tie it with. We'd seen few newspapers through the winter, but even so, the level of disagreement between the Governor and the Assembly was clear; he'd resorted to a practice of continuous proroguing, repeatedly dismissing the Assembly in order to prevent them passing legislation at odds with his desires.

I could well imagine what the public response would be to the revelation that he contemplated arming the Cherokee, Catawba, and Creek, and inciting them against his own people.

"I'm guessing that he isn't actually going to do that," I said, finding the blue ribbon I was looking for, "because if he had—does, I mean—the Revolution would have got going in North Carolina right now, rather than in Massachusetts or Philadelphia two years from now. But why on earth is he publishing these letters in the newspaper?"

Jamie laughed. He shook his head, pushing back the disheveled hair from his face.

"He's not. Evidently, the Governor's mail is being intercepted. He's no verra pleased about it, MacDonald says."

"I daresay not." Mail was notoriously insecure, and always had been. In fact, we had originally acquired Fergus when Jamie hired him as a pickpocket, in order to steal letters in Paris. "How is Fergus doing?" I asked.

Jamie made a small grimace, pulling on his stockings.

"Better, I think. Marsali says he's staying more to home, which is good. And he's earning a wee bit, teaching French to Hiram Crombie. But—"

"Hiram? *French?*"

"Oh, aye." He grinned at me. "Hiram's set upon the idea that he must go and preach to the Indians, and he thinks he'll be best equipped to manage if he's got some French as well as English. Ian's teaching him a bit of the Tsalagi, too, but there are so many Indian tongues, he'd never learn them all."

"Will wonders never cease," I murmured. "Do you think—"

I was interrupted at this point by Mrs. Bug bellowing up the stairs, "If Certain Persons are wantin' to let a good breakfast be spoilt, I'm sure they're welcome!"

Like clockwork, Major MacDonald's door popped open, and his feet clattered eagerly down the stairs.

"Ready?" I said to Jamie. He seized my hairbrush and tidied himself with a few licks, then came to open the door and bowed, ushering me ceremoniously out.

"What ye said, Sassenach," he said as he followed me down the stair. "About it starting in two years. It's already well begun. Ye know that, aye?"

"Oh, yes," I said, rather grimly. "But I don't want to think about it on an empty stomach."

Roger stood up straight, measuring. The edge of the kiln pit he stood in came just under his chin. Six feet would be just about at eye level; only a few more inches, then. That was heartening. Setting the shovel against the dirt wall, he stooped, grabbed a wooden bucket full of earth, and heaved it up over the rim.

"Dirt!" he yelled. There was no response to his shout. He rose on his toes, peering balefully round for his so-called assistants. Jemmy and Germain were meant to be taking it in turn to empty the buckets and pass them back down to him, but had a tendency to vanish abruptly.

"Dirt!" he shouted as loudly as he could. The wee buggers couldn't have gone far; it took him less than two minutes to fill a bucket.

This call was answered, but not by the boys. A cold shadow fell over him, and he squinted up to see the silhouette of his father-in-law, stooping to grab the handle of the bucket. Jamie strode two paces and flung the dirt onto the slowly mounting heap, then came back, hopping down into the pit to return it.

"A tidy wee hole ye have here," he said, turning round to survey it. "Ye could barbecue an ox in it."

"I'll need one. I'm starving." Roger wiped a sleeve across his forehead; the spring day was cool and crisp, but he was drenched with sweat.

Jamie had picked up his shovel and was examining the blade with interest.

"I've never seen the like. Is it the lass's work?"

"With a bit of help from Dai Jones, aye." It had taken roughly thirty seconds' work with an eighteenth-century shovel to convince Brianna that improvements could be made. It had taken three months to acquire a chunk of iron that could be shaped to her directions by the blacksmith and to persuade Dai Jones—who was Welsh and thus by definition stubborn—into doing it. The normal spade was made of wood, and looked like nothing so much as a roof shingle attached to a pole.

"May I try?" Enchanted, Jamie drove the pointed end of the new spade into the dirt at his feet.

"Be my guest."

Roger scrambled up out of the deep part of the pit into the shallower end of the kiln. Jamie stood in the part where the fire would go, according to Brianna, with a chimney to be raised over it. Items to be fired would sit in the longer, relatively shallow part of the pit and be covered over. After a week of shoveling, Roger was less inclined to think the distant possibility of plumbing was worth all the labor involved, but Bree wanted it—and like her father, Bree was difficult to resist, though their methods varied.

Jamie shoveled briskly, tossing spadesful of dirt into the bucket, with small exclamations of delight and admiration at the ease and speed with which dirt could be dug. Despite his dim view of the occupation, Roger felt a sense of pride in his wife's implement.

"First the wee matchsticks," Jamie said, making a joke of it, "now shovels. What will she think of next?"

"I'm afraid to ask," Roger said, with a tinge of rue that made Jamie laugh.

The bucket filled, Roger picked it up and took it to empty, while Jamie filled the second. And without spoken agreement, they continued the job, Jamie digging, Roger carrying, finishing in what seemed no time at all.

Jamie climbed out of the pit and joined Roger on the edge, looking down at their handiwork in satisfaction.

"And if it doesna work well as a kiln," Jamie observed, "she can make a root cellar of it."

"Waste not, want not," Roger agreed. They stood looking down into the hole, the breeze chilly through their damp shirts now that they'd stopped moving.

"D'ye think ye might go back, you and the lass?" Jamie said. He spoke so casually that Roger missed his meaning at first, not catching on until he saw his father-in-law's face, set in the imperturbable calm that—he'd learned to his cost—generally covered some strong emotion.

"Back," he repeated uncertainly. Surely he didn't mean—but of course he did. "Through the stones, do you mean?"

Jamie nodded, seeming to find some fascination in the walls of the pit, where drying grass rootlets hung in tangles, and the jagged edges of stones protruded from the patchy damp dirt.

"I've thought of it," Roger said, after a pause. "*We've* thought. But . . ." He let his voice trail off, finding no good way to explain.

Jamie nodded again, though, as if he had. He supposed Jamie and Claire must have discussed it, even as he and Bree had, playing over the pros and cons. The dangers of the passage—and he did not underestimate those dangers, the more so in light of what Claire had told him about Donner and his comrades; what if he made it through—and Bree and Jem didn't? It didn't bear thinking.

Beyond that, if they all survived the passage, was the pain of separation—and he would admit that it would be painful for him, as well. Whatever its limitations or inconveniences, the Ridge was home.

Against those considerations, though, stood the dangers of the present time, for the four horsemen of the apocalypse rode widely here; it was no trick to catch a glimpse of pestilence or famine from the corner of your eye. And the pale horse and its rider were inclined to show up unexpectedly—and often.

But that's what Jamie meant, of course, he realized belatedly. "Because of the war, ye mean."

"The O'Brians," Jamie said quietly. "That will happen again, ken? Many times."

It was spring now, not autumn, but the cold wind that touched his bones was the same as the one that had blown brown and golden leaves across the face of the little girl. Roger had a sudden vision of the two of them, Jamie and himself, standing now at the edge of this cavernous hole, like bedraggled mourners at a graveside. He turned his back on the pit, looking instead into the budding green of the chestnut trees.

"Ye know," he said, after a moment's silence, "when I first learned what—what Claire is, what we are, all about it—I thought, 'How fascinating!' To actually see history in the making, I mean. In all honesty, I maybe came as much for that as for Bree. Then, I mean."

Jamie laughed shortly, turning round as well.

"Oh, aye, and is it? Fascinating?"

"More than I ever thought," Roger assured him, with extreme

dryness. "But why are ye asking now? I told ye a year ago that we'd stay."

Jamie nodded, pursing his lips.

"Ye did. The thing is—I am thinking I must sell one or more of the gemstones."

That brought Roger up a bit. He'd not consciously thought it, of course—but the knowledge that the gems were there, in case of need . . . He hadn't realized what a sense of security that knowledge had held, until this moment.

"They're yours to sell," he replied, cautious. "Why now, though? Are things difficult?"

Jamie gave him an exceedingly wry look.

"Difficult," he repeated. "Aye, ye could say that." And proceeded to lay out the situation succinctly.

The marauders had destroyed not only a season's whisky in the making, but also the malting shed, only now rebuilding. That meant no surplus of the lovely drink this year to sell or trade for necessities. There were twenty-two more tenant families on the Ridge to be mindful of, most of them struggling with a place and a profession that they could never have imagined, trying merely to keep alive long enough to learn how to stay that way.

"And then," Jamie added grimly, "there's MacDonald—speak o' the devil."

The Major himself had come out onto the stoop, his red coat bright in the morning sun. He was dressed for travel, Roger saw, booted and spurred, and wearing his wig, laced hat in hand.

"A flying visit, I see."

Jamie made a small, uncouth noise.

"Long enough to tell me I must try to arrange the purchase of thirty muskets, with shot and powder—at my own expense, mind—to be repaid by the Crown, eventually," he added, in a cynic tone that made it obvious how remote he considered this eventuality to be.

"Thirty muskets." Roger contemplated that, pursing his own lips in a soundless whistle. Jamie had not been able even to afford to replace the rifle he had given Bird for his help in the matter of Brownsville.

Jamie shrugged.

"And then there are wee matters like the dowry I've promised Lizzie Wemyss—she'll be wed this summer. And Marsali's mother, Laoghaire—" He glanced warily at Roger, unsure how much he might know regarding Laoghaire. More than Jamie would be comfortable knowing, Roger thought, and tactfully kept his face blank.

"I owe a bit to her, for maintenance. We can live, aye, with what we've got—but for the rest . . . I must sell land, or the stones. And I willna give up the land." His fingers drummed restlessly against his thigh, then stopped, as he raised his hand to wave to the Major, who had just spotted them across the clearing.

"I see. Well, then . . ." Plainly, it had to be done; it was foolish to sit on a fortune in gems, merely because they might one day be needed for a far-fetched and risky purpose. Still, the notion made Roger feel slightly hollow, like rappelling down a cliff and having someone cut your safety line.

Jamie blew out his breath.

"Well, so. I'll send one wi' Bobby Higgins to his Lordship in Virginia. He'll get me a good price, at least."

"Aye, that's a—" Roger halted, his attention deflected by the scenario unfolding before him.

The Major, obviously well-breakfasted and cheerful, had come down the steps and was strolling toward them—oblivious of the white sow, who had emerged from her den beneath the foundation and was ambling along the side of the house, bent on her own breakfast. It would be a matter of seconds before she spotted the Major.

"Hoy!" Roger bellowed, and felt something tear in his throat. The pain was so sharp that it stopped him cold, and he clutched at his throat, struck suddenly mute.

"'Ware the pig!" Jamie was shouting, waving and pointing. The Major thrust his head forward, hand behind his ear—then caught the repeated bellows of "Pig!" and looked wildly round, just in time to see the white sow break into a ponderous trot, scything her tusks from side to side.

He would have been best served by wheeling and sprinting back to the safety of the stoop, but instead panic struck him and he ran—away from the pig, coming straight for Jamie and Roger, who promptly ran in different directions.

Glancing back, Roger saw the Major gaining on the pig with long-legged leaps, his goal evidently the cabin. Between the Major and the cabin, though, lay the open hole of the groundhog kiln, masked by the heavy growth of long spring grass through which the Major bounded.

"Pit!" Roger shouted, only the word came out in a strangled croak. Nonetheless, MacDonald seemed to hear him, for a bright red face turned in his direction, eyes bulging. It must have sounded like "Pig!" for the Major glanced back over his shoulder then to see the sow trot faster, small pink eyes fixed on him with murderous intent.

The distraction proved nearly fatal, for the Major's spurs caught and tangled, and he sprawled headlong in the grass, losing his grip on the laced hat—which he had held throughout the chase—and sending it pinwheeling through the air.

Roger hesitated for an instant, but then ran back to help, with a smothered oath. He saw Jamie running back, too, spade held at the ready—though even a metal shovel seemed pitifully inadequate to deal with a five-hundred-pound hog.

MacDonald was already scrambling to his feet, though; before either of them could reach him, he took off running as though the devil himself were breathing on his coattails. Arms pumping and face set in puce determination, he ran for his life, bounding like a jackrabbit through the grass and disappeared. One instant he was there, and the next he had vanished, as though by magic.

Jamie looked wide-eyed at Roger, then at the pig, who had stopped short on the far side of the kiln pit. Then, moving gingerly, one eye always on the pig, he sidled toward the pit, glancing sideways, as though afraid to see what lay at the bottom.

Roger moved to stand at Jamie's shoulder, looking down. Major MacDonald had fallen into the deeper hole at the end, where he lay curled up like a hedgehog, arms clasped protectively over his wig—which had remained in place by some miracle, though now much bespattered with dirt and bits of grass.

"MacDonald?" Jamie called down. "Are ye damaged, man?"

"Is she there?" quavered the Major, not emerging from his ball.

Roger glanced across the pit at the pig, now some distance away, snout down in the long grass.

"Er . . . aye, she is." To his surprise, his voice came easy, if a little hoarse. He cleared his throat and spoke a little louder. "Ye needna worry, though. She's busy eating your hat."

The Gun-Smith

Jamie accompanied MacDonald as far as Coopersville, where he set the Major on the road back to Salisbury, equipped with food, a disreputable slouched hat against the weather, and a small bottle of whisky to fortify his bruised spirits. Then, with an internal sigh, he turned into the McGillivrays' place.

Robin was at work in his forge, surrounded by the smells of hot metal, wood shavings, and gun oil. A lanky young man with a hatchet face was working the leather bellows, though his dreamy expression showed a certain lack of attention to the job.

Robin caught the shadow of Jamie's entrance and glanced up, gave a quick nod, and returned to his work.

He was hammering bar iron into flat bands; the iron cylinder he meant to wrap them round to form a gun barrel was waiting, propped between two blocks. Jamie moved carefully out of range of flying sparks and sat down on a bucket to wait.

That was Senga's betrothed at the bellows . . . Heinrich. Heinrich Strasse. He picked the name unerringly out of the hundreds he carried in his mind, and along with it came automatically all he knew of young Heinrich's history, family, and connections, these appearing in his imagination round the boy's long, dreamy face in a constellation of social affinities, orderly and complex as the pattern of a snowflake.

He always saw people in this way, but seldom thought of it consciously. There was something about the shape of Strasse's face, though, that reinforced the mental imagery—the long axis of forehead, nose, and chin, emphasized by a horsey upper lip, deeply grooved, the horizontal axis shorter, but no less sharply defined by long, narrow eyes and flat dark brows above them.

He could see the boy's origins—the middle of nine children, but the eldest boy, son of an overbearing father and a mother who dealt with this by means of subterfuge and quiet malice—sprouting in a delicate array from the rather pointed top of his head, his religion—Lutheran, but slack about it—a lacy spray under an equally pointed chin, his relation with Robin—cordial, but wary, as befitted a new son-in-law who was also an apprentice—extending like a fanned spike from his right ear, that with Ute—a mix of terror and helpless abashment—from the left.

This notion entertained him very much, and he was obliged to look away, affecting interest in Robin's workbench, in order to keep from staring and rendering the lad uncomfortable.

The gunsmith was not tidy; scraps of wood and metal lay among a jumble of spikes, scribes, hammers, blocks of wood, bits of filthy garnet cloth and sticks of charcoal on the bench. A few papers were weighted down with a spoiled gunstock that had split in the making, their dirty edges fluttering in the hot breath of the forge. He would have taken no notice, save that he recognized the style of the drawing, would have known that boldness and delicacy of line anywhere.

Frowning, he rose and pulled the papers from under the gunstock. Drawings of a gun, executed from different angles—a rifle, there was the cutaway interior of the barrel, the grooves and landings clear—but most peculiar. One drawing showed it whole, reasonably familiar, bar the odd hornlike growths on the barrel. But the next . . . the gun seemed as though someone had broken it over his knee; it was snapped through, stock and barrel pointing downward in opposite directions, joined only by . . . what sort of hinge was that? He closed one eye, considering.

The cessation of clamor from the forge and the loud hiss of hot metal in the sump broke his fascination with the drawings and made him look up.

"Did your lass show ye those?" Robin asked, with a nod at the papers. He pulled the tail of his shirt up from behind his leather apron, and mopped steam from his sweating face, looking amused.

"No. What is she about? Is she wanting ye to make her a gun?" He relinquished the sheets to the gunsmith, who shuffled through them, sniffing with interest.

"Oh, she's no way of paying for that, *Mac Dubh*, unless Roger Mac's discovered a pot o' fairy gold since last week. No, she's only been telling me her notions of improvement in the art of riflery, asking what it might cost to make such a thing." The cynic smile that had been lurking in the corner of Robin's mouth broadened into a grin, and he shoved the papers back at Jamie. "I can tell she's yours, *Mac Dubh*. What other lass would spend her time thinking of guns, rather than gowns and bairns?"

There was more than a little implied criticism in this remark—Brianna had undoubtedly been a good deal more forthright in manner than was becoming—but he let it pass for the moment. He needed Robin's goodwill.

"Well, any woman has her fancies," he observed mildly. "Even wee Lizzie, I suppose—but Manfred will see to that, I'm sure. He'll be in Salisbury just now? Or Hillsboro?"

Robin McGillivray was by no means a stupid man. The abrupt transition of subject made him arch one brow, but he passed no remark. Instead, he sent Heinrich off to the house to fetch them some beer, waiting for the lad to disappear before turning back to Jamie, expectant.

"I need thirty muskets, Robin," he said without preamble. "And I'll need them quickly—within three months."

The gunsmith's face went comically blank with astonishment, but only for a moment. He blinked then, and closed his mouth with a snap, resuming his usual expression of sardonic good humor.

"Starting your own army, are ye, *Mac Dubh*?"

Jamie merely smiled at that without answering. If word got around that he meant to arm his tenantry and muster his own Committee of Safety in answer to Richard Brown's banditry, that would do nay harm and might do good. Letting word get out that the Governor was working secretly to arm the savages, in case he required to suppress an armed rising in the backcountry, and that he, Jamie Fraser, was the agent of such action—that was an excellent way to get himself killed and his house burnt to the ground, to say nothing of what other trouble might ensue.

"How many can ye find for me, Robin? And how fast?"

The gunsmith squinted, thinking, then darted a sideways glance at him.

"Cash?"

He nodded, seeing Robin's lips purse in a soundless whistle of astonishment. Robin kent as well as anyone that he had no money to speak of—let alone the small fortune required to assemble that many guns.

He could see the speculation in Robin's eyes, as to where he might be planning to acquire that sort of money—but the gunsmith said nothing aloud. McGillivray's upper teeth sank into his lower lip in concentration, then relaxed.

"I can find six, maybe seven, betwixt Salisbury and Salem. Brugge"—naming the Moravian gunsmith—"would do one or two, if he kent it was for you. . . ." Seeing the infinitesimal shake of Jamie's head he nodded in resignation. "Aye, well, maybe seven, then. And Manfred and I can manage maybe three more—it's only muskets you're wanting, nothing fancy?" He tilted his head toward Brianna's drawing with a small flash of his earlier humor.

"Nothing fancy," Jamie said, smiling. "That's ten, then." He waited. Robin sighed, settling himself.

"I'll ask about," he said. "But it's no an easy matter. Particularly if ye dinna mean your name to be heard in connection—and I gather ye don't."

"Ye're a man o' rare wit and discretion, Robin," Jamie assured him gravely, making him laugh. It was true, for all that; Robin McGillivray had fought beside him at Culloden, lived three years with him in Ardsmuir; Jamie would trust him with his life—and was. He began to wish the pig had eaten MacDonald after all, but put the unworthy thought from his mind and drank the beer Heinrich brought, chatting of inconsequence and trivia until it was polite to take his leave.

He had ridden Gideon, to bear MacDonald company on his horse, but meant to leave him in Dai Jones's barn. Through a complex bit of bargaining, Gideon would cover John Woolam's spotted mare—to be brought up when Woolam returned from Bear Creek—and when the harvest was in come autumn, Jamie would collect a hundredweight of barley, with a bottle of whisky to Dai for his assistance.

Exchanging a bit of conversation with Dai—he could never decide whether the blacksmith was truly a man of few words, or was it only that he despaired of making the Scots understand his Welsh singsong—Jamie slapped Gideon encouragingly on the neck and left him to eat grain and fettle his loins against the coming of the spotted mare.

Dai had offered him food, but he declined; he was peckish, but looked forward to the peace of the five-mile walk home. The day was fine and pale blue, with the spring leaves murmuring to themselves overhead, and a bit of solitude would be welcome.

The decision had been made when he asked Robin to find him guns. But the situation bore thought.

There were sixty-four villages of the Cherokee; each with its own headman, its own peace chief and war chief. Only five of those villages were within his power to influence—the three villages of the Snowbird people, and two that belonged to the Overhill Cherokee. Those, he thought, would follow the leaders of the Overhill, regardless of his words.

Roger Mac had known relatively little of the Cherokee, or what their role might be in the looming fight. He had been able to say only that the Cherokee had not acted *en masse*; some villages chose to fight, some did not—some fought for one side, some for another.

Well, so. It was not likely that anything he said or did would turn the tide of war, and that was a comfort. But he could not escape the knowledge that his own time to jump was coming. So far as anyone knew now, he was a loyal subject to His Majesty, a Tory beavering away in Geordie's interest, suborning savages and distributing guns with an eye to suppressing the riotous passions of Regulators, Whigs, and would-be republicans.

At some point, this facade must necessarily crumble to reveal him as a dyed-in-the-wool rebel and a traitor. But when? He wondered idly whether he might have a price on his head this time, and how much it would be.

It might be not so difficult, with the Scots. Grudge-bearing and hardheaded as they were, he was one of them, and personal liking might moderate the sense of outrage at his turning rebel, when the time came.

No, it was the Indians he worried over—for he came to them as the agent of the King. How suddenly to explain his change of heart? And further, do it in such a way that they might share it? Surely they would see this as treachery at worst, grossly suspicious behavior at best. He thought they would not kill him, but how in God's name to induce them to fall in with the cause of rebellion, when they enjoyed a stable and prosperous relation with His Majesty?

Oh, God, and there was John. What could he say to his friend, when the time came? Convince him by logic and rhetoric to change his coat as well? He hissed through his teeth and shook his head in consternation, trying—and failing utterly—to envision John Grey, lifelong soldier, ex-Royal Governor, that very soul of loyalty and honor, suddenly declaring himself for rebellion and republic.

He passed on, fretting in this fashion for some time, but gradually found the walking soothe his mind, and the peace of the day lighten his heart. There would be time before supper to take wee Jem fishing, he thought; the sun was bright, but there was a certain dampness to the air under the trees that was promising for a first hatch of flies on the water. He had a feeling in his bones that the trout would rise near sunset.

In this more pleasant frame of mind, he was glad to meet his daughter, some little way below the Ridge. His heart lifted at sight of her hair, streaming wanton down her back in ruddy glory.

"Ciamar a tha thu, a nighean?" he said, kissing her cheek in greeting.

"Tha mi gu math, mo athair," she said, and she smiled, but he noted a small frown that troubled the smooth flesh of her forehead like the hatch of mayfly on a trout pond.

"I've been waiting for you," she said, taking his arm. "I wanted to talk to you before you go to the Indians tomorrow." And there was that in her tone that drove all thought of fish from his mind upon the instant.

"Oh, aye?"

She nodded, but seemed to have some difficulty in finding words—an occurrence that alarmed him still further. But he could not help her, without some notion what it was about, and so kept pace with her, silent but encouraging. A mockingbird was busy nearby, practicing its repertoire of calls. It was the bird who lived in the red spruce behind the house; he knew because it paused now and then in the midst of its chatter and trilling to give a fine imitation of Adso the cat's midnight yowl.

"When you talked to Roger about the Indians," Brianna said finally, and turned her head to look at him, "did he mention something called the Trail of Tears?"

"No," he said, curious. "What is that?"

She grimaced, hunching her shoulders in a way that seemed disconcertingly familiar.

"I thought maybe he hadn't. He said he'd told you all he knew about the Indians and the Revolution—not that he knows all that much, it wasn't his specialty—but this happened—will happen later, after the Revolution. So he maybe didn't think it was important. Maybe it's not."

She hesitated, as though wanting him to tell her that it wasn't. He only waited, though, and she sighed, looking at her feet as she paced along. She was wearing sandals without stockings, and her long, bare toes were grimed with the soft dust of the wagon road. The sight of her feet always filled him with an odd mixture of pride at their elegant shape and a faint sense of shame at their size—but as he was responsible for both, he supposed he had no grounds for complaint.

"About sixty years from now," she said at last, eyes on the ground, "the American government will take the Cherokee from their land and move them. A long way—to a place called Oklahoma. It's a thousand miles, at least, and hundreds and hundreds of them will starve and die on the way. That's why they called it—will call it—the Trail of Tears."

He was impressed to hear that there should be a government capable of doing such a thing, and said so. She shot him an angry glance.

"They'll do it by cheating. They'll talk some of the Cherokee leaders into agreeing by promising them things and not keeping their bargain."

He shrugged.

"That's how most governments behave," he observed mildly. "Why are ye telling me this, lass? I will—thank God—be safely dead before any of it happens."

He saw a flicker cross her face at mention of his death, and was sorry to have caused her distress by his levity. Before he could apologize, though, she squared her shoulders and went on.

"I'm telling you because I thought you should know," she said. "Not all of the Cherokee went—some of them went farther up into the mountains and hid; the army didn't find them."

"Aye?"

She turned her head and gave him a look from those eyes that were his own, touching in their earnestness.

"Don't you see? Mama told you what would happen—about Culloden. You couldn't stop it, but you saved Lallybroch. And your men, your tenants. Because you knew."

"Oh, Christ," he said, realizing with a shock what she meant. Recollection washed through him in a flood, the terror and desperation and uncertainty of that time—the numb despair that had carried him through that last fatal day. "Ye want me to tell Bird."

She rubbed a hand over her face, and shook her head.

"I don't know. I don't know if you *should* tell him—or if you do, whether he'll listen. But Roger and I talked about it, after you asked him about the Indians. And I kept thinking about it . . . and, well, it just didn't seem *right*, to know and not do anything. So I thought I'd better tell you."

"Aye, I see," he said a little bleakly.

He had noticed before the inclination of persons with tender consciences to ease their discomfort by handing the necessity of taking action on to someone else, but forbore to mention it. She could hardly be telling Bird herself, after all.

As though the situation he faced with the Cherokee were not sufficiently difficult already, he thought wryly—now he must deal with saving unknown future generations of savages? The mockingbird zoomed past his ear, unnervingly close, clucking like a hen, of all things.

It was so incongruous that he laughed. And then realized that there was nothing else to do. Not now.

Brianna was looking at him curiously.

"What are you going to do?"

He stretched himself, slowly, luxuriously, feeling the muscles of his back pull upon his bones, feeling each of them, alive and solid. The sun was coming down the sky, supper was beginning to cook, and for now, for this one last night, he need do nothing. Not yet.

"I'm going fishing," he said, smiling at his lovely, unlikely, problematical daughter. "Fetch the wee lad, aye? I'll get the poles."

James Fraser, Esq. from Fraser's Ridge

*To my Lord John Grey, Mount Josiah Plantation,
this 2nd day of April, Anno Domini 1774*

My lord,

*I depart in the morning to visit the Cherokee, and so
leave this with my wife, to be entrusted to Mr. Higgins
when he shall next arrive, to be delivered with its
accompanying parcel into your hands.*

*I presume upon your kindness and your solicitude for
my family in asking your favor to help in selling the
object I entrust to you. I suspect that your connexions
might enable you to obtain a better price than I might do
myself—and to do so discreetly.*

*I shall hope upon my return to confide in you the
reasons for my action, as well as certain philosophical
reflections which you may find of interest. In the
meantime, believe me ever*

Your most affectionate friend and humble servant,
J. Fraser

42

Dress Rehearsal

Bobby Higgins looked uneasily at me over his mug of
beer.

"Beg pardon, mum," he said. "But you wouldn't be
a-thinking of practicing some type of physic upon me, would

you? The worms are gone, I'm sure of it. And the—the other"—he blushed slightly and squirmed upon the bench—"that's quite all right, too. I've et so many beans, I fart quite regular, and not a touch of the fiery knives about it!"

Jamie had frequently remarked upon the transparency of my features, but this was surprising perspicacity on Bobby's part.

"I'm thrilled to hear it," I said, evading his question momentarily. "You look quite in the pink of health, Bobby."

He did; the hollow, wasted look had left him, and his flesh was firm and solid, his eyes bright. The blind one hadn't gone milky, nor did it wander perceptibly; he must have some residual ability to detect light and shape, which strengthened my original diagnosis of a partially detached retina.

He nodded warily, and took a sip of beer, still keeping his eyes fixed on me.

"I'm very well indeed, mum," he said.

"Splendid. You don't happen to know how much you weigh, do you, Bobby?"

The look of wariness vanished, replaced by modest pride.

"Happen I do, mum. I took some fleeces to the river port for his Lordship last month, and was a mercer there what had a scale for weighing out—tobacco or rice, or blocks of indigo as it might be. Some of us fellows got to wagering for sport what this or that might weigh, and . . . well, ten stone four it is, mum."

"Very nice," I said with approval. "Lord John's cook must be feeding you well." I thought he couldn't have weighed more than a hundred and ten pounds when I first saw him; a hundred and forty-four was still on the light side for a man of nearly six feet, but it was a major improvement. And a real stroke of luck, that he should have known his weight exactly.

Of course, if I didn't act fast, he might easily gain a stone or two; Mrs. Bug had set herself to outdo Lord John's Indian cook (of whom we had heard much), and to this end was shoveling eggs, onions, venison, and a slice of leftover pork pie onto Bobby's plate, to say nothing of the basket of fragrant muffins already in front of him.

Lizzie, seated beside me, took one of these and spread it with butter. I noted with approval that she, too, was looking healthier, delicately flushed—though I must remember to take a sample to check the malarial parasites in her blood. That would be an excellent thing to do while she was out. No way of getting an exact weight for her, unfortunately—but she couldn't weigh more than seven stone, small and light-boned as she was.

Now, Bree and Roger at the other end of the scale . . . Roger had to weigh at least a hundred and eighty-five; Bree probably one-fifty. I took a muffin myself, thinking how best to bring up my plan. Roger would do it if I asked, of course, but Bree . . . I'd have to be careful there. She'd had her tonsils out under ether at the age of ten, and hadn't liked the experience. If she found out what I was up to and began expressing her opinions freely, she might arouse alarm in the rest of my guinea pigs.

Enthused by my success at making ether, I had seriously underestimated the difficulty of inducing anyone to let me use it on them. Mr. Christie might well be an awkward bugger, as Jamie on occasion called him—but he was not alone in his resistance to the notion of being rendered suddenly unconscious.

I would have thought that the appeal of painlessness was universal—but not to people who had never experienced it. They had no context in which to place such a notion, and while they presumably didn't all think ether was a Papist plot, they did view an offer to remove pain from them as being in some way contrary to the divine vision of the universe.

Bobby and Lizzie, though, were sufficiently under my sway that I was fairly sure I could coax—or bully—them into a brief trial. If they then reported the experience in a positive light . . . but improved public relations was only the half of it.

The real necessity was to try my ether out on a variety of subjects, taking careful note of the results. The scare of Henri-Christian's birth had shown me how woefully unprepared I was. I needed to have some idea of how much to administer per unit of body weight, how long such-and-such a dose might last, and how deep the resulting stupor might be. The last thing I wanted was to be up to my elbows in someone's abdomen, only to have them come suddenly round with a shriek.

"You're doing it again, mum." Bobby's brow creased as he chewed slowly, eyes narrowed at me.

"What? What am I doing?" I feigned innocence, helping myself to a bit of the pork pie.

"Watching me. Same as a sparrer hawk watches a mouse, just afore she stoops. I'n't she?" he appealed to Lizzie.

"Aye, she is," Lizzie agreed, dimpling at me. "But it's only her way, ken. Ye'd make a big mouse, Bobby." Being Scottish, she pronounced it "moose," which made Bobby laugh and choke over his muffin.

Mrs. Bug paused to pound him helpfully on the back, leaving him purple and gasping.

"Well, wha's amiss wi' him, then?" she asked, coming round to squint critically at Bobby's face. "Ye've no got the shits again, have ye, lad?"

"Again?" I said.

"Oh, no, mum," he croaked. "Perish the thought! 'Twas only eating green apples, the once." He choked, coughed, and sat up straight, clearing his throat.

"Can we please not talk about me bowels, mum?" he asked plaintively. "Not over breakfast, at least?"

I could feel Lizzie vibrating with amusement next to me, but she kept her eyes demurely on her plate, not to embarrass him further.

"Certainly," I said, smiling. "I hope you'll be staying for a few days, Bobby?" He'd come the day before, bearing the usual assortment of letters and newspapers from Lord John—along with a package containing a marvelous present for Jemmy: a musical jack-in-the-box, sent specially from London by the good offices of Lord John's son, Willie.

"Oh, I s'all, mum, yes," he assured me, mouth full of muffin. "His Lordship said I was to see if Mr. Fraser had a letter for me to carry back, so I must wait for him, mustn't I?"

"Of course." Jamie and Ian had gone to the Cherokee a week before; it was likely to be another week before they returned. Plenty of time to make my experiments.

"Is there anything I might do, mum, in the way of service to you?" Bobby asked. "Seeing as I'm here, I mean, and Mr. Fraser and Mr. Ian not." There was a small tone of satisfaction in this; he got on all right with Ian, but there was no doubt that he preferred to have Lizzie's attention to himself.

"Why, yes," I said, scooping up a bit of porridge. "Now that you mention it, Bobby . . ."

By the time I had finished explaining, Bobby still looked healthy, but a good deal less in bloom.

"Put me asleep," he repeated uncertainly. He glanced at Lizzie, who looked a little uncertain, too, but who was much too used to being told to do unreasonable things to protest.

"You'll only be asleep for a moment," I assured him. "Likely you won't even notice."

His face expressed considerable skepticism, and I could see him shifting about for some excuse. I'd foreseen that ploy, though, and now played my trump card.

"It's not only me needing to judge the dose," I said. "I can't operate on someone and give the ether at the same time—or not easily. Malva Christie will be assisting me; she'll need the practice."

"Oh," Bobby said thoughtfully. "Miss Christie." A sort of soft, dreamy expression spread across his face. "Well. I s'ouldn't want to put Miss Christie out, of course."

Lizzie made one of those economical Scottish noises in the back of her throat, managing to convey scorn, derision, and abiding disapproval in the space of two glottal syllables.

Bobby looked up in inquiry, a bit of pie poised on his fork. "Did you say something?"

"Who, me?" she said. "O' course not." She got up abruptly and, carrying her apron before her, neatly shook crumbs into the fire, and turned to me.

"When d'ye mean to do it?" she demanded, adding a belated, "ma'am."

"Tomorrow morning," I said. "It needs to be done on an empty stomach, so we'll do it first thing, before breakfast."

"Fine!" she said, and stamped out.

Bobby blinked after her, then turned to me, bewildered.

"Did I say something?"

Mrs. Bug's eye met mine in perfect understanding.

"Not a thing, lad," she said, depositing a fresh spatulaful of scrambled eggs onto his plate. "Eat up. Ye'll need your strength."

Brianna, clever with her hands, had made the mask to my specifications, woven of oak splits. It was simple enough, a sort of double cage, hinged so that the two halves of it swung apart for the insertion of a thick layer of cotton wool between them, and then back together, the whole thing shaped to fit like a catcher's mask over the patient's nose and mouth.

"Put enough ether on to dampen the cotton wool all through," I instructed Malva. "We'll want it to take effect quickly."

"Aye, ma'am. Oh, it does smell queer, doesn't it?" She sniffed cautiously, face turned half away as she dripped ether onto the mask.

"Yes. Do be careful not to breathe too much of it yourself," I said. "We don't want you falling over in the midst of an operation."

She laughed, but dutifully held the mask further away.

Lizzie had bravely offered to go first—with the clear intent of deflecting Bobby's attention from Malva to her. This was working; she lay in a languid pose on the table, cap off, and her soft, pale hair displayed to best advantage on the pillow. Bobby sat beside her, earnestly holding her hand.

"All right, then." I had a tiny minute-glass to hand, the best I could do by way of keeping accurate time. "Put it gently over her face. Lizzie, just breathe deeply, and count with me, one . . . two . . . goodness, that didn't take long, did it?"

She'd taken one long breath, rib cage rising high—and then gone limp as a dead flounder as the breath went out. I hastily flipped the glass, and came to take her pulse. All well there.

"Wait for a bit; you can feel it, when they start to come round, a sort of vibration in the flesh," I instructed Malva, keeping one eye on Lizzie and the other on the glass. "Put your hand on her shoulder. . . . There, do you feel it?"

Malva nodded, nearly trembling with excitement.

"Two or three drops then." She added these, her own breath held, and Lizzie relaxed again with a sigh like an escape of air from a punctured tire.

Bobby's blue eyes were absolutely round, but he clung fiercely to Lizzie's other hand.

I timed the period to arousal once or twice more, then let Malva put her under a little more deeply. I picked up the lancet I had ready, and pricked Lizzie's finger. Bobby gasped as the blood welled up, looking back and forth from the crimson drop to Lizzie's angelically peaceful face.

"Why, she don't feel it!" he exclaimed. "Look, she's never moved a muscle!"

"Exactly," I said, with a profound feeling of satisfaction. "She won't feel anything at all, until she comes round."

"Mrs. Fraser says we could cut someone quite open," Malva informed Bobby, self-importantly. "Slice into them, and get at what's ailing—and they'd never feel a thing!"

"Well, not until they woke up," I said, amused. "They'd feel it then, I'm afraid. But it really is quite a marvelous thing," I added more softly, looking down at Lizzie's unconscious face.

I let her stay under whilst I checked the fresh blood sample, then told Malva to take the mask off. Within a minute, Lizzie's eyelids began to flutter. She looked curiously round, then turned to me.

"When are ye going to start it, ma'am?"

Despite assurances from both Bobby and Malva that she had been to all appearances dead as a doornail for the last quarter hour, she refused to believe it, asserting indignantly that she couldn't have been—though at a loss to explain the prick on her finger and the slide of freshly smeared blood.

"You remember the mask on your face?" I asked. "And my telling you to take a deep breath?"

She nodded uncertainly.

"Aye, I do, then, and it felt for a moment as though I were choking—but then ye were all just staring down at me, next thing!"

"Well, I suppose the only way to convince her is to show her," I said, smiling at the three flushed young faces. "Bobby?"

Eager to demonstrate the truth of the matter to Lizzie, he hopped up on the table and laid himself down with a will, though the pulse in his slender throat was hammering as Malva dripped ether on the mask. He drew a deep, convulsive gasp the moment she put it on his face. Frowning a bit, he took another—one more—and went limp.

Lizzie clapped both hands to her mouth, staring.

"Jesus, Joseph, and Mary!" she exclaimed. Malva giggled, thrilled at the effect.

Lizzie looked at me, eyes wide, then back at Bobby. Stooping to his ear, she called his name, to no effect, then picked up his hand and wiggled it gingerly. His arm waggled limply, and she made a soft exclamation and set his hand down again. She looked quite agitated.

"Can he no wake up again?"

"Not until we take away the mask," Malva told her, rather smug.

"Yes, but you don't want to keep someone under longer than you need to," I added. "It's not good for them to be anesthetized too long."

Malva obediently brought Bobby back to the edge of consciousness and put him back under several times, while I made note of times and dosages. During the last of these notes, I glanced up, to see her looking down at Bobby with an intent sort of expression, seeming to concentrate on something. Lizzie had withdrawn to a corner of the surgery, plainly made uneasy by seeing Bobby unconscious, and sat on a stool, plaiting her hair and twisting it up under her cap.

I stood up and took the mask from Malva's hand, setting it aside.

"You did a wonderful job," I told her, speaking quietly. "Thank you."

She shook her head, face glowing.

"Oh, ma'am! It was . . . I've never seen the like. It's such a feeling, is it not? Like as we killed him, and brought him alive again." She spread her hands out, looking at them half-unconsciously, as though wondering how she had done such a marvel, then closed them into small fists, and smiled at me, conspiratorially.

"I think I see why my faither says it's devil's work. Were he to see what it's like"—she glanced at Bobby, who was beginning to stir—"he'd say no one but God has a right to do such things."

"Really," I said, rather dryly. From the gleam in her eye, her father's likely reaction to what we had been doing was one of the chief attractions of the experiment. For an instant, I rather pitied Tom Christie.

"Um . . . perhaps you'd better not tell your father, then," I suggested. She smiled, showing small, sharp white teeth, and rolled her eyes.

"Don't you think it, ma'am," she assured me. "He'd stop me coming, as quick as—"

Bobby opened his eyes, turned his head to one side, and threw up, putting a stop to the discussion. Lizzie gave a cry and hurried to his side, fussing over him, wiping his face and fetching him brandy to drink. Malva, looking slightly superior, stood aside and let her.

"Oh, that's queer," Bobby repeated, for perhaps the tenth time, rubbing a hand across his mouth. "I saw the most terrible thing—

just for a moment, there—and then I felt sick, and here it was all over."

"What sort of terrible thing?" Malva asked, interested. He glanced at her, looking wary and uncertain.

"I scarcely know, tell 'ee true, miss. Only as it was . . . dark, like. A form, as you might say; I thought 'twas a woman's. But . . . terrible," he finished, helpless.

Well, that was too bad. Hallucination wasn't an uncommon side effect, but I hadn't expected it with such a brief dose.

"Well, I imagine it was just a bit of nightmare," I said soothingly. "You know, it's a form of sleep, so it's not surprising that you might get the odd bit of dreaming now and then."

To my surprise, Lizzie shook her head at this.

"Oh, no, ma'am," she said. "It's no sleep at all. When ye sleep, ken, ye give your soul up to the angels' keeping, so as no ghoulies shall come near. But this . . ." Frowning, she eyed the bottle of ether, now safely corked again, then looked at me.

"I did wonder," she said, "where does your soul go?"

"Er . . ." I said. "Well, I should think it simply stays with your body. It must. I mean—you aren't dead."

Both Lizzie and Bobby were shaking their heads decidedly.

"No, it doesn't," Lizzie said. "When ye're sleepin', ye're still *there*. When ye do *that*"—she gestured toward the mask, a faint uneasiness on her small features—"ye're not."

"That's true, mum," Bobby assured me. "You're not."

"D'ye think maybe ye go to limbo, wi' the unbaptized babes and all?" Lizzie asked anxiously.

Malva gave an unladylike snort.

"Limbo's no real place," she said. "It's only a notion thought up by the Pope."

Lizzie's mouth dropped open in shock at this blasphemy, but Bobby luckily distracted her by feeling dizzy and requiring to lie down.

Malva seemed inclined to go on with the argument, but beyond repeating, "The Pope . . ." once or twice, simply stood, swaying to and fro with her mouth open, blinking a little. I glanced at Lizzie, only to find her glassy-eyed as well. She gave an enormous yawn and blinked at me, eyes watering.

It occurred to me that I was beginning to feel a trifle light-headed myself.

"Goodness!" I snatched the ether mask from Malva's hand, and guided her hastily to a stool. "Let me get rid of this, or we'll all be giddy."

I flipped open the mask, pulled the damp wad of cotton wool out of it, and carried it outside at arm's length. I'd opened both the surgery windows, to provide ventilation and save us all being gassed, but ether was insidious. Heavier than air, it tended to sink toward the floor of a room and accumulate there, unless there was a fan or some other device to remove it. I might have to operate in the open air, I thought, were I using it for any length of time.

I laid the cotton-wool pad on a stone to dry out, and came back, hoping that they were all too groggy now to continue their philosophical speculations. I didn't want them following *that* line of thought; let it get around the Ridge that ether separated people from their souls, and I'd never get anyone to let me use it on them, no matter how dire the situation.

"Well, thank you all for helping," I said, smiling as I entered the room, relieved to find them all looking reasonably alert. "You've done something very useful and valuable. You can all go along about your business now, though—I'll tidy up."

Malva and Lizzie hesitated for a moment, neither girl wanting to leave Bobby to the other, but under the impetus of my shooing, drifted toward the door.

"When are ye to be wed, Miss Wemyss?" Malva asked casually—and loudly enough for Bobby to hear—though she certainly knew; everyone on the Ridge did.

"In August," Lizzie replied coolly, lifting her small nose half an inch. "Right after the haying—*Miss* Christie." *And then I shall be Mrs. McGillivray,* her satisfied expression said. *And you—* Miss *Christie—without an admirer to your name.* Not that Malva attracted no notice from young men; only that her father and brother were assiduous in keeping them away from her.

"I wish ye great joy of it," Malva said. She glanced at Bobby Higgins, then back at Lizzie, and smiled, demure beneath her starched white cap.

Bobby stayed sitting on the table for a moment, looking after the girls.

"Bobby," I said, struck by the deeply thoughtful expression on his face, "the figure you saw under the anesthetic—did you recognize it?"

He looked at me, then his eyes slid back to the empty doorway, as though unable to keep away.

"Oh, no, mum," he said, in such a tone of earnest conviction that I knew he lied. "Not at all!"

Displaced Persons

They had stopped to water the horses by the edge of the small lake the Indians called Thick Rushes. It was a warm day, and they hobbled the horses, stripped, and waded into the water, spring-fed and gloriously cold. Cold enough to shock the senses and, for a moment at least, drive away Jamie's moody contemplation of the note MacDonald had delivered him from John Stuart, the Indian Superintendent of the Southern Department.

It had been complimentary enough, praising his celerity and enterprise in drawing the Snowbird Cherokee into the British sphere of influence—but had gone on to urge more vigorous involvement, pointing out Stuart's own coup in directing the choice of leaders among the Choctaws and the Chickasaw, at a congress he had himself convened two years before.

> . . . *The competition and anxiety of the candidates for medals and commissions was as great as can be imagined and equalled the struggles of the most aspiring and ambitious for honours and preferment in great states. I took every step to be informed of characters and filled the vacancies with the most worthy and likely to answer the purposes of maintaining order and the*

attachment of this nation to the British interest. I urge
you to strive for similar good results to be achieved
among the Cherokee.

"Oh, aye," he said aloud, popping up among the rushes and shaking water from his hair. "I'm to depose Tsisqua, nay doubt by assassination, and bribe them all to install Pipestone Carver"— the smallest and most self-effacing Indian Jamie had ever seen— "as peace chief. Heugh!" He sank again, in a rush of bubbles, entertaining himself by cursing Stuart's presumption, watching his words rise up in wavering quicksilver balls, to disappear magically at the bright light of the surface.

He rose again, gasping, then gulped air and held his breath.

"What was that?" said a startled voice nearby. "Is it them?"

"No, no," said another, low and urgent. "There are only two; I see them both, over there, do you see?"

He opened his mouth and breathed like a zephyr, striving to hear over the pounding of his heart.

He had understood them, but for an instant, could not put a name to their tongue. Indians, aye, but not Cherokee, they were . . . Tuscarora, that was it.

He hadn't spoken with any Tuscarora for years; most of them had gone north in the wake of the measles epidemic that had destroyed so many—going to join their Mohawk "fathers" in the lands ruled by the Iroquois League.

These two were arguing in whispers, but near enough that he made out most of what they said; they were no more than a few feet from him, hidden by a thick growth of rushes and cattail plants that stood nearly as high as a man's head.

Where was Ian? He could hear distant splashing, at the far end of the lake, and turning his head gently, saw from the corner of his eye that Ian and Rollo were sporting in the water, the dog submerged to his ruff, paddling to and fro. If one didn't know—and the beast didn't sense the intruders and bark—it looked very much like two men swimming.

The Indians had concluded that this was likely the case—two horses, thus two men, and both safely distant. With much creaking and rustling, they began to make their way stealthily in the direction of the horses.

Jamie was half-inclined to let them try to take Gideon and see how far they got with such an enterprise. But they might only make off with Ian's horse and the pack mule—and Claire would be fashit, did he let them take Clarence. Feeling himself very much at a disadvantage, he slithered naked through the reeds, grimacing at the rasp of them on his skin, and crawled up among the cattails, into the mud of the shore.

Had they the wit to look back, they must have seen the cattails shaking—and he hoped Ian *would* see—but they were intent on their errand. He could glimpse them now, skulking in the tall grass at the forest edge, glancing to and fro—but never in the right direction.

Only two, he was sure of that now. Young, from the way they moved, and unsure. He couldn't see if they were armed.

Slimed with mud, he crept further, sinking onto his belly in the rank grasses near the lake, squirming rapidly toward the shelter of a sumac bush. What he wanted was a club, and quickly.

In such circumstances, of course, nothing came to hand but twigs and long-rotted branches. For lack of better, he seized a good-sized stone, but then found what he wanted: a dogwood branch cracked by wind and hanging in reach, still attached to the tree. They were approaching the grazing horses now; Gideon saw them and lifted his head abruptly. He went on chewing, but his ears lay half back in patent suspicion. Clarence, the ever-sociable, took notice and raised his head, as well, ears twitching to alertness.

Jamie seized the chance, and as Clarence emitted a welcoming bray, he ripped the branch from the tree and charged the intruders, roaring, *"Tulach Ard!"* at the top of his voice.

Wide eyes met his, and one man bolted, long hair flying. The other followed, but limping badly, going down on one knee as something gave way. He was up again at once, but too slow; Jamie swept the branch at his legs with a two-handed fury that knocked him flat, and leapt on his back, driving a vicious knee into his kidney.

The man made a strangled noise and froze, paralyzed by pain. Jamie had dropped his rock—no, there it was. He snatched it up and thumped the man solidly behind the ear, for luck. Then he was off and running after the other, who had made for the wood but sheered off, blocked by a rock-bound streamlet in his path. Now the man was bounding through the sedges; Jamie saw him cast a terrified look toward the water, where Ian and Rollo were making their way toward him, swimming like beaver.

The Indian might have made it to the sanctuary of the forest, had one foot not suddenly sunk in soft mud. He staggered sideways, and Jamie was on him, feet sliding in the mud, grappling.

The man was young and wiry and fought like an eel. Jamie, with the advantage of size and weight, managed to push him over, and they fell together and rolled about in the sedges and mud, clawing and thumping. The Indian caught Jamie's long hair and yanked, bringing tears to his eyes; he punched the man hard in the ribs to make him let go, and when he did, butted him in the face.

Their foreheads met with a dull thunk, and blinding pain shot through his head. They fell apart, gasping, and Jamie rolled up onto his knees, head spinning and eyes watering, trying to see.

There was a blur of gray and a shriek of terror. Rollo gave one deep-chested, snarling bark, then settled into a rumbling, continuous growl. Jamie shut one eye, a hand to his throbbing forehead, and made out his opponent lying flat in the mud, Rollo poised over him, black lips drawn back to show all his teeth.

The splash of feet running through the shallows, and Ian was there, gasping for breath.

"Are ye all right, Uncle Jamie?"

He took his hand away and looked at his fingers. No blood, though he would have sworn his head was split open.

"No," he said, "but better than him. Oh, Jesus."

"Did ye kill the other one?"

"Probably not. Oh, God."

Lowering himself to his hands and knees, he crawled a short distance away and threw up. Behind him, he could hear Ian sharply demanding to know who the men were and whether there were others with them, in Cherokee.

"They're Tuscarora," he said. His head still throbbed, but he felt a little better.

"Oh, aye?" Ian was surprised, but at once shifted into the tongue of the Kahnyen'kehaka. The young captive, already terrorized by Rollo, looked as though he might die of fright, seeing Ian's tattoos and hearing him speak Mohawk. Kahnyen'kehaka was of the same family as Tuscarora, and plainly the young man could make out what Ian said, for he replied, stammering with fear. They were alone. Was his brother dead?

Jamie rinsed his mouth with water, splashed it on his face. That was better, though a lump like a duck's egg was swelling over his left eye.

"Brother?"

Yes, the young man said, his brother. If they did not mean to kill him now, might he go and see? His brother was wounded.

Ian glanced at Jamie for agreement, then called Rollo off with a word. The bedraggled captive struggled painfully to his feet, staggering, and set off back along the shore, followed by the dog and the two naked Scots.

The other man was indeed wounded; blood was seeping through a crude bandage round his leg. He had made the bandage of his shirt, and was bare-chested, scrawny, and starved-looking. Jamie glanced from one to the other; neither could be older than twenty, he thought, and likely younger than that, with their faces pinched by hunger and ill-usage, their clothes little more than rags.

The horses had moved off a little, nervous of the fighting, but the clothes the Scots had left hanging from the bushes were still there. Ian pulled on his breeches and went to fetch food and drink from the saddlebags, while Jamie dressed more slowly, interrogating the young man as the latter anxiously examined his brother.

They were Tuscarora, the young man confirmed. His name was a long one, meaning roughly "the gleam of light on water in a spring"; this was his brother, "the goose that encourages the leader when they fly," more simply known as Goose.

"What happened to him?" Jamie pulled his shirt over his head and nodded—wincing at the movement—at the gash in Goose's leg, quite obviously made by something like an ax.

Light on Water took a deep breath and closed his eyes for a moment. He had a substantial knot on his head, as well.

"Tsalagi," he said. "We were two score in number; the rest are dead, or taken. You will not give us to them, Lord? Please?"

"Tsalagi? Which?"

Light shook his head; he could not say. His band had chosen to stay when his village moved north, but they had not prospered; there were not enough men to defend a village and hunt, and without defenders, others stole their crops, took their women.

Growing poorer, they, too, had taken to stealing and to begging to survive through the winter. More had died of cold and sickness, and the remnants moved from place to place, now and then finding a place to settle for a few weeks, but then driven out by the much stronger Cherokee.

A few days past, they had been set upon by a party of Cherokee warriors, who had taken them by surprise, killed most of them, and taken some women.

"They took my wife," Light said, his voice unsteady. "We came to—to take her back."

"They will kill us, of course," said Goose weakly, but with a fair amount of cheerfulness. "But that doesn't signify."

"Of course not," Jamie said, smiling despite himself. "Do you know where they took her?"

The brothers knew the direction taken by the raiders, and had been following, to track them to their village. That way, they said, pointing toward a notch. Ian glanced at Jamie, and nodded.

"Bird," he said. "Or Fox, I should say," for Running Fox was war chief of the village; a good warrior, though somewhat lacking in imagination—a trait Bird possessed in quantity.

"Shall we help them, then?" Ian said in English. His feathery brows arched in question, but Jamie could see that it was a question in form only.

"Oh, aye, I expect we will." He rubbed gingerly at his forehead; the skin over the lump was already stretched and tender. "Let's eat first, though."

It was not a question of whether the thing might be done; only how. Jamie and Ian both dismissed out of hand any suggestion that the brothers might steal back Light's wife.

"They *will* kill ye," Ian assured them.

"We don't mind," Light said stoutly.

"Of course ye don't," said Jamie. "But what of your wife? She'd be left alone, then, and in no better case."

Goose nodded judiciously.

"He's right, you know," he said to his glowering brother.

"We could ask for her," Jamie suggested. "A wife for you, Ian. Bird thinks well of ye; he'd likely give her to you."

He was only half-joking. If no one had yet taken the young woman to wife, the person who had her as slave might be persuaded to give her to Ian, who was deeply respected.

Ian gave a perfunctory smile, but shook his head.

"Nay, we'd best ransom her. Or—" He looked consideringly at the two Indians, industriously eating their way through the remainder of the food in the saddlebags. "Might we ask Bird to adopt them?"

That was a thought, to be sure. For once they had got the young woman back, by whatever means, she and the brothers would be in the same dire case—wandering and hungry.

The brothers frowned, though, and shook their heads.

"Food is a good thing," Goose said, licking his fingers. "But we saw them kill our family, our friends. If we hadn't seen it ourselves, it would be possible. But—"

"Aye, I see," Jamie said, and was struck for an instant by mild astonishment that he *did* see; evidently, he had spent longer among the Indians than he supposed.

The brothers exchanged glances, obviously communicating something. Decision made, Light made a gesture of respect to Jamie.

"We are *your* slaves," he pointed out with some diffidence. "It is yours to decide what to do with us." He paused delicately, waiting.

Jamie rubbed a hand over his face, considering that perhaps he hadn't spent quite enough time with Indians after all. Ian didn't smile, but seemed to emit a low vibration of amusement.

MacDonald had told him stories of campaigns during the French and Indian War; soldiers who took Indian prisoners commonly either killed them for scalp money or sold them as slaves. Those campaigns lay a scant ten years in the past; the peace since had been frequently uneasy, and God knew the various Indians made slaves of their prisoners, unless they chose—for whatever inscrutable Indian motive—to adopt or kill them, instead.

Jamie had captured the two Tuscarora; ergo, by custom, they were now his slaves.

He understood quite well what Light was suggesting—that *he* adopt the brothers, and doubtless the young woman, too, once he'd rescued her—and how in God's name had he suddenly become responsible for doing that?

"Well, there's nay market for their scalps just now," Ian pointed out. "Though I suppose ye could *sell* the two of them to Bird. Though they're no worth a great deal, scrawny and ill-feckit as they are."

The brothers stared at him, impassive, awaiting his decision. Light belched suddenly, and looked surprised at the sound. Ian *did* laugh at that, a low creaking noise.

"Oh, I couldna do any such thing, and the three of ye ken that perfectly well," Jamie said crossly. "I should have hit ye harder and saved myself trouble," he said to Goose, who grinned at him, with gap-toothed good nature.

"Yes, Uncle," he said, bowing low in deep respect.

Jamie made a displeased sound in response, but the two Indians took no notice.

It would have to be the medals, then. MacDonald had brought him a chest bulging with medals, gilt buttons, cheap brass compasses, steel knife blades, and other bits of attractive rubbish. Since the chiefs derived their power from their popularity, and their popularity increased in direct proportion to their ability to give gifts, the British Indian agents exerted influence by distributing largesse to those chiefs who indicated a willingness to ally themselves to the Crown.

He'd brought only two small bags of such bribery; the rest left at home for future use. What he had on hand would, he was sure, be sufficient to ransom Mrs. Light, but to expend it all in such fashion would leave him empty-handed with respect to the other village chiefs—and that wouldn't do.

Well, and he supposed he must send Ian back, then, to fetch more. But not until he'd arranged the ransom; he wanted Ian's help in that matter.

"Fine, then," he said, standing up. He fought off a wave of dizziness. "But I am *not* adopting them." The last thing he needed just this minute was three more mouths to feed.

44

Scotchee

A rranging the ransom was, as he had supposed, a simple matter of bargaining. And in the end, Mrs. Light came fairly cheap, at the price of six medals, four knives, and a compass. Granted, he hadn't seen her until the conclusion of the dealing—if he had, he might have offered even less; she was a small, pockmarked lass of perhaps fourteen, with a slight walleye.

Still, he reflected, there was no accounting for taste, and both Light and Goose had been willing to die for her. Doubtless she had a kind heart, or some other excellent quality of character, such as a talent and affinity for bed.

He was quite shocked to find himself thinking such a thing, and looked at her more closely. It was in no way obvious—and yet, now that he *did* look—she did radiate that strange appeal, that remarkable gift, held by a few women, that bypassed such superficial appreciations as looks, age, or wit, and caused a man simply to wish to seize her and—

He choked the sprouting image off at the root. He'd known a few such women, most of them French. And had thought more than once that perhaps it was his own wife's French heritage that was responsible for her possession of that most desirable but very dangerous gift.

He could see Bird eyeing the girl thoughtfully, quite obviously regretting that he had let her go for so little. Fortunately, a distraction occurred to drive the matter from his attention—the return of a hunting party, bringing with them guests.

The guests were Cherokee of the Overhill Band, far from their home in the Tennessee mountains. And with them was a man Jamie had often heard of, but never met until this day—one

Alexander Cameron, whom the Indians called "Scotchee."

A dark, weathered man of middle-age, Cameron was distinguishable from the Indians only by his heavy beard and the long, inquisitive shape of his nose. He had lived with the Cherokee since the age of fifteen, had a Cherokee wife, and was much esteemed among them. He was also an Indian agent, thick with John Stuart. And his presence here, two hundred miles from home, caused Jamie's own long, inquisitive nose to twitch with interest.

The interest was frankly mutual; Cameron examined him with deep-set eyes in which intelligence and wiliness showed in equal measure.

"The redheided Bear-Killer, och, och!" he exclaimed, shaking Jamie warmly by the hand, and then embracing him in the Indian fashion. "I've heard such tales of ye, ken, and fair dyin' to meet ye to see were they true."

"I doubt it," Jamie said. "The last one I heard myself, I'd done for three bears at once, killin' the last of them high in a tree, where he'd chased me after chewin' off my foot."

Despite himself, Cameron looked down at Jamie's feet, then looked up and hooted with laughter, all the lines of his face curving in such irresistible merriment that Jamie felt his own laughter bubble up.

It was not, of course, proper to speak of business yet awhile. The hunting party had brought down one of the woods buffaloes, and a great feast was preparing: the liver taken away to be singed and devoured at once, the strap of tender meat from the back roasted with whole onions, and the heart—so Ian told him—to be shared among the four of them: Jamie, Cameron, Bird, and Running Fox, a mark of honor.

After the liver had been eaten, they retired to Bird's house to drink beer for an hour or two, while the women made ready the rest of the food. And in the course of nature, he found himself outside, having a comfortable piss against a tree, when a quiet footfall came behind him, and Alexander Cameron stepped up alongside, undoing the fall of his breeches.

It seemed natural—though plainly Cameron had intended it—to walk about together for a bit then, the cool air of the evening a respite from the smoke inside the house, and speak of things of common interest—John Stuart, for one, and the ways and means of the Southern Department. Indians, for another; comparing the personalities and means of dealing with the various village chiefs, speculating as to who would make a leader, and whether there might be a great congress called within the year.

"Ye'll be wondering, I expect," Cameron said quite casually, "at my presence here?"

Jamie made a slight motion of the shoulders, admitting interest, but indicating a polite lack of inquisition into Cameron's affairs.

Cameron chuckled.

"Aye, well. It's no secret, to be sure. It's James Henderson, is what it is—ye'll ken the name, maybe?"

He did. Henderson had been Chief Justice of the Superior Court in North Carolina—until the Regulation had caused him to leave, climbing out the window of his courthouse and fleeing for his life from a mob bent on violence.

A wealthy man, and one with a due regard for the value of his skin, Henderson had retired from public life and set about increasing his fortune. To which end, he proposed now to buy an enormous tract of land from the Cherokee, this located in Tennessee, and establish townships there.

Jamie gave Cameron an eye, apprehending at once the complexity of the situation. For the one thing, the lands in question lay far, far inside the Treaty Line. For Henderson to instigate such dealings was an indication—had any been needed—of just how feeble the grasp of the Crown had grown of late. Plainly, Henderson thought nothing of flouting His Majesty's treaty, and expected no interference with his affairs as a result of doing so.

That was one thing. For another, though—the Cherokee held land in common, as all the Indians did. Leaders could and did sell land to whites, without such legal niceties as clear title, but were still subject to the *ex post facto* approval or disapproval of their people. Such approval would not affect the sale, which would be already accomplished, but could result in the fall of a leader, and in a good deal of trouble for the man who tried to take possession of land paid for in good faith—or what passed for good faith, in such dealings.

"John Stuart knows of this, of course," Jamie said, and Cameron nodded, with a small air of complacency.

"Not officially, mind," he said.

Naturally not. The Superintendent of Indian Affairs could hardly countenance such an arrangement officially. At the same time, it would be smiled on unofficially, as such a purchase could not help but further the department's goal of bringing the Indians further under the sway of British influence.

Jamie wondered idly whether Stuart profited in any personal way from the sale. Stuart had a good reputation and was not known to be corrupt—but he might well have a silent interest in the matter. Then again, he might have no financial interest himself, and be turning an officially blind eye to the arrangement only in furtherance of the department's purposes.

Cameron, though . . . He couldn't say, of course, but would be most surprised if Cameron had no finger in the pie.

He did not know where Cameron's natural interest lay, whether with the Indians among whom he lived or with the British to whom he had been born. He doubted that anyone did—perhaps not even Cameron. Regardless of his abiding interests, though, Cameron's immediate goals were clear. He wished the sale to be met with approval—or at least indifference—by the surrounding Cherokee, thus keeping his own pet chiefs in good odor with their followers, and allowing Henderson to go forward with his plans with no undue harassment by Indians in the area.

"I shall not, of course, say anything for a day or two," Cameron told him, and he nodded. There was a natural rhythm to such business. But of course, Cameron had told him now so that he might be of help when the subject arose in due course.

Cameron took it for granted that he *would* help. There was no explicit promise of a bit of Henderson's pie for himself, but no need; it was the sort of opportunity that was a perquisite of being an Indian agent—the reason that such appointments were considered plums.

Given what Jamie knew of the near future, he had neither expectation nor interest in Henderson's purchase—but the subject did give him a welcome opportunity for a useful *quid pro quo*.

He coughed gently.

"Ye ken the wee Tuscarora lassie I bought from Bird?"

Cameron laughed.

"Aye. And he's most perplexed what ye mean to do with her; he says ye willna take any of the lasses he sends to warm your bed. She's no so much to look at—but still . . ."

"Not that," Jamie assured him. "She's marrit, for the one thing. I brought two Tuscaroran lads with me; she belongs to one of them."

"Oh, aye?" Cameron's nose twitched with interest, scenting a story. Jamie had been waiting for this opportunity since the sight of Cameron first gave him the notion, and he told it well, with the satisfactory outcome that Cameron agreed to take the three displaced young Tuscaroras with him, and sponsor their adoption into the Overhill Band.

"It'll no be the first time," he told Jamie. "There are more and more of them—wee scraps of what were villages, even whole peoples—wandering about the country starved and wretched. Heard of the Dogash, have ye?"

"No."

"Nor are ye like to," Cameron said, shaking his head. "There's no but ten or so of them left. They came to us last winter; offered themselves as slaves, only so that they might survive the cold. No—dinna fash yourself, man," he assured Jamie, catching sight of Jamie's expression. "Your wee lads and the lass won't be slaves; my word on it."

Jamie nodded his thanks, pleased with the business. They had wandered some distance outside the village, and stood talking near the edge of a gorge, where the wood opened suddenly over a vista of mountain ranges, rolling away and away like furrows plowed in some endless field of the gods, their backs dark and brooding beneath a starlit sky.

"How can there ever be people enough to settle such a wilderness?" he said, moved suddenly by the sight of it. And yet the smell of woodsmoke and cooking meat hung heavy in the air. People did inhabit it, few and scattered as they were.

Cameron shook his head in contemplation.

"They come," he said, "and they keep on coming. My ain folk came from Scotland. You have," he added, teeth a brief gleam in his beard. "And dinna mean to go back, I'll warrant."

Jamie smiled at that, but made no answer, though a queer feeling rose in his wame at the thought. He did not mean to go back. Had said goodbye to Scotland at the rail of the *Artemis,* knowing full well it was likely his last sight of the place. And yet, the notion that he would never set foot there again had never fully settled on him 'til this moment.

Calls of "Scotchee, Scotchee" summoned them, and he turned to follow Cameron back to the village, conscious all the time of the glorious, terrifying emptiness behind him—and the more terrifying emptiness within.

They smoked that night, after feasting, in ceremonious observance of Jamie's bargain with Bird, in welcome to Cameron. When the pipe had gone twice around the fire, they began to tell stories.

Stories of raids, of battles. Exhausted from the day, head still throbbing, mellowed by food and spruce beer, and slightly intoxicated by the smoke, Jamie had meant only to listen. Perhaps it was the thought of Scotland, so casually evoked by Cameron's remark. But at some point, a memory had stirred, and when the next expectant silence fell, he was surprised to hear his own voice, telling them of Culloden.

"And there near a wall I saw a man I knew, named MacAllister, besieged by a horde of enemies. He fought with gun and sword, but both failed him—his blade was broken, his shield shattered upon his breast."

The fume of the pipe reached him and he raised it and drew deep, as though he drank the air of the moor, hazed with rain and the smoke of the day.

"Still they came, his enemies, to kill him, and he seized up a piece of metal, the tongue of a wagon, and with it, killed six"—he held up both hands, fingers stuck up in illustration—"six of them, before he was at last brought down."

Sounds of awe and tongue clicks of approval greeted this recounting.

"And you yourself, Bear-Killer, how many men did you kill in this battle?"

The smoke burned in his chest, behind his eyes, and for an instant he tasted the bitter smoke of cannon fire, not sweet tobacco. He saw—he *saw*—Alistair MacAllister, dead at his feet among the red-clothed bodies, the side of his head crushed in and the round curve of his shoulder shining solid through the cloth of the shirt, so wetly did it cling to him.

He was there, on the moor, the wet and cold no more than a shimmer on his skin, rain slick on his face, his own shirt sopping and steaming on him with the heat of his rage.

And then he no longer stood on Drumossie, and became aware a second too late of the indrawn breaths around him. He saw Robert Talltree's face, the wrinkles all turned up in astonishment, and only then looked down, to see all ten of his fingers flex and fold, and the four fingers of the right extend again, quite without his meaning it. The thumb wavered, indecisive. He watched this with fascination, then, coming finally to his wits, balled his right hand as well as he could and wrapped the left around it, as though to throttle the memory that had been thrust with such unnerving suddenness into the palm of his hand.

He looked up to see Talltree glance sharply at his face, and he saw the dark old eyes harden, then narrow under a frown—and then the old man took the pipe, drank deep, and blew the smoke across him, bowing forward. Talltree did this twice more, and a hum of hushed approval at the honor came from the clustered men.

He took the pipe and returned the honor of the gesture, then passed it to the next man, refusing to speak further.

They didn't push him to, seeming to recognize and respect the shock he felt.

Shock. Not even that. What he felt was the blankest astonishment. Cautiously, unwilling, he stole a keek at that picture of Alistair. God, it was there.

He realized that he was holding his breath, not wanting to breathe the reek of blood and spilled bowels. He breathed, soft smoke and a copper tang of seasoned bodies, and could have wept, swept with sudden longing for the cold, sharp air of the Highlands, pungent with the scents of peat and gorse.

Alexander Cameron said something to him, but he couldn't reply. Ian, seeing the difficulty, leaned forward to answer, and they all laughed. Ian gave him a curious look, but then turned back to the conversation, beginning a story of a famous game of lacrosse he had played among the Mohawk. Leaving Jamie to sit still, wreathed in the smoke.

Fourteen men. And he did not remember a single face. And that random thumb, hovering uncertainly. Whatever did he mean

by that? That he had fought yet another, but not made certain of
the fellow?

He was afraid even to think of the memory. Unsure what to do
with it. But at the same time, conscious of a sense of awe. And despite everything, grateful to have this small thing back.

It was very late, and most of the men had gone to their own
houses, or lay comfortably asleep around the fire. Ian had left the
fire, but hadn't come back. Cameron was still there, smoking his
own pipe now, though he shared this with Bird, taking turn and
turn about.

"There is a thing I would tell you," Jamie said abruptly, in the
midst of a drowsy silence. "Both of you." Bird raised his brows in
slow question, drugged with tobacco.

He hadn't known he meant to say it. Had thought to wait, judge
his time—if he spoke at all. Perhaps it was the closeness of the
house, the dark intimacy of the fireside, or the intoxication of tobacco. Perhaps only the kinship of an exile for those who would
suffer the same fate. But he'd spoken; had no choice now but to
tell them what he knew.

"The women of my family are . . ." He groped, not knowing the
Cherokee word. "Those who see in dreams what is to come." He
darted a look at Cameron, who appeared to take this in his stride, for
he nodded, and closed his eyes to draw smoke into his lungs.

"Have they the Sight, then?" he asked, mildly interested.

Jamie nodded; it was as good an explanation as any.

"They have seen a thing concerning the Tsalagi. Both my wife
and my daughter have seen this thing."

Bird's attention sharpened, hearing this. Dreams were important; for more than one person to share a dream was extraordinary,
and therefore most important.

"It grieves me to tell you," Jamie said, and meant it. "Sixty
years from this time, the Tsalagi will be taken from their lands, removed to a new place. Many will die on this journey, so that the
path they tread will be called . . ." He groped for the word for
"tears," did not find it, and ended, "the trail where they wept."

Bird's lips pursed, as though to draw smoke, but the pipe
fumed unnoticed in his hands.

"Who will do this?" he asked. "Who *can*?"

Jamie drew a deep breath; here was the difficulty. And yet—so much less difficult than he had thought, now that it came to the matter.

"It will be white men," he said. "But it will not be King George's men."

"The French?" Cameron spoke with a hint of incredulity, but frowned, nonetheless, trying to see how this might come to pass. "Or the Spanish, do they mean? The Spanish are a good deal closer—but none sae many." Spain still held the country south of Georgia, and parts of the Indies, but the English held Georgia firmly; there was little apparent chance of any northward movement by the Spaniards.

"No. Not Spanish, not French." He could wish Ian had stayed, for more than one reason. But the lad had not, and so he would have to struggle with the Tsalagi, which was an interesting tongue, but one in which he could talk fluently only of solid things—and of a very limited future.

"What they tell me—what my women say—" He struggled to find sensible words. "A thing that they see in their dreams, this thing will come to pass, if it concerns many people. But they think it may *not* come to pass, if it concerns a few, or one."

Bird blinked, confused—and no wonder. Grimly, Jamie tried again to explain.

"There are large things, and there are small things. A large thing is a thing like a great battle, or the raising up of a notable chief—though he is one man, he is raised up by the voices of many. If my women dream of these large things, then they will happen. But in any large thing, there are many people. Some say do this; others, do that." He zigzagged his hand to and fro, and Bird nodded.

"So. If many people say, 'Do *this*'"—he stabbed his fingers sharply to the left—"then this happens. But what of the people who said, 'do that'?" And he jerked a thumb back the other way. "These people may choose a different way."

Bird made the hm-hm-*hm!* sound he used when startled.

"So it may be that some will not go?" Cameron asked sharply. "They might escape?"

"I hope so," Jamie said simply.

They sat in silence for a bit, each man staring into the fire, each seeing his own visions—of the future, or the past.

"This wife you have," Bird said at last, deeply contemplative, "did you pay a great deal for her?"

"She cost me almost everything I had," he said, with a wry tone that made the others laugh. "But worth it."

It was very late when he went to the guesthouse; the moon had set, and the sky had that look of deep serenity, the stars singing to themselves in endless night. His body ached in every muscle, and he was so tired that he stumbled on the threshold. His instincts were still working, though, and he felt, rather than saw, someone move in the shadows of the sleeping-couch.

God, Bird was still at it. Well, tonight it wouldn't matter; he could lie naked with a covey of young women, and sleep sound. Too exhausted to be annoyed by her presence, he struggled for some polite acknowledgment of the woman. Then she stood up.

The firelight showed him an elderly woman, her hair in grizzled plaits, her dress of white buckskin decorated with paint and porcupine quills. He recognized Calls-in-the-Forest, dressed in her best. Bird's sense of humor had finally got completely out of hand; he had sent Jamie his mother.

All grasp of Tsalagi deserted him. He opened his mouth, but merely gaped at her. She smiled, very slightly, and held out her hand.

"Come and lie down, Bear-Killer," she said. Her voice was kind and gruff. "I've come to comb the snakes from your hair."

She drew him unresisting to the couch, and made him lie down with his head in her lap. Sure enough; she unplaited his hair and spread it out across her knees, her touch soothing to his throbbing head and the painful knot on his brow.

He had no idea how old she might be, but her fingers were muscular and tireless, making small, rhythmic circles in his scalp, on his temples, behind his ears, near to the bone at the base of his skull. She had thrown sweet grass and some other herb on the fire; the chimney hole was drawing well and he could see white smoke rising upward in a wavering pillar, very calm, but a sense of constant movement in it.

She was humming to herself, or rather whispering some song, the words too indistinct to make out. He watched the silent shapes stream upward in the smoke, and felt his body growing heavy, limbs filled with wet sand, his body a sandbag placed in the path of a flood.

"Talk, Bear-Killer," she said very softly, breaking off her chant. She had a wooden comb in her hand; he felt the teeth of it caress his scalp, rounded with wear.

"I cannot call your words to me," he said, searching for each word in Tsalagi, and thus speaking very slowly. She made a small snorting noise in reply.

"The words don't matter, nor the tongue in which you speak," she said. "Only talk. I will understand."

And so he began haltingly to speak—in Gaelic, as it was the only tongue that didn't seem to require any effort. He understood that he was to speak of what filled his heart, and so began with Scotland—and Culloden. Of grief. Of loss. Of fear.

And in the speaking turned from past to future, where he saw these three specters loom again, cold creatures coming toward him out of the fog, looking through their empty eyes.

Another stood among them—Jack Randall—confusingly on both sides of him. Those eyes were not empty, but alive, intent in a misty face. Had he killed the man, or not? If he had, did the ghost follow at his heels? Or if he had not, was it the thought of vengeance unsatisfied that haunted him, taunted him with its imperfect memory?

But in the speaking, he seemed somehow to rise a little way above his body, and see himself at rest, eyes open, fixed upward, his hair darkly flaming in a halo round his head, streaked with the silver of his age. And here he saw that he merely *was,* in a place between, apart. And quite alone. At peace.

"I hold to no evil in my heart," he said, hearing his voice come slow, from a long way off. "This evil does not touch me. More may come, but not this. Not here. Not now."

"I understand," whispered the old woman, and went on combing his hair as the white smoke rose silent toward the hole to the sky.

45

A Taint in the Blood

June 1774

I sat back on my heels and stretched, tired but pleased. My back ached, my knees creaked like hinges, my fingernails were caked with dirt, and strands of hair stuck to my neck and cheeks—but the new crops of pole beans, onions, turnips, and radishes were planted, the cabbages weeded and culled, and a dozen large peanut bushes had been pulled up and hung to dry on the garden palisades, safe from marauding squirrels.

I glanced up at the sun; still above the chestnut trees. Time enough then before supper for a last chore or two. I stood up and surveyed my small kingdom, debating where best to spend my remaining time. Rooting up the catmint and lemon balm that threatened to engulf the far corner of the garden? Carting baskets of nicely rotted manure up from the heap behind the barn? No, that was man's work.

Herbs? My three French lavender bushes stood knee-high, thick with deep blue swabs on slender stalks, and the yarrow was well in bloom, with lacy umbels of white and pink and yellow. I rubbed a finger under my itching nose, trying to recall whether this was the proper phase of the moon in which to cut yarrow. Lavender and rosemary should be cut in the morning, though, when the volatile oils had risen with the sun; it wasn't as potent if taken later in the day.

Down with the mint, then. I reached for the hoe I had left leaning against the fence, saw a face leering through the palisades, and started back, my heart leaping into my throat.

"Oh!" My visitor had jumped back, too, equally startled. "*Bitte,* ma'am! Didn't mean to fright ye."

It was Manfred McGillivray, peeping shyly through the drooping vines of morning glory and wild yam. He'd come earlier in the day, bringing a canvas-wrapped bundle containing several muskets for Jamie.

"That's all right." I stooped to pick up the hoe I had dropped. "Are you looking for Lizzie? She's in—"

"Ach, no, ma'am. That is, I—do ye think I might have a word, ma'am?" he asked abruptly. "Alone, like?"

"Of course. Come along in; we can talk while I hoe."

He nodded, and went round to let himself in by the gate. What might he want with me? I wondered. He had on a coat and boots, both covered in dust, and his breeches were badly creased. He'd been riding some way, then, not just from his family's cabin—and he hadn't been into the house yet; Mrs. Bug would have dusted him off, forcibly.

"Where have you come from?" I asked, offering him the gourd dipper from my water bucket. He accepted it, drinking thirstily, then wiped his mouth politely on his sleeve.

"Thank ye, ma'am. I've been to Hillsboro, for to fetch the . . . er . . . the things for Mr. Fraser."

"Really? That seems a long way," I said mildly.

A look of profound uneasiness crossed his face. He was a nice-looking boy, tanned and handsome as a young faun under his crop of dark, curly hair, but he looked almost furtive now, glancing back over his shoulder toward the house, as though fearful of interruption.

"I . . . um . . . well, ma'am, that's to do, a bit, with what I meant to speak to ye about."

"Oh? Well . . ." I made a cordial gesture, indicating that he should feel free to unburden himself, and turned away to begin my hoeing, so that he might feel less self-conscious. I was beginning to suspect what he wanted to ask me, though I wasn't sure what Hillsboro had to do with it.

"It's . . . ah . . . well, it's to do with Mrs. Lizzie," he began, folding his hands behind him.

"Yes?" I said encouragingly, nearly sure that I was right in my suppositions. I glanced toward the western end of the garden, where the bees were buzzing happily among the tall yellow umbels of the *dauco* plants. Well, it was better than the eighteenth-century notion of condoms, at least.

"I can't marry her," he blurted.

"What?" I stopped hoeing and straightened up, staring at him. His lips were pressed tightly together, and I saw now that what I had taken for shyness had been his attempt to mask a deep unhappiness that now showed plainly in the lines of his face.

"You'd better come and sit down." I led him to the small bench Jamie had made me, set beneath the shade of a black gum tree that overhung the north side of the garden.

He sat, head drooping and hands trapped between his knees. I took off my broad-brimmed sun hat, wiped my face on my apron, and pinned up my hair more neatly, breathing in the cool freshness of the spruce and balsam trees that grew on the slope above.

"What is it?" I asked gently, seeing that he did not know how to start. "Are you afraid that perhaps you don't love her?"

He gave me a startled look, then turned his head back to the studied contemplation of his knees.

"Oh. No, ma'am. I mean—I don't, but that's no matter."

"It isn't?"

"No. I mean—I'm sure we *should* grow to be fond of one another, *meine Mutter* says so. And I like her well enough now, to be sure," he added hastily, as though fearing this might sound insulting. "Da says she's a tidy wee soul, and my sisters are verra fond of her indeed."

I made a noncommittal sound. I had had my doubts about this match to begin with, and it was beginning to sound as though they were justified.

"Is there . . . perhaps someone else?" I asked delicately.

Manfred shook his head slowly, and I heard him swallow hard.

"No, ma'am," he said in a low voice.

"You're sure?"

"Aye, ma'am." He drew a deep breath. "I mean—there was. But that's all done with now."

I was puzzled by this. If he had decided to renounce this mysterious other girl—whether out of fear of his mother, or for some other reason—then what was stopping him from going through with the marriage to Lizzie?

"The other girl—is she by chance from Hillsboro?" Things

were coming a little clearer. When I had first met him and his family at the Gathering, his sisters had exchanged knowing glances at mention of Manfred's visits to Hillsboro. They had known about it then, even if Ute had not.

"Aye. That's why I went to Hillsboro—I mean, I had to go, for the . . . er . . . But I meant to see . . . Myra . . . and tell her that I would be married to Miss Wemyss and couldna come to see her anymore."

"Myra." So she had a name, at least. I sat back, tapping my foot meditatively. "You meant to—so you didn't see her, after all?"

He shook his head again, and I saw a tear drop and spread suddenly on the dusty homespun of his breeches.

"No, ma'am," he said, his voice half-choked. "I couldn't. She was dead."

"Oh, dear," I said softly. "Oh, I am so sorry." The tears were falling on his knees, making spots on the cloth, and his shoulders shook, but he didn't make a sound.

I reached out and gathered him into my arms, holding him tight against my shoulder. His hair was soft and springy and his skin flushed with heat against my neck. I felt helpless to deal with his grief; he was too old to comfort with mere touch, too young— perhaps—to find any solace in words. There was nothing I could do for the moment save hold him.

His arms went round my waist, though, and he clung to me for several minutes after his weeping was spent. I held him quietly, patting his back and keeping watch through the flickering green shadows of the vine-twined palisades, lest anyone else come looking for me in the garden.

At last he sighed, let go, and sat up. I groped for a handkerchief, and not finding one, pulled off my apron and handed it to him to wipe his face.

"You needn't marry right away," I said, when he seemed to have regained possession of himself. "It's only right that you should take a little time to—to heal. But we can find some excuse to put the wedding off; I'll speak to Jamie—"

But he was shaking his head, a look of sad determination taking the place of tears.

"No, ma'am," he said, low-voiced but definite. "I can't."

"Why not?"

"Myra was a whore, ma'am. She died of the French disease."

He looked up at me then, and I saw the terror in his eyes, behind the grief.

"And I think I've got it."

"Ye're sure?" Jamie set down the hoof he had been trimming, and looked bleakly at Manfred.

"*I'm* sure," I said tartly. I had obliged Manfred to show me the evidence—in fact, I had taken scrapings from the lesion to examine microscopically—then took him straight to find Jamie, barely waiting for the boy to do up his breeches.

Jamie looked fixedly at Manfred, plainly trying to decide what to say. Manfred, purple-faced from the double stress of confession and examination, dropped his own eyes before this basilisk gaze, staring at a crescent of black hoof paring that lay on the ground.

"I'm that sorry, sir," he murmured. "I—I didna mean to . . ."

"I shouldna suppose anyone does," Jamie said. He breathed deeply and made a sort of subterranean growling noise that caused Manfred to hunch his shoulders and try to withdraw his head, turtlelike, into the safer confines of his clothing.

"He did do the right thing," I pointed out, trying to put the best face possible on the situation. "Now, I mean—telling the truth."

Jamie snorted.

"Well, he couldna be poxing wee Lizzie, now, could he? That's worse than only going wi' a whore."

"I suppose some men would just keep quiet about it, and hope for the best."

"Aye, some would." He narrowed his eyes at Manfred, evidently looking for overt indications that Manfred might be a villain of this description.

Gideon, who disliked having his feet messed about and was consequently in bad temper, stamped heavily, narrowly missing Jamie's own foot. He tossed his head, and emitted a rumbling noise that I thought was roughly the equivalent of Jamie's growl.

"Aye, well." Jamie left off glaring at Manfred, and grabbed Gideon's halter. "Go along to the house with him, Sassenach. I'll finish here, and then we'll have Joseph in and see what's to do."

"All right." I hesitated, unsure whether to speak in front of

Manfred. I didn't want to raise his hopes too much, until I'd had a chance to look at the scrapings under the microscope.

The spirochetes of syphilis were very distinctive, but I didn't think I had a stain that would allow me to see them with a simple light microscope such as mine was. And while I thought my homemade penicillin could likely eliminate the infection, I would have no way of knowing for certain, unless I *could* see them, and then see that they had disappeared from his blood.

I contented myself with saying, "I have got penicillin, mind."

"I ken that well enough, Sassenach." Jamie switched his baleful look from Manfred to me. I'd saved his life with the penicillin—twice—but he hadn't enjoyed the process. With a Scottish noise of dismissal, he bent and picked up Gideon's enormous hoof again.

Manfred seemed a bit shell-shocked, and said nothing on the way to the house. He hesitated at the door to the surgery, glancing uneasily from the gleaming microscope to the open box of surgical tools, and then toward the covered bowls lined up on the counter, in which I grew my penicillin colonies.

"Come in," I said, but was obliged to reach out and take him by the sleeve before he would step across the threshold. It occurred to me that he hadn't been to the surgery before; it was a good five miles to the McGillivrays' place, and *Frau* McGillivray was entirely capable of dealing with her family's minor ills.

I wasn't feeling terribly charitable toward Manfred at the moment, but gave him a stool and asked if he would like a cup of coffee. I thought he could probably use a stiff drink, if he was about to have an interview with Jamie and Joseph Wemyss, but supposed I had better keep him clear-headed.

"No, ma'am," he said, and swallowed, white-faced. "I mean, thank ye, no."

He looked extremely young, and very frightened.

"Roll up your sleeve then, please. I'm going to draw a bit of blood, but it won't hurt much. How did you come to meet the, er, young lady? Myra, that was her name?"

"Aye, ma'am." Tears welled in his eyes at her name; I suppose he really had loved her, poor boy—or thought he had.

He had met Myra in a tavern in Hillsboro. She had seemed kind, he said, and was very pretty, and when she asked the young gunsmith to buy her a glass of geneva, he had obliged, feeling dashing.

"So we drank a bit together, and she laughed at me, and . . ." He seemed rather at a loss to explain how matters had progressed from there, but he had waked up in her bed. That had sealed the matter, so far as he was concerned, and he had seized every excuse to go to Hillsboro thereafter.

"How long did this affair go on?" I asked, interested. Lacking a decent syringe for drawing blood, I'd merely pierced the vein inside his elbow with a fleam, and drained off the welling blood into a small vial.

For the better part of two years, apparently.

"I kent I couldna wed her," he explained earnestly. "*Meine Mutter* would never . . ." He trailed off, assuming the look of a startled rabbit hearing hounds in its immediate vicinity. "*Gruss Gott!*" he said. "My mother!"

I'd been wondering about that particular aspect of the affair myself. Ute McGillivray wasn't going to be at all pleased to hear that her pride and joy, her only son, had contracted a disreputable disease, and furthermore, one which was about to lead to the breaking of his carefully engineered engagement and very likely to a scandal that the entire backcountry would hear about. The fact that it was generally a fatal disease would probably be a secondary concern.

"She'll kill me!" he said, sliding off his stool and rolling his sleeve down hastily.

"Probably not," I said mildly. "Though I suppose—"

At this fraught moment came the sound of the back door opening and voices in the kitchen. Manfred stiffened, dark curls quivering with alarm. Then heavy footsteps started down the hall toward the surgery, and he dived across the room, flung a leg across the windowsill, and was off, running like a deer for the trees.

"Come back here, you ass!" I bellowed through the open window.

"Which ass is that, Auntie?" I turned to see that the heavy footsteps belonged to Young Ian—heavy, because he was carrying Lizzie Wemyss in his arms.

"Lizzie! What's the matter? Here, put her on the table." I could see at once what the matter was: a return of the malarial fever. She was limp, but shivered nonetheless with chill, the contracting muscles shaking her like jelly.

"I found her in the dairy shed," Ian said, laying her gently on the table. "The deaf Beardsley came rushin' out as though the devil was chasing him, saw me, and dragged me in. She was on the floor, wi' the churn overturned beside her."

This was very worrying—she hadn't had an attack for some time, but for a second time, the attack had come upon her too suddenly for her to go for help, causing almost immediate collapse.

"Top shelf of the cupboard," I said to Ian, hastily rolling Lizzie on her side and undoing her laces. "That bluish jar—no, the big one."

He grabbed it without question, removing the lid as he brought it to me.

"Jesus, Auntie! What's that?" He wrinkled his nose at the smell from the ointment.

"Gallberries and cinchona bark in goose grease, among other things. Take some and start rubbing it into her feet."

Looking bemused, he gingerly scooped up a dollop of the purplish-gray cream and did as I said, Lizzie's small bare foot nearly disappearing between the large palms of his hands.

"Will she be all right, d'ye think, Auntie?" He glanced at her face, looking troubled. The look of her was enough to trouble anyone—the clammy color of whey, and the flesh gone slack so that her delicate cheeks juddered with the chills.

"Probably. Close your eyes, Ian." I'd got her clothes loosened, and now pulled off her gown, petticoats, pocket, and stays. I threw a ratty blanket over her before working the shift off over her head—she owned only two, and wouldn't want one spoiled with the reek of the ointment.

Ian had obediently closed his eyes, but was still rubbing the ointment methodically into her feet, a small frown drawing his brows together, the look of concern lending him for a moment a brief but startling resemblance to Jamie.

I drew the jar toward me, scooped up some ointment, and, reaching under the blanket, began to rub it into the thinner skin beneath her armpits, then over her back and belly. I could feel the outlines of her liver distinctly, a large, firm mass beneath her ribs. Swollen, and tender from the way she grimaced at my touch; there was some ongoing damage there, certainly.

"Can I open my eyes now?"

"Oh—yes, of course. Rub more up her legs, please, Ian."

Shoving the jar back in his direction, I caught a glimpse of movement in the doorway. One of the Beardsley twins stood there, clinging to the jamb, dark eyes fixed on Lizzie. Kezzie, it must be; Ian had said "the deaf Beardsley" had come to fetch help.

"She'll be all right," I said to him, raising my voice, and he nodded once, then disappeared, with a single burning glance at Ian.

"Who was it ye were shouting at, Auntie Claire?" Ian looked up at me, clearly as much to preserve Lizzie's modesty as from courtesy to me; the blanket was turned back and his big hands were smoothing ointment into the skin above her knee, thumbs gently circling the small rounded curves of her patella, her skin so thin that the pearly bone seemed almost visible through it.

"Who—oh. Manfred McGillivray," I said, suddenly recollecting. "Damn! The blood!" I leapt up and wiped my hands hurriedly on my apron. Thank God, I'd corked the vial; the blood inside was still liquid. It wouldn't keep long, though.

"Do her hands and arms, would you please, Ian? I've got to manage this quickly."

He moved obligingly to do as I said, while I hastily spilled a drop of blood on each of several slides, dragging a clean slide across each one to make a smear. What sort of stain might work on spirochetes? No telling; I'd try them all.

I explained the matter disjointedly to Ian, as I pulled stain bottles out of the cupboard, made up the solutions, and set the slides to soak.

"The pox? Poor lad; he must be nearly mad wi' fright." He eased Lizzie's arm, gleaming with ointment, under the blanket and tucked it gently round her.

I was momentarily surprised at this show of sympathy, but then remembered. Ian had been exposed to syphilis some years before, after his abduction by Geillis Duncan; I hadn't been sure that he had the disease, but had dosed him with the last of my twentieth-century penicillin, just in case.

"Did ye not tell him ye could cure him, though, Auntie?"

"I hadn't the chance. Though I'm not absolutely sure that I can, to be honest." I sat down on a stool, and took Lizzie's other hand, feeling for her pulse.

"Ye're not?" His feathery brows went up at that. "Ye told me I was cured."

"You are," I assured him. "If you ever had the disease in the first place." I gave him a sharp look. "You've never had a sore on your prick, have you? Or anywhere else?"

He shook his head, mute, a dark wave of blood staining his lean cheeks.

"Good. But the penicillin I gave you—that was some that I'd brought from . . . well, from before. That was purified—very strong and certainly potent. I'm never sure, when I use this stuff"—I gestured at the culturing bowls on the counter—"whether it's strong enough to work, or even the right strain. . . ." I rubbed the back of my hand under my nose; the gallberry ointment, had a most *penetrating* smell.

"It doesn't always work." I had had more than one patient with an infection that didn't respond to one of my penicillin concoctions—though in those cases, I had often succeeded with another attempt. In a few instances, the person had recovered on his own before the second brew was ready. In one instance, the patient had died, despite applications of two different penicillin mixtures.

Ian nodded slowly, his eyes on Lizzie's face. The first bout of chills had spent itself and she lay quiet, the blanket barely moving over the slight round of her chest.

"If ye're no sure, then . . . ye'd not let him marry her, surely?"

"I don't know. Jamie said he'd speak to Mr. Wemyss, see what he thought of the matter."

I rose and took the first of the slides from its pinkish bath, shook off the clinging drops, and, wiping the bottom of the slide, placed it carefully on the platform of my microscope.

"What are ye looking for, Auntie?"

"Things called spirochetes. Those are the particular kind of germ that causes syphilis."

"Oh, aye." Despite the seriousness of the situation, I smiled, hearing the note of skepticism in his voice. I'd shown him microorganisms before, but—like Jamie—like almost everyone—he simply couldn't believe that something so nearly invisible was capable of harm. The only one who had seemed to accept the notion wholeheartedly was Malva Christie, and in her case, I thought the acceptance was due simply to her faith in me. If I told *her* something, she believed me; very refreshing, after years of assorted Scots looking at me with varying degrees of squiggle-eyed suspicion.

"Has he gone home, d'ye think? Manfred?"

"I don't know." I spoke absently, slowly moving the slide to and fro, searching. I could make out the red blood cells, pale pink discs that floated past my field of view, drifting lazily in the watery stain. No deadly spirals visible—but that didn't mean they weren't there, only that the stain I had used might not reveal them.

Lizzie stirred and moaned, and I looked round to see her eyes flutter open.

"There, lass," Ian said softly, and smiled at her. "Better, is it?"

"Is it?" she said faintly. Still, the corners of her mouth lifted slightly, and she put a hand out from under her blanket, groping. He took it in his, patting it.

"Manfred," she said, turning her head to and fro, eyes half-lidded. "Is Manfred here?"

"Um . . . no," I said, exchanging a quick glance of consternation with Ian. How much had she heard? "No, he was here, but he's—he's gone now."

"Oh." Seeming to lose interest, she closed her eyes again. Ian looked down at her, still stroking her hand. His face showed deep sympathy—with perhaps a tinge of calculation.

"Shall I maybe carry the lassie up to her bed?" he asked softly, as though she might be sleeping. "And then maybe go and find . . . ?" He tilted his head toward the open window, raising one eyebrow.

"If you would, please, Ian." I hesitated, and his eyes met mine, deep hazel and soft with worry and the shadow of remembered pain. "She'll be all right," I said, trying to infuse a sense of certainty into the words.

"Aye, she will," he said firmly, and stooped to gather her up, tucking the blanket under her. "If I've anything to say about it."

46

In Which Things Gang Agley

Manfred McGillivray did not come back. Ian did, with a blackened eye, skinned knuckles, and the terse report that Manfred had declared a set intention of going off and hanging himself, and good riddance to the fornicating son of a bitch, and might his rotten bowels gush forth like Judas Iscariot's, the traitorous, stinking wee turd. He then stamped upstairs, to stand silent over Lizzie's bed for a time.

Hearing this, I hoped that Manfred's statement was merely the counsel of temporary despair—and cursed myself for not having told him at once and in the strongest terms that he could be cured, whether it was absolutely true or not. Surely he wouldn't . . .

Lizzie was half-conscious, prostrated with the burning fevers and shaking agues of malaria, and in no fit state to be told of her betrothed's desertion, nor the cause of it. I would have to make some delicate inquiries, though, so soon as she was fit, because there was the possibility that she and Manfred had anticipated their marriage vows, and if so . . .

"Well, there's the one thing about it," Jamie observed grimly. "The Beardsley twins were making ready to track our poxed lad down and castrate him, but now they've heard he means to hang himself, they've magnanimously decided that will do."

"Thank the Lord for small blessings," I said, sinking down at the table. "They might really do it." The Beardsleys, particularly Josiah, were excellent trackers—and not given to idle threats.

"Oh, they would," Jamie assured me. "They were most seriously sharpening their knives when I found them at it and told them not to trouble themselves."

I suppressed an involuntary smile at the image of the Beardsleys, bent side by side over a grindstone, their lean, dark faces set in identical scowls of vengeance, but the momentary flash of humor faded.

"Oh, God. We'll have to tell the McGillivrays."

Jamie nodded, looking pale at the thought, but pushed back his bench.

"I'd best go straightaway."

"Not 'til ye've had a bite." Mrs. Bug put a plate of food firmly in front of him. "Ye dinna want to be dealing wi' Ute McGillivray on an empty stomach."

Jamie hesitated, but evidently found her argument to have merit, for he picked up his fork and addressed himself to the ragoo'd pork with grim determination.

"Jamie . . ."

"Aye?"

"Perhaps you *should* let the Beardsleys track Manfred down. Not to hurt him, I don't mean—but we need to find him. He *will* die of it, if he isn't treated."

He paused, a forkful of ragoo halfway to his mouth, and regarded me under lowered brows.

"Aye, and if they find him, he'll die of *that,* Sassenach." He shook his head, and the fork completed its journey. He chewed and swallowed, evidently completing his plan as he did so.

"Joseph's in Bethabara, courting. He'll have to be told, and by rights, I should fetch him to go with me to the McGillivrays'. But . . ." He hesitated, clearly envisioning Mr. Wemyss, that mildest and shyest of men, and no one's notion of a useful ally. "No. I'll go and tell Robin. May be as he'll start searching for the lad himself—or Manfred may have thought better of it and run for home already."

That was a cheering thought, and I saw him off with hope in mind. But he returned near midnight, grim-faced and silent, and I knew that Manfred had not come home.

"You told them both?" I asked, turning back the coverlet for him to crawl in beside me. He smelled of horse and night, cool and pungent.

"I asked Robin to walk outside wi' me, and told him. I hadna the nerve to tell Ute to her face," he admitted. He smiled at me, snuggling under the quilt. "Ye dinna think me too much a coward, I hope, Sassenach."

"No, indeed," I assured him, and leaned to blow out the candle. "Discretion is the better part of valor."

We were roused just before dawn by a thunderous pounding on the door. Rollo, who had been sleeping on the landing, shot down the stair, roaring threats. He was closely followed by Ian, who had been sitting up by Lizzie's bed, keeping watch while I slept. Jamie leapt out of bed and, seizing a loaded pistol from the top of the wardrobe, rushed to join the fray.

Shocked and dazed—I had been asleep for less than an hour—I sat up, heart pounding. Rollo stopped barking for a moment, and I heard Jamie shout, "Who is it?" through the door.

This query was answered by a renewed pounding that echoed up the stairwell and seemed to shake the house, accompanied by an upraised feminine voice that would have done credit to Wagner in one of his more robust moods. Ute McGillivray.

I began to struggle out of the bedclothes. Meanwhile, a confusion of voices, renewed barking, the grate of the bolt being lifted—and then more confused voices, all much louder. I ran to the window and looked out; Robin McGillivray was standing in the dooryard, having evidently just dismounted from one of a pair of mules.

He looked much older, and somehow deflated, as though the spirit had gone out of him, taking all his strength and leaving him flabby. He turned his head away from whatever riot was taking place on the stoop, closing his eyes. The sun was just up now, and the pure clear light showed up all the lines and hollows of exhaustion and a desperate unhappiness.

As though he sensed me looking at him, he opened his eyes and raised his face toward the window. He was red-eyed, disheveled. He saw me, but didn't respond to my tentative wave of greeting. Instead, he turned away, closing his eyes again, and stood, waiting.

The riot below had moved inside, and appeared to be progressing up the stairs, borne on a wave of Scottish expostulations and

Germanic shrieks, punctuated by enthusiastic barking from Rollo, always willing to lend his efforts to further the festivities.

I seized my wrapper from its peg, but had barely got one arm into it before the door of the bedchamber was flung open, crashing into the wall so hard that it rebounded and hit her in the chest. Nothing daunted, she slammed it open again and advanced on me like a juggernaut, cap awry and eyes blazing.

"You! *Weibchen!* How you dare, such insult, such lies to say my son about! You I kill, I tear off your hair, *nighean na galladh!* You—"

She lunged at me and I flung myself sideways, narrowly avoiding her grab at my arm.

"Ute! *Frau* McGillivray! Listen to—"

The second grab was more successful; she got hold of the sleeve of my night rail and wrenched, dragging the garment off my shoulder with a rending noise of torn cloth, even as she clawed at my face with her free hand.

I jerked back, and screamed with all my strength, my nerves recalling for one dreadful instant a hand striking at my face, hands pulling at me. . . .

I struck at her, the strength of terror flooding through my limbs, screaming, screaming, some tiny remnant of rationality in my brain watching this, bemused, appalled—but completely unable to stop the animal panic, the unreasoning rage that geysered up from some deep and unsuspected well.

I hit out, hammering blindly, screaming—wondering even as I did so, why, why was I doing this?

An arm grabbed me round the waist and I was lifted off the ground. A fresh spurt of panic ripped through me, and then I found myself suddenly alone, untouched. I was standing in the corner by the wardrobe, swaying drunkenly, panting. Jamie stood in front of me, shoulders braced and elbows raised, shielding me.

He was talking, very calmly, but I had lost the capacity to make sense of words. I pressed my hands back against the wall, and felt some sense of comfort from its solid bulk.

My heart was still hammering in my ears, the sound of my own breathing scaring me, it was so like the gasping sound when Harley Boble had broken my nose. I shut my mouth hard, trying to stop. Holding my breath seemed to work, allowing only small inhalations through my now-functioning nose.

The movement of Ute's mouth caught my eye and I stared at it, trying to fix myself once more in time and space. I was hearing words, but couldn't quite make the jump of comprehension. I breathed, letting the words flow over me like water, taking emotion from them—anger, reason, protest, placation, shrillness, growling—but no explicit meaning.

Then I took a deep breath, wiped my face—I was surprised to find it wet—and suddenly everything snapped back to normal. I could hear, and understand.

Ute was staring at me, anger and dislike clear on her face, but muted by a lurking horror.

"You are mad," she said, nodding. "I see." She sounded almost calm at this point. "Well, then."

She turned to Jamie, automatically twisting up untidy handsful of grizzled blond hair, stuffing them under her enormous cap. The ribbon had been torn; a loop of it dangled absurdly over one eye.

"So, she is mad. I will say so, but still, my son—my son!—is gone. So." She stood heaving, surveying me, and shook her head, then turned again to Jamie.

"Salem is closed to you," she said curtly. "My family, those who know us—they will not trade with you. Nor anyone else I speak to, to tell them the wicked thing she has done." Her eye drifted back to me, a cold, gelid blue, and her lip curled in a heavy sneer under the loop of torn ribbon.

"You are shunned," she said. "You do not exist, you." She turned on her heel and walked out, forcing Ian and Rollo to side-step hastily out of her way. Her footfalls echoed heavily on the stair, a ponderous, measured tread, like the tolling of a passing bell.

I saw the tension in Jamie's shoulders relax, little by little. He was still wearing his nightshirt—there was a damp patch between his shoulder blades—and had the pistol still in his hand.

The front door boomed shut below. Everyone stood still, struck silent.

"You wouldn't really have shot her, would you?" I asked, clearing my throat.

"What?" He turned, staring at me. Then he caught the direction of my glance, and looked at the pistol in his hand as though wondering where *that* had come from.

"Oh," he said, "no," and shook his head, reaching up to put it back on top of the wardrobe. "I forgot I had it. Though God kens well enough that I should *like* to shoot the besotted auld besom," he added. "Are ye all right, Sassenach?"

He stooped to look at me, his eyes soft with worry.

"I'm all right. I don't know what—but it's all right. It's gone now."

"Ah," he said softly, and looked away, lashes coming down to hide his eyes. Had he felt it, too, then? Found himself suddenly . . . back? I knew he had sometimes. Remembered waking from sleep in Paris to see him braced in an open window, pressing so hard against the frame that the muscles stood out in his arms, visible by moonlight.

"It's all right," I repeated, touching him, and he gave me a brief, shy smile.

"Ye should have bitten her," Ian was saying earnestly to Rollo. "She's got an arse the size of a hogshead of tobacco—how could ye miss?"

"Probably afraid of being poisoned," I said, coming out of my corner. "Do you suppose she meant it—or no, she meant it, certainly. But do you suppose she can do it? Stop anyone trading with us, I mean."

"She can stop Robin," Jamie said, a certain grimness returning to his expression. "For the rest . . . we'll see."

Ian shook his head, frowning, and rubbed his knuckled fist gingerly against his thigh.

"I kent I should have broken Manfred's neck," he said with real regret. "We could ha' told *Frau* Ute he fell off a rock, and saved a deal of trouble."

"Manfred?" The small voice made everyone turn as one, to see who had spoken.

Lizzie stood in the doorway, thin and pale as a starveling ghost, her eyes huge and glassy with recent fever.

"What about Manfred?" she said. She swayed dangerously, and put out a hand to the jamb, to save herself falling. "What's happened to him?"

"Poxed and gone," Ian said curtly, drawing himself up. "Ye didna give him your maidenheid, I hope."

In the event, Ute McGillivray was not quite able to fulfill her threat—but she did enough damage. Manfred's dramatic disappearance, the breaking of his engagement to Lizzie, and the reason for it was a fearful scandal, and word of it spread from Hillsboro and Salisbury, where he had worked now and then as an itinerant gunsmith, to Salem and High Point.

But thanks to Ute's efforts, the story was even more confused than would be normal for such gossip; some said that he was poxed, others that I had maliciously and falsely accused him of being poxed, because of some fancied disagreement with his parents. Others, more kindly, did not believe Manfred was poxed, but said that doubtless I had been mistaken.

Those who believed him to be poxed were divided as to how he had achieved that condition, half of them convinced that he had got it from some whore, and a good many of the rest speculating that he had got it from poor Lizzie, whose reputation suffered terribly—until Ian, Jamie, the Beardsley twins, and even Roger took to defending her honor with their fists, at which point people did not, of course, stop talking—but stopped talking where any of her champions might hear directly.

All of Ute's numerous relatives in and around Wachovia, Salem, Bethabara, and Bethania of course believed her version of the story, and tongues wagged busily. All of Salem did not cease trading with us—but many people did. And more than once, I had the unnerving experience of greeting Moravians I knew well, only to have them stare past me in stony silence, or turn their backs upon me. Often enough that I no longer went to Salem.

Lizzie, beyond a certain initial mortification, seemed not terribly upset at the rupture of her engagement. Bewildered, confused, and sorry—she said—for Manfred, but not desolated by his loss. And since she seldom left the Ridge anymore, she didn't hear what people said about her. What *did* trouble her was the loss of the McGillivrays—particularly Ute.

"D'ye see, ma'am," she told me wistfully, "I'd never had a mother, for my own died when I was born. And then *Mutti*—she asked me to call her so when I said I'd marry Manfred—she said I was her daughter, just like Hilda and Inga and Senga. She'd fuss over me, and bully me and laugh at me, just as she did them. And it was . . . just so *nice*, to have all that family. And now I've lost them."

Robin, who had been sincerely attached to her, had sent her a short, regretful note, sneaked out through the good offices of Ronnie Sinclair. But since Manfred's disappearance, neither Ute nor the girls had come to see her, nor sent a single word.

It was Joseph Wemyss, though, who was most visibly affected by the affair. He said nothing, plainly not wishing to make matters worse for Lizzie—but he drooped, like a flower deprived of rain. Beyond his pain for Lizzie, and his distress at the blackening of her reputation, he, too, missed the McGillivrays, missed the joy and comfort of suddenly being part of a large, exuberant family, after so many years of loneliness.

Worse, though, was that while Ute had not been able to carry out her threat entirely, she *had* been able to influence her near relatives—including Pastor Berrisch, and his sister, Monika, who, Jamie told me privately, had been forbidden to see or speak to Joseph again.

"The Pastor's sent her away to his wife's relatives in Halifax," he said, shaking his head sadly. "To forget."

"Oh, dear."

And of Manfred, there was no slightest trace. Jamie had sent word through all his usual avenues, but no one had seen him since his flight from the Ridge. I thought of him—and prayed for him— daily, haunted by pictures of him skulking in the woods alone, the deadly spirochetes multiplying in his blood day by day. Or, much worse, working his way to the Indies on some ship, pausing in every port to drown his sorrows in the arms of unsuspecting whores, to whom he would pass on the silent, fatal infection—and they, in turn . . .

Or sometimes, the nightmare image of a bundle of rotting clothes hanging from a tree limb, deep in the forest, with no mourners save the crows who came to pick the flesh from his bones. And despite everything, I could not find it in my heart to hate Ute McGillivray, who must be thinking the same thoughts.

The sole bright spot in this ruddy quagmire was that Thomas Christie, quite contrary to my expectations, had allowed Malva to continue to come to the surgery, his sole stipulation being that if I proposed to involve his daughter in any further use of the ether, he was to be told ahead of time.

"There." I stood back, gesturing to her to look through the eyepiece of the microscope. "Do you see them?"

Her lips pursed in silent fascination. It had taken no little effort to find a combination of staining and reflected sunlight that would reveal the spirochetes, but I had succeeded at last. They weren't strongly visible, but you could see them, if you knew what you were looking for—and despite my complete conviction in my original diagnosis, I was relieved to see them.

"Oh, yes! Wee spirals. I see them plain!" She looked up at me, blinking. "D'ye mean seriously to tell me that these bittie things are what's poxed Manfred?" She was too polite to express open skepticism, but I could see it in her eyes.

"I do indeed." I had explained the germ theory of disease a number of times, to a variety of disbelieving eighteenth-century listeners, and in the light of this experience had little expectation of finding a favorable reception. The normal response was either a blank stare, indulgent laughter, or a sniff of dismissal, and I was more or less expecting a polite version of one of these reactions from Malva.

To my surprise, though, she seemed to grasp the notion at once—or at least pretended to.

"Well, so." She put both hands on the counter and peered again at the spirochetes. "These wee beasties cause the syphilis, then. However do they do that? And why is it that the bittie things ye showed me from my teeth don't make me ill?"

I explained, as best I could, the notion of "good bugs" or "indifferent bugs" versus "bad bugs," which she seemed to grasp easily—but my explanation of cells, and the concept of the body being composed of these, left her frowning at the palm of her hand in confusion, trying to make out the individual cells. She shook off her doubt, though, and folding up her hand in her apron, returned to her questions.

Did the bugs cause all disease? The penicillin—why did it work on some of the germs, but not all? And how did the bugs get from one person to another?

"Some travel by air—that's why you must try to avoid people coughing or sneezing on you—and some by water— which is why you mustn't drink from a stream that someone's been using as a privy—and some . . . well, by other means." I didn't know how much she might know about sex in humans— she lived on a farm, clearly she knew how pigs, chickens, and horses behaved—and I was wary of enlightening her, lest her father hear about it. I rather thought he'd prefer her to be dealing with ether.

Naturally, she pounced on my evasion.

"Other means? What other means are there?" With an internal sigh, I told her.

"They do *what*?" she said, incredulous. "Men, I mean. Like an animal! Whyever would a woman let a man do that to her?"

"Well, they *are* animals, you know," I said, suppressing an urge to laugh. "So are women. As to why one would let them . . ." I rubbed my nose, looking for a tasteful way of putting it. She was moving rapidly ahead of me, though, putting two and two together.

"For money," she said, looking thunderstruck. "*That's* what a whore does! She lets them do such things to her for money."

"Well, yes—but women who aren't whores—"

"The bairns, aye, ye said." She nodded, but was plainly thinking of other things; her small, smooth forehead was wrinkled in concentration.

"How much money do they get?" she asked. "I should want a lot, I think, to let a man—"

"I don't know," I said, somewhat taken aback. "Different amounts, I expect. Depending."

"Depending . . . oh, if he was maybe ugly, ye mean, ye could make him pay more? Or if *she* were ugly . . ." She gave me a quick, interested look. "Bobby Higgins told me of a whore he kent in London, that her looks was spoilt by vitriol." She looked up at the cupboard where I kept the sulfuric acid under lock and key, and shivered, her delicate shoulders quivering with revulsion at the thought.

"Yes, he told me about her, too. Vitriol is what we call a caustic—a liquid that burns. That's why—"

But her mind had already returned to the subject of fascination.

"To think of Manfred McGillivray doing such a thing!" She turned round gray eyes on me. "Well, and Bobby. He must have been, mustn't he?"

"I do believe soldiers are inclined—"

"But the Bible," she said, squinting thoughtfully. "It says ye mustna be whoring after idols. Does that mean men went about sticking their pricks into—did the idols look like women, d'ye think?"

"I'm sure that's not what it means, no," I said hastily. "More a metaphor, you know. Er . . . lusting after something, I think it means, not, er . . ."

"Lust," she said thoughtfully. "That's to want something sinful bad, is it not?"

"Yes, rather." Heat was wavering over my skin, dancing in tiny veils. I needed cool air, quickly, or I'd be flushed as a tomato and drenched with sweat. I rose to go out, but felt I really mustn't leave her with the impression that sex had to do only with money or babies—even though it well might, for some women.

"There *is* another reason for intercourse, you know," I said, speaking over my shoulder as I headed for the door. "When you love someone, you want to give them pleasure. And they want to do the same for you."

"Pleasure?" Her voice rose behind me, incredulous. "Ye mean some women *like* it?"

47

Bees and Switches

I was by no means spying. One of my hives had swarmed, and I was looking for the fugitive bees.

New swarms usually didn't travel far, and stopped frequently, often resting for hours in a tree fork or open log, where they formed a ball of humming conference. If they could be located before making up their collective mind about where to settle, they could often be persuaded into a temptingly empty basket hive, and thus hauled back into captivity.

The trouble with bees is that they don't leave footprints. Now I was casting to and fro on the mountainside, nearly a mile from the house, an empty basket hive slung on a rope over my shoulder, trying to follow Jamie's instructions regarding hunting, and think like a bee.

There were huge blooming patches of galax, fire-weed, and other wildflowers on the hillside far above me, but there was a very attractive dead snag—if one was a bee—poking out of the heavy growth some way below.

The basket hive was heavy, and the slope was steep. It was easier to go down than up. I hitched up the rope, which was beginning to rub the skin off my shoulder, and began sidling downward through sumac and hobble-bush, bracing my feet against rocks and grabbing at branches to keep from slipping.

Concentrating on my feet, I didn't take particular notice of where I was. I emerged into a gap in the bushes from which the roof of a cabin was visible, some distance below me. Whose was that? The Christies', I thought. I wiped a sleeve across the sweat dripping from the point of my chin; the day was warm, and I hadn't brought a canteen. Perhaps I would stop and ask for water on the way home.

Making my way at last to the snag, I was disappointed to find no sign of the swarm. I stood still, blotting sweat from my face and listening, in hopes of picking up the bees' telltale deep drone. I heard the hum and whine of assorted flying insects, and the genial racket of a flock of foraging pygmy nuthatches on the slope above—but no bees.

I sighed and turned to make my way around the snag, but then paused, my eye caught by a glimpse of white below.

Thomas Christie and Malva were in the small clearing at the back of their cabin. I had caught the flash of his shirt as he moved, but now he stood motionless, arms crossed.

His attention appeared to be fixed on his daughter, who was cutting branches from one of the mountain ash trees at the side of the clearing. What for? I wondered.

There seemed something very peculiar about the scene, though I couldn't think exactly what. Some attitude of body? Some air of tension between them?

Malva turned and walked toward her father, several long, slender branches in her hand. Her head was bent, her step dragging, and when she handed him the branches, I understood abruptly what was going on.

They were too far away for me to hear them, but he apparently said something to her, gesturing brusquely toward the stump they used as a chopping block. She knelt down by it, bent forward, and lifted up her skirts, exposing her bare buttocks.

Without hesitation, he raised the switches and slashed them hard across her rump, then whipped them back in the other direction, crisscrossing her flesh with vivid lines that I could see even at such a distance. He repeated this several times, whipping the springy twigs back and forth with a measured deliberation whose violence was the more shocking for its lack of apparent emotion.

It hadn't even occurred to me to look away. I stood stock-still in the shrubbery, too stunned even to brush away the gnats that swarmed around my face.

Christie had thrown down the switches, turned on his heel, and gone into the house before I could do more than blink. Malva sat back on her heels and shook down her skirts, smoothing the fabric gingerly over her bottom as she rose. She was red-faced, but not weeping or distraught.

She's used to it. The thought came unbidden. I hesitated, not knowing what to do. Before I could decide, Malva had settled her cap, turned, and walked into the woods with an air of determination—headed straight toward me.

I ducked behind a big tulip poplar, before I was even aware of making a decision. She wasn't injured, and I was sure she wouldn't like to know that anyone had seen the incident.

Malva passed within a few feet of me, puffing a little on the climb, and snorting through her nose and muttering in a way that made me think she was very angry, rather than upset.

I peered cautiously round the poplar, but caught no more than a glimpse of her cap, bobbing through the trees. There were no cabins up there, and she hadn't carried a basket or any tools for foraging. Perhaps she only wanted to be alone, to recover herself. No surprise, if so.

I waited until she was safely out of sight, then made my own way slowly down the slope. I didn't stop at the Christie cabin, thirsty as I was, and had quite lost interest in errant bees.

I met Jamie at a stiled fence, some little distance from home, in conversation with Hiram Crombie. I nodded in greeting, and waited in some impatience for Crombie to finish his business, so I could tell Jamie what I had just witnessed.

Luckily, Hiram showed no inclination to linger; I made him nervous.

I told Jamie at once what I had seen, and was annoyed to find that he didn't share my concern. If Tom Christie thought it necessary to whip his daughter, that was his affair.

"But he might be . . . it might be—perhaps it doesn't stop with a switching. Perhaps he does . . . other things to her."

He shot me a look of surprise.

"Tom? D'ye have any reason to think so?"

"No," I admitted reluctantly. The Christie ménage gave me an uncomfortable feeling, but that was likely only because I didn't get on with Tom. I wasn't so foolish as to think that a tendency toward Bible-thumping meant a person wouldn't engage in wickedness—but in all fairness, it didn't mean he *did*, either. "But surely he shouldn't be whipping her like that—at her age?"

He glanced at me in mild exasperation.

"Ye dinna understand a thing, do ye?" he said, echoing my thought exactly.

"I was about to say just that, to *you,*" I said, giving him look for look. He didn't look away, but held my gaze, his own slowly taking on a wry amusement.

"So it will be different?" he said. "In your world?" There was just enough edge in his voice to remind me forcibly that we were not in my world—nor ever would be. Sudden gooseflesh ran up my arm, lifting the fine blond hairs.

"A man wouldna beat a woman, then, in your time? Not even for good cause?"

And what was I to say to that? I couldn't lie, even if I wanted to; he knew my face much too well.

"Some do," I admitted. "But it's not the same. There—then, I mean—a man who beat his wife would be a criminal. But," I added in fairness, "a man who beat his wife then would most often be using his fists."

A look of astonished disgust crossed his face.

"What sort of man would do that?" he asked incredulously.

"A bad one."

"So I should think, Sassenach. And ye dinna think there's a difference?" he asked. "Ye'd see it the same, if I were to smash your face, rather than only take a tawse to your bum?"

Blood flared abruptly in my cheeks. He once *had* taken a strap to me, and I hadn't forgotten it. I had wanted to kill him at the time—and didn't feel kindly toward him at the memory. At the same time, I wasn't stupid enough to equate his actions with those of a modern-day wife-beater.

He glanced at me, raised one eyebrow, then understood what I was recalling. He grinned.

"Oh," he said.

"Oh, indeed," I said very cross. I had succeeded in putting that extremely humiliating episode out of mind, and didn't at all like having it recalled.

He, on the other hand, was plainly enjoying the recollection. He eyed me in a manner I found grossly insufferable, still grinning.

"God, ye screamed like a *ban-sidhe*."

I began to feel a distinct throbbing of blood in my temples.

"I bloody well had cause to!"

"Oh, aye," he said, and the grin widened. "Ye did. Your own fault, mind," he added.

"*My* f—"

"It was," he said firmly.

"You apologized!" I said completely outraged. "You know you did!"

"No, I didn't. And it was still your fault to begin with," he said, with complete lack of logic. "Ye wouldna have got nearly such a wicked tanning, if ye'd only minded me in the first place, when I told ye to kneel and—"

"Minded you! You think I would have just meekly given in and let you—"

"I've never seen ye do *anything* meek, Sassenach." He took my arm to help me over the stile, but I jerked free, puffing with indignation.

"You beastly *Scot*!" I dropped the hive on the ground at his feet, picked up my skirts, and scrambled over the stile.

"Well, I havena done it again," he protested, behind me. "I promised, aye?"

I whirled round on the other side and glared at him.

"Only because I threatened to cut your heart out if you ever tried!"

"Well, even so. I *could* have—and ye ken that well, Sassenach. Aye?" He'd quit grinning, but there was a distinct glint in his eye.

I took several deep breaths, trying simultaneously to control my annoyance and think of some crushing rejoinder. I failed in both attempts, and with a briefly dignified "Hmph!" turned on my heel.

I heard the rustle of his kilt as he picked up the hive, hopped over the stile, and came after me, catching up within a stride or two. I didn't look at him; my cheeks were still flaming.

The infuriating fact was that I *did* know that. I remembered all too well. He had used his sword belt to such effect that I hadn't been able to sit comfortably for several days—and if he should ever decide to do it again, there was absolutely nothing to stop him.

I was, for the most part, able to ignore the fact that I was legally his property. That didn't alter the fact that it *was* a fact—and he knew it.

"What about Brianna?" I demanded. "Would you feel the same way about it, if young Roger suddenly decided to take his belt or a switch to your daughter?"

He appeared to find something amusing in the notion.

"I think he'd have the devil of a fight on his hands if he tried," he said. "That's a braw wee lassie, no? And she has your notions of what constitutes wifely obedience, I'm afraid. But then," he added, swinging the hive's rope across his shoulder, "ye never ken what goes on in a marriage, do ye? Perhaps she'd be pleased if he tried."

"Pleased?!" I gawked at him in astonishment. "How can you think that any woman would *ever*—"

"Oh, aye? What about my sister?"

I stopped dead in the middle of the path, staring at him.

"What *about* your sister? Surely you aren't telling me—"

"I am." The glint was back, but I didn't think he was joking.

"Ian *beat* her?"

"I do wish ye'd stop calling it that," he said mildly. "It sounds as though Ian took his fists to her, or blackened her eyes. I gave ye a decent skelping, but I didna bloody ye, for God's sake." His eyes flicked briefly toward my face; everything had healed, at least outwardly; the only trace left was a tiny scar through one eyebrow—invisible, unless one parted the hairs there and looked closely. "Neither would Ian."

I was completely flabbergasted to hear this. I had lived in close proximity with Ian and Jenny Murray for months at a time, and had never seen the slightest indication that he possessed a violent nature. For that matter, it was impossible to imagine anyone trying such a thing on Jenny Murray, who had—if such a thing was possible—an even stronger personality than her brother.

"Well, what *did* he do? And why?"

"Well, he'd only take his belt to her now and then," he said, "and only if she made him."

I took a deep breath.

"If she *made* him?" I asked calmly, under the circumstances.

"Well, ye ken Ian," he said, shrugging. "He's no the one to be doing that sort of thing unless Jenny deviled him into it."

"I never saw anything of that sort going on," I said, giving him a hard look.

"Well, she'd scarcely do it in front of ye, would she?"

"And she would, in front of *you*?"

"Well, not precisely, no," he admitted. "But I wasna often in the house, after Culloden. Now and then, though, I'd come down for a visit, and I'd see that she was . . . brewing for something." He rubbed his nose and squinted against the sun, searching for words. "She'd devil him," he said at last, shrugging. "Pick at him over nothing, make wee sarcastic remarks. She'd—" His face cleared a bit, as he came up with a suitable description. "She'd act like a spoilt wee lassie in need of the tawse."

I found this description completely incredible. Jenny Murray had a sharp tongue, and few inhibitions about using it on anyone, her husband included. Ian, the soul of good nature, merely laughed at her. But I simply couldn't countenance the notion of her behaving in the manner described.

"Well, so. I'd seen that a time or two, as I say. And Ian would give her an eye, but held his peace. But then the once, I was out hunting, near sunset, and took a small deer on the hill just behind the broch—ye ken the place?"

I nodded, still feeling stunned.

"It was close enough to carry the carcass to the house without help, so I brought it down to the smoke shed and hung it. There was no one about—I found out later the children had all gone to the market in Broch Mhorda, and the servants with them. So I thought the house was empty altogether, and stepped into the kitchen to find a bite and a cup of buttermilk before I left."

Thinking the house empty, he had been startled by noises in the bedchamber overhead.

"What sort of noises?" I asked, fascinated.

"Well . . . shrieks," he said, shrugging. "And giggling. A bit of shoving and banging, with a stool or some such falling over. If it weren't for the yaffling, I should have thought there were thieves in the house. But I kent it was Jenny's voice, and Ian's, and—" He broke off, his ears going pink at the memory.

"So then . . . there was a bit more—raised voices, like—and then the crack of a belt on a bum, and the sort of skelloch ye could hear across six fields."

He took a deep breath, shrugging.

"Well, I was taken back a bit, and couldna think what to do at once."

I nodded, understanding that, at least.

"I expect it would be a bit of an awkward situation, yes. It . . . er . . . went on, though?"

He nodded. His ears were a deep red by now, and his face flushed, though that might only be from heat.

"Aye, it did." He glanced at me. "Mind, Sassenach, if I'd thought he meant harm to her, I should have been up the stairs in an instant. But . . ." He brushed away an inquisitive bee, shaking his head. "There was—it felt—I canna even think how to say it. It wasna really that Jenny kept laughing, because she didna—but that I felt she wanted to. And Ian . . . well, Ian *was* laughing. Not out loud, I dinna mean; it was just . . . in his voice."

He blew out his breath, and swiped his knuckles along his jaw, wiping sweat.

"I stayed quite frozen there, wi' a bit of pie in my hand, listening. I came to myself only when the flies started lighting in my open mouth, and by that time, they'd . . . ah . . . they were . . . mmphm." He hunched his shoulders, as though his shirt were too tight.

"Making it up, were they?" I asked very dryly.

"I expect so," he replied, rather primly. "I left. Walked all the way to Foyne, and stayed the night with Grannie MacNab." Foyne was a tiny hamlet, some fifteen miles from Lallybroch.

"Why?" I asked.

"Well, I had to," he said logically. "I couldna ignore it, after all. It was either walk about and think of things, or else give in and abuse myself, and I couldna verra well do *that*—it was my own sister, after all."

"You mean to say you can't think and engage in sexual activity at the same time?" I asked, laughing.

"Of course not," he said—thus confirming a long-held private opinion of mine—and gave me a look as though I were crazy. "Can you?"

"I *can*, yes."

He raised one eyebrow, plainly unconvinced.

"Well, I'm not saying I *do,* always," I admitted, "but it's possible. Women are used to doing more than one thing at once—they have to, because of the children. Anyway, go back to Jenny and Ian. Why on earth—"

"Well, I did walk about and think of it," Jamie admitted. "I couldna seem to stop thinking of it, to be honest. Grannie MacNab could see I'd something on my mind, and pestered me over the supper until . . . ah . . . well, until I told her about it."

"Really. What did she say?" I asked, fascinated. I'd known Grannie MacNab, a sprightly old person with a highly forthright manner—and a lot of experience with human weakness.

"She cackled like thorns under a pot," he said, one side of his mouth turning up. "I thought she'd fall into the fire wi' merriment."

Recovered to some extent, though, the old lady had wiped her eyes and explained matters to him, kindly, as though addressing a simpleton.

"She said it was because of Ian's leg," Jamie said, glancing at me to see whether this made sense to me. "She said that such a thing would make no difference to Jenny, but it would to *him*. She said," he added, his color heightening, "that men havena got any idea what women think about bed, but they always think they have, so it causes trouble."

"I knew I liked Grannie MacNab," I murmured. "What else?"

"Well, so. She said it was likely that Jenny was only makin' it clear to Ian—and maybe to herself, as well—that she still thought he was a man, leg or no."

"What? Why?"

"Because, Sassenach," he said, very dryly indeed, "when ye're a man, a good bit of what ye have to do is to draw up lines and fight other folk who come over them. Your enemies, your tenants, your children—your wife. Ye canna always just strike them or take a strap to them, but when ye can, at least it's clear to everyone who's in charge."

"But that's perfectly—" I began, and then broke off, frowning as I considered this.

"And if ye're a man, you're in charge. It's you that keeps order, whether ye like it or not. It's true," he said, then touched my elbow as he nodded toward an opening in the wood. "I'm thirsty. Shall we stop a bit?"

I followed him up a narrow path through the wood to what we called the Green Spring—a bubbling flow of water over pale serpentine stone, set in a cool, shady bowl of surrounding moss. We knelt, splashed our faces, and drank, sighing with grateful relief. Jamie tipped a handful of water down inside his shirt, closing his eyes in bliss. I laughed at him, but unpinned my sweat-soaked kerchief and doused it in the spring, using it to wipe my neck and arms.

The walk to the spring had caused a break in the conversation, and I wasn't sure quite how—or whether—to resume it. Instead, I merely sat quietly in the shade, arms about my knees, idly wriggling my toes in the moss.

Jamie, too, seemed to feel no need of speech for the moment. He leaned comfortably back against a rock, the wet fabric of his shirt plastered to his chest, and we sat still, listening to the wood.

I wasn't sure what to say, but that didn't mean I had stopped thinking about the conversation. In an odd way, I thought I understood what Grannie MacNab had meant—though I wasn't quite sure I agreed with it.

I was thinking more about what Jamie had said, though, regarding a man's responsibility. Was it true? Perhaps it was, though I had never thought of it in that light before. It *was* true that he was a bulwark—not only for me, and for the family, but for the tenants, as well. Was that really how he did it, though? *"Draw up lines, and fight other folk who come over them"?* I rather thought it was.

There were lines between him and me, surely; I could have drawn them on the moss. Which was not to say we did not "come across" each other's lines—we did, frequently, and with varying results. I had my own defenses—and means of enforcement. But he had only beaten me once for crossing his lines, and that was early on. So, had he seen that as a necessary fight? I supposed he had; that was what he was telling me.

But he had been following his own train of thought, which was running on a different track.

"It's verra odd," he said thoughtfully. "Laoghaire drove me mad wi' great regularity, but it never once occurred to me to thrash her."

"Well, how very thoughtless of you," I said, drawing myself up. I disliked hearing him refer to Laoghaire, no matter what the context.

"Oh, it was," he replied seriously, taking no notice of my sarcasm. "I think it was that I didna care enough for her to think of it, let alone do it."

"You didn't care enough to beat her? Wasn't she the lucky one, then?"

He caught the tone of pique in my voice; his eyes sharpened and fixed on my face.

"Not to hurt her," he said. Some new thought came to him; I saw it cross his face.

He smiled a little, got up, and came toward me. He reached down and pulled me to my feet, then took hold of my wrist, which he lifted gently over my head and pinned against the trunk of the pine I had been sitting under, so that I was obliged to lean back flat against it.

"Not to hurt her," he said again, speaking softly. "To own her. I didna want to possess her. You, *mo nighean donn*—you, I would own."

"*Own* me?" I said. "And what, exactly, do you mean by that?"

"What I say." There was still a gleam of humor in his eyes, but his voice was serious. "Ye're mine, Sassenach. And I would do anything I thought I must to make that clear."

"Oh, indeed. Including beating me on a regular basis?"

"No, I wouldna do that." The corner of his mouth lifted slightly, and the pressure of his grip on my trapped wrist increased. His eyes were deep blue, an inch from mine. "I dinna need to—because I *could*, Sassenach—and ye ken that well."

I pulled against his grip, by sheer reflex. I remembered vividly that night in Doonesbury: the feeling of fighting him with all my strength—to no avail whatever. The horrifying feeling of being pinned to the bed, defenseless and exposed, realizing that he could do anything whatever that he liked to me—and would.

I squirmed violently, trying to escape the grip of memory, as much as his grasp on my flesh. I didn't succeed, but did turn my wrist so as to be able to sink my nails into his hand.

He didn't flinch or look away. His other hand touched me lightly—no more than a brush of my earlobe, but that was quite enough. He *could* touch me anywhere—in any way.

Evidently, women *are* capable of experiencing rational thought and sexual arousal simultaneously, because I appeared to be doing precisely that.

My brain was engaged in indignant rebuttal of all kinds of things, including at least half of everything he'd said in the course of the last few minutes.

At the same time, the other end of my spinal cord was not merely shamefully aroused at the thought of physical possession; it was bloody deliriously weak-kneed with desire at the notion, and was causing my hips to sway outward, brushing his.

He was still ignoring the dig of my nails. His other hand came up and took my free hand before I could do anything violent with it; he folded his fingers around mine and held them captive, down at my side.

"If ye asked me, Sassenach, to free ye—" he whispered, "d'ye think I'd do so?"

I took a deep breath; deep enough that my breasts brushed his chest, he stood so close, and realization welled up in me. I stood still, breathing, watching his eyes, and felt my agitation fade slowly away, mutating into a sense of conviction, heavy and warm in the pit of my belly.

I had thought my body swayed in answer to his—and it did. But his moved unconsciously with mine; the rhythm of the pulse I saw in his throat was the pounding of the heartbeat that echoed in my wrist, and the sway of his body followed mine, barely touching, moving scarcely more than the leaves above, sighing on the breeze.

"I wouldn't ask," I whispered. "I'd tell you. And you'd do it. You'd do as I said."

"Would I?" His grip on my wrist was still firm, and his face so close to mine that I felt his smile, rather than saw it.

"Yes," I said. I had stopped pulling at my trapped wrist; instead, I pulled my other hand from his—he made no move to stop me—and brushed a thumb from the lobe of his ear down the side of his neck. He took a short, sharp breath, and a tiny shudder ran through him, stippling his skin with goosebumps in the wake of my touch.

"Yes, you would," I said again very softly. "Because I own you, too . . . man. Don't I?"

His hand released its grip abruptly and slid upward, long fingers intertwining with mine, his palm large and warm and hard against my own.

"Oh, aye," he said, just as softly. "Ye do." He lowered his head the last half-inch and his lips brushed mine, whispering, so that I felt the words as much as heard them.

"And I ken that verra well indeed, *mo nighean donn*."

48

Woodears

Despite his dismissal of her worries, Jamie had promised his wife to look into the matter, and found opportunity to speak with Malva Christie a few days later.

Coming back from Kenny Lindsay's place, he met a snake curled up in the dust of the path before him. It was a largish creature, but gaily striped—not one of the venomous vipers. Still, he couldn't help it; snakes gave him the grue, and he did not wish to pick it up with his hands, nor yet to step over it. It might not be disposed to lunge up his kilt—but then again, it might. For its part, the snake remained stubbornly curled among the leaves, not budging in response to his "Shoo!" or the stamping of his foot.

He took a step to the side, found an alder, and cut a good stick from it, with which he firmly escorted the wee beastie off the path and into the wood. Affronted, the snake writhed off at a good rate of speed into a hobble-bush, and next thing, a loud shriek came from the other side of the bush.

He darted round it to find Malva Christie, making an urgent, though unsuccessful, effort to squash the agitated snake with a large basket.

"It's all right, lass, let him go." He seized her arm, causing a number of mushrooms to cascade out of her basket, and the snake decamped indignantly in search of quieter surroundings.

He crouched and scooped up the mushrooms for her, while she gasped and fanned herself with the end of her apron.

"Oh, thank ye, sir," she said, bosom heaving. "I'm that terrified o' snakes."

"Och, well, that's no but a wee king snake," he said, affecting nonchalance. "Great ratters—or so I'm told."

"Maybe so, but they've a wicked bite." She shuddered briefly.

"Ye've no been bitten, have ye?" He stood up and dumped a final handful of fungus into her basket, and she curtsied in thanks.

"No, sir." She straightened her cap "But Mr. Crombie was. Gully Dornan brought one of those things in a box, to Sunday meeting last, just for mischief, for he kent the text was *For they shall take up poisonous serpents and suffer no harm.* I think he meant to let it out in the midst of the prayin'." She grinned at the telling, clearly reliving the event.

"But Mr. Crombie saw him with the box, and took it from him, not knowing what was in it. Well, so—Gully was shaking of the box, to keep the snake awake, and when Mr. Crombie opened it, the snake came out like a jack-i'-the-box and bit Mr. Crombie on the lip."

Jamie couldn't help smiling in turn.

"Did it, then? I dinna recall hearing about that."

"Well, Mr. Crombie was that furious," she said, trying for tact. "I imagine no one wanted to spread the story, sir, for fear he'd maybe pop with rage."

"Aye, I see," he said dryly. "And that's why he wouldna come to have my wife see to the wound, I suppose."

"Oh, he wouldna do that, sir," she assured him, shaking her head. "Not if he was to have cut off his nose by mistake."

"No?"

She picked up the basket, glancing shyly up at him.

"Well . . . no. Some say may be as your wife's a witch, did ye ken that?"

He felt an unpleasant tightness in his wame, though he was not surprised to hear it.

"She is a Sassenach," he answered, calm. "Folk will always say such things of a stranger, especially a woman." He glanced sideways at her, but her eyes were modestly cast down to the contents of her basket. "Think so yourself, do ye?"

She looked up at that, gray eyes wide.

"Oh, no, sir! Never!"

She spoke with such earnestness that he smiled, despite the seriousness of his errand.

"Well, I suppose ye'd have noticed, so much time as ye spend in her surgery."

"Oh, I should wish nothing but to be just like her, sir!" she assured him, clutching the handle of her basket in worshipful enthusiasm. "She is so kind and lovely, and she kens so much! I want to know all she can teach me, sir."

"Aye, well. She's said often how good it is to have such a pupil as yourself, lass. Ye're a great help to her." He cleared his throat, wondering how best to work round from these cordialities to a rude inquiry as to whether her father was interfering with her. "Ah . . . your Da doesna mind that ye spend so much time with my wife?"

A cloud fell upon her countenance at that, and her long black lashes swept down, hiding the dove-gray eyes.

"Oh. Well. He . . . he doesna say I mustna go."

Jamie made a noncommittal sound in his throat, and gestured her ahead of him back to the path, where he strode along for a bit without further question, allowing her to regain her composure.

"What d'ye think your father will do," he inquired, swishing his stick casually through a patch of toadflax, "once ye've wed and left his house? Is there a woman he might consider? He'd need someone to do for him, I expect."

Her lips tightened at that, to his interest, and a faint flush rose in her cheeks.

"I dinna mean to be wed anytime soon, sir. We'll manage well enough."

Her answer was short enough to cause him to probe a bit.

"No? Surely ye've suitors, lass—the lads swoon after ye in droves; I've seen them."

The flush on her skin bloomed brighter.

"Please, sir, ye'll say no such thing to my faither!"

That rang a small alarm bell in him—but then, she might mean only that Tom Christie was a strict parent, vigilant of his daughter's virtue. And he would have been astonished to the marrow to learn that Christie was soft, indulgent, or in any way delinquent in such responsibilities.

"I shall not," he said mildly. "I was only teasin', lass. Is your father sae fierce, then?"

She did look at him then, very direct.

"Thought ye kent him, sir."

He burst out laughing at that, and after a moment's hesitation, she joined him, with a small titter like the sound of the wee birds in the trees above.

"I do," he said, recovering. "He's a good man, Tom—if a bit dour."

He looked to see the effect of this. Her face was still flushed, but there was a tiny residual smile on her lips. That was good.

"Well, so," he resumed casually, "have ye enough of the woodears there?" He nodded at her basket. "I saw a good many yesterday, up near the Green Spring."

"Oh, did ye?" She glanced up, interested. "Where?"

"I'm headed that way," he said. "Come if ye like, I'll show ye."

They made their way along the Ridge, talking of inconsequent things. He led her now and then back to the subject of her father, and noted that she seemed to have no reservations concerning him—only a prudent regard for his foibles and temper.

"Your brother, then," he said thoughtfully, at one point. "Is he content, d'ye think? Or will he be wanting to leave, maybe go down to the coast? I ken he's no really a farmer at heart, is he?"

She snorted a bit, but shook her head.

"No, sir, that he's not."

"What did he do, then? I mean, he grew up on a plantation, did he not?"

"Oh, no, sir." She looked up at him, surprised. "He grew up in Edinburgh. We both did."

He was taken back a bit at that. It was true, both she and Allan had an educated accent, but he had thought it only that Christie was a schoolmaster, and strict of such things.

"How is that, lass? Tom said he'd married here, in the Colonies."

"Oh, so he did, sir," she assured him hastily. "But his wife was not a bond servant; she went back to Scotland."

"I see," he said mildly, seeing her face grow much pinker and her lips press tight. Tom had said his wife had died—well, and he supposed she had, but in Scotland, after she'd left him. Proud as Christie was, he could hardly wonder that the man hadn't confessed to his wife's desertion. But—

"Is it true, sir, that your grandsire was Lord Lovat? Him they called the Old Fox?"

"Oh, aye," he said, smiling. "I come from a long line of traitors, thieves, and bastards, ken?"

She laughed at that, and very prettily urged him to tell her more of his sordid family history—quite obviously, as a means of avoiding his asking more questions regarding hers.

The "but" lingered in his mind, though, even as they talked, with increasing desultoriness as they climbed through the dark, scented forest.

But. Tom Christie had been arrested two or three days after the Battle of Culloden, and imprisoned for the next ten years, before being transported to America. He did not know Malva's exact age, but he thought she must be eighteen or so—though she often seemed older, her manner was so poised.

She must have been conceived, then, quite soon after Christie's arrival in the Colonies. No great wonder, if the man had seized the first chance he had to marry, after living without a woman for so long. And then the wife had thought better of her bargain, and gone. Christie had told Roger Mac his wife had died of influenza—well, a man had his pride, and God knew Tom Christie had more than most.

But Allan Christie . . . where had *he* come from? The young man was somewhere in his twenties; it was possible that he had been conceived before Culloden. But if so—who was his mother?

"You and your brother," he said abruptly, at the next break in conversation. "Did ye have the same mother?"

"Yes, sir," she said, looking startled.

"Ah," he said, and let the subject drop. Well, now. So

Christie had been wed before Culloden. And then the woman, whoever she was, had come to find him in the Colonies. That argued a high degree of determination and devotion, and made him regard Christie with a good deal more interest. But that devotion had not been proof against the hardships of the Colonies—or else she found Tom so changed by time and circumstance that the devotion had been drowned in disappointment, and she had left again.

He could see that, easily—and felt an unexpected bond of sympathy with Tom Christie. He recalled his own feelings, all too well, when Claire came back to find him. The disbelieving joy of her presence—and the bone-deep fear that she would not recognize the man she had known, in the man who stood before her.

Worse, if she had discovered something that made her flee— and well as he knew Claire, he still was not sure that she would have stayed, if he'd told her at once about his marriage to Laoghaire. For that matter, if Laoghaire hadn't shot him and nearly killed him, Claire might well have run away, and been lost for good. The thought of it was a black pit, gaping at his feet.

Of course, had she gone, he *would* have died, he reflected. And never come to this place and got his land, nor seen his daughter, nor held his grandson in his arms. Come to think, perhaps being nearly killed wasn't always a misfortune—so long as you didn't actually die of it.

"Does your arm trouble ye, sir?" He was jerked back from his thoughts to realize that he was standing like a fool, one hand clutching the spot on his upper arm where Laoghaire's pistol ball had gone through and Malva squinting at him in concern.

"Ah, no," he said hastily, dropping his hand. "A midgie bite. The bittie things are out early. Tell me"—he groped for some neutral topic of conversation—"d'ye like it here in the mountains?"

Inane as the question was, she appeared to consider it seriously.

"It's lonely, sometimes," she said, and glanced into the forest, where falling shafts of sunlight splintered on leaves and needles, shrubs and rocks, filling the air with a shattered green light. "But it *is* . . ." she groped for a word. "Pretty," she said, with a small smile at him, acknowledging the inadequacy of the word.

They had reached the small clearing where the water bubbled out over a ledge of what his daughter said was serpentine—the rock whose soft green gave the spring its name; that, and the thick layer of vivid moss that grew around it.

He gestured to her to kneel and drink first. She did, cupping her hands to her face and closing her eyes in bliss at the taste of the cold, sweet water. She gulped, cupped her hands and drank again, almost greedily. She was very pretty herself, he thought in amusement, and the word was much more appropriate to the wee lassie, with that delicate chin and the lobes of her tender pink ears peeping from her cap, than to the spirit of the mountains. Her mother must have been lovely, he thought—and it was fortunate for the lass that she had not taken much of her father's grim looks, save those gray eyes.

She sat back on her heels, breathing deep, and scooted to the side, nodding at him to kneel and take his turn. The day wasn't hot, but it was a steep climb to the spring, and the cold water went down gratefully.

"I've never seen the Highlands," Malva said, dabbing the end of her kerchief over her wet face. "Some say this place is like it, though. D'ye think so yourself, sir?"

He shook the water from his fingers and wiped the back of his hand across his mouth.

"Something like. Some parts. The Great Glen, and the forest—aye, that's verra like this." He pointed his chin up at the trees surrounding them, murmurous and resin-scented. "But there's nay bracken here. And nay peat, of course. And nay heather; that's the biggest difference."

"Ye hear the stories—of men hiding in the heather. Did ye ever do so yourself, sir?" She dimpled slightly, and he didn't know whether she meant to tease, or was only making conversation.

"Now and then," he said, and smiled at her as he rose, brushing pine needles from his kilt. "Stalking the deer, aye? Here, I'll show ye the woodears."

The fungus grew in thick shelves at the foot of an oak, no more than ten feet from the spring. Some of the things had opened their gills already, begun to darken and curl; the ground nearby was scattered with the spores, a dark brown powder that lay upon the glossy crackle of last year's dry leaves. The fresher fungi were still bright, though, deep orange and meaty.

He left her there with a cordial word, and went back down the narrow trail, wondering about the woman who had loved and left Tom Christie.

49

The Venom of the North Wind

July 1774

B rianna drove the sharp end of the spade into the muddy bank and pulled out a chunk of clay the color of chocolate fudge. She could have done without the reminder of food, she thought, flinging it aside into the current with a grunt. She hitched up her soggy shift and wiped a forearm across her brow. She hadn't eaten since mid-morning, and it was nearly teatime. Not that she meant to stop until supper. Roger was up the mountain, helping Amy McCallum rebuild her chimney stack, and the little boys had gone up to the Big House to be fed bread and butter and honey and generally spoiled by Mrs. Bug. She'd wait to eat; there was too much to do here.

"D'ye need help, lass?"

She squinted, shading her eyes against the sun. Her father was standing on the bank above, viewing her efforts with what looked like amusement.

"Do I *look* like I need help?" she asked irritably, swiping the back of a mud-streaked hand across her jaw.

"Ye do, aye."

He'd been fishing; barefoot and wet to mid-thigh. He laid his rod against a tree and swung the creel from his shoulder, woven reeds creaking with the weight of the catch. Then he grasped a sapling for balance, and started to edge down the slippery bank, bare toes squelching in the mud.

"Wait—take your shirt off!" She realized her mistake an instant too late. A startled look flitted across his face, only for a moment, and then was gone.

"I mean . . . the mud . . ." she said, knowing it was too late. "The washing."

"Oh, aye, to be sure." Without hesitation, he pulled the shirt over his head and turned his back to her, hunting for a convenient branch from which to hang it.

His scars were not really shocking. She'd glimpsed them before, imagined them many times, and the reality was much less vivid. The scars were old, a faint silvered net, moving easily over the shadows of his ribs as he reached upward. He moved naturally. Only the tension in his shoulders suggested otherwise.

Her hand closed involuntarily, feeling for an absent pencil, feeling the stroke of the line that would capture that tiny sense of unease, the jarring note that would draw the observer closer, closer still, wondering what it was about this scene of pastoral grace. . . .

Thou shalt not uncover thy father's nakedness, she thought, and spread her hand flat, pressing it hard against her thigh. But he had turned back and was coming down the bank, eyes on the tangled rushes and protruding stones underfoot.

He slid the last two feet and arrived beside her with a splash, arms flailing to keep his balance. She laughed, as he'd intended, and he smiled. She'd thought for an instant to speak of it, make some apology—but he would not meet her eyes.

"So, then, move it, or go round?" His attention focused on the boulder embedded in the bank, he leaned his weight against it and shoved experimentally.

"*Can* we move it, do you think?" She waded up beside him, retucking the hem of her shift, which she had pulled between her legs and fastened with a belt. "Going round would mean digging another ten feet of ditch."

"That much?" He glanced at her in surprise.

"Yes. I want to cut a notch here, to cut through to that bend—then I can put a small water-wheel here and get a good fall." She leaned past him, pointing downstream. "The next-best place would be down there—see where the banks rise?—but this is better."

"Aye, all right. Wait a bit, then." He made his way back to the bank, scrambled up, and disappeared into the wood, from whence he returned with several stout lengths of fresh oak sapling, still sporting the remnants of their glossy leaves.

"We dinna need to get it out of the creekbed, aye?" he asked. "Only move it a few feet, so ye can cut through the bank beyond it?"

"That's it." Rivulets of sweat, trapped by her thick eyebrows, ran tickling down the sides of her face. She'd been digging for the best part of an hour; her arms ached from heaving shovelsful of heavy mud, and her hands were blistered. With a sense of profound gratitude, she surrendered the spade and stepped back in the creek, stooping to splash cold water on her scratched arms and flushed face.

"Heavy work," her father observed, grunting a little as he briskly finished undermining the boulder. "Could ye not have asked Roger Mac to do it?"

"He's busy," she said, perceiving the shortness of her tone, but not inclined to disguise it.

Her father darted a sharp glance at her, but said no more, merely busying himself with the proper placement of his oak staves. Attracted like iron filings to the magnetism of their grandfather's presence, Jemmy and Germain appeared like magic, loudly wanting to help.

She'd asked them to help, and they'd helped—for a few minutes, before being drawn away by the glimpse of a porcupine high up in the trees. With Jamie in charge, of course, they leaped to the task, madly scooping dirt from the bank with flat bits of wood, giggling, pushing, getting in the way, and stuffing handsful of mud down the back of each other's breeches.

Jamie being Jamie, he ignored the nuisance, merely directing their efforts and finally ordering them out of the creek, so as not to be crushed.

"All right, lass," he said, turning to her. "Take a grip there." The boulder had been loosened from the confining clay, and now protruded from the bank, oak staves thrust into the mud beneath, sticking up on either side, and another behind.

She seized the one he indicated, while he took the other two.

"On the count of three . . . one . . . two . . . heave!"

Jem and Germain, perched above, chimed in, chanting "One . . . two . . . *heave!*" like a small Greek chorus. There was a splinter in her thumb and the wood rasped against the waterlogged creases of her skin, but she felt suddenly like laughing.

"One . . . two . . . *hea*—" With a sudden shift, a swirl of mud, and a cascade of loose dirt from the bank above, the boulder gave way, falling into the stream with a splash that soaked them both to the chest and made both little boys shriek with joy.

Jamie was grinning ear-to-ear and so was she, wet shift and muddy children notwithstanding. The boulder now lay near the opposite bank of the stream, and—just as she had calculated—the diverted current was already eating into the newly created hollow in the near bank, a strong eddy eating away the fine-grained clay in streams and spirals.

"See that?" She nodded at it, dabbing her mud-spattered face on the shoulder of her shift. "I don't know how far it will erode, but if I let it go for a day or two, there won't be much digging left to do."

"Ye kent that would happen?" Her father glanced at her, face alight, and laughed. "Why, ye clever, bonnie wee thing!"

The glow of recognized achievement did quite a bit to dampen her resentment of Roger's absence. The presence of a bottle of cider in Jamie's creel, keeping cold amongst the dead trout, did a lot more. They sat companionably on the bank, passing the bottle back and forth, admiring the industry of the new eddy pool at work.

"This looks like good clay," she observed, leaning forward to scoop a little of the wet stuff out of the crumbling bank. She squeezed it in her hand, letting grayish water run down her arm, and opened her hand to show him how it kept its shape, showing clearly the prints of her fingers.

"Good for your kiln?" he asked, peering dutifully at it.

"Worth a try." She had made several less-than-successful experiments with the kiln so far, producing a succession of malformed plates and bowls, most of which had either exploded in the kiln or shattered immediately upon removal. One or two survivals, deformed and scorched round the edges, had been pressed into dubious service, but it was precious little reward for the effort of stoking the kiln and minding it for days.

What she needed was advice from someone who knew about kilns and making earthenware. But with the strained relations now existent between the Ridge and Salem, she couldn't seek it. It had been awkward enough, her speaking directly to Brother Mordecai about his ceramic processes—a Popish woman, and speaking to a man she wasn't married to, the scandal!

"Damn wee Manfred," her father agreed, hearing her complaint. He'd heard it before, but didn't mention it. He hesitated. "Would it maybe help was I to go and ask? A few o' the Brethren will still speak to me, and it might be that they'd let me talk wi' Mordecai. If ye were to tell me what it is ye need to know . . . ? Ye could maybe write it down."

"Oh, Da, I love you!" Grateful, she leaned to kiss him, and he laughed, clearly gratified to be doing her a service.

Elated, she took another drink of cider, and rosy visions of hardened clay pipes began to dance in her brain. She had a wooden cistern already built, with a lot of complaint and obstruction from Ronnie Sinclair. She needed help to heave that into place. Then, if she could get only twenty feet of reliable pipe . . .

"Mama, come *look*!" Jem's impatient voice cut through the fog of calculation. With a mental sigh, she made a hasty note of where she had been, and pushed the process carefully into a corner of her mind, where it would perhaps helpfully ferment.

She handed the bottle back to her father, and made her way down the bank to where the boys squatted, expecting to be shown frog spawn, a drowned skunk, or some other wonder of nature appealing to small boys.

"What is it?" she called.

"Look, look!" Jemmy spotted her and popped upright, pointing to the rock at his feet.

They were standing on the Flat Rock, a prominent feature of the creek. As the name suggested, it was a flat shelf of granite, large enough for three men to occupy at once, undercut by the water so that it jutted out over the boiling stream. It was a favorite spot for fishing.

Someone had built a small fire; there was a blackened smudge on the rock, with what looked like the remnants of charred sticks in the center. It was much too small for a cooking fire, but still, she would have thought nothing of it. Her father was frowning at the fire site, though, in a way that made her walk out onto the rock and stand beside him, looking.

The objects in the ashes weren't sticks.

"Bones," she said at once, and squatted down to look closer. "What kind of animal are those from?" Even as she said it, her mind was analyzing and rejecting—squirrel, possum, rabbit, deer, pig—unable to make sense of the shapes.

"They're finger bones, lass," he said, lowering his voice as he glanced at Jemmy—who had lost interest in the fire and was now sliding down the muddy bank, to the further detriment of his breeches. "Dinna touch them," he added—unnecessarily, as she had drawn back her hand in instant revulsion.

"From a human, you mean?" Instinctively, she wiped her hand on the side of her thigh, though she had touched nothing.

He nodded, and squatted beside her, studying the charred remains. There were blackened lumps there, too—though she thought these were the remains of some plant material; one was greenish, maybe a stem of something, incompletely burned.

Jamie bent low, sniffing at the burned remains. Instinctively, Brianna drew a deep breath through her nose in imitation—then snorted, trying to get rid of the smell. It was disconcerting: a reek of char, overlaid with something bitter and chalky—and that in turn overlaid with a sort of pungent scent that reminded her of medicine.

"Where could they have come from?" she asked, also low-voiced—though Jemmy and Germain had begun pelting each other with mudballs, and wouldn't have noticed if she'd shouted.

"I havena noticed anyone missing a hand, have you?" Jamie glanced up, giving her a half-smile. She didn't return it.

"Not walking around, no. But if they aren't walking around—" She swallowed, trying to ignore the half-imagined taste of bitter herbs and burning. "Where's the rest? Of the body, I mean."

That word, "body," seemed to bring the whole thing into a new and nasty focus.

"Where's the rest of that finger, I wonder?" Jamie was frowning at the blackened smudge. He moved a knuckle toward it, and she saw what he had seen: a paler smudge within the circle of the fire, where part of the ashes had been swept away. There were three fingers, she saw, still swallowing repeatedly. Two were intact, the bones gray-white and spectral among the ashes. Two joints of the third were gone, though; only the slender last phalanx remained.

"An animal?" She glanced round for traces, but there were no pawprints on the surface of the rock—only the muddy smudges left by the little boys' bare feet.

Vague visions of cannibalism were beginning to stir queasily in the pit of her stomach, though she rejected the notion at once.

"You don't think Ian—" She stopped abruptly.

"Ian?" Her father looked up, astonished. "Why should Ian do such a thing?"

"I don't think he would," she said, taking hold of common sense. "Not at all. It was just a thought—I'd heard that the Iroquois sometimes . . . sometimes . . ." She nodded at the charred bones, unwilling to articulate the thought further. "Um . . . maybe a friend of Ian's? Uh . . . visiting?"

Jamie's face darkened a little, but he shook his head.

"Nay, there's the smell of the Highlands about this. The Iroquois will burn an enemy. Or cut bits off him, to be sure. But not like that." He pointed at the bones with his chin, in the Highland way. "This is a private business, ken? A witch—or one of their shamans, maybe—might do a thing like that; not a warrior."

"I haven't seen any Indians of any kind lately. Not on the Ridge. Have you?"

He looked at the burned smudge a moment longer, frowning, then shook his head.

"No, nor anyone missing a few fingers, either."

"You're *sure* they're human?" She studied the bones, trying for other possibilities. "Maybe from a small bear? Or a big coon?"

"Maybe," he said flatly, but she could tell he said it only for her sake. He was sure.

"Mama!" The patter of bare feet on the rock behind her was succeeded by a tug at her sleeve. "Mama, we're hungry!"

"Of course you are," she said, rising to meet the demand, but still gazing abstractedly at the charred remnants. "You haven't eaten in nearly an hour. What did you—" Her gaze drifted slowly from the fire to her son, then snapped abruptly, focusing on the two little boys, who stood grinning at her, covered from head to foot in mud.

"*Look* at you!" she said, dismay tempered by resignation.

"How could you possibly get that filthy?"

"Oh, it's easy, lass," her father assured her, grinning as he rose to his feet. "Easy cured, too, though." He bent, and seizing Germain by the back of shirt and seat of breeks, heaved him neatly off the rock and into the pool below.

"Me, too, me, too! Me, too, Grandda!" Jemmy was dancing up and down in excitement, spattering clods of mud in all direction.

"Oh, aye. You, too." Jamie bent and grabbed Jem round the waist, launching him high into the air in a flutter of shirt before Brianna could cry out.

"He can't swim!"

This protest coincided with a huge splash, as Jem hit the water and promptly sank like a rock. She was striding toward the edge, prepared to dive in after him, when her father put a hand on her arm to stop her.

"Wait a bit," he said. "How will ye ken whether he swims or not, if ye dinna let him try?"

Germain was already arrowing his way toward shore, his sleek blond head dark with water. Jemmy popped up behind him, though, splashing and spluttering, and Germain dived, turned like an otter, and came up alongside.

"Kick!" he called to Jemmy, churning up a huge spray in illustration. "Go on your back!"

Jemmy ceased flailing, went on his back, and kicked madly. His hair was plastered over his face and the spray of his efforts must have obscured any remnants of vision—but he went on valiantly kicking, to encouraging whoops from Jamie and Germain.

The pool was no more than ten feet across, and he reached the shallows on the opposite bank within seconds, beaching among the rocks by virtue of crashing headfirst into one. He stopped, thrashing feebly in the shallows, then bounced to his feet, showering water, and shoved the wet hair out of his face. He looked amazed.

"I can swim!" he shouted. "Mama, I can *swim*!"

"That's wonderful!" she called, torn between sharing his ecstatic pride, the urge to rush home and tell Roger about it—and dire visions of Jemmy now leaping heedlessly into bottomless ponds and rock-jagged rapids, under the reckless delusion that he could indeed swim. But he'd gotten his feet wet, in no uncertain terms; there was no going back.

"Come here!" She bent toward him, clapping her hands. "Can you swim back to me? Come on, come here!"

He looked blankly at her for an instant, then around him at the rippling water of the pool. The blaze of excitement in his face died.

"I forget," he said, and his mouth curled down, fat with sudden woe. "I forget how!"

"Fall down and kick!" Germain bellowed helpfully, from his perch on the rock. "You can do it, *cousin*!"

Jemmy took one or two blundering steps into the water, but stopped, lip trembling, terror and confusion starting to overwhelm him.

"Stay there, *a chuisle*! I'm coming!" Jamie called, and dove cleanly into the pool, a long pale streak beneath the water, bubbles streaming from hair and breeks. He popped up in front of Jemmy in an explosion of breath and shook his head, flinging strands of wet red hair out of his face.

"Come along then, man," he said, scooting round on his knees in the shallows, so that his back was to Jemmy. He looked back, patting his own shoulder. "Take hold of me here, aye? We'll swim back together."

And they did, kicking and splashing in ungainly dog paddle, Jemmy's shrieks of excitement echoed by Germain, who had leaped into the water to paddle alongside.

Hauled out onto the rock, the three of them lay puddled, gasping and laughing at her feet, water spreading in pools around them.

"Well, you are cleaner," she said judiciously, moving her foot away from a spreading streamlet. "I'll admit that much."

"Of course we are." Jamie sat up, wringing out the long tail of his hair. "It occurs to me, lass, that there's maybe a better way to do what ye want."

"What I w—oh. You mean the water?"

"Aye, that." He sniffed, and rubbed the back of his hand under his nose. "I'll show ye, if ye come up to the house after supper."

"What's that, Grandda?" Jemmy had got to his feet, wet hair standing up in red spikes, and was looking curiously at Jamie's back. He put out a tentative finger and traced one of the long, curving scars.

"What? Oh . . . that." Jamie's face went quite blank for a moment. "It's . . . ah . . ."

"Some bad people hurt Grandda once," she interrupted firmly, bending down to pick Jemmy up. "But that was a long time ago. He's all right now. You weigh a ton!"

"Papa says *Grandpère* is perhaps a silkie," Germain remarked, viewing Jamie's back with interest. "Like his papa before him. Did the bad people find you in your silkie skin, *Grandpère,* and try to cut it from you? He would then of course become a man again," he explained matter-of-factly, looking up at Jemmy, "and could kill them with his sword."

Jamie was staring at Germain. He blinked, and wiped his nose again.

"Oh," he said. "Aye. Um. Aye, I expect that was the way of it. If your papa says so."

"What's a silkie?" asked Jemmy, bewildered but interested. He wiggled in Brianna's arms, wanting to be put down, and she lowered him back to the rock.

"I don't know," Germain admitted. "But they have fur. What's a silkie, *Grandpère*?"

Jamie closed his eyes against the sinking sun, and rubbed a hand over his face, shaking his head a little. Brianna thought he was smiling, but couldn't tell for sure.

"Ah, well," he said, sitting up straighter, opening his eyes, and throwing back his wet hair. "A silkie is a creature who is a man upon the land, but becomes a seal within the sea. And a seal," he added, cutting off Jemmy, who had been opening his mouth to ask, "is a great sleek beastie that barks like a dog, is as big as an ox, and beautiful as the black of night. They live in the sea, but come out onto the rocks near the shore sometimes."

"Have you seen them, *Grandpère*?" Germain asked, eager.

"Oh, many a time," Jamie assured him. "There are a great many seals who live on the coasts of Scotland."

"Scotland," Jemmy echoed. His eyes were round.

"*Ma mère* says Scotland is a good place," Germain remarked. "She cries sometimes, when she talks of it. I am not so sure I would like it, though."

"Why not?" Brianna asked.

"It's full of giants and water horses and . . . things," Germain replied, frowning. "I don't want to meet any of those. And parritch, *Maman* says, but we have parritch here."

"So we have. And I expect it's time we were going home to eat some." Jamie got to his feet and stretched, groaning in the pleasure of it. The late-afternoon sun washed rock and water with a golden light, gleaming on the boys' cheeks and the bright hairs on her father's arms.

Jemmy stretched and groaned, too, in worshipful imitation, and Jamie laughed.

"Come on, wee fishie. D'ye want a ride home?" He bent so that Jemmy could scramble onto his back, then straightened up, settling the little boy's weight, and put out a hand to take Germain's.

Jamie saw her attention turn momentarily back toward the blackened smudge at the edge of the rock.

"Leave it, lass," he said quietly. "It's a charm of some kind. Ye dinna want to touch it."

Then he stepped off the rock and made for the trail, Jemmy on his back and Germain clutched firmly by the back of the neck, both boys giggling as they made their way through the slippery mud of the path.

Brianna retrieved her spade and Jamie's shirt from the creekbank, and caught the boys up on the trail to the Big House. A breeze had begun to breathe through the trees, chilly in the damp cloth of her shift, but the heat of walking was enough to keep her from being cold.

Germain was singing softly to himself, still hand-in-hand with his grandfather, his small blond head tilting back and forth like a metronome.

Jemmy sighed in exhausted bliss, legs wrapped round Jamie's middle, arms about his neck, and leaned his sun-reddened cheek against the scarred back. Then he thought of something, for he raised his head and kissed his grandfather with a loud smacking noise, between the shoulder blades.

Her father jerked, nearly dropping Jem, and made a high-pitched noise that made her laugh.

"Is that make it better?" Jem inquired seriously, pulling himself up and trying to look over Jamie's shoulder into his face.

"Oh. Aye, lad," his grandfather assured him, face twitching. "Much better."

The gnats and midges were out in force now. She beat a cloud of them away from her face, and slapped a mosquito that lit on Germain's neck.

"Ak!" he said, hunching his shoulders, but then resumed singing "Alouette," undisturbed.

Jemmy's shirt was thin, worn linen, cut down from one of Roger's old ones. The cloth had dried to the shape of his body, square-rumped and solid, the breadth of his small, tender shoulders echoing the wide set of the older, firmer ones he clung to. She glanced from the redheads to Germain, walking reed-thin and graceful through shadows and light, still singing, and thought how desperately beautiful men were.

"Who were the bad people, Grandda?" Jemmy asked drowsily, head nodding with the rhythm of Jamie's steps.

"Sassunaich," Jamie replied briefly. "English soldiers."

"English *canaille,*" Germain amplified, breaking off his song. "They are the ones who cut off my papa's hand, too."

"They were?" Jemmy's head lifted in momentary attention, then fell back between Jamie's shoulder blades with a thump that made his grandfather grunt. "Did you kill them with your sword, Grandda?"

"Some of them."

"I will kill the rest, when I am big," Germain declared. "If there are any left."

"I suppose there might be." Jamie hitched Jem's weight a little higher, letting go Germain's hand in order to hold Jemmy's slackening legs tight to his body.

"Me, too," Jemmy murmured, eyelids drooping. "I'll kill them, too."

At the fork in the trail, Jamie surrendered her son to her, sound asleep, and took back his shirt. He pulled it on, brushing disheveled hair out of his face as his head came through. He smiled at her, then leaned forward and kissed her forehead, gently, putting one hand on Jemmy's round, red head where it lay against her shoulder.

"Dinna fash yourself, lass," he said softly. "I'll speak to Mordecai. And your man. Take care of this one."

"This is a private business," her father had said. The general implication being that she should leave it alone. And she might have, save for a couple of things. One, that Roger had come

home well after dark, whistling a song he said Amy McCallum had taught him. And two, that other offhand remark her father had made about the fire on the Flat Rock—that there was a smell of the Highlands about it.

Brianna had a very keen nose, and she smelled a rat. She also had recognized—belatedly—what had made Jamie say what he had. The odd smell of the fire, that tang of medicine—it was iodine; the smell of burned seaweed. She'd smelled a fire built of sea wrack on the shore near Ullapool, in her own time, when Roger had taken her up there for a picnic.

There was certainly seaweed on the coast, and it wasn't impossible that someone, sometime, had brought some inland. But it also wasn't impossible that some of the fisher-folk had brought bits of it from Scotland, in the way that some exiles might bring earth in jar, or a handful of pebbles to remind them of the land left behind.

A charm, her father had said. And the song Roger had learned from Amy McCallum was called "The Deasil Charm," he said.

All of which was no particular evidence of anything. Still, she mentioned the small fire and its contents to Mrs. Bug, just from curiosity. Mrs. Bug knew a good deal about Highland charms of all sorts.

Mrs. Bug frowned thoughtfully at her description, lips pursed.

"Bones, ye say? What sort—the bones of an animal, were they, or a man?"

Brianna felt as though someone had dropped a slug down her back.

"A man?"

"Oh, aye. There's some charms that take grave dust, ken, and some the dust of bones, or the ashes of a body." Evidently reminded by the mention of ashes, Mrs. Bug pulled a big pottery mixing bowl from the warm ashes of the hearth, and peered into it. The bread starter had died a few days before, and the bowl of flour, water, and honey had been set out in hopes of snaring a wild yeast from the passing air.

The round little Scotswoman frowned at the bowl, shook her head, and put it back with a brief muttered verse in Gaelic. Naturally, Brianna thought, slightly amused, there *would* be a prayer for catching yeast. Which patron saint was in charge of that?

"What ye said, though," Mrs. Bug said, returning both to her chopping of turnips and to the original subject of conversation. "About it bein' on the Flat Rock. Seaweed, bones, and a flat rock. That's a love charm, lass. The one they call the Venom o' the North Wind."

"What a really peculiar name for a love charm," she said, staring at Mrs. Bug, who laughed.

"Och, now, do I remember it at all?" she asked rhetorically. She wiped her hands upon her apron, and folding them at her waist with a vaguely theatrical air, recited:

> *"A love charm for thee,*
> *Water drawn through a straw,*
> *The warmth of him thou lovest,*
> *With love to draw on thee.*
>
> *"Arise betimes on Lord's day,*
> *To the flat rock of the shore*
> *Take with thee the butterbur*
> *And the foxglove.*
>
> *"A small quantity of embers*
> *In the skirt of thy kirtle,*
> *A special handful of seaweed*
> *In a wooden shovel.*
>
> *"Three bones of an old man,*
> *Newly torn from the grave,*
> *Nine stalks of royal fern,*
> *Newly trimmed with an ax.*
>
> *"Burn them on a fire of faggots*
> *And make them all into ashes;*
> *Sprinkle in the fleshy breast of thy lover,*
> *Against the venom of the north wind.*
>
> *"Go round the rath of procreation,*
> *The circuit of the five turns,*
> *And I will vow and warrant thee*
> *That man shall never leave thee."*

Mrs. Bug unfolded her hands and took another turnip, quartering it with neat, quick chops and tossing the pieces into the pot. "Ye're not wanting such a thing yourself, I hope?"

"No," Brianna murmured, feeling the small cold feeling continue down her back. "Do you think—would the fisher-folk use a charm like that?"

"Well, as to that, I canna say *what* they'd do—but surely a few would ken that charm; it's weel enough known, though I havena kent anyone myself has done it. There are easier ways to make a lad fall in love wi' ye, lass," she added, pointing a stubby finger at Brianna in admonition. "Cook him up a nice plate o' neeps boiled in milk and served wi' butter, for one."

"I'll remember," Brianna promised, smiling, and excused herself.

She had meant to go home; there were dozens of things needing to be done, from spinning yarn and weaving cloth, to plucking and drawing the half dozen dead geese she had shot and hung in the lean-to. But instead she found her footsteps turning up the hill, along the overgrown trail that led to the graveyard.

Surely it wasn't Amy McCallum who'd made that charm, she thought. It would have taken her hours to walk down the mountain from her cabin, and her with a small baby to tend. But babies could be carried. And no one would know whether she had left her cabin, save perhaps Aidan—and Aidan didn't talk to anyone but Roger, whom he worshipped.

The sun was nearly down, and the tiny cemetery had a melancholy look to it, long shadows from its sheltering trees slanting cold and dark across the needle-strewn ground and the small collection of crude markers, cairns, and wooden crosses. The pines and hemlocks murmured uneasily overhead in the rising breeze of evening.

The sense of cold had spread from her backbone, making a wide patch between her shoulder blades. Seeing the earth grubbed up beneath the wooden marker with *Ephraim* on it didn't help.

50

Sharp Edges

He should have known better. *Did* know better. But what could he have done? Much more important, what was he to do now?

Roger made his way slowly up the mountainside, nearly oblivious to its beauty. Nearly, but not quite. Desolate in the bleakness of winter, the secluded notch where Amy McCallum's ramshackle cabin perched among the laurels was a blaze of color and life in spring and summer—so vivid that even his worry couldn't stop his noticing the blaze of pinks and reds, interrupted by soft patches of creamy dogwood and carpets of bluets, their tiny blue flowers nodding on slender stems above the torrent of the stream that bounded down beside the rocky trail.

They must have chosen the site in summer, he reflected cynically. It would have seemed charming then. He hadn't known Orem McCallum, but plainly the man hadn't been any more practical than his wife, or they would have realized the dangers of their remoteness.

The present situation wasn't Amy's fault, though; he shouldn't blame her for his own lack of judgment.

He didn't precisely blame himself, either—but he should have noticed sooner what was going on; what was being said.

"Everybody kens ye spend more time up at the notch wi' the widow McCallum than ye do with your own wife."

That's what Malva Christie had said, her little pointed chin raised in defiance. *"Tell my father, and I'll tell everyone I've seen you kiss Amy McCallum. They'll all believe me."*

He felt an echo of the astonishment he'd felt at her words—an astonishment succeeded by anger. At the girl and her silly threat, but much more at himself.

He'd been working at the whisky clearing and, heading back to the cabin for dinner, had rounded a turn in the trail and surprised the two of them, Malva and Bobby Higgins, locked in an embrace. They'd sprung apart like a pair of startled deer, eyes wide, so alarmed as to be funny.

He'd smiled, but before he could either apologize or fade tactfully into the underbrush, Malva had stepped up to him, eyes still wide, but blazing with determination.

"Tell my father," she'd said, *"and I'll tell everyone I've seen you kiss Amy McCallum."*

He'd been so taken aback by her words that he'd scarcely noticed Bobby, until the young soldier had put a hand on her arm, murmuring something to her, drawing her away. She'd turned reluctantly, with a last, wary, meaningful glance at Roger, and a parting shot that left him staggered.

"Everybody kens ye spend more time up at the notch wi' the widow McCallum than ye do with your own wife. They'll all believe me."

God damn it, they would, too, and it was his own bloody fault. Bar one or two sarcastic remarks, Bree hadn't protested his visits; she'd accepted—or seemed to—that *someone* had to go now and then to see the McCallums, make sure they had food and fire, provide a few moments' company, a small respite in the monotony of loneliness and labor.

He'd done such things often, going with the Reverend to call on the aged, the widowed, the ill of the congregation; take them food, stop for a bit to talk—to listen. It was just what you *did* for a neighbor, he told himself; a normal kindness.

But he should have taken more notice. Now he recalled Jamie's thoughtful glance over the supper table, the breath taken as though to say something, when Roger had asked Claire for a salve for wee Orrie McCallum's rash—and then Claire's glance at Brianna, and Jamie's closing his mouth, whatever he'd thought of saying left unspoken.

"They'll all believe me." For the girl to have said that, there must have been talk already. Likely Jamie had heard it; he could only hope that Bree hadn't.

The crooked chimney came in sight above the laurels, the

smoke a nearly transparent wisp that made the clear air above the rooftree seem to quiver, as though the cabin were enchanted, might vanish with a blink.

The worst of it was that he knew precisely how it had happened. He had a weakness for young mothers, a terrible tenderness toward them, a desire to take care of them. The fact that he knew exactly *why* he harbored such an urge—the memory of his own young mother, who had died saving his life during the Blitz—didn't help.

It was a tenderness that had nearly cost him his life at Alamance, when that bloody-minded fool William Buccleigh MacKenzie had mistaken Roger's concern for Morag MacKenzie for . . . well, all right, he'd kissed her, but only on the forehead, and for God's sake, she was his own many-times-great-grannie . . . and the thundering idiocy of nearly being killed by your own great-great-etc.-grandfather for molesting his wife . . . it had cost him his voice, and he should have learned his lesson, but he hadn't, not well enough.

Suddenly furious with himself—and with Malva Christie, the malicious little chit—he picked up a stone from the trail and flung it down the mountain, into the stream. It struck another in the water, bounced twice, and vanished into the rushing gurgle.

His visits to the McCallums had to stop, at once. He saw that clearly. Another way would have to be found for them . . . but he had to come once more, to explain. Amy would understand, he thought—but how to explain to Aidan what reputation was, and why gossip was a deadly sin, and why Roger couldn't come anymore to fish or show him how to build things. . . .

Cursing steadily under his breath, he made the last short, steep ascent and came into the ragged, overgrown little dooryard. Before he could call out to announce his presence, though, the door flew open.

"Roger Mac!" Amy McCallum half-fell down the step and into his arms, gasping and weeping. "Oh, you came, you came! I prayed for someone to come, but I didna think anyone would, in time, and he'd die, but ye've come, God be thankit!"

"What is it? What's wrong? Is wee Orrie taken sick?" He got hold of her arms, steadying her, and she shook her head, so violently that her cap slid half off.

"Aidan," she gasped. "It's Aidan."

Aidan McCallum lay doubled up on my surgery table, white as a sheet, making little gasping groans. My first hope—green apples or gooseberries—vanished with a closer look at him. I was fairly sure what I had here, but appendicitis shares symptoms with a number of other conditions. A classic case does, however, have one striking aspect.

"Can you unfold him, just for a moment?" I looked at his mother, hovering over him on the verge of tears, but it was Roger who nodded and came to put his hands on Aidan's knees and shoulders, gently persuading him to lie flat.

I put a thumb in his navel, my little finger on his right hipbone, and pressed his abdomen sharply with my middle finger, wondering for a second as I did so whether McBurney had yet discovered and named this diagnostic spot. Pain in McBurney's Spot was a specific diagnostic symptom for acute appendicitis. I pressed Aidan's stomach there, then I released the pressure, he screamed, arched up off the table, and doubled up like a jackknife.

A hot appendix for sure. I'd known I'd encounter one sometime. And with a mixed sense of dismay and excitement, I realized that the time had come for me finally to use the ether. No doubt about it, and no choice; if the appendix wasn't removed, it would rupture.

I glanced up; Roger was supporting little Mrs. McCallum with a hand under her elbow; she clutched the baby close to her chest, wrapped in its bundle. She'd need to stay; Aidan would need her.

"Roger—get Lizzie to come mind the baby, will you? And then run as fast as you can to the Christies'; I'll need Malva to come and help."

The most extraordinary expression flitted across his face; I couldn't interpret it, but it was gone in an instant, and I didn't have time to worry about it. He nodded and left without a word, and I turned my attention to Mrs. McCallum, asking her the questions I needed answered before I cut into her small son's belly.

It was Allan Christie who opened the door to Roger's brusque knock. A darker, leaner version of his owl-faced father, he blinked slowly at the question as to Malva's whereabouts.

"Why . . . she's gone to the stream," he said. "Gathering rushes, she said." He frowned. "Why do ye want her?"

"Mrs. Fraser needs her to come and help with—with something." Something moved inside; the back door opening. Tom Christie came in, a book in his hand, the page he'd been reading caught between two fingers.

"MacKenzie," he said, with a short jerk of the head in acknowledgment. "Did ye say Mrs. Fraser is wanting Malva? Why?" He frowned as well, the two Christies looking exactly like a pair of barn owls contemplating a questionable mouse.

"Only that wee Aidan McCallum's taken badly, and she'd be glad of Malva's help. I'll go and find her."

Christie's frown deepened, and he opened his mouth to speak, but Roger had already turned, hurrying into the trees before either of them could stop him.

He found her fairly quickly, though every moment spent searching seemed an eternity. How long did it take an appendix to burst? She was knee-deep in the stream, skirts kirtled high and her rush basket floating beside her, tethered by an apron string. She didn't hear him at first, deafened by the flow of the water. When he called her name more loudly, her head jerked up in alarm, and she raised the rush knife, gripped tightly in her hand.

The look of alarm faded when she saw who it was, though she kept a wary eye on him—and a good grip on the knife, he saw. His summons was received with a flash of interest.

"The ether? Really, she's going to cut him?" she asked eagerly, wading toward him.

"Yes. Come on; I've already told your father Mrs. Fraser needs you. We needn't stop."

Her face changed at that.

"Ye told him?" Her brow creased for a moment. Then she bit her lip and shook her head.

"I can't," she said, raising her voice above the sound of the stream.

"Yes, ye can," he said, as encouragingly as possible, and stretched out a hand to help her. "Come on; I'll give ye a hand with your things."

She shook her head more decidedly, pink lower lip poking out a bit.

"No. My father—he'll no have it." She glanced in the direction of the cabin, and he turned to look, but it was all right; neither Allan nor Tom had followed him. Yet.

He kicked off his shoes and stepped into the icy creek, the stones rolling, hard and slippery under his feet. Malva's eyes widened and her mouth fell open as he bent and grabbed her basket, ripped it from her apron string, and tossed it onto the bank. Then he took the knife from her hand, thrust it through his belt, grabbed her round the waist, and picking her up, splashed ashore with her, disregarding the kicking and squealing.

"You're coming with me," he said, grunting as he set her down. "Ye want to walk, or do I carry you?"

He thought she seemed more intrigued than horrified at this proposal, but she shook her head again, backing away from him.

"I can't—truly! He'll—he'll beat me if he finds out I've been meddling wi' the ether."

That checked him momentarily. Would he? Perhaps. But Aidan's life was at stake.

"He won't find out, then," he said. "Or if he does, I'll see to it that he does ye no harm. Come, for God's sake—there's no time to be wasting!"

Her small pink mouth compressed itself in stubbornness. No time for scruples, then. He leaned down to bring his face close to hers and stared her in the eye.

"You'll come," he said, fists curling, "or I tell your father and your brother about you and Bobby Higgins. Say what ye like about me—I don't care. But if ye think your father would beat you for helping Mrs. Fraser, what's he likely to do if he hears ye've been snogging Bobby?"

He didn't know what the eighteenth-century equivalent of snogging was, but plainly she understood him. And if she'd been anywhere near his own size, she would have knocked him down, if he read the dangerous light in those big gray eyes correctly.

But she wasn't, and after an instant's consideration, she bent, dried her legs on her skirts, and shuffled hurriedly into her sandals.

"Leave it," she said briefly, seeing him stoop for the basket. "And give me back my knife."

It might have been simply an urge to keep some influence over her until she was safely in the surgery—surely he wasn't afraid of her. He put a hand to the knife at his belt, though, and said, "Later. When it's done."

She didn't bother arguing, but scampered up the bank ahead of him and headed for the Big House, the soles of her sandals flapping against her bare heels.

I had my fingers on the brachial pulse in Aidan's armpit, counting. His skin was very hot to the touch, maybe a temperature of 101, 102. The pulse was strong, though rapid . . . slowing as he went further under. I could feel Malva counting under her breath, so many drops of ether, so long a pause before the next . . . I lost my own count of the pulse, but it didn't matter; I was taking it into myself, feeling my own pulse begin to beat in the same rhythm, and it was normal, steady.

He was breathing well. The little abdomen rose and fell slightly under my hand, and I could feel the muscles relaxing by the moment, everything except the tense, distended belly, the visible ribs arching high above it as he breathed. I had the sudden illusion that I could push my hand straight through the wall of his abdomen and touch the swollen appendix, could see it in my mind, throbbing malignantly in the dark security of its sealed world. Time, then.

Mrs. McCallum made a small sound when I took up the scalpel, a louder one when I pressed it down into the pale flesh, still gleaming wet with the alcohol I'd swabbed it with, like a fish's belly yielding to the gutting knife.

The skin parted easily, blood welling in that odd, magical way, seeming to appear from nowhere. He had almost no fat beneath it; the muscles were right there, dark red, resilient to the touch. There were other people in the room; I felt them vaguely. I had no attention to spare, though. Every sense I had was focused on the small body under my hands. Someone stood at my shoulder, though— Bree?

"Give me a retractor—yes, that thing." Yes, it was Bree; a long-fingered hand, wet with disinfectant, picked up the claw-shaped thing and put it in my waiting left hand. I missed the services of a good surgical nurse, but we'd manage.

"Hold that, just there." I nosed the blade between the muscle fibers, splitting them easily, and then pinched up the thick soft gleam of the peritoneum, lifted it and sliced it.

His innards were very warm, sucking wet around two probing fingers. Soft squish of intestine, small half-firm lumps of matter felt through their walls, the brush of bone against my knuckle—he was so small, there wasn't much room to feel around. I had my eyes closed, concentrating on touch alone. The cecum *had* to be right under my fingers, that was the curve of the large intestine I could feel, inert but live, like a sleeping snake. Behind? Below? I probed carefully, opened my eyes, and peered closely into the wound. He wasn't bleeding badly, but the wound was still awash. Ought I take the time to cauterize the small bleeders? I glanced at Malva; she was frowning in concentration, her lips moving silently, counting—and she had one hand on the pulse in his neck, keeping track.

"Cautery iron—a small one." A moment's pause; with the flammability of ether in mind, I had doused the hearth and put the brazier across the hall, in Jamie's study. Bree was quick, though; I had it in my hand in seconds. A wisp of smoke rose from his belly and the sizzle of seared flesh struck into the thick warm smell of blood. I glanced up to hand the iron back to Bree, and saw Mrs. McCallum's face, all eyes, staring.

I blotted away the blood with a handful of lint, looked again—my fingers were still holding what I thought . . . all right.

"All right," I said out loud, triumphant. "Got you!" Very carefully, I hooked a finger under the curve of the cecum and pulled a section of it up through the wound, the inflamed appendix sticking out from it like an angry fat worm, purple with inflammation.

"Ligature."

I had it now. I could see the membrane down the side of the appendix and the blood vessels feeding it. Those had to be tied off first; then I could tie off the appendix itself and cut it away. Difficult only because of the small size, but no real problem . . .

The room was so still, I could hear the tiny hisses and pops from the charcoal in the brazier across the hall. Sweat was running down behind my ears, between my breasts, and I became dimly aware that my teeth were sunk in my lower lip.

"Forceps." I pulled the purse-string stitch tight, and taking the forceps, poked the tied-off stump of the appendix neatly up into the cecum. I pressed this firmly back into his belly and took a breath.

"How long, Malva?"

"A bit more than ten minutes, ma'am. He's all right." She took her eyes off the ether mask long enough to dart a quick smile at me, then took up the dropping bottle, lips resuming her silent count.

Closing up was quick. I painted the sutured wound with a thick layer of honey, wrapped a bandage tightly round his body, tucked warm blankets over him and breathed.

"Take off the mask," I said to Malva, straightening up. She made no reply, and I looked at her. She had raised the mask, was holding it in both hands before her, like a shield. But she wasn't watching Aidan anymore; her eyes were fixed on her father, standing rigid in the doorway.

Tom Christie looked back and forth from the small naked body on the table to his daughter. She took an uncertain step back, still clutching the ether mask. His head twisted, piercing me with a fierce gray look.

"What's to do here?" he demanded. "What are ye doing to that child?"

"Saving his life," I replied tartly. I was still vibrating from the intensity of the surgery, and in no mood for rannygazoo. "Did you want something?"

Christie's thin lips pressed tight, but before he could reply, his son, Allan, pushed his way past into the room, and reaching his sister in a couple of strides, grabbed her by the wrist.

"Come away, ye wee gomerel," he said roughly, jerking at her. "Ye've no business here."

"Let go of her." Roger spoke sharply, and took hold of Allan's shoulder, to pull him away. Allan whirled on his heel and punched Roger in the stomach, short and sharp. Roger made a hollow crowing noise, but didn't crumple. Instead, he slugged Allan Christie in the jaw. Allan reeled backward, knocking over the little table of instruments—blades and retractors clattered over the floor in a swash of falling metal, and the jar of catgut ligatures in alcohol smashed on the boards, spraying glass and liquid everywhere.

A soft thump from the floor made me look down. Amy McCallum, overcome by ether fumes and emotion, had passed out.

I hadn't time to do anything about that; Allan bounced back with a wild swing, Roger ducked, caught the rush of the younger Christie's body, and the two of them staggered backward, hit the sill, and fell out of the open window, entangled.

Tom Christie made a low growling noise and hurried toward the window. Malva, seizing her chance, ran out the door; I heard her footsteps pattering hastily down the hall toward the kitchen—and, presumably, the back door.

"What on *earth* . . . ?" Bree said, looking at me.

"Don't look at me," I said, shaking my head. "I have *no* idea." Which was true; I did, however, have a sinking feeling that my involving Malva in the operation had a lot to do with it. Tom Christie and I had reached something like rapprochement, following my operation on his hand—but that didn't mean he had altered his views on the ungodliness of ether.

Bree drew herself abruptly upright, stiffening. A certain amount of grunting, gasping, and incoherent half-insults outside indicated that the fight was continuing—but Allan Christie's raised voice had just called Roger an adulterer.

Brianna glanced sharply at the huddled form of Amy McCallum, and I said a very bad word to myself. I'd heard a few sidelong remarks about Roger's visits to the McCallums—and Jamie had come close to saying something to Roger about it, but I had dissuaded him from interfering, telling him that I'd take up the matter tactfully with Bree. I hadn't had the chance, though, and now—

With a last unfriendly look at Amy McCallum, Bree strode out the door, plainly intending to take a hand in the fight. I clutched my brow and must have moaned, for Tom Christie turned sharply from the window.

"Are ye ill, mistress?"

"No," I said, a little wanly. "Just . . . look, Tom. I'm sorry if I've caused trouble, asking Malva to help me. She has a real gift for healing, I think—but I didn't mean to persuade her into doing something you didn't approve of."

He gave me a bleak look, which he then transferred to Aidan's slack body. The look sharpened suddenly.

"Is that child dead?" he asked.

"No, no," I said. "I gave him ether; he's just gone aslee—"

My voice dried in my throat, as I noticed that Aidan had chosen this inconvenient moment to stop breathing.

With an incoherent cry, I shoved Tom Christie out of the way and fell on Aidan, gluing my mouth over his and pressing the heel of my hand hard in the center of his chest.

The ether in his lungs flowed over my face as I took my mouth away, making my head swim. I gripped the edge of the table hard with my free hand, putting my mouth back on his. I could *not* black out, I couldn't.

My vision swam and the room seemed to be revolving slowly round me. I clung doggedly to consciousness, though, urgently blowing into his lungs, feeling the tiny chest under my hand rise gently, then fall.

It couldn't have been more than a minute, but a minute filled with nightmare, everything spinning round me, the feel of Aidan's flesh the only solid anchor in a whirl of chaos. Amy McCallum stirred on the floor beside me, rose swaying to her knees—then fell on me with a shriek, pulling at me, trying to get me off her son. I heard Tom Christie's voice, raised in command, trying to calm her; he must have pulled her away, for suddenly her grip on my leg was gone.

I blew into Aidan once more—and this time, the chest under my hand twitched. He coughed, choked, coughed again, and started simultaneously to breathe and to cry. I stood up, head spinning, and had to hold on to the table to avoid falling.

I saw a pair of figures before me, black, distorted, with gaping mouths that opened toward me, filled with sharp fangs. I blinked, staggering, and took deep gulps of air. Blinked again, and the figures resolved themselves into Tom Christie and Amy McCallum. He was holding her round the waist, keeping her back.

"It's all right," I said, my own voice sounding strange and far off. "He's all right. Let her come to him."

She flung herself at Aidan with a sob, pulling him into her arms. Tom Christie and I stood staring at each other over the wreckage. Outside, everything had gone quiet.

"Did ye just raise that child from the dead?" he asked. His voice was almost conversational, though his feathery brows arched high.

I wiped a hand across my mouth, still tasting the sickly sweetness of the ether.

"I suppose so," I said.

"Oh."

He stared at me, blank-faced. The room reeked of alcohol, and it seemed to sear my nasal lining. My eyes were watering a little; I wiped them on my apron. Finally, he nodded, as though to himself, and turned to go.

I had to see to Aidan and his mother. But I couldn't let him go without trying to mend things for Malva, so far as I could.

"Tom—Mr. Christie." I hurried after him, and caught him by the sleeve. He turned, surprised and frowning.

"Malva. It's my fault; I sent Roger to bring her. You won't—" I hesitated, but couldn't think of any tactful way to put it. "You won't punish her, will you?"

The frown deepened momentarily, then lifted. He shook his head, very slightly, and with a small bow, detached his sleeve from my hand.

"Your servant, Mrs. Fraser," he said quietly, and with a last glance at Aidan—presently demanding food—he left.

Brianna dabbed the wet corner of a handkerchief at Roger's lower lip, split on one side, swollen and bleeding from the impact of some part of Allan Christie.

"It's my fault," he said, for the third time. "I should have thought of something sensible to tell them."

"Shut up," she said, beginning to lose her precarious grip on her patience. "If you keep talking, it won't stop bleeding." It was the first thing she'd said to him since the fight.

With a mumbled apology, he took the handkerchief from her and pressed it to his mouth. Unable to keep still, though, he got up and went to the open door of the cabin, looking out.

"He's not still hanging around, is he? Allan?" She came to look over his shoulder. "If he is, leave him alone. I'll go—"

"No, he's not," Roger interrupted her. Hand still pressed to his mouth, he nodded toward the Big House, at the far end of the sloped clearing. "It's Tom."

Sure enough, Tom Christie was standing on the stoop. Just standing, apparently deep in thought. As they watched, he shook his head like a dog shedding water, and set off with decision in the direction of his own place.

"I'll go and talk to him." Roger tossed the handkerchief at the table.

"Oh, no, you won't." She grabbed him by the arm as he turned toward the door. "You stay out of it, Roger!"

"I'm not going to fight him," he said, patting her hand in what he plainly thought a reassuring manner. "But I've got to talk to him."

"No, you don't." She tightened her grip on his arm, and pulled, trying to bring him back to the hearth. "You'll just make it worse. Leave them alone."

"No, I won't," he said, irritation beginning to show on his face. "What do ye mean, I'll make it worse? What d'ye think I am?"

That wasn't a question she wanted to answer right this minute. Vibrating with emotion from the tension of Aidan's surgery, the explosion of the fight, and the niggling bur of Allan's shouted insult, she barely trusted herself to speak, let alone be tactful.

"Don't go," she repeated, forcing herself to lower her voice, speak calmly. "Everyone's upset. At least wait until they've settled down. Better yet, wait 'til Da comes back. He can—"

"Aye, he can do everything better than I can, I know that fine," Roger replied caustically. "But it's me that promised Malva she'd come to no harm. I'm going." He yanked at his sleeve, hard enough that she felt the underarm seam give way.

"Fine!" She let go, and slapped him hard on the arm. "Go! Take care of everybody in the world but your own family. Go! Bloody *go*!"

"What?" He stopped, scowling, caught between anger and puzzlement.

"You heard me! Go!" She stamped her foot, and the jar of *dauco* seeds, left too near the edge of the shelf, fell off and smashed on the floor, scattering tiny black seeds like pepper grains. "Now look what you've done!"

"What *I've*—"

"Never mind! Just never mind. Get out of here." She was puffing like a grampus with the effort not to cry. Her cheeks were hot with blood and her eyeballs felt red, bloodshot, so hot that she felt she might sear him with a look—certainly she wished she could.

He hovered, clearly trying to decide whether to stay and

conciliate his disgruntled wife, or rush off in chivalrous protection of Malva Christie. He took a hesitant step toward the door,
and she dived for the broom, making stupid, high-pitched squeaks
of incoherent rage as she swung it at his head.

He ducked, but she got him on the second swing, catching him
across the ribs with a *thwack*. He jerked in surprise at the impact,
but recovered fast enough to catch the broom on the next swing.
He yanked it out of her hand, and with a grunt of effort, broke it
over his knee with a splintering crack.

He threw the pieces clattering at her feet and glared at her,
angry but self-possessed.

"What in the name of God is the matter with you?"

She drew up tall and glared back.

"What I said. If you're spending so much time with Amy
McCallum that it's common talk you're having an affair with
her—"

"I'm *what*?" His voice broke with outrage, but there was a
shifty look in his eyes that gave him away.

"So you've heard it, too—haven't you?" She didn't feel triumphant at having caught him out; more a sense of sick fury.

"You can't possibly think that's true, Bree," he said, his voice
pitched uncertainly between angry repudiation and pleading.

"I know it isn't true," she said, and was furious to hear her own
voice as shaky and cracked as his was. "That's not the effing
point, Roger!"

"The point," he repeated. His black brows were drawn down,
his eyes sharp and dark beneath them.

"The point," she said, gulping air, "is that you're always *gone*.
Malva Christie, Amy McCallum, Marsali, Lizzie—you even go
help Ute McGillivray, for God's sake!"

"Who else is to do it?" he asked sharply. "Your father or your
cousin might, aye—but they've to be gone to the Indians. I'm
here. And I'm not always gone," he added, as an afterthought.
"I'm home every night, am I not?"

She closed her eyes and clenched her fists, feeling the nails dig
into her palms.

"You'll help any woman but me," she said, opening her eyes.
"Why is that?"

He gave her a long, hard look, and she wondered for an instant
whether there was such a thing as a black emerald.

"Maybe I didn't think ye needed me," he said. And turning on his heel, he left.

51

The Calling

The water lay calm as melted silver, the only movement on it the shadows of the evening clouds. But the hatch was about to rise; you could feel it. Or perhaps, Roger thought, what he felt was the expectation in his father-in-law, crouched like a leopard on the bank of the trout pool, pole and fly at the ready for the first sign of a ripple.

"Like the pool at Bethesda," he said, amused.

"Oh, aye?" Jamie answered, but didn't look at him, his attention fixed on the water.

"The one where an angel would go down into the pool and trouble the water now and then. So everyone sat about waiting, so as to plunge in the minute the water began to stir."

Jamie smiled, but still didn't turn. Fishing was serious business.

That was good; he'd rather not have Jamie look at him. But he'd have to hurry if he meant to say something; Fraser was already paying out the line to make a practice cast or two.

"I think—" He stopped himself, correcting. "No, I don't think. I know. I want—" His air ran out in a wheeze, annoying him; the last thing he wanted was to sound in any way doubtful about what he was saying. He took a huge breath, and the next words shot out as though fired from a pistol. "I mean to be a minister."

Well, then. He'd said it out loud. He glanced upward, involuntarily, but sure enough, the sky hadn't fallen. It was hazed and riffled with mare's tails, but the blue calm of it showed through and the ghost of an early moon floated just above the mountain's shoulder.

Jamie glanced thoughtfully at him, but didn't seem shocked or taken aback. That was some small comfort, he supposed.

"A minister. A preacher, d'ye mean?"

"Well . . . aye. That, too."

The admission disconcerted him. He supposed he *would* have to preach, though the mere notion of it was terrifying.

"That, *too*?" Fraser repeated, looking at him sideways.

"Aye. I mean—a minister does preach, of course." Of course. What about? How? "But that's not—I mean, that's not the main thing. Not why I—I have to do it." He was getting flustered, trying to explain clearly something that he could not even explain properly to himself.

He sighed, and rubbed a hand over his face.

"Aye, look. Ye recall Grannie Wilson's funeral, of course. And the McCallums?"

Jamie merely nodded, but Roger thought perhaps a flicker of understanding showed in his eyes.

"I've done . . . a few things. A bit like that, when it was needed. And—" He twitched a hand, unsure even how to begin describing things like his meeting with Hermon Husband on the banks of the Alamance, or the conversations had with his dead father, late at night.

He sighed again, made to toss a pebble into the water, and stopped himself, just in time, when he saw Jamie's hand tense round his fishing pole. He coughed, feeling the familiar choke and rasp in his throat, and closed his hand around the pebble.

"The preaching, aye, I suppose I'll manage. But it's the other things—oh, God, this sounds insane, and I do believe I may be. But it's the burying and the christening and the—the—maybe just being able to *help,* even if it's only by listening and praying."

"Ye want to take care of them," Jamie said softly, and it wasn't a question, but rather an acceptance.

Roger laughed a little, unhappily, and closed his eyes against the sparkle of the sun off the water.

"I don't want to do it," he said. "It's the last thing I thought of, and me growing up in a minister's house. I mean, I ken what it's like. But someone *has* to do it, and I am thinking it's me."

Neither of them spoke for a bit. Roger opened his eyes and watched the water. Algae coated the rocks, wavering in the current like locks of mermaid's hair. Fraser stirred a little, drawing back his rod.

"Do Presbyterians believe in the sacraments, would ye say?"

"Yes," Roger said, surprised. "Of course we do. Have ye never—" Well, no. He supposed in fact Fraser never *had* spoken to anyone not a Catholic, regarding such matters. "We do," he repeated. He dipped a hand gently in the water, and wiped it across his brow, so the coolness ran down his face and down his neck inside his shirt.

"It's Holy Orders I mean, ken?" The drowned fly swam through the water, a tiny speck of red. "Will ye not need to be ordained?"

"Oh, I see. Aye, I would. There's a Presbyterian academy in Mecklenburg County. I'll go there and speak with them about it. Though I'm thinking it willna take such a time; I've the Greek and Latin already, and for what it's worth"—he smiled, despite himself—"I've a degree from Oxford University. Believe it or not, I was once thought an educated man."

Jamie's mouth twitched at the corner as he drew back his arm and snapped his wrist. The line sailed out, a lazy curve, and the fly settled. Roger blinked; sure enough—the surface of the pool was beginning to pucker and shiver, tiny ripples spreading out from the rising hatch of mayflies and damselflies.

"Have ye spoken to your wife about it?"

"No," he said, staring across the pool.

"Why not?" There was no tone of accusation in the question; more curiosity. Why, after all, should he have chosen to talk to his father-in-law first, rather than his wife?

Because you know what it is to be a man, he thought, *and she doesn't.* What he said, though, was another version of the truth.

"I don't want her to think me a coward."

Jamie made a small "hmph" noise, almost surprise, but didn't reply at once, concentrating on reeling in his line. He took the sodden fly from the hook, then hesitated over the collection on his hat, finally choosing a delicate green thing with a curving wisp of black feather.

"D'ye think she would?" Not waiting for an answer, Fraser stood and whipped the line up and back, sending the fly out to

drift down over the center of the pool, lighting like a leaf on the
water.

Roger watched as he brought it in, playing it over the water in
a jerky dance. The Reverend had been a fisherman. All at once, he
saw the Ness and its sparkling riffles, running clear brown over
the rocks, Dad standing in his battered waders, reeling in his line.
He was choked with longing. For Scotland. For his father. For one
more day—just one—of peace.

The mountains and the green wood rose up mysterious and
wild around them, and the hazy sky unfurled itself over the hollow like angel's wings, silent and sunlit. But not peaceful; never
peace, not here.

"Do you believe us—Claire and Brianna and me—about the
war that's coming?"

Jamie laughed shortly, gaze fixed on the water.

"I've eyes, man. It doesna take either prophet or witch to see it
standing on the road."

"That," said Roger, giving him a curious look, "is a very odd
way of putting it."

"Is it, so? Is that no what the Bible says? *When ye shall see the
abomination of desolation, standing where it ought not, then let
them in Judaea flee to the mountains?*"

Let him who readeth understand. Memory supplied the missing part of the verse, and Roger became aware, with a small sense
of cold in the bone, that Jamie did indeed see it standing on
the road, and recognized it. Nor was he using figures of speech;
he was describing, precisely, what he saw—because he had seen
it before.

The sound of small boys yelling in joy drifted across the water,
and Fraser turned his head a little, listening. A faint smile touched
his mouth, then he looked down into the moving water, seeming
to grow still. The ropes of his hair stirred against the sunburned
skin of his neck, in the same way that the leaves of the mountain
ash moved above.

Roger wanted suddenly to ask Jamie whether he was afraid,
but kept silence. He knew the answer, in any case.

It doesn't matter. He breathed deep, and felt the same answer,
to the same question, asked of himself. It didn't seem to come
from anywhere, but was just there inside him, as though he had
been born with it, always known it.

It doesn't matter. You will do it anyway.

They stayed for some time in silence. Jamie cast twice more with the green fly, then shook his head and muttered something, reeled it in, changed it for a Dun Fly, and cast again. The little boys charged past on the other bank, naked as eels, giggling, and disappeared through the bushes.

Really odd, Roger thought. He felt all right. Still having not the slightest idea what he meant to do, exactly, still seeing the drifting cloud coming toward them, and now knowing much more about what lay within it. But still all right.

Jamie had a fish on the line. He brought it in fast, and jerked it shining and flapping onto the bank, where he killed it with a sharp blow on a rock before tucking it into his creel.

"D'ye mean to turn Quaker?" Jamie asked seriously.

"No." Roger was startled by the question. "Why do you ask that?"

Jamie made the odd little half-shrugging gesture that he sometimes used when uncomfortable about something, and didn't speak again until he'd made the new cast.

"Ye said ye didna want Brianna to think ye coward. I've fought by the side of a priest before." One side of his mouth turned up, wry. "Granted, he wasna much of a swordsman, the Monsignor, and he couldna hit the broad side of a barn wi' a pistol—but he was game enough."

"Oh." Roger scratched the side of his jaw. "Aye, I take your meaning. No, I can't fight with an army, I don't think." Saying it, he felt a sharp pang of regret. "But take up arms in defense of— of those who need it . . . I can square that with my conscience, aye."

"That's all right, then."

Jamie reeled in the rest of the line, shook water from the fly, and stuck the hook back into his hat. Laying the line aside, he rummaged in the creel and pulled out a stoneware bottle. He sat down with a sigh, pulled the cork with his teeth, spat it into his hand, and offered Roger the bottle.

"It's a thing Claire says to me, now and again," he explained, and quoted: *"Malt does more than Milton can, to justify God's ways to man."*

Roger lifted an eyebrow.

"Ever read Milton?"

"A bit. She's right about it."

"Ye ken the next lines?" Roger lifted the bottle to his lips. *"Ale, man, ale's the stuff to drink, For fellows whom it hurts to think."*

A subterranean laugh moved through Fraser's eyes.

"This must be whisky, then," he said. "It only smells like beer."

It was cool and dark and pleasantly bitter, and they passed the bottle to and fro, not saying much of anything, until the ale was gone. Jamie put the cork thriftily back in, and tucked the empty bottle away in the creel.

"Your wife," he said thoughtfully, rising and hitching the strap of the creel onto his shoulder.

"Aye?" Roger picked up the battered hat, bestrewn with flies, and gave it to him. Jamie nodded thanks, and set it on his head.

"She has eyes, too."

52

M-I-C-

Fireflies lit the grass, the trees, and floated through the heavy air in a profusion of cool green sparks. One lighted on Brianna's knee; she watched it pulse, on-off, on-off, and listened to her husband telling her he meant to be a minister.

They were sitting on the stoop of their cabin as the dusk thickened into night. Across the big clearing, the whoops of small children at play sounded in the bushes, high and cheerful as hunting bats.

"You . . . uh . . . could say something," Roger suggested. His head was turned, looking at her. There was enough light yet to see his face, expectant, slightly anxious.

"Well . . . give me a minute. I sort of wasn't expecting this, you know?"

That was true, and it wasn't. Certainly, she hadn't consciously thought of such a thing, yet now that he'd stated his intentions—and he had, she thought; he wasn't asking her permission—she wasn't at all surprised. It was less a change than a recognition of something that had been there for some time—and in a way, it was a relief to see it and know it for what it was.

"Well," she said, after a long moment of consideration, "I think that's good."

"Ye do." The relief in his voice was palpable.

"Yes. If you're helping all these women because God told you to, that's better than doing it because you'd rather be with them than with me."

"Bree! Ye can't think that, that I—" He leaned closer, looking anxiously into her face. "Ye don't, do you?"

"Well, only sometimes," she admitted. "In my worse moments. Not most of the time." He looked so anxious that she reached up and cupped her hand to the long curve of his cheek; the stubble of his beard was invisible in this light, but she could feel it, soft and tickling against her palm.

"You're sure?" she said softly. He nodded, and she saw his throat move as he swallowed.

"I'm sure."

"Are you afraid?"

He smiled a little at that.

"Yeah."

"I'll help," she said firmly. "You tell me how, and I'll help."

He took a deep breath, his face lightening, though his smile was rueful.

"I don't know how," he said. "How to do it, I mean. Let alone what *you* might do. That's what scares me."

"Maybe not," she said. "But you've *been* doing it, anyway, haven't you? Do you need to do anything formal about this, though? Or can you just announce you're a minister, like those TV preachers, and start taking up the collection right away?"

He smiled at the joke, but answered seriously.

"Bloody Romanist. Ye always think no one else has any claim to sacraments. We do, though. I'm thinking I'll go to the Presbyterian Academy, see what I need to do about ordination. As for taking up the collection—I expect this means I'll never be rich."

"I sort of wasn't expecting that, anyway," she assured him gravely. "Don't worry; I didn't marry you for your money. If we need more, I'll make it."

"How?"

"I don't know. Not selling my body, probably. Not after what happened to Manfred."

"Don't even joke about that," he said. His hand came down over hers, large and warm.

Aidan McCallum's high, piercing voice floated through the air, and a sudden thought struck her.

"Your—your, um, flock . . ." The word struck her funny bone, and she giggled, despite the seriousness of the question. "Will they mind that I'm a Catholic?" She turned to him suddenly, another thought coming rapidly in its wake. "You don't—you aren't asking me to convert?"

"No, I'm not," he said quickly, firmly. "Not in a million years. As for what they might think—or say—" His face twitched, caught between dismay and determination. "If they're not willing to accept it, well . . . they can just go to hell, that's all."

She burst out laughing, and he followed her, his laugh cracked, but without restraint.

"The Minister's Cat is an irreverent cat," she teased. "And how do you say *that* in Gaelic?"

"I've no idea. But the Minister's Cat is a relieved cat," he added, still smiling. "I didn't know what ye might think about it."

"I'm not totally sure what I *do* think about it," she admitted. She squeezed his hand lightly. "But I see that you're happy."

"It shows?" He smiled, and the last of the evening light glowed briefly in his eyes, a deep and lambent green.

"It shows. You're sort of . . . lighted up inside." Her throat felt tight. "Roger—you won't forget about me and Jem, will you? I don't know that I can compete with God."

He looked thunderstruck at that.

"No," he said, his hand tightening on hers, hard enough to make her ring cut into her flesh. "Not ever."

They sat silent for a little, the fireflies drifting down like slow green rain, their silent mating song lighting the darkening grass and trees. Roger's face was fading as the light failed, though she still saw the line of his jaw, set in determination.

"I swear to ye, Bree," he said. "Whatever I'm called to now—and God knows what that is—I was called to be your husband first. Your husband and the father of your bairns above all things—and that I always shall be. Whatever I may do, it will not ever be at the price of my family, I promise you."

"All I want," she said softly to the dark, "is for you to love me. Not because of what I can do or what I look like, or because I love you—just because I am."

"Perfect, unconditional love?" he said just as softly. "Some would tell ye only God can love that way—but I can try."

"Oh, I have faith in you," she said, and felt the glow of him reach her own heart.

"I hope ye always will," he said. He raised her hand to his lips, kissed her knuckles in formal salutation, his breath warm on her skin.

As though to test the resolution of his earlier declaration, Jem's voice rose and fell on the evening breeze, a small, urgent siren. "DadddeeeDaaaddeeeDAAADDDEEE . . ."

Roger sighed deeply, leaned over, and kissed her, a moment's soft, deep connection, then rose to deal with the emergency of the moment.

She sat for a bit, listening. The sound of male voices came from the far end of the clearing, high and low, demand and question, reassurance and excitement. No emergency; Jem wanted to be lifted into a tree too high for him to climb alone. Then laughter, mad rustling of leaves—oh, good grief, Roger was in the tree, too. They were all up there, hooting like owls.

"What are ye laughing at, *a nighean*?" Her father loomed out of the night, smelling of horses.

"Everything," she said, scooching over to make room for him to sit beside her. It was true. Everything seemed suddenly bright, the candlelight from the windows of the Big House, the fireflies in the grass, the glow of Roger's face when he told her his desire. She could still feel the touch of his mouth on hers; it fizzed in her blood.

Jamie reached up and fielded a passing firefly, holding it for a moment cupped in the dark hollow of his hand, where it flashed on and off, the cool light seeping through his fingers. Far off, she heard a brief snatch of her mother's voice, coming through an open window; Claire was singing "Clementine."

Now the boys—and Roger—were howling at the moon, though it was no more than a pale sickle on the horizon. She felt her father's body shake with silent laughter, too.

"It reminds me of Disneyland," she said on impulse.

"Oh, aye? Where's that?"

"It's an amusement park—for children," she added, knowing that while there were such things as amusement parks in places like London and Paris, these were purely adult places. No one ever thought of entertaining children now, beyond their own games and the occasional toy.

"Daddy and Mama took me there every summer," she said, slipping back without effort to the hot, bright days and warm California nights. "The trees all had little sparkling lights in them—the fireflies reminded me."

Jamie spread his palm; the firefly, suddenly free, pulsed to itself once or twice, then spread its wings with a tiny whir and lifted into the air, floating up and away.

"Dwelt a miner, forty-niner, and his daugh-ter, Clementine . . ."

"What was it like, then?" he asked curiously.

"Oh . . . it was wonderful." She smiled to herself, seeing the brilliant lights of Main Street, the music and mirrors and beautiful, beribboned horses of King Arthur's Carrousel. "There were . . . rides, we called them. A boat, where you could float through the jungle on a river, and see crocodiles and hippopotamuses and head-hunters . . ."

"Headhunters?" he said, intrigued.

"Not real ones," she assured him. "It's all make-believe—but it's . . . well, it's a world to itself. When you're there, the real world sort of disappears; nothing bad can happen there. They call it 'The Happiest Place on Earth'—and for a little while, it really seems that way."

"Light she was, and like a fairy, and her shoes were number nine, Herring boxes without topses, sandals were for Clementine."

"And you'd hear music everywhere, all the time," she said, smiling. "Bands—groups of musicians playing instruments, horns and drums and things—would march up and down the streets, and play in pavilions. . . ."

"Aye, that happens in amusement parks. Or it did, the once I was in one." She could hear a smile in his voice, as well.

"Mm-hm. And there are cartoon characters—I told you about cartoons—walking around. You can go up and shake hands with Mickey Mouse, or—"

"With what?"

"Mickey Mouse." She laughed. "A big mouse, life-size—human-size, I mean. He wears gloves."

"A giant rat?" he said, sounding slightly stunned. "And they take the weans to play with it?"

"Not a rat, a mouse," she corrected him. "And it's really a person dressed up like a mouse."

"Oh, aye?" he said, not sounding terribly reassured.

"Yes. And an enormous carousel with painted horses, and a railroad train that goes through the Rainbow Caverns, where there are big jewels sticking out of the walls, and colored streams with red and blue water . . . and orange-juice bars. Oh, orange-juice bars!" She moaned softly in ecstatic remembrance of the cold, tart, overwhelming sweetness.

"It was nice, then?" he said softly.

"Thou art lost and gone forever, Dreadful sor-ry . . . Clementine."

"Yes," she said, sighed, and was silent for a moment. Then she leaned her head against his shoulder, and wrapped her hand around his arm, big and solid.

"You know what?" she said, and he made a small interrogatory noise in reply.

"It *was* nice—it was great—but what I really, really loved about it was that when we were there, it was just the three of us, and everything was perfect. Mama wasn't worrying about her patients, Daddy wasn't working on a paper—they weren't ever silent or angry with each other. Both of them laughed—we all laughed, all the time . . . while we were there."

He made no reply, but tilted his head so it rested against hers. She sighed again, deeply.

"Jemmy won't get to go to Disneyland—but he'll have that. A family that laughs—and millions of little lights in the trees."

PART SEVEN

Rolling Downhill

53

Principles

From Fraser's Ridge, North Carolina,
on the Third day of July, Anno Domini 1774,
James Fraser, Esq.

To his Lordship, John Grey, at Mount Josiah
Plantation, in the colony of Virginia

My Dear Friend,

I cannot begin to express our Gratitude for your
kind Behavior in sending a Draft drawn upon your own
Bank, as advance Payment against the eventual Sale of
the Objects I confided to your disposition. Mr. Higgins,
in delivering this Document, was of course most tactful—and yet, I gathered from his anxious Demeanor
and his efforts at Discretion that you may perhaps
believe us to be in dire Straits. I hasten to assure you
that this is not the Case; we will do well enough, so far
as Matters of Victuals, Clothes, and the Necessities of
Life.

I said that I would tell you the Details of the Affair,
and I see that I must, if only to disabuse you of the
Vision of rampant Starvation among my family and
tenants.

Beyond a small legal Obligation requiring Cash, I
have a Matter of Business in Hand, involving the
acquisition of a Number of Guns. I had been in Hopes
of acquiring these through the good offices of a Friend,
but find that this Arrangement will no longer answer; I
must look further abroad.

I and my Family are invited to a Barbecue in honor

*of Miss Flora MacDonald, the Heroine of the Rising—
you are familiar with the Lady, I believe? I recall your
telling me once of your meeting with her in London,
whilst she was imprisoned there—to take place next
month at my aunt's Plantation, River Run. As this Affair
will be attended by a great many Scots, some coming
from considerable Distances, I am in Hopes that with
Cash in Hand, I may make Arrangements to procure the
requisite Weapons via other Avenues. In re which,
should your own Connexions suggest any such useful
Avenues, I should be grateful to
hear of them.*

*I write quickly, as Mr. Higgins has other Errands, but
my Daughter bids me send herewith a box of Matchsticks,
her own Invention. She has schooled Mr. Higgins most
carefully in their Use, so if he does not burst inadvertently
into Flame on the way back, he will be able to demonstrate them to you.*

> *Your humble and ob't. servant,*
> *James Fraser*

*P.S. I require thirty Muskets, with as much Powder and
Ammunition as may be possible. These need not be of the
latest Manufacture, but must be well-kept and functional.*

"'Other avenues?'" I said, watching him sand the letter before
folding it. "You mean smugglers? And if so, are you sure that
Lord John will understand what you mean?"

"I do, and he will," Jamie assured me. "I ken a few smugglers
myself, who bring things in through the Outer Banks. He'll know
the ones who come through Roanoke, though—and there's more
business there, because of the blockade in Massachusetts. Goods
come in through Virginia, and go north overland."

He took a half-burned beeswax taper from the shelf and held
it to the coals in the hearth, then dripped soft brown wax in a puddle over the seam of the letter. I leaned forward and pressed the
back of my left hand into the warm wax, leaving the mark of my
wedding ring in it.

"Damn Manfred McGillivray," he said, with no particular heat. "It will be three times the cost, and I must get them from a smuggler."

"Will you ask about him, though? At the barbecue, I mean?" Flora MacDonald, the woman who had saved Charles Stuart from the English after Culloden, dressing him in her maid's clothes and smuggling him to a rendezvous with the French on the Isle of Skye, was a living legend to the Scottish Highlanders, and her recent arrival in the colony was the subject of vast excitement, news of it coming even as far as the Ridge. Every well-known Scot in the Cape Fear valley—and a good many from farther away—would be present at the barbecue to be held in her honor. No better place to spread the word for a missing young man.

He glanced up at me, surprised.

"Of course I will, Sassenach. What d'ye think I am?"

"I think you're very kind," I said, kissing him on the forehead. "If a trifle reckless. And I notice you carefully didn't tell Lord John why you need thirty muskets."

He gave a small snort, and swept the grains of sand carefully off the table into the palm of his hand.

"I dinna ken for sure myself, Sassenach."

"Whatever do you mean by that?" I asked, surprised. "Do you not mean to give them to Bird, after all?"

He didn't answer at once, but the two stiff fingers of his right hand tapped gently on the tabletop. Then he shrugged, reached to the stack of journals and ledgers, and pulled out a paper, which he handed to me. A letter from John Ashe, who had been a fellow commander of militia during the War of the Regulation.

"The fourth paragraph," he said, seeing me frown at a recounting of the latest contretemps between the Governor and the Assembly. I obligingly skimmed down the page, to the indicated spot, and felt a small, premonitory shiver.

"A Continental Congress is proposed," I read, *"with delegates to be sent from each colony. The lower house of the Connecticut Assembly has moved already to propose such men, acting through Committees of Correspondence. Some gentlemen with whom you are well-acquainted propose that North Carolina shall do likewise, and will meet to accomplish the matter in mid-August. I could wish that you would join us, friend, for I am*

convinced that your heart and mind must lie with us in the matter of liberty; surely such a man as yourself is no friend to tyranny.

"Some gentlemen with whom you are well-acquainted," I repeated, putting down the letter. "Do you know who he means?"

"I could guess."

"Mid-August, he says. Before the barbecue, do you think, or after?"

"After. One of the others sent me the date of the meeting. It's to be in Halifax."

I put down the letter. The afternoon was still and hot, and the thin linen of my shift was damp, as were the palms of my hands.

"One of the others," I said. He shot me a quick glance, with a half-smile, and picked up the letter.

"In the Committee of Correspondence."

"Oh, naturally," I said. "You might have told me." Naturally, he would have found a means of inveigling himself into the North Carolina Committee of Correspondence—the center of political intrigue, where the seeds of rebellion were being sown—meanwhile holding a commission as Indian agent for the British Crown and ostensibly working to arm the Indians, in order to suppress precisely those seeds of rebellion.

"I am telling ye, Sassenach," he said. "This is the first time they've asked me to meet wi' them, even in private."

"I see," I said softly. "Will you go? Is it—is it time?" Time to make the leap, declare himself openly as a Whig, if not yet a rebel. Time to change his public allegiance, and risk the brand of treason. Again.

He sighed deeply and rubbed a hand through his hair. He'd been thinking; the short hairs of several tiny cowlicks were standing on end.

"I don't know," he said finally. "It's two years yet, no? The fourth of July, 1776—that's what Brianna said."

"No," I said. "It's two years until they declare independence— but, Jamie, the fighting will have started already. That will be much too late."

He stared at the letters on the desk, and nodded bleakly.

"Aye, it will have to be soon, then."

"It would be likely safe enough," I said hesitantly. "What you told me about Henderson buying land in Tennessee: if no one's stopping him, I can't see anyone in the government being agitated enough to come up here and try to force us out. And surely not if you were only known to have *met* with the local Whigs?"

He gave me a small, wry smile.

"It's no the government I'm worrit by, Sassenach. It's the folk nearby. It wasna the Governor who hanged the O'Brians and burnt their house, ken? Nor was it Richard Brown, nor Indians. That wasna done for the sake of law nor profit; it was done for hate, and verra likely by someone who knew them."

That made a more pronounced chill skitter down my spine. There was a certain amount of political disagreement and discussion on the Ridge, all right, but it hadn't reached the stage of fisticuffs yet, let alone burning and killing.

But it would.

I remembered, all too well. Bomb shelters and ration coupons, blackout wardens and the spirit of cooperation against a dreadful foe. And the stories from Germany, France. People reported on, denounced to the SS, dragged from their houses—others hidden in attics and barns, smuggled across borders.

In war, government and their armies were a threat, but it was so often the neighbors who damned or saved you.

"Who?" I said baldly.

"I could guess," he said, with a shrug. "The McGillivrays? Richard Brown? Hodgepile's friends—if he had any. The friends of any of the other men we killed? The Indian ye met—Donner?—if he's still alive. Neil Forbes? He's a grudge against Brianna, and she and Roger Mac would do well to remember it. Hiram Crombie and his lot?"

"Hiram?" I said dubiously. "Granted, he doesn't like you very much—and as for me—but . . ."

"Well, I do doubt it," he admitted. "But it's possible, aye? His people didna support the Jacobites at all; they'll no be pleased at an effort to overthrow the King from this side of the water, either."

I nodded. Crombie and the rest would of necessity have taken an oath of loyalty to King George, before being allowed to travel to America. Jamie had—of necessity—taken the same oath, as part of his pardon. And must—of an even greater necessity—break it. But when?

He'd stopped drumming his fingers; they rested on the letter before him.

"I do trust ye're right, Sassenach," he said.

"About what? What will happen? You know I am," I said, a little surprised. "Bree and Roger told you, too. Why?"

He rubbed a hand slowly through his hair.

"I've never fought for the sake of principle," he said, reflecting, and shook his head. "Only necessity. I wonder, would it be any better?"

He didn't sound upset, merely curious, in a detached sort of way. Still, I found this vaguely disturbing.

"But there is principle to it, this time," I protested. "In fact, it may be the first war ever fought over principle."

"Rather than something sordid like trade, or land?" Jamie suggested, raising one eyebrow.

"I don't say trade and land haven't anything to do with it," I replied, wondering precisely how I'd managed to become a defender of the American Revolution—an historical period I knew only from Brianna's school textbooks. "But it goes well beyond that, don't you think? *We hold these truths to be self-evident, that all men are created equal, that they are endowed by their Creator with certain unalienable Rights, that among these are Life, Liberty, and the pursuit of Happiness.*"

"Who said that?" he asked, interested.

"Thomas Jefferson will say it—on behalf of the new republic. The Declaration of Independence, it's called. Will be called."

"All men," he repeated. "Does he mean Indians, as well, do ye think?"

"I can't say," I said, rather irritated at being forced into this position. "I haven't met him. If I do, I'll ask, shall I?"

"Never mind." He lifted his fingers in brief dismissal. "I'll ask him myself, and I have the opportunity. Meanwhile, I'll ask Brianna." He glanced at me. "Though as to principle, Sassenach—"

He leaned back in his chair, folded his arms over his chest, and closed his eyes.

"As long as but a hundred of us remain alive," he said precisely, *"never will we on any conditions be brought under English rule. It is in truth not for glory, nor riches, nor honours that we are fighting, but for freedom—for that alone, which no honest man gives up but with life itself."*

"The Declaration of Arbroath," he said, opening his eyes. He gave me a lopsided smile. "Written some four hundred years ago. Speaking o' principles, aye?"

He stood up then, but still remained standing by the battered table he used as a desk, looking down at Ashe's letter.

"As for my own principles . . ." he said, as though to himself, but then looked at me, as though suddenly realizing that I was still there.

"Aye, I think I mean to give Bird the muskets," he said. "Though I may have cause to regret it, and I find them pointing at me, two or three years hence. But he shall have them, and do with them what seems best, to defend himself and his people."

"The price of honor, is it?"

He looked down at me, with the ghost of a smile.

"Call it blood money."

54

Flora MacDonald's Barbecue

River Run Plantation
August 6, 1774

Whatever did one say to an icon? Or an icon's husband, for that matter?

"Oh, I shall faint, I know I shall." Rachel Campbell was fluttering her fan hard enough to create a perceptible breeze. "Whatever shall I say to her?"

"'Good day, Mrs. MacDonald'?" suggested her husband, a

faint smile lurking at the corner of his withered mouth.

Rachel hit him sharply with her fan, making him chuckle as he dodged away. For all he was thirty-five years her senior, Farquard Campbell had an easy, teasing way with his wife, quite at odds with his usual dignified demeanor.

"I shall faint," Rachel declared again, having evidently decided upon this as a definite social strategy.

"Well, ye must please yourself, of course, *a nighean*, but if ye do, it will have to be Mr. Fraser picking you up from the ground; my ancient limbs are scarcely equal to the task."

"Oh!" Rachel cast a quick glance at Jamie, who smiled at her, then hid her blushes behind her fan. While plainly fond of her own husband, she made no secret of her admiration for mine.

"Your humble servant, madam," Jamie gravely assured her, bowing.

She tittered. I shouldn't like to wrong the woman, but she definitely tittered. I caught Jamie's eye, and hid a smile behind my own fan.

"And what will *you* say to her, then, Mr. Fraser?"

Jamie pursed his lips and squinted thoughtfully at the brilliant sun streaming through the elm trees that edged the lawn at River Run.

"Oh, I suppose I might say that I'm glad the weather has kept fine for her. It was raining the last time we met."

Rachel's jaw dropped, and so did her fan, bouncing on the lawn. Her husband bent to pick it up for her, groaning audibly, but she had no attention to spare for him.

"You've *met* her?" she cried, eyes wide with excitement. "When? Where? With the prin—with *him*?"

"Ah, no," Jamie said, smiling. "On Skye. I'd gone wi' my father—a matter of sheep, it was. We chanced to meet Hugh MacDonald of Armadale in Portree—Miss Flora's stepfather, aye?—and he'd brought the lass into the town with him, for a treat."

"Oh!" Rachel was enchanted. "And was she beautiful and gracious as they say?"

Jamie frowned, considering.

"Well, no," he said. "But she'd a terrible grippe at the time, and no doubt would have looked much improved without the red nose.

Gracious? Well, I wouldna say so, really. She snatched a bridie right out of my hand and ate it."

"And how old were you both at the time?" I asked, seeing Rachel's mouth sag in horror.

"Oh, six, maybe," he said cheerfully. "Or seven. I doubt I should remember, save I kicked her in the shin when she stole my bridie, and she pulled my hair."

Recovering somewhat from the shock, Rachel was pressing Jamie for further reminiscences, a pressure he was laughingly deflecting with jokes.

Of course, he had come prepared to this occasion; all over the grounds, there were stories being exchanged—humorous, admiring, longing—of the days before Culloden. Odd, that it should have been the defeat of Charles Stuart, and his ignominious flight, that made a heroine of Flora MacDonald and united these Highland exiles in a way that they could never have achieved—let alone sustained—had he actually won.

It struck me suddenly that Charlie was likely still alive, quietly drinking himself to death in Rome. In any real way, though, he was long since dead to these people who had loved or hated him. The amber of time had sealed him forever in that one defining moment of his life—*Bliadha Tearlach*; "Charlie's Year," it meant, and even now, I heard people call it that.

It was Flora's coming that was causing this flood of sentiment, of course. How strange for her, I thought, with a pang of sympathy—and for the first time, wondered what on earth I might say to her myself.

I had met famous people before—not the least of them the Bonnie Prince himself. But always before, I had met them when they—and I—were in the midst of their normal lives, not yet past the defining events that would make them famous, and thus still just people. Bar Louis—but then, he was a king. There are rules of etiquette for dealing with kings, since after all, no one ever does approach them as normal people. Not even when—

I snapped my own fan open, hot blood bursting through my face and body. I breathed deeply, trying not to fan quite as frantically as Rachel, but wanting to.

I had not once, in all the years since it happened, ever specifically recalled those two or three minutes of physical intimacy with Louis of France. Not deliberately, God knew, and not by accident, either.

Yet suddenly, the memory of it had touched me, as suddenly as a hand coming out of the crowd to seize my arm. Seize my arm, lift my skirts, and penetrate me in a way much more shockingly intrusive than the actual experience had been.

The air around me was suffused with the scent of roses, and I heard the creak of the dress cage as Louis's weight pressed upon it, and heard his sigh of pleasure. The room was dark, lit by one candle; it flickered at the edge of vision, then was blotted out by the man between my—

"Christ, Claire! Are ye all right?" I hadn't actually fallen down, thank God. I had reeled back against the wall of Hector Cameron's mausoleum, and Jamie, seeing me go, had leapt forward to catch hold of me.

"Let go," I said, breathless, but imperative. "Let go of me!"

He heard the note of terror in my voice, and slackened his grip, but couldn't bring himself to let go altogether, lest I fall. With the energy of sheer panic, I pulled myself upright, out of his grasp.

I still smelled roses. Not the cloying scent of rose oil—fresh roses. Then I came to myself, and realized that I was standing next to a huge yellow brier rose, trained to climb over the white marble of the mausoleum.

Knowing that the roses were real was comforting, but I felt as though I stood still on the edge of a vast abyss, alone, separate from every other soul in the universe. Jamie was close enough to touch, and yet it was as though he stood an immeasurable distance away.

Then he touched me and spoke my name, insistently, and just as suddenly as it had opened, the gap between us closed. I nearly fell into his arms.

"What is it, *a nighean*?" he whispered, holding me against his chest. "What's frightened ye?" His own heart was thumping under my ear; I'd scared him, too.

"Nothing," I said, and an overwhelming wave of relief went over me, at the realization that I was safely in the present; Louis had gone back into the shadows, an unpleasant but harmless memory once more. The staggering sense of violation, of loss and grief and isolation, had receded, no more than a shadow on my mind. Best of all, Jamie was there; solid and physical and smelling of sweat and whisky and horses . . . and *there*. I hadn't lost him.

Other people were clustering round, curious, solicitous. Rachel fanned me earnestly, and the breeze of it felt soothing; I was drenched with sweat, wisps of hair clinging damply to my neck.

"Quite all right," I murmured, suddenly self-conscious. "Just a bit faint . . . hot day . . ."

A chorus of offers to fetch me wine, a glass of syllabub, lemon shrub, a burned feather, were all trumped by Jamie's production of a flask of whisky from his sporran. It was the three-year-old stuff, from the sherry casks, and I felt a qualm as the scent of it reached me, remembering the night we had got drunk together after he had rescued me from Hodgepile and his men. God, was I about to be hurled back into *that* pit?

But I wasn't. The whisky was merely hot and consoling, and I felt better with the first sip.

Flashback. I'd heard colleagues talk about it, arguing as to whether this was the same phenomenon as shell shock, and if it was, whether it truly existed, or should be dismissed as simply "nerves."

I shuddered briefly, and took another sip. It most assuredly existed. I felt much better, but I had been shaken to the core, and my bones still felt watery. Beyond the faint echoes of the experience itself was a much more unsettling thought. It had happened once before, when Ute McGillivray attacked me. Was it likely to happen again?

"Shall I carry ye inside, Sassenach? Perhaps ye should lie down a bit."

Jamie had shooed away the well-wishers, had a slave fetch me a stool, and was now hovering over me like an anxious bumble-bee.

"No, I'm all right now," I assured him. "Jamie . . ."

"Aye, lass?"

"You—when you—do you . . ."

I took a deep breath—and another sip of whisky—and tried again.

"Sometimes, I wake up during the night and see you—struggling—and I think it's with Jack Randall. Is it a dream that you have?"

He stared down at me for a moment, face blank, but trouble moving in his eyes. He glanced from side to side, but we were quite alone now.

"Why?" he asked, low-voiced.

"I need to know."

He took a breath, swallowed, and nodded.

"Aye. Sometimes it's dreams. That's . . . all right. I wake, and ken where I am, say a wee prayer, and . . . it's all right. But now and then—" He shut his eyes for a moment, then opened them. "I *am* awake. And yet I am there, with Jack Randall."

"Ah." I sighed, feeling at once terribly sad for him, and at the same time somewhat reassured. "Then I'm not losing my mind."

"Ye think so?" he said dryly. "Well, I'm that glad to hear it, Sassenach."

He stood very close, the cloth of his kilt brushing my arm, so that I should have him for support, if I suddenly went faint again. He looked searchingly at me, to be sure that I wasn't going to keel over, then touched my shoulder and with a brief "Sit still" went off.

Not far; just to the tables set up under the trees at the edge of the lawn. Ignoring the slaves arranging food for the barbecue, he leaned across a platter of boiled crayfish and picked up something from a tiny bowl. Then he was back, leaning down to take my hand. He rubbed his fingers together, and a pinch of salt sprinkled into my open palm.

"There," he whispered. "Keep it by ye, Sassenach. Whoever it is, he'll trouble ye no more."

I closed my hand over the damp grains, feeling absurdly comforted. Trust a Highlander to know precisely what to do about a case of daylight haunting! Salt, they said, kept a ghost in its grave. And if Louis was still alive, the other man, whoever he had been, that pressing weight in the dark, was surely dead.

There was a sudden rush of excitement, as a call came from the river—the boat had been sighted. As one, the crowd drew itself up on tiptoe, breathless with anticipation.

I smiled, but felt the giddy contagion of it touch me nonetheless. Then the pipes began to skirl, and my throat at once was tight with unshed tears.

Jamie's hand tightened on my shoulder, unconsciously, and I looked up to see him rub his knuckles hard across his upper lip, as he, too, turned toward the river.

I looked down, blinking to control myself, and as my vision cleared, I saw the grains of salt on the ground, carefully scattered before the gates of the mausoleum.

She was much smaller than I'd thought. Famous people always are. Everyone—dressed in their best, and an absolute sea of tartan—pressed close, awed past courtesy. I caught a glimpse of the top of her head, dark hair dressed high with white roses, and then it disappeared behind the thronged backs of well-wishers.

Her husband, Allan, was visible. A stoutly handsome man with gray-streaked black hair tied neatly back, he was standing—I assumed—behind her, bowing and smiling, acknowledging the flood of Gaelic compliment and welcome.

Despite myself, I felt the urge to rush forward and stare, with everyone else. I held firm, though. I was standing with Jocasta on the terrace; Mrs. MacDonald would come to us.

Sure enough; Jamie and Duncan were pushing their way firmly through the crowd, forming a flying wedge with Jocasta's black butler, Ulysses.

"That's really her?" Brianna murmured at my shoulder, eyes fixed with interest on the seething multitude, from which the men had now extracted the guest of honor, escorting her from the dock, up the lawn, toward the terrace. "She's smaller than I thought. Oh, it's too bad Roger isn't here—he'd just die to see her!" Roger was spending a month at the Presbyterian Academy at Charlotte, having his qualifications for ordination examined.

"He may get to see her another time," I murmured back. "I hear they've bought a plantation near Barbecue Creek, by Mount Pleasant." And they would stay in the colony for at least another year or two, but I didn't say that out loud; so far as the people here knew, the MacDonalds had immigrated permanently.

But I had seen the tall memorial stone on Skye—where Flora MacDonald had been born, and would someday die, disillusioned with America.

It wasn't the first time I'd met someone and known their fate, of course—but it was always unsettling. The crowd opened and she stepped out, small and pretty, laughing up at Jamie. He had a hand under her elbow, guiding her up onto the terrace, and made a gesture of introduction toward me.

She looked up, expectant, met my gaze dead on, and blinked, her smile momentarily fading. It was back in an instant, and she was bowing to me and I to her, but I did wonder what she had seen in my face?

But she turned at once to greet Jocasta, and introduce her grown daughters, Anne and Fanny, a son, a son-in-law, her husband—by the time she had accomplished the confusion of introduction, she was perfectly in command of herself, and greeted me with a charming, gentle smile.

"Mrs. Fraser! I am so much obliged to meet you at last. I have heard such stories of your kindness and skill, I confess I am in awe to be in your presence."

It was said with so much warmth and sincerity—she seizing me by the hands—that I found myself responding, in spite of a cynical wonder as to who she'd been talking to about me. My reputation in Cross Creek and Campbelton was notorious, but not universally lauded, by any means.

"I had the honor of Dr. Fentiman's acquaintance at the subscription ball held for us in Wilmington—so kind, so amazingly kind of everyone! We have been so well treated, since our arrival—and he was quite in raptures regarding your—"

I should have liked to hear what had enraptured Fentiman— our relations were still marked by a certain wariness, though we had reached a rapprochement—but at this point, her husband spoke in her ear, desiring her to come and meet Farquard Campbell and some other prominent gentlemen, and with a regretful grimace, she squeezed my hands and departed, the brilliant public smile back in place.

"Huh," Bree remarked, *sotto voce*. "Lucky for her she's still got most of her teeth."

That was in fact exactly what I'd been thinking, and I laughed, converting it into a hasty coughing fit as I saw Jocasta's head turn sharply toward us.

"So that's her." Young Ian had come up on my other side, and was watching the guest of honor with an expression of deep interest. He was dressed in kilt, waistcoat, and coat for the occasion, his brown hair done up in a proper queue, and he looked quite civilized, bar the tattoos that looped across his cheekbones and over the bridge of his nose.

"That's her," Jamie agreed. *"Fionnaghal*—the Fair One." There was a surprising note of nostalgia in his voice, and I glanced at him in surprise.

"Well, it's her proper name," he said mildly. *"Fionnaghal.* It's only the English call her Flora."

"Did you have a crush on her when you were little, Da?" Brianna asked, laughing.

"A what?"

"A *tendresse*," I said, batting my eyelashes delicately at him over my fan.

"Och, dinna be daft!" he said. "I was seven years old, for God's sake!" Nonetheless, the tips of his ears had gone quite pink.

"I was in love when I was seven," Ian remarked, rather dreamily. "Wi' the cook. Did ye hear Ulysses say as she's brought a looking glass, Uncle? Given to her by Prince *Tearlach*, with his arms upon the back. Ulysses put it in the parlor, wi' two of the grooms to stand guard over it."

Sure enough, those people who weren't in the swirling crowd surrounding the MacDonalds were all pressing through the double doors into the house, forming a line of animated chatter down the hall to the parlor.

"Seaumais!"

Jocasta's imperious voice put a stop to the teasing. Jamie gave Brianna an austere look, and went to join her. Duncan was detained in conversation with a small knot of prominent men—I recognized Neil Forbes, the lawyer, as well as Cornelius Harnett and Colonel Moore—and Ulysses was nowhere in sight—most likely dealing with the backstage logistics of a barbecue for two hundred people—thus leaving Jocasta temporarily marooned. Her hand on Jamie's arm, she sailed off the terrace, heading for Allan MacDonald, who had become detached from his wife by the press of people round her, and was standing under a tree, looking vaguely affronted.

I watched them go across the lawn, amused by Jocasta's sense of theatrics. Her body servant, Phaedre, was dutifully following—and could plainly have guided her mistress. That wouldn't have had at all the same effect, though. The two of them together made heads turn—Jocasta tall and slender, graceful despite her age and striking with her white hair piled high and her blue silk gown, Jamie with his Viking height and crimson Fraser tartan, both with those bold MacKenzie bones and catlike grace.

"Colum and Dougal would be proud of their little sister," I said, shaking my head.

"Oh, aye?" Ian spoke absently, not attending. He was still watching Flora MacDonald, now accepting a bunch of flowers from one of Farquard Campbell's grandchildren, to general applause.

"Not jealous, are you, Mama?" Brianna teased, seeing me glance in the same direction.

"Certainly not," I said with a certain amount of complacence. "After all, I have all *my* teeth, too."

I had missed him in the initial crush, but Major MacDonald was among the revelers, looking very flash in a brilliantly scarlet uniform coat and a new hat, lavish with gold lace. He removed this object and bowed low to me, looking cheerful—no doubt because I was unaccompanied by livestock, Adso and the white sow being both safely on Fraser's Ridge.

"Your servant, mum," he said. "I saw that ye had a word with Miss Flora—so charming, is she not? And a canty, handsome woman, as well."

"Indeed she is," I agreed. "Do you know her, then?"

"Oh, aye," he said, a look of profound satisfaction spreading across his weathered face. "I should not dare to the presumption of friendship—but believe I may stake a modest claim to acquaintancy. I accompanied Mrs. MacDonald and her family from Wilmington, and have had the great honor to assist in settling them in their present situation."

"Did you really?" I gave him an interested eye. The Major wasn't the type to be awed by celebrity. He *was* the type to appreciate its uses. So was Governor Martin, evidently.

The Major was watching Flora MacDonald now with a proprietary eye, noting with approval the way in which people clustered round her.

"She has most graciously agreed to speak today," he told me, rocking back a little on his bootheels. "Where would be the best place, do you think, mum? From the terrace, as being the point of highest elevation? Or perhaps near the statue on the lawn, as being more central and allowing the crowd to surround her, thus increasing the chance of everyone hearing her remarks?"

"I think she'll have a sunstroke, if you put her out on the lawn in this weather," I said, tilting my own broad-brimmed straw hat to shade my nose. It was easily in the nineties, in terms both of temperature and humidity, and my thin petticoats clung soddenly to my lower limbs. "What sort of remarks is she going to make?"

"Just a brief address upon the subject of loyalty, mum," he said blandly. "Ah, there is your husband, talking to Kingsburgh; if you'll excuse me, mum?" Bowing, he straightened, put his hat back on, and strode down the lawn to join Jamie and Jocasta, who were still with Allan MacDonald—styled "Kingsburgh," in the Scottish fashion, for the name of his estate on Skye.

Food was beginning to be brought out: tureens of powsowdie and hotchpotch—and an enormous tub of soup à la Reine, a clear compliment to the guest of honor—platters of fried fish, fried chicken, fried rabbit; venison collops in red wine, smoked sausages, Forfar bridies, inky-pinky, roast turkeys, pigeon pie; dishes of colcannon, stovies, turnip purry, roasted apples stuffed with dried pumpkin, squash, corn, mushroom pasties; gigantic baskets overflowing with fresh baps, rolls, and other breads . . . all this, I was well aware, merely as prelude to the barbecue whose succulent aroma was drifting through the air: a number of hogs, three or four beeves, two deer, and, the *pièce de résistance*, a wood bison, acquired God knew how or where.

A hum of pleasant anticipation rose around me, as people began metaphorically to loosen their belts, squaring up to the tables with a firm determination to do their duty in honor of the occasion.

Jamie was still stuck fast to Mrs. MacDonald, I saw; he was helping her to a dish of what looked from the distance to be broccoli salad. He looked up and saw me, beckoned me to join them— but I shook my head, gesturing with my fan toward the buffet tables, where the guests were setting to in the businesslike manner of grasshoppers in a barley field. I didn't want to lose the opportunity of inquiring about Manfred McGillivray, before the stupor of satiety settled over the crowd.

I made my way purposefully into the fray, accepting tidbits offered to me by assorted servants and slaves, pausing to chat with any acquaintance I saw, particularly those from Hillsboro. Manfred had spent a great deal of time there, I knew, taking commissions for guns, delivering the finished products, and doing small jobs of repair. That was the most likely place for him to go, I thought. But no one I talked to had seen him, though most knew him.

"Nice lad," one gentleman told me, pausing momentarily in his potations. "And sore missed, too. Besides Robin, there's few gun-smiths closer than Virginia."

I knew that, and knowing, wondered whether Jamie was having any luck in locating the muskets he needed. Perhaps Lord John's smuggling connections would be necessary.

I accepted a small pie from a passing slave's tray, and wandered on, munching and chatting. There was much talk about a series of fiery articles that had appeared recently in the *Chronicle*, the local newspaper, whose proprietor, one Fogarty Simms, was spoken of with considerable sympathy.

"A rare plucked 'un, is Simms," said Mr. Goodwin, shaking his head. "But I doubt me he'll stand. I spoke with him last week, and he told me he's in some fear of his skin. There've been threats, aye?"

From the tone of the gathering, I assumed that Mr. Simms must be a Loyalist, and this appeared to be true, from the various accounts I was given. There was talk, apparently, of a rival paper setting up, this to support the Whiggish agenda, with its incautious talk of tyranny and the overthrow of the King. No one knew quite who was behind the new venture, but there was talk—and much indignation at the prospect—that a printer was to be brought down from the north, where folk were notably given to such perverse sentiments.

The general consensus was that such persons wanted their backsides kicked, to bring them to their senses.

I hadn't sat down to eat formally, but after an hour of moving slowly through fields of champing jaws and wandering herds of hors d'oeuvre trays, I felt as though I'd sat through a French royal banquet—those occasions lasting so long that chamber pots were discreetly placed beneath the guests' chairs, and where the occasional guest giving way and sliding beneath the table was discreetly ignored.

The present occasion was less formal, but not much less prolonged. After an hour's preliminary eating, the barbecue was raised steaming from the pits near the stable, and brought to the lawns on wooden trestles, mounted on the shoulders of slaves. The sight of immense sides of beef, pork, venison, and buffalo, gleaming with oil and vinegar and surrounded by the smaller charred carcasses of hundreds of pigeons and quail, was greeted with applause by the guests, all by this time drenched with the sweat of their efforts, but nothing daunted.

Jocasta, seated by her guest, looked deeply gratified by the sound of her hospitality being so warmly accepted, and leaned toward Duncan, smiling, putting a hand on his arm as she said something to him. Duncan had left off looking nervous—the effect of a quart or two of beer, followed by most of a bottle of whisky—and seemed to be enjoying himself, too. He smiled broadly at Jocasta, then essayed a remark to Mrs. MacDonald, who laughed at whatever he said.

I had to admire her; she was besieged on all sides by people wanting a word, but she kept her poise admirably, being kind and gracious to everyone—though this meant sitting sometimes for ten minutes, a forkful of food suspended in air as she listened to some interminable story. At least she was in the shade—and Phaedre, dressed in white muslin, stood dutifully behind her with a huge fan made of palmetto fronds, making a breeze and keeping off the flies.

"Lemon shrub, ma'am?" A wilting slave, gleaming with sweat, offered me yet another tray, and I took a glass. I was dripping with perspiration, my legs aching and my throat dried with talking. At this point, I didn't care what was in the glass, provided it was wet.

I changed my opinion instantly upon tasting it; it was lemon juice and barley water, and while it *was* wet, I was much more inclined to pour it down the neck of my gown than to drink it. I edged unobtrusively toward a laburnum bush, intending to pour the drink into it, but was forestalled by the appearance of Neil Forbes, who stepped out from behind it.

He was as startled to see me as I was to see him; he jerked back, and glanced hastily over his shoulder. I looked in the same direction, and caught sight of Robert Howe and Cornelius Harnett, making off in the opposite direction. Clearly, the three of them had been conferring secretly behind the laburnum bush.

"Mrs. Fraser," he said, with a short bow. "Your servant."

I curtsied in return, with a vague murmur of politeness. I

would have slithered past him, but he leaned toward me, preventing my exit.

"I hear that your husband is collecting guns, Mrs. Fraser," he said, his voice at a low and rather unfriendly pitch.

"Oh, really?" I was holding an open fan, as was every other woman there. I waved it languidly before my nose, hiding most of my expression. "Who told you such a thing?"

"One of the gentlemen whom he approached to that end," Forbes said. The lawyer was large and somewhat overweight; the unhealthy shade of red in his cheeks might be due to that, rather than to displeasure. Then again . . .

"If I might impose so far upon your good nature, ma'am, I would suggest that you exert your influence upon him, so as to suggest that such a course is not the wisest?"

"To begin with," I said, taking a deep breath of hot, damp air, "just what course do you think he's embarked upon?"

"An unfortunate one, ma'am," he said. "Putting the best complexion upon the matter, I assume that the guns he seeks are intended to arm his own company of militia, which is legitimate, though disturbing; the desirability of that course would rest upon his later actions. But his relations with the Cherokee are well-known, and there are rumors about that the weapons are destined to end in the hands of the savages, to the end that they may turn upon His Majesty's subjects who presume to offer objection to the tyranny, abuse, and corruption so rife among the officials who govern—if so loose a word may be employed to describe their actions—this colony."

I gave him a long look over the edge of my fan.

"If I hadn't already known you were a lawyer," I remarked, "that speech would have done it. I *think* that you just said that you suspect my husband of wanting to give guns to the Indians, and you don't like that. On the other hand, if he's wanting to arm his own militia, that might be all right—providing that said militia acts according to *your* desires. Am I right?"

A flicker of amusement showed in his deep-set eyes, and he inclined his head toward me in acknowledgment.

"Your perception astounds me, ma'am," he said.

I nodded, and shut the fan.

"Right. And what *are* your desires, may I ask? I won't ask why you think Jamie ought to take heed of them."

He laughed, his heavy face, already flushed with the heat, going a deeper shade of red beneath his neat tie-wig.

"I desire justice, ma'am; the downfall of tyrants and the cause of liberty," he said. "As must any honest man."

. . . freedom alone—which any honest man surrenders only with his life. The line echoed in my head, and must have shown on my face, for he looked keenly at me.

"I esteem your husband deeply, ma'am," he said quietly. "You will tell him what I have said?" He bowed and turned away, not waiting for my nod.

He hadn't guarded his voice when speaking of tyrants and liberty; I saw heads nearby turn, and here and there, men drew together, murmuring as they watched him go.

Distracted, I took a mouthful of lemon shrub, and was then obliged to swallow the nasty stuff. I turned to find Jamie; he was still near Allan MacDonald, but had moved a little aside, and was in private conversation with Major MacDonald.

Things were moving faster than I had thought. I had thought republican sentiment was still a minority in this part of the colony, but for Forbes to speak so openly in a public gathering, it was obviously gaining ground.

I turned back to look after the lawyer, and saw two men confront him, their faces tight with anger and suspicion. I was too far away to hear what was said, but their postures and expressions were eloquent. Words were exchanged, growing in heat, and I glanced toward Jamie; the last time I had attended a barbecue like this at River Run, in the prelude to the War of the Regulation, there had been a fistfight on the lawn, and I rather thought such an occurrence might be about to happen again. Alcohol, heat, and politics made for explosions of temper in any gathering, let alone one composed largely of Highlanders.

Such an explosion might have happened—more men were gathering round Forbes and his two opponents, fists curling in readiness—had the boom of Jocasta's large gong not sounded from the terrace, making everyone look up in startlement.

The Major was standing on an upturned tobacco hogshead, hands raised in the air, beaming at the multitudes, face shining red with heat, beer, and enthusiasm.

"*Ceud mile fàilte!*" he called, and was greeted by enthusiastic applause. "And we wish a hundred thousand welcomes to our honored guests!" he continued in Gaelic, sweeping a hand toward the MacDonalds, who were now standing side by side near him, nodding and smiling at the applause. From their demeanor, I rather thought they were accustomed to this sort of reception.

A few more introductory remarks—half-drowned in the enthusiastic cheers—and Jamie and Kingsburgh lifted Mrs. MacDonald carefully up onto the barrel, where she swayed a little, but regained her balance, grabbing the heads of both men for stability, and smiling at the laughter of the audience.

She beamed at the crowd, who beamed back, *en masse*, and immediately quieted themselves in order to hear her.

She had a clear, high voice, and was obviously accustomed to speaking in public—a most unusual attribute in a woman of the time. I was too far away to hear every word, but had no trouble picking up the gist of her speech.

After graciously thanking her hosts, the Scottish community who had welcomed her family so warmly and generously, and the guests, she commenced an earnest exhortation against what she called "factionalism," urging her hearers to join in suppressing this dangerous movement, which could not but cause great unrest, threatening the peace and prosperity that so many of them had achieved in this fair land, they having risked everything to attain it.

And she was, I realized with a small shock, exactly right. I'd heard Bree and Roger arguing the point—why any of the Highlanders, who had suffered so much under English rule, should have fought on the English side, as many of them eventually would.

"Because," Roger had said patiently, "they had something to lose, and damn little to gain. And—of all people—they knew exactly what it was like to fight *against* the English. Ye think folk who lived through Cumberland's cleansing of the Highlands, made it to America, and rebuilt their lives from nothing were eager to live through all that *again*?"

"But surely they'll want to fight for freedom," Bree had protested. He looked at her cynically.

"They *have* freedom, a great deal more than they've ever seen in Scotland. They risk losing it in the event of a war—and they know that very well. And then, of course," he'd added, "nearly all of them have sworn an oath of loyalty to the Crown. They'd not break it lightly, surely not for something that looked like one more wild-eyed—and doubtless short-lived—political upheaval. It's like—" His brow had furrowed as he looked for a suitable analogy.

"Like the Black Panthers, or the civil-rights movement. Anyone could see the idealistic point—but a lot of middle-class people found the whole thing threatening or frightening and just wished it would go away, so life could be peaceful."

The trouble, of course, was that life never *was* peaceful—and this particular wild-eyed movement wasn't *going* to go away. I could see Brianna on the far side of the crowd, eyes narrowed in thoughtful speculation as she listened to Flora MacDonald's high, clear voice, talking of the virtues of loyalty.

I heard a low sort of "Hmph!" just to the side, behind me, and turning, saw Neil Forbes, his heavy features set in disapproval. He had reinforcements now, I saw; three or four other gentlemen stood close beside him, glancing to and fro but trying not to look as though they were. Gauging the mood of the crowd, I thought they were outnumbered by roughly two hundred to one, and the two hundred were growing steadily more entrenched in their opinions as the drink took hold and the speech went on.

Looking away, I caught sight again of Brianna, and realized that she was now looking at Neil Forbes, too—and he was looking back. Both taller than the people around them, they stared at each other over the heads of the intervening crowd, he with animosity, she with aloofness. She had rejected his suit a few years before, and had done so without tact. Forbes certainly hadn't been in love with her—but he was a man with a fair degree of self-esteem, and not the sort to suffer such a public slight with philosophical resignation.

Brianna turned away, coolly, as though she had taken no notice of him, and spoke to the woman beside her. I heard him grunt again, say something in a low tone to his compatriots—and then the knot of them were leaving, rudely turning their backs on Mrs. MacDonald, who was still speaking.

Gasps and murmurs of indignation followed them, as they shoved their way through the thick-packed crowd, but no one offered to stop them, and the offense of their leaving was drowned by the outburst of prolonged applause that greeted the conclusion of the speech—this accompanied by the starting up of bagpipes, the random firing of pistols into the air, organized cheering of

"Hip, hip, huzzay!" led by Major MacDonald, and such a general hullabaloo that no one would have noticed the arrival of an army, let alone the departure of a few disaffected Whigs.

I found Jamie in the shade of Hector's mausoleum, combing out his hair with his fingers, preparatory to retying it.

"That went with a bang, didn't it?" I asked.

"Several of them," he said, keeping a wary eye on one obviously inebriated gentleman in the act of trying to reload his musket. "Watch that man, Sassenach."

"He's too late to shoot Neil Forbes. Did you see him leave?"

He nodded, deftly knotting the leather thong at his nape.

"He couldna have come much closer to an open declaration, save he'd got up on the barrel next to Fionnaghal."

"And that would have made him an *excellent* target." I squinted at the red-faced gentleman, presently spilling gunpowder on his shoes. "I don't think he has any bullets."

"Oh, well, then." Jamie dismissed him with a wave of the hand. "Major MacDonald's in rare form, no? He told me he's arranged for Mrs. MacDonald to give such speeches here and there about the colony."

"With himself as impresario, I take it." I could just catch the gleam of MacDonald's red coat among the press of well-wishers on the terrace.

"I daresay." Jamie didn't seem pleased at the prospect. In fact, he seemed rather sober, his face shadowed by dark thoughts. His mood would not be improved by hearing about my conversation with Neil Forbes, but I told him anyway.

"Well, it couldna be helped," he said with a small shrug. "I'd hoped to keep the matter quiet, but wi' things as they are wi' Robin McGillivray, I've no real choice save to ask where I may, though that lets the matter be known. And talked about." He moved again, restless.

"Are ye well, Sassenach?" he asked suddenly, looking at me.

"Yes. But *you* aren't. What is it?"

He smiled faintly.

"Och, it's nothing. Nothing I didna ken already. But it's different, no? Ye think ye're ready, and then ye meet it face to face, and would give anything to have it otherwise."

He looked out at the lawn, lifting his chin to point at the crowd. A sea of tartan flowed across the grass, the ladies' parasols raised against the sun, a field of brightly colored flowers. In the shade of the terrace, a piper played on, the sound of his *piobreachd* a thin, piercing descant to the hum of conversation.

"I kent I should have to stand one day against a good many of them, aye? To fight friends and kin. But then I found myself standing there, wi' Fionnaghal's hand upon my head like a blessing, face to face wi' them all, and watching her words fall upon them, see the resolve growing in them . . . and all of a sudden, it was as though a great blade had come down from heaven between them and me, to cleave us forever apart. The day is coming—and I can not stop it."

He swallowed, and looked down, away from me. I reached out to him, wanting to help, wanting to ease him—and knowing that I couldn't. It was, after all, by my doing that he found himself here, in this small Gethsemane.

Nonetheless, he took my hand, not looking at me, and squeezed it hard, so the bones pressed together.

"Lord, that this cup might pass from me?" I whispered.

He nodded, his gaze still resting on the ground, the fallen petals of the yellow roses. Then he looked at me, with a small smile but such pain in his eyes that I caught my breath, stricken to the heart.

Still, he smiled, and wiping his hand across his forehead, examined his wet fingers.

"Aye, well," he said. "It's only water, not blood. I'll live."

Perhaps you won't, I thought suddenly, appalled. To fight on the winning side was one thing; to survive, quite another.

He saw the look on my face, and released the pressure on my hand, thinking he was hurting me. He was, but not physically.

"But not my will be done, but Thine," he said very softly. "I chose my way when I wed ye, though I kent it not at the time. But I chose, and cannot now turn back, even if I would."

"Would you?" I looked into his eyes as I asked, and read the answer there. He shook his head.

"Would you? For you have chosen, as much as I."

I shook my head, as well, and felt the small relaxation of his body as his eyes met mine, clear now as the brilliant sky. For the space of a heartbeat, we stood alone together in the universe. Then a knot of chattering girls drifted within earshot, and I changed the subject to something safer.

"Have you heard anything about poor Manfred?"

"Poor Manfred, is it?" he gave me a cynical look.

"Well, he may be an immoral young hound, and have caused any amount of trouble—but that doesn't mean he ought to die for it."

He looked as though he might not be in complete agreement with this sentiment, but let the matter lie, saying merely that he'd asked, but so far without result.

"He'll turn up, though," he assured me. "Likely in the most inconvenient place."

"Oh! Oh! Oh! That I should live to see such a day! I thank ye, sir, thank ye indeed!" It was Mrs. Bug, flushed with heat, beer, and happiness, fanning herself fit to burst. Jamie smiled at her.

"So, were ye able to hear everything, then, *mo chridhe*?"

"Oh, indeed I was, sir!" she assured him fervently. "Every word! Arch found me a lovely place, just by one of they tubs o' wee flowers, where I could hear and not be trampled." She had nearly died of excitement when Jamie had offered to bring her down to the barbecue. Arch was coming, of course, and would go on to do errands in Cross Creek, but Mrs. Bug hadn't been off the Ridge since their arrival several years before.

Despite my disquiet over the profoundly Loyalist atmosphere that surrounded us, her bubbling delight was infectious, and I found myself smiling, Jamie and myself taking it in turns to answer her questions: she hadn't seen black slaves close-to before, and thought them exotically beautiful—did they cost a great deal? And must they be taught to wear clothes and speak properly? For she had heard that Africa was a heathen place where folk went entirely naked and killed one another with spears, like as one would do with a boar, and if one wanted to speak of naked, that statue of the soldier laddie on the lawn was shocking, did we not think? And him wi' not a stitch behind his shield! And whyever was that woman's heid at his feet? And had I looked—her hair was made to look as if 'twere snakes, of all horrid things! And who was Hector Cameron, whose tomb this was?—and made all of white marble, same as the tombs in Holyrood, imagine! Oh, Mrs. Innes's late husband? And when had she married Mr. Duncan, whom she had met, and such a sweet, kind-eyed man as he was, such a shame as he had lost his arm, was that in a battle of some type? And—oh, look! Mrs. MacDonald's husband—and a fine figure of man he was, too—was going to talk, as well!

Jamie gave the terrace a bleak look. Sure enough, Allan MacDonald was stepping up—merely onto a stool; no doubt the hogshead seemed extreme—and a number of people—far fewer than had attended his wife, but a respectable number—were clustering round attentively.

"Will ye no come and hear him?" Mrs. Bug was already in flight, hovering above the ground like a hummingbird.

"I'll hear well enough from here," Jamie assured her. "You go along then, *a nighean.*"

She bumbled off, buzzing with excitement. Jamie gingerly touched both hands to his ears, testing to be sure they were still attached.

"It was kind of you to bring her," I said, laughing. "The dear old thing probably hasn't had such fun in half a century."

"No," he said, grinning. "She likely—"

He stopped abruptly, frowning as he caught sight of something over my shoulder. I turned to look, but he was already moving past me, and I hurried to catch up.

It was Jocasta, white as milk, and disheveled in a way I had never seen her. She swayed unsteadily in the side doorway, and might have fallen, had Jamie not come up and taken quick hold of her, one arm about her waist to support her.

"Jesus, Auntie. What's amiss?" He spoke quietly, not to draw attention, and was moving her back inside the house even as he spoke.

"Oh, God, oh, merciful God, my head," she whispered, hand spread over her face like a spider, so that her fingers barely touched the skin, cupping her left eye. "My eye."

The linen blindfold that she wore in public was creased and blotched with moisture; tears were leaking out from under it, but she wasn't crying. Lacrimation: one eye was watering terribly. Both eyes were tearing, but much worse on the left; the edge of the linen was soaked, and wetness shone on that cheek.

"I need to look at her eye," I said to Jamie, touching his elbow, and looking round in vain for any of the servants. "Get her to her sitting room." That was closest, and all the guests were either outside or traipsing through the parlor to see the Prince's looking glass.

"No!" It was almost a scream. "No, not there!"

Jamie glanced at me, one brow raised in puzzlement, but spoke soothingly to her.

"Nay, Auntie, it's all right. I'll bring ye to your own chamber. Come, then." He stooped, and lifted her in his arms as though she were a child, her silk skirts falling over his arm with the sound of rushing water.

"Take her; I'll be right there." I'd spotted the slave named Angelina passing through the far end of the hall, and hurried to catch her up. I gave my orders, then rushed back toward the stairs—pausing momentarily to glance into the small sitting room as I did so.

There was no one there, though the presence of scattered punch cups and the strong scent of pipe tobacco indicated that Jocasta had likely been holding court there earlier. Her workbasket stood open, some half-knitted garment dragged out and left to dangle carelessly down the side like a dead rabbit.

Children perhaps, I thought; several balls of thread had been pulled out, too, and lay scattered on the parquet floor, trailing their colors. I hesitated—but instinct was too much for me, and I hastily scooped up the balls of thread and dropped them back into the workbasket. I stuffed the knitting in on top, but jerked my hand back with an exclamation.

A small gash on the side of my thumb was welling blood. I put it in my mouth and sucked hard to apply pressure to the wound; meanwhile, I groped more cautiously in the depths of the basket with my other hand, to see what had cut me.

A knife, small but businesslike. Likely used to cut embroidery threads; there was a tooled-leather sheath for it, loose in the bottom of the basket. I slipped the knife back into its sheath, seized the needle case I'd come for, and closed the folding tabletop of the workbasket before hurrying for the stairs.

Allan MacDonald had finished his brief speech; there was a loud clatter of applause outside, with shouts and whoops of Gaelic approval.

"Bloody Scots," I muttered under my breath. "Don't they *ever* learn?"

But I hadn't time to consider the implications of the MacDonalds' rabble-rousing. By the time I reached the top of the stair, one slave was close behind me, puffing under the weight of my medicine box, and another was at the bottom, starting more cautiously up with a pan of hot water from the kitchen.

Jocasta was bent double in her big chair, moaning, lips pressed into invisibility. Her cap had come off and both hands moved restlessly to and fro through her disordered hair, as though looking helplessly for something to seize. Jamie was stroking her back, murmuring to her in Gaelic; he looked up with obvious relief as I came in.

I had long suspected that the cause of Jocasta's blindness was glaucoma—rising pressure inside the eyeball that if untreated eventually damages the optic nerve. Now I was quite sure of it. More than that, I knew what form of the disease she had; she was plainly having an acute attack of closed-angle glaucoma, the most dangerous type.

There was no treatment for glaucoma now; the condition itself wouldn't be recognized for some time. Even if there had been, it was far too late; her blindness was permanent. There was, however, something I could do about the immediate situation—and I was afraid I'd have to.

"Put some of this to steep," I said to Angelina, grabbing the jar of goldenseal from my box and thrusting it into her hands. "And you"—I turned to the other slave, a man whose name I didn't know—"set the water to boil again, fetch me some clean rags, and put them in the water."

Even as I talked, I'd got out the tiny spirit lamp I carried in my case. The fire had been allowed to burn down on the hearth, but there were still live coals; I bent and lit the wick, then opened the needle case I'd taken from the sitting room and abstracted the largest needle in it, a three-inch length of steel, used for mending carpets.

"You aren't . . ." Jamie began, then broke off, swallowing.

"I have to," I said briefly. "There's nothing else. Hold her hands."

He was nearly as pale as Jocasta, but he nodded and took hold of the clutching fingers, pulling her hands gently away from her head.

I lifted away the linen bandage. The left eye bulged noticeably beneath its lid, vividly bloodshot. Tears welled up round it and overflowed in a constant stream. I could *feel* the pressure inside the eyeball, even without touching it, and clenched my teeth in revulsion.

No help for it. With a quick prayer to Saint Clare—who was, after all, patroness of sore eyes, as well as my own patron saint—I ran the needle through the flame of the lamp, poured pure alcohol onto a rag, and wiped the soot from the needle.

Swallowing a sudden excess of saliva, I spread the eyelids of the affected eye apart with one hand, commended my soul to God, and shoved the needle hard into the sclera of the eye, near the edge of the iris.

There was a cough and a splattering on the floor nearby, and the stink of vomit, but I had no attention to spare. I withdrew the needle carefully, though as fast as I could. Jocasta had stiffened abruptly, frozen stiff, hands clawed over Jamie's. She didn't move at all, but made small, shocked panting sounds, as though afraid to move enough even to breathe.

There was a trickle of fluid from the eye, vitreous humor, faintly cloudy, just thick enough to be distinguishable as it flowed sluggishly across the wet surface of the sclera. I was still holding the eyelids apart; I plucked a rag from the goldenseal tea with my free hand, squeezed out the excess liquid, careless of where it went, and touched it gently to her face. Jocasta gasped at the touch of the warmth on her skin, pulled her hands free, and grasped at it.

I let go then, and allowed her to seize the warm rag, pressing it against her closed left eye, the heat of it some relief.

Light feet pounded up the stairs again, and down the hall; Angelina, panting, a handful of salt clutched to her bosom, a spoon in her other hand. I brushed the salt from her damp palm into the pan of warm water, and set her to stir it while it dissolved.

"Did you bring laudanum?" I asked her quietly. Jocasta was lying back in her chair, eyes closed—but rigid as a statue, her eyelids squeezing tight, fists clenched in knots on her knees.

"I couldna find the laudanum, missus," Angelina murmured to me, with a frightened glance at Jocasta. "I dinna ken who could be takin' it—hain't nobody got the key but Mr. Ulysses and Miz Cameron herself."

"Ulysses let you into the simples closet, then—so he knows that Mrs. Cameron is ill?"

She nodded vigorously, setting the ribbon on her cap a-flutter.

"Oh, yes, missus! He be bleezin', if he find out and I hain't told him. He say come fetch him quick, she want him—otherwise, I tell

Miz Cameron she hain't to worry none, he take care every single thing."

Jocasta let out a long sigh at this, her clenched fists relaxing a little.

"God bless the man," she murmured, eyes closed. "He *will* take care of everything. I should be lost without him. Lost."

Her white hair was soaked at the temples, and sweat dripped from the ends of the tendrils that lay over her shoulder, making spots on the dark blue silk of her gown.

Angelina unlaced Jocasta's gown and stays and got them off. Then I had Jamie lay her down on the bed in her shift, with a thick layer of towels tucked round her head. I filled one of my rattlesnake syringes with the warm salt water, and with Jamie gingerly holding the lids of her eye apart, I was able to gently irrigate the eye, in hopes of perhaps preventing infection to the puncture wound. The wound itself showed as a tiny scarlet spot on the sclera, a small conjunctival bleb above it. Jamie couldn't look at it without blinking, I saw, and smiled at him.

"She'll be all right," I said. "You can go, if you like."

Jamie nodded, turning to go, but Jocasta's hand shot out to stop him.

"No, be staying, *a chuisle*—if ye will." This last was strictly for form's sake; she had him clutched by the sleeve, hard enough to turn her fingers white.

"Aye, Auntie, of course," he said mildly, and put his hand over hers, squeezing in reassurance. Still, she didn't let go until he had sat down beside her.

"Who else is there?" she asked, turning her head fretfully from side to side, trying to hear the telltale sounds of breathing and movement that would inform her. "Have the slaves gone?"

"Yes, they've gone back to help with the serving," I told her. "It's only me and Jamie left."

She closed her eyes and drew a deep, shuddering breath, only then beginning to relax a little.

"Good. I must tell ye a thing, Nephew, and no one else must hear. Niece"—she lifted a long white hand toward me—"go and be seeing as we're truly alone."

I went obediently to look out into the hall. No one was visible, though there were voices coming from a room down the hall— laughter, and tremendous rustlings and thumpings, as young women chattered and rearranged their hair and clothing. I pulled my head back in and closed the door, and the sounds from the rest of the house receded at once, muffled into a distant rumble.

"What is it, then, Auntie?" Jamie was still holding her hand, one big thumb gently stroking the back of it, over and over, in the soothing rhythm I'd seen him use on skittish animals. It was less effective on his aunt than on the average horse or dog, though.

"It was him. He's here!"

"Who's here, Auntie?"

"I don't know!" Her eyes rolled desperately to and fro, as though in a vain attempt to see through not only darkness, but walls, as well.

Jamie raised his brows at me, but he could see as well as I that she wasn't raving, incoherent as she sounded. She realized what she sounded like; I could see the effort in her face as she pulled herself together.

"He's come for the gold," she said, lowering her voice. "The Frenchman's gold."

"Oh, aye?" Jamie said cautiously. He darted a glance at me, one eyebrow raised, but I shook my head. She wasn't having hallucinations.

Jocasta sighed with impatience and shook her head, then stopped abruptly, with a muffled "Och!" of pain, putting both hands to her head as though to keep it on her shoulders.

She breathed deeply for a moment or two, her lips pressed tight together. Then she slowly lowered her hands.

"It started last night," she said. "The pain in my eye."

She'd waked in the night to a throbbing in her eye, a dull pain that spread slowly to the side of her head.

"It's come before, ken," she explained. She had pushed herself up to a sitting position now, and was beginning to look a little better, though she still held the warm cloth to her eye. "It began when I started to lose my sight. Sometimes it would be one eye, sometimes both. But I kent what was coming."

But Jocasta MacKenzie Cameron Innes was not a woman to allow mere bodily indisposition to interfere with her plans, let alone interrupt what promised to be the most scintillating social affair in Cross Creek's history.

"I was that disgusted," she said. "And here Miss Flora MacDonald coming!"

But the arrangements had all been made; the barbecued carcasses were roasting in their pits, hogsheads of ale and beer stood ready by the stables, and the air was full of the fragrance of hot bread and beans from the cookhouse. The slaves were well-trained, and she had full faith that Ulysses would manage everything. All she must do, she'd thought, was to stay on her feet.

"I didna want to take opium or laudanum," she explained. "Or I'd fall asleep for sure. So I made do wi' the whisky."

She was a tall woman, and thoroughly accustomed to an intake of liquor that would have felled a modern man. By the time the MacDonalds arrived, she'd had the better part of a bottle—but the pain was getting worse.

"And then my eye began to water so fierce, everyone would ha' seen something was wrong, and I didna want *that*. So I came into my sitting room; I'd taken care to put a wee bottle of laudanum in my workbasket, in case the whisky should be not enough.

"Folk were swarming thick as lice outside, trying to catch a glimpse or a word with Miss MacDonald, but the sitting room was deserted, so far as I could tell, what wi' my head pounding and my eye fit to explode." She said this last quite casually, but I saw Jamie flinch, the memory of what I'd done with the needle obviously still fresh. He swallowed and wiped his knuckles hard across his mouth.

Jocasta had quickly abstracted the bottle of laudanum, swallowed a few gulps, and then sat for a moment, waiting for it to take effect.

"I dinna ken if ye've ever had the stuff, Nephew, but it gives ye an odd feeling, as though ye might be starting to dissolve at the edges. Take a drop too much, and ye begin to see things that aren't there—blind or not—and hear them, too."

Between the effects of laudanum and liquor and the noise of the crowd outside, she hadn't noticed footsteps, and when the voice spoke near her, she'd thought for a moment that it was a hallucination.

" 'So here ye are, lass,' he said," she quoted, and her face, already pale, blanched further at the memory. " 'Remember me, do ye?' "

"I take it ye did, Aunt?" Jamie asked dryly.

"I did," she replied just as dryly. "I'd heard that voice twice before. Once at the Gathering where your daughter was wed—and once more than twenty years ago, in an inn near Coigach, in Scotland."

She lowered the wet cloth from her face and put it unerringly back into the bowl of warm water. Her eyes were red and swollen, raw against the pale skin, and looking terribly vulnerable in their blindness—but she had command of herself once more.

"Aye, I did ken him," she repeated.

She had recognized the voice at once as one known—but for a moment, could not place it. Then realization had struck her, and she had clutched the arm of her chair for support.

"Who are ye?" she'd demanded, with what force she could summon. Her heart was pounding in time to the throbbing in her head and eye, and her senses swimming in whisky and laudanum. Perhaps it was the laudanum that seemed to transform the sound of the crowd outside into the sound of a nearby sea, the noise of a slave's footsteps in the hall to the thump of the landlord's clogs on the stairs of the inn.

"I was there. Truly there." Despite the sweat that still ran down her face, I saw gooseflesh pebble the pale skin of her shoulders. "In the inn at Coigach. I smelt the sea, and I heard the men—Hector and Dougal—I could *hear* them! Arguing together, somewhere behind me. And the man wi' the mask—I could *see* him," she said, and a ripple went up the back of my own neck as she turned her blind eyes toward me. She spoke with such conviction that for an instant, it seemed she *did* see.

"Standing at the foot of the stair, just as he'd been twenty-five years ago, a knife in his hand and his eyes upon me through the holes in his mask."

And, "Ye ken well enough who I am, lass," he'd said, and she had seemed to see his smile, though dimly she had known she only heard it in his voice; she'd never seen his face, even when she had her sight.

She was sitting up, half doubled over, arms crossed over her breast as though in self-defense and her white hair wild and tangled down her back.

"He's come back," she said, and shook with a sudden convulsive shudder. "He's come for the gold—and when he finds it, he will kill me."

Jamie laid a hand on her arm, in an attempt to calm her.

"No one will kill ye while I'm here, Aunt," he said. "So this man came to ye in your sitting room, and ye kent him from his voice. What else did he say to ye?"

She was still shivering, but not so badly. I thought it was as much reaction to massive amounts of laudanum and whisky as from fear.

She shook her head in the effort of recollection.

"He said—he said he had come to take the gold to its rightful owner. That we'd held it in trust, and while he didna grudge me what we'd spent of it, Hector and me—it wasna mine, had never been mine. I should tell him where it was, and he would see to the rest. And then he put his hand on me." She ceased clutching herself, and held out one arm toward Jamie. "On my wrist. D'ye see the marks there? D'ye see them, Nephew?" She sounded anxious, and it occurred to me suddenly that she might doubt the existence of the visitor herself.

"Aye, Auntie," Jamie said softly, touching her wrist. "There are marks."

There were; three purplish smudges, small ovals where fingers had grippcd.

"He squeezed, and then twisted my wrist so hard I thought it had snapped. Then he let go, but he didna step back. He stayed over me, and I could feel the heat of his breath and the stink of tobacco ᵟn my face."

I had hold of her other wrist, feeling the pulse beat there. It was strong and rapid, but every once in a while would skip a beat. Hardly surprising. I did wonder how often she took laudanum—and how much.

"So I reached down into my workbasket, took my wee knife from its sheath, and went for his balls," she concluded.

Taken by surprise, Jamie laughed.

"Did ye get him?"

"Yes, she did," I said, before Jocasta could answer. "I saw dried blood on the knife."

"Well, that will teach him to terrorize a helpless blind woman, won't it?" Jamie patted her hand. "Ye did well, Auntie. Did he go, then?"

"He did." The recounting of her success had steadied her a lot; she pulled her hand from my grip, in order to push herself up straighter against the pillows. She pulled away the towel still draped around her neck, and dropped it on the floor with a brief grimace of distaste.

Seeing that she was plainly feeling better, Jamie glanced at me, then rose to his feet.

"I'll go and see is anyone limping about the place, then." At the door, he paused, though, turning back to Jocasta.

"Auntie. Ye said ye'd met this fellow *twice* before? At the inn in Coigach where the men brought the gold ashore—and at the Gathering four years ago?"

She nodded, brushing back the damp hair from her face.

"I did. 'Twas on the last day. He came into my tent, while I was alone. I kent someone was there, though he didna speak at first, and I asked who was it? He gave a bit of a laugh, then, and said, 'It's true what they said, then—you're blind entirely?'"

She had stood up, facing the invisible visitor, recognizing the voice, but not quite knowing yet why.

"'So ye dinna ken me, Mrs. Cameron? I was a friend to your husband—though it's been a good many years since last we met. On the coast of Scotland—on a moonlicht nicht.'"

She licked dry lips at the memory.

"So then it came to me, all on the sudden. And I said, 'Blind I may be, but I ken ye well, sir. What d'ye want?' But he was gone. And the next instant, I heard Phaedre and Ulysses talking as they came toward the tent; he'd seen them, and fled away. I asked them, but they'd been ta'en up wi' their arguing, and hadna seen him leave. I kept someone by me all the time, then, until we left—and he didna come near me again. Until now."

Jamie frowned and rubbed a knuckle slowly down the long, straight bridge of his nose.

"Why did ye not tell me then?"

A trace of humor touched her ravaged face, and she wrapped her fingers round her injured wrist.

"I thought I was imagining things."

Phaedre had found the bottle of laudanum where Jocasta had dropped it, under her chair in the sitting room. Likewise, a trail of tiny blood spots that I had missed in my hurry. These disappeared before reaching the door, though; whatever wound Jocasta had inflicted on the intruder had been minor.

Duncan, summoned discreetly, had hurried in to comfort Jocasta—only to be sent directly out again, with instructions to see to the guests; neither injury nor illness was going to mar such an occasion!

Ulysses met with a slightly more cordial reception. In fact, Jocasta sent for him. Peering into her room to check on her, I found him sitting by the bed, holding his mistress's hand, with such an expression of gentleness on his usually impassive face that I was quite moved by it, and stepped quietly back into the hall, not to disturb them. He saw me, though, and nodded.

They were talking in low voices, his head in its stiff white wig bending toward hers. He seemed to be arguing with her, in a most respectful fashion; she shook her head, and gave a small cry of pain. His hand tightened on hers, and I saw that he had taken off his white gloves; her hand lay long and frail, pallid in his powerful dark grasp.

She breathed deeply, steadying herself. Then she said something definite, squeezed his hand, and lay back. He rose, and stood for a moment beside the bed, looking down at her. Then he drew himself up, and taking his gloves from his pocket, came out into the hall.

"If you will fetch your husband, Mrs. Fraser?" he said, low-voiced. "My mistress wishes me to tell him something."

The party was still in full swing, but had shifted to a lower, digestive sort of gear. People greeted Jamie or me as we followed Ulysses into the house, but no one stopped us.

He led us downstairs to his butler's pantry, a tiny room that lay off the winter kitchen, its shelves crammed with silver ornaments, bottles of polish, vinegar, blacking, and bluing, a housewife with needles, pins, and threads, small tools for mending, and what looked like a substantial private stock of brandy, whisky, and assorted cordials.

He removed these from their shelf, and reaching back into the empty space where they had stood, pressed upon the wood of the wall with both white-gloved hands. Something clicked, and a small panel slid aside with a soft rasping sound.

He stood aside, silently inviting Jamie to look. Jamie raised one eyebrow and leaned forward, peering into the recess. It was dark and shadowy in the butler's pantry, with only a dim light filtering in from the high basement windows that ran around the top of the kitchen walls.

"It's empty," he said.

"Yes, sir. It should not be." Ulysses's voice was low and respectful, but firm.

"What *was* there?" I asked, glancing out of the pantry to be sure we were not overheard. The kitchen looked as though a bomb had gone off in it, but only a scullion was there, a half-witted boy who was washing pots, singing softly to himself.

"Part of an ingot of gold," Ulysses replied softly.

The French gold Hector Cameron had brought away from Scotland, ten thousand pounds in bullion, cast in ingots and marked with the royal fleur-de-lis, was the foundation of River Run's wealth. But it would not do, of course, for that fact to be known. First Hector, and then, after Hector's death, Ulysses, had taken one of the gold bars and scraped bits of the soft yellow metal into a small, anonymous heap. This could then be taken to the river warehouses—or for additional safety, sometimes as far as the coastal towns of Edenton, Wilmington, or New Bern—and there carefully changed, in small amounts that would cause no comment, into cash or warehouse certificates, which could safely be used anywhere.

"There was about half of the ingot left," Ulysses said, nodding toward the cavity in the wall. "I found it gone a few months ago. Since then, of course, I have contrived a new hiding place."

Jamie looked into the empty cavity, then turned to Ulysses.

"The rest?"

"Safe enough, last time I checked, sir." The bulk of the gold was concealed inside Hector Cameron's mausoleum, hidden in a coffin and guarded, presumably, by his spirit. One or two of the slaves besides Ulysses might know about it, but the very lively fear of ghosts was enough to keep everyone away. I remembered the line of salt spread on the ground in front of the mausoleum, and shivered a little, in spite of the stifling heat in the basement.

"I could not, of course, make shift to look today," the butler added.

"No, of course not. Duncan knows?" Jamie nodded toward the recess, and Ulysses nodded.

"The thief might have been anyone. So many people come to this house. . . . " The butler's massive shoulders moved in a small shrug. "But now that this man from the sea has come again—it puts a different face upon the matter, does it not, sir?"

"Aye, it does." Jamie contemplated the matter for a moment, tapping two fingers softly against his leg.

"Well, then. Ye'll need to stay for a bit, Sassenach, will ye not? To look after my aunt's eye?"

I nodded. Provided no infection resulted from my crude intervention, there was little or nothing I could do for the eye itself. But it should be watched, kept clean and irrigated, until I could be sure it was healed.

"We'll stay, then, for a bit," he said, turning to Ulysses. "I'll send the Bugs back to the Ridge, to mind things and see to the haying. We'll stay, and watch."

The house was full of guests, but I slept in Jocasta's dressing room, so that I might keep an eye on her. The easing of pressure in her eye had relieved the excruciating pain, and she had fallen soundly asleep, her vital signs reassuring enough that I felt I could sleep, too.

Knowing I had a patient, though, I slept lightly, waking at intervals to tiptoe into her room. Duncan was sleeping on a pallet at the foot of her bed, dead to the world from the exhaustions of the day. I could hear his heavy breathing, as I lit a taper from the hearth and came to stand by the bed.

Jocasta was still soundly asleep, lying on her back, arms crossed gracefully over the coverlet and her head thrown back, sternly long-nosed and aristocratic as the tomb figures in the chapel of St. Denys. All she wanted was a crown, and a small dog of some kind crouched at her feet.

I smiled at the thought, thinking as I did how odd it was: Jamie slept in exactly that fashion, lying flat on his back, hands crossed, straight as an arrow. Brianna didn't; she was a wild sleeper, and had been from a child. Like me.

The thought gave me a small, unexpected feeling of pleasure. I knew I had given her some parts of me, of course, but she resembled Jamie so strongly, it was always something of a surprise to notice one.

I blew out the taper, but didn't at once return to bed. I had taken Phaedre's cot in the dressing room, but it was a hot, airless little space. The hot day and the consumption of alcohol had left me cotton-mouthed, with a vague headache; I picked up the carafe from Jocasta's bedside, but it was empty.

No need to relight the taper; one of the sconces in the hallway was still burning, and a dim glow outlined the door. I pushed it open quietly and looked out. The corridor was lined with bodies—servants sleeping by the doors of the bedrooms—and the air throbbed gently with the snoring and heavy breathing of a great many people sunk in slumber of varying degrees.

At the end of the corridor, though, one pale figure stood upright, looking out through the tall casement window toward the river.

She must have heard me, but didn't turn around. I came to stand beside her, looking out. Phaedre was undressed to her shift, her hair free of its cloth and falling in a soft thick mass around her shoulders. Rare for a slave to have such hair, I thought; most women kept their hair very short under turban or headcloth, lacking both time and tools for dressing it. But Phaedre was a body servant; she would have some leisure—and a comb, at least.

"Would you like your bed back?" I asked, low-voiced. "I'll be up for a while—and can sleep on the divan."

She glanced at me, and shook her head.

"Oh, no, ma'am," she said softly. "Thankee kindly; I ain't sleepy." She saw the carafe I carried, and reached for it. "I fetch you some water, ma'am?"

"No, no, I'll do it. I'd like the air." Still, I stood beside her, looking out.

It was a beautiful night, thick with stars that hung low and bright over the river, a faint silver thread that wound its way through the dark. There was a moon, a slender sickle, riding low on its way below the curve of the earth, and one or two small campfires burned in the trees beside the river.

The window was open, and bugs were swarming in; a small cloud of them danced around the candle in the sconce behind us, and tiny winged things brushed my face and arms. Crickets sang, so many of them that their song was a high, constant sound, like a bow drawn over violin strings.

Phaedre moved to shut it—to sleep with a window open was considered most unhealthy, and likely *was,* given the various mosquito-borne diseases in this swampish atmosphere.

"I thought I heard something. Out there," she said, nodding toward the dark below.

"Oh? Probably my husband," I said. "Or Ulysses."

"Ulysses?" she said, looking startled.

Jamie, Ian, and Ulysses had organized a system of patrol, and were doubtless out somewhere in the night, gliding round the house and keeping an eye on Hector's mausoleum, just in case. Knowing nothing of the disappearing gold nor Jocasta's mysterious visitor, though, Phaedre wouldn't be aware of the increased vigilance, save in the indirect way in which slaves always knew things—the instinct that had doubtless roused her to look out the window.

"They're just keeping an eye out," I said, as reassuringly as I could. "With so many people here, you know." The MacDonalds had gone to Farquard Campbell's plantation to spend the night, and a goodly number of guests had gone with them, but there were still a lot of people on the premises.

She nodded, but looked troubled.

"It just feel like something ain't right," she said. "Don't know what 'tis."

"Your mistress's eye—" I began, but she shook her head.

"No. No. I don't know, but there's something in the air; I be feelin' it. Not just tonight, I don't mean—something goin' on. Something coming." She looked at me, helpless to express what she meant, but her mood communicated itself to me.

It might be in part simply the heightened emotions of the oncoming conflict. One could in fact feel that in the air. But there might be something else, too—something subterranean, barely sensed, but there, like the dim form of a sea serpent, glimpsed for only a moment, then gone, and so put down to legend.

"My grannie, she taken from Africa," Phaedre said softly, staring out at the night. "She talk to the bones. Say they tell her when bad things comin'."

"Really?" In such an atmosphere, quiet save the night sounds, so many souls adrift around us, there seemed nothing unreal about such a statement. "Did she teach you to . . . talk to bones?"

She shook her head, but the corner of her mouth tucked in, a small, secret expression, and I thought she might know more about it than she was willing to say.

One unwelcome thought had occurred to me. I didn't see how Stephen Bonnet could be connected to present events—surely he was not the man who had spoken to Jocasta out of her past, and just as surely, stealthy theft was not his style. But he did have some reason to believe there might be gold somewhere at River Run—and from what Roger had told us of Phaedre's encounter with the big Irishman in Cross Creek . . .

"The Irishman you met, when you were out with Jemmy," I said, changing my grip on the slick surface of the carafe, "have you ever seen him again?"

She looked surprised at that; clearly Bonnet was the farthest thing from her mind.

"No, ma'am," she said. "Ain't seen him again, ever." She thought for a moment, big eyes hooded. She was the color of strong coffee with a dash of cream, and her hair—there had been a white man in her family tree at some time, I thought.

"No, ma'am," she repeated softly, and turned her troubled gaze back to the quiet night and the sinking moon. "All I know—something ain't right."

Out by the stables, a rooster began to crow, the sound out of place and eerie in the dark.

Wendigo

The light in the morning room was perfect.

"We began with this room," Jocasta had told her great-niece, raising her face to the sun that poured through the open double doors to the terrace, lids closed over her blind eyes. "I wanted a room to paint in, and chose this spot, where the light would come in, bright as crystal in the morning, like still water in the afternoon. And then we built the house around it." The old woman's hands, still long-fingered and strong, touched the easel, the pigment pots, the brushes, with affectionate regret, as she might caress the statue of a long-dead lover—a passion recalled, but accepted as forever gone.

And Brianna, sketching block and pencil in hand, had drawn as quickly, as covertly as she could, to catch that fleeting expression of grief outlived.

That sketch lay with the others in the bottom of her box, against the day when she might try it in more finished form, try to catch that merciless light, and the deep-carved lines of her aunt's face, strong bones stark in the sun she could not see.

For now, though, the painting at hand was a matter of business, rather than love or art. Nothing suspicious had happened since Flora MacDonald's barbecue, but her parents meant to stay for a little longer, just in case. With Roger still in Charlotte—he had written to her; the letter was secreted in the bottom of her box, with the private sketches—there was no reason why she shouldn't stay, too. Hearing of her continued presence, two or three of Jocasta's acquaintances, wealthy planters, had commissioned portraits of themselves or their families; a welcome source of income.

"I will never understand how ye do that," Ian said, shaking his head at the canvas on her easel. "It's wonderful."

In all honesty, she didn't understand how she did it, either; it didn't seem necessary. She'd said as much in answer to similar compliments before, though, and realized that such an answer generally struck the hearer either as false modesty or as condescension.

She smiled at him, instead, letting the glow of pleasure she felt show in her face.

"When I was little, my father would take me walking on the Common, and we'd see an old man there often, painting with an easel. I used to make Daddy stop so I could watch, and he and the old man would chat. I mostly just stared, but once I got up the nerve to ask him how he did that and he looked down at me and smiled, and said, 'The only trick, sweetie, is to see what you're looking at.'"

Ian looked from her to the picture, then back, as though comparing the portrait with the hand that had made it.

"Your father," he said, interested. He lowered his voice, glancing toward the door into the hallway. There were voices, but not close. "Ye dinna mean Uncle Jamie?"

"No." She felt the familiar small ache at the thought of her first father, but put it aside. She didn't mind telling Ian about him—but not here, with slaves all over the place and a constant flow of visitors who might pop in at any moment.

"Look." She glanced over her shoulder to be sure no one was near, but the slaves were talking loudly in the foyer, arguing over a misplaced boot scraper. She lifted the cover of the small compartment that held spare brushes, and reached under the strip of felt that lined it.

"What do you think?" She held the pair of miniatures out for his inspection, one in either palm.

The look of expectation on his face changed to outright fascination, and he reached slowly for one of the tiny paintings.

"I will be damned," he said. It was the one of her mother, her hair long and curling loose on bare shoulders, the small firm chin raised with an authority that belied the generous curve of the mouth above.

"The eyes—I don't think those are quite right," she said, peering into his hand. "Working so small . . . I couldn't get the color, exactly. Da's were much easier."

Blues just *were* easier. A tiny dab of cobalt, highlighted with white and that faint green shadow that intensified the blue while vanishing itself . . . well, and that was Da, too. Strong, vivid, and straightforward.

To get a brown with true depth and subtlety, though, let alone something that even approximated the smoky topaz of her mother's eyes—always clear, but changing like the light on a peat-brown trout stream—that needed more underpainting than was really possible in the tiny space of a miniature. She'd have to try again sometime, with a larger portrait.

"Are they like, do you think?"

"They're wonderful." Ian looked from one to the other, then he put the portrait of Claire gently back into its place. "Have your parents seen them yet?"

"No. I wanted to be sure they were right, before I showed them to anybody. But if they are—I'm thinking I can show them to the people who come to sit, and maybe get commissions for more miniatures. Those I could work on at home, on the Ridge; all I'd need is my paint box and the little ivory discs. I could do the painting from the sketches; I wouldn't need the sitter to keep coming."

She made a brief, explanatory gesture toward the large canvas she was working on, which showed Farquard Campbell, looking rather like a stuffed ferret in his best suit, surrounded by numerous children and grandchildren, most of these mere whitish blobs at the moment. Her strategy was to have their mothers drag the small ones in one at a time, to have each child's limbs and features hastily sketched into the appropriate blob before natural wriggliness or tantrums obtruded.

Ian glanced at the canvas, but his attention returned to the miniatures of her parents. He stood looking at them, a slight smile on his long, half-homely face. Then, feeling her eyes on him, he glanced up, alarmed.

"Oh, no, ye don't!"

"Oh, come on, Ian, let me just sketch you," she coaxed. "It won't hurt, you know."

"Och, that's what you think," he countered, backing away as though the pencil she had taken up might be a weapon. "The Kahnyen'kehaka think to have a likeness of someone gives ye power over them. That's why the medicine society wear false faces—so the demons causing the illness willna have their true likeness and willna ken who to hurt, aye?"

This was said in such a serious tone that she squinted at him, to see whether he was joking. He didn't seem to be.

"Mmm. Ian—Mama explained to you about germs, didn't she?"

"Aye, she did, o' course," he said, in a tone exhibiting no conviction at all. "She showed me things swimmin' about, and said they were livin' in my teeth!" His face showed momentary repugnance at the notion, but he left the matter to return to the subject at hand.

"There was a traveling Frenchman came to the village once, a natural philosopher—he'd drawings he'd made of birds and animals, and that astonished them—but then he made the mistake of offering to make a likeness of the war chief's wife. I barely got him out in one piece."

"But you aren't a Mohawk," she said patiently, "and if you were—you're not afraid of me having power over you, are you?"

He turned his head and gave her a sudden queer look that went through her like a knife through butter.

"No," he said. "No, of course not." But his voice had little more conviction than when discussing germs.

Still, he moved to the stool she kept for sitters, set in good light from the open doors that led to the terrace, and sat down, chin lifted and jaw set like one about to be heroically executed.

Suppressing a smile, she took up the sketching block and drew as quickly as she could, lest he change his mind. He was a difficult subject; his features lacked the solid, clear-cut bone structure that both her parents and Roger had. And yet it was in no way a soft face, even discounting the stippled tattoos that curved from the bridge of his nose across his cheeks.

Young and fresh, and yet the firmness of his mouth—it was slightly crooked, she saw with interest; how had she never noticed that before?—belonged to someone much older, bracketed by lines that would cut much deeper with age, but were already firmly entrenched.

The eyes . . . she despaired of getting those right. Large and hazel, they were his one claim to beauty, and yet, beautiful was the last thing you would call them. Like most eyes, they weren't one color at all, but many—the colors of autumn, dark wet earth and crackling oak leaves, and the touch of setting sun on dry grass.

The color was a challenge, but one she could meet. The expression, though—it changed in an instant from something so guilelessly amiable as to seem almost half-witted to something you wouldn't want to meet in a dark alley.

The expression at present was somewhere between these two extremes, but shifted suddenly toward the latter as his attention focused on the open doors behind her, and the terrace beyond.

She glanced over her shoulder, startled. Someone was there; she saw the edge of his—or her—shadow, but the person who threw it was keeping out of sight. Whoever it was began to whistle, a tentative, breathy sound.

For an instant, everything was normal. Then the world shifted. The intruder was whistling "Yellow Submarine."

All the blood rushed from her head, and she swayed, grabbing the edge of an occasional table to keep from falling. Dimly, she sensed Ian rising like a cat from his stool, seizing one of her palette knives, and sliding noiselessly out of the room into the hallway.

Her hands had gone cold and numb; so had her lips. She tried to whistle a phrase in reply, but nothing but a little air emerged. Straightening up, she took hold of herself, and sang the last few words instead. She could barely manage the tune, but there was no doubt of the words.

Dead silence from the terrace; the whistling had stopped.

"Who are you?" she said clearly. "Come in."

The shadow lengthened slowly, showing a head like a lion's, light shining through the curls, glowing on the terrace stones. The head itself poked cautiously into sight around the corner of the door. It was an Indian, she saw, with astonishment, though his dress was mostly European—and ragged—bar a wampum necklet. He was lean and dirty, with close-set eyes, which were fixed on her with eagerness and something like avidity.

"You alone, man?" he asked, in a hoarse whisper. "Thought I heard voices."

"You can see I am. Who on earth are you?"

"Ah . . . Wendigo. Wendigo Donner. Your name's Fraser, right?" He had edged all the way into the room now, though still glancing warily from side to side.

"My maiden name, yes. Are you—" She stopped, not sure how to ask.

"Yeah," he said softly, looking her up and down in a casual way that no man of the eighteenth century would have employed to a lady. "So are you, aren't you? You're her daughter, you have to be." He spoke with a certain intensity, moving closer.

She didn't think he meant her harm; he was just very interested. Ian didn't wait to see, though; there was a brief darkening of the light from the door, and then he had Donner from behind, the Indian's squawk of alarm choked off by the arm across his throat, the point of the palette knife jabbing him under the ear.

"Who are ye, arsebite, and what d'ye want?" Ian demanded, tightening the arm across Donner's throat. The Indian's eyes bulged, and he made small mewling noises.

"How do you expect him to answer you, if you're choking him?" This appeal to reason caused Ian to relax his grip, albeit reluctantly. Donner coughed, rubbing his throat ostentatiously, and shot Ian a resentful look.

"No need for that, man, I wasn't doin' nothin' to her." Donner's eyes went from her to Ian and back. He jerked his head toward Ian. "Is he . . . ?"

"No, but he knows. Sit down. You met my mother when she—when she was kidnapped, didn't you?"

Ian's feathery brows shot up at this, and he took a firmer grip on the palette knife, which was flexible but had a definite point.

"Yeah." Donner lowered himself gingerly onto the stool, keeping a wary eye on Ian. "Man, they nearly got me. Your mother, she told me her old man was gnarly and I didn't want to be there when he showed up, but I didn't believe her. Almost, I didn't. But when I heard those drums, man, I bugged out, and a damn good thing I did, too." He swallowed, looking pale. "I went back, in the morning. Jeez, man."

Ian said something under his breath, in what Brianna thought was Mohawk. It sounded unfriendly in the extreme, and Donner evidently discerned enough of the meaning to make him scoot his stool a little farther away, hunching his shoulders.

"Hey, man, I didn't do nothin' to her, okay?" He looked pleadingly at Brianna. "I didn't! I was gonna help her get away—ask her, she'll tell you! Only Fraser and his guys showed up before I could. Christ, why would I hurt her? She's the first one I found back here—I needed her!"

"The first one?" Ian said, frowning. "The first—"

"The first . . . traveler, he means," Brianna said. Her heart was beating fast. "What did you need her for?"

"To tell me how to get—back." He swallowed again, his hand going to the wampum ornament around his neck. "You—did you come through, or were you born here? I'm figuring you came through," he added, not waiting for an answer. "They don't grow 'em as big as you now. Little bitty girls. Me, I like a big woman." He smiled, in what he plainly intended to be an ingratiating manner.

"I came," Brianna said shortly. "What the hell are you doing here?"

"Trying to get close enough to talk to your mother." He glanced uneasily over his shoulder; there were slaves in the kitchen garden, their voices audible. "I hid out with the Cherokee for a while, then I figured to come down and talk to her at Fraser's Ridge when it was safe, but the old lady there told me you were all down here. Heck of a long way to walk," he added, looking vaguely resentful.

"But then that big black dude ran me off twice, when I tried to get in before. Guess I didn't meet the dress code." His face flickered, not quite managing a smile.

"I been sneaking around for the last three days, trying to catch a glimpse of her, find her alone outside. But I saw her talking to you, out on the terrace, and heard you call her Mama. Seeing how big you are, I figured you must be . . . well, I figured if you didn't pick up on the song, no harm done, huh?"

"So ye want to go back where ye came from, do ye?" Ian asked. Plainly he thought this was an excellent idea.

"Oh, yeah," Donner said fervently. "*Oh,* yeah!"

"Where did you come through?" Brianna asked. The shock of his appearance was fading, subsumed by curiosity. "In Scotland?"

"No, is that where you did it?" he asked eagerly. Scarcely waiting for her nod, he went on. "Your mother said she came and then went back and came again. Can you all go back and forth, like, you know, a revolving door?"

Brianna shook her head violently, shuddering in recollection.

"God, no. It's horrible, and it's so dangerous, even with a gemstone."

"Gemstone?" He pounced on that. "You gotta have a gemstone to do it?"

"Not absolutely, but it seems to be some protection. And it may be that there's some way to use gemstones to—to steer, sort of, but we don't really know about that." She hesitated, wanting to ask more questions, but wanting still more to fetch Claire. "Ian—could you go get Mama? I think she's in the kitchen garden with Phaedre."

Her cousin gave the visitor a flat, narrow look, and shook his head.

"I'll not leave ye alone wi' this fellow. You go; I'll watch him."

She would have argued, but long experience with Scottish males had taught her to recognize intractable stubbornness when she saw it. Besides, Donner's eyes were fixed on her in a way that made her slightly uncomfortable—he was looking at her hand, she realized, at the cabochon ruby in her ring. She was reasonably sure she could fight him off, if necessary, but still . . .

"I'll be right back," she said, hastily stabbing a neglected brush into the pot of turps. "Don't go anywhere!"

I was shocked, but less so than I might have been. I had felt that Donner was alive. Hoped he was, in spite of everything. Still, seeing him face to face, sitting in Jocasta's morning room, struck me dumb. He was talking when I came in, but stopped when he saw me. He didn't stand up, naturally, nor yet offer any observations on my survival; just nodded at me, and resumed what he'd been saying.

"To stop whitey. Save our lands, save our people."

"But you came to the wrong time," Brianna pointed out. "You were too late."

Donner gave her a blank look.

"No, I didn't—1766, that's when I was supposed to come, and that's when I came." He pounded the heel of his hand violently against the side of his head. "Crap! What was *wrong* with me?"

"Congenital stupidity?" I suggested politely, having regained my voice. "That, or hallucinogenic drugs."

The blank look flickered a little, and Donner's mouth twitched. "Oh. Yeah, man. There was some of that."

"But if you came to 1766—and meant to"—Bree objected—"what about Robert Springer—Otter-Tooth? According to the story Mama heard about him, he meant to warn the native tribes against white men and prevent them colonizing the place. Only he arrived too *late* to do that—and even so, he must have arrived forty or fifty years before you did!"

"That wasn't the plan, man!" Donner burst out. He stood up, rubbing both hands violently through his hair in agitation, making it stand out like a bramble bush. "Jeez, no!"

"Oh, it wasn't? What the bloody hell *was* the plan, then?" I demanded. "You did have one."

"Yeah. Yeah, we did." He dropped his hands, glancing round as though fearing to be overheard. He licked his lips.

"Bob did want to do what you said—only the rest said, nah, that wouldn't work. Too many different groups, too much pressure to trade with the whiteys . . . just no way it would fly, you know? We couldn't stop it all, just maybe make it better."

The official plan of the group had been somewhat less ambitious in scope. The travelers would arrive in the 1760s, and over the course of the next ten years, in the confusion and reshuffling, the movement of tribes and villages attendant upon the end of the French and Indian War, would infiltrate themselves into various Indian groups along the Treaty Line in the Colonies and up into the Canadian territories.

They would then use such persuasive powers as they had gained to sway the Indian nations to fight on the British side in the oncoming Revolution, with the intent of insuring a British victory.

"See, the English, they act like the Indians are sovereign nations," he explained, with a glibness suggesting this was a theory learned by rote. "They won, they'd go on doing trade and like that, which is okay, but they wouldn't be trying to push the Indians back and stomp 'em out. The colonists"—he waved scornfully toward the open door—"greedy sons o' bitches been shoving their way into Indian lands for the last hundred years; *they* ain't going to stop."

Bree raised her brows, but I could see that she found the notion intriguing. Evidently, it wasn't quite as insane as it sounded.

"How could you think you'd succeed?" I demanded. "Only a few men to—oh, my God," I said, seeing his face change. "Jesus H. Roosevelt Christ—you weren't the only ones, were you?"

Donner shook his head, wordless.

"How many?" Ian asked. He sounded calm, but I could see that his hands were clenched on his knees.

"I dunno." Donner sat down abruptly, slumping into himself like a bag of grain. "There were like, two or three hundred in the group. But most of 'em couldn't hear the stones." His head lifted a little, and he glanced at Brianna. "Can you?"

She nodded, ruddy brows drawn together.

"But you think there were more . . . travelers . . . than you and your friends?"

Donner shrugged, helpless.

"I got the idea there were, yeah. But Raymond said only five at a time could pass through. So we trained in, like, cells of five. We kept it secret; nobody in the big group knew who could travel and who couldn't, and Raymond was the only one who knew all of 'em."

I had to ask.

"What did Raymond look like?" A possibility had been stirring in the back of my mind, ever since I'd heard that name.

Donner blinked, having not expected that question.

"Jeez, I dunno," he said helplessly "Short dude, I think. White hair. Wore it long, like we all did." He raked a hand through his knotted locks in illustration, brows furrowed in the search for memory.

"A rather . . . wide . . . forehead?" I knew I oughtn't to prompt him, but couldn't help myself, and drew both index fingers across my own brow in illustration.

He stared at me in confusion for a moment.

"Man, I don't remember," he said, shaking his head helplessly. "It was a long time ago. How would I remember something like that?"

I sighed.

"Well, tell me what happened, when you came through the stones."

Donner licked his lips, blinking in the effort of recall. It wasn't just native stupidity, I saw; he didn't like thinking about it.

"Yeah. Well, there were five of us, like I said. Me, and Rob, and Jeremy and Atta. Oh, and Jojo. We came through on the island, and—"

"What island?" Brianna, Ian, and I all chorused together.

"Ocracoke," he said, looking surprised. "It's the northmost portal in the Bermuda Triangle group. We wanted to be as close as we could get to—"

"The Ber—" Brianna and I began, but broke off, looking at each other.

"You know where a number of these portals are?" I said, striving for calm.

"How many are there?" Brianna chimed in, not waiting for his answer.

The answer, in any event, was confused—no surprise there. Raymond had told them that there were many such places in the world, but that they tended to occur in groups. There was such a group in the Caribbean, another in the Northeast, near the Canadian border. Another in the Southwestern desert—Arizona, he thought, and down through Mexico. Northern Britain and the coast of France, as far as the tip of the Iberian peninsula. Probably more, but that's all he'd mentioned.

Not all of the portals were marked with stone circles, though those in places where people had lived for a long time tended to be. "Raymond said those were safer," he said, shrugging. "I dunno why."

The spot on Ocracoke hadn't been bounded by a full circle of stones, though it *was* marked. Four stones, he said. One of them had marks on it Raymond said were African—maybe made by slaves.

"It's kind of in the water," he said, shrugging. "A little stream runs through it, I mean. Ray said he didn't know about water, whether that made any difference, but he thought it might. But we didn't know what *kind* of difference. You guys know?"

Brianna and I shook our heads, round-eyed as a pair of owls. Ian's brow, already furrowed, drew further down at this, though. Had he heard something, during his time with Geillis Duncan?

The five of them—and Raymond—had driven as far as they could; the road that led down the Outer Banks was a poor one, which tended to wash away in storms, and they were obliged to leave the car several miles away from the spot, struggling through the scrub pines of the coastal forest and patches of unexpected quicksand. It was late fall—

"Samhain," Brianna said softly, but softly enough that Donner was not distracted from the flow of his story.

Late fall, he said, and the weather was bad. It had been raining for days, and the footing was uncertain, slippery and boggy by turns. The wind was high, and the storm surge pounded the beaches; they could hear it, even in the secluded spot where the portal lay.

"We were all scared—maybe all but Rob—but it was way exciting, man," he said, beginning to show a glimmer of enthusiasm. "The trees were just about layin' down flat, and the sky, it was green. The wind was so bad, you could taste salt, all the time, because little bits of ocean were flying through the air, mixed with the rain. We were, like, soaked through to our choners."

"Your what?" Ian said, frowning.

"Underpants—you know, drawers. Smallclothes," Brianna said, flapping an impatient hand. "Go on."

Once arrived at the place, Raymond had checked them all, to see that they carried the few necessities they might need—tinderboxes, tobacco, a little money of the time—and then given each one a wampum necklet, and a small leather pouch, which he said was an amulet of ceremonial herbs.

"Oh, you know about that," he said, seeing the expression on my face. "What kind did you use?"

"I didn't," I said, not wanting him to wander from his story. "Go on. How did you plan to hit the right time?"

"Oh. Well." He sighed, hunching on his stool. "We didn't. Ray said it would be just about two hundred years, give or take a couple. It wasn't like we could steer—that's what I was hoping you guys would know. How to get to a specific time. 'Cuz, boy, I'd sure like to go back and get there *before* I got messed up with Ray and them."

They had, at Raymond's direction, walked a pattern among the stones, chanting words. Donner had no idea what the words meant, nor even what the language was. At the conclusion of the pattern, though, they had walked single file toward the stone with African markings, passing carefully to the left of it.

"And, like—pow!" He smacked a fist into the palm of his other hand. "First guy in line—he's *gone*, man! We were just freaked out. I mean, that's what was s'posed to happen, but . . . gone," he repeated, shaking his head. "Just . . . *gone*."

Agog at this evidence of effectiveness, they had repeated the pattern and the chant, and at each repetition, the first man to pass the stone had vanished. Donner had been the fourth.

"Oh, God," he said, going pale at the memory. "Oh, God, I never felt anything like that before and I hope I never do again."

"The amulet—the pouch you had," Brianna said, ignoring his pallor. Her own face was intense, blazing with interest. "What happened to that?"

"I dunno. I maybe dropped it, maybe it went someplace else. I passed out, and when I came to, it wasn't with me." The day was warm and close, but he began to shiver. "Jojo. He was with me. Only he was dead."

That statement struck me like a knife blow, just under the ribs. Geillis Duncan's notebooks had held lists of people found near stone circles—some alive, some dead. I hadn't needed anything to tell me that the journey through the stones was a perilous passage—but this reminder made me feel weak in the knees, and I sat down on Jocasta's tufted ottoman.

"The others," I said, trying to keep my voice steady. "Did they . . ."

He shook his head. He was still clammy and shivering, but sweat glazed his face; he looked very unwell.

"Never saw 'em again," he said.

He didn't know what had killed Jojo; didn't pause to look, though he had a vague notion that there might have been burn marks on his shirt. Finding his friend dead, and none of the others nearby, he had stumbled off in a panic through scrub forest and salt marsh, collapsing after several hours of wandering, lying in the sand dunes among stiff grass all night. He had starved for three days, found and eaten a nest of turtle eggs, eventually made his way to the mainland on a stolen canoe, and thereafter had drifted haplessly, working here and there at menial jobs, seeking refuge in drink when he could afford it, falling into company with Hodgepile and his gang a year or so past.

The wampum necklets, he said, were to allow the conspirators to identify each other should they meet at some point—but he had never seen anybody else wearing one.

Brianna wasn't paying attention to this rambling part of the story, though; she had jumped ahead.

"Do you think Otter-Tooth—Springer—screwed up your group by deliberately trying to go to a different time?"

He looked at her, mouth hanging open a little.

"I never thoughta that. He went first. He went first," he repeated, in a wondering sort of way.

Brianna began to ask another question, but was interrupted by the sound of voices in the hall, coming toward the morning room. Donner was on his feet in an instant, eyes wide with alarm.

"Crap," he said. "It's him. You gotta help me!"

Before I could inquire exactly why he thought so, or who "him" was, the austere form of Ulysses appeared in the doorway.

"You," he said to the cowering Donner, in awful tones. "Did I not tell you to begone, sirrah? How dare you to enter Mrs. Innes's house and pester her relations?"

He stepped aside, then, with a nod to whomever stood beside him, and a small, round, cross-looking gentleman in a rumpled suit peered in.

"That's him," he said, pointing an accusatory finger. "That's the blackguard what stole my purse at Jacobs's ordinary this morning! Took it right out my pocket whilst I was eatin' ham for breakfast!"

"It wasn't me!" Donner made a poor attempt at a show of outrage, but guilt was written all over his face, and when Ulysses seized him by the scruff of the neck and unceremoniously rummaged his clothing, the purse was discovered, to the outspoken gratification of the owner.

"Thief!" he cried, shaking his fist. "I been a-following of you all the morning. Damn' tick-bellied, louse-ridden, dog-eatin' savage—oh, I do beg pardon, ladies," he added, bowing to me and Brianna as an afterthought before resuming his denunciation of Donner.

Brianna glanced at me, eyebrows raised, but I shrugged. There was no way of preserving Donner from the righteous wrath of his victim, even had I really wanted to. At the gentleman's behest, Ulysses summoned a pair of grooms and a set of manacles—the sight of which made Brianna grow somewhat pale—and Donner was marched off, protesting that he hadn't done it, he'd been framed, wasn't him, he was a friend of the ladies, really, man, ask 'em! . . . to be conveyed to the gaol in Cross Creek.

There was a deep silence in the wake of his removal. At last, Ian shook his head as though trying to rid himself of flies, and putting down the palette knife at last, picked up the sketching block, where Brianna had made Donner try to draw the pattern he said the men had walked. A hopeless scrawl of circles and squiggles, it looked like one of Jemmy's drawings.

"What kind of name is Weddigo?" Ian asked, putting it down.

Brianna had been clutching her pencil so tightly that her knuckles were white. She unfolded her hand and put it down, and I saw that her hands were shaking slightly.

"Wendigo," she said. "It's an Ojibway cannibal spirit that lives in the wood. It howls in storms and eats people."

Ian gave her a long look.

"Nice fellow," he said.

"Wasn't he, just." I felt more than a little shaken myself. Apart from the shock of Donner's appearance and revelations, and then his arrest, small jolts of memory—vivid images of my first meeting with him—kept shooting uncontrollably through my mind, despite my efforts to shut them out. I could taste blood in my mouth, and the stink of unwashed men drowned the scent of flowers from the terrace.

"I suppose it's what one would call a *nom de guerre*," I said, with an attempt at nonchalance. "He can't have been christened that, surely."

"Are you all right, Mama?" Bree was frowning at me. "Shall I get something? A glass of water?"

"Whisky," Ian and I said in unison, and I laughed, despite the shakiness. By the time it arrived, I was in command of myself again.

"What do you think will happen to him, Ulysses?" I asked, as he held the tray for me. The butler's stolidly handsome face showed nothing beyond a mild distaste for the recent visitor; I saw him frown at the scumbled bits of dirt that Donner's shoes had left on the parquet floor.

"I suppose they will hang him," he said. "Mr. Townsend—that was the gentleman's name—had ten pound in the purse he stole." More than enough to merit hanging. The eighteenth century took a dim view of thievery; as little as a pound could incur a capital sentence.

"Good," said Ian, with obvious approval.

I felt a small lurch of the stomach. I disliked Donner, distrusted him, and to be honest, really didn't feel that his death would be a great loss to humanity, by and large. But he was a fellow traveler; did that impose any obligation on our part to help him? More importantly, perhaps—did he have any more information that he hadn't told us yet?

"Mr. Townsend has gone to Campbelton," the butler added, offering the tray to Ian. "To ask Mr. Farquard to attend to the case promptly, as he is bound for Halifax, and wishes to give his witness at once." Farquard Campbell was a justice of the peace—and likely the only thing approaching a judge within the county, since the Circuit Court had ceased to operate.

"They won't hang him before tomorrow, though, I don't suppose," Brianna said. She didn't normally drink whisky, but had taken a glass now; the encounter had shaken her, too. I saw she had turned the ring around upon her finger, rubbing the big ruby absentmindedly with her thumb.

"No," said Ian, looking at her suspiciously. "Ye dinna mean to—" He glanced at me. "No!" he said in horror at the indecision he saw on my face. "Yon fellow's a thief and a blackguard, and if ye didna see him burning and killing wi' your own eyes, Auntie, ye ken well enough he did it. For God's sake, let them hang him and have done!"

"Well . . ." I said, wavering. The sound of footsteps and voices in the hall saved me answering. Jamie and Duncan had been in Cross Creek; now they were back. I felt an overwhelming flood of relief at sight of Jamie, who loomed up in the doorway, sunburned and ruddy, dusty from riding.

"Hang who?" he inquired cheerfully.

Jamie's opinion was the same as Ian's; let them hang Donner, and good riddance. He was reluctantly persuaded that either Brianna or I must talk to the man at least once more, though, to be sure there was nothing further he could tell us.

"I'll speak to the gaoler," he said without enthusiasm. "Mind, though"—he pointed a monitory finger at me—"neither of ye is to go anywhere near the man, save Ian or I am with ye."

"What do you think he'd do?" Brianna was ruffled, annoyed at his tone. "He's about half my size, for heaven's sake!"

"And a rattlesnake is smaller yet," her father replied. "Ye wouldna walk into a room with one of those, only because ye outweigh him, I hope?"

Ian snickered at that, and Brianna gave him an elbow, hard in the ribs.

"Anyway," Jamie said, ignoring them, "I've a bit of news. And a letter from Roger Mac," he said. He pulled it out of his shirt, smiling at Bree. "If ye're no too distracted to read it?"

She lit up like a candle and grabbed it. Ian made a teasing snatch at it, and she slapped his hand away, laughing, and ran out of the room to read it in privacy.

"What sort of news?" I asked. Ulysses had left the tray and decanter; I poured a tot into my empty glass and gave it to Jamie.

"Someone's seen Manfred McGillivray," he replied. *"Slàinte."* He drained the glass, looking contented.

"Oh, aye? Where?" Ian looked less than pleased at this news. For myself, I was thrilled.

"In a brothel, where else?"

Unfortunately, his informant had not been able to supply the exact location of said brothel—having likely been too drunk at the time to know precisely where he was, as Jamie cynically observed—but had been reasonably sure that it was in Cross Creek or Campbelton. Also unfortunately, the sighting was several weeks old. Manfred might well have moved on.

"It's a start, though," I said, hopeful. Penicillin was effective, even against more advanced cases of syphilis, and I had some brewing in the winter kitchen, even now. "I'll go with you, when you go to the gaol. Then after we've spoken with Donner, we can go look for the brothel."

Jamie's look of contentment lessened appreciably.

"What? Why?"

"I dinna think Manfred would be still there, Auntie," Ian said, patently amused. "I doubt he'd have the money, for one thing."

"Oh, ha ha," I said. "He might have said where he was staying, mightn't he? Besides, I want to know whether he was showing any symptoms." In my own time, it might be ten, twenty, or even thirty years after the appearance of the initial chancre before further syphilitic symptoms developed; in this time, though, syphilis was a much more fulminant disease—a victim could die within a year of infection. And Manfred had been gone for more than three months; God knew how long since he had first contracted the infection.

Jamie looked distinctly unenthused about the idea of searching for brothels; Ian seemed rather more interested.

"I'll help look," he volunteered. "Fergus can come, too; he kens a great deal about whores—they'd likely talk to him."

"Fergus? Fergus is here?"

"He is," Jamie said. "That was the other bit of news. He's payin' his respects to my aunt at the moment."

"Why is he here, though?"

"Well, ye heard the talk at the barbecue, aye? About Mr. Simms, the printer, and his troubles? It seems they've got worse, and he thinks of selling up, before someone burns his shop to the ground and him in it. It struck me that perhaps it would suit Fergus and Marsali, better than the farming. So I sent word for him to come down, and maybe have a word wi' Simms."

"That's a brilliant idea!" I said. "Only . . . what would Fergus use for money to buy it?"

Jamie coughed and looked evasive.

"Aye, well. I imagine some sort of bargain might be struck. Particularly if Simms is anxious to sell up."

"All right," I said, resigned. "I don't suppose I want to know the gory details. But Ian—" I turned to him, fixing him with a beady eye. "Far be it from me to offer you moral advice. But you are *not*—repeat, not—to be questioning whores in any deeply personal manner. Do I make myself clear?"

"Auntie!" he said, pretending shock. "The idea!" But a broad grin spread across his tattooed face.

56

Tar and Feathers

In the event, I let Jamie go alone to the gaol to make arrangements for seeing Donner. He had assured me that this would be simpler without my presence, and I had several errands in Cross Creek. Besides the usual salt, sugar, pins, and other household goods needing replenishment, I urgently needed more cinchona bark for Lizzie. The gallberry ointment worked to treat malarial attacks, but was not nearly so effective as Jesuit bark in preventing them.

The British trade restrictions were having their effect, though. There was, of course, no tea to be found—I had expected that; there had been none for nearly a year—but neither was there any sugar, save at an exorbitant price, and steel pins were not to be found at all.

Salt, I could get. With a pound of this in my basket, I made my way up from the docks. The day was hot and humid; away from the slight breeze off the river, the air was motionless and thick as treacle. The salt had solidified in its burlap bags, and the merchant had had to chip off lumps of it with a chisel.

I wondered how Ian and Fergus were coming with their researches; I had a scheme in mind regarding the brothel and its inhabitants, but first, we had to find it.

I hadn't mentioned the idea to Jamie. If anything came of it, that would be time enough. A side street offered shade, in the form of a number of large elms that had been planted so as to overhang the street. I stepped into the welcome shadow of one of these, and found myself at the edge of the fashionable district—about ten houses, all told—of Cross Creek. From where I stood, I could see Dr. Fentiman's fairly modest abode, distinguished by a small hanging shingle decorated with a caduceus. The doctor was not in when I called, but his servant, a neat, plain young woman with badly crossed eyes, admitted me and showed me to the consulting room.

This was a surprisingly cool and pleasant room, with large windows and a worn canvas cloth on the floor, painted in blue and yellow chequers, and furnished with a desk, two comfortable chairs, and a chaise longue on which patients might recline for examination. He had a microscope standing on the desk, through which I peered with interest. It was a fine one, though not quite so good as my own, I thought with some complacency.

I was possessed of a strong curiosity about the rest of his equipment, and was debating with myself as to whether it would be an abuse of the doctor's hospitality to snoop through his cupboards, when the doctor himself arrived, borne on the wings of brandywine.

He was humming a little tune to himself, and carrying his hat under one arm, his battered medical case in the crook of the other. Seeing me, he dropped these carelessly on the floor and hastened to grasp me by the hand, beaming. He bowed over my hand and pressed moistly fervent lips to my knuckles.

"Mrs. Fraser! My dear lady, I am so pleased to see you! You are in no physical distress, I trust?"

I was in some danger of being overwhelmed by the fumes of alcohol on his breath, but kept as cordial a countenance as possible, unobtrusively wiping my hand upon my gown, whilst assuring him that I was entirely well, as were all the members of my immediate family.

"Oh, splendid, splendid," he said, plumping down quite suddenly upon a stool and giving me an enormous grin, revealing tobacco-stained molars. His oversize wig had slid round sideways, causing him to peer out from under it like a dormouse under a tea cozy, but he seemed not to have noticed. "Splendid, splendid, splendid."

I took his rather vague wave as invitation and sat down, as well. I had brought a small present in order to sweeten the good doctor, and now removed this from my basket—though in all truth, I rather thought he was so well-marinated as to require little more attention before I broached the subject of my errand.

He was, however, thrilled with my gift—a gouged-out eyeball, which Young Ian had thoughtfully picked up for me following a fight in Yanceyville, hastily preserved in spirits of wine. Having heard something of Doctor Fentiman's tastes, I thought he might appreciate it. He did, and went on saying, "Splendid!" at some length.

Eventually trailing off, he blinked, held the jar up to the light, and turned it round, viewing it with great admiration.

"Splendid," he said once more. "It will have a most particularly honorable place in my collection, I do assure you, Mrs. Fraser!"

"You have a collection?" I said, affecting great interest. I'd heard about his collection.

"Oh, yes, oh, yes! Would you care to see it?"

There was no possibility of refusal; he was already up and staggering toward a door at the back of his study. This proved to lead into a large closet, the shelves of which held thirty or forty glass containers, filled with alcoholic spirits—and a number of objects which could indeed be described as "interesting."

These ranged from the merely grotesque to the truly startling. One by one, he brought out a big toe sporting a wart the size and color of an edible mushroom, a preserved tongue which had been split—apparently during the owner's lifetime, as the two halves were quite healed—a cat with six legs, a grossly malformed brain ("Removed from a hanged murderer," as he proudly informed me. "I shouldn't wonder," I murmured in reply, thinking of Donner and wondering what *his* brain might look like), and several infants, presumably stillborn, and exhibiting assorted atrocious deformities.

"Now, *this*," he said, lifting down a large glass cylinder in trembling hands, "is quite the prize of my collection. There is a most distinguished physician in Germany, a *Herr Doktor* Blumenbach, who has a world-renowned collection of skulls, and he has been pursuing me—nay, absolutely *pestering* me, I assure you!—in an effort to persuade me to part with it."

"This" was the defleshed skulls and spinal column of a double-headed infant. It was, in fact, fascinating. It was also something that would cause any woman of childbearing age to swear off sex immediately.

Grisly as the doctor's collection was, though, it offered me an excellent opportunity for approaching my true errand.

"That is truly amazing," I said, leaning forward as though to examine the empty orbits of the floating skulls. They were separate and complete, I saw; it was the spinal cord that had divided, so that the skulls hung side by side in the fluid, ghostly white and leaning toward each other so that the rounded heads touched gently, as though sharing some secret, only separating when a movement of the jar caused them momentarily to float apart. "I wonder what causes such a phenomenon?"

"Oh, doubtless some dreadful shock to the mother," Doctor Fentiman assured me. "Women in an expectant condition are fearfully vulnerable to any sort of excitement or distress, you know. They must be kept quite sequestered and confined, well away from any injurious influences."

"I daresay," I murmured. "But you know, some malformations—that one, for instance?—I believe are the result of syphilis in the mother."

It was; I recognized the typical malformed jaw, the narrow skull, and the caved-in appearance of the nose. This child had been preserved with flesh intact, and lay curled placidly in its bottle. By the size and lack of hair, it had likely been premature; I hoped for its own sake that it had not been born alive.

"Shiphi—syphilis," the doctor repeated, swaying a little. "Oh, yes. Yes, yes. I got that particular little creature from a, um . . ." It occurred to him belatedly that syphilis was perhaps not a topic suitable to discuss with a lady. Murderer's brains and two-headed children, yes, but not venereal disease. There was a jar in the closet that I was reasonably sure contained the scrotum of a Negro male who had suffered from elephantiasis; I noticed he hadn't shown me *that* one.

"From a prostitute?" I inquired sympathetically. "Yes, I suppose such misfortunes must be common among such women."

To my annoyance, he slithered away from the desired topic.

"No, no. In fact—" He darted a look over his shoulder, as though fearing to be overheard, then leaned near me and whispered hoarsely, "I received that specimen from a colleague in London, some years ago. It is reputed to be the child of a foreign nobleman!"

"Oh, dear," I said, taken aback. "How . . . interesting."

At this rather inconvenient point, the servant came in with tea—or rather, with a revolting concoction of roasted acorns and chamomile, stewed in water—and the conversation turned in-eluctably toward social trivia. I was afraid that the tea might sober him up before I could inveigle him back in the right direction, but luckily the tea tray also included a decanter of fine claret, which I dispensed liberally.

I had a fresh try at drawing him back into medical subjects, by leaning over to admire the jars left out on his desk. The one nearest me contained the hand of a person who had had such an advanced case of Dupuytren's contracture as to render the appendage little more than a knot of constricted fingers. I wished Tom Christie could see it. He had avoided me since his surgery, but so far as I knew, his hand was still functional.

"Isn't it remarkable, the variety of conditions that the human body displays?" I said.

He shook his head. He had discovered the state of his wig and turned it round; his wizened countenance beneath it looked like that of a solemn chimpanzee—bar the flush of broken capillar-ies that lit his nose like a beacon.

"Remarkable," he echoed. "And yet, what is quite as remark-able is the resilience a body may show in the face of quite terrible injury."

That was true, but it wasn't at all the line I wished to work upon.

"Yes, quite. But—"

"I am very sorry not to be able to show you one specimen—it would have been a notable addition to my collection, I assure you! But alas, the gentleman insisted upon taking it with him."

"He—what?" Well, after all, I had in my time presented vari-ous children with their appendixes or tonsils in a bottle, following surgery. I supposed it wasn't entirely unreasonable for someone to wish to retain an amputated limb.

"Yes, most astonishing." He took a meditative sip of claret. "A testicle, it was—I trust you will pardon my mentioning it," he added belatedly. He hesitated for an instant, but in the end, simply couldn't resist describing the occurrence. "The gentleman had suffered a wound to the scrotum, a most unfortunate accident."

"Most," I said, feeling a sudden tingle at the base of my spine. Was this Jocasta's mysterious visitor? I had been keeping off the claret, in the interests of a clear head, but now poured a tot, feeling it needed. "Did he say how this unfortunate incident transpired?"

"Oh, yes. A hunting accident, he said. But they all say that, don't they?" He twinkled at me, the end of his nose bright red. "I expect it was a *duello*. The work of a jealous rival, perhaps!"

"Perhaps." A *duello*? I thought. But most duels of the time were fought with pistols, not swords. It really was good claret, and I felt a little steadier. "You—er—removed the testicle?" He must have, if he had been contemplating adding it to his ghastly collection.

"Yes," he said, and was not too far gone to give a small sympathetic shudder at the memory. "The gun-shot had been seriously neglected; he said it had occurred some days previous. I was obliged to remove the injured testicle, but fortunately preserved the other."

"I'm sure he was pleased about that." *Gun-shot? Surely not,* I was thinking. *It can't be . . . and yet . . .* "Did this happen quite recently?"

"Mmm, no." He tilted back in his chair, eyes crossing slightly with the effort of recall. "It was in the spring, two years ago— May? Perhaps May."

"Was the gentleman named Bonnet, by chance?" I was surprised that my voice sounded quite casual. "I believe I had heard that a Stephen Bonnet was involved in some such . . . accident."

"Well, you know, he would not give his name. Often patients will not, if the injury is one that might cause public embarrassment. I do not insist in such cases."

"But you do remember him." I found that I was sitting on the edge of my chair, claret cup clenched in my fist. With a little effort, I set it down.

"Mm-hmm." Damn, he was getting sleepy; I could see his lids begin to droop. "A tall gentleman, well-dressed. He had a . . . a most beautiful *horse*. . . ."

"A bit more tea, Doctor Fentiman?" I urged a fresh cup upon him, willing him to stay awake. "Do tell me more about it. The surgery must have been quite delicate?"

In fact, men never like to hear that the removal of testicles is a simple matter, but it is. Though I would admit that the fact of the patient's being conscious during the whole procedure had likely added to the difficulty.

Fentiman regained a bit of his animation, telling me about it.

" . . . and the ball had gone straight *through* the testicle; it had left the most perfect hole. . . . You could look quite through it, I assure you." Plainly he regretted the loss of this interesting specimen, and it was with some difficulty that I got him to tell me what had become of the gentleman to whom it belonged.

"Well, that was odd. It was the horse, you see . . ." he said vaguely. "Lovely animal . . . long hair, like a woman's, so unusual . . ."

A Friesian horse. The doctor had recalled that the planter Phillip Wylie was fond of such horses, and had said as much to his patient, suggesting that as the man had no money—and would not be capable of riding comfortably for some time, in any case—he might think of selling his animal to Wylie. The man had agreed to this, and had requested the doctor to make inquiry of Wylie, who was in town for the Court Sessions.

Doctor Fentiman had obligingly gone out to do so, leaving his patient cozily tucked up on the chaise with a draught of tincture of laudanum.

Phillip Wylie had professed himself most interested in the horse ("Yes, I'll wager he was," I said, but the doctor didn't notice), and had hastened round to see it. The horse was present, but the patient was not, having absconded on foot in the doctor's absence—taking with him half a dozen silver spoons, an enameled snuffbox, the bottle of laudanum, and six shillings, which happened to be all the money the doctor had in the house.

"I cannot imagine how he managed it," Fentiman said, eyes quite round at the thought. "In such condition!" To his credit, he appeared more distressed at the notion of his patient's condition than his own loss. He was a terrible drunkard, Fentiman, I thought; I'd never seen him completely sober—but not a bad doctor.

"Still," he added philosophically, "all's well as ends well, is it not, my dear lady?"

By which he meant that Phillip Wylie had purchased the horse from him for a price sufficient to more than compensate for his losses, and leave him with a tidy profit.

"Quite," I said, wondering just how Jamie would take this news. He had won the stallion—for it must of course be Lucas—from Phillip Wylie in the course of an acrimonious card game at River Run, only to have the horse stolen by Stephen Bonnet a few hours later.

On the whole, I expected that Jamie would be pleased that the stallion was back in good hands, even if they weren't his. As for the news about Bonnet . . . *"A bad penny always turns up,"* had been his cynical opinion, expressed when Bonnet's body had failed to be discovered after Brianna had shot him.

Fentiman was openly yawning by now. He blinked, eyes watering, patted about his person in search of a handkerchief, then bent to rummage in his case, which he had dropped on the floor near his chair.

I had pulled out my own handkerchief and leaned across to hand it to him, when I saw them in the open case.

"What are those?" I asked, pointing. I could see what they were, of course; what I wanted to know was where he'd got them. They were syringes, two of them, lovely little syringes, made of brass. Each one was composed of two bits: a plunger with curled handles, and a cylindrical barrel, drawn out at the narrowed end into a very long, blunt-tipped needle.

"I—why—that is . . . ah . . ." He was terribly taken aback, and stammered like a schoolboy caught sneaking cigarettes behind the toilets. Then something occurred to him, and he relaxed.

"Ears," he declared, in ringing tones. "For cleansing ears. Yes, that is what they are, indubitably. Ear clysters!"

"Oh, are they really?" I picked one up; he tried to stop me, but his reflexes were delayed, and he succeeded only in grabbing at the ruffle of my sleeve.

"How ingenious," I said, working the plunger. It was a little stiff, but not bad at all—particularly not when the alternative was a makeshift hypodermic composed of a leather tube with a rattlesnake's fang attached. Of course a blunt tip wouldn't do, but it would be a simple matter to cut it to a sharp angle. "Where did you get them? I should like very much to order one myself."

He stared at me in abject horror, jaw agape.

"I—er—I really do not think . . ." he protested feebly. Just then, in a perfect miracle of bad timing, his housemaid appeared in the doorway.

"Mr. Brennan's come; it's his wife's time," she said briefly.

"Oh!" Doctor Fentiman leapt to his feet, slammed shut his case, and snatched it up.

"My apologies, dear Mrs. Fraser . . . must go . . . matter of great urgency—so pleasant to have seen you!" He rushed out, case clutched to his bosom, stepping on his hat in his haste.

The maid picked up the crushed chapeau with an air of resignation, and punched it indifferently back into shape.

"Will you be wanting to leave now, ma'am?" she inquired, with an intonation making it clear that I ought to be leaving, whether I wanted to or not.

"I will," I said, rising. "But tell me"—I held out the brass syringe on the palm of my hand—"do you know what this is, and where Doctor Fentiman got it?"

It was difficult to tell in which direction she was looking, but she bent her head as though to examine it, with no more interest than had it been a two-day old smelt offered her for sale in the market.

"Oh, that. Aye, ma'am, it's a penis syringe. I b'lieve he had it sent him from Philadelphia."

"A, um, penis syringe. I see," I said, blinking a little.

"Yes, ma'am. It's for treating of the drip, or the clap. The doctor does a deal of business for the men what goes to Mrs. Silvie's."

I took a deep breath.

"Mrs. Silvie's. Ah. And would you know where Mrs. Silvie's . . . establishment is?"

"Behind Silas Jameson's ordinary," she replied, giving me for the first time a faintly curious look, as though wondering what sort of blockhead didn't know *that*. "Will you be needing anything else, ma'am?"

"Oh, no," I said. "That will do nicely, thank you!" I made to hand her back the penis syringe, but then was struck by impulse. The doctor had two, after all.

"Give you a shilling for it," I said, meeting the eye that seemed most likely to be pointed in my direction.

"Done," she said promptly. She paused for a moment, then added, "If you're going to use it on your man, best be sure he's dead drunk first."

My primary mission was thus accomplished, but now I had a new possibility to explore, before mounting an assault on Mrs. Silvie's house of ill-repute.

I had planned to visit a glassmaker and attempt to explain by means of drawings how to make the barrel and plunger for a hypodermic syringe, leaving up to Bree the problem of making a hollow needle and attaching it. Unfortunately, while the single glassblower operating in Cross Creek was capable of producing any manner of everyday bottles, jugs, and cups, a glance at his stock had made it obvious that my requirements were well beyond his capabilities.

But now I needn't worry about that! While metal syringes lacked some desirable qualities of glass, they also had an undeniable advantage, insofar as they wouldn't break—and while a disposable needle was nice, I could simply sterilize the entire item after each use.

Doctor Fentiman's syringes had very thick, blunt-tipped needle ends. It would be necessary to heat them, and draw the tips out much further in order to narrow them. But any idiot with a forge could do that, I thought. Then to cut the brass tip at an angle and file the point smooth enough to puncture skin cleanly . . . child's play, I thought blithely, and narrowly refrained from skipping down the sandy walk. Now, all I required was a good stock of cinchona bark.

My hopes of obtaining the bark were dashed, though, as soon as I turned into the main street and glimpsed Mr. Bogues's apothecary's shop. The door stood open, letting in flies, and the usually immaculate stoop was marred with such a multitude of muddy footprints as to suggest that some hostile army had descended upon the shop.

The impression of sacking and looting was furthered by the scene inside; most of the shelves were empty, scattered with remnants of dried leaf and broken pottery. The Bogueses' ten-year-old daughter, Miranda, stood mournful watch over a small collection of jars and bottles and an empty tortoiseshell.

"Miranda!" I said. "Whatever has happened?"

She brightened at sight of me, small pink mouth momentarily reversing its downward droop.

"Mrs. Fraser! D'you want some horehound? We've nearly a pound of that left—and it's cheap, only three farthings the ounce."

"I'll have an ounce," I said, though in fact I had plenty growing in my own garden. "Where are your parents?"

The mouth went down again, and the lower lip quivered.

"Mama's in the back, packing. And Papa's gone to sell Jack to Mr. Raintree."

Jack was the apothecary's wagon horse, and Miranda's particular pet. I bit the inside of my lip.

"Mr. Raintree's a very kind man," I said, striving for what comfort there might be. "And he has a nice pasture for his horses, and a warm stable; I think Jack might be happy there. He'll have friends."

She nodded, mouth pinched tight, but two fat tears escaped to roll down her cheeks.

With a quick glance behind me, to assure that no one was coming in, I stepped round the counter, sat down on an upturned keg, and drew her onto my lap, where she melted at once, clinging to me and crying, though making an obvious effort not to be heard in the living quarters behind the shop.

I patted her and made small soothing noises, feeling an unease beyond mere sympathy for the girl. Clearly the Bogueses were selling up. Why?

So infrequently as I came down the mountain, I had no idea what Ralston Bogues's politics might be these days. Not being Scottish, he hadn't come to the barbecue in Flora MacDonald's honor. The shop had always been prosperous, though, and the family decently off, judging by the children's clothes—Miranda and her two little brothers always had shoes. The Bogueses had lived here all of Miranda's life, at least, and likely longer. For them to be leaving in this manner meant that something serious had happened—or was about to.

"Do you know where you're going?" I asked Miranda, who was now sitting on my knee, sniffing and wiping her face on my apron. "Perhaps Mr. Raintree can write to you, to tell you how Jack is faring."

She looked a little more hopeful at that. .

"Can he send a letter to England, do you think? It's a terrible long way."

England? It *was* serious.

"Oh, I should think so," I said, tucking wisps of hair back under her cap. "Mr. Fraser writes a letter every night, to his sister in Scotland—and that's much further away even than England!"

"Oh. Well." Looking happier, she scrambled off my lap and

smoothed down her dress. "Can I write to Jack, do you think?"

"I'm sure Mr. Raintree will read the letter to him if you do," I assured her. "Can you write well, then?"

"Oh, yes, ma'am," she said earnestly. "Papa says I read and write better than he ever did when he was my age. *And* in Latin. He taught me to read all the names of the simples, so I could fetch him what he wanted—see that one?" She pointed with some pride to a large china apothecary's jar, elegantly decorated with blue and gold scrolls. "*Electuary Limonensis.* And that one is *Ipecacuanha!*"

I admired her prowess, thinking that at least I now knew her father's politics. The Bogueses must be Loyalists, if they were returning to England. I would be sorry to see them go, but knowing what I knew of the immediate future, I was glad that they would be safe. At least Ralston would likely have got a decent price for his shop; a short time hence, Loyalists would have their property confiscated, and be lucky to escape arrest— or worse.

"Randy? Have you seen Georgie's shoe? I've found one under the chest, but—oh, Mrs. Fraser! Your pardon, ma'am, I didn't know anyone was here." Melanie Bogues's sharp glance took in my position behind the counter, her daughter's pink-rimmed eyes, and the damp spots on my apron, but she said nothing, merely patting Miranda's shoulder as she passed.

"Miranda tells me you're leaving for England," I said, rising and moving unobtrusively out from behind the counter. "We'll be sorry to see you go."

"That's kind of you, Mrs. Fraser." She smiled unhappily. "We're sorry to go, as well. And I'm not looking forward to the voyage, I can tell you!" She spoke with the heartfelt emotion of someone who had made such a voyage before and would strongly prefer to be boiled alive before doing it again.

I sympathized very much, having done it myself. Doing it with three children, two of them boys under five . . . the imagination boggled.

I wanted to ask her what had caused them to make such a drastic decision, but couldn't think how to broach the matter in front of Miranda. Something had happened; that was clear. Melanie was jumpy as a rabbit, and somewhat more harried than even packing up a household containing three children might account for. She kept darting glances over her shoulder, as though fearing something sneaking up on her.

"Is Mr. Bogues—" I began, but was interrupted by a shadow falling across the stoop. Melanie started, hand to her chest, and I whirled round to see who had come.

The doorway was filled by a short, stocky woman, dressed in a very odd combination of garments. For an instant, I thought she was an Indian, for she wore no cap, and her dark hair was braided—but then she came into the shop, and I saw that she was white. Or rather, pink; her heavy face was flushed with sunburn and the tip of her pug nose was bright red.

"Which one of you is Claire Fraser?" she demanded, looking from me to Melanie Bogues.

"I am," I said, repressing an instinctive urge to take a step backward. Her manner wasn't threatening, but she radiated such an air of physical power that I found her rather intimidating. "Who are you?" I spoke from astonishment, rather than rudeness, and she did not seem offended.

"Jezebel Hatfield Morton," she said, squinting intently at me. "Some geezer at the docks tellt me that you was headin' here." In marked contrast to Melanie Bogue's soft English accent, she had the rough speech I associated with people who had been in the backcountry for three or four generations, speaking to no one in the meantime save raccoons, possums, and one another.

"Er . . . yes," I said, seeing no point in denying it. "Did you need help of some kind?"

She didn't look it; had she been any healthier, she would have burst the seams of the man's shirt she was wearing. Melanie and Miranda were staring at her, wide-eyed. Whatever danger Melanie had been afraid of, it wasn't Miss Morton.

"Not to say help," she said, moving further into the shop. She tilted her head to one side, examining me with what looked like fascination. "I was thinkin' you might know where'bouts that skunk Isaiah Morton be, though."

My mouth dropped open, and I shut it quickly. Not Miss Morton, then—*Mrs.* Morton. The *first* Mrs. Isaiah Morton, that is. Isaiah Morton had fought with Jamie's militia company in the War of the Regulation, and he had mentioned his first wife— breaking out in a cold sweat as he did so.

"I . . . ah . . . believe he's working somewhere upcountry," I said. "Guilford? Or was it Paleyville?"

Actually, it was Hillsboro, but that scarcely mattered, since at the moment, he wasn't *in* Hillsboro. He was, in fact, in Cross Creek, come to take delivery of a shipment of barrels for his employer, a brewster. I'd seen him at the cooper's shop barely an hour earlier, in company with the *second* Mrs. Morton and their infant daughter. Jezebel Hatfield Morton did not look like the sort of person to be civilized about such things.

She made a low noise in her throat, indicative of disgust.

"He's a dang slippery little weasel. But I'll kotch up to him yet, don't you trouble none about that." She spoke with a casual assurance that boded ill for Isaiah.

I thought silence was the wiser course, but couldn't stop myself asking, "Why do you want him?" Isaiah possessed a certain uncouth amiability, but viewed objectively, he scarcely seemed the sort to inflame one woman, let alone two.

"Want him?" She looked amused at the thought, and rubbed a solid fist under her reddened nose. "I don't want him. But ain't no man runs out on *me* for some whey-faced trollop. Once I kotch up to him, I mean to stave his head in and nail his fly-bit hide to my door."

Spoken by another person, this statement might have passed for rhetoric. As spoken by the lady in question, it was an unequivocal declaration of intent. Miranda's eyes were round as a frog's, and her mother's nearly so.

Jezebel H. Morton squinted at me, and scratched thoughtfully beneath one massive breast, leaving the fabric of her shirt pasted damply to her flesh.

"I heerd tell as how you saved the little toad-sucker's life at Alamance. That true?"

"Er . . . yes." I eyed her warily, watching for any offensive movement. She was blocking the door; if she made for me, I would dive across the counter and dash through the door into the Bogueses' living quarters.

She was wearing a large pig-sticker of a knife, unsheathed. This was thrust through a knotted wampum belt that was doing double duty, holding up a kilted mass of what I thought might originally have been red flannel petticoats, hacked off at the knee. Her very solid legs were bare, as were her feet. She had a pistol and powder horn slung from the belt, as well, but made no move to reach for any of her weapons, thank God.

"Too bad," she said dispassionately. "But then, if he'd died, I'd not have the fun of killin' him, so I s'pose it's as well. Don't worry me none; if'n I don't find him, one of my brothers will."

Business apparently disposed of for the moment, she relaxed a bit, and looked around, noticing for the first time the empty shelves.

"What-all's goin' on here?" she demanded, looking interested.

"We're selling up," Melanie murmured, attempting to shove Miranda safely behind her. "Going to England."

"That so?" Jezebel looked mildly interested. "What happened? They kill your man? Or tar and feather him?"

Melanie went white.

"No," she whispered. Her throat moved as she swallowed, and her frightened gaze went toward the door. So that was the threat. I felt suddenly cold, in spite of the sweltering heat.

"Oh? Well, if you care whether they do, maybe you best move on down to Center Street," she suggested helpfully. "They're fixin' to make roast chicken out of *somebody,* sure as God made little green apples. You can smell hot tar all over town, and they's a boiling of folks comin' forth from the taverns."

Melanie and Miranda uttered twin shrieks, and ran for the door, shoving past the unflappable Jezebel. I was moving rapidly in the same direction, and narrowly avoided a collision, as Ralston Bogues stepped through the door, just in time to catch his hysterical wife.

"Randy, you go mind your brothers," he said calmly. "Be still, Mellie, it's all right."

"Tar," she panted, clutching him. "She said—she said—"

"Not me," he said, and I saw that his hair dripped and his face shone pale through its sweat. "They're not after me. Not yet. It's the printer."

Gently, he disengaged his wife's hands from his arm, and stepped round the counter, casting a brief glance of curiosity at Jezebel.

"Take the children, go to Ferguson's," he said, and pulled a fowling piece from its hiding place beneath the counter. "I'll come so soon as I may." He reached into a drawer for the powder horn and cartridge box.

"Ralston!" Melanie spoke in a whisper, glancing after Miranda's retreating back, but the entreaty was no less urgent for its lack of volume. "Where are you going?"

One side of his mouth twitched, but he didn't reply.

"Go to Ferguson's," he repeated, eyes fixed on the cartridge in his hand.

"No! No, don't go! Come with us, come with me!" She seized his arm, frantic.

He shook her off, and went doggedly about the business of loading the gun.

"Go, Mellie."

"I will not!" Urgent, she turned to me. "Mrs. Fraser, tell him! Please, tell him it's a waste—a terrible waste! He mustn't go."

I opened my mouth, unsure what to say to either of them, but had no chance to decide.

"I don't imagine Mistress Fraser will think it a waste, Mellie," Ralston Bogues said, eyes still on his hands. He slung the strap of the cartridge box over his shoulder and cocked the gun. "Her husband is holding them off right now—by himself."

He looked up at me then, nodded once, and was gone.

Jezebel was right: you *could* smell tar all over town. This was by no means unusual in the summertime, especially near the warehouse docks, but the hot thick reek now took on an atmosphere of threat, burning in my nostrils. Tar—and fear—aside, I was gasping from the effort to keep up with Ralston Bogues, who was not precisely running, but was moving as fast as it was possible to go without breaking into a lope.

Jezebel had been right about the people boiling out of taverns, too; the corner of Center Street was choked with an excited crowd. Mostly men, I saw, though there were a few women of the coarser type among them, fishwives and bond servants.

The apothecary hesitated when he saw them. A few faces turned toward him; one or two plucked at their neighbors' sleeves, pointing—and with not very friendly expressions on their faces.

"Get away, Bogues!" one man yelled. "It's not your business—not yet!"

Another stooped, picked up a stone, and hurled it. It clacked harmlessly on the wooden walk, a few feet short of Bogues, but it drew more attention. Bits of the crowd were beginning to turn, surging slowly in our direction.

"Papa!" said a small, breathless voice behind me. I turned to see Miranda, cap lost and pigtails unraveling down her back, her face the color of beetroot from running.

There wasn't time to think about it. I picked her up and swung her off her feet, toward her father. Taken off guard, he dropped the gun and caught her under the arms.

A man lunged forward, reaching for the gun, but I swooped down and got it first. I backed away from him, clutching it to my chest, daring him with my eyes.

I didn't know him, but he knew me; his eyes flicked over me, hesitating, then he glanced back over his shoulder. I could hear Jamie's voice, and a lot of others, all trying to shout each other down. The breath was still whistling in my chest; I couldn't make out any words. The tone of it was argument, though; confrontation, not bloodshed. The man wavered, glanced at me, away—then turned and shoved his way back into the gathering crowd.

Bogues had had the sense to keep hold of his daughter, who had her arms wrapped tightly round his neck, face buried in his shirt. He darted his eyes at me, and made a small gesture, as though to take back the gun. I shook my head and held it tighter. The stock was warm and slick in my hands.

"Take Miranda home," I said. "I'll—do something."

It was loaded and primed. One shot. The best I could do with that was to create a momentary distraction—but that *might* help.

I pushed my way through the crowd, the gun pointed carefully down not to spill the powder, half-hidden in my skirts. The smell of tar was suddenly much stronger. A cauldron of the stuff lay overturned in front of the printer's shop, a black sticky puddle smoking and reeking in the sun.

Glowing embers and blackened chunks of charcoal were scattered across the street, under everyone's feet; a solid citizen whom I recognized as Mr. Townsend was kicking the bejesus out of a hastily built fire, thwarting the attempts of a couple of young men to rebuild it.

I looked for Jamie and found him precisely where Ralston Bogues had said he was—in front of the door to the printer's shop, clutching a tar-smeared broom and with the light of battle in his eye.

"That your man?" Jezebel Morton had caught up, and was peering interestedly over my shoulder. "Big 'un, ain't he?"

Tar was spattered all over the front of the shop—and Jamie. A large glob was stuck in his hair, and I could see the flesh of his arm reddened where a long string of hot tar had struck. Despite this, he was grinning. Two more tar-daubed brooms lay on the ground nearby, one broken—almost certainly over someone's head. At least for the moment, he was having fun.

I didn't at once see the printer, Fogarty Simms. Then a frightened face showed briefly at the window, but ducked out of sight as a rock flung from the crowd crashed into the window frame, cracking the glass.

"Come out, Simms, you slinkin' coward!" bellowed a man nearby. "Or shall we smoke you out?"

"Smoke him! Smoke him!" Enthusiastic shouts came from the crowd, and a young man near me bent, scrabbling after a burning brand scattered from the fire. I stamped viciously on his hand as he grasped it.

"Jesus *God*!" He let go and fell to his knees, clutching his hand between his thighs, open-mouthed and gasping with pain. "Oh, oh, Jesus!"

I edged away, shouldering my way through the press. Could I get near enough to give Jamie the gun? Or would that make matters worse?

"Get away from the door, Fraser! We've no quarrel with you!"

I recognized that cultivated voice; it was Neil Forbes, the lawyer. He wasn't dressed in his usual natty suiting, though; he wore rough homespun. So it wasn't an impromptu attack—he'd come prepared for dirty work.

"Hey! You speak for yourself, Forbes! *I've* a quarrel with him!" That was a burly man in a butcher's apron, red-faced and indignant, sporting a swollen and empurpled eye. "Look what he did to me!" He waved a meaty hand at the eye, then at the front of his clothing, where a tar-clotted broom had quite evidently caught him square in the chest. He shook a massive fist at Jamie. "You'll pay for this, Fraser!"

"Aye, but I'll pay ye in the same coin, Buchan!" Jamie feinted, broom held like a lance. Buchan yelped and skittered backward, face comically alarmed, and the crowd burst into laughter.

"Come back, man! Ye want to play savage, ye'll need a bit more paint!" Buchan had turned to flee, but was blocked by the crowd. Jamie lunged with the broom, smudging him neatly on the seat of his breeches. Buchan leaped in panic at the jab, causing more laughter and hoots of derision as he shoved and stumbled out of range.

"The rest of ye want to play savage, too, do ye?" Jamie shouted. He swiped his broom through the steaming puddle and swung it hard in a wide arc before him. Droplets of hot tar flew through the air, and men yelled and pushed to get out of the way, stepping on each other and knocking each other down.

I was shoved to one side and fetched up hard against a barrel standing in the street. I would have fallen, save for Jezebel, who caught me by the arm and hauled me up, with no apparent effort.

"Yon feller's right rumbustious," she said with approval, eyes fixed on Jamie. "I could admire me a man like that!"

"Yes," I said, nursing a bruised elbow. "So could I. Sometimes."

Such sentiments appeared not to be universal.

"Give him up, Fraser, or wear feathers with him! Frigging Tories!"

The shout came from behind me, and I turned to see that the speaker had come prepared; he clutched a feather pillow in one hand, the end of it already ripped open, so that down feathers flew in spurts with each gesture.

"Tar and feather 'em all!"

I turned again at the shout from above, and looked up in time to see a young man fling wide the shutters in the upper story of the house on the other side of the street. He was trying to stuff a feather bed through the window but was being substantially impeded in this endeavor by the housewife whose property it was. This lady had leaped on his back and was beating him about the head with a spurtle, uttering shrieks of condemnation.

A young man near me started clucking like a chicken, flapping his elbows—to the intense amusement of his friends, who all began to do it, too, drowning out any attempts at reason—not that there was much of that.

A chant started up at the far side of the street.

"Tory, Tory, Tory!"

The tenor of the situation was changing, and not for the better. I half-lifted the fowling piece, unsure what to do, but knowing that I must do *something*. Another moment, and they'd rush him.

"Give me the gun, Auntie," said a soft voice at my shoulder, and I whirled round to find Young Ian there, breathing hard. I gave it to him without the slightest hesitation.

"Reste d'retour!" Jamie shouted in French. *"Oui, le tout!* Stay back, all of you!" He might have been shouting at the crowd, but he was looking at Ian.

What the devil did he—then I caught sight of Fergus, elbowing viciously to keep his place near the front of the crowd. Young Ian, who had been about to raise the gun, hesitated, holding it close.

"He's right, stay back!" I said urgently. "Don't fire, not yet." I saw now that a hasty shot might do more harm than good. Look at Bobby Higgins and the Boston Massacre. I didn't want any massacres taking place in Cross Creek—particularly not with Jamie at the center of them.

"I won't—but I'm no going to let them take him, either," Ian muttered. "If they go for him—" He broke off, but his jaw was set, and I could smell the sharp scent of his sweat, even above the reek of tar.

A momentary distraction had intervened, thank God. Yells from above made half the crowd turn to see what was happening.

Another man—evidently the householder—had popped up in the window above, jerking the first man back and punching him. Then the struggling pair disappeared from view, and within a few seconds, the sounds of altercation ceased and the woman's shrieks died away, leaving the feather bed hanging in limp anticlimax, half in and half out of the window.

The chant of "Tory Tory Tory!" had died out during the fascination with the conflict overhead, but was now starting up again, punctuated by bellows for the printer to come out and give himself up.

"Come out, Simms!" Forbes bellowed. I saw that he had equipped himself with a fresh broom, and was edging closer to the print shop's door. Jamie saw him, too, and I saw his mouth twist with derision.

Silas Jameson, the proprietor of a local ordinary, was behind Forbes, crouched like a wrestler, his broad face wreathed in a vicious grin.

"Come out, Simms!" he echoed. "What kind of man takes shelter beneath a Scotsman's skirts, eh?"

Jameson's voice was loud enough that everyone heard that, and most laughed—including Jamie.

"A wise one!" Jamie shouted back, and shook the end of his plaid at Jameson. "This tartan's sheltered many a poor lad in its time!"

"And many a lassie, too, I'll wager!" shouted some ribald soul in the crowd.

"What, d'ye think I've your wife under my plaid?" Jamie was breathing hard, shirt and hair pasted to him with sweat, but still grinning as he seized the hem of his kilt. "Ye want to come and have a look for her, then?"

"Is there room under there for me, too?" called one of the fish-wives promptly.

Laughter rolled through the crowd. Fickle as any mob, their mood was changing back from threat to entertainment. I took a deep, trembling breath, feeling sweat roll down between my breasts. He was managing them, but he was walking a razor's edge.

If he'd made up his mind to protect Simms—and he had—then no power on earth would make him give the printer up. If the mob wanted Simms—and they did—they'd have to go through Jamie. And they *would*, I thought, any minute.

"Come out, Simms!" yelled a voice from the Scottish Lowlands. "Ye canny be hidin' up Fraser's backside all day!"

"Better a printer up my arse than a lawyer!" Jamie shouted back, waving his broom at Forbes in illustration. "They're smaller, aye?"

That made them roar; Forbes was a beefily substantial sort, while Fogarty Simms was a pinched starveling of a man. Forbes went very red in the face, and I saw sly looks being cast in his direction. Forbes was in his forties, never married, and there was talk . . .

"I wouldna have a lawyer up my backside at all," Jamie was shouting happily, poking at Forbes with his broom. "He'd steal your shite and charge ye for a clyster!"

Forbes's mouth opened, and his face went purple. He backed up a step, and seemed to be shouting back, but no one could hear his response, drowned as it was by the roar of laughter from the crowd.

"And then he'd sell it back to ye for night soil!" Jamie bellowed, the instant he could be heard. Neatly reversing his broom, he jabbed Forbes in the belly with the handle.

The crowd whooped in glee, and Forbes, no kind of a fighter, lost his head and charged Jamie, his own broom held like a shovel. Jamie, who had quite obviously been waiting for some such injudicious move, stepped aside like a dancer, tripped Forbes, and smacked him across the shoulders with the tar-smeared broom, sending him sprawling into the cooling tar puddle, to the raucous delight of the whole street.

"Here, Auntie, hold this!" The fowling piece was thrust suddenly back into my hands.

"What?" Completely taken aback, I whirled round to see Ian moving fast behind the crowd, beckoning to Fergus. In seconds, unnoticed by the crowd—whose attention was riveted on the fallen Forbes—they had reached the house where the feather bed hung from the window.

Ian stooped and cupped his hands; as though they had rehearsed it for years, Fergus stepped into this improvised stirrup and launched himself upward, swiping at the feather bed with his hook. It caught; he dangled for a moment, grabbing frantically with his sound hand at the hook, to keep it from coming off.

Ian sprang upward and seized Fergus round the waist, yanking downward. Then the fabric of the bed gave way under their combined weight, Fergus and Ian tumbled to the ground, and a perfect cascade of goose feathers poured out on top of them, only to be caught at once by the thick, damp air and whirled up into a delirious snowstorm that filled the street and plastered the surprised mob with clumps of sticky down.

The air seemed filled with feathers; they were everywhere, tickling eyes and nose and throat, sticking to hair and clothes and lashes. I wiped a bit of down from a watering eye and stepped hastily back, away from the half-blind people staggering near me, yelling and bumping into one another.

I had been watching Fergus and Ian, but when the featherstorm struck, I—unlike everyone else in the street—looked back at the print shop, in time to see Jamie reach through the door, seize Fogarty Simms by the arm, and snatch him out of the shop like a winkle on a pin.

Jamie gave Simms a shove that sent him staggering, then whirled back to snatch up his broom and cover the printer's escape. Ralston Bogues, who had been lurking in the shadow of a tree, popped out, a club in his hand, and ran after Simms to protect him, glancing back and brandishing the club to discourage pursuers.

This action had not gone totally unnoticed; though most of the men were distracted, batting and clawing at the bewildering cloud of feathers that surrounded them, a few had seen what was going on, and raised a halloo, yelping like hounds as they tried to push through the crowd in pursuit of the fleeing printer.

If ever there was a moment . . . I'd shoot above their heads and they'd duck, giving Simms time to get away. I raised the gun with decision, reaching for the trigger.

The fowling piece was snatched from my grasp so deftly that I didn't realize for an instant that it was gone, but stood staring in disbelief at my empty hands. Then a bellow came from behind me, loud enough to stun everyone nearby into silence.

"Isaiah Morton! You gonna *die*, boy!"

The fowling piece went off by my ear with a deafening *bwoom!* and a cloud of soot that blinded me. Choking and coughing, I scrubbed at my face with my apron, recovering sight in time to see the short, pudgy figure of Isaiah Morton a block away, running as fast as his legs would carry him. Jezebel Hatfield Morton was after him in an instant, ruthlessly flattening anyone in her way. She leapt nimbly over a besmeared and befeathered Forbes, who was still on his hands and knees, looking dazed, then pushed through the remnants of the mob and hared down the street, short flannel petticoats flying, moving at a surprising rate of speed for someone of her build. Morton careened round a corner and disappeared, implacable Fury close on his tail.

I felt a trifle dazed myself. My ears were still ringing, but I looked up at a touch on my arm.

Jamie was squinting down at me, one eye closed, as though unsure he was seeing what he thought he was seeing. He was saying something I couldn't make out, but the gestures he was making toward my face—coupled with a telltale twitching of the corner of his mouth—made his probable meaning *quite* clear.

"Ha," I said coldly, my own voice sounding tinny and far off. I swiped at my face again with the apron. "*You* should talk!"

He looked like a piebald snowman, with black splotches of tar on his shirt, and clumps of white goose down clinging to his brows, his hair, and the stubble of his beard. He said something else, but I couldn't hear him clearly. I shook my head and twisted a finger in my ear, indicating temporary deafness.

He smiled, took me by the shoulders, and leaned his head forward until his forehead met mine with a small *thunk!* I could feel him trembling slightly, but wasn't sure whether it was laughter or exhaustion. Then he straightened up, kissed my forehead, and took me by the arm.

Neil Forbes sat in the middle of the street, legs splayed and careful hair disheveled. He was black with tar from the shoulder to the knee on one side. He'd lost a shoe, and helpful parties were trying to pick the feathers off him. Jamie led me in a wide circle round him, nodding pleasantly as we passed.

Forbes looked up, glowering, and said something muffled, heavy face twisting in dislike. On the whole, I thought it was just as well I couldn't hear him.

Ian and Fergus had gone off with the majority of the rioters, no doubt to commit mayhem elsewhere. Jamie and I retired to the Sycamore, an inn on River Street, to seek refreshment and make repairs. Jamie's hilarity gradually subsided as I picked tar and feathers off him, but was significantly quenched by hearing an account of my visit to Dr. Fentiman.

"Ye do *what* with it?" Jamie had flinched slightly during my recounting of the tale of Stephen Bonnet's testicle. When I reached a description of the penis syringes, he crossed his legs involuntarily.

"Well, you work the needlelike bit down in, of course, and then flush a solution of something like mercuric chloride through the urethra, I suppose."

"Through the, er . . ."

"Do you want me to show you?" I inquired. "I left my basket at the Bogueses', but I can get it, and—"

"No." He leaned forward and planted his elbows firmly on his knees. "D'ye suppose it burns much?"

"I can't think it's at all pleasant."

He shuddered briefly.

"No, I shouldna think so."

"I don't think it's really effective, either," I added thoughtfully. "Pity to go through something like that, and not be cured. Don't you think?"

He was watching me with the apprehensive air of a man who has just realized that the suspicious-looking parcel sitting next to him is ticking.

"What—" he began, and I hurried to finish.

"So you won't mind going round to Mrs. Sylvie's and making the arrangements for me to treat the girls, will you?"

"Who is Mrs. Sylvie?" he asked suspiciously.

"The owner of the local brothel," I said, taking a deep breath. "Dr. Fentiman's maid told me about her. Now, I realize that there might be more than one brothel in town, but I think that Mrs. Sylvie must certainly know the competition, if there is any, so she can tell you—"

Jamie drew a hand down over his face, pulling down his lower eyelids so that the bloodshot appearance of his eyes was particularly emphasized.

"A brothel," he repeated. "Ye want me to go to a brothel."

"Well, I'll go with you if you like, of course," I said. "Though I think you might manage better alone. I'd do it myself," I added, with some asperity, "but I think they might not pay any attention to me."

He closed one eye, regarding me through the other, which looked as though it had been sandpapered.

"Oh, I rather think they would," he said. "So this is what ye had in mind when ye insisted on coming to town with me, is it?" He sounded a trifle bitter.

"Well . . . yes," I admitted. "Though I really did need cinchona bark. Besides," I added logically, "if I hadn't come, you wouldn't have found out about Bonnet. Or Lucas, for that matter."

He said something in Gaelic, which I interpreted roughly as an indication that he could have lived quite happily in ignorance of either party.

"Besides, you're quite accustomed to brothels," I pointed out. "You had a room in one, in Edinburgh!"

"Aye, I did," he agreed. "But I wasna marrit, then—or rather I was, but I—aye, well, I mean it quite suited me, at the time, to have folk think that I—" He broke off and looked at me pleadingly. "Sassenach, d'ye honestly want everyone in Cross Creek to think that I—"

"Well, they won't think that if I go with you, will they?"

"Oh, God."

At this point, he dropped his head into his hands and massaged his scalp vigorously, presumably under the impression that this would help him figure out some means of thwarting me.

"Where is your sense of compassion for your fellow man?" I demanded. "You wouldn't want some hapless fellow to be facing a session with Dr. Fentiman's syringe, just because you—"

"As long as I'm no required to face it myself," he assured me, raising his head, "my fellow man is welcome to the wages of sin, and serve him just right, too."

"Well, I'm rather inclined to agree," I admitted. "But it isn't only them. It's the women. Not just the whores; what about all the wives—*and* the children—of the men who get infected? You can't let all of them die of the pox, if they can be saved, surely?"

He had by this time assumed the aspect of a hunted animal, and this line of reasoning did not improve it.

"But—the penicillin doesna always work," he pointed out. "What if it doesna work on the whores?"

"It's a possibility," I admitted. "But between trying something that might not work—and not trying at all . . ." Seeing him still looking squiggle-eyed, I dropped the appeal to reason and re-sorted to my best weapon.

"What about Young Ian?"

"What about him?" he replied warily, but I could see that my words had caused an instant vision to spring up in his mind. Ian was not a stranger to brothels—thanks to Jamie, inadvertent and involuntary as the introduction had been.

"He's a good lad, Ian," he said, stoutly. "He wouldna . . ."

"He might," I said. "And you know it."

I had no idea of the shape of Young Ian's private life—if he had one. But he was twenty-one, unattached, and so far as I could see, a completely healthy young male of the species. Hence . . .

I could see Jamie coming reluctantly to the same conclusions. He had been a virgin when I married him, at the age of twenty-three. Young Ian, owing to factors beyond everyone's control, had been introduced to the ways of the flesh at a substantially earlier age. And that particular innocence could not be regained.

"Mmphm," he said.

He picked up the towel, rubbed his hair ferociously with it, then flung it aside, and gathered back the thick, damp tail, reaching for a thong to bind it.

"If it were done when 'tis done, 'twere well it were done quickly," I said, watching with approval. "I think I'd best come, too, though. Let me fetch my box."

He made no response to this, merely setting grimly about the task of making himself presentable. Luckily he hadn't been wearing his coat or waistcoat during the contretemps in the street, so was able to cover the worst of the damage to his shirt.

"Sassenach," he said, and I turned to find him regarding me with a bloodshot glint.

"Yes?"

"Ye'll pay for this."

Mrs. Sylvie's establishment was a perfectly ordinary-looking two-storied house, small and rather shabby. Its shingles were curling up at the ends, giving it a slight air of disheveled surprise, like a woman taken unawares with her hair just out of rollers.

Jamie made disapproving Scottish noises in his throat at sight of the sagging stoop and overgrown yard, but I assumed that this was merely his way of covering discomfiture.

I was not quite sure what I had been expecting Mrs. Sylvie to be —the only madam of my acquaintance having been a rather elegant French émigré in Edinburgh—but the proprietor of Cross Creek's most popular bawdy house was a woman of about twenty-five, with a face as plain as piecrust, and extremely prominent ears.

In fact, I had momentarily assumed her to be the maid, and only Jamie's greeting her politely as "Mrs. Sylvie" informed me that the madam herself had answered the door. I gave Jamie a sideways look, wondering just how he came to be acquainted with her, but then looked again and realized that he had noted the good quality of her gown and the large brooch upon her bosom.

She looked from him to me, and frowned.

"May we come in?" I said, and did so, not waiting for an answer.

"I'm Mrs. Fraser, and this is my husband," I said, gesturing toward Jamie, who was looking pink around the ears already.

"Oh?" Mrs. Sylvie said warily. "Well, it'll be a pound extra, if it's the two of you."

"I beg your—oh!" Hot blood flooded my face as I belatedly

grasped her meaning. Jamie had got it instantly, and was the color of beetroot.

"It's quite all right," she assured me. "Not the usual, to be sure, but Dottie wouldn't mind a bit, she being summat partial to women, you see."

Jamie made a low growling noise, indicating that this was my idea and it was up to me to be carrying it out.

"I'm afraid we didn't make ourselves clear," I said, as charmingly as possible. "We ... er ... we merely wish to inter- view your—" I stopped, groping for an appropriate word. Not "employees," surely.

"Girls," Jamie put in tersely.

"Um, yes. Girls."

"Oh, you do." Her small bright eyes darted back and forth be- tween us. "Methody, are you? Or Bright Light Baptists? Well, that'll be *two* pound, then. For the nuisance."

Jamie laughed.

"Cheap at the price," he observed. "Or is that per girl?"

Mrs. Sylvie's mouth twitched a little.

"Oh, per girl, to be sure."

"Two pound per soul? Aye, well, who would put a price on sal- vation?" He was openly teasing now, and she—having plainly made out that we were neither potential clients nor door-to-door missionaries—was amused, but taking care not to seem so.

"I would," she replied dryly. "A whore knows the price of everything but the value of nothing—or so I've been told."

Jamie nodded at this.

"Aye. What's the price of one of your girls' lives, then, Mrs. Sylvie?"

The look of amusement vanished from her eyes, leaving them just as bright, but fiercely wary.

"Do you threaten me, sir?" She drew herself up tall, and put her hand on a bell that stood on the table near the door. "I have protection, sir, I assure you. You would be well-advised to leave at once."

"If I wished to damage ye, woman, I should scarcely bring my wife along to watch," Jamie said mildly. "I'm no so much a per- vert as all that."

Her hand, tight on the bell's handle, relaxed a bit.

"You'd be surprised," she said. "Mind," she said, pointing a finger at him, "I don't deal in such things—never think it—but I've seen them."

"So have I," said Jamie, the teasing tone gone from his voice. "Tell me, have ye maybe heard of a Scotsman called *Mac Dubh*?"

Her face changed at that; clearly she had. I was bewildered, but had the sense to keep quiet.

"I have," she said. Her gaze had sharpened. "That was you, was it?"

He bowed gravely.

Mrs. Sylvie's mouth pursed briefly, then she seemed to notice me again.

"Did he tell you?" she asked.

"I doubt it," I said, giving him an eye. He sedulously avoided my glance.

Mrs. Sylvie uttered a short laugh.

"One of my girls went with a man to the Toad"—naming a low sort of dive near the river, called the Toad and Spoon—"and he dealt badly with her. Then dragged her out to the taproom and offered her to the men there. She said she knew she was dead—you know it is possible to be raped to death?" This last was addressed to me, in a tone that mingled aloofness with challenge.

"I do," I said, very shortly. A brief qualm ran through me and my palms began to sweat.

"A big Scotchman was there, though, and he took issue with the proposal, apparently. It was him alone, though, against a mob—"

"Your specialty," I said to Jamie, under my breath, and he coughed.

"—but he suggested that they deal cards for the girl. Played a game of brag, and won."

"Really?" I said politely. Cheating at cards was another of his specialties, but one I tried to discourage his using, convinced that it would get him killed one day. No wonder he hadn't told me about this particular adventure.

"So he picked up Alice, wrapped her in his plaid, and brought her home—left her at the door."

She looked at Jamie with grudging admiration.

"So. Have you come to claim a debt, then? You have my thanks, for what they may be worth."

"A great deal, madam," he said quietly. "But no. We've come to try to save your girls from worse than drunken raparees."

Her thin brows arched high in question.

"From the pox," I said baldly. Her mouth fell open.

For all her relative youth, Mrs. Sylvie was a hard customer, and no easy sell. While fear of the pox was a constant factor in the life of a whore, talk of spirochetes cut no ice with her, and my proposition that I inject her staff—there were only three girls, it appeared—with penicillin met with a firm refusal.

Jamie allowed the wrangling to go on until it became clear we had reached a stone wall. Then he came in on a different tack.

"My wife isna proposing such a course only from the goodness of her heart, ken?" he said. By now, we had been invited to sit, in a neat little parlor adorned with gingham curtains, and he leaned forward gingerly, so as not to strain the joints of the delicate chair he was sitting on.

"The son of a friend came to my wife, saying he'd contracted the syphilis from a whore in Hillsboro. She saw the sore; there is no question but that the lad is poxed. He panicked, though, before she was able to treat him, and ran. We have been looking for him ever since—and heard just yesterday that he had been seen here, in your establishment."

Mrs. Sylvie lost control of her face for an instant. It was back in a moment, but there was no mistaking the look of horror.

"Who?" she said hoarsely. "A Scotch lad? What did he look like?"

Jamie exchanged a brief, quizzical glance with me, and described Manfred McGillivray. By the time he had finished, the young madam's face was white as a sheet.

"I had him," she said. "Twice. Oh, Jesus." She took a couple of deep breaths, though, and rallied.

"He was clean, though! I made him show me—I always do."

I explained that while the chancre healed, the disease remained in the blood, only to emerge later. After all, had she not known of whores who contracted syphilis, without any exhibition of a previous sore?

"Yes, of course—but they can't have taken proper care," she said, jaw set stubbornly. "I always do, and my girls, too. I insist upon it."

I could see denial setting in. Rather than admit she might be harboring a deadly infection, she would insist it was not possible, and within moments would have talked herself into believing it and would throw us out.

Jamie could see it, too.

"Mrs. Sylvie," he said, interrupting her flow of justifications. She looked at him, blinking.

"Have ye a deck of cards in the house?"

"What? I—yes, of course."

"Bring them, then," he said with a smile. "Gleek, loo, or brag, your choice."

She gave him a long, hard look, her mouth pressed tight. Then it relaxed a little.

"Honest cards?" she asked, and a small gleam showed in her eye. "And for what stakes?"

"Honest cards," he assured her. "If I win, my wife injects the lot of ye."

"And if you lose?"

"A cask of my best whisky."

She hesitated a moment longer, eyeing him narrowly, estimating the odds. There was still a blob of tar in his hair, and feathers on his coat, but his eyes were deep blue and guileless. She sighed, and put out a hand.

"Done," she said.

"Did you cheat?" I asked, grasping his arm to keep from stumbling. It was well after dark by now, and the streets of Cross Creek were not lighted, save by starlight.

"Didna have to," he said, and yawned hugely. "She may be a good whore, but she's no hand at cards. She should have chosen loo; that's mostly luck, while brag takes skill. Easier to cheat at loo, though," he added, blinking.

"What, exactly, constitutes a good whore?" I asked curiously. I had never considered the question of qualifications anent that profession, but supposed there must be some, beyond possession of the requisite anatomy and a willingness to make it available.

He laughed at that, but scratched his head, considering.

"Well, it helps if she has a genuine liking for men, but doesna take them verra serious. And if she likes to go to bed, that's as well, too. Ouch." I had stepped on a rock, and tightening my grip on his arm, had got him on the patch of skin burned by tar earlier in the day.

"Oh, sorry. Is it bad? I have a bit of balm I can put on it, when we get to the inn."

"Och, no. Just blisters; it will bide." He rubbed his arm gingerly, but shrugged off the discomfort, and taking me by the elbow, led me round the corner, toward the main street. We had decided earlier that since we might be late, we would stay at McLanahan's King's Inn, rather than make the long drive back to River Run.

The smell of hot tar still permeated this end of town, and the evening breeze swirled feathers into small drifts at the side of the road; now and then, a down feather floated past my ear like a slow-moving moth.

"I wonder, are they still picking the feathers off Neil Forbes?" Jamie said, a grin in his voice.

"Maybe his wife will just put a bolster cover on him and use him as a pillow," I suggested. "No, wait, he hasn't got a wife. They'll have to—"

"Call him a rooster, and put him out in the yard to serve the hens," Jamie suggested, giggling. "He's a fine cock-a-doodle, if no much in the way of a cock."

He wasn't drunk—we had drunk weak coffee with Mrs. Sylvie, after the injections—but he was desperately tired; we both were, and suddenly in the state of exhaustion where the lamest joke seems immensely funny, and we staggered, bumping together and laughing at worse and worse jokes until our eyes teared.

"What's that?" Jamie said suddenly, drawing a deep, startled breath through his nose. "What's burning?"

Something substantial; there was a glow in the sky, visible over the roofs of the nearby houses, and the sharp scent of burning wood suddenly overlaid the thicker smell of hot tar. Jamie ran toward the corner of the street, with me hot on his heels.

It was Mr. Simms's print shop; well ablaze. Evidently his political enemies, balked of their prey, had decided to vent their animosity on his premises.

A knot of men was milling in the street, much as they had earlier in the day. Again, there were calls of "Tory!" and a few were brandishing torches. More men were running down the street toward the scene of the fire, shouting. I caught a bellow of "Goddamn Whigs!" and then the two groups collided in a flurry of shoving and punching.

Jamie grabbed my arm and propelled me back the way we had come, out of sight around the corner. My heart was pounding, and I was short of breath; we ducked under a tree and stood panting.

"Well," I said, after a short silence, filled with the shouts of the riot, "I suppose Fergus will have to find a different occupation. There's an apothecary's shop going cheap, I know."

Jamie made a small sound, not quite a laugh.

"He'd do better to go into partnership wi' Mrs. Sylvie," he said. "There's a business not subject to politics. Come on, Sassenach— we'll go the long way round."

When at length we reached the inn, we found Young Ian fidgeting on the porch, watching out for us.

"Where in the name of Bride have you *been*?" he demanded severely, in a manner that made me think suddenly of his mother. "We've been combin' the town for ye, Uncle Jamie, and Fergus sure ye'd been caught up in the collieshangie yonder and maimed or killed." He nodded toward the print shop; the blaze was beginning to die, though there was still enough light from it to see his face, set in a disapproving frown.

"We've been doing good deeds," Jamie assured him piously. "Visiting the sick, as Christ commands us."

"Oh, aye?" Ian responded, with considerable cynicism. "He said ye should visit those in prison, too. Too bad ye didna start wi' that."

"What? Why?"

"Yon bugger Donner's escaped, that's for why," Ian informed him, seeming to take a grim pleasure in imparting bad news. "During the fight this afternoon. The gaoler came to join in the fun, and left the door on the latch; the bugger just walked out and awa'."

Jamie inhaled deeply, then let his breath out slowly, coughing slightly from the smoke.

"Aye, well," he said. "So we're down by one print shop and one thief—but four whores to the good. D'ye think that a fair exchange, Sassenach?"

"Whores?" Ian exclaimed, startled. "What whores?"

"Mrs. Sylvie's," I said, peering at him. He looked shifty, though perhaps it was only the light. "Ian! You didn't!"

"Well, of course he did, Sassenach," Jamie said, resigned. "Look at him." A guilty expression was spreading over Ian's features like an oil slick on water, easy to make out, even by the flickering, ruddy light of the dying fire.

"I found out about Manfred," Ian offered hastily. "He went downriver, meaning to find a ship in Wilmington."

"Yes, we found that out, too," I said a little testily. "Who was it? Mrs. Sylvie or one of the girls?"

His large Adam's apple bobbed nervously.

"Mrs. Sylvie," he said in a low voice.

"Right," I said. "Fortunately, I have some penicillin left—and a nice, dull syringe. Inside with you, Ian, you abandoned wretch, and down with your breeks."

Mrs. McLanahan, emerging onto the porch to inquire whether we would like a bit of late supper, overheard this and gave me a startled look, but I was well past caring.

Sometime later, we lay at last in the haven of a clean bed, safe from the upheavals and turmoils of the day. I had pried the window open, and the faintest of breezes disturbed the heaviness of the thick, hot air. Several soft gray flecks drifted in, feathers or bits of ash, spiraling like snowflakes toward the floor.

Jamie's arm lay across me, and I could make out the soft, glaucous shapes of the blisters that covered most of his forcarm. The air was harsh with burning, but the smell of tar lay like an abiding threat beneath. The men who had burned Simms's shop—and come so close to burning Simms, and likely Jamie, as well—were rebels in the making, men who would be called patriots.

"I can hear ye thinking, Sassenach," he said. He sounded peaceful, on the verge of sleep. "What is it?"

"I was thinking of tar and feathers," I said softly, and very gently touched his arm. "Jamie—it's time."

"I know," he answered just as softly.

Some men went by in the street outside, singing drunkenly, with torches; the flickering light flowed across the ceiling and was gone. I could feel Jamie watch it go, listening to the raucous voices as they faded down the street, but he said nothing, and after a bit, the big body that cradled me began to relax, sinking once again toward sleep.

"What are you thinking?" I whispered, not sure whether he could still hear me. He could.

"I was thinking that ye'd make a really good whore, Sassenach, were ye at all promiscuous," he replied drowsily.

"What?" I said, quite startled.

"But I'm glad ye're not," he added, and began to snore.

57

The Minister's Return

September 4, 1774

Roger steered clear of Coopersville on his way home. It wasn't that he feared Ute McGillivray's wrath, but he didn't want to tarnish the happiness of his homecoming with coldness nor confrontation. Instead, he took the long way round, winding his way gradually up the steep slope toward the Ridge, pushing through overgrown parts where the forest had taken back the path, and fording small streams.

His mule splashed out of the last of these at the base of the trail, shaking itself and scattering droplets from its belly. Pausing to wipe sweat from his face, he spotted a movement on a large stone by the bank. Aidan, fishing, affecting not to have seen him.

Roger reined Clarence up alongside and watched for a moment, saying nothing. Then he asked, "Are they biting well?"

"Tolerable," Aidan replied, squinting hard at his line. Then he looked up, a huge grin splitting his face from ear to ear, and flinging down his pole, sprang up, reaching with both hands, so that Roger could grasp his skinny wrists and swing him up onto the saddle in front of him.

"Ye're back!" he exclaimed, throwing his arms about Roger and burying his face happily in Roger's chest. "I waited for ye. Are ye a real minister now, then?"

"Amost. How'd ye know I'd be along today?"

Aidan shrugged. "I've been waitin' the best part of a week, have I no?" He looked up into Roger's face, round-eyed and quizzical. "Ye dinna look any different."

"I'm not," Roger assured him, smiling. "How's the belly?"

"Prime. Ye want to see my scar?" He leaned back, pulling up his ratty shirttail to display a neat red four-inch weal across the pallid skin.

"Well done," Roger approved. "Taking care of your Mam and wee Orrie, then, now ye're mended, I suppose."

"Oh, aye." Aidan puffed his narrow chest. "I brought home *six* trout for supper last night, and the biggest one the size of me arm!" He stuck out a forearm in illustration.

"Ah, get on wi' ye."

"I *did*, then!" Aidan said indignantly, then twigged that he was being teased, and grinned.

Clarence was becoming restive, wanting home, and turned in little circles, stamping his feet and twitching at the reins.

"Best go. Ye want to ride up wi' me?"

Aidan looked tempted, but shook his head.

"Nah, then. I promised Mrs. Ogilvie as I should come tell her, the minute ye came."

Roger was surprised at that.

"Oh, aye? Why's that?"

"She's had a wean last week, what she wants ye to baptize."

"Oh?" His heart rose a little at that, and the bubble of happiness he carried inside him seemed to expand a little. His first christening! Or rather—his first official baptism, he thought, with a small pang at the memory of the small O'Brian girl he had buried without a name. He wouldn't be able to do it until after his ordination, but it was something to look forward to.

"Tell her I'll be glad to christen the wean," he said, lowering Aidan to the ground. "Have her send to tell me when. And dinna forget your wee fish!" he called.

Aidan grabbed up his pole and the string of silvery fish—none of them longer than the length of a hand—and plunged off into the wood, leaving Roger to turn Clarence's head toward home.

He smelled smoke from a good way down the trail. Stronger than chimney smoke. With all the talk he had heard on his way, regarding the recent events in Cross Creek, he couldn't help a small feeling of uneasiness, and urged Clarence on with a nudge of the heels. Clarence, scenting home even through the smoke, took the hint with alacrity, and trotted briskly up the steep incline.

The smell of smoke grew stronger, mixed with an odd musty sort of scent that seemed vaguely familiar. A visible haze grew among the trees, and when they burst out of the undergrowth into the clearing, he was nearly standing in his stirrups with agitation.

The cabin stood, weathered and solid, and relief dropped him back in the saddle with a force that made Clarence grunt in protest. Smoke rose around the house in thick swirls, though, and the figure of Brianna, swathed like a Muslim with a scarf around her head and face, was dimly visible in the midst of it. He dismounted, took a breath to call out to her, and immediately suffered a coughing fit. The damned groundhog kiln was open, belching smoke like hell's chimney, and now he recognized the musty scent—scorched earth.

"Roger! Roger!" She'd seen him, and came running, skirts and scarf ends flying, leaping a stack of cut turves like a mountain goat to hurl herself into his arms.

He grabbed her and held on, thinking that nothing in life had ever felt better than the weight of her against him and the taste of her mouth, in spite of the fact that she'd plainly eaten onions for lunch.

She emerged beaming and wet-eyed from the embrace, long enough to say, "I love you!" then grabbed his face and kissed him again. "I missed you. When did you shave last? I love you."

"Four days ago, when I left Charlotte. I love you, too. Is everything all right?"

"Sure. Well, actually no. Jemmy fell out of a tree and knocked out a tooth, but it was a baby tooth and Mama says she doesn't think it will hurt the permanent one coming in. And Ian got exposed to syphilis, maybe, and we're all disgusted with him, and Da was nearly tarred and feathered in Cross Creek, and we met Flora MacDonald, and Mama stuck a needle in Aunt Jocasta's eye, and—"

"Eugh!" Roger said in instinctive revulsion. "Why?"

"So it wouldn't burst. And I got paid six pounds in painting commissions!" she concluded triumphantly. "I bought some fine wire and silk to make paper screens with, and enough wool for a winter cloak for you. It's green. The biggest thing, though, is we met another—well, I'll tell you about that later; it's complicated. How did it go with the Presbyterians? Is it all right? Are you a minister?"

He shook his head, trying to decide which part of this cataract to respond to, and ended up choosing the last bit, only because he could remember it.

"Sort of. Have you been taking lessons in incoherence from Mrs. Bug?"

"How can you be sort of a minister? Wait—tell me in a minute, I have to open it up some more."

With that, she was flitting back across the broken ground toward the gaping hole of the kiln. The tall clay-brick chimney stack rose at one end, looking like a headstone. The scorched turves that had covered it in operation were scattered round it, and the general impression was that of an enormous, smoking grave from which something large, hot, and doubtless demonic had just arisen. Had he been Catholic, he would have crossed himself.

As it was, he advanced carefully toward the edge, where Brianna was kneeling, reaching across with her shovel to remove another layer of turves from the willow-work frame that arched across the top of the pit.

Looking down through a roiling haze of smoke, he could see irregularly shaped objects, lying on the earthen shelves that lined the pit. A few he could make out as being bowls or platters. Most of them, though, were vaguely tubular objects, two or three feet long, tapered and rounded at one end, the other slightly flared. They were a dark pinkish color, streaked and darkened with smoke, and looked like nothing so much as a collection of giant barbecued phalluses, a notion that he found nearly as disturbing as the story of Jocasta's eyeball.

"Pipes," Brianna said proudly, pointing her shovel at one of these objects. "For water. Look—they're perfect! Or they will be, if they don't crack while they're cooling."

"Terrific," Roger said, with a decent show of enthusiasm. "Hey—I brought ye a present." Reaching into the side pocket of his coat, he brought out an orange, which she seized with a cry of delight, though she paused for an instant before digging her thumb into the peel.

"No, you eat it; I've got another for Jem," he assured her.

"I love you," she said again, fervently, juice running down her chin. "What about the Presbyterians? What did they say?"

"Oh. Well, basically, it's all right. I have got the university degree, and enough Greek and Latin to impress them. The Hebrew was a bit lacking, but if I mug that up in the meantime—Reverend Caldwell gave me a book." He patted the side of his coat.

"Yes, I can just see you preaching in Hebrew to the Crombies and Buchanans," she said grinning. "So? What else?"

There was a fleck of orange pulp stuck to her lip, and he bent on impulse and kissed it off, the tiny burst of sweetness rich and tart on his tongue.

"Well, they examined me as to doctrine and understanding, and we talked a great deal; prayed together for discernment." He felt somewhat shy talking to her about it. It had been a remarkable experience, like returning to a home he'd never known he'd missed. To confess his calling had been joyful; to do it among people who understood and shared it . . .

"So I'm provisionally a minister of the Word," he said, looking down at the toes of his boots. "I'll need to be ordained before I can administer sacraments like marriage and baptism, but that will have to wait until there's a Presbytery Session held somewhere. In the meantime, I can preach, teach, and bury."

She was looking at him, smiling, but a little wistfully.

"You're happy?" she said, and he nodded, unable to speak for a moment.

"Very happy," he said at last, his voice hardly audible.

"Good," she said softly, and smiled a little more genuinely. "I understand. So now you're sort of handfast with God, is that it?"

He laughed, and felt his throat ease. God, he'd have to do something about that; he couldn't be preaching drunk every Sunday. Talk of giving scandal to the faithful . . .

"Aye, that's it. But I'm properly married to *you*—I'll not forget it."

"See that you don't." Her smile now was wholehearted. "Since we *are* married . . ." She gave him a very direct look, one that went through him like a mild electric shock. "Jem's at Marsali's, playing with Germain. And I've never made love to a minister before. It seems kind of wicked and depraved, don't you think?"

He took a deep breath, but it didn't help; he still felt giddy and light-headed, doubtless from the smoke.

"Behold, thou art fair, my beloved, yea, pleasant," he said, *"and our bed is green. The joints of thy thighs are like jewels, the work of the hands of a cunning workman. Thy navel is like a*

round goblet, which wanteth not liquor: thy belly is like an heap of wheat set about with lilies." He reached out and touched her, gently.

"Thy two breasts are like two young roes that are twins."

"They are?"

"It's in the Bible," he assured her gravely. "It must be so, aye?"

"Tell me more about my navel," she said, but before he could, he saw a small form bounding out of the woods and haring toward them. Aidan, now fishless and panting.

"Mrs. Ogil . . . vie says . . . come *now!*" he blurted. He gasped a little, recovering enough breath for the rest of the message. "The wean—she's poorly, and they want her christened, in case she should die."

Roger clapped a hand to his other side; *The Book of Common Worship* that they'd given him in Charlotte was a small, reassuring weight in his pocket.

"Can you?" Brianna was looking at him worriedly. "Catholics can—I mean, a lay person can baptize somebody if it's an emergency."

"Yes, in that case—yes," he said, more breathless than he'd been a moment before. He glanced at Brianna, smudged with soot and dirt, her garments reeking of smoke and baked clay rather than myrrh and aloes.

"D'ye want to come?" He urgently wanted her to say yes.

"Wouldn't miss it for the world," she assured him, and discarding the filthy scarf, shook out her hair, bright as banners on the wind.

It was the Ogilvies' first child, a tiny girl whom Brianna—with the experience of long motherhood—diagnosed as suffering from a vicious colic, but basically in good health. The frighteningly young parents—they both looked about fifteen—were pathetically grateful for everything: Brianna's reassurances and advice, her offer to have Claire visit (for they were much too scared to think of approaching the laird's wife themselves, leave alone the stories they had heard of her) with medicine and food, and most of all, for Roger's coming to baptize the baby.

That a real minister—for they could not be convinced otherwise—should appear in this wilderness, and condescend to come confer the blessing of God upon their child—they were over-whelmed by their good fortune.

Roger and Brianna stayed for some time, and left as the sun was going down, glowing with the faintly self-conscious pleasure of doing good.

"Poor things," Brianna said, voice trembling between sympathy and amusement.

"Poor wee things," Roger agreed, sharing her sentiments. The christening had gone beautifully; even the screaming, purple-faced infant had suspended operations long enough for him to pour the water on her bald head and claim heaven's protection for her soul. He felt the greatest joy in it, and immense humility at having been allowed to perform the ceremony. There was only the one thing—and his feelings were still confused between embarrassed pride and deep dismay.

"Her name—" Brianna said, and stopped, shaking her head.

"I tried to stop them," he said, trying to control his voice. "I did *try*—you're my witness. Elizabeth, I said. Mairi. Elspeth, perhaps. You heard me!"

"Oh, now," she said, and her voice trembled. "I think Rogerina is a perfectly *beautiful* name." Then she lost control, sat down in the grass, and laughed like a hyena.

"Oh, God, the poor wee lassie," he said, trying—and failing—not to laugh himself. "I've heard of Thomasina, and even Jamesina, but . . . oh, God."

"Maybe they'll call her Ina for short," Brianna suggested, snuffling and wiping her face on her apron. "Or they can spell it backward—Aniregor—and call her Annie."

"Oh, *you're* a great comfort," Roger said dryly, and reached down to haul her to her feet.

She leaned against him and put her arms round him, still vibrating with laughter. She smelled of oranges and burning, and the light of the setting sun rippled in her hair.

Finally, she stopped, and lifted her head from his shoulder.

"I am my beloved's, and my beloved is mine," she said, and kissed him. "You did good, Reverend. Let's go home."

PART EIGHT

The Call

58

Love One Another

Roger took the deepest breath he could, and shouted as loudly as he could. Which was not very damn loud. Again. And again.

It hurt. It was aggravating, too; the feeble, choked sound of it made him want to shut up and never open his mouth again. He breathed, shut his eyes, and screamed with all his might, or tried to.

A searing flash of pain shot down inside his throat on the right, and he broke off, gasping. All right. He breathed gingerly for a moment, swallowing, then did it again.

Jesus, that hurt.

He rubbed a sleeve across his watering eyes and braced himself for another go. As he inflated his chest, fists curling, he heard voices, and let the breath out.

The voices were calling to each other, not far from him, but the wind was away and he couldn't make out the words. Likely hunters, though. It was a fine fall day, with air like blue wine and the forest restless with dappled light.

The leaves had just begun to turn, but some were already falling, a silent, constant flicker at the edge of vision. Any movement could look like game in such surroundings, he knew that well. He drew breath to call out, hesitated, and said, "Shit," under his breath. Great. He'd rather be shot in mistake for a deer than embarrass himself by calling out.

"Ass," he said to himself, drew breath, and shouted, "Halloooo!" at the top of his voice—reedy and without volume as it was. Again. Again. And yet again. By the fifth time, he was beginning to think he'd rather be shot than go on trying to make them hear him, but at last a faint "Halloooo!" drifted back to him on the crisp, light air.

He stopped, relieved, and coughed, surprised not to be bringing up blood; his throat felt like raw meat. But he essayed a quick hum, then, cautiously, a rising arpeggio. An octave. Just barely, and it was a strain that sent shooting pains through his larynx—but a full octave. The first time he'd managed that much of a range in pitch since the injury.

Encouraged by this small evidence of progress, he greeted the hunters cheerfully when they came in view: Allan Christie and Ian Murray, both with long rifles in hand.

"Preacher MacKenzie!" Allan greeted him, grinning, like an incongruously friendly owl. "What are you doing out here all on your owney-o? Rehearsing your first sermon?"

"As a matter of fact, yes," Roger said pleasantly. It was true, in a way—and there was no other good explanation for what he was doing out in the woods by himself, lacking weapons, snare, or fishing pole.

"Well, best make it good," Allan said, wagging his head. "Everyone will be coming. Da's had Malva hard at it from dawn to dusk, sweeping and cleaning."

"Ah? Well, do tell her I appreciate it, will ye?" After a good deal of thought, he'd asked Thomas Christie whether the Sunday services might be held in the schoolmaster's home. It was no more than a rude cabin, like most on the Ridge, but since lessons were held there, the main room was somewhat more commodious than the average. And while Jamie Fraser would certainly have allowed the use of the Big House, Roger felt that his congregation—what a daunting word—might well be uneasy at holding their services in the house of a Papist, accommodating and tolerant though said Papist might be.

"Ye're coming, are ye not?" Allan was asking Ian. Ian looked surprised at the invitation, and rubbed an uncertain knuckle beneath his nose.

"Och, well, but I was baptized Romish, eh?"

"Well, ye're a Christian, at least?" Allan said with some impatience. "Or no? Some folk do say as how ye turned pagan, with the Indians, and didna turn back."

"Do they?" Ian spoke mildly, but Roger saw his face tighten a little at that. He noticed with interest that Ian didn't answer the question, though, instead asking him, "Will your wife come to hear ye, cousin?"

"She will," he said, mentally crossing his fingers against the day, "and wee Jem, too."

"How's this?" Bree had asked him, fixing him with a look of rapt intensity, chin slightly lifted, lips just a fraction of an inch apart. *"Jackie Kennedy. That about right, do you think, or shall I aim for Queen Elizabeth reviewing the troops?"* Her lips compressed, the chin drew in a bit, and her mobile face altered from rapt attention to dignified approbation.

"Oh, Mrs. Kennedy, by all means," he'd assured her. He'd be pleased if she kept a straight face, let alone anyone else's.

"Aye, well, I'll come along then—if ye dinna think anyone would take it amiss," Ian added formally to Allan, who dismissed the notion with a hospitable flap of the hand.

"Oh, everyone will be there," he repeated. The notion made Roger's stomach contract slightly.

"Out after deer, are ye?" he asked with a nod toward the rifles, in hopes of turning the conversation toward something other than his own impending debut as a preacher.

"Aye," Allan answered, "but then we heard a painter screech, off this way." He nodded, indicating the wood just around them. "Ian said if there's a painter about, the deer will be long gone."

Roger shot a narrow glance at Ian, whose unnaturally blank expression told him more than he wanted to know. Allan Christie, born and raised in Edinburgh, *might* not know a panther's scream from a man's, but Ian most assuredly did.

"Too bad if it's frightened away the game," he said, lifting one brow at Ian. "Come on, then; I'll walk back with ye."

He'd chosen "Love thy neighbor as thyself" as the text for his first sermon. "An oldie but a goodie," as he'd told Brianna, causing her to fizz slightly. And having heard at least a hundred variations on that theme, he was reasonably sure of having sufficient material to go on for the requisite thirty or forty minutes.

A standard church service was a great deal longer—several readings of psalms, discussion of the lesson of the day, intercessions for members of the congregation—but his voice wouldn't take that yet. He was going to have to work up to the full-bore service, which could easily run three hours. He'd arrange with Tom Christie, who was an elder, to do the readings and the earliest prayers, to start with. Then they'd see how things went.

Brianna was sitting modestly off to one side now, watching him—not like Jackie Kennedy, thank God, but with a hidden smile that warmed her eyes whenever he met her gaze.

He'd brought notes, in case he should dry up or inspiration fail, but found that he didn't need them. He'd had a moment's breathlessness, when Tom Christie, who had read the lesson, snapped shut his Bible and looked significantly at him—but once launched, he felt quite at home; it was a lot like lecturing at university, though God knew the congregation was more attentive by far than his university students usually were. They didn't interrupt with questions or argue with him, either—at least not while he was talking.

He was intensely conscious for the first few moments of his surroundings: the faint fug of bodies and last night's fried onions in the air, the scuffed boards of the floor, scrubbed and smelling of lye soap, and the close press of people, ranged on benches, but so many that they crammed into every bit of standing space, as well. Within a few minutes, though, he lost all sense of anything beyond the faces in front of him.

Allan Christie hadn't exaggerated; everyone had come. It was nearly as crowded as it had been during his last public appearance, presiding at old Mrs. Wilson's untimely resurrection.

He wondered how much that occasion had to do with his present popularity. A few people were watching him covertly, with a faint air of expectation, as though he might turn water into wine for an encore, but for the most part, they appeared satisfied with the preaching. His voice was hoarse, but loud enough, thank God.

He believed in what he was saying; after the start he found himself talking more easily, and without the need of concentrating on his speech was able to glance from one person to another, making it seem he spoke to each one personally—meanwhile making fleeting observations in the back of his mind.

Marsali and Fergus hadn't come—no surprise there—but Germain was present; he sat with Jem and Aidan McCallum next to Brianna. All three boys had poked each other excitedly and pointed at him when he began to speak, but Brianna had quelled this behavior with some muttered threat of sufficient force to reduce them to simple squirming. Aidan's mother sat on his other side, looking at Roger with a sort of open adoration that made him uneasy.

The Christies had the place of honor in the center of the first bench: Malva Christie, demure in a lacy cap, her brother sitting protectively on one side, her father on the other, apparently unaware of the occasional looks shot her way by some of the young men.

Rather to Roger's surprise, Jamie and Claire had come, as well, though they stood at the very back. His father-in-law was calmly impassive, but Claire's face was an open book; she clearly found the proceedings amusing.

". . . and if we are truly considering the love of Christ as it is . . ." It was instinct, honed by innumerable lectures, that made him aware that something was amiss. There was some slight disturbance in the far corner, where several half-grown lads had congregated. A couple of the numerous McAfee boys, and Jacky Lachlan, widely known as a limb of Satan.

No more than a nudge, the glint of an eye, some sense of subterranean excitement. But he sensed it, and kept glancing back at that corner with a narrowed eye, in hopes of keeping them subdued. And so happened to be looking when the serpent slithered out between Mrs. Crombie's shoes. It was a largish king snake, brightly striped with red, yellow, and black, and it seemed fairly calm, all things considered.

"Now, ye may say, 'Who's my neighbor, then?' And a good question, coming to live in a place where half the folk ye meet are strangers—and plenty of them more than a bit strange, too."

A titter of appreciation ran through the congregation at that. The snake was casting about in a leisurely sort of way, head raised and tongue flickering with interest as it tested the air. It must be a tame snake; it wasn't bothered by the crush of people.

The reverse was not true; snakes were rare in Scotland, and most of the immigrants were nervous of them. Beyond the natural association with the devil, most folk couldn't or wouldn't distinguish a poison snake from any other, since the only Scottish snake, the adder, *was* venomous. They'd have fits, Roger thought grimly, were they to look down and see what was gliding silently along the floorboards by their feet.

A strangled giggle, cut short, rose from the corner of guilty parties, and several heads in the congregation turned, uttering a censorious "Shoosh!" in unison.

". . . when I was hungry, ye gave me to eat; when I was thirsty, ye gave me to drink. And who d'ye ken here who would ever turn away even . . . even a Sassenach, say, who came to your door hungry?"

A ripple of amusement, and slightly scandalized glances at Claire, who was rather pink, but with suppressed laughter, he thought, not offense.

A quick glance down; the snake, having paused for a rest, was on the move again, snooving its way gently round the end of a bench. A sudden movement caught Roger's eye; Jamie had seen the snake, and jerked. Now he was standing rigid, eyeing it as though it were a bomb.

Roger had been sending up brief prayers, in the interstices of his sermon, suggesting that heavenly benevolence might see fit to shoo the snake quietly out the open door at the back. He intensified these prayers, at the same time unobtrusively unbuttoning his coat to allow for freer action.

If the damned thing came toward the front of the room instead of the back, he'd have to dive forward and try to catch it before it got out in full sight of everyone. That would cause a disturbance, but nothing to what might happen if . . .

". . . now ye'll have noticed what Jesus said, when He spoke to the Samaritan woman at the well . . ."

The snake was still wrapped halfway round the bench leg, making up its mind. It was no more than three feet from his father-in-law. Jamie was watching it like a hawk, and a visible gloss of sweat had appeared on his brow. Roger was aware that his father-in-law had a fixed dislike of snakes—and no wonder, given that a big rattler had nearly killed him three years before.

Too far now for Roger to reach the thing; there were three benches of bodies between him and the snake. Bree, who could have dealt with it, was right away on the far side of the room. No help for it, he decided, with an inward sigh of resignation. He'd have to stop the proceedings, and in a very calm voice, call upon someone dependable—who? He cast hastily round, and spotted Ian Murray, who was within reach, thank God, to grasp the thing and take it out.

He was opening his mouth to do just this, in fact, when the snake, bored with the scenery in its view, slid rapidly round the bench and headed straight along the back row.

Roger's eye was on the snake, so he was as surprised as anyone—including the snake, no doubt—when Jamie suddenly stooped and snatched it from the floor, whipping the startled serpent under his plaid.

Jamie was a large man, and the stir of his movement made several people look over their shoulders to see what had happened. He shifted, coughed, and endeavored to look passionately interested in Roger's sermon. Seeing that there was nothing to look at, everyone turned back, settling themselves more comfortably.

". . . Now, we come across the Samaritans again, do we not, in the story of the Good Samaritan? Ye'll most of ye ken that one, but for the weans who may not have heard it yet—" Roger smiled at Jem, Germain, and Aidan, who all wriggled like worms and made small, ecstatic squeaks at the thrill of being singled out.

From the corner of his eye, he could see Jamie, standing frozen and pale as his best linen sark. Something was moving about inside said sark, and the barest hint of bright scales showed in his clenched hand—the snake was evidently trying to escape up his arm, being restrained from popping through the neck of the shirt only by Jamie's desperate grip on its tail.

Jamie was sweating badly; so was Roger. He saw Brianna frown a little at him.

". . . and so the Samaritan told the innkeeper to mind the poor fellow, bind up his wounds, and feed him, and he'd stop to settle the account on his way back from his business. So . . ."

Roger saw Claire lean close to Jamie, whispering something. His father-in-law shook his head. At a guess, Claire had noticed the snake—she could scarcely fail to—and was urging Jamie to go outside with it, but Jamie was nobly refusing, not wanting to further disrupt the sermon, as he couldn't go out without pushing past a number of other standees.

Roger paused to wipe his face with the large handkerchief Brianna had provided for the purpose, and under cover of this, saw Claire reach into the slit of her skirt and draw out a large calico pocket.

She appeared to be arguing with Jamie in a whisper; he was shaking his head, looking like the Spartan with the fox at his vitals.

Then the snake's head appeared suddenly under Jamie's chin, tongue flicking, and Jamie's eyes went wide. Claire stood instantly on tiptoe, seized it by the neck, and whipping the astonished reptile out of her husband's shirt like a length of rope, crammed the writhing ball headfirst into her pocket and jerked shut the drawstring.

"Praise the Lord!" Roger blurted, to which the congregation obligingly chorused "Amen!" though looking a little puzzled at the interjection.

The man next to Claire, who had witnessed this rapid sequence of events, stared at her bug-eyed. She stuffed the pocket—now heaving with marked agitation—back into her skirt, dropped her shawl over it, and giving the gentleman beside her a "What are *you* looking at, mate?" sort of stare, faced front and adopted a look of pious concentration.

Roger made it somehow to the end, sufficiently relieved at having the snake in custody that even leading the final hymn—an interminable back-and-forth "line hymn" in which he was obliged to chant each line, this echoed by the congregation—didn't disconcert him too much, though he had almost no voice left and what there was creaked like an unoiled hinge.

His shirt was clinging to him and the cool air outside was a balm as he stood shaking hands, bowing, accepting the kind words of his flock.

"A grand sermon, Mr. MacKenzie, grand!" Mrs. Gwilty assured him. She nudged the wizened gentleman who accompanied her, who might be either her husband or her father-in-law. "Was it no the grand sermon, then, Mr. Gwilty?"

"Mmphm," said the wizened gentleman judiciously. "No bad, no bad. Bit short, and ye left out the fine story aboot the harlot, but nay doot ye'll get the way of it in time."

"Nay doubt," Roger said, nodding and smiling, wondering, *What harlot?* "Thank ye for coming."

"Oh, wouldna have missed it for the world," the next lady informed him. "Though the singing wasna quite what one might have hoped for, was it?"

"No, I'm afraid not. Perhaps next time—"

"I never did care for Psalm 109, it's that dreary. Next time, perhaps ye'll give us one o' the mair sprightly ones, aye?"

"Aye, I expect—"

"DaddyDaddyDaddy!" Jem cannoned into his legs, clutching him affectionately round the thighs and nearly knocking him over.

"Nice job," said Brianna, looking amused. "What was going on in the back of the room? You kept looking back there, but I couldn't see anything, and—"

"Fine sermon, sir, fine sermon!" The older Mr. Ogilvie bowed to him, then walked off, his wife's hand in his arm, saying to her, "The puir lad canna carry a tune in his shoe, but the preaching wasna sae bad, all things considered."

Germain and Aidan joined Jemmy, all trying to hug him at once, and he did his best to encompass them, smile at everyone, and nod agreeably to suggestions that he speak louder, preach in the Gaelic, refrain from Latin (what Latin?) and Popish references, try to look more sober, try to look happier, try not to twitch, and put in more stories.

Jamie came out, and gravely shook his hand.

"Verra nice," he said.

"Thanks." Roger struggled to find words. "You—well. Thanks," he repeated.

"Greater love hath no man," Claire observed, smiling at him from behind Jamie's elbow. The wind lifted her shawl, and he could see the side of her skirt moving oddly.

Jamie made a small amused sound.

"Mmphm. Ye might drop by, maybe, and have a word wi' Rab McAfee and Isaiah Lachlan—perhaps a short sermon on the text, *'He who loveth his son chasteneth him betimes?'"*

"McAfee and Lachlan. Aye, I'll do that." Or perhaps he'd just get the McAfees and Jacky Lachlan alone and see to the chastening himself.

He saw off the last of the congregation, took his leave of Tom Christie and his family with thanks, and headed for home and luncheon, his own family in tow. Normally, there would be another service in the afternoon, but he wasn't up to that yet.

Old Mrs. Abernathy was a little way before them on the path, being assisted by her friend, the slightly less-ancient Mrs. Coinneach.

"A nice-looking lad," Mrs. Abernathy was remarking, her cracked old voice floating back on the crisp fall air. "But nervous, och! Sweating rivers, did ye see?"

"Aye, well, shy, I suppose," Mrs. Coinneach replied comfortably. "I expect he'll settle, though, in time."

Roger lay in bed, savoring the lingering sense of the day's accomplishments, the relief of disasters averted, and the sight of his wife, the light from the embers glowing through the thin linen of her shift as she knelt by the hearth, touching her skin and the ends of her hair with light, so that she looked illuminated from within.

The fire banked for the night, she rose and peered at Jemmy, curled up in his trundle and looking deceptively angelic, before coming to bed.

"You look contemplative," she said, smiling as she climbed onto the mattress. "What are you thinking about?"

"Trying to think what on earth I might have said that Mr. MacNeill could possibly have thought was Latin, let alone a Catholic reference," he replied, companionably making room for her.

"You didn't start singing 'Ave Maria' or anything," she assured him. "I would have noticed."

"Mm," he said, and coughed. "Don't mention the singing, aye?"

"It'll get better," she said firmly, and turned, pushing and squirming, to make a nest for herself. The mattress was stuffed with wool, much more comfortable—and a hell of a lot quieter—than corn shucks, but very prone to lumps and odd hollows.

"Aye, maybe," he said, though thinking, *Maybe. But it will never be what it was.* No point in thinking of that, though; he'd grieved as much as he meant to. It was time to make the best of things and get on.

Comfortable at last, she turned to him, sighing in contentment as her body seemed to melt momentarily and remold itself around him—one of her many small, miraculous talents. She had put her hair in a thick plait for sleeping, and he ran his hand down its length, recalling the snake with a brief shudder. He wondered what Claire had done with it. Likely set it free in her garden to eat mice, pragmatist that she was.

"Did you figure out which harlot story it was you left out?" Brianna murmured, moving her hips against his in a casual but definitely nonaccidental sort of way.

"No. There are a terrible lot of harlots in the Bible." He took the tip of her ear very gently between his teeth and she drew a deep, sudden breath.

"Whassa harlot?" said a small, sleepy voice from the trundle.

"Go to sleep, mate—I'll tell ye in the morning," Roger called, and slid a hand down over Brianna's very round, very solid, very warm hip.

Jemmy would almost certainly be asleep in seconds, but they contented themselves with small, secret touches beneath the bed-clothes, waiting to be sure he was *soundly* asleep. He slept like the dead, once firmly in dreamland, but had more than once roused from the drowsy foreshore at very awkward moments, disturbed by his parents' unseemly noises.

"Is it like you thought it would be?" Bree asked, putting a thoughtful thumb on his nipple and rotating it.

"Is what—oh, the preaching. Well, bar the snake . . ."

"Not just that—the whole thing. Do you think . . ." Her eyes searched his, and he tried to keep his mind on what she was saying, rather than what she was doing.

"Ah . . ." His hand clamped over hers, and he took a deep breath. "Yeah. Ye mean am I still sure? I am; I wouldna have done such a thing if I weren't."

"Dad—Daddy—always said it was a great blessing to have a calling, to *know* that you were meant to be something in parti-cular. Do you think you've always had a—a calling?"

"Well, for a time, I had the fixed notion that I was meant to be a deep-sea diver," he said. "Don't laugh; I mean it. What about you?"

"Me?" She looked surprised, then pursed her lips, thinking. "Well, I went to a Catholic school, so we were all urged to think about becoming priests or nuns—but I was pretty sure I didn't have a religious vocation."

"Thank God," he said, with a fervency that made her laugh.

"And then for quite a while, I thought I should be a historian—that I wanted to be one. And it *was* interesting," she said slowly. "I could do it. But—what I really wanted was to build things. To make things." She pulled her hand out from under his and wag-gled her fingers, long and graceful. "But I don't know that that's a calling, really."

"Do ye not think motherhood is a calling, of sorts?" He was on delicate ground here. She was several days late, but neither of them had mentioned it—or was going to, yet.

She cast a quick glance over her shoulder at the trundle bed, and made a small grimace, whose import he couldn't read.

"Can you call something that's accidental for most people a calling?" she asked. "I don't mean it isn't important—but shouldn't there be some choice involved?"

Choice. Well, Jem had been thoroughly an accident, but this one—if there was one—they'd chosen, all right.

"I don't know." He smoothed the long rope of her braid against her spine, and she pressed closer in reflex. He thought she felt somehow riper than usual; something about the feel of her breasts. Softer. Bigger.

"Jem's asleep," she said softly, and he heard the surprisingly deep, slow breathing from the trundle. She put her hand back on his chest, the other somewhat lower.

A little later, drifting toward dreamland himself, he heard her say something, and tried to rouse enough to ask her what it was, but managed only a small interrogative "Mm?"

"I've always thought I *do* have a calling," she repeated, looking upward at the shadows in the beamed ceiling. "Something I was meant to do. But I don't know yet what it is."

"Well, ye definitely weren't meant to be a nun," he said drowsily. "Beyond that—I couldna say."

The man's face was in darkness. He saw an eye, a wet shine, and his heart beat in fear. The bodhrana were talking.

There was wood in his hand, a tipper, a club—it seemed to change in size, immense, yet he handled it lightly, part of his hand, it beat the drumhead, beat in the head of the man whose eyes turned toward him, shining with terror.

Some animal was with him, something large and half-seen, brushing eager past his thighs into the dark, urgent for blood, and he after it, hunting.

The club came down, and down, and upanddown, upanddown, upanddown with the waggle of his wrist, the bodhran live and talking in his bones, the thud that shivered through his arm, a skull breaking inward with a wet, soft sound.

Joined for that instant, joined closer than man and wife, hearts one, terror and bloodlust both yielding to that soft, wet thud and the empty night. The body fell, and he felt it go away from him, a rending loss, felt earth and pine needles rough against his cheek as he fell.

The eyes shone wet and empty, and the face slack-lipped in firelight, one he knew, but he knew not the name of the dead, and the animal was breathing in the night behind him, hot breath on his nape. Everything was burning: grass, trees, sky.

The bodhrana were talking in his bones, but he could not make it out what they said, and he beat the ground, the soft limp body, the burning tree in a rage that made sparks fly, to make the drums leave his blood, speak clearly. Then the tipper flew free, his hand struck the tree and burst into flame.

He woke with his hand on fire, gasping. He brought his knuckles to his mouth by instinct, tasting silver blood. His heart was hammering so that he could scarcely breathe, and he fought the notion, trying to slow his heart, keep breathing, keep panic at bay, stop his throat closing up and strangling him.

The pain in his hand helped, distracting him from the thought of suffocation. He'd thrown a punch in his sleep, and hit the log wall of the cabin square. Jesus, it felt like his knuckles had burst. He pressed the heel of his other hand against them, hard, gritting his teeth.

Rolled onto his side and saw the wet shine of eyes in the ghost of firelight and would have screamed, if he'd had any breath.

"Are you all right, Roger?" Brianna whispered, voice urgent. Her hand touched his shoulder, his back, the curve of his brow, quickly seeking injury.

"Yeah," he said, fighting for breath. "Bad . . . dream." He wasn't dreaming of suffocation; his chest was tight, every breath a conscious effort.

She threw back the covers and rose in a rustle of sheets, pulling him up.

"Sit up," she said, low-voiced. "Wake all the way up. Breathe slow; I'll make you some tea—well, something hot, at least."

He hadn't any breath to protest. The scar on his throat was a vise. The first agony in his hand had subsided; now it began to throb in time to his heart—fine, that was all he needed. He fought back the dream, the sense of drums beating in his bones, and in the struggle, found his breath start to ease. By the time Brianna brought him a mug of hot water poured over something foul-smelling, he was breathing almost normally.

He declined to drink whatever it was, whereupon she thriftily used it to bathe his scraped knuckles instead.

"Do you want to tell me about the dream?" She was heavy-eyed, still yearning for sleep, but willing to listen.

He hesitated, but he could feel the dream hovering in the night-still air, just behind him; to keep silent and lie back in the dark was to invite its return. And perhaps she should know what the dream had told him.

"It was a muddle, but to do with the fight—when we went to bring Claire back. The man—the one I killed—" The word stuck in his throat like a bur, but he got it out. "I was smashing in his head, and he fell, and I saw his face again. And suddenly I realized I'd seen him before; I—I know who he was." The faint horror of knowing the man showed in his voice, and her heavy lashes rose, her eyes suddenly alert.

Her hand covered his injured knuckles, lightly, questioning.

"Do ye recall a wretched little thieftaker named Harley Boble? We met him, just the once, at the Gathering at Mount Helicon."

"I remember. Him? You're sure? It was dark, you said, and all confused—"

"I'm sure. I didn't know, when I hit him, but I saw his face when he fell—the grass was on fire, I saw it clearly—and I saw it again, just now, in the dream, and the name was in my mind when I woke up." He flexed his hand slowly, grimacing. "It seems a lot worse, somehow, to kill someone ye know." And the knowledge of having killed a stranger was quite bad enough. It obliged him to think of himself as one capable of murder.

"Well, you *didn't* know him, at the time," she pointed out. "Didn't recognize him, I mean."

"No, that's true." It was, but didn't help. The fire was smoored for the night, and the room was chilly; he noticed the gooseflesh on her bare forearms, the gold hairs rising. "You're cold; let's go back to bed."

The bed still held a faint warmth, and it was unutterable comfort to have her curl close to his back, the heat of her body penetrating his bone-deep chill. His hand still throbbed, but the pain had dulled to a negligible ache. Her arm settled firmly round him, a loose fist curled under his chin. He bent his head to kiss her own knuckles, smooth and hard and round, felt her warm breath on his neck, and had the oddest momentary recollection of the animal in his dream.

"Bree . . . I did *mean* to kill him."

"I know," she said softly, and tightened her arm around him, as though to save him falling.

59

Froggy Goes A-Courting

From Lord John Grey
Mount Josiah Plantation

My dear Friend,

I write in some Perturbation of Spirit.

You will recall Mr. Josiah Quincy, I am sure. I should not have provided him with a Letter of Introduction to you, had I had any Notion of the eventual Outcome of his Efforts: For I am sure that it is by his Action that your Name is associated with the so-called Committee of Correspondence in North Carolina. A Friend, knowing of my Acquaintance with you, showed me a Missive yesterday, purporting to originate from this Body, and containing a List of its presumed Recipients. Your Name was among these, and the Sight of it in such Company caused me such Concern as to compel me to write at once to inform you of the Matter.

I should have burned the Missive at once, was it not

apparent that it was only one of several Copies. The
Others are doubtless in transit through various of the
Colonies. You must move at once to disassociate yourself
from any such Body, and take Pains that your Name does
not appear in Future in such Contexts.

For be warned: the Mail is not safe. I have received
more than one official Document—even some bearing
royal Seals!—that not only show Signs of having been
opened, but that in some Cases are blatantly marked with
the Initials or Signatures of those Men who have
intercepted and inspected them. Such Inspection may be
imposed either by Whig or Tory, there is no telling, and I
hear that Governor Martin himself is now having his
Mail directed to his Brother in New York, thus to be
brought to him by private Messenger—one of these was a
recent Guest at my table—as he cannot trust its secure
Delivery within North Carolina.

I can only hope that no incriminating Document
containing your Name falls into the Hands of Persons
with the Power to arrest or instigate other Proceedings
against the Speakers of such Sedition as appears in it. I
apologize most sincerely, if my Inadvertence in introducing Mr. Quincy should in any way have endangered or
inconvenienced you, and I will, I assure you, lend my
every Effort to correct the Situation so far as may be in
my Power.

Meanwhile, I offer you the Services of Mr. Higgins,
should you require secure Delivery of any Document, not
merely Letters addressed to myself. He is completely
trustworthy, and I will send him regularly to you, in case
you may require him.

Still, I am in Hopes that the Situation overall may yet be
retrieved. I think those Hotheads who urge Rebellion must
be for the most Part ignorant of the Nature of War, or surely
they would not risk its Terrors and Hardships, nor yet think
lightly of shedding Blood or the Sacrifice of their own Lives
for the sake of so Small a Disagreement with their Parent.

Feeling in London at present is that the Matter will
amount to no more than "a few bloody Noses," as Lord
North puts it, and I trust it may be so.

This News has also a personal Aspect; my son William has purchased a Lieutenant's Commission, and will join his Regiment almost immediately. I am of course proud of him—and yet, knowing the Dangers and Hardships of a Soldier's Life, I confess that I should have preferred him to adopt another Course, either devoting himself to the Conduct of his considerable Estates, or, if he felt this too tame a Life, perhaps entering the Realm of Politics or Commerce—for he has much natural Ability to add to the Power of his Resources, and might well achieve some Influence in such Spheres.

Those Resources are of course still within my Control, until William shall attain his Majority. But I could not gainsay him, so exigent was his Desire—and so vivid my Memories of myself at that Age, and my Determination to serve. It may be that he will have his Fill of Soldiering quickly, and adopt another Course. And I will admit that the military Life has many Virtues to recommend it, stern as these Virtues may sometimes be.

On a less alarming Note—

I find myself returned unexpectedly to the Role of Diplomat. Not, I hasten to add, on behalf of His Majesty, but rather on behalf of Robert Higgins, who begs that I will employ what small Influence I possess in advancing his Prospects for Marriage.

I have found Mr. Higgins a good and faithful Servant, and am pleased to offer what Assistance I may; I hope you will find yourself similarly disposed, for as you will see, your Advice and Counsel is most urgently desired and, in fact, quite indispensable.

There is some small Delicacy involved in this Matter, and upon this Point, I would beg your Consideration; your Discretion I of course trust implicitly. It would appear that Mr. Higgins has formed some Attachment to two young Ladies, both resident on Fraser's Ridge. I have pointed out to him the Difficulty of fighting on two Fronts, as it were, and advised him to concentrate his Forces so as to provide the best chance of Success in his Attack upon a single Object—with, perhaps, the Possibility of falling back to regroup, should his initial Essay fail.

The two Ladies in question are Miss Wemyss and Miss
Christie, both possessed of Beauty and Charm in
Abundance, according to Mr. Higgins, who is most elo-
quent in their Praises. Pressed to choose between them,
Mr. Higgins protested that he could not—but after some
little Discussion on the matter, has at length settled upon
Miss Wemyss as his first Choice.

This is a practical Decision, and the Reasons for his
Choice concern not only the Lady's undoubted
Attractions, but a more mundane Consideration: viz, that
the Lady and her Father are both Bond Servants, indentured to you. I am, by Reason of Mr. Higgins's devoted
Service, offering to purchase both Indentures, should this
be agreeable to you, upon Miss Wemyss's Agreement to
wed Mr. Higgins.

I should not wish to deprive you thus of two valued
Servants, but Mr. Higgins feels that Miss Wemyss will not
wish to leave her Father. By the same Token, he hopes
that my offering to free Father and Daughter from
Servitude (for I have agreed that I would do so, provided
that Mr. Higgins's Employment with me shall continue)
would be sufficient Inducement to overcome any
Objections which Mr. Wemyss might present on Account
of Mr. Higgins's lack of Connexions and personal
Property, or such other small Impediments to the
Marriage as might present themselves.

I collect that Miss Christie, while equally attractive,
has a Father who may be somewhat more difficult of
Persuasion, and her social Situation is somewhat higher
than that of Miss Wemyss. Still, should Miss Wemyss or
her father decline Mr. Higgins's Offer, I will do my Best,
with your Assistance, to devise some Inducement that
might appeal to Mr. Christie.

What think you of this Plan of Attack? I beg you to
consider the Prospects carefully, and if you feel that the
Proposal might be received favorably, to broach the
Matter to Mr. Wemyss and his Daughter—if possible, with
such Discretion as not to prejudice a secondary
Expedition, should that prove necessary.

Mr. Higgins is most sensible of his inferior Position,

*viewed as a potential Groom, and thus most conscious of
the Favor he seeks, as is*

> *Your most humble and obedient Servant,*
> John Grey

". . . *such other small Impediments to the Marriage as might present themselves,*" I read, over Jamie's shoulder. "Like being a convicted murderer with a brand on his cheek, no family, and no
money, do you think he means?"

"Aye, like that," Jamie agreed, straightening out the sheets of
paper and tapping the edges straight. He was clearly amused by
Lord John's letter, but his brows had drawn together, though I
didn't know whether this was a sign of concern over Lord John's
news about Willie, or merely concentration on the delicate question of Bobby Higgins's proposal.

The latter, evidently, for he glanced upward, toward the room
that Lizzie and her father shared. No sound of movement came
through the ceiling, though I'd seen Joseph go upstairs a little
earlier.

"Asleep?" Jamie asked, eyebrows raised. He looked involuntarily at the window. It was mid-afternoon, and the yard was
cheerfully awash in mellow light.

"Common symptom of depression," I said, with a small shrug.
Mr. Wemyss had taken the dissolution of Lizzie's betrothal hard—
much more so than had his daughter. Frail-looking to begin with,
he had noticeably lost weight, and had withdrawn into himself,
speaking only when spoken to, and becoming increasingly hard to
rouse from sleep in the mornings.

Jamie struggled momentarily with the concept of depression,
then dismissed it with a brief shake of the head. He tapped the
stiff fingers of his right hand thoughtfully on the table.

"What d'ye think, Sassenach?"

"Bobby's a lovely young man," I said dubiously. "And Lizzie
obviously likes him."

"And if the Wemysses were still indentured, Bobby's proposal
would likely have some appeal," Jamie agreed. "But they're not."
He had given Joseph Wemyss his papers of indenture some years
earlier, and Brianna had hastily freed Lizzie from her own bond
nearly as soon as it was made. That was not a matter of public

knowledge, though, since Joseph's presumed status as a bondsman protected him from service in the militia. Likewise, as a
bondmaid, Lizzie benefited from Jamie's overt protection, as she
was considered his property; no one would dare to trouble her or
treat her with open disrespect.

"Perhaps he'd be willing to engage them as paid servants," I
suggested. "Their combined salary would likely be a good deal
less than the price of two indentures." We paid Joseph, but his
salary was only three pounds a year, though with room, board, and
clothing supplied.

"I will suggest as much," Jamie said, but with an air of dubiousness. "But I'll have to speak with Joseph." He glanced upward
once more, and shook his head.

"Speaking of Malva . . ." I said, glancing across the hall and
lowering my voice. She was in the surgery, straining liquid from
the bowls of mold that provided our supply of penicillin. I had
promised to send more to Mrs. Sylvie, with a syringe; I hoped she
would use it.

"Do you think Tom Christie would be receptive, if Joseph
isn't? I think both girls are rather partial to Bobby."

Jamie made a mildly derisive noise at the thought.

"Tom Christie marry his daughter to a murderer, and a penniless murderer at that? John Grey doesna ken the man at all, or he
wouldna be suggesting such a thing. Christie's proud as
Nebuchadnezzar, if not more so."

"Oh, as proud as all that, is he?" I said, amused despite myself.
"Who do you think he *would* find suitable, here in the wilderness?"

Jamie lifted one shoulder in a shrug.

"He hasna honored me with his confidences in the matter," he
said dryly. "Though he doesna let his daughter walk out wi' any of
the young lads hereabouts; I imagine none seems worthy to him. I
shouldna be surprised at all, if he were to contrive some means of
sending her to Edenton or New Bern to make a match, and he can
contrive a way to do it. Roger Mac says he's mentioned such a
course."

"Really? He's getting quite thick with Roger these days, isn't
he?"

A reluctant smile crossed his face at that.

"Aye, well. Roger Mac takes the welfare of his flock to heart—
with an eye to his own, nay doubt."

"Whatever do you mean by that?"

He eyed me for a moment, evidently judging my capacity for keeping secrets.

"Mmphm. Well, ye mustna mention it to Brianna, but Roger Mac has it in mind to make a match between Tom Christie and Amy McCallum."

I blinked, but then considered. It wasn't really a bad idea, though not one that would have occurred to me. Granted, Tom was likely more than twenty-five years older than Amy McCallum, but he was still healthy and strong enough to provide for her and her sons. And she plainly needed a provider. Whether she and Malva could share a house was another question; Malva had had the running of her father's house since she could manage it. She was amiable, certainly, but I rather thought she had as much pride as her father, and wouldn't take kindly to being supplanted.

"Mmm," I said dubiously. "Perhaps. What do you mean about Roger's own welfare, though?"

Jamie raised one thick eyebrow.

"Have ye not seen the way the widow McCallum looks at him?"

"No," I said, taken aback. "Have you?"

He nodded.

"I have, and so has Brianna. She bides her time for the moment—but mark my words, Sassenach: if wee Roger doesna see the widow safely marrit soon, he'll find hell nay hotter than his own hearth."

"Oh, now. Roger isn't looking *back* at Mrs. McCallum, is he?" I demanded.

"No, he is not," Jamie said judiciously, "and that's why he's still in possession of his balls. But if ye think my daughter is one to stand—"

We had been speaking in low voices and, at the sound of the surgery door opening, stopped abruptly. Malva poked her head into the study, her cheeks flushed and wispy tendrils of dark hair floating round her face. She looked like a Dresden figurine, despite the stains on her apron, and I saw Jamie smile at her look of eager freshness.

"Please, Mrs. Fraser, I've strained off all the liquid and bottled it—ye did say that we must feed the slops left over to the pig at once . . . did ye mean the big white sow that lives under the house?" She looked rather doubtful at the prospect, and no wonder.

"I'll come and do it," I said, rising. "Thank you, dear. You go along to the kitchen and ask Mrs. Bug for a bit of bread and honey before you go home, why don't you?"

She curtsied and went off toward the kitchen; I could hear Young Ian's voice, teasing Mrs. Bug, and saw Malva stop for an instant to pat her cap, twirl a wisp of hair around her finger to make it curl against her cheek, and straighten her slender back before going in.

"Well, Tom Christie may propose all he likes," I murmured to Jamie, who had come out into the hall with me and seen her go, "but yours isn't the only daughter with a mind of her own and strong opinions."

He gave a small, dismissive grunt and went back to his study, while I continued across the hall, to find a large basin of soggy garbage, the remnants of the latest batch of penicillin-making, neatly collected and standing on the counter.

Opening the window at the side of the house, I peered out and down. Four feet below was the mound of dirt that marked the white sow's den beneath the foundation.

"Pig?" I said, leaning out. "Are you at home?" The chestnuts were ripe and falling from the trees; she might well be out in the wood, gorging herself on chestnut mast. But no; there were hoof-marks in the soft soil, leading in, and the sound of stertorous breathing was audible below.

"Pig!" I said, louder and more peremptorily. Hearing the stir-ring and scraping of an enormous bulk beneath the floorboards, I leaned out and dropped the wooden basin neatly into the soft dirt, spilling only a little of its contents.

The thump of its landing was followed at once by the protru-sion of an immense white-bristled head, equipped with a large and snuffling pink nose, and followed by shoulders the width of a hogshead of tobacco. With eager grunts, the rest of the sow's great body followed, and she fell upon the treat at once, curly tail coiled tightly with delight.

"Yes, well, just you remember who's the source from whom all blessing flows," I told her, and withdrew, taking pains to shut the window. The sill showed considerable splintering and gouging—the result of leaving the slop basin too long on the counter; the sow was an impatient sort, who was quite willing to try to come into the house and claim her due, if it wasn't forthcoming promptly enough to suit.

While partly occupied with the pig, my mind had not yet left the question of Bobby Higgins's proposal, with all its potential complications. To say nothing of Malva. Granted, she was undoubtedly sensible of Bobby's blue eyes; he was a very handsome young man. But she wasn't insensible to Young Ian's charms, either, less striking as they might be.

And what would Tom Christie's opinion of Ian as a son-in-law be, I wondered. He wasn't *quite* penniless; he had ten acres of mostly uncleared land, though no income to speak of. Were tribal tattoos more socially acceptable than a murderer's brand? Probably—but then, Bobby was a Protestant, while Ian was at least nominally Catholic.

Still, he was Jamie's nephew—a fact that might cut both ways. Christie was intensely jealous of Jamie; I knew that. Would he see an alliance between his family and ours as a benefit, or as something to be avoided at all costs?

Of course, if Roger succeeded in getting him to marry Amy McCallum, that might distract his mind a bit. Brianna hadn't said anything to me about the widow—but now that I thought back, I realized that the fact that she hadn't said *anything* might be an indication of suppressed feeling.

I could hear voices and laughter from the kitchen; obviously, everyone was having fun. I thought to go and join them, but glancing into Jamie's study, saw that he was standing by his desk, hands clasped behind him, looking down at Lord John's letter, a small frown of abstraction on his face.

His thoughts weren't with his daughter, I thought, with a small, queer pang—but with his son.

I came into the study and put my arm round his back, leaning my head against his shoulder.

"Have you thought, perhaps, of trying to convince Lord John?" I said, a little hesitantly. "That the Americans may possibly have a point, I mean—convert him to your way of thinking." Lord John himself would not be fighting in the coming conflict; Willie well might, and on the wrong side. Granted, fighting on either side was likely to be as dangerous—but the fact remained that the Americans would win, and the only conceivable way of swaying Willie was through his putative father, whose opinions he respected.

Jamie snorted, but put an arm around me.

"John? D'ye recall what I told ye about Highlanders, when Arch Bug came to me wi' his wee ax?"

"They live by their oath; they will die by it, too."

I shivered a little, and pressed closer, finding some comfort in his solidness. He was right; I had seen it myself, that brutal tribal fealty—and yet it was so hard to grasp, even when I saw it right under my nose.

"I remember," I said.

He nodded at the letter, his eyes still fixed on it.

"He is the same. Not all Englishmen are—but he is." He looked down at me, ruefulness tinged with begrudging respect. "He is the King's man. It wouldna matter if the Angel Gabriel appeared before him and told him what will pass; he wouldna abandon his oath."

"Do you think so?" I said, emboldened. "I'm not so sure."

His brows went up in surprise, and I went on, hesitating as I groped for words.

"It's—I do know what you mean; he's an honorable man. But that's just it. I don't think he *is* sworn to the King—not in the same way Colum's men swore to him, nor the way your men from Lallybroch swore to you. What matters to him   what he'd sell his life for—it's honor."

"Well, aye—it is," he said slowly, brows knit in concentration. "But for a soldier, such as he is, honor lies in his duty, no? And that comes from his fealty to the King, surely?"

I straightened and rubbed a finger beneath my nose, trying to put into words what I thought.

"Yes, but that's not quite what I mean. It's the *idea* that matters to him. He follows an ideal, not a man. Of all the people you know, he may be the only one who *would* understand—this will be a war fought about ideals; maybe the first."

He closed one eye and regarded me quizzically out of the other.

"Ye've been talking to Roger Mac. Ye'll never have thought that on your own, Sassenach."

"I gather you have, too," I said, not bothering to refute the implied insult. Besides, he was right. "So you understand?"

He made a small Scottish noise, indicating dubious agreement.

"I did ask him what about the Crusades, did he not think that was fought for an ideal? And he was obliged to admit that ideals were involved, at least—though even there he said it was money and politics, and I said it always was, and surely it would be now, as well. But, aye, I understand," he added hastily, seeing my nostrils flare. "But with regard to John Grey—"

"With regard to John Grey," I said, "you do have a chance of convincing him, because he's both rational and idealistic. You'd have to convince him that honor doesn't lie in following the King—but in the ideal of freedom. But it's possible."

He made another Scottish noise, this one deep-chested and filled with uneasy doubt. And finally, I realized.

"*You* aren't doing it for the sake of ideals, are you? Not for the sake of—of liberty. Freedom, self-determination, all that."

He shook his head.

"No," he said softly. "Nor yet for the sake of being on the winning side—for once. Though I expect that will be a novel experience." He gave me a sudden rueful smile, and, caught by surprise, I laughed.

"Why, then?" I asked, more gently.

"For you," he said without hesitation. "For Brianna and the wee lad. For my family. For the future. And if that is not an ideal, I've never heard of one."

Jamie did his best in the office of ambassador, but the effect of Bobby's brand proved insuperable. While admitting that Bobby was a nice young man, Mr. Wemyss was unable to countenance the notion of marrying his daughter to a murderer, no matter what the circumstances that had led to his conviction.

"Folk would take against him, sir, ye ken that fine," he said, shaking his head in response to Jamie's arguments. "They dinna stop to ask the why and wherefore, if a man's condemned. His eye—he did nothing, I am sure, to provoke such a savage attack. How could I expose my dear Elizabeth to the possibility of such reprisals? Even if she should escape herself, what of her fate— and that of her children—if he is knocked over in the street one day?" He wrung his hands at the thought.

"And if he should one day lose his Lordship's patronage, he could not look for decent employment elsewhere, not with yon mark of shame upon his face. They would be beggared. I have been left in such straits myself, sir—and would not for the world risk my daughter's sharing such a fate again."

Jamie rubbed a hand over his face.

"Aye. I understand, Joseph. A pity, but I canna say as ye're wrong. For what the observation be worth, I dinna believe that Lord John would cast him off, though."

Mr. Wemyss merely shook his head, looking pale and unhappy.

"Well, then." Jamie pushed himself back from his desk. "I'll have him in, and ye can give him your decision." I rose, as well, and Mr. Wemyss sprang up in panic.

"Oh, sir! Ye will not leave me alone with him!"

"Well, I scarcely think he'll try to knock ye down or pull your nose, Joseph," Jamie said mildly.

"No," Mr. Wemyss said dubiously. "Nooo . . . I suppose not. But still, I should take it *very* kindly if you would—would remain while I speak with him? And you, Mrs. Fraser?" He turned pleading eyes upon me. I looked at Jamie, who nodded in resignation.

"All right," he said. "I'll go and fetch him, then."

"I am sorry, sir." Joseph Wemyss was nearly as unhappy as Bobby Higgins. Small in stature and shy in manner, he was unaccustomed to conducting interviews, and kept glancing at Jamie for moral support, before returning his attention to his daughter's importunate suitor.

"I *am* sorry," he repeated, meeting Bobby's eyes with a sort of helpless sincerity. "I like ye, young man, and so does Elizabeth, I am sure. But her welfare, her happiness, is my responsibility. And I cannot think . . . I really do not suppose . . ."

"I should be kind to her," Bobby said anxiously. "You know I should, zur. She should have a new gown once a year, and I should sell anything I have to keep her in shoes!" He, too, glanced at Jamie, presumably in hopes of reinforcement.

"I'm sure Mr. Wemyss has the highest regard for your intentions, Bobby," Jamie said as gently as possible. "But he's right, aye? It is his duty to make the best match he can for wee Lizzie. And perhaps . . ."

Bobby swallowed hard. He had groomed himself to the nines

for this interview, and wore a starched neckcloth that threatened to choke him, with his livery coat, a pair of clean woolen breeches, and a pair of carefully preserved silk stockings, neatly darned in only a few places.

"I know I ha'n't got a great deal of money," he said. "Nor property. But I have got a good situation, zur! Lord John pays me ten pound a year, and has been so kind as to say I may build a small cottage on his grounds, and 'til it is ready, we might have quarters in his house."

"Aye, so ye said." Mr. Wemyss looked increasingly wretched. He kept looking away from Bobby, perhaps in part from natural shyness and unwillingness to refuse him eye-to-eye—but also, I was sure, to avoid seeming to look at the brand upon his cheek.

The discussion went on for a bit, but to no effect, as Mr. Wemyss could not bring himself to tell Bobby the real reason for his refusal.

"I—I—well, I will think further." Mr. Wemyss, unable to bear the tension any longer, got abruptly to his feet and nearly ran out of the room—forcing himself to a stop at the door, though, to turn and say, "Mind, I do not think I shall change my mind!" before disappearing.

Bobby looked after him, nonplussed, then turned to Jamie.

"Have I hopes, zur? I know you will be honest."

It was a pathetic plea, and Jamie himself glanced away from those large blue eyes.

"I do not think so," he said. It was said kindly, but definitely, and Bobby sagged a little. He had slicked down his wavy hair with water; now dried, tiny curls were popping up from the thick mass, and he looked absurdly like a newborn lamb that has just had its tail docked, shocked and dismayed.

"Does she—do ye know, zur, or ma'am"—turning to me—"are Miss Elizabeth's affections given elsewhere? For if that was to be the case, sure I would bide. But if not . . ." He hesitated, glancing toward the door where Joseph had so abruptly disappeared.

"D'ye think I might have some chance of overcoming her father's objections? Perhaps—perhaps if I was to find some way of coming by a bit o' money . . . or if it was to be a question of religion . . ." He looked a little pale at this, but squared his shoulders resolutely. "I—I think I should be willing to be baptized Romish and he required it. I meant to tell him so, but forgot. Would ye maybe say so to him, zur?"

"Aye . . . aye, I will," Jamie said reluctantly. "Ye've quite made up your mind as it's Lizzie, then, have ye? Not Malva?"

Bobby was taken back by that.

"Well, to be honest, zur—I'm that fond of them both, I'm sure I should be happy with either one. But—well, truth to tell, I be mortal feared of Mr. Christie," he confessed, blushing. "And I think he don't like you, zur, while Mr. Wemyss does. If you could . . . speak for me, zur? Please?"

In the end, even Jamie was not proof against this guileless begging.

"I'll try," he conceded. "But I promise ye nothing, Bobby. How long will ye stay now, before ye go back to Lord John?"

"His Lordship's given me a week for my wooing, zur," Bobby said, looking much happier. "But I suppose ye'll be going yourself tomorrow or next day?"

Jamie looked surprised.

"Going where?"

Bobby looked surprised in turn.

"Why . . . I don't rightly know, zur. But I thought *you* must."

After a bit more cross-talk, we succeeded in disentangling the tale. He had, it seemed, fallen in with a small group of travelers on the road, farmers driving a herd of pigs to market. Given the nature of pigs as traveling companions, he hadn't stayed with them for more than one night, but over supper, in the course of casual talk, had heard them make reference to a meeting of sorts and speculate as to who might come to it.

"Your name was mentioned, zur—'James Fraser,' they said, and they mentioned the Ridge, too, so as I was sure 'twas you they meant."

"What sort of meeting was it?" I asked curiously. "And where?"

He shrugged, helpless.

"Took no notice, ma'am. Only they said 'twas Monday next."

Neither did he recall the names of his hosts, having been too much occupied in trying to eat without being overcome by the presence of the pigs. He was plainly too occupied at the moment with the results of his unsuccessful courtship to give much mind to the details, and after a few questions and confused answers, Jamie sent him off.

"Have you any idea—" I began, but then saw that his brows were furrowed; he obviously did.

"The meeting to choose delegates for a Continental Congress," he said. "It must be that."

He had had word after Flora MacDonald's barbecue that the initial meeting place and time were to be abandoned, the organizers fearing interference. A new place and time would be established, John Ashe had told him—word would be sent.

But that was before the contretemps in downtown Cross Creek.

"I suppose a note might have gone astray," I suggested, but the suggestion was a feeble one.

"One might," he agreed. "Not six."

"Six?"

"When I heard nothing, I wrote myself, to the six men I know personally within the Committee of Correspondence. No answer from any of them." His stiff finger tapped once against his leg, but he noticed, and stilled it.

"They don't trust you," I said, after a moment's silence, and he shook his head.

"Little wonder, I suppose, after I rescued Simms and tarred Neil Forbes in the public street." Despite himself, a small smile flitted across his face at the memory. "And poor wee Bobby didna help, I expect; he would have told them he carried letters betwixt me and Lord John."

That was probably true. Friendly and garrulous, Bobby *was* capable of keeping a confidence—but only if you told him explicitly which confidence to keep. Otherwise, anyone who shared a meal with him would know all his business by the time the pudding came.

"Can you do anything else to find out? Where the meeting is, I mean?"

He blew out his breath in mild frustration.

"Aye, maybe. But if I did, and went there—there's a great chance they would put me out. If not worse. I think the risk of such a breach isna worth it." He glanced at me, with a wry expression. "I suppose I should have let them roast the printer."

I disregarded that, and came to stand beside him.

"You'll think of something else," I said, trying to be encouraging.

The big hour candle stood on his desk, half-burned, and he touched it. No one seemed ever to notice that the candle was never consumed.

"Perhaps . . ." he said meditatively. "I may find a way. Though I should hate to take another for the purpose."

Another gem, he meant.

I swallowed a small lump in my throat at the thought. There were two left. One each, if Roger, or Bree, and Jemmy—but I choked that thought off firmly.

"What does it profit a man to gain the world," I quoted, "if he lose his soul? It won't do us any good to be secretly rich, if *you* get tarred and feathered." I didn't like that thought any better, but it wasn't one I could avoid.

He glanced at his forearm; he had rolled up his sleeves for writing, and the fading burn still showed, a faint pink track among the sunbleached hairs. He sighed, went round his desk, and picked a quill from the jar.

"Aye. Perhaps I'd best write a few more letters."

60

The Pale Horseman Rides

On the twentieth of September, Roger preached a sermon on the text, *God hath chosen the weak things of the world to confound the things which are mighty.* On the twenty-first of September, one of those weak things set out to prove the point.

Padraic and Hortense MacNeill and their children hadn't come to church. They always did, and their absence aroused comment—enough that Roger asked Brianna next morning if she might walk round and visit, to see that there was nothing wrong.

"I'd go myself," he said, scraping the bottom of his porridge bowl, "but I've promised to ride with John MacAfee and his father to Brownsville; he means to offer for a girl there."

"Does he mean you to make them handfast on the spot if she says yes?" I asked. "Or are you just there to keep assorted Browns from assassinating him?" There had been no open violence since we had returned Lionel Brown's body, but there were occasional small clashes, when a party from Brownsville happened to meet men from the Ridge now and then in public.

"The latter," Roger said with a small grimace. "Though I've some hopes that a marriage or two betwixt the Ridge and Brownsville might help to mend matters, over time."

Jamie, reading a newspaper from the most recent batch, looked up at that.

"Oh, aye? Well, it's a thought. Doesna always work out just so, though." He smiled. "My uncle Colum thought to mend just such a matter wi' the Grants, by marrying my mother to the Grant. Unfortunately," he added, turning over a page, "my mother wasna inclined to cooperate. She snubbed Malcolm Grant, stabbed my uncle Dougal, and eloped wi' my father, instead."

"Really?" Brianna hadn't heard that particular story; she looked enchanted. Roger gave her a sidelong glance, and coughed, ostentatiously removing the sharp knife with which she'd been cutting up sausages.

"Well, be that as it may," he said, pushing back from the table, knife in hand. "If ye wouldn't mind having a look-in on Padraic's family, just to see they're all right?"

In the event, Lizzie and I came along with Brianna, meaning to call on Marsali and Fergus, whose cabin was a little way beyond the MacNeills'. We met Marsali on the way, though, coming back from the whisky spring, and so there were four of us when we came to the MacNeills' cabin.

"Why are there so many flies, of a sudden?" Lizzie slapped at a large bluebottle that had landed on her arm, then waved at two more, circling round her face.

"Something's dead nearby," Marsali said, lifting her nose to sniff the air. "In the wood, maybe. Hear the crows?"

There were crows, cawing in the treetops nearby; looking up, I saw more circling, black spots against the brilliant sky.

"Not in the wood," Bree said, her voice suddenly strained. She was looking toward the cabin. The door was tightly shut, and a mass of flies milled over the hide-covered window. "Hurry."

The smell in the cabin was unspeakable. I saw the girls gasp and clamp their mouths tight shut, as the door swung open. Unfortunately, it was necessary to breathe. I did so, very shallowly, as I moved across the dark room and ripped down the hide that had been tightly nailed across the window.

"Leave the door open," I said, ignoring a faint moan of complaint from the bed at the influx of light. "Lizzie—go and start a smudge fire near the door and another outside the window. Start it with grass and kindling, then add something—damp wood, moss, wet leaves—to make it smoke."

Flies had begun to come in within seconds of my opening the window, and were whizzing past my face—deerflies, bluebottles, gnats. Drawn by the smell, they had been clustered on the sunwarmed logs outside, seeking entrance, avid for food, desperate to lay their eggs.

The room would be a buzzing hell in minutes—but we needed

light and air, and would just have to deal with the flies as best we might. I pulled off my kerchief and folded it into a makeshift fly-swatter, slapping to and fro with it as I turned to the bed.

Hortense and the two children were there. All naked, their pallid limbs glimmering with the sweat of the sealed cabin. They were clammy white where the sunlight struck, legs and bodies streaked with reddish-brown. I hoped that it was only diarrhea, and not blood.

Someone had moaned; someone moved. Not dead then, thank God. The bedcoverings had been thrown to the floor in a tangled heap—that was fortunate, as they were still mostly clean. I thought we had better burn the straw mattress, as soon as we got them off it.

"Do *not* put your fingers in your mouth," I murmured to Bree, as we began to work, sorting the feebly twitching heap of humanity into its component parts.

"You have *got* to be kidding," she said, speaking through her teeth while smiling at a pale-faced child of five or six, who lay half-curled in the exhausted aftermath of a diarrhetic attack. She worked her hands under the little girl's armpits. "Come on, lovey, let me lift you."

The child was too weak to make any protest at being moved; her arms and legs hung limp as string. Her sister's state was even more alarming; no more than a year old, the baby didn't move at all, and her eyes were sunk deep, a sign of severe dehydration. I picked up the tiny hand and gently pinched the skin between thumb and forefinger. It stayed for a moment, a tiny peak of grayish skin, then slowly, slowly, began to disappear.

"Bloody fucking hell," I said softly to myself and bent swiftly to listen, hand on the child's chest. She wasn't dead—I could barely feel the bump of her heart—but wasn't far from it. If she were too far gone to suck or drink, there was nothing that would save her.

Even as the thought passed through my mind, I was rising, looking about the cabin. No water; a hollowed gourd lay on its side by the bed, empty. How long had they been like this, with nothing to drink?

"Bree," I said, my voice level but urgent. "Go and get some water—quickly."

She had laid the older child on the floor, and was wiping the filth from her body; she glanced up, though, and the sight of my face made her drop the rag she was using and stand up at once. She grabbed the kettle I thrust into her hand and vanished; I heard her footsteps, running across the dooryard.

The flies were settling on Hortense's face; I flapped the kerchief close to shoo them away. The cloth skimmed her nose, but her slack features barely twitched. She was breathing; I could see her belly, distended with gas, moving slightly.

Where was Padraic? Hunting, perhaps.

I caught a whiff of something under the overwhelming stench of voided bowels and leaned over, sniffing. A sweet, pungently fermented scent, like rotted apples. I put a hand under Hortense's shoulder and pulled, rolling her toward me. There was a bottle—empty—under her body. A whiff of it was enough to tell me what it had contained.

"Bloody, bloody fucking hell," I said, under my breath. Desperately ill and with no water to hand, she had drunk applejack, either to quench her thirst or to soothe the pain of the cramps. A logical thing to do—save that alcohol was a diuretic. It would leach even more water from a body that was already seriously dehydrated, to say nothing of further irritating a gastrointestinal tract that scarcely needed it.

Bloody Christ, had she given it to the children, too?

I stooped to the elder child. She was limp as a ragdoll, head lolling on her shoulders, but there was still some resilience to her flesh. A pinch of the hand; the skin stayed peaked, but returned to normal faster than the baby's had.

Her eyes had opened when I pinched her hand. That was good. I smiled at her, and brushed the gathering flies away from her half-open mouth. The soft pink membranes were dry and stickylooking.

"Hallo, darling," I said softly. "Don't worry now. I'm here."

And was that going to help? I wondered. Damn it all; if only I had been a day earlier!

I heard Bree's hurrying steps and met her at the door.

"I need—" I began, but she interrupted me.

"Mr. MacNeill's in the woods!" she said. "I found him on the way to the spring. He's—"

The kettle in her hands was still empty. I seized it with a cry of exasperation.

"Water! I need water!"

"But I—Mr. MacNeill, he's—"

I thrust the kettle back into her hands and shoved past her.

"I'll find him," I said. "Get water! Give it to them—the baby first! Make Lizzie help you—the fires can wait! Run!"

I heard the flies first, a buzzing noise that made my skin crawl with revulsion. Out in the open, they had found him quickly, attracted by the smell. I took a hasty gulp of air and shoved through the buckbrush to where Padraic lay, collapsed in the grass beneath a sycamore.

He wasn't dead. I saw that at once; the flies were a cloud, not a blanket—hovering, lighting, flicking away again as he twitched.

He lay curled on the ground, wearing only a shirt, a water jug lying near his head. I knelt by him, peering as I touched him. His shirt and legs were stained, as was the grass where he lay. The excrement was very watery—most had soaked into the soil by now—but there was some solid matter. He'd been stricken later than Hortense and the children, then; his guts hadn't been griping long, or there would be mostly water, tinged with blood.

"Padraic?"

"Mrs. Claire, thank the Lord ye've come." His voice was so hoarse I could scarcely make out words. "My bairnies. Have ye got my bairnies safe?"

He raised himself on one elbow, shaking, sweat plastering strands of gray hair to his cheeks. His eyes cracked open, trying to see me, but they were swelled to mere slits by the bites of deerflies.

"I have them." I put a hand on him at once, squeezing to force reassurance into him. "Lie down, Padraic. Wait a moment while I tend them, then I'll see to you." He was very ill, but not in immediate danger; the children were.

"Dinna mind me," Padraic muttered. "Dinna . . . mind . . ." He swayed, brushed at the flies that crawled on his face and chest, then groaned as cramp seized his belly again, doubling as though some massive hand had crushed him in its grip.

I was already running back to the house. There were splashes of water in the dust of the path—good, Brianna had come this way, hurrying.

Amoebic dysentery? Food poisoning? Typhoid? Typhus? Cholera—please God, not that. All of those, and a lot more, were currently lumped together simply as "the bloody flux" in this time, and for obvious reasons. Not that it mattered in the short term.

The immediate danger of all the diarrhetic diseases was simple dehydration. In the effort to expel whatever microbial invader was irritating the gut, the gastrointestinal tract simply flushed itself repeatedly, depleting the body of the water necessary to circulate blood, to eliminate wastes, to cool the body by means of sweat, to maintain the brain and membranes—the water necessary to maintain *life*.

If one could keep a patient sufficiently hydrated by means of intravenous saline and glucose infusions, then the gut would, most likely, heal itself eventually and the patient would recover. Without intravenous intervention, the only possibility was to administer fluids by mouth, or rectum as quickly and as constantly as possible, for as long as it took. If one could.

If the patient couldn't keep down even water—I didn't think the MacNeills were vomiting; I didn't recall *that* smell among the others in the cabin. Probably not cholera, then; that was something.

Brianna sat on the floor by the elder child, the little girl's head in her lap, pressing a cup against her mouth. Lizzie knelt by the hearth, face red with exertion as she kindled the fire. The flies were settling on the motionless body of the woman on the bed, and Marsali crouched over the limp form of the baby on her lap, frantically trying to rouse it to drink.

Spilled water streaked her skirt. I could see the tiny head lolled back on her lap, water dribbling down a slack and horribly flattened cheek.

"She can't," Marsali was saying, over and over. "She can't, she can't!"

Disregarding my own advice about fingers, I ruthlessly thrust an index finger into the baby's mouth, prodding the palate for a gag reflex. It was there; the baby choked on the water in its mouth and gasped, and I felt the tongue close hard against my finger for an instant.

Sucking. She was an infant, still breastfed—and suckling is the first of the instincts for survival. I whirled to look at the woman, but a glance at her flat breasts and sunken nipples was enough; even so, I grabbed one breast, squeezing my fingers toward the nipple. Again, again—no, no droplets of milk showed on the brownish nipples, and the breast tissue was flabby in my hand. No water, no milk.

Marsali, grasping what I was about, seized the neck of her blouse and ripped it down, pressing the child to her own bared breast. The tiny legs were limp against her dress, toes bruised and curled like wilted petals.

I was tipping back Hortense's face, dribbling water into her open mouth. From the corner of my eye, I saw Marsali rhythmically squeezing her breast with one hand, an urgent massage to make the milk let down, even as my own fingers moved in an echo of the motion, massaging the unconscious woman's throat, urging her to swallow.

Her flesh was slick with sweat, but most of it was mine. Trickles of perspiration were running down my back, tickling between my buttocks. I could smell myself, a strange metallic scent, like hot copper.

The throat moved in sudden peristalsis, and I took my hand away. Hortense choked and coughed, then her head rolled to the side and her stomach heaved, sending its meager contents rocketing back up. I wiped the trace of vomit from her lips, and pressed the cup to her mouth again. Her lips didn't move; the water filled her mouth and dribbled down her face and neck.

Among the buzzing of the flies, I heard Lizzie's voice behind me, calm but abstracted, as though she spoke from a long way off.

"Can ye stop cursing, ma'am? It's only that the weans can hear ye."

I jerked round at her, only then realizing that I had in fact been repeating "Bloody fucking *hell*!" out loud, over and over as I worked.

"Yes," I said. "Sorry." And turned back to Hortense.

I got some water down her now and then, but not enough. Not nearly enough, given that her bowels were still trying to rid themselves of whatever troubled them. Bloody flux.

Lizzie was praying.

"Hail Mary, full of grace, the Lord is with thee . . ."

Brianna was murmuring something under her breath, urgent sounds of maternal encouragement.

"Blessed is the fruit of thy womb, Jesus . . ."

My thumb was on the pulse of the carotid artery. I felt it bump, skip, and go on, jerking along like a cart with a missing wheel. Her heart was beginning to fail, arrhythmic.

"Holy Mary, Mother of God . . ."

I slammed my fist down on the center of her chest, and then again, and again, hard enough that the bed and the pale splayed body quivered under the blows. Flies rose in alarm from the soaked straw, buzzing.

"Oh, no," said Marsali softly behind me. "Oh, no, no, please." I had heard that tone of disbelief before, of protest and appeal denied—and knew what had happened.

"Pray for us sinners . . ."

As though she, too, had heard, Hortense's head rolled suddenly to one side, and her eyes sprang open, staring toward the place where Marsali sat, though I thought she saw nothing. Then the eyes closed and she doubled suddenly, onto one side, legs drawn up nearly to her chin. Her head wrenched back, body tight in spasm, and then she suddenly relaxed. She would not let her child go alone. Bloody flux.

'Now and at the hour of our death, amen. Hail Mary, full of grace . . ."

Lizzie's soft voice went on mechanically, repeating her words of prayer as mindlessly as I had said mine earlier. I held Hortense's wrist, checking for the pulse, but it was mere formality. Marsali curled over the tiny body in grief, rocking it against her breast. Milk dripped from the swollen nipple, coming slowly, then faster, falling like white rain on the small still face, futilely eager to nourish and sustain.

The air was still stifling, still thick with odor and flies and the sound of Lizzie's prayers—but the cabin seemed empty, and curiously silent.

There was a shuffling noise outside; the sound of something being dragged, a grunt of pain and dreadful exertion. Then the soft sound of falling, a gasp of breath. Padraic had made it back to his own doorstep. Brianna looked to the door, but she still held the older girl in her arms, still alive.

I set down the limp hand that I held, carefully, and went to help.

61

A Noisome Pestilence

The days were growing shorter, but light still came early. The windows at the front of the house faced east, and the rising sun glowed on the scrubbed white oak of my surgery floor. I could see the brilliant bar of light advancing across the hand-hewn boards; had I had an actual timepiece, I could have calibrated the floor like a sundial, marking the seams between the boards in minutes.

As it was, I marked them in heartbeats, waiting through the moments until the sun should have reached the counter where my microscope stood ready, slides and beaker beside it.

I heard soft footsteps in the corridor, and Jamie pushed the door open with his shoulder, a pewter mug of something hot held in each hand, wrapped with rags against the heat.

"Ciamar a tha thu, mo chridhe," he said softly, and handed one to me, brushing a kiss across my forehead. "How is it, then?"

"It could be worse." I gave him a smile of gratitude, though it was interrupted by a yawn. I didn't need to tell him that Padraic and his elder daughter still lived; he would have known at once by my face if anything dire had happened. In fact, bar any complications, I thought both would recover; I had stayed with them all night, rousing them hourly to drink a concoction of honeyed water, mixed with a little salt, alternating with a strong infusion of peppermint leaf and dogwood bark to calm the bowels.

I lifted the mug—goosefoot tea—closing my eyes as I inhaled the faint, bitter perfume, and feeling the tight muscles of my neck and shoulders relax in anticipation.

He had seen me twist my head to ease my neck; Jamie's hand came down on my nape, large and wonderfully warm from holding the hot tea. I gave a small moan of ecstasy at the touch, and he laughed low in his throat, massaging my sore muscles.

"Should ye not be abed, Sassenach? Ye'll not have slept at all the night."

"Oh, I did . . . a bit." I had dozed fitfully, sitting up by the open window, roused periodically by the startling touch on my face of the moths that flew in, drawn to the light of my candle. Mrs. Bug had come at dawn, though, fresh and starched, ready to take over the heavy nursing.

"I'll go lie down in a bit," I promised. "But I wanted to have a quick look first." I waved vaguely toward my microscope, which stood assembled and ready on the table. Next to it were several small glass bottles, plugged with twists of cloth, each containing a brownish liquid. Jamie frowned at them.

"Look? At what?" he said. He lifted his long, straight nose, sniffing suspiciously. "Is that shit?"

"Yes, it is," I said, not bothering to stifle a jaw-cracking yawn. I had—as discreetly as possible—collected samples from Hortense and the baby and, later, from my living patients, as well. Jamie eyed them.

"Exactly *what*," he inquired cautiously, "are ye looking for?"

"Well, I don't know," I admitted. "And in fact, I may not find anything—or anything I can recognize. But it's possible that it was either an amoeba or a bacillus that made the MacNeills sick—and I think I *would* recognize an amoeba; they're quite big. Relatively speaking," I added hastily.

"Oh, aye?" His ruddy brows drew together, then lifted. "Why?"

That was a better question than he knew.

"Well, partly for the sake of curiosity," I admitted. "But also, if I do find a causative organism that I can recognize, I'll know a bit more about the disease—how long it lasts, for instance, and whether there are any complications to look out for specially. And how contagious it is."

He glanced at me, cup half-raised to his mouth.

"Is it one *you* can catch?"

"I don't know," I admitted. "Though I'm fairly sure it is. I've been vaccinated against typhus and typhoid—but this doesn't look like either one of those. And there are no vaccines for dysentery or *Giardia* poisoning."

The brows drew together and stayed that way, knotted as he

sipped his tea. His fingers gave my neck a final squeeze and dropped away.

I sipped cautiously at my own tea, sighing in pleasure as it gently scalded my throat and ran hot and comforting down into my stomach. Jamie lounged on his stool, long legs thrust out. He glanced down into the steaming cup between his hands.

"D'ye think this tea is hot, Sassenach?" he asked.

I raised my own brows at that. Both cups were still wrapped in rags, and I could feel the heat seeping through to my palms.

"I do," I said. "Why?"

He lifted the mug and took a mouthful of tea, which he held for a moment before swallowing; I could see the long muscles move in his throat.

"Brianna came into the kitchen whilst I was brewing the pot," he said. "She took down the basin, and the pannikin of soap—and then she took a dipper of water steaming from the kettle, and poured it over her hands, one and then the other." He paused a moment. "The water was boiling when I took it off the fire a moment before."

The mouthful of tea I had taken went down crooked, and I coughed.

"Did she burn herself?" I said, when I had got my breath back.

"She did," he said, rather grimly. "She scrubbed herself from fingertips to elbows, and I saw the blister on the side of her hand where the water fell." He paused for a moment, and his eyes met mine over the mugs, dark blue with worry.

I took another sip of my un-honeyed tea. The room was cool enough, just past dawn, that my hot breath made tiny wisps of steam as I sighed.

"Padraic's baby died in Marsali's arms," I said quietly. "She held the other child. She knows it's contagious." And knowing, could not touch or pick up her own child without doing her best to wash away her fear.

Jamie moved uneasily.

"Aye," he began. "But still . . ."

"It's different," I said, and put a hand on his wrist, as much for my own comfort as his.

The transient coolness of the morning air touched face and mind alike, dispelling the warm tangle of dreams. The grass and trees were still lit with a chilly dawn glow, blue-shadowed and mysterious, and Jamie seemed a solid point of reference, fixed in the shifting light.

"Different," I repeated. "For her, I mean." I took a breath of the sweet morning air, smelling of wet grass and morning glories.

"I was born at the end of a war—the Great War, they called it, because the world had never seen anything like it. I told you about it." My voice held a slight question, and he nodded, eyes fixed on mine, listening.

"The year after I was born," I said, "there was a great epidemic of influenza. All over the world. People died in hundreds and thousands; whole villages disappeared in the space of a week. And then came the other, my war."

The words were quite unconscious, but hearing them, I felt the corner of my mouth twitch with irony. Jamie saw it and a faint smile touched his own lips. He knew what I meant—that odd sense of pride that comes of living through a terrible conflict, leaving one with a peculiar feeling of possession. His wrist turned, his fingers wrapping tight around my own.

"And she has never seen plague or war," he said, beginning to understand. "Never?" His voice held something odd. Nearly incomprehensible, to a man born a warrior, brought up to fight as soon as he could lift a sword; born to the idea that he must—he would—defend himself and his family by violence. An incomprehensible notion—but a rather wonderful one.

"Only as pictures. Films, I mean. Television." That one he would never understand, and I could not explain. The way in which such pictures focused on war itself; bombs and planes and submarines, and the thrilling urgency of blood shed on purpose; a sense of nobility in deliberate death.

He knew what battlefields were really like—battlefields, and what came after them.

"The men who fought in those wars—and the women—they didn't die of the killing, most of them. They died like this—" A lift of my mug toward the open window, toward the peaceful mountains, the distant hollow where Padraic MacNeill's cabin lay hidden. "They died of illness and neglect, because there wasn't any way to stop it."

"I have seen that," he said softly, with a glance at the stoppered bottles. "Plague and ague run rampant in a city, half a regiment dead of flux."

"Of course you have."

Butterflies were rising among the flowers in the dooryard, cabbage whites and sulfur yellows, here and there the great, lazy sail of a late tiger swallowtail out of the shadow of the wood. My thumb still rested on his wrist, feeling his heartbeat, slow and powerful.

"Brianna was born seven years after penicillin came into common use. She was born in America—not this one"—I nodded toward the window again—"but *that* one, that will be. There, it isn't usual for lots of people to die of contagious illness." I glanced at him. The light had reached his waist, and glowed on the metal cup in his hand.

"Do you remember the first person you knew of who had died?"

His face went blank with surprise, then sharpened, thinking. After a moment, he shook his head.

"My brother was the first who was important, but I kent others before him, surely."

"I can't remember, either." My parents, of course; their deaths had been personal—but born in England, I had lived in the shadow of cenotaphs and memorials, and people just beyond the bounds of my own family died regularly; I had a sudden vivid memory, of my father putting on a homburg and dark coat to go to the baker's wife's funeral. Mrs. Briggs, her name had been. But she hadn't been the first; I knew already about death and funerals. How old had I been then—four, perhaps?

I was very tired. My eyes felt grainy from lack of sleep, and the delicate early light was brightening to full sun.

"I think Frank's was the first death Brianna ever experienced personally. Maybe there were others; I can't be sure. But the point is—"

"I see the point." He reached to take the empty cup from my hand, and set it on the counter, then drained his own and set it down, too.

"But it's no herself she fears for, aye?" he asked, his eyes penetrating. "It's the wean."

I nodded. She would have known, of course, in an academic sort of way, that such things were possible. But to have a child die suddenly before you, from something like a simple case of diarrhea . . .

"She's a good mother," I said, and yawned suddenly. She was. But it would never have struck her in any visceral way that something so negligible as a germ could suddenly snatch away her child. Not until yesterday.

Jamie stood up suddenly, and pulled me to my feet.

"Go to bed, Sassenach," he said. "That will wait." He nodded at the microscope. "I've never known shit spoil with keeping."

I laughed, and collapsed slowly against him, my cheek pressed against his chest.

"Maybe you're right." Still, I didn't push away. He held me, and we watched the sunlight grow, creeping slowly up the wall.

62

Amoeba

I turned the mirror of the microscope a fraction of an inch further, to get as much light as I could.

"There." I stepped back, motioning Malva to come and look. "Do you see it? The big, clear thing in the middle, lobed, with the little flecks in it?"

She frowned, squinting one-eyed into the ocular, then drew in her breath in a gasp of triumph.

"I see it plain! Like a currant pudding someone's dropped on the floor, no?"

"That's it," I said, smiling at her description in spite of the general seriousness of our investigation. "It's an amoeba—one of the bigger sorts of microorganisms. And I very much think it's our villain."

We were looking at slides made from the stool samples I had retrieved from all the sick so far—for Padraic's family was not the only one affected. There were three families with at least one person ill with a vicious bloody flux—and in all of the samples I had looked at so far, I had found this amoebic stranger.

"Is it really?" Malva had looked up when I spoke, but now returned to the eyepiece, absorbed. "However can something so small cause such *a stramash* in something so big as a person?"

"Well, there *is* an explanation," I said, swishing another slide gently through the dye bath and setting it to dry. "But it would take me a bit of time to tell you, all about cells—you remember, I showed you the cells from the lining of your mouth?"

She nodded, frowning slightly, and ran her tongue along inside her cheek.

"Well, the body makes all kinds of different cells, and there are special kinds of cells whose business it is to fight bacteria—the small, roundish sorts of things, you remember those?" I gestured at the slide, which being fecal matter, had the usual vast quantities of *Escherichia coli* and the like.

"But there are millions of different sorts, and sometimes a microorganism comes along that the special cells aren't able to deal with. You know—I showed you the *Plasmodium* in Lizzie's blood?" I nodded toward the stoppered vial on the counter; I had taken blood from Lizzie only a day or two before, and shown the malarial parasites in the cells to Malva. "And I do think that this amoeba of ours may well be one like that."

"Oh, well. Will we give the sick folk the penicillin, then?" I smiled a little at the eager "we," though there was little enough to smile at in the situation overall.

"No, I'm afraid penicillin isn't effective against amoebic dysentery—that's what you call a very bad flux, a dysentery. No, I'm afraid we've nothing much to be going on with save herbs." I opened the cupboard and ran an eye over the ranks of bottles and gauze-wrapped bundles, puzzling.

"Wormwood, for a start." I took the jar down and handed it to Malva, who had come to stand beside me, looking with interest into the mysteries of the cupboard. "Garlic, that's generally useful for infections of the digestive tract—but it makes quite a good poultice for skin things, as well."

"What about onions? My grannie would steam an onion, and put it to my ear, when I was a wee bairn and had the earache. It smelt something dreadful, but it did work!"

"It can't hurt. Run out to the pantry, then, and fetch . . . oh, three big ones, and several heads of garlic."

"Oh, at once, ma'am!" She set down the wormwood and dashed out, sandals flapping. I turned back to the shelves, trying to calm my own sense of urgency.

I was torn between the urge to be with the sick, nursing them, and the need to make medicines that *might* be of help. But there were other people who could do the nursing, and no one but me who knew enough to try to compound an antiparasitic remedy.

Wormwood, garlic . . . agrimony. And gentian. Anything with a very high content of copper or sulfur—oh, rhubarb. We were past the growing season, but I'd had a fine crop and had put up several dozen bottles of the boiled pulp and syrup, as Mrs. Bug liked it for pies, and it provided some vitamin C for the winter months. That would make a splendid base for the medicine. Add perhaps slippery elm, for its soothing effects on the intestinal tract—though such effects were likely to be so slight as to be unnoticeable against the ravages of such a virulent onslaught.

I began pounding wormwood and agrimony in my mortar, meanwhile wondering where the bloody hell the thing had come from. Amoebic dysentery was normally a disease of the tropics, though God knew, I'd seen any number of peculiar tropical diseases on the coast, brought in with the slave and sugar trade from the Indies—and not a few further inland, too, since any such disease that wasn't instantly fatal tended to become chronic and move along with its victim.

It wasn't impossible that one of the fisher-folk had contracted it during the journey from the coast, and while being one of the fortunate persons who suffered only a mild infection, was now carrying the encysted form of the amoeba around in his or her digestive tract, all ready to shed infective cysts right and left.

Why this sudden outbreak? Dysentery was almost always spread via contaminated food or water. What—

"Here, ma'am." Malva was back, breathless from her hurry, several large brown onions in hand, crackling and glossy, and a dozen garlic heads bundled in her apron. I set her to slicing them up, and had the happy inspiration of telling her to stew them in honey. I didn't know whether the antibacterial effect of honey would be likewise effective against an amoeba, but it couldn't hurt—and might conceivably make the mixture a little more palatable; it was shaping up to be more than a trifle eye-watering, between the onions, the garlic, and the rhubarb.

"Phew! What are you guys *doing* in here?" I looked up from my macerating to see Brianna in the door, looking deeply suspicious, nose wrinkled against the smell.

"Oh. Well . . ." I'd become habituated to it myself, but in fact, the air in the surgery was fairly thick with the smell of fecal samples, now augmented by waves of onion fumes. Malva looked up, eyes streaming, and sniffed, wiping her nose on her apron.

"We're magking bedicine," she informed Bree, with considerable dignity.

"Is anyone else fallen sick?" I asked anxiously, but she shook her head and edged into the room, fastidiously avoiding the counter where I had been making slides of fecal material.

"No, not that I've heard. I took some food over to the McLachlans' this morning, and they said only the two little ones had it. Mrs. Coinneach said she'd had diarrhea a couple of days ago, but not bad, and she's all right now."

"They're giving the little ones honey water?"

She nodded, a small frown between her eyebrows.

"I saw them. They look pretty sick, but nothing like the MacNeills." She looked rather sick herself, at the memory, but shook it off, turning to the high cupboard.

"Can I borrow a little sulfuric acid, Mama?" She'd brought an earthenware cup with her, and the sight of it made me laugh.

"Ordinary people borrow a cup of sugar," I told her, nodding at it. "Of course. Be careful with it, though—you'd best put it in one of those vials with a waxed cork. You do *not* want to chance tripping and spilling it."

"I definitely don't," she assured me. "I only need a few drops, though; I'm going to dilute it down pretty far. I'm making paper."

"Paper?" Malva blinked, red-eyed, and sniffed. "How?"

"Well, you squish up anything fibrous you can get your hands on," Bree told her, making squishing motions with both hands in illustrations. "Old bits of used paper, old rags of cloth, bits of yarn or thread, some of the softer sorts of leaves or flowers. Then you soak the mash for days and days in water and—if you happen to have some—dilute sulfuric acid." One long finger tapped the square bottle affectionately.

"Then once the mash is all digested down to a sort of pulp, you can spread a thin layer of it on screens, press out the water, let it dry, and hey-presto, paper!"

I could see Malva mouthing "hey-presto" to herself, and turned away a little, so she couldn't see me smile. Brianna uncorked the big square bottle of acid and, very carefully, poured a few drops into her cup. Immediately, the hot smell of sulfur rose like a demon amidst the miasma of feces and onions.

Malva stiffened, eyes still streaming but wide.

"What is that?" she said.

"Sulfuric acid," Bree said, looking at her curiously.

"Vitriol," I amended. "Have you seen—er, smelled it before?"

She nodded, put the sliced onions into a pot, and put the lid neatly on.

"Aye, I have." She came to look at the green glass bottle, dabbing at her eyes. "My mother—she died when I was young—she had some of that. I remember the smell of it, and how she'd say as I mustn't touch it, ever. Brimstone, folk called the smell—a whiff o' brimstone."

"Really? I wonder what she used it for." I *did* wonder, and with a certain sense of unease. An alchemist or an apothecary might have the stuff; the only reason that I knew of for a common citizen to keep it was as a means of aggression—to throw at someone.

But Malva only shook her head, and turning, went back to the onions and garlic. I'd caught the look on her face, though; a queer expression of hostility and longing that rang a small, unsuspected bell somewhere inside me.

Longing for a mother long dead—and the fury of a small girl, abandoned. Bewildered and alone.

"What?" Brianna was watching *my* face, frowning slightly. "What's wrong?"

"Nothing," I said, and put a hand on her arm, just to feel the strength and joy of her presence, the years of her growth. Tears stung my eyes, but that could be put down to onions. "Nothing at all."

I was getting terribly tired of funerals. This was the third, in as many days. We had buried Hortense and the baby together, then the older Mrs. Ogilvie. Now it was another child, one of Mrs.

MacAfee's twins. The other twin, a boy, stood by his sister's grave, in a shock so profound that he looked like a walking ghost himself, though the disease hadn't touched him.

We were later than intended—the coffin hadn't been quite ready—and the night was rising around us. All the gold of the autumn leaves had faded into ash, and white mist was curling through the dark wet trunks of the pines. One could hardly imagine a more desolate scene—and yet it was in a way more fitting than the bright sunshine and fresh breeze that had blown when we buried Hortense and little Angelica.

"The Lord is my shepherd. He leadeth me beside—" Roger's voice cracked painfully, but no one seemed to notice. He struggled for a moment, swallowing hard, and went on, doggedly. He held the little green Bible in his hands, but wasn't looking at it; he was speaking from memory, and his eyes went from Mr. MacAfee, standing alone, for his wife and his sister were both sick, to the little boy beside him—a little boy about Jemmy's age.

"Though I walk . . . though I walk through the valley of death, I shall . . . shall fear no evil—" His voice was trembling audibly, and I saw that tears were running down his face. I looked for Bree; she was standing a little way behind the mourners, Jem half-swaddled in the folds of her dark cloak. The hood of it was drawn up, but her face was visible, pale in the gloaming, Our Lady of Sorrows.

Even Major MacDonald's red coat was muted, charcoal-gray in the last vestiges of light. He had arrived in the afternoon, and helped to carry up the little coffin; he stood now, hat somberly tucked beneath his arm, wigged head bowed, his face invisible. He, too, had a child—a daughter, somewhere back in Scotland with her mother.

I swayed a little, and felt Jamie's hand under my elbow. I had been without sleep for most of the last three days, and had taken precious little food. I didn't feel either hungry or tired, though; I felt remote and unreal, as though the wind blew through me.

The father uttered a cry of inconsolable grief, and sank suddenly down upon the heap of dirt thrown up by the grave. I felt Jamie's muscles contract in instinctive compassion toward him, and pulled away a little, murmuring, "Go."

I saw him cross swiftly to Mr. MacAfee, bend to whisper to him, put an arm around him. Roger had stopped talking.

My thoughts would not obey me. Try as I might to fix them on the proceedings, they strayed away. My arms ached; I had been pounding herbs, lifting patients, carrying water . . . I felt as though I were doing all these things over and over, could feel the repetitive thud of pestle in mortar, the dragging weight of fainting bodies. I was seeing in vivid memory the slides of *Entameba*, greedy pseudopodia flowing in slow-motion appetite. Water, I heard water flowing; it lived in water, though only the cystic form was infective. It was passed on by means of water. I thought that very clearly.

Then I was lying on the ground, with no memory of falling, no memory of ever being upright, the smell of fresh, damp dirt and fresh, damp wood strong in my nose, and a vague thought of worms. There was a flutter of motion before my eyes; the small green Bible had fallen and lay on the dirt in front of my face, the wind turning over its pages, one by one by one in a ghostly game of *sortes Virgilianae*—where would it stop? I wondered dimly.

There were hands and voices, but I could not pay attention. A great amoeba floated majestically in darkness before me, pseudopodia flowing slowly, slowly, in welcoming embrace.

63

Moment of Decision

Fever rolled across my mind like a thunderstorm, jagged forks of pain crackling through my body in bursts of brilliance, each a lightning bolt that glowed for a vivid moment along some nerve or plexus, lighting up the hidden hollows of my joints, burning down the length of muscle fibers. A merciless brilliance, it struck again, and again, the fiery sword of a destroying angel who gave no quarter.

I seldom knew whether my eyes were open or closed, nor whether I woke or slept. I saw nothing but a roiling gray, turbulent and shot with red. The redness pulsed in veins and patches, shrouded in the cloud. I seized upon one crimson vein and followed its path, clinging to the track of its sullen glow amid the buffeting of thunder. The thunder grew louder as I penetrated deeper and deeper into the murk that boiled around me, becoming hideously regular, like the beating of a kettledrum, so that my ears rang with it, and I felt myself a hollow skin, tight-stretched, vibrating with each crash of sound.

The source of it was now before me, throbbing so loudly that I felt I must shout, only to hear some other sound—but though I felt my lips draw back and my throat swell with effort, I heard nothing but the pounding. In desperation, I thrust my hands—if they were my hands—through the misty gray and seized some warm, moist object, very slippery, that throbbed, convulsing in my hands.

I looked down and knew it all at once to be my own heart.

I dropped it in horror, and it crawled away in a trail of reddish slime, shuddering with effort, the valves all opening and closing like the mouths of suffocating fish, each popping open with a hollow click, closing again with a small, meaty thud.

Faces sometimes appeared in the clouds. Some seemed familiar, though I could put no name to them. Others were the faces of strangers, the half-seen, unknown faces that flit sometimes through the mind on the verge of sleep. These looked at me with curiosity or indifference—then turned away.

The others, the ones I knew, bore looks of sympathy or worry; they would seek to fix my gaze with theirs, but my glance slid guiltily off, giddily away, unable to gain traction. Their lips moved, and I knew they spoke to me, but I heard nothing, their words drowned by the silent thunder of my storm.

I felt quite odd—but, for the first time in uncountable days, not ill. The fever clouds had rolled back; still grumbling softly somewhere near, but for the moment, gone from sight. My eyes were clear; I could see the raw wood in the beams overhead.

In fact, I saw the wood with such clarity that I was struck with awe at the beauty of it. The loops and whorls of the polished grain seemed at once static and alive with grace, the colors of it shimmering with smoke and the essence of the earth, so that I could see how the beam was transformed and yet held still the spirit of the tree.

I was so entranced by this that I reached out my hand to touch it—and did. My fingers brushed the wood with delight at the cool surface and the grooves of the axmarks, wing-shaped and regular as a flight of geese along the beam. I could hear the beating of powerful wings, and at the same time, feel the flex and swing of my shoulders, the vibration of joy through my forearms as the ax fell on the wood. As I explored this fascinating sensation, it occurred to me, dimly, that the beam was eight feet above the bed.

I turned—with no sense whatever of effort—and saw that I lay upon the bed below.

I lay on my back, the quilts rumpled and scattered, as though I had tried at some point to throw them off but lacked the strength to do so. The air in the room was strangely still, and the blocks of color in the fabric glowed through it like jewels at the bottom of the sea, rich but muted.

By contrast, my skin was the color of pearls, bloodless pale and shimmering. And then I saw that this was because I was so thin that the skin of face and limb pressed hard upon the bone, and it was the gleam of bone and cartilage below that gave that luster to my face, smooth hardness shining through transparent skin.

And such bones as they were! I was filled with wonder at the marvel of their shaping. My eyes followed the delicacy of the arching ribs, the heartbreaking beauty of the sculptured skull with a sense of awed astonishment.

My hair was tumbled, matted, and snarled . . . and yet I felt myself drawn to it, tracing its curves with eye and . . . finger? For I had no consciousness of moving, and yet I felt the softness of the strands, the cool silk of brown and the springing vibrancy of silver, heard the hairs chime softly past each other, a rustle of notes cascading like a harp's.

My God, I said, and heard the words, though no sound stirred the air, *you are so lovely!*

My eyes were open. I looked deep and met a gaze of amber and soft gold. The eyes looked through me, to something far beyond—and yet they saw me, too. I saw the pupils dilate slightly, and felt the warmth of their darkness embrace me with knowledge and acceptance. *Yes*, said those knowing eyes. *I know you. Let us go.* I felt a sense of great peace, and the air around me stirred, like wind rushing through feathers.

Then some sound turned me toward the window and I saw the man who stood there. I had no name for him, and yet I loved him. He stood with his back turned to the bed, arms braced on the sill, and his head sunk on his chest, so the dawn light glowed red on his hair and traced his arms with gold. A spasm of grief shook him; I felt it, like the temblors of a distant quake.

Someone moved near him. A dark-haired woman, a girl. She came close, touched his back, murmuring something to him. I saw the way she looked at him, the tender inclination of her head, the intimacy of her body swaying toward him.

No, I thought, with great calm. *That won't do.*

I looked once more at myself lying on the bed, and with a feeling that was at once firm decision and incalculable regret, I took another breath.

64

I Am the Resurrection,
Part 2

I still slept for long periods, waking only briefly to take nourishment. Now the fever dreams were gone, though, and sleep was a lake of deep black water, where I breathed oblivion and drifted past the waving waterweed, mindless as a fish.

I would float sometimes just below the surface, aware of people and things in the air-breathing world, but incapable of joining them. Voices spoke near me, muffled and meaningless. Now and then some phrase would penetrate the clear liquid around me and float into my head, where it would hang like a tiny jellyfish, round and transparent, yet pulsating with some mysterious inner meaning, its words a drifting net.

Each phrase hung for a time in my purview, folding and unfolding in its curious rhythms, and then drifted quietly up and away, leaving silence.

And in between the small jellyfish came open spaces of clear water, some filled with radiant light, some the darkness of utter peace. I drifted upward and downward, suspended between the surface and the depths, at the whim of unknown currents.

"Physician, look." Fizz. A stirring there, some dormant spore of consciousness, disturbed by carbonation, splits and blooms. Then a stab as sharp as metal, *Who is calling me?* "Physician, look."

I opened my eyes.

It was no great shock, for the room was filled with twilight, still light, like being underwater, and I had no sense of disruption.

"O Lord Jesus Christ, Thou great Physician: Look with Thy gracious favor upon this Thy servant; give wisdom and discretion to those who minister to her in her sickness; bless all the means used for her recovery . . ."

The words flowed past me in a whispering stream, cool on my skin. There was a man before me, dark head bent over a book. The light in the room embraced him and he seemed part of it.

"Stretch forth Thy hand," he whispered to the pages, in a voice that cracked and broke, "and according to Thy will, restore her to health and strength, that she may live to praise Thee for Thy goodness and Thy grace; to the glory of Thy holy name. Amen."

"Roger?" I said, groping for his name. My own voice was hoarse from disuse; speaking was an intolerable effort.

His eyes were closed in prayer; they sprang open, unbelieving, and I thought how vivid they were, the green of wet serpentine and summer leaves.

"Claire?" His voice cracked like a teenaged boy's, and he dropped the book.

"I don't know," I said, feeling the dreamlike sense of submergence threatening to engulf me again. "Am I?"

I could lift a hand for a moment or two, but was too weak even to lift my head, let alone sit up. Roger helpfully dragged me semi-upright against piled pillows, and put his hand at the back of my head to prevent wobbling, holding a cup of water to my dry lips. It was the odd feel of his hand on the bare skin of my neck that began a dim process of realization. Then I felt the warmth of his hand, vivid and immediate, at the back of my head, and jerked like a gaffed salmon, sending the cup flying.

"What? What?" I spluttered, clutching my head, too shocked to formulate a complete sentence, and oblivious to the cold water soaking through the sheets. "WHAT?!"

Roger looked nearly as shocked as I felt. He swallowed, searching for words. "I . . . I . . . I thought you knew," he stammered, voice breaking. "Didn't you . . . ? I mean . . . I thought . . . look, it'll grow!"

I could feel my mouth working, vainly trying different shapes that might approximate words, but there was no connection between tongue and brain—there was room for nothing but the realization that the accustomed soft, heavy weight of my hair was gone, replaced by a fuzz of bristles.

"Malva and Mrs. Bug cut it off, day before yesterday," Roger said, all in a rush. "They—we weren't here, Bree nor I, we wouldn't have let them, of course we wouldn't—but they thought it's what you do for someone with a terrible fever, it *is* what people do now. Bree was furious with them, but they thought—they truly thought they were helping save your life—oh, God, Claire, don't look like that, please!"

His face had disappeared in a starburst of light, a curtain of shimmering water suddenly coming down to protect me from the gaze of the world.

I wasn't conscious of crying, at all. Grief simply burst from me, like wine spraying from a wineskin stabbed with a knife. Purple-red as bone marrow, splattering and dripping everywhere.

"I'll fetch Jamie!" he croaked.

"NO!" I seized him by the sleeve, with more strength than I would have imagined I possessed. "God, no! I don't want him to see me like this!"

His momentary silence told me, but I kept stubborn hold of his sleeve, unable to think how else to prevent the unthinkable. I blinked, water sliding over my face like a stream over rock, and Roger wavered once more into visibility, blurred around the edges.

"He's . . . er . . . he's seen you," Roger said gruffly. He looked down, not wanting to meet my eyes. "It. Already. I mean—" He waved a hand vaguely in the vicinity of his own black locks. "He saw it."

"He did?" This was nearly as much a shock as the initial discovery. "What—what did he say?"

He took a deep breath and looked back up, like someone fearing to see a Gorgon. Or the anti-Gorgon, I thought bitterly.

"He didn't say anything," Roger said quite gently, and put a hand on my arm. "He—he just cried."

I was still crying, too, but in a more orthodox fashion now. Less of the gasping note. The sense of bone-deep cold had passed, and my limbs felt warm now, though I still felt a disconcertingly chilly breeze on my scalp. My heart was slowing again, and a faint sense that I was standing outside my body came over me.

Shock? I thought, dimly surprised as the word formed itself in my mind, rubbery and melting. I supposed that one *could* suffer true physical shock as the result of emotional wounds—of course one could, I knew that. . . .

"Claire!" I became aware that Roger was calling my name with increasing urgency, and shaking my arm. With immense effort, I brought my eyes to focus on him. He was looking truly alarmed, and I wondered, vaguely, whether I had started to die again. But no—it was too late for that.

"What?"

He sighed—with relief, I thought.

"You looked funny for a moment." His voice was cracked and husky; he sounded as though it hurt him to talk. "I thought—d'ye want another drink of water?"

The suggestion seemed so incongruous that I nearly laughed. But I *was* terribly thirsty—and all at once, a cup of cold water seemed the most desirable thing in the world.

"Yes." The tears continued to flow down my face, but now seemed almost soothing. I made no attempt to stop them—that seemed much too difficult—but blotted my face with a corner of the damp sheet.

It was beginning to dawn on me that I might not have made the wisest—or at least not the easiest—choice, when I decided not to die. Things outside the limits and concerns of my own body were starting to come back. Troubles, difficulties, dangers . . . sorrow. Dark, frightening things, like a swarm of bats. I didn't want to look too closely at the images that lay in a disorderly pile at the bottom of my brain—things I had jettisoned in the struggle to stay afloat.

But if I had come back, I had come back to be what I was—and I was a doctor.

"The . . . sickness." I blotted the last of the tears and let Roger wrap his hands around mine, helping me to hold the new cup. "Is it still—?"

"No." He spoke gently, and guided the rim of the cup to my lips. What was it? I wondered vaguely. Water, but with something in it—mint and something stronger, more bitter . . . angelica?

"It's stopped." Roger held the cup, letting me sip slowly. "No one's fallen sick in the last week."

"A week?" I bobbled the cup, spilling a little down my chin. "How long have I—"

"Just about that." He cleared his throat. Roger's eyes were intent on the cup; he skimmed a thumb lightly along my chin, removing the drops I had spilled. "You were among the last to fall sick."

I took a long breath, then drank a bit more. The liquid had a soft, sweet taste, too, floating over the bitter tang . . . honey. My mind located the word and I felt a sense of relief at having located this small missing piece of reality.

I knew from his manner that some of the sick had died, but asked no more for the moment. Deciding to live was one thing. Rejoining the world of the living was a struggle that would take strength I didn't have right now. I had pulled up my roots, and lay like a wilted plant; sinking them back into the earth was beyond me for the moment.

The knowledge that people I knew—perhaps had loved—had died seemed an equal grief to the loss of my hair—and either was more than I could cope with.

I drank two further cups of honey-sweetened water, despite the underlying bitterness, then lay back with a sigh, my stomach feeling like a small, cold balloon.

"Ye want to take a bit of rest," Roger advised me, putting down the cup on the table. "I'll fetch Brianna, aye? But you sleep if ye want to."

I hadn't strength to nod, but managed a twitch of the lips that seemed to pass muster as a smile. I reached up a trembling hand and brushed it gingerly over the top of my shorn head. Roger flinched, very slightly.

He rose, and I saw how thin and strained he looked—he would have been helping tend the sick all week, I supposed, not only me. And bury the dead. He was licensed to conduct funerals.

"Roger?" It was a terrible effort to speak; so terribly hard to find the words, separate them from the tangle in my head. "Have you eaten anything recently?"

His face changed then, a look of relief lightening the lines of strain and worry.

"No," he said, cleared his throat again, and smiled. "Not since last night."

"Oh. Well," I said, and lifted one hand, heavy as lead. "Do. Get something. Won't you?"

"Yes," he said. "I will." Instead of leaving, though, he hesitated, then took several rapid strides back, bent over the bed, and seizing my face between his palms, kissed me on the forehead.

"You're beautiful," he said fiercely, and with a final squeeze of my cheeks, left.

"What?" I said faintly, but the only answer was the bellying of the curtain as the breeze came in, scented with apples.

In point of fact, I looked like a skeleton with a particularly unflattering crew cut, as I learned when I finally gained sufficient strength as to force Jamie to bring me a looking glass.

"I dinna suppose ye'd think of wearing a cap?" he suggested, diffidently fingering a muslin specimen that Marsali had brought me. "Only until it grows out a bit?"

"I don't suppose I bloody would."

I had some difficulty in saying this, shocked as I was by the horrifying vision in the glass. In fact, I had a strong impulse to seize the cap from his hands, put it on and pull it down to my shoulders.

I had rejected earlier offers of a cap from Mrs. Bug—who had been volubly congratulating herself on my survival as the obvious result of her fever treatment—and from Marsali, Malva, and every other woman who'd come to visit me.

This was simple contrariness on my part; the sight of my unrestrained hair outraged their Scottish sense of what was proper in a woman, and they'd been trying—with varying degrees of subtlety—to force me into a cap for years. I was damned if I'd let circumstance accomplish it for them.

Having now seen myself in a mirror, I felt somewhat less adamant about it. And my scalped head did feel a bit chilly. On the other hand, I realized that if I were to give in, Jamie would be terribly alarmed—and I thought I'd frightened him quite enough, judging by the hollow look of his face and the deep smudges under his eyes.

As it was, his face had lightened considerably when I rejected the cap he was holding, and he tossed it aside.

I carefully turned the looking glass over and set it on the counterpane, repressing a sigh.

"Always good for a laugh, I suppose, seeing the expressions on people's faces when they catch sight of me."

Jamie glanced at me, the corner of his mouth twitching.

"Ye're verra beautiful, Sassenach," he said gently. Then he burst out laughing, snorting through his nose and wheezing. I raised one eyebrow at him, picked up the glass and looked again—which made him laugh harder.

I leaned back against the pillows, feeling a bit better. The fever had quite gone, but I still felt wraithlike and weak, barely able to sit up unassisted, and I fell asleep almost without warning, after the least exertion.

Jamie, still snorting, took my hand, raised it to his mouth, and kissed it. The sudden warm immediacy of the touch rippled the fair hairs of my forearm, and my fingers closed involuntarily on his.

"I love you," he said very softly, his shoulders still trembling with laughter.

"Oh," I said, suddenly feeling quite a lot better. "Well, then. I love you, too. And it *will* grow, after all."

"So it will." He kissed my hand again, and set it gently on the quilt. "Have ye eaten?"

"A bit," I said, with what forbearance I could muster. "I'll have more later."

I had realized many years before why "patients" are called that; it's because a sick person is generally incapacitated, and thus obliged to put up with any amount of harassment and annoyance from persons who are *not* sick.

The fever had broken and I had regained consciousness two days before; since then, the invariable response of everyone who saw me was to gasp at my appearance, urge me to wear a cap— and then try to force food down my throat. Jamie, more sensitive to my tones of voice than were Mrs. Bug, Malva, Brianna, or Marsali, wisely desisted after a quick glance at the tray by the bed to see that I actually *had* eaten something.

"Tell me what's happened," I said, settling and bracing myself. "Who's been ill? How are they? And who—" I cleared my throat. "Who's died?"

He narrowed his eyes at me, obviously trying to guess whether I would faint, die, or leap out of bed if he told me.

"Ye're sure ye feel well enough, Sassenach?" he asked dubiously. "It's news that wilna spoil with keeping."

"No, but I have to hear sooner or later, don't I? And knowing is better than worrying about what I *don't* know."

He nodded, taking the point, and took a deep breath.

"Aye, then. Padraic and his daughter are well on the mend. Evan—he's lost his youngest, wee Bobby, and Grace is still ill, but Hugh and Caitlin didna fall sick at all." He swallowed, and went on. "Three of the fisher-folk have died; there's maybe a dozen still ailing, but most are on the mend." He knit his brows, considering. "And then there's Tom Christie. He's still bad, I hear."

"Is he? Malva didn't mention it." But then, Malva had refused to tell me anything when I'd asked earlier, insisting that I must just rest, and not worry myself.

"What about Allan?"

"No, he's fine," Jamie assured me.

"How long has Tom been sick?"

"I dinna ken. The lass can tell ye."

I nodded—a mistake, as the light-headedness had not left me yet, and I was obliged to shut my eyes and let my head fall back, illuminated patterns flashing behind my lids.

"That's very odd," I said, a little breathlessly, hearing Jamie start up in response to my small collapse. "When I close my eyes, often I see stars—but not like stars in the sky. They look just like the stars on the lining of a doll's suitcase—a portmanteau, I mean—that I had as a child. Why do you suppose that is?"

"I havena got the slightest idea." There was a rustle as he sat back down on the stool. "Ye're no still delirious, are ye?" he asked dryly.

"Shouldn't think so. *Was* I delirious?" Breathing deeply and carefully, I opened my eyes and gave him my best attempt at a smile.

"Ye were."

"Do I want to know what I said?"

The corner of his mouth twitched.

"Probably not, but I may tell ye sometime, anyway."

I considered closing my eyes and floating off to sleep, rather than contemplate future embarrassments, but rallied. If I was going to live—and I was—I needed to gather up the strands of life that tethered me to the earth, and reattach them.

"Bree's family, and Marsali's—they're all right?" I asked only for form's sake; both Bree and Marsali had come to hover anxiously over my prostrate form, and while neither one would tell me anything they thought might upset me in my weakened condition, I was reasonably sure that neither one could have kept it secret if the children were seriously ill.

"Aye," he said slowly, "aye, they're fine."

"What?" I said, picking up the hesitation in his voice.

"They're fine," he repeated quickly. "None of them has fallen ill at all."

I gave him a cold look, though careful not to move too much while doing it.

"You may as well tell me," I said. "I'll get it out of Mrs. Bug if you don't."

As though mention of her name had invoked her, I heard the distinctive thump of Mrs. Bug's clogs on the stair, approaching. She was moving more slowly than usual, and with a care suggesting that she was laden with something.

This proved to be true; she negotiated sideways through the door, beaming, a loaded tray in one hand, the other wrapped round

Henri-Christian, who clung to her, monkeylike.

"I've brought ye a wee bit to eat, *a leannan*," she said briskly, nudging the barely touched bowl of parritch and plate of cold toast aside to make room for the fresh provisions. "Ye're no catching, are ye?"

Barely waiting for my shake of the head, she leaned over the bed and gently decanted Henri-Christian into my arms. Undiscriminatingly friendly as always, he butted his head under my chin, nuzzled into my chest, and began mouthing my knuckles, his sharp little baby teeth making small dents in my skin.

"Hallo, what's happened here?" I frowned, smoothing the soft brown licks of baby hair off his rounded brow, where the yellowing stain of an ugly bruise showed at his hairline.

"The spawn of the de'il tried to kill the poor wean," Mrs. Bug informed me, mouth pulled tight. "And would have done, too, save for Roger Mac, bless him."

"Oh? Which spawn was this?" I asked, familiar with Mrs. Bug's methods of description.

"Some of the fishers' weans," Jamie said. He put out a finger and touched Henri Christian's nose, snatched it away as the baby grabbed for it, then touched his nose again. Henri-Christian giggled and grabbed his own nose, entranced by the game.

"The wicked creatures tried to drown him," Mrs. Bug amplified. "Stole the puir wee laddie in his basket and set him adrift in the creek!"

"I shouldna think they meant to drown him," Jamie said mildly, still absorbed in the game. "If so, they wouldna have troubled wi' the basket, surely."

"Hmph!" was Mrs. Bug's response to this piece of logic. "They didna mean to do him any good," she added darkly.

I had been taking a quick inventory of Henri-Christian's physique, finding several more healing bruises, a small scabbed cut on one heel, and a scraped knee.

"Well, you've been bumped about a bit, haven't you?" I said to him.

"Ump. Heeheehee!" said Henri-Christian, vastly entertained by my explorations.

"Roger saved him?" I asked, glancing up at Jamie.

He nodded, one side of his mouth turning up a little.

"Aye. I didna ken what was going on, 'til wee Joanie rushed up to me, shouting as they'd taken her brother—but I got there in time to see the end of the matter."

The boys had set the baby's basket afloat in the trout pool, a wide, deep spot in the creek, where the water was fairly quiet. Made of stoutly woven reeds, the basket had floated—long enough for the current to push it toward the outfall from the pool, where the water ran swiftly through a stretch of rocks, before plunging over a three-foot fall, down into a tumbling churn of water and boulders.

Roger had been building a rail fence, within earshot of the creek. Hearing boys shouting and Félicité's steam-whistle shrieks, he had dropped the rail he was holding and rushed down the hill, thinking that she was being tormented.

Instead, he had burst from the trees just in time to see Henri-Christian, in his basket, tip slowly over the edge of the outfall and start bumping crazily from rock to rock, spinning in the current and taking on water.

Running down the bank and launching himself in a flat dive, Roger had landed full-length in the creek just below the fall, in time for Henri-Christian, bawling with terror, to drop from his sodden basket, plummet down the fall, and land on Roger, who grabbed him.

"I was just in time to see it," Jamie informed me, grinning at the memory. "And then to see Roger Mac rise out o' the water like a triton, wi' duckweed streaming from his hair, blood runnin' from his nose, and the wee lad clutched tight in his arms. A terrible sight, he was."

The miscreant boys had followed the basket's career, yelling along the banks, but were now struck dumb. One of them moved to flee, the others starting up like a flight of pigeons, but Roger had pointed an awful finger at them and bellowed, *"Sheas!"* in a voice loud enough to be heard over the racket of the creek.

Such was the force of his presence, they *did* stay, frozen in terror.

Holding them with his glare, Roger had waded almost to the shore. There, he squatted and cupped a handful of water, which he poured over the head of the shrieking baby—who promptly quit shrieking.

"I baptize thee, Henri-Christian," Roger had bellowed, in his hoarse, cracked voice. "In the name of the Father, and the Son, and the Holy Ghost! D'ye hear me, wee bastards? His name is *Christian*! He belongs to the Lord! Trouble him again, ye lot of scabs, and Satan will pop up and drag ye straight down screaming—TO HELL!"

He stabbed an accusing finger once more at the boys, who this time did break and run, scampering wildly into the brush, pushing and falling in their urge to escape.

"Oh, dear," I said, torn between laughter and dismay. I looked down at Henri-Christian, who had lately discovered the joys of thumb-sucking and was absorbed in further study of the art. "That must have been impressive."

"It impressed *me*, to be sure," Jamie said, still grinning. "I'd no notion Roger Mac had it in him to preach hellfire and damnation like that. The lad's a great roar to him, cracked voice and all. He'd have a good audience, did he do it for a Gathering, aye?"

"Well, that explains what happened to his voice," I said. "I wondered. Do you think it *was* only mischief, though? Them putting the baby in the creek?"

"Oh, it was mischief, sure enough," he said, and cupped a big hand gently round Henri-Christian's head. "Not just boys' mischief, though."

Jamie had caught one of the fleeing boys as they hurtled past him, grabbing him by the neck and quite literally scaring the piss out of the lad. Walking the boy firmly into the wood, he'd pinned him hard against a tree and demanded to know the meaning of this attempted murder.

Trembling and blubbering, the boy had tried to excuse it, saying that they hadn't meant any harm to the wean, truly! They'd only wanted to see him float—for their parents all said he was demon-born, and everyone kent that those born of Satan floated, because the water would reject their wickedness. They'd taken the baby in his basket and put that into the water, because they were afraid to touch him, fearing his flesh would burn them.

"I told him I'd burn him myself," Jamie said with a certain grimness, "and did." He'd then dismissed the smarting lad, with instructions to go home, change his breeks, and inform his confederates that they were expected in Jamie's study before supper

to receive their own share of retribution—or else Himself would
be coming round to their houses after supper, to thrash them before their parents' eyes.

"Did they come?" I asked, fascinated.

He gave me a look of surprise.

"Of course. They took their medicine, and then we went to the
kitchen and had bread and honey. I'd told Marsali to bring the wee
lad, and after we'd eaten, I took him on my knee, and had them all
come and touch him, just to see."

He smiled lopsidedly.

"One of the lads asked me was it true, what Mr. Roger said,
about the wean belonging to the Lord? I told him I certainly
wouldna argue with Mr. Roger about that—but whoever else he
belonged to, Henri-Christian belongs to me, as well, and best they
should remember it."

His finger trailed slowly down Henri-Christian's round,
smooth cheek. The baby was nearly asleep now, heavy eyelids
closing, a tiny, glistening thumb half in, half out of his mouth.

"I'm sorry I missed that," I said softly, so as not to wake him.
He'd grown much warmer, as sleeping babies did, and heavy in
the curve of my arm. Jamie saw that I was having difficulty holding him, and took him from me, handing him back to Mrs. Bug,
who had been bustling quietly round the room, tidying, all the
while listening with approval to Jamie's account.

"Oh, 'twas something to see," she assured me in a whisper,
patting Henri-Christian's back as she took him. "And the lads all
poking their fingers out to touch the bairnie's wee belly, ginger-
like, as if they meant to prod a hot potato, and him squirmin' and
giggling like a worm wi' the fits. The wicked little gomerels' eyes
were big as sixpences!"

"I imagine they were," I said, amused.

"On the other hand," I remarked *sotto voce* to Jamie as she left
with the baby, "if their parents think he's demon-born, and you're
his grandfather . . ."

"Well, you're his grannie, Sassenach," Jamie said dryly. "It
might be you. But aye, I'd prefer not to have them dwell on that
aspect of the matter."

"No," I agreed. "Though—do any of them know, do you think,
that Marsali isn't your daughter by blood? They must know about
Fergus."

"It wouldna much matter," he said. "They think wee Henri's a changeling, in any case."

"How do you know that?"

"People talk," he said briefly. "Are ye feeling well in yourself, Sassenach?"

Relieved of the baby's weight, I had put back the covers a bit to let in air. Jamie stared at me in disapproval.

"Christ, I can count all your ribs! Right through your shift!"

"Enjoy the experience while you can," I advised him tartly, though I felt a sharp pang of hurt. He seemed to sense this, for he took my hand, tracing the lines of the deep blue veins that ran across the back of it.

"Dinna fash yourself, Sassenach," he said, more gently. "I didna mean it that way. Here, Mrs. Bug's brought ye something tasty, I expect." He lifted the lid off a small covered dish, frowned at the substance in it, then stuck a cautious finger in and licked it.

"Maple pudding," he announced, looking happy.

"Oh?" I had no appetite at all yet, but maple pudding sounded at least innocuous, and I made no objection as he scooped up a spoonful, guiding it toward my mouth with the concentration of a man flying an airliner.

"I *can* feed myself, you kn—" He slipped the spoon between my lips, and I resignedly sucked the pudding off it. Amazing revelations of creamy sweetness immediately exploded in my mouth, and I closed my eyes in minor ecstasy, recalling.

"Oh, God," I said. "I'd forgotten what good food tastes like."

"I *knew* ye hadn't been eating," he said with satisfaction. "Here, have more."

I insisted upon taking the spoon myself, and managed half the dish; Jamie ate the other half, at my urging.

"You may not be as thin as I am," I said, turning my hand over and grimacing at the sight of my protruding wrist bones, "but you haven't been eating a lot, either."

"I suppose not." He scraped the spoon carefully round the bowl, retrieving the last bits of pudding, and sucked the spoon clean. "It's been . ... busy."

I watched him narrowly. He was being patently cheerful, but my rusty sensibilities were beginning to come back. For some unknowable span of time, I'd had neither energy nor attention for anything that lay outside the fever-racked shell of my body; now I was seeing the small familiarities of Jamie's body, voice and manner, and becoming reattuned to him, like a slack violin string being tightened in the presence of a tuning fork.

I could feel the vibration of some strain in him, and I was beginning to think it wasn't all due to my recent near-demise.

"What?" I said.

"What?" He raised his eyebrows in question, but I knew him too well for that. The question alone gave me confidence that I was right.

"What aren't you telling me?" I asked, with what patience I could muster. "Is it Brown again? Have you got news of Stephen Bonnet? Or Donner? Or has the white sow eaten one of the children and choked to death?"

That made him smile, at least, though only for a moment.

"Not that," he said. "She went for MacDonald, when he called a few days ago, but he made it onto the porch in time. Verra agile the Major is, for a man of his age."

"He's younger than you are," I objected.

"Well, I'm agile, too," he said logically. "The sow hasna got me yet, has she?"

I felt a qualm of unease at his mention of the Major, but it wasn't news of political unrest or military rumblings that was troubling Jamie; he would have told me that at once. I narrowed my eyes at him again, but didn't speak.

He sighed deeply.

"I am thinking I must send them away," he said quietly, and took my hand again.

"Send who away?"

"Fergus and Marsali and the weans."

I felt a sharp, sudden jolt, as though someone had struck me just below the breastbone, and found it suddenly difficult to draw breath.

"What? Why? And—and *where*?" I managed to ask.

He rubbed his thumb lightly over my knuckles, back and forth, his eyes focused on the small motion.

"Fergus tried to kill himself, three days ago," he said very quietly.

My hand gripped his convulsively.

"Holy God," I whispered. He nodded, and I saw that he was unable to speak for the moment; his teeth were set in his lower lip.

Now it was I who took his hand in both of mine, feeling coldness seep through my flesh. I wanted to deny it, reject the notion utterly—but couldn't. It sat there between us, an ugly thing like a poisonous toad that neither of us wished to touch.

"How?" I said at last. My voice seemed to echo in the room. I wanted to say, "Are you *sure*?" but I knew he was.

"With a knife," he replied literally. The corner of his mouth twitched again, but not with humor. "He said he would have hanged himself, but he couldna tie the rope with one hand. Lucky, that."

The pudding had formed a small, hard ball, like rubber, that lay in the bottom of my stomach.

"You . . . found him? Or was it Marsali?"

He shook his head.

"She doesna ken. Or rather, I expect she does, but she's no admitting it—to either of them."

"He can't have been badly wounded, then, or she'd have to know for sure." My chest still hurt, but the words were coming more easily.

"No. I saw him go past, whilst I was scraping a deer's hide up on the hill. He didna see me, and I didna call out—I dinna ken what it was that struck me queer about him . . . but something did. I went on wi' my work for a bit—I didna want to go far from the house, in case—but it niggled at me." He let go of my hand and rubbed his knuckles underneath his nose.

"I couldna seem to let go of the thought that something was amiss, and finally I put down my work and went after him, thinking myself all kinds of a fool for it."

Fergus had headed over the end of the Ridge, and down the wooded slope that led to the White Spring. This was the most remote and secluded of the three springs on the Ridge, called "white" because of the large pale boulder that stood near the head of the pool.

Jamie had come down through the trees in time to see Fergus lie down by the spring, sleeve rolled up and coat folded beneath his head, and submerge his handless left arm in the water.

"I should maybe ha' shouted then," he said, rubbing a distracted hand through his hair. "But I couldna really believe it, ken?"

Then Fergus had taken a small boning knife in his right hand, reached down into the pool, and neatly opened the veins of his left elbow, blood blooming in a soft, dark cloud around the whiteness of his arm.

"I shouted *then*," Jamie said. He closed his eyes, and scrubbed his hands hard over his face, as though trying to erase the memory of it.

He had run down the hill, grabbed Fergus, jerked him to his feet, and hit him.

"You *hit* him?"

"I did," he said shortly. "He's lucky I didna break his neck, the wee bastard." Color had begun to rise in his face as he talked, and he pressed his lips tight together.

"Was this after the boys took Henri-Christian?" I asked, my memory of the conversation in the stable with Fergus vividly in mind. "I mean—"

"Aye, I ken what ye mean," he interrupted. "And it was the day after the lads put Henri-Christian in the creek, aye. It wasna only that, though—not only all the trouble over the wee laddie being a dwarf, I mean." He glanced at me, his face troubled.

"We talked. After I'd bound up his arm and brought him round. He said he'd been thinking of it for some time; the thing wi' the bairn only pushed him into it."

"But . . . how *could* he?" I said, distressed. "To leave Marsali, and the children—how?"

Jamie looked down, hands braced on his knees, and sighed. The window was open, and a soft breeze came in, lifting the hairs on the crown of his head like tiny flames.

"He thought they would do better without him," he said flatly. "If he was dead, Marsali could wed again—find a man who could care for her and the weans. Provide for them. Protect wee Henri."

"He thinks—thought—he couldn't?"

Jamie glanced sharply at me.

"Sassenach," he said, "he kens damn well he can't."

I drew breath to protest this, but bit my lip instead, finding no immediate rebuttal.

Jamie stood up and moved restlessly about the room, picking things up and putting them down.

"Would you do such a thing?" I asked, after a bit. "In the same circumstances, I mean."

He paused for a moment, his back to me, hand on my hairbrush.

"No," he said softly. "But it's a hard thing for a man to live with."

"Well, I see that . . ." I began, slowly, but he swung round to face me. His own face was strained, filled with a weariness that had little to do with lack of sleep.

"No, Sassenach," he said. "Ye don't." He spoke gently, but with such a tone of despair in his voice that tears came to my eyes.

It was as much sheer physical weakness as emotional distress, but I knew that if I gave way to it, the end would be complete soggy disintegration, and no one needed that just now. I bit my lip hard and wiped my eyes with the edge of the sheet.

I heard the thump as he knelt down beside me, and I reached out blindly for him, pulling his head against my breast. He put his arms round me and sighed deeply, his breath warm on my skin through the linen of my shift. I stroked his hair with one trembling hand, and felt him give way suddenly, all the tension going out of him like water running from a jug.

I had the oddest feeling, then—as though the strength he had clung to had now been let go . . . and was flowing into me. My tenuous grip on my own body firmed as I held his, and my heart ceased wavering, taking up instead its normal solid, tireless beating.

The tears had retreated, though they were precariously near the surface. I traced the lines of his face with my fingers, ruddy bronze and lined with sun and care; the high forehead with its thick auburn brows, and the broad planes of his cheek, the long straight nose, straight as a blade. The closed eyes, slanted and mysterious with those odd lashes of his, blond at the root, so deep an auburn at the tips as to seem almost black.

"Don't you know?" I said very softly, tracing the small, neat line of his ear. Tiny, stiff blond hairs sprouted in a tiny whorl from the tagus, tickling my finger. "Don't *any* of you know? That it's *you*. Not what you can give, or do, or provide. Just you."

He took a deep, shuddering breath, and nodded, though he didn't open his eyes.

"I know. I said that to him, to Fergus," he said very softly. "Or at least I think I did. I said a terrible lot of things."

They had knelt together by the spring, embracing, wet with

blood and water, locked together as though he could hold Fergus to the earth, to his family, by force of will alone, and he had no notion at all what he had said, lost in the passion of the moment—until the end.

"You must continue, for their sakes—though you would not for your own," he had whispered, Fergus's face pressed into his shoulder, the black hair wet with sweat and water, cold against his cheek. *"Tu comprends, mon enfant, mon fils? Comprends-tu?"*

I felt his throat move as he swallowed.

"See, I kent ye were dying," he said very softly. "I was sure ye'd be gone when I came back to the house, and I should be alone. I wasna speaking to Fergus then, I think, so much as to myself."

He raised his head then, and looked at me through a blur of tears and laughter.

"Oh, God, Claire," he said, "I would have been so angry, if ye'd died and left me!"

I wanted to laugh or cry, or both, myself—and had I still harbored regrets regarding the loss of eternal peace, I would have surrendered them now without hesitation.

"I didn't," I said, and touched his lip. "I won't. Or at least I'll try not." I slid my hand behind his head and drew him back to me. He was a good deal larger and heavier than Henri-Christian, but I felt I could hold him forever, if necessary.

It was early afternoon, and the light just beginning to shift, slanting in through the tops of the west-facing windows so that the room filled with a clean, bright light that glowed on Jamie's hair and the worn creamy linen of his shirt. I could feel the knobs at the top of his spine, and the yielding flesh in the narrow channel between shoulder blade and backbone.

"Where will you send them?" I asked, and tried to smooth the whorled hair of the cowlick on his crown.

"To Cross Creek, maybe—or to Wilmington," he replied. His eyes were half-closed, watching the shadows of leaves flicker on the side of the armoire he had built me. "Wherever seems best for the printing trade."

He shifted a little, tightening his grip on my buttocks, then frowned.

"Christ, Sassenach, ye havena got any bum left at all!"

"Well, never mind," I said with resignation. "I'm sure *that* will grow back soon enough."

65

Moment of Declaration

Jamie met them near Woolam's Mill, five men on horseback. Two were strangers; two were men from Salisbury that he knew—ex-Regulators named Green and Wherry; avid Whigs. The last was Richard Brown, whose face was cold, save for his eyes.

He silently cursed his love of conversation. If not for that, he would have parted from MacDonald as usual, at Coopersville. But they had been talking of poetry—poetry, for God's sake!—and amusing each other in declamation. Now here he stood in the empty road, holding two horses, while MacDonald, whose guts were in disagreement with him, busied himself deep in the wood.

Amos Green tipped him a nod, and would have passed, but Kitman Wherry reined up; the strangers did likewise, staring curiously.

"Where are Thou bound, friend James?" Wherry, a Quaker, asked pleasantly. "Does Thee come to the meeting at Halifax? For Thee are welcome to ride with us, and that be so."

Halifax. He felt a trickle of sweat run down the crease of his back. The meeting of the Committee of Correspondence to elect delegates to the Continental Congress.

"I am seeing a friend upon his road," he replied courteously, with a nod toward MacDonald's horse. "I will follow, though; perhaps I shall catch ye up along the way." *Fat chance of that*, he thought, carefully not looking at Brown.

"I'd not be so sure of your welcome, Mr. Fraser." Green spoke civilly enough, but with a certain coldness in his manner that made Wherry glance at him in surprise. "Not after what happened in Cross Creek."

"Oh? And would ye see an innocent man burnt alive, or tarred and feathered?" The last thing he wished was an argument, but something must be said.

One of the strangers spat in the road.

"Not so innocent, if that's Fogarty Simms you're speakin' of. Little Tory pissant," he added as an afterthought.

"That's the fellow," Green said, and spat in agreement. "The committee in Cross Creek set out to teach him a lesson; seems Mr. Fraser here was in disagreement. Quite a scene it was, from what I hear," he drawled, leaning back a little in his saddle to survey Jamie from his superior height. "Like I said, Mr. Fraser—you ain't all that popular, right this minute."

Wherry was frowning, glancing to and fro between Jamie and Green. "To save a man from tar and feathers, no matter what his politics, seems no more than common humanity," he said sharply.

Brown laughed unpleasantly.

"Might seem so to you, I reckon. Not to other folk. You know a man by the company he keeps. And beyond that, there's your auntie, eh?" he said, redirecting his speech to Jamie. "And the famous Mrs. MacDonald. I read that speech she gave—in the final edition of Simms's newspaper," he added, repeating the unpleasant laugh.

"My aunt's guests have naught to do wi' me," Jamie said, striving for simple matter-of-factness.

"No? How 'bout your aunt's husband—your uncle, would he be?"

"Duncan?" His incredulity plainly showed in his voice, for the strangers exchanged glances, and their manner relaxed a little. "No, he's my aunt's fourth husband—and a friend. Why d'ye speak of him?"

"Why, Duncan Innes is cheek-by-jowl with Farquard Campbell, and a good many other Loyalists. The two of 'em have been putting money enough to float a ship into pamphlets preachin' reconciliation with Mother England. Surprised you didn't know that, Mr. Fraser."

Jamie was not merely surprised but thunderstruck at this revelation, but hid it.

"A man's opinions are his own," he said with a shrug.

"Duncan must do as he likes, and I shall do the same."

Wherry was nodding agreement with this, but the others were regarding him with expressions ranging from skepticism to hostility.

Wherry was not unaware of his companions' responses.

"What *is* thy opinion, then, friend?" he asked politely.

Well, he'd known it was coming. Had now and then tried to imagine the circumstances of his declaration, in situations ranging from the vaingloriously heroic to the openly dangerous, but as usual in such matters, God's sense of humor trumped all imagination. And so he found himself taking that final step into irrevocable and public commitment to the rebel cause—just incidentally being required to ally himself with a deadly enemy in the process—standing alone in a dusty road, with a uniformed officer of the Crown squatting in the bushes directly behind him, breeches round his ankles.

"I am for liberty," he said, in a tone indicating mild astonishment that there could be any question regarding his position.

"Are you so?" Green looked hard at him, then lifted his chin in the direction of MacDonald's horse, where MacDonald's regimental sword hung from the saddle, gilt and tassels gleaming in the sun. "How come you to be in company with a redcoat, then?"

"He is a friend," Jamie replied evenly.

"A redcoat?" One of the strangers reared back in his saddle as though stung by a bee. "How come redcoats *here*?" The man sounded flabbergasted, and looked hastily to and fro, as though expecting a company of the creatures to burst from the wood, muskets firing.

"Only the one, so far as I know," Brown assured him. "Name's MacDonald. He's not a real soldier; retired on half-pay, works for the Governor."

His companion didn't seem noticeably reassured.

"What are you doing with this MacDonald?" he demanded of Jamie.

"As I said—he is a friend." The attitude of the men had changed in an instant, from skepticism and mild hostility to open offense.

"He's the Governor's spy, is what he is," Green declared flatly.

This was no more than the truth, and Jamie was reasonably sure that half the backcountry knew it; MacDonald made no effort to hide either his appearance nor his errands. To deny the fact was to ask them to believe Jamie a dunce, duplicitous, or both.

There was a stirring among the men now, glances exchanged, and the smallest of motions, hands touching knife hilts and pistol grips.

Very fine, Jamie thought. Not satisfied with the irony of the situation, God had now decided that he should fight to the death against the allies he had declared himself to moments earlier, in defense of an officer of the Crown he had just declared himself against.

As his son-in-law was fond of remarking—great.

"Bring him out," Brown ordered, nudging his horse to the forefront. "We'll see what he has to say for himself, this friend of yours."

"And then might be we'll learn him a lesson he can carry back to the Governor, eh?" One of the strangers took off his hat and tucked it carefully beneath the edge of his saddle, preparing.

"Wait!" Wherry drew himself up, trying to quell them with a hand, though Jamie could have told him he was several minutes past the point where such an attempt might have had any effect. "You cannot lay violent hands upon—"

"Can't we, though?" Brown grinned like a death's head, eyes fixed on Jamie, and began to undo the leather quirt coiled and fastened to his saddle. "No tar to hand, alas. But a good beating, say, and send 'em both squealing home to the Governor stark naked—that'd answer."

The second stranger laughed, and spat again, so the gob landed juicily at Jamie's feet.

"Aye, that'll do. Hear you held off a mob by yourself in Cross Creek, Fraser—only five to two now, how you like them odds?"

Jamie liked them fine. Dropping the reins he held, he turned and flung himself between the two horses, screeching and slapping hard at their flanks, then dived headlong into the brush at the roadside, scrabbling through roots and stones on hands and knees as fast as he could.

Behind him, the horses were rearing and wheeling, whinnying loudly and spreading confusion and fright through the other

men's mounts; he could hear cries of anger and alarm, as they
tried to gain control of the plunging horses.

He slid down a short slope, dirt and uprooted plants spraying
up around his feet, lost his balance and fell at the bottom,
bounded up and dashed into an oak copse, where he plastered
himself behind a screen of saplings, breathing hard.

Someone had had wit—or fury—enough to jump off his horse
and follow on foot; he could hear crashing and cursing near at
hand, over the fainter cries of the commotion on the road. Glancing
cautiously through the leaves, he saw Richard Brown, disheveled
and hatless, looking wildly round, pistol in hand.

Any thought he might have had of confrontation vanished;
he was unarmed, save a small knife in his stocking, and it was
clear to him that Brown would shoot him instantly, claiming
self-defense when the others eventually caught up.

Up the slope, toward the road, he caught a glimpse of red.
Brown, turning in the same direction, saw it, too, and fired.
Whereupon Donald MacDonald, having thoughtfully hung up his
coat in a tree, stepped out of cover behind Richard Brown in his
shirtsleeves, and hit Brown over the head with a solid length of
tree branch.

Brown fell on his knees, momentarily stunned, and Jamie
slipped out of the copse, beckoning to MacDonald, who ran heavily to meet him. Together they made their way deeper into the forest, waiting by a stream until prolonged silence from the road
indicated that it might be safe to go back for a look.

The men were gone. So was MacDonald's horse. Gideon, the
whites of his eyes showing and ears laid flat, rolled back his upper lip and squealed fiercely at them, big yellow teeth bared and
slobber flying. Brown and company had wisely thought twice
about stealing a rabid horse, but had tied him up to a tree and
managed to spoil his harness, which hung in bits around his neck.
MacDonald's sword lay in the dust, torn from its scabbard, blade
broken in two.

MacDonald picked up the pieces, viewed them for a moment,
then, shaking his head, tucked them through his belt.

"D'ye think Jones could mend it?" he asked. "Or better to go
down to Salisbury?"

"Wilmington or New Bern," Jamie said, wiping a hand across
his mouth. "Dai Jones hasna the skill to mend a sword, but ye'll

find few friends in Salisbury, from what I hear." Salisbury had been at the heart of the Regulation, and antigovernment sentiment still ran high there. His own heart had gone back to its usual way of beating, but he still felt weak-kneed in the aftermath of flight and anger.

MacDonald nodded bleakly, then glanced at Gideon.

"Is yon thing safe to ride?"

"No."

In Gideon's present state of agitation, Jamie wouldn't risk riding him alone, let alone double-mounted and with no bridle. They'd left the rope on his saddle, at least. He got a loop over the stallion's head without being bitten, and they set off without comment, returning to the Ridge on foot.

"Verra unfortunate," MacDonald observed thoughtfully at one point. "That they should have met us together. D'ye think it's dished your chances of worming your way into their councils? I should give my left ball to have an eye and an ear in that meeting they spoke of, I'll tell ye that for nothing!"

With a dim sense of wonder, Jamie realized that having made his momentous declaration, overheard by the man whose cause he sought to betray, and then nearly killed by the new allies whose side he sought to uphold—neither side had believed him.

"D'ye ever wonder what it sounds like when God laughs, Donald?" he asked thoughtfully.

MacDonald pursed his lips and glanced at the horizon, where dark clouds swelled just beyond the shoulder of the mountain.

"Like thunder, I imagine," he said. "D'ye not think so?"

Jamie shook his head.

"No. I think it's a verra small, wee sound indeed."

66

The Dark Rises

I heard all the sounds of the household below, and the rumble of Jamie's voice outside, and felt entirely peaceful. I was watching the sun shift and glow on the yellowing chestnut trees outside, when the sound of feet came marching up the stairs, steady and determined.

The door flung open and Brianna came in, wind-tousled and bright-faced, wearing a steely expression. She halted at the foot of my bed, leveled a long forefinger at me, and said, "You are not allowed to die."

"Oh?" I said, blinking. "I didn't think I was going to."

"You tried!" she said, accusing. "You know you did!"

"Well, not to say tried, exactly . . ." I began weakly. If I hadn't exactly tried to die, though, it was true that I hadn't quite tried not to, and I must have looked guilty, for her eyes narrowed into blue slits.

"Don't you dare do that again!" she said, and wheeling in a sweep of blue cloak, stomped out, pausing at the door to say, "BecauseIloveyouandIcan'tdowithoutyou," in a strangled voice, before running down the stairs.

"I love you too, darling!" I called, the always-ready tears coming to my eyes, but there was no reply, save the sound of the front door closing.

Adso, drowsing in a puddle of sun on the counterpane at my feet, opened his eyes a fraction of an inch at the noise, then sank his head back into his shoulders, purring louder.

I lay back on the pillow, feeling a good deal less peaceful, but somewhat more alive. A moment later, I sat up, put back the quilts, and swung my legs out of bed. Adso abruptly quit purring.

"Don't worry," I told him. "I'm not going to keel over; your supply of milk and scraps is perfectly safe. Keep the bed warm for me."

I had been up, of course, and even allowed on short, intensely supervised excursions outside. But no one had let me try to go anywhere alone since before I fell ill, and I was reasonably sure they wouldn't let me do it now.

I therefore stole downstairs in stockinged feet, shoes in hand, and instead of going through the front door, whose hinges squeaked, or through the kitchen, where Mrs. Bug was working, I slipped into my surgery, opened the window, and—having checked to be sure the white sow was not hanging about below—climbed carefully out.

I felt quite giddy at my escape, a rush of spirits that sustained me for a little way down the path. Thereafter, I was obliged to stop every few hundred feet, sit down, and gasp a bit while my legs recovered their strength. I persevered, though, and at last came to the Christie cabin.

No one was in sight, nor was there any response to my tentative "Hallo!", but when I knocked at the door, I heard Tom Christie's voice, gruff and dispirited, bid me enter.

He was at the table, writing, but from the looks of him, ought still to have been in bed. His eyes widened in surprise at sight of me, and he hastily tried to straighten the grubby shawl round his shoulders.

"Mrs. Fraser! Are you—that is—what in the name of God . . ." Deprived of speech, he pointed at me, eyes round as saucers. I had taken off my broad-brimmed hat when I entered, forgetting momentarily that I looked like nothing so much as an excited bottle brush.

"Oh," I said, passing a self-conscious hand over my head. "That. You ought to be pleased; I'm not going about outraging the public by a wanton display of my flowing locks."

"You look like a convict," he said bluntly. "Sit down."

I did, being rather in need of the stool he offered me, owing to the exertions of the walk.

"How are you?" I inquired, peering at him. The light in the cabin was very bad; he had been writing with a candle, and had put it out upon my appearance.

"How am I?" He seemed both astonished and rather put out at

the inquiry. "You have walked all the way here, in a dangerously enfeebled condition, to ask after my health?"

"If you care to put it that way," I replied, rather nettled by that "dangerously enfeebled." "I don't suppose you would care to step out into the light, so that I can get a decent look at you, would you?"

He drew the ends of the shawl protectively across his chest.

"Why?" He frowned at me, peaked brows drawing together so that he looked like an irritable owl.

"Because I want to know a few things regarding your state of health," I replied patiently, "and examining you is likely the best way of finding them out, since you don't seem able to tell me anything."

"You are most unaccountable, madam!"

"No, I am a doctor," I countered. "And I want to know—" A brief wave of giddiness came over me, and I leaned on the table, holding on 'til it passed.

"You are insane," he stated, having scrutinized me for a moment. "You are also still ill, I believe. Stay there; I shall call my son to go and fetch your husband."

I flapped a hand at him and took a deep breath. My heart was racing, and I was a trifle pale and sweaty, but essentially all right

"The fact of the matter, Mr. Christie, is that while I've certainly *been* ill, I wasn't ill with the same sickness that's been afflicting people on the Ridge—and from what Malva was able to tell me, I don't think you were, either."

He had risen to go and call Allan; at this, he froze, staring at me with his mouth open. Then he slowly lowered himself back into his chair.

"What do you mean?"

Having finally got his attention, I was pleased to lay out the facts before him; I had them neatly to hand, having given them considerable thought over the last few days.

While several families on the Ridge had suffered the depredations of amoebic dysentery, I hadn't. I had had a dangerously high fever, accompanied by dreadful headache and—so far as I could tell from Malva's excited account—convulsions. But it certainly wasn't dysentery.

"Are you certain of this?" He was twiddling his discarded quill, frowning.

"It's rather hard to mistake bloody flux for headache and fever," I said tartly. "Now—did you have flux?"

He hesitated a moment, but curiosity got the better of him.

"No," he said. "It was as you say—a headache fit to split the skull, and fever. A terrible weakness, and . . . and extraordinarily unpleasant dreams. I had no notion that it was not the same illness afflicting the others."

"No reason you should, I suppose. You didn't see any of them. Unless—did Malva describe the illness to you?" I asked only from curiosity, but he shook his head.

"I do not wish to hear of such things; she does not tell me. Still, why have you come?" He tilted his head to one side, narrowing his eyes. "What difference does it make whether you and I suffered an ague, rather than a flux? Or anyone else, for that matter?"

He seemed rather agitated, and got up, moving about the cabin in an unfocused, bumbling sort of way, quite unlike his usual decisive movements.

I sighed, rubbing a hand over my forehead. I'd got the basic information I came for; explaining why I'd wanted it was going to be uphill work. I had enough trouble getting Jamie, Young Ian, and Malva to accept the germ theory of disease, and that was with the evidence visible through a microscope to hand.

"Disease is catching," I said a little tiredly. "It passes from one person to another—sometimes directly, sometimes by means of food or water shared between a sick person and a healthy one. All of the people who had the flux lived near a particular small spring; I have some reason to think that it was the water of that spring that carried the amoeba—that made them ill.

"You and I, though—I haven't seen you in weeks. Nor have I been near anyone else who's had the ague. How is it that we should both fall ill of the same thing?"

He stared at me, baffled and still frowning.

"I do not see why two persons cannot fall ill without seeing each other. Certainly I have known such illnesses as you describe: gaol fever, for instance, spreads in close quarters—but surely not all illnesses behave in the same fashion?"

"No, they don't," I admitted. I wasn't in a fit state to try to get across the basic notions of epidemiology or public health, either. "It's possible, for instance, for some diseases to be spread by mosquitoes. Malaria, for one." Some forms of viral meningitis, for another—my best guess as to the illness I'd just recovered from.

"Do you recall being bitten by a mosquito any time recently?"

He stared at me, then uttered a brief sort of bark I took for laughter.

"My dear woman, everyone in this festering climate is bitten repeatedly during the hot weather." He scratched at his beard, as though by reflex.

That was true. Everyone but me and Roger. Now and then, some desperate insect would have a go, but for the most part, we escaped unbitten, even when there were absolute plagues of the creatures and everyone around us was scratching. As a theory, I suspected that blood-drinking mosquitoes had evolved so closely with mankind through the years that Roger and I simply didn't smell right to them, having come from too far away in time. Brianna and Jemmy, who shared my genetic material but also Jamie's, were bitten, but not as frequently as most people.

I didn't recall having been bitten any time recently, but it was possible that I had been and had simply been too busy to notice.

"Why does it matter?" Christie asked, seeming now merely baffled.

"I don't know. I just—need to find things out." I'd also needed both to get away from the house and to make some move to reclaim my life by the most direct means I knew—the practice of medicine. But that wasn't anything I meant to share with Tom Christie.

"Hmph," he said. He stood looking down at me, frowning and undecided, then suddenly extended a hand—the one I had operated on, I saw; the "Z" of the incision had faded to a healthy pale pink, and the fingers lay straight.

"Come outside, then," he said, resigned. "I will see you home, and if ye insist upon asking intrusive and bothersome questions regarding my health along the way, I suppose I cannot stop you."

Startled, I took his hand, and found his grip solid and steady, despite the haggard look of his face and the slump of his shoulders.

"You needn't walk me home," I protested. "You ought to be in bed, by the looks of you!"

"So should you," he said, leading me to the door with a hand beneath my elbow. "But if ye choose to risk your health and your life by undertaking such inappropriate exertion—why, so can I. Though you must," he added sternly, "put on your hat before we go."

We made it back to the house, stopping frequently for rest, and arrived panting, dripping with sweat, and generally exhilarated by the adventure. No one had missed me, but Mr. Christie insisted upon delivering me inside, which meant that everyone observed my absence *ex post facto*, and in the irrational way of people, at once became very annoyed.

I was scolded by everyone in sight, including Young Ian, frog-marched upstairs virtually by the scruff of the neck, and thrust forcibly back into bed, where, I was given to understand, I should be lucky to be given bread and milk for my supper. The most annoying aspect of the whole situation was Thomas Christie, standing at the foot of the stairs with a mug of beer in his hand, watching as I was led off, and wearing the only grin I had ever seen on his hairy face.

"What in the name of God possessed ye, Sassenach?" Jamie jerked back the quilt and gestured peremptorily at the sheets.

"Well, I felt quite well, and—"

"Well! Ye're the color of bad buttermilk, and trembling so ye can scarcely—here, let me do that." Making snorting noises, he pushed my hands away from the laces of my petticoats, and had them off me in a trice.

"Have ye lost your mind?" he demanded. "And to sneak off like that without telling anyone, too! What if ye'd fallen? What if ye got ill again?"

"If I'd told anyone, they wouldn't have let me go out," I said mildly. "And I *am* a physician, you know. Surely I can judge my own state of health."

He gave me a look, strongly suggesting that he wouldn't trust me to judge a flower show, but merely gave a louder than usual snort in reply.

He then picked me up bodily, carried me to the bed, and placed me gently into it—but with enough demonstration of restrained strength as to let me know that he would have preferred to drop me from a height.

He then straightened up, giving me a baleful look.

"If ye didna look as though ye were about to faint, Sassenach, I swear I would turn ye over and smack your bum for ye."

"You can't," I said, rather faintly. "I haven't got one." I was in fact a little tired . . . well, to be honest, my heart was beating like a kettledrum, my ears were ringing, and if I didn't lie down flat at once, I likely *would* faint. I did lie down, and lay with my eyes closed, feeling the room spin gently round me, like a merry-go-round, complete with flashing lights and hurdy-gurdy music.

Through this confusion of sensations, I dimly sensed hands on my legs, then a pleasant coolness on my heated body. Then something warm and cloudlike enveloped my head, and I flailed my hands about wildly, trying to get it off before I smothered.

I emerged, blinking and panting, to discover that I was naked. I glanced at my pallid, sagging, skeletal remains, and snatched the sheet up over myself. Jamie was bending to collect my discarded gown, petticoat, and jacket from the floor, adding these to the shift he had folded over his arm. He picked up my shoes and stockings and added these to his bag.

"You," he said, pointing a long accusatory finger at me, "are going nowhere. You are not allowed to kill yourself, do I make myself clear?"

"Oh, so that's where Bree gets it," I murmured, trying to stop my head from swimming. I closed my eyes again.

"I seem to recall," I said, "a certain abbey in France. And a very stubborn young man in ill health. And his friend Murtagh, who took his clothes in order to prevent his getting up and wandering off before he was fit."

Silence. I opened one eye. He was standing stock still, the fading light from the window striking sparks in his hair.

"Whereupon," I said conversationally, "if memory serves, you promptly climbed out a window and decamped. Naked. In the middle of winter."

The stiff fingers of his right hand tapped twice against his leg.

"I was four-and-twenty," he said at last, sounding gruff. "I wasna meant to have any sense."

"I wouldn't argue with *that* for an instant," I assured him. I opened the other eye and fixed him with both. "But you do know why I did it. I had to."

He drew a very deep breath, sighed, and set down my clothes.

He came and sat down on the bed beside me, making the wooden frame creak and groan beneath his weight.

He picked up my hand, and held it as though it were something precious and fragile. It was, too—or at least it *looked* fragile, a delicate construct of transparent skin and the shadow of the bones within it. He ran his thumb gently down the back of my hand, tracing the bones from phalange to ulna, and I felt an odd, small tingle of distant memory; the vision of my own bones, glowing blue through the skin, and Master Raymond's hands, cupping my inflamed and empty womb, saying to me through the mists of fever, "Call him. Call the red man."

"Jamie," I said very softly. Sunlight flashed on the metal of my silver wedding ring. He took hold of it between thumb and forefinger, and slid the little metal circlet gently up and down my finger, so loose that it didn't even catch on the bony knuckle.

"Be careful," I said. "I don't want to lose it."

"Ye won't." He folded my fingers closed, his own hand closing large and warm around mine.

He sat silent for a time, and we watched the bar of sun creep slowly across the counterpane. Adso had moved with it, to stay in its warmth, and the light tipped his fur with a soft silver glow, the fine hairs that edged his ears tiny and distinct.

"It's a great comfort," he said at last, "to see the sun come up and go down. When I dwelt in the cave, when I was in prison, it gave me hope, to see the light come and go, and know that the world went about its business."

He was looking out the window, toward the blue distance where the sky darkened toward infinity. His throat moved a little as he swallowed.

"It gives me the same feeling, Sassenach," he said, "to hear ye rustling about in your surgery, rattling things and swearin' to yourself." He turned his head, then, to look at me, and his eyes held the depths of the coming night.

"If ye were no longer there—or somewhere—" he said very softly, "then the sun would no longer come up or go down." He lifted my hand and kissed it, very gently. He laid it, closed around my ring, upon my chest, rose, and left.

I slept lightly now, no longer flung into the agitated world of fever dreams, nor sucked down into the deep well of oblivion as my body sought the healing of sleep. I didn't know what had wakened me, but I *was* awake, quite suddenly, alert and fresh-eyed, with no interval of drowsiness.

The shutters were closed, but the moon was full; soft light striped the bed. I ran a hand over the sheet beside me, lifted my hand far above my head. My arm was a slender pale stem, bloodless and fragile as a toadstool's stalk; my fingers flexed gently and spread, a web, a net to catch the dark.

I could hear Jamie breathing, in his accustomed spot on the floor beside the bed.

I brought my arm down, stroked my body lightly with both hands, assessing. A tiny swell of breast, ribs I could count, one, two, three, four, five, and the smooth concavity of my stomach, slung like a hammock between the uprights of my hipbones. Skin, and bones. Not much else.

"Claire?" There was a stirring in the dark beside the bed, and Jamie's head rose up, a presence more sensed than seen, so dark was the shadow there by contrast with the moonlight.

A large dark hand groped across the quilt, touched my hip.

"Are ye well, *a nighean*?" he whispered. "D'ye need anything?"

He was tired; his head lay on the bed beside me, his breath warm through my shift. If he hadn't been warm, his touch, his breath, perhaps I wouldn't have had the courage, but I felt cold and bodiless as the moonlight itself, and so I closed my spectral hand on his and whispered, "I need you."

He was quite still for a moment, slowly making sense of what I'd said.

"I'll not trouble your sleep?" he said, sounding doubtful. I pulled on his wrist in answer, and he came, rising up from the pool of dark on the floor, the thin lines of moonlight rippling over him like water.

"Kelpie," I said softly.

He snorted briefly in answer, and awkwardly, gingerly, eased himself beneath the quilt, the mattress giving under his weight.

We lay very shyly together, barely touching. He was breathing shallowly, clearly trying to make as little obtrusion of his presence as possible. Aside from a faint rustling of sheets, the house was silent.

Finally, I felt one large finger nudge gently against my thigh.

"I missed ye, Sassenach," he whispered.

I rolled onto my side facing him, and kissed his arm in answer. I wanted to move closer, lay my head in the curve of his shoulder, and lie in the circle of his arm—but the idea of my short, bristly hair against his skin kept me from it.

"I missed you, too," I said, into the dark solidness of his arm.

"Will I take ye, then?" he said softly. "D'ye want it, truly?" One hand caressed my arm; the other went downward, starting the slow, steady rhythm to ready himself.

"Let me," I whispered, stilling his hand with my own. "Lie still."

I made love to him at first like a sneak thief, hasty strokes and tiny kisses, stealing scent and touch and warmth and salty taste. Then he put a hand on the back of my neck, pressing me closer, deeper.

"Dinna hurry yourself, lass," he said in a hoarse whisper. "I'm no going anywhere."

I let a quiver of silent amusement pass through me and he drew in a deep, deep breath as I closed my teeth very gently round him and slid my hand up under the warm, musky weight of his balls.

Then I rose up over him, light-headed at the sudden movement, needing urgently. We both sighed deeply as it happened, and I felt the breath of his laughter on my breasts as I bent over him.

"I missed ye, Sassenach," he whispered again.

I was shy of his touching me, changed as I was, and leaned with my hands on his shoulders, keeping him from pulling me down to him. He didn't try, but slid his hand curled between us.

I felt a brief pang at the thought that the hair on my privates was longer than that on my head—but the thought was driven out by the slow pressure of the big knuckle pressing deep between my legs, rocking gently back and forth.

I seized his other hand and brought it to my mouth, sucked his fingers hard, one by one, and shuddered, gripping his hand with all my strength.

I was still gripping it sometime later, as I lay beside him. Or rather, holding it, admiring the unseen shapes of it, complex and graceful in the dark, and the hard, smooth layer of callus on palms and knuckles.

"I've the hands of a bricklayer," he said, laughing a little as I passed my lips lightly over the roughened knuckles and the still-sensitive tips of his long fingers.

"Calluses on a man's hands are deeply erotic," I assured him.

"Are they, so?" His free hand passed lightly over my shorn head and down the length of my back. I shivered and pressed closer to him, self-consciousness beginning to be forgotten. My own free hand roamed down the length of his body, toying with the soft, wiry bush of his hair, and the damply tender, half-hard cock.

He arched his back a little, then relaxed.

"Well, I'll tell ye, Sassenach," he said. "If I havena got calluses *there*, it's no fault of yours, believe me."

67

The Last Laugh

I t was an old musket, made perhaps twenty years before, but well-kept. The stock was polished with wear, the wood beautiful to the touch, and the metal of the barrel mellow and clean.

Standing Bear clutched it in ecstasy, running awed fingers up and down the gleaming barrel, bringing them to his nose to sniff the intoxicating perfume of oil and powder, then beckoning his friends to come and smell it, too.

Five gentlemen had received muskets from the beneficent hand of Bird-who-sings-in-the-morning, and a sense of delight ran through the house, spreading in ripples through the village. Bird himself, with twenty-five muskets still to give, was drunk with the sense of inestimable wealth and power, and thus in a mood to welcome anyone and anything.

"This is Hiram Crombie," Jamie said to Bird, in Tsalagi, indicating Mr. Crombie, who had stood by him, white-faced with nerves, throughout the preliminary talk, the presentation of the muskets, the summoning of the braves, and the general rejoicing over the guns. "He has come to offer his friendship, and to tell you stories of the Christ."

"Oh, your Christ? The one who went to the lower world and came back? I always wondered, did he meet Sky-woman there, or Mole? I am fond of Mole; I would like to know what he said." Bird touched the stone pendant at his neck, a small red carving of Mole, the guide to the underworld.

Mr. Crombie's brow was furrowed, but luckily he had not yet developed any sense of ease in Tsalagi; he was still in the stage of mentally translating each word into English, and Bird was a rapid speaker. And Ian had found no occasion to teach Hiram the word for Mole.

Jamie coughed.

"I am sure he will be happy to tell you all the stories he knows," he said. "Mr. Crombie," he said, switching momentarily to English, "Tsisqua offers you welcome."

Bird's wife Penstemon's nostrils flared delicately; Crombie was sweating with nervousness, and smelled like a goat. He bowed earnestly, and presented Bird with the good knife he had brought as a present, slowly reciting the complimentary speech he had committed to memory. Reasonably well, too, Jamie thought; he'd mispronounced only a couple of words.

"I come to b-bring you great joy," he finished, stammering and sweating.

Bird looked at Crombie—small, stringy, and dripping wet— for a long, inscrutable moment, then back at Jamie.

"You're a funny man, Bear-Killer," he said with resignation. "Let us eat!"

It was autumn; the harvest was in and the hunting was good. And so the Feast of the Guns was a notable occasion, with wapiti and venison and wild pig raised steaming from pits and roasted over roaring fires, with overflowing platters of maize and roasted squash and dishes of beans spiced with onion and coriander, dishes of pottage, and dozen upon dozen of small fish rolled in cornmeal, fried in bear grease, their flesh crisp and sweet.

Mr. Crombie, very stiff to begin with, began to unbend under the influence of food, spruce beer, and the flattering attention paid him. A certain amount of the attention, Jamie thought, was due to the fact that Ian, a wide grin on his face, stayed by his pupil for a time, prompting and correcting, 'til Hiram should feel more at ease in the tongue, and able to manage on his own. Ian was extremely popular, particularly with the young women of the village.

For himself, he enjoyed the feasting very much; relieved of responsibility, there was nothing to do save to talk and listen and eat—and in the morning he would go.

It was an odd feeling, and one he was not sure he had ever had before. He had had many leavetakings, most regretful—a few taken with a sense of relief—some that wrenched the heart from his chest and left him aching. Not tonight. Everything seemed strangely ceremonious, something consciously done for the last time, and yet there was no sadness in it.

Completion, he supposed, was the sense of it. He had done what he could do, and now must leave Bird and the others to make their own way. He might come again, but never again by duty, in his role as the agent of the King.

That was a peculiar thought in itself. He had never lived without the consciousness of allegiance—whether willing or not, witting or not—to a king, whether that be German Geordie's house or the Stuarts. And now he did.

For the first time, he had some glimmer of what his daughter and his wife had tried to tell him.

Hiram was trying to recite one of the psalms, he realized. He was doing a good job of it, because he had asked Ian to translate it, and had then carefully committed it to memory. However . . .

"Oil runs down over the head and the beard . . ."

Penstemon cast a wary glance at the small pot of melted bear grease that they were using as a condiment, and narrowed her eyes at Hiram, plainly intending to snatch the dish from him if he tried to pour it over his head.

"It's a story of his ancestors," Jamie said to her, with a brief shrug. "Not his own custom."

"Oh. Hm." She relaxed a little, though continuing to keep a close eye on Hiram. He was a guest, but not all guests could be trusted to behave well.

Hiram did nothing untoward, though, and with many protests

of sufficiency, and awkward compliments toward his hosts, was persuaded to eat until his eyes bulged, which pleased them.

Ian would stay for a few days, to be sure that Hiram and Bird's people were in some sort of mutual accord. Jamie was not quite sure that Ian's sense of responsibility would overcome his sense of humor, though—in some ways, Ian's sense of humor tended toward the Indians'. A word from Jamie might therefore not come amiss, just by way of precaution.

"He has a wife," Jamie said to Bird, with a nod toward Hiram, now engaged in close discourse with two of the older men. "I think he would not welcome a young woman in his bed. He might be rude to her, not understanding the compliment."

"Don't worry," said Penstemon, overhearing this. She glanced at Hiram, and her lip curled with scorn. "Nobody would want a child from *him*. Now, a child from *you*, Bear-Killer . . ." She gave him a long look beneath her lashes, and he laughed, saluting her with a gesture of respect.

It was a perfect night, cold and crisp, and the door was left open that the air might come in. The smoke from the fire rose straight and white, streaming toward the hole above, its moving wraiths like spirits ascending in joy.

Everyone had eaten and drunk to the point of a pleasant stupor, and there was momentary silence and a pervading sense of peace and happiness.

"It is good for men to eat as brothers," Hiram observed to Standing Bear, in his halting Tsalagi. Or rather, tried to. And after all, Jamie reflected, feeling his ribs creak under the strain, it was really a very minor difference between "as brothers" and "their brothers."

Standing Bear gave Hiram a thoughtful look, and edged slightly farther away from him.

Bird observed this, and after a moment's silence, turned to Jamie.

"You're a very funny man, Bear-Killer," he repeated, shaking his head. "You win."

To Mr. John Stuart,
Superintendent of the Southern
Department of Indian Affairs

From Fraser's Ridge,
on the First Day of November,
Anno Domini 1774,
James Fraser, Esq.

My dear sir,

    This is to notify you of my Resignation as Indian Agent, as I find that my personal Convictions will no longer allow me to perform my Office on behalf of the Crown in good Conscience.
    In thanks for your kind Attention and many Favors, and wishing you well in future, I remain

                    Your most humble Servant,
                        J. Fraser

PART NINE

The Bones of Time

68

Savages

Only two left. The pool of liquid wax glowed with the light of the flaming wick above it, and the jewels slowly came into view, one green, one black, glowing with their own inner fire. Jamie dipped the feather end of a quill gently into the melted wax and scooped the emerald up, raising it into the light.

He dropped the hot stone into the handkerchief I held waiting, and I rubbed it quickly, to get off the wax before it should harden.

"Our reserves are getting rather low," I said, in uneasy jest. "Let's hope there aren't any more expensive emergencies."

"I shallna touch the black diamond, regardless," he said definitely, and blew out the wick. "That one is for you."

I stared at him.

"What do you mean by that?"

He shrugged a little, and reached to take the emerald in its handkerchief from me.

"If I should be killed," he said very matter-of-factly. "Ye'll take it and go. Back through the stones."

"Oh? I don't know that I would," I said. I didn't like talking about any contingency that involved Jamie's death, but there was no point in ignoring the possibilities. Battle, disease, imprisonment, accident, assassination . . .

"You and Bree were going about forbidding *me* to die," I said. "I'd do the same thing, if I had the faintest hope of your paying the least attention."

He smiled at that.

"I always mind your words, Sassenach," he assured me gravely.

"But ye do tell me that man proposes and God disposes, and should He see fit to dispose of *me*—ye'll go back."

"Why would I?" I said, nettled—and unsettled. The memories of his sending me back through the stones on the eve of Culloden were not ones I ever wished to recall, and here he was, prying open the door to that tightly sealed chamber of my mind. "I'd stay with Bree and Roger, wouldn't I? Jem, Marsali and Fergus, Germain and Henri-Christian and the girls—everyone's here. What is there to go back to, after all?"

He took the stone from its cloth, turning it over between his fingers, and looked thoughtfully at me, as though making up his mind whether to tell me something. Small hairs began to prickle on the back of my neck.

"I dinna ken," he said at last, shaking his head. "But I've seen ye there."

The prickling ran straight down the back of my neck and down both arms.

"Seen me *where*?"

"There." He waved a hand in a vague gesture. "I dreamt of ye there. I dinna ken where it was; I only know it was *there*—in your proper time."

"How do you know that?" I demanded, my flesh creeping briskly. "What was I doing?"

His brow furrowed in the effort of recollection.

"I dinna recall, exactly," he said slowly. "But I knew it was *then,* by the light." His brow cleared suddenly. "That's it. Ye were sitting at a desk, with something in your hand, maybe writing. And there was light all round ye, shining on your face, on your hair. But it wasna candlelight, nor yet firelight or sunlight. And I recall thinking to myself as I saw ye, *Oh, so that's what electric light is like."*

I stared at him, open-mouthed.

"How can you recognize something in a dream that you've never seen in real life?"

He seemed to find that funny.

"I dream of things I've not seen all the time, Sassenach—don't you?"

"Well," I said uncertainly. "Yes. Sometimes. Monsters, odd plants, I suppose. Peculiar landscapes. And certainly *people* that I don't know. But surely that's different? To see something you know about, but haven't seen?"

"Well, what I saw may not be what electric light *does* look like," he admitted, "but that's what I said to myself when I saw it. And I was quite sure that ye were in your own time.

"And after all," he added logically, "I dream of the past; why would I not dream of the future?"

There was no good answer to a thoroughly Celtic remark of that nature.

"Well, *you* would, I suppose," I said. I rubbed dubiously at my lower lip. "How old was I, in this dream of yours?"

He looked surprised, then uncertain, and peered closely at my face, as though trying to compare it with some mental vision.

"Well . . . I dinna ken," he said, sounding for the first time unsure. "I didna think anything about it—I didna notice that ye had white hair, or anything of the sort—it was just . . . you." He shrugged, baffled, then looked down at the stone in my hand.

"Does it feel warm to your touch, Sassenach?" he asked curiously.

"Of course it does," I said, rather crossly. "It's just come out of hot wax, for heaven's sake." And yet the emerald *did* seem to pulse gently in my hand, warm as my own blood and beating like a miniature heart. And when I handed it to him, I felt a small, peculiar reluctance—as though it did not want to leave me.

"Give it to MacDonald," I said, rubbing my palm against the side of my skirt. "I hear him outside, talking to Arch; he'll be wanting to be off."

MacDonald had come pelting up to the Ridge in the midst of a rainstorm the day before, weathered face nearly purple with cold, exertion, and excitement, to inform us that he had found a printing establishment for sale in New Bern.

"The owner has already left—somewhat involuntarily," he told us, dripping and steaming by the fire. "His friends seek to sell the premises and equipment promptly, before they might be seized or destroyed, and thus provide him with funds to reestablish himself in England."

By "somewhat involuntarily," it turned out, he meant that the print shop's owner was a Loyalist, who had been kidnapped off the street by the local Committee of Safety and shoved willy-nilly onto a ship departing for England. This form of impromptu deportation was becoming popular, and while it was more humane than tar and feathers, it did mean that the printer would arrive penniless in England, and owing money for his passage, to boot.

"I happened to meet wi' some of his friends in a tavern, tearin' their hair over his sad fate and drinking to his welfare—whereupon I told them that I might be able to put them in the way of an advantage," the Major said, swelling with satisfaction. "They were all ears, when I said that ye might—just might, mind—have ready cash."

"What makes ye think I do, Donald?" Jamie asked, one eyebrow cocked.

MacDonald looked surprised, then knowing. He winked and laid a finger beside his nose.

"I hear the odd bit, here and there. Word has it that ye've got a wee cache of gems—or so I hear, from a merchant in Edenton whose bank dealt wi' one."

Jamie and I exchanged looks.

"Bobby," I said, and he nodded in resignation.

"Well, as for me, mum's the word," MacDonald said, observing this. "Ye can rely upon my discretion, to be sure. And I doubt the matter's widely known. But then—a poor man doesna go about buying muskets by the dozen, now, does he?"

"Oh, he might," Jamie said, resigned. "Ye'd be surprised, Donald. But as it is . . . I imagine a bargain might be struck. What are the printer's friends asking—and will they offer insurance, in case of fire?"

MacDonald had been empowered to negotiate on behalf of the printer's friends—they being anxious to get the problematical real estate sold before some patriotic soul came and burned it down—and so the bargain was concluded on the spot. MacDonald was sent hurtling back down the mountain to change the emerald into money, conclude payment on the printer's shop, leaving the residue of the money with Fergus for ongoing expenses—and let it be known as quickly as possible in New Bern that the premises were shortly to be under new management.

"And if anyone asks about the politics of the new owner . . ." Jamie said. To which MacDonald merely nodded wisely, and laid his finger alongside his red-veined nose once more.

I was reasonably sure that Fergus had no personal politics to speak of; beyond his family, his sole allegiance was to Jamie. Once the bargain was made, though, and the frenzy of packing begun—Marsali and Fergus would have to leave at once, to have any chance of making it to New Bern before winter set in in earnest— Jamie had had a serious talk with Fergus.

"Now, it'll no be like it was in Edinburgh. There's no but one other printer in the town, and from what MacDonald says, he's an elderly gentleman, and sae much afraid o' the committee and the Governor both, he willna print a thing but books of sermons and handbills advertising horseraces."

"*Très bon,*" said Fergus, looking even happier, if such a thing was possible. He'd been going about lit up like a Chinese lantern since hearing the news. "We will have all of the newspaper and broadsheet business, to say nothing of the printing of scandalous plays and pamphlets—there is nothing like sedition and unrest for the printing business, milord, you know that yourself."

"I do know that," Jamie said very dryly. "Which is why I mean to beat the need for care into your thick skull. I dinna wish to hear that ye've been hanged for treason, nor yet tarred-and-feathered for no being treasonous enough."

"Oh, la." Fergus waved an airy hook. "I know well enough how this game is played, milord."

Jamie nodded, still looking dubious.

"Aye, ye do. But it's been some years; ye may be out of practice. And ye'll not know who's who in New Bern; ye dinna want to find yourself buying meat from the man ye've savaged in the morning's paper, aye?"

"I'll mind that, Da." Marsali sat by the fire, nursing Henri-Christian, and taking close heed. If anything, she looked happier than Fergus, upon whom she looked adoringly. She switched the look of adoration to Jamie, and smiled. "We'll take good care, I promise."

Jamie's frown softened as he looked at her.

"I'll miss ye, lass," he said softly. Her look of happiness dimmed, but didn't go out entirely.

"I'll miss ye, too, Da. All of us will. And Germain doesna want to leave Jem, o' course. But . . ." Her eyes drifted back to Fergus, who was making a list of supplies, whistling "Alouette" under his breath, and she hugged Henri-Christian closer, making him kick his legs in protest.

"Aye, I know." Jamie coughed, to cover his emotion, and wiped a knuckle underneath his nose. "Now then, wee Fergus. Ye'll have a bit of money over; be sure to bribe the constable and the watch first of all. MacDonald's given me the names o' the Royal Council, and the chief Assemblymen—he'll be of help wi' the council, as he's the Governor's man. Be tactful, aye? But see he's taken care of; he's been a great help in the matter."

Fergus nodded, head bent over his paper.

"Paper, ink, lead, bribes, shammy leather, brushes," he said, writing busily, and resumed absently singing, *"Alouette, gentil alouette . . ."*

It was impossible to get a wagon up to the Ridge; the only approach was by the narrow trail that wound up the slope from Coopersville—one of the factors that had led to the development of that minor crossroads into a small hamlet, as itinerant peddlers and other travelers tended to stop there, making brief forays on foot upward into the mountain.

"Which is all very well for discouraging hostile invasion onto the Ridge," I told Bree, panting as I set down a large canvas-wrapped bundle of candlesticks, chamber pots, and other small household belongings at the side of the trail. "But it unfortunately makes it rather difficult to get *off* the bloody Ridge, too."

"I suppose it never occurred to Da that anyone would want to leave," Bree said, grunting as she lowered her own burden—Marsali's cauldron, packed with cheeses, sacks of flour, beans, and rice, plus a wooden box full of dried fish and a string bag of apples. "This thing weighs a *ton*."

She turned and bellowed, "GERMAIN!" up the trail behind us. Dead silence. Germain and Jemmy were meant to be shepherding

Mirabel the goat down to the wagon. They had left the cabin with us, but had been dropping steadily behind.

Neither a call nor a *mehhhh* came from the trail, but Mrs. Bug came into view, trundling slowly under the weight of Marsali's spinning wheel, which she bore on her back, and holding Mirabel's halter in one hand. Mirabel, a small, neat white goat with gray markings, blatted happily at sight of us.

"I found the puir wee lassie tethered to a bush," Mrs. Bug said, setting down the spinning wheel with a wheeze and wiping her face with her apron. "No sign o' the lads, the wicked wee creatures."

Brianna made a low growling noise that boded ill for either Jemmy or Germain, if she caught them. Before she could stomp back up the trail, though, Roger and Young Ian came down, each carrying one end of Marsali's loom, collapsed for the occasion into a large bundle of heavy timbers. Seeing the traffic jam in the road, though, they stopped, setting down their burden with sighs of relief.

"What's amiss, then?" Roger asked, glancing from face to face, and settling on the goat with a frown. "Where are Jem and Germain?"

"Dollars to donuts the little fiends are hiding somewhere," Bree said, smoothing tumbled red hair out of her face. Her plait had come undone, and straggling wisps of hair were sticking damply to her face. I was momentarily grateful for my short thicket of curls; no matter what it looked like, it was certainly convenient.

"Shall I go and look?" Ian asked, emerging from the wooden pudding basin he'd been carrying upside down on his head. "They'll no have gone far."

Sounds of hasty feet from below made everyone turn expectantly in that direction—but it was not the boys, but Marsali, breathless and wide-eyed.

"Henri-Christian," she gasped, her eyes flicking rapidly round the group. "Have ye got him, Mother Claire? Bree?"

"I thought *you* had him," Bree said, catching Marsali's sense of urgency.

"I did. Wee Aidan McCallum was minding him for me, whilst I loaded things into the wagon. But then I stopped to feed him"—a hand went briefly to her bosom—"and they were both vanished! I thought perhaps . . ." Her words died away as she began

scanning the bushes along the trail, her cheeks flushed with exertion and annoyance.

"I'll strangle him," she said through gritted teeth. "And
where's Germain, then?" she cried, catching sight of Mirabel,
who had taken advantage of the stop to nibble tasty thistles by the
path.

"This is beginning to have the look of a plan about it," Roger
observed, obviously amused. Ian, too, seemed to be finding
something funny in the situation, but vicious glares from the
frazzled females present wiped the smirks off their faces.

"Yes, do go and find them, please," I said, seeing that Marsali
was about to either burst into tears or go berserk and throw things.

"Aye, do," she said tersely. "And beat them, while ye're at it."

"Ye ken where they are?" Ian asked, shading his eyes to look
up a trough of tumbled rock.

"Aye, likely. This way." Roger pushed through a tangle of
yaupon and redbud, with Ian after him, and emerged onto the
bank of the small creek that paralleled the trail here. Below, he
caught a glimpse of Aidan's favorite fishing place near the ford,
but there was no sign of life down there.

Instead, he turned upward, making his way through thick dry
grass and loose rocks along the creekbank. Most of the leaves had
fallen from the chestnuts and poplars, and lay in slippery mats of
brown and gold underfoot.

Aidan had shown him the secret place some time ago; a shallow cave, barely three feet high, hidden at the top of a steep slope
overgrown by a thicket of oak saplings. The oaks were bare now,
and the cave's opening easily visible, if you knew to look for it. It
was particularly noticeable at the moment, because smoke was
coming out of it, slipping veil-like up the face of the rock above,
leaving a sharp scent in the cold, dry air.

Ian raised one eyebrow. Roger nodded, and made his way up
the slope, making no effort to be quiet about it. There was a mad
scuffle of noises inside the cave, thumpings and low cries, and the
veil of smoke wavered and stopped, replaced by a loud hiss and a
puff of dark gray from the cave mouth as someone threw water on
the fire.

Ian, meanwhile, had made his way silently up the side of the rockface above the cave, seeing a small crevice from which a tiny plume of smoke issued. Clinging one-handed to a dogwood that grew out of the rock, he leaned perilously out, and cupping a hand near his mouth, let out a frightful Mohawk scream, directed into the crevice.

Terror-stricken shrieks, much higher-pitched, issued from the cave, followed in short order by a tumble of little boys, pushing and tripping over each other in their haste.

"Ho, there!" Roger snagged his own offspring neatly by the collar as he rushed past. "The jig's up, mate."

Germain, with Henri-Christian's sturdy form clutched to his midsection, was attempting to escape down the slope, but Ian leapt past him, springing pantherlike down the rocks, and grabbed the baby from him, bringing him to a reluctant stop.

Only Aidan remained at large. Seeing his comrades in captivity, he hesitated at the edge of the slope, obviously wanting to flee, but nobly gave in, coming back with dragging step to share their fate.

"Right, lads; sorry, it's not on." Roger spoke with some sympathy; Jemmy had been upset for days at the prospect of Germain's leaving.

"But we do not want to go, Uncle Roger," Germain said, employing his most effective look of wide-eyed pleading. "We will stay here, we can live in the cave, and hunt for our food."

"Aye, sir, and me and Jem, we'll share our dinners wi' them," Aidan piped up in anxious support.

"I brought some of Mama's matches, so they've got a fire to keep warm," Jem chipped in eagerly, "and a loaf of bread, too!"

"So ye see, Uncle—" Germain spread his hands gracefully in demonstration, "we shall be no trouble to anyone!"

"Oh, nay trouble, is it?" Ian said, with no less sympathy. "Tell your mother that, aye?"

Germain put his hands behind him, clutching his buttocks protectively by reflex.

"And what were ye thinking, dragging your wee brother up here?" Roger said a little more severely. "He can barely walk yet! Two steps out of there"—he nodded at the cave—"and he'd be tumbling down the burn and his neck broken."

"Oh, no, sir!" Germain said, shocked. He fumbled in his pocket and drew out a piece of string. "I should tie him up, when I was not there, so he shouldna wander or fall. But I couldna be leaving him; I promised *Maman,* when he was born, I said I would never leave him."

Tears were beginning to trickle down Aidan's thin cheeks. Henri-Christian, totally confused, began to howl in sympathy, which made Jem's lower lip tremble, as well. He wriggled out of Roger's grasp, ran to Germain, and clutched him passionately about the middle.

"Germain can't go, Daddy, please don't make him go!"

Roger rubbed his nose, exchanged brief looks with Ian, and sighed.

He sat down on a rock, and motioned to Ian, who was having a certain amount of difficulty in deciding which way up to hold Henri-Christian. Ian gave him the baby with a noticeable air of relief, and Henri-Christian, feeling the need of security, seized Roger's nose with one hand and his hair with the other.

"Look, *a bhailach,*" he said, detaching Henri-Christian's grasp with some difficulty. "Wee Henri-Christian needs his mother to feed him. He's barely got teeth, for God's sake—he canna be living up here in the wild, eating raw meat wi' you savages."

"He has too got teeth!" Aidan said stoutly, extending a bitten forefinger in proof. "Look!"

"He eats pap," Germain said, but with some uncertainty to his tone. "We would mash up biscuits for him with milk."

"Henri-Christian needs his mother," Roger repeated firmly, "and your mother needs *you.* Ye dinna expect her to manage a wagon and two mules *and* your sisters, all the way to New Bern alone, do ye?"

"But Papa can help," Germain protested. "The girls mind him, when they mind no one else!"

"Your papa's gone already," Ian informed him. "He's ridden ahead, to find a place for ye all to live, once ye've got there. Your mother's to follow on, wi' all your things. Roger Mac's right, *a bhailach*—your mother needs ye."

Germain's small face paled a little. He looked helplessly down at Jemmy, still clinging to him, then up the hill at Aidan, and gulped. The wind had come up, and blew his blond fringe back from his face, making him look very small and fragile.

"Well, then," he said, and stopped, swallowing. Very gently, he put his arms round Jemmy's shoulders and kissed the top of his round red head.

"I'll come back, cousin," he said. "And you will come and visit me by the sea. You'll come, too," he assured Aidan, looking up. Aidan sniffed, nodding, and made his way slowly down the slope.

Roger reached out a free hand and gently detached Jemmy. "Get on my back, *mo chuisle*," he said. "It's a steep slope; I'll take ye down pick-a-back."

Not waiting to be asked, Ian leaned down and picked up Aidan, who wrapped his legs round Ian's middle, hiding his tear-streaked face in Ian's buckskin shirt.

"D'ye want to ride, too?" Roger asked Germain, standing up carefully under the weight of his double burden. "Ian can carry ye, if ye like."

Ian nodded and held out a hand, but Germain shook his head, blond hair flying.

"*Non*, Uncle Roger," he said, almost too softly to hear. "I'll walk." And turning round, began to make his way gingerly down the precipitous slope.

69

A Stampede of Beavers

October 25, 1774

They had been walking for an hour before Brianna began to realize that they weren't after game. They'd cut the trail of a small herd of deer, with droppings so fresh that the pellets were still patchy with moisture, but Ian ignored the sign, pushing up the slope in single-minded determination.

Rollo had come with them, but after several fruitless attempts to draw his master's attention to promising scents, abandoned them in disgust and bounded off through the flurrying leaves to do his own hunting.

The climb was too steep to permit conversation, even had Ian seemed inclined. With a mental shrug, she followed, but kept gun in hand and an eye on the brush, just in case.

They had left the Ridge at dawn; it was well past noon when they paused at last, on the bank of some small and nameless stream. A wild grapevine wrapped itself round the trunk of a persimmon that overhung the bank; animals had taken most of the grapes, but a few bunches still hung out over the water, out of reach for any but the most daring of squirrels—or a tall woman.

She shucked her moccasins and waded into the stream, gasping at the icy shock of the water on her calves. The grapes were ripe to bursting, so purple as to be nearly black, and sticky with juice. The squirrels hadn't got to them, but the wasps had, and she kept a cautious eye on the dagger-bellied foragers as she twisted the tough stem of a particularly succulent bunch.

"So, do you want to tell me what we're really looking for?" she asked, back turned to her cousin.

"No," he said, a smile in his voice.

"Oh, a surprise, is it?" She popped the stem, and turned to toss the grapes to him.

He caught the bunch one-handed, and set them down on the bank beside the ragged knapsack in which he carried provisions.

"Something o' the sort."

"As long as we aren't just out for a walk, then." She twisted off another bunch, and sloshed ashore, to sit down beside him.

"No, not that." He flipped two grapes into his mouth, crushed them, and spat the skins and pips with the ease of long custom. She nibbled hers more daintily, biting one in half and flicking the seeds out with a fingernail.

"You ought to eat the skins, Ian; they have vitamins."

He raised one shoulder in skepticism, but said nothing. Both she and her mother had explained the concept of vitamins—numerous times—to little or no effect. Jamie and Ian had reluctantly been obliged to admit the existence of germs, because Claire could show them teeming seas of microorganisms in her microscope. Vitamins, however, were unfortunately invisible and thus could be safely ignored.

"Is it much farther, this surprise?" The grape skins were, in fact, very bitter. Her mouth puckered involuntarily as she bit into one. Ian, industriously eating and spitting, noticed and grinned at her.

"Aye, a bit farther."

She cast an eye at the horizon; the sun was coming down the sky. If they were to turn back now, it would be dark before they reached home.

"How *much* farther?" She spit the mangled grape skin into her palm and flicked it away into the grass.

Ian glanced at the sun, too, and pursed his lips.

"Well . . . I should think we'll reach it by midday tomorrow."

"We'll *what*? Ian!" He looked abashed, and ducked his head.

"I'm sorry, coz. I ken I should have told ye before—but I thought ye maybe wouldn't come, if I said how far."

A wasp lighted on the bunch of grapes in her hand, and she slapped it irritably away.

"You *know* I wouldn't. Ian, what were you thinking? Roger will have a fit!"

Her cousin seemed to find the notion funny; his mouth turned up at the corner.

"A fit? Roger Mac? I shouldna think so."

"Well, all right, he won't throw a fit—but he'll be worried. And Jemmy will miss me!"

"No, they'll be all right," Ian assured her. "I told Uncle Jamie we'd be gone three days, and he said he'd bring the wean up to the Big House. With your Mam and Lizzie and Mrs. Bug to fuss him, wee Jem won't even notice you're gone."

This was likely true, but did nothing to assuage her annoyance.

"You told *Da*? And he just said fine, and both of you thought it was perfectly all right to—to—lug me off into the woods for three days, without telling me what was going on? You—you—"

"High-handed, insufferable, beastly *Scots*," Ian said, in such a perfect imitation of her mother's English accent that she burst out laughing, despite her annoyance.

"Yes," she said, wiping spluttered grape juice off her chin. "Exactly!"

He was still smiling, but his expression had changed; he wasn't teasing anymore.

"Brianna," he said softly, with that Highland lilt that made of her name something strange and graceful. "It's important, aye?"

He wasn't smiling at all now. His eyes were fixed on hers, warm, but serious. His hazel eyes were the only feature of any beauty about Ian Murray's face, but they held a gaze of such frank, sweet openness that you felt he had let you look inside his soul, just for an instant. She had had occasion before to wonder whether he was aware of this particular effect—but even if he was, it was difficult to resist.

"All right," she said, and waved away a circling wasp, still cross but resigned. "All *right*. But you still should have told me. And you won't tell me, even now?"

He shook his head, looking down at the grape he was thumbing loose from its stem.

"I can't," he said simply. He flipped the grape into his mouth and turned to open his bag—which, now that she noticed, bulged suspiciously. "D'ye want some bread, coz, or a bit of cheese?"

"No. Let's go." She stood up and brushed dead leaves from her breeches. "The sooner we get there, the sooner we'll be back."

They stopped an hour before sunset, while enough light remained to gather wood. The bulging knapsack had proved to contain two blankets, as well as food and a jug of beer—welcome, after the day's walking, which had been mostly uphill.

"Oh, this is a good batch," she said approvingly, sniffing at the neck of the jug after a long, aromatic, hop-edged swallow. "Who made it?"

"Lizzie. She caught the knack of it from *Frau* Ute. Before the . . . er . . . mphm." A delicate Scottish noise encompassed the painful circumstances surrounding the dissolution of Lizzie's betrothal.

"Mmm. That was too bad, wasn't it?" She lowered her lashes, watching him covertly to see whether he would say anything further about Lizzie. Lizzie and Ian had seemed fond of each other once—but first he had gone to the Iroquois, and then she had been engaged to Manfred McGillivray when he returned. Now that both of them were free once more . . .

He dismissed her comment about Lizzie with nothing more than a shrug of agreement, though, concentrating on the tedious process of fire-making. The day had been warm and an hour of daylight remained, but the shadows under the trees were already blue; the night would be chilly.

"I'm going to have a look at the stream," she announced, plucking a coiled line and hook from the small pile of effects Ian had unloaded from his bag. "It looked like there's a trout pool just below the bend, and the flies will be rising."

"Oh, aye." He nodded, but paid her little attention, patiently scraping the pile of kindling a little higher before striking the next shower of sparks from his flint.

As she made her way around the bend of the little creek, she saw that it wasn't merely a trout pool—it was a beaver pond. The humped mound of the lodge was reflected in still water, and on the far bank she could see the agitated judderings of a couple of willow saplings, evidently in the process of being consumed.

She moved slowly, a wary eye out. Beavers wouldn't trouble her, but they *would* make a dash for the water if they saw her, not only splashing, but smacking the water with their tails in alarm. She'd heard it before; it was amazingly loud, sounding like a fusillade of gunshots, and guaranteed to scare every fish within miles into hiding.

Gnawed sticks littered the near bank, the white inner wood chiseled as neatly as any carpenter could do, but none was fresh, and she heard nothing nearby but the sigh of wind in the trees. Beavers were not stealthy; none was close.

With a cautious eye on the far bank, she baited the hook with a small chunk of cheese, whirled it slowly overhead, picked up speed as she let the line out, then let it fly. The hook landed with a small *plop!* in the middle of the pond, but the noise wasn't sufficient to alarm the beavers; the willow saplings on the far bank continued to shake and heave under the assault of industrious teeth.

The evening hatch was rising, just as she'd told Ian. The air was soft, cool on her face, and the surface of the water dimpled and glimmered like gray silk shaken in light. Small clouds of gnats drifted in the still air under the trees, prey for the rising of the carnivorous caddis flies, stone flies, and damselflies breaking free of the surface, new-hatched and ravenous.

It was a pity that she hadn't a casting rod or tied flies—but still worth a try. Caddis flies weren't the only things that rose hungry at twilight, and voracious trout had been known to strike at almost anything that floated in front of them—her father had once taken one with a hook adorned with nothing more than a few knotted strands of his own bright hair.

That was a thought. She smiled to herself, brushing back a wisp of hair that had escaped from its plait, and began to draw the line slowly back toward shore. But there were likely more than trout here, and cheese was—

A strong tug came on the line, and she jerked in surprise. A snag? The line jerked back, and a thrill from the depths shot up her arm like electricity.

The next half hour passed without conscious thought, in the single-minded pursuit of finny prey. She was wet to mid-thigh, rashed with mosquito bites, and her wrist and shoulder ached, but she had three fat fish gleaming in the grass at her feet, a hunter's sense of profound satisfaction—and a few more crumbs of cheese left in her pocket.

She was drawing back her arm to throw the hook again, when a sudden chorus of squeaks and hisses shattered the evening calm, and a stampede of beavers broke from cover, trundling down the opposite bank of the pond like a platoon of small, furry tanks. She stared at them open-mouthed, and took a step back in reflex.

Then something big and dark appeared among the trees behind the beavers, and further reflex shot adrenaline through her limbs as she whirled to flee. She would have been into the trees and away in an instant, had she not stepped on one of her fish, which slid under her foot like greased butter and dumped her unceremoniously on her backside. From which position she was ideally placed to see Rollo race from the trees in a long, low streak and launch himself in an arching parabola from the top of the bank. Graceful as a comet, he soared through the air and landed in the pond among the beavers, with a splash like a fallen meteor.

Ian looked up at her, open-mouthed. Slowly, his eyes traveled from her dripping hair, over her sopping, mud-smeared clothes, and down to the fish—one slightly squashed—that dangled from a leather string in her hand.

"The fish put up a good fight, did they?" he asked, nodding at the string. The corners of his mouth began to twitch.

"Yes," she said, and dropped them on the ground in front of him. "But not nearly as good a fight as the beavers."

"Beavers," he said. He rubbed a knuckle meditatively down the bridge of his long, bony nose. "Aye, I heard them slapping. Ye've been fighting beavers?"

"I've been rescuing your wretched *dog* from beavers," she said, and sneezed. She sank to her knees in front of the new-made fire and closed her eyes in momentary bliss at the touch of heat on her shivering body.

"Oh, Rollo's back, then? Rollo! Where are ye, hound?" The big dog slunk reluctantly out of the shrubbery, tail barely twitching in response to his master's call.

"What's this I hear about beavers, then, *a madadh*?" Ian said sternly. In response, Rollo shook himself, though no more than a fine mist of water droplets rose from his coat. He sighed, dropped to his belly, and put his nose morosely on his paws.

"Maybe he was only after fish, but the beavers didn't see it that way. They ran from him on shore, but once he was in the water—" Brianna shook her head, and wrung out the soggy tail of her hunting shirt. "I tell you what, Ian—*you* clean those damn fish."

He was already doing so, gutting one with a single neat slice up the belly and a scoop of the thumb. He tossed the entrails toward Rollo, who merely let out another sigh, and seemed to flatten against the dead leaves, ignoring the treat.

"He's no hurt, is he?" Ian asked, frowning at his dog.

She glared at him.

"No, he isn't. I expect he's embarrassed. You could ask whether *I'm* hurt. Do you have any idea what kind of *teeth* beavers have?"

The light was nearly gone, but she could see his lean shoulders shaking.

"Aye," he said, sounding rather strangled. "I have. They, um, didna bite ye, did they? I mean—I should think it would be noticeable, if ye'd been gnawed." A small wheeze of amusement escaped him, and he tried to cover it with a cough.

"No," she said, rather coldly. The fire was going well, but not nearly well enough. The evening breeze had come up, and was reaching through the soaked fabric of shirt and breeches to fondle her backside with ice-cold fingers.

"It wasn't so much the teeth as the tails," she said, shuffling round on her knees to present her back to the fire. She rubbed a hand gingerly over her right arm, where one of the muscular paddles had struck flat on her forearm, leaving a reddened bruise that stretched from wrist to elbow. For a few moments, she'd thought the bone was broken.

"It was like being hit with a baseball bat—er . . . with a club, I mean," she amended. The beavers hadn't attacked her directly, of course, but being in the water with a panicked wolf-dog and half a dozen sixty-pound rodents in a state of extreme agitation had been rather like walking through an automated car wash on foot—a maelstrom of blinding spray and thrashing objects. A chill struck her and she wrapped both arms around herself, shivering.

"Here, coz." Ian stood up and skinned the buckskin shirt off over his head. "Put this on."

She was much too cold and battered to refuse the offer. Retiring modestly behind a bush, she stripped off the wet things and emerged a moment later, clad in Ian's buckskin, one of the blankets wrapped around her waist sarong-style.

"You don't eat enough, Ian," she said, sitting down by the fire again, and eyeing him critically. "All your ribs show."

They did. He'd always been lean to the point of thinness, but in his younger years, his teenage scrawniness had seemed quite normal, merely the result of his bones outstripping the growth of the rest of him.

Now he had reached his full growth and had had a year or two to let his muscles catch up. They had—she could see every sinew in his arms and shoulders—but the knobs of his spine bulged against the tanned skin of his back, and she could see the shadows of his ribs like rippled sand underwater.

He raised a shoulder, but made no reply, intent on skewering the cleaned fish on peeled willow twigs for broiling.

"And you don't sleep very well, either." She narrowed her eyes at him across the fire. Even in this light, the shadows and hollows in his face were obvious, despite the distraction of the Mohawk tattoos that looped across his cheekbones. The shadows had been obvious to everyone for months; her mother had wanted to say something to Ian, but Jamie had told her to let the lad be; he would speak when he was ready.

"Oh, well enough," he murmured, not looking up.

Whether he was ready now or not, she couldn't say. But he'd brought her here. If he wasn't ready, he could bloody well get that way fast.

She had—of course—wondered all day about the mysterious goal of their journey, and why *she* was his necessary companion. For a matter of hunting, Ian would have taken one of the men; good as she was with a gun, several of the men on the Ridge were better, including her father. And any one of them would be better suited than she to something like digging out a bear's den or packing home meat or hides.

They were in the Cherokee lands at the moment; she knew Ian visited the Indians frequently, and was on good terms with several villages. But if it had been a matter of some formal arrangement to be made, surely he would have asked Jamie to accompany him, or Peter Bewlie, with his Cherokee wife to interpret.

"Ian," she said, with the tone in her voice that could bring almost any man up short. "Look at me."

His head jerked up, and he blinked at her.

"Ian," she said, a little more gently, "is this to do with your wife?"

He stayed frozen for a moment, eyes dark and unfathomable. Rollo, in the shadows behind him, suddenly raised his head and let out a small whine of inquiry. That seemed to rouse Ian; he blinked and looked down.

"Aye," he said, sounding quite matter-of-fact. "It is."

He adjusted the angle of the stick he had driven into the earth by the fire; the pale flesh of the fish curled and sizzled, browning on the green wood.

She waited for him to say more, but he didn't speak—just broke off the edge of a piece of half-cooked fish and held it out to the dog, clicking his tongue in invitation. Rollo rose and sniffed Ian's ear in concern, but then deigned to take the fish, and lay down again, licking the hot tidbit delicately before scooping it up with his tongue, gathering enough spirit then to engulf the discarded heads and fish guts as well.

Ian pursed his lips a little, and she could see the thoughts flickering half-formed across his face, before he made up his mind to speak.

"I did once think of marrying you, ye ken."

He gave her a quick, direct glance, and she felt an odd little jolt of realization. He'd thought about it, all right. And while she had no doubt that his offer then had been made from the purest of motives . . . he was a young man. She hadn't until this moment realized that he would of course have contemplated every detail of what that offer entailed.

His eyes held hers in wry acknowledgment of the fact that he had indeed imagined the physical details of sharing her bed—and had not found the prospect in any way objectionable. She resisted the impulse to blush and look away; that would discredit them both.

She was suddenly—and for the first time—aware of him *as* a man, rather than as an endearing young cousin. And aware of the heat of his body that had lingered in the soft buckskin when she pulled it on.

"It wouldn't have been the worst thing in the world," she said, striving to match his matter-of-fact tone. He laughed, and the stippled lines of his tattoos lost their grimness.

"No," he said. "Maybe not the best—that would be Roger Mac, aye? But I'm glad to hear I wouldna have been the worst, either. Better than Ronnie Sinclair, d'ye think? Or worse than Forbes the lawyer?"

"Ha, bloody ha." She refused to be discomposed by his teasing. "You would have been at least third on the list."

"Third?" That got his attention. "What? Who was second?" He actually seemed miffed at the notion that someone might precede him, and she laughed.

"Lord John Grey."

"Oh? Oh, well. Aye, I suppose he'd do," Ian admitted grudgingly. "Though of course, he—" He stopped abruptly, and darted a cautious look in her direction.

She felt an answering stab of caution. Did Ian know about John Grey's private tastes? She thought he must, from the odd expression on his face—but if not, it was no place of hers to be revealing Lord John's secrets.

"Have you met him?" she asked curiously. Ian had gone with her parents to rescue Roger from the Iroquois, before Lord John had appeared at her aunt's plantation, where she had met the nobleman herself.

"Oh, aye." He was still looking wary, though he had relaxed a little. "Some years ago. Him and his . . . son. Stepson, I mean.

They came to the Ridge, traveling through to Virginia, and stopped a bit. I gave him the measle." He grinned, quite suddenly. "Or at least he *had* the measle. Auntie Claire nursed him through it. Ye've met the man yourself, though?"

"Yes, at River Run. Ian, the fish is on fire."

It was, and he snatched the stick from the flames with a small Gaelic exclamation, waving scorched fingers to cool them. Extinguished in the grass, the fish proved to be quite edible, if a little crispy round the edges, and a tolerably good supper, with the addition of bread and beer.

"Did ye meet Lord John's son, then, at River Run?" he asked, resuming their conversation. "Willie, his name is. A nice wee lad. He fell into the privy," he added thoughtfully.

"Fell in the privy?" she said, laughing. "He sounds like an idiot. Or was he just quite small?"

"No, a decent size for his age. And sensible enough, for an Englishman. See, it wasna quite his fault, ken. We were looking at a snake, and it came up the branch toward us, and . . . well, it was an accident," he concluded, handing Rollo another piece of fish. "Ye've not seen the lad yourself, though?"

"No, and I think you are deliberately changing the subject."

"Aye, I am. D'ye want a bit more beer?"

She raised an eyebrow at him—he needn't think he was going to escape that easily—but nodded, accepting the jug.

They were quiet for a bit, drinking beer and watching the last of the light fade into darkness as the stars came out. The scent of the pine trees strengthened, their sap warmed from the day, and in the distance she heard the occasional gunshot warning slap of a beaver's tail on the pond—evidently the beavers had posted sentries, in case she or Rollo should sneak back after dark, she thought wryly.

Ian had wrapped his own blanket round his shoulders against the growing chill, and was lying flat in the grass, staring upward into the vault of heaven overhead.

She didn't make any pretense of not watching him, and was quite sure he was aware of it. His face was quiet for the moment, minus its usual animation—but not guarded. He was thinking, and she was content to let him take his time; it was autumn now and night would be long enough for many things.

She wished she had thought to ask her mother more about the

girl Ian called Emily—the Mohawk name was something multi-syllabic and unpronounceable. Small, her mother had said. Pretty, in a neat, small-boned sort of way, and very clever.

Was she dead, Emily the small and clever? She thought not. She'd been in this time long enough to have seen many men deal with the death of wives. They showed loss and grief—but they didn't do what Ian had been doing.

Could he be taking her to *meet* Emily? That was a staggering thought, but one she rejected almost immediately. It would be a month's journey, at least, to reach the Mohawks' territory—probably more. But then . . .

"I wondered, ken?" he said suddenly, still looking up at the sky. "D'ye feel sometimes . . . wrong?" He glanced at her helplessly, not sure whether he'd said what he meant—but she understood him perfectly.

"Yes, all the time." She felt a sense of instant, unexpected relief at the admission. He saw the slump of her shoulders, and smiled a little, crookedly.

"Well . . . maybe not *all* the time," she amended. "When I'm out in the woods, alone, it's fine. Or with Roger, by ourselves. Though even then . . ." She saw Ian's eyebrow lift, and hurried to explain. "Not that. Not being with him. It's just that we . . . we talk about what was."

He gave her a look in which sympathy was mingled with interest. Plainly, he would like to know about "what was," but put that aside for the moment.

"The woods, aye?" he said. "I see that. When I'm awake, at least. Sleeping, though . . ." He turned his face back toward the empty sky and the brightening stars.

"Are you afraid—when the dark comes on?" She'd felt that now and then; a moment of deep fear at twilight—a sense of abandonment and elemental loneliness as night rose from the earth. A feeling that sometimes remained, even when she had gone inside the cabin, the bolted door secure behind her.

"No," he said, frowning a little at her. "You are?"

"Just a little," she said, waving it away. "Not all the time. Not now. But what is it about sleeping in the woods?"

He sat up, and rocked back a little, big hands linked around one knee, thinking.

"Aye, well . . ." he said slowly. "Sometimes I think of the

auld tales—from Scotland, aye? And ones I've heard now and then, living wi' the Kahnyen'kehaka. About . . . things that may come upon a man while he sleeps. To lure away his soul."

"Things?" Despite the beauty of the stars and the peace of the evening, she felt something small and cold slide down her back. "*What* things?"

He took a deep breath and blew it out, brows puckered.

"Ye call them *sidhe* in the Gaelic. The Cherokee call them the Nunnahee. And the Mohawk have names for them, too—more than one. But when I heard Eats Turtles tell of them, I kent at once what they were. It's the same—the Old Folk."

"Fairies?" she said, and her incredulity must have been clear in her voice, for he glanced up sharply at her, a glint of irritation in his eyes.

"No, I ken what *you* mean by that—Roger Mac showed me the wee picture ye drew for Jem, all tiny things like dragonflies, prinking in the flowers. . . ." He made an uncouth noise in the back of his throat. "Nay. These things are . . ." He made a helpless gesture with one big hand, frowning at the grass.

"Vitamins," he said suddenly, looking up.

"Vitamins," she said, and rubbed a hand between her brows. It had been a long day; they had likely walked fifteen or twenty miles and fatigue had settled like water in her legs and back. The bruises from her battle with the beavers were beginning to throb.

"I see. Ian . . . are you sure that your head isn't still a bit cracked?" She said it lightly, but her real anxiety lest it be true must have shown in her voice, for he gave a low, rueful chuckle.

"No. Or at least—I dinna think so. I was only—well, d'ye see, it's like that. Ye canna see the vitamins, but you and Auntie Claire ken weel that they're there, and Uncle Jamie and I must take it on faith that ye're right about it. I ken as much about the—the Old Ones. Can ye no believe me about *that*?"

"Well, I—" She had begun to agree, for the sake of peace between them—but a feeling swept over her, sudden and cold as a cloud-shadow, that she wished to say nothing to acknowledge the notion. Not out loud. And not here.

"Oh," he said, catching sight of her face. "So ye *do* know."

"I don't *know*, no," she said. "But I don't know it's not, either. And I don't think it's a good idea to talk about things like that, in a wood at night, a million miles away from civilization. All right?"

He smiled a little at that, and nodded in acceptance.

"Aye. And it's no what I meant to say, really. It's more . . ." His feathery brows knitted in concentration. "When I was a bairn, I'd wake in my bed, and I'd ken at once where I was, aye? There was the window"—he flung out a hand—"and there was the basin and ewer on the table, wi' a blue band round the top, and *there*"—he pointed toward a laurel bush—"was the big bed where Janet and Michael were sleepin', and Jocky the dog at the bed fit, farting like a beetle, and the smell of peat smoke from the fire and . . . well, even if I should wake at midnight and the house all still around me, I should ken at once where I was."

She nodded, the memory of her own old room in the house on Furey Street rising around her, vivid as a vision in the smoke. The striped wool blanket, itchy under her chin, and the mattress with the indentation of her body in the middle, cupping her like a huge, warm hand. Angus, the stuffed Scottie with the ragged tam-o-shanter who shared her bed, and the comforting hum of her parents' conversation from the living room below, punctuated by the baritone sax of the theme music from *Perry Mason*.

Most of all, the sense of absolute security.

She had to close her eyes, and swallow twice before answering.

"Yes. I know what you mean."

"Aye. Well. For some time after I left home, I might find myself sleeping rough, wi' Uncle Jamie in the heather, or here and there in inns and pothouses. I'd wake wi' no notion where I was—and still, I'd ken I was in Scotland. It was all right." He paused, lower lip caught between his teeth as he struggled to find the right words.

"Then . . . things happened. I wasna in Scotland any longer, and home was . . . gone." His voice was soft, but she could hear the echo of loss in it.

"I would wake, with no idea where I might be—or who."

He was hunched over now, big hands hanging loose between his thighs as he gazed into the fire.

"But when I lay wi' Emily—from the first time. I knew. Kent who I was again." He looked up at her then, eyes dark and shadowed by loss. "My soul didna wander while I slept—when I slept wi' her."

"And now it does?" she asked quietly, after a moment.

He nodded, wordless. The wind whispered in the trees above. She tried to ignore it, obscurely afraid that if she listened closely, she might hear words.

"Ian," she said, and touched his arm, very lightly. "Is Emily dead?"

He sat quite still for a minute, then took a deep, shuddering breath, and shook his head.

"I dinna think so." He sounded very doubtful, though, and she could see the trouble in his face.

"Ian," she said very softly. "Come here."

He didn't move, but when she scooted close and put her arms around him, he didn't resist. She pulled him down with her, insisting that he lie beside her, his head pillowed in the curve between shoulder and breast, her arm around him.

Mother instinct, she thought, wryly amused. Whatever's wrong, the first thing you do is pick them up and cuddle them. And if they're too big to lift . . . and if his warm weight and the sound of his breathing in her ear kept the voices in the wind at bay, so much the better.

She had a fragmentary memory, a brief vivid image of her mother standing behind her father in the kitchen of their house in Boston. He lay back in a straight chair, his head against her mother's stomach, eyes closed in pain or exhaustion, as she rubbed his temples. What had it been? A headache? But her mother's face had been gentle, the lines of her own day's stress smoothed away by what she was doing.

"I feel a fool," Ian said, sounding shy—but didn't pull away.

"No, you don't."

He took a deep breath, squirmed a little, and settled cautiously into the grass, his body barely touching hers.

"Aye, well. I suppose not, then," he murmured. He relaxed by wary degrees, his head growing heavier on her shoulder, the muscles of his back yielding slowly, their tension subsiding under her hand. Very tentatively, as though expecting her to slap him away, he lifted one arm and laid it over her.

It seemed the wind had died. The firelight shone on his face, the dark dotted lines of his tattoos standing out against the young skin. His hair smelled of woodsmoke and dust, soft against her cheek.

"Tell me," she said.

He sighed, deeply.

"Not yet," he said. "When we get there, aye?"

He would not say more, and they lay together, quiet in the grass, and safe.

Brianna felt sleep come, the waves of it gentle, lifting her toward peace, and did not resist. The last thing she recalled was Ian's face, cheek heavy on her shoulder, his eyes still open, watching the fire.

Walking Elk was telling a story. It was one of his best stories, but Ian wasn't paying proper attention. He sat across the fire from Walking Elk, but it was the flames he was watching, not his friend's face.

Very odd, he thought. He'd been watching fires all his life, and never seen the woman in them, until these winter months. Of course, peat fires had no great flame to speak of, though they had a good heat and a lovely smell . . . oh. Aye, so she was there, after all, the woman. He nodded slightly, smiling. Walking Elk took this as an expression of approval at his performance and became even more dramatic in his gestures, scowling horrendously and lurching to and fro with bared teeth, growling in illustration of the glutton he had carefully tracked to its lair.

The noise distracted Ian from the fire, drawing his attention to the story again. Just in time, for Walking Elk had reached the climax, and the young men nudged each other in anticipation. Walking Elk was short and heavily built—not so much unlike a glutton himself, which made his imitations that much more entertaining.

He turned his head, wrinkling up his nose and growling through his teeth, as the glutton caught the hunter's scent. Then he changed in a flash, became the hunter, creeping carefully through the brush, pausing, squatting low—and springing upward with a sharp yelp, as his buttock encountered a thorny plant.

The men around the fire whooped as Walking Elk became the glutton, who looked at first astonished at the noise, and then thrilled to have seen its prey. It leaped from its lair, uttering growls and sharp yips of rage. The hunter fell back, horrified, and turned to run. Walking Elk's stubby legs churned the pounded earth of the longhouse, running in place. Then he threw up his arms and sprawled forward with a despairing "Ay-YIIIIII!" as the glutton struck him in the back.

The men shouted encouragement, slapping their palms on their thighs, as the beleaguered hunter managed to roll onto his back, thrashing and cursing, grappling with the glutton that sought to tear out his throat.

The firelight gleamed on the scars that decorated Walking Elk's chest and shoulders—thick white gouges that showed briefly at the gaping neck of his shirt as he writhed picturesquely, arms straining upward against his invisible enemy. Ian found himself leaning forward, his breath short and his own shoulders knotted with effort, though he knew what was coming next.

Walking Elk had done it many times, but it never failed. Ian had tried it himself, but couldn't do it at all. The hunter dug his heels and shoulders into the dirt, his body arched like a bow at full stretch. His legs trembled, his arms shook—surely they would give way at any moment. The men by the fire held their breath.

Then it came: a soft, sudden click. *Distinct and somehow muffled, it was exactly the sound made by the breaking of a neck. The snap of bone and ligament, muffled in flesh and fur. The hunter stayed arched a moment, unbelieving, and then slowly, slowly, lowered himself to the ground and sat up, staring at the body of his enemy, clutched limp in his hands.*

He cast up his eyes in prayerful thanks, then stopped, wrinkling his nose. He glanced down, face screwed into a grimace, and rubbed fastidiously at his leggings, soiled by the odorous voidings of the glutton. The hearth rocked with laughter.

A small bucket of spruce beer was making the rounds; Walking Elk beamed, his face shining with sweat, and accepted it. His short, thick throat worked industriously, sucking the sharp drink down as though it was water. He lowered the bucket at last and looked about in dreamy satisfaction.

"You, Wolf's Brother. Tell us a story!" He threw the half-empty bucket across the fire; Ian caught it, only sloshing a little over his wrist. He sucked the liquid from his sleeve, laughed, and shook his head. He took a quick mouthful of beer and passed the bucket to Sleeps with Snakes, beside him.

Eats Turtles, on his other side, poked Ian in the ribs, wanting him to talk, but he shook his head again and shrugged, jerking his chin toward Snake.

Snake, nothing loath, set the bucket neatly before him and leaned forward, the firelight dancing on his face as he began to talk. He was no actor like Walking Elk, but he was an older man—perhaps thirty—and had traveled much in his youth. He had lived with the Assiniboin and the Cayuga, and had many stories from them, which he told with great skill—if less sweat.

"Will you talk later, then?" Turtle said in Ian's ear. "I want to hear more tales of the great sea and the woman with green eyes."

Ian nodded, a little reluctant. He had been very drunk the first time, or he would never have spoken of Geillis Abernathy. It was only that they had been drinking trader's rum, and the spinning sensation it caused in his head was very like that caused by the stuff she'd given him to drink, though the taste was different. That caused a giddiness that made his eyes blur, so candle flames streaked and ran like water, and the flames of the fire seemed to overflow and leap the hearthstones, glimmering all round her lavish room, small separate blazes springing up in all the rounded surfaces of silver and glass, gems and polished wood— flickering brightest behind green eyes.

He glanced around. There were no shining surfaces here. Clay pots, rough firewood, and the smooth poles of bed frames, grinding stones and woven baskets; even the cloth and furs of their clothes were soft dull colors that drowned the light. It must have been only the memory of those times of light-glazed dizziness that had brought her to mind.

He seldom thought of the Mistress—that was how the slaves and the other boys spoke of her; she needed no more name than that, for no one could imagine another of her sort. He did not value his memories of her, but Uncle Jamie had told him not to hide from them, and he obeyed, finding it good counsel.

He stared intently into the fire, only half-hearing Snake's recounting of the story about Goose and how he had outwitted the Evil One to bring tobacco to the People and save Old Man's life. Was it her, then, the witch Geillis, that he saw in the fire?

He thought it was not. The woman in the fire gave him a warm feeling when he saw her that ran from his heated face down through his chest and curled up low and hot in his belly. The woman in the fire had no face; he saw her limbs, her curving back, a sweep of long, smooth hair, twisting toward him, gone in a flicker; he heard her laugh, soft and breathy, far away—and it was not Geillis Abernathy's laugh.

Still, Turtle's words had brought her to his mind, and he could see her there. He sighed to himself and thought what story he might tell, when it came his turn. Perhaps he would tell about Mrs. Abernathy's twin slaves, the huge black men who did her every bidding; he had once seen them kill a crocodile, and carry it up from the river between them to lay it at her feet.

He didn't mind so much. He had found—after that first drunken telling—that to speak of her in such a way caused him to think of her in the same way—as though she was a story, interesting but unreal. Perhaps she had happened, as perhaps Goose had brought tobacco to Old Man—but it did not seem so much as though she had happened to him.

And after all, he had no scars, like Walking Elk's, that would remind either his hearers or himself that he spoke truth.

In truth, he was growing bored with drinking and stories. The real truth was that he longed to escape to the furs and cool darkness of his bed platform, shed his clothes, and curl his hot nakedness around his wife. Her name meant "Works with Her Hands," but in the privacy of bed, he called her Emily.

Their time was growing short; in two moons more, she would leave, to go to the women's house, and he would not see her. Another moon before the child came, one more after that for cleansing . . . The thought of two months spent cold and alone, without her next to him at night, was enough to make him reach for the beer as it came around, and drink deep.

Only the bucket was empty. His friends giggled as he held it upside down above his open mouth, a single amber drop splattering on his surprised nose.

A small hand reached over his shoulder and took the bucket from his grasp, as its partner reached over his other shoulder, holding a full one.

He took the bucket and twisted, smiling up at her. Works with Her Hands smiled smugly back; it gave her great pleasure to anticipate his wants. She knelt behind him, the curve of her belly pressing warm against his back, and swatted away Turtle's hand as he reached for the beer.

"*No, let my husband have it! He tells much better stories when he's drunk.*"

Turtle closed one eye, fixing her with the other. He was swaying slightly.

"*Is it that he tells better stories when he's drunk?*" *he asked.* "*Or do we just* think *they're better, because* we're *drunk?*"

Works with Her Hands ignored this philosophical inquiry and proceeded to make room for herself at the hearth, swinging her solid little bum deftly back and forth like a battering ram. She settled comfortably next to Ian, folding her arms atop her mound.

Other young women had come in with her, bringing more beer. They nudged their way in among the young men, murmuring, poking, and laughing. He'd been wrong, Ian thought, watching them. The firelight shone on their faces, glanced from their teeth, caught the moist shine of eyes and the soft dark flesh inside their mouths as they laughed. The fire gleamed on their faces more than it had ever shone from the crystal and silver of Rose Hall.

"*So, husband,*" *Emily said, lowering her eyelids demurely.* "*Tell us about this woman with green eyes.*"

He took a thoughtful swallow of beer, then another.

"*Oh,*" *he said.* "*She was a witch, and a very wicked woman—but she did make good beer.*"

Emily's eyes flew open wide, and everyone laughed. He looked into her eyes and saw it, clearly; the image of the fire behind him, tiny and perfect—welcoming him in.

"*But not as good as yours,*" *he said. He lifted the bucket in salute, and drank deep.*

Brianna woke in the morning stiff and sore, but with one clear thought in mind. *Okay. I know who I am.* She had no clear idea *where* she was, but that didn't matter. She lay still for a moment, feeling oddly peaceful, despite the urge to get up and pee.

How long had it been, she wondered, since she *had* wakened alone and peaceful, with no company but her own thoughts? Really, not since she had stepped through the stones, she thought, in search of her family. And found them.

"In spades," she murmured, stretching gingerly. She groaned, staggered to her feet, and shuffled into the brush to pee and change back into her own clothes before returning to the blackened fire ring.

She unplaited her draggled hair, and began groggily combing her fingers through it. There was no sign of Ian or the dog nearby, but she wasn't concerned. The wood around her was filled with the racket of birds, but not alarm calls, just the daily business of flutter and feeding, a cheerful chatter that didn't alter when she rose. The birds had been watching her for hours; they weren't concerned, either.

She never woke easily, but the simple pleasure of not being dragged from sleep by the insistent demands of those who did made the morning air seem particularly sweet, in spite of the bitter tang of ashes from the dead fire.

Mostly awake, she wiped a handful of dew-wet poplar leaves over her face by way of a morning toilette, then squatted by the fire ring and began the chore of fire-starting. They had no coffee to boil, but Ian would be hunting. With luck, there'd be something to cook; they'd eaten everything in the knapsack, save a heel of bread.

"Heck with this," she muttered, whacking flint and steel together for the dozenth time, and seeing the spatter of sparks wink out without catching. If Ian had only told her they were camping, she would have brought her fire-striker, or some matches—though on second thought, she was not sure that would be safe. The things could easily burst into flame in her pocket.

"How did the Greeks do it?" she said aloud, scowling at the tiny mat of charred cloth on which she was attempting to catch a spark. "They must have had a way."

"The Greeks had what?"

Ian and Rollo were back, having captured, respectively, half a dozen yams and a blue-gray waterbird of some kind—a small heron? Rollo refused to allow her to look at it, and took his prey off to devour under a bush, its long, limp yellow legs dragging on the ground.

"The Greeks had what?" Ian repeated, turning out a pocket full of chestnuts, red-brown skins gleaming from the remnants of their prickly hulls.

"Had stuff called phosphorus. You ever heard of it?"

Ian looked blank, and shook his head.

"No. What is it?"

"Stuff," she said, finding no better word to hand. "Lord John sent me some, so I could make matches."

"Matches between whom?" Ian inquired, regarding her warily.

She stared at him for a moment, her morning-sodden mind making slow sense of the conversation.

"Oh," she said, having at last discovered the difficulty. "Not that kind of match. Those fire-starters I made. Phosphorus burns by itself. I'll show you, when we get home." She yawned, and gestured vaguely at the small pile of unlit kindling in the fire ring.

Ian made a tolerant Scottish noise and took up the flint and steel himself.

"I'll do it. Do the nuts, aye?"

"Okay. Here, you should put your shirt back on." Her own clothes had dried, and while she missed the comfort of Ian's buckskin, the worn thick wool of her fringed hunting shirt was warm and soft on her skin. It was a bright day, but chilly so early in the morning. Ian had discarded his blanket while starting the fire, and his bare shoulders were pebbled with gooseflesh.

He shook his head slightly, though, indicating that he'd put on his shirt in a bit. For now . . . his tongue stuck out of the corner of his mouth in concentration as he struck flint and steel again, then disappeared as he muttered something under his breath.

"What did you say?" She paused, a half-hulled nut in her fingers.

"Oh, it's no but a—" He'd struck once more and caught a spark, glowing like a tiny star on the square of char. Hastily, he touched a wisp of dry grass to it, then another, and as a tendril of smoke rose up, added a bark chip, more grass, a handful of chips, and finally a careful crisscross of pine twigs.

"No but a fire charm," he finished, grinning at her over the infant blaze that had sprung up before him.

She applauded briefly, then proceeded to cut the skin of the chestnut she was holding, crosswise, so it wouldn't burst in the fire.

"I haven't heard that one," she said. "Tell me the words."

"Oh." He didn't blush easily, but the skin of his throat darkened a little. "It's . . . it's no the Gaelic, that one. It's the Kahnyen'kehaka."

Her brows went up, as much at the easy sound of the word on his tongue as at what he'd said.

"Do you ever think in Mohawk, Ian?" she asked curiously.

He shot her a glance of surprise, almost, she thought, of fright.

"No," he said tersely, and rose off his heels. "I'll fetch a bit of wood."

"I have some," she said, holding him with a stare. She reached behind her and thrust a fallen pine bough into the kindling fire. The dry needles burst in a puff of sparks and were gone, but the ragged bark began to catch and burn at the edges.

"What is it?" she said. "What I said, about thinking in Mohawk?"

His lips pressed tight together, not wanting to answer.

"You asked me to come," she said, not sharp with him, but firm.

"So I did." He took a deep breath, then looked down at the yams he was burying in the heating ashes to bake.

She worked on the nuts slowly, watching him make up his

mind. Loud chewing sounds and intermittent puffs of blue-gray feathers drifted out from under Rollo's bush, behind him.

"Did ye dream last night, Brianna?" he asked suddenly, his eyes still on what he was doing.

She wished he had brought something coffeelike to boil, but still, she was sufficiently awake by now as to be able to think and respond coherently.

"Yes," she said. "I dream a lot."

"Aye, I ken that. Roger Mac told me ye write them down sometimes."

"He did?" That was a jolt, and one bigger than a cup of coffee. She'd never *hidden* her dreambook from Roger, but they didn't really discuss it, either. How much of it had he read?

"He didna tell me anything about them," Ian assured her, catching the tone of her voice. "Only that ye wrote things down, sometimes. So I thought, maybe, those would be important."

"Only to me," she said, but cautiously. "Why . . . ?"

"Well, d'ye see—the Kahnyen'kehaka set great store by dreams. More even than Highlanders." He glanced up with a brief smile, then back at the ashes where he had buried the yams. "What did ye dream of last night, then?"

"Birds," she said, trying to recall. "Lots of birds." Reasonable enough, she thought. The forest around her had been live with birdsong since well before dawn; of course it would seep into her dreams.

"Aye?" Ian seemed interested. "Were the birds alive, then?"

"Yes," she said, puzzled. "Why?"

He nodded, and picked up a chestnut to help her.

"That's good, to dream of live birds, especially if they sing. Dead birds are a bad thing, in a dream."

"They were definitely alive, and singing," she assured him, with a glance up at the branch above him, where some bird with a bright yellow breast and black wings had lighted, viewing their breakfast preparations with interest.

"Did any of them talk to ye?"

She stared at him, but he was clearly serious. And after all, she thought, why *wouldn't* a bird talk to you, in a dream?

She shook her head, though.

"No. They were—oh." She laughed, unexpectedly recalling. "They were building a nest out of toilet paper. I dream about toilet paper all the time. That's a thin, soft kind of paper that you use to wipe your, er, behind with," she explained, seeing his incomprehension.

"Ye wipe your arse with *paper*?" He stared at her, jaw dropped in horror. "Jesus God, Brianna!"

"Well." She rubbed a hand under her nose, trying not to laugh at his expression. He might well be horrified; there were no paper mills in the Colonies, and aside from tiny amounts of handmade paper such as she made herself, every sheet had to be imported from England. Paper was hoarded and treasured; her father, who wrote frequently to his sister in Scotland, would write a letter in the normal fashion—but then would turn the paper sideways, and write additional lines perpendicularly, to save space. Little wonder that Ian was shocked!

"It's very cheap then," she assured him. "Really."

"Not as cheap as a cob o' maize, I'll warrant," he said, narrow-eyed with suspicion.

"Believe it or not, most people then won't have cornfields to hand," she said, still amused. "And I tell you what, Ian—toilet paper is *much* nicer than a dry corncob."

"'Nicer,'" he muttered, obviously still shaken to the core. "Nicer. Jesus, Mary, and Bride!"

"You were asking me about dreams," she reminded him. "Did you dream last night?"

"Oh. Ah . . . no." He turned his attention from the scandalous notion of toilet paper with some difficulty. "Or at least if I did, I dinna recall it."

It came to her suddenly, looking at his hollowed face, that one reason for his sleeplessness might be that he was afraid of what dreams might come to him.

In fact, he seemed afraid now that she might press him on the subject. Not meeting her eye, he picked up the empty beer jug and clicked his tongue for Rollo, who followed him, blue-gray feathers sticking to his jaws.

She had cut the last of the chestnut skins and buried the gleaming marrons in the ashes to bake with the yams, by the time he came back.

"Just in time," she called, seeing him. "The yams are ready."

"Just in time, forbye," he answered, smiling. "See what I've got?"

What he had was a chunk of honeycomb, thieved from a bee tree and still chilled enough that the honey ran slow and thick, drizzled over the hot yams in glorious blobs of gold sweetness. Garnished with roasted, peeled, sweet chestnuts and washed down with cold creek water, she thought it was possibly the best breakfast she'd eaten since leaving her own time.

She said as much, and Ian lifted one feathery brow in derision.

"Oh, aye? And what would ye eat then that's better?"

"Oooh . . . chocolate donuts, maybe. Or hot chocolate, with marshmallows in it. I really miss chocolate." Though it was hard to miss it much at the moment, licking honey off her fingers.

"Och, get on wi' ye! I've had chocolate." He squinched his eyes and pinched his lips in exaggerated distaste. "Bitter, nasty stuff. Though they did charge a terrible lot of money just for a wee cup of it, in Edinburgh," he added practically, unsquinching.

She laughed.

"They put sugar in it, where I come from," she assured him. "It's sweet."

"Sugar in your chocolate? That's the most decadent thing I've ever heard of," he said severely. "Even worse than the arse-wiping paper, aye?" She saw the teasing glint in his eye, though, and merely snorted, nibbling the last shreds of orange yam flesh from the blackened skin.

"Someday I'll get hold of some chocolate, Ian," she said, discarding the limp peel and licking her fingers like a cat. "I'll put sugar in it and feed it to you, and see what you think then!"

It was his turn to snort, good-naturedly, but he made no further remarks, concentrating instead on licking his own hands clean.

Rollo had appropriated the remnants of honeycomb, and was noisily gnawing and slurping at the wax, with complete enjoyment.

"That dog must have the digestion of a crocodile," Brianna said, shaking her head. "Is there anything he won't eat?"

"Well, I've no tried him on nails, yet." Ian smiled briefly, but didn't take up the conversation. The unease that had lain upon him when he talked of dreams had disappeared over breakfast, but seemed now to have returned. The sun was well up, but he made no move to rise. He merely sat, arms wrapped about his knees, gazing thoughtfully into the fire as the rising sun stole the light from the flames.

In no great hurry to start moving herself, Brianna waited patiently, eyes fixed on him.

"And what would you eat for breakfast when you lived with the Mohawk, Ian?"

He looked at her then, and his mouth tucked in at one corner. Not a smile, but a wry acknowledgment. He sighed, and laid his head on his knees, face hidden. He sat slumped that way for a bit, then slowly straightened up.

"Well," he said, in a matter-of-fact tone of voice. "It was to do wi' my brother-in-law. At least to start."

Ian Murray thought that before too long, he would be obliged to do something about his brother-in-law. Not that "brother-in-law" was precisely the word for it. Still, Sun Elk was the husband of Looking at the Sky, who was in turn the sister of his own wife. By the notions of the Kahnyen'kehaka this implied no relation between the men beyond that of clansmen, but Ian still thought of Sun Elk with the white part of his mind.

That was the secret part. His wife had English, but they did not speak it, even when most private. He spoke no word of Scots or English aloud, had heard not a syllable of either tongue in the year since he had chosen to stay, to become Kahnyen'kehaka. It was assumed he had forgotten what he had been. But each day he found some moment to himself, and, lest he lose the words, would silently name the objects around him, hearing their English names echo in the hidden white part of his mind.

Pot, he thought to himself, squinting at the blackened earthenware warming in the ashes. In fact he was not alone at the moment. He was, however, feeling distinctly alien.

Corn, he thought, leaning back against the polished tree trunk that formed one upright of the longhouse. Several clusters of dried maize hung above him, festively colored by comparison with the sacks of grain sold in Edinburgh—and yet *corn* nonetheless. *Onions*, he thought, eyes passing down the braided chain of yellow globes. *Bed. Furs. Fire.*

His wife leaned toward him, smiling, and the words ran suddenly together in his mind. *BlackravenblackhairshiningbreastbudsthighssoroundohyesohyesohEmily* . . .

She set a warm bowl in his hand, and the rich aroma of rabbit and corn and onion rose up into his nose. *Stew*, he thought, the slippery flow of words coming to a sudden halt as his mind focused on food. He smiled at her, and laid his hand over hers, holding it for a moment, small and sturdy under his, curved around the wooden bowl. Her smile deepened; then she pulled away, rising up to go and fetch more food.

He watched her go, appreciating the sway of her walk. Then his eye caught Sun Elk—watching, too, from the doorway of his own apartment.

Bastard, Ian thought, very clearly.

"See, we got on well enough to start," Ian explained. "He's a bonny man, for the most part, Sun Elk."

"For the most part," Brianna echoed. She sat still, watching him. "And which part was that?"

Ian rubbed a hand through his hair, making it stand up like the bushy quills on a porcupine.

"Well . . . the friend part. We *were* friends, to begin with, aye? Brothers, in fact; we were of the same clan."

"And you stopped being friends because of—of your wife?"

Ian sighed deeply.

"Well, ye see . . . the Kahnyen'kehaka, they've a notion of marriage that—it's like what ye see in the Highlands, often enough. That is, the parents have a good deal to do wi' arranging it. Often enough, they've watched the weans as they grew, and seen if maybe there was a lad and a lassie that seemed well-matched. And if they were—and if they came from the proper clans—now, that bit's different, see?" he added, breaking off.

"The clans?"

"Aye. In the Highlands, ye'd mostly marry within your own clan, save it was to make an alliance wi' another. Among the Iroquois nations, though, ye canna ever marry someone from your own clan, and ye can only marry someone from particular clans, not just any other."

"Mama said the Iroquois reminded her a lot of Highlanders," Brianna said, mildly amused. "Ruthless, but entertaining, was how she put it, I think. Bar some of the torturing, maybe, and the burning your enemies alive."

"Your mother's no heard some of Uncle Jamie's stories about his grandsire, then," he replied with a wry smile.

"What, Lord Lovat?"

"No, the other—*Seaumais Ruaidh*—Red Jacob, him Uncle Jamie's named for. A wicked auld bugger, my Mam always said; he'd put any Iroquois to shame for pure cruelty, from all I've heard of him." He dismissed this tangent with a wave of the hand, though, returning to his explanation.

"Well, so, when the Kahnyen'kehaka took me, and named me, I was adopted to the Wolf clan, aye?" he said, with an explanatory nod at Rollo, who had consumed the honeycomb, dead bees and all, and was now meditatively licking his paws.

"Very appropriate," she murmured. "What clan was Sun Elk?"

"Wolf, of course. And Emily's mother and grandmother and sisters were Turtle. But what I was saying—if a lad and lassie from properly different clans seemed maybe suited to each other, then the mothers would speak—they call all the aunties 'mother,' too," he added. "So there might be a good many mothers involved in the matter. But if all the mothers and grandmothers and aunties were to agree that it would be a good match . . ." He shrugged. "They'd marry."

Brianna rocked back a little, arms around her knees.

"But you didn't have a mother to speak for you."

"Well, I did wonder what my Mam would ha' said, if she'd been there," he said, and smiled, despite his seriousness.

Brianna, having met Ian's mother, laughed at the thought.

"Aunt Jenny would be a match for any Mohawk, male *or* female," she assured him. "But what happened, then?"

"I loved Emily," he said very simply. "And she loved me."

This state of affairs, which rapidly became apparent to everyone in the village, caused considerable public comment. Wakyo'teyehsnonhsa, Works with Her Hands, the girl Ian called Emily, had been widely expected to marry Sun Elk, who had been a visitor to her family's hearth since childhood.

"But there it was." Ian spread his hands and shrugged. "She loved me, and she said so."

When Ian had been taken into the Wolf clan, he had been given to foster parents, as well—the parents of the dead man in whose stead he had been adopted. His foster mother had been somewhat taken aback by the situation, but after discussing the matter with the other women of the Wolf clan, had gone to speak formally with Tewaktenyonh, Emily's grandmother—and the most influential woman in the village.

"And so we married." Dressed in their best, and accompanied by their parents, the two young people had sat together on a bench before the assembled people of the village, and exchanged baskets—his containing the furs of sable and beaver, and a good knife, symbolizing his willingness to hunt for her and protect her; hers filled with grain and fruit and vegetables, symbolizing her willingness to plant, gather, and provide for him.

"And four moons later," Ian added, "Sun Elk wed Looking at the Sky, Emily's sister."

Brianna raised one eyebrow.

"But . . . ?"

"Aye, but."

Ian had the gun Jamie had left with him, a rare and valued item among the Indians, and he knew how to use it. He also knew how to track, to lie in ambush, to think like an animal—other things of value that Uncle Jamie had left with him.

In consequence, he was a good hunter, and rapidly gained respect for his ability to bring in meat. Sun Elk was a decent hunter—not the best, but capable. Many of the young men would joke and make remarks, denigrating each other's skills and making fun; he did it himself. Still, there was a tone to Sun Elk's jests to Ian that now and then made one of the other men glance sharply at him, then away with the faintest of shrugs.

He had been inclined to ignore the man. Then he had seen Sun Elk look at Wakyo'teyehsnonhsa, and everything became at once clear to him.

She had been going to the forest with some other girls, one day in late summer. They carried baskets for gathering; Wakyo'teyehsnonhsa had an ax through her belt. One of the other girls had asked her whether she meant to find wood for another bowl like the one she had made for her mother; Works With Her Hands had said—with a quick, warm look toward Ian, who lounged nearby with the other young men—that no, she wished to find a good red cedar, for wood to make a cradleboard.

The girls had giggled and embraced Wakyo'teyehsnonhsa; the young men had grinned and prodded Ian knowingly in the ribs. And Ian had caught a glimpse of Sun Elk's face, hot eyes fixed on Emily's straight back as she walked away.

Within one moon, Sun Elk had moved into the longhouse, husband to his wife's sister, Looking at the Sky. The sisters' compartments were across from each other; they shared a hearth. Ian had seldom seen Sun Elk look at Emily again—but he had seen him look carefully away, too many times.

"There is a person who desires you," he said to Emily one night. It was long past the hour of the wolf, deep night, and the longhouse slept around them. The child she carried obliged her to rise and make water; she had come back to their furs skin-chilled and with the fresh smell of pines in her hair.

"Oh? Well, why not? Everyone else is asleep." She had stretched luxuriously and kissed him, the small bulge of her belly smooth and hard against his.

"Not me. I mean—of course this person desires you, too!" he'd said hastily, as she drew back a bit, offended. He wrapped his arms about her in quick illustration. "I mean—there is someone else."

"Hmf." Her voice was muffled, her breath warm against his chest. "There are many who desire me. I am very, very good with my hands." She gave him a brief demonstration, and he gasped, causing her to chuckle with satisfaction.

Rollo, who had accompanied her outside, crawled under the bed platform and curled up in his accustomed spot, chewing noisily at an itching spot near his tail.

A little later, they lay with the furs thrown back. The hide that hung over their doorway was pulled back, so the heat of the fire could come in, and he could see the shine of light on the moist gold skin of her shoulder, where she lay turned away from him. She reached back and put one of her clever hands on his, took his palm, and pressed it against her belly. The child inside had begun to stir; he felt a soft, sudden push against his palm, and his breath stilled in his throat.

"You shouldn't worry," Emily said very softly. "This person desires only you."

He had slept well.

In the morning, though, he had sat by the hearth eating corn-meal mush, and Sun Elk, who had already eaten, walked by. He stopped and looked down at Ian.

"This person dreamed about you, Wolf's Brother."

"Did you?" Ian said pleasantly. He felt the warmth rise up his throat, but kept his face relaxed. The Kahyen'kehaka set great store by dreams. A good dream would have everyone in the longhouse discussing it for days. The look on Sun Elk's face didn't indicate that his dream about Ian had been a good one.

"That dog—" He nodded at Rollo, who lay sprawled inconveniently in the doorway of Ian's compartment, snoring. "I dreamed that it rose up over your couch, and seized you by the throat."

That was a menacing dream. A Kahnyen'kehaka who believed such a dream might decide to kill the dog, lest it be a foretelling of ill fortune. But Ian was not—not quite—Kahnyen'kehaka.

Ian raised both brows, and went on eating. Sun Elk waited for a moment, but as Ian said nothing, eventually nodded and turned away.

"Ahkote'ohskennonton," Ian said, calling his name. The man turned back, expectant.

"This person dreamed of you, too." Sun Elk glanced sharply at him. Ian didn't speak further, but let a slow and evil smile grow upon his face.

Sun Elk stared at him. He kept smiling. The other man turned away with a snort of disgust, but not before Ian had seen the faint look of unease in Sun Elk's eyes.

"Well, so." Ian took a deep breath. He closed his eyes briefly, then opened them. "Ye ken the child died, aye?"

He spoke with no emotion at all in his voice. It was that dry, controlled tone that seared her heart, and choked her so that she could do no more than nod in reply.

He couldn't keep it up, though. He opened his mouth as though to speak, but the big, bony hands clenched suddenly on his knees, and instead, he rose abruptly to his feet.

"Aye," he said. "Let's go. I'll—I'll tell ye the rest, walking."

And he did, his back resolutely turned, as he led her higher up the mountain, then across a narrow ridge, and down the path of a stream that fell in a series of small, enchanting waterfalls, each encircled with a mist of miniature rainbows.

Works with Her Hands had conceived again. That child was lost just after her belly began to swell with life.

"They say, the Kahnyen'kehaka," Ian explained, his voice muffled as he shoved his way through a screen of brilliant red creeper, "that for a woman to conceive, her husband's spirit does battle with hers, and must overcome it. If his spirit isna strong enough"—his voice came clear as he ripped a handful of creeper down, breaking the branch it hung from, and cast it viciously away—"then the child canna take root in the womb."

After this second loss, the Medicine Society had taken the two of them to a private hut, there to sing and beat drums and to dance in huge painted masks, meant to frighten away whatever evil entities might be hampering Ian's spirit—or unduly strengthening Emily's.

"I wanted to laugh, seeing the masks," Ian said. He didn't turn round; yellow leaves spangled the shoulders of his buckskin and stuck in his hair. "They call it the Funny-Face Society, too—and for a reason. Didna do it, though."

"I don't . . . suppose Em-Emily laughed." He was going so fast that she was pressed to keep up with him, though her legs were nearly as long as his own.

"No," he said, and uttered a short, bitter laugh himself. "She didna."

She had gone into the medicine hut beside him silent and gray, but had come out with a peaceful face, and reached for him in their bed that night with love. For three months, they had made love with tenderness and ardor. For another three, they had made love with a sense of increasing desperation.

"And then she missed her courses again."

He had at once ceased his attentions, terrified of causing a further mishap. Emily had moved slowly and carefully, no longer going into the fields to work, but staying in the longhouse, working, always working, with her hands. Weaving, grinding, carving, boring beads of shell for wampum, hands moving ceaselessly, to compensate for the waiting stillness of her body.

"Her sister went to the fields. It's the women who do, ken?" He paused to slash an outreaching brier with his knife, tossing the severed branch out of the way so it wouldn't snap back and hit Brianna in the face.

"Looking at the Sky brought us food. All the women did, but her most of all. She was a sweet lass, Karònya."

There was a slight catch in his voice at this, the first in his harsh recitation of facts.

"What happened to her?" Brianna hastened her step a little as they came out onto the top of a grass-covered bank, so that she drew up nearly even with him. He slowed a little, but didn't turn to look at her—kept his face forward, chin raised as though confronting enemies.

"Taken." Looking at the Sky had been in the habit of staying later in the fields than the other women, gathering extra corn or squash for her sister and Ian, though she had a child of her own by then. One evening, she did not return to the longhouse, and when the villagers had gone out to search for her, neither she nor the child was anywhere to be found. They had vanished, leaving only one pale moccasin behind, tangled in the squash vines at the edge of a field.

"Abenaki," Ian said tersely. "We found the sign next day; it was full dark before we began to search in earnest."

It had been a long night searching, followed by a week of the same—a week of growing fear and emptiness—and Ian had returned to his wife's hearth at dawn on the seventh day, to learn that she had miscarried once more.

He paused. He was sweating freely from walking so fast, and wiped a sleeve across his chin. Brianna could feel the sweat trickling down her own back, dampening the hunting shirt, but disregarded it. She touched his back, very gently, but said nothing.

He heaved a deep sigh, almost of relief, she thought—perhaps that the dreadful tale was nearly done.

"We tried a bit longer," he said, back to the matter-of-fact tone. "Emily and I. But the heart had gone out of her. She didna trust me any longer. And . . . Ahkote'ohskennonton was there. He ate at our hearth. And he watched her. She began to look back."

Ian had been shaping wood for a bow one day, concentrating on the flow of the grain beneath his knife, trying to see those things in the swirls that Emily saw, to hear the voice of the tree, as she had told him. It wasn't the tree that spoke behind him, though.

"Grandson," said a dry old voice, lightly ironic.

He dropped the knife, narrowly missing his own foot, and swung round, bow in hand. Tewaktenyonh stood six feet away, one eyebrow lifted in amusement at having sneaked up on him unheard.

"Grandmother," he said, and nodded in wry acknowledgment of her skill. Ancient she might be, but no one moved more softly. Hence her reputation; the children of the village lived in respectful dread of her, having heard that she could vanish into air, only to rematerialize in some distant spot, right before the guilty eyes of evil-doers.

"Come with me, Wolf's Brother," she said, and turned away, not waiting for his response. None was expected.

She was already out of sight by the time he had laid the half-made bow under a bush, taken up his fallen knife, and whistled for Rollo, but he caught her up with no difficulty.

She had led him away from the village, through the forest, to the head of a deer trail. There she had given him a bag of salt and an armlet of wampum and bade him go.

"And you went?" Brianna asked, after a long moment of silence. "Just—like that?"

"Just like that," he said, and looked at her for the first time since they had left their campsite that morning. His face was gaunt, hollow with memories. Sweat gleamed on his cheekbones, but he was so pale that the dotted lines of his tattoos stood out sharp—perforations, lines along which his face might come apart.

She swallowed a few times before she could speak, but managed a tone much like his own when she did.

"Is it much farther?" she asked. "Where we're going?"

"No," he said softly. "We're nearly there." And turned to walk again before her.

Half an hour later, they had reached a place where the stream cut deep between its banks, widening into a small gorge. Silver birch and hobblebush grew thick, sprouting from the rocky walls, smooth-skinned roots twisting through the stones like fingers clawing at the earth.

The notion gave Brianna a slight prickle at the neck. The

waterfalls were far above them now, and the noise of the water had lessened, the creek talking to itself as it purled over rocks and shushed through mats of cress and duckweed.

She thought the going might be easier above, on the lip of the gorge, but Ian led her down into it without hesitation, and she followed likewise, scrambling over the tumble of boulders and tree roots, hampered by her long gun. Rollo, scorning this clumsy exertion, plunged into the creek, which was several feet deep, and swam, ears clamped back against his head so that he looked like a giant otter.

Ian had recovered his self-possession in the concentration of navigating the rough ground. He paused now and then, reaching back to help her down a particularly tricky fall of rock, or over a tree uprooted in some recent flood—but he didn't meet her eyes, and the shuttered planes of his face gave nothing away.

Her curiosity had reached fever pitch, but clearly he had done speaking for the moment. It was just past midday, but the light under the birches was a shadowed gold that made everything seem somehow hushed, almost enchanted. She could make no sensible guess as to the purpose of this expedition, in light of what Ian had told her—but the place was one where almost anything seemed possible.

She thought suddenly of her first father—of Frank Randall—and felt a small, remembered warmth at the thought. She would like so much to show him this place.

They had taken holidays often in the Adirondacks; different mountains, different trees—but something of the same hush and mystery in the shadowed glades and rushing water. Her mother had come sometimes, but more often it was just the two of them, hiking far up into the trees, not talking much, but sharing a deep content in the company of the sky.

Suddenly, the sound of the water rose again; there was another fall nearby.

"Just here, coz," Ian said softly, and beckoned her to follow with a turn of the head.

They stepped out from under the trees and she saw that the gorge dropped suddenly away, the water falling twenty feet or more into a pool below. Ian led her past the head of the falls; she could hear the water rushing past below, but the top of the bank was thick with sedges, and they had to push their way through, tramping down the yellowing stems of goldenrod and dodging the panicked whir of grasshoppers rocketing up underfoot.

"Look," Ian said, glancing back, and reached to part the screen of laurel in front of her.

"Wow!"

She recognized it immediately. There was no mistaking it, in spite of the fact that much of it was invisible, still buried in the crumbling bank on the far side of the gorge. Some recent flood had raised the level of the creek, undercutting the bank so that a huge block of stone and dirt had fallen away, revealing its buried mystery.

The raked arches of ribs rose huge from the dirt, and she had the impression of a scatter of things half-buried in the rubble at the foot of the bank: enormous things, knobbed and twisted. They might be bones or simply boulders—but it was the tusk that caught her eye, jutting from the bank in a massive curve, intensely familiar, and the more startling for its very familiarity.

"Ye ken it?" Ian asked eagerly, watching her face. "Ye've seen something like it?"

"Oh, yes," she said, and though the sun was warm on her back, she shivered, gooseflesh pebbling her forearms. Not from fear, but sheer awe at sight of it, and a kind of incredulous joy. "Oh, yes. I have."

"What?" Ian's voice was still pitched low, as though the creature might hear them. "What is it?"

"A mammoth," she said, and found that she was whispering, too. The sun had passed its zenith; already the bottom of the creekbed lay in shadow. Light struck the stained curve of ancient ivory, and threw the vault of the high-crowned skull that held it into sharp relief. The skull was fixed in the soil at a slight angle, the single visible tusk rising high, the eye socket black as mystery.

The shiver came again, and she hunched her shoulders. Easy to feel that it might at any moment wrench itself free of the clay and turn that massive head toward them, empty-eyed, clods of dirt raining from tusks and bony shoulders as it shook itself and began to walk, the ground vibrating as long toes struck and sank in the muddy soil.

"That's what it's called—mammoth? Aye, well . . . it *is* verra big." Ian's voice dispelled the illusion of incipient movement, and she was able finally to take her eyes off it—though she felt she must glance back, every second or so, to be sure it was still there.

"The Latin name is *Mammuthus*," she said, clearing her throat. "There's a complete skeleton in a museum in New York. I've seen it often. And I've seen pictures of them in books." She glanced back at the creature in the bank.

"A museum? So it's not a thing ye've got where—when"—he stumbled a bit—"where ye come from? Not alive then, I mean?" He seemed rather disappointed.

She wanted to laugh at the picture of mammoths roaming Boston Common, or wallowing on the bank of the Cambridge River. In fact, she had a moment's pang of disappointment that they *hadn't* been there; it would have been so wonderful to see them.

"No," she said regretfully. "They all died thousands and thousands of years ago. When the ice came."

"Ice?" Ian was glancing back and forth between her and the mammoth, as though afraid one or the other might do something untoward.

"The Ice Age. The world got colder, and sheets of ice spread down from the north. A lot of animals went extinct—I mean, they couldn't find food, and all died."

Ian was pale with excitement.

"Aye. Aye, I've heard such stories."

"You have?" She was surprised at that.

"Aye. But ye say it's real." He swung his head to look at the mammoth's bones once more. "An animal, aye, like a bear or a possum?"

"Yes," she said, puzzled by his attitude, which seemed to alternate between eagerness and dismay. "Bigger, but yes. What else would it be?"

"Ah," he said, and took a deep breath. "Well, d'ye see, that's what I needed ye to tell me, coz. See, the Kahnyen'kehaka—they have stories of . . . things. Animals that are really spirits. And if ever I saw a thing that might *be* a spirit—" He was still looking at the skeleton, as though it might walk out of the earth, and she saw a slight shiver pass through him.

She couldn't prevent a similar shiver, looking at the massive creature. It towered above them, grim and awful, and only her knowledge of what it was kept her from wanting to cower and run.

"It's real," she repeated, as much to reassure herself as him. "And it's dead. *Really* dead."

"How d'ye know these things?" he asked, intently curious. "It's auld, ye say. You'd be much further away from—that"—he jerked his chin at the giant skeleton—"in your own time than we are now. How can ye ken more about it than folk do now?"

She shook her head, smiling a little, and helpless to explain. "When did you find this, Ian?"

"Last month. I came up the gorge"—he gestured with his chin—"and there it was. I near beshit myself."

"I can imagine," she said, stifling an urge to laugh.

"Aye," he said, not noticing her amusement in his desire to explain. "I should have been sure that it was Rawenniyo—a spirit, a god—save for the dog."

Rollo had climbed out of the stream, and having shaken the water from his fur, was squirming on his back in a patch of crushed turtlehead, tail wagging in pleasure, and clearly oblivious to the silent giant in the cliff above.

"What do you mean? That Rollo wasn't afraid of it?"

Ian nodded.

"Aye. He didna behave as though there were anything there at all. And yet . . ." He hesitated, darting a glance at her. "Sometimes, in the wood. He—he *sees* things. Things I canna see. Ken?"

"I ken," she said, a ripple of unease returning. "Dogs do see . . . things." She remembered her own dogs; in particular, Smoky, the big Newfoundland, who would sometimes in the evening suddenly raise his head, listening, hackles rising as his eyes followed . . . something . . . that passed through the room and disappeared.

He nodded, relieved that she knew what he was talking about.

"They do. I ran, when I saw that"—he nodded at the cliff—"and ducked behind a tree. But the dog went on about his business, paying it no mind. And so I thought, well, just maybe it's no what I think, after all."

"And what did you think?" she asked. "A Rawenniyo, you said?" As the excitement of seeing the mammoth began to recede, she remembered what they were theoretically doing here. "Ian— you said what you wanted to show me had to do with your wife. Is this—" She gestured toward the cliff, brows raised.

He didn't answer directly, but tilted his head back, studying the jut of the giant tusks.

"I heard stories, now and then. Among the Mohawk, I mean. They'd speak of strange things that someone found, hunting. Spirits trapped in the rock, and how they came to be there. Evil things, for the most part. And I thought to myself, if that should be what this is . . ."

He broke off and turned to her, serious and intent.

"I needed ye to tell me, aye? Whether that's what it is or no. Because if it was, then perhaps what I've been thinking is wrong."

"It's not," she assured him. "But what on earth have you been thinking?"

"About God," he said, surprising her again. He licked his lips, unsure how to go on.

"Yeksa'a—the child. I didna have her christened," he said. "I couldna. Or perhaps I could—ye can do it yourself, ken, if there's no priest. But I hadna the courage to try. I—never saw her. They'd wrapped her already. . . . They wouldna have liked it, if I'd tried to . . ." His voice died away.

"Yeksa'a," she said softly. "Was that your—your daughter's name?"

He shook his head, his mouth twisting wryly.

"It only means 'wee girl.' The Kahnyen'kehaka dinna give a name to a child when it's born. Not until later. If . . ." His voice trailed off, and he cleared his throat. "If it lives. They wouldna think of naming a child unborn."

"But you did?" she asked gently.

He raised his head and took a breath that had a damp sound to it, like wet bandages pulled from a fresh wound.

"Iseabail," he said, and she knew it was the first—perhaps would be the only—time he'd spoken it aloud. "Had it been a son, I would ha' called him Jamie." He glanced at her, with the shadow of a smile. "Only in my head, ken."

He let out all his breath then with a sigh and put his face down upon his knees, back hunched.

"What I am thinking," he said after a moment, his voice much too controlled, "is this. Was it me?"

"Ian! You mean your fault that the baby died? How could it be?"

"I left," he said simply, straightening up. "Turned away. Stopped being a Christian, being Scots. They took me to the stream, scrubbed me wi' sand to take away the white blood. They gave me my name—Okwaho'kenha—and said I was Mohawk. But I wasna, not really."

He sighed deeply again, and she put a hand on his back, feeling the bumps of his backbone press through the leather of his shirt. He didn't eat nearly enough, she thought.

"But I wasna what I had been, either," he went on, sounding almost matter-of-fact. "I tried to be what they wanted, ken? So I left off praying to God or the Virgin Mother, or Saint Bride. I listened to what Emily said, when she'd tell me about *her* gods, the spirits that dwell in the trees and all. And when I went to the sweat lodge wi' the men, or sat by the hearth and heard the stories . . . they seemed as real to me as Christ and His saints ever had."

He turned his head and looked up at her suddenly, half-bewildered, half-defiant.

"I am the Lord thy God," he said. *"Thou shalt have no other gods before me.* But I did, no? That's mortal sin, is it not?"

She wanted to say no, of course not. Or to protest weakly that she was not a priest, how could she say? But neither of those would do; he was not looking for easy reassurance, and a weak-minded abnegation of responsibility would not serve him.

She took a deep breath and blew it out. It had been a good many years since she'd been taught the Baltimore Catechism, but it wasn't the sort of thing you forget.

"The conditions of mortal sin are these," she said, reciting the words precisely from memory. "First, that the action be grievously wrong. Secondly, that you know the action is wrong. And thirdly—that you give full consent to it."

He was watching her intently.

"Well, it was wrong, and I suppose I kent that—aye, I *did* ken that. Especially—" His face darkened further, and she wondered what he was recalling.

"But . . . how should I serve a God who would take a child for her father's sins?" Without waiting for an answer, he glanced toward the cliff face, where the remains of the mammoth lay frozen in time. "Or was it them? Was it not my God at all, but the Iroquois spirits? Did they ken I wasna really Mohawk—that I held back a part of myself from them?"

He looked back at her, dead serious.

"Gods are jealous, are they no?"

"Ian . . ." She swallowed, helpless. But she had to say something.

"What you did—or didn't do—that wasn't wrong, Ian," she said firmly. "Your daughter . . . she was half-Mohawk. It wasn't wrong to let her be buried according to her mother's ways. Your wife—Emily—she would have been terribly upset, wouldn't she, if you'd insisted on baptizing the baby?"

"Aye, maybe. But . . ." He closed his eyes, hands clenched hard into fists on his thighs. "Where is she, then?" he whispered, and she could see tears trembling on his lashes. "The others—they were never born; God will have them in His hand. But wee Iseabail—she'll not be in heaven, will she? I canna bear the thought that she—that she might be . . . lost, somewhere. Wandering."

"Ian . . ."

"I hear her, greeting. In the night." His breath was coming in deep, sobbing gasps. "I canna help, I canna find her!"

"Ian!" The tears were running down her own cheeks. She gripped his wrists fiercely, squeezed as hard as she could. "Ian, listen to me!"

He drew a deep, trembling breath, head bent. Then he nodded, very slightly.

She rose onto her knees and gathered him tight against her, his head cradled on her breasts. Her cheek pressed against the top of his head, his hair warm and springy against her mouth.

"Listen to me," she said softly. "I had another father. The man who raised me. He's dead now." For a long time now, the sense of desolation at his loss had been muted, softened by new love, distracted by new obligations. Now it swept over her, newly fresh, and sharp as a stab wound in its agony. "I know—I know he's in heaven."

Was he? Could he be dead and in heaven, if not yet born? And yet he was dead to her, and surely heaven took no heed of time.

She lifted her face toward the cliff, but spoke to neither bones nor God.

"Daddy," she said, and her voice broke on the word, but she held her cousin hard. "Daddy, I need you." Her voice sounded small, and pathetically unsure. But there was no other help to be had.

"I need you to find Ian's little girl," she said, as firmly as she could, trying to summon her father's face, to see him there among the shifting leaves at the clifftop. "Find her, please. Hold her in your arms, and make sure that she's safe. Take—please take care of her."

She stopped, feeling obscurely that she should say something else, something more ceremonious. Make the sign of the cross? Say "amen"?

"Thank you, Daddy," she said softly, and cried as though her father were newly dead, and she bereft, orphaned, lost, and crying in the night. Ian's arms were wrapped around her, and they clung tight together, squeezing hard, the warmth of the late sun heavy on their heads.

She stood still within his arms when she stopped crying, her head resting on his shoulder. He patted her back, very gently, but didn't push her away.

"Thank you," he whispered in her ear. "Are ye all right, Brianna?"

"Uh-huh." She straightened and stood away from him, swaying a little, as though she were drunk. She felt drunk, too, her bones gone soft and malleable, everything around her faintly out of focus, save for certain things that caught her eye: a brilliant patch of pink lady's slipper, a stone fallen from the cliff face, its surface streaked red with iron. Rollo, almost sitting on Ian's foot, big head pressed anxiously against his master's thigh.

"Are *you* all right, Ian?" she asked.

"I will be." His hand sought Rollo's head, and gave the pointed ears a cursory rub of reassurance. "Maybe. Just . . ."

"What?"

"Are ye . . . are ye sure, Brianna?"

She knew what he was asking; it was a question of faith. She drew herself up to her full height, wiping her nose on her sleeve.

"I'm a Roman Catholic and I believe in vitamins," she declared stoutly. "And I knew my father. Of course I'm sure."

He took a deep, sighing breath and his shoulders slumped as he let it out. He nodded then, and the lines of his face relaxed a little.

She left him sitting on a rock, and made her way down to the stream to splash cold water on her face. The shadow of the cliff fell across the creek and the air was cold with the scents of earth and pine trees. In spite of the chill, she remained there for a while, on her knees.

She could still hear the voices murmuring in trees and water, but paid no attention to them. Whoever they were, they were no threat to her or hers—and not at odds with the presence that she felt so strongly nearby.

"I love you, Daddy," she whispered, closing her eyes, and felt at peace.

Ian must be better, too, she thought, when she made her way at length back through the rocks to where he sat. Rollo had left him to investigate a promising hole at the foot of a tree, and she knew the dog wouldn't have left Ian, had he considered his master to be in distress.

She was about to ask him whether their business here was complete, when he stood up, and she saw that it wasn't.

"Why I brought ye here," he said abruptly. "I wanted to know about that—" He nodded at the mammoth. "But I meant to ask ye a question. Advice, like."

"Advice? Ian, I can't give you any advice! How could I tell you what to do?"

"I think ye're maybe the only one who can," he said with a lop-sided smile. "You're my family, you're a woman—and ye care for me. Yet ye ken more even than Uncle Jamie, perhaps, because of who or what"—his mouth twisted a little—"ye are."

"I don't know more," she said, and looked up at the bones in the rock. "Only—different things."

"Aye," he said, and took a deep breath.

"Brianna," he said very softly. "We're no wed—we never shall be." He looked away for an instant, then back. "But if we *had* been marrit, I should have loved ye and cared for ye, so well as I could. I trust you, that ye'd have done the same by me. Am I right?"

"Oh, Ian." Her throat was still thick, raspy with grief; the words came out in a whisper. She touched his face, cool-skinned and bony, and traced the line of tattooed dots with a thumb. "I love you now."

"Aye, well," he said still softly. "I ken that." He lifted a hand and put it over her own, big and hard. He pressed her palm against his cheek for a moment, then his fingers closed over hers and he brought their linked hands down, but didn't let go.

"So tell me," he said, his eyes not leaving hers. "If ye love me, tell me what I shall do. Shall I go back?"

"Back," she repeated, searching his face. "Back to the Mohawk, you mean?"

He nodded.

"Back to Emily. She loved me," he said quietly. "I ken that. Did I do wrong, to let the old woman send me away? Ought I to go back, maybe fight for her, if I had to? Perhaps see if she would come away wi' me, back to the Ridge."

"Oh, Ian." She felt the same sense of helplessness as before, though this time it came without the burden of her own grief. But who was she to tell him anything? How could she be responsible for making that decision for him—for saying to him, stay, or go?

His eyes stayed steady on her face, though, and it came over her—she was his family. And so the responsibility lay in her hands, whether she felt adequate to it or not.

Her chest felt tight, as though she might burst if she took a deep breath. She took it anyway.

"Stay," she said.

He stood looking into her eyes for a long time, his own deep hazel, gold-flecked and serious.

"You could fight him—Ahk . . ." She fumbled for the syllables of the Mohawk name. "Sun Elk. But you can't fight her. If she's made up her mind that she doesn't want to be with you anymore . . . Ian, you can't change it."

He blinked, dark lashes cutting off his gaze, and kept his eyes closed, whether in acknowledgement or denial of what she'd said, she didn't know.

"But it's more than that," she said, her voice growing firmer. "It isn't only her, *or* him. Is it?"

"No," he said. His voice sounded distant, almost uncaring, but she knew it wasn't that.

"It's them," she said more softly. "All the mothers. The grandmothers. The women. The—the children." Clan and family and tribe and nation; custom, spirit, tradition—the strands that wrapped Works with Her Hands and held her to the earth, secure. And above all, children. Those loud small voices that drowned the voices of the wood, and kept a soul from wandering through the night.

No one knew the strength of such bonds better than one who had walked the earth without them, outcast and alone. She had, and he had, and they both knew the truth.

"It's them," he echoed softly, and opened his eyes. They were dark with loss, the color of shadows in the deepest wood. "And them." He turned his head, to look upward, into the trees beyond the creek, above the bones of the mammoth that lay trapped in the earth, stripped to the sky and mute to all prayer. He turned back, raised a hand, and touched her cheek.

"I'll stay, then."

They camped for the night on the far side of the beaver pond. The litter of wood chips and debarked saplings made good kindling for their fire.

There was little to eat; no more than a hatful of bitter fox-grapes and the heel of bread, so hard by now that it had to be dunked in water to chew. It didn't matter; neither one of them was hungry, and Rollo had disappeared to hunt for himself.

They sat silently, watching the fire die down. There was no need to keep it going; the night was not cold, and they would not linger in the morning—home was too near.

At last, Ian stirred a bit, and Brianna glanced at him.

"What was your father's name?" he asked very formally.

"Frank—er . . . Franklin. Franklin Wolverton Randall."

"An Englishman, then?"

"Very," she said, smiling in spite of herself.

He nodded, murmuring "Franklin Wolverton Randall" to himself, as though to commit it to memory, then looked at her seriously.

"If ever I find myself in a church again, then, I shall light a candle to his memory."

"I expect . . . he'd like that."

He nodded, and leaned back, back braced against a longleaf pine. The ground nearby was littered with the cones; he picked up a handful and tossed them, one by one, into the fire.

"What about Lizzie?" she asked after a little while. "She's always been fond of you." To put it mildly: Lizzie had wilted and pined for weeks, when he had been lost to the Iroquois. "And now that she's not marrying Manfred . . ."

He tilted back his head, eyes closed, and rested it against the trunk of the pine.

"I've thought of it," he admitted.

"But . . . ?"

"Aye, but." He opened his eyes and gave her a wry look. "I'd ken where I was, if I woke beside her. But where I'd be is in bed wi' my wee sister. I think I'm maybe not so desperate as that. Yet," he added as an obvious afterthought.

71

Black Pudding

I was in the middle of a black pudding when Ronnie Sinclair appeared in the yard, carrying two small whisky casks. Several more were bound in a neatly corrugated cascade down his back, which made him look like some exotic form of caterpillar, balanced precariously upright in mid-pupation. It was a chilly day, but he was sweating freely from the long walk uphill—and cursing in similar vein.

"Why in the name of Bride did Himself build the frigging house up here in the godforsaken clouds?" he demanded without ceremony. "Why not where a bloody wagon could reach the yard?" He set the casks down carefully, then ducked his head through the straps of the harness to shed his wooden carapace. He sighed in relief, rubbing at his shoulders where the straps had dug.

I ignored the rhetorical questions, and kept stirring, tilting my head toward the house in invitation.

"There's fresh coffee made," I said. "And bannocks with honey, too." My own stomach recoiled slightly at the thought of eating. Once spiced, stuffed, boiled, and fried, black pudding was delicious. The earlier stages, involving as they did arm-deep manipulations in a barrel of semi-coagulated pig's blood, were substantially less appetizing.

Sinclair, though, looked happier at mention of food. He wiped a sleeve across his sweating forehead and nodded to me, turning toward the house. Then he stopped and turned back.

"Ah. I'd forgot, missus. I've a wee message for yourself, as well." He patted gingerly at his chest, then lower, probing around his ribs until he at length found what he was looking for and extracted it from the layers of his sweat-soaked clothing. He pulled out a damp wad of paper and held it out to me in expectation, ignoring the fact that my right arm was coated with blood nearly to the shoulder, and the left in scarcely better case.

"Put it in the kitchen, why don't you?" I suggested. "Himself's inside. I'll come as soon as I've got this lot sorted. Who—" I started to ask whom the letter was from, but tactfully altered this to, "Who gave it to you?" Ronnie couldn't read—though I saw no marks on the outside of the note, in any case.

"A tinker on his way to Belem's Creek handed it to me," he said. "He didna say who gave it him—only that it was for the healer."

He frowned at the wadded paper, but I saw his eyes slide sideways toward my legs. In spite of the chill, I was barefoot and stripped to my chemise and stays, no more than a smeared apron wrapped around my waist. Ronnie had been looking for a wife for some little time, and in consequence had formed the unconscious habit of appraising the physical attributes of every woman he encountered, without regard to age or availability. He noticed my noticing, and hastily jerked his gaze away.

"That was all?" I asked. "The healer? He didn't give my name?"

Sinclair rubbed a hand through thinning ginger hair, so two spikes stood up over his reddened ears, increasing his naturally sly, foxy look.

"Didna have to, did he?" Without further attempts at conversation, he disappeared into the house, in search of food and Jamie, leaving me to my sanguinary labors.

The worst part was cleaning the blood: swishing an arm through the dark, reeking depths of the barrel to collect the threads of fibrin that formed as the blood began to clot. These clung to my arm and could then be pulled out and rinsed away—repeatedly. At that, it was slightly less nasty than the job of washing out the intestines to be used for the sausage casings; Brianna and Lizzie were doing that, down at the creek.

I peered at the latest results; no fibers visible in the clear red liquid that dripped from my fingers. I dunked my arm again in the water cask that stood beside the blood barrel, balanced on boards laid across a pair of trestles under the big chestnut tree. Jamie and Roger and Arch Bug had dragged the pig—not the white sow, but one of her many offspring from a prior year—into the yard, clubbed it between the eyes with a maul, then swung it up into the branches, slit the throat, and let the blood drain into the barrel.

Roger and Arch had then taken the disemboweled carcass away to be scalded and the bristles scraped off; Jamie's presence was required to deal with Major MacDonald, who had appeared suddenly, puffing and wheezing from the climb up to the Ridge. Between the two, I thought Jamie would much have preferred to deal with the pig.

I finished washing my hands and arms—wasted labor, but necessary to my peace of mind—and dried off with a linen towel. I shoveled double handsful into the barrel from the waiting bowls of barley, oatmeal, and boiled rice, smiling slightly at memory of the Major's plum-red face, and Ronnie Sinclair's complaints. Himself had picked his building site on the Ridge with a great deal of forethought—precisely *because* of the difficulties involved in reaching it.

I ran my fingers through my hair, then took a deep breath and plunged my clean arm back into the barrel. The blood was cooling rapidly. Doused by the cereal, the smell was less immediate now than the metallic reek of fresh, hot blood. The mixture was still warm to the touch, though, and the grains made graceful swirls of white and brown, pale whirlpools drawn down into the blood as I stirred.

Ronnie was right; it hadn't been necessary to identify me further than "the healer." There wasn't another closer than Cross Creek, unless one counted the shamans among the Indians—which most Europeans wouldn't.

I wondered who had sent the note, and whether the matter was urgent. Probably not—at least it was not likely to be a matter of imminent childbirth or serious accident. Word of such events was likely to arrive in person, carried urgently by a friend or relative. A written message entrusted to a tinker couldn't be counted on to be delivered with any sort of promptitude; tinkers wandered or stayed, depending on what work they found.

For that matter, tinkers and tramps seldom came so far as the Ridge, though we had seen three within the last month. I didn't know whether that was the result of our growing population—Fraser's Ridge boasted nearly sixty families now, though the cabins were scattered over ten miles of forested mountain slopes—or something more sinister.

"It's one of the signs, Sassenach," Jamie had told me, frowning after the departing form of the last such temporary guest. "When there is war in the air, men take to the roads."

I thought he was right; I remembered wanderers on the Highland roads, carrying rumors of the Stuart Rising. It was as though the tremors of unrest jarred loose those who were not firmly attached to a place by love of land or family, and the swirling currents of dissension bore them onward, the first premonitory fragments of a slow-motion explosion that would shatter everything. I shivered, the light breeze touching cold through my shift.

The mass of gruel had reached the necessary consistency, something like a very thick, dark-red cream. I shook clumps of clotted grain from my fingers and reached with my clean left hand for the wooden bowl of minced and sauteed onions, standing ready. The strong smell of the onions overlaid the scent of butchery, pleasantly domestic.

The salt was ground, so was the pepper. All I needed now . . . as if on cue, Roger appeared around the corner of the house, a large basin in his hands, filled with fine-chopped pork fat.

"Just in time!" I said, and nodded toward the barrel. "No, don't dump it in, it has to be measured—roughly." I'd used ten double handsful of oatmeal, ten of rice, ten of barley. Half that total, then—fifteen. I shook back the hair from my eyes again, and carefully scooped up a double handful of the basin's content, dropping it into the barrel with a splat.

"All right, are you?" I asked. I gestured toward a stool with my chin, beginning to work the fat into the mixture with my fingers. Roger was still a trifle pale and tight around the mouth, but he gave me a wry smile as he sat.

"Fine."

"You didn't have to do it, you know."

"Yes, I did." The note of wryness in his voice deepened. "I only wish I'd done it better."

I shrugged, one-shouldered, and reached into the basin he held out for me.

"It takes practice."

Roger had volunteered to kill the pig. Jamie had simply handed him the maul and stood back. I had seen Jamie kill pigs before; he said a brief prayer, blessed the pig, then crushed the skull with one tremendous blow. It had taken Roger five tries, and the memory of the squealing raised gooseflesh on my shoulders even now. Afterward, he had set down the maul, gone behind a tree, and been violently sick.

I scooped another handful. The mix was thickening, developing a greasy feel.

"He should have shown you how."

"I shouldn't think there's anything technically difficult about it," Roger said dryly. "Straightforward enough, after all, to bash an animal on the head."

"Physically, perhaps," I agreed. I scooped more fat, working with both hands now. "There's a prayer for it, you know. For slaughtering an animal, I mean. Jamie should have told you."

He looked faintly startled.

"No, I didn't know." He smiled, a little better now. "Last rites for the pig, aye?"

"I don't think it's for the pig's benefit," I said tartly. We lapsed into silence for a few moments, as I creamed the rest of the fat into the grain mixture, pausing to flick away occasional bits of gristle. I could feel Roger's eyes on the barrel, watching the curious alchemy of cookery, that process of making the transfer of life from one being to another palatable.

"Highland drovers sometimes drain a cup or two of blood from one of their beasts, and mix it with oatmeal to eat on the road," I said. "Nutritious, I suppose, but less tasty."

Roger nodded, abstracted. He had set down the nearly empty basin and was cleaning dried blood from under his nails with the point of his dirk.

"Is it the same as the one for deer?" he asked. "The prayer. I've seen Jamie say that one, though I didn't catch all of the words."

"The gralloch prayer? I don't know. Why don't you ask him?"

Roger worked industriously on a thumbnail, eyes fixed on his hand.

"I wasn't sure if he thought it right for me to know it. Me not being a Catholic, I mean."

I looked down into the mixture, hiding a smile.

"I don't think it would make a difference. That particular prayer is a lot older than the Church of Rome, if I'm not mistaken."

A flicker of interest lit Roger's face, the buried scholar coming to the surface.

"I did think the Gaelic was a very old form—even older than what you hear these days—I mean . . . now." He flushed a little, realizing what he had said. I nodded, but didn't say anything.

I remembered what it was like, that feeling that one was living in an elaborate make-believe. The feeling that reality existed in another time, another place. I remembered, and with a small shock, realized that it *was* now only memory—for me, time had shifted, as though my illness had pushed me through some final barrier.

Now was my time, reality the scrape of wood and slick of grease beneath my fingers, the arc of the sun that set the rhythm of my days, the nearness of Jamie. It was the other world, of cars and ringing telephones, of alarm clocks and mortgages, that seemed unreal and remote, the stuff of dreams.

Neither Roger nor Bree had made that transition, though. I could see it in the way they behaved, hear it in the echoes of their private conversations. Likely it was because they had each other; they could keep the other time alive, a small shared world between them. For me, the change was easier. I had lived here before, had come this time on purpose, after all—and I had Jamie. No matter what I told him of the future, he could never see it as other than a fairy tale. Our small shared world was built of different things.

I worried now and then about Bree and Roger, though. It was dangerous to treat the past as they sometimes did—as picturesque or curious, a temporary condition that could be escaped. There was no escape for them—whether it was love or duty, Jemmy held them both, a small redheaded anchor to the present. Better—or safer, at least—if they could wholly accept this time as theirs.

"The Indians have it, too," I said to Roger. "The gralloch prayer, or something like it. That's why I said I thought it older than the Church."

He nodded, interested.

"I think that kind of thing is common to all primitive cultures—anyplace where men kill to eat."

Primitive cultures. I caught my lower lip between my teeth, forbearing to point out that primitive or not, if his family were to survive, he personally would very likely be obliged to kill for them. But then I caught sight of his hand, idly rubbing at the dried blood between his fingers. He knew that already. *"Yes, I did,"* he'd said, when I'd told him he need not.

He looked up then, caught my eye, and gave me a faint, tired smile. He understood.

"I think maybe . . . it's that killing without ceremony seems like murder," he said slowly. "If you have the ceremony—some sort of ritual that acknowledges your necessity . . ."

"Necessity—and also sacrifice." Jamie's voice came softly from behind me, startling me. I turned my head sharply. He was standing in the shadow of the big red spruce; I wondered how long he'd been there.

"Didn't hear you come out," I said, turning up my face to be kissed as he came to me. "Has the Major gone?"

"No," he said, and kissed my brow, one of the few clean spots left. "I've left him wi' Sinclair for a bit. He's exercised about the Committee of Safety, aye?" He grimaced, then turned to Roger.

"Aye, ye've the right of it," he said. "Killing's never a pleasant business, but it's needful. If ye must spill blood, though, it's right to take it wi' thanks."

Roger nodded, glancing at the mixture I was working, up to my elbows in spilled blood.

"Ye'll tell me the proper words for the next time, then?"

"Not too late for this time, is it?" I said. Both men looked slightly startled. I raised an eyebrow at Jamie, then Roger. "I did say it wasn't for the pig."

Jamie's eyes met mine with a glint of humor, but he nodded gravely.

"Well enough."

At my direction, he took up the heavy jar of spices: the ground mixture of mace and marjoram, sage and pepper, parsley and thyme. Roger held out his hands, cupped, and Jamie poured them full. Then Roger rubbed the herbs slowly between his palms, showering the dusty, greenish crumbs into the barrel, their pungent scent mingling with the smell of the blood, as Jamie spoke the words slowly, in an ancient tongue come down from the days of the Norsemen.

"Say it in English," I said, seeing from Roger's face that while he spoke the words, he did not recognize them all.

"O Lord, bless the blood and the flesh of this the creature that You gave me," Jamie said softly. He scooped a pinch of the herbs himself, and rubbed them between thumb and forefinger, in a rain of fragrant dust.

> *"Created by Your hand as You created man,*
> *Life given for life.*
> *That me and mine may eat with thanks for the gift,*
> *That me and mine may give thanks for Your own*
> *   sacrifice of blood and flesh,*
> *Life given for life."*

The last crumbs of green and gray disappeared into the mixture under my hands, and the ritual of the sausage was complete.

"That was good of ye, Sassenach," Jamie said, drying my clean, wet hands and arms with the towel afterward. He nodded toward the corner of the house, where Roger had disappeared to help with the rest of the butchering, looking somewhat more peaceful. "I did think to tell him before, but I couldna see how to do it."

I smiled and moved close to him. It was a cold, windy day, and now that I had stopped working, the chill drove me closer to seek his warmth. He wrapped his arms around me, and I felt both the reassuring heat of his embrace, and the soft crackle of paper inside his shirt.

"What's that?"

"Oh, a bittie letter Sinclair's brought," he said, drawing back a bit to reach into his shirt. "I didna want to open it while Donald was there, and didna trust him not to be reading it when I went out."

"It's not your letter, anyway," I said, taking the smudged wad of paper from him. "It's mine."

"Oh, is it? Sinclair didna say, just handed it to me."

"He would!" Not unusually, Ronnie Sinclair viewed me—all women, for that matter—as simply a minor appendage of a husband. I rather pitied the woman he might eventually induce to marry him.

I unfolded the note with some difficulty; it had been worn so long next to sweaty skin that the edges had frayed and stuck together.

The message inside was brief and cryptic, but unsettling. It had been scratched into the paper with something like a sharpened stick, using an ink that looked disturbingly like dried blood, though it was more likely berry juice.

"What does it say, Sassenach?" Seeing me frowning at the paper, Jamie moved to the side to look. I held it out to him.

Far down, in one corner, scratched in faint and tiny letters, as though the sender had hoped by this means to escape notice, was the word "Faydree." Above, in bolder scratchings, the message read

> YU
> CUM

"It must be her," I said, shivering as I drew my shawl closer. It was cold in the surgery, despite the small brazier glowing in the corner, but Ronnie Sinclair and MacDonald were in the kitchen, drinking cider and waiting while the sausages boiled. I spread the note open on my surgery table, its minatory summons dark and peremptory above the timid signature. "Look. Who else could it be?"

"She canna write, surely?" Jamie objected. "Though I suppose it might be that someone wrote it for her," he amended, frowning.

"No, she could have written this, I think." Brianna and Roger had come into the surgery, too; Bree reached out and touched the ragged paper, one long finger gently tracing the staggered letters. "I taught her."

"You did?" Jamie looked surprised. "When?"

"When I stayed at River Run. When you and Mama went to find Roger." Her wide mouth pressed thin for a moment; it wasn't an occasion she wished much to remember.

"I taught her the alphabet; I meant to teach her to read and write. We did all the letters—she knew how they sounded, and she could draw them. But then one day she said she couldn't anymore, and she wouldn't sit down with me." She glanced up, a troubled frown between her thick, red brows. "I thought maybe Aunt Jocasta found out, and stopped her."

"More likely Ulysses. Jocasta would have stopped *you,* lass." Jamie's frown matched hers as he glanced at me. "Ye do think it's Phaedre, then? My aunt's body slave?"

I shook my head, and bit one corner of my lip in doubt.

"The slaves at River Run do say her name like that—Faydree. And I certainly don't know anyone else by that name."

Jamie had questioned Ronnie Sinclair—casually, to give no occasion for alarm or gossip—but the cooper knew no more than he had told me: the note had been handed to him by a tinker, with the simple direction that it was "for the healer."

I leaned over the table, lifting a candle high to look at the note once more. The "F" of the signature had been made with a hesitant, repeated stroke—more than one try before the writer had committed herself to signing it. The more evidence, I thought, of its origin. I didn't know whether it was against the law in North Carolina to teach a slave to read or write, but it was certainly discouraged. While there were marked exceptions—slaves educated to their owners' ends, like Ulysses himself—it was on the whole a dangerous skill, and one a slave would go some way to conceal.

"She wouldn't have risked sending word like this, unless it was a serious matter," Roger said. He stood behind Bree, one hand on her shoulder, looking down at the note she held flattened on the table. "But what?"

"Have you heard from your aunt lately?" I asked Jamie, but I knew the answer before he shook his head. Any word from River Run that reached the Ridge would have been a matter of public knowledge within hours.

We had not gone to the Gathering at Mt. Helicon this year; there was too much to do on the Ridge and Jamie wished to avoid the heated politics involved. Still, Jocasta and Duncan had meant to be there. Anything wrong would surely have been a matter of general gossip, which would have reached us long since.

"So it is not only serious, but a private matter to the slave, too," Jamie said. "Otherwise, my aunt would have written, or Duncan sent word." His two stiff fingers tapped once, softly, against his thigh.

We stood around the table, staring at the note as though it were a small white slab of dynamite. The scent of boiling sausages filled the cold air, warm and comforting.

"Why you?" Roger asked, looking up at me. "Do you think it might be a medical matter? If she were ill, say—or pregnant?"

"Not illness," I said. "Too urgent." It was a week's ride to River Run at least—in good weather, and barring accident. Heaven knew how long it had taken the note to make its way up to Fraser's Ridge.

"But if she was pregnant? Maybe." Brianna pursed her lips, still frowning at the paper. "I think she thinks of Mama as a friend. She'd tell you before she'd tell Aunt Jocasta, I think."

I nodded, but reluctantly. Friendship was too strong a word; people situated as Phaedre and I could not be friends. Liking was constrained by too many things—suspicion, mistrust, the vast chasm of difference that slavery imposed.

And yet there was a certain feeling of sympathy between us, that much was true. I had worked with her, side by side, planting herbs and harvesting them, making simples for the stillroom, explaining their uses. We had buried a dead girl together and plotted to protect a runaway slave accused of her murder. She had a certain talent with the sick, did Phaedre, and some knowledge of herbs. Any minor matter, she could deal with herself. But something like an unexpected pregnancy . . .

"What does she think I could do, though, I wonder?" I was thinking out loud, and my fingertips felt cold in contemplation. An unexpected child born to a slave would be of no concern to an owner—to the contrary, it would be welcomed as additional property; but I had heard stories of slave women who killed a child at birth, rather than have the babe brought up in slavery. Phaedre was a house slave, though, well-treated, and Jocasta did not separate slave families, I knew that. If it were that, Phaedre's situation was surely not so dire—and yet, who was I to judge?

I blew out a cloud of smoky breath, uncertain.

"I just can't see why—I mean, she couldn't possibly expect that I'd help her to get rid of a child. And for anything else . . . why me? There are midwives and healers much closer. It just doesn't make sense."

"What if—" Brianna said, and stopped. She pursed her lips in speculation, looking from me to Jamie and back. "What if," she said carefully, "she was pregnant, but the father was . . . someone it shouldn't be?"

A wary but humorous speculation sprang up in Jamie's eyes, increasing the resemblance between him and Brianna.

"Who, lass?" he said. "Farquard Campbell?"

I laughed out loud at the thought, and Brianna snorted with mirth, white wisps of breath floating round her head. The notion of the very upright—and quite elderly—Farquard Campbell seducing a house slave was . . .

"Well, no," Brianna said. "Though he *does* have all those children. But I just thought suddenly—what if it was Duncan?"

Jamie cleared his throat, and avoided catching my eye. I bit my lip, feeling my face start to go red. Duncan had confessed his chronic impotence to Jamie before Duncan's wedding to Jocasta— but Brianna didn't know.

"Oh, I shouldna think it likely," Jamie said, sounding a trifle choked. He coughed, and fanned smoke from the brazier away from his face. "What gives ye that notion, lass?"

"Nothing about Duncan," she assured him. "But Aunt Jocasta *is*—well, old. And you know what men can be like."

"No, what?" asked Roger blandly, making me cough with the effort to suppress a laugh.

Jamie eyed her with a certain amount of cynicism.

"A good deal better than you do, *a nighean*. And while I wouldna wager much on some men, I think I should feel safe in laying odds that Duncan Innes isna the man to be breaking his marriage vows with his wife's black slave."

I made a small noise, and Roger lifted one eyebrow at me.

"Are you all right?"

"Fine," I said, sounding strangled. "Just—fine." I put a corner of the shawl over my no-doubt purple face and coughed ostentatiously. "It's . . . smoky in here, isn't it?"

"Maybe so," Brianna conceded, addressing Jamie. "It might not be that at all. It's just that Phaedre sent the note to 'the healer,' probably because she didn't want to use Mama's name, in case anybody saw the note before it got here. I just thought, maybe it wasn't really Mama she wants—maybe it's you."

That sobered both Jamie and me, and we glanced at each other. It was a definite possibility, and one that hadn't occurred to either of us.

"She couldn't send a note direct to you without rousing all kinds of curiosity," Bree went on, frowning at the note. "But she could say 'the healer' without putting a name on it. And she'd know that if Mama came, you'd probably come with her, at this time of year. Or if you didn't, Mama could send for you openly."

"It's a thought," Jamie said slowly. "But why in God's name might she want *me*?"

"Only one way to find out," said Roger, practical. He looked at Jamie. "Most of the outside work is done; the crops and the hay are in, the slaughtering's finished. We can manage here, if you want to go."

Jamie stood still for a moment, frowning in thought, then crossed to the window and raised the sash. A cold wind blew into the room, and Bree pinned the fluttering note to the table to keep it from taking wing. The coals in the small brazier smoked and flamed higher, and the bunches of dried herbs rustled uneasily overhead.

Jamie thrust his head out the window and breathed in deeply, eyes closed like one savoring the bouquet of fine wine.

"Cold and clear," he announced, drawing in his head and closing the window. "Clear weather for three days, at least. We could be off the mountain by that time, and we ride briskly." He smiled at me; the tip of his nose was red with the cold. "In the meantime, d'ye think those sausages are ready yet?"

72

Betrayals

A slave I didn't recognize opened the door to us, a broad-built woman in a yellow turban. She eyed us severely, but Jamie gave her no chance to speak, pushing rudely past her into the hall.

"He's Mrs. Cameron's nephew," I felt obliged to explain to her, as I followed him.

"I can see *that*," she muttered, in a lilt that came from Barbados. She glared after him, making it evident that she detected a family resemblance in terms of high-handedness, as well as physique.

"I'm his wife," I added, overcoming the reflexive urge to shake her hand, and bowing slightly instead. "Claire Fraser. Nice to meet you."

She blinked, disconcerted, but before she could reply, I had whisked past her, following Jamie toward the small drawing room where Jocasta was inclined to sit in the afternoons.

The door to the drawing room was closed, and as Jamie set his hand on the knob, a sharp yelp came from inside—the prelude to a barrage of frenzied barking as the door swung wide.

Stopped in his tracks, Jamie paused, hand on the door, frowning at the small brown bundle of fur that leaped to and fro at his feet, eyes bulging in hysteria as it barked its head off.

"What is *that*?" he said, edging his way into the room as the creature made abortive dashes at his boots, still yapping.

"It's a wee dog, what d'ye think?" Jocasta said acerbically. She lifted herself from her chair, frowning in the direction of the noise. "*Sheas,* Samson."

"Samson? Oh, to be sure. The hair." Smiling despite himself,

Jamie squatted and extended a closed fist toward the dog. Throttling back to a low growl, the dog extended a suspicious nose toward his knuckles.

"Where's Delilah?" I asked, edging into the room behind him.

"Ah, ye've come, as well, Claire?" Jocasta's face swiveled in my direction, lit by a smile. "A rare treat, to have the both of ye. I dinna suppose Brianna or the bittie lad have come along—no, I would have heard them." Dismissing that, she sat down again, and waved toward the hearth.

"As for Delilah, the lazy creature's asleep by the fire; I can hear her snoring."

Delilah was a large whitish hound of indeterminate breed but plentiful skin; it drooped around her in folds of relaxation as she lay on her back, paws curled over a freckled belly. Hearing her name, she snorted briefly, opened one eye a crack, then closed it again.

"I see ye've had a few changes since I was last here," Jamie observed, rising to his feet. "Where is Duncan? And Ulysses?"

"Gone. Looking for Phaedre." Jocasta had lost weight; the high MacKenzie cheekbones stood out sharp, and her skin looked thin and creased.

"Looking for her?" Jamie glanced sharply at her. "What's become of the lass?"

"Run away." She spoke with her usual self-possession, but her voice was bleak.

"Run away? But—are you sure?" Her workbox had been upset, the contents spilled on the floor. I knelt and began to tidy the confusion, picking up the scattered reels of thread.

"Weel, she's gone," Jocasta said with some acerbity. "Either she's run, or someone's stolen her. And I canna think who would have the gall or the skill to snatch her from my house, and no one seeing."

I exchanged a quick glance with Jamie, who shook his head, frowning. Jocasta was rubbing a fold of her skirt between thumb and forefinger; I could see small worn spots in the nap of the fabric near her hand, where she had done it repeatedly. Jamie saw it, too.

"When did she go, Auntie?" he asked quietly.

"Four weeks past. Duncan and Ulysses have been gone for two."

That fitted well enough with the arrival of the note. No telling how long before her disappearance the note had actually been written, given the vagaries of delivery.

"I see Duncan took pains to leave ye some company," Jamie observed. Samson had abandoned his watchdog role, and was sniffing assiduously at Jamie's boots. Delilah rolled onto her side with a luxurious groan and opened two luminous brown eyes, through which she regarded me with utmost tranquillity.

"Oh, aye, they're that." Half-grudgingly, Jocasta leaned out from her chair and located the hound's head, scratching behind the long, floppy ears. "Though Duncan meant them for my protection, or so he said."

"A sensible precaution," Jamie said mildly. It was; we had had no further word of Stephen Bonnet, nor had Jocasta heard the voice of the masked man again. But lacking the concrete reassurance of a corpse, either one could presumably pop up at any time.

"Why would the lassie run, Aunt?" Jamie asked. His tone was still mild, but persistent.

Jocasta shook her head, lips compressed.

"I dinna ken at all, Nephew."

"Nothing's happened of late? Nothing out of the ordinary?" he pressed.

"Do ye not think I should have said at once?" she asked sharply. "No. I woke late one morning, and couldna hear her about my room. There was nay tea by my bed, and the fire had gone out; I could smell the ashes. I called for her, and there was no answer. Gone, she was—vanished without a trace." She tilted her head toward him with a grim sort of "so there" expression.

I raised a brow at Jamie and touched the pocket I wore at my waist, containing the note. Ought we to tell her?

He nodded, and I drew the note from my pocket, unfolding it on the arm of her chair, as he explained.

Jocasta's look of displeasure faded into one of puzzled astonishment.

"Whyever should she send for you, *a nighean*?" she asked, turning to me.

"I don't know—perhaps she was with child?" I suggested. "Or had contracted a—disease of some sort?" I didn't want to suggest syphilis openly, but it was a possibility. If Manfred had infected Mrs. Sylvie, and she had then passed the infection on to one or more of her customers in Cross Creek, who then had visited River

Run . . . but that would mean, perhaps, that Phaedre had had some kind of relationship with a white man. *That* was something a slave woman would go to great lengths to keep secret.

Jocasta, no fool, was rapidly coming to similar conclusions, though her thoughts ran parallel to mine.

"A child, that would be no great matter," she said, flicking a hand. "But if she had a lover . . . aye," she said thoughtfully. "She might have gone off with a lover. But then, why send for you?"

Jamie was growing restive, impatient with so much unprovable speculation.

"Perhaps she might think ye meant to sell her, Aunt, if ye discovered such a thing?"

"To *sell* her?"

Jocasta broke out laughing. Not her usual social laughter, nor even the sound of genuine amusement; this was shocking—loud and crude, almost vicious in its hilarity. It was her brother Dougal's laugh, and the blood ran momentarily cold in my veins.

I glanced at Jamie, to find him looking down at her, face gone blank. Not in puzzlement; it was the mask he wore to hide strong feeling. So he'd heard that grisly echo, too.

She seemed unable to stop. Her hands clutched the carved arms of her chair and she leaned forward, face turning red, gasping for breath between those unnerving deep guffaws.

Delilah rolled onto her belly and uttered a low *"wuff"* of unease, looking anxiously round, unsure what the matter was, but convinced that something wasn't right. Samson had backed under the settee, growling.

Jamie reached out and took her by the shoulder—not gently.

"Be still, Aunt," he said. "Ye're frightening your wee dogs."

She stopped, abruptly. There was no sound but the faint wheeze of her breathing, nearly as unnerving as the laughter. She sat still, bolt upright in her chair, hands on the arms, the blood ebbing slowly from her face and her eyes gone dark and bright, fixed as though on something that only she could see.

"Sell her," she murmured, and her mouth creased as though the laughter were about to break out of her again. She didn't laugh, though, but stood up suddenly. Samson yapped once, in astonishment.

"Come with me."

She was through the door before either of us could say anything.

Jamie lifted an eyebrow at me, but motioned me through the door before him.

She knew the house intimately; she made her way down the hall toward the door to the stables with no more than an occasional touch of the wall to keep her bearings, walking as fast as though she could see. Outside, though, she paused, feeling with one extended foot for the edge of the brick-laid path.

Jamie stepped up beside her and took her firmly by the elbow. "Where d'ye wish to go?" he asked, a certain resignation in his tone.

"To the carriage barn." The peculiar laughter had left her, but her face was still flushed, her strong chin lifted with an air of defiance. Who was she defying? I wondered.

The carriage barn was shadowed and tranquil, dust motes drifting gold in the stir of air from the opened doors. A wagon, a carriage, a sledge, and the elegant two-wheeled trap sat like large, placid beasts on the straw-covered floor. I glanced at Jamie, whose mouth curled slightly as he looked at me; we had taken temporary refuge in that carriage, during the chaos of Jocasta's wedding to Duncan, almost four years before.

Jocasta paused in the doorway, one hand braced on the jamb and breathing deeply, as though orienting herself. She made no move to enter the barn herself, though, but instead nodded toward the depths of the building.

"Along the back wall, *an mhic mo peather*. There are boxes there; I want the large chest made of wickerwork, the one as high as your knee, with a rope tied round it."

I had not really noticed during our earlier excursion into the carriage barn, but the back wall was stacked high with boxes, crates, and bundles, piled two and three deep. With such explicit direction, though, Jamie made short work of finding the desired container, and dragged it out into the light, covered with dust and bits of straw.

"Shall I carry it into the house for ye, Auntie?" he asked, rubbing a finger under a twitching nose.

She shook her head, stooping and feeling for the knot of the rope that bound it.

"No. I shallna have it the house. I swore I should not."

"Let me." I laid a hand on hers to still her fumbling, then took charge of the knot myself. Whoever had tied it had been thorough, but not skilled; I had it loose within a minute, and the catch undone.

The wicker chest was filled with pictures. Bundles of loose drawings, done in pencil, ink, and charcoal, neatly tied with faded ribbons of colored silk. Several bound sketchbooks. And a number of paintings: a few large unframed squares, and two smaller boxes of miniatures, all framed, stacked on edge like a deck of cards.

I heard Jocasta sigh, above me, and looked up. She stood still, eyes closed, and I could tell that she was inhaling deeply, breathing in the smell of the pictures—the smell of oils and charcoal, gesso, paper, canvas, linseed and turpentine, a full-bodied ghost that floated out of its wicker casket, transparently vivid against the background scents of straw and dust, wood and wicker.

Her fingers curled, thumb rubbing against the tips of her other fingers, unconsciously rolling a brush between them. I had seen Bree do that, now and then, looking at something she wanted to paint. Jocasta sighed again, then opened her eyes and knelt down beside me, reaching in to run her fingers lightly over the cache of buried art, searching.

"The oils," she said. "Fetch those out."

I had already taken out the boxes of miniatures. Jamie squatted on the other side of the casket, lifting the bundles of loose drawings and the sketchbooks, so that I could pull out the larger oils, laid on edge along the side of the container.

"A portrait," she said, head on one side to listen to the flat, hollow sound as I laid each one against the side of the wicker box. "An old man."

It was plain which one she meant. Two of the large canvases were landscapes, three, portraits. I recognized Farquard Campbell, much younger than his present age, and what must be a self-portrait of Jocasta herself, done perhaps twenty years before. I had no time to look at these, though, interesting as they were.

The third portrait looked to have been done much more recently than the others, and showed the effects of Jocasta's failing eyesight.

The edges were blurred, the colors muddy, shapes just slightly distorted, so that the elderly gentleman who looked out of the clouded oil seemed somehow disturbing, as though he belonged to some race not quite human, in spite of the orthodoxy of his wig and high white stock.

He wore a black coat and waistcoat, old-fashioned in style, with the folds of a tartan plaid draped over his shoulder, caught up with a brooch whose golden gleam was echoed by the ornamental knurl atop the dirk the old man held, his fingers bent and gnarled with arthritis. I recognized that dirk.

"So that is Hector Cameron." Jamie recognized it, too. He looked at the painting with fascination.

Jocasta reached out a hand, touching the surface of the paint as though to identify it by touch.

"Aye, that's him," she said dryly. "Never saw him in life, did ye, Nephew?"

Jamie shook his head.

"Once perhaps—but I was nay more than a babe at the time." His gaze traced the old man's features with deep interest, as though looking for clues to Hector Cameron's character. Such clues were evident; the man's force of personality fairly vibrated from the canvas.

He had strong bones, the man in the portrait, though the flesh hung from them in the infirmity of age. The eyes were still sharp, but one was half-closed—it might have been only a drooping eyelid caused by a small stroke, but the impression was that of an habitual manner of looking at the world; one eye always narrowed in cynical appraisal.

Jocasta was searching through the contents of the chest, fingers darting lightly here and there, like hunting moths. She touched one box of miniatures, and lifted it with a small grunt of satisfaction.

She ran a finger slowly along the edge of each miniature, and I saw that the frames were patterned differently; squares and ovals, smooth gilded wood, tarnished silver laid in a rope border, another studded with tiny rosettes. She found one she recognized, and plucked it from the box, handing it absently to me as she went back to her search.

The miniature was also of Hector Cameron—but this portrait done many years before the other. Dark wavy hair lay loose on his shoulders, a small ornamental braid down one side sporting two grouse's feathers, in the ancient Highland style. The same solid bones were there, but the flesh was firm; he had been handsome, Hector Cameron.

It *was* an habitual expression; whether by inclination or accident of birth, the right eye was narrowed here, as well, though not as much as in the older portrait.

My scrutiny was interrupted by Jocasta, who laid a hand on my arm.

"Is this the lass?" she asked, thrusting another of the miniatures at me.

I took it, puzzled, and gasped when I turned it over. It was Phaedre, done when the girl was in her early teens. Her usual cap was missing; she wore a simple kerchief bound over her hair that threw the bones of her face into bold relief. Hector Cameron's bones.

Jocasta nudged the box of paintings with her foot.

"Give those to your daughter, Nephew. Tell her to paint them over—it would be shame to waste the canvas." Without waiting for response, she set off back toward the house alone, hesitating only briefly at the fork in the path, steering by scent and memory.

There was a profound silence in the wake of Jocasta's departure, broken only by the singing of a mockingbird in a nearby pine.

"I will be damned," Jamie said at last, taking his eyes off the figure of his aunt as she vanished into the house, alone. He didn't look shocked, so much as deeply bemused. "Did the girl know, d'ye think?"

"Almost certainly," I said. "The slaves would surely have known; some must have been here when she was born; they'd have told her, if she wasn't quick enough to have worked it out herself—and I certainly think she is."

He nodded, and leaned back against the wall of the carriage house, looking meditatively down his long nose at the wicker chest of paintings. I felt a strong reluctance to go back to the house, myself. The buildings were beautiful, a mellow gold in the late-fall sun, and the grounds were peaceful, well-ordered. The sound of cheerful voices came from the kitchen garden, several horses grazed contentedly in the paddock nearby, and far away down the distant silver river, a small boat came down, a four-oared piretta, its oars stroking the surface, brisk and graceful as a water strider.

"Where every prospect pleases, and only man is vile," I re-marked. Jamie gave me a brief glance of incomprehension, then returned to his thoughts.

So Jocasta would by no means sell Phaedre, and thought Phaedre knew it. I wondered exactly why. Because she felt some duty to the girl, as the child of her husband? Or as a subtle form of revenge on that long-dead husband, keeping his illegitimate daughter as a slave, a body servant? I supposed that the two were not entirely exclusive, come to that—I had known Jocasta long enough to realize that her motives were rarely simple.

There was a chill in the air, with the sun low in the sky. I leaned against the carriage house beside Jamie, feeling the stored warmth of the sun soak from its bricks into my body, and wished that we could step into the old farm wagon and drive posthaste back to the Ridge, leaving River Run to deal with its own legacies of bitterness.

But the note was in my pocket, crackling when I moved. *YU CUM.* Not an appeal I could dismiss. But I *had* come—and now what?

Jamie straightened suddenly, looking toward the river. I looked, too, and saw that the boat had drawn into the dock there. A tall figure sprang up onto the dock, then turned to help another out of the boat. The second man was shorter, and moved in an odd fashion, off-kilter and out of rhythm.

"Duncan," I said at once, seeing this. "And Ulysses. They're back!"

"Aye," Jamie said, taking my arm and starting toward the house. "But they havena found her."

RUNAWAY or STOLEN on the 31st of October, a Negro Wench, twenty-two years of Age, above middling Height and comely in Appearance, with a Scar on the left Forearm in the shape of an Oval, caused by a Burn. Dressed in an indigo Gown, with a green-striped Apron, white Cap, brown Stockings, and leather Shoes. No miss-ing Teeth. Known by the Name of "FAYDREE." Communicate Particulars to D. Innes, River Run Plantation, in the vicinity of Cross Creek. Substantial Reward will be paid for good Information.

I smoothed the crumpled broadsheet, which also sported a crude drawing of Phaedre, looking vaguely cross-eyed. Duncan had emptied his pockets and dropped a handful of these sheets on the table in the hall when he had come in the afternoon before, exhausted and dispirited. They had, he said, posted the bills in every tavern and public house between Campbelton and Wilmington, making inquiries as they went—but to no avail. Phaedre had vanished like the dew.

"May I have the marmalade, please?" Jamie and I were taking breakfast alone, neither Jocasta nor Duncan having appeared this morning. I was enjoying it, despite the gloomy atmosphere. Breakfast at River Run was normally a lavish affair, extending even to a pot of real tea—Jocasta must be paying her pet smuggler an absolute fortune for it; there was none to be found between Virginia and Georgia, to the best of my knowledge.

Jamie was frowning at another of the broadsheets, deep in thought. He didn't take his eyes off it, but his hand roamed vaguely over the table, settled on the cream jug, and passed it across to me.

Ulysses, showing little sign of his long journey beyond a certain heaviness of the eyes, stepped silently forward, took the cream jug, replaced it neatly, and set the pot of marmalade beside my plate.

"Thank you," I said, and he graciously inclined his head.

"Will you require further bloaters, madam?" he inquired. "Or more ham?"

I shook my head, my mouth being full of toast, and he glided off, picking up a loaded tray by the door, this presumably intended for Jocasta, Duncan, or both.

Jamie watched him go, with a sort of abstracted expression.

"I have been thinking, Sassenach," he said.

"I would never have guessed it," I assured him. "About what?"

He looked momentarily surprised, but then smiled, realizing.

"Ye kent what I told ye, Sassenach, about Brianna and the widow McCallum? That she wouldna scruple long to act, if Roger Mac were to be taking heed where he shouldn't?"

"I do," I said.

He nodded, as though verifying something to himself.

"Well, the lass comes by it honestly enough. The MacKenzies

of Leoch are proud as Lucifer, all of them, and black jealous with it. Ye dinna want to cross one—still less to betray one."

I regarded him warily over my cup of tea, wondering where this was leading.

"I thought their defining trait was charm, allied with cunning. And as for betrayal, both your uncles were past hands at it."

"The two go together, do they not?" he asked, reaching across to dip a spoon in the marmalade. "Ye must beguile someone before ye can betray them, no? And I am inclined to think that a man who would betray is all the quicker to resent betrayal himself. Or a woman," he added delicately.

"Oh, really," I said, sipping with pleasure. "Jocasta, you mean." Put in those terms, I could see it. The MacKenzies of Leoch had powerful personalities—I did wonder what Jamie's maternal grandfather, the notorious Red Jacob, had been like— and I'd noted small commonalities of behavior between Jocasta and her elder brothers before.

Colum and Dougal had had an unshakable loyalty to each other—but to no one else. And Jocasta was essentially alone, separated from her family since her first marriage at fifteen. Being a woman, it was natural that the charm should be more apparent in her—but that didn't mean the cunning wasn't there. Nor yet the jealousy, I supposed.

"Well, plainly she knew that Hector betrayed her—and I do wonder whether she painted that portrait of Phaedre as a means of indicating to the world at large that she knew it, or merely as a private message to Hector—but what has that got to do with the present situation?"

He shook his head.

"Not Hector," he said. "Duncan."

I stared at him, absolutely open-mouthed. All other considerations aside, Duncan was impotent; he had told Jamie so, on the eve of his wedding to Jocasta. Jamie smiled crookedly, and reaching across the table, put a thumb under my chin and pushed my mouth gently shut.

"It's a thought, Sassenach, is all I'm saying. But I think I must go and have a word wi' the man. Will ye come?"

Duncan was in the small room he used as a private office, tucked away above the stables, along with the tiny rooms that housed the grooms and stable-lads. He was slumped in a chair, looking hopelessly at the untidy stacks of papers and undusted ledgers that had accumulated on every horizontal surface.

He looked desperately tired, and a great deal older than when I had last seen him, at Flora MacDonald's barbecue. His gray hair was thinning, and when he turned to greet us, the light of the sun shone across his face, and I saw the thin line of the hare-lip scar Roger had mentioned, hidden in the luxuriant growth of his mustache.

Something vital seemed to have gone out of him, and when Jamie delicately broached the subject upon which we had come, he made no attempt at all to deny it. In fact, he seemed glad, rather than otherwise, to have it out.

"Ye did lie wi' the lass, then, Duncan?" Jamie asked directly, wanting to have the fact established.

"Well, no," he said vaguely. "I should have liked to, o' course—but what wi' her sleeping in Jo's dressing room . . ." At this reference to his wife, his face flushed a deep, unhealthy red.

"I mean, ye've had carnal knowledge of the woman, have ye not?" Jamie said, keeping a grip on his patience.

"Oh, aye." He gulped. "Aye. I did."

"How?" I asked bluntly.

The flush deepened, to such a degree that I feared he might have an apoplexy on the spot. He breathed like a grampus for a bit, though, and finally, his complexion began to fade back to something like normal.

"She fed me," he said at last, rubbing a hand tiredly across his eyes. "Every day."

Jocasta rose late and breakfasted in her sitting room, attended by Ulysses, to make plans for the day. Duncan, who had risen before dawn every day of his life, usually in the expectation of a dry crust or at most, a bit of drammach—oatmeal mixed with water—woke now to find a steaming pot of tea beside his bed, accompanied by a bowl of creamy parritch, liberally garnished with honey and cream, toast drenched in butter, eggs fried with ham.

"Sometimes a wee fish, rolled in cornmeal, crisp and sweet," he added, with mournful reminiscence.

"Well, that's verra seductive, to be sure, Duncan," Jamie said, not without sympathy. "A man's vulnerable when he's hungry." He gave me a wry glance. "But still . . ."

Duncan had been grateful to Phaedre for her kindness, and had—being a man, after all—admired her beauty, though in a purely disinterested sort of way, he assured us.

"To be sure," Jamie said with marked skepticism. "What happened?"

Duncan had dropped the butter, was the answer, whilst struggling to butter his toast one-handed. Phaedre had hastened to retrieve the pieces of the fallen dish, and then hurried to fetch a cloth and wipe the streaks of butter from the floor—and then from Duncan's chest.

"Well, I was in my nightshirt," he murmured, starting to go red again. "And she was—she had—" His hand rose and made vague motions in the vicinity of his chest, which I took to indicate that Phaedre's bodice had displayed her bosom to particular advantage while in such close proximity to him.

"And?" Jamie prompted ruthlessly.

And, it appeared, Duncan's anatomy had taken note of the fact—a circumstance admitted with such strangulated modesty that we could barely hear him

"But I thought you couldn't—" I began.

"Oh, I couldna," he assured me hastily. "Only at night, like, dreaming. But not waking, not since I had the accident. Perhaps it was being so early i' the morning; my cock thought I was still asleep."

Jamie made a low Scottish noise expressing considerable doubt as to this supposition, but urged Duncan to continue, with a certain amount of impatience.

Phaedre had taken notice in her turn, it transpired.

"She was only sorry for me," Duncan said frankly. "I could tell as much. But she put her hand on me, soft. So soft," he repeated, almost inaudibly.

He had been sitting on his bed—and had gone on sitting there in dumb amazement, as she took away the breakfast tray, lifted his nightshirt, climbed on the bed with her skirts neatly tucked above her round brown thighs, and with great tenderness and gentleness, had welcomed back his manhood.

"Once?" Jamie demanded. "Or did ye keep doing it?"

Duncan put his head in his hand, a fairly eloquent admission, under the circumstances.

"How long did this . . . er . . . liaison go on?" I asked more gently.

Two months, perhaps three. Not every day, he hastened to add—only now and then. And they had been very careful.

"I wouldna ever have wanted to shame Jo, ken," he said very earnestly. "And I kent weel I shouldna be doing it, 'twas a great sin, and yet I couldna keep from—" He broke, off, swallowing. "It's all my fault, what's happened, let the sin be on me! Och, my puir darling lass . . ."

He fell silent, shaking his head like an old, sad, flea-ridden dog. I felt terribly sorry for him, regardless of the morality of the situation. The collar of his shirt was turned awkwardly under, strands of his grizzled hair trapped beneath his coat; I gently pulled them out and straightened it, though he took no heed.

"D'ye think she's dead, Duncan?" Jamie asked quietly, and Duncan blanched, his skin going the same gray as his hair.

"I canna bring myself to think it, *Mac Dubh*," he said, and his eyes filled with tears. "And—and yet . . ."

Jamie and I exchanged uneasy glances. And yet. Phaedre had taken no money when she disappeared. How could a female slave travel very far without detection, advertised and hunted, lacking a horse, money, or anything beyond a pair of leather shoes? A man might possibly make it to the mountains, and manage to survive in the woods, if he were tough and resourceful—but a girl? A house slave?

Someone had taken her—or else she was dead.

None of us wanted to voice that thought, though. Jamie heaved a great sigh, and taking a clean handkerchief from his sleeve, put it in Duncan's hand.

"I shall pray for her, Duncan—wherever she may be. And for you, *a charaid* . . . and for you."

Duncan nodded, not looking up, the handkerchief clutched tight. It was clear that any attempt at comfort would be futile, and so at last we left him sitting there, in his tiny, landlocked room, so far from the sea.

We made our way back slowly, not speaking, but holding hands, feeling the strong need to touch each other. The day was bright, but there was a storm coming up; ragged clouds were streaming in from the east, and the breeze came in gusts that whirled my skirts about like a twirling parasol.

The wind was less on the back terrace, sheltered as it was by its waist-high wall. Looking up from here, I could just see the window that Phaedre had been looking out of when I'd found her there, the night of the barbecue.

"She told me that something wasn't right," I said. "The night of Mrs. MacDonald's barbecue. Something was troubling her then."

Jamie shot me an interested glance.

"Oh, aye? But she didna mean Duncan, surely?" he objected.

"I know." I shrugged helplessly. "She didn't seem to know what was wrong herself—she just kept saying, 'Something ain't right.'"

Jamie took a deep breath and blew it out again, shaking his head.

"In a way, I suppose I hope that whatever it was, it had to do with her going. For if it wasna to do with her and Duncan . . ." He trailed off, but I had no difficulty in finishing the thought.

"Then it wasn't to do with your aunt, either," I said. "Jamie— do you really think Jocasta might have had her killed?"

It should have sounded ridiculous, spoken aloud like that. The horrible thing was that it didn't.

Jamie made that small, shrugging gesture he used when very uncomfortable about something, as though his coat was too tight.

"Had she her sight, I should think it—possible, at least," he said. "To be betrayed by Hector—and she blamed him already, for the death of her girls. So her daughters are dead, but there is Phaedre, alive, every day, a constant reminder of insult. And then to be betrayed yet again, by Duncan, *with* Hector's daughter?"

He rubbed a knuckle under his nose. "I should think any woman of spirit might be . . . moved."

"Yes," I said, imagining what I might think or feel under the same circumstances. "Certainly. But to murder—that *is* what we're talking about, isn't it? Couldn't she simply have sold the girl?"

"No," he said thoughtfully. "She couldn't. We made provision to safeguard her money when she wed—but not the property. Duncan is the owner of River Run—and all that goes with it."

"Including Phaedre." I felt hollow, and a little sick.

"As I said. Had she her sight, I shouldna be astonished at all by the thought. As it is . . ."

"Ulysses," I said, with certainty, and he nodded reluctantly. Ulysses was not only Jocasta's eyes, but her hands, as well. I didn't think he would have killed Phaedre at his mistress's command—but if Jocasta had poisoned the girl, for instance, Ulysses might certainly have helped to dispose of the body.

I felt an odd air of unreality—even with what I knew of the MacKenzie family, calmly discussing the possibility of Jamie's aged aunt having murdered someone . . . and yet . . . I *did* know the MacKenzies.

"*If* my aunt had any hand at all in the matter," Jamie said. "After all, Duncan said they were discreet. And it may be the lass was taken off—perhaps by the man my aunt recalls from Coigach. It could be he'd think Phaedre might help him to the gold, no?"

That was a somewhat happier thought. And it *did* fit with Phaedre's premonition—if that's what it was—which had occurred the same day that the man from Coigach came.

"I suppose all we *can* do is pray for her, poor thing," I said. "I don't suppose there's a patron saint of abducted persons, is there?"

"Saint Dagobert," he replied promptly, causing me to stare at him.

"You're making that up."

"Indeed I am not," he said with dignity. "Saint Athelais is another one—and perhaps better, now I think. She was a young Roman lass, who was abducted by the Emperor Justinian, who wished to have his way wi' her, and she vowed to chastity. But she escaped and went off to live with her uncle in Benevento."

"Good for her. And Saint Dagobert?"

"A king of some sort—Frankish? Anyway, his guardian took against him as a child, and had him kidnapped away to England, so the guardian's son might reign instead."

"Where do you learn these things?" I demanded.

"From Brother Polycarp, at the Abbey of St. Anne," he said, the corner of his mouth tucking back in a smile. "When I couldna sleep, he'd come and tell me stories of the saints, hours on end. It didna always put me to sleep, but after an hour or so of hearing about holy martyrs having their breasts amputated or being flogged wi' iron hooks, I'd close my eyes and make a decent pretense of it."

Jamie took my cap off and set it on the ledge. The air blew

through my inch of hair, ruffling it like meadow grass, and he
smiled as he looked at me.

"Ye look like a boy, Sassenach," he said. "Though damned if
I've ever seen a lad with an arse like yours."

"Thanks so much," I said, absurdly pleased. I had eaten like a
horse in the last two months, slept well and deeply through the
nights, and knew I was much improved in looks, hair notwithstanding. Never hurt to hear it, though.

"I want ye verra much, *mo nighean donn*," he said softly, and
curled his fingers round my wrist, letting the pads rest gently on
my pulse.

"So the MacKenzies of Leoch are all prone to black jealousy,"
I said. I could feel my pulse, steady under his fingers. "Charming,
cunning, and given to betrayal." I touched his lip, ran my thumb
lightly along it, the tiny prickles of beard pleasant to the touch.
"All of them?"

He looked down, fixing me suddenly with a dark blue gaze in
which humor and ruefulness were mingled with a good many
other things I couldn't read.

"Ye think I am not?" he said, and smiled a little sadly. "God
and Mary bless ye, Sassenach." And bent to kiss me.

We could not tarry at River Run. The fields down here on the
piedmont had long since been harvested and turned under, the
remnants of dried stalks flecking the fresh dark earth; snow would
fly soon in the mountains.

We had discussed the matter round and round—but came to no
useful conclusion. There was nothing further we could do to help
Phaedre—except to pray. Beyond that, though . . . there was
Duncan to think of.

For it had occurred to both of us that if Jocasta *had* found out
about his liaison with Phaedre, her wrath was not likely to be
limited to the slave girl. She might bide her time—but she would
not forget the injury. I'd never met a Scot who *would*.

We took our leave of Jocasta after breakfast the next day, finding her in her private parlor, embroidering a table runner. The
basket of silk threads sat in her lap, the colors carefully arrayed
in a spiral, so that she could choose the one she wanted by touch,

and the finished linen fell to one side, five feet of cloth edged with an intricate design of apples, leaves, and vines—or no, I realized, when I picked up the end of the cloth to admire it. Not vines. Black-eyed serpents, coiling slyly, slithering, green and scaly. Here and there one gaped to show its fangs, guarding scattered red fruit.

"Garden of Eden," she explained to me, rubbing the design lightly betwixt her fingers.

"How beautiful," I said, wondering how long she'd been working on it. Had she begun it before Phaedre's disappearance?

A bit of casual talk, and then Josh the groom appeared to say that our horses were ready. Jamie nodded, dismissing him, and stood.

"Aunt," he said to Jocasta matter-of-factly, "I should take it verra much amiss were any harm to come to Duncan."

She stiffened, fingers halting in their work.

"Why should any harm come to him?" she asked, lifting her chin.

Jamie didn't reply at once, but stood regarding her, not without sympathy. Then he leaned down, so that she could feel his presence close, his mouth near her ear.

"I know, Aunt," he said softly. "And if ye dinna wish anyone else to share that knowledge . . . then I think I shall find Duncan in good health when I return."

She sat as though turned to salt. Jamie stood up, nodding toward the door, and we took our leave. I glanced back from the hallway, and saw her still sitting like a statue, face as white as the linen in her hands and the little balls of colored thread all fallen from her lap, unraveling across the polished floor.

73

Double-dealing

With Marsali gone, the whisky-making became more difficult. Among us, Bree and Mrs. Bug and I had managed to get off one more malting before the weather became too cold and rainy, but it was a near thing, and it was with great relief that I saw the last of the malted grain safely decanted into the still. Once set to ferment, the stuff became Jamie's responsibility, as he trusted no one else with the delicate job of judging taste and proof.

The fire beneath the still had to be kept at exactly the right level, though, to keep fermentation going without killing the mash, then raised for the distillings once fermentation was complete. This meant that he lived—and slept—beside the still for the few days necessary for each batch to come off. I generally brought him supper and stayed until the dark came, but it was lonely without him in my bed, and I was more than pleased when we poured the last of the new making into casks.

"Oh, that smells good." I sniffed beatifically at the inside of an empty cask; it was one of the special casks Jamie had obtained through one of Lord John's shipping friends—charred inside like a normal whisky cask, but previously used to store sherry. The sweet mellow ghost of the sherry mingled with the faint scent of char and the hot, raw reek of the new whisky were together enough to make my head spin pleasantly.

"Aye, it's a small batch, but no bad," Jamie agreed, inhaling the aroma like a perfume connoisseur. He lifted his head and eyed the sky overhead; the wind was coming up strong, and thick clouds were racing past, dark-bellied and threatening.

"There's only the three casks," he said. "If ye think ye might manage one, Sassenach, I'll take the others. I should like to have them safe, rather than dig them out of a snowbank next week."

A half-mile walk in a roaring wind, carrying or rolling a six-gallon cask, was no joke, but he was right about the snow. It wasn't quite cold enough for snow yet, but it would be soon. I sighed, but nodded, and between us, we managed to lug the casks slowly up to the whisky cache, hidden among rocks and ragged grapevines.

I had quite regained my strength, but even so, every muscle I had was trembling and jerking in protest by the time we had finished, and I made no objection at all when Jamie made me sit down to rest before heading back to the house.

"What do you plan to do with these?" I asked, nodding back toward the cache. "Keep, or sell?"

He wiped a flying strand of hair out of his face, squinting against a blast of flying dust and dead leaves.

"I'll have to sell one, for the spring seed. We'll keep one to age—and I think perhaps I can put the last to good purpose. If Bobby Higgins comes again before the snow, I shall send a half-dozen bottles to Ashe, Harnett, Howe, and a few others—a wee token of my abiding esteem, aye?" He grinned wryly at me.

"Well, I've heard of worse bona fides," I said, amused. It had taken him a good deal of work to worm his way back into the good graces of the North Carolina Committee of Correspondence, but several members had begun answering his letters again—cautiously, but with respect.

"I shouldna think anything important will happen over the winter," he said thoughtfully, rubbing his cold-reddened nose.

"Likely not." Massachusetts, where most of the uproar had been taking place, was now occupied by a General Gage, and the latest we had heard was that he had fortified Boston Neck, the narrow spit of land that connects the city to the mainland—which meant that Boston was now cut off from the rest of the colony, and under seige.

I felt a small pang, thinking of it; I had lived in Boston for nearly twenty years, and was fond of the city—though I knew I would not recognize it now.

"John Hancock—he's a merchant there—is heading the Committee of Safety, Ashe says. They've voted to recruit twelve thousand militia, and are looking to purchase five *thousand* muskets—with the trouble I had to find thirty, good luck to them, is all I can say."

I laughed, but before I could reply, Jamie stiffened.

"What's that?" His head turned sharply, and he laid a hand on my arm. Silenced abruptly, I held my breath, listening. The wind stirred the drying leaves of wild grapevines with a papery rustle behind me, and in the distance a murder of crows passed, squabbling in shrill cries.

Then I heard it, too: a small, desolate, and very human sound. Jamie was already on his feet, making his way with care between the fallen rocks. He ducked beneath the lintel made by a leaning slab of granite, and I made to follow him. He stopped abruptly, nearly making me run into him.

"Joseph?" he said incredulously.

I peered around him as best I could. To my equal astonishment, it *was* Mr. Wemyss, sitting hunched on a boulder, a stone jug between his bony knees. He'd been crying; his nose and eyes were red, making him look even more like a white mouse than usual. He was also extremely drunk.

"Oh," he said, blinking in dismay at us. "Oh."

"Are ye . . . quite well, Joseph?" Jamie came closer, extending a hand gingerly, as though afraid that Mr. Wemyss might crack into pieces if touched.

This instinct was sound; when he touched the little man, Mr. Wemyss's face crumpled like paper, and his thin shoulders began to shake uncontrollably.

"I am so sorry, sir," he kept saying, quite dissolved in tears. "I'm *so* sorry!"

Jamie gave me a "do something, Sassenach" look of appeal, and I knelt swiftly, putting my arms round Mr. Wemyss's shoulders, patting his slender back.

"Now, now," I said, giving Jamie a "now *what*?" sort of look over Mr. Wemyss's matchstick shoulder in return. "I'm sure it will be all right."

"Oh, no," he said, hiccuping. "Oh, no, it can't." He turned a face streaming with woe toward Jamie. "I can't bear it, sir, truly I can't."

Mr. Wemyss's bones felt thin and brittle, and he was shivering. He was wearing only a thin shirt and breeches, and the wind was beginning to whine through the rocks. Clouds thickened overhead, and the light went from the little hollow, suddenly, as though a blackout curtain had been dropped.

Jamie unfastened his own cloak and wrapped it rather awkwardly round Mr. Wemyss, then lowered himself carefully onto another boulder.

"Tell me the trouble, Joseph," he said quite gently. "Is someone dead, then?"

Mr. Wemyss sank his face into his hands, head shaking to and fro like a metronome. He muttered something, which I understood to be "Better if she were."

"Lizzie?" I asked, exchanging a puzzled glance with Jamie. "Is it Lizzie you mean?" She'd been perfectly all right at breakfast; what on earth—

"First Manfred McGillivray," Mr. Wemyss said, raising his face from his hands, "and then Higgins. As though a degenerate and a murderer were not bad enough—now this!"

Jamie's brows shot up and he looked at me. I shrugged slightly. The gravel was jabbing sharply into my knees; I rose stiffly and brushed it away.

"Are you saying that Lizzie is, er . . . in love with someone . . . unsuitable?" I asked carefully.

Mr. Wemyss shuddered.

"Unsuitable," he said, in a hollow tone. "Jesus Christ. Unsuitable!"

I'd never heard Mr. Wemyss blaspheme before; it was unsettling.

He turned wild eyes on me, looking like a crazed sparrow, huddled in the depths of Jamie's cloak.

"I gave up everything for her!" he said. "I sold myself—and gladly!—to save her from dishonor. I left home, left Scotland, knowing I should never see it more, that I should leave my bones in the soil of the strangers. And yet I've said nay word of reproach to her, my dear wee lassie, for how should it be her fault? And now . . ." He turned a hollow, haunted gaze on Jamie.

"My God, my God. What shall I do?" he whispered. A blast of wind thundered through the rocks and whipped the cloak around him, momentarily obliterating him in a shroud of gray, as though distress had quite engulfed him.

I kept tight hold of my own cloak, to prevent it being torn off me; the wind was strong enough that I nearly lost my footing. Jamie squinted against the spray of dust and fine gravel that blasted us, setting his teeth in discomfort. He wrapped his arms around himself, shivering.

"Is the lass with child, then, Joseph?" he said, obviously wanting to get to the bottom of things and go home.

Mr. Wemyss's head popped out of the folds of cloak, fair hair tousled into broomstraw. Blinking reddened eyes, he nodded, then excavated the jug and, raising it in trembling hands, took several gulps. I saw the single "X" marked on the jug; with his characteristic modesty, he had taken a jug of the raw new whisky, not the cask-aged higher quality.

Jamie sighed, reached out a hand, and taking the jug from him, took a healthy gulp himself.

"Who?" he said, handing it back. "Is it my nephew?"

Mr. Wemyss stared at him, owl-eyed.

"Your nephew?"

"Ian Murray," I put in helpfully. "Tall brown-haired lad? Tattoos?"

Jamie gave me a look suggesting that I was perhaps not being quite so helpful as I thought, but Mr. Wemyss went on looking blank.

"Ian Murray?" Then the name appeared to penetrate through the alcoholic fog. "Oh. No. Christ, if it were! I should bless the lad," he said fervently.

I exchanged another look with Jamie. This looked like being serious.

"Joseph," he said with just a touch of menace. "It's cold." He wiped his nose on the back of his hand. " Who's debauched your daughter? Give me his name, and I'll see him wed to her in the morning or dead at her feet, whichever ye like. But let's do it inside by the fire, aye?"

"Beardsley," Mr. Wemyss said, in a tone suggesting visions of utter despair.

"Beardsley?" Jamie repeated. He raised one eyebrow at me. It wasn't what I would have expected—but hearing it came as no great shock, either.

"Which Beardsley was it?" he asked, with relative patience. "Jo? Or Kezzie?"

Mr. Wemyss heaved a sigh that came from the bottoms of his feet.

"She doesn't know," he said flatly.

"Christ," said Jamie involuntarily. He reached for the whisky again, and drank heavily.

"Ahem," I said, giving him a meaningful look as he lowered the jug. He surrendered it to me without comment, and straightened himself on his boulder, shirt plastered against his chest by the wind, his hair whipped loose behind him.

"Well, then," he said firmly. "We'll have the two of them in, and find out the truth of it."

"No," said Mr. Wemyss, "we won't. They don't know, either."

I had just taken a mouthful of raw spirit. At this, I choked, spluttering whisky down my chin.

"They *what*?" I croaked, wiping my face with a corner of my cloak. "You mean . . . *both* of them?"

Mr. Wemyss looked at me. Instead of replying, though, he blinked once. Then his eyes rolled up into his head and he fell headlong off the boulder, poleaxed.

I managed to restore Mr. Wemyss to semiconsciousness, but not to the point of his being able to walk. Jamie was therefore obliged to carry the little man slung across his shoulders like a deer carcass; no mean feat, considering the broken ground that lay between the whisky cache and the new malting floor, and the wind that pelted us with bits of gravel, leaves, and flying pinecones. Clouds had boiled up over the shoulder of the mountain, dark and dirty as laundry suds, and were spreading rapidly across the sky. We were going to get drenched, if we didn't hurry.

The going became easier once we reached the trail to the house, but Jamie's temper was not improved by Mr. Wemyss's suddenly coming to at this point and vomiting down the front of his shirt. After a hasty attempt at swabbing off the mess, we reorganized our strategy, and made our way with Mr. Wemyss precariously balanced between us, each firmly gripping one elbow as he slipped and stumbled, his spindly knees giving way at unexpected moments, like Pinocchio with his strings cut.

Jamie was talking to himself volubly in Gaelic under his breath during this phase of the journey, but desisted abruptly when we came into the dooryard. One of the Beardsley twins was there, catching chickens for Mrs. Bug before the storm; he had two of them, held upside down by the legs like an ungainly bouquet of brown and yellow. He stopped when he saw us, and stared curiously at Mr. Wemyss.

"What—" began the boy. He got no further. Jamie dropped Mr. Wemyss's arm, took two strides, and punched the Beardsley twin in the stomach with sufficient force that he doubled over, dropped the chickens, staggered back, and fell down. The chickens flapped off in a cloud of scattered feathers, squawking.

The boy writhed about on the ground, mouth opening and closing in a vain search for air, but Jamie paid no attention. He stooped, seized the lad by the hair, and spoke loudly and directly into his ear—in case it was Kezzie, I supposed.

"Fetch your brother. To my study. Now."

Mr. Wemyss had been watching this interesting tableau, one arm draped across my shoulders for support and his mouth hanging open. It continued to hang open as he turned his head, following Jamie as he strode back toward us. He blinked, though, and shut it, as Jamie seized his other arm and, removing him neatly from me, propelled him into the house without a backward glance.

I gazed reproachfully at the Beardsley on the ground.

"How *could* you?" I said.

He made soundless goldfish mouths at me, his eyes completely round, then managed a long *heeeeee* sound of inhalation, his face dark purple.

"Jo? What's the matter, are ye hurt?" Lizzie came out of the trees, a pair of chickens clutched by the legs in either hand. She was frowning worriedly at—well, I supposed it *was* Jo; if anyone could tell the difference, it would surely be Lizzie.

"No, he's not hurt," I assured her. "Yet." I pointed a monitory finger at her. "You, young lady, go and put those chickens in their coop and then—" I hesitated, glancing at the boy on the ground, who had recovered enough breath to gasp and was gingerly sitting up. I didn't want to bring her into my surgery, not if Jamie and Mr. Wemyss were going to be eviscerating the Beardsleys right across the hall.

"I'll go with you," I decided hastily, gesturing her away from Jo. "Shoo."

"But—" She cast a bewildered glance at Jo—yes, it was Jo; he ran a hand through his hair to get it out of his face, and I saw the scarred thumb.

"He's fine," I said, turning her toward the chicken coop with a firm hand on her shoulder. "Go."

I glanced back, to see that Jo Beardsley had made it to his feet and, with a hand pressed to his tender middle, was making off toward the stable, presumably to fetch his twin as ordered.

I glanced back at Lizzie, giving her a narrow eye. If Mr. Wemyss had the right end of the stick and she *was* pregnant, she was evidently one of those fortunate persons who doesn't suffer from morning sickness or the usual digestive symptoms of early pregnancy; she was, in fact, very healthy-looking.

That in itself should have alerted me, I supposed, pale and green-stick as she normally was. Now that I looked carefully, there seemed to be a soft pink glow about her, and her pale blond hair was shiny where it peeped out under her cap.

"How far along are you?" I asked, holding back a branch for her. She gave me a quick look, gulped visibly, then ducked under the branch.

"About four months gone, I think," she said meekly, not looking at me. "Um . . . Da told ye, did he?"

"Yes. Your poor father," I said severely. "Is he right? *Both* of the Beardsleys?"

She hunched her shoulders a little, head bowed, but nodded, almost imperceptibly.

"What—what will Himself do to them?" she asked, her voice small and tremulous.

"I really don't know." I doubted that Jamie himself had formed any specific notions—though he *had* mentioned having the miscreant responsible for Lizzie's pregnancy dead at her feet if her father wished it.

Now that I thought, the alternative—having her wed by morning—was likely to be somewhat more problematic than simply killing the twins would be.

"I don't know," I repeated. We had reached the coop, a stoutly built edifice that sheltered under a spreading maple. Several of the hens, slightly less stupid than their sisters, were roosting like huge, ripe fruits in the lower branches, heads buried in their feathers.

I pulled open the door, releasing a gust of ripe ammonia from the dark interior, and holding my breath against the stink, pulled the hens from the tree and tossed them brusquely inside. Lizzie ran into the woods nearby, snatching chickens out from under bushes and rushing back to shove them in. Large drops were beginning to plummet from the clouds, heavy as pebbles, making small, audible splats as they struck the leaves above.

"Hurry!" I slammed the door behind the last of the squawking chickens, threw the latch, and seized Lizzie by the arm. Borne on a whoosh of wind, we ran for the house, skirts whirling up round us like pigeons' wings.

The summer kitchen was nearest; we burst through the door just as the rain came down with a roar, a solid sheet of water that struck the tin roof with a sound like anvils falling.

We stood panting inside. Lizzie's cap had come off in flight, and her plait had come undone, so that her hair straggled over her shoulders in strands of shining, creamy blond; a noticeable change from the wispy, flyaway look she usually shared with her father. If I had seen her without her cap, I should have known at once. I took time to recover my breath, trying to decide what on earth to say to her.

She was making a great to-do over tidying herself, panting and pulling at her bodice, smoothing her skirts—all the while trying not to meet my eye.

Well, there was one question that had been niggling at me since Mr. Wemyss's shocking revelation; best to get that one out of the way at once. The initial roar of the rain had slackened to a regular drumbeat; it was loud, but conversation was at least possible.

"Lizzie." She looked up from her skirt-settling, slightly startled. "Tell me the truth," I said. I put my hands on either side of her face, looking earnestly into her pale blue eyes. "Was it rape?"

She blinked, the look of absolute amazement that suffused her features more eloquent than any spoken denial could have been.

"Oh, no, ma'am!" she said just as earnestly. "Ye couldna think Jo or Kezzie would do such a thing?" Her small pink lips twitched slightly. "What, did ye think they maybe took it in turns to hold me down?"

"No," I said tartly, releasing her. "But I thought I'd best ask, just in case."

I hadn't really thought so. But the Beardsleys were such an odd mix of the civil and the feral that it was impossible to say definitely *what* they might or might not do.

"But it *was* . . . er . . . both of them? That's what your father said. Poor man," I added, with a tone of some reproach.

"Oh." She cast down her pale lashes, pretending to find a loose thread on her skirt. "Ummm . . . well, aye, it was. I do feel something terrible about shaming Da so. And it wasna really that we did it a-purpose . . ."

"Elizabeth Wemyss," I said, with no little asperity, "rape aside—and we've ruled that out—it is not possible to engage in sexual relations with two men without meaning to. One, maybe, but not two. Come to that . . ." I hesitated, but vulgar curiosity was simply too much. "Both at *once?*"

She did look shocked at that, which was something of a relief.

"Oh, no, ma'am! It was . . . I mean, I didna ken that it . . ." She trailed off, quite pink in the face.

I pulled two stools out from under the table and pushed one toward her.

"Sit down," I said, "and tell me about it. We aren't going anywhere for a bit," I added, glancing through the half-open door at the downpour outside. A silver haze rose knee-high over the yard, as the raindrops struck the grass in small explosions of mist, and the sharp smell of it washed through the room.

Lizzie hesitated, but took the stool; I could see her making up her mind to it that there was really nothing to do now but explain—assuming that the situation *could* be explained.

"You, um, said you didn't know," I said, trying to offer her an opening. "You mean—you thought it was only one twin, but they, er, fooled you?"

"Well, aye," she said, and took a huge breath of the chilly air. "Something like that. See, 'twas when you and Himself went to Bethabara for the new goat. Mrs. Bug was down wi' the lumbago, and it was only me and Da in the house—but then he went down to Woolam's for to fetch the flour, and so it was just me."

"To Bethabara? That was six months ago! And you're four months gone—you mean all this time you've been—well, never mind. What happened, then?"

"The fever," she said simply. "It came back."

She had been gathering firewood when the first malarial chill struck her. Recognizing it for what it was, she had dropped the wood and tried to reach the house, only to fall halfway there, her muscles going slack as string.

"I lay upon the ground," she explained, "and I could feel the fever comin' for me. It's like a great beast, aye? I can feel it seize me in its jaws and bite—'tis like my blood runs hot and then cold, and the teeth of it sink into my bones. I can feel it set in then, to try to break them in twa, and suck the marrow." She shuddered in memory.

One of the Beardsleys—she thought it was Kezzie, but had been in no state of mind to ask—had discovered her lying in a disheveled heap in the dooryard. He'd run to fetch his brother, and the two of them had raised her, carried her between them into the house, and fetched her upstairs to her bed.

"My teeth were clackin' so hard together I thought they'd break, surely, but I told them to fetch the ointment, wi' the gall-berries, the ointment ye'd made."

They had rummaged through the surgery cupboard until they found it, and then, frantic as she burned hotter and hotter, had stripped off her shoes and stockings and begun to rub the ointment into her hands and feet.

"I told them—I told them they must rub it all over," she said, her cheeks going a deep peony. She looked down, fiddling with a strand of hair. "I was—well, I was quite oot my mind wi' the fever, ma'am, truly I was. But I kent I needed my medicine bad."

I nodded, beginning to understand. I didn't blame her; I'd seen the malaria overpower her. And so far as that went, she'd done the right thing; she did need the medicine, and couldn't have managed to apply it herself.

Frantic, the two boys had done as she'd said, got her clothes awkwardly off, and rubbed the ointment thoroughly into every inch of her naked body.

"I was goin' in and oot a bit," she explained, "wi' the fever dreams walkin' oot my heid and about the room, so it's all a bit mixed, what I recall. But I do think one o' the lads said to the other as he was getting the ointment all over, and would spoil his shirt, best take it off."

"I see," I said, seeing vividly. "And then . . ."

And then she had quite lost track of what was happening, save that whenever she drifted to the surface of the fever, the boys were still there, talking to her and each other, the murmur of their voices a small anchor to reality and their hands never leaving her, stroking and smoothing and the sharp smell of gallberries cutting through the woodsmoke from the hearth and the scent of beeswax from the candle.

"I felt . . . safe," she said, struggling to express it. "I dinna remember much in particular, only opening my eyes once and seein' his chest right before my face, and the dark curlies all round his paps, and them wee and brown and wrinkled, like raisins." She turned her face to me, eyes still rounded at the memory. "I can still see that, like as it was right in front o' me this minute. That's queer, no?"

"Yes," I agreed, though in fact it was not; there was something about high fever that blurred reality but at the same time could sear certain images so deeply into the mind that they never left. "And then . . . ?"

Then she had begun to shake violently with chills, which neither more quilts nor a hot stone at her feet had helped. And so one of the boys, in desperation, had crawled under the quilts beside her and held her against him, trying to drive out the cold from her bones with his own heat—which, I thought cynically, must have been considerable, at that point.

"I dinna ken which it was, or if it was the same one all night, or if they changed now and then, but whenever I woke, he was there, wi' his arms about me. And sometimes he'd put back the blanket and rub more ointment down my back and, and, round . . ." She stumbled, blushing. "But when I woke in the morning, the fever was gone, like it always is on the second day."

She looked at me, pleading for understanding.

"D'ye ken how that is, ma'am, when a great fever's broken? 'Tis the same every time, so I'm thinking it may be so for everyone. But it's . . . peaceful. Your limbs are sae heavy ye canna think of moving, but ye dinna much care. And everything ye see—all the wee things ye take nay notice of day by day—ye notice, and they're beautiful," she said simply. "I think sometimes that will be how it is when I'm dead. I shall just wake, and everything will be like that, peaceful and beautiful—save I shall be able to move."

"But you woke this time, and couldn't," I said. "And the boy—whichever it was—he was still there, with you?"

"It was Jo," she said, nodding. "He spoke to me, but I didna pay much mind to what he said, and I dinna think he did, either."

She bit her lower lip momentarily, the small teeth sharp and white.

"I—I hadna done it before, ma'am. But I came close, a time or two wi' Manfred. And closer still wi' Bobby Higgins. But Jo hadna ever even kissed a lass, nor his brother had, either. So ye see, 'twas really my fault, for I kent well enough what was happening, but . . . we were both slippery wi' the ointment, still, and naked under the quilts, and it . . . happened."

I nodded, understanding precisely and in detail.

"Yes, I can see how it happened, all right. But then it . . . er . . . went on happening, I suppose?"

Her lips pursed up and she went very pink again.

"Well . . . aye. It did. It—it feels sae *nice*, ma'am," she whispered, leaning a little toward me as though imparting an important secret.

I rubbed a knuckle hard across my lips.

"Um, yes. Quite. But—"

The Beardsleys had washed the sheets at her direction, and there were no incriminating traces left by the time her father returned, two days later. The gallberries had done their work, and while she was still weak and tired, she told Mr. Wemyss only that she had had a mild attack.

Meanwhile, she met with Jo at every opportunity, in the deep summer grass behind the dairy shed, in the fresh straw in the stable—and when it rained, now and then on the porch of the Beardsleys' cabin.

"I wouldna do it inside, for the stink o' the hides," she explained. "But we put an old quilt on the porch, so as I shouldna have splinters in my backside, and the rain comin' down just a foot away . . ." She looked wistfully through the open door, where the rain had softened into a steady whisper, the needles trembling on the pine trees as it fell.

"And what about Kezzie? Where was he, while all this was going on?" I asked.

"Ah. Well, Kezzie," she said, taking a deep breath.

They had made love in the stable, and Jo had left her lying on her cloak in the straw, watching as he rose and dressed himself. Then he had kissed her and turned to the door. Seeing that he had forgotten his canteen, she called softly after him.

"And he didna answer, nor turn round," she said. "And it came to me sudden, as he didna hear me."

"Oh, I see," I said softly. "You, um, couldn't tell the difference?"

She gave me a direct blue look.

"I can *now*," she said.

In the beginning, though, sex was so new—and the brothers both sufficiently inexperienced—that she hadn't noticed any differences.

"How long . . . ?" I asked. "I mean, do you have any idea when they, er . . . ?"

"Not for certain," she admitted. "But if I was to guess about it, I think the first time it was Jo—no, I ken for sure that was Jo, for I saw his thumb—but the second time, it was likely Kezzie. They share, ken?"

They *did* share—everything. And so it was the most natural thing in the world—to all three of them, evidently—that Jo should wish his brother to share in this new marvel.

"I ken it seems . . . strange," she said, shrugging a little. "And I suppose I ought to have said something, or done something—but I couldna think what. And really"—she raised her eyes to me, helpless—"it didna seem *wrong* at all. They're different, aye, but at the same time, they're sae close to each other . . . well, it's just as if I was touching the one lad, and talking to him—only he's got the twa bodies."

"Twa bodies," I said, a little bleakly. "Well, yes. There's just the difficulty, you see, the two bodies part." I eyed her closely. Despite the history of malaria and her fine-boned build, she had definitely filled out; she had a plump little bosom swelling over the edge of her bodice, and, while she was sitting on it so I couldn't tell for sure, very likely a bottom to match. The only real wonder was that it had taken her three months to fall pregnant.

As though reading my mind, she said, "I took the seeds, aye? The ones you and Miss Bree take. I had a store put by, from when I was betrothed to Manfred; Miss Bree gave me them. I meant to gather more, but I didna always remember, and—" She shrugged again, putting her hands across her belly.

"Whereupon you proceeded to say nothing," I observed. "Did your father find out by accident?"

"No, I told him," she said. "I thought I best had, before I began to show. Jo and Kezzie came with me."

This explained Mr. Wemyss's resort to strong drink, all right. Perhaps we should have brought the jug back with us.

"Your poor father," I said again, but abstractedly. "Had the three of you worked out any sort of plan?"

"Well, no," she admitted. "I hadna told the lads I was in a family way 'til this morning, either. They seemed taken back a bit," she added, biting her lip again.

"I daresay." I glanced outside; it was still raining, but the downpour had slackened momentarily, dimpling the puddles on the path. I rubbed a hand over my face, feeling suddenly rather tired.

"Which one will you choose?" I asked.

She gave me a sudden, startled look, the blood draining from her cheeks.

"You can't have them both, you know," I said gently. "It doesn't work that way."

"Why?" she said, trying for boldness—but her voice trembled. "It's no harming anyone. And it's no one's business but ours."

I began to feel the need of a stiff drink myself.

"Hoho," I said. "Try telling your father that. Or Mr. Fraser. In a big city, perhaps you could get away with it. But here? Everything that happens is everybody's business, and you know it. Hiram Crombie would stone you for fornication as soon as look at you, if he found out about it." Without waiting for a reply, I got to my feet.

"Now, then. We'll go back to the house and see whether they're both still alive. Mr. Fraser may have taken matters into his own hands, and solved the problem for you."

The twins were still alive, but didn't look as though they were particularly glad of the fact. They sat shoulder to shoulder in the center of Jamie's study, pressed together as though trying to re-unite into a single being.

Their heads jerked toward the door in unison, looks of alarm and concern mingling with joy at seeing Lizzie. I had her by the arm, but when she saw the twins, she pulled loose and hurried to them with a small exclamation, putting an arm about each boy's neck to draw him to her bosom.

I saw that one of the boys had a fresh black eye, just beginning to puff and swell; I supposed it must be Kezzie, though I didn't know whether this was Jamie's notion of fairness, or merely a convenient means of ensuring that he could tell which twin was which while talking to them.

Mr. Wemyss was also alive, though he didn't look any more pleased about it than the Beardsleys. He was red-eyed, pale, and still slightly green about the gills, but was at least upright and reasonably sober, seated beside Jamie's table. There was a cup of chicory coffee in front of him—I could smell it—but it seemed so far untouched.

Lizzie knelt on the floor, still clinging to the boys, the three heads drawn together like the lobes of a clover leaf as they murmured to one another.

"Are ye hurt?" she was saying, and "Are ye all right?" they were asking, an absolute tangle of hands and arms meanwhile searching, patting, stroking, and embracing. They reminded me of nothing so much as a tenderly solicitous octopus.

I glanced at Jamie, who was viewing this behavior with a jaundiced eye. Mr. Wemyss emitted a low moan, and buried his head in his hands.

Jamie cleared his throat with a low Scottish noise of infinite menace, and the proceedings in the middle of the room stopped as though hit with some sort of paralyzing death ray. Very slowly, Lizzie turned her head to look at him, chin held high, her arms still locked protectively about the Beardsleys' necks.

"Sit down, lass," Jamie said with relative mildness, nodding toward an empty stool.

Lizzie rose, and turned, her eyes still fixed on him. She made no move to take the offered stool, though. Instead, she walked deliberately round behind the twins and stood between them, putting her hands upon their shoulders.

"I'll stand, sir," she said, her voice high and thin with fear, but filled with determination. Like clockwork, each twin reached up and grasped the hand upon his shoulder, their faces assuming similar expressions of mingled apprehension and steadfastness.

Jamie wisely decided not to make an issue of it, instead nodding to me in an offhand way. I took the stool myself, surprisingly glad to sit down.

"The lads and I have been talking wi' your father," he said, addressing Lizzie. "I take it it's true, what ye told your Da? Ye are with child, and ye dinna ken which is the father?"

Lizzie opened her mouth, but no words came out. Instead, she bobbed her head in an awkward nod.

"Aye. Well, then, ye'll need to be wed, and the sooner the better," he said, in a matter-of-fact tone of voice. "The lads couldna quite decide which of them it should be, so it's up to you, lass. Which one?"

All six hands tightened in a flash of white knuckles. It was really quite fascinating—and I couldn't help feeling sorry for the three of them.

"I can't," Lizzie whispered. Then she cleared her throat and tried again. "I can't," she repeated more strongly. "I don't—I don't want to choose. I love them both."

Jamie looked down at his clasped hands for a moment, lips pursing as he thought. Then he raised his head and looked at her, very levelly. I saw her draw herself upright, lips pressed together, trembling but resolute, determined to defy him.

Then, with truly diabolical timing, Jamie turned to Mr. Wemyss.

"Joseph?" he said mildly.

Mr. Wemyss had been sitting transfixed, eyes on his daughter, pale hands wrapped round his coffee cup. He didn't hesitate, though, or even blink.

"Elizabeth," he said, his voice very soft, "do you love *me*?"

Her facade of defiance broke like a dropped egg, tears welling from her eyes.

"Oh, Da!" she said. She let go the twins and ran to her father, who stood up in time to clasp her tightly in his arms, cheek pressed to her hair. She clung to him, sobbing, and I heard a brief sigh from one of the twins, though I couldn't tell which one.

Mr. Wemyss swayed gently with her, patting and soothing her, his murmured words indistinguishable from her sobs and broken utterances.

Jamie was watching the twins—not without sympathy. Their hands were knotted together, and Kezzie's teeth were fixed in his lower lip.

Lizzie separated herself from her father, sniffling and groping vaguely for a handkerchief. I pulled one from my pocket, got up, and gave it to her. She blew her nose hard, and wiped her eyes, trying not to look at Jamie; she knew very well where the danger lay.

It was, however, a fairly small room, and Jamie was not a person who could be easily ignored, even in a large one. Unlike my surgery, the windows of the study were small and placed high in the wall, which gave the room under normal circumstances a pleasant dim coziness. At the moment, with the rain still coming down outside, a gray light filled the room and the air was chill.

"It's no a matter of whom ye love, now, lass," Jamie said very gently. "Not even your father." He nodded toward her stomach. "Ye've a child in your belly. Nothing else matters, but to do right by it. And that doesna mean painting its mother a whore, aye?"

Her cheeks flamed, a patchy crimson.

"I'm not a whore!"

"I didna say ye were," Jamie replied calmly. "But others will, and it gets around what ye've been up to, lass. Spreading your legs for two men, and married to neither of them? And now with a wean, and ye canna name its father?"

She looked angrily away from him—and saw her own father, head bowed, his own cheeks darkening in shame. She made a small, heartbroken sound, and buried her face in her hands.

The twins stirred uneasily, glancing at each other, and Jo got his feet under him to rise—then caught a look of wounded reproach from Mr. Wemyss, and changed his mind.

Jamie sighed heavily and rubbed a knuckle down the bridge of his nose. He stood then, stooped to the hearth, and pulled two straws from the basket of kindling. Holding these in his fist, he held them out to the twins.

"Short straw weds her," he said with resignation.

The twins gaped at him, open-mouthed. Then Kezzie swallowed visibly, closed his eyes, and plucked a straw, gingerly, as though it might be attached to something explosive. Jo kept his eyes open, but didn't look at the straw he'd drawn; his eyes were fixed on Lizzie.

Everyone seemed to exhale at once, looking at the straws.

"Verra well, then. Stand up," Jamie said to Kezzie, who held the short one. Looking dazed, he did so.

"Take her hand," Jamie told him patiently. "Now, d'ye swear

before these witnesses"—he nodded at me and Mr. Wemyss—
"that ye take Elizabeth Wemyss as your wife?"

Kezzie nodded, then cleared his throat and drew himself up.

"I do, so," he said firmly.

"And do you, ye wee besom, accept Keziah—ye *are* Keziah?"
he asked, squinting dubiously at the twin. "Aye, all right, Keziah.
Ye'll take him as your husband?"

"Aye," Lizzie said, sounding hopelessly confused.

"Good," Jamie said briskly. "You're handfast. Directly we find
a priest, we'll have it properly blessed, but ye're married." He
looked at Jo, who had risen to his feet.

"And you," he said firmly, "ye'll leave. Tonight. Ye'll not come
back 'til the child is born."

Jo was white to the lips, but nodded. He had both hands
pressed to his body—not where Jamie had hit him, but higher,
over his heart. I felt a sharp answering pain in the same place, seeing his face.

"Well, then." Jamie took a deep breath, his shoulders slumping
a little. "Joseph—have ye still got the marriage contract ye drew
for your daughter and young McGillivray? Fetch it out, aye, and
we'll change the name."

Looking like a snail poking its head out after a thunderstorm, Mr. Wemyss nodded cautiously. He looked at Lizzie,
still standing hand-in-hand with her new bridegroom, the two
of them resembling Lot and Mrs. Lot, respectively. Mr. Wemyss
patted her softly on the shoulder, and hurried out, his feet tapping on the stairs.

"You'll need a fresh candle, won't you?" I said to Jamie, tilting
my head meaningfully toward Lizzie and the twins. The stub in
his candlestick had half an inch to go, but I thought it only decent
to give them a few moments of privacy.

"Oh? Oh, aye," he said, catching my meaning. He coughed.
"I'll, ah, come and get it."

The moment we entered my surgery, he closed the door, leaned
against it, and let his head fall, shaking it.

"Oh, God," he said.

"Poor things," I said, with some sympathy. "I mean—you do
have to feel sorry for them."

"I do?" He sniffed at his shirt, which had dried but still had a
distinct stain of vomit down the front, then straightened up,

stretching 'til his back creaked. "Aye, I suppose I do," he admitted. "But—oh, God! Did she tell ye how it happened?"

"Yes. I'll tell you the gory details later." I heard Mr. Wemyss's feet coming down the stairs. I took down a fresh pair of candles from the array that hung near the ceiling and held them out, stretching the long wick that joined them. "Do you have a knife handy?"

His hand went automatically to his waist, but he wasn't wearing his dirk.

"No. There's a penknife on my desk, though."

He opened the door just as Mr. Wemyss reached the office. Mr. Wemyss's exclamation of shock reached me simultaneously with the smell of blood.

Jamie pushed Mr. Wemyss unceremoniously aside, and I rushed in after him, heart in my throat.

The three of them were standing by the desk, close together. A spray of fresh blood stained the desk, and Kezzie was holding my bloodied handkerchief wrapped round his hand. He looked up at Jamie, his face ghostly in the guttering light. His teeth were gritted tight together, but he managed a smile.

A small movement caught my eye, and I saw Jo, carefully holding the blade of Jamie's penknife over the candle flame. Acting as though no one was there, he took his brother's hand, pulled off the handkerchief, and pressed the hot metal against the raw oval of the wound on Kezzie's thumb.

Mr. Wemyss made a small choking noise, and the smell of seared flesh mixed with the scent of rain. Kezzie drew breath deeply, then let it out, and smiled crookedly at Jo.

"Godspeed, Brother," he said, his voice a little loud and flat.

"Much happiness to you, Brother," Jo said—in the same voice.

Lizzie stood between them, small and disheveled, her reddened eyes fixed on Jamie. And smiled.

74

So Romantic

Brianna drove the little car slowly up the slope of the quilt over Roger's leg, across his stomach, and into the center of his chest, where he captured both the car and her hand, giving her a wry grin.

"That's a really good car," she said, pulling her hand loose and rolling comfortably onto her side beside him. "All four wheels turn. What kind is it? A Morris Minor, like that little orange thing you had in Scotland? That was the cutest thing I ever saw, but I never understood how you managed to squeeze into it."

"With talcum powder," he assured her. He lifted the toy and set a front wheel spinning with a flick of his thumb. "Aye, it *is* a good one, isn't it? It isn't really meant to be a particular model, but I suppose I was remembering that Ford Mustang of yours. Remember driving down out of the mountains that time?" His eyes softened with memory, the green of them nearly black in the dim light of the banked fire.

"I do. I nearly drove off the road when you kissed me at eighty-five miles per hour."

She moved closer to him by reflex, nudging him with a knee. He rolled obligingly to face her, and kissed her again, meanwhile running the car swiftly backward down the length of her spine and over the curve of her buttocks. She yelped and squirmed against him, trying to escape the tickling wheels, then punched him in the ribs.

"Cut that out!"

"I thought ye found speed erotic. Vroom," he murmured, steering the toy up her arm—and suddenly down the neck of her shift.

She grabbed for the car, but he snatched it away, then plunged his hand under the covers, running the wheels down her thigh—then madly up again.

A furious wrestling match for possession of the car ensued, which ended with both of them on the floor in a tangle of bedding and nightclothes, gasping for breath and helpless with giggling.

"Ssh! You'll wake up Jemmy!" She heaved and wriggled, trying to get out from under Roger's weight. Secure in his fifty pounds' advantage, he merely relaxed on top of her, pinning her to the floor.

"You couldn't wake him with cannon fire," Roger said, with a certainty born of experience. It was true; once past the stage of waking to be fed every few hours, Jem had always slept like a particularly comatose log.

She subsided, puffing hair out of her eyes and biding her time.

"Do you think you'll ever go anywhere at eighty-five miles per hour again?"

"Only if I fall off the edge of a very deep gorge. Ye're naked, did ye know that?"

"Well, so are you!"

"Aye, but I started out that way. Where's the car?"

"I have no idea," she lied. It was, in fact, under the small of her back, and very uncomfortable, but she wasn't about to give him any further advantages. "What do you want it for?"

"Oh, I was going to explore the terrain a bit," he said, raising himself on one elbow and walking his fingers slowly across the upper slope of one breast. "I suppose I could do it on foot, though. Takes more time, but ye do enjoy the scenery more. They say."

"Mmm." He could hold her down with his weight, but couldn't restrain her arms. She extended one index finger, and placed the nail of it precisely on his nipple, making him breathe in deeply. "Did you have a long journey in mind?" She glanced at the small shelf near the bed, where she kept her contraceptive materials.

"Long enough." He followed her glance, then looked back to meet her eyes, a question in his own.

She wriggled to make herself more comfortable, unobtrusively dislodging the miniature car.

"They say a journey of a thousand miles begins with a single step," she said, and raising her head, put her mouth on his nipple, and closed her teeth gently. A moment later, she let go.

"Be quiet," she said reproachfully. "You'll wake up Jemmy."

"Where are your scissors? I'm cutting it off."

"I'm not telling you. I like it long." She pushed the soft dark hair back from his face and kissed the end of his nose, which appeared to disconcert him slightly. He smiled, though, and kissed her briefly back before sitting up, swiping the hair out of his face with one hand.

"That can't be comfortable," he said, eyeing the cradle. "Surely I should move him to his own bed?"

Brianna glanced up at the cradle from her position on the floor. Jemmy, aged four, had long since graduated to a trundle bed, but now and then insisted upon sleeping in his cradle for old times' sake, wedging himself stubbornly into it, despite the fact that he couldn't get all four limbs and his head inside at once. He was invisible at the moment, save for two chubby bare legs sticking straight up in the air at one end.

He was getting so big, she thought. He couldn't quite read yet, but knew all his letters, and could count to a hundred and write his name. And he knew how to load a gun; his grandfather had taught him.

"Do we tell him?" she asked suddenly. "And if so, when?"

Roger must have been thinking something along the same lines, for he appeared to understand exactly what she meant.

"Christ, how do you tell a kid something like that?" he said. He rose and picked up a handful of bedding, shaking it in apparent hopes of finding the leather string with which he bound his hair.

"Wouldn't you tell a kid if he were adopted?" she objected, sitting up and running both hands through her own bountiful hair. "Or if there's some family scandal, like his father's not dead, he's in prison? If you tell them early, it doesn't mean all that much to them, I don't think; they're comfortable with it as they get older. If they find out later, it's a shock."

He gave her a wry, sidelong look. "You'd know."

"So would you." She spoke dryly, but she felt the echo of it, even now. Disbelief, anger, denial—and then the sudden collapse of her world as she began, against her will, to believe. The sense of hollowness and abandonment—and the sense of black rage and betrayal at discovering how much of what she had taken for granted was a lie.

"At least for you, it wasn't a choice," she said, squirming into a more comfortable position against the edge of the bed. "Nobody knew about you; nobody *could* have told you what you were—but didn't."

"Oh, and ye think they should have told you about the time travel early on? Your parents?" He lifted one black brow, cynically amused. "I can see the notes coming home from your school—*Brianna has a most creative imagination, but should be encouraged to recognize situations where it is not appropriate to employ it.*"

"Ha." She kicked away the remaining tangle of clothes and bedding. "I went to a Catholic school. The nuns would have called it lying, and put a stop to it, period. Where's my shift?" She had wriggled completely out of it in the struggle, and while she was still warm from their struggle, she felt uncomfortably exposed, even in the dim shadows of the room.

"Here it is." He plucked a wad of linen from the mess and shook it out. "Do you?" he repeated, looking up at her with one brow raised.

"Think they should have told me? Yes. And no," she admitted reluctantly. She reached for the shift and pulled it over her head. "I mean—I see why they didn't. Daddy didn't believe it, to start with. And what he *did* believe . . . well, whatever it was, he did ask Mama to let me think he was my real father. She gave him her word; I guess I don't think she should have broken it, no." To the best of her knowledge, her mother had broken her word only once—unwillingly, but to staggering effect.

She smoothed the worn linen over her body and fished for the ends of the drawstring that gathered the neck. She was covered now, but felt just as much exposed as if she were still naked. Roger was sitting on the mattress, methodically shaking out the blankets, but his eyes were still fixed on her, green and questioning.

"It was still a lie," she burst out. "I had a right to know!"

He nodded slowly.

"Mmphm." He picked up a rope of twisted sheet and began unwinding it. "Aye, well. I can see telling a kid he's adopted or his dad's in prison. This is maybe more along the lines of telling a kid his father murdered his mother when he found her screwing the postie and six good friends in the kitchen, though. Maybe it doesn't mean that much to him if you tell him early on—but it's definitely going to get the attention of his friends when he starts telling *them*."

She bit her lip, feeling unexpectedly cross and prickly. She hadn't thought her own feelings were still so near the surface, and didn't like either the fact that they were—or that Roger could see that they were.

"Well . . . yes." She glanced at the cradle. Jem had moved; he was curled up like a hedgehog now, with his face pressed to his knees, and nothing visible save the curve of his bottom under his nightshirt, rising over the edge of the cradle like the moon rising above the horizon. "You're right. We'd have to wait until he's old enough to realize that he can't tell people; that it's a secret."

The leather thong fell out of a shaken quilt. He bent to pick it up, dark hair falling round his face.

"Would ye want to tell Jem someday that I'm not his real father?" he asked quietly, not looking at her.

"Roger!" All her crossness disappeared in a flood of panic. "I wouldn't do that in a hundred million years! Even if I thought it was true," she added hastily, "and I don't. Roger, I don't! I know you're his father." She sat down beside him, gripping his arm urgently. He smiled, a little crookedly, and patted her hand—but he wouldn't meet her eyes. He waited a moment, then moved, gently disengaging himself in order to tie up his hair.

"What ye said, though. Has he not got a right to know who he is?"

"That's not—it's different." It was; and yet it wasn't. The act that had resulted in her own conception hadn't been rape—but it had been just as unintended. On the other hand, there had been no doubt, either: both—well, all three—of her parents had known that she was Jamie Fraser's child, beyond doubt.

With Jem . . . she looked again at the cradle, instinctively wanting to find some stamp, some undeniable clue to his paternity. But he looked like her, and like her father, in terms both of coloring and feature. He was big for his age, long-limbed and broad-backed—but so were both of the men who might have fathered him. And both, damn them, had green eyes.

"I'm not telling him that," she said firmly. "Not ever, and neither are you. You *are* his father, in any way that matters. And there wouldn't be any good reason for him to even know that Stephen Bonnet exists."

"Save that he *does* exist," Roger pointed out. "And *he* thinks the wean is his. What if they should meet someday? When Jem's older, I mean."

She had not grown up with the habit of crossing herself at moments of stress as her father and cousin did—but she did it now, making him laugh.

"I am not being funny," she said, sitting up straight. "It's not happening. And if it did—if I ever saw Stephen Bonnet anywhere near my child, I'd . . . well, next time, I'll aim higher, that's all."

"Ye're determined to give the lad a good story for his classmates, aren't you?" He spoke lightly, teasing, and she relaxed a little, hoping that she had succeeded in easing any doubt he might have about what she might tell Jemmy regarding his paternity.

"Okay, but he does have to know the rest, sooner or later. I don't want him to find out by accident."

"You didna find out by accident. Your mother *did* tell you." *And look where we are now.* That bit went unspoken, but rang loud inside her head, as he gave her a long, straight look.

If she hadn't felt compelled to come back, go through the stones to find her real father—none of them would be here now. They'd be safe in the twentieth century, perhaps in Scotland, perhaps in America—but in a place where children didn't die of diarrhea and sudden fevers.

In a place where sudden danger didn't lurk behind every tree and war wasn't hiding under the bushes. A place where Roger's voice still sang pure and strong.

But maybe—just maybe—she wouldn't have Jem.

"I'm sorry," she said, feeling choked. "I know it's my fault—all of it. If I hadn't come back . . ." She reached out, tentatively, and touched the ragged scar that circled his throat. He caught her hand and pulled it down.

"Christ," he said softly, "if I could have gone anywhere to find either of my parents—including hell—Brianna, I would have done it." He looked up, his eyes bright green, and squeezed her hand hard. "If there's anyone in this world who understands that, hen, it's me."

She squeezed back with both hands, hard. Relief that he didn't blame her loosened the cords of her body, but sorrow for his own losses—and hers—still filled throat and chest, heavy as wet feathers, and it hurt to breathe.

Jemmy stirred, rose suddenly upright, then fell back, still sound asleep, so that one arm flopped out of the cradle, limp as a noodle. She'd frozen at his sudden movement, but now relaxed and rose to try to tuck the arm back in. Before she could reach the cradle, though, a knock came at the door.

Roger grabbed hastily for his shirt with one hand, his knife with the other.

"Who is it?" she called, heart thumping. People didn't pay calls after dark, save in emergency.

"It's me, Miss Bree," said Lizzie's voice through the wood. "Can we come in, please?" She sounded excited, but not alarmed. Brianna waited to be sure that Roger was decently covered, then lifted the heavy bolt.

Her first thought was that Lizzie looked excited, too; the little bondmaid's cheeks were flushed as apples, the color visible even in the darkness of the stoop.

"We" was herself and the two Beardsleys, who bowed and nodded, murmuring apologies for the lateness of the hour.

"Not at all," Brianna said automatically, glancing around for a shawl. Not only was her linen shift thin and ratty, it had an incriminating stain on the front. "Er, come in!"

Roger came forward to greet the unexpected guests, magnificently disregarding the fact that he was wearing nothing but a shirt, and she scuttled hastily into the dark corner behind her loom, groping for the ancient shawl she kept there as comfort for her legs while working.

Safely wrapped in this, she kicked a log to break the fire, and stooped to light a candle from the fiery coals. In the wavering glow of the candlelight, she could see that the Beardsleys were dressed with unaccustomed neatness, their hair combed and firmly plaited, each with a clean shirt and a leather vest; they didn't own coats. Lizzie was dressed in her best, too—in fact, she was wearing the pale peach woolen dress they had made for her wedding.

Something was up, and it was fairly obvious what, as Lizzie buzzed earnestly into Roger's ear.

"Ye want me to *marry* you?" Roger said, in tones of astonishment. He glanced from one twin to the other. "Er . . . to whom?"

"Aye, sir." Lizzie bobbed a respectful curtsey. "It's me and Jo, sir, if ye'd be sae kind. Kezzie's come to be witness."

Roger rubbed a hand over his face, looking baffled.

"Well . . . but . . ." He gave Brianna a pleading look.

"Are you in trouble, Lizzie?" Brianna asked directly, lighting a second candle and putting it in the sconce by the door. With more light, she could see that Lizzie's eyelids were reddened and swollen, as though she had been crying—though her attitude was one of excited determination, rather than fear.

"Not to say trouble, exactly. But I—I'm wi' child, aye." Lizzie crossed her hands on her belly, protective. "We—we wanted to be marrit, before I tell anyone."

"Oh. Well . . ." Roger gave Jo a disapproving look, but appeared no more than half-convinced. "But your father—won't he—"

"Da would want us to be marrit by a priest," Lizzie explained earnestly. "And so we will be. But ye ken, sir, it'll be months—maybe years—before we can find one." She cast down her eyes, blushing. "I—I should like to be marrit, with proper words, ken, before the babe comes."

"Yes," he said, eyes drawn ineluctably to Lizzie's midsection. "I grasp that. But I dinna quite understand the rush, if ye take my meaning. I mean, ye won't be noticeably more pregnant tomorrow than ye are tonight. Or next week."

Jo and Kezzie exchanged glances over Lizzie's head. Then Jo put his hand on Lizzie's waist and drew her gently to him.

"Sir. It's only—we want to do right by each other. But we'd like it to be private, see? Just me and Lizzie, and my brother."

"Just us," Kezzie echoed, drawing close. He looked earnestly at Roger. "Please, sir?" He seemed to have injured his hand somehow; there was a handkerchief wound round it.

Brianna found the three of them touching almost beyond bearing; they were so innocent, and so young, the three scrubbed faces turned earnestly up to Roger in supplication. She moved closer and touched Roger's arm, warm through the cloth of his sleeve.

"Do it for them," she said softly. "Please? It's not a marriage, exactly—but you can make them handfast"

"Aye, well, but they ought to be counseled . . . her father . . ."

His protests trailed off as he glanced from her toward the trio, and she could see that he was as much touched by their innocence as she was. And, she thought, privately amused, he was also very much drawn by the thought of performing his first wedding, unorthodox as it might be. The circumstances would be romantic and memorable, here in the quiet of the night, vows exchanged by the light of fire and candle, with the memory of their own lovemaking warm in the shadows and the sleeping child a silent witness, both blessing and promise for the new marriage to be made.

Roger sighed deeply, then smiled at her in resignation, and turned away.

"Aye, all right, then. Let me put my breeches on, though; I'm not conducting my first wedding bare-arsed."

Roger held a spoon of marmalade over his slice of toast, staring at me.

"They *what*?" he said, in a strangled tone.

"Oh, she *didn't*!" Bree clapped a hand to her mouth, eyes wide above it, removing it at once to ask, "*Both* of them?"

"Evidently so," I said, suppressing a most disgraceful urge to laugh. "You really married her to Jo last night?"

"God help me, I did," Roger muttered. Looking thoroughly rattled, he put the spoon in his coffee cup and stirred mechanically. "But she's handfast with Kezzie, too?"

"Before witnesses," I assured him, with a wary glance at Mr. Wemyss, who was sitting across the breakfast table, mouth open and apparently turned to stone.

"Do you think—" Bree said to me, "I mean—both of them at *once*?"

"Er, she said not," I replied, cutting my eyes toward Mr. Wemyss as an indication that perhaps this was not a suitable question to be considering in his presence, fascinating as it was.

"Oh, God," Mr. Wemyss said, in a voice from the sepulchre. "She is damned."

"Holy Mary, Mother of God." Mrs. Bug, saucer-eyed, crossed herself. "May Christ have mercy!"

Roger took a gulp of his coffee, choked, and put it down, spluttering. Brianna pounded him helpfully on the back, but he motioned her away, eyes watering, and pulled himself together.

"Now, it's maybe not so bad as it seems," he said to Mr. Wemyss, trying to find a bright side to look on. "I mean, one could maybe make a case that the twins are one soul that God's put into two bodies for purposes of His own."

"Aye, but—two bodies!" Mrs. Bug said. "Do ye think—both at *once*?"

"I don't know," I said, giving up. "But I imagine—" I glanced at the window, where the snow whispered at the closed shutter. It had begun to snow heavily the night before, a thick, wet snow; by now, there was nearly a foot of it on the ground, and I was reasonably sure that everyone at the table was imagining exactly what I was: a vision of Lizzie and the Beardsley twins, tucked up cozily in a warm bed of furs by a blazing fire, enjoying their honeymoon.

"Well, I don't suppose there's actually much anybody can *do* about it," Bree said practically. "If we say anything in public, the Presbyterians will probably stone Lizzie as a Papist whore, and—"

Mr. Wemyss made a sound like a stepped-on pig's bladder.

"Certainly no one will say anything." Roger fixed Mrs. Bug with a hard look. "Will they?"

"Well, I'll have to tell Arch, mind, or I'll burst," she said frankly. "But no one else. Silent as the grave, I swear it, de'il take me if I lie." She put both hands over her mouth in illustration, and Roger nodded.

"I suppose," he said dubiously, "that the marriage I performed isna actually valid as such. But then—"

"It's certainly as valid as the handfasting Jamie did," I said. "And besides, I think it's too late to force her to choose. Once Kezzie's thumb heals, no one will be able to tell . . ."

"Except Lizzie, probably," Bree said. She licked a smear of honey from the corner of her mouth, regarding Roger thoughtfully. "I wonder what it would be like if there were two of you?"

"We'd both of us be thoroughly bamboozled," he assured her. "Mrs. Bug—is there any more coffee?"

"Who's bamboozled?" The kitchen door opened in a swirl of snow and frigid air, and Jamie came in with Jem, both fresh from a visit to the privy, ruddy-faced, their hair and lashes thick with melting snowflakes.

"You, for one. You've just been done in the eye by a nineteen-year-old bigamist," I informed him.

"What's a bigamiss?" Jem inquired.

"A very large young lady," Roger said, taking a piece of buttered toast and thrusting it into Jem's mouth. "Here. Why don't ye take that, and . . ." His voice died away as he realized that he couldn't send Jem outside.

"Lizzie and the twins came round to Roger's last night, and she married her to Jo," I told Jamie. He blinked, water from the melting snow on his lashes running down his face.

"I will be damned," he said. He took a long breath, then realized he was still covered with snow, and went to shake himself at the hearth, bits of snow falling into the fire with a sputter and hiss.

"Well," he said, coming back to the table and sitting down beside me, "at least your grandson will have a name, Joseph. It's Beardsley, either way."

This ridiculous observation seemed actually to comfort Mr. Wemyss a bit; a small bit of color came back to his cheeks, and he allowed Mrs. Bug to put a fresh bannock on his plate.

"Aye, I suppose that's something," he said. "And I really cannot see—"

"Come *look*," Jemmy was saying, tugging impatiently on Bree's arm. "Come see, Mama!"

"See what?"

"I wrote my name! Grandda showed me!"

"Oh, you did? Well, good for you!" Brianna beamed at him, then her brow furrowed. "What—just now?"

"Yes! Come see afore it's covered up!"

She looked at Jamie under lowered brows.

"Da, you *didn't.*"

He took a piece of fresh toast from the platter, and spread it neatly with butter.

"Aye, well," he said, "there's got to be *some* advantage still to being a man, even if no one pays a bit of heed to what ye say. Will ye pass the marmalade, Roger Mac?"

J em put his elbows on the table, chin on his fists, following the path of the spoon through the batter with the intent expression of a lion watching an appetizing wildebeest on its way to the water hole.

"Don't even think about it," I said, with a glance at his grubby fingers. "They'll be done in a few minutes; you can have one then."

"But I like 'em raw, Grandma," he protested. He widened his dark-blue eyes in wordless pleading.

"You oughtn't to eat raw things," I said sternly. "They can make you sick."

"You do, Grandma." He poked a finger at my mouth, where a smudge of brownish batter remained. I cleared my throat and wiped the incriminating evidence on a towel.

"You'll spoil your supper," I said, but with the acuity of any jungle beast, he sensed the weakening of his prey.

"Promise I won't. I'll eat everything!" he said, already reaching for the spoon.

"Yes, that's what I'm afraid of," I said, relinquishing it with some reluctance. "Just a taste, now—leave some for your daddy and grandda."

He nodded, wordless, and licked the spoon with a long, slow swipe of the tongue, closing his eyes in ecstasy.

I found another spoon and set about dropping the cookies onto the tin sheets I used for baking. We ended in a dead heat, the sheets full and the bowl quite empty, just as footsteps came down the hallway toward the door. Recognizing Brianna's tread, I snatched the empty spoon from Jemmy and rubbed a quick towel across his smudgy mouth.

Bree stopped in the doorway, her smile turning to a look of suspicion.

"What are you guys doing?"

"Making molasses cookies," I said, lifting the sheets in evidence, before sliding them into the brick oven set in the wall of the fireplace. "Jemmy's been helping me."

One neat red brow arched upward. She glanced from me to Jemmy, who was wearing a look of sublimely unnatural innocence. I gathered my own expression was no more convincing.

"So I see," she said dryly. "How much batter did you eat, Jem?"

"Who, me?" Jemmy said, eyes going wide.

"Mmm." She leaned forward, and picked a speck out of his wavy red hair. "What's this, then?"

He frowned at it, crossing his eyes slightly in the attempt to focus.

"A real big louse?" he suggested brightly. "Reckon I got it from Rabbie McLeod."

"Rabbie McLeod?" I said, uneasily aware that Rabbie had been curled up on the kitchen settle a few days ago, his unruly black curls flowing into Jemmy's bright locks as the boys slept, waiting for their fathers. I recalled thinking at the time how charming the little boys looked, curled up head to head, their faces soft with dreaming.

"Has Rabbie got lice?" Bree demanded, flicking the bit of batter away from her as though it were indeed a loathsome insect.

"Oh, aye, he's crawlin'," Jemmy assured her cheerfully. "His Mam says she's gonna get his daddy's razor and shave off ever bit of his hair, him and his brothers and his daddy and his uncle Rufe too. She says they got lice hoppin' all over their bed. She's tired of bein' ate up alive." Quite casually, he lifted a hand to his head and scratched, fingers raking through his hair in a characteristic gesture I had seen all too often before.

Bree and I exchanged a brief look of horror, then she seized Jemmy by the shoulders, dragging him over to the window.

"Come here!"

Sure enough. Exposed to the brilliant light bouncing off the snow, the tender skin behind his ears and on the back of his neck showed the characteristic pinkness caused by scratching for lice, and a quick inspection of his head revealed the worst: tiny nits clinging to the base of the hairs, and a few reddish-brown adult lice, half the size of rice grains, who scrambled madly away into the thickets. Bree caught one and cracked it between her thumbnails, tossing the remains into the fire.

"Eugh!" She rubbed her hands on her skirt, then pulled off the ribbon that tied back her hair, scratching vigorously. "Have I got them?" she asked anxiously, thrusting the crown of her head toward me.

I ruffled quickly through the thick mass of auburn and cinnamon, looking for the telltale whitish nits, then stepped back, bending my own head.

"No, have I?"

The backdoor opened, and Jamie stepped in, looking only mildly surprised to find Brianna picking through my hair like a crazed baboon. Then his head jerked up, sniffing the air.

"Is something burning?"

"I got 'em, Grandda!"

The exclamation reached me together with the scent of singeing molasses. I jerked upright and banged my head on the edge of the dish shelf, hard enough to make me see stars.

These cleared just in time for me to see Jemmy, standing on tiptoe as he reached into the smoking oven in the wall of the hearth, well over his head. His eyes were squinched shut with concentration, his face turned away from the waves of heat coming off the brick, and he had a towel wound clumsily round the groping hand.

Jamie reached the boy with two strides, jerking him back by the collar. He reached into the oven bare-handed and yanked out a tin sheet of smoking cookies, flinging the hot sheet away with such force that it struck the wall. Small brown disks flew off and scattered over the floor.

Adso, who had been perched in the window, helping with the louse hunt, saw what looked like prey and pounced fiercely on a fleeing cookie, which promptly burned his paws. Uttering a startled yowl, he dropped it and raced under the settle.

Jamie, shaking his scorched fingers and making extremely vulgar remarks in Gaelic, had seized a stick of kindling in his other hand and was poking into the oven, trying to extract the remaining cookie-sheet amid clouds of smoke.

"What's going—hey!"

"Jemmy!"

Roger's cry coincided with Bree's. Coming in on Jamie's heels, Roger's expression of bewilderment had changed at once to alarm at sight of his offspring crouched on the floor, industriously collecting cookies, and oblivious of the fact that his trailing towel was smoldering in the ashes of the cookfire.

Roger lunged for Jemmy, colliding with Bree on the same course. The two of them cannoned into Jamie, who had just maneuvered the second sheet of cookies to the edge of the oven. He reeled, staggering off balance, and the sheet clanged into the hearth, scattering lumps of smoking, molasses-scented charcoal. The cauldron, knocked askew, swung and shifted perilously on its hook, splashing soup into the coals and sending up clouds of hissing, savory steam.

I didn't know whether to laugh or run out of the door, but settled for snatching up the towel, which had burst into flames, and beating it out on the stone-flagged hearth.

I stood up, panting, to find that my family had now managed to extricate itself from the fireplace. Roger had a squirming Jemmy in a death grip against his chest, while Bree frisked the child for burns, flames, and broken bones. Jamie, looking rather annoyed, was sucking on a blistered finger, waving smoke away from his face with his free hand.

"Cold water," I said, addressing the most immediate exigency. I grasped Jamie by the arm, pulled the finger out of his mouth, and stabbed it into the washbowl.

"Is Jemmy all right?" I asked, turning to the Happy Families tableau by the window. "Yes, I see he is. Do put him down, Roger, the child has lice."

Roger dropped Jemmy like a hot potato, and—in the usual adult reaction to hearing the word "lice"—scratched himself. Jemmy, unaffected by the recent commotion, sat down on the floor and began to eat one of the cookies he had kept clutched in his hand throughout.

"You'll spoil your—" Brianna began automatically, then caught sight of the spilled cauldron and the puddled hearth, glanced at me, and shrugged. "Got any more cookies?" she asked Jemmy. Mouth full, he nodded, reached into his shirt, and handed her one. She viewed it critically, but took a bite anyway.

"Not bad," she said, through crumbs. "Hm?" She held the remnant out to Roger, who wolfed it one-handed, using the other to poke through Jemmy's hair.

"It's going round," he said. "At least, we saw half a dozen lads near Sinclair's, all shaved like convicts. Shall we have to shave your head, then?" he asked, smiling at Jemmy and ruffling the boy's hair.

The boy's face lighted up at the suggestion.

"Will I be bald like Grandma?"

"Yes, even balder," I assured him tartly. I had in fact got a good two-inch crop at the moment, though the curliness made it look shorter, little waves and swirls hugging the curves of my skull.

"Shave his *head*?" Brianna looked aghast. She turned to me. "Isn't there any other good way to get rid of lice?"

I looked consideringly at Jemmy's head. He had the same thick, slightly wavy hair as his mother and grandfather. I glanced at Jamie, who grinned at me, one hand in the washbowl. He knew from experience just how long it took to nit-comb that sort of hair; I'd done it for him many times. He shook his head.

"Shave him," he said. "Ye'll not get a lad that size to sit still long enough to comb."

"We *could* use lard," I suggested dubiously. "You plaster his head with lard or bear grease and leave it for a few days. It suffocates the lice. Or at least you hope so."

"Ack." Brianna viewed her son's head with disfavor, obviously envisioning the havoc he could wreak on clothes and linens, if allowed to roam at large while plastered with lard.

"Vinegar and a fine-comb will get out the big ones," I said, coming to peer down at the fine white line of the parting through Jemmy's ruddy hair. "It doesn't get the nits, though; you have to scrape those off with your fingernails—or else wait 'til they hatch and comb them out."

"Shave him," Roger said, shaking his head. "Ye never get all the nits; you have to do it over again every few days, and if ye miss a few that grow big enough to hop . . ." He grinned and flicked a cookie crumb off his thumbnail; it bounced off Bree's skirt and she slapped it away, glowering at Roger.

"You're a big help!" She bit her lip, frowning, then nodded reluctantly. "All right, then, I suppose there's no help for it."

"It will grow back," I assured her.

Jamie went upstairs to fetch his razor; I went to the surgery to get my surgical scissors and·a bottle of oil of lavender for Jamie's burned finger. By the time I came back, Bree and Roger had their heads together over what looked like a newspaper.

"What's that?" I asked, coming to peer over Brianna's shoulder.

"Fergus's maiden effort." Roger smiled up at me, and moved the paper so I could see. "He sent it up with a trader who left it at Sinclair's for Jamie."

"Really? That's wonderful!"

I craned my neck to see, and a small thrill went through me at sight of the bold headline across the top of the page:

THE NEW BERN UNION

Then I looked closer.

"Onion?" I said, blinking. "*The Onion*?"

"Well, he explains that," Roger said, pointing to an ornately embellished *Remarks by the Proprietor* in the center of the page, the legend upheld by a couple of floating cherubim. "It's to do with onions having layers—complexity, you see—and the . . . er"—his finger ran down the line—"*the Pungency and Savor of the Reasoned Discourse always to be exercised herein for the compleat Information and Amusement of our Purchasers and Readers.*"

"I notice he makes a distinction between purchasers and readers," I remarked. "Very French of him!"

"Well, yes," Roger agreed. "There's a distinctly Gallic tone to some of the pieces, but you can see that Marsali must have had a hand in it—and, of course, most of the advertisements were written by the people who placed them." He pointed to one small item, headed, *Lost, a hat. If found in good condition, please return to the subscriber, S. Gowdy, New Bern. If not in good condition, wear it yourself.*

Jamie arrived with his razor in time to hear this, and joined in the laughter. He poked a finger down the page, at another item.

"Aye, that's good, but I think the 'Poet's Corner' is maybe my favorite. Fergus couldna have done it, I dinna think; he's no ear for rhyme at all—was it Marsali, d'ye think, or someone else?"

"Read it out loud," Brianna said, reluctantly relinquishing the paper to Roger. "I'd better clip Jemmy before he gets away and spreads lice all over Fraser's Ridge."

Once resigned to the prospect, Brianna didn't hesitate, but tied a dishcloth round Jemmy's neck and set to with the scissors in a determined fashion that sent strands of red-gold and auburn falling to the floor like shimmering rain. Meanwhile, Roger read out, with dramatic flourishes,

> *"On the late Act against retailing*
> *Spirituous Liquors, etc.—*
> *Tell me—can it be understood,*
> *This Act intends the Publick Good?*
> *No truly; I deny it:*
> *For if, as all allow, 'tis best,*
> *Of Evils Two, to chose the least,*
> *Then my Opinion's right.*
> *Suppose on Search—it should appear,*
> *Ten Bunters dy'd in every year—*
>
> *"—By drinking to Excess*
> *Should thousands innocent be led*
> *Into Despair, and lose their Bread,*
> *Such folly to redress?*
> *I'd not be thought t'encourage sin,*
> *Or be an Advocate of Gin;*
> *But humbly do conceive,*
> *This scheme, tho' drawn with nicest care*
> *Don't with Almighty Justice square*
> *If Scriptures we believe*
> *When Sodom's Sin for Vengeance call'd*
> *Ten righteous had its Doom forestall'd*
> *And mov'd e'en God to Pity.*
> *But now Ten bare-fac'd Debauchees*
> *Some private Epicures displease,*
> *And ruin half a City."*

"*I'd not be thought t'encourage sin/Or be an Advocate of Gin,*" Bree repeated, giggling. "You notice he—or she—doesn't mention whisky. What's a Bunter, though? Oops, hold still, baby!"

"A harlot," Jamie said absently, stropping his razor while still reading over Roger's shoulder.

"What's a harlot?" Jemmy asked, his radar naturally picking up the single indelicate word in the conversation. "Is it Richie's sister?"

Richard Woolam's sister Charlotte was a most attractive young person; she was also a most devout Quaker. Jamie exchanged glances with Roger, and coughed.

"No, I shouldna think it, lad," he said. "And for God's sake, don't say so, either! Here, are ye ready to be shaved?" Not waiting for an answer, he picked up the shaving brush and lathered Jemmy's polled head, to the accompaniment of delighted squeals.

"Barber, barber, shave a pig," Bree said, watching. "How many hairs to make a wig?"

"Lots," I replied, sweeping up the drifts of fallen hair and throwing them into the fire, hopefully to the destruction of all resident lice. It *was* rather a pity; Jemmy's hair was beautiful. Still, it would grow again—and the clipping showed off the lovely shape of his head, roundly pleasing as a cantaloupe.

Jamie hummed tunelessly under his breath, drawing the razor over the skin of his grandson's head with as much delicacy as if he had been shaving a honeybee.

Jemmy turned his head slightly, and I caught my breath, struck by a fleeting memory—Jamie, his hair clipped short against his skull in Paris, readying himself to meet Jack Randall; readying himself to kill—or be killed. Then Jemmy turned again, squirming on his stool, and the vision vanished—to be replaced by something else.

"Whatever is that?" I leaned forward to look, as Jamie drew his razor down with a flourish and flicked away the last dollop of lather into the fire.

"What?" Bree leaned in beside me, and her eyes widened at sight of the small brown blotch. It was about the size of a farthing, quite round, just above the hairline toward the back of his head, behind the left ear.

"What is it?" she asked, frowning. She touched it gently, but Jemmy scarcely noticed; he was squirming even more, wanting to get down.

"I'm fairly sure it's all right," I assured her, after a quick inspection. "It looks like what's called a nevus—it's something like a flat mole, usually quite harmless."

"But where did it come from? He wasn't born with it, I know!" she protested.

"Babies very seldom have any sort of mole," I explained, untying my dishcloth from round Jemmy's neck. "All right, yes, you're done! Go and be good now—we'll have supper as soon as I can manage. No," I added, turning back to Bree, "moles usually start to develop around three years of age—though of course people can get more as they grow older."

Freed from restraint, Jemmy was rubbing his naked head with both hands, looking pleased and chanting, "Char-lotte the Har-lot, Char-lotte the Har-lot," quietly under his breath.

"You're sure it's all right?" Brianna was still frowning, worried. "It isn't dangerous?"

"Oh, aye, it's nothing," Roger assured her, glancing up from the newspaper. "I've had one just like that myself, ever since I was a kid. Just . . . here." His face changed abruptly as he spoke, and his hand rose, very slowly, to rest on the back of his head—just above the hairline, behind the left ear.

He looked at me, and I saw his throat move as he swallowed, the jagged rope scar dark against the sudden paleness of his skin. The down hairs rose silently on my arms.

"Yes," I said, answering the look, and hoping my voice didn't shake too noticeably. "That sort of mark is . . . often hereditary."

Jamie said nothing, but his hand closed on mine, squeezing tight.

Jemmy was on his hands and knees now, trying to coax Adso out from under the settle. His neck was small and fragile, and his shaven head looked unearthly white and shockingly naked, like a mushroom poking out of the earth. Roger's eyes rested on it for a moment; then he turned to Bree.

"I do believe perhaps I've picked up a few lice myself," he said, his voice just a tiny bit too loud. He reached up, pulled off the thong that bound his thick black hair, and scratched his head vigorously with both hands. Then he picked up the scissors, smiling, and held them out to her. "Like father, like son, I suppose. Give us a hand here, aye?"

PART TEN

Where's Perry Mason When You Need Him?

76

Dangerous
Correspondence

From Mount Josiah Plantation in the Colony of Virginia,
Lord John Grey to Mr. James Fraser, Esq.,
Fraser's Ridge, North Carolina,
upon the Sixth of March, Anno Domini 1775

Dear Mr. Fraser—

*What in the Name of God are you about? I have
known you in the course of our long Acquaintance to be
many Things—Intemperate and Stubborn being two of
them—but have always known you for a Man of
Intelligence and Honor.*

*Yet despite explicit Warnings, I find your Name upon
more than one List of suspected Traitors and Seditionists,
associated with illegal Assemblies, and thus subject to
Arrest. The Fact that you are still at Liberty, my Friend,
reflects nothing more than the Lack of Troops at present
available in North Carolina—and that may change rapidly. Josiah Martin has implored London for Help, and it
will be forthcoming, I assure you.*

*Was Gage not more than sufficiently occupied in
Boston, and Lord Dunsmore's Virginia troops still in
process of Assembly, the Army would be upon you within
a few Months. Do not delude yourself; the King may be
misguided in his Actions, but the Government perceives—
if belatedly—the Level of Turmoil in the Colonies, and is*

moving as rapidly as may be to suppress it, before greater Harm can ensue.

Whatever else you may be, you are no Fool, and so I must assume you realize the Consequences of your Actions. But I would be less than a Friend did I not put the Case to you bluntly: you expose your Family to the utmost Danger by your Actions, and you put your own Head in a Noose.

For the Sake of whatever Affection you may yet bear me, and for the Sake of those dear Connexions between your Family and myself—I beg you to renounce these most dangerous Associations while there is still Time.

John

I read the letter through, then looked up at Jamie. He was sitting at his desk, papers strewn in every direction, scattered with the small brown fragments of broken sealing wax. Bobby Higgins had brought a good many letters, newspapers, and packages—Jamie had put off reading Lord John's letter 'til the last.

"He's very much afraid for you," I said, putting the single sheet of paper down on top of the rest.

Jamie nodded.

"For a man of his parts to refer to the King's actions as possibly 'misguided' is verra close to treason, Sassenach," he observed, though I *thought* he was joking.

"These lists he mentions—do you know anything about that?"

He shrugged at that, and poked through one of the untidy piles with a forefinger, pulling out a smeared sheet that had obviously been dropped in a puddle at some point.

"Like that, I suppose," he said, handing it over. It was unsigned, and nearly illegible, a misspelt and vicious denunciation of various *Outrages and Debached Persons*—here listed—whose speech, action, and appearance was a threat to all who valued peace and prosperity. These, the writer felt, should be *shown whats what,* presumably by being beaten, skinned alive, *rold in boiling Tar and plac'd on a Rail,* or in particularly pernicious cases, *Hanged outright from there own Rooftrees.*

"Where did you pick *that* up?" I dropped it on the desk, using two fingers.

"In Campbelton. Someone sent it to Farquard, as Justice of the Peace. He gave it to me, because my name is on it."

"It is?" I squinted at the straggling letters. "Oh, so it is. *J. Frayzer.* You're sure it's you? There are quite a few Frasers, after all, and not a few named John, James, Jacob, or Joseph."

"Relatively few who could be described as a *Red-haired dejenerate Pox-ridden Usuring Son of a Bitch who skulks in Brothels when not drunk and comitting Riot in the Street,* I imagine."

"Oh, I missed that part."

"It's in the exposition at the bottom." He gave the paper a brief, indifferent glance. "I think Buchan the butcher wrote it, myself."

"Always assuming that 'usuring' is a word, I don't see where he gets that bit; you haven't any money to lend."

"I wouldna suppose a basis in truth is strictly required, under the circumstances, Sassenach," he said very dryly. "And thanks to MacDonald and wee Bobby, there are a good many folk who think I *do* have money—and if I am not inclined to lend it to them, why then, plainly it's a matter of my having put my fortune all in the hands of Jews and Whig speculators, as I am intent upon ruining trade for my own profit."

"What?"

"That was a somewhat more literary effort," he said, shuffling through the pile and pulling out an elegant parchment sheet, done in a copperplate hand. This one had been sent to a newspaper in Hillsboro, and was signed, *A Friend to Justice*; and while it didn't name Jamie, it was clear who the subject of the denunciation was.

"It's the hair," I said, looking critically at him. "If you wore a wig, they'd have a much harder time of it."

He lifted one shoulder in a sardonic shrug. The commonly held view of red hair as an indicator of low character and moral coarseness, if not outright demonic possession, was by no means limited to anonymous ill-wishers. The knowledge of that view—together with personal disinclination—had quite a bit to do with the fact that he never *did* wear either wig or powder, even in situations where a proper gentleman would.

Without asking, I reached for a stack of the papers and began to leaf through them. He made no move to stop me, but sat quietly watching, listening to the thrum of the rain.

A heavy spring storm was washing down outside, and the air

was cold and damp, thick with the green scents of the forest insinuating themselves through the crevices of door and window. I sometimes had the sudden feeling, hearing the wind coming through the trees, that the wilderness outside meant to come in, march through the house, and obliterate it, erasing all trace of us.

The letters were a mixed bag. Some were from the members of the North Carolina Committee of Correspondence, with bits of news, most of it from the north. Continental Association Committees had sprung up in New Hampshire and New Jersey, these bodies now beginning to virtually take over the functions of government, as the royal governors lost their grip on assemblies, courts, and Customs, the remnants of organization falling ever deeper into disarray.

Boston was still occupied by Gage's troops, and some of the letters continued the appeals for food and supplies to be sent to the succor of her citizens—we had sent two hundredweight of barley during the winter, which one of the Woolams had undertaken to get into the city, along with three wagonloads of other foodstuffs contributed by the inhabitants of the Ridge.

Jamie had picked up his quill, and was writing something, slowly, to accommodate the stiffness of his hand.

Next up was a note from Daniel Putnam, circulated through Massachusetts, noting the rising of militia companies in the countryside, and asking for arms and powder. It was signed by a dozen other men, each one bearing witness to the truth of the situation in his own township.

A Second Continental Congress was proposed, to meet in Philadelphia, the date yet undecided.

Georgia had formed a Provincial Congress, but as the Loyalist letter-writer—plainly assuming Jamie to be like-minded—triumphantly noted, *There is no Sense of Grievance toward Great Britain here, as elsewhere; Loyalist Sentiment is so strong that only five Parishes of twelve have sent anyone to this upstart and illegal Congress.*

A much-bedraggled copy of the *Massachusetts Gazette*, dated February 6, containing a letter, circled in ink and titled *The Rule of Law and the Rule of Men*. It was signed *Novanglus*—which I took to be a sort of hog-Latin for "new Englishman"—and to be a response to previous letters by a

Tory who signed himself *Massachusettensis*, of all things.

I had no idea who Massachusettensis might be, but I recognized a few phrases from Novanglus's letter, from long-ago bits of Bree's schoolwork—John Adams, in good form.

"A government of laws, not of men," I murmured. "What sort of pen name would you use, if you were going to write this sort of thing?" Glancing up, I caught sight of him, looking sheepish to a degree.

"You've been doing it *already*?"

"Well, just the odd bittie letter here or there," he said defensively. "No pamphlets."

"Who are you?"

He shrugged, deprecating.

"Scotus Americanus, but only 'til I think of something better. There are a few others using that name, that I ken."

"Well, that's something. The King will have a harder time picking you out of the crowd." Muttering "Massachusettensis" to myself, I picked up the next document.

A note from John Stuart, much affronted by Jamie's abrupt resignation, noting that the *most illegal and prodigal Congress, as they call it* of Massachusetts had formally invited the Stockbridge Indians to enlist in the service of the colony, and informing Jamie that should any of the Cherokee follow suit, he, John Stuart, would take the greatest pleasure in personally ensuring that he, Jamie Fraser, was hanged for treason.

"And I don't suppose John Stuart even knows you have red hair," I observed, laying it aside. I felt a trifle shaky, in spite of my attempts to joke about it. Seeing it all laid out in black and white solidified the clouds that had been gathering round us, and I felt the first chilling drop of icy rain on my skin, despite the woolen shawl around my shoulders.

There was no hearth in the study; only a small brazier that we used for heat. It was burning now in the corner, and Jamie rose, picked up a stack of letters, and began to feed them to the fire, one by one.

I had a sudden rush of déjà vu, and saw him standing by the hearth in the drawing room of his cousin Jared's house in Paris, feeding letters to the fire. The stolen letters of Jacobite conspirators, rising in white puffs of smoke, the gathering clouds of a storm long past.

I remembered what Fergus had said, in answer to Jamie's

instructions: *"I remember how this game is played."* So did I, and spicules of ice began to form in my blood.

Jamie dropped the last flaming fragment into the brazier, then sanded the page he had been writing, shook the sand off, and handed it to me. He had used one of the sheets of the special paper Bree had made by pressing a digested pulp of rags and plant matter between silk screens. It was thicker than the usual, with a soft, glossy texture, and she had mixed berries and tiny leaves into the pulp, so that here and there a small red stain spread like blood beneath the shadow of a leaf's silhouette.

> *From Fraser's Ridge, in the Colony of North*
> *Carolina,*
> *this 16th day of March, Anno Domini 1775,*
> *James Fraser to Lord John Grey, of Mount Josiah*
> *Plantation,*
> *in the Colony of Virginia*
>
> *My dear John—*
>
>   *It is too late.*
>   *Our continued Correspondence cannot but prove a*
> *Danger to you, but it is with the greatest Regret that I*
> *sever this Link between us.*
>   *Believe me ever*
>
> > *Your most humble and affectionate Friend,*
> > *Jamie*

I read it in silence, and handed it back. As he poked about in search of the sealing wax, I noticed a small wrapped parcel on the corner of his desk that had been hidden by the drifts of paper.

"What's this?" I picked it up; it was amazingly heavy for its size.

"A present from his Lordship, for wee Jemmy." He lit the beeswax taper from the brazier and held it over the seam of the folded letter. "A set of lead soldiers, Bobby says."

77

The Eighteenth of April

R oger came awake quite suddenly, with no notion what had wakened him. It was full dark, but the air had the still, inward feel of the small hours; the world holding its breath, before dawn comes on a rising wind.

He turned his head on the pillow and saw that Brianna was awake, too; she lay looking upward, and he caught the brief flicker of her eyelids as she blinked.

He moved a hand to touch her, and hers closed over it. An adjuration to silence? He lay very still, listening, but heard nothing. An ember broke in the hearth with a muffled crack and her hand tightened. Jemmy flung himself over in bed with a rustle of quilts, let out a small yelp, and fell silent. The night was undisturbed.

"What is it?" he said, low-voiced.

She didn't turn to look at him; her eyes were fixed now on the window, a dark gray rectangle, barely visible.

"Yesterday was the eighteenth of April," she said. "It's here." Her voice was calm, but there was something in it that made him move closer, so they lay side by side, touching from shoulder to foot.

Somewhere to the north of them, men were gathering in the cold spring night. Eight hundred British troops, groaning and cursing as they dressed by candlelight. Those who had gone to bed rousing to the beat of the drum passing by the houses and warehouses and churches where they quartered, those who hadn't, stumbling from dice and drink, the warm hearths of taverns, the warm arms of women, hunting lost boots and seizing weapons, turning out by twos and threes and fours, clanking and mumbling through the streets of frozen mud to the muster point.

"I grew up in Boston," she said, her voice softly conversational. "Every kid in Boston learned that poem, somewhere along the line. I learned it in fifth grade."

"Listen, my children, and you shall hear/Of the midnight ride of Paul Revere." Roger smiled, envisioning her in the uniform of Saint Finbar's parochial school, blue overall jumper, white blouse, and knee socks. He'd seen her fifth-grade school photograph once; she looked like a small, fierce, disheveled tiger that some maniac had dressed in doll's clothes.

"That's the one. *On the eighteenth of April, in Seventy-five/Hardly a man is now alive/Who remembers that famous day and year."*

"Hardly a man," Roger echoed softly. Someone—who? A householder, eavesdropping on the British commanders quartered in his house? A barmaid, bringing mugs of pokered hot rum to a couple of sergeants? There was no keeping of secrets, not with eight hundred men on the move. It was all a matter of time. Someone had sent word from the occupied city, word that the British meant to seize the stored arms and powder in Concord, and at the same time, arrest Hancock and Samuel Adams—the founder of the Committee of Safety, the inflammatory speaker, the leaders of *this treasonous rebellion*—reported to be in Lexington.

Eight hundred men to capture two? Good odds. And a silversmith and his friends, alarmed at the news, had set out into that cold night. Bree continued:

> *"He said to his friend, 'If the British march*
> *By land or sea from the town tonight,*
> *Hang a lantern aloft in the belfry arch*
> *Of the North Church tower as a signal light—*
> *One if by land, and two if by sea;*
> *And I on the opposite shore will be,*
> *Ready to ride and spread the alarm*
> *Through every Middlesex village and farm,*
> *For the country folk to be up and to arm.'"*

"They don't write poems like *that* anymore," Roger said. But in spite of his cynicism, he couldn't bloody help seeing it: the steam of a horse's breath, white in darkness, and across the black water, the tiny star of a lantern, high above the sleeping town. And then another.

"What happened next?" he said.

> *"Then he said 'Good-night!' and with muffled oar*
> *Silently rowed to the Charlestown shore,*
> *Just as the moon rose over the bay,*
> *Where swinging wide at her moorings lay*
> *The Somerset, British man-of-war;*
> *A phantom ship, with each mast and spar*
> *Across the moon like a prison bar,*
> *And a huge black hulk, that was magnified*
> *By its own reflection in the tide."*

"Well, that's not too bad," he said judiciously. "I like the bit about the *Somerset*. Rather a painterly description."

"Shut up." She kicked him, though without real violence. "It goes on about his friend, who *wanders and watches, with eager ears—*" Roger snorted, and she kicked him again. *"Till in the silence around him he hears/The muster of men at the barrack door/The sound of arms, and the tramp of feet/And the measured tread of the grenadiers/Marching down to their boats on the shore."*

He had visited her in Boston in the spring. In mid-April, the trees would have no more than a haze of green, their branches still mostly bare against pale skies. The nights were still frigid, but the cold was somehow touched with life, a freshness moving through the icy air.

"Then there's a boring part about the friend climbing the stairs of the church tower, but I like the next verse." Her voice, already soft, dropped a little, whispering.

> *"Beneath, in the churchyard, lay the dead,*
> *In their night encampment on the hill,*
> *Wrapped in silence so deep and still*
> *That he could hear, like a sentinel's tread,*
> *The watchful night-wind, as it went*
> *Creeping along from tent to tent,*

> *And seeming to whisper, 'All is well!'*
> *A moment only he feels the spell*
> *Of the place and the hour, and the secret dread*
> *Of the lonely belfry and the dead;*
> *For suddenly all his thoughts are bent*
> *On a shadowy something far away,*
> *Where the river widens to meet the bay—*
> *A line of black that bends and floats*
> *On the rising tide like a bridge of boats."*

"Then there's a lot of stuff with old Paul killing time waiting for the signal," she said, abandoning the dramatic whisper for a more normal tone of voice. "But it finally shows up, and then . . .

> *"A hurry of hoofs in a village street,*
> *A shape in the moonlight, a bulk in the dark,*
> *And beneath, from the pebbles, in passing, a spark*
> *Struck out by a steed flying fearless and fleet;*
> *That was all! And yet, through the gloom and the light,*
> *The fate of a nation was riding that night;*
> *And the spark struck out by that steed, in his flight,*
> *Kindled the land into flame with its heat."*

"That's actually pretty good." His hand curved over her thigh, just above the knee, in case she might kick him again, but she didn't. "Do you remember the rest?"

"'So he goes along by the Mystic River," Brianna said, ignoring him, "and then there are three verses, as he passes through the townships:

> *"It was twelve by the village clock*
> *When he crossed the bridge into Medford town.*
> *He heard the crowing of the cock,*
> *"And the barking of the farmer's dog,*
> *And felt the damp of the river fog,*
> *That rises after the sun goes down.*
>
> *"It was one by the village clock,*
> *When he galloped into Lexington.*
> *He saw the gilded weathercock*

> *Swim in the moonlight as he passed,*
> *And the meeting-house windows, blank and bare,*
> *Gaze at him with a spectral glare,*
> *As if they already stood aghast*
> *At the bloody work they would look upon.*

"*It was two by the village clock*—and yes, I hear the clock chiming in the first lines, be quiet!" He had in fact drawn breath, but not to interrupt, only because he'd suddenly realized he'd been holding it. "*It was two by the village clock,*" she repeated,

> "*When he came to the bridge in Concord town.*
> *He heard the bleating of the flock,*
> *And the twitter of birds among the trees,*
> *And felt the breath of the morning breeze*
> *Blowing over the meadow brown.*
> *And one was safe and asleep in his bed*
> *Who at the bridge would be first to fall,*
> *Who that day would be lying dead,*
> *Pierced by a British musket ball.*

"*You know the rest.*" She stopped abruptly, her hand tight on his.

From one moment to the next, the character of the night had changed. The stillness of the small hours had ceased, and a breath of wind moved through the trees outside. All of a sudden, the night was alive again, but dying now, rushing toward dawn.

If not actively twittering, the birds were wakeful; something called, over and over, in the nearby wood, high and sweet. And above the stale, heavy scent of the fire, he breathed the wild clean air of morning, and felt his heart beat with sudden urgency.

"Tell me the rest," he whispered.

He saw the shadows of men in the trees, the stealthy knocking on doors, the low-voiced, excited conferences—and all the while, the light growing in the east. The lap of water and creak of oars, the sound of restless kine lowing to be milked, and on the rising breeze the smell of men, stale with sleep and empty of food, harsh with black powder and the scent of steel.

And without thinking, pulled his hand from his wife's grasp, rolled over her, and pulling up the shift from her thighs, took her hard and fast, in vicarious sharing of that mindless urge to spawn that attended the imminent presence of death.

Lay on her trembling, the sweat drying on his back in the breeze from the window, heart thumping in his ears. For the one, he thought. The one who would be the first to fall. The poor sod who maybe hadn't swived his wife in the dark and taken the chance to leave her with child, because he had no notion what was coming with the dawn. This dawn.

Brianna lay still under him; he could feel the rise and fall of her breath, powerful ribs that lifted even under his weight.

"You know the rest," she whispered.

"Bree," he said very softly. "I would sell my soul to be there now."

"Shh," she said, but her hand rose, and settled on his back in what might be benediction. They lay still, watching the light grow by degrees, keeping silence.

This silence was broken a quarter of an hour later, by the sound of rushing footsteps and a pounding at the door. Jemmy popped out of his blankets like a cuckoo from a clock, eyes round, and Roger heaved himself up, hurriedly brushing down his nightshirt.

It was one of the Beardsleys, face pinched and white in the gray light. He paid no attention to Roger, but cried out to Brianna, "Lizzie's having the baby, come quick!", before dashing off in the direction of the Big House, where the figure of his brother could be seen gesticulating wildly on the porch.

Brianna flung on her clothes and burst out of the cabin, leaving Roger to deal with Jemmy. She met her mother, similarly disheveled but with a neatly packed medical kit slung over her shoulder, hurrying toward the narrow path that led past spring house and stable, into the distant woods where the Beardsleys' cabin lay.

"She should have come down last week," Claire gasped. "I told her . . ."

"So did I. She said . . ." Brianna gave up the attempt to speak. The Beardsley twins had long outdistanced them, sprinting through the wood like deer, whooping and yelling—whether from sheer excitement at their impending fatherhood, or to let Lizzie know help was on the way, she couldn't tell.

Claire had worried about Lizzie's malaria, she knew. And yet the yellow shadow that so often hung over her erstwhile bond-maid had all but disappeared during her pregnancy; Lizzie bloomed.

Nonetheless, Brianna felt her stomach clench in fear as they came into sight of the Beardsleys' cabin. The hides had been moved outside, stacked round the tiny house like a barricade, and the smell of them gave her a moment's terrible vision of the MacNeills' cabin, filled with death.

The door hung open, though, and there were no flies. She forced herself to hang back an instant, to let Claire go in first, but hurried in on her heels—to find that they were too late.

Lizzie sat up in a blood-smeared bower of furs, blinking with amazed stupefaction at a small, round, blood-smeared baby, who was regarding her with the exact same expression of open-mouthed astonishment.

Jo and Kezzie were clutching each other, too excited and afraid to speak. From the corner of her eye, Brianna saw their mouths opening and closing in syncopation, and wanted to laugh, but instead followed her mother to the bedside.

"He just popped out!" Lizzie was saying, glancing momentarily at Claire, but then jerking her fascinated gaze back to the baby, as though she expected him—yes, it was a him, Brianna saw—to disappear as suddenly as he had arrived.

"My back hurt something dreadful, all last night, so I couldna sleep, and the lads took it in turns to rub me, but it didna really help, and then when I got up to go to the privy this morning, all the water burst forth from betwixt my legs—just as ye said it would, ma'am!" she said to Claire. "And so I said to Jo and Kezzie they must run fetch ye, but I didna ken quite what to do next. So I set about to mix up batter for to make hoecake for breakfast"—she waved at the table, where a bowl of flour sat with a jug of milk and two eggs—"and next thing, I had this terrible urge to—to—" She blushed, a deep, becoming peony color.

"Well, I couldna even reach the chamber-pot. I just squatted there by the table, and—and—pop! There he was, right on the ground beneath me!"

Claire had picked the new arrival up, and was cooing reassurances to him, while deftly checking whatever it was one checked about new babies. Lizzie had made a blanket in preparation, carefully knitted of lamb's wool, dyed with indigo. Claire glanced at the pristine blanket, then pulled a length of stained, soft flannel from her kit. Wrapping the baby in it, she handed him to Brianna.

"Hold him a moment while I deal with the cord, will you, darling?" she said, pulling scissors and thread from her kit. "Then you can clean him off a bit—there's a bottle of oil in here—while I take care of Lizzie. And you lot," she added, glancing sternly at the Beardsleys, "go outside."

The baby moved suddenly inside his wrappings, startling Brianna with the sudden vivid recollection of tiny, solid limbs pushing from inside: a kick to the liver, the liquid swell and shift as head or buttocks pressed up in a hard, smooth curve beneath her ribs.

"Hallo, little guy," she said softly, cuddling him against her shoulder. He smelled strongly and strangely of the sea, she thought, and oddly fresh against the acrid pungency of the hides outside.

"Ooh!" Lizzie gave a startled squeal, as Claire kneaded her belly, and there was a juicy, slithering sort of sound. Brianna remembered that vividly, too; the placenta, that liverish, slippery afterthought of birth, almost soothing as it passed over the much-abused tissues with a sense of peaceful completion. All over, and the stunned mind began to comprehend survival.

There was a gasp from the doorway, and she looked up to see the Beardsleys, side by side and saucer-eyed.

"Shoo!" she said firmly, and flipped a hand at them. They promptly disappeared, leaving her to the entertaining task of cleaning and oiling the flailing limbs and creased body. He was a small baby, but round: round-faced, very round-eyed for a newborn—he hadn't cried at all, but was plainly awake and alert—and with a round little belly, from which the stump of his umbilical cord protruded, dark purple and fresh.

His look of astonishment had not faded; he goggled up at her, solemn as a fish, though she could feel the huge smile on her own face.

"You are so cute!" she told him. He smacked his lips in a thoughtful sort of way, and crinkled his brow.

"He's hungry!" she called over her shoulder. "Are you ready?"

"Ready?" Lizzie croaked. "Mother of God, how can ye be

ready for something like *this*?", which made Claire and Brianna both laugh like loons.

Nonetheless, Lizzie reached for the little blue-wrapped bundle and put it uncertainly to her breast. There was a certain amount of fumbling and increasingly anxious grunts from the baby, but at last a suitable connection was established, making Lizzie utter a brief shriek of surprise, and everyone breathed a sigh of relief.

At this point, Brianna became aware that there had been conversation going on outside for some time—a mutter of male voices, deliberately pitched low, in a confusion of speculation and puzzlement.

"I imagine you can let them in now. Then put the griddle in the fire, if you would." Claire, beaming fondly at mother and child, was mixing the neglected batter.

Brianna poked her head out of the cabin door, to find Jo, Kezzie, her own father, Roger, and Jemmy, clustered in a knot a little distance away. They all glanced up when they saw her, with expressions ranging from vaguely shamefaced pride to simple excitement.

"Mama! Is the baby here?" Jem rushed up, pushing to get past her into the cabin, and she grabbed him by the collar.

"Yes. You can come see him, but you have to be quiet. He's very new, and you don't want to scare him, all right?"

"Him?" one of the Beardsleys asked, excited. "It's a boy?"

"I told ye so!" his brother said, nudging him in the ribs. "I said I saw a wee prick!"

"You don't say things like 'prick' in front of ladies," Jem informed him severely, turning to frown at him. "And Mama says be quiet!"

"Oh," said the Beardsley twin, abashed. "Oh, aye, to be sure."

Moving with an exaggerated caution that made her want to laugh, the twins tiptoed into the cabin, followed by Jem, Jamie's hand firm on his shoulder, and Roger.

"Is Lizzie all right?" he asked softly, pausing to kiss her briefly in passing.

"A little overwhelmed, I think, but fine."

Lizzie was in fact sitting up, soft blond hair now combed and shining around her shoulders, glowing with happiness at Jo and Kezzie, who knelt at her bedside, grinning like apes.

"May the blessing of Bride and of Columba be on you, young woman," Jamie said formally in Gaelic, bowing to her, "and may the love of Christ sustain you always in your motherhood. May milk spring from your breasts like water from the rock and may you rest secure in the arms of your"—he coughed briefly, glancing at the Beardsleys—"husband."

"If you can't say 'prick,' why can you say 'breasts'?" Jemmy inquired, interested.

"Ye can't, unless it's a prayer," his father informed him. "Grandda was giving Lizzie a blessing."

"Oh. Are there any prayers with pricks in them?"

"I'm sure there are," Roger replied, carefully avoiding Brianna's eye, "but ye don't say them out loud. Why don't ye go and help Grannie with the breakfast?"

The iron griddle was sizzling with fat, and the fragrant smell of fresh batter filled the room as Claire began to pour spoonfuls onto the hot metal.

Jamie and Roger, having presented their compliments to Lizzie, had stepped back a bit, to give the little family a moment to themselves—though the cabin was so small, there was barely room for everyone to fit inside.

"You are so beautiful," Jo—or possibly Kezzie—whispered, touching her hair with an awed forefinger. "Ye look like the new moon, Lizzie."

"Did it hurt ye very much, sweetheart?" murmured Kezzie—or maybe Jo—stroking the back of her hand.

"Not so much," she said, stroking Kezzie's hand, then lifting her palm to cup Jo's cheek. "Look. Is he no the bonniest wee creature ye've ever seen?" The baby had drunk his fill and fallen asleep; he let go the nipple with an audible *pop!* and rolled back in his mother's arm like a dormouse, mouth a little open.

The twins made identical soft sounds of awe, and looked doe-eyed at their—well, what else could one say? Brianna thought—their son.

"Oh, such dear wee fingers!" Kezzie—or Jo—breathed, touching the little pink fist with a dirty forefinger.

"Is he all there?" Jo—or Kezzie—asked. "Ye've looked?"

"I have," Lizzie assured him. "Here—d'ye want to hold him?" Not pausing for assent, she put the bundle into his arms.

Whichever twin it was looked at once thrilled and terrified, and glanced wildly at his brother for support.

Brianna, enjoying the tableau, felt Roger close behind her.

"Aren't they sweet?" she whispered, reaching back for his hand.

"Oh, aye," he said, a smile in his voice. "Enough to make ye want another, isn't it?"

It was an innocent remark; she could tell he had meant nothing by it—but he heard the echo, even as she did, and coughed, letting go her hand.

"Here—that's for Lizzie." Claire was handing a plate of fragrant cakes, drizzled with butter and honey, to Jem. "Is anyone else hungry?"

The general stampede in response to this enabled Brianna to hide her feelings, but they were still there—and painfully clear, if still tangled.

Yes, she *did* want another baby, thank you, she thought fiercely at Roger's oblivious back. In the instant of holding the newborn child, she wanted it with a yearning of flesh that surpassed hunger or thirst. And she would have loved to blame him for the fact that it hadn't happened yet.

It had taken a true leap of faith, across the vertiginous abyss of knowledge, for her to put aside her *dauco* seeds, those fragile pellets of protection. But she'd done it. And nothing. Lately, she'd been thinking uneasily of what Ian had told her about his wife and their struggles to conceive. True, she had suffered no miscarriage, and was profoundly grateful for that. But the part he had told her, where their lovemaking became more mechanical and desperate—*that* was beginning to loom like a specter in the distance. It hadn't gotten that bad yet—but more often than not, she turned into Roger's arms, thinking, *Now? Will it be this time?* But it never was.

The twins were becoming more comfortable with their offspring, their dark heads pressed close together, tracing the chubby outlines of his sleeping features and wondering aloud who he most resembled, of all idiotic things.

Lizzie was single-mindedly devouring her second plate of hoecakes, accompanied by grilled sausages. The smell was wonderful, but Brianna wasn't hungry.

It was a good thing that they knew for sure, she told herself, watching Roger take his turn to hold the baby, his dark, lean face softening. If there had still been any doubt that Jemmy was Roger's child, he would have blamed himself as Ian did, thought there was something wrong with him. As it was . . .

Had something happened to *her*? she wondered uneasily. Had Jemmy's birth damaged something?

Jamie was holding the new baby now, one big hand cradling the round little head, smiling down with that look of soft affection so peculiar—and endearing—to men. She did long to see that look on Roger's face, holding his own newborn child.

"Mr. Fraser." Lizzie, filled at last with sausages, put aside her empty plate and leaned forward, looking earnestly up at Jamie. "My father. Does—does he know?" She couldn't help glancing at the empty doorway behind him.

Jamie looked momentarily disconcerted.

"Ah," he said, and handed the baby carefully to Roger, clearly taking advantage of the pause to try to think of some less-hurtful way to phrase the truth.

"Aye, he kens the babe was on the way," he said carefully. "I told him."

And he had not come. Lizzie's lips pressed together, and a shadow of unhappiness crossed the new-moon glow of her face.

"Had we—had I—one of us—best go and tell him, sir?" one of the twins asked hesitantly. "That the child's here, I mean, and . . . and that Lizzie's all right."

Jamie hesitated, clearly uncertain whether that would be a good idea or not. Mr. Wemyss, pale and ill-looking, had not referred to his daughter, his putative sons-in-law, or his theoretical grandchild since the imbroglio surrounding Lizzie's multiple weddings. Now that the grandchild was a concrete fact, though . . .

"Whatever he thinks he *ought* to do," Claire said, her face slightly troubled, "he'll *want* to know that they're all right, surely."

"Oh, aye," Jamie agreed. He glanced dubiously at the twins. "I'm just no entirely sure it should be Jo or Kezzie to tell him, though."

The twins exchanged a long glance, in which some decision seemed to be reached.

"It should, sir," one of them said firmly, turning to Jamie. "The baby's ourn, but it's his blood, too. That's a link between us; he'll know that."

"We don't want him to be crosswise with Lizzie, sir," his brother said, more soft-spoken. "It hurts her. Might be the baby would . . . ease things, d'ye think?"

Jamie's face betrayed nothing other than a studied attention to the matter at hand, but Brianna saw him dart a quick glance at Roger before returning his gaze to the bundle in Roger's arm, and she hid a smile. He had certainly not forgotten his own acrimonious first response to Roger, but it had been Roger's claiming of Jem that had established the first—and very fragile—link in the chain of acceptance that she thought now bound Roger nearly as close to Jamie's heart as she herself.

"Aye, then," Jamie said, still reluctant. He very much disliked being involved in this situation, she could tell—but hadn't yet succeeded in figuring out any way of dealing with it. "Go and tell him. Just the one of ye, though! And should he come, t'other of ye keep well out of his sight, d'ye hear me?"

"Oh, aye, sir," both of them assured him in unison. Jo—or Kezzie—frowned a little at the bundle, and hesitantly extended his arms. "Should I—"

"No, don't." Lizzie was sitting bolt upright, her arms braced to keep her weight off her tender nether parts. Her small fair brow was set in a frown of determination. "Tell him we're well, aye. But if he wants to see the bairn—he'll come, and welcome. But if he'll no set foot upon my threshold . . . well, then, he's no welcome to see his grandson. Tell him," she repeated, easing herself back upon her pillows.

"Now give my bairnie to me." She held out her arms, and clutched the sleeping baby to her, closing her eyes against any possibility of argument or reproach.

78

The Universal
Brotherhood of Man

Brianna lifted the waxed cloth covering one of the big earthenware basins, and sniffed, taking pleasure in the musty, turned-earth smell. She stirred the pale mess with a stick, lifting it out periodically in order to assess the texture of the pulp that dripped from it.

Not bad. Another day, and it would be dissolved enough to press. She considered whether to add more of the dilute sulfuric acid solution, but decided against it, and instead reached into the bowl at her side, filled with the limp petals of dogwood and redbud flowers gathered for her by Jemmy and Aidan. She scattered a handful of these delicately over the grayish pulp, stirred them in, then covered the bowl again. By tomorrow, they'd be no more than faint outlines, but still visible as shadows in the finished sheets of paper.

"I'd always heard that paper mills stank." Roger made his way through the bushes toward her. "Perhaps they use something else in the making?"

"Be glad I'm not tanning hides," she advised him. "Ian says the Indian women use dog turds for that."

"So do European tanners; they just call the stuff 'pure.'"

"Pure what?"

"Pure dog turds, I suppose," he said with a shrug. "How's it going?"

Coming up beside her, he looked with interest at her own small paper factory: a dozen big, fired-clay basins, each filled with scraps of used paper, worn-out scraps of silk and cotton, flax fibers, the soft pith of cattail reeds, and anything else she could get her hands on that might be useful, torn to shreds or ground small in a quern. She'd dug out a small seep, and laid one of her broken water pipes as a catch basin, to provide a convenient water supply; nearby, she'd built a platform of stone and wood, on which stood the framed silk screens in which she pressed the pulp.

There was a dead moth floating in the next bowl, and he reached to take it out, but she waved him away.

"Bugs drown in it all the time, but as long as they're soft-bodied, it's okay. Enough sulfuric acid"—she nodded at the bottle, stoppered with a bit of rag—"and they all just become part of the pulp: moths, butterflies, ants, gnats, lacewings . . . wings are the only things that won't dissolve all the way. Lacewings look sort of pretty embedded in the paper, but not roaches." She fished one of these out of a bowl and flicked it away into the bushes, then added a little more water from the gourd dipper, stirring.

"I'm not surprised. I stamped on one of them this morning; he flattened out, then popped back up and strolled off, smirking." He paused a moment; he wanted to ask her something, she could tell, and she made an interrogative hum to encourage him.

"I was only wondering—would ye mind taking Jem up to the Big House after supper? Perhaps the two of ye spending the night?"

She looked at him in astonishment.

"What are you planning to do? Throw a stag party for Gordon Lindsay?" Gordon, a shy boy of about seventeen, was betrothed to a Quaker girl from Woolam's Mill; he'd been round the day before to "thig"—beg small bits of household goods in preparation for his marriage.

"No girls popping out of cakes," he assured her, "but it's definitely men only. It's the first meeting of the Fraser's Ridge Lodge."

"Lodge . . . what, Freemasons?" She squinted dubiously at him, but he nodded. The breeze had come up, and it whipped his black hair up on end; he smoothed it back with one hand.

"Neutral ground," he explained. "I didna want to suggest holding meetings in either the Big House or Tom Christie's place—not wanting to favor either side, ye might say."

She nodded, seeing that.

"Okay. But why Freemasons?" She knew nothing whatever about Freemasons, save that they were some sort of secret society and that Catholics weren't allowed to join.

She mentioned this particular point to Roger, who laughed.

"True," he said "The Pope forbade it about forty years ago."

"Why? What does the Pope have against Freemasons?" she asked, interested.

"It's rather a powerful body. A good many men of power and influence belong—and it crosses international lines. I imagine the Pope's actual concern is competition in terms of power-broking—though if I recall aright, his stated reason was that Freemasonry is too much like a religion itself. Oh, that, and they worship the Devil."

He laughed.

"Ye did know your father started a Lodge at Ardsmuir, in the prison there?"

"Maybe he mentioned it; I don't remember."

"I did bring up the Catholic thing with him. He gave me one of those looks of his and said, 'Aye, well, the Pope wasna in Ardsmuir Prison, and I was.'"

"Sounds reasonable to me," she said, amused. "But then, I'm not the Pope. Did he say why? Da, I mean, not the Pope."

"Sure—as a means of uniting the Catholics and Protestants imprisoned together. One of the principles of Freemasonry being the universal brotherhood of man, aye? And another being that ye don't talk religion or politics in Lodge."

"Oh, you don't? What do you do in Lodge, then?"

"I can't tell you. Not worshipping the Devil, though."

She raised her eyebrows at him, and he shrugged.

"I can't," he repeated. "When ye join, you take an oath not to talk outside the Lodge about what's done there."

She was mildly miffed at that, but dismissed it, going back to add more water to one bowl. It looked as though someone had thrown up in it, she thought critically, and reached for the acid bottle.

"Sounds pretty fishy to me," she remarked. "And kind of silly. Isn't there something about secret handshakes, that sort of thing?"

He merely smiled, not bothered by her tone.

"I'm not saying there isn't a bit of stage business involved. It's more or less medieval in origin, and it's kept quite a bit of the original trappings—rather like the Catholic Church."

"Point taken," she said dryly, picking up a ready bowl of pulp. "Okay. So, is it Da's idea to start a Lodge here?"

"No, mine." His voice lost its humorous tone, and she looked at him sharply.

"I need a way to give them common ground, Bree," he said. "The women have it—the fishers' wives sew and spin and knit and quilt wi' the others, and if they privately think you or your mother or Mrs. Bug are heretics damned to hell, or goddamned Whigs, or whatever, it seems to make no great difference. But not the men."

She thought of saying something about the relative intelligence and common sense of the two sexes, but feeling that this might be counterproductive just at the moment, nodded understanding. Besides, he obviously had no notion of the kind of gossip that went on in sewing circles.

"Hold that screen steady, will you?"

He obligingly grasped the wooden frame, pulling taut the edges of the finely drawn wire threaded through it, as instructed.

"So," she said, spooning the thin gruel of the pulp onto the silk, "do you want me to provide milk and cookies for this affair tonight?"

She spoke with considerable irony, and he smiled across the screen at her.

"That'd be nice, aye."

"I was joking!"

"I wasn't." He was still smiling, but with complete seriousness behind his eyes, and she realized suddenly that this wasn't a whim. With an odd small twist of the heart, she saw her father standing there.

One had known the care of other men from his earliest years, a part of the duty of his birthright; the other had come to it later, but both felt that burden to be the will of God, she had no doubt at all—both accepted that duty without question, would honor it, or die in trying. She only hoped it wouldn't come to that—for either of them.

"Give me one of your hairs," she said, looking down to hide what she felt.

"Why?" he asked, but was plucking a strand from his head even as he spoke.

"The paper. The pulp shouldn't be spread any thicker than a hair." She laid the black thread at the edge of the silk screen, then spread the creamy liquid thin and thinner, so it flowed past the hair but did not cover it. It flowed with the liquid, a sinuous dark line through the white, like the tiny crack on the surface of her heart.

79

Alarms

L'OIGNON–INTELLIGENCER

A MARRIAGE IS ANNOUNCED. The NEW BERN INTELLIGENCER, founded by Jno. Robinson, has ceased publication with the removal of its founder to Great Britain, but we assure its Customers that this Newspaper shall not vanish altogether, as its Premises, Stock, and Subscription Lists have been acquired by the Proprietors of THE ONION, that esteemed, popular, and Preeminent Journal. The New Periodical, Much Improved and Expanded, will henceforth appear as the L'OIGNON– INTELLIGENCER, distributed upon a Weekly Basis, with Extra Editions as events demand, these provided at a modest cost of One Penny. . . .

*To Mr. and Mrs. James Fraser, of the Ridge,
North Carolina, from Mr. and Mrs. Fergus Fraser,
Thorpe Street, New Bern
Dear Father and Mother Claire:*

*I write to acquaint you with the latest Change in
our Fortunes. Mr. Robinson, who had owned the other
Newspaper in the town, found himself removed to
Great Britain. Literally removed, as some Persons
unknown, disguised as Savages, invaded his Shop in
the early Hours of the Morning, and pulled him from
his Bed, hurrying him to the Harbor and there thrusting him aboard a Ship, clad only in his Nightclothes
and Cap.*

*The Captain promptly cast off his Tethers and made
Sail, leaving the Town in some Uproar, as you may imagine.*

*Within a Day of Mr. Robinson's abrupt Departure,
though, we were visited by two separate Parties (I cannot write their Names, being discreet as you will appreciate). One of these was a Member of the local
Committee of Safety—which everyone knows was behind
Mr. Robinson's Removal, but no one says so. He was
civil in his Speech, but his manner was not so much. He
wished, he said, to assure himself that Fergus did not
share the Willfully Wrongheaded Sentiments so oft
expressed by Mr. Robinson, regarding recent Events and
Particulars.*

*Fergus told him with a very straight face that he
would not chuse to share so much as a Glass of Wine with
Mr. Robinson (which he could not, Mr. Robinson being
Methody and against Drink), and the Gentleman took this
to mean what he wished, and went away satisfied, and
gave Fergus a Purse of Money.*

*Next thing comes another Gentleman, fat and most
Important in the Affairs of the Town, and a Member of the
Royal Council, though I did not know it at the time. His
Errand was the Same—or rather, the Opposite: he wished
to inquire whether Fergus was inclined to acquire Mr.
Robinson's Assets, so to continue his work on behalf of
the King—that being the printing of some Letters, and the
Suppression of Others.*

*Fergus says to this Gentleman, most grave, that he has
always found Much to admire in Mr. Robinson (chiefly*

*his horse, which is gray and very amiable, and the curi-
ous Buckles on his Shoes), but adding that we have
barely Means to buy Ink and Paper, and so he feared we
must resign ourselves to the Acquisition of Mr.
Robinson's Shop by a Person of no great Sensitivity in
Politickal Matters.*

*I was myself in Terror, a State not improved when the
Gentleman uttered a Laugh and took a fat Purse from his
Pocket, remarking that one must not "spoil the ship for a
happeny's worth of tar." He seemed to think this most
amusing, and laughed quite immoderate, then patted
Henri-Christian on the Head and went away.*

*So our Prospects are at once enlarged and alarming. I
am fair sleepless, thinking on the Future, but Fergus is so
much Improved in Spirits that I cannot regret it.*

*Pray for us, as we pray for you always, my Dear
Parents.*

> *Your Obedient and Loving Daughter,*
> *Marsali*

"You taught him well," I remarked, trying to keep my voice casual.

"Evidently so." Jamie looked slightly worried, but much more amused. "Dinna fash yourself over it, Sassenach. Fergus has some skill at this game."

"It is not a game," I said, with enough vehemence that he looked at me in surprise.

"It's not," I repeated, a little more calmly.

He raised his brows at me, and pulling a small sheaf of papers from the mess on his desk, handed them across.

WEDNESDAY MORNING
NEAR 10 OF THE CLOCK—WATERTOWN

*To all the friends of American liberty be it known that
this morning before break of day, a brigade, consisting
of about 1,000 to 1,200 men landed at Phip's Farm at
Cambridge and marched to Lexington, where they found*

*a company of our colony militia in arms, upon whom
they fired without any provocation and killed six men
and wounded four others. By an express from Boston, we
find another brigade are now upon their march from
Boston supposed to be about 1,000. The Bearer, Israel
Bissell, is charged to alarm the country quite to
Connecticut and all persons are desired to furnish him
with fresh horses as they may be needed. I have spoken
with several persons who have seen the dead and
wounded. Pray let the delegates from this colony to
Connecticut see this.*

     J. Palmer, one of the Committee of Safety.

    *They know Col. Foster of Brookfield one of the
Delegates.*

Beneath this message was a list of signatures, though most
were done in the same handwriting. The first read *A true copy
taken from the original per order of the Committee of
Correspondence for Worcester—April 19, 1775. Attest. Nathan
Baldwin, Town Clerk.* All the others were preceded by similar
statements.

"I will be damned," I said. "It's the Lexington Alarm." I
glanced up at Jamie, wide-eyed. "Where did you get it?"

"One of Colonel Ashe's men brought it." He shuffled to the
end of the last sheet, pointing out John Ashe's endorsement.
"What is the Lexington Alarm?"

"That." I looked at it with fascination. "After the battle at
Lexington, General Palmer—he's a general of militia—wrote
this and sent it through the countryside by an express rider, to bear
witness to what had happened; to notify the militias nearby that
the war had started.

"Men along the way took copies of it, endorsed them to swear
that they were true copies, and sent the message along to other
townships and villages; there were probably hundreds of copies
made at the time, and quite a few survived. Frank had one that
someone gave him as a present. He kept it in a frame, in the front
hall of our house in Boston."

Then a quite extraordinary shudder went through me, as I realized that the familiar letter I was looking at had in fact been written only a week or two before—not two hundred years.

Jamie was looking a little pale, too.

"This—it's what Brianna told me would happen," he said, a tone of wonder in his voice. "Upon the nineteenth of April, a fight in Lexington—the start of the war." He looked straight at me, and I saw that his eyes were dark, with a combination of awe and excitement.

"I did believe ye, Sassenach," he said. "But . . ."

He didn't finish the sentence, but sat down, reaching for his quill. With slow deliberation, he signed his name at the foot of the page.

"Ye'll make me a fair copy, Sassenach?" he said. "I'll send it on."

80

The World Turned Upside Down

Colonel Ashe's man had also brought word of a congress to be held in Mecklenberg County, to take place in mid-May, with the intent to declare the county's official independence from the King of England.

Aware of the fact that he was still viewed with skepticism by not a few leaders of what had now suddenly become "the rebellion," despite the stout personal support of John Ashe and a few other friends, Jamie made up his mind to attend this congress and speak openly in support of the measure.

Roger, absolutely blazing with suppressed excitement at this,

his first chance to witness recorded history in the making, was to go with him.

A few days before their scheduled departure, though, everyone's attention was distracted from the prospect of history by the more immediate present: the entire Christie family arrived suddenly at the front door, soon after breakfast.

Something had happened; Allan Christie was flushed with agitation, Tom grim and gray as an old wolf. Malva had clearly been crying, and her face went red and white by turns. I greeted her, but she looked away from me, lips trembling, as Jamie invited them into his study, gesturing them to sit.

"What is it, Tom?" He glanced briefly at Malva—plainly she was the focus of this family emergency—but gave his attention to Tom, as patriarch.

Tom Christie's mouth was pressed so tight that it was barely visible in the depths of his neatly clipped beard.

"My daughter finds herself with child," he said abruptly.

"Oh?" Jamie cast another brief glance at Malva—who stood with capped head bowed, looking down at her clasped hands—then looked at me with a raised eyebrow. "Ah. Well . . . there's a good bit of it going about, to be sure," he said, and smiled kindly, in an effort to ease the Christies, all of whom were quivering like beads on a tight-pulled wire.

I was myself less than startled to hear the news, though naturally concerned. Malva had always attracted a great deal of attention from young men, and while both her brother and father had been vigilant in preventing any open courting, the only way of keeping young men away altogether would have been to lock her in a dungeon.

Who had the successful suitor been? I wondered. Obadiah Henderson? Bobby, perhaps? One of the McMurchie brothers? Not—please God—both of them, I hoped. All of these—and not a few others—had been obvious in their admiration.

Tom Christie received Jamie's attempt at pleasantry with stony silence, though Allan made a poor attempt at a smile. He was nearly as pale as his sister.

Jamie coughed.

"Well, so. Is there some way in which I might help, then, Tom?"

"She says," Christie began gruffly, with a piercing look at his daughter, "that she will not name the man, save in your presence." He turned the look on Jamie, thick with dislike.

"In my presence?" Jamie coughed again, clearly embarrassed at the obvious implication—that Malva thought her male relatives would either beat her or proceed to do violence upon her lover, unless the presence of the landlord constrained them. Personally, I thought that particular fear was probably well founded, and gave Tom Christie a narrow look of my own. Had he already tried, and failed, to beat the truth out of her?

Malva was not making any attempt at divulging the name of the father of her child, Jamie's presence notwithstanding. She merely pleated her apron between her fingers, over and over, eyes fixed on her hands.

I cleared my throat delicately.

"How—um—how far gone are you, my dear?"

She didn't answer directly, but pressed both hands, shaking, against her apron front, smoothing down the cloth so that the round bulge of her pregnancy was suddenly visible, smooth and melonlike, surprisingly large. Six months, perhaps; I was startled. Clearly, she'd delayed telling her father for as long as she possibly could—and hidden it well.

The silence was well beyond awkward. Allan shifted uncomfortably on his stool, and leaned forward to murmur reassuringly to his sister.

"It'll be all right, Mallie," he whispered. "Ye've got to say, though."

She took a huge gulp of air at that, and raised her head. Her eyes were reddened, but still very beautiful, and wide with apprehension.

"Oh, sir," she said, but then stopped dead.

Jamie was by now looking nearly as uncomfortable as the Christies, but did his best to keep his air of kindness.

"Will ye not tell me, then, lass?" he said, as gently as possible. "I promise ye'll not suffer for it."

Tom Christie made an irritable noise, like some beast of prey disturbed at its meal, and Malva went very pale indeed, but her eyes stayed fixed on Jamie.

"Oh, sir," she said, and her voice was small but clear as a bell, ringing with reproach. "Oh, sir, how can ye say that to me, when ye ken the truth as well as I do?" Before anyone could react to that, she turned to her father, and lifting a hand, pointed directly at Jamie.

"It was him," she said.

I have never been so grateful for anything in life as for the fact that I was looking at Jamie's face when she said it. He had no warning, no chance to control his features—and he didn't. His face showed neither anger nor fear, denial or surprise; nothing save the open-mouthed blankness of absolute incomprehension.

"What?" he said, and blinked, once. Then realization flooded into his face.

"WHAT?" he said, in a tone that should have knocked the little trollop flat on her lying little bottom.

She blinked then, and cast down her eyes, the very picture of virtue shamed. She turned, as though unable to bear his gaze, and stretched out a tremulous hand toward me.

"I'm *so* sorry, Mrs. Fraser," she whispered, tears trembling becomingly on her lashes. "He—we—we didna mean to hurt ye."

I watched with interest from somewhere outside my body, as my arm lifted and drew back, and felt a sense of vague approval as my hand struck her cheek with enough force that she stumbled backward, tripped over a stool, and fell, her petticoats tumbled up to her waist in a froth of linen, wool-stockinged legs sticking absurdly up in the air.

"Can't say the same, I'm afraid." I hadn't even thought of saying anything, and was surprised to feel the words in my mouth, cool and round as river stones.

Suddenly, I was back in my body. I felt as though my stays had tightened during my temporary absence; my ribs ached with the effort to breathe. Liquid surged in every direction; blood and lymph, sweat and tears—if I did draw breath, my skin would give way and let it all spurt out, like the contents of a ripe tomato, thrown against a wall.

I had no bones. But I had will. That alone held me upright and saw me out the door. I didn't see the corridor or realize that I had pushed open the front door of the house; all I saw was a sudden blaze of light and a blur of green in the dooryard and then I was running, running as though all the demons of hell coursed at my heels.

In fact, no one pursued me. And yet I ran, plunging off the trail and into the wood, feet sliding in the layers of slippery needles down the runnels between stones, half-falling down the slope of the hill, caroming painfully off fallen logs, wrenching free of thorns and brush.

I arrived breathless at the bottom of a hill and found myself in a dark, small hollow walled by the towering black-green of rhododendrons. I paused, gasping for breath, then sat down abruptly. I felt myself wobble, and let go, ending on my back among the dusty layers of leathery mountain laurel leaves.

A faint thought echoed in my mind, under the sound of my gasping breath. *The guilty flee, where no man pursues.* But *I* surely wasn't guilty. Nor was Jamie; I knew that. Knew it.

But Malva was certainly pregnant. Someone was guilty.

My eyes were blurred from running and the sunlight starred into fractured slabs and streaks of color—dark blue, light blue, white and gray, pinwheels of green and gold as the cloudy sky and the mountainside spun round and round above me.

I blinked hard, unshed tears sliding down my temples.

"Bloody, bloody, fucking hell," I said very softly. "Now what?"

Jamie stooped without thought, seized the girl by the elbows, and hauled her unceremoniously to her feet. Her one cheek bore a crimson patch where Claire had struck her, and for an instant, he had a strong urge to give her one to match on the other side.

He hadn't the chance either to quell that desire or to execute it; a hand seized his shoulder to yank him round, and it was reflex alone that made him dodge aside as Allan Christie's fist glanced off the side of his head, catching him painfully on the tip of the ear. He pushed the young man hard in the chest with both hands, then hooked a heel behind his calf as he staggered, and Allan dropped on his backside with a thud that shook the room.

Jamie stepped back, a hand to his throbbing ear, and glared at Tom Christie, who was standing staring at him like Lot's wife.

Jamie's free left hand was clenched in a fist, and he raised it a little, in invitation. Christie's eyes narrowed further, but he made no move toward Jamie.

"Get up," Christie said to his son. "And keep your fists to yourself. There's nay need for that now."

"Isn't there?" cried the lad, scrambling to his feet. "He's made a whore of your daughter, and you'll let him stand? Well, and ye'll play coward, auld man, I'll not!"

He lunged at Jamie, wild-eyed, hands grabbing for his throat. Jamie stepped to the side, shifted weight back on one leg, and hooked the lad in the liver with a vicious left that drove his wame into his backbone and doubled him over with a *whoof.* Allan stared up at him, open-mouthed and the whites of his eyes showing all round, then subsided onto his knees with a thud, mouth opening and closing like a fish's.

It might have been comical under other circumstances, but Jamie felt no disposition to laugh. He wasted no more time on either of the men, but swung round on Malva.

"So, what mischief is this ye're about, *nighean na galladh?*" he said to her. It was a serious insult, and Tom Christie knew what it meant, Gaelic or not; Jamie could see Christie stiffen, in the corner of his eye.

The girl herself was already in tears, and burst into sobs at this.

"How can ye speak to me so?" she wailed, and clutched her apron to her face. "How can ye be so cruel?"

"Oh, for God's sake," he said crossly. He shoved a stool in her direction. "Sit, ye wee loon, and we'll hear the truth of whatever ye think ye're up to. Mr. Christie?" He glanced at Tom, nodded toward another stool, and went to take his own chair, ignoring Allan, who had collapsed onto the floor and was curled up on his side like a kitten, holding his belly.

"Sir?"

Mrs. Bug, hearing the racket, had come out from her kitchen, and was standing in the doorway, eyes wide under her cap.

"Will ye . . . be needin' anything, sir?" she asked, making no pretense of not staring from Malva, red-faced and sobbing on her stool, to Allan, white and gasping on the floor.

Jamie thought that he needed a strong dram—or maybe two—but that would have to wait.

"I thank ye, Mrs. Bug," he said politely, "but no. We'll bide." He lifted his fingers in dismissal, and she faded reluctantly from view. She hadn't gone far, though, he knew, just round the edge of the door.

He rubbed a hand over his face, wondering what it was about young girls these days. It was a full moon tonight; perhaps they truly did run lunatic.

On the other hand, the wee bitch had undoubtedly been playing the loon with *someone*; with her apron up like that, the bairn was showing plainly, a hard round swell like a calabash under her thin petticoat.

"How long?" he asked Christie, with a nod toward her.

"Six months gone," Christie said, and sank reluctantly onto the offered stool. He was dour as Jamie had ever seen him, but in control of himself, that was something.

"It was when the sickness came late last summer; when I was here, helping to nurse his wife!" Malva burst out, lowering her apron and staring reproachfully at her father, full lip a-tremble. "And not just the once, either!" She switched her gaze back to Jamie, wet-eyed and pleading. "Tell them, sir, please—tell them the truth!"

"Oh, I mean to," he said, giving her a black look. "And ye'll do the same, lass, I assure ye."

The shock of it was beginning to fade, and while his sense of irritation remained—in fact, it was growing by the moment—he was beginning to think, and furiously.

She was pregnant by someone grossly unsuitable; that much was clear. Who? Christ, he wished Claire had stayed; she listened to the gossip on the Ridge and she took interest in the lass; she'd know which young men were likely prospects. He'd seldom noticed young Malva particularly himself, save she was always about, helping Claire.

"The first time was when Herself was so ill as we despaired of her life," Malva said, snapping him back to attention. "I told ye, Faither. It wasna rape—only Himself being off his heid wi' the sorrow of it, and me, as well." She blinked, a pearly tear sliding down the unmarked cheek. "I came down from her room late at night, to find him in here, sitting in the dark, and grieving. I felt so sorry for him. . . ." Her voice shook, and she stopped, swallowing.

"I asked could I fetch him a wee bite, maybe something to drink—but he'd drink taken already, there was whisky in a glass before him. . . ."

"And I said no, thank ye kindly, and that I'd be alone," Jamie broke in, feeling the blood begin to surge in his temples at her re-counting. "Ye left."

"No, I didn't." She shook her head; the cap had come half off when she fell and she hadn't settled it again; dark tendrils of hair hung down, framing her face. "Or rather, ye did say that to me, that ye'd be alone. But I couldn't bear to see ye in such straits, and—I know 'twas forward and unseemly, but I did pity ye so much!" she burst out, looking up and then immediately dropping her gaze again.

"I . . . I came and touched him," she whispered, so low that he had trouble hearing her. "Put my hand on his shoulder, like, only to comfort him. But he turned then, and put his arms round me, all of a sudden and grasped me to him. And—and then . . ." She gulped, audibly.

"He . . . he took me. Just . . . there." The toe of one small buskin stretched out, pointing delicately at the rag rug just in front of the table. Where there was, in fact, a small and ancient brown stain, which might have been blood. It *was* blood—Jemmy's, left when the wee lad had tripped on the rug and bumped his nose so it bled.

He opened his mouth to speak, but was so choked by outraged amazement that nothing emerged but a sort of gasp.

"So ye've not the balls to deny it, eh?" Young Allan had recovered his breath; he was swaying on his knees, hair hanging in his face, and glaring. "Balls enough to do it, though!"

Jamie gave Allan a quelling look, but didn't bother replying to him. He turned his attention instead to Tom Christie.

"Is she mad?" he inquired. "Or only clever?"

Christie's face might have been carved in stone, save for the pouchy flesh quivering beneath his eyes, and the eyes themselves, bloodshot and narrowed.

"She's not mad," Christie said.

"A clever liar, then." Jamie narrowed his own eyes at her. "Clever enough to ken no one would believe a tale of rape."

Her mouth opened in horror.

"Oh, no, sir," she said, and shook her head so hard the dark curls danced by her ears. "I should *never* say such a thing of ye, never!" She swallowed, and timidly raised her eyes to meet his—swollen with weeping, but a soft dove gray, guileless with inno-cence.

"Ye needed comfort," she said, softly but clearly. "I gave it ye."

He pinched the bridge of his nose hard betwixt thumb and forefinger, hoping the sensation would wake him from what was plainly nightmare. This failing to occur, he sighed and looked at Tom Christie.

"She's with child by someone, and not by me," he said bluntly. "Who might it have been?"

"It *was* you!" the girl protested, letting her apron fall as she sat bolt upright on her stool. "There's no one else!"

Christie's eyes slid reluctantly toward his daughter, then came back to meet Jamie's. They were the same dove gray, but they'd never possessed any trace of either guilelessness or innocence.

"I know of no one," he said. He took a deep breath, squaring his stocky shoulders. "She says it wasn't just the once. That ye had her a dozen times or more." His voice was nearly colorless, but not from lack of feeling, rather, from the grip he had upon his feelings.

"Then she's lied a dozen times or more," Jamie said, keeping his own voice under as much control as Christie's.

"Ye know I have not! Your wife believes me," Malva said, and a steely note had entered her voice. She lifted a hand to her cheek, where the flaming color had subsided but where the print of Claire's fingers was still clear, livid in outline.

"My wife has better sense," he said coldly, but was conscious all the same of a sinking sensation at the mention of Claire. Any woman might find such an accusation shock enough to make her flee—but he did wish that she'd stayed. Her presence, stoutly denying any misbehavior by him and personally rebuking Malva's lies, would have helped.

"Does she?" The vivid color had faded from the girl's face altogether, but she had stopped weeping. She was white-faced, her eyes huge and brilliant. "Well, I've sense, as well, sir. Sense enough to prove what I say."

"Oh, aye?" he said skeptically. "How?"

"I've seen the scars on your naked body; I can describe them."

That declaration brought everyone up short. There was silence for a moment, broken by Allan Christie's grunt of satisfaction. He rose to his feet, one hand still pressed to his middle, but an unpleasant smile upon his face.

"So, then?" he said. "Nay answer to that one, have ye?"

Irritation had long since given way to a monstrous anger. Under that, though, was the barest thread of something he would not—not yet—call fear.

"I dinna put my scars on display," he said mildly, "but there are a number of folk who've seen them, nonetheless. I havena lain with any of *them,* either."

"Aye, folk speak sometimes of the scars on your back," Malva shot back. "And everyone kens the great ugly one up your leg, that ye took at Culloden. But what of the crescent-shaped one across your ribs? Or the wee one on your left hurdie?" She reached a hand behind her, cupping her own buttock in illustration.

"Not in the center, quite—a bit down, on the outer side. About the size of a farthing." She didn't smile, but something like triumph blazed in her eyes.

"I havena got—" he began, but then stopped, appalled. Christ, he did. A spider's bite, taken in the Indies, that festered for a week, made an abscess, then burst, to his great relief. Once healed, he'd never thought of it again—but it was there.

Too late. They'd seen the realization cross his face.

Tom Christie closed his eyes, jaw working under his beard. Allan grunted again with satisfaction, and crossed his arms.

"Want to show us she's wrong?" the young man inquired sarcastically. "Take down your breeks, and gie us a look at your backside, then!"

With a good deal of effort, he kept himself from telling Allan Christie what he could do with his own backside. He took a long, slow breath, hoping that by the time he let it out again, some useful thought would have come to him.

It didn't. Tom Christie opened his eyes with a sigh.

"So," he said flatly. "I suppose ye'll not intend to put aside your wife and marry her?"

"I should never do such a thing!" The suggestion filled him with fury—and something like panic at the mere notion of being without Claire.

"Then we'll draw a contract." Christie rubbed a hand over his face, shoulders slumped with exhaustion and distaste. "Maintenance for her and the bairn. Formal acknowledgment of the child's rights as one of your heirs. Ye can decide, I suppose, if ye wish to take it for your wife to rear, but that—"

"Get out." He rose, very slowly, and leaned forward, hands on the table, eyes fixed on Christie's. "Take your daughter and leave my house."

Christie stopped speaking and looked at him, black-browed. The girl had started grieving again, making whimpering noises into her apron. He'd the odd feeling that time had stopped, somehow; they would all just be trapped here forever, himself and Christie staring each other down like dogs, unable to look down but knowing that the floor of the room had vanished beneath their feet and they hung suspended over some dreadful abyss, in the endless moment before the fall.

It was Allan Christie who broke it, of course. The movement of the young man's hand going to his knife freed Jamie's gaze from Christie's, and his fingers tightened, digging into the wood of the table. An instant before, he'd felt bodiless; now blood hammered in his temples and pulsed through his limbs and his muscles trembled with an urgent need to damage Allan Christie. And wring his sister's neck to stop her noise, as well.

Allan Christie's face was black with anger, but he'd sense enough—barely, Jamie thought—not to draw the knife.

"I should like nothing better, wee man, than to gie ye your heid in your hands to play with," he said softly. "Leave now, before I do it."

Young Christie licked his lips and tensed himself, knuckle-bones going white on the hilt—but his eyes wavered. He glanced at his father, who sat like a stone, grim-jowled and square. The light had changed; it shone from the side and through the grizzled tufts of Christie's beard, so his own scar showed, a thin pink rope that curled like a snake above his jaw.

Christie straightened slowly, pushing himself up with his hands on his thighs, then shook his head suddenly like a dog shaking off water and stood up. He gripped Malva by the arm, lifted her from her stool, and pushed her before him, weeping and stumbling on the way out.

Allan followed them, making occasion to brush so near to Jamie as he left that Jamie could smell the younger man's stink, ripe with fury. Young Christie cast a single angry glance back over his shoulder, hand still on his knife—but left. Their tread in the hall made the floorboards tremble under Jamie's feet, and then came the heavy slam of the door.

He looked down, then, vaguely surprised to see the battered

surface of his table and his own hands still flattened there as if they'd grown to it. He straightened up and his fingers curled, the stiff joints painful as they made themselves into fists. He was drenched with sweat.

Lighter footsteps came down the hall then, and Mrs. Bug came in with a tray. She set it down before him, curtsied to him, and went out. The single crystal goblet that he owned was stood on it, and the decanter that held the good whisky.

He felt obscurely that he wanted to laugh, but couldn't quite remember how it was done. The light touched the decanter and the drink within glowed like a chrysoberyl. He touched the glass gently in acknowledgment of Mrs. Bug's loyalty, but that would have to wait. The Devil was loose in the world and there'd be hell to pay, surely. Before he did aught else, he must find Claire.

After a time, the drifting clouds boiled up into thunderheads, and a cold breeze moved over the top of the hollow, shaking the laurels overhead with a rattling like dry bones. Very slowly, I got to my feet and began to climb.

I had no sure destination in mind; didn't care, really, if I were wet or not. I only knew that I couldn't go back to the house. As it was, I came to the trail that led to the White Spring, just as rain began to fall. Huge drops splattered on the leaves of pokeweed and burdock, and the firs and pines let go their long-held breath in a fragrant sigh.

The patter of drops on leaves and branches was punctuated by the muffled thud of heavier drops striking deep into soft earth— hail was coming with the rain, and suddenly there were tiny white particles of ice bouncing crazily on the packed needles, peppering my face and neck with stinging cold.

I ran, then, and took shelter beneath the drooping branches of a balsam fir that overhung the spring. The hail pocked the water and made it dance, but melted on impact, disappearing at once into the dark water. I sat still, arms wrapped around myself against the chill, shivering.

You could almost understand, said the part of my mind that had begun talking somewhere on the journey up the hill. *Everyone thought you were dying—including you. You know what happens . . . you've seen it.* People under the terrible strain of grief, those dealing with the presence of overwhelming death— I'd seen it. It was a natural seeking of solace; an attempt to hide, only for a moment, to deny death's coldness by taking comfort in the simple warmth of bodily contact.

"But he didn't," I said stubbornly, out loud. "If he *had*, and that was it—I could forgive him. But God damn it, he *didn't*!"

My subconscious subsided in the face of this certainty, but I was aware of subterranean stirrings—not suspicions, nothing strong enough to be called doubts. Only small, cool observations that poked their heads above the surface of my own dark well like spring peepers, high, thin pipings that were barely audible individually but that together might eventually form a racket of sound to shake the night.

You're an old woman.

See how the veins stand out on your hands.

The flesh has fallen away from your bones; your breasts sag.

If he were desperate, needing comfort . . .

He might reject her, but could never turn away from a child of his blood.

I closed my eyes and fought a rising sense of nausea. The hail had passed, succeeded by heavy rain, and cold steam began to rise from the ground, vapor drifting upward, disappearing like ghosts into the downpour.

"No," I said aloud. "No!"

I felt as though I had swallowed several large rocks, jagged and dirt-covered. It wasn't just the thought that Jamie might—but that Malva *had* most certainly betrayed me. Had betrayed me if it were true—and still more, if it were not.

My apprentice. My daughter of the heart.

I was safe from the rain, but the air was thick with water; my garments grew damp and hung heavy on me, clammy on my skin. Through the rain, I could see the big white stone that stood at the head of the spring, that gave the pool its name. Here it was that Jamie had shed his blood in sacrifice, and dashed it on that rock, asking the help of the kinsman he had slain. And here it was that Fergus had lain down, opening his veins in despair for his son, his blood blooming dark in the silent water.

And I began to realize why I had come here, why the place had called me. It was a place to meet oneself, and find truth.

The rain passed, and the clouds broke. Slowly, the light began to fade.

It was nearly dark when he came. The trees were moving, restless with twilight and whispering among themselves; I didn't hear his footsteps on the sodden trail. He was just there, suddenly, at the edge of the clearing.

He stood searching; I saw his head lift when he saw me, and then he strode round the pool and ducked under the overhanging branches of my shelter. He'd been out for some time, I saw; his coat was wet and the cloth of his shirt plastered to his chest with rain and sweat. He'd brought a cloak with him, bundled under his arm, and he unfolded this and wrapped it round my shoulders. I let him.

He sat quite close to me then, arms wrapped about his knees, and stared into the darkening pool of the spring. The light had reached that point of beauty, just before all color fades, and the hairs of his eyebrows arched auburn and perfect over the solid ridges of his brows, each hair distinct, like the shorter, darker hairs of his sprouting beard.

He breathed long and deep, as though he had been walking for some time, and rubbed away a drop of moisture that dripped from the end of his nose. Once or twice, he took a shorter breath, as though about to say something, but didn't.

The birds had come out briefly after the rain. Now they were going to their rest, cheeping softly in the trees.

"I *do* hope you were planning to say something," I said finally, politely. "Because if you don't, I'll probably start screaming, and I might not be able to stop."

He made a sound somewhere between amusement and dismay, and sank his face into the palms of his hands. He stayed that way for a moment, then rubbed his hands hard over his face and sat up, sighing.

"I have been thinking all the time I was searching for ye, Sassenach, what in God's name I should say when I found ye. I thought of one thing and another—and . . . there seemed nothing whatever I *could* say." He sounded helpless.

"How is that?" I asked, a distinct edge in my voice. "I could think of a few things to say, I daresay."

He sighed, and made a brief gesture of frustration.

"What? To say I was sorry—that's not right. I *am* sorry, but to say so—it sounds as though I've done something to be sorry for, and that I have not. But I thought to start off so would make ye maybe think . . ." He glanced at me. I was keeping a tight grip on both my face and my emotions, but he knew me very well. The instant he'd said, "I'm sorry," my stomach had plunged toward my feet.

He looked away.

"There's naught I can say," he said quietly, "that doesna sound as though I try to defend or excuse myself. And I willna do that."

I made a small sound, as though someone had punched me in the stomach, and he glanced sharply at me.

"I won't do it!" he said fiercely. "There is no way to deny such a charge that doesna carry the stink of doubt about it. And nothing I can say to you that doesna sound like some groveling apology for—for—well, I willna apologize for something I havena done, and if I did, ye'd only doubt me more."

I was beginning to breathe a little easier.

"You don't seem to have a lot of faith in my faith in *you*."

He gave me a wary look.

"If I hadna got quite a lot of it, Sassenach, I wouldna be here."

He watched me for a moment, then reached out and touched my hand. My fingers turned at once and curved to meet his, and our hands clasped tight. His fingers were big and cold and he held mine so tightly that I thought my bones would break.

He took a deep breath, almost a sob, and his shoulders, tight in his sodden coat, relaxed all at once.

"Ye didna think it true?" he asked. "Ye ran away."

"It *was* a shock," I said. And I'd thought, dimly, that if I stayed, I might just kill her.

"Aye, it was," he said very dryly. "I expect I might have run away myself—if I could."

A small twinge of guilt was added to the overload of emotions; I supposed my hasty exit couldn't have helped the situation. He didn't reproach me, though, but merely said again, "Ye didna think it true, though?"

"I don't."

"Ye don't." His eyes searched mine. "But ye did?"

"No." I pulled the cloak closer round me, settling it on my shoulders. "I didn't. But I didn't know why."

"And now ye do."

I took a deep, deep breath of my own and let it go, then turned to face him, straight on.

"Jamie Fraser," I said, with great deliberation. "If you could do such a thing as that—and I don't mean lying with a woman, I mean doing it and lying to *me* about it—then everything I've done and everything I've been—my whole life—has been a lie. And I am not prepared to admit such a thing."

That surprised him a little; it was nearly dark now, but I saw his eyebrows rise.

"What d'ye mean by that, Sassenach?"

I waved a hand up the trail, where the house lay invisible above us, then toward the spring, where the white stone stood, a blur in the dark.

"I don't belong here," I said softly. "Brianna, Roger . . . they don't belong here. Jemmy shouldn't be here; he should be watching cartoons on television, drawing pictures of cars and airplanes with crayons—not learning to shoot a gun as big as he is and cut the entrails from a deer."

I lifted my face and closed my eyes, feeling the damp settle on my skin, heavy on my lashes.

"But we *are* here, all of us. And we're here because I loved you, more than the life that was mine. Because I believed you loved me the same way."

I took a deep breath, so that my voice wouldn't tremble, opened my eyes and turned to him.

"Will you tell me that's not true?"

"No," he said after a moment, so softly I could barely hear him. His hand tightened harder on mine. "No, I willna tell ye that. Not ever, Claire."

"Well, then," I said, and felt the anxiety and fury and fear of the afternoon run out of me like water. I rested my head on his shoulder, and breathed the rain and sweat on his skin. He smelled acrid, pungent with the musk of fear and curdled anger.

It was entirely dark by now. I could hear sounds in the distance, Mrs. Bug calling to Arch from the stable where she'd been milking the goats, and his cracked old voice hallooing back. A bat flittered past, silent and hunting.

"Claire?" Jamie said softly.

"Hm?"

"I've got to tell ye something."

I froze. After a moment, I carefully detached myself from him and sat upright.

"Don't do that," I said. "It makes me feel as though I've been punched in the stomach."

"I'm sorry."

I wrapped my arms around myself, trying to swallow the sudden feeling of nausea.

"You said you wouldn't start off by saying you were sorry, because it felt as though there must be something to be sorry for."

"I did," he said, and sighed.

I felt the movement between us as the two stiff fingers of his right hand thrummed against his leg.

"There isna any good way," he said finally, "of telling your wife ye've lain wi' someone else. No matter what the circumstances. There's just not."

I felt suddenly dizzy, and short of breath. I closed my eyes momentarily. He didn't mean Malva; he'd made that clear.

"Who?" I said as evenly as possible. "And when?"

He stirred uneasily.

"Oh. Well . . . when ye . . . when ye were . . . gone, to be sure."

I managed to take a short breath.

"Who?" I said.

"Just the once," he said. "I mean—I hadna the slightest intention of—"

"Who?"

He sighed, and rubbed hard at the back of his neck.

"Christ. The last thing I want is to upset ye, Sassenach, by sounding as though it—but I dinna want to malign the puir woman by makin' it seem that she was—"

"WHO?" I roared, seizing him by the arm.

"Jesus!" he said, thoroughly startled. "Mary MacNab."

"Who?" I said again, blankly this time.

"Mary MacNab," he repeated, and sighed. "Can ye let go, Sassenach? I think ye've drawn blood."

I had, my fingernails digging hard enough into his wrist as to pierce the skin. I flung his hand away, and folded my own into fists, wrapping my arms around my body by way of stopping myself from strangling him.

"Who. The. Hell. Is. Mary. MacNab?" I said, through my teeth.

My face was hot, but cold sweat prickled along my jaw and rolled down my ribs.

"Ye ken her, Sassenach. She was wife to Rab—him that died when his house was burnt. They had the one bairn, Rabbie; he was stable-lad at Lallybroch when—"

"Mary MacNab. *Her?*" I could hear the astonishment in my own voice. I did recall Mary MacNab—barely. She'd come to be a maid at Lallybroch after the death of her nasty husband; a small, wiry woman, worn with work and hardship, who seldom spoke, but went about her business like a shadow, never more than half-noticed in the rowdy chaos of life at Lallybroch.

"I scarcely noticed her," I said, trying—and failing—to remember whether she had been there on my last visit. "But I gather you *did*?"

"No," he said, and sighed. "Not like ye mean, Sassenach."

"Don't call me that," I said, my voice sounding low and venomous to my own ears.

He made a Scottish noise in his throat, of frustrated resignation, rubbing his wrist.

"Aye. Well, see, 'twas the night before I gave myself up to the English—"

"You never told me that!"

"Never told ye what?" He sounded confused.

"That you gave yourself up to the English. We thought you'd been captured."

"I was," he said briefly. "But by arrangement, for the price on my head." He flipped a hand, dismissing the matter. "It wasna important."

"They might have hanged you!" *And a good thing, too,* said the small, furiously hurt voice inside.

"No, they wouldn't." A faint tinge of amusement showed in his voice. "Ye'd told me so, Sass—mmphm. I didna really care, though, if they did."

I had no idea what he meant by saying I'd told him so, but *I* certainly didn't care at the moment.

"Forget that," I said tersely. "I want to know—"

"About Mary. Aye, I ken." He rubbed a hand slowly through his hair. "Aye, well. She came to me, the night before I—I went. I was in the cave, ken, near Lallybroch, and she brought me supper. And then she . . . stayed."

I bit my tongue, not to interrupt. I could feel him gathering his thoughts, searching for words.

"I tried to send her away," he said at last. "She . . . well, what she said to me . . ." He glanced at me; I saw the movement of his head. "She said she'd seen me with ye, Claire—and that she kent the look of a true love when she saw it, for all she'd not had one herself. And that it wasna in her mind to make me betray that. But she would give me . . . some small thing. That's what she said to me," he said, and his voice had grown husky, "'*some small thing, that maybe ye can use.*'"

"It was—I mean, it wasna . . ." He stopped, and made that odd shrugging motion of his, as though his shirt were tight across his shoulders. He bowed his head for a moment on his knees, hands linked round them.

"She gave me tenderness," he said finally, so softly that I barely heard him. "I—I hope I gave her the same."

My throat and chest were too tight to speak, and tears prickled behind my eyes. I remembered, quite suddenly, what he had said to me the night I mended Tom Christie's hand, about the Sacred Heart—"*so wanting—and no one to touch him.*" And he had lived in a cave for seven years, alone.

There was no more than a foot of space between us, but it seemed an unbridgeable gulf.

I reached across it and laid my hand on his, the tips of my fingers on his big, weathered knuckles. I took a breath, then two, trying to steady my voice, but it cracked and broke, nonetheless.

"You gave her . . . tenderness. I know you did."

He turned to me, suddenly, and my face was pressed into his coat, the cloth of it damp and rough on my skin, my tears blooming in tiny warm patches that vanished at once into the chill of the fabric.

"Oh, Claire," he whispered into my hair. I reached up, and could feel wetness on his cheeks. "She said—she wished to keep ye alive for me. And she meant it; she didna mean to take anything for herself."

I cried then, holding nothing back. For empty years, yearning for the touch of a hand. Hollow years, lying beside a man I had betrayed, for whom I had no tenderness. For the terrors and doubts and griefs of the day. Cried for him and me and for Mary MacNab, who knew what loneliness was—and what love was, as well.

"I would have told ye, before," he whispered, patting my back as though I were a small child. "But it was . . . it was the once." He shrugged a little, helpless. "And I couldna think how. How to say it, that ye'd understand."

I sobbed, gulped air, and finally sat up, wiping my face carelessly on a fold of my skirt.

"I understand," I said. My voice was thick and clogged, but fairly steady now. "I do."

And I did. Not only about Mary MacNab and what she had done—but why he'd told me now. There was no need; I would never have known. No need but the need for absolute honesty between us—and that I must know it was there.

I had believed him, about Malva. But now I had not only certainty of mind—but peace of heart.

We sat close together, the folds of my cloak and skirts flowing over his legs, his simple presence a comfort. Somewhere nearby, a very early cricket began to chirp.

"The rain's past, then," I said, hearing it. He nodded, with a small sound of assent.

"What shall we do?" I said at last. My voice sounded calm.

"Find out the truth—if I can."

Neither of us mentioned the possibility that he might not. I shifted, gathering the folds of my cloak.

"Will we go home, then?"

It was too dark to see now, but I felt him nod as he got to his feet, putting down a hand to help me.

"Aye, we will."

The house was empty when we returned, though Mrs. Bug had left a covered dish of shepherd's pie on the table, the floor swept, and the fire neatly smoored. I took off my wet cloak and hung it on the peg, but then stood, unsure quite what to do next, as though I stood in a stranger's house, in a country where I did not know the custom.

Jamie seemed to feel the same way—though after a moment, he stirred, fetched down the candlestick from the shelf over the hearth, and lit it with a spill from the fire. The wavering glow seemed only to emphasize the odd, echoing quality of the room, and he stood holding it for a minute, at a loss, before finally setting it down with a thump in the middle of the table.

"Are ye hungry, S . . . Sassenach?" He had begun to speak by habit, but then interrupted himself, looking up to be sure the name was once more allowed. I did my best to smile at him, though I could feel the corners of my mouth tremble.

"No. Are you?"

He shook his head, silent, and dropped his hand from the dish. Looking round for something else to do, he took up the poker and stirred the coals, breaking up the blackened embers and sending a swirl of sparks and soot up the chimney and out onto the hearth. It would ruin the fire, which would need to be rebuilt before bed, but I said nothing—he knew that.

"It feels like a death in the family," I said at last. "As though something terrible has happened, and this is the shocked bit, before you begin to send round and tell all the neighbors."

He gave a small, rueful laugh, and put the poker down.

"We'll not need to. They'll all ken well enough by daybreak what's happened."

Rousing at last from my immobility, I shook out my damp skirts and came to stand beside him by the fire. The heat of it seared at once through the wet cloth; it should have been comforting, but there was an icy weight in my abdomen that wouldn't melt. I put a hand on his arm, needing the touch of him.

"No one will believe it," I said. He put a hand over mine, and smiled a little, his eyes closed, but shook his head.

"They'll all believe it, Claire," he said softly. "I'm sorry."

81

Benefit of the Doubt

"I t isn't freaking true!"

"No, of course not." Roger watched his wife warily; she was exhibiting the general symptoms of a large explosive device with an unstable timing mechanism, and he had the distinct feeling that it was dangerous to be in her vicinity.

"That little *bitch*! I want to just grab her and choke the truth out of her!" Her hand closed convulsively on the neck of the syrup bottle, and he reached to take it from her before she should break it.

"I understand the impulse," he said, "but on the whole—better not."

She glared at him, but relinquished the bottle.

"Can't *you* do something?" she said.

He'd been asking himself that since he'd heard the news of Malva's accusation.

"I don't know," he said. "But I thought I'd go and talk to the Christies, at least. And if I can get Malva alone, I will." Thinking of his last tête-à-tête with Malva Christie, though, he had an uneasy feeling that she wouldn't be easily shaken from her story.

Brianna sat down, scowling at her plate of buckwheat cakes, and began slathering them with butter. Her fury was beginning to give way to rational thought; he could see ideas darting behind her eyes.

"If you can get her to admit that it's not true," she said slowly, "that's good. If not, though—the next best thing is to find out who's been with her. If some guy will admit in public that he *could* be the father—that would cast a lot of doubt on her story, at least."

"True." Roger poured syrup sparingly over his own cakes, even in the midst of uncertainty and anxiety enjoying the thick dark smell of it and the anticipation of rare sweetness. "Though there would still be those who'd be convinced Jamie's guilty. Here."

"I saw her kissing Obadiah Henderson in the woods," Bree said, accepting the bottle. "Late last fall." She shuddered fastidiously. "If it was him, no wonder she doesn't want to say."

Roger eyed her curiously. He knew Obadiah, who was large and uncouth, but not at all bad looking and not stupid. Some women would consider him a decent match; he had fifteen acres, which he farmed competently, and was a good hunter. He'd never seen Bree so much as speak to the man, though.

"Can you think of anybody else?" she asked, still frowning.

"Well . . . Bobby Higgins," he replied, still wary. "The Beardsley twins used to eye her now and then, but of course . . ." He had a nasty feeling that this line of inquiry was going to culminate in her adjuring *him* to go and ask awkward questions of any putative fathers—a process that struck him as likely being both pointless and dangerous.

"Why?" she demanded, cutting viciously into her stack of pancakes. "Why would she *do* it? Mama's always been so kind to her!"

"One of two reasons," Roger replied, and paused for a moment, closing his eyes, the better to savor the decadence of melted butter and velvet-smooth maple syrup on fresh, hot buckwheat. He swallowed, and reluctantly opened his eyes.

"Either the real father is someone she doesn't want to marry—for whatever reason—or she's decided to try to get hold of your father's money or property, by getting him to settle a sum on her or, failing that, on the child."

"Or both. I mean, she doesn't want to marry whoever it is, *and* wants Da's money—not that he has any."

"Or both," he agreed.

They ate in silence for a few minutes, forks scraping on the wooden plates, each absorbed in thought. Jem had spent the night at the Big House; in the wake of Lizzie's marriage, Roger had suggested that Amy McCallum take over Lizzie's work as housemaid, and since she and Aidan had moved in, Jem spent even more time over there, finding solace for the loss of Germain in Aidan's companionship.

"It isn't true," she repeated stubbornly. "Da simply *wouldn't* . . ."

But he saw the faint doubt at the back of her eyes—and a slight glaze of panic at the thought.

"No, he wouldn't," he said firmly. "Brianna—you can't possibly think there's any truth to it?"

"No, of course not!" But she spoke too loudly, too definitely. He laid down his fork and looked at her levelly.

"What's the matter? Do ye know something?"

"Nothing." She chased the last bite of pancake round her plate, speared and ate it.

He made a skeptical sound, and she frowned at the sticky puddle left on her plate. She always poured too much honey or syrup; he, more sparing, always ended with a clean plate.

"I don't," she said. She bit her lower lip, though, and put the tip of her finger into the puddle of syrup. "It's only . . ."

"What?"

"Not Da," she said slowly. She put the tip of her finger in her mouth and sucked the syrup off. "And I don't *know* for sure about Daddy. It's only—looking back at things I didn't understand at the time—now I see—" She stopped abruptly, and closed her eyes, then opened them, fixing him directly.

"I was looking through his wallet one day. Not snooping, just having fun, taking all the cards and things out and putting them back. There was a note tucked away, between the dollar bills. It was asking him to meet somebody for lunch—"

"Innocent enough."

"It started out with *Darling*—, and it wasn't my mother's handwriting," she said tersely.

"Ah," he said, and after a moment, "how old were you?"

"Eleven." She drew small patterns on the plate with the tip of her finger. "I just put the note back and kind of blotted it out of my mind. I didn't want to think about it—and I don't think I ever did, from that day to this. There were a few other things, things I saw and didn't understand—it was mostly the way things were between them, my parents . . . Every now and then, *something* would happen, and I never knew what, but I always knew something was really wrong."

She trailed off, sighed deeply, and wiped her finger on her napkin.

"Bree," he said gently. "Jamie's an honorable man, and he loves your mother deeply."

"Well, see, that's the thing," she said softly. "I would have sworn Daddy was, too. And did."

It wasn't impossible. The thought kept returning, to niggle Roger uncomfortably, like a pebble in his shoe. Jamie Fraser *was* an honorable man, he *was* deeply uxorious—and he had been in the depths of despair and exhaustion during Claire's illness. Roger had feared for him nearly as much as for Claire; he'd gone hollow-eyed and grim-jawed through the hot, endless days of reeking death, not eating, not sleeping, held together by nothing more than will.

Roger had tried to speak to him then, of God and eternity, reconcile him with what seemed the inevitable, only to be repulsed with a hot-eyed fury at the mere idea that God might think to take his wife—this followed by complete despair as Claire lapsed into a stupor near death. It wasn't impossible that the offer of a moment's physical comfort, made in that void of desolation, had gone further than either party intended.

But it was early May now, and Malva Christie was six months gone with child. Which meant that she'd got that way in November. The crisis of Claire's illness had been in late September; he remembered vividly the smell of burnt-over fields in the room when she'd wakened from what looked like certain death, her eyes huge and lambent, startlingly beautiful in a face like an androgynous angel's.

Right, then, it frigging *was* impossible. No man was perfect, and any man might yield in extremis—once. But not repeatedly. And not Jamie Fraser. Malva Christie was a liar.

Feeling more settled in mind, Roger made his way down the creekside toward the Christies' cabin.

Can't you do something? Brianna had asked him, anguished. Damn little, he thought, but he had to try. It was Friday; he could—and would—preach an ear-blistering sermon on the evils of gossip, come Sunday. Knowing what he did of human nature, though, any benefit derived from that was likely to be short-lived.

Beyond that—well, Lodge meeting was Wednesday night. It had been going really well, and he hated to jeopardize the fragile amity of the newborn Lodge by risking unpleasantness at a meeting . . . but if there was a chance of it helping . . . would it be useful to encourage both Jamie and the two Christie men to attend? It would get the matter out in the open, and no matter how bad, open public knowledge was always better than the festering weed of whispered scandal. He thought Tom Christie would observe the proprieties and be civil, notwithstanding the delicacy of the situation—but he wasn't all that sure of Allan. The son shared his father's features and his sense of self-righteousness, but lacked Tom's iron will and self-control.

But now he was at the cabin, which seemed deserted. He heard the sound of an ax, though, the slow *klop!* of kindling being split, and went round to the back.

It was Malva, who turned at his greeting, her face wary. There were lavender smudges beneath her eyes, he saw, and the bloom of her skin was clouded. Guilty conscience, he hoped, as he greeted her cordially.

"If ye've come to try to get me to take it back, I won't," she said flatly, ignoring his greeting.

"I came to ask if ye wanted someone to talk to," he said. That surprised her; she set down the ax, and wiped her face with her apron.

"To talk to?" she said slowly, eyeing him. "What about?"

He shrugged and offered her a very slight smile.

"Anything ye like." He let his accent relax, broadening toward her own Edinburgh tinge. "I doubt ye've been able to talk to anyone of late, save your Da and brother—and they might not be able to listen just the noo."

A matching small smile flitted across her features, and disappeared.

"No, they don't listen," she said. "But it's all right; I've naught much to say, ken? I'm a hoor; what else is there?"

"I dinna think ye're a hoor," Roger said quietly.

"Oh, ye don't?" She rocked back a little on her heels, surveying him mockingly. "What else would ye call a woman that spreads her legs for a marrit man? Adulteress, of course—but hoor, as well, or so I'm told."

He thought she meant to shock him with deliberate coarseness. She did, rather, but he kept it to himself.

"Mistaken, maybe. Jesus didna speak harshly to the woman who *was* a harlot; it's no my business to be doing it to someone who isn't."

"And if ye've come to quote the Bible to me, save your breath to cool your parritch with," she said, a look of distaste pulling down the delicate corners of her mouth. "I've heard a deal more of it than I care to."

That, he reflected, was probably true. Tom Christie was the sort who knew a verse—or ten—for every occasion, and if he didn't beat his daughter physically, had almost certainly been doing it verbally.

Not sure what to say next, he held out his hand.

"If ye'll give me the hatchet, I'll do the rest."

One eyebrow raised, she put it into his hand and stepped back. He put up a chunk of kindling and split it clean in two, stooped for another. She watched for a moment, then sat down, slowly, on a smaller stump.

The mountain spring was still cool, touched with the last winter breath of the high snows, but the work warmed him. He didn't by any means forget she was there, but he kept his eyes on the wood, the bright grain of the fresh-split stick, the tug of it as he pulled the ax blade free, and found his thoughts move back to his conversation with Bree.

So Frank Randall had been—perhaps—unfaithful to his wife, on occasion. In all justice, Roger wasn't sure he could be blamed, knowing the circumstances of the case. Claire had disappeared completely, without trace, leaving Frank to hunt desperately, to mourn, and then, at last, to begin to put the pieces of his life back together and move on. Whereupon the missing wife pops back up, distraught, mistreated—and pregnant by another man.

Whereupon Frank Randall, whether from a sense of honor, of love, or simply of—what? curiosity?—had taken her back. He recalled Claire's telling them the story, and it was clear that she hadn't particularly *wanted* to be taken back. It must have been damned clear to Frank Randall, too.

Little wonder, then, if outrage and rejection had led him occasionally—and little wonder, too, that the echoes of the hidden conflicts between her parents had reached Brianna, like seismic disturbances that travel through miles of earth and stone, jolts from an upwelling of magma, miles deep beneath the crust.

And little wonder, he realized with a sense of revelation, that she'd been so upset by his friendship with Amy McCallum.

He realized, quite suddenly, that Malva Christie was crying. Silently, without covering her face. Tears ran down her cheeks and her shoulders quivered, but her lower lip was caught hard between her teeth; she made no sound.

He cast down the ax and went to her. Put an arm gently round her shoulders, and cradled her capped head, patting her.

"Hey," he said softly. "Don't worry, aye? It's going to be all right."

She shook her head, and the tears washed down her face.

"Can't be," she whispered. "Can't be."

Beneath his pity for her, Roger was aware of a sense of growing hope. Whatever reluctance he might have to exploit her desperation was well overcome by a determination to get to the bottom of her trouble. Mostly for the sake of Jamie and his family—but for her own, as well.

He mustn't push too hard, though, mustn't rush. She had to trust him.

So he patted her, rubbed her back as he did for Jem when he woke with nightmare, said small soothing things, all meaningless, and felt her begin to yield. Yield, but in a strangely physical fashion, as though her flesh were somehow opening, blossoming slowly under his touch.

Strange, and at the same time, oddly familiar. He'd felt it now and then with Bree, when he'd turned to her in the dark, when she hadn't time to think but responded to him with her body alone. The physical recollection jarred him, and he drew back a little. He meant to say something to Malva, but the sound of a footfall interrupted him, and he looked up to see Allan Christie coming toward him out of the trees, fast, with a face like black thunder.

"Get away from her!"

He straightened, heart pounding as he realized quite suddenly what this might look like.

"What d'ye mean, slinkin' round like a rat after a rind o' cheese?" Allan cried. "D'ye think since she's shamed, she's meat for any whoreson bastard that cares to take her?"

"I came to offer counsel," Roger said as coolly as he could manage. "And comfort, if I might."

"Oh, aye." Allan Christie's face was flushed, the tufts of his hair standing on end like the bristles on a hog about to charge. "Comfort me with apples and stay me with raisins, is it? Ye can stick your comfort straight up your arse, MacKenzie, and your goddamned stiff prick, too!"

Allan's hands were clenched at his sides, trembling with rage.

"Ye're no better than your wicked good-father—or perhaps"— he rounded suddenly on Malva, who had stopped crying, but was sitting white-faced and frozen on her stump—"perhaps it was him, too? Is that it, ye wee bitch, did ye take them both? Answer me!" His hand shot out to slap her, and Roger caught his wrist by reflex.

Roger was so angry that he could barely speak. Christie was strong, but Roger was bigger; he would have broken the young man's wrist, if he could. As it was, he dug his fingers hard into the space between the bones, and was gratified to see Christie's eyes pop and water from the pain of it.

"Ye'll not speak to your sister that way," he said, not loudly, but very clearly. "Nor to me." He shifted his grip suddenly and bent Christie's wrist sharply backward. "D'ye hear me?"

Allan's face went white and the breath hissed out of him. He didn't answer, but managed to nod. Roger released his hold, almost flinging the younger man's wrist away, with a sudden feeling of revulsion.

"I do not wish to hear that ye've abused your sister in any way," he said, as evenly as he could. "If I do—ye'll regret it. Good day, Mr. Christie. Miss Christie," he added, with a brief bow to Malva. She didn't respond, only stared at him from eyes gray as storm clouds, huge with shock. The memory of them followed him as he strode from the clearing and plunged into the darkness of the wood, wondering whether he'd made things better, or much, much worse.

The next meeting of the Fraser's Ridge Lodge was on Wednesday. Brianna went as usual to the Big House, taking Jemmy and her workbasket, and was surprised to find Bobby Higgins seated at the table, finishing his supper.

"Miss Brianna!" He half-rose at sight of her, beaming, but she waved him back to his seat, and slid into the bench opposite.

"Bobby! How nice to see you again! We thought—well, we thought you wouldn't come again."

He nodded, looking rueful.

"Aye, happen I might not, at least not for a bit. But his Lordship had some things, things come in from England, and he says to me as I shall bring 'em." He ran a piece of bread carefully round the inside of his bowl, sopping up the last of Mrs. Bug's chicken gravy.

"And then . . . well, I did wish to come on my own account. For to see Miss Christie, aye?"

"Oh." She glanced up and caught Mrs. Bug's eye. The older woman rolled her eyes, helpless, and shook her head. "Um. Yes, Malva. Er . . . is my mother upstairs, Mrs. Bug?"

"Nay, *a nighean.* She was called to Mr. MacNeill; he's bad wi' the pleurisy." Barely pausing for breath, she whipped off her apron and hung it on its hook, reaching for her cloak with the other hand. "I'll be along, then, *a leannan*; Arch will be wanting his supper. If there's aught wanting, Amy's about." And with the briefest of farewells, she vanished, leaving Bobby staring after her in puzzlement at this uncharacteristic behavior.

"Is something amiss?" he asked, turning back to Brianna with a small frown.

"Ahh . . . well." With a few uncharitable thoughts toward Mrs. Bug, Brianna girded up her loins and told him, grimacing inwardly at the sight of his sweet young face as it turned white and rigid in the firelight.

She couldn't bring herself to mention Malva's accusation, only told him that the girl was with child. He'd hear about Jamie, soon enough, but please God, not from her.

"I see, miss. Aye . . . I see." He sat for a moment, staring at the bit of bread in his hand. Then he dropped it into his bowl, rose suddenly, and rushed outside; she heard him retching into the blackberry bushes outside the back door. He didn't come back.

It was a long evening. Her mother was plainly spending the night with Mr. MacNeill and his pleurisy. Amy McCallum came down for a little while, and they made awkward conversation over their sewing, but then the maid escaped upstairs. Aidan and Jemmy, allowed to stay up late and play, wore themselves out and fell asleep on the settle.

She fidgeted, abandoned her sewing, and paced up and down, waiting for Lodge to finish. She wanted her own bed, her own house; her parents' kitchen, normally so welcoming, seemed strange and uncomfortable, and she a stranger in it.

At long, long last, she heard footsteps and the creak of the door, and Roger came in, looking bothered.

"There you are," she said with relief. "How was Lodge? Did the Christies come?"

He shook his head.

"No. It . . . went all right, I suppose. A bit of awkwardness, of course, but your father carried it off as well as anyone might, in the circumstances."

She grimaced, imagining it.

"Where is he?"

"He said he thought he'd go and walk by himself for a bit—maybe do a little night fishing." Roger put his arms round her and hugged her close, sighing. "Did ye hear the ruckus?"

"No! What happened?"

"Well, we'd just had a wee blether on the universal nature of brotherly love, when a clishmaclaver broke out, over by your kiln. Well, so, everyone streamed out to see what was to do, and here's your cousin Ian and wee Bobby Higgins, rolling in the dirt and trying to kill each other."

"Oh, dear." She felt a spasm of guilt. Probably someone had told Bobby everything, and he had gone in search of Jamie, meeting Ian instead, and thrown Malva's accusations of Jamie at him. If she'd told him herself . . .

"What happened?"

"Well, Ian's bloody dog took a hand, for the one thing—or a paw. Your father barely stopped him tearing out Bobby's throat, but it did stop the fight. We dragged them apart, then, and Ian tore free and loped off into the woods, with the dog beside him. Bobby's . . . well, I cleaned him up a bit, then gave him Jemmy's trundle for the night," he said apologetically. "He said he couldna stay up here—" He looked round at the shadowed kitchen; she'd already smoored the fire and carried the little boys up to bed; the room was empty, lit only by a faint hearth glow.

"I'm sorry. Will ye sleep here, then?"

She shook her head emphatically.

"Bobby or no Bobby, I want to go home."

"Aye, all right. You go on, then; I'll fetch Amy down to bar the door."

"No, that's okay," she said quickly. "I'll get her." And before he could protest, she was down the hall and up the stair, the empty house strange and silent below.

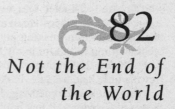

82

Not the End of the World

There is a great deal of satisfaction in wresting weeds out of the earth. Backbreaking and endless as the chore may be, there is a tiny but unassailable sense of triumph in it, feeling the soil give suddenly, yielding the stubborn root, and the foe lying defeated in your hand.

It had rained recently and the earth was soft. I ripped and tore with ferocious concentration; dandelions, fireweed, rhododendron sprouts, bunchgrass, muhly, smartweed, and the creeping mallow known locally as "cheese." Paused for an instant, narrow-eyed at a bull thistle, and prised it from the ground with a vicious stab of my pruning knife.

The grapevines that ran up the palisades had just begun their spring rush, and sprouts and ruffles of a delicate green tinged with rust cascaded from the woody stems, eager tendrils curling like my own new-grown hair—God damn her, she'd taken my hair on purpose to disfigure me! The shade they cast provided refuge for immense bushy growths of the pernicious thing I called "jewelweed," not knowing its real name, for the tiny white flowers that winked like diamond clusters in the feathery green fronds. It was likely a fennel of some sort, but formed neither a useful bulb nor edible seeds;

pretty, but useless—and thus the sort of thing that spreads like wildfire.

There was a small swishing sound, and a ball of rags came to rest by my foot. This was followed immediately by the rush of a much larger body, and Rollo swept past me, snatching the ball adroitly and galloping away, the wind of his passage stirring my skirts. Startled, I looked up, to see him bounding toward Ian, who'd come soft-footed into the garden.

He made a small gesture of apology, but I sat back on my heels and smiled at him, making an effort to quell the vicious sentiments surging to and fro in my bosom.

Evidently, the quelling wasn't all that successful, for I saw him frown a little, and hesitate, looking at my face.

"Did you want something, Ian?" I said shortly, dropping the facade of welcome. "If that hound of yours knocks over one of my hives, I'll make a rug of him."

"Rollo!" Ian snapped his fingers at the dog, who leapt gracefully over the row of bee gums and basket hives that sat at the far end of the garden, trotted up to his master, dropped the ball at his feet, and stood genially panting, yellow wolf-eyes fixed with apparent interest on me.

Ian scooped up the ball, and turning, flung it out through the open gate, Rollo after it like the tail of a comet.

"I did want to ask ye something, Auntie," he said, turning back to me. "It would wait, though."

"No, that's all right. Now's as good a time as any." Getting awkwardly to my feet, I waved him to the little bench Jamie had made for me in a shady nook beneath a flowering dogwood that overhung the corner of the garden.

"So?" I settled myself beside him, brushing crumbs of dirt from the bottom of my skirt.

"Mmphm. Well . . ." He stared at his hands, linked over his knee, big-knuckled and bony. "I . . . ah . . ."

"You haven't been exposed to syphilis again, have you?" I asked, with a vivid memory of my last interview with an awkward young man in this garden. "Because if you have, Ian, I swear I will use Dr. Fentiman's syringe on you and I won't be gentle with it. You—"

"No, no!" he said hastily. "No, of course not, Auntie. It's about—about Malva Christie." He tensed as he said it, in case I should lunge for the pruning knife, but I merely drew a deep breath and let it out again, slowly.

"What about her?" I said, my voice deliberately even.

"Well . . . no really her, exactly. More what she said—about Uncle Jamie." He stopped, swallowing, and I drew another slow breath. Disturbed as I was by the situation myself, I'd scarcely thought about its impact on anyone else. But Ian had idolized Jamie from the time he was a tiny boy; I could well imagine that the widespread suggestions that Jamie might have feet of clay were deeply upsetting to him.

"Ian, you mustn't worry yourself." I put a consoling hand—dirt-stained as it was—on his arm. "It will . . . work itself out, somehow. Such things always do." They did—generally with the maximum of uproar and catastrophe. And if Malva's child should by some horrid cosmic joke be born with red hair . . . I closed my eyes for a moment, feeling a wave of dizziness.

"Aye, I suppose they will," Ian said, sounding uncertain in the extreme. "It's only—what they're sayin', about Uncle Jamie. Even his own Ardsmuir men, folk that should know better! That he must have—well, I'll no repeat any of it, Auntie—but . . . I canna bear to hear it!"

His long, homely face was twisted with unhappiness, and it suddenly occurred to me that he might be having his own doubts about the matter.

"Ian," I said, with as much firmness as I could muster, "Malva's child could not possibly be Jamie's. You do believe that, don't you?"

He nodded, very slowly, but wouldn't meet my eyes.

"I do," he said softly, and then swallowed hard. "But, Auntie . . . it could be mine."

A bee had lighted on my arm. I stared at it, seeing the veins in its glassy wings, the dust of yellow pollen that clung to the minuscule hairs of its legs and abdomen, the gentle pulsing of its body as it breathed.

"Oh, Ian," I said as softly as he'd spoken himself. "Oh, Ian."

He was strung tight as a marionette, but when I spoke, a little of the tension left the arm under my hand, and I saw that he had closed his eyes.

"I'm sorry, Auntie," he whispered.

Wordless, I patted his arm. The bee flew off, and I wished

passionately that I could exchange places with it. It would be so
wonderful, simply to be about the business of gathering, single-
minded in the sun.

Another bee lighted on Ian's collar, and he brushed it absently
away.

"Well, so," he said, taking a deep breath and turning his head
to look at me. "What must I do, Auntie?"

His eyes were dark with misery and worry—and something
very like fear, I thought.

"Do?" I said, sounding as blank as I felt. "Jesus H. Roosevelt
Christ, Ian."

I hadn't meant to make him smile, and he didn't, but he did
seem to relax very slightly.

"Aye, I've done it already," he said, very rueful. "But—it's
done, Auntie. How can I mend it?"

I rubbed my brow, trying to think. Rollo had brought back his
ball, but seeing that Ian was in no mood to play, dropped it by his
feet and leaned against his leg, panting.

"Malva," I said finally. "Did she tell you? Before, I mean."

"Ye think I scorned her, and that's what made her accuse Uncle
Jamie?" He gave me a wry look, absently scratching Rollo's ruff.
"Well, I wouldna blame ye if ye did, Auntie, but no. She said not
a word to me about the matter. If she had, I should ha' marrit her
at once."

The hurdle of confession overcome, he was talking more easily now.

"You didn't think of marrying her *first*?" I said, with perhaps a
slight tinge of acerbity.

"Ah . . . no," he said, very sheepish. "It wasna precisely a matter of—well, I wasna thinking at all, Auntie. I was drunk. The first
time, anyway," he added as an afterthought.

"The first—? How many— No, don't tell me. I don't want to
know the gory details." I shut him up with a brusque gesture, and
sat up straight, struck by a thought. "Bobby Higgins. Was that—"

He nodded, lowering his lashes so I couldn't see his eyes. The
blood had come up under his tan.

"Aye. That was why—I mean, I didna really wish to marry her,
to begin with, but still, I would have asked, after we . . . but I put
it off a bit, and—" He scrubbed a hand across his face, helpless.
"Well, I didna want her to wife, but I couldna keep from wanting

her, nonetheless, and I ken well enough how awful it must seem—but I've got to tell the truth, Auntie, and that's it." He took a gulp of air, and continued.

"I'd—wait for her. In the woods, when she came to gather. She'd not speak when she saw me, only smile, and raise her skirts a bit, then turn quick and run and . . . God, I should be after her like a dog after a bitch in heat," he said bitterly. "But then one day I came late, and she wasna there where we usually met. But I heard her laughing, far off, and when I went to see . . ."

He twisted his hands hard enough to dislocate a finger, grimacing, and Rollo whined softly.

"Let us just say that yon bairn might well be Bobby Higgins's, too," he said, biting off the words.

I felt suddenly exhausted, as I had when recovering from my illness, as though it was too much effort even to breathe. I leaned back against the palisades, feeling the cool papery rustle of grape leaves against my neck, fanning softly over my heated cheeks.

Ian bent forward, head in his hands, the dappled green shadows playing over him.

"What shall I do?" he asked at last, voice muffled. He sounded as tired as I felt. "I dinna mind saying that I—that the child might be mine. But would it help, d'ye think?"

"No," I said bleakly. "It wouldn't." Public opinion would not be changed in the slightest; everyone would simply assume that Ian was lying for his uncle's sake. Even if he were to marry the girl, it wouldn't—

A thought struck me and I pulled myself upright again.

"You said you didn't want to marry her, even before you knew about Bobby. Why?" I asked curiously.

He lifted his head from his hands with a helpless gesture.

"I dinna ken how to say it. She was—well, she was bonnie enough, aye, and a proper spirit to her, as well. But she . . . I dinna ken, Auntie. It was only that I always had the feeling, lying wi' her—that I dare not fall asleep."

I stared at him.

"Well, that would be off-putting, I imagine."

He had dismissed that, though, and was frowning, digging the heel of his moccasin into the soil.

"There's no means of telling which of two men has fathered a bairn, is there?" he asked abruptly. "Only—if it's mine, I should want it. I would wed her for the child's sake, no matter what else. If it's mine."

Bree had told me the bare bones of his history; I knew about his Mohawk wife, Emily, and the death of his daughter, and I felt the small presence of my own first child, Faith, stillborn but always with me.

"Oh, Ian," I said softly, and touched his hair. "You might be able to tell, by the way the child looked—but probably not, or not right away."

He nodded, and sighed. After a moment, he said, "If I say it's mine, and I wed her—folk might still talk, but after a time . . ." His voice died away. True, talk might eventually die down. But there would still be those who thought Jamie responsible, others who would call Malva a whore, a liar, or both—which she bloody well *was,* I reminded myself, but not a nice thing to hear about one's wife. And what might Ian's life be like, married under such circumstances, to a woman he could not trust and—I thought—did not especially like?

"Well," I said, rising to my feet and stretching, "don't do anything drastic just yet awhile. Let me talk with Jamie; you don't mind if I tell him?"

"I wish ye would, Auntie. I dinna think I could face him, myself." He still sat on the bench, bony shoulders slumped. Rollo lay on the ground at his feet, the big wolf head resting on Ian's moccasined foot. Moved with pity, I put my arms round Ian, and he leaned his head against me, simply, like a child.

"It isn't the end of the world," I said.

The sun was touching the edge of the mountain, and the sky burned red and gold, the light of it falling in blazing bars through the palisades.

"No," he said, but there was no conviction in his voice.

83

Declarations

Charlotte, Mecklenberg County
May 20, 1775

The one thing Roger had not envisioned about the making of history was the sheer amount of alcohol involved. He should have, he thought; if there was anything a career in academia had taught him, it was that almost all worthwhile business was conducted in the pub.

The public houses, taverns, ordinaries, and pothouses in Charlotte were doing a roaring business, as delegates, spectators, and hangers-on seethed through them, men of Loyalist sentiments collecting in the King's Arms, those of rabidly opposing views in the Blue Boar, with shifting currents of the unallied and undecided eddying to and fro, purling through the Goose and Oyster, Thomas's ordinary, the Groats, Simon's, Buchanan's, Mueller's, and two or three nameless places that barely qualified as shebeens.

Jamie visited all of them. And drank in all of them, sharing beer, ale, rum punch, shandy, cordial, porter, stout, cider, brandywine, persimmon beer, rhubarb wine, blackberry wine, cherry bounce, perry, merry brew, and scrumpy. Not all of them were alcoholic, but the great majority were.

Roger confined himself largely to beer, and found himself glad of his restraint, when he happened to meet with Davy Caldwell in the street, turning from a fruiterer's stall with a handful of early apricots.

"Mr. MacKenzie!" Caldwell cried, his face lighting with welcome. "I had nay thought to meet you here, but what blessing that I have!"

"Blessing indeed," Roger said, shaking the minister's hand with cordial fervor. Caldwell had married him and Brianna, and had examined him at the Presbyterian Academy regarding his own calling, some months before. "How d'ye do, Mr. Caldwell?"

"Och, for myself, well enough—but my heart misgives me for the fate of my poor brethren!" Caldwell shook his head in dismay, gesturing at a group of men crowding into Simon's ordinary, laughing and talking. "What is to come of this, I ask ye, Mr. MacKenzie—what's to come?"

Roger was, for an unbalanced instant, tempted to tell him what was to come of it, exactly. As it was, though, he gestured to Jamie—who had been stopped by an acquaintance in the street—to go along without him, and turned away to walk a bit with Caldwell.

"Have ye come for the conference, then, Mr. Caldwell?" he asked.

"I have that, Mr. MacKenzie, I have that. Little hope have I that my words will make the slightest difference, but it is my duty to speak as I find, and so I shall."

What Davy Caldwell found was a shocking condition of human slothfulness, for which he blamed the entire current situation, convinced that unreflective apathy and "a stupid concern with personal comfort" on the part of the colonists both tempted and provoked the exercise of tyrannical powers on the part of Crown and Parliament.

"It's a point, sure," Roger said, aware that Caldwell's impassioned gestures were attracting a certain amount of notice, even amongst the crowds in the street, most of them reasonably argumentative themselves.

"A point!" Caldwell cried. "Aye, it is, and *the* point entirely. The ignorance, disregard of moral obligation, and the supreme love of ease of the groveling sluggard corresponds exactly—exactly!—with a tyrant's appetite and cynicism."

He glowered at one gentleman who had subsided against the side of a house, taking a brief respite from the noonday heat with his hat over his face.

"The spirit of God must redeem the slothful, fill the human frame with activity, poise, and libertarian consciousness!"

Roger wondered, rather, whether Caldwell would view the

escalating war as the result of God's intervention—but upon reflection, thought that he likely would. Caldwell was a thinker, but a staunch Presbyterian, and thus a believer in predestination.

"The slothful encourage and facilitate oppression," Caldwell explained, with a scornful gesture toward a family of tinkers enjoying an alfresco luncheon in the yard of a house. "Their own shame and sinking spirits, their own pitiful compliance and submission—these become self-made chains of slavery!"

"Oh, aye," Roger said, and coughed. Caldwell was a famous preacher, and rather inclined to want to keep in practice. "Will ye take a whet, Mr. Caldwell?" It was a warm day, and Caldwell's rather round, cherubic face was becoming very red.

They went into Thomas's ordinary, a fairly respectable house, and sat down with tankards of the house beer—for Caldwell, like most, did not regard beer as being in any way "drink," like rum or whisky. What else, after all, would one drink? Milk?

Out of the sun, and with a cooling draught to hand, Davy Caldwell became less heated in his expressions, as well as his countenance.

"Praise God for the fortune of meeting ye here, Mr. MacKenzie," he said, breathing deep after lowering his tankard. "I had sent a letter, but doubtless ye will have left home before it could come. I wished to inform ye of the gladsome news—there is to be a Presbytery."

Roger felt a sudden leap of the heart.

"When? And where?"

"Edenton, early next month. The Reverend Doctor McCorkle is coming from Philadelphia. He'll remain for a time, before departing on his further journey—he is going to the Indies, to encourage the efforts of the church there. I am, of course, presuming to know your mind—I apologize for the forwardness of my address, Mr. MacKenzie—but is it still your desire to seek ordination?"

"With all my heart."

Caldwell beamed, and grasped him strongly by the hand.

"Give ye joy of it, dear man—great joy."

He then plunged into a close description of McCorkle, whom he had met in Scotland, and speculations regarding the state of religion in the colony—he spoke of Methodism with some respect, but considered the New Light Baptists "somewhat unregulated" in their effusions of worship, though doubtless well-meaning—and surely sincere belief was an improvement over unbelief, whatever the form it might take. In due course, though, he came back round to their present circumstances.

"Ye've come with your father-in-law, have ye?" he asked. "I thought I saw him, in the road."

"I have, and ye did," Roger assured him, fumbling in his pocket for a coin. The pocket itself was full of coiled horsehair; with his academic experience as guide, he had made provision against possible boredom by bringing the makings of a new fishing line.

"Ah." Caldwell looked at him keenly. "I've heard things of late—is it true, he's turned Whig?"

"He is a firm friend to liberty," Roger said, cautious, and took a breath. "As am I." He'd not had occasion to say it out loud before; it gave him a small, breathless feeling, just under the breastbone.

"Aha, aha, very good! I had heard of it, as I say—and yet there are a great many who say otherwise: that he is a Tory, a Loyalist like his relations, and that this protestation of support for the independency movement is but a ruse." It wasn't phrased as a question, but Caldwell's bushy eyebrow, cocked like a swell's hat, made it clear that it was.

"Jamie Fraser is an honest man," Roger said, and drained his tankard. "And an honorable one," he added, setting it down. "And speaking of the same, I think I must go and find him."

Caldwell glanced around; there was an air of restlessness around them, of men calling their accounts and settling up. The official meeting of the convention was to begin at two o'clock, at MacIntyre's farmhouse. It was past noon now, delegates, speakers, and spectators would be slowly gathering, girding themselves for an afternoon of conflict and decision. The breathless feeling came back.

"Aye, then. Give him my regards, if ye will—though perhaps I may see him myself. And may the Holy Spirit penetrate the encrustations of habit and lethargy, and convert the souls and rouse the consciences of those who gather here today!"

"Amen," said Roger, smiling in spite of the glances from the men—and not a few women—around them.

He found Jamie in the Blue Boar, in the company of a number of men in whom the Holy Spirit had already been hard at work on the encrustations, judging from the volume. The chatter near the door died away, though, as he made his way through the room— not in cause of his own presence, but because there was something more interesting going on near the center.

To wit: Jamie Fraser and Neil Forbes, both red with heat, passion, and a gallon or two of mixed spirits, head to head over a table, and hissing like snakes in the Gaelic.

Only a few of the spectators were Gaelic speakers; these were hastily translating the high points of the dialogue for the rest of the crowd.

Gaelic insult was an art, and one at which his father-in-law excelled, though Roger was obliged to admit that the lawyer was no slouch at it, himself. The translations rendered by the onlookers fell far short of the original; nonetheless, the taproom was rapt, with occasional admiring whistles or whoops from the spectators, or laughter as a particularly pungent point was made.

Having missed the beginning, Roger had no idea how the conflict had begun, but so far into it as they were, the exchange was focused on cowardice and arrogance, Jamie's remarks aimed at Forbes's leading the attack on Fogarty Simms as a low-minded and cowardly attempt to make himself look the big man at the price of a defenseless man's life, Forbes—shifting into English here, as he realized that they had become the cynosure of the room—taking the view that Jamie's presence here was an unwarrantable affront to those who truly held the ideals of liberty and justice, as everyone knew he was in truth the King's man, but he, the puffed-up cock o' the walk, thought that he could pull the wool over everyone's eyes long enough to betray the whole boiling, but if he, Fraser, thought he, Forbes, was fool enough to be gulled by antic tricks in the public street and a lot of talk with nay more substance than the shrieking of gulls, he, Fraser, had best think again!

Jamie slapped a hand flat on the table, making it boom like a drum, and rattling the cups. He rose, glaring down at Forbes.

"Do ye libel my honor, sir?" he cried, also shifting to English. "For if ye do, let us go out, and we shall settle the matter at once, yea or nay!"

Sweat was streaming down Forbes's broad, flushed face, and his eyes were gleaming with anger, but even overheated as he was, Roger saw belated caution pluck at his sleeve. Roger hadn't seen the fight in Cross Creek, but Ian had told him the details, meanwhile laughing his head off. The last thing Neil Forbes could desire was a duel.

"Have ye honor to libel, sir?" Forbes demanded, standing in turn, and drawing himself up as though about to address the jury. "Ye come here acting the great one, carousing and showing away like a sailor come ashore with prize money in his pocket—but have we any evidence that your words are more than puffery? Puffery, I say, sir!"

Jamie stood, both hands braced on the tabletop, surveying Forbes through narrowed eyes. Roger had once seen that expression focused on himself. It had been followed rapidly by the sort of mayhem customary in a Glasgow pub on Saturday night—only more so. The only thing to be thankful for was that Forbes had clearly not heard any whiff of Malva Christie's accusation, or there would be blood on the floor already.

Jamie straightened slowly, and his left hand went toward his waist. There were gasps, and Forbes paled. But Jamie had reached for his sporran, not his dirk, and plunged his hand inside.

"As to that . . . *sir* . . ." he said in a low, even voice that carried through the room, "I have made myself clear. I am for liberty, and to that end, I pledge my name, my fortune"—here he withdrew his hand from his sporran and slammed it on the table; a small purse, two golden guineas, and a jewel—"and my sacred honor."

The room was silent, all eyes focused on the black diamond, which shimmered with a baleful light. Jamie paused for the space of three heartbeats, then drew breath.

"Is there any man here who gives me the lie?" he said. It was ostensibly addressed to the room at large, but his eyes were fixed on Forbes. The lawyer had gone a mottled red and gray, like a bad oyster, but said nothing.

Jamie paused again, looked once round the room, then picked up purse, money, and jewel, and stalked out the door. Outside, the town clock chimed two, the strokes slow and heavy in the humid air.

L'OIGNON–INTELLIGENCER

Upon the 20th of this month, a Congress met in Charlotte, composed of Delegates from Mecklenberg County, for the purpose of discussion upon the issue of current Relations with Great Britain. After due Deliberation, a Declaration was proposed and accepted, whose Provisions are Herewith Shown:

1. *That whosoever directly or indirectly abetted or in any way, form or manner countenanced to unchartered & dangerous invasion of our rights as claimed by G. Britain is an enemy to this County—to America & to the inherent & inaliable rights of man.*
2. *We the Citizens of Mecklenburg County do hereby desolve the political bands which have connected us to the Mother Country & hereby absolve ourselves from all allegiance to the British crown & abjure all political connection, contract or association with that nation who have wantonly trampled on our rights & liberties & inhumanely shed the innocent blood of American patriots at Lexington.*
3. *We do hereby declare ourselves a free and independent people—are & of right ought to be a sovereign & self-governing association, under the controul of no power other than that of our God & the general government of the congress, to the maintainence of which independence civil & religious we solemnly pledge to each other our mutual cooperation, our lives, our fortunes & our most sacred honor.*
4. *As we now acknowledge the existence & controul of no law or legal officers, civil or military, within this County, we do hereby ordain & adopt as a rule of life, all, each & every of our former laws—wherein nevertheless the crown of Great Britain never can be considered as holding rights, privileges, immunities, or authority therein.*
5. *It is also further decreed that all, each & every military officer in this County is hereby reinstated in his former*

command & authority, he acting conformably to these regulations. And that every member present of this delegation shall henceforth be a civil officer, viz. a Justice of the peace in the character of a "Committee-man" to issue process, hear & determine all matters of controversy according to sd. adopted laws—to preserve peace, union & harmony in sd. County & to use every exertion to spread the love of country & fire of freedom throughout America until a more general & organized government be established in this province. A selection from the members present shall constitute a Committee of public safety for sd. County.

6. *That a copy of these resolutions be transmitted by express to the President of the Continental Congress assembled in Philadelphia, to be laid before that body.*

84

Among the Lettuces

S ome idiot—or child—had left the gate of my garden open. I hurried up the path, hoping that it hadn't been that way for long. If it had been open overnight, the deer would have eaten every lettuce, onion, and bulb plant in the plot, to say nothing of ruining the—

I jerked, letting out a small cry. Something like a red-hot hat pin had stabbed me in the neck, and I smacked the place by reflex. An electric jab in the temple made my vision go white, then blur with water, and a fiery stab in the crook of my elbow—bees.

I blundered off the path, suddenly aware that the air was full of them, frenzied and stinging. I plunged through the brush, barely able to see for the watering of my eyes, aware too late of the low-pitched thrum of a hive at war.

Bear! God damn it, a bear had got in! In the half-second between the first sting and the next, I had glimpsed one of the bee gums lying on its side in the dirt just inside the gate, combs and honey spilling out of it like entrails.

I ducked under branches and flung myself into a patch of poke-weed, gasping and cursing incoherently. The sting on my neck throbbed viciously, and the one on my temple was already puffing up, pulling at the eyelid on that side. I felt something crawling on my ankle, and batted it away by reflex before it could sting.

I wiped tears away, blinking. A few bees sailed past through the yellow-flowered stems above me, aggressive as Spitfires. I crawled a little farther, trying at once to get away, slap at my hair, and shake out my skirts, lest any more of them be trapped in my clothes.

I was breathing like a steam engine, shaking with adrenaline and fury.

"Bloody hell . . . frigging bear . . . God damn it . . ."

My strong impulse was to rush in screaming and flapping my skirts, in hopes of panicking the bear. An equally strong impulse of self-preservation overcame it.

I scrambled to my feet, and keeping low in case of enraged bees, thrust my way through the brush uphill, meaning to circle the garden and come down on the other side, away from the ravaged hives. I could get back to the path that way and down to the house, where I could recruit help—preferably armed—to drive away the monster before it destroyed the rest of the hives.

No point in keeping quiet, and I crashed through bushes and stumbled over logs, panting with rage. I tried to see the bear, but the growth of grapevines over the palisades was too thick to show me anything but rustling leaves and sun shadows. The side of my face felt as though it were on fire, and jolts of pain shot through the trigeminal nerve with each heartbeat, making the muscles twitch and the eye water terribly.

I reached the path just below the spot where the first bee had stung me—my gardening basket lay where I'd dropped it, tools spilled out. I grabbed the knife I used for everything from pruning to digging roots; it was a stout thing, with a six-inch blade, and while it might not impress the bear, I felt better for having it.

I glanced at the open gate, ready to run—but saw nothing. The ruined hive lay just as I'd seen it, the wax combs broken and squashed, the smell of honey thick in the air. But the combs were not scattered; shattered pillars of wax still stuck to the exposed wooden base of the hive.

A bee zoomed menacingly past my ear and I ducked, but didn't run. It was quiet. I tried to stop panting, trying to hear over the thunder of my own racing pulse. Bears weren't quiet; they didn't need to be. I should hear snufflings and gulping noises, at least— rustlings of broken foliage, the lap of a long tongue. I didn't.

Cautiously, I moved sideways up the path, a step at a time, ready to run. There was a good-size oak, about twenty feet away. Could I make that, if the bear popped out?

I listened as hard as I could, but heard nothing beyond the soft rustle of the grapevines and the sound of angry bees, now dropped to a whining hum as they gathered thick on the remnants of their combs.

It was gone. Had to be. Still wary, I edged closer, knife in hand.

I smelled the blood and saw her in the same instant. She was lying in the salad bed, her skirt flown out like some gigantic, rusty flower blooming amid the young lettuces.

I was kneeling by her, with no memory of reaching her, and the flesh of her arm was warm when I grasped her wrist—such small, fragile bones—but slack, there was no pulse—*Of course not,* said the cold small watcher inside, *her throat is cut, there's blood everywhere, but you can see the artery isn't pumping; she's dead.*

Malva's gray eyes were open, blank with surprise, and her cap had fallen off. I clutched her wrist harder, as though I must be able to find the buried pulse, to find some trace of life . . . and did. The bulge of her belly moved, very slightly, and I dropped the flaccid arm at once and seized my knife, scrabbling for the hem of her skirt.

I acted without thought, without fear, without doubt—there wasn't anything but the knife and the pressure, the flesh parting and the faint possibility, the panic of absolute *need* . . .

I slit the belly from navel to pubis, pushing hard through slack muscle, nicked the womb but no matter, cut quick but careful through the wall of the womb, dropped the knife, and thrust my hands into the depths of Malva Christie, still blood-warm, and seized the child, cupping, turning, wrenching hard in my frenzy to pull it free, bring it out from sure death, bring it into the air, help it breathe. . . . Malva's body flopped and heaved as I jerked, limp limbs flailing with the force of my yanking.

It came free with the suddenness of birth, and I was swiping blood and mucus from the tiny sealed face, blowing into its lungs, gently, gently, you have to blow gently, the alveoli of the lungs are like cobwebs, so small, compressing its chest, no more than a hand's span, two fingers pressing, no more, and felt the tiny spring of it, delicate as a watch spring, felt the movement, small squirms, a faint instinctive struggling—and felt it fade, that flicker, that tiny spark of life, cried out in anguish and clutched the tiny, doll-like body to my breast, still warm, still warm.

"Don't go," I said, "don't go, don't go, please don't go." But the vibrancy faded, a small blue glow that seemed to light the palms of my hands for an instant, then dwindle like a candle flame, to the coal of a smoldering wick, to the faintest trace of brightness—then everything was dark.

I was still sitting in the brilliant sun, crying and blood-soaked, the body of the little boy in my lap, the butchered corpse of my Malva beside me, when they found me.

85

The Stolen Bride

A week passed after Malva's death, and there was no slightest hint of who had killed her. Whispering, sidelong glances, and a palpable fog of suspicion hung about the Ridge, but despite Jamie's every effort, no one could be located who knew—or would say—anything at all useful.

I could see the tension and frustration building up in Jamie, day by day, and knew it must find an outlet. I had no idea what he might do, though.

After breakfast on the Wednesday, Jamie stood glowering at the window in his study, then slammed down his fist on the table, with a suddenness that made me jump.

"I have reached the mortal limit of endurance," he informed me. "One moment more of this, and I shall run mad. I must do something, and I will." Without waiting for any response to this statement, he strode to the office door, flung it open, and bellowed, "Joseph!" into the hall.

Mr. Wemyss appeared out of the kitchen, where he had been sweeping the chimney at Mrs. Bug's direction, looking startled, pale, soot-smudged, and generally unkempt.

Jamie ignored the black footprints on the study floor—he had burned the rug—and fixed Mr. Wemyss with a commanding gaze.

"D'ye want that woman?" he demanded.

"Woman?" Mr. Wemyss was understandably bewildered. "What—oh. Are you—might you be referring to Fraulein Berrisch?"

"Who else? D'ye want her?" Jamie repeated.

It had plainly been a long time since anyone had asked Mr. Wemyss what he wanted, and it took him some time to gather his wits from the shock of it.

Brutal prodding by Jamie forced him past deprecating murmurs about the Fraulein's friends no doubt being the best judge of her happiness, his own unsuitability, poverty, and general unworthiness as a husband, and into—at long last—a reckless admission that, well, if the Fraulein should not be terribly averse to the prospect, perhaps . . . well . . . in a word . . .

"Aye, sir," he said, looking terrified at his own boldness. "I do. Very much!" he blurted.

"Good." Jamie nodded, pleased. "We'll go and get her, then."

Mr. Wemyss was open-mouthed with astonishment; so was I. Jamie swung round to me, issuing orders with the confidence and *joie de vivre* of a sea-captain with a fat prize in view.

"Go and find Young Ian for me, will ye, Sassenach? And tell Mrs. Bug to put up food, enough for a week's travel for four men. And then fetch Roger Mac; we'll need a minister."

He rubbed his hands together in satisfaction, then clapped Mr. Wemyss on the shoulder, causing a small puff of soot to rise from his clothes.

"Go fettle yourself, Joseph," he said. "And comb your hair. We're going to go and steal ye a bride."

". . . and put a pistol to his breest, his breest," Young Ian chanted, "Marry me, marry me, minister, or else I'll be your priest, your priest—or else I'll be your priest!"

"Of course," Roger said, dropping the song, in which a bold young man named Willie rides with his friends to abduct and forcibly marry a young woman who proves bolder yet, "we'll hope ye prove a wee bit more capable than Willie upon the night, aye, Joseph?"

Mr. Wemyss, scrubbed, dressed, and fairly vibrating with excitement, gave him a glance of complete incomprehension. Roger grinned, tightening the strap of his saddlebag.

"Young Willie obliges a minister to marry him to the young woman at gunpoint," he explained to Mr. Wemyss, "but then, when he takes his stolen bride to bed, she'll have none of him— and his best efforts will not avail to force her."

"And so return me, Willie, to my hame, as virgin as I came, I came—as virgin as I came!" Ian caroled.

"Now, mind," Roger said warningly to Jamie, who was heaving his own saddlebags over Gideon's back. "If the Fraulein is at all unwilling . . ."

"What, unwilling to be wed to Joseph?" Jamie clapped Mr. Wemyss on the back, then bent to give him a foot up and fairly heaved the smaller man into the saddle. "I canna see any woman of sense turning from such an opportunity, can you, *a charaid*?"

He took a quick look round the clearing, to see all was well, then ran up the steps and kissed me in quick farewell, before running down again to mount Gideon, who for once seemed amenable and made no effort to bite him.

"Keep well, *mo nighean donn*," he said, smiling into my eyes. And then they were gone, thundering out of the clearing like a gang of Highland raiders, Ian's ear-splitting whoops ringing from the trees.

Oddly enough, the departure of the men seemed to ease things slightly. The talk, of course, went merrily on—but without Jamie or Ian there to serve as a lightning-rod, it merely crackled to and fro like St. Elmo's fire; spitting, fizzing, and making everyone's hair stand on end, but essentially a harmless phenomenon, unless touched directly.

The house felt less an embattled fortress, and more the eye of a storm.

Also, with Mr. Wemyss out of the house, Lizzie came to visit, bringing little Rodney Joseph, as the baby was called—Roger having set his face firmly against the young fathers' enthusiastic suggestions of Tilgath-pileser and Ichabod. Wee Rogerina had come out of it all right, being now commonly known as Rory, but Roger declined entirely to hear of a child being christened anything that might result in his being known to the world at large as Icky.

Rodney seemed a very congenial child, in part because he had never quite lost that air of round-eyed astonishment that made him seem agog to hear what you had to say. Lizzie's astonishment at his birth had mutated into an enchantment that might have completely eclipsed Jo and Kezzie, were it not for the fact that they shared it.

Either one of them would—unless forcibly stopped—spend half an hour discussing Rodney's bowel habits with the intensity heretofore reserved for new snares and the peculiar things found inside the stomachs of animals they had killed. Pigs, it seemed, really would eat anything; so would Rodney.

A few days after the men's departure on their bride-stealing expedition, Brianna had come up from her cabin with Jemmy to visit, and Lizzie likewise had brought Rodney. The two of them joined Amy McCallum and me in the kitchen, where we were spending a pleasant evening sewing by the light of the fire, admiring Rodney, keeping a negligent eye on Jemmy and Aidan—and after a certain amount of cautious exploration, devoting ourselves wholeheartedly to a rundown of the male population of the Ridge, viewed in the light of suspects.

I, of course, had a more personal and painful interest in the topic, but all three of the young women were solidly on the side of justice—i.e., the side that refused even to contemplate the notion that either Jamie or I might have had anything to do with the murder of Malva Christie.

For myself, I found such open speculation rather a comfort. I had, of course, been engaging in private conjecture nonstop—and an exhausting business it was, too. Not only was it unpleasant to visualize every man I knew in the role of cold-blooded murderer—the process obliged me continuously to reimagine the murder itself, and relive the moment when I had found her.

"I'd really hate to think it might have been Bobby," Bree said, frowning as she pushed a wooden darning egg into the heel of a sock. "He seems just such a nice boy."

Lizzie drew down her chin at this, pursing her lips.

"Oh, aye, he's a sweet lad," she said. "But what ye might call warm-blooded."

All of us looked at her.

"Well," she said mildly, "I didna let him, but he tried hard enough. And when I said no, he did go off and kick a tree."

"My husband would do that sometimes, if I refused him," Amy said, thoughtful. "But I'm sure he wouldna have cut my throat."

"Well, but Malva didn't refuse whoever it was," Bree pointed out, squinting as she threaded her darning needle. "That was the problem. He killed her because she was pregnant, and he was afraid she'd tell everyone."

"Ho!" Lizzie said, triumphant. "Well, then—it canna have been Bobby at all, can it? For when my Da turned him awa'—" A brief shadow crossed her face at mention of her father, who still had not spoken a word to her nor acknowledged the birth of little Rodney. "Did he not think of speiring for Malva Christie? Ian said he meant to. And if she were with child by him—well, then, her father would be obliged to agree, would he not?"

Amy nodded, finding this convincing, but Bree had objections.

"Yes—but she was insisting that it *wasn't* his baby. And he threw up in the blackberry bushes when he heard that she was"—her lips compressed momentarily—"well, he wasn't happy at all. So he might have killed her out of jealousy, don't you think?"

Lizzie and Amy hmm'd dubiously at this—both of them were fond of Bobby—but were obliged to admit the possibility.

"What I wonder about," I said a little hesitantly, "is the older men. The married ones. Everyone knows about the young men who were interested in her—but I've certainly seen more than one married man glance at her in passing."

"I nominate Hiram Crombie," Bree said at once, stabbing her needle into the heel of the sock. Everyone laughed, but she shook her head.

"No, I'm serious. It's always the really religious, very uptight ones that turn out to have secret drawers full of women's underwear, and slink around molesting choirboys."

Amy's jaw dropped.

"Drawers full of women's underwear?" she said. "What . . . shifts and stays? Whatever would he do wi' them?"

Brianna flushed at that, having forgotten her audience. She coughed, but there was no good way out.

"Er . . . well. I was thinking more of French women's underwear," she said weakly. "Um . . . lacy sorts of things."

"Oh, French," Lizzie said, nodding wisely. Everyone knew about the notorious reputation of French ladies—though I doubted that any woman on Fraser's Ridge save myself had ever seen one. In the interests of covering Bree's lapse, though, I obligingly told them about La Nestlé, the King of France's mistress, who had had her nipples pierced and appeared at court with her breasts exposed, sporting gold hoops through them.

"Another few months o' this," Lizzie said darkly, looking down at Rodney, who was nursing fiercely at her breast, tiny fists clenched with effort, "and I shall be able to do the same. I'll tell Jo and Kezzie to fetch me back some hoops when they sell their hides, aye?"

In the midst of the laughter at this, the sound of a knock at the front door passed unnoticed—or would have, if not for Jemmy and Aidan, who had been playing in Jamie's study, rushing into the kitchen to tell us about it.

"I'll get it." Bree set down her darning, but I was already on my feet.

"No, I'll go." I waved her back, picked up a candlestick, and went down the dark hallway, heart beating fast. Visitors after dark were almost always an emergency of one kind or another.

So was this one, though not any kind I might have expected. For a moment, I didn't even recognize the tall woman who stood swaying on the stoop, white-faced and gaunt. Then she whispered, "Frau Fraser? I may—may I komm?" and fell into my arms.

The noise of it brought all the young women rushing to help, and we had Monika Berrisch—for it was indeed Mr. Wemyss's putative bride—laid on the settle, covered with quilts, and plied with hot toddy in nothing flat.

She recovered quickly—there was nothing wrong with her, really, save exhaustion and hunger—she said she hadn't eaten in three days—and within a short time, was able to sit up eating soup, and explain her astonishing presence.

"It wass my husband's sister," she said, closing her eyes in momentary bliss at the aroma of split-pea soup with ham. "She did not want me, effer, and when her husband had the bad accident and lost his wagon, so there was not so much money to keep us all, she did not want me more."

She had, she said, yearned for Joseph, but had not had either the strength nor yet the means to withstand her family's opposition and insist upon returning to him.

"Oh?" Lizzie was examining her in a close, but not unfriendly manner. "What happpened, then?"

Fraulein Berrisch turned large, gentle eyes on her.

"I could not bear it more," she said simply. "I wish so much to be with Joseph. My husband's sister, she wish me to be gone, so she will give a small bit of money. So I came," she concluded, with a shrug, and took another small, greedy spoonful of soup.

"You . . . walked?" Brianna said. "From Halifax?"

Fraulein Berrisch nodded, licking the spoon, and put out a foot from under the quilts. Her shoes had worn entirely through at the sole; she had wrapped them with random scraps of leather and strips of fabric torn from her shift, so her feet looked like bundles of filthy rags.

"Elizabeth," she said, looking earnestly at Lizzie. "I hope you do not mind I komm. Your father—he is hier? I hope so much he does not mind, too."

"Umm, no," I said, exchanging a glance with Lizzie. "He isn't here—but I'm sure that he'll be delighted to see you!"

"Oh?" Her gaunt face, which had shown alarm at hearing that Mr. Wemyss was not here, grew radiant when we told her where he was.

"Oh," she breathed, clasping the spoon to her bosom as though it were Mr. Wemyss's head. "Oh, *mein Kavalier*!" Beaming with joy, she looked round at all of us—and for the first time, noticed Rodney, snoozing in his basket at Lizzie's feet.

"But who is this?" she cried, and leaned forward to look at him. Not quite asleep, Rodney opened round, dark eyes and regarded her with a solemn, sleepy interest.

"This is my wee bairnie. Rodney Joseph, he's called—for my Da, ken?" Lizzie hoisted him out of his basket, chubby knees pulled up under his chin, and laid him gently in Monika's arms.

She cooed over him in German, face alight.

"Granny lust," Bree muttered to me, out of the side of her mouth, and I felt laughter bubble up under my stays. I hadn't laughed since before Malva's death, and found it balm to the spirit.

Lizzie was explaining earnestly to Monika the estrangement resulting from her unorthodox marriage, to which Monika was nodding, clicking her tongue in sympathetic understanding—and I did wonder how much of it she grasped—and talking baby-talk to Rodney all at once.

"Fat chance of Mr. Wemyss staying estranged," I said out of the side of my own mouth. "Keep his new wife from her new grand-son? Ha!"

"Yes, what's a little matter of dual sons-in-law?" Bree agreed.

Amy was regarding the tender scene with a slight sense of wistfulness. She reached out and put an arm round Aidan's skinny shoulders.

"Well, they do say, the more, the merrier," she said.

86

Priorities

Three shirts, an extra pair of decent breeches, two pair of stockings, one lisle, one silk—wait, where were the silk ones?

Brianna stepped to the door and called to her husband, who was industriously laying segments of clay pipe into the trench he had dug, assisted by Jemmy and Aidan.

"Roger! What have you done with your silk stockings?"

He paused, frowning, and rubbed his head. Then, handing the shovel to Aidan, he came across to the house, leaping over the open trench.

"I wore them last Sunday to preach, no?" he asked, reaching her. "What did I . . . oh."

"Oh?" she said suspiciously, seeing his face change from puzzlement to guilt. "What's 'oh'?"

"Ahh . . . well, you'd stayed to home with Jem and his stomachache"—a tactically helpful ailment, greatly exaggerated in order to keep her from having to sit through two hours of staring and whispering—"so when Jocky Abernathy asked me would I care to go fishing with him . . ."

"Roger MacKenzie," she said, fixing him with a look of wrath, "if you put your good silk stockings in a creel full of smelly fish and forgot them—"

"I'll just nip up to the house and borrow a pair from your Da, shall I?" he said hurriedly. "I'm sure mine will turn up, somewhere."

"So will your head," she said. "Probably under a rock!"

That made him laugh, which was not what she had intended, but which had the effect of easing her temper.

"I'm sorry," he said, leaning forward to kiss her forehead. "It's probably Freudian."

"Oh? And what does leaving your stockings wrapped around a dead trout symbolize?" she demanded.

"Generalized guilt and divided loyalties, I imagine," he said, still joking, but not so much. "Bree—I've been thinking. I really don't think I should go. I don't need to—"

"Yes, you do," she said, as firmly as possible. "Da says so, Mama says so, *and so do I.*"

"Oh, well, then." He smiled, but she could see the uneasiness under his humor—the more so because she shared it. Malva Christie's murder had caused an uproar on the Ridge—alarm, hysteria, suspicion, and finger-pointing in every direction. Several young men—Bobby Higgins among them—had simply disappeared from the Ridge, whether from a sense of guilt, or merely from a sense of self-preservation.

There had been accusations enough to go around; even she herself had come in for her share of gossip and suspicion, some of her unguarded remarks about Malva Christie having been repeated. But by far the greatest weight of suspicion rested squarely on her parents.

Both of them were doing their best to go about their daily business, grimly ignoring the gossip and the pointed looks—but it was getting harder; anyone could see that.

Roger had gone at once to visit the Christies—had gone every day since Malva's death save for his hasty expedition to Halifax— had buried the girl with simplicity and tears—and had since worn himself out with being reasonable and soothing and firm to everyone else on the Ridge. He had immediately put aside his plan to go to Edenton for ordination, but Jamie, hearing of it, had insisted.

"You've done everything here you could possibly do," Brianna said, for the hundredth time. "There's nothing else you can do to help—and it might be years before you have another chance."

She knew how urgently he wished to be ordained, and would have done anything to further that wish. For herself, she wished that she could see it; but without a great deal of talk, they had agreed that it was best for her and Jem to go to River Run, and wait there for Roger to make the trip to Edenton and then return. It couldn't do a candidate for ordination any good to turn up with a Catholic wife and child.

The guilt of leaving, though, with her parents standing in the eye of the whirlwind . . .

"You have to go," she repeated. "But maybe I—"

He stopped her with a look.

"No, we've done that." His argument was that her presence couldn't affect public opinion, which was probably true. She realized that his real reason—shared by her parents—was a desire to get her and Jem away from the situation on the Ridge, out of the uproar and safe, preferably before Jem realized that a good many of the neighbors thought that one, if not both, of his grandparents was a cold-blooded murderer.

And, to her private shame, she was eager to go.

Someone had killed Malva—and her baby. Every time she thought of it, the possibilities swam before her, the litany of names. And every time, she was forced to see her cousin's name among them. Ian had not run away, and she couldn't—could *not*—think that it had been him. And yet every day she was obliged to see Ian, and to contemplate the possibility.

She stood staring into the bag she was packing, folding and re-folding the shirt in her hands, looking for reasons to go, reasons to stay—and knowing that no reason had any power at all, not now.

A dull *thunk!* from outside jerked her from her mire of indecision.

"What—" She reached the door in two steps, fast enough to see Jem and Aidan disappearing into the woods like a pair of rabbits. On the edge of the trench lay the cracked pieces of the pipe segment they had just dropped.

"You little *snot*-rags!" she bellowed, and grabbed for a broom—intending what she didn't know, but violence seemed the only outlet for the frustration that had just erupted like a volcano, searing through her.

"Bree," Roger said softly, and put a hand on her back. "It's not important."

She jerked away and rounded on him, the blood roaring in her ears.

"Do you have any idea how long it takes to make one of those? How many firings it takes to get one that's not cracked? How—"

"Yes, I do know," he said, his voice level. "And it's still not important."

She stood trembling, breathing hard. Very gently, he reached out and took the broom from her, standing it neatly back in its place.

"I need—to go," she said, when she could form words again, and he nodded, his eyes tinged with the sadness he had carried ever since the day of Malva's death.

"Aye, ye do," he said quietly.

He came behind her, put his arms around her, his chin resting on her shoulder, and gradually she stopped shaking. Across the clearing, she saw Mrs. Bug come down the path from the garden with an apron full of cabbages and carrots; Claire had not set foot in her garden since . . .

"Will they be all right?"

"We'll pray that they will," he said, and tightened his arms around her. She was comforted by his touch, and didn't notice until later that he had not in fact reassured her that they would.

87

Justice Is Mine,
Sayeth the Lord

I poked at the last package from Lord John, trying to work up enough enthusiasm to open it. It was a small wooden crate; perhaps more vitriol. I supposed I should make a fresh batch of ether—but then, what was the point? People had stopped coming to my surgery, even for the treatment of minor cuts and bruises, let alone the odd appendectomy.

I ran a finger through the dust on the counter, and thought that I should at least take care of that; Mrs. Bug kept the rest of the house spotless, but wouldn't come into the surgery. I added dusting to the long list of things that I should do, but made no move to go and find a dust cloth.

Sighing, I got up and went across the hall. Jamie was sitting at his desk, twiddling a quill and staring at a half-finished letter. He put down the quill when he saw me, smiling.

"How is it, Sassenach?"

"All right," I said, and he nodded, accepting it at face value. His face showed the lines of strain, and I knew that he was no more all right than I was. "I haven't seen Ian all day. Did he say he was going?" To the Cherokee, I meant. Little wonder if he wanted to get away from the Ridge; I thought it had taken a good deal of fortitude for him to stay as long as he had, bearing the stares and murmurs—and the outright accusations.

Jamie nodded again, and dropped the quill back into its jar.

"Aye, I told him to go. No purpose to him staying any longer; there'd only be more fights." Ian didn't say anything about the fights, but had more than once turned up to supper with the marks of battle on him.

"Right. Well, I'd better tell Mrs. Bug before she starts the supper." Still, I made no motion to get up, finding some small sense of comfort in Jamie's presence, some surcease from the constant memory of the small, bloody weight in my lap, inert as a lump of meat—and the sight of Malva's eyes, so surprised.

I heard horses in the yard, several of them. I glanced at Jamie, who shook his head, brows raised, then rose to go and meet the visitors, whoever they were. I followed him down the hall, wiping my hands on my apron and mentally revising the supper menu to accommodate what sounded like at least a dozen guests, from the whickering and murmuring I heard in the dooryard.

Jamie opened the door, and stopped dead. I looked over his shoulder, and felt terror seize me. Horsemen, black against the sinking sun, and in that moment, I was back in the whisky clearing, damp with sweat and clad in nothing but my shift. Jamie heard my gasp, and put back a hand, to keep me away.

"What d'ye want, Brown?" he said, sounding most unfriendly.

"We've come for your wife," said Richard Brown. There was an unmistakable note of gloating in his voice, and hearing it, the down hairs on my body rippled with cold, and black spots floated in my field of vision. I stepped back, hardly feeling my feet, and took hold of the doorjamb to my surgery, clinging to it for support.

"Well, ye can just be on your way, then," Jamie replied, with the same unfriendly tone. "Ye've nothing to do with my wife, nor she with you."

"Ah, now, there you're wrong, *Mister* Fraser." My vision had cleared, and I saw him urge his horse up closer to the stoop. He leaned down, peering through the door, and evidently saw me, for he smiled, in a most unpleasant fashion.

"We've come to arrest your wife, for the dastard crime of murder."

Jamie's hand tensed where he gripped the door, and he drew himself slowly to his fullest height, seeming to expand as he did so.

"Ye'll leave my land, sir," he said, and his voice had dropped to a level just above the rustlings of horses and harness. "And ye'll go now."

I felt, rather than heard, footsteps behind me. Mrs. Bug, coming to see what was afoot.

"Bride save us," she whispered, seeing the men. Then she was gone, running back through the house, light-footed as a deer. I should follow her, I knew, escape through the back door, run up into the forest, hide. But my limbs were frozen. I could barely breathe, let alone move.

And Richard Brown was looking at me over Jamie's shoulder, open dislike mingling with triumph.

"Oh, we'll leave," he said, straightening up. "Hand her over, and we'll be gone. Vanished like the morning dew," he said, and laughed. Dimly, I wondered whether he was drunk.

"By what right do you come here?" Jamie demanded. His left hand rose, rested on the hilt of his dirk in plain threat. The sight of it galvanized me, finally, and I stumbled down the hall, toward the kitchen where the guns were kept.

". . . Committee of Safety." I caught those words in Brown's voice, raised in threat, and then was through into the kitchen. I grabbed the fowling piece from its hooks above the hearth, and wrenching open the drawer of the sideboard, hastily bundled the three pistols there into the large pockets of my surgical apron, made to hold instruments while I worked.

My hands were shaking. I hesitated—the pistols were primed and loaded; Jamie checked them every night—should I take the shot pouch, the powder horn? No time. I heard Jamie's voice and Richard Brown's, shouting now at the front of the house.

The sound of the back door opening jerked my head up, and I saw an unfamiliar man pause in the doorway, looking round. He saw me and started toward me, grinning, hand out to seize my arm.

I lifted a pistol from my apron and shot him, point-blank. The grin didn't leave his face, but took on a slightly puzzled air. He blinked once or twice, then put a hand to his side, where a reddening spot was beginning to spread on his shirt. He looked at his blood-smeared fingers, and his jaw dropped.

"Well, goddamn!" he said. "You shot me!"

"I did," I said, breathless. "And I'll bloody do it again, if you don't get out of here!" I dropped the empty pistol on the floor with a crash, and scrabbled one-handed in my apron pocket for another, still holding the fowling piece in a death grip.

He didn't wait to see if I meant it, but whirled and crashed into the door frame, then stumbled through it, leaving a smear of blood on the wood.

Wisps of black-powder smoke floated in the air, mingling oddly with the scent of roasting fish, and I thought for an instant that I might throw up, but managed despite my nausea to set down the fowling piece for a moment and bar the door, my hands shaking so that it took several tries.

Sudden sounds from the front of the house drove nerves and everything else from my mind, and I was running down the hall, gun in hand, before I had made a conscious decision to move, the heavy pistols in my apron banging against my thighs.

They'd dragged Jamie off the porch; I caught a brief glimpse of him in the midst of a surging melee of bodies. They'd stopped shouting. There wasn't any noise at all, save for small grunts and the impact of flesh, the scuffling of myriad feet in the dust. It was deadly earnest, that struggle, and I knew at once that they meant to kill him.

I leveled the fowling piece at the edge of the crowd farthest from Jamie, and pulled the trigger. The crash of the gun and the startled screams seemed to come together, and the scene before me flew apart, the knot of men dissolving, peppered with bird shot. Jamie had kept hold of his dirk; with a little room around him now, I saw him drive it into one man's side, wrench it back and lash sideways in the same motion, scoring a bloody furrow across the forehead of a man who had fallen back a little.

Then I caught a glimpse of metal to one side and by reflex shrieked "DUCK!" an instant before Brown's pistol fired. There was a small *tchoong* past my ear, and I realized, in a very calm sort of way, that Brown had fired at me, not Jamie.

Jamie had, however, ducked. So had everyone else in the yard, and men were now scrambling to their feet, confused, the impetus of the attack dispersed. Jamie had dived toward the porch; he was up and stumbling toward me, striking viciously with the hilt of his dirk at a man who grabbed at his sleeve, so the man fell back with a cry.

We might have rehearsed it a dozen times. He took the steps of the porch in one leap and flung himself into me, carrying us both through the door, then spun on his heel and slammed the door, throwing himself against it and holding it against the frenzied impact of bodies for the instant it took me to drop the fowling piece, seize the bolt, and lift it into place.

It fell into its hooks with a thunk.

The door vibrated to the blows of fists and shoulders, and the shouting had started up again, but with a different sound. No gloating, no taunting. Cursing still, but with a set, malign intent.

Neither of us paused to listen.

"I barred the kitchen door," I gasped, and Jamie nodded, diving into my surgery to secure the bolts of the inside shutters there. I heard the crash of breaking glass in the surgery behind me as I ran into his study; the windows there were smaller, and not glass, placed high in the wall. I slammed the shutters to and bolted them, then ran back into the suddenly darkened hallway to find the gun.

Jamie had it already; he was in the kitchen, grabbing things, and as I started toward the kitchen door, he came out of it, hung about with shot pouches, powder horns, and the like, fowling piece in his hand, and with a jerk of the head, motioned me before him up the stairs.

The rooms above were still filled with light; it was like bursting up from underwater, and I gulped the light as though it were air, dazzled and eyes watering as I rushed to bolt the shutters in the boxroom and Amy McCallum's room. I didn't know where Amy and her sons were; I could only be grateful that they weren't in the house at the moment.

I ran into the bedroom, gasping. Jamie was kneeling by the window, methodically loading guns and saying something under his breath in Gaelic—prayer or cursing, I couldn't tell.

I didn't ask if he was hurt. His face was bruised, his lip was split, and blood had run down his chin onto his shirt, he was covered with dirt and what I assumed to be smears of other peoples' blood, and the ear on the side closest me was swollen. But he was steady in his movements, and anything short of a fractured skull would have to wait.

"They mean to kill us," I said, and didn't mean it as a question.

He nodded, eyes on his work, then handed me a spare pistol to load.

"Aye, they do. Good job the weans are all safe away, isn't it?" He smiled at me suddenly, bloody-toothed and fierce, and I felt steadier than I had for a long time.

He'd left one side of the shutter ajar. I moved carefully back behind him and peered out, the loaded pistol primed and in my hand.

"No bodies lying in the dooryard," I reported. "I suppose you didn't kill any of them."

"Not for want of trying," he replied. "God, what I'd give for a rifle!" He rose cautiously to his knees, the barrel of the fowling piece protruding over the sill, and surveyed the state of the attack.

They had withdrawn for the moment; a small group was visible under the chestnut trees at the far side of the clearing, and they'd taken the horses down toward Bree and Roger's cabin, safely out of range of flying bullets. Brown and his minions were clearly planning what to do next.

"What do you suppose they would have done, if I'd agreed to go with them?" I could feel my heart again, at least. It was going a mile a minute, but I could breathe, and some feeling was coming back into my extremities.

"I should never ha' let ye go," he replied shortly.

"And quite possibly Richard Brown knows that," I said. He nodded; he'd been thinking along the same lines. Brown had never intended actually to arrest me; only to provoke an incident in which we could both be killed under circumstances dubious enough as to prevent wholesale retaliation by Jamie's tenants.

"Mrs. Bug got out, did she?" he asked.

"Yes. If they didn't catch her outside the house." I narrowed my eyes against the brilliant afternoon sun, searching for a short, broad figure in skirts among the group by the chestnut trees, but I saw only men.

Jamie nodded again, hissing gently through his back teeth as he swiveled the gun barrel slowly through an arc that covered the dooryard.

"We'll see, then" was all he said. "Come that wee bit closer, man," he murmured, as one man started cautiously across the yard toward the house. "One shot; that's all I ask. Here, Sassenach, take this." He pushed the fowling piece into my hands, and selected his favorite of the pistols, a long-barreled Highland dag with a scroll butt.

The man—it was Richard Brown, I saw—stopped some distance away, pulled a handkerchief from the waist of his breeches, and waved it slowly overhead. Jamie snorted briefly, but let him come on.

"Fraser!" he called, coming to a stop at a distance of forty yards or so. "Fraser! D'ye hear me?"

Jamie sighted carefully and fired. The ball struck the ground a few feet in front of Brown, raising a sudden puff of dust from the path, and Brown leapt in the air as though stung by a bee.

"What's the matter with you?" he yelled indignantly. "Have ye never heard of a flag o' truce, you horse-stealin' Scotcher?"

"If I wanted ye dead, Brown, ye'd be coolin' this minute!" Jamie shouted back. "Speak your piece." What he did want was plain: he wanted them wary of coming closer to the house; it was impossible to hit anything accurately with a pistol at forty yards, and not that easy with a musket.

"You know what I want!" Brown called. He took off his hat, wiping sweat and dirt from his face. "I want that goddamn murderous witch of yours."

The answer to that was another carefully aimed pistol ball. Brown jumped again, but not so high.

"Look you," he tried again, with a conciliating note in his voice. "We ain't going to hurt her. We mean to take her to Hillsboro for trial. A fair trial. That's all."

Jamie handed me the second pistol to reload, took another, and fired.

You had to give Brown credit for persistence, I thought. Of course, it had probably dawned on him that Jamie either couldn't or wouldn't actually hit him, and he doggedly stood his ground through two more shots, yelling that they meant to take me to Hillsboro, and surely to God if I were innocent, Jamie should *want* a trial, shouldn't he?

It was hot upstairs, and sweat was trickling down between my breasts. I blotted the fabric of my shift against my chest.

With no answer save the whine of pistol balls, Brown threw up his hands in exaggerated pantomime of a reasonable man tried beyond endurance, and stamped back to his men beneath the chestnut trees. Nothing had changed, but seeing the narrow back of him made me breathe a little easier.

Jamie was still crouched in the window, pistol at the ready, but seeing Brown go back, he relaxed and sat back on his heels, sighing.

"Is there water, Sassenach?"

"Yes." The bedroom ewer was full; I poured him a cup and he drank it thirstily. We had food, water, and a fair amount of shot and powder. I did not, however, foresee a long siege ahead.

"What do you suppose they'll do?" I didn't go near the window, but by standing to one side, I could see them clearly, gathered in conference under the trees. The air was still and heavy, and the leaves above them hung like damp rags.

Jamie came to stand behind me, dabbing at his lip with the tail of his shirt.

"Fire the house as soon as it's dark, I suppose," he said matter-of-factly. "I would. Though I suppose they might try draggin' Gideon out and threatening to put a ball through his head, and I didna give ye up." He seemed to think this last was a joke, but I failed to see the humor in it.

He saw my face and put a hand behind my back, drawing me close for a moment. The air was hot and sticky, and we were both wringing wet, but the nearness of him was a comfort, nonetheless.

"So," I said, taking a deep breath. "It all depends on whether Mrs. Bug got away—and who she's told."

"She'll ha' gone for Arch, first thing." Jamie patted me gently, and sat down on the bed. "If he's to home, he'll run for Kenny Lindsay; he's nearest. After that . . ." He shrugged, and closed his eyes, and I saw that his face was pale under the sunburn and the smears of dirt and blood.

"Jamie—are you hurt?"

He opened his eyes and gave me a small, one-sided smile, trying not to stretch his torn lip.

"No, I've broken my bloody finger again, is all." He raised a shoulder in deprecation, but let me lift his right hand to look.

It was a clean break; that was all that could be said for it. The fourth finger was stiff, the joints fused from being so badly broken long ago, in Wentworth Prison. He couldn't bend it, and it therefore stuck out awkwardly; this wasn't the first time he'd snapped it.

He swallowed as I felt gently for the break, and closed his eyes again, sweating.

"There's laudanum in the surgery," I said. "Or whisky." I knew he would refuse, though, and he did.

"I'll want a clear head," he said, "whatever happens." He opened his eyes and gave me the ghost of a smile. The room was sweltering and airless, despite the open shutter. The sun was more than halfway down the sky, and the first shadows were gathering in the corners of the room.

I went down to the surgery to fetch a splint and bandage; it wouldn't help a lot, but it was something to do.

The surgery was dark, with the shutters closed, but with the windows broken, air came through them, making the room seem oddly exposed and vulnerable. I walked in like a mouse, quiet, stopping abruptly, listening for danger, whiskers twitching. Everything was quiet, though.

"*Too* quiet," I said aloud, and laughed. Moving with purpose and ignoring the noise, I set my feet down firmly and opened cupboard doors with abandon, banging instruments and rattling bottles as I looked out what I needed.

I stopped into the kitchen before returning upstairs. Partly to reassure myself that the back door *was* firmly bolted, and partly to see what bits of food Mrs. Bug might have left out. He hadn't said so, but I knew the pain of the broken finger was making Jamie mildly nauseated—and in him, food generally quelled that sort of disturbance, and made him feel more settled.

The cauldron was still over the coals, but the fire, untended, had burned down so far that the soup had luckily not boiled away. I poked up the embers and put on three sticks of fat pine, as much by way of thumbing my nose at the besiegers outside as from the long-ingrained habit of never letting a fire die. Let them see the spray of sparks from the chimney, I thought, and imagine us sitting peacefully down to eat by our hearth. Or better yet, imagine us sitting by the blazing fire, melting lead and molding bullets.

In this defiant frame of mind, I went back upstairs, equipped with medical supplies, an alfresco lunch, and a large bottle of black ale. I couldn't help but notice, though, the echo of my footsteps on the stair, and the silence that settled quickly back into place behind me, like water when one steps out of it.

I heard a shot, just as I approached the head of the stair, and took the last steps so fast that I tripped and would have fallen headlong, save for reeling into the wall.

Jamie appeared from Mr. Wemyss's room, fowling piece in hand, looking startled.

"Are ye all right, Sassenach?"

"Yes," I said crossly, wiping spilled soup off my hand with my apron. "What in the name of God are you shooting at?"

"Nothing. I only wanted to make the point that the back of the house is nay safer than the front, if they thought of creeping up that way. Just to ensure that they *do* wait for dark to fall."

I bound up his finger, which seemed to help a little. The food, as I'd hoped, helped considerably more. He ate like a wolf, and rather to my surprise, so did I.

"The condemned ate a hearty meal," I observed, picking up crumbs of bread and cheese. "I'd always thought being in danger of death would make one too nervous to eat, but apparently not."

He shook his head, took a swallow of ale, and passed me the bottle.

"A friend once told me, 'The body has nay conscience.' I dinna ken that that's entirely so—but it is true that the body doesna generally admit the possibility of nonexistence. And if ye exist—well, ye need food, that's all." He grinned one-sided at me, and tearing the last of the sweet rolls in half, gave one to me.

I took it, but didn't eat it immediately. There was no sound outside, save the buzzing of cicadas, though the air had a sultry thickness to it that often presaged rain. It was early in the summer for storms, but one could only hope.

"You've thought of it, too, haven't you?" I said quietly.

He made no pretense of misunderstanding me.

"Well, it *is* the twenty-first o' the month," he said.

"It's *June*, for heaven's sake! And the wrong year, as well. That newspaper clipping said January, of 1776!" I was absurdly indignant, as though I had somehow been cheated.

He found that funny.

"I was a printer myself, Sassenach," he said, laughing through a mouthful of sweet roll. "Ye dinna want to believe everything ye read in the newspapers, aye?"

When I looked out again, only a few men were visible under the chestnut trees. One of them saw my movement; he waved his arm slowly to and fro above his head—then drew the edge of his hand flat across his throat.

The sun was just above the treetops; two hours, perhaps, to nightfall. Two hours surely was enough time for Mrs. Bug to have summoned help, though—always assuming she had found anyone who would come. Arch might have gone to Cross Creek—he went once a month; Kenny might be hunting. As for the newer tenants . . . without Roger to keep them in order, their suspicion and dislike of me had become blatant. I had the feeling that they might come if summoned—but only to cheer as I was dragged away.

If anyone *did* come—what then? I didn't want to be dragged away, much less shot or burnt alive in the ashes of my house—but I didn't want anyone else injured or killed in an effort to prevent it, either.

"Come away from the window, Sassenach," Jamie said. He held out a hand to me, and I went, sitting on the bed beside him. I felt all at once exhausted, the adrenaline of emergency having burned away, leaving my muscles feeling like heat-softened rubber.

"Lie down, *a Sorcha*," he said softly. "Lay your head in my lap."

Hot as it was, I did so, finding it a comfort to stretch out, even more to hear his heart, thumping slow and solid above my ear, and feel his hand, light on my head.

All the weapons were laid out, ranged on the floor beside the window, all loaded, primed, and ready for use. He'd taken his sword down from the armoire; it stood by the door, a last resort.

"There's nothing we can do now, is there?" I said after a little. "Nothing but wait."

His fingers moved idly through the damp curls of my hair; it fell to just above my shoulders now, long enough—barely—to tie back or pin up.

"Well, we might say an Act of Contrition," he said. "We did that, always, the night before a battle. Just in case," he added, smiling down at me.

"All right," I said after a pause. "Just in case."

I reached up and his good hand closed round mine.

"Mon Dieu, je regrette . . ." he began, and I remembered that he said this prayer in French, harking back to those days as a mercenary in France; how often had he said it then, a necessary precaution, cleansing the soul at night in expectation of the possibility of death in the morning?

I said it, too, in English, and we fell silent. The cicadas had stopped. Far, far away, I thought I heard a sound that might be thunder.

"Do you know," I said after a long while, "I'm sorry for a great many things and people. Rupert, Murtagh, Dougal . . . Frank. Malva," I added softly, with a catch in my throat. "But speaking only for myself . . ." I cleared my throat.

"I don't regret anything," I said, watching the shadows creep in from the corners of the room. "Not one bloody thing."

"Nor do I, *mo nighean donn*," he said, and his fingers stilled, warm against my skin. "Nor do I."

I woke from a doze with the smell of smoke in my nostrils. Being in a state of grace is all very well, but I imagine even Joan of Arc had qualms when they lit the first brand. I sat bolt upright, heart pounding, to see Jamie at the window.

It wasn't quite dark yet; streaks of orange and gold and rose lit the sky to the west, and touched his face with a fiery light. He looked long-nosed and fierce, the lines of strain cut deep.

"Folk are coming," he said. His voice was matter-of-fact, but his good hand was clenched hard round the edge of the shutter, as though he would have liked to slam and bolt it.

I came to stand by him, combing my fingers hastily through my hair. I could still make out figures under the chestnut trees, though they now were no more than silhouettes. They'd built a bonfire there, at the far edge of the dooryard; that's what I'd smelled. There were more people coming into the dooryard, though; I was sure I made out the squat figure of Mrs. Bug among them. The sound of voices floated up, but they weren't talking loudly enough to make out words.

"Will ye plait my hair, Sassenach? I canna manage, wi' this." He gave his broken finger a cursory glance.

I lit a candle, and he moved a stool to the window, so he could keep watch while I combed his hair and braided it into a tight, thick queue, which I clubbed at the base of his neck and tied with a neat black ribbon.

I knew his reasons were twofold: not only to appear well-groomed and gentlemanly, but to be ready to fight if he had to. I was less worried about someone seizing me by the hair as I attempted to cleave them in half with a sword, but supposed that if this were my last appearance as the lady of the Ridge, I should not appear unkempt.

I heard him mutter something under his breath, as I brushed my own hair by candlelight, and turned on my stool to look at him.

"Hiram's come," he informed me. "I hear his voice. That's good."

"If you say so," I said dubiously, recollecting Hiram Crombie's denunciations in church a week before—thinly veiled remarks clearly aimed at us. Roger hadn't mentioned them; Amy McCallum had told me.

Jamie turned his head to look at me, and smiled, an expression of extraordinary sweetness coming over his face.

"Ye're verra lovely, Sassenach," he said as though surprised. "But, aye, it's good. Whatever he thinks, he wouldna countenance Brown hanging us in the dooryard, nor yet setting the house afire to drive us out."

There were more voices outside; the crowd was growing quickly.

"Mr. Fraser!"

He took a deep breath, took the candle from the table, and threw open the shutter, holding the candle near his face so they could see him.

It was almost full dark, but several of the crowd were holding torches, which gave me uneasy visions of the mob coming to burn Dr. Frankenstein's monster—but did at least allow me to make out the faces below. There were at least thirty men—and not a few women—there, in addition to Brown and his thugs. Hiram Crombie was indeed there, standing beside Richard Brown, and looking like something out of the Old Testament.

"We require ye to come down, Mr. Fraser," he called. "And your wife—if ye please."

I caught sight of Mrs. Bug, plump and clearly terrified, her face streaked with tears. Then Jamie closed the shutters, gently, and offered me his arm.

Jamie had worn both dirk and sword, and had not changed his clothes. He stood on the porch, bloodstained and battered, and dared them to harm us further.

"Ye'll take my wife over my dead body," he said, raising his powerful voice enough to be heard across the clearing. I was rather afraid they would. He'd been right—so far—about Hiram not countenancing lynching, but it was clear that public opinion was not in our favor.

"Thou shalt not suffer a witch to live!" someone shouted from the back of the crowd, and a stone whistled through the air, bouncing off the front of the house with a sharp report, like a gunshot. It struck no more than a foot from my head, and I flinched, instantly regretting it.

Angry murmurs had risen from the moment Jamie had opened the door, and this encouraged them. There were shouts of "Murderers!" and "Heartless! Heartless!" and a number of Gaelic insults that I didn't try to understand.

"If she didn't do it, *breugaire*, who did?" someone bellowed. "Liar" it meant.

The man Jamie had slashed across the face with his dirk was in the forefront of the crowd; the open wound gaped, still oozing, and his face was a mask of dried blood.

"If 'twasn't her, 'twas him!" he shouted, pointing at Jamie. *"Fear-siùrsachd!"* Lecher.

There was an ugly rumble of agreement at that, and I saw Jamie shift his weight and set his hand to his sword, ready to draw if they charged him.

"Be still!" Hiram's voice was rather shrill, but penetrating. "Be still, I tell ye!" He pushed Brown aside and came up the steps, very deliberately. At the top, he gave me a look of revulsion, but then turned to the crowd.

"Justice!" one of Brown's men yelled, before he could speak. "We want justice!"

"Aye, we do!" Hiram shouted back. "And justice we shall have, for the puir raped lass and her bairn unborn!"

A satisfied growl greeted this, and icy terror ran down my legs, so that I feared my knees would give way.

"Justice! Justice!" Various people were taking up the chant, but Hiram stopped them, raising both hands as though he were bloody Moses parting the Red Sea.

"*Justice is mine*, sayeth the Lord," Jamie remarked, in a voice just loud enough to be generally heard. Hiram, who had evidently been about to say the same thing, gave him a furious look, but couldn't very well contradict him.

"And justice you'll have, Mister Fraser!" Brown said very loudly. He lifted his face, narrow-eyed and malicious with triumph. "I wish to take her for trial. Anyone accused is entitled to that, nay? If she is innocent—if *you* are innocent—how can you refuse?"

"Certainly a point," Hiram observed, very dry. "If your wife be clean o' the crime, she's naught to fear. How say ye, sir?"

"I say that should I surrender her to the hands of this man, she willna live to stand a trial," Jamie replied hotly. "He holds me to blame for the death of his brother—and some of ye here will ken well enough the truth o' *that* affair!" he added, lifting his chin to the crowd.

Here and there, heads nodded—but they were few. No more than a dozen of his Ardsmuir men had been on the expedition that rescued me; in the wake of gossip following it, many of the new tenants would have known only that I had been abducted, assaulted in some scandalous fashion, and that men had died on my account. The mind of the times being what it was, I was well aware that an obscure sense of blame attached to the victim of any sexual crime—unless the woman died, in which case she became at once a spotless angel.

"He will slaughter her out of hand, for the sake of revenge upon me," Jamie said, raising his voice. He changed abruptly to Gaelic, pointing at Brown. "Look at yon man, and see the truth of the matter writ upon his face! He has no more to do with justice than with honor, and he would not recognize honor by the smell of its arse!"

That made a few of them laugh, in sheer surprise. Brown, disconcerted, looked round to see what they were laughing at, which made more of them laugh.

The mood of the assembly was still against us, but they were not yet with Brown—who was, after all, a stranger. Hiram's narrow brow creased in consideration.

"What would ye offer by way of guarantee for the woman's safety?" Hiram asked Brown.

"A dozen hogsheads of beer and three dozen prime hides," Brown replied promptly. "Four dozen!" His eagerness gleamed in his eyes, and it was all he could do to keep his voice from shaking with the lust to take me. I had a sudden, unpleasant conviction that while my death was his ultimate goal, he didn't intend that it should be a quick one, unless circumstances demanded it.

"It would be worth far more than that to ye, *breugaire*, to have your revenge upon me with her death," Jamie said evenly.

Hiram glanced from one to the other, unsure what to do. I

looked out into the crowd, keeping my face impassive. In truth, it was not difficult to do; I felt completely numb.

There were a few friendly faces, glancing anxiously to Jamie, to see what to do. Kenny and his brothers, Murdo and Evan, stood in a tight group, hands on their dirks and faces set. I didn't know whether Richard Brown had chosen his timing, or merely been lucky. Ian was gone, hunting with his Cherokee friends. Arch was plainly gone, as well, or he would be visible—Arch and his ax would be uncommonly handy just now, I thought.

Fergus and Marsali were gone—they, too, would have helped to stem the tide. But the most important absence was Roger's. He alone had been keeping the Presbyterians more or less under control since the day of Malva's accusation, or at least keeping a lid on the simmering pot of gossip and animosity. He might have cowed them now—had he been here.

The conversation had devolved from high drama to a three-way wrangle among Jamie, Brown, and Hiram, the former two adamant in their positions, and poor Hiram, quite unsuited to the task, trying to adjudicate. Insofar as I had feelings to spare, I felt rather sorry for him.

"Take him!" a voice called suddenly. Allan Christie pushed his way to the front of the crowd, and pointed at Jamie. His voice trembled and broke with emotion. "It's him debauched my sister, him that kilt her! If ye'll put someone to the trial, take him!"

There was a subterranean rumble of agreement at that, and I saw John MacNeill and young Hugh Abernathy draw close together, glancing uneasily from Jamie to the three Lindsay brothers, and back again.

"Nay, it's her!" a woman's voice called in contradiction, high and shrill. One of the fishers' wives; she stabbed a finger at me, face pinched with malevolence. "A man might kill a lass he'd got wi' child—but no man would do sich wickedness as to steal a babe unborn frae the womb! No but a witch would do that—and she found wi' the puir wee corpse in her hands!"

A higher susurrus of condemnation greeted that. The men might possibly give me the benefit of doubt—no woman would.

"By the name of the Almighty!" Hiram was losing his grip on the situation, and becoming panicky. The situation was perilously close to degenerating into riot; anyone could feel the currents of hysteria and violence in the air. He cast his eyes up to heaven, looking for inspiration—and found some.

"Take them both!" he said suddenly. He looked at Brown, then Jamie. "Take them both," he repeated, testing the notion and finding it good. "Ye'll go along, to see that nay harm comes to your wife," he said reasonably to Jamie. "And if it should be proved that she is innocent . . ." His voice died away on that, as it dawned on him that what he was saying was that if I were proven innocent, Jamie must be guilty, and what a good idea it would be to have him on the spot to be hanged instead.

"She is innocent; so am I." Jamie spoke without heat, doggedly repeating it. He had no real hope of convincing anyone; the only doubt among the crowd was whether he or I was the guilty party—or whether we had plotted together to destroy Malva Christie.

He turned suddenly to face the crowd, and cried out to them in Gaelic.

"If you will deliver us into the stranger's hand, then our blood be upon your heads, and you will answer for our lives upon the Day of Judgment!"

A sudden hush fell on the crowd at that. Men glanced uncertainly at their neighbors, measured Brown and his cohort with doubtful eyes.

They were known to the community, but strangers— Sassenachs—in the Scottish sense. So was I, and a witch, to boot. Lecher, rapist, and Papist murderer he might be—but Jamie at least was not a stranger.

The man I had shot was grinning at me evilly over Brown's shoulder; evidently, I had no more than grazed him, worse luck. I gave him stare for stare, sweat gathering between my breasts, moisture slick and hot beneath the veil of my hair.

A murmur was rising among the crowd; argument and disputation, and I could see the Ardsmuir men begin to make their way slowly toward the porch, pushing through the mob. Kenny Lindsay's eyes were fixed on Jamie's face, and I felt Jamie take a deep breath beside me.

They would fight for him, if he called them. But there were too few of them, and poorly armed, by contrast with Brown's mob. They would not win—and there were women and children in the crowd. To call his men would provoke only bloody riot, and leave the deaths of innocents upon his conscience. That was not a burden he could bear; not now.

I saw him come to this conclusion, and his mouth tighten. I had no idea what he might be about to do, but he was forestalled. There was a disturbance at the edge of the crowd; people turned to look, then froze, stricken silent.

Thomas Christie came through the crowd; in spite of the darkness and wavering torchlight, I knew at once it was him. He walked like an old man, hunched and halting, looking at no one. The crowd gave way before him at once, deeply respectful of his grief.

The grief was plainly marked on his face. He had let his beard and hair go untrimmed, uncombed, and both were matted. His eyes were pouched and bloodshot, the lines from nose to mouth black furrows through his beard. His eyes were alive, though, alert and intelligent. He walked through the crowd, past his son, as though he were alone, and came up the steps onto the porch.

"I will go with them to Hillsboro," he said quietly to Hiram Crombie. "Let them both be taken, if ye will—but I will travel with them, as surety that no further evil may be done. Surely justice is mine, if it be anyone's."

Brown looked much taken aback by this declaration; plainly it wasn't what he'd had in mind at all. But the crowd was in instant sympathy, murmuring agreement at the proposed solution. Everyone had the greatest compassion and respect for Tom Christie in the wake of his daughter's murder, and the general feeling seemed to be that this gesture was one of the greatest magnanimity.

It was, too, as he had in all likelihood just saved our lives—at least for the moment. From the look in his eye, Jamie would strongly have preferred simply to take his chances on killing Richard Brown, but realized that beggars could not be choosers, and acquiesced as gracefully as possible, with a nod of the head.

Christie's gaze rested on me for a moment, then turned to Jamie.

"If it will suit your convenience, Mr. Fraser, perhaps we will leave in the morning? There is no reason why you and your wife should not rest in your own beds."

Jamie bowed to him.

"I thank ye, sir," he said with great formality. Christie nodded back, then turned and went back down the steps, completely ignoring Richard Brown, who was looking at once irritated and confounded.

I saw Kenny Lindsay close his eyes, shoulders slumping in relief. Then Jamie put his hand under my elbow, and we turned, going into our house for what might be the final night spent under its roof.

88

In the Wake of Scandal

T he rain that had threatened arrived in the night, and the day dawned gray, bleak, and wet. Mrs. Bug was in a similar state, sniffling into her apron and repeating over and over, "Oh, if only Arch had been here! But I couldna find anyone save Kenny Lindsay, and by the time he'd run for MacNeill and Abernathy—"

"Dinna fash yourself for it, *a leannan*," Jamie said, and kissed her affectionately on the brow. "It may be for the best. No one was damaged, the house is still standing"—he cast a wistful eye toward the rafters, every beam shaped by his own hand— "and it may be we'll have this wretched matter settled soon, God willing."

"God willing," she echoed fervently, crossing herself. She sniffed and wiped her eyes. "And I've packed a wee bit of food, that ye shouldna starve on the way, sir."

Richard Brown and his men had sheltered under the trees as best they could; no one had offered them hospitality, which was as damning an indication of their unpopularity as could be imagined, Highland standards being what they were in such matters. And as clear an indication of our own unpopularity, that Brown should be permitted to take us into custody.

In consequence, Brown's men were soaking wet, ill-fed, sleepless, and short-tempered. I hadn't slept, either, but I was at least full of breakfast, warm, and—for the moment—dry, which made me feel a little better, though my heart felt hollow and my bones filled with lead as we reached the head of the trail and I looked back across the clearing at the house, with Mrs. Bug standing waving on the porch. I waved back, and then my horse plunged into the darkness of the dripping trees.

It was a grim journey, and silent for the most part. Jamie and I rode close together, but couldn't speak of anything important, in hearing of Brown's men. As for Richard Brown, he was seriously out of countenance.

It was reasonably clear that he had never intended to take me anywhere for trial, but had merely seized upon the pretext as a means of revenging himself on Jamie for Lionel's death—and God knew what he would have done, I reflected, had he known what had really happened to his brother, and Mrs. Bug there within arm's length of him. With Tom Christie along, though, there was nothing he could do; he was obliged to take us to Hillsboro, and he did so with bad grace.

Tom Christie rode like a man in a dream—a bad dream—his face closed and inward-looking, speaking to no one.

The man Jamie had slashed was not there; I supposed he had gone home to Brownsville. The gentleman I had shot was still with us, though.

I couldn't tell how bad the wound was, nor yet whether the bullet had gone into him or merely grazed his side. He wasn't incapacitated, but it was plain from the way he hunched to one side, his face contorting now and then, that he was in pain.

I hesitated for some time. I had brought a small medical kit with me, as well as saddlebags and bedroll. Under the circumstances, I felt relatively little sense of compassion for the man. On the other hand, instinct was strong—and as I said to Jamie in an undertone when we stopped to make camp for the evening, it wouldn't help matters if he died of infection.

I steeled myself to offer to examine and dress the wound, as soon as the opportunity should occur. The man—his name seemed to be Ezra, though under the circumstances, no formal introductions had been made—was in charge of distributing bowls of food at supper, and I waited under the pine where Jamie and I had taken shelter, intending to speak kindly to him when he brought our food.

He came over, a bowl in each hand, shoulders hunched under a leather coat against the rain. Before I could speak, though, he grinned nastily, spat thickly in one bowl, and handed it to me. The other he dropped at Jamie's feet, spattering his legs with dried-venison stew.

"Oops," he said mildly, and turned on his heel.

Jamie contracted sharply, like a big snake coiling, but I got hold of his arm before he could strike.

"Never mind," I said, and raising my voice just a little, said, "Let him rot."

The man's head snapped round, wide-eyed.

"Let him rot," I repeated, staring at him. I'd seen the flush of fever in his face when he came near, and smelled the faint sweet scent of pus.

Ezra looked completely taken back. He hurried back to the sputtering fire, and refused to look in my direction.

I was still holding the bowl he'd given me, and was startled to have it taken from my hand. Tom Christie threw the contents of the bowl into a bush, and handed me his own, then turned away without speaking.

"But—" I started after him, meaning to give it back. We wouldn't starve, thanks to Mrs. Bug's "wee bit of food," which filled one entire saddlebag. Jamie's hand on my arm stopped me, though.

"Eat it, Sassenach," he said softly. "It's kindly meant."

More than kind, I thought. I was aware of hostile eyes upon me, from the group around the fire. My throat was tight, and I had no appetite, but I took my spoon from my pocket and ate.

Beneath a nearby hemlock tree, Tom Christie had wrapped himself in a blanket and lain down alone, his hat pulled down over his face.

It rained all the way to Salisbury. We found shelter in an inn there, and seldom had a fire seemed so welcome. Jamie had brought what cash we had, and in consequence, we could afford a room to ourselves. Brown posted a guard on the stair, but that was merely for show; after all, where would we go?

I stood in front of the fire in my shift, my wet cloak and gown spread over a bench to dry.

"You know," I observed, "Richard Brown hasn't thought this out at all." Not surprising, that, since he hadn't actually intended to take me or us to trial. "Who, exactly, does he mean to hand us over to?"

"The sheriff of the county," Jamie replied, untying his hair and shaking it out over the hearth, so that droplets of water sizzled and popped in the fire. "Or failing that, a justice of the peace, perhaps."

"Yes, but what then? He's got no evidence—no witnesses. How can there be any semblance of a trial?"

Jamie looked at me curiously.

"Ye've never been tried for anything, have ye, Sassenach?"

"You know I haven't."

He nodded.

"I have. For treason."

"Yes? And what happened?"

He ran a hand through his damp hair, considering.

"They made me stand up, and asked my name. I gave it, the judge muttered to his friend for a bit, and then he said, 'Condemned. Imprisonment for life. Put him in irons.' And they took me out to the courtyard and had a blacksmith hammer fetters onto my wrists. The next day we began walking to Ardsmuir."

"They made you *walk* there? From Inverness?"

"I wasna in any great hurry, Sassenach."

I took a deep breath, trying to stem the sinking feeling in the pit of my stomach.

"I see. Well . . . but surely—wouldn't m-murder"—I could just about say it without stammering, but not quite, yet—"be a matter for a jury trial?"

"It might, and certainly I shall insist upon it—if things go so far. Mr. Brown seems to think they may; he's telling everyone in the taproom the story, making us out to be monsters of depravity. Which I must say is no great feat," he added ruefully, "considering the circumstances."

I pressed my lips tight together, to avoid giving a hasty answer.

I knew he knew that I had had no choice—he knew that I knew he had had nothing to do with Malva in the first place—but I could not help but feel a sense of blame in both directions, for this desperate muddle in which we found ourselves. Both for what had happened afterward, and for Malva's death itself—though God knew I would give anything to have her alive again.

He was right about Brown, I realized. Cold and wet, I'd paid little attention to the noises from the taproom below, but I could hear Brown's voice, echoing up the chimney, and from the random words that came through, it was apparent that he was doing exactly what Jamie said—blackening our characters, making it out that he and his Committee of Safety had undertaken the ignoble but necessary job of apprehending us and committing us to justice. And, just incidentally, carefully prejudicing any potential jury members by making sure the story spread abroad in all its scandalous detail.

"Is there anything to be done?" I asked, having listened to as much of this nonsense as I could stomach.

He nodded, and pulled a clean shirt from his saddlebag.

"Go down for supper, and look as little like depraved murderers as possible, *a nighean*."

"Right," I said, and with a sigh, withdrew the ribbon-trimmed cap I had packed.

I shouldn't have been surprised. I had lived long enough to have a fairly cynical view of human nature—and lived long enough in this time to know how directly public opinion expressed itself. And yet I was still shocked, when the first stone hit me in the thigh.

We were some distance south of Hillsboro. The weather continued wet, the roads muddy, and the travel difficult. I think Richard Brown would have been pleased to relinquish us to the sheriff of Rowan county—if such a person had been available. The office, he was informed, was currently unfilled, the last occupant having decamped hurriedly overnight and no one yet found willing to replace him.

A matter of politics, I gathered, the recent sheriff having leaned toward independency, whilst the majority of persons in the county were still strongly Loyalist. I didn't learn the specifics of the incident that had triggered the recent sheriff's hasty departure, but the taverns and inns near Hillsboro were buzzing like hornets' nests in the wake of it.

The Circuit Court had ceased to meet some months before, Brown was informed, the justices who attended it feeling it too dangerous to appear in the present unsettled state of things. The sole justice of the peace he was able to discover felt similarly, and declined point-blank to take custody of us, informing Brown that it was more than his life was worth, to be involved in anything even faintly controversial at the moment.

"But it's nothing to do with politics!" Brown had shouted at him, frustrated. "It's murder, for God's sake—black murder!"

"Anything and everything's political these days, sir," the JP, one Harvey Mickelgrass, informed him sadly, shaking his head. "I should not venture to address even a case of drunk and disorderly, for fear of having my house pulled down around my ears and my wife left widowed. The sheriff attempted to sell his office, but could find no one willing to purchase it. No, sir—you will have to go elsewhere."

Brown would by no means take us to Cross Creek or Campbelton, where Jocasta Cameron's influence was strong, and where the local justice was her good friend, Farquard Campbell. And so we headed south, toward Wilmington.

Brown's men were disedified; they had expected a simple lynching and house-burning, perhaps the odd bit of looting—not this long-drawn-out and tedious plodding from place to place. Their spirits were further lowered when Ezra, who had been clinging to his horse in a dogged daze of fever, fell suddenly into the road and was picked up dead.

I didn't ask to examine the body—and wouldn't have been given leave in any case—but I rather thought from the lolling looks of him that he had simply lost consciousness, tumbled off, and broken his neck.

Not a few of the others cast looks of open fear toward me in the wake of this occurrence, though, and their sense of enthusiasm for the venture diminished visibly.

Richard Brown was not deterred; he would, I was sure, have shot us without mercy long since, had it not been for Tom Christie, silent and gray as the morning fog on the roads. He said little, and that little confined to necessities. I should have thought him moving mechanically, in the numb haze of grief—had I not turned one evening as we camped by the road, to see his eyes fixed upon me, with a look of such naked anguish in them that I glanced hastily away, only to see Jamie, sitting beside me, watching Tom Christie with a very thoughtful expression.

For the most part, though, he kept his face impassive—what could be seen of it, under the shade of his leather slouch hat. And Richard Brown, prevented by Christie's presence from doing us active harm, took every opportunity to spread his version of the tale of Malva's murder—perhaps as much to harrow Tom Christie in the hearing of it, over and over again, as for its effect on our reputations.

At any rate, I should not have been surprised when they stoned us, in a small, nameless hamlet south of Hillsboro—but I was. A young boy had seen us on the road, stared as we rode by—then vanished like a fox, scampering down a bank with the news. And ten minutes later, we rode around a bend in the road and into a fusillade of stones and shrieks.

One struck my mare on the shoulder and she shied violently. I kept my seat narrowly, but was off-balance; another hit me in the thigh, and another high in the chest, knocking the breath from me, and when one more bounced painfully off my head, I lost my grip on the reins, and as the horse, panicked, curvetted and spun, I flew off, landing on the ground with a bone-shaking thud.

I should have been terrified; in fact, I was furious. The stone that had hit me in the head had glanced off—thanks to the thickness of my hair and the cap I wore—but with the infuriating sting of a slap or a pinch, rather than true impact. I was on my feet by reflex, staggering, but caught sight of a jeering boy on the bank above me, hooting and dancing in triumph. I lunged, caught him by the foot and jerked.

He yelped, slipped, and fell on top of me. We crashed to the ground together, and rolled in a tangle of skirts and cloak. I was older, heavier, and completely berserk. All the fear, misery, and uncertainty of the last weeks came to an instant boil, and I punched his sneering face, twice, as hard as I could. I felt something crack in my hand, and pain shot up my arm.

He bellowed, and wriggled to escape—he was smaller than I was, but strong with panic. I struggled to keep a grip on him, got him by the hair—he struck out at me, flailing, and knocked off my cap, getting one hand in my hair and yanking hard.

The pain reignited my fury and I jammed a knee into him, anywhere I could, again, and once more, blindly seeking his soft parts. His mouth opened in a soundless "O" and his eyes bulged; his fingers relaxed and let go of my hair, and I reared up over him and slapped him as hard as I possibly could.

A big rock struck my shoulder with a numbing blow and I was knocked sideways by the impact. I tried to hit him again, but couldn't lift my arm. Panting and sobbing, he writhed free of my cloak and scrambled away on hands and knees, nose bleeding. I whirled on my knees to look after him, and looked straight into the eyes of a young man, his face intent and blazing with excitement, rock at the ready.

It hit me in the cheekbone and I swayed, my vision gone blurry. Then something very large hit me from behind, and I found myself flat on my face, pressed into the ground, the weight of a body on top of mine. It was Jamie; I could tell by the breathless "Holy Mother." His body jerked as the stones hit him; I could hear the horrifying thud of them into his flesh.

There was a lot of shouting going on. I heard Tom Christie's hoarse voice, then the firing of a single shot. More yelling, but of a different character. One or two soft thumps, stones striking earth nearby, a last grunt from Jamie as one slammed into him.

We lay pressed flat for a few moments, and I became aware of the uncomfortably spiky plant squashed under my cheek, the scent of its leaves harsh and bitter in my nose.

Then Jamie sat up, slowly, drawing in his breath with a catch, and I rose in turn on a shaky arm, nearly falling. My cheek was puffed and my hand and shoulder throbbed, but I had no attention to spare for that.

"Are you all right?" Jamie had got halfway to his feet, then sat down again, suddenly. He was pale, and a trickle of blood ran down the side of his face from a cut in his scalp, but he nodded, a hand pressed to his side.

"Aye, fine," he said, but with a breathlessness that told me he likely had cracked ribs. "Ye're all right, Sassenach?"

"Fine." I managed to get to my feet, trembling. Brown's men were scattered, some chasing the horses who had fled in the melee, others cursing, gathering up scattered bits of belongings from the road. Tom Christie was vomiting into the bushes by the road. Richard Brown stood under a tree, watching, his face white. He glanced at me sharply, then away.

We stopped at no more taverns on the way.

89

A Moonlicht Flicht

"W hen ye go to hit someone, Sassenach, ye want to do it in the soft parts. Faces have too many bones. And then there's the teeth to be thinkin' of."

Jamie spread her fingers, gently pressing the scraped, swollen knuckles, and air hissed between her own teeth.

"Thanks so much for the advice. And you've broken your hand *how* many times, hitting people?"

He wanted to laugh; the vision of her pounding that wee boy in a fury of berserk rage, hair flying in the wind and a look of blood in her eye, was one he would treasure. He didn't, though.

"Your hand's not broken, *a nighean*." He curled her fingers, cupping her loose fist with both of his.

"How would you know?" she snapped. "*I'm* the doctor here."

He stopped trying to hide his smile.

"If it were broken," he said, "ye'd be white and puking, not red-faced and crankit."

"Crankit, my arse!" She pulled her hand free, glaring at him as she nursed it against her bosom. She was in fact only slightly flushed, and most attractive, with her hair curling out in a wild mass round her head. One of Brown's men had picked up her fallen cap after the attack, timidly offering it to her. Enraged, she had snatched it from him and stuffed it violently into a saddlebag.

"Are ye hungry, lass?"

"Yes," she admitted grudgingly, as aware as he was that folk with broken bones generally had little appetite immediately, though they ate amazingly, once the pain had backed a bit.

He rummaged in the saddlebag, blessing Mrs. Bug as he came out with a handful of dried apricots and a large wrapped wedge of goat's cheese. Brown's men were cooking something over their fire, but he and Claire had not touched any food but their own, not since the first night.

How much longer might this farce go on? he wondered, breaking off a bit of cheese and handing it to his wife. They had food for perhaps a week, with care. Long enough, maybe, to reach the coast, and the weather held good. And what then?

It had been plain to him from the first that Brown had no plan, and was attempting to deal with a situation that had been out of his control since the first moment. Brown had ambition, greed, and a respectable sense of revenge, but almost no capacity of forethought, that much was clear.

Now, here he was, saddled with the two of them, forced to travel on and on, the unwelcome responsibility dragging like a worn-out shoe tied to a dog's tail. And Brown the hindered dog, snarling and turning in circles, snapping at the thing that hampered him, and biting his own tail in consequence. Half his men had been wounded by the flung stones. Jamie thoughtfully touched a large, painful bruise on the point of his elbow.

He himself had had no choice; now Brown hadn't, either. His men were growing restive; they had crops to tend, and hadn't bargained for what they must see now as a fool's errand.

It would be a simple matter to escape by himself. But then what? He could not leave Claire in Brown's hands, and even were he able to get her safe away, they could not return to the Ridge with matters as they were; to do so would be to find themselves straight back in the pot.

He sighed, then caught his breath and let it out gingerly. He didn't think his ribs were cracked, but they hurt.

"Ye've a bit of ointment, I expect?" he said, nodding at the bag that held her bits of medicine.

"Yes, of course." She swallowed her bite of cheese, reaching for the bag. "I'll put some on that cut on your head."

He let her do that, but then insisted upon anointing her hand in turn. She objected, insisting that she was perfectly fine, needed no such thing, they should save the ointment in case of future need—and yet she let him take her hand and smooth the sweet-smelling cream into her knuckles, the small fine bones of her hand hard under his fingers.

She so hated being helpless in any way—but the armor of righteous fury was wearing off, and while she kept a fierce face for Brown and the rest, he knew she was afraid. Not without reason, either.

Brown was uneasy, unable to settle. He moved to and fro, talking aimlessly with one man or another, needlessly checking the hobbled horses, pouring a cup of chicory coffee and holding it undrunk until it grew cold, then flinging it into the weeds. And all the time, his restless gaze returned to them.

Brown was hasty, impetuous, and half-baked. He was not entirely stupid, Jamie thought. And clearly he had realized that his strategy of spreading gossip and scandal concerning his prisoners in order to endanger them had severe defects, so long as he was himself obliged to continue in close proximity to said prisoners.

Their simple meal finished, Jamie lay down, carefully, and Claire curled herself into him spoonwise, wanting comfort.

Fighting was an exhausting business, and so was fear; she was asleep in moments. Jamie felt the pull of sleep, but would not yield to it yet. He occupied himself instead in reciting some of the poems Brianna had told him—he quite liked the one about the silversmith in Boston, riding to spread the alarm to Lexington, which he considered a handsome piece.

The company was beginning to settle for the night. Brown was still a-fidget, sitting staring darkly at the ground, then leaping to his feet to stride up and down. By contrast, Christie had barely stirred, though he made no move to go to bed. He sat on a rock, his supper barely touched.

A flicker of movement near Christie's boot; a wee small mouse, making feints toward the neglected plate that sat on the ground, filled with bounty.

It had occurred to Jamie a couple of days before, in the vague way that one recognizes a fact unconsciously known for some time, that Tom Christie was in love with his wife.

Poor bugger, he thought. Surely Christie did not believe that

Claire had had aught to do with the death of his daughter; if so, he would not be here. Did he think that Jamie, though . . . ?

He lay in the shelter of the darkness, watching the fire play across Christie's haggard features, his eyes half-hooded, giving no hint of his thoughts. There were men who could be read like books; Tom Christie wasn't one of them. But if ever he had seen a man being eaten alive before his eyes . . .

Was it the fate of his daughter, alone—or also the desperate need of a woman? He'd seen that need before, that gnawing at the soul, and knew it personally. Or *did* Christie think that Claire had killed wee Malva, or been in some way involved? There would be a quandary for an honorable man.

The need of a woman . . . the thought brought him back to the moment, and the awareness that the sounds he had been listening for in the wood behind him were now there. He had known for the past two days that they were followed, but last night they had camped in an open meadow, with no cover at all.

Moving slowly, but with no attempt at furtiveness, he rose, covered Claire with his cloak, and stepped into the wood, like one called by nature.

The moon was pale and hunchbacked and there was little light beneath the trees. He closed his eyes to damp the fire shadow and opened them again to the dark world, that place of shapes that lacked dimension and air that held spirits.

It was no spirit that stepped out from behind the blur of a pine tree, though.

"Blessed Michael defend us," he said softly.

"The blessed host of angels and archangels be with ye, Uncle," said Ian, in the same soft tone. "Though I am thinking that a few thrones and dominations wouldna come amiss, either."

"Well, I wouldna argue, if Divine Intervention chose to take a hand," Jamie said, heartened most amazingly by his nephew's presence. "I'm sure I've no notion how else we shall escape this foolish coil."

Ian grunted at that; Jamie saw his nephew's head turn, checking the faint glow of the camp. Without discussion, they moved further into the wood.

"I canna be gone for long, without they come after me," he said. "First, then—is all well wi' the Ridge?"

Ian lifted a shoulder.

"There's talk," he said, the tone of his voice indicating that "talk" covered everything from auld wives' gossip to the sort of insult that must be settled by violence. "No one killed yet, though. What shall I do, Uncle Jamie?"

"Richard Brown. He's thinking, and God only kens what *that* will lead to."

"He thinks too much; such men are dangerous," Ian said, and laughed. Jamie, who had never known his nephew to read a book willingly, gave him a look of disbelief, but dismissed questions in favor of the pressing concerns of the moment.

"Aye, he is," he said dryly. "He's been spreading the story in pothouses and inns as we go—at a guess, in hopes of rousing public indignation to the point that some poor fool of a constable can be pushed into taking us off his hands, or better yet, that a mob might be stirred up to seize us and hang us out of hand, thus resolving his difficulty."

"Oh, aye? Well, if that's what he had in mind, Uncle, it's working. Ye wouldna countenance some of the things I've heard, following in your tracks."

"I know." Jamie stretched gently, easing his painful ribs. It was only the mercy of God that it hadn't been worse—that, and Claire's rage, which had interrupted the attack, as everyone stopped to watch the engrossing spectacle of her hatcheling her assailant like a bundle of flax.

"It's come home to him, though, that if ye mean to pin a target on someone, it's wise to step away smartly thereafter. He's thinking, as I say. Should he go off, then, or send someone . . ."

"I'll follow, aye, and see what's to do."

He sensed rather than saw Ian's nod; they stood in black shadow, the faint haze of moonlight like fog in the space between the trees. The lad moved, as though to go, then hesitated.

"Ye're sure, Uncle, as it wouldna be better to wait a bit, then creep away? There's nay bracken, but there's decent cover in the hills nearby; we could be safe hidden by dawn."

It was a great temptation. He felt the pull of the dark wild forest, above all, the lure of freedom. If he could but walk away into the greenwood, and stay there . . . But he shook his head.

"It wouldna do, Ian," he said, though he let regret show in his voice. "We should be fugitives, then—and doubtless wi' a price on our heads. With the countryside already roused against us—

broadsides, posted bills? The public would do Brown's work for him, promptly. And then, to run would seem an admission of guilt, forbye."

Ian sighed, but nodded agreement.

"Well, then," he said. He stepped forward and embraced Jamie, squeezing hard for an instant, and then was gone.

Jamie let out a long, tentative breath against the pain of his injured ribs.

"God go with ye, Ian," he said to the dark, and turned back.

When he lay down again beside his wife, the camp was silent. The men lay like logs, wrapped in their blankets. Two figures, though, remained by the embers of the dying fire: Richard Brown and Thomas Christie, each alone on a rock with his thoughts.

Ought he to wake Claire, tell her? He considered for a moment, his cheek against the warm softness of her hair, and reluctantly decided no. It might hearten her a little to know of Ian's presence—but he dare not risk rousing Brown's suspicion; and if Brown were to perceive by any change in Claire's mood or face that something had happened . . . no, best not. At least not yet.

He glanced along the ground at Christie's feet, and saw the faint pale scurry of movement in the dark; the mouse had brought friends to share her feast.

90

Forty-Six Beans
to the Good

At dawn, Richard Brown was gone. The rest of the men seemed grim, but resigned, and under the command of a squatty, morose sort of fellow named Oakes, we resumed our push south.

Something had changed in the night; Jamie had lost a little of the tension that had infused him since our departure from the Ridge. Stiff, sore, and disheartened as I was, I found this change some comfort, though wondering what had caused it. Was it the same thing that had caused Richard Brown to leave on his mysterious errand?

Jamie said nothing, though, beyond inquiring after my hand—which was tender, and so stiff that I couldn't immediately flex my fingers. He continued to keep a watchful eye on our companions, but the lessening of tension had affected them, too; I began to lose my fear that they might suddenly lose patience and string us up, Tom Christie's dour presence notwithstanding.

As though in accord with this more relaxed atmosphere, the weather suddenly cleared, which heartened everyone further. It would have been stretching things to say that there was any sense of rapprochement, but without Richard Brown's constant malevolence, the other men at least became occasionally civil. And as it always did, the tedium and hardships of travel wore everyone down, so that we rolled down the rutted roads like a pack of marbles, occasionally caroming off one another, dusty, silent, and united in exhaustion, if nothing else, by the end of each day.

This neutral state of affairs changed abruptly in Brunswick. For a day or two before, Oakes had been plainly anticipating something, and when we reached the first houses, I could see him beginning to draw great breaths of relief.

It was therefore no surprise when we stopped to refresh ourselves at a pothouse on the edge of the tiny, half-abandoned settlement, to find Richard Brown awaiting us. It *was* a surprise when, without more than a murmured word from Brown, Oakes and two others suddenly seized Jamie, knocking the cup of water from his hand and slamming him against the wall of the building.

I dropped my own cup and flung myself toward them, but Richard Brown grabbed my arm in a viselike grip and dragged me toward the horses.

"Let go! What are you doing? Let go, I say!" I kicked him, and had a good go at scratching out his eyes, but he got hold of both my wrists, and shouted for one of the other men to help. Between the two of them, they got me—still screaming at the top of my lungs—on a horse in front of another of Brown's men. There was a deal of shouting from Jamie's direction, and general hubbub, as a few people came out of the pothouse, staring. None of them seemed disposed to interfere with a large group of armed men, though.

Tom Christie was shouting protests; I glimpsed him hammering on the back of one man, but to no avail. The man behind me wrapped an arm round my middle and jerked it tight, knocking out what breath I had left.

Then we were thundering down the road, Brunswick—and Jamie—disappearing in the dust.

My furious protests, demands, and questions brought no response, of course, beyond an order to be quiet, this accompanied by another warning squeeze of the restraining arm around me.

Shaking with rage and terror, I subsided, and at that point, saw that Tom Christie was still with us, looking shaken and disturbed.

"Tom!" I shouted. "Tom, go back! Don't let them kill him! Please!"

He looked in my direction, startled, rose in his stirrups, and looked back toward Brunswick, then turned toward Richard Brown, shouting something.

Brown shook his head, reined his mount in so that Christie could come up alongside, and leaning over, yelled something at him that must have passed for explanation. Christie clearly didn't like the situation, but after a few impassioned exchanges, he subsided, scowling, and dropped back. He pulled his horse's head aside and circled back to come within speaking distance of me.

"They will not kill nor harm him," he said, raising his voice to be heard over the rumble of hooves and rattle of harness. "Brown's word of honor upon it, he says."

"And you *believe* him, for God's sake?"

He looked disconcerted at that, glanced again at Brown, who had spurred up to ride ahead, then back at Brunswick. Indecision played across his features, but then his lips firmed and he shook his head.

"It will be all right," he said. But he would not meet my eyes, and in spite of my continued entreaties to him to go back, to stop them, he slackened his pace, falling back so that I couldn't see him anymore.

My throat was raw from screaming, and my stomach hurt, bruised and clenched in a knot of fear. Our speed had slowed, now that we had left Brunswick behind, and I concentrated on breathing; I wouldn't speak until I was sure I could do so without my voice trembling.

"Where are you taking me?" I asked finally. I sat stiff in the saddle, enduring an unwanted intimacy with the man behind me.

"New Bern," he said, with a note of grim satisfaction. "And then, thank God, we'll be shut of you at last."

The journey to New Bern passed in a blur of fear, agitation, and physical discomfort. While I did wonder what was about to happen to me, all such speculations were drowned by my anxiety about Jamie.

Tom Christie was plainly my only hope of finding out anything, but he avoided me, keeping his distance—and I found *that* as alarming as anything else. He was clearly troubled, even more so than he had been since Malva's death, but he no longer bore a look of dull suffering; he was actively agitated. I was terribly afraid that he knew or suspected Jamie was dead, but would not admit it—either to me, or to himself.

All of the men clearly shared my captor's urge to be rid of me as soon as possible; we stopped only briefly, when absolutely necessary for the horses to rest. I was offered food, but could not eat. By the time we reached New Bern, I was completely drained from the sheer physical exertion of the ride, but much more so from the constant strain of apprehension.

Most of the men remained at a tavern on the outskirts of the town; Brown and one of the other men took me through the streets, accompanied by a silent Tom Christie, arriving at last at a large house of whitewashed brick. The home, as Brown informed me with a sense of lively pleasure, of Sheriff Tolliver—also, the town gaol.

The sheriff, a darkly handsome sort, viewed me with a sort of interested speculation, mingled with a growing disgust as he heard the crime of which I was accused. I made no attempt at rebuttal or defense; the room was going in and out of focus, and all my attention was required to keep my knees from giving way.

I barely heard most of the exchange between Brown and the sheriff. At the last, though, just before I was led away into the house, I found Tom Christie suddenly beside me.

"Mrs. Fraser," he said, very low. "Believe me, he is safe. I would not have his death on my conscience—nor yours." He was looking at me directly, for the first time in . . . days? weeks? . . . and I found the intensity of his gray eyes both disconcerting and oddly comforting.

"Trust in God," he whispered. "He will deliver the righteous out of all his dangers." And with a sudden hard and unexpected squeeze of my hand, he was gone.

As eighteenth-century gaols went, it could have been worse. The women's quarters consisted of a small room at the back of the sheriff's house, which had likely been a storeroom of sorts originally. The walls were roughly plastered, though some escape-minded former occupant had chipped away a large chunk of the plaster, before discovering that beneath it lay a layer of lath, and beneath *that* an impenetrable wall of baked-clay brick, which confronted me at once with its bland impenetrability when the door was opened.

There was no window, but an oil dip burned on a ledge by the door, casting a faint circle of light that illuminated the daunting bare patch of brick, but left the corners of the room in deep shadow. I couldn't see the night-soil bucket, but knew there was one; the thick, acrid tang of it stung my nose, and I automatically began breathing through my mouth as the sheriff pushed me into the room.

The door closed firmly behind me, and a key grated in the lock.

There was a single, narrow bedstead in the shadows, occupied by a large lump under a threadbare blanket. The lump took its time, but eventually stirred and sat up, resolving itself into a small, plump woman, capless and frowsy with sleep, who sat blinking at me like a dormouse.

"Ermp," she said, and rubbed her eyes with her fists, like a small child.

"So sorry to disturb you," I said politely. My heart had slowed a bit by now, though I was still shaking and short of breath. I pressed my hands flat against the door to stop them trembling.

"Think nothing of it," she said, and yawned suddenly, like a hippopotamus, showing me a set of worn but serviceable molars. Blinking and smacking her lips absently, she reached down beside her, pulled out a battered pair of spectacles, and set them firmly on her nose.

Her eyes were blue, and hugely magnified by the lenses, enormous with curiosity.

"What's your name?" she asked.

"Claire Fraser," I said, watching her narrowly, in case she too might already have heard all about my supposed crime. The bruise on my breast left by the stone that had struck me was still visible, beginning to yellow above the edge of my gown.

"Oh?" She squinted, as though trying to place me, but evidently failed, for she shrugged away the effort. "Got any money?"

"A bit." Jamie had forced me to take almost all the money— not a great deal, but there was a small weight of coin at the bottom of each of the pockets tied around my waist, and a couple of proclamation notes tucked inside my stays.

The woman was a good deal shorter than I, and pillowy in aspect, with large, drooping breasts and several comfortable rolls corrugating her uncorseted middle; she was in her shift, with her gown and stays hung from a nail in the wall. She seemed harmless—and I began to breathe a little more easily, beginning to grasp the fact that at least I was safe for the moment, no longer in danger of sudden, random violence.

The other prisoner made no offensive moves toward me, but hopped down off the bed, bare feet thumping softly in what I realized now was a matted layer of moldy straw.

"Well, call the old bizzom and send for some Holland, then, why don't you?" she suggested cheerfully.

"The . . who?"

Instead of answering, she trundled to the door and banged on it, shouting, "Mrs. Tolliver! Mrs. Tolliver!"

The door opened almost immediately, revealing a tall, thin woman, looking like an annoyed stork.

"Really, Mrs. Ferguson," she said. "You are the most dreadful nuisance. I was just coming to pay my respects to Mrs. Fraser, in any case." She turned her back on Mrs. Ferguson with magisterial dignity and inclined her head a bare inch toward me.

"Mrs. Fraser. I am Mrs. Tolliver."

I had a split second in which to decide how to react, and chose the prudent—if galling—course of genteel submission, bowing to her as though she were the Governor's lady.

"Mrs. Tolliver," I murmured, careful not to meet her eyes. "How kind of you."

She twitched, sharp-eyed, like a bird spotting the stealthy progress of a worm through the grass—but I had firm control of my features by now, and she relaxed, detecting no sarcasm.

"You are welcome," she said with chilly courtesy. "I am to see to your welfare, and acquaint you with our custom. You will receive one meal each day, unless you wish to send to the ordinary for more—at your own expense. I will bring you a basin for washing once each day. You'll carry your own slops. And—"

"Oh, stuff your custom, Maisie," said Mrs. Ferguson, butting into Mrs. Tolliver's set speech with the comfortable assumption of long acquaintance. "She's got some money. Fetch us a bottle of geneva, there's a good girl, and then if you must, you can tell her what's what."

Mrs. Tolliver's narrow face tightened in disapproval, but her eyes twitched toward me, bright in the dim light of the rush dip. I ventured a hesitant gesture toward my pocket, and her lower lip sucked in. She glanced over her shoulder, then took a quick step toward me.

"A shilling, then," she whispered, hand held open between us. I dropped the coin into her palm, and it disappeared at once beneath her apron.

"You've missed supper," she announced in her normal disapproving tones, stepping backward. "However, as you've just come, I shall make an allowance and bring you something."

"How kind of you," I said again.

The door closed firmly behind her, shutting out light and air, and the key turned in the lock.

The sound of it set off a tiny spark of panic, and I stamped on it hard. I felt like a dried skin, stuffed to the eyeballs with the tinder of fear, uncertainty, and loss. It would take no more than a spark to ignite that and burn me to ashes—and neither I nor Jamie could afford that.

"She drinks?" I asked, turning back to my new roommate with an assumption of coolness.

"Do you know anyone who doesn't, given the chance?" Mrs. Ferguson asked reasonably. She scratched her ribs. "Fraser, she said. You aren't the—"

"I am," I said, rather rudely. "I don't want to talk about it."

Her eyebrows shot up, but she nodded equably.

"Just as you like," she said. "Any good at cards?"

"Loo or whist?" I asked warily.

"Know a game called brag?"

"No." Jamie and Brianna played it now and then, but I had never acquainted myself with the rules.

"That's all right; I'll teach you." Reaching under the mattress, she pulled out a rather limp deck of pasteboards and fanned them expertly, waving them gently under her nose as she smiled at me.

"Don't tell me," I said. "You're in here for cheating at cards?"

"Cheat? Me? Not a bit of it," she said, evidently unoffended. "Forgery."

Rather to my own surprise, I laughed. I was still feeling shaky, but Mrs. Ferguson was definitely proving a welcome distraction.

"How long have you been in here?" I asked.

She scratched at her head, realized that she wasn't wearing a cap, and turned to pull one out of the rumpled bedding.

"Oh—a month, just about." Putting on the crumpled cap, she nodded at the doorpost beside me. Turning to look, I saw that it was crosshatched with dozens of small nicks, some old and dark with dirt, some freshly scratched, showing raw yellow wood. The sight of the marks made my stomach plunge again, but I took a deep breath and turned my back on them.

"Have you had a trial yet?"

She shook her head, light glinting off her spectacles.

"No, praise God. I hear from Maisie that the court's shut down; all the justices gone into hiding. Hasn't been anybody tried in the last two months."

This was not good news. Evidently the thought showed on my face, for she leaned forward and patted my arm sympathetically.

"I wouldn't be in a hurry, dearie. Not in your shoes, I wouldn't. If they've not tried you, they can't hang you. And while I have met those as say the waiting's like to kill them, I've not seen anybody die of it. And I *have* seen them die at the end of a rope. Nasty business, that is."

She spoke almost negligently, but her own hand rose, as though by itself, and touched the soft white flesh of her neck. She swallowed, the tiny bump of her Adam's apple bobbing.

I swallowed, too, an unpleasantly constricted feeling in my own throat.

"But I'm innocent," I said, wondering even as I said it how I could sound so uncertain.

"'Course you are," she said stoutly, giving my arm a squeeze. "You stick to it, dearie—don't you let 'em bully-whack you into admitting the least little thing!"

"I won't," I assured her dryly.

"One of these days, a mob's like to come *here*," she said, nodding. "String up the sheriff, if he don't look sharp. He's not popular, Tolliver."

"I can't imagine why not—a charming fellow like that." I wasn't sure how I felt about the prospect of a mob storming the house. Stringing up Sheriff Tolliver was all very well, so far as that went—but with the memory of the hostile crowds in Salisbury and Hillsboro fresh in mind, I wasn't sure at all that they'd stop with the sheriff. Dying at the hands of a lynch mob wasn't at all preferable to the slower sort of judicial murder I likely faced. Though I supposed there was always a possibility of escaping in the riot.

And go where, if you did? I wondered.

With no good answer to that question, I shoved it to the back of my mind and turned my attention back to Mrs. Ferguson, who was still holding out the cards invitingly.

"All right," I said. "But not for money."

"Oh, no," Mrs. Ferguson assured me. "Perish the thought. But we must have some sort of stake to make it interesting. We'll play for beans, shall we?" She set down the cards, and digging under the pillow, withdrew a small pouch, from which she poured a handful of small white beans.

"Splendid," I said. "And when we're finished, we'll plant them, shall we, and hope for a giant beanstalk to spring up and burst through the roof, so we can escape up it."

She burst into giggles at that, which somehow made me feel very slightly better.

"From your mouth to God's ear, dearie!" she said. "I'll deal first, shall I?"

Brag appeared to be a form of poker. And while I had lived with a cardsharp long enough to know one when I saw one, Mrs. Ferguson appeared to be playing honestly—for the moment. I was forty-six beans to the good, by the time Mrs. Tolliver returned.

The door opened without ceremony, and she came in, holding a three-legged stool and a chunk of bread. This latter appeared to be both my supper and her ostensible excuse for visiting the cell, for she shoved it at me with a loud, "This will have to keep you 'til tomorrow, Mrs. Fraser!"

"Thank you," I said mildly. It was fresh, and appeared to have been hastily dragged through bacon drippings, in lieu of butter. I bit into it without hesitation, having sufficiently recovered from shock now as to feel very hungry indeed.

Mrs. Tolliver, glancing over her shoulder to be sure the coast was clear, shut the door quietly, put down the stool, and drew a squat bottle from her pocket, blue glass and filled with some clear liquid.

She pulled the cork from it, tilted it, and drank deeply, her long, lean throat moving convulsively.

Mrs. Ferguson said nothing, but watched the process with a sort of analytic attention, light glinting from her spectacles, as though comparing Mrs. Tolliver's behavior with that of previous occasions.

Mrs. Tolliver lowered the bottle and stood for a moment grasping it, then handed it abruptly to me and sat down suddenly on the stool, breathing heavily.

I wiped the neck of the bottle as inconspicuously as possible on my sleeve, then took a token sip. It was gin, all right—heavily flavored with juniper berries to hide the poor quality, but powerfully alcoholic.

Mrs. Ferguson took a healthy guzzle in her turn, and so we continued, passing the bottle from hand to hand, exchanging small cordialities with it. Her first thirst slaked, Mrs. Tolliver became almost affable, her frosty manner thawing substantially. Even so, I waited until the bottle was nearly empty before asking the question foremost in my mind.

"Mrs. Tolliver, the men who brought me—did you happen to hear them say anything about my husband?"

She put a fist to her mouth to stifle a belch.

"Say anything?"

"About where he is," I amended.

She blinked a little, looking blank.

"I didn't hear," she said. "But I suppose they may have told Tolly."

Mrs. Ferguson handed down the bottle to her—we were sitting side by side on the bed, that being the only place to sit in the small room—nearly falling off the bed in the process.

"S'pose you could ask him, could you, Maisie?" she said.

An uneasy look came into Mrs. Tolliver's eyes, glazed as they were.

"Oh, no," she said, shaking her head. "He doesn't talk to me about such things. Not my business."

I exchanged a glance with Mrs. Ferguson, and she shook her head slightly; best not to press the matter now.

Worried as I was, I found it difficult to abandon the subject, but plainly there was nothing to be done. I gathered what shreds of patience I had, estimating how many bottles of gin I could afford before my money ran out—and what I might accomplish with them.

I lay still that night, breathing the damp, thick air with its scents of mold and urine. I could smell Sadie Ferguson next to me, too: a faint miasma of stale sweat, overlaid with a strong perfume of gin. I tried to close my eyes, but every time I did, small waves of claustrophobia washed over me; I could feel the sweating plaster walls draw closer, and gripped my fists in the cloth of the mattress ticking, to keep from throwing myself at the locked door. I had a nasty vision of myself, pounding and shrieking, my nails torn and bloody from clawing at the unyielding wood, my cries unheard in the darkness—and no one ever coming.

I thought it a distinct possibility. I had heard more from Mrs. Ferguson regarding Sheriff Tolliver's unpopularity. If he were to be attacked and dragged from his home by a mob—or to lose his nerve and run—the chances of him or his wife remembering the prisoners were remote.

A mob might find us—and kill us, in the madness of the moment. Or not find us, and fire the house. The storeroom was clay brick, but the adjoining kitchen was timber; damp or not, the place would burn like a torch, leaving nothing but that bloody brick wall standing.

I took an especially deep breath, smell notwithstanding, exhaled, and shut my eyes with decision.

Sufficient unto the day is the evil thereof. That had been one of Frank's favorite expressions, and by and large, a good sentiment.

Depends a bit on the day, though, doesn't it? I thought in his direction.

Does it? You tell me. The thought was there, vivid enough that I might have heard it—or only imagined it. If I had imagined it, though, I had imagined also a tone of dry amusement that was particularly Frank's.

Fine, I thought. *Reduced to having philosophical arguments with a ghost. It's been a worse day than I thought.*

Imagination or not, the thought had succeeded in wrenching my attention off the single-minded track of worry. I felt a sense of invitation—or temptation, perhaps. The urge to talk to him. The need to escape into conversation, even if one-sided . . . and imaginary.

No. I won't use you that way, I thought, a little sadly. *Not right that I should only think of you when I need distraction, and not for your own sake.*

And do you never think of me, for my own sake? The question floated in the darkness of my eyelids. I could see his face, quite clearly, the lines of it curved in humor, one dark eyebrow raised. I was dimly surprised; it had been so long since I thought of him in any focused way that I should have long since forgotten exactly what he looked like. But I hadn't.

And I suppose that's the answer to your question, then, I thought silently to him. *Good night, Frank.*

I turned onto my side, facing the door. I felt a little calmer now. I could just make out the outlines of the door, and being able to see it lessened that feeling of being buried alive.

I closed my eyes again, and tried to concentrate on the processes of my own body. That often helped, bringing me a sense of quiet, listening to the purling of blood through my vessels and the subterranean gurglings of organs all carrying peacefully on without the slightest need of my conscious direction. Rather like sitting in the garden, listening to the bees hum in their hives—

I stopped *that* thought in its tracks, feeling my heart jolt in memory, electric as a bee sting.

I thought quite fiercely about my heart, the physical organ, its thick soft chambers and delicate valves—but what I felt was a soreness there. There were hollow places in my heart.

Jamie. A gaping, echoing hollow, cold and deep as the crevasse of a glacier. Bree. Jemmy. Roger. And Malva, like a tiny, deep-drilled sore, an ulcer that wouldn't heal.

I had managed so far to ignore the rustlings and heavy breathings of my companion. I couldn't ignore the hand that brushed my neck, then slipped down my chest and rested lightly, cupped around my breast.

I stopped breathing. Then, very slowly, exhaled. Entirely without my intent, my breast settled into her cupped palm. I felt a touch on my back; a thumb, gently tracing the groove of my spine through my shift.

I understood the need of human comfort, the sheer hunger for touch. I had taken it, often, and given it, part of the fragile web of humanity, constantly torn, constantly made new. But there was that in Sadie Ferguson's touch that spoke of more than simple warmth, or the need of company in the dark.

I took hold of her hand, and lifting it from my breast, squeezed the fingers gently shut, and put it firmly away from me, folded back against her own bosom.

"No," I said softly.

She hesitated, moved her hips so that her body curved behind me, thighs warm and round against mine, offering encompassment and refuge.

"No one would know," she whispered, still hopeful. "I could make you forget—for a bit." Her hand stroked my hip, gentle, insinuating.

If she could, I thought wryly, I might be tempted. But that pathway was not one I could take.

"No," I said more firmly, and shifted, rolling onto my back, as far away as I could get—which was roughly an inch and a half. "I'm sorry—but no."

She was silent for a moment, then sighed heavily.

"Oh, well. Perhaps a bit later."

"No!"

The noises from the kitchen had ceased, and the house settled into silence. It wasn't the silence of the mountains, though, that cradle of boughs and whispering winds and the vast deep of the starry sky. It was the silence of a town, disturbed by smoke and the fogged dim glow of hearth and candle; filled with slumbering thoughts unleashed from waking reason, roaming and uneasy in the dark.

"Could I hold you?" she asked wistfully, and her fingers brushed my cheek. "Only that."

"No," I said again. But I reached for her hand, and held it. And so we fell asleep, hands chastely—and firmly—linked between us.

We were roused by what I thought at first was the wind, moaning in the chimney whose back bulged into our cubbyhole. The moaning grew louder, though, broke into a full-throated scream, then stopped abruptly.

"Ye gods and little fishes!" Sadie Ferguson sat up, eyes wide and blinking, groping for her spectacles. "What was that?"

"A woman in labor," I said, having heard that particular pattern of sounds fairly often. The moaning was starting up again. "And *very* near her time." I slid off the bed and shook my shoes, dislodging a small roach and a couple of silverfish who had taken shelter in the toes.

We sat for nearly an hour, listening to the alternate moaning and screaming.

"Shouldn't it stop?" Sadie said, swallowing nervously. "Shouldn't the child be birthed by now?"

"Perhaps," I said absently. "Some babies take longer than others." I had my ear pressed to the door, trying to make out what was going on on the other side. The woman, whoever she was, was in the kitchen, and no more than ten feet away from me. I heard Maisie Tolliver's voice now and then, muffled and sounding doubtful. But for the most part, only the rhythmic panting, moaning, and screaming.

Another hour of it, and my nerves were becoming frayed. Sadie was on the bed, the pillow pressed down hard over her head, in hopes of blocking the noise.

Enough of this, I thought, and when next I heard Mrs. Tolliver's voice, I banged on the door with the heel of my shoe, shouting, "Mrs. Tolliver!" as loudly as I could, to be heard over the noise.

She did hear me, and after a moment, the key grated in the lock and a wave of light and air fell into the cell. I was momentarily blinded by the daylight, but blinked and made out the shape of a woman on her hands and knees by the hearth, facing me. She was black, bathed in sweat, and, raising her head, howled like a wolf. Mrs. Tolliver started as though someone had run a pin into her from behind.

"Excuse me," I said, pushing past her. She made no move to stop me, and I caught a strong blast of juniper-scented gin fumes as I brushed by her.

The black woman sank down on her elbows, panting, her uncovered rear in the air. Her belly hung like a ripe guava, pale in the sweat-soaked shift that clung to it.

I asked sharp questions in the brief interval before the next howl, and ascertained that this was her fourth child and that she had been laboring since her water had broken the night before. Mrs. Tolliver contributed the information that she was also a prisoner, and a slave. I might have guessed that, from the purplish weals on her back and buttocks.

Mrs. Tolliver was of little other use, swaying glassy-eyed over me, but had managed to provide a small pile of rags and a basin of water, which I used to mop the woman's sweating face. Sadie Ferguson poked her bespectacled nose cautiously out of the cell, but drew back hastily when the next howl broke forth.

It was a breech birth, which accounted for the difficulty, and the next quarter-hour was hair-raising for all concerned. At length, though, I eased a small baby into the world, feet first, slimy, motionless, and the most unearthly shade of pale blue.

"Oh," said Mrs. Tolliver, sounding disappointed. "It's dead."

"Good," said the mother, in a hoarse, deep voice, and closed her eyes.

"Damned if he is," I said, and turned the child hastily face-down, tapping its back. No movement, and I brought the sealed, waxy face to my own, covered nose and mouth with my own mouth, and sucked hard, then turned my head to spit away the mucus and fluid. Face slimy and the taste of silver in my mouth, I blew gently into him, paused, holding him, limp and slippery as a fresh fish, blew—and saw his eyes open, a deeper blue than his skin, vaguely interested.

He took a startled, gasping breath and I laughed, a sudden wellspring of joy bubbling up from my depths. The nightmare memory of another child, a flicker of life blinking out between my hand, faded away. This child was well and truly lit, burning like a candle with a soft, clear flame.

"Oh!" said Mrs. Tolliver, again. She leaned forward to look, and an enormous smile spread across her face. "Oh, oh!"

The baby started crying. I cut the cord, wrapped him in some of the rags, and with some reservation, handed him to Mrs. Tolliver, hoping she wouldn't drop him in the fire. Then I turned my attention to the mother, who was drinking thirstily from the basin, water spilling down her front and soaking the already wet shift further.

She lay back and allowed me to tend her, but without speaking, rolling her eyes occasionally toward the child with a brooding, hostile look.

I heard footsteps coming through the house, and the sheriff appeared, looking surprised.

"Oh, Tolly!" Mrs. Tolliver, smeared with birth fluids and reeking of gin, turned to him happily, holding out the baby to him. "Look, Tolly, it's alive!"

The sheriff looked quite taken aback, and his brow furrowed as he looked at his wife, but then he seemed to catch the scent of her happiness, above the gin. He leaned forward and touched the little bundle gently, his stern face relaxing.

"That's good, Maisie," he said. "Hallo, little fellow." He caught sight of me, then, kneeling on the hearth, doing my best to clean up with a rag and what was left of the water.

"Mrs. Fraser brought the child," Mrs. Tolliver explained eagerly. "It was laid catty-wumpus, but she brought it so cleverly, and made it breathe—we thought 'twas dead, it was so still, but it wasn't! Isn't that wonderful, Tolly?"

"Wonderful," the sheriff repeated a little bleakly. He gave me a hard look, then transferred the same look to the new mother, who gazed back with a sullen indifference. He beckoned me to my feet, then, and with a curt bow, gestured me back into the cell and shut the door.

Only then did I recall what it was he thought I'd done. Little wonder if my juxtaposition with a newborn child made him a trifle nervous, I supposed. I was wet and filthy, and the cell seemed particularly hot and airless. Nonetheless, the miracle of birth was still tingling through my synapses, and I sat down on the bed, still smiling, a wet rag in my hand.

Sadie was regarding me with respect, mingled with a slight revulsion.

"That's the messiest business I ever did see," she said. "Heavens above, is it always like that?"

"More or less. Haven't you ever seen a child born? You've never had one yourself?" I asked curiously. She shook her head vigorously, and made the sign of the horns, which made me laugh, giddy as I was.

"Had I ever been disposed to let a man near me, the thought of *that* would dissuade me," she assured me fervently.

"Oh, yes?" I said, belatedly recalling her overtures of the night before. It *wasn't* merely comfort she'd been offering, then. "And what about *Mister* Ferguson?"

She gave me a demure look, blinking through her spectacles.

"Oh, he was a farmer—*much* older than I. Dead of the pleurisy, these five years gone."

And totally fictitious, I was inclined to think. But a widow had a great deal more freedom than did a maid or a wife, and if ever I saw a woman capable of taking care of herself . . .

I had been paying no attention to the sounds in the kitchen, but at this point, there was a heavy crash and the sheriff's voice, cursing. No sound of the child or Mrs. Tolliver.

"Taking the black bitch back to her quarters," Sadie said, with such a hostile intonation that I glanced at her in amazement.

"Didn't you know?" she said, seeing my surprise. "She's killed her babies. They can hang her, now she's borne this one."

"Oh," I said a little blankly. "No. I didn't know." The noises in the kitchen receded, and I sat staring at the rush dip, the sense of life still moving in my hands.

91

A Reasonably Neat Scheme

W ater lapped just under Jamie's ear, Jamie's ear, the mere sound of it making him feel queasy. The reek of decaying mud and dead fish didn't help, nor did the dunt he'd taken when he fell against the wall.

He shifted, trying to find some position that would ease head, stomach, or both. They'd trussed him like a boiled fowl, but he managed with some effort to roll onto his side and bring his knees up, which helped a bit.

He was in a dilapidated boat shed of some sort; he'd seen it in the last of the twilight, when they'd brought him down to the shore—he'd thought at first they meant to drown him—and carried him inside, dropping him on the floor like a sack of flour.

"Hurry up, Ian," he muttered, shifting again, in increasing discomfort. "I'm a great deal too old for this sort of nonsense."

He could only hope his nephew had been close enough when Brown moved to have been able to follow, and to have some notion where he was now; certainly the lad would be looking. The shore where the shed stood was open, no cover, but there was plenty among the brush below Fort Johnston, standing on the headland a little way above him.

The back of his head throbbed dully, giving him a nasty taste in the back of the mouth, and a disquieting echo of the shattering headaches he used to suffer in the wake of an ax wound that had cracked his skull, many years before. He was shocked at how easily the recollection of those headaches came back; it had happened a lifetime ago, and he had thought even the memory of it dead and buried. His skull clearly had a much more vivid memory of its own, though, and was determined to make him sick by way of revenge for his forgetfulness.

The moon was up, and bright; the light shone soft through the cracks between the crude boards of the wall. Dim as it was, it seemed to shift, wavering in a disturbingly qualmish fashion, and he shut his eyes, concentrating grimly on what he might do to Richard Brown, and he got the man alone someday.

Where in the name of Michael and all the saints had he taken Claire, and why? Jamie's only comfort was that Tom Christie had gone with them. He was fairly sure that Christie wouldn't let them kill her—and if Jamie could find him, he would lead him to her.

A sound reached him above the nauseating lapping of the tide. Faint whistling—then singing. He could just make out the words, and smiled a little, in spite of everything. *"Marry me, marry me, minister—or else I'll be your priest, your priest—or else I'll be your priest."*

He shouted, though it hurt his head, and within a few moments, Ian, the dear wee lad, was beside him, cutting through the ropes. He rolled over, unable for a moment to make his cramped muscles work, then managed to get his hands under him and rise enough to vomit.

"All right, Uncle Jamie?" Ian sounded vaguely amused, damn him.

"I'll do. D'ye ken where Claire is?" He got to his feet, swaying, and was fumbling at his breeches; his fingers felt like sausages, and the broken one was throbbing, the pins and needles of returning circulation stabbing through the jagged ends of bone. All discomfort was forgotten for an instant, though, in the rush of over-whelming relief.

"Jesus, Uncle Jamie," Ian said, impressed. "Aye, I do. They've taken her to New Bern. There's a sheriff there that Forbes says might take her."

"Forbes?" He swung round in his astonishment, and nearly fell, saving himself with a hand on the creaking wood wall. "Neil Forbes?"

"The very same." Ian caught him with a hand beneath his elbow to steady him; the flimsy board had cracked under his weight. "Brown went here and there and talked to this one and that—but it was Forbes he did business with at last, in Cross Creek."

"Ye heard what they said?"

"I heard." Ian's voice was casual, but with an underlying ex-citement—and no little pride in his accomplishment.

Brown's aim was simple at this point—to rid himself of the en-cumbrance the Frasers had become. He knew of Forbes and his relations with Jamie, owing to all the gossip after the tar incident in the summer of last year, and the confrontation at Mecklenberg in May. And so he offered to hand the two of them over to Forbes, for what use the lawyer might make of the situation.

"So he strode to and fro a bit, thinking—Forbes, I mean—they were in his warehouse, ken, by the river, and me hiding behind the barrels o' tar. And then he laughs, as though he's just thought of something clever."

Forbes's suggestion was that Brown's men should take Jamie, suitably bound, to a small landing that he owned, near Brunswick. From there, he would be taken onto a ship headed for England, and thus safely removed from interference in the affairs of either Forbes or Brown—and, incidentally, rendered unable to defend his wife.

Claire, meanwhile, should be committed to the mercies of the law. If she were to be found guilty, well, that would be the end of her. If not, the scandal attendant upon a trial would both occupy the attention of anyone connected to her and destroy any influ-ence they might have—thus leaving Fraser's Ridge ripe for the pickings, and Neil Forbes a clear field toward claiming leadership of the Scottish Whigs in the colony.

Jamie listened to this in silence, torn between anger and a re-luctant admiration.

"A reasonably neat scheme," he said. He was feeling steadier now, the queasiness disappearing with the cleansing flow of anger through his blood.

"Oh, it gets better, Uncle," Ian assured him. "Ye recall a gentleman named Stephen Bonnet?"

"I do. What about him?"

"It's Mr. Bonnet's ship, Uncle, that's to take ye to England." Amusement was beginning to show in his nephew's voice again. "It seems Lawyer Forbes has had a verra profitable partnership with Bonnet for some time—him and some merchant friends in Wilmington. They've shares in both the ship and its cargoes. And since the English blockade, the profits have been greater still; I take it that our Mr. Bonnet is a most experienced smuggler."

Jamie said something extremely foul in French, and went quickly to look out of the shed. The water lay calm and beautiful, a moon path stretching silver out to sea. There was a ship out there; small and black and perfect as a spider on a sheet of paper. Bonnet's?

"Christ," he said. "When will they come in, d'ye think?"

"I dinna ken," Ian said, sounding unsure for the first time. "Is the tide coming in, would ye say, Uncle? Or going out?"

Jamie glanced down at the water rippling under the boathouse, as though it might offer some clue.

"How would I know, for God's sake? And what difference would it make?" He rubbed a hand hard over his face, trying to think. They'd taken his dirk, of course. He had a *sgian dhu,* carried in his stocking, but somehow doubted that its three-inch blade would offer much help in the present situation.

"What have ye got by way of weapons, Ian? Ye dinna have your bow with ye, I don't suppose?"

Ian shook his head regretfully. He had joined Jamie in the door of the boathouse, and the moon showed the hunger in his face as he eyed the ship.

"I've two decent knives, a dirk, and a pistol. There's my rifle, but I left it with the horse." He jerked his head toward the dark line of the distant wood. "Shall I fetch it? They might see me."

Jamie thought for a moment, tapping his fingers against the jamb of the door, 'til the pain of the broken one made him stop. The urge to lie in wait for Bonnet and take him was a physical thing; he understood Ian's hunger, and shared it. But his rational mind was busy reckoning the odds, and would insist upon presenting them, little as the vengefully animal part of him wished to know them.

There was not yet any sign of a boat coming from the ship. Always assuming that the ship out there was indeed Bonnet's—and that, they didn't know for sure—it might still be hours before anyone came to fetch him away. And when they did, what odds that Bonnet himself would come? He was the ship's captain; would he come on such an errand, or send minions?

With a rifle, if Bonnet *were* in the boat, Jamie would wager any amount that he could shoot the man from ambush. If he were in the boat. If he were recognizable in the dark. And while he could hit him, he might not kill him.

If Bonnet were not in the boat, though . . . then it would be a matter of waiting 'til the boat came close enough, leaping aboard, and overpowering whoever was aboard—how many would come on such an errand? Two, three, four? They must all be killed or disabled, and then it would be a matter of rowing the damn boat back out to the ship—where all aboard would doubtless have noticed the stramash taking place on shore, and be prepared either to drop a cannonball through the bottom of the boat or to wait for them to haul alongside and then pick them off from the rail with small-arms fire, like sitting ducks.

And if they should somehow succeed in getting aboard without notice—then searching the goddamn ship for Bonnet himself, hunting him down, and killing him, without attracting undue notice from the crew . . .

This laborious analysis ran through his mind in the time it took to breathe, and was as quickly dismissed. If they were to be captured or killed, Claire would be alone and defenseless. He could not risk it. Still, he thought, trying to comfort himself, he could find Forbes—and would, when the time came.

"Aye, well, then," he said, and turned away with a sigh. "Have ye but the one horse, Ian?"

"Aye," Ian said with a matching sigh. "But I ken where we can maybe steal another."

92

Amanuensis

Two days passed. Hot, damp days in the sweltering dark, and I could feel various kinds of mold, fungus, and rot trying to take hold in my crevices—to say nothing of the omnivorous, omnipresent cockroaches, who seemed determined to nibble my eyebrows the moment the light was put out. The leather of my shoes was clammy and limp, my hair hung lank and dirty, and—like Sadie Ferguson—I took to spending most of my time in my shift.

When Mrs. Tolliver appeared and ordered us to come assist with the washing, therefore, we abandoned the latest game of loo—she was winning—and nearly pushed each other over in our haste to oblige.

It was much hotter in the yard, with the laundry fire roaring, and quite as damp as it had been in the cell, with the thick clouds of moisture boiling off the big kettle of clothes and plastering strands of hair to our faces. Our shifts already clung to our bodies, the grubby linen almost transparent with sweat—laundry was heavy work. There were, however, no bugs, and if the sun shone blinding, and fierce enough to redden my nose and arms—well, it shone, and that was something to be grateful for.

I asked Mrs. Tolliver about my erstwhile patient and her child, but she merely pressed her lips tight and shook her head, looking pinched and severe. The sheriff had been absent the night before; there had been no sound of his booming voice in the kitchen. And from the green-gilled looks of Maisie Tolliver herself, I diagnosed a long and solitary night with the gin bottle, followed by a fairly ghastly dawn.

"You'll feel much better if you sit in the shade and sip . . . water," I said. "Lots of water." Tea or coffee would be better, but these substances were more costly than gold in the colony, and I doubted a sheriff's wife would have any. "If you have any ipecacuanha . . . or perhaps some mint . . ."

"I thank you for your valuable opinion, Mrs. Fraser!" she snapped, though she swayed, rather, and her cheeks were pale and glossy with sweat.

I shrugged, and bent my attention to the task of levering a wad of sopping, steaming clothes from the filthy suds with a five-foot wooden laundry spoon, so worn with use that my sweaty hands slipped on the smooth wood.

We got the lot laboriously washed, rinsed, scaldingly wrung, and hung upon a line to dry, then sank gasping into the thin line of shade afforded by the side of the house, and took turns passing a tin dipper back and forth, gulping lukewarm water from the well bucket. Mrs. Tolliver, disregarding her elevated social position, sat down, too, very suddenly.

I turned to offer her the dipper, only to see her eyes roll back into her head. She didn't so much fall as dissolve backward, sub-siding slowly into a heap of damp, checked gingham.

"Is she dead?" Sadie Ferguson inquired with interest. She glanced to and fro, obviously estimating the chances of making a run for it.

"No. Bad hangover, possibly aggravated by a slight case of sunstroke." I'd got hold of her pulse, which was light and fast, but quite steady. I was myself debating the wisdom of abandoning Mrs. Tolliver to the dangers of aspirating her own vomit and ab-sconding, even barefoot and in my shift, but was forestalled by male voices coming round the corner of the house.

Two men—one was Tolliver's constable, whom I'd seen briefly when Brown's men had delivered me to the gaol. The other was a stranger, very well dressed, with silver coat buttons and a silk waistcoat, rather the worse for sweat stains. This gentleman, a heavyset sort of about forty, frowned at the scene of dissipation before him.

"Are these the prisoners?" he asked in tones of distaste.

"Aye, sir," the constable said. "Leastwise, the two in their shifts is. 'Tother one's the sheriff's wife."

Silver Buttons's nostrils pinched in briefly in receipt of this in-telligence, then flared.

"Which is the midwife?"

"That would be me," I said, straightening up and trying for an air of dignity. "I am Mrs. Fraser."

"Are you," he said, his tone indicating that I might have said I was Queen Charlotte, for all it mattered to him. He looked me up and down in a disparaging fashion, shook his head, then turned to the sweating constable.

"What is she charged with?"

The constable, a rather dim young man, pursed his lips at this, looking dubiously back and forth between us.

"Ahh . . . well, one of 'em's a forger," he said, "and 'tother's a murderess. But as to which bein' which . . ."

"I'm the murderess," Sadie said bravely, adding loyally, "She's a very fine midwife!" I looked at her in surprise, but she shook her head slightly and compressed her lips, adjuring me to keep quiet.

"Oh. Hmm. All right, then. Have you a gown . . . madam?" At my nod, he said briefly, "Get dressed," and turned to the constable, taking out a vast silk handkerchief from his pocket, with which to wipe his broad pink face. "I'll take her, then. You'll tell Mr. Tolliver."

"I will, sir," the constable assured him, more or less bowing and scraping. He glanced down at the unconscious form of Mrs. Tolliver, then frowned at Sadie.

"You, there. Take her inside and see to her. Hop!"

"Oh, yes, sir," Sadie said, and gravely pushed up her sweat-fogged spectacles with one forefinger. "Right away, sir!"

I had no opportunity to speak with Sadie, and barely time enough to struggle into my bedraggled gown and stays and seize my small bag before being escorted into a carriage—rather bedraggled itself, but once of good quality.

"Would you mind telling me who you are, and where you're taking me?" I inquired, after we had rattled through two or three cross streets, my companion gazing out the window with an abstracted sort of frown.

My question roused him, and he blinked at me, only then seeming to realize that I was not in fact an inanimate object.

"Oh. Beg pardon, madam. We are going to the Governor's Palace. Have you not a cap?"

"No."

He grimaced, as though he'd expected nothing else, and resumed his private thoughts.

They'd finished the place, and very nicely, too. William Tryon, the previous governor, had built the Governor's Palace, but had been sent to New York before construction had been finished. Now the enormous brick edifice with its graceful spreading wings was complete, even to the lawns and ivy beds that lined the drive, though the stately trees that would eventually surround it were mere saplings. The carriage pulled up on the drive, but we did not—of course—enter by the imposing front entrance, but rather scuttled round the back and down the stairs to the servants' quarters in the basement.

Here I was hastily shoved into a maid's room, handed a comb, basin, and ewer, and a borrowed cap, and urged to make myself look less like a slattern, as quickly as possible.

My guide—Mr. Webb was his name, as I learned from the cook's respectful greeting to him—waited with obvious impatience while I made my hasty ablutions, then grasped my arm and urged me upstairs. We ascended by a narrow back stair to the second floor, where a very young and frightened-looking maidservant was waiting.

"Oh, you've come, sir, at last!" She bobbed a curtsy to Mr. Webb, giving me a curious glance. "Is this the midwife?"

"Yes. Mrs. Fraser—Dilman." He nodded at the girl, giving only her surname, the English fashion for house servants. She curtsied to me in turn, then beckoned me toward a door that stood ajar.

The room was large and gracious, furnished with a canopied bed, a walnut commode, armoire, and armchair, though the air of elegant refinement was somewhat impaired by a heap of mending, a ratty sewing basket overturned and spilling its threads, and a basket of children's toys. In the bed was a large mound, which—given the evidence to hand—I rather supposed must be Mrs. Martin, the Governor's wife.

This proved to be the case when Dilman curtsied again, murmuring my name to her. She was round—very round, given her advanced state of pregnancy—with a small, sharp nose and a nearsighted way of peering that reminded me irresistibly of Beatrix Potter's Mrs. Tiggy-Winkle. In terms of personality, not quite so much.

"Who the devil is this?" she demanded, poking a frowsy, capped head out of the bedclothes.

"Midwife, mum," Dilman said, bobbing again. "Have you slept well, mum?"

"Of course not," Mrs. Martin said crossly. "This beastly child's kicked my liver black and blue, I've puked all night, I've sweated through my sheets, and I have a shaking ague. I was told there was no midwife to be found within the county." She gave me a dyspeptic look. "Where did you discover this person, the local prison?"

"Actually, yes," I said, unslinging my bag from my shoulder. "How far gone are you, how long have you been ill, and when's the last time you moved your bowels?"

She looked marginally more interested, and waved Dilman out of the room.

"What did she say your name was?"

"Fraser. Are you experiencing any symptoms of early labor? Cramping? Bleeding? Intermittent pain in the back?"

She gave me a sideways look, but did begin to answer my questions. From which, in the fullness of time, I eventually was able to diagnose an acute case of food poisoning, likely caused by a leftover slice of oyster pie, consumed—with quite a lot of other edibles—in a fit of pregnancy-induced greed the day before.

"I have not an ague?" She withdrew the tongue she had allowed me to inspect, frowning.

"You have not. Not yet, anyway," honesty compelled me to add. It was no wonder she thought she had; I had learned in the course of the examination that a particularly virulent sort of fever was abroad in the town—and in the palace. The Governor's secretary had died of it two days before, and Dilman was the only upstairs servant still on her feet.

I got her out of bed, and helped her to the armchair, where she subsided, looking like a squashed cream cake. The room was hot and stuffy, and I opened the window in hopes of a breeze.

"God's teeth, Mrs. Fraser, do you mean to kill me?" She clutched her wrapper tight around her belly, hunching her shoulders as though I had admitted a howling blizzard.

"Probably not."

"But the miasma!" She waved a hand at the window, scandalized.

In all truth, mosquitoes *were* a danger. But it was still several hours 'til sunset, when they would begin to rise.

"We'll close it in a bit. For the moment, you need air. And possibly something light. Could you stomach a bit of dry toast, do you think?"

She thought that one over, tasting the corners of her mouth with a tentative tongue tip.

"Perhaps," she decided. "And a cup of tea. Dilman!"

Dilman dismissed to fetch the tea and toast—how long was it since I had even seen real tea? I wondered—I settled down to take a more complete medical history.

How many earlier pregnancies? Six, but a shadow crossed her face, and I saw her glance involuntarily at a wooden puppet, lying near the hearth.

"Are your children in the palace?" I asked, curious. I had heard no sign of any children, and even in a place the size of the palace, it would be difficult to hide six of them.

"No," she said with a sigh, and put her hands on her belly, holding it almost absently. "We sent the girls to my sister in New Jersey, a few weeks ago."

A few more questions, and the tea and toast arrived. I left her to eat it in peace, and went to shake out the damp, crumpled bed-clothes.

"Is it true?" Mrs. Martin asked suddenly, startling me.

"Is what true?"

"They say you murdered your husband's pregnant young mistress, and cut the baby from her womb. Did you?"

I put the heel of my hand against my brow and pressed, closing my eyes. How on earth had she heard that? When I thought I could speak, I lowered my hands and opened my eyes.

"She wasn't his mistress, and I didn't kill her. As for the rest— yes, I did," I said as calmly as I could.

She stared at me for a moment, her mouth hanging open. Then she shut it with a snap and crossed her forearms over her belly.

"Trust George Webb to choose me a proper midwife!" she said—and much to my surprise, began to laugh. "He doesn't know, does he?"

"I would assume not," I said with extreme dryness. "I didn't tell him. Who told you?"

"Oh, you are quite notorious, Mrs. Fraser," she assured me.

"Everyone has been talking of it. George has no time for gossip, but even he must have heard of it. He has no memory for names, though. I do."

A little color was coming back into her face. She took another nibble of toast, chewed, and swallowed gingerly.

"I was not sure that it was you, though," she admitted. "Not until I asked." She closed her eyes, grimacing doubtfully, but evidently the toast hit bottom, for she opened them and resumed her nibbling.

"So now that you *do* know . . . ?" I asked delicately.

"I don't know. I've never known a murderess before." She swallowed the last of the toast and licked the tips of her fingers before wiping them on the napkin.

"I am *not* a murderess," I said.

"Well, of course you'd say so," she agreed. She took up the cup of tea, surveying me over it with interest. "You don't look depraved—though I must say, you don't look quite respectable, either." She raised the fragrant cup and drank, with a look of bliss that made me conscious that I hadn't eaten anything since the rather meager bowl of unsalted, unbuttered porridge provided for breakfast by Mrs. Tolliver.

"I'll have to think about it," Mrs. Martin said, setting down her cup with a clink. "Take that back to the kitchen," she said, waving at the tray, "and have them send me up some soup, and perhaps a few sandwiches. I do believe my appetite has come back!"

Well, *now* bloody what? I had been whisked so abruptly from gaol to palace that I felt like a sailor decanted onto land after months at sea, staggering and off-balance. I went obediently down to the kitchen, as instructed, obtained a tray—with a most delectable-smelling bowl of soup—and took it back to Mrs. Martin, walking like an automaton. By the time she dismissed me, my brain had begun to function again, if not yet at full capacity.

I was in New Bern. And, thanks be to God and Sadie Ferguson, out of Sheriff Tolliver's noisome gaol. Fergus and Marsali were in New Bern. Ergo, the obvious—in fact, the only—thing to do was plainly to escape and find my way to them. They could help me to find Jamie. I clung firmly to Tom Christie's promise that Jamie wasn't dead and to the notion that he *was* findable, because nothing else was tolerable.

Escaping from the Governor's Palace, though, proved more difficult than I had anticipated. There were guards posted at all the doors, and my attempt to talk my way past one of them failed utterly, leading to the abrupt appearance of Mr. Webb, who took me by the arm and escorted me firmly up the stairs to a hot, stuffy little garret, where he locked me in.

It was better than the gaol, but that was all that could be said for it. There was a cot, a chamber pot, a basin, ewer, and chest of drawers, the latter containing meager bits of clothing. The room showed signs of recent occupancy—but not immediately recent. A film of fine summer dust lay over everything, and while the ewer was full of water, it had obviously been there for some time; a number of moths and other small insects had drowned in it, and a film of the same fine dust floated on the surface.

There was also a small window, painted shut, but determined banging and heaving got it open, and I breathed a heady lungful of hot, muggy air.

I stripped off, removed the dead moths from the pitcher, and washed, a blissful experience that made me feel immensely better, after the last week of unalloyed grime, sweat, and filth. After a moment's hesitation, I helped myself to a worn linen shift from the chest of drawers, unable to bear the thought of putting my own filthy, sweat-soaked chemise back on.

I could do only so much without soap or shampoo, but even so, felt much improved, and stood by the window, combing out my wet hair—there had been a wooden comb on the chest, though no looking glass—and surveying what I could see from my perch.

There were more guards, posted round the edge of the property. Was that usual? I wondered. I thought perhaps it was not; they seemed uneasy, and very alert; I saw one challenge a man who approached the gate, presenting his weapon in rather belligerent fashion. The man seemed startled and backed up, then turned and walked away fast, glancing backward as he went.

There were a number of uniformed guards—I thought they were perhaps Marines, though I wasn't sufficiently familiar with uniforms as to be sure of it—clustered round six cannon, these situated on a slight rise before the palace, commanding the town and the harbor's edge.

There were two nonuniformed men among them; leaning out a bit, I made out the tall, heavyset figure of Mr. Webb, and a shorter man beside him. The shorter man was strolling along the line of cannon, hands folded beneath his coattails, and the Marines, or whatever they were, were saluting him. At a guess, this was the Governor, then: Josiah Martin.

I watched for a little while, but nothing of interest happened, and I found myself overwhelmed with sudden sleepiness, borne down by the strains of the last month and the hot, still air that seemed to press upon me like a hand.

I lay down on the cot in my borrowed shift, and fell instantly asleep.

I slept until the middle of the night, when I was again called to attend Mrs. Martin, who seemed to be having a relapse of her digestive difficulties. A slightly pudgy, long-nosed man in nightshirt and cap lurked in the doorway with a candle, looking worried; I took this to be the Governor. He looked hard at me, but made no move to interfere, and I had no time to take much notice of him. By the time the crisis had passed, the Governor—if indeed it was he—had disappeared. The patient now safely asleep, I lay down like a dog on the rug beside her bed, with a rolled-up petticoat as pillow, and went thankfully back to sleep.

It was full daylight when I woke again, and the fire was out. Mrs. Martin was out of bed, calling fretfully into the passage for Dilman.

"Wretched girl," she said, turning back as I got awkwardly to my feet. "Got the ague, I suppose, like the rest. Or run away."

I gathered that while several servants were down with the fever, a good many of the others had simply decamped out of fear of contagion.

"You're quite sure I have not got the tertian ague, Mrs. Fraser?" Mrs. Martin squinted at herself in her looking glass, putting out her tongue and surveying it critically. "I do believe I look yellow."

In fact, her complexion was a soft English pink, though rather pale from throwing up.

"Keep off the cream cakes and oyster pie in hot weather, don't eat anything larger than your head at one sitting, and you should be quite all right," I said, suppressing a yawn. I caught a look at myself in the glass, over her shoulder, and shuddered. I was nearly as pale as she was, with dark circles under my eyes, and my hair . . . well, it was almost clean, that was all that could be said for it.

"I should be let blood," Mrs. Martin declared. "That is the proper treatment for a plethory; dear Dr. Sibelius always says so. Three or four ounces, perhaps, to be followed by the black draught. Dr. Sibelius says he finds the black-draught answer very well in such cases." She moved to an armchair and reclined, her belly bulging under her wrapper. She pulled up the sleeve of the wrapper, extending her arm in languorous fashion. "There is a fleam and bowl in the top left drawer, Mrs. Fraser. If you would oblige me?"

The mere thought of letting blood first thing in the morning was enough to make *me* want to vomit. As for Dr. Sibelius's black draught, that was laudanum—an alcoholic tincture of opium, and not *my* treatment of choice for a pregnant woman.

The subsequent acrimonious discussion over the virtues of blood-letting—and I began to think, from the anticipatory gleam in her eye, that the thrill of having a vein opened by a murderess was what she actually desired—was interrupted by the unceremonious entry of Mr. Webb.

"Do I disturb you, mum? My apologies." He bowed perfunctorily to Mrs. Martin, then turned to me. "You—put on your cap and come with me."

I did so without protest, leaving Mrs. Martin indignantly unperforated.

Webb ushered me down the gleamingly polished front stair this time, and into a large, gracious, book-lined room. The Governor, now properly wigged, powdered, and elegantly suited, was seated behind a desk overflowing with papers, dockets, scattered quills, blotters, sand-shakers, sealing wax, and all the other impedimenta of an eighteenth-century bureaucrat. He looked hot, bothered, and quite as indignant as his wife.

"What, Webb?" he demanded, scowling at me. "I need a secretary, and you bring me a midwife?"

"She's a forger," Webb said baldly. That stopped whatever

complaint the Governor had been going to bring forth. He paused, mouth slightly open, still frowning at me.

"Oh," he said in an altered tone. "Indeed."

"*Accused* of forgery," I said politely. "I haven't been tried, let alone convicted, you know."

The Governor's eyebrows went up, hearing my educated accent.

"Indeed," he said again, more slowly. He looked me up and down, squinting dubiously. "Where on earth did you get her, Webb?"

"From the gaol." Webb cast me an indifferent glance, as though I might be some unprepossessing yet useful bit of furniture, like a chamber pot. "When I made inquiries for a midwife, someone told me that this woman had done prodigies with a slave, another prisoner, having a difficult lying-in. And as the matter was urgent, and no other cunning woman to be found . . ." He shrugged, with a faint grimace.

"Hmmmm." The Governor pulled a handkerchief from his sleeve and dabbed thoughtfully at the plump flesh beneath his chin. "Can you write a fair hand?"

I supposed it would be a poor forger who couldn't, but contented myself with saying, "Yes." Fortunately, it was true; in my own time, I had scribbled ball-point prescriptions with the best of them, but now I had trained myself to write clearly with a quill, so that my medical records and case notes should be legible, for the benefit of whoever should read them after me. Once again, I felt a sharp pang at the thought of Malva—but there was no time to think of her.

Still eyeing me speculatively, the Governor nodded toward a straight-backed chair and a smaller desk at the side of the room.

"Sit." He rose, scrabbled among the papers on his desk, and deposited one in front of me. "Let me see you make a fair copy of that, if you please."

It was a brief letter to the Royal Council, outlining the Governor's concerns regarding recent threats to that body, and postponing the next scheduled meeting of the council. I chose a quill from the cut-glass holder on the desk, found a silver penknife by it, trimmed the quill to my liking, uncorked the inkwell, and set about the business, deeply aware of the scrutiny of the two men.

I didn't know how long my imposture might hold up—Mrs.

Governor could blow the gaff at any time—but for the nonce, I thought I probably had a better chance of escape as an accused forger than as an accused murderer.

The Governor took my finished copy, surveyed it, and laid it on the desk with a small grunt of satisfaction.

"Good enough," he said. "Make eight further copies of that, and then you can go on with these." Turning back to his own desk, he shuffled together a large sheaf of correspondence, which he deposited in front of me.

The two men—I had no notion of Webb's office, but he was obviously the Governor's close friend—returned to a discussion of current business, ignoring me completely.

I went about my assigned task mechanically, finding the scratch of the quill, the ritual of sanding, blotting, shaking, soothing. Copying occupied a very small part of my mind; the rest was free to worry about Jamie, and to think how best to engineer an escape.

I could—and doubtless should—make an excuse after a bit to go and see how Mrs. Martin did. If I could make shift to do so unaccompanied, I would have a few moments of unobserved freedom, during which to make a surreptitious dash for the nearest exit. So far, though, every door I'd seen had been guarded. The Governor's Palace had a very well-stocked simples closet, alas; it would be hard to invent a need for anything from an apothecary—and even then, unlikely that they'd let me go alone to fetch it.

Waiting for nightfall seemed the best notion; at least if I did get out of the palace, I would have several hours before my absence was noted. If they locked me in again, though . . .

I scratched away assiduously, turning over various unsatisfactory plans, and trying very hard not to envision Jamie's body turning slowly in the wind, hanging from a tree in some lonely hollow. Christie had given me his word; I clung to that, having nothing else to cling to.

Webb and the Governor murmured together, but their talk was of things I had no notion of, and for the most part, it washed over me like the sound of the sea, meaningless and soothing. After some time, though, Webb came over to instruct me in the sealing and direction of those letters to be sent. I thought of asking why he didn't lend a hand himself in this clerical emergency, but then saw his hands—both badly twisted with arthritis.

"You write a very fair hand, Mrs. Fraser," he unbent enough to say, at one point, and gave me a brief, wintry smile. "It is unfortunate that you should have been the forger, rather than the murderess."

"Why?" I asked, rather astonished at that.

"Why, you are plainly literate," he said, surprised in turn at my astonishment. "If convicted of murder, you could plead benefit of clergy, and be let off with a public whipping and branding in the face. Forgery, though—" He shook his head, pursing his lips. "Capital crime, no pardon possible. If convicted of forgery, Mrs. Fraser, I am afraid you must be hanged."

My feelings of gratitude toward Sadie Ferguson underwent an abrupt reappraisal.

"Indeed," I said as coolly as possible, though my heart had given a convulsive leap and was now trying to burrow out of my chest. "Well, we'll hope that justice is served then, and I am released, won't we?"

He made a choked sound that I thought passed for a laugh.

"To be sure. If only for the Governor's sake."

After that, we resumed work silently. The gilded clock behind me struck noon, and as though summoned by the sound, a servant whom I took to be the butler came in, to inquire whether the Governor would receive a delegation of the town's citizens?

The Governor's mouth compressed a bit, but he nodded in resignation, and a group of six or seven men came in, all attired in their best coats, but plainly tradesmen, rather than merchants or lawyers. None I recognized, thank God.

"We have come, sir," said one, who introduced himself as George Herbert, "to ask the meaning of this movement of the cannon."

Webb, sitting next to me, stiffened a little, but the Governor seemed to have been prepared for this.

"The cannon?" he said with every evidence of innocent surprise. "Why—the mountings are being repaired. We shall fire a royal salute—as usual—in honor of the Queen's birthday, later in the month. Upon inspecting the cannon in anticipation of this, though, it was discovered that the wood of the caissons had rotted away in spots. Firing the cannon is of course impossible until repairs shall be effected. Would you wish to inspect the mountings for yourself, sir?"

He half-rose from his seat as he said this, as though personally to escort them outside, but spoke with such a tinge of irony to his courtesy that they flushed and muttered refusals.

There was a bit more back and forth, in the name of courtesy, but the delegation then left, exhibiting only marginally less suspicion than that with which they'd come in. Webb closed his eyes and exhaled audibly, as the door closed behind them.

"God damn them," said the Governor very softly. I didn't think he meant it to be heard, and pretended I hadn't, busying myself with the papers and keeping my head lowered.

Webb got up and went to the window that overlooked the lawn, presumably to assure himself that the cannon were where he thought they should be. By craning a bit, I could see past him; sure enough, the six cannon had been removed from their mountings and lay on the grass, harmless logs of bronze.

From the subsequent conversation—salted with strong remarks regarding rebellious dogs who had the temerity to put the question to a Royal Governor as though he were a bootblack, by God!—I gathered that in fact, the cannon had been removed because of a very real fear that the townspeople might seize them and turn them upon the palace itself.

It dawned on me, listening to all this, that things had gone further and moved faster than I had expected. It was mid-July, but of 1775—nearly a year before a larger and more forceful version of the Mecklenberg Declaration would flower into an official declaration of independence for the united colonies. And yet here was a Royal Governor, in obvious fear of open revolt.

If what we had seen on our journey south from the Ridge had not been enough to convince me that war was now upon us, a day spent with Governor Martin left no doubt.

I did go up in the afternoon—accompanied by the watchful Webb, alas—to check my patient, and to make inquiries regarding anyone else who might be ill. Mrs. Martin was torpid and low in spirits, complaining of the heat and the pestilential, wretched climate, missing her daughters, and suffering severely from a lack of personal service, having been obliged to brush her own hair in the absence of Dilman, who had vanished. She was, however, in good health, as I was able to report to the Governor, who asked me of it upon my return.

"Would she stand a journey, do you think?" he asked, frowning a bit.

I considered for a moment, then nodded.

"I think so. She's a bit wobbly, still, from the digestive upset— but she should be quite well again by tomorrow. I see no difficulties with the pregnancy—tell me, had she any trouble with previous confinements?"

The Governor's face flushed rosily at that, but he shook his head.

"I thank you, Mrs. Fraser," he said with a slight inclination of the head. "You will excuse me, George—I must go and speak to Betsy."

"Is he thinking of sending his wife away?" I asked Webb, in the wake of the Governor's departure. Despite the heat, a small qualm of uneasiness stirred beneath my skin.

For once, Webb seemed quite human; he was frowning after the Governor, and nodded absently.

"He has family in New York and New Jersey. She'll be safe there, with the girls. Her three daughters," he explained, catching my eye.

"Three? She said she'd had six—ah." I stopped abruptly. She said she had borne six children, not that she had six living children.

"They have lost three small sons to the fevers here," Webb said, still looking after his friend. He shook his head, sighing. "It hasn't been a fortunate place for them."

He seemed then to recover himself, and the man disappeared back behind the mask of the chilly bureaucrat. He handed me another sheaf of papers, and went out, not bothering to bow.

93

In Which I Impersonate
a Lady

I ate supper alone in my room; the cook seemed still to be functioning, at least, though the atmosphere of disorder in the house was a palpable thing. I could feel the uneasiness, bordering on panic—and had the thought that it wasn't fear of fever or ague that had caused the servants to leave, but more likely that sense of self-preservation that causes rats to flee a sinking ship.

From my tiny window, I could see a small portion of the town, apparently serene in the gathering twilight. The light was very different here from that in the mountains—a flat, dimensionless light that limned the houses and the fishing boats in the harbor with a hard-edged clarity, but faded into a haze that hid the farther shore completely, so that I looked beyond the immediate prospect into featureless infinity.

I shook off the notion, and took from my pocket the ink, quill, and paper I had abstracted from the library earlier. I had no idea whether or how I might get a note out of the palace—but I did have a little money, still, and if the opportunity offered . . .

I wrote quickly to Fergus and Marsali, telling them briefly what had happened, urging Fergus to make inquiries for Jamie in Brunswick and Wilmington.

I thought myself that if Jamie *was* alive, that he was most likely in the Wilmington gaol. Brunswick was a tiny settlement, dominated by the looming presence of the log-built Fort Johnston, but the fort was a militia garrison; there would be no good reason to take Jamie there—though if they *had* . . . the fort was under the command of a Captain Collet, a Swiss emigrant who knew him. At least he would be safe there.

Who else did he know? He had a good many acquaintances on the coast, from the days of the Regulation. John Ashe, for one; they had marched side by side to Alamance, and Ashe's company had camped next to ours every night; we had entertained him at our campfire many times. And Ashe was from Wilmington.

I had just finished a brief plea to John Ashe, when I heard footsteps coming down the hallway toward my room. I folded it hastily, not worrying about smearing, and thrust it with the other note into my pocket. There was no time to do anything with the contraband ink and paper, save push it under the bed.

It was Webb, of course, my customary jailer. Evidently, I was now considered the general dogsbody of the establishment; I was escorted to Mrs. Martin's room and desired to pack her things.

I might have expected complaint or hysteria, but in fact, she was not only dressed but pale-faced and composed, directing and even assisting the process with a sense of clear-minded order.

The reason for her self-possession was the Governor, who came in midway through the packing, his face drawn with worry. She went at once to him, and put her hands affectionately on his shoulders.

"Poor Jo," she said softly. "Have you had any supper?"

"No. It doesn't matter. I'll have a bite later." He kissed her briefly on the forehead, his look of worry lightening a little as he looked at her. "You're quite well now, Betsy? You're sure of it?" I realized suddenly that he was Irish—Anglo-Irish, at least; he had no hint of an accent, but his unguarded speech held a faint lilt.

"Entirely recovered," she assured him. She took his hand and pressed it to her bulge, smiling. "See how he kicks?"

He smiled back, raised her hand to his lips, and kissed it.

"I'll miss you, darling," she said very softly. "You will take very great care?"

He blinked rapidly, and looked down, swallowing.

"Of course," he said gruffly. "Dear Betsy. You know I could not bear to part with you, unless—"

"I do know. That's why I fear so greatly for you. I—" At this point, she looked up, and realized suddenly that I was there. "Mrs.

Fraser," she said in quite a different tone. "Go down to the kitchen, please, and have a tray prepared for the Governor. You may take it to the library."

I bobbed slightly, and went. Was this the chance I had been waiting for?

The halls and stairway were deserted, lit only by flickering tin sconces—burning fish oil, by the smell. The brick-walled kitchen was, of course, in the basement, and the eerie silence in what should ordinarily be a hive of activity made the unlighted kitchen stairway seem like the descent into a dungeon.

There was no light in the kitchen now save the hearth fire, burning low—but it *was* burning, three servants clustered near it despite the smothering heat. They turned at my footsteps, startled and faceless in silhouette. With steam rising from the cauldron behind them, I had the momentary delusion that I was facing Macbeth's three witches, met in dreadful prophecy.

"Double, double, toil and trouble," I said pleasantly, though my heart beat a little faster as I approached them. "Fire burn, and cauldron bubble."

"Toil and trouble, *that* be right," said a soft female voice, and laughed. Closer now, I could see that they had appeared faceless in the shadows because they were all black; slaves, likely, and thus unable to flee the house.

Unable also to carry a message for me. Still, it never hurt to be friendly, and I smiled at them.

They smiled shyly back, looking at me with curiosity. I had not seen any of them before—nor they me, though "downstairs" being what it was, I thought it likely they knew who I was.

"Governor be sendin' his lady away?" asked the one who had laughed, moving to fetch down a tray from a shelf in response to my request for something light.

"Yes," I said. I realized the value of gossip as currency, and related everything that I decently could, as the three of them moved efficiently about, dark as shadows, their darting hands slicing, spreading, arranging.

Molly, the cook, shook her head, her white cap like a sunset cloud in the fire's glow.

"Bad times, bad times," she said, clicking her tongue, and the other two murmured assent. I thought, from their attitude, that they liked the Governor—but then, as slaves, their fate was inextricably linked with his, regardless of their feelings.

It occurred to me, as we chatted, that even if they could not reasonably flee the house altogether, they might at least leave the premises now and again; someone had to do the marketing, and there seemed to be no one else left. In fact, this proved to be the case; Sukie, the one who had laughed, went out to buy fish and fresh vegetables in the mornings, and tactfully approached, was not averse to delivering my notes to the printshop—she said she knew where it was, the place with all the books in the window—for a small consideration.

She tucked away the paper and money in her bosom, giving me a knowing look, and winked. God knew what she thought it was, but I winked back, and hefting the loaded tray, made my way back up into the fishy-smelling realms of light.

I found the Governor alone in the library, burning papers. He nodded absently at the tray I set on the desk, but did not touch it. I wasn't sure what to do, and after a moment's awkward standing about, sat down at my accustomed place.

The Governor thrust a final sheaf of documents into the fire, then stood looking bleakly after them, as they blackened and curled. The room had cooled a little, with the setting sun, but the windows were tightly shut—of course—and rivulets of condensing moisture rolled down the ornamental panes of glass. Blotting a similar condensation from my cheeks and nose, I got up and threw open the window closest to me, drawing in a deep gulp of the evening air, cloyingly warm, but fresh, and sweet with honeysuckle and roses from the garden, undercut with dankness from the distant shore.

Woodsmoke, too; there were fires burning outside. The soldiers who guarded the palace had watch fires burning, evenly spaced around the perimeter of the grounds. Well, that would help with the mosquitoes—and we would not be completely surprised, if an attack should come.

The Governor came to stand behind me. I expected him to tell me to shut the window, but he merely stood, looking out across his lawns and the long, graveled drive. The moon had risen, and the dismounted cannon were dimly visible, lying in the shadows like dead men in a row.

After a moment, the Governor moved back to his desk, and calling me over, handed me a sheaf of official correspondence for copying, another for sorting and filing. He left the window open;

I thought that he wished to hear, if anything should happen.

I wondered where the omnipresent Webb was. There was no sound from elsewhere in the Palace; presumably Mrs. Martin had finished her packing alone, and gone to bed.

We worked on, through the intermittent chiming of the clock, the Governor getting up now and then to commit another batch of papers to the fire, taking my copies and bundling them into large leather folders that he bound with tape, stacking them on his desk. He had taken off his wig; his hair was brown, short but curly—rather like my own had been, after the fever. Now and then he paused, head turned, listening.

I had faced a mob, and knew what he was listening for. I didn't know what to hope for, at this point, or to fear. And so I worked on, welcoming the work for the numbing distraction it was, though my hand had grown desperately cramped, and I had to pause every few moments to rub it.

The Governor was writing now; he shifted in his chair, grimacing with discomfort in spite of the cushion. Mrs. Martin had told me that he suffered from a fistula. I doubted very much that he'd let me treat it.

He eased himself onto one buttock, and rubbed a hand down his face. It was late, and he was plainly tired, as well as uncomfortable. I was tired, too, stifling yawns that threatened to dislocate my jaw and left my eyes watering. He kept doggedly working, though, with occasional glances at the door. Who was he expecting?

The window at my back was still open, and the soft air caressed me, warm as blood, but moving enough to stir the wisps of hair on my neck and make the candle flame waver wildly. It bent to one side and flickered, as though it would go out, and the Governor reached quickly to shelter it with a cupped hand.

The breeze passed and the air fell still again, save for the sound of crickets outside. The Governor's attention seemed focused on the paper before him, but suddenly his head turned sharply, as though he had seen something dart past the open door.

He looked for a moment, then blinked, rubbed his eyes, and returned his attention to the paper. But he couldn't keep it there. He glanced again at the empty doorway—I couldn't help looking, too—then back, blinking.

"Did you . . . see someone pass, Mrs. Fraser?" he asked.

"No, sir," I said, nobly swallowing a yawn.

"Ah." Seeming somehow disappointed, he took up his quill, but didn't write anything, just held it between his fingers, as though he had forgotten it was there.

"Were you expecting anyone, Your Excellency?" I asked politely, and his head jerked up, surprised to be directly addressed.

"Oh. No. That is . . ." His voice died away as he glanced once more at the doorway that led to the back of the house.

"My son," he said. "Our darling Sam. He—died here, you know—late last year. Only eight years old. Sometimes . . . sometimes I think I see him," he ended quietly, and bent his head once more over his paper, lips pressed tight.

I moved impulsively, meaning to touch his hand, but his tight-lipped air prevented me.

"I am sorry," I said quietly, instead. He didn't speak, but gave one quick, short nod of acknowledgment, not raising his head. His lips tightened further, and he went back to his writing, as did I.

A little later, the clock struck the hour, then two. It had a soft, sweet chime, and the Governor stopped to listen, a distant look in his eyes.

"So late," he said, as the last chime died away. "I have kept you intolerably late, Mrs. Fraser. Forgive me." He motioned to me to leave the papers I was working on, and I rose, stiff and aching from sitting so long.

I shook my skirts into some order and turned to go, realizing only then that he had made no move to put away his ink and quills.

"You should go to bed, too, you know," I said to him, turning and pausing at the door.

The palace was still. Even the crickets had ceased, and only the soft snore of a sleeping soldier in the hall disturbed the quiet.

"Yes," he said, and gave me a small, tired smile. "Soon." He shifted his weight to the other buttock, and picked up his quill, bending his head once more over the papers.

No one woke me in the morning, and the sun was well up when I stirred on my own. Listening to the silence, I had a momentary fear that everyone had decamped in the night, leaving me locked in to starve. I rose hastily, though, and looked out. The red-coated soldiers were still patrolling the grounds, just as usual. I could see small groups of citizens outside the perimeter, mostly strolling past in twos or threes, but sometimes stopping to stare at the palace.

Then I began to hear small thumps and homely noises on the floor below, and felt relieved; I was not entirely abandoned. I was, however, extremely hungry by the time the butler came to let me out.

He brought me to Mrs. Martin's bedchamber, but to my surprise it was empty. He left me there, and within a few moments, Merilee, one of the kitchen slaves, came in, looking apprehensive at being in this unfamiliar part of the house.

"Whatever is going on?" I asked her. "Where is Mrs. Martin, do you know?"

"Well, I know *that*," she said, in a dubious tone indicating that it was the only thing she *did* know for certain. "She lef' just afore dawn this mornin'. That Mr. Webb, he took her away, secret-like, in a wagon with her boxes."

I nodded, perplexed. It was reasonable that she should have left quietly; I imagined the Governor didn't want to give any indication that he felt threatened, for fear of provoking exactly the violence he feared.

"But if Mrs. Martin is gone," I said, "why am I here? Why are *you* here?"

"Oh. Well, I know that, too," Merilee said, gaining a bit of confidence. "I s'posed to hep you dress, ma'am."

"But I don't need any . . ." I began, and then saw the garments laid out on the bed: one of Mrs. Martin's day gowns, a pretty printed floral cotton, done in the newly popular "polonaise" fashion, complete with voluminous petticoats, silk stockings, and a large straw hat to shade the face.

Evidently, I was meant to impersonate the Governor's wife. There was no real point in protesting; I could hear the Governor and the butler talking in the hall, and after all—if it got me out of the palace, so much the better.

I was only two or three inches taller than Mrs. Martin, and my lack of a bulge made the gown hang lower. There was no hope of my fitting into any of her shoes, but my own were not completely disreputable, in spite of all my adventures since leaving home.

Merilee cleaned them and rubbed them with a bit of grease to make the leather shine; they were at least not so crude as to draw attention immediately.

With the broad-brimmed hat slanting forward to hide my face, and my hair twisted up and firmly pinned under a cap beneath it, I was probably a reasonable approximation, at least to people who did not know Mrs. Martin well. The Governor frowned when he saw me, and walked slowly round me, tugging here and there to adjust the fit, but then nodded, and with a small bow, offered me his arm.

"Your servant, mum," he said politely. And with me slumping slightly to disguise my height, we went out the front door, to find the Governor's carriage waiting in the drive.

94

Absquatulation

Jamie Fraser observed the quantity and quality of books in the window of the printshop—*F. Fraser, Proprietor*—and allowed himself a momentary sense of pride in Fergus; the establishment, though small, was apparently thriving. Time, however, was pressing, and he pushed through the door without stopping to read the titles.

A small bell over the door rang at his entrance, and Germain popped up behind the counter like an ink-smeared jack-in-the-box, emitting a whoop of joy at sight of his grandfather and his uncle Ian.

"Grandpère, Grandpère!" he shouted, then dived under the flap in the counter, clutching Jamie about the hips in ecstasy. He'd grown; the top of his head now reached Jamie's lower ribs. Jamie

ruffled the shiny blond hair gently, then detached Germain and told him to fetch his father.

No need; aroused by the shouting, the whole family came boiling out from the living quarters behind the shop, exclaiming, yelling, squealing, and generally carrying on like a pack of wolves, as Ian pointed out to them, Henri-Christian riding on his shoulders in red-faced triumph, clinging to his hair.

"What has happened, milord? Why are you here?" Fergus disengaged Jamie easily from the riot and drew him aside, into the alcove where the more expensive books were kept—and those not suitable for public display.

He could see from the look on Fergus's face that some news had come down from the mountains; while surprised to see him, Fergus was not astonished, and his pleasure covered a worried mind. He explained the matter as quickly as he could, stumbling now and then over his words from haste and weariness; one of the horses had broken down some forty miles from town, and unable to find another, they had walked for two nights and a day, taking it in turns to ride, the other trotting alongside, clinging to the stirrup leathers.

Fergus listened with attention, wiping his mouth with the handkerchief he had taken from his collar; they had arrived in the middle of dinner.

"The sheriff—that would be Mr. Tolliver," he said. "I know him. Shall we—"

Jamie made an abrupt gesture, cutting him short.

"We went there to begin with," he said. They had found the sheriff gone, and no one in the house save a very drunken woman with a face like a discontented bird, collapsed and snoring on the settle with a small Negro baby clutched in her arms.

He had taken the baby and thrust it into Ian's arms, bidding him grimly to mind it while he sobered the woman enough to talk. He had then dragged her out into the yard and poured buckets of well water over her until she gasped and blinked, then dragged her dripping and stumbling back into the house, where he obliged her to drink water poured over the black, burned dregs of chicory coffee he had found in the pot. She had vomited profusely and disgustingly, but regained some vague sense of language.

"At first, all she could say was that all of the female prisoners were gone—run off or hanged." He said nothing of the fright that had lanced through his belly at that last. He had shaken the woman thoroughly, though, demanding particulars, and eventually, after further applications of water and vile coffee, got them.

"A man came, the day before yesterday, and took her away. That was all she knew—or all she remembered. I made her tell me what she could of how he looked—it wasna Brown, nor yet Neil Forbes."

"I see." Fergus glanced behind him; his family were all gathered round Ian, pestering and caressing him. Marsali, though, was looking toward the alcove, worry on her face, obviously wanting to come and join the conversation, but detained by Joan, who was tugging on her skirt.

"Who would take her, I wonder?"

"Joanie, *a chuisle*, will ye not leave go? Help Félicité for a moment, aye?"

"But, Mama—"

"Not *now*. In a moment, aye?"

"I dinna ken," Jamie said, the frustration of helplessness welling up like black bile at the back of his throat. A sudden, more horrible thought struck him. "God, d'ye suppose it might have been Stephen Bonnet?"

The woman's slurred description had not sounded like the pirate—but she had been far from certain in it. Could Forbes have learned of his own escape, and determined simply to reverse the roles in the drama he had conceived—deport Claire forcibly to England, and try to pin the guilt of Malva Christie's death to Jamie's coat?

He found it hard to breathe, and had to force air into his chest. If Forbes had given Claire to Bonnet, he would slit the lawyer from wishbone to cock, rip the guts from his belly, and strangle him with them. And the same for the Irishman, once he laid hands upon him.

"Papi, Pa-pee . . ." Joan's singsong voice penetrated dimly through the red cloud that filled his head.

"What, *chérie*?" Fergus lifted her with the ease of long practice, balancing her fat little bottom on his left arm, to leave his right hand free.

She put her arms round his neck and hissed something into his ear.

"Oh, did you?" he said, plainly abstracted. "*Très bien.* Where did you put it, *chérie*?"

"With the naughty-lady pictures."

She pointed at the upper shelf, where several volumes lay, leather-bound but discreetly untitled. Glancing in the direction she indicated, Jamie saw a smudged paper sticking out from between two of the books.

Fergus clicked his tongue in displeasure, and smacked her lightly on the bottom with his good hand.

"You know you are not to climb up there!"

Jamie reached over and pulled the paper out. And felt all the blood leave his head, at sight of the familiar writing on it.

"What?" Fergus, alarmed at his appearance, set Joanie down. "Sit, milord! Run, *chérie*, get the smelling bottle."

Jamie waved a hand, speechless, trying to indicate that he was all right, and succeeded at last in finding his tongue.

"She's in the Governor's Palace," he said. "Christ be thanked, she's safe."

Seeing a stool pushed under the shelf, he pulled it out and sat on it, feeling exhaustion pulse through the quivering muscles of thigh and calf, ignoring the confusion of question and explanation, how Joanie had found the note pushed under the door—anonymous submissions to the newspaper often were delivered in this fashion, and the children knew they were to bring such things to their father's attention. . . .

Fergus read the note, his dark eyes assuming the expression of interested intent that he always had when contemplating the abstraction of something difficult and valuable.

"Well, that is good," he said. "We will go and fetch her. But I think first you must eat a little, milord."

He wished to refuse, to say that there was not a moment to be lost, that he could eat nothing in any case; his wame was knotted, hurting him.

But Marsali was already hurrying the girls back to the kitchen, calling out things about hot coffee and bread, and Ian following her, Henri-Christian still wrapped lovingly about his ears, Germain yapping eagerly at his heels. And he knew that should it come to a fight, he had nothing left to fight with. Then the succulent sizzle and scent of eggs frying in butter reached him, and he was up and moving toward the back, like iron drawn by a magnet.

Over their hasty meal, various plans were offered and rejected. At length, he reluctantly accepted Fergus's suggestion that either

Fergus or Ian should go openly to the palace, asking to see Claire, saying that he was a kinsman, wishing to assure himself of her welfare.

"They have no reason to deny her presence, after all," Fergus said, shrugging. "If we can see her, so much the better; but even if not, we will learn whether she is still there, and perhaps where she is likely to be within the palace."

Fergus clearly wished to undertake the errand, but yielded when Ian pointed out that Fergus was widely known in New Bern, and it might be suspected that he was merely hunting scandal for the newspaper.

"For I am pained to say, milord," Fergus said apologetically, "that the matter—the crime—is known here already. There are broadsheets . . . the usual nonsense. *L'Oignon* was obliged to print something regarding the matter, of course, to keep our countenance, but we did so in a most repressive fashion, mentioning only the bald facts of the matter." His long, mobile mouth compressed briefly, in illustration of the repressive nature of his article, and Jamie smiled faintly.

"Aye, I see," he said. He pushed back from the table, pleased to feel some strength returned to his limbs, and heartened anew by food, coffee, and the comforting knowledge of Claire's whereabouts. "Well, then, Ian, comb your hair. Ye dinna want the Governor to think ye a savage."

Jamie insisted upon going with Ian, despite the danger of being recognized. His nephew eyed him narrowly.

"Ye're no going to do anything foolish, Uncle Jamie?"

"When was the last time ye kent me to do anything foolish?"

Ian gave him an old-fashioned look, held up one hand, and began to fold the fingers down, one by one.

"Oh, well, let me reckon, then . . . Simms the printer? Tarring Forbes? Roger Mac told me what ye did in Mecklenberg. And then there was—"

"Ye would have let them kill wee Fogarty?" Jamie inquired. "And if we're mentioning fools, who was it got his arse pricked for wallowing in mortal sin with—"

"What I mean is," Ian said severely, "ye're no going to walk into the Governor's Palace and try to take her by force, no matter what happens. Ye'll wait quietly wi' your hat on until I come back, and then we'll see, aye?"

Jamie pulled down the brim of his hat, a floppy, weathered felt affair such as a pig farmer might wear, with his hair tucked up beneath it.

"What makes ye think I wouldn't?" he asked, as much from curiosity as natural contention.

"The look on your face," Ian replied briefly. "I want her back as much as you do, Uncle Jamie—well," he amended, with a wry grin, "perhaps not *quite* sae much—but I mean to have her back, nonetheless. You"——he poked his uncle emphatically in the chest—"bide your time."

And leaving Jamie standing under a heat-stricken elm, he strode purposefully toward the gates of the palace.

Jamie took several deep breaths, trying to maintain a sense of annoyance with Ian as an antidote to the anxiety that wrapped itself round his chest like a snake. As the annoyance had been purely manufactured, it evaporated like steam from a kettle, leaving the anxiety squirming and writhing.

Ian had reached the gate, and was in palaver with the guard who stood there, musket at the ready. Jamie could see the man shaking his head emphatically.

This was nonsense, he thought. The need of her was a physical thing, like the thirst of a sailor becalmed for weeks on the sea. He'd felt that need before, often, often, in their years apart. But why now? She was safe; he knew where she was—was it only the exhaustion of the past weeks and days, or perhaps the weakness of creeping age that made his bones ache, as though she had in fact been torn from his body, as God had made Eve from Adam's rib?

Ian was arguing, making persuasive gestures toward the guard. The sound of wheels on gravel drew his attention from them; a carriage was coming down the drive, a small open conveyance with two people and a driver, drawn by a team of nice dark bays.

The guard had pushed Ian back with the barrel of his musket, gesturing him to keep away while the guard and his fellow opened the gates. The carriage rattled through without stopping, turned into the street, and came past him.

He had never seen Josiah Martin, but thought the plump, self-important-looking gentleman must surely be the— His eye caught the merest glimpse of the woman, and his heart clenched like a fist. Without an instant's thought, he was pelting after the carriage, as hard as he could run.

In his prime, he could not have outrun a team of horses. Even so, he came within a few feet of the carriage, would have called, but had no breath, no sight, and then his foot struck a misplaced cobble and he fell headlong.

He lay stunned and breathless, vision dark and his lungs afire, hearing only the receding clatter of hooves and carriage wheels, until a strong hand seized his arm and jerked.

"We'll avoid notice, he says," Ian muttered, bending to get his shoulder under Jamie's arm. "Your hat's flown off, did ye notice *that*? Nay, of course not, nor the whole street staring, ye crack-brained gomerel. God, ye weigh as much as a three-year bullock!"

"Ian," he said, and paused to gulp for breath.

"Aye?"

"Ye sound like your mother. Stop." Another gulp of air. "And let go my arm; I can walk."

Ian gave a snort that sounded even more like Jenny, but did stop, and did let go. Jamie picked up his fallen hat and limped toward the printshop, Ian following in urgent silence through the staring streets.

Safely away from the palace, we trotted sedately through the streets of New Bern, provoking only mild interest from the citizenry, some of whom waved, a few of whom called out vaguely hostile things, most of whom simply stared. At the edge of town, the groom turned the team onto the main road, and we bowled pleasantly along, apparently bound for an outing in the countryside, an illusion bolstered by the wicker picnic hamper visible behind us.

Once past the congestion of heavy wagons, cattle, sheep, and the other traffic of commerce, though, the groom whipped up, and we were flying again.

"Where are we going?" I shouted over the noise of the team, holding on to my hat to prevent it blowing off. I had thought we were merely providing a diversion, so that no one would notice Mrs. Martin's quiet removal until she was safely out of the colony. Evidently, though, we were *not* merely out for a picnic.

"Brunswick!" the Governor shouted back.

"Where?"

"Brunswick," he repeated. He looked grim, and grimmer still as he cast a last look back toward New Bern. "God damn them," he said, though I was sure he meant this observation only for himself. He turned round then, and settled himself, leaning slightly forward, as though to speed the carriage, and said no more.

95

The Cruizer

I woke every morning, just before dawn. Worn out from worry and the Governor's late hours, I slept like the dead, through all the thumps and rattlings and bell-ringings of the watch, shouts from boats nearby, occasional musket-fire from the shore, and the whine of the offshore wind as it passed through the rigging. But in that moment before the light, the silence woke me.

Today? was the single thought in my mind, and I seemed to hang bodiless for a moment, just above my pallet beneath the forecastle. Then I drew breath, heard my heart beating, and felt the gentle heave of the deck beneath me. Would turn my face to the shore, watching, as the light began to touch the waves and reach toward land. We had first gone to Fort Johnston, but had stayed there barely long enough for the Governor to meet with local Loyalists who had assured him how unsafe it was, before retreating further.

We had been aboard His Majesty's sloop *Cruizer* for nearly a week, anchored off Brunswick. Lacking any troops save the Marines aboard the sloop, Governor Martin was unable to seize back control of his colony, and was reduced to writing frenzied letters, attempting to keep up some semblance of a government in exile.

Lacking anyone else to fill the office, I remained in my role as *ad hoc* secretary, though I had moved up from mere copyist to amanuensis, taking down some letters by dictation when Martin grew too tired to write himself. And cut off from land and information alike, I spent every spare moment watching the shore.

Today, a boat was coming, out of the fading dark.

One of the watch hailed it, and an answering "halloo" came up, in tones of such agitation that I sat up abruptly, groping for my stays.

Today, there would be news.

The messenger was already in the Governor's cabin, and one of the Marines barred my way—but the door was open, and the man's voice clearly audible.

"Ashe's done it, sir, he's moving against the fort!"

"Well, God damn him for a treasonous dog!"

There was a sound of footsteps, and the Marine stepped hastily out of the way, just in time to avoid the Governor, who came popping out of his cabin like a jack out of the box, still attired in a billowing nightshirt and minus his wig. He seized the ladder and scampered up it like a monkey, affording me an unwanted view from below of his chubby bare buttocks. The Marine caught my eye and quickly averted his own gaze.

"What are they doing? Do you see them?"

"Not yet." The messenger, a middle-aged man in the dress of a farmer, had followed the Governor up the ladder; their voices floated down from the rail.

"Colonel Ashe ordered all the ships in Wilmington Harbor to take on troops yesterday and float them down to Brunswick. They were mustering just outside the town this morning; I heard the roll calls whilst I was doing the morning milking—nigh onto five hundred men, they must have. When I saw that, sir, I slipped away down to the shore and found a boat. Thought you ought to know, Your Excellency." The man's voice had lost its agitation now, and taken on a rather self-righteous tone.

"Oh, yes? And what do you expect me to do about it?" The Governor sounded distinctly cranky.

"How should I know?" said the messenger, replying in like vein. "*I* ain't the Governor, now, am I?"

The Governor's response to this was drowned out by the striking of the ship's bell. As it died away, he strode past the companionway, and looking down, saw me below.

"Oh, Mrs. Fraser. Will you fetch me some tea from the galley?"

I hadn't much choice, though I would have preferred to stay and eavesdrop. The galley fire had been banked for the night in its small iron pot, and the cook was still abed. By the time I had poked up the fire, boiled water, brewed a pot of tea, and assembled a tray with teapot, cup, saucer, milk, and toast, butter, biscuits, and jam, the Governor's informant had gone; I saw his boat heading for the shore, a dark arrowhead against the slowly brightening surface of the sea.

I paused for a moment on deck and rested my tea tray on the rail, looking inland. It was just light now, and Fort Johnston was visible, a blocky log building that stood exposed on top of a low rise, surrounded by a cluster of houses and outbuildings. There was a fair amount of activity around it; men were coming and going like a trail of ants. Nothing that looked like an imminent invasion, though. Either the commander, Captain Collet, had decided to evacuate—or Ashe's men had not yet begun their march from Brunswick.

Had John Ashe received my message? If he had . . . would he have acted? It wouldn't have been a popular thing to do; I couldn't blame him if he had decided that he simply couldn't afford to be seen aiding a man widely suspected of being a Loyalist—let alone one accused of such a hideous crime.

He might have, though. With the Governor marooned at sea, the Council disbanded, and the court system evaporated, there was no effective law in the colony now—save for the militias. If Ashe chose to storm the Wilmington jail and remove Jamie, he would have faced precious little opposition.

And if he had . . . if Jamie were free, he would be looking for me. And surely he would hear quickly where I was. If John Ashe came to Brunswick and Jamie were free, he would surely come with Ashe's men. I looked toward shore, seeking movement, but saw only a boy driving a cow desultorily along the road to Brunswick. But the shadows of the night were still cold around my feet; it was barely dawn.

I took a deep breath, and noticed the aromatic scent of the tea, mixed with the shore's morning breath—the smell of tide flats and piney scrub. I hadn't drunk tea in months, if not years. Thoughtfully, I poured a cup, and sipped it slowly, watching the shore.

When I arrived in the surgeon's cabin, which the Governor had taken for his office, he was dressed, and alone.

"Mrs. Fraser." He nodded briefly to me, scarcely looking up. "I am obliged. Will you write, please?"

He had been writing himself, already; quills and sand and blotter were scattered about the desk, and the inkwell stood open. I picked out a decent quill and a sheet of paper, and began to write as per his dictation, with a sense of growing curiosity.

The note—dictated between bites of toast—was to a General Hugh MacDonald, and referred to the General's safe arrival upon the mainland with a Colonel McLeod. Receipt of the General's report was acknowledged, and request made for continuing information. Mention was also made of the Governor's request for support—which I knew about—and assurances he had received regarding the arrival of that support, which I didn't.

"Enclosure, a letter of credit—no, wait." The Governor darted a look in the direction of the shore—to no particular avail, as the surgeon's cabin boasted no porthole—and scowled in concentration. Evidently, it had occurred to him that in light of recent events, a letter of credit issued by the Governor's office was possibly worth less than one of Mrs. Ferguson's forgeries.

"Enclosure, twenty shillings," he amended with a sigh. "If you will make the fair copy at once, Mrs. Fraser? These, you may do at your leisure." He pushed across an untidy stack of notes, done in his own crabbed hand.

He got up then, groaning as he stretched, and went up, no doubt to peer over the railing at the fort again.

I made the copy, sanded it, and set it aside, wondering who on earth *this* MacDonald was, and what he was doing? Unless Major MacDonald had undergone a change of name and an extraordinary promotion of late, it couldn't be he. And from the tone of the Governor's remarks, it appeared that General MacDonald and his friend McLeod were traveling alone—and on some particular mission.

I flipped quickly through the waiting stack of notes, but saw nothing else of interest; just the usual administrative trivia. The Governor had left his writing desk on the table, but it was closed. I debated trying to pick the lock and rummage through his private correspondence, but there were too many people about: seamen, Marines, ship's boys, visitors—the place was seething.

There was a sense of nervous tension aboard, as well. I'd noticed many times before how a sense of danger communicates itself among people in a confined setting: hospital emergency room, surgical suite, train car, ship; urgency flashes from one person to the next without speech, like the impulse down a neuron's axon to the dendrites of another. I didn't know whether anyone beyond the Governor and myself knew about John Ashe's movements yet—but the *Cruizer* knew that something was up.

The sense of nervous anticipation was affecting me, too. I was fidgeting, toe tapping absently, fingers moving restlessly up and down the shaft of the quill, unable to concentrate enough to write with it.

I stood up, with no idea what I meant to do; only the fixed notion that I would suffocate with impatience if I stayed below any longer.

On the shelf beside the door to the cabin stood the usual half-tidy clutter of shipboard, jammed behind a rail: a candlestick, extra candles, a tinderbox, a broken pipe, a bottle with a twist of flax stopping it, a bit of wood that someone had tried to carve and made a mess of. And a box.

The *Cruizer* had no surgeon aboard. And surgeons tended to take their personal implements with them, unless they died. This must be a kit belonging to the ship itself.

I glanced out the door; there were voices nearby, but no one in sight. I hastily flipped open the box, wrinkling my nose at the scent of dried blood and stale tobacco. There wasn't much there, and what there was was thrown in higgledy-piggledy, rusted, crusted, and of little use. A tin of Blue Pills, so labeled, and a bottle, not labeled, but recognizable, of black draught—laudanum, that is. A dried-up sponge and a sticky cloth stained with something yellow.

And the one thing certain to be in any surgeon's kit of the times—blades.

There were footsteps coming down the companionway, and I heard the Governor's voice, talking to someone. Without pausing to consider the wisdom of my conduct, I grabbed a small jointing knife and thrust it down the front of my stays.

I slammed shut the lid of the box. There was no time to sit down again, though, before the Governor arrived, with another visitor in tow.

My heart was hammering in my throat. I pressed my palms, damp with sweat, against my skirt, and nodded to the new arrival, who was regarding me, open-mouthed, behind the Governor.

"Major MacDonald," I said, hoping that my voice wouldn't tremble. "Fancy meeting *you* here!"

MacDonald's mouth snapped shut and he drew himself more firmly upright.

"Mrs. Fraser," he said, bowing warily. "Your servant, mum."

"You know her?" Governor Martin glanced from MacDonald to me and back, frowning.

"We've met," I said, nodding politely. It had occurred to me that it might not profit either of us for the Governor to think there was some connection between us—if indeed there was one.

The same thought had clearly struck MacDonald; his face betrayed nothing beyond faint courtesy, though I could see the thoughts darting to and fro behind his eyes like a swarm of gnats. I was entertaining a similar swarm, myself—and knowing that my own face was naturally revealing, I cast down my eyes demurely, and murmuring an excuse about refreshment, made off toward the galley.

I threaded my way through clumps of seamen and Marines, mechanically acknowledging their salutes, mind working furiously.

How? How was I going to speak to MacDonald alone? I *had* to find out what he knew about Jamie—if anything. Would he tell me, if he did know anything? But yes, I thought, he would; soldier he might be, but MacDonald was also a confirmed gossip—and he was plainly dying of curiosity at the sight of me.

The cook, a chubby young free black named Tinsdale, who wore his hair in three stubby braids that stuck out of his head like the horns of a triceratops, was at work in the galley, dreamily toasting bread over the fire.

"Oh, hullo," he said amiably, seeing me. He waved the toasting fork. "Want a bit of toast, Mrs. Fraser? Or is it the hot water, again?"

"Love some toast," I said, seized by inspiration. "But the Governor has company; he wants coffee sent. And if you have a few of those nice almond biscuits to go with it . . ."

Armed with a loaded coffee tray, I made my way toward the surgeon's cabin a few minutes later, heart pounding. The door was open for air; evidently it wasn't a secret meeting.

They were huddled together over the small desk, the Governor frowning at a wad of papers, these clearly having traveled some distance in MacDonald's dispatch case, judging from the creases and stains upon them. They appeared to be letters, written in a variety of hands and inks.

"Oh, coffee," the Governor said, looking up. He seemed vaguely pleased, plainly not recalling that he hadn't ordered any. "Splendid. Thank you, Mrs. Fraser."

MacDonald hastily picked up the papers, making room for me to set the tray down on the desk. The Governor had one in his hand; he kept hold of this, and I caught a quick glimpse of it as I bent to place the tray in front of him. It was a list of some sort— names on one side, numbers beside them.

I managed to knock a spoon to the floor, enabling a better look as I stooped for it. *H. Bethune, Cook's Creek, 14. Jno. McManus, Boone, 3. F. Campbell, Campbelton, 24?*

I darted a look at MacDonald, who had his eyes fixed on me. I dropped the spoon on the desk, then took a hasty step back, so that I stood directly behind the Governor. I pointed a finger at MacDonald, then in rapid succession clutched my throat, tongue protruding, grabbed my stomach with crossed forearms, then jabbed the finger again at him, then at myself, all the while giving him a monitory stare.

MacDonald viewed this pantomime with subdued fascination, but—with a veiled glance at the Governor, who was stirring his coffee with one hand, frowning at the paper he held in the other— gave me a tiny nod.

"How many can you be quite sure of?" the Governor was saying, as I curtsied and backed out.

"Oh, at least five hundred men, sir, even now," MacDonald replied confidently. "A great many more to come, as word spreads. Ye should see the enthusiasm with which the General has been received so far! I cannot speak for the Germans, of course, but depend upon it, sir, we shall have all the Highlanders of the backcountry, and not a few of the Scotch–Irish, too."

"God knows I hope you are right," the Governor said, sounding hopeful, but still dubious. "Where is the General now?"

I would have liked to hear the answer to that—and a good many other things—but the drum was beating overhead for mess, and thundering feet were already pounding down the decks and companionways. I couldn't lurk about eavesdropping in plain sight of the mess, so was obliged to go back up top, hoping that MacDonald had indeed got my message.

The captain of the *Cruizer* was standing by the rail, his first mate beside him, both scanning the shore with their telescopes.

"Is anything happening?" I could see more activity near the fort, people coming and going—but the shore road was still empty.

"Can't say, ma'am." Captain Follard shook his head, then lowered the telescope and shut it, reluctantly, as though afraid something might happen if he didn't keep his eyes fixed on the shore. The first mate didn't move, still squinting fixedly toward the fort on its bluff.

I remained there by his side, staring silently toward the shore. The tide shifted; I had been on the ship long enough to feel it, a barely perceptible pause, the sea taking breath as the invisible moon yielded its pull.

There is a tide in the affairs of men. . . . Surely Shakespeare had stood upon a deck, at least once, and felt that same faint shift, deep in the flesh. A professor had told me once, in medical school, that the Polynesian seafarers dared their vast journeys through the trackless sea because they had learned to sense the currents of the ocean, the shifts of wind and tide, registering these changes with that most delicate of instruments—their testicles.

It didn't take a scrotum to feel the currents that were swirling round us now, I reflected, with a sideways glance at the first mate's securely fastened white breeches. I could feel them in the pit of my stomach, in the damp of my palms, in the tenseness of the muscles at the back of my neck. The mate had lowered his telescope, but still looked toward the shore, almost absently, his hands resting on the rail.

It occurred to me suddenly that if something drastic were to happen on land, the *Cruizer* would at once lift sail and head out to sea, carrying the Governor to safety—and me farther from Jamie. Where on earth might we end up? Charlestown? Boston? Either was as likely. And no one on that seething shore would have any notion where we had gone.

I'd met displaced persons during the war—my war. Driven or taken from their homes, their families scattered, their cities destroyed, they thronged refugee camps, stood in lines besieging embassies and aid stations, asking, always asking for the names of the vanished, describing the faces of the loved and lost, grasping at any scrap of information that might lead them back to whatever might be left. Or, failing that, preserve for a moment longer what they had once been.

The day was warm, even on the water, and my clothes clung to me with humid damp, but my muscles convulsed and my hands on the rail shook with sudden chill.

I might have seen them all for the last time, not knowing it: Jamie, Bree, Jemmy, Roger, Ian. That's how it happened: I had not even said goodbye to Frank, had had no faintest inkling when he left that last night that I would never see him alive again. What if—

But no, I thought, steadying myself with a tighter grip on the wooden rail. We would find each other again. We had a place to return to. Home. And if I remained alive—as I most firmly intended to do—I *would* go back home.

The mate had shut his telescope and left; I hadn't noticed his departure, absorbed in morbid thoughts, and was quite startled when Major MacDonald hove to alongside me.

"Too bad the *Cruizer* has nay long-range guns," he said with a nod at the fort. "'Twould put a crimp in the plans o' those wee heathen, eh?"

"Whatever those plans might be," I replied. "And speaking of plans—"

"I've a kind of a griping in the wame," he interrupted blandly. "The Governor suggested that ye might possibly have some sort of medicine to soothe it."

"Did he indeed?" I said. "Well, come down to the galley; I'll brew you a cup of something that will set you right, I expect."

"Did ye ken, he thought ye were a forger?" MacDonald, hands wrapped around a mug of tea, jerked his head in the direction of the main cabin. The Governor was nowhere in sight, and the cabin's door closed.

"I did, yes. Does he know better now?" I asked with a sense of resignation.

"Well, aye." MacDonald looked apologetic. "I supposed he knew already, or I wouldna have said. Though if I hadn't," he added, "he would have kent it sooner or later. The story's spread all the way to Edenton by now, and the broadsheets . . ."

I flapped a hand, dismissing this.

"Have you seen Jamie?"

"I have not." He glanced at me, curiosity warring with wariness. "I'd heard . . . aye, well, I've heard a great many things, and all different. But the meat of the matter is that ye've both been arrested, aye? For the murder of Miss Christie."

I nodded briefly. I wondered whether one day I would grow used to that word. The sound of it was still like a punch in the stomach, short and brutal.

"Need I tell you that there is no truth to it?" I said bluntly.

"Not the slightest need, mum," he assured me, with a fair assumption of confidence. But I sensed the hesitation in him, and saw the sideways glance, curious and somehow avid. Perhaps one day I'd get used to that, too.

My hands were cold; I wrapped them round my own mug, taking what comfort I could in its heat.

"I need to get word to my husband," I said. "Do you know where he is?"

MacDonald's pale blue eyes were fixed on my face, his own showing no more now than courteous attention.

"No, mum. But you do, I assume?"

I gave him a sharp look.

"Don't be coy," I advised him shortly. "You know as well as I do what's going on on shore—probably much better."

"Coy." His thin lips pursed in brief amusement. "I dinna believe anyone's called me that before. Aye, I know. And so?"

"I think that he *may* be in Wilmington. I tried to send word to John Ashe, and asked him to get Jamie out of the gaol in Wilmington, if possible—if he was there—and to tell him where I was. But I don't know—" I waved a hand in frustration toward the shore.

He nodded, native caution at odds with his obvious desire to ask me for the gory details of Malva's death.

"I shall be going back through Wilmington. I'll make such inquiries as may be possible. If I find Mr. Fraser—shall I tell him anything, beyond your present situation?"

I hesitated, thinking. I had been holding a constant conversation with Jamie, ever since they took him away from me. But none of what I said to him in the wide black nights or the lonely dawns seemed appropriate to confide to MacDonald. And yet . . . I couldn't forgo the opportunity; God knew when I might have another.

"Tell him that I love him," I said softly, my eyes on the table-top. "I always will."

MacDonald made a small sound that made me look up at him.

"Even though he—" he began, then stopped himself.

"He didn't kill her," I said sharply. "And neither did I. I told you so."

"Of course not," he said hurriedly. "No one could imagine . . . I only meant . . . but of course, a man's but a man, and . . . mmphm." He broke off and looked away, the color high in his face.

"He didn't do that, either," I said through my teeth.

There was a marked silence, during which we avoided each other's gaze.

"Is General MacDonald a kinsman of yours?" I asked abruptly, needing either to change the course of the conversation or to leave.

The Major glanced up, surprised—and relieved.

"Aye, a distant cousin. The Governor's mentioned him?"

"Yes," I said. It was the truth, after all; Martin simply hadn't mentioned the General to *me*. "You're, um, assisting him, are you? It sounded as though you've been having some success."

Relieved to have escaped the social awkwardness of dealing

with the question as to whether I were a murderess, and Jamie
only a philanderer, or he a murderer and I his scorned and de-
luded dupe, MacDonald was only too eager to take the offered
bait.

"Great success, indeed," he said heartily. "I've gathered
pledges from many of the most prominent men in the colony; they
stand ready to do the Governor's bidding at the slightest word!"

Jno. McManus, Boone, 3. Prominent men. I happened to know
Jonathan McManus, whose gangrenous toes I had removed the
winter before. He likely *was* the most prominent man in Boone, if
by that, MacDonald meant that the other twenty inhabitants all
knew him for a drunkard and a thief. It was also probably true that
he had three men who would go to fight with him if called: his
one-legged brother and his two feeble-minded sons. I took a sip of
tea to hide my expression. Still, MacDonald had Farquard
Campbell on his list; had Farquard really made a formal commitment?

"I gather the General is not presently anywhere near Brunswick,
though," I said, "given the, er, present circumstances?" If he was,
the Governor would be much less nervous than he was.

MacDonald shook his head.

"No. But he is not ready to muster his forces yet; he and
McLeod do but discover the readiness of the Highlanders to rise.
They will not call muster until the ships come."

"Ships?" I blurted. "What ships?"

He knew he oughtn't to speak further, but couldn't resist. I saw
it in his eyes; after all, what danger could there be in telling me?

"The Governor has asked for aid from the Crown in subduing
the factionalism and unrest that runs rampant in the colony. And
has received assurances that it will be forthcoming—should he be
able to raise enough support on the ground to reinforce the government troops who will arrive by ship.

"That is the plan, ye see," he went on, warming to it. "We are
notified"—*Oh, "we" indeed,* I thought—"that my Lord
Cornwallis begins to gather troops in Ireland, who will take ship
shortly. They should arrive in the early autumn, and join wi' the
General's militia. Between Cornwallis on the coast and the
General comin' doon frae the hills—" He closed thumb and fingers in a pinching movement. "They'll crush the Whiggish
whoresons like a pack o' lice!"

"Will they?" I said, endeavoring to sound impressed. Possibly they would; I had no idea, nor did I much care, being in no position to see far beyond the present moment. If I ever got off this frigging boat and out of the shadow of a noose, I'd worry about it.

The sound of the main cabin's door opening made me look up. The Governor was closing it behind him. Turning, he saw us, and came to inquire as to MacDonald's presumed indisposition.

"Oh, I am a great deal better," the Major assured him, hand pressed to the waistcoat of his uniform. He belched in illustration. "Mrs. Fraser is a capital hand at such things. Capital!"

"Oh, good," Martin said. He seemed a trifle less harassed than he had earlier. "You will be wanting to go back, then." He signaled to the Marine standing at the foot of the companionway, who knuckled his forehead in acknowledgment and disappeared up the ladder.

"The boat will be ready for you in a few minutes' time." With a nod at MacDonald's half-drunk tea, and a punctilious bow to me, the Governor turned and went into the surgeon's cabin, where I could see him standing beside the desk, frowning at the heap of crumpled papers.

MacDonald hastily swallowed the rest of his tea, and with a lift of the eyebrows, invited me to accompany him to the upper deck. We were standing on deck, waiting as a local fishing boat made its way out to the *Cruizer* from shore, when he suddenly laid a hand on my arm.

This startled me; MacDonald was not a casual toucher.

"I will do my utmost to discover your husband's whereabouts, mum," he said. "It occurs to me, though—" He hesitated, eyes on my face.

"What?" I said cautiously.

"I said I had heard considerable speculation?" he said delicately. "Regarding . . . erm . . . the unfortunate demise of Miss Christie. Would it not be . . . desirable . . . that I know the truth of the matter, so that I might put any ill-natured rumors firmly to rest, should I encounter them?"

I was torn between anger and laughter. I should have known that curiosity would be too much for him. But he was right; given the rumors I had heard—and I knew they were but a fraction of those circulating—the truth was certainly more desirable. On the other hand, I was entirely sure that the telling of the truth would do nothing to quell the rumors.

And still. The urge to be justified was a strong one; I understood those poor wretches who cried their innocence from the gallows—and I bloody hoped I wasn't going to be one.

"Fine," I said crisply. The first mate was back by the rail, keeping an eye on the fort, and within earshot, but I supposed it didn't matter whether he heard.

"The truth is this: Malva Christie was got with child by *someone,* but rather than name the real father, insisted that it was my husband. I know this to be false," I added, fixing him with a gimlet stare. He nodded, mouth a little open.

"A few days later, I went out to tend my garden and found the little—Miss Christie lying in my lettuce patch with her throat freshly cut. I thought . . . there was some chance that I might save her unborn child. . . ." Despite my assumption of bravado, my voice trembled a little. I stopped, clearing my throat. "I couldn't. The child was born dead."

Much better not to say *how* it was born; that weltering image of severed flesh and dirt-smeared blade was not one I wished the Major to have in mind, if it could be prevented. I had told no one—not even Jamie—about the faint flicker of life, that tingle that I still held secret in the palms of my hands. To say that the child had been born alive was to arouse immediate suspicion that I had killed it, and I knew as much. Some would think that anyway; Mrs. Martin plainly had.

MacDonald's hand was still resting on my arm, his gaze on my face. For once, I blessed the transparency of my countenance; no one watching my face ever doubted what I said.

"I see," he said quietly, and gently squeezed my arm.

I took a deep breath, and told him the rest—circumstantial details might convince some hearers.

"You know that there were bee gums at the edge of my garden? The murderer kicked two of them over in fleeing; he must have been stung several times- -I was, when I came into the garden. Jamie— Jamie had no stings. It wasn't him." And under the circumstances, I had not been able to find out which man—or woman? For the first time, it occurred to me that it could have been a woman—*had* been stung.

At this, he gave a deep "hum!" of interest. He stood for a moment in contemplation, then shook his head, as though waking from a dream, and let go my arm.

"I thank ye, mum, for telling me," he said formally, and bowed to me. "Be assured, I will speak in your behalf, whenever the occasion shall arise."

"I appreciate that, Major." My voice was husky, and I swallowed. I hadn't realized how much it would hurt to speak of.

The wind stirred around us, and the reefed sails rustled in their ropes overhead. A shout from below announced the presence of the boat that would carry MacDonald back to the shore.

He bowed low over my hand, breath warm on my knuckles. For an instant, my fingers tightened on his; I was surprisingly reluctant to let him go. But let him go I did, and watched him all the way to the shore; a diminishing silhouette against the brightness of the water, back straight with resolution. He didn't look back.

The mate moved at the rail, sighing, and I glanced at him, then at the fort.

"What are they doing?" I asked. Some of the antlike forms seemed to be dropping lines from the walls to their fellows on the ground; I saw the ropes, fine as spiderwebs from this distance.

"I do believe the fort's commander is preparing to remove the cannon, madam," he said, snapping shut his brass telescope with a click. "If you will excuse me, I need to go inform the captain."

96

Gunpowder, Treason, and Plot

I f the Governor's attitude toward me was altered by the news that I was not in fact a forger but rather a notorious—if merely accused—murderess, I had no opportunity to find out. He, like the rest of the officers and half the men aboard, rushed to the rail, and the rest of the day passed in a flurry of observation, speculation, and largely fruitless activity.

The lookout at the masthead called down periodic observations—men were leaving the fort, carrying things . . . the fort's weaponry, it looked like.

"Are they Collet's men?" the Governor bellowed, shading his eyes to look aloft.

"Can't say, sir," came the unhelpful reply from above.

At last, the *Cruizer*'s two launches were sent ashore, with orders to collect what information they could. They came back several hours later, with the news that Collet had abandoned the fort, in the face of threats, but had taken pains to remove the guns and powder, lest these fall into rebel hands.

No, sir, they had not spoken with Colonel Collet, who was—by rumor—on his way upriver with his militia forces. They had sent two men down the road toward Wilmington; it was true that a large force was gathering in the fields outside the town, under Colonels Robert Howe and John Ashe, but no word of what was planned.

"No word of what's planned, God's ballocks!" muttered the Governor, having been ceremoniously informed of this by Captain

Follard. "They mean to burn the fort, what else would Ashe be planning, for the love of Jesus?"

His instincts were quite sound; just before sunset, the scent of smoke came across the water, and we could just make out the antlike scurrying of men, piling heaps of flammable debris around the base of the fort. It was a simple, square building, made of logs. And despite the dampness of the humid air, it *would* burn, eventually.

It took them no little time to get the fire going, though, with neither powder nor oil to hasten its burning; as night fell, we could clearly see flaming torches, streaming in the breeze as they were carried to and fro, passed from hand to hand, dipping to touch off a pile of kindling, coming back a few minutes later, as the kindling went out.

Around nine o'clock, someone found a few barrels of turpentine, and the blaze took a sudden, lethal hold of the fort's log walls. Sheets of wavering flame rose pure and brilliant, orange and crimson billows against the night-black sky, and we heard scraps of cheering and snatches of ribald song, borne with the smell of smoke and the tang of turpentine on the offshore breeze.

"At least we needn't worry about the mosquitoes," I observed, waving a cloud of whitish smoke away from my face.

"Thank you, Mrs. Fraser," said the Governor. "I had not considered that particular positive aspect of the matter." He spoke with some bitterness, his fists resting impotently on the rail.

I took the hint, and said no more. For myself, the leaping flames and the column of smoke that rose wavering toward the stars were cause for celebration. Not for any benefit that the burning of Fort Johnston might be to the rebel cause—but because Jamie might be there, by one of the campfires that had sprung up on the shore below the fort.

And if he was . . . he would come tomorrow.

He did. I was awake well before dawn—in fact, I had not slept—and standing at the rail. There was little of the usual boat traffic this morning, in the wake of the fort's burning; the bitter smell of wood ash mingled with the marshy smell of the nearby mud flats, and the water was still and oily-looking. It was a gray day, heavily overcast, and a deep bank of haze hung over the water, hiding the shore.

I kept watching, though, and when a small boat came out of the haze, I knew at once that it was Jamie. He was alone.

I watched the long, smooth reach of his arms and the pull of the oars, and felt a sudden deep, calm happiness. I had no notion what might happen—and all the horror and anger connected with Malva's death still lurked at the back of my mind, a great dark shape under very thin ice. But he was *there*. Near enough now to see his face, as he looked back over his shoulder toward the ship.

I lifted a hand to wave; his eyes were already fixed on me. He didn't stop rowing, but turned round and came on. I stood clinging to the rail, waiting.

The rowboat passed out of sight for a moment, under the lee of the *Cruizer*, and I heard the watch hail him, the deep half-audible answer, and felt something that had been knotted inside me for a long time let go at the sound of his voice.

I stood rooted, though, not able to move. Then there were footsteps on deck, and a murmur of voices—someone going to fetch the Governor—and I turned blindly, into Jamie's arms.

"Knew you'd come," I whispered into the linen of his shirt. He reeked of fire: smoke and pinesap and scorched cloth, and the bitter tang of turpentine. Reeked of stale sweat and horses, the weariness of a man who has not slept, who has labored all night, the faint yeasty smell of long hunger.

He held me close, ribs and breath and warmth and muscle, then put me away from him a little and looked down into my face. He had been smiling since I saw him. It lit his eyes, and without a word, he pulled the cap off my head and threw it over the rail. He ran his hands through my hair, fluffing it out into abandon, then cupped my head in his hands and kissed me, fingers digging into my scalp. He had a three-day beard, which rasped my skin like sandpaper, and his mouth was home and safety.

Somewhere behind him, one of the Marines coughed, and said loudly, "You wished to see the Governor, I believe, sir?"

He let go, slowly, and turned.

"I do indeed," he said, and put out a hand to me. "Sassenach?"

I took it, and followed the Marine, heading for the companionway. I glanced back over the rail, to see my cap bobbing in the swell, puffed with air and tranquil as a jellyfish.

The momentary illusion of peace vanished directly, though, once we were below.

The Governor had been up most of the night, as well, and didn't look much better than Jamie, though he was not, of course, besmeared with soot. He was, however, unshaven, bloodshot, and in no mood to be trifled with.

"Mr. Fraser," he said with a short nod. "You are James Fraser, I collect? And you dwell in the mountain backcountry?"

"I am the Fraser, of Fraser's Ridge," Jamie said courteously. "And I have come for my wife."

"Oh, have you." The Governor gave him a sour look and sat down, gesturing indifferently at a stool. "I regret to inform you, sir, that your wife is a prisoner of the Crown. Though perhaps you were aware of this?"

Jamie ignored this bit of sarcasm and took the proffered seat.

"In fact, she is not," he said. "It is true, is it not, that you have declared martial law upon the colony of North Carolina?"

"It is," Martin said shortly. This was rather a sore point, since while he *had* declared martial law, he was in no position actually to enforce it, but was obliged to float impotently off-shore, fuming, until and unless England chose to send him re-inforcements.

"Then in fact, all customary legal usage is suspended," Jamie pointed out. "You alone have control over the custody and dispo-sition of any prisoners—and my wife has in fact been in your cus-tody for some little time. Ye therefore have also the power to release her."

"Hm," said the Governor. Plainly he hadn't thought of that, and wasn't sure of its ramifications. At the same time, the notion that he was in control of anything at all at the moment was likely soothing to his inflamed spirits.

"She has not been committed for trial, and in fact, there has been no evidence whatever adduced against her," Jamie said firmly.

I found myself uttering a silent prayer of thanks that I had told MacDonald the gory details *after* his visit with the Governor—it might not be what a modern court called evidence, but being found with a knife in my hand and two warm, bloody corpses was very damned circumstantial.

"She is accused, but there is no merit to the charge. Surely, having had her acquaintance for even so short a time as you have, ye will have drawn your own conclusions as to her character?" Not waiting for an answer to this, he pressed on.

"When accusation was made, we did not resist the attempt to bring my wife—or myself, for I also have been accused in the matter—to trial. What better indication is there that we should hold such conviction of her innocence as to wish for a speedy trial to establish it?"

The Governor had narrowed his eyes, and appeared to be thinking intently.

"Your arguments are not entirely lacking in virtue, sir," he said at last, with formal courtesy. "However, I understand that the crime of which your wife stands accused was a most heinous one. For me to release her must necessarily cause public outcry—and I have had rather enough of public unrest," he added, with a bleak look at the scorched cuffs of Jamie's coat.

Jamie took a deep breath and had another go.

"I quite understand Your Excellency's reservations," he said. "Perhaps some . . . surety might be offered, which would overcome them?" ·

Martin sat bolt upright in his chair, receding jaw thrust out.

"What do you suggest, sir? Have you the impertinence, the—the—unspeakable bloody face to try to *bribe* me?" He slapped both hands down on the desk and glared from Jamie to me and back. "God damn it, I should hang the two of you, out of hand!"

"Very nice, Mr. Ohnat," I muttered to Jamie under my breath. "At least we're already married."

"Oh, ah," he replied, giving me a brief glance of incomprehension before returning his attention to the Governor, who was muttering "Swing them from the bloody yardarm . . . the infernal cheek of it, the creatures!"

"I had no such intent, sir." Jamie kept his voice level, his eyes direct. "What I offer is a bond, against my wife's appearance in court to answer the charge against her. When she does so appear, it would be returned to me."

Before the Governor could respond to this, he reached into his pocket and withdrew something small and dark, which he set on the desk. The black diamond.

The sight of it stopped Martin in mid-sentence. He blinked, once, his long-nosed face going almost comically blank. He rubbed a finger slowly across his upper lip, considering.

Having seen a great deal of the Governor's private correspondence and accounts by now, I was well aware that he had few private means, and was obliged to live far beyond his modest income in order to maintain the appearances necessary for a Royal Governor.

The Governor in turn was well aware that in the current state of unrest, there was little chance of my being brought to trial in any sort of timely manner. It could be months—and possibly years—before the court system was restored to anything like routine function. And for however long it took, he would have the diamond. He couldn't in honor simply sell the thing—but could most assuredly borrow a substantial sum against it, in the reasonable expectation that he might redeem it later.

I saw his eyes flicker toward the sooty marks on Jamie's coat, narrowing in speculation. There was also a good possibility of Jamie's being killed or arrested for treason—and I saw the impulse to do just that pop momentarily into his mind—which would leave the diamond perhaps in legal limbo, but certainly in Martin's possession. I had to force myself to keep on breathing.

But he wasn't stupid, Martin—nor was he venal. With a small sigh, he pushed the stone back toward Jamie.

"No, sir," he said, though his voice had now lost its earlier outrage. "I will not accept this as bond for your wife. But the notion of surety . . ." His gaze went to the stack of papers on his desk, and returned to Jamie.

"I will make you a proposition, sir," he said abruptly. "I have an action in train, an operation by which I hope to raise a considerable body of the Scottish Highlanders, who will march from the backcountry to the coast, there to meet with troops sent from England, and in the process, to subdue the countryside on behalf of the King."

He paused for breath, eyeing Jamie closely to assess the effect of his speech. I was standing close behind Jamie, and couldn't see his face, but didn't need to. Bree, joking, called it his "brag face"; no one looking at him would ever know whether he held four aces, a full house, or a pair of threes. I was betting on the pair of threes, myself—but Martin didn't know him nearly as well as I did.

"General Hugh MacDonald and a Colonel Donald McLeod came into the colony some time ago, and have been traversing the countryside, rallying support—which they have gained in gratifying numbers, I am pleased to say." His fingers drummed briefly on the letters, then stopped abruptly as he leaned forward.

"What I propose, then, sir, is this: you will return to the back-country, and gather such men as you can. You will then report to General MacDonald and commit your troops to his campaign. When I receive word from MacDonald that you have arrived—with, let us say, two hundred men—then, sir, I will release your wife to you."

My pulse was beating fast, and so was Jamie's; I could see it throbbing in his neck. Definitely a pair of threes. Obviously, MacDonald hadn't had time to tell the Governor—or hadn't known—just how widespread and acrimonious the response had been to Malva Christie's death. There were still men on the Ridge who would follow Jamie, I was sure—but many more who would not, or who would, but only if he repudiated me.

I was trying to think logically about the situation, as a means of distracting myself from the crushing disappointment of realizing that the Governor was not going to let me go. Jamie must go without me, leave me here. For an overwhelming instant, I thought I could not bear it; I would run mad, scream and leap across the desk to claw Josiah Martin's eyes out.

He glanced up, caught a glimpse of my face, and started back, half-rising from his chair.

Jamie put back a hand and gripped my forearm, hard.

"Be still, *a nighean*," he said softly.

I had been holding my breath without realizing it. Now I let it out in a gasp, and made myself breathe slowly.

Just as slowly, the Governor—a wary gaze still fixed on me—lowered himself back into his seat. Clearly, the accusation against me had just become a lot more likely, in his mind. *Fine,* I thought fiercely, to keep from crying. *See how easily you sleep, with me never more than a few feet away from you.*

Jamie drew a long, deep breath, and his shoulders squared beneath his tattered coat.

"You will give me leave, sir, to consider your proposal," he said formally, and letting go of my arm, rose to his feet.

"Do not despair, *mo chridhe*," he said to me in Gaelic. "I will see you when the morning comes."

He lifted my hand to his lips and kissed it, then, with the barest of nods to the Governor, strode out, without looking back.

There was an instant's silence in the cabin, and I heard his feet going away, climbing the ladder of the companionway. I didn't pause to consider, but reached down into my stays and withdrew the small knife I had taken from the surgeon's kit.

I jabbed it down with all my strength, so that it stuck in the wood of the desk and stood there, quivering before the Governor's astonished eyes.

"You fucking *bastard*," I said evenly, and left.

97

For the Sake of One Who Is

I was waiting at the rail again before dawn the next day. The smell of ashes was strong and acrid on the wind, but the smoke had gone. An early-morning haze still shrouded the shore, though, and I felt a small thrill of *déjà vu*, mingled with hope, as I saw the small boat come out of the mist, pulling slowly toward the ship.

As it grew closer, though, my hands tightened on the rail. It wasn't Jamie. For a few moments, I tried to convince myself that it was, that he had merely changed his coat—but with each stroke of the oars, it became more certain. I closed my eyes, stinging with tears, all the while telling myself that it was absurd to be so upset; it meant nothing.

Jamie would be here; he'd said so. The fact that someone else was coming early to the ship had nothing to do with him or me.

It did, though. Opening my eyes and wiping them on my wrist, I looked again at the rowboat, and felt a start of disbelief. It couldn't be. It was, though. He looked up at the watch's hail, and saw me at the rail. Our eyes met for an instant, then he bowed his head, reaching to the oars. Tom Christie.

The Governor was not amused at being roused from his bed at dawn for the third day running; I could hear him below, ordering one of the Marines to tell the fellow, whoever he was, to wait to a more reasonable hour—this followed by a peremptory slam of the cabin door.

I was not amused, either, and in no mood to wait. The Marine at the head of the companionway refused to allow me below, though. Heart pounding, then, I turned and made my way to the stern, where they had put Christie to wait the Governor's pleasure.

The Marine there hesitated, but after all, there were no orders to prevent me speaking with visitors; he let me pass.

"Mr. Christie." He was standing at the rail, staring back at the coast, but turned at my words.

"Mrs. Fraser." He was very pale; his grizzled beard stood out nearly black. He had trimmed it, though, and his hair, as well. While he still looked like a lightning-blasted tree, there was life in his eyes once more when he looked at me.

"My husband—" I began, but he cut me off.

"He is well. He awaits you on the shore; you will see him presently."

"Oh?" The boil of fear and fury inside me reduced itself slightly, as though someone had turned down the flame, but a sense of impatience was still steaming. "Well, what in bloody hell is going on, will you tell me that?"

He looked at me for a long moment in silence, then licked his lips briefly, and turned to look over the rail at the smooth gray swell. He glanced back at me and drew a deep breath, obviously bracing himself for something.

"I have come to confess to the murder of my daughter."

I simply stared at him, unable to make sense of his words. Then I assembled them into a sentence, read it from the tablet of my mind, and finally grasped it.

"No, you haven't," I said.

The faintest shadow of a smile seemed to stir in his beard, though it vanished almost before I had seen it.

"You remain contrary, I see," he said dryly.

"Never mind what I remain," I said, rather rudely. "Are you insane? Or is this Jamie's latest plan? Because if so—"

He stopped me with a hand on my wrist; I started at the touch, not expecting it.

"It is the truth," he said very softly. "And I will swear to it by the Holy Scriptures."

I stood looking at him, not moving. He looked back, directly, and I realized suddenly how seldom he had ever met my eyes; all through our acquaintance, he had glanced away, avoided my gaze, as though he sought to escape any real acknowledgment of me, even when obliged to speak to me.

Now that was gone, and the look in his eyes was nothing I had ever seen before. The lines of pain and suffering cut deep around them, and the lids were heavy with sorrow—but the eyes themselves were deep and calm as the sea beneath us. That sense he had carried through our nightmare journey south, that atmosphere of mute horror, numb pain, had left him, replaced by resolve and something else—something that burned, far down in his depths.

"Why?" I said at last, and he let go his grip on my wrist, stepping back a pace.

"D'ye remember once"—from the reminiscent tone of his voice, it might have been decades before—"ye asked me, did I think ye a witch?"

"I remember," I replied guardedly. "You said—" Now I remembered that conversation, all right, and something small and icy fluttered at the base of my spine. "You said that you believed in witches, all right—but you didn't think I was one."

He nodded, dark gray eyes fixed on me. I wondered whether he was about to revise that opinion, but apparently not.

"I believe in witches," he said with complete matter-of-fact seriousness. "For I've kent them. The girl was one, as was her mother before her." The icy flutter grew stronger.

"The girl," I said. "You mean your daughter? Malva?"

He shook his head a little, and his eyes took on a darker hue. "No daughter of mine," he said.

"Not—not yours? But—her eyes. She had your eyes." I heard myself say it, and could have bitten my tongue. He only smiled, though, grimly.

"And my brother's." He turned to the rail, put his hands on it, and looked across the stretch of sea, toward land. "Edgar was his name. When the Rising came, and I declared for the Stuarts, he would have none of it, saying 'twas folly. He begged me not to go." He shook his head slowly, seeing something in memory, that I knew was not the wooded shore.

"I thought—well, it doesna matter what I thought, but I went. And asked him, would he mind my wife, and the wee lad." He drew a deep breath, let it slowly out. "And he did."

"I see," I said very quietly. He turned his head sharply at the tone of my voice, gray eyes piercing.

"It was not his fault! Mona was a witch—an enchantress." His lips compressed at the expression on my face. "Ye don't believe me, I see. It is the truth; more than once, I caught her at it—working her charms, observing times—I came once to the roof o' the house at midnight, searching for her. I saw her there, stark naked and staring at the stars, standing in the center of a pentacle she'd drawn wi' the blood of a strangled dove, and her hair flying loose, mad in the wind."

"Her hair," I said, looking for some thread to grasp in this, and suddenly realizing. "She had hair like mine, didn't she?"

He nodded, looking away, and I saw his throat move as he swallowed.

"She was . . . what she was," he said softly. "I tried to save her—by prayer, by love. I could not."

"What happened to her?" I asked, keeping my voice as low as his. With the wind as it was, there was little chance of our being overheard here, but this was not the sort of thing I thought anyone should hear.

He sighed, and swallowed again.

"She was hangit," he said, sounding almost matter-of-fact about it. "For the murder of my brother."

This, it seemed, had happened while Tom was imprisoned at Ardsmuir; she had sent him word, before her execution, telling him of Malva's birth, and that she was confiding care of the children to Edgar's wife.

"I suppose she thought that funny," he said, sounding abstracted. "She'd the oddest sense of humor, Mona had."

I felt cold, beyond the chill of the early-morning breeze, and hugged my elbows.

"But you got them back—Allan and Malva."

He nodded; he had been transported, but had the good fortune to have his indenture bought by a kind and wealthy man, who had given him the money for the children's passage to the Colonies. But then both his employer and the wife he had taken here had died in an epidemic of the yellow fever, and casting about for some new opportunity, he had heard of Jamie Fraser's settling in North Carolina and that he would help those men he had known in Ardsmuir to land of their own.

"I would to God I had cut my own throat before I came," he said, turning back abruptly to me. "Believe me in that."

He seemed entirely sincere. I didn't know what to say in response, but he seemed to require none, and went on.

"The girl . . . she was nay more than five years old when I first saw her, but already she had it—the same slyness, the charm—the same darkness of soul."

He had tried to the best of his ability to save Malva, as well—to beat the wickedness out of her, to constrain the streak of wildness, above all, to keep her from working her wiles upon men.

"Her mither had that, too." His lips tightened at the thought. "Any man. It was the curse of Lilith that they had, the both of them."

I felt a hollowness in the pit of my stomach, as he came back now to the matter of Malva.

"But she was with child . . ." I said.

His face paled further, but his voice was firm.

"Aye, she was. I do not think it wrong to prevent yet another witch from entering the world."

Seeing my face, he went on before I could interrupt.

"Ye ken she tried to kill ye? You and me, both."

"What do you mean? Tried to kill me, how?"

"When ye told her about the invisible things, the—the germs. She took great interest in that. She told me, when I caught her wi' the bones."

"What bones?" I asked, a sliver of ice running down my back.

"The bones she took from Ephraim's grave, to work her charms upon your husband. She didna use them all, and I found them in her workbasket later. I beat her, badly, and she told me then."

Accustomed to wander alone in the woods in search of food plants and herbs, she had been doing so during the height of the dysentery epidemic. And in her wanderings, had come upon the isolated cabin of the sin-eater, that strange, damaged man. She had found him near death, burning with fever and sunk in coma, and while she stood there undecided whether to run for help, or only run, he had in fact died.

Whereupon, seized by inspiration—and bearing my careful teachings in mind—she had taken mucus and blood from the body and put it into a little bottle with a bit of broth from the kettle on the hearth, nurturing it inside her stays with the warmth of her own body.

And had slipped a few drops of this deadly infusion into my food, and that of her father, in the hope that if we fell sick, our deaths would be seen as no more than a part of the sickness that plagued the Ridge.

My lips felt stiff and bloodless.

"You're sure of this?" I whispered. He nodded, making no effort to convince me, and that alone gave me conviction that he spoke the truth.

"She wanted—Jamie?" I asked.

He closed his eyes for a moment; the sun was coming up, and while the brilliance of it was behind us, the gleam off the water was bright as silver plate.

"She . . . wanted," he said at last. "She lusted. Lusted for wealth, for position, for what she saw as freedom, not seeing it as license—never seeing!" He spoke with sudden violence, and I thought it was not Malva alone who had never seen things as he did.

But she had wanted Jamie, whether for himself or only for his property. And when her love charm failed, and the epidemic of sickness came, had taken a more direct way toward what she wanted. I could not yet find a way to grasp that—and yet I knew it was true.

And then, finding herself inconveniently with child, she had come up with a new scheme.

"Do you know who the father really was?" I asked, my throat tightening again—I thought it always would—at the memory of the sunlit garden and the two neat, small bodies, ruined and wasted. Such a waste.

He shook his head, but would not look at me, and I knew that he had some idea, at least. He would not tell me, though, and I supposed it didn't matter just now. And the Governor would be up soon, ready to receive him.

He, too, heard the stirrings down below, and took a deep breath.

"I could not let her destroy so many lives; could not let her go on. For she was a witch, make no mistake; that she failed to kill either you or me was no more than luck. She would have killed someone, before she finished. Perhaps you, if your husband clung to you. Perhaps him, in the hope of inheriting his property for the child." He took a ragged, painful breath.

"She was not born of my loins, and yet—she was my daughter, my blood. I could not . . . could not allow . . . I was responsible." He stopped, unable to finish. In this, I thought, he told the truth. And yet . . .

"Thomas," I said firmly, "this is twaddle, and you know it."

He looked at me, surprised, and I saw that tears stood in his eyes. He blinked them back and answered fiercely.

"Say you so? You know nothing, nothing!"

He saw me flinch, and looked down. Then, awkwardly, he reached out and took my hand. I felt the scars of the surgery I had done, the flexible strength of his gripping fingers.

"I have waited all my life, in a search . . ." He waved his free hand vaguely, then closed his fingers, as though grasping the thought, and continued more surely, "No. In hope. In hope of a thing I could not name, but that I knew must exist."

His eyes searched my face, intent, as though he memorized my features. I raised a hand, uncomfortable under this scrutiny, intending, I suppose, to tidy my mad hair—but he caught my hand and held it, surprising me.

"Leave it," he said.

Standing with both hands in his, I had no choice.

"Thomas," I said, uncertain. "Mr. Christie . . ."

"I became convinced that it was God I sought. Perhaps it was. But God is not flesh and blood, and the love of God alone could not sustain me.

"I have written down my confession." He let go, and poked a hand into his pocket, fumbling a little, and pulled out a folded paper, which he clutched in his short, solid fingers.

"I have sworn here that it was I who killed my daughter, for the shame she had brought upon me by her wantonness." He spoke firmly enough, but I could see the working of his throat above the wilted stock.

"You didn't," I said positively. "I know you didn't."

He blinked, gazing at me.

"No," he said, quite matter-of-fact. "But perhaps I should have.

"I have written a copy of this confession," he said, tucking the document back into his coat, "and have left it with the newspaper in New Bern. They will publish it. The Governor will accept it— how can he not?—and you will go free."

Those last four words struck me dumb. He was still gripping my right hand; his thumb stroked gently over my knuckles. I wanted to pull away, but forced myself to keep still, compelled by the look in his eyes, clear gray and naked now, without disguise.

"I have yearned always," he said softly, "for love given and returned; have spent my life in the attempt to give my love to those who were not worthy of it. Allow me this: to give my life for the sake of one who is."

I felt as though someone had knocked the wind from me. I hadn't any breath, but struggled to form words.

"Mr. Chr—Tom," I said. "You mustn't. Your life has—has value. You can't throw it away like this!"

He nodded, patient.

"I know that. If it did not, this would not matter."

Feet were coming up the companionway, and I heard the Governor's voice below, in cheerful conversation with the Captain of Marines.

"Thomas! Don't do this!"

He only looked at me, and smiled—had I ever seen him smile?—but did not speak. He raised my hand and bent over it; I felt the prickle of his beard and the warmth of his breath, the softness of his lips.

"I am your servant, madam," he said very softly. He squeezed my hand and released it, then turned and glanced toward the shore. A small boat was coming, dark against the glitter of the silver sea. "Your husband is coming for you. *Adieu*, Mrs. Fraser."

He turned and walked away, back steady in spite of the swell that rose and fell beneath us.

PART

ELEVEN

In the Day of Vengeance

98

To Keep a Ghost at Bay

J amie groaned, stretched, and sat down heavily on the bed.

"I feel as though someone's stepped on my cock."

"Oh?" I opened one eye to look at him. "Who?"

He gave me a bloodshot look.

"I dinna ken, but it feels as though it was someone heavy."

"Lie down," I said, yawning. "We haven't got to leave right away; you can rest a bit more."

He shook his head.

"Nay, I want to be home. We've been gone too long as it is." Nonetheless, he didn't get up and finish dressing, but continued to sit on the swaybacked inn bed in his shirt, big hands hanging idle between his thighs.

He looked tired to death, in spite of just having risen, and no wonder. I didn't think he could have slept at all for several days, what with his search for me, the burning of Fort Johnston, and the events attending my release from the *Cruizer*. Remembering, I felt a pall settle over my own spirits, in spite of the joy in which I had wakened, realizing that I was free, on land, and with Jamie.

"Lie down," I repeated. I rolled toward him, and put a hand on his back. "It's barely dawn. At least wait for breakfast; you can't travel without rest *or* food."

He glanced at the window, still shuttered; the cracks had begun to pale with the growing light, but I was right; there was no sound below of fires being stoked or pots banged in preparation. Capitulating suddenly, he collapsed slowly sideways, unable to repress a sigh as his head settled back on the pillow.

He didn't protest when I flung the ratty quilt over him, nor yet when I curved my body to fit round him, wrapping an arm about his waist and laying my cheek against his back. He still smelled of smoke, though both of us had washed hastily the night before, before falling into bed and a dearly bought oblivion.

I could feel how tired he was. My own joints still ached with fatigue—and from the lumps in the flattened, wool-stuffed mattress. Ian had been waiting with horses when we came ashore, and we had ridden as far as we could before darkness fell, finally fetching up at a ramshackle inn in the middle of nowhere, a crude roadside accommodation for wagoneers on their way to the coast.

"Malcolm," he'd said, with the slightest of hesitations, when the innkeeper had asked his name. "Alexander Malcolm."

"And Murray," Ian had said, yawning and scratching his ribs. "John Murray."

The innkeeper had nodded, not particularly caring. There was no reason why he should associate three nondescript, bedraggled travelers with a notorious case of murder—and yet I had felt panic well up under my diaphragm when he glanced at me.

I had sensed Jamie's hesitation in giving the name, his distaste for reassuming one of the many aliases he had once lived under. More than most men, he valued his name—I only hoped that given time, it would once more *have* value.

Roger might help. He would be a full-fledged minister by now, I thought, smiling at the thought. He had a true gift for soothing the divisions among the inhabitants of the Ridge, easing acrimony—and having the additional authority of being an ordained minister, his influence would be increased.

It would be good to have him back. And to see Bree and Jemmy again—I had a moment's longing for them, though we would see them soon; we meant to go through Cross Creek and collect them on the way. But of course, neither Bree nor Roger had any notion what had happened in the last three weeks—nor what life might now be like, in the wake of it.

The birds were in full voice in the trees outside; after the constant screeching of gulls and terns that formed the background of life on the *Cruizer,* the sound of them was tender, a homely conversation that made me long suddenly for the Ridge. I understood Jamie's strong urge to be home—even knowing that what we would find there was not the same life we had left. The Christies would be gone, for one thing.

I hadn't had the chance to ask Jamie about the circumstances of my rescue; I had finally been put ashore just before sunset, and we had ridden off at once, Jamie wanting to put as much distance as possible between me and Governor Martin—and, perhaps, Tom Christie.

"Jamie," I said softly, my breath warm in the folds of his shirt. "Did you make him do it? Tom?"

"No." His voice was soft, too. "He came to Fergus's printshop, the day after ye left the palace. He'd heard that the gaol had burned—"

I sat up in bed, shocked.

"What? Sheriff Tolliver's house? No one told me that!"

He rolled onto his back, looking up at me.

"I dinna suppose anyone ye've spoken to in the last week or two would know," he said mildly. "No one was killed, Sassenach—I asked."

"You're sure of it?" I asked with uneasy thoughts of Sadie Ferguson. "How did it happen? A mob?"

"No," he said, yawning. "From what I hear, Mrs. Tolliver got stinking drunk, stoked her laundry fire too high, then lay down in the shade and fell asleep. The wood collapsed, the embers set fire to the grass, it spread to the house, and . . ." He flipped a hand in dismissal. "The neighbor smelt smoke, though, and rushed over in time to drag Mrs. Tolliver and the bairn safe away. He said there was no one else in the place."

"Oh. Well . . ." I let him persuade me to lie down again, my head resting in the hollow of his shoulder. I couldn't feel strange with him, not after spending the night pressed close against him in the narrow bed, each of us aware of the other's every small movement. Still, I was very conscious of him.

And he of me; his arm was round me, his fingers unconsciously exploring the length of my back, lightly reading the shapes of me like braille as he talked.

"So, then, Tom. He kent about *L'Onion,* of course, and so went there, when he found ye'd disappeared from the gaol. By then, of course, ye'd gone from the palace, as well—it had taken him some time to part company wi' Richard Brown, without rousing their suspicions.

"But he found us there, and he told me what he meant to do." His fingers stroked the back of my neck, and I felt the tightness there begin to relax. "I told him to bide; I should have a go at getting ye back on my own—but if I could not . . ."

"So you know he didn't do it." I spoke with certainty. "Did he tell you he had?"

"He only said that he had kept silent while there was any chance of ye being tried and acquitted—but that had ye ever seemed in urgent danger, then he'd meant to speak up at once; that's why he insisted upon coming with us. I, ah, didna wish to ask him questions," he said delicately.

"But he didn't do it." I prodded, insistent. "Jamie, you *know* he didn't!"

I felt the rise of his chest under my cheek as he breathed.

"I know," he said softly.

We were silent for a bit. There was a sudden, muffled rapping outside, and I jerked—but it was only a woodpecker, hunting insects in the wormy timbers of the inn.

"Will they hang him, do you think?" I asked at last, staring up at the splintered beams above.

"I expect they will, aye." His fingers had resumed their half-unconscious motion, smoothing strands of my hair behind my ear. I lay still, listening to the slow thump of his heart, not wanting to ask what came next. But I had to.

"Jamie—tell me that he didn't do it—that he didn't make that confession—for me. Please." I didn't think I could bear that, not on top of everything else.

His fingers stilled, just touching my ear.

"He loves you. Ye ken that, aye?" He spoke very quietly; I heard the reverberation of the words in his chest, as much as the words themselves.

"He said he did." I felt a tightness in the throat, recalling that very direct gray look. Tom Christie was a man who said what he meant, and meant what he said—a man like Jamie, in that regard at least.

Jamie was quiet for what seemed a long time. Then he sighed, and turned his head so his cheek rested against my hair; I heard the faint rasp of his whiskers.

"Sassenach—I would have done the same, and counted my life well lost, if it saved ye. If he feels the same, then ye've done nay wrong to him, to take your life from his hand."

"Oh, dear," I said. "Oh, dear." I didn't want to think of any of it—not Tom's clear gray look and the calling of gulls, not the lines of affliction that carved his face into pieces, not the thought of what he had suffered, in loss, in guilt, in suspicion—in fear. Nor did I want to think of Malva, going unwitting to that death among the lettuces, her son heavy and peaceful in her womb. Nor the dark rusty blood drying in gouts and splashes among the leaves of the grapevines.

Above all, I didn't want to think that I had had any part in this tragedy—but that was inescapable.

I swallowed, hard.

"Jamie—can it ever be made right?"

He held my hand now, in his other hand, stroking his thumb gently back and forth under my fingers.

"The lass is dead, *mo chridhe*."

I closed my hand on his thumb, stilling it.

"Yes, and someone killed her—and it wasn't Tom. Oh, God, Jamie—who? Who was it?"

"I dinna ken," he said, and his eyes grew deep with sadness. "She was a lass who craved love, I think—and took it. But she didna ken how to give it back again."

I took a deep breath and asked the question that had lain unspoken between us since the murder.

"You don't think it was Ian?"

He nearly smiled at that.

"If it had been, *a nighean*, we'd know. Ian could kill; he couldna let you or me suffer for it."

I sighed, shifting my shoulders to ease the knot between them. He was right, and I felt comforted, on Ian's account—and still more guilty, on Tom Christie's.

"The man who fathered her child—if that wasn't Ian, and I so hope it wasn't—or someone who wanted her and killed her from jealousy when he found she was pregnant—"

"Or someone already wed. Or a woman, Sassenach."

That stopped me cold. "A woman?"

"She took love," he repeated, and shook his head. "What makes ye think it was only the young men she took it from?"

I closed my eyes, envisioning the possibilities. If she had had an affair with a married man—and they had looked at her, too, only more discreetly—yes, he might have killed her to keep it undiscovered. Or a scorned wife . . . I had a brief, shocking glimpse of Murdina Bug, face contorted with effort as she pressed the pillow over Lionel Brown's face. Arch? God, no. Once again, with a sense of utter hopelessness, I turned away from the question, seeing in mind the myriad faces of Fraser's Ridge—one of them hiding a murderer's soul.

"No, I know it can't be fixed for them—not Malva, or Tom. Or—or even Allan." For the first time, I spared a thought for Tom's son, so suddenly bereft of his family and in such dreadful circumstances. "But the rest . . ." The Ridge, I meant. Home. The life we had had. Us.

It had grown warm under the quilt, lying together—too warm, and I felt the heat of a hot flush wash over me. I sat up abruptly, throwing off the quilt, and leaned forward, lifting the hair off my neck in hopes of an instant's coolness.

"Stand up, Sassenach."

Jamie rolled out of bed, stood up, and took me by the hand, pulling me to my feet. Sweat had already broken out on my body like dew, and my cheeks were flushed. He bent and, taking the hem of my shift in both hands, stripped it off over my head.

He smiled faintly, looking at me, then bent and blew softly over my breasts. The coolness was a tiny but blessed relief, and my nipples rose in silent gratitude.

He opened the shutters for more air, then stepped back and pulled off his own shirt. Day had broken fully now, and the flood of pure morning light glimmered on the lines of his pale torso, on the silver web of his scars, the red-gold dusting of hair on his arms and legs, the rust and silver hairs of his sprouting beard. Likewise on the darkly suffused flesh of his genitals in their morning state, standing stiff against his belly and gone the deep, soft color one would find in the heart of a shadowed rose.

"As to putting things right," he said, "I canna say—though I mean to try." His eyes moved over me—stark naked, slightly salt-encrusted, and noticeably grimy about the feet and ankles. He smiled. "Shall we make a start, Sassenach?"

"You're so tired you can barely stand up," I protested. "Um— with certain exceptions," I added, glancing down. It was true; there were dark hollows under his eyes, and while the lines of his body were still long and graceful, they were also eloquent of deep fatigue. I felt as though I'd been run over by a steamroller myself, and *I* hadn't been up all night burning down forts.

"Well, seeing as we've a bed to hand, I didna plan to stand up for it," he replied. "Mind, I may never get back on my feet again, but I think I might be able to stay awake for the next ten minutes or so, at least. Ye can pinch me if I fall asleep," he suggested, smiling.

I rolled my eyes at him, but didn't argue. I lay down upon the grubby but now-cool sheets, and with a small tremor in the pit of my stomach, opened my legs for him.

We made love like people underwater, heavy-limbed and slow. Mute, able to speak only through crude pantomime. We had barely touched one another in this way since Malva's death—and the thought of her was still with us.

And not only her. For a time, I tried to focus only on Jamie, fixing my attention on the small intimacies of his body, so well known—the tiny white cicatrice of the triangular scar at his throat, the whorls of auburn hair and the sunburned skin beneath—but I was so tired that my mind refused to cooperate, and persisted in showing me instead random bits of memory or, even more disturbing, imagination.

"It's no good," I said. My eyes were shut tight, and I was clinging to the bedclothes with both hands, sheets knotted in my fingers. "I can't."

He made a small sound of surprise, but at once rolled away, leaving me damp and trembling.

"What is it, *a nighean*?" he said softly. He didn't touch me, but lay close.

"I don't know," I said, close to panic. "I keep seeing—I'm sorry, I'm sorry, Jamie. I see other people; it's like I'm making love to other m-men."

"Oh, aye?" He sounded cautious, but not upset. There was a whish of fabric, and he drew the sheet up over me. That helped a little, but not much. My heart was pounding hard in my chest, I felt dizzy and couldn't seem to take a full breath; my throat kept closing.

Bolus hystericus, I thought, quite calmly. *Do stop, Beauchamp.* Easier said than done, but I did stop worrying that I was having a heart attack.

"Ah . . ." Jamie's voice was cautious. "Who? Hodgepile and—"

"No!" My stomach clenched in revulsion at the thought. I swallowed. "No, I—I hadn't even thought of that."

He lay quietly beside me, breathing. I felt as though I were literally coming apart.

"Who is it that ye see, Claire?" he whispered. "Can ye tell me?"

"Frank," I said, fast, before I could change my mind. "And Tom. And—and Malva." My chest heaved, and I felt that I would never have air enough to breathe again.

"I could—all of a sudden, I could feel them all," I blurted. "Touching me. Wanting to come in." I rolled over, burying my face in the pillow, as though I could seal out everything.

Jamie was silent for a long time. Had I hurt him? I was sorry that I'd told him—but I had no defenses anymore. I could not lie, even for the best of reasons; there was simply no place to go, nowhere to hide. I felt beset by whispering ghosts, their loss, their need, their desperate love pulling me apart. Apart from Jamie, apart from myself.

My entire body was clenched and rigid, trying to keep from dissolution, and my face was pushed so deep into the pillow, trying to escape, that I felt I might suffocate, and was obliged to turn my head, gasping for breath.

"Claire." Jamie's voice was soft, but I felt his breath on my face and my eyes popped open. His eyes were soft, too, shadowed with sorrow. Very slowly, he lifted a hand and touched my lips.

"Tom," I blurted. "I feel as though he's already dead, because of me, and it's so terrible. I can't bear it, Jamie, I really can't!"

"I know." He moved his hand, hesitated. "Can ye bear it if I touch ye?"

"I don't know." I swallowed the lump in my throat. "Try it and see."

That made him smile, though I'd spoken with complete seriousness. He put his hand gently on my shoulder and turned me, then gathered me against him, moving slowly, so that I might pull back. I didn't.

I sank into him, and clung to him as though he was a floating spar, the only thing keeping me from drowning. He was.

He held me close and stroked my hair for a long time.

"Can ye weep for them, *mo nighean donn*?" he whispered into my hair at last. "Let them come in."

The mere idea made me go rigid with panic again. "I can't."

"Weep for them," he whispered, and his voice opened me deeper than his cock. "Ye canna hold a ghost at bay."

"I can't. I'm afraid," I said, but I was already shaking with grief, tears wet on my face. "I can't!"

And yet I did. Gave up the struggle and opened myself, to memory and sorrow. Sobbed as though my heart would break—and let it break, for them, and all I could not save.

"Let them come, and grieve them, Claire," he whispered. "And when they've gone, I'll take ye home."

99

Old Master

River Run

It had rained hard the night before, and while the sun had come out bright and hot, the ground was soggy and steam seemed to rise from it, adding to the thickness of the air. Brianna had put her hair up, to keep it off her neck, but wisps escaped constantly, clinging damply to forehead and cheeks, always in her eyes. She wiped a strand away crossly with the back of her hand; her fingers were smeared with the pigment she was grinding—and the humidity wasn't doing *that* any good, making the powder clump and cling to the sides of the mortar.

She needed it, though; she had a new commission, due to start this afternoon.

Jem was hanging round, too, bored and poking his fingers into everything. He was singing to himself, half under his breath; she paid no attention, until she happened to catch a few words.

"*What* did you say?" she asked, rounding on him incredulously. He couldn't have been singing "Folsom Prison Blues"—could he?

He blinked at her, lowered his chin to his chest, and said—in the deepest voice he could produce—"Hello. I'm Johnny Cash."

She narrowly stopped herself laughing out loud, feeling her cheeks go pink with the effort of containment.

"Where did you get that?" she asked, though she knew perfectly well. There was only one place he *could* have gotten it, and her heart rose up at the thought.

"Daddy," he said logically.

"Has Daddy been singing?" she asked, trying to sound casual. He had to have been. And, just as obviously, had to have been trying Claire's advice, to shift the register of his voice so as to loosen his frozen vocal cords.

"Uh-huh. Daddy sings a lot. He teached me the song about Sunday morning, and the one about Tom Dooley, and . . . and lots," he ended, rather at a loss.

"Did he? Well, that's—put that down!" she said, as he idly picked up an open pouch of rose madder.

"Oops." He looked guiltily at the blob of paint that had erupted from the leather pouch and landed on his shirt, then at her, and made a tentative move toward the door.

"Oops, he says," she said darkly. "Don't you move!" Snaking out a hand, she grabbed him by the collar and applied a turpentine-soaked rag vigorously to the front of his shirt, succeeding only in producing a large pink blotch rather than a vivid red line.

Jem was silent during this ordeal, head bobbing as she pulled him to and fro, swabbing.

"What are you doing in here, anyway?" she demanded crossly. "Didn't I tell you to go find something to do?" There was no shortage of things to do at River Run, after all.

He hung his head and muttered something, in which she made out the word "scared."

"Scared? Of what?" A little more gently, she pulled the shirt off over his head.

"The ghost."

"What ghost?" she asked warily, not sure yet how to handle this. She was aware that all of the slaves at River Run believed implicitly in ghosts, simply as a fact of life. So did virtually all of the Scottish settlers in Cross Creek, Campbelton, and the Ridge. And the Germans from Salem and Bethania. So, for that matter, did her own father.

She could not simply inform Jem that there was no such thing as a ghost—particularly as she was not entirely convinced of that herself.

"*Maighistear àrsaidh*'s ghost," he said, looking up at her for the first time, his dark blue eyes troubled. "Josh says he's been walkin'."

Something skittered down her back like a centipede. *Maighistear àrsaidh* was Old Master—Hector Cameron. Involuntarily, she glanced toward the window. They were in the small room above the stable block where she did the messier bits of paint preparation, and Hector Cameron's white marble mausoleum was clearly visible from here, gleaming like a tooth at the side of the lawn below.

"What makes Josh say that, I wonder?" she said, stalling for time. Her first impulse was to observe that ghosts didn't walk in broad daylight—but the obvious corollary to that was that they *did* walk by night, and the last thing she wanted to do was give Jem nightmares.

"He says Angelina saw him, night before last. A *big* ol' ghost," he said, stretching up, hands clawed, and widening his eyes in obvious imitation of Josh's account.

"Yeah? What was he doing?" She kept her tone light, only mildly interested, and it seemed to be working; Jem was more interested than scared, for the moment.

"Walkin'," Jem said with a small shrug. What else did ghosts do, after all?

"Was he smoking a pipe?" She'd caught sight of a tall gentleman strolling under the trees on the lawn below, and had an idea.

Jem looked somewhat taken aback at the notion of a pipe-smoking ghost.

"I dunno," he said dubiously. "Do ghosts smoke pipes?"

"I sort of doubt it," she said. "But Mr. Buchanan does. See him down there on the lawn?" She moved aside, gesturing toward the window with her chin, and Jem rose up on his toes to look out over the sill. Mr. Buchanan, an acquaintance of Duncan's who was staying at the house, was in fact smoking a pipe at this very moment; the faint aroma of his tobacco reached them through the open window.

"I think probably Angelina saw Mr. Buchanan walking around in the dark," she said. "Maybe he was in his nightshirt, going out to the necessary, and she just saw the white and *thought* he was a ghost."

Jem giggled at the thought. He seemed willing to be reassured, but hunched his skinny shoulders, peering closely at Mr. Buchanan.

"Josh says Angelina says the ghost was comin' out of old Mr. Hector's tomb," he said.

"I expect Mr. Buchanan just walked round it, and she saw him coming along the side, and *thought* he was coming out of it," she said, carefully avoiding any question as to why a middle-aged Scottish gentleman should be walking round tombs in his nightshirt; obviously, that wasn't a notion that struck Jemmy as odd.

It did occur to her to ask just what Angelina was doing outside in the middle of the night seeing ghosts, but on second thought, better not. The most likely reason for a maid's stealing out at night wasn't something a boy of Jemmy's age needed to hear about, either.

Her lips tightened a little at the thought of Malva Christie, who had perhaps gone to a rendezvous of her own in Claire's garden. Who? she wondered for the thousandth time, even as she automatically crossed herself, with a brief prayer for the repose of Malva's soul. Who had it been? If ever there were a ghost that should walk . . .

A small shiver passed over her, but that in turn gave her a new idea.

"I think it was Mr. Buchanan Angelina saw," she said firmly. "But if you ever *should* be afraid of ghosts—or anything else—you just make the Sign of the Cross, and say a quick prayer to your guardian angel."

The words gave her a slight sense of dizziness—perhaps it was *déjà vu*. She thought that someone—her mother? her father?—had said exactly that to her, sometime in the distant past of her childhood. What had she been afraid of? She no longer remembered that, but did remember the sense of security that the prayer had given her.

Jem frowned uncertainly at that; he knew the Sign of the Cross, but wasn't so sure about the angel prayer. She rehearsed it with him, feeling slightly guilty as she did so.

It was only a matter of time before he did something overtly

Catholic—like make the Sign of the Cross—in front of someone who mattered to Roger. For the most part, people either assumed that the minister's wife was Protestant, as well—or knew the truth, but were in no position to make a fuss about it. She was aware of a certain amount of muttering amongst Roger's flock, particularly in the wake of Malva's death and the talk about her parents—she felt her lips press tight again, and consciously relaxed them—but Roger steadfastly refused to hear any such remarks.

She felt a deep pang of longing for Roger, even with the worrying thought of potential religious complications fresh in her mind. He'd written; Elder McCorkle had been delayed, but should be in Edenton within the week. A week more, maybe, before the Presbytery Session convened—and then he'd be coming to River Run for her and Jem.

He was so happy at the thought of his ordination; surely once he *was* ordained, they couldn't defrock him—if that's what happened to miscreant ministers—for having a Catholic wife, could they?

Would she convert, if she had to, for Roger to be what he so clearly wanted—and needed—to be? The thought made her feel hollow, and she put her arms round Jemmy for reassurance. His skin was damp and still baby-soft, but she could feel the hardness of his bones pressing through, giving promise of a size that would likely one day match his father and grandfather. His father—there was a small, glowing thought that calmed all her anxieties, and even soothed the ache of missing Roger.

Jemmy's hair had long since grown again, but she kissed the spot behind his left ear where the hidden mark was, making him hunch his shoulders and giggle at the tickle of her breath on his neck.

She sent him off then, to take the paint-stained shirt to Matilda the laundress to see what might be done, and went back to her grinding.

The mineral smell of the malachite in her mortar seemed vaguely wrong; she lifted it and sniffed, even as she did so aware that that was ridiculous: ground stone couldn't go bad. Maybe the mixture of turpentine and the fumes from Mr. Buchanan's pipe was affecting her sense of smell. She shook her head, and scraped the soft green powder carefully out into a vial, to be mixed with walnut oil or used in an egg tempera later.

She cast an appraising eye over the selection of boxes and

pouches—some supplied by Aunt Jocasta, others courtesy of John Grey, sent specially from London—and the vials and drying trays of the pigments she'd ground herself, to see what else might be needed.

This afternoon, she'd only be making preliminary sketches— the commission was for a portrait of Mr. Forbes's ancient mother—but she might have only a week or two to finish the job before Roger's return; she couldn't waste—

A wave of dizziness made her sit down suddenly, and black spots flickered through her vision. She put her head between her knees, breathing deep. That didn't help; the air was raw with turps, and thick with the meaty, decaying animal smells of the stables below.

She lifted her head, and grabbed for the edge of the table. Her insides seemed to have turned abruptly to a liquid substance that shifted with her movement like water in a bowl, sloshing from belly to throat and back, leaving the bitter yellow smell of bile at the back of her nose.

"Oh, God."

The liquid in her belly rushed up her throat, and she had barely time to seize the washbasin from the table and dump the water on the floor before her stomach turned inside out in the frantic effort to empty itself.

She set the basin down, very carefully, and sat panting, staring at the wet blotch on the floor, as the world beneath her shifted on its axis and settled at a new, uneasy angle.

"Congratulations, Roger," she said out loud, her voice sounding faint and uncertain in the close, damp air. "I *think* you're going to be a daddy. Again."

She sat still for some time, cautiously exploring the sensations of her body, looking for certainty. She hadn't been sick with Jemmy—but she remembered the oddly altered quality of her senses; that odd state called synesthesia, where sight, smell, taste, and even sometimes hearing occasionally and weirdly took on characteristics of each other.

It had gone away as abruptly as it had happened; the tang of Mr. Buchanan's tobacco was much stronger, but now it was only the mellow burning of cured leaves, not a mottled green-brown thing that writhed through her sinuses and rattled the membranes of her brain like a tin roof in a hailstorm.

She had been concentrating so hard on her bodily sensations and what they might or might not mean that she hadn't really noticed the voices in the next room. That was Duncan's modest lair, where he kept the ledgers and accounts of the estate and—she thought—went to hide, when the grandeur of the house became too much for him.

Mr. Buchanan was in there with Duncan now, and what had started out as a genial thrum of conversation was now showing signs of strain. She got up, relieved to feel only a slight residual clamminess now, and picked up the basin. She had the natural human inclinations toward eavesdropping, but lately, she had been careful not to hear anything but what she must.

Duncan and her aunt Jocasta were stout Loyalists, and nothing she could say by way of tactful urging or logical argument would sway them. She had overheard more than one of Duncan's private conversations with local Tories that made her heart go small with apprehension, knowing as she did what would be the outcome of the present events.

Here in the piedmont, in the heart of the Cape Fear country, most of the solid citizens *were* Loyalists, convinced that the violence taking place to the north was an overblown rumpus that might be unnecessary, and if it was not, had little to do with them—and that what was most needed here was a firm hand to rein in the wild-eyed Whigs, before their excesses provoked a ruinous retaliation. Knowing that exactly such a ruinous retaliation was coming—and to people she liked, or even loved—gave her what her father called the grue: a cold sense of oppressive horror, coiling through the blood.

"When, then?" Buchanan's voice came clearly as she opened the door, sounding impatient. "They will not wait, Duncan. I must have the money by Wednesday week, or Dunkling will sell the arms elsewhere; ye ken it's a seller's market the noo. For gold, he'll wait—but not for long."

"Aye, I ken that fine, Sawny." Duncan sounded impatient—and very uneasy, Brianna thought. "If it can be done, it will be."

"IF?" Buchanan cried. "What is this 'if'? 'Til now, it's been, oh, aye, Sawny, nay difficulty, to be sure, Sawny, tell Dunkling it's on, oh, of *course*, Sawny—"

"I said, Alexander, that if it can be done, it will." Duncan's voice was low, but suddenly had a note of steel in it that she had never heard before.

Buchanan said something rude in the Gaelic, and suddenly the door of Duncan's office burst open and the man himself popped out, in so great a huff that he barely saw her, and gave her no more than a brusque nod in passing.

Which was just as well, she thought, since she was standing there holding a bowl full of vomit.

Before she could move to dispose of it, Duncan came out in turn. He looked hot, cross—and extremely worried. He did, however, notice her.

"How d'ye fare, lass?" he asked, squinting at her. "Ye're that bit green; have ye eaten aught amiss?"

"I think so. But I'm all right now," she said, hastily turning to put the basin back in the room behind her. She set it on the floor and closed the door on it. "Are you, er, all right, Duncan?"

He hesitated for an instant, but whatever was bothering him was too overwhelming to keep it bottled up. He glanced about, but none of the slaves was up here at this time of day. He leaned close, nonetheless, and lowered his voice.

"Have ye by chance . . . seen anything peculiar, *a nighean*?"

"Peculiar, how?"

He rubbed a knuckle under his drooping mustache, and glanced round once more.

"Near Hector Cameron's tomb, say?" he asked, his voice pitched only just above a whisper.

Her diaphragm, still sore from vomiting, contracted sharply at that, and she put a hand to her middle.

"Ye have, then?" Duncan's expression sharpened.

"Not me," she said, and explained about Jemmy, Angelina, and the supposed ghost.

"I thought perhaps it was Mr. Buchanan," she finished, nodding toward the stair down which Alexander Buchanan had vanished.

"Now, there's a thought," Duncan muttered, rubbing distractedly at his grizzled temple. "But no . . . surely not. He couldna—but it's a thought." Brianna thought that he looked very slightly more hopeful.

"Duncan—can you tell me what's wrong?"

He took a deep breath, shaking his head—not in refusal, but in perplexity—and let it out again, his shoulders slumping.

"The gold," he said simply. "It's gone."

Seven thousand pounds in gold bullion was a substantial amount, in all senses of the word. She had no idea how much such a sum might weigh, but it had completely lined Jocasta's coffin, standing chastely next to Hector Cameron's in the family mausoleum.

"What do you mean 'gone'?" she blurted. "*All* of it?"

Duncan clutched her arm, features contorted in the urge to shush her.

"Aye, all of it," he said, looking round yet again. "For God's sake, lass, keep your voice down!"

"When did it go? Or rather," she amended, "when did you find it gone?"

"Last night." He looked round yet again, and jerked his chin toward his office. "Come in, lass; I'll tell ye about it."

Duncan's agitation subsided a little as he told her the story; by the time he had finished, he had regained a certain amount of outward calm.

The seven thousand pounds was what was left of the original ten thousand, which in turn was one-third of the thirty thousand sent—too late, but sent nonetheless—from Louis of France in support of Charles Stuart's doomed attempt on the thrones of England and Scotland.

"Hector was careful, aye?" Duncan explained. "He lived as a rich man, but always within such means as a place like this"—he waved his one hand around, indicating the grounds and messuages of River Run—"might provide. He spent a thousand pound acquiring the land and building the house, then over the years, another thousand in slaves, cattle, and the like. And a thousand pound he put to the bankers—Jo said he couldna bear the thought of all that money sitting, earning nay interest"—he gave her a small, wry smile—"though he was too clever to at-tract attention by putting it all out. I suppose he meant, maybe, to invest the rest, a bit at a time—but he died before that was done."

Leaving Jocasta as a very wealthy widow—but even more cau-tious than her husband had been about attracting undue attention. And so the gold had sat, safe in its hiding place, save for the one ingot being gradually whittled away and disposed of by Ulysses. Which had disappeared, she remembered with a qualm. *Someone* knew there was gold here.

Perhaps whoever had taken that ingot had guessed that there was more—and hunted, quietly, patiently, until they found it.

But now—

"Ye'll have heard about General MacDonald?"

She'd heard the name frequently of late, in conversation—he was a Scottish general, more or less retired, she'd assumed—who had been staying here and there, the guest of various prominent fami-lies. She *hadn't* heard of his purpose, though.

"He means to raise men—three thousand, four—among the Highlanders, to march to the coast. The Governor's sent for aid; troopships are coming. So the General's men will come down through the Cape Fear valley"—he made a graceful swooping gesture with his hand—"meet the Governor and his troops—and pincer the rebel militias that are a-building."

"And you meant to give him the gold—or no," she corrected herself. "You meant to give him arms and powder."

He nodded and chewed his mustaches, looking unhappy.

"A man named Dunkling; Alexander knows him. Lord Dunsmore is gathering a great store of powder and arms in Virginia, and Dunkling is one of his lieutenants—and willing to give up some of that store, in return for gold."

"Which is now gone." She took a deep breath, feeling sweat trickle down between her breasts, further dampening her shift.

"Which is now gone," he agreed bleakly. "And I'm left to won-der what about this ghost of wee Jem's, aye?"

Ghost, indeed. For someone to have entered a place like River Run, teeming with people, and to have moved several hundred pounds by weight of gold, completely unnoticed . . .

The sound of feet on the stairs caused Duncan to jerk his head sharply toward the door, but it was only Josh, one of the black grooms, his hat in his hand.

"Best we be going, Miss Bree," he said, bowing respectfully. "If ye be wanting the light, like?"

For her drawings, he meant. It was a good hour's trip into Cross Creek to lawyer Forbes's house, and the sun was rising fast toward noon.

She glanced at her green-smeared fingers, and recalled the hair straggling untidily down from its makeshift bun; she'd have to tidy herself a bit first.

"Go, lass." Duncan waved her toward the door, his lean face still creased with worry but lightened a little by having shared it.

She kissed him affectionately on the forehead and went down after Josh. She *was* worried, and not only about missing gold and prowling ghosts. General MacDonald, indeed. For if he meant to raise fighting men among the Highlanders, one of the natural places for him to go was to her father.

As Roger had noted to her sometime earlier, *"Jamie can walk the tightrope between Whigs and Tories better than any man I know—but when push comes to shove . . . he'll have to jump."*

The push had come at Mecklenberg. But shove, she thought, was named MacDonald.

100

A Trip to the Seaside

Neil Forbes, thinking it prudent to be absent from his usual haunts for a time, had removed to Edenton, with the excuse of taking his aged mother to visit her even more aged sister. He had enjoyed the long journey, in spite of his mother's complaints about the clouds of dust raised by another carriage that preceded them.

He had been loath to sacrifice his sight of that carriage—a small, well-sprung affair, whose windows were sealed and heavily curtained. But he had always been a devoted son, and at the next post stop, he went to speak to the driver. The other coach obligingly dropped back, following them at a convenient distance.

"Whatever are ye lookin' at, Neil?" his mother demanded, looking up from fastening her favorite garnet brooch. "That's the third time ye've had a peek out thon window."

"Not a thing, Mam," he said, inhaling deeply. "Only taking pleasure in the day. Such beautiful weather, is it not?"

Mrs. Forbes sniffed, but obligingly settled her spectacles on her nose and leaned to peer out.

"Aye, weel, it's fair enough," she admitted dubiously. "Hot, though, and damp enough to wring buckets from your shirt."

"Never mind, *a leannan*," he said, patting her black-clad shoulder. "We'll be in Edenton afore ye know. It'll be cooler there. Nothing like a sea-breeze, so they say, to put the roses in your cheeks!"

101

Nightwatch

Edenton

The Reverend McMillan's house was on the water. A blessing in the hot, muggy weather. The offshore breeze in the evening swept everything away—heat, hearth smoke, mosquitoes. The men sat on the big porch after supper, smoking their pipes and enjoying the respite.

Roger's enjoyment was spiced by the guilty awareness that Mrs. Reverend McMillan and her three daughters were sweating to and fro, washing dishes, clearing away, sweeping floors, boiling up the leftover ham bones from supper with lentils for tomorrow's soup, putting children to bed, and generally slaving away in the stuffy, sweltering confines of the house. At home, he would have felt obliged to help with such work, or face Brianna's wrath; here, such an offer would have been received with drop-jawed incredulity, followed by deep suspicion. Instead, he sat peacefully in the cool evening breeze, watching fishing boats come in across the water of the sound and sipping something that passed for coffee, engaged in pleasant male conversation.

There was, he thought, occasionally something to be said for the eighteenth-century model of sexual roles.

They were talking over the news from the south: the flight of Governor Martin from New Bern, the burning of Fort Johnston. The political climate of Edenton was strongly Whiggish, and the company was largely clerical—the Reverend Doctor McCorkle, his secretary Warren Lee, the Reverend Jay McMillan, Reverend Patrick Dugan, and four "inquirers" awaiting ordination besides Roger—but there were still currents of political disagreement flowing beneath the outwardly cordial surface of the conversation.

Roger himself said little; he didn't wish to offend McMillan's hospitality by contributing to any argument—and something inside him wished for quiet, to contemplate tomorrow.

Then the conversation took a new turn, though, and he found himself paying rapt attention. The Continental Congress had met in Philadelphia two months before, and given General Washington command of the Continental army. Warren Lee had been in Philadelphia at the time, and was giving the company a vivid account of the battle at Breed's Hill, at which he had been present.

"General Putnam, he brought up wagonloads of dirt and brush, to the neck of the Charlestown peninsula—you said you knew it, sir?" he asked, courteously turning toward Roger. "Well, Colonel Prescott, he's there already, with two militia comp'nies from Massachusetts, and parts of another from Connecticut—was mebbe a thousand men in all, and dear Lord, was they a stench from the camps!"

His soft Southern accent—Lee was a Virginian—held a slight
touch of amusement, but this faded as he went on.

"General Ward, he'd give orders to fortify this one hill, Bunker
Hill, they call it, for an old redoubt atop. But Colonel Prescott, he
goes up it and don't care so much for the looks, him and Mr.
Gridley, the engineer. So they leave a detachment there, and go on
to Breed's Hill, what they think is maybe better to the purpose,
bein' closer to the harbor.

"Now, this is all at night, mind. I was with one of the
Massachusetts companies, and we marched right smart, then spent
the whole night through, 'twixt midnight and dawn, diggin'
trenches and raising up six-foot walls about the perimeter.

"Come the dawn, and we skulked down behind our fortifications, and just in time, too, for there's a British ship in the harbor—the *Lively*, they said—and she opens fire the minute the
sun's up. Looked right pretty, for the fog was still on the water and
the cannon lit it up in red flashes. Did no harm, though; most all
the balls fell short into the harbor—did see one whaleboat at the
docks hit, though; stove it like kindling. The crew, they'd hopped
out like fleas when the *Lively* took to firing. From where I was, I
could just see 'em, hoppin' up and down on the dock, a-shakin'
their fists—then the *Lively* let off another broadside, and they all
fell flat or run like rabbits."

The light was nearly gone, and Lee's young face invisible in
the shadows, but the amusement in his voice made a small rumble
of laughter run among the other men.

"They was some firin' from a little battery up on Copp's
Hill, and one or two of the other ships, they let off a pop or two,
but they could see 'twan't no earthly use and ceased. Then
come in some fellows from New Hampshire to join up with us,
and that was purely heartening. But General Putnam, he sends a
good many men back to work on the fortifications at Bunker,
and the New Hampshire folk, they're crouched way down on
the left, where they's got no cover beyond rail fences stuffed
with mown grass. Lookin' at 'em down there, I was pleased as
punch to have four feet of solid earthwork in front of me, I tell
you, gentlemen."

The British troops had set out across the Charles River, bold as
brass under the midday sun, with the warships behind them and
the batteries on shore all providing covering fire.

"We didn't fire back, of course. Had no cannon," Lee said with an audible shrug.

Roger, listening intently, couldn't keep from asking a question at this point.

"Is it true that Colonel Stark said, 'Don't fire until you see the whites of their eyes'?"

Lee coughed discreetly.

"Well, sir. I couldn't say for sure as no one said that, but I didn't hear it myself. Mind, I *did* hear one colonel call out, 'Any whoreson fool wastes his powder afore the bastards are close enough to kill is gonna get his musket shoved up his arse butt-first!'"

The assembly erupted into laughter. An inquiry from Mrs. McMillan, who had come out to offer further refreshment, as to the source of this merriment shut them all up sharp, though, and they listened with a fair assumption of sober attention to the rest of Lee's account.

"Well, so, then, on they come, and I will say 'twas a daunting sight. They'd several regiments, and all in their different colors, fusiliers and grenadiers, Royal Marines, and a proper boiling of light infantry, all comin' on over the ground like a horde of ants, and just as mean.

"I wouldn't make great claim to bravery myself, gentlemen, but I would say the fellows standin' with me had some nerve. We did let 'em come, and the first ranks weren't no more than ten feet away when our volley cut into them.

"They rallied, came back on, and we cut them down again—like ninepins. And the officers—there was a powerful lot of the officers went; they were on their horses, see? I—I shot one such. He keeled over, but he didn't fall off—his horse carried him away. Kind of lolling, with his head loose. But he didn't fall."

Lee's voice had lost some of its color, and Roger saw the burly form of the Reverend Doctor McCorkle lean toward his secretary, touching his shoulder.

"They rallied a third time, and came on. And . . . we were most of us out of ammunition. They came on over the earthworks and through the fences. With their bayonets fixed."

Roger was sitting on the steps of the porch, Lee above him and several feet away, but could hear the young man swallow.

"We fell back. That's how they say it. We ran, is what we did. So'd they."

He swallowed again.

"A bayonet—it makes a terrible sound, goin' into a man. Just—terrible. I can't say how it is, describe it properly. Heard it, though, and more'n once. Was a good many run straight through the body that day—skewered and then the steel pulled out, and they left to die on the ground, floppin' like fish."

Roger had seen—handled—eighteenth-century bayonets, often. A seventeen-inch triangular blade, heavy and brutal, with a blood groove down one side. He thought, quite suddenly, of the furrowed scar that ran up Jamie Fraser's thigh, and rose to his feet. Murmuring a brief excuse, he left the porch, and walked down the shore, pausing only for a moment to shed his shoes and stockings.

The tide was going out; sand and shingle were wet and cool under his bare feet. The breeze rattled faintly among palmetto leaves behind him, and a line of pelicans flew down the shore, solemn against the last of the light. He walked a little way into the surf, small rippling waves that tugged at his heels, sucking the sand away beneath him, making him shift and sway to keep his balance.

Far out on the water of Albemarle Sound, he could see lights; fishing boats, with small fires built in sandboxes aboard, to light the torches the fishermen swung over the side. These seemed to float in the air, swinging to and fro, their reflections in the water winking slowly in and out like fireflies.

The stars were coming out. He stood looking up, trying to empty his mind, his heart, open himself to the love of God.

Tomorrow, he would be a minister. *Thou art a priest forever,* said the ordination service, quoting from the Bible, *after the order of Melchizedek.*

"Are you afraid?" Brianna had asked him, when he'd told her. "Yeah," he said softly, aloud.

He stood until the tide left him, then followed it, walking into the water, wanting the rhythmic touch of the waves.

"Will you do it anyway?"

"Yeah," he said, more softly still. He had no idea what he was agreeing to, but said it, anyway. Far down the beach behind him, the breeze brought him now and then a snatch of laughter, a few words from the Reverend McMillan's porch. They had moved on, then, from the talk of war and death.

Had any of them ever killed a man? Lee, perhaps. The

Reverend Doctor McCorkle? He snorted a little at the thought, but did not dismiss it. He turned and walked a little further, until the only sounds were those of the waves and the offshore wind.

Soul-searching. It was what squires used to do, he thought, smiling a little wryly at the thought. The night before he became a knight, a young man would keep vigil in church or chapel, watching through the dark hours, lighted only by the glow of a sanctuary lamp, praying.

For what? he wondered. Purity of mind, singleness of purpose. Courage? Or perhaps forgiveness?

He hadn't meant to kill Randall Lillington; that had been almost accident, and what wasn't had been self-defense. But he had been hunting when he did it, had gone out looking for Stephen Bonnet, meaning to kill him in cold blood. And Harley Boble; he could still see the shine of the thieftaker's eyes, feel the echo of the blow, the shards of the man's skull reverberating through the bones of his own arm. He'd meant that, yes. Could have stopped. Didn't.

Tomorrow, he would swear before God that he believed in the doctrine of predestination, that he had been meant to do what he had done. Perhaps.

Maybe I don't believe that, so much, he thought, doubt stealing in. *But maybe I do. Christ—oh, sorry*—he apologized mentally—*can I be a proper minister, with doubts? I think everyone's got them, but if I've got too many—maybe ye'd best let me know now, before it's too late.*

His feet had gone numb, and the sky was ablaze with a glory of stars, thick in the black velvet night. He heard the crunch of footsteps among the shingle and the sea wrack nearby.

It was Warren Lee—tall and gangly by starlight, the Reverend Doctor McCorkle's secretary, erstwhile militiaman.

"Thought I'd take a bit of air," Lee said, his voice hardly audible above the hiss of the sea.

"Aye, well, there's a lot of it, and it's free," Roger said as amiably as he could. Lee chuckled briefly in response, but luckily didn't seem disposed to talk.

They stood for some time, watching the fishing boats. Then, by unspoken consent, turned to go back. The house was dark, the porch deserted. A single candle burned in the window, though, lighting them home.

"That officer, the one I shot," Lee blurted suddenly. "I pray for him. Every night."

Lee shut up abruptly, embarrassed. Roger breathed slow and deep, feeling the jerk of his own heart. Had he ever prayed for Lillington, or Boble?

"I will, too," he said.

"Thank you," said Lee very softly, and side by side, they made their way back up the beach, pausing to pick up their shoes, going back barefooted, sand drying on their feet.

They had sat down on the steps to brush it off before going in, when the door behind them opened.

"Mr. MacKenzie?" said the Reverend McMillan, and something in his voice pulled Roger to his feet, heart pounding. "You have a visitor."

He saw the tall silhouette behind McMillan, and knew, even before Jamie Fraser's pale, fierce face appeared, eyes black in the candlelight.

"He's taken Brianna," Jamie said without preamble. "Ye'll come."

102

Anemone

Feet trampled back and forth overhead, and she could hear voices, but most of the words were too muffled to make out. There was a chorus of jovial shouts on the side nearest shore, and cordial feminine shrieks in reply.

The cabin had a wide, paned window—did you call it a window on a ship, she wondered, or had it some special nautical name?—that ran behind the bunk, raked back with the angle of the stern. It was made in small, thick panes, set in leading. No hope there of escape, but it did offer the possibility of air, and perhaps information regarding their whereabouts.

Repressing a qualm of nauseated distaste, she clambered across the stained and rumpled sheets of the bed. She pressed close to the window and pushed her face into one of the open panes, taking deep breaths to dispel the aromas of the cabin, though the smell of the harbor was no great improvement, rife as it was with the smell of dead fish, sewage, and baking mud.

She could see a small dock, and moving figures on it. A fire was burning on the shore outside a low, whitewashed building roofed with palmetto leaves. It was too dark to see what, if anything, lay beyond the building. There must be at least a small town, though, judging from the noise of the people on the dock.

There were voices outside the cabin door, coming closer. ". . . meet him on Ocracoke, the dark o' the moon," said one, to which the other replied in an indistinct mumble, before the door flew open.

"Care to join the party, sweetheart? Or have ye started without me?"

She whirled on her knees, heart hammering in her throat. Stephen Bonnet stood inside the door to the cabin, a bottle in one hand and a slight smile on his face. She took a deep breath to quell the shock, and nearly gagged on the stale scent of sex that wafted from the sheets under her knees. She scrambled off the bed, heedless of her clothes, and felt a rip at the waist as her knee caught in her skirt.

"Where are we?" she demanded. Her voice sounded shrill, panicked to her own ears.

"On the *Anemone*," he said patiently, still smiling.

"You know that isn't what I mean!" The neck of her gown and chemise had torn in the struggle when the men pulled her from her horse, and most of one breast was exposed; she put up a hand, pushing the fabric back in place.

"Do I?" He set the bottle on the desk, and reached to unfasten the stock from his neck. "Ah, that's better." He rubbed at the dark red line across his throat, and she had a sudden, piercing vision of Roger's throat, with its ragged scar.

"I wish to know what this town is called," she said, deepening her voice and fixing him with a gimlet eye. She didn't expect that what worked on her father's tenants would work on him, but the assumption of an air of command helped to steady her a bit.

"Well, that's an easily gratified wish, to be sure." He waved a casual hand toward the shore. "Roanoke." He shucked his coat, tossing it carelessly over the stool. The linen of his shirt was crumpled, and clung damply to his chest and shoulders.

"Ye'd best take off the gown, darlin'; it's hot."

He reached for the strings that tied his shirt, and she moved abruptly away from the bed, glancing round the cabin, searching the shadows for something that could be used as a weapon. Stool, lamp, logbook, bottle . . . there. A piece of wood showed among the rubble on the desk, the blunt end of a marlinespike.

He frowned, attention fastened momentarily on a knot in the string. She took two long steps and seized the marlinespike, yanking it off the desk in a shower of rubbish and clanging oddments.

"Stand back." She held the thing like a baseball bat, gripped in both hands. Sweat streamed down the hollow of her back, but her hands felt cold and her face went hot and cold and hot again, ripples of heat and terror rolling down her skin.

Bonnet looked at her as though she had gone mad.

"Whatever will ye be after doing with that, woman?" He left off fiddling with his shirt and took a step toward her. She took one back, raising the club.

"Don't fucking touch me!"

He stared at her, eyes fixed wide, pale green and unblinking above a small, odd smile. Still smiling, he took another step toward her. Then another, and the fear boiled off in a surge of rage. Her shoulders bunched and lifted, ready.

"I mean it! Stand back or I'll kill you. I'll know who this baby's father is, if I die for it!"

He had raised a hand, as though to grasp the club and jerk it away from her, but at this, he stopped abruptly.

"Baby? You are with child?"

She swallowed, her breath still thick in her throat. The blood hammered in her ears, and the smooth wood was slick with sweat from her palms. She tightened her grip, trying to keep the rage alive, but it was already dying.

"Yes. I think so. I'll know for sure in two weeks."

His sandy eyebrows lifted.

"Hm!" With a short grunt, he stepped back, surveying her with interest. Slowly, his eyes traveled over her, appraising her one bared breast.

The sudden spurt of rage had drained away, leaving her breathless and empty-bellied. She kept hold of the marlinespike, but her wrists quivered, and she lowered it.

"Is that the way of it, then?"

He leaned forward and reached out, quite without lascivious intent now. Startled, she froze for an instant, and he weighed the breast in one hand, kneading thoughtfully, as though it were a grapefruit he meant to buy at market. She gasped and hit at him one-handed with the club, but she had lost what readiness she had, and the blow bounced off his shoulder, rocking him but having little other effect. He grunted and stepped back, rubbing at his shoulder.

"Could be. Well, then." He frowned, and tugged at the front of his breeches, adjusting himself without the slightest embarrassment. "Lucky we're in port, I suppose."

She made no sense whatever of this remark, but didn't care; apparently he had changed his mind upon hearing her revelation, and the feeling of relief made her knees go weak and her skin prickle with sweat. She sat down, quite suddenly, upon the stool, the club clanking to the floor beside her.

Bonnet had put his head out into the corridor, and was bellowing for someone named Orden. Whoever Orden was, he didn't come into the cabin, but within a few moments, a voice mumbled interrogatively outside.

"Fetch me down a whore from the docks," Bonnet said, in the casual tone of one ordering a fresh pint of bitter. "Clean, mind, and fairly young."

He shut the door then, and turned to the table, scrabbling through the debris until he unearthed a pewter cup. He poured a drink, quaffed half of it, and then—seeming belatedly to realize that she was still there—offered her the bottle with a vague "Eh?" of invitation.

She shook her head, wordless. A faint hope had sprung up in the back of her mind. He did have some faint streak of gallantry, or at least decency; he had come back to rescue her from the burning warehouse, and he had left her the stone for what he assumed to be his child. Now he had abandoned his advances, upon hearing that she was with child again. Perhaps he would let her go, then, particularly if she was of no immediate use to him.

"So . . . you don't want me?" she said, edging her feet under her, ready to leap up and run, as soon as the door opened to admit her replacement. She hoped she *could* run; her knees were still trembling with reaction.

Bonnet glanced at her, surprised.

"I've split your quim once already, sweetheart," he said, and grinned. "I recall the red hair—a lovely sight, sure—but it wasn't so memorable an experience otherwise that I can't be waitin' to repeat it. Time enough, darlin', time enough." He chucked her negligently under the chin, and gulped more of his drink. "For now, though, LeRoi's needing a bit of a gallop."

"Why am I here?" she demanded.

Distracted, he pulled once more at the crotch of his breeches, quite unselfconscious of her presence.

"Here? Why, because a gentleman paid me to take ye to London-town, darlin'. Didn't ye know?"

She felt as though someone had hit her in the stomach, and sat down on the bed, folding her arms protectively across her midsection.

"What gentleman? And for God's sake—why?"

He considered for a moment, but evidently concluded that there was no reason not to tell her.

"A man named Forbes," he said, and threw back the rest of his drink. "Know him, do you?"

"I most certainly do," she said, amazement vying with fury. "That bloody *bastard*!" So they were Forbes's men, the masked bandits that had stopped her and Josh, dragged them from their horses, and shoved them both into a sealed carriage, bumping over unseen roads for days on end, until they reached the coast, and then been pulled out, disheveled and reeking, and bundled aboard the ship.

"Where's Joshua?" she asked abruptly. "The young black man who was with me?"

"Was there?" Bonnet looked quizzical. "If they brought him aboard, I imagine they've put him in the hold with the other cargo. A bonus, I suppose," he added, and laughed.

Her fury at Forbes had been tinged with relief at finding out he was the motive behind her abduction; Forbes might be a lowdown, sneaking scoundrel, but he wouldn't be intending to murder her. That laugh of Stephen Bonnet's, though, made a cold qualm run through her, and she felt suddenly light-headed.

"What do you mean, a bonus?"

Bonnet scratched his cheek, gooseberry eyes roaming over her in approval.

"Oh, well, then. Mr. Forbes only wanted ye out of the way, he said. Whatever did ye do to the man, darlin'? But he's paid your fare already, and I've the impression that he's no great interest in where ye end up."

"Where I end up?" Her mouth had been dry; now saliva was pouring from her membranes, and she had to swallow repeatedly.

"Well, after all, darlin', why bother takin' ye all the way to London, where ye'd be of no particular use to anyone? Besides, it rains quite a bit in London; I'm sure ye wouldn't like it."

Before she could draw breath to ask any more questions, the door opened, and a young woman slid through, closing it behind her.

She was likely in her twenties, though with a missing molar that showed when she smiled. She was plump and plain-faced, brown-haired, and clean by local standards, though the scent of her sweat and waves of freshly applied cheap cologne wafted across the cabin, making Brianna want to throw up again.

"Hallo, Stephen," the newcomer said, standing on tiptoe to kiss Bonnet's cheek. "Give us a drink to be starting with, eh?"

Bonnet grabbed her, gave her a deep and lingering kiss, then let her go and reached for the bottle.

Coming down onto her heels, she looked at Brianna with detached professional interest, then back at Bonnet, and scratched at her neck.

"You'll have the two of us, Stephen, or shall it be me and her to start? It's a quid more, either way."

Bonnet didn't bother answering, but thrust the bottle into her hand, whipped off the kerchief that hid the swell of her heavy breasts, and began at once to undo his flies. He dropped the breeches on the floor, and without ado, seized the woman by the hips and pressed her against the door.

Guzzling from the bottle she held in one hand, the young woman snatched up her skirts with the other, whisking skirt and petticoat out of the way with a practiced motion that bared her to the waist. Brianna caught a glimpse of sturdy thighs and a patch of dark hair, before they were obscured by Bonnet's buttocks, blond-furred and clenched with effort.

She turned her head away, cheeks burning, but morbid fascination compelled her to glance back. The whore was standing balanced on her toes, squatting slightly to accommodate him, gazing placidly over his shoulder as he thrust and grunted. One hand still held the bottle; the other stroked Bonnet's shoulders in a practiced way. She caught Brianna's eye on her, and winked, still saying, "Ooh, yes . . . oh, YES! That's good, love, so good . . ." in her client's ear.

The cabin door quivered with each meaty thump of the whore's backside, and Brianna could hear laughter in the corridor outside, both male and female; evidently Orden had brought back enough to supply crew as well as captain.

Bonnet heaved and grunted for a minute or two, then gave a loud groan, his movements suddenly jerky and uncoordinated. The whore put a helpful hand on his buttocks and pulled him close, then relaxed her grip as his body went limp, leaning heavily against her. She supported him for a moment, patting his back matter-of-factly, like a mother burping a baby, then pushed him off.

His face and neck were flushed dark red, and he was breathing heavily. He nodded to the whore, and stooped, fumbling for his breeches. He stood up with them and waved toward the littered desk.

"Help yourself to your pay, darlin', but give me back the bottle, aye?"

The whore pouted slightly, but took a final deep gulp of the liquor and handed him the bottle, now no more than a quarter full. She pulled a wadded cloth from the pocket at her waist and clapped it between her thighs, then shook down her skirts and minced across to the desk, poking delicately among the litter for scattered coins, which she picked out with two fingers, dropping them one by one into the depths of her pocket.

Bonnet, clothed once more, went out without a backward glance at the two women. The air in the cabin was hot and thick with the scent of sex, and Brianna felt her stomach clench. Not with revulsion, but with panic. The strong male reek had triggered an instinctive flush of response that tingled across her breasts and gripped her inwardly; for a brief, disorienting moment, she felt Roger's skin, slick with sweat against her own, and her breasts tingled, swollen and wanting.

She pressed both lips and legs tight together, and curled her hands into fists, breathing shallowly. The last thing she could stand right now, she thought—the *very* last thing—was to think of Roger and sex, while anywhere within miles of Stephen Bonnet. She resolutely pushed the thought aside, and edged closer to the whore, searching for some remark with which to open conversation.

The whore sensed the movement, and glanced at Brianna, taking in both the torn dress and its quality, but then dismissed her in favor of finding more coins. Once she had her pay, the woman would leave, going back to the docks. It was a chance to get word to Roger and her parents. Not much, perhaps, but a chance.

"You . . . um . . . know him well?" she said.

The whore glanced at her, eyebrows lifted.

"Who? Oh, Stephen? Aye, he's a good 'un, Stephen." She shrugged. "Don't take more than two or three minutes, no bones about the money, never wants nothin' but a simple swive. He's rough now and then, but he don't hit unless you cross him, and no one's fool enough to do that. Not more than once, anyroad." Her gaze lingered for a moment on Brianna's torn dress, one brow lifting sardonically.

"I'll remember that," Brianna said dryly, and pulled the edge of her ripped chemise up higher. She glimpsed a glass bottle amid the rubble on the desk, filled with a clear liquid, containing a small round object. She leaned closer to look at it, frowning. It couldn't be . . . but it was. A round, fleshy object, rather like a hard-boiled egg, a pinkish-gray in color—with a neat round hole drilled completely through it.

She crossed herself, feeling faint.

"I was that surprised," the whore went on, eyeing Brianna with open curiosity. "He's never had two girls together, so far as I know, and he's not one as wants someone to watch while he's at his pleasure."

"I'm not—" Brianna began, but then stopped, not wanting to offend the woman.

"Not a whore?" The young woman grinned broadly, exposing the black gap of her missing tooth. "I might ha' guessed as much, chickie. Not as it would make no never mind to Stephen. He sows as he likes, and I can see as how he might like you. Most men would." She looked at Brianna with dispassionate assessment, nodding at her disheveled hair, flushed face, and tidy figure.

"I expect they like you, too," Brianna said politely, with a faint feeling of surreality. "Er . . . what's your name?"

"Hepzibah," the woman said with an air of pride. "Or Eppie, for short, like." There were coins still on the desk, but the whore left them alone. Bonnet might be generous, but evidently the whore didn't want to take advantage of him—more likely a sign of fear than of friendship, Brianna thought. She took a deep breath and pressed on.

"What a lovely name. Pleased to meet you, Eppie." She held out a hand. "My name is Brianna Fraser MacKenzie." She gave all three names, hoping the whore would remember at least one of them.

The woman glanced at the extended hand in puzzlement, then gingerly shook it, dropping it like a dead fish. She pulled up her skirt, and began to clean herself with the rag, fastidiously wiping away all trace of the recent encounter.

Brianna leaned closer, bracing herself against the odors of the stained rag, the woman's body, and the hot smell of liquor on her breath.

"Stephen Bonnet kidnapped me," she said.

"Oh, aye?" said the whore, indifferent. "Well, he takes as he likes, does Stephen."

"I want to get away," Brianna said, keeping her voice low, with a glance at the cabin door. She could hear the sound of feet on the deck overhead, and hoped voices wouldn't carry through the heavy planks.

Eppie wadded up the rag and dropped it on the desk. She rummaged in her pocket, coming out with a small bottle stoppered with a plug of wax. She still held her skirts up, and Brianna could see the silvery streaks of stretch marks across her plump belly.

"Well, give him what he wants, then," the whore advised, taking out the plug and pouring a bit of the bottle's contents—a surprisingly mild scent of rosewater—into her hand. "Chances are he'll tire of ye in a few days and put ye ashore." She wiped the rosewater lavishly over her pubic hair, then sniffed critically at her hand and made a face.

"No. I mean, that's not what he kidnapped me for. I don't think," she added.

Eppie recorked the bottle, and dropped both it and the rag into her pocket.

"Oh, he means to ransom you?" Eppie eyed her with a little more interest. "Still, I've never known scruples interfere with the man's appetite. He'd take a virgin's maidenhead and sell her back to her father before her belly started swelling." She pursed her lips, a belated thought coming to her.

"So how did you talk him out of havin' you, then?"

Brianna put a hand on her stomach.

"I told him I was pregnant. That stopped him. I wouldn't have thought—a man like that—but it did. Perhaps he's better than you think?" she asked with a wisp of hope.

Eppie laughed at that, small eyes squeezing half-shut with hilarity at the thought.

"Stephen? God, no!" She sniffed with amusement, and smoothed down her skirts.

"No," she went on, more matter-of-factly, "best story you could tell, though, if you don't want him at you. He called me down to him once, then put me off when he saw I'd a cake in the oven—when I joked him about it, he said he'd once taken a whore with her belly the size of a cannonball, and right in the midst of it, she give a groan and the blood come spurting out of her fit to drench the room. Put him right off, he said, and no wonder. Left our Stephen with a horror of swiving girls what are up the spout. He's takin' no chances, see."

"I see." A trickle of sweat ran down Brianna's cheek, and she wiped it away with the back of her hand. Her mouth felt dry, and she sucked the inside of her cheek for moisture. "The woman—what happened to her?"

Hepzibah looked blank for a moment.

"Oh, the whore? Why, she died, of course, poor cow. Stephen said as how he was struggling to get into his wet breeches, all soused with blood like they were, and he looked up and saw her layin' still as stone on the floor, but with her belly still wriggling and twitching like a bag full o' snakes. Said it come to him sudden that the babe meant to come out and take its revenge on him, and he fled the house right then in his shirt, leavin' his breeches behind."

She chortled at this amusing vision, then snorted and settled herself, brushing down her skirts. "But then, Stephen's Irish," she added tolerantly. "They take morbid fancies, the Irish, especially when they're gone in drink." The tip of her tongue came out and passed reminiscently over her lower lip, tasting the lingering traces of Bonnet's liquor.

Brianna leaned closer, holding out her hand.

"Look."

Hepzibah glanced into her hand, then looked again, riveted. The thick gold band with its big cabochon ruby winked and glowed in the lantern light.

"I'll give it to you," Brianna said, lowering her voice, "if you'll do something for me."

The whore licked her lips again, a sudden look of alertness coming into her heavy face.

"Aye? Do what?"

"Get word to my husband. He's in Edenton, at the Reverend McMillan's house—anyone will know where it is. Tell him where I am, and tell him—" She hesitated. What should she say? There was no telling how long the *Anemone* would stay here, or where Bonnet would choose to go next. The only clue she had was what she had overheard in his conversation with his mate, just before he came in.

"Tell them I think he has a hiding place on Ocracoke. He means to rendezvous with someone there at the dark of the moon. Tell him that."

Hepzibah cast an uneasy glance at the cabin door, but it stayed shut. She looked back at the ring, longing for it warring in her face with an obvious fear of Bonnet.

"He won't know," Brianna urged. "He won't find out. And my father will reward you."

"He's a rich man, then, your father?" Brianna saw the look of calculation in the whore's eyes, and felt a moment's misgiving— what if she should simply take the ring and betray her to Bonnet? Still, she hadn't taken more money than her due; perhaps she was honest. And there was no choice, after all.

"Very rich," she said firmly. "His name is Jamie Fraser. My aunt is rich, too. She has a plantation called River Run, just above Cross Creek in North Carolina. Ask for Mrs. Innes—Jocasta Cameron Innes. Yes, if you don't find Ro—my husband, send word there."

"River Run." Hepzibah repeated it obediently, eyes still fixed on the ring.

Brianna twisted it off and dropped it into the whore's palm before she could change her mind. The woman's hand closed tight around it.

"My father's name is Jamie Fraser; my husband is Roger MacKenzie," she repeated. "At the Reverend McMillan's house. Can you remember?"

"Fraser and MacKenzie," Hepzibah repeated uncertainly. "Oh, aye, to be sure." She was already moving toward the door.

"Please," Brianna said urgently.

The whore nodded but without looking at her, then sidled through the door, shutting it behind her.

The ship creaked and swayed underfoot, and she heard the rattle of wind through the trees on the shore, over the shouts of drunken men. Her knees gave way then and she sat down on the bed, careless of the sheets.

They left with the tide; she heard the anchor chain rumble and felt the ship quicken, taking life as her sails took wind. Glued to the window, she watched the dark green mass of Roanoke recede. A hundred years before, the first English colony had landed here—and disappeared without trace. The governor of the colony, returning from England with supplies, had found everyone gone, leaving no clue save the word "Croatan" carved into the trunk of a tree.

She wasn't even leaving that much. Heartsick, she watched until the island sank into the sea.

No one came for some hours. Empty-bellied, she grew nauseated, and threw up in the chamber pot. She could not bear the thought of lying down on those revolting sheets, but instead pulled them off, remade the bed with only the quilts, and lay down.

The windows were open, and the fresh air of the sea stirred her hair and lifted the clamminess from her skin, making her feel a little better. She was unbearably conscious of her womb, a small, heavy, tender weight, and what was likely happening inside it: that orderly dance of dividing cells, a sort of peaceful violence, implacably wresting lives and wrenching hearts.

When had it happened? She tried to think back, remember. It might have been the night before Roger left for Edenton. He had been excited, almost exalted, and they had made love with lingering joy, spiced by longing, for they both knew the morrow would bring separation. She had fallen asleep in his arms, feeling loved.

But then she had waked alone, in the middle of the night, to find him sitting by the window, bathed in the light of a gibbous moon. She had been reluctant to disturb his private contemplation, but he had turned, feeling her eyes on him, and something in his look had made her get out of bed and go to him, taking his head against her bosom, holding him.

He had risen then, laid her on the floor, and had her again, wordless and urgent.

Catholic that she was, she had found it terribly erotic, the notion of seducing a priest on the eve of his ordination, stealing him—if only for a moment—from God.

She swallowed, hands clasped over her belly. *Be careful what you pray for.* The nuns at school had always told the children that.

The wind was growing cold, chilling her, and she pulled the edge of one quilt—the cleanest over her. Then, concentrating fiercely, she began very carefully to pray.

103

Put to the Question

Neil Forbes sat in the parlor of the King's Inn, enjoying a glass of hard cider and the feeling that all was right with the world. He had had a most fruitful meeting with Samuel Iredell and his friend, two of the most prominent rebel leaders in Edenton—and an even more fruitful meeting with Gilbert Butler and William Lyons, local smugglers.

He had a great fondness for jewels, and in private celebration of his elegant disposal of the threat of Jamie Fraser, he had bought a new stickpin, topped with a beautiful ruby. He contemplated this with quiet satisfaction, noting the lovely shadows that the stone cast on the silk of his ruffle.

His mother was safely planted at her sister's house, he had an appointment for luncheon with a local lady, and an hour to spare beforehand. Perhaps a stroll to stimulate appetite; it was a beautiful day.

He had in fact pushed back his chair and begun to rise when a large hand planted itself in the center of his chest and shoved him back into it.

"What—?" He looked up in indignation—and took great care to keep that expression on his face, despite a sudden deep qualm. A tall, dark man was standing over him, wearing a most unfriendly expression. MacKenzie, the chit's husband.

"How dare you, sir?" he said, belligerent. "I must demand apology!"

"You demand what ye like," MacKenzie said. He was pale under his tan, and grim. "Where is my wife?"

"How should I know?" Forbes's heart was beating fast, but with glee as much as trepidation. He lifted his chin and made to rise. "You will excuse me, sir."

A hand on his arm stopped him, and he turned, looking into the face of Fraser's nephew, Ian Murray. Murray smiled, and Forbes's sense of self-satisfaction diminished slightly. They said the boy had lived with the Mohawk, become one of them—that he dwelt with a vicious wolf who spoke to him and obeyed his commands, that he had cut a man's heart out and eaten it in some heathen ritual.

Looking at the lad's homely face and disheveled dress, though, Forbes was not impressed.

"Remove your hand from my person, sir," he said with dignity, straightening in his chair.

"No, I think I won't," Murray said. The hand tightened on his arm like the bite of a horse, and Forbes's mouth opened, though he made no sound.

"What have ye done with my cousin?" Murray said.

"I? Why, I—I have nothing whatever to do with Mrs. MacKenzie. Let go, God damn you!"

The grip relaxed, and he sat breathing heavily. MacKenzie had pulled up a chair to face him and sat down.

Forbes smoothed the sleeve of his coat, avoiding MacKenzie's stare and thinking rapidly. How had they found out? Or had they? Perhaps they were only trying a venture, with no sure knowledge.

"I am grieved to hear that any misfortune might have befallen Mrs. MacKenzie," he said politely. "Am I to take it that you have somehow misplaced her?"

MacKenzie looked him up and down for a moment without answering, then made a small sound of contempt.

"I heard ye speak in Mecklenberg," he said, his tone conversational. "Very glib ye were. A great deal about justice, I heard, and protection of our wives and children. Such eloquence."

"Fine talk," Ian Murray put in, "for a man who would abduct a helpless woman." He was still crouching on the floor like a savage, but had moved round a little, so as to stare directly into Forbes's face. The lawyer found it slightly unnerving, and chose instead to meet MacKenzie's eyes, man to man.

"I regret your misfortune extremely, sir," he said, striving for a tone of concern. "I should be pleased to help, in any way possible, of course. But I do not—"

"Where is Stephen Bonnet?"

The question struck Forbes like a blow to the liver. He gaped for a moment, thinking that he had made a mistake in choosing MacKenzie to look at; that flat green gaze was like a snake's.

"Who is Stephen Bonnet?" he asked, licking his lips. His lips were dry, but the rest of him was heavily bedewed; he could feel sweat pooling in the creases of his neck, soaking the cambric of his shirt beneath his oxters.

"I heard ye, ken," Murray remarked pleasantly. "When ye made the bargain wi' Richard Brown. In your warehouse, it was."

Forbes's head snapped round. He was so shocked that it was a moment before he realized that Murray was holding a knife, laid casually across his knee.

"What? You say—what? I tell you, sir, you are mistaken—mistaken!" He half-rose, stammering. MacKenzie shot to his feet and seized him by the shirtfront, twisting.

"No, sir," he said very softly, his face so close that Forbes felt the heat of his breath. "It is yourself has been mistaken. Most grievously mistaken, in choosing my wife to serve your wicked ends."

There was a ripping sound as the fine cambric tore. MacKenzie shoved him back violently into the chair, then leaned forward, seizing his neckcloth in a grip that threatened to choke him on the spot. His mouth opened, gasping, and black spots flickered in his vision—but not sufficiently as to obscure those brilliant, cold green eyes.

"Where has he taken her?"

Forbes gripped the arms of his chair, breathing heavily.

"I know nothing about your wife," he said, his voice pitched low and venomous. "And as for grievous error, sir, you are in the process of committing one. How dare you assault me? I shall prefer charges, I do assure you!"

"Oh, assault, forbye," Murray said, scoffing. "We havena done any such thing. Yet." He sat back on his haunches, tapping the knife thoughtfully against his thumbnail and regarding Forbes with an air of estimation, like one planning to carve a suckling pig on a platter.

Forbes set his jaw and glared up at MacKenzie, who was still standing, looming over him.

"This is a public place," he pointed out. "You cannot harm me without notice being taken." He glanced behind MacKenzie, hoping that someone would come into the parlor and interrupt this grossly uncomfortable tête-à-tête, but it was a quiet morning, and all the chambermaids and ostlers inconveniently about their duties elsewhere.

"Do we care if anyone notices, *a charaid*?" Murray inquired, glancing up at MacKenzie.

"Not really." Nonetheless, MacKenzie resumed his seat and resumed his stare. "We can wait a bit, though." He glanced at the case clock by the mantel, its pendulum moving with a serene ticktock. "It won't be long."

Belatedly, it occurred to Forbes to wonder where Jamie Fraser was.

Elspeth Forbes was rocking gently on the veranda of her sister's house, enjoying the coolness of the morning air, when a visitor was announced.

"Why, Mr. Fraser!" she exclaimed, sitting up. "What brings ye to Edenton? Is it Neil ye're in search of? He's gone to—"

"Ah, no, Mistress Forbes." He swept her a low bow, the morning sun gleaming off his hair as though it were bronze metal. "It is yourself I've come for."

"Oh? Oh!" She sat up in her chair, hastily brushing away crumbs of toast on her sleeve, and hoping her cap was on straight. "Why, sir, what could ye possibly want with an old woman?"

He smiled—such a nice-looking lad he was, so fine in his gray coatie, and that look of mischief in his eyes—and leaned close to whisper in her ear.

"I've come to steal ye away, Mistress."

"Och, awa' with ye!" She flapped a hand at him, laughing, and he took it, kissing her knuckles.

"I shallna take 'no' for answer, now," he assured her, and gestured toward the edge of the porch, where he had left a large, promising-looking basket, covered with a checkered cloth. "I've a mind to eat my luncheon in the country, under a tree. I've the very tree in mind—a braw, fine tree—but it's a poor meal, taken without company."

"Surely to goodness ye could find better company than mine, lad," she said, thoroughly charmed. "And where's your dear wife, then?"

"Ah, she's left me," he said, affecting sorrow. "Here's me, with a wonderful picnic planned, and her off to a birthing. So I said to myself, well, Jamie, it's shame to waste such a feast—who might be at liberty to share it with ye? And what should I see next but your most elegant self, taking your ease. An answer to prayer, it was; surely ye wouldna go against heavenly guidance, Mistress Forbes?"

"Hmph," she said, trying not to laugh at him. "Och, well. If it's a matter of wasting . . ."

Before she could say more, he had stooped down and plucked her from her chair, lifting her in his arms. She whooped with surprise.

"If it's a proper abduction, I must carry ye away, aye?" he said, smiling down at her.

To her mortification, the sound she made could be called nothing but a giggle. He seemed not to mind, though, and bending to sweep up the basket in one strong hand, carried her like a bit of thistledown out to his carriage.

"You cannot keep me prisoner here! Let me pass, or I will shout for help!"

They had, in fact, held him for more than an hour, blocking all attempts on his part to rise and leave. He was right, though, Roger thought; traffic was beginning to pick up in the street outside, and he could hear—as could Forbes—the noises of a maid setting out the tables for dinner in the next room.

He glanced at Ian. They had discussed it; if word hadn't come within an hour, they would have to try to remove Forbes from the inn, take him to a more private place. That could be a dicey business; the lawyer was intimidated, but stubborn as a ball bearing. And he *would* call for help.

Ian pursed his lips thoughtfully, and drew the knife he had been playing with down the side of his breeches, polishing the blade.

"Mr. MacKenzie?" A small boy had popped up beside him like a mushroom, dirt-smeared and round-faced.

"I am," he said, a wave of thankfulness washing through him. "Have ye got something for me?"

"Aye, sir." The urchin handed over a small twist of paper, accepted a coin in return, and was gone, in spite of Forbes's call of "Wait, boy!"

The lawyer had half-risen from his seat in agitation. Roger made a sharp move toward him, though, and he sank back at once, not waiting to be pushed. Good, Roger thought grimly, he was learning.

Undoing the twist of paper, he found himself holding a large brooch in the shape of a bunch of flowers, done in garnets and silver. It was a good piece of workmanship, but rather ugly. Its impression on Forbes, though, was substantial.

"You wouldn't. He wouldn't." The lawyer was staring at the brooch in Roger's hand, his heavy face gone pale.

"Oh, I expect he would, if ye mean Uncle Jamie," Ian Murray said. "He's fond of his daughter, aye?"

"Nonsense." The lawyer was making a game attempt to bluff it out, but he couldn't keep his eyes off the brooch. "Fraser is a gentleman."

"He's a Highlander," Roger said brutally. "Like your father, aye?" He'd heard stories about the elder Forbes, who by all accounts had escaped Scotland just ahead of the hangsman.

Forbes chewed his lower lip.

"He would not harm an old woman," he said, with as much bravado as he could summon.

"Would he not?" Ian's sketchy brows lifted. "Aye, perhaps not. He might just send her awa', though—to Canada, maybe? Ye seem to ken him fair weel, Mr. Forbes. What d'ye think?"

The lawyer drummed his fingers on the arm of the chair, breathing through his teeth, evidently reviewing what he knew of Jamie Fraser's character and reputation.

"All right," he said suddenly. "All right!"

Roger felt the tension running through him snap like a cut wire. He'd been strung like a puppet since Jamie had come to fetch him last night.

"Where?" he said, feeling breathless. "Where is she?"

"She's safe," Forbes said hoarsely. "I wouldn't have her harmed." He looked up, wild-eyed. "For God's sake, I wouldn't harm her!"

"Where?" Roger clamped the brooch tight, not caring that its edges cut into his hand. "Where is she?"

The lawyer sagged like a half-filled bag of meal.

"Aboard a ship called *Anemone*, Captain Bonnet." He swallowed hard, unable to keep his eyes away from the brooch. "She— I told—they are bound for England. But she is safe, I tell you!"

Shock tightened Roger's grip, and he felt the sudden slick of blood on his fingers. He flung the brooch onto the floor, wiping his hand on his breeches, struggling for words. The shock had tightened his throat, as well; he felt as though he were strangling.

Seeing his trouble, Ian stood abruptly and pressed his knife against the lawyer's throat.

"When did they sail?"

"I—I—" The lawyer's mouth opened and closed at random, and he looked helplessly from Ian to Roger, eyes bulging.

"Where?" Roger forced the word past the blockage in his throat, and Forbes flinched at the sound.

"She—she was put aboard here. In Edenton. Two—two days ago."

Roger nodded abruptly. Safe, he said. In Bonnet's hands. Two days, in Bonnet's hands. But he had sailed with Bonnet, he thought, trying to steady himself, keep a grip on his rationality. He knew how the man worked. Bonnet was a smuggler; he would not sail for England without a full cargo. He might—*might*—be going down the coast, picking up small shipments before turning to the open sea and the long voyage for England.

And if not—he might still be caught, with a fast ship.

No time to be lost; people on the docks might know where the *Anemone* was headed next. He turned and took a step toward the door. Then a red wave washed through him and he whirled back, smashing his fist into Forbes's face with the full weight of his body behind it.

The lawyer gave a high-pitched scream, and clutched both hands to his nose. All noises in the inn and in the street seemed to stop; the world hung suspended. Roger took a short, deep breath, rubbing his knuckles, and nodded once more.

"Come on," he said to Ian.

"Oh, aye."

Roger was halfway to the door when he realized that Ian was not with him. He looked back, and was just in time to see his cousin-by-marriage take Forbes gently by one ear and cut it off.

104

Sleeping with a Shark

S tephen Bonnet was as good as his word—if that's how one would describe it. He made no sexual advances toward her, but did insist that she share his bed.

"I like a warm body in the night," he said. "And I think ye might prefer my bed to the cargo hold, sweetheart."

She would most emphatically have preferred the cargo hold, though her explorations—once free of land, she was allowed out of the cabin—had revealed the hold as a dark and comfortless hole, in which several hapless slaves were chained among a collection of boxes and barrels, in constant danger of being crushed should the cargo shift.

"Where are we going, miss? And what will happen when we get there?" Josh spoke in Gaelic, his handsome face small and frightened in the shadows of the hold.

"I think we're going to Ocracoke," she said in the same language. "Beyond that—I don't know. Do you still have your rosary?"

"Oh, yes, miss." He touched his chest, where the crucifix hung. "It's the only thing that keeps me from despair."

"Good. Keep praying." She glanced at the other slaves: two women, two men, all with slender bodies and delicate, fine-boned faces. She had brought food for Josh from her own supper, but had nothing to offer them, and was troubled.

"Do they feed you down here?"

"Yes, miss. Fairly well," he assured her.

"Do they"—she moved her chin a little, delicately indicating the other slaves—"know anything? About where we're going?"

"I don't know, miss. I can't talk to them. They're African—

Fulani, I can see that from the way they look, but that's all I know."

"I see. Well . . ." She hesitated, eager to be out of the dark, clammy hold, but reluctant to leave the young groom there.

"You go along, miss," he said quietly in English, seeing her doubt. "I be fine. We all be fine." He touched his rosary, and did his best to give her a smile, though it wavered round the edges. "Holy Mother see us safe."

Having no words of comfort to impart, she nodded, and climbed the ladder into the sunlight, feeling five sets of eyes upon her.

Bonnet, thank God, spent most of his time on deck during the day. She could see him now, coming down the rigging like a nimble ape.

She stood very still, no movement save the brush of windblown hair, of skirts against her frozen limbs. He was as sensitive to the movements of her body as was Roger—but in his own way. The way of a shark, signaled to and drawn by the flappings of its prey.

She had spent one night in his bed so far, sleepless. He had pulled her casually against himself, said, "Good night, darlin'," and fallen instantly asleep. Whenever she had tried to move, to extricate herself from his grip, though, he had shifted, moving with her, to keep her firmly by him.

She was obliged to an unwelcome intimacy with his body, an acquaintance that awoke memories she had with great difficulty put away—the feel of his knee pushing her thighs apart, the rough joviality of his touch between her legs, the sun-bleached blond hairs that curled crisply on his thighs and forearms, the unwashed, musky male smell of him. The mocking presence of LeRoi, rising at intervals during the night, pressed in firm and mindless hunger against her buttocks.

She had a moment of intense thankfulness, both for her present pregnancy—for she was in no doubt of it now—and for her certain knowledge that Stephen Bonnet had not fathered Jemmy.

He dropped from the rigging with a thud, saw her, and smiled. He said nothing, but squeezed her bottom familiarly as he passed, making her clench her teeth and cling to the rail.

Ocracoke, at the dark of the moon. She looked up into the brilliant sky, wheeling with clouds of terns and gulls; they could not be far offshore. How long, for God's sake, 'til the dark of the moon?

105

The Prodigal

They had no trouble in finding persons familiar with *Anemone* and her captain. Stephen Bonnet was well-known on the Edenton docks, though his reputation varied, depending on his associations. An honest captain was the usual opinion, but hard in his dealings. A blockade runner, a smuggler, said others—and whether that was good or bad depended on the politics of the person saying it. He'd get you anything, they said—for a price.

Pirate, said a few. But those few spoke in low tones, looking frequently over their shoulders, and strongly desired not to be quoted.

The *Anemone* had left quite openly, with a homely cargo of rice and fifty barrels of smoked fish. Roger had found one man who recalled seeing the young woman go aboard with one of Bonnet's hands: "Great huge doxy, with flaming hair a-loose, flowing down to her arse," the man had said, smacking his lips. "Mr. Bonnet's a good-size man himself, though; expect he can handle her."

Only Ian's hand on his arm had stopped him hitting the man.

What they had not yet found was anyone who knew for sure where *Anemone* was headed.

"London, I think," said the harbormaster, dubious. "But not directly; he's not yet got a full cargo. Likely he'll be going down the coast, trading here and there—perhaps sail for Europe from Charlestown. But then again," the man added, rubbing his chin, "could be he's bound for New England. Terrible risky business, getting anything into Boston these days—but well worth it if you do. Rice and smoked fish like to be worth their weight in gold up there, if you can get it ashore without the navy's warships blowing you out of the water."

Jamie, looking a little pale, thanked the man. Roger, unable to speak for the knot in his throat, merely nodded, and followed his father-in-law out of the harbormaster's office, back into the sun of the docks.

"Now what?" Ian asked, stifling a belch. He had been trawling through the dockside taverns, buying beer for casual laborers who might have helped load *Anemone*, or who might have spoken with her hands regarding her destination.

"The best I can think of is maybe for you and Roger Mac to take ship down the coast," Jamie said, frowning at the masts of the sloops and packet boats rocking at anchor. "Claire and I could go up, toward Boston."

Roger nodded, still unable to speak. It was far from being a good plan, particularly in light of the disruption the undeclared war was having on shipping—but the need of doing *something* was acute. He felt as though the marrow of his bones was burning; only movement would quench it.

To hire a small ship—even a fishing smack—or take passage on a packet boat, though, was expensive business.

"Aye, well." Jamie curled his hand in his pocket, where the black diamond still lay. "I'll go and see Judge Iredell; he can maybe put me in touch with an honest banker who'll advance me money against the sale of the stone. Let's go and tell Claire what's to do, first."

As they turned off the docks, though, a voice hailed Roger.

"Mr. MacKenzie!"

He turned, to find the Reverend Doctor McCorkle, his secretary, and the Reverend McMillan, carrying bags, all staring at him.

There was a brief scuffle of introduction—they had of course met Jamie when he came to fetch Roger, but not Ian—and then a slightly awkward pause.

"You—" Roger cleared his throat, addressing the elder. "You are leaving, then, sir? For the Indies?"

McCorkle nodded, his large, kindly face set in concern.

"I am, sir. I regret so much that I must go—and that you were not able to—well." Both McCorkle and the Reverend McMillan had tried to persuade him to return to them the day before, to take his place at the service of ordination. But he could not. Could not spare hours to such a thing, could not possibly engage himself to undertake the commitment with anything less than a single mind—and while his mind was in fact single just now, it was not toward God. There was room in his heart just now for only one thing—Brianna.

"Well, doubtless it is God's will," McCorkle said with a sigh. "Your wife, Mr. MacKenzie? There is no word of her?"

He shook his head, and muttered acknowledgment of their concern, their promises to pray for him and for the safe return of his wife. He was too much worried to find this much solace, yet still, he was touched by their kindness, and parted from them with many good wishes in both directions.

Roger, Jamie, and Ian walked silently back toward the inn where they had left Claire.

"Just by way of curiosity, Ian, what did ye do with Forbes's ear?" Jamie asked, breaking the silence as they turned into the wide street where the inn was.

"Oh, I have it safe, Uncle," Ian assured him, patting the small leather pouch at his belt.

"What in the name of G—" Roger stopped abruptly, then resumed. "What d'ye mean to do with it?"

"Keep it with me until we find my cousin," Ian said, seeming surprised that this was not obvious. "It will help."

"It will?"

Ian nodded, serious.

"When ye set about a difficult quest—if ye're Kahnyen'kehaka, I mean—ye generally go aside for a time, to fast and pray for guidance. We havena time to be doing that now, of course. But often, while ye're doing that, ye choose a talisman—or to be right about it, it chooses you—" He sounded completely matter-of-fact about this procedure, Roger noted.

"And ye carry it with ye through the quest, to keep the attention of the spirits upon your desire and ensure your success."

"I see." Jamie rubbed the bridge of his nose. He appeared—like Roger—to be wondering what the Mohawk spirits might make of Neil Forbes's ear. It would, probably, ensure their attention, at least. "The ear . . . did ye pack it in salt, I hope?"

Ian shook his head.

"Nay, I smoked it over the kitchen fire at the inn last night. Dinna fash yourself, Uncle Jamie; it will keep."

Roger found a perverse sort of comfort in this conversation. Between the prayers of the Presbyterian clergy and the support of the Mohawk spirits, perhaps they had a chance—but it was the presence of his two kinsmen, stalwart and determined on either side of him, that kept him in hope. They would not give up until Brianna was found, no matter what it took.

He swallowed the lump in his throat for the thousandth time since hearing the news, thinking of Jemmy. The little boy was safe at River Run—but how could he tell Jem that his mother was gone? Well . . . he wouldn't, that was all. They'd find her.

In this mood of resolution, he led the way through the door of the Brewster, only to be hailed again.

"Roger!"

This time, it was Claire's voice, sharp with excitement. He turned at once, to see her rising from a bench in the taproom. Seated across the table from her were a plump young woman and a slightly built young man with a cap of tightly curled black hair. Manfred McGillivray.

"I saw ye before, sir, two days ago." Manfred bobbed his head apologetically toward Jamie. "I . . . er . . . well, I hid myself, sir, and I do regret it. But of course, I'd no way of knowing, until Eppie came back from Roanoke and showed me the ring. . . ."

The ring lay on the table, its cabochon ruby casting a tiny, calm pool of ruddy light on the boards. Roger picked it up and turned it in his fingers. He barely heard the explanations—that Manfred lived with the whore, who made periodic expeditions to the ports near Edenton, and upon seeing the ring had overcome his sense of shame and come to find Jamie—too much overcome by this small, hard, tangible evidence of Brianna.

Roger closed his fingers over it, finding the warmth of it a comfort, and came to himself in time to hear Hepzibah say earnestly, "Ocracoke, sir. At the dark of the moon." She coughed modestly, ducking her head. "The lady did say, sir, as you might feel some gratitude for the news of her whereabouts. . . ."

"Ye'll be paid, and paid well," Jamie assured her, though he was clearly giving her no more than a fraction of his attention. "The dark of the moon," he said, turning to Ian. "Ten days?"

Ian nodded, his face shining with excitement.

"Aye, about that. She didna ken whereabouts on Ocracoke Island this was?" he asked the whore.

Eppie shook her head.

"Nay, sir. I ken Stephen's got a house there, a large one, hidden in the trees, but that's all."

"We'll find it." Roger's own voice surprised him; he hadn't meant to speak aloud.

Manfred had been looking uneasy throughout. He leaned forward, putting his hand on top of Eppie's.

"Sir—when ye do find it . . . ye'll not say to anybody, will ye, about Eppie telling ye? Mr. Bonnet's a dangerous man, and I wouldna have her imperiled from him." He glanced at the young woman, who blushed and smiled at him.

"No, we won't say anything about her," Claire assured him. She had been scrutinizing both Manfred and Hepzibah carefully while they talked, and now leaned across the table to touch Manfred's forehead, which showed a stippling of some sort of rash. "Speaking of peril . . . she's in a great deal more danger from *you,* young man, than from Stephen Bonnet. Did you tell her?"

Manfred went a little paler, and for the first time, Roger noticed that the young man looked truly ill, his face thin and deeply lined.

"I did, *Frau* Fraser. From the first."

"Oh, about the pox?" Hepzibah affected nonchalance, though Roger could see her hand tighten on Manfred's. "Aye, he did tell me. But I says to him as it makes no difference. I daresay I've had a few men what are poxed before, not knowing. If I should get it . . . well. God's will, innit?"

"No," Roger said to her quite gently. "It isn't. But you'll go with Mrs. Claire, you and Manfred both, and do exactly what she tells you. Ye'll be all right, and so will he. Won't they?" he asked, turning to Claire, suddenly a little uncertain.

"Yes, they will," she said dryly. "Fortunately, I have quite a bit of penicillin with me."

Manfred's face was a study in confusion.

"But—do ye mean, *meine Frau,* that ye can—can *cure* it?"

"That is exactly what I mean," Claire assured him, "as I tried to tell you before you ran away."

His mouth hung open, and he blinked. Then he turned to Hepzibah, who was staring at him in puzzlement.

"*Liebchen!* I can go home! *We* can go home," he amended quickly, seeing her face change. "We will be married. We will go home," he repeated, in the tones of one seeing a beatific vision but not quite trusting in its reality yet.

Eppie was frowning in uncertainty.

"I'm a whore, Freddie," she pointed out. "And from the stories you tell about your mother . . ."

"I rather think that *Frau* Ute will be so happy to have Manfred back that she won't be disposed to ask too many questions," Claire said, with a glance at Jamie. "The Prodigal Son, you know?"

"Ye won't need to be a whore any longer," Manfred assured her. "I'm a gunsmith; I'll earn a good living. Now that I know I *shall* be living!" His thin face was suddenly suffused with joy, and he flung his arms around Eppie and kissed her.

"Oh," she said, flustered, but looking pleased. "Well. Hm. This . . . er . . . this penny—?" She looked inquiringly at Claire.

"The sooner, the better," Claire said, standing up. "Come with me." Her own face was a little flushed, Roger saw, and she put out a quick hand to Jamie, who took it and pressed it hard.

"We'll go and see to things," he said, glancing at Ian and Roger in turn. "With luck, we'll sail this evening."

"Oh!" Eppie had already stood up to follow Claire, but at this reminder of their business, she turned to Jamie, a hand to her mouth. "Oh. I've thought of the one more thing." Her pleasant round face was puckered in concentration. "There are wild horses that run near the house. On Ocracoke. I heard Stephen speak o' them once." She looked from one man to the other. "Might that help?"

"It might," Roger said. "Thank you—and God bless you."

It wasn't until they were outside, heading for the docks again, that he realized the ring was still clutched tight in his hand. What was it Ian had said?

"Ye choose a talisman—or to be right about it, it chooses you."

His hands were slightly bigger than Brianna's, but he pushed the ring onto his finger, and closed his hand around it.

She woke from a damp and restless sleep, mother-sense at once aroused. She was halfway out of bed, moving by instinct toward Jemmy's trundle, when a hand grabbed her wrist, a convulsive grip like the bite of a crocodile.

She jerked back, groggy and alarmed. The sound of footsteps came to her from the deck overhead and she realized belatedly that the sound of distress that had wakened her had not come from Jemmy, but from the darkness at her side.

"Don't go," he whispered, and the fingers dug deep into the soft flesh of her inner wrist.

Unable to wrench free, she reached out with the other hand, to push him away. She touched damp hair, hot skin—and a trickle of wetness, cool and surprising on her fingers.

"What is it?" she whispered back, and leaned toward him by instinct. She reached again, touched his head, smoothed his hair—all the things she had waked prepared to do. She felt her hand rest on him and thought to stop, but did not. It was as though the spurt of maternal comfort, once called forth, could not be pressed back into her, no more than the spurt of breast milk summoned by an infant's cry could be recalled to its source.

"Are you all right?" She kept her voice low, and as impersonal as the words allowed. She lifted her hand, and he moved, rolling toward her, pressing his head hard against the curve of her thigh.

"Don't go," he said again, and caught his breath in what might have been a sob. His voice was low and rough, but not as she had ever heard it before.

"I'm here." Her trapped wrist was growing numb. She laid her free hand on his shoulder, hoping he would let go if she seemed willing to stay.

He did relax his grip, but only to reach out and seize her by the waist, pulling her back into bed. She went, because there was no choice, and lay in silence, Bonnet's breathing harsh and warm on the back of her neck.

At length, he let go and rolled onto his back with a sigh, allowing her to move. She rolled onto her own back, cautious, trying to keep a few inches between them. Moonlight came through the stern windows in a silver flood, and she could see the silhouette of his face, catch the glint of light from forehead and cheek as he turned his head.

"Bad dream?" she ventured. She'd meant to sound sarcastic,

but her own heart was still tripping fast from the alarm of the awakening, and the words had a tentative sound.

"Aye, aye," he said with a shuddering sigh. "The same. It comes to me over and over again, see? Ye'd think I'd know what it was about and wake, but I never do. Not 'til the waters close over my head." He rubbed a hand under his nose, sniffing like a child.

"Oh." She didn't want to ask for details, didn't want to encourage any further sense of intimacy. What she wanted, though, had nothing much to do with things anymore.

"Since I was a lad, I've dreamed of drowning," he said, and his voice, normally so assured, was unsteady. "The sea comes in, and I cannot move—not at all. The tide's risin', and I know it will kill me, but there's no way to move." His hand clutched the sheet convulsively, pulling it away from her.

"It's gray water, full of mud, and there are blind things swimmin' in it. They're waitin' on the sea to finish its business wit' me, see—and then they've business of their own."

She could hear the horror of it in his voice, and was torn between wanting to edge farther away from him and the ingrained habit of offering comfort.

"It was only a dream," she said at last, staring up at the boards of the deck, no more than three feet above her head. If only *this* were a dream!

"Ah, no," he said, and his voice had dropped to little more than a whisper in the darkness beside her. "Ah, no. It's the sea herself. Callin' me, see?"

Quite suddenly, he rolled toward her, seizing her and pressing her hard against him. She gasped, stiffening, and he pressed harder, responding, sharklike, to her struggles.

To her own horror, she felt LeRoi rising, and forced herself to be still. Panic and the need to escape his dream might all too easily make him forget his aversion to having sex with pregnant women, and that was the very last thing, the *very* last thing . . .

"Sshh," she said firmly, and clutched him round the head, forcing his face down into her shoulder, patting him, stroking his back. "Shh. It will be all right. It was only a dream. I won't let it hurt you—I won't let anything hurt you. Hush, hush now."

She went on patting him, her eyes closed, trying to imagine herself holding Jemmy after such a nightmare, quiet in their cabin, the hearth fire low, Jem's little body relaxing in trust, the sweet little-boy smell of his hair near her face. . . .

"I won't let you drown," she whispered. "I promise. I won't let you drown."

She said it over and over, and slowly, slowly, his breathing eased, and his grip on her slackened as sleep overcame him. Still she repeated it, a soft, hypnotic murmur, her words half-lost in the sound of water, hissing past the side of the ship, and she spoke no longer to the man beside her, but to the slumbering child within.

"I won't let anything hurt you. *Nothing* will hurt you. I promise."

106

Rendezvous

Roger paused to wipe the sweat out of his eyes. He'd tied a folded kerchief round his head, but the humidity in the thick growth of the tidal forest was so high that sweat formed in his eye sockets, stinging and blurring his vision.

From a taproom in Edenton, the knowledge that Bonnet was—or would be—on Ocracoke had seemed all heady conviction; the search narrowed suddenly to one tiny sandbar, versus the millions of other places the pirate could have been; how difficult could it be? Once *on* the bloody sandbar, the perspective had altered. The frigging island was narrow, but several miles long, with large patches of scrub forest, and most of its coastline fraught with hidden bars and dangerous eddies.

The skipper of the fishing boat they'd hired had got them there in good time; then they'd spent two days sailing up and down the length of the damn thing, looking for possible landing spots, likely pirate hideouts, and herds of wild horses. So far, none of these had appeared.

Having spent long enough retching over the side—Claire hadn't brought her acupuncture needles, having not foreseen the need of them—Jamie had insisted upon being put ashore. He would walk the length of the island, he said, keeping an eye out for anything untoward. They could pick him up at sundown.

"And what if you run smack into Stephen Bonnet, all on your own?" Claire had demanded, when he refused to allow her to accompany him.

"I'd rather be run through than puke to death," was Jamie's elegant reply, "and besides, Sassenach, I need ye to stay here and make sure yon misbegotten son of a—of a captain doesna sail away without us, aye?"

So they had rowed him ashore and left him, watching as he strode away, staggering only slightly, into the thicket of scrub pines and palmetto.

Another day of frustration, spent sailing slowly up and down the coast, seeing nothing but the occasional ramshackle fishing shack, and Roger and Ian had begun to see the wisdom of Jamie's approach, as well.

"See yon houses?" Ian pointed at a tiny cluster of shacks on the shore.

"If ye want to call them that, yes." Roger shaded his hand over his eyes to look, but the shacks looked deserted.

"If they can get boats off there, we can get one on. Let's go ashore and see will the folk there tell us anything."

Leaving Claire glowering behind them, they had rowed ashore to make inquiries—to no avail. The only inhabitants of the tiny settlement were a few women and children, all of whom heard the name "Bonnet" and scuttled into their homes like clams digging into the sand.

Still, having felt solid ground under their feet, they were less than eager to admit defeat and go back to the fishing shack. "Let's have a look, then," Ian had said, gazing thoughtfully into the sun-striped forest. "We'll crisscross, aye?" He drew a quick series of X's in the sand in illustration. "We'll cover more ground, and meet up every so often. Whoever reaches the shore first each time will wait on the other."

Roger had nodded agreement, and with a cheery wave at the

fishing boat and the small, indignant figure on its bow, had turned inland.

It was hot and still under the pines, and his progress was impaired by all sorts of low bushes, creepers, patches of sandburs and other stickery things. The going was a little easier near the shore, as the forest thinned and gave way to stretches of coarse sea oats, with dozens of tiny crabs that scuttled out of his way—or occasionally crunched under his feet.

Still, it was a relief to move, to feel that somehow he was doing something, was making progress toward finding Bree—though he admitted to himself that he wasn't sure exactly what they were looking for. Was she here? Had Bonnet arrived on the island already? Or would he be coming in a day or two, at the dark of the moon, as Hepzibah had said?

Despite the worry, the heat, and the millions of gnats and mosquitoes—they didn't bite, for the most part, but insisted upon crawling into his ears, eyes, nose, and mouth—he smiled at the thought of Manfred. He'd been praying for the boy ever since his disappearance from the Ridge, that he might be restored to his family. Granted, to find him firmly attached to an ex-prostitute was likely not quite the answer to prayer that Ute McGillivray had been hoping for, but he'd learned before that God had His own methods.

Lord, let her be safe. He didn't care how that prayer was answered, provided only that it was. *Let me have her back, please.*

It was well past mid-afternoon, and his clothes stuck to him with sweat, when he came to one of the dozens of small tidal inlets that cut into the island like the holes in Swiss cheese. It was too wide to leap across, so he made his way down the sandy bank and into the water. It was deeper than he'd thought—he was up to his neck by mid-channel, and had to swim a few strokes before he found solid footing on the other side.

The water pulled at him, rushing toward the sea; the tide had begun to turn. Likely the inlet would be much shallower when the tide was out—but he thought a boat could make it up the inlet easily, with the tide coming in.

That was promising. Encouraged, he crawled out on the far side and began to follow the channel inland. Within minutes, he heard a sound in the distance and stopped dead, listening.

Horses. He would swear it was the sound of neighing, though

so far away he couldn't be sure of it. He turned in a circle, trying to locate it, but the sound had vanished. Still, it seemed a sign, and he pushed on with renewed vigor, frightening a family of raccoons washing their meal in the water of the channel.

But then the inlet began to narrow, the water level dropping to no more than a foot—and then less, only a few inches of water running clear over dusky sand. He was loath to give up, though, and shoved his way under a low canopy of pine and twisted scrub oak. Then he stopped dead, skin tingling from scalp to sole.

Four of them. Crude stone pillars, pale in the shadow of the trees. One stood actually in the channel itself, tilted drunkenly by the action of the water. Another, on the bank, had carvings on its face, abstract symbols that he didn't recognize. He stood frozen, as though they were live things that might see him if he moved.

It seemed abnormally silent; even the insects seemed temporarily to have deserted him. He had no doubt that this was the circle the man Donner had described to Brianna. Here, the five men had chanted, walked their pattern, and turned, passing to the left of the inscribed stone. And here at least one of them had died. A profound shiver ran through him, despite the oppressive heat.

He moved at last, very carefully, backing away, as though the stones might wake, but did not turn his back on them until he was a good distance away—so far away that the stones were lost to sight, buried in the heavy growth. Then he turned and walked back toward the sea, fast, and then faster, 'til the breath burned in his throat, feeling as though invisible eyes bored into his back.

I sat in the shade of the forecastle, sipping cool beer and watching the shore. Just like bloody men, I thought, frowning at the tranquil stretch of sand. Charge in pigheaded, leaving the women to mind the store. Still . . . I wasn't so sure that I would have wanted to slog the length of the beastly island on foot myself. By repute, Blackbeard and a number of his confederates had used the place as a lair, and the reason why was obvious. A less hospitable shore I'd seldom seen.

The chance of finding anything in that secretive, wooded place by randomly poking into holes was low. Still, sitting on my bum in a boat while Brianna was dealing with Stephen Bonnet was making me twitch with anxiety and the urgent desire to *do* something.

But there was nothing *to* do, and the afternoon wore slowly away. I watched the shore steadily; now and then, I would see Roger or Ian pop out of the undergrowth, then the two of them would confer briefly before popping back in. Now and then, I looked to the north—but there was no sign of Jamie.

Captain Roarke, who *was* in fact a misbegotten son of a poxed whore, as he cheerfully admitted himself, sat down with me for a time and accepted a bottle of beer. I congratulated myself on my forethought in having brought a few dozen, a few of which I'd put over the side in a net to keep cool; the beer was doing a lot to soothe my impatience, though my stomach was still knotted with worry.

"None o' your men are what ye might call sailing men, are they?" Captain Roarke observed, after a thoughtful silence.

"Well, Mr. MacKenzie's spent a bit of time on fishing boats in Scotland," I said, dropping an empty bottle into the net. "But I wouldn't say he's an able seaman, no."

"Ah." He drank a bit more.

"All right," I said finally. "Why?"

He lowered his bottle and belched loudly, then blinked.

"Oh. Well, ma'am—I believe I did hear one o' the young men say as how there was a rondayvooz to occur, at dark o' moon?"

"Yes," I said a little guardedly. We had told the captain as little as possible, not knowing whether he might have some association with Bonnet. "The dark of the moon is tomorrow night, isn't it?"

"It is," he agreed. "But what I mean to say is—when one says 'dark o' moon,' most likely one *does* mean nighttime, aye?" He peered into the empty neck of his bottle, then lifted it and blew thoughtfully across it, making a deep *woooog* sound.

I took the hint and handed him another.

"Thank you kindly, ma'am," he said, looking happy. "See, the tide turns about half-eleven, this time o' month—and it's going *out*," he added with emphasis.

I gave him a blank look.

"Well, if you look careful, ma'am, you'll see the tide is half out now"—he pointed toward the south—"yet there's middling deep water close to shore all along o' here. Come the nighttime, though, it won't be."

"Yes?" I was still missing his point, but he was patient.

"Well, with the tide out, it's easier to see the bars and inlets, sure—and were you coming in with a boat with a shallow draft, that would be the time to choose. But was the rondayvooz to be with something bigger, maybe anything that draws more than four feet . . . well, then." He took a gulp, and pointed the bottom of his bottle toward a spot far down the shore. "The water there is deep, ma'am—see the color of it? Was I a ship of any size, that would be the safest place to anchor, when the tide is on the ebb."

I regarded the spot he'd indicated. The water *was* distinctly darker there, a deeper blue-gray than the waves surrounding it.

"You could have told us that earlier," I said with a certain note of reproach.

"So I could, ma'am," he agreed cordially, "save for not knowin' as you'd like to hear it." He got up then and wandered toward the stern, an empty bottle in hand, absently going *woog-woog-woog,* like a distant foghorn.

As the sun sank into the sea, Roger and Ian appeared on the shore, and Captain Roarke's hand, Moses, rowed ashore to fetch them off. Then we hoisted sail and made our way slowly up the coast of Ocracoke, until we found Jamie, waving from a tiny spit of sand.

Anchored offshore for the night, we exchanged notes of our findings—or lack of them. All the men were drained, exhausted from heat and searching and with little appetite for supper, despite their exertions. Roger, in particular, looked drawn and pale, and said almost nothing.

The last sliver of the waning moon rose in the sky. With a minimum of conversation, the men took their blankets and lay down on deck, asleep within minutes.

Quantities of beer notwithstanding, I was wide awake. I sat beside Jamie, my own blanket wrapped about my shoulders against the coolness of the night wind, watching the low black mystery of the island. The anchorage Captain Roarke had pointed out to me was invisible in the darkness. Would we know, I wondered, if a ship were to come tomorrow night?

In fact, it came that night. I woke in the very early morning, dreaming of corpses. I sat up, heart pounding, to see Roarke and

Moses at the rail, and a dreadful smell in the air. It wasn't a smell one would ever forget, and when I got to my feet and went to the rail to look, I was not at all surprised to hear Roarke murmur, "Slaver," nodding toward the south.

The ship was anchored half a mile or so away, its masts black against the paling sky. Not a huge ship, but definitely too big to make its way into the small channels of the island. I watched a long time, joined by Jamie, Roger, and Ian as they woke—but no boats were lowered.

"What d'ye suppose it's doing there?" Ian said. He spoke in a low voice; the slave ship made everyone nervous.

Roarke shook his head; he didn't like it, either.

"Damned if I know," he said. "Wouldn't expect such a thing in such a place. Not at all."

Jamie rubbed a hand across his unshaven chin. He hadn't shaved in days, and, green-faced and hollow-eyed beneath the stubble—he'd vomited over the rail within minutes of rising, though the swell was very gentle—looked even more disreputable than Roarke himself.

"Can ye lay us alongside her, Mr. Roarke?" he said, eyes on the slave ship. Roger glanced at him sharply.

"Ye don't suppose Brianna's aboard?"

"If she is, we'll find out. If she's not—we'll maybe find out who yon ship has come to see."

It was full daylight by the time we came along the ship, and there were a number of hands on deck, all of whom peered curiously down over the rail at us.

Roarke hallooed up, asking permission to come aboard. There was no immediate response to this, but after a few minutes, a large man with an air of authority and an ill-tempered face appeared.

"What d'ye want?" he called down.

"To come aboard," Roarke bellowed back.

"No. Shove off."

"We are in search of a young woman!" Roger called up. "We should like to ask you a few questions!"

"Any young women on this ship are mine," the captain—if that's what he was—said definitely. "Bugger off, I said." He turned and gestured to his hands, who scattered at once, reappearing in moments with muskets.

Roger cupped his hands to his mouth.

"BRIANNA!" he bellowed. "BRIANNAAAA!"

One man raised his gun and fired, the ball whistling safely over our heads, and ripping through the mainsail.

"Oi!" shouted Roarke, incensed. "What's the matter of you?"

The only answer to this was a fusillade of further shots, followed by the opening of the port lids nearest us, and the sudden appearance of the long black noses of several cannon, along with a more intense gust of stink.

"Jesus God," said Roarke, astonished. "Well, if that's how you feel about—well, God damn you!" he shouted, brandishing a fist. "God damn you, I say!"

Moses, less interested in rhetoric, had made sail with the first shot and was already at the tiller; we slid past the slave ship and into clean water within moments.

"Well, *something's* going on," I remarked, looking back at the ship. "Whether it's to do with Bonnet or not."

Roger was clinging to the rail, his knuckles white.

"It is," Jamie said. He wiped a hand across his mouth, and grimaced. "Can ye keep in sight of her, but out of range, Mr. Roarke?" A fresh wave of the smell of sewage, corruption, and hopelessness hit us, and he turned the color of rancid suet. "And maybe upwind, too?"

We were obliged to sail well out into the ocean and tack to and fro in order to meet these various conditions, but at length had beaten our way back and anchored a safe distance away, the slave ship barely visible. Here we lay through the rest of the day, taking it in turns to keep an eye on the strange ship through Captain Roarke's telescope.

Nothing happened, though; no boats came from the ship, nor from the shore. And as we all sat silent on deck, watching the stars come out in a moonless sky, the ship was swallowed by the dark.

107

The Dark of the Moon

They anchored long before dawn, and a small boat took them ashore.

"Where is *this*?" she asked, voice rusty with disuse—Bonnet had wakened her in the dark. They had made three stops along the way, at nameless coves where mysterious men came out of the shrubbery, rolling barrels or carrying bales, but she had not been taken off at any of them. This was a long, low island, thick with scrub forest and hazy with mist, looking haunted under a dying moon.

"Ocracoke," he answered, leaning forward to peer into the fog. "A bit farther to port, Denys." The seaman at the oars leaned harder to the side, and the nose of the boat turned slowly, drawing nearer to the shore.

It was cold on the water; she was grateful for the thick cloak he had wrapped around her before handing her into the boat. Even so, the chill of the night and the open sea had little to do with the small, constant shiver that made her hands tremble and numbed her feet and fingers.

Soft murmurs between the pirates, further direction. Bonnet jumped off into waist-deep, muddy water, and waded into the shadows, pushing aside the heavy growth so that the water of the hidden inlet showed suddenly, a smooth dark gleam before them. The boat nosed its way under the overhanging trees, then paused, so that Bonnet could pull himself over the gunwales, splashing and dripping.

A shattering cry sounded near them, so close that she jerked, heart pounding, before realizing that it was only a bird somewhere in the swamp around them. Otherwise, the night was quiet, save for the muted, regular splash of the oars.

They had put Josh and the Fulani men into the boat, too; Josh sat at her feet, a hunched black form. He was shivering; she could feel it. Disengaging a fold of the cloak, she put it over him, and put a hand on his shoulder under it, meaning to give him what encouragement she could. A hand rose and settled softly over hers, squeezing, and thus linked, they sailed slowly into the dark unknown beneath the dripping trees.

The sky was lightening by the time the boat reached a small landing, and streaks of rose-tinted cloud reached across the horizon. Bonnet hopped out, and reached down to take her hand. Reluctantly, she let go of Josh, and stood up.

There was a house, half-hidden in the trees. Made of gray clapboards, it seemed to sink into the remnants of fog, as though it weren't quite real and might disappear at any moment.

The wind-borne stink, though, was real enough. She'd never smelled it before herself, but had heard her mother's vivid description of it, and recognized it instantly—the smell of a slaver, anchored offshore. Josh recognized it, too; she heard his sudden gasp, and then a hasty murmur—he was saying the Hail Mary in Gaelic, as fast as he could.

"Take these to the barracoon," Bonnet said to the seaman, pushing Josh in his direction and waving at the Fulani. "Then go back to the ship. Tell Mr. Orden we sail for England in four days' time; he'll see to the rest of the provisioning. Come for me Saturday, an hour before high tide."

"Josh!" She called after him, and he looked back, eyes white with fear, but the seaman hustled him along, and Bonnet dragged her in the other direction, up the path toward the house.

"Wait! Where is he taking him? What are you going to do with him?" She dug her feet into the mud, and grabbed hold of a mangrove, refusing to move.

"Sell him, what else?" Bonnet was matter-of-fact about that, and also about her refusal to move. "Come along, darlin'. Ye know I can make ye, and ye know ye won't like it if I do." He reached out, flipped back the edge of her cloak, and pinched her nipple, hard, in illustration.

Burning with anger, she snatched the cloak back and wrapped

it tight around her, as though that might soothe the pain. He had already turned, and was making his way up the path, quite certain that she would follow. To her everlasting shame, she did.

The door was opened by a black man, nearly as tall as Bonnet himself, and even wider through the chest and shoulder. A thick vertical scar between his eyes ran nearly from his hairline to the bridge of his nose, but it had the clean look of a deliberate tribal scar, not the result of accident.

"Emmanuel, me man!" Bonnet greeted the man cheerfully, and pushed Brianna ahead of him into the house. "Look what the cat dragged in, will ya?"

The black man looked her up and down with an expression of doubt.

"She damn tall," he said, in a voice that held an African lilt. He took her by the shoulder and turned her round, running a hand down her back and cupping her buttocks briefly through the cloak. "Nice fat arse, though," he admitted grudgingly.

"Isn't it, though? Well, be seeing to her, then come tell me how it is here. The hold's near full—oh, and I've picked up four—no, five—more blacks. The men can go to Captain Jackson, but the women—ah, now, those are somethin' special." He winked at Emmanuel. "Twins."

The black man's face went rigid.

"Twins?" he said in a tone of horror. "You bring them in the house?"

"I will," Bonnet said firmly. "Fulani, and gorgeous things they are, too. No English, no training—but they'll go for fancies, sure. Speakin' of which, have we word from *Signor* Ricasoli?"

Emmanuel nodded, though his brow was furrowed; the scar pulled the frown lines into a deep "V."

"He be here on Thursday. *Monsieur* Houvener comes then, too. Mister Howard be here tomorrow, though."

"Splendid. I'm wanting me breakfast now—and I imagine you're hungry as well, aren't ye, darlin'?" he asked, turning to Brianna.

She nodded, torn between fear, outrage, and morning sickness. She had to eat something, and fast.

"Fine, then. Take her somewhere"—he flipped a hand toward the ceiling, indicating rooms upstairs—"and feed her. I'll eat in me office; come find me there."

Without acknowledgment of the order, Emmanuel clamped a hand like a vise on the back of her neck, and shoved her toward the stairs.

The butler—if one could describe something like Emmanuel with such a domestic term—pushed her into a small room and shut the door behind her. It was furnished, but sparsely: a bed frame with a bare mattress, one woolen blanket, and a chamber pot. She made use of the latter object with relief, then made a rapid reconnaissance of the room itself.

There was only one window, a small one, set with metal bars. There was no glass, only inside shutters, and the breath of sea and scrub forest filled the room, vying with dust and the stale smell of the stained mattress. Emmanuel might be a factotum, but he wasn't much of a housekeeper, she thought, trying to keep her spirits up.

A familiar sound came to her, and she craned her neck to see. Not much was visible from the window—only the white crushed shells and sandy mud that surrounded the house, and the tops of stunted pines. If she pressed her face to the side of the window, though, she could see a small slice of a distant beach, with white breakers rolling in. As she watched, three horses galloped across it, vanishing out of her view—but with the wind-borne sound of neighing, then came five more, and then another group of seven or eight. Wild horses, the descendants of Spanish ponies left here a century ago.

The sight of them charmed her, and she watched for a long time, hoping they would come back, but they didn't; only a flight of pelicans passed by, and a few gulls, diving for fish.

The sight of the horses had made her feel less alone for a few moments, but no less empty. She had been in the room for half an hour, at least, and there were no sounds of footsteps in the hall outside, bringing food. Cautiously, she tried the door, and was surprised to find it unlocked.

There *were* sounds downstairs; someone was here. And the warm, grainy aromas of porridge and baking bread were faint in the air.

Swallowing to keep her stomach down, she moved soft-footed through the house and down the stairs. There were male voices in a room at the front of the house—Bonnet and Emmanuel. The sound of them made her diaphragm tighten, but the door was closed, and she tiptoed past.

The kitchen was a cookshack, a separate small building outside, connected to the house by a short breezeway and surrounded by a fenced yard that also enclosed the back of the house. She gave the fence—very tall, and spiked—a glance, but first things first: she had to have food.

There was someone in the kitchen; she could hear the movements of pots, and a woman's voice, muttering something. The smell of food was strong enough to lean against. She pushed open the door and went in, pausing to let the cook see her. Then she saw the cook.

She was so battered by circumstance at this point that she only blinked, certain she was seeing things.

"Phaedre?" she said uncertainly.

The girl swung around, wide-eyed and open-mouthed with shock.

"Oh, sweet Jesus!" She glanced wildly behind Brianna, then, seeing that she was alone, grabbed Brianna's arm and pulled her out into the yard.

"What you doing here?" she demanded, sounding fierce. "How do you come to be *here*?"

"Stephen Bonnet," Brianna said briefly. "How on earth did you—did he kidnap you? From River Run?" She couldn't think how—or why—but everything from the moment she had learned she was pregnant had had the surreal feel of hallucination, and how much of this was due to pregnancy alone she had no real idea.

Phaedre was shaking her head, though.

"No, miss. That Bonnet, he got me a month ago. From a man name Butler," she added, mouth twisting in an expression that made clear her loathing of Butler.

The name seemed vaguely familiar to Brianna. She thought it was the name of a smuggler; she had never met him, but had heard the name now and then. He wasn't the smuggler who provided her aunt with tea and other contraband luxuries, though—she *had* met that man, a disconcertingly effete and dainty gentleman named Wilbraham Jones.

"I don't understand. But—wait, is there anything to eat?" she asked, the floor of her stomach dropping suddenly.

"Oh. Surely. You wait here." Phaedre vanished back into the kitchen, light-footed, and was back in an instant with half a loaf of bread and a crock of butter.

"Thank you." She grabbed the bread and ate some hastily, not bothering to butter it, then put down her head between her knees and breathed for a few minutes, until the nausea subsided.

"Sorry," she said, raising her head at last. "I'm pregnant."

Phaedre nodded, plainly unsurprised.

"Who by?" she asked.

"My husband," Brianna answered. She'd spoken tartly, but then realized, with a small lurch of her unsettled innards, that it could so easily be otherwise. Phaedre had been gone from River Run for months—God only knew what had happened to her in that span of time.

"He's not had you long, then." Phaedre glanced at the house.

"No. You said a month—have you tried to get away?"

"Once." The girl's mouth twisted again. "You see that man Emmanuel?"

Brianna nodded.

"He an Ibo. Track a haunt through a cypress swamp, and make it sorry when he catch it." She wrapped her arms around herself, though the day was warm.

The yard was fenced with eight-foot pointed pine stakes, laced with rope. She might get over them, with a foot up from Phaedre . . . but then she saw the shadow of a man pass by on the other side, a gun across his shoulder.

She would have guessed as much, had she been capable of organized thought. This was Bonnet's hideaway—and judging from the piles of boxes, bundles, and casks stacked haphazardly in the yard, it was also where he kept valuable cargo before selling it. Naturally, it would be guarded.

A faint breeze wafted through the pickets of the fence, carrying the same vile stench she had smelled when they came ashore. She took another quick bite of bread, forcing it down as ballast for her queasy stomach.

Phaedre's nostrils flared, then pinched at the reek.

"Be a slave ship, anchored past the breakers," she said very quietly, and swallowed. "Captain come in yesterday, see if Mr.

Bonnet have something for him, but he ain't back yet. Captain Jackson say he come again tomorrow."

Brianna could feel Phaedre's fear, like a pale yellow miasma wavering over her skin, and took another bite of bread.

"He won't—he wouldn't sell you to this Jackson?" She wouldn't put anything at all past Bonnet. But she did by now understand things about slavery. Phaedre was a prime item: light-skinned, young, and pretty—and trained as a body servant. Bonnet could get a very good price for her almost anywhere, and from what little she knew of slavers, they dealt in raw slaves from Africa.

Phaedre shook her head, her lips gone pale.

"I don't think so. He say I'm what he call a 'fancy.' That's why he's kept me so long; he got some men he know, come up from the Indies this week. Planters." She swallowed again, looking ill. "They buy pretty women."

The bread Brianna had eaten melted suddenly into a soggy, slimy mass in her stomach, and with a certain feeling of fatality, she got up and took a few steps away before throwing up over a bale of raw cotton.

Stephen Bonnet's voice echoed in her head, cheerfully jovial.

"Why bother takin' ye all the way to London, where ye'd be of no particular use to anyone? Besides, it rains quite a bit in London; I'm sure ye wouldn't like it."

"They buy pretty women," she whispered, leaning against the palisades, waiting for the sense of clamminess to fade. But *white* women?

Why not? said the coldly logical part of her brain. Women are property, black or white. If you can be owned, you can be sold. She herself had owned Lizzie, for a time.

She wiped her sleeve over her mouth, and went back to Phaedre, who was sitting on a roll of copper, her fine-boned face thin and drawn with worry.

"Josh—he took Josh, too. When we came ashore, he told them to take Josh to the barracoon."

"Joshua?" Phaedre sat up straight, eyes huge. "Joshua, Miss Jo's groom? He's *here*?"

"Yes. Where's the barracoon, do you know?"

Phaedre had hopped to her feet and was striding to and fro, agitated.

"I ain't knowing for sure. I cook up food for the slaves there, but be one of the seamen takes it. Can't be far from the house, though."

"Is it a big one?"

Phaedre shook her head emphatically at that.

"No'm. Mr. Bonnet, he ain't really in the slaving business. He pick up a few, here and there—and then he got his 'fancies'"— she grimaced at that—"but can't be more'n a dozen here, amount of food they eat. Three girls in the house—five, counting they Fulani he say he's bringing."

Feeling better, Brianna began to cast about the yard, searching for anything that might be of use. It was a hodgepodge of valuable things—everything from bolts of Chinese silk, wrapped in linen and oiled cloth, and crates of porcelain dishes, to rolls of copper, casks of brandy, bottles of wine packed in straw, and chests of tea. She opened one of these, breathing in the soft perfume of the leaves and finding it wonderfully soothing to her internal distress. She'd give almost anything for a hot cup of tea just now.

Even more interesting, though, were a number of small barrels, thick-walled and tightly sealed, containing gunpowder.

"If only I had a few matches," she muttered to herself, looking at them longingly. "Or even a striker." But fire was fire, and there was certainly one in the kitchen. She looked at the house carefully, thinking exactly where to place the barrels—but she couldn't blow the place up, not with the other slaves inside, and not without knowing what she'd do next.

The sound of the door opening galvanized her; by the time Emmanuel looked out, she had jumped away from the gunpowder, and was examining an enormous box enclosing a grandfather clock, the gilded face—decorated with three animated sailing ships on a sea of silver—peeping out behind the protective laths nailed over it.

"You, girl," he said to Brianna, and jerked his chin. "You come wash yourself." He gave Phaedre a hard look—Brianna saw that she wouldn't meet his eyes, but hastily began to pick up sticks of kindling from the ground.

The hand clamped hard on her neck again, and she was marched ignominiously back into the house.

This time, Emmanuel *did* lock the door. He brought her a basin and ewer, a towel, and a clean shift. Much, much later, he came back, bringing a tray of food. But he ignored all questions, and locked the door again upon leaving.

She pulled the bed over to the window and knelt on it, elbows wedged between the bars. There was nothing to do but think—and that was something she would as soon put off a little longer. She watched the forest and the distant beach, the shadows of the scrub pines creeping over the sand, the oldest of sundials, marking the snaillike progress of the hours.

After a long time, her knees grew numb and her elbows hurt, and she spread the cloak over the nasty mattress, trying not to consider the various stains on it, nor the smell. Lying on her side, she watched the sky through the window, the infinitesimal changes of the light from one moment to the next, and considered in detail the specific pigments and the exact brushstrokes she would use to paint it. Then she got up and began pacing to and fro, counting her steps, estimating distance.

The room was about eight feet by ten; 5,280 feet in a mile. Five hundred and twenty-eight laps. She really hoped Bonnet's office was underneath her.

Nothing, though, was enough, and as the room darkened and she reached two miles, she found Roger in her mind—where he had been all along, unacknowledged.

She sank down on the bed, hot from the exercise, and watched the last of the flaming color fade from the sky.

Had he been ordained, as he wanted so much? He had been worried about the question of predestination, not sure that he could take the Holy Orders he desired, if he were not able to subscribe wholeheartedly to that notion—well, *she* called it a notion; to Presbyterians, it was dogma. She smiled wryly, thinking of Hiram Crombie.

Ian had told her about Crombie earnestly attempting to explain the doctrine of predestination to the Cherokee. Most of them had listened politely, then ignored him. Bird's wife, Penstemon, though, had been interested by the argument, and followed Crombie about during the day, playfully pushing him, then crying out, 'Did your God know I would do *that*? How could he know that—*I* didn't know I would do that!', or in more thoughtful mood, trying to get him to explain how the idea of predestination might work in terms of gambling—like most of the Indians, Penstemon would bet on almost anything.

She thought Penstemon had probably had a lot to do with the shortness of Crombie's initial visit to the Indians. She had to give him credit, though: he'd gone back. And back again. He believed in what he was doing.

As did Roger. Damn, she thought wearily, there he was again, those soft moss-green eyes of his dark with thought, running a finger slowly down the bridge of his nose.

"Does it really matter?" she'd said at last, tiring of the discussion of predestination, and privately pleased that Catholics weren't required to believe any such thing and were content to let God work in mysterious ways. "Doesn't it matter more that you can help people, that you can offer comfort?"

They'd been in bed, the candle extinguished, talking by the glow of the hearth. She could feel the shift of his body as he moved, his hand playing with a strand of her hair as he considered.

"I don't know," he'd said at last. He'd smiled a little then, looking up at her.

"Do ye not think any time-traveler must be a bit of a theologian, though?"

She'd taken a deep, martyred breath, and he'd laughed then, and let it go, kissing her instead and descending to far earthier matters.

He'd been right, though. No one who had traveled through the stones could help asking it: why me? And who would answer that question, if not God?

Why me? And the ones who didn't make it—why them? She felt a small chill, thinking of those. The anonymous bodies, listed in Geillis Duncan's notebook; Donner's companions, dead on arrival. And speaking of Geillis Duncan . . . the thought came to her suddenly; the witch had died *here*, out of her own time.

Putting metaphysics aside and looking at the matter purely in terms of science—and it *must* have a scientific basis, she argued stubbornly, it wasn't magic, no matter what Geilie Duncan had thought—the laws of thermodynamics held that neither mass nor energy could be created nor destroyed. Only changed.

Changed how, though? Did movement through time constitute change? A mosquito whined past her ear, and she flapped her hand to drive it away.

You could go both ways; they knew that for a fact. The obvious implication—which neither Roger nor her mother had mentioned, so perhaps they hadn't seen it—was that one could go into the future from a starting point, rather than only into the past and back.

So perhaps if someone traveled to the past and died there, as Geillis Duncan and Otter-Tooth had both demonstrably done . . . perhaps that must be balanced by someone traveling to the future and dying *there*?

She closed her eyes, unable—or unwilling—to follow that train of thought any further. Far in the distance, she heard the sound of the surf, pounding on the sand, and thought of the slave ship. Then she realized that the smell of it was *here,* and rising suddenly, went to the window. She could just see the far end of the path that led to the house; as she watched, a big man in a dark-blue coat and hat stumped rapidly out of the trees, followed by two others, shabbily dressed. *Sailors,* she thought, seeing the roll of their gait.

This must be Captain Jackson, then, come to conduct his business with Bonnet.

"Oh, Josh," she said out loud, and had to sit down on the bed, a wave of faintness washing over her.

Who had it been? One of the Saint Theresas—Theresa of Avila? Who'd said in exasperation to God, *"Well, if this is how You treat Your friends, no wonder You have so few of them!"*

She had fallen asleep thinking of Roger. She waked in the morning thinking of the baby.

For once, the nausea and the odd sense of dislocation were absent. All she felt was a deep peace, and a sense of . . . curiosity?

Are you there? she thought, hands across her womb. Nothing so definite as an answer; but knowledge was there, as sure as the beating of her own heart.

Good, she thought, and fell asleep again.

Noises from below awakened her sometime later. She sat up suddenly, hearing loud voices raised, then swayed, feeling faint, and lay down again. The nausea had returned, but if she closed her eyes and kept very still, it lay dormant, like a sleeping snake.

The voices continued, rising and falling, with the occasional loud thud for punctuation, as though a fist had struck a wall or table. After a few minutes, though, the voices ceased, and she heard nothing further until light footsteps came to her door. The lock rattled, and Phaedre came in, with a tray of food.

She sat up, trying not to breathe; the smell of anything fried . . .

"What's going on down there?" she asked.

Phaedre pulled a face.

"That Emmanuel, he's not best pleased with they Fulani women. Ibo, they think twins are bad, bad luck—any woman bear twins, she take them out in the forest, leave them there to die. Emmanuel want to send the Fulani off with Captain Jackson first thing, get them out the house, but Mr. Bonnet, he say he waiting on the gentlemen from the Indies, get a lots better price."

"Gentlemen from the Indies—what gentlemen?"

Phaedre lifted her shoulders.

"I ain't knowing. Gentlemen he think he sell things to. Sugar planters, I reckon. You eat that; I be back later."

Phaedre turned to go, but Brianna suddenly called after her.

"Wait! You didn't tell me yesterday—who took you from River Run?"

The girl turned back, looking reluctant.

"Mr. Ulysses."

"Ulysses?" Brianna said, disbelieving. Phaedre heard the doubt in her voice, and gave her a flat, angry look.

"What, you don't believe me?"

"No, no," Brianna hastily assured her. "I do believe you. Only—why?"

Phaedre breathed in deeply through her nose.

"Because I am one damn stupid nigger," she said bitterly. "My mama told me, she say never, ever cross Ulysses. But did I listen?"

"Cross him," Brianna said warily. "How did you cross him?" She gestured to the bed, inviting Phaedre to sit down. The girl hesitated for a moment, but then did, smoothing a hand over the white cloth tied round her head, over and over, while she searched for words.

"Mr. Duncan," she said at last, and her face softened a little. "He a nice, nice man. You know he never been with a woman? He got kicked by a horse when he young, hurt his balls, think he can't do nothing that way."

Brianna nodded; she'd heard something of Duncan's trouble from her mother.

"Well," Phaedre said with a sigh. "He wrong about that." She glanced at Brianna, to see how she might take this admission. "He wasn't meaning no harm, and nor was I. It just—happened." She shrugged. "But Ulysses, he find it out; he find out every single thing goes on at River Run, sooner or later. Maybe one of the girls told him, maybe some other way, but he knew. And he told me that ain't right, I put a stop to it this minute."

"But you didn't?" Brianna guessed.

Phaedre shook her head slowly, lips pushed out.

"Told him I'd stop when Mr. Duncan didn't want to no more—not *his* business. See, I thought Mr. Duncan, he the master. Ain't true, though; Ulysses be the master at River Run."

"So he—he took you away—sold you?—to stop you sleeping with Duncan?" *Why would he care?* she wondered. *Was he afraid Jocasta would discover the affair and be hurt?*

"No, he sell me because I told him if he don't leave me and Mr. Duncan be, then I tell about him and Miss Jo."

"Him and . . ." Brianna blinked, not believing what she was hearing. Phaedre looked at her, and gave a small, ironic smile.

"He share Miss Jo's bed these twenty years and more. Since before Old Master die, my mama said. Every slave there knows it; ain't one stupid enough to say so to his face, 'cept me."

Brianna knew she was gaping like a goldfish, but couldn't help it. A hundred tiny things she'd seen at River Run, myriad small intimacies between her aunt and the butler, suddenly took on new significance. No wonder her aunt had gone to such lengths to get him back after the death of Lieutenant Wolff. And no wonder, either, that Ulysses had taken instant action. Phaedre might have been believed, or not; the mere accusation would have destroyed him.

Phaedre sighed, and rubbed a hand over her face.

"He ain't waste no time. That very night, he and Mr. Jones come take me from my bed, wrap me up tight in a blanket, and carry me away in a wagon. Mr. Jones, he say he ain't no slaver, but he do it as a favor for Mr. Ulysses. So he don't keep me; he take me way downriver, though, sell me in Wilmington to a man what owns an ordinary. That's not too bad, but then a couple months later, Mr. Jones comes and takes me back—Wilmington's not far enough away to suit Ulysses. So he give me to Mr. Butler, and Mr. Butler, he take me to Edenton."

She looked down, pleating the quilt between long, graceful fingers. Her lips were tight, and her face slightly flushed. Brianna forbore to ask what she had done for Butler in Edenton, thinking that she had likely been employed in a brothel.

"And . . . er . . . Stephen Bonnet found you there?" she hazarded.

Phaedre nodded, not looking up.

"Won me in a card game," she said succinctly. She stood up. "I got to go; I had me enough of crossing black men—ain't risking no more beatings from that Emmanuel."

Brianna was beginning to emerge from the shock of hearing about Ulysses and her aunt. A sudden thought occurred to her, and she jumped out of bed, hurrying to catch Phaedre before she reached the door.

"Wait, wait! Just one more thing—do you—do the slaves at River Run—know anything about the gold?"

"What, in Old Master's tomb? Surely." Phaedre's face expressed a cynical surprise that there could be any doubt about it. "Ain't nobody touch it, though. Everybody know there a curse on it."

"Do you know anything about its disappearing?"

Phaedre's face went blank.

"Disappearing?"

"Oh, wait—no, you wouldn't know; you . . . left, long before it disappeared. I just wondered, you know, whether maybe Ulysses had something to do with that."

Phaedre shook her head.

"I don't know nothing about that. But I ain't put one thing past Ulysses, curse or no." There was a sound of heavy footsteps on the stair, and she paled. Without a word or gesture of farewell, she slipped out the door and closed it; Brianna heard the frantic fumbling of the key on the other side, and then the click of the closing lock.

Emmanuel, silent as a lizard, brought her a dress in the afternoon. It was too short by a good bit, and too tight in the bosom, but a heavy blue watered silk, and well-made. It had plainly been worn before; there were sweat stains on it and it smelled—of fear, she thought, repressing a shudder as she struggled into it.

She was sweating herself as Emmanuel led her downstairs, though a pleasant breeze swept through the open windows, stirring the curtains. The house was very simple, for the most part, with bare wooden floors and little more than stools and bed frames by way of furniture. The room downstairs to which Emmanuel showed her was such a contrast that it might have belonged to a different house entirely.

Rich Turkey rugs covered the floor in a overlapping riot of color, and the furniture, while of several different styles, was all heavy and elaborate, carved wood and silk upholstery. Silver and crystal glittered from every available surface, and a chandelier—much too large for the room—hung with crystal pendants sprayed the room with tiny rainbows. It was a pirate's idea of a rich man's room—lavish abundance, displayed with no sense of style or taste.

The rich man seated by the window appeared not to mind his surroundings, though. A thin man in a wig, with a prominent Adam's apple, he looked to be in his thirties, though his skin was lined and yellowed by some tropical disease. He glanced sharply at the door as she entered, then rose to his feet.

Bonnet had been entertaining his guest; there were glasses and a decanter on the table, and the smell of brandy was sweet and heavy in the air. Brianna felt her stomach shift queasily, and wondered what they'd do if she were to vomit on the Turkey rug.

"There ye are, darlin'," Bonnet said, coming to take her by the hand. She pulled it away from him, but he affected not to notice, and instead pushed her toward the thin man, a hand in the small of her back. "Come and make your bob to Mr. Howard, sweetheart."

She drew herself to her full height—she was a good four inches taller than Mr. Howard, whose eyes widened at sight of her—and glowered down at him.

"I am being held against my will, Mr. Howard. My husband and my father will—ow!" Bonnet had gripped her wrist and twisted it, hard.

"Lovely, is she not?" he said conversationally, as though she had not spoken.

"Oh, yes. Yes, indeed. Very *tall*, though . . ." Howard walked round her, examining her dubiously. "And red hair, Mr. Bonnet? I do really prefer blond."

"Oh, do you indeed, you little pissant!" she snapped, in spite of Bonnet's grip on her arm. "Where do you get off, preferring things?" With a wrench, she pulled away from Bonnet and rounded on Howard.

"Now, look," she said, trying to sound reasonable—he was blinking at her in a faintly bewildered fashion— "I am a woman of good—of *excellent*—family, and I have been kidnapped. My father's name is James Fraser, my husband is Roger MacKenzie, and my aunt is Mrs. Hector Cameron, of River Run Plantation."

"Is she really of good family?" Howard addressed this question to Bonnet, appearing to be more interested.

Bonnet bowed slightly in affirmation.

"Oh, indeed she is, sir. The finest blood!"

"Hmmm. And good health, I see." Howard had resumed his examination, leaning close to peer at her. "Has she bred before?"

"Aye, sir, a healthy son."

"Good teeth?" Howard rose on his toes, looking inquisitive, and Bonnet obligingly yanked one arm behind her back to hold her still, then took a handful of her hair and jerked her head back, making her gasp.

Howard took her chin in one hand and pried at the corner of her mouth with the other, poking experimentally at her molars.

"Very nice," he said approvingly. "And I will say the skin is very fine. But—"

She jerked her chin out of his grasp, and bit down as hard as she could on Howard's thumb, feeling the meat of it shift and tear between her molars with a sudden copper taste of blood.

He shrieked and struck at her; she let go and dodged, enough so his hand glanced off her cheek. Bonnet let go, and she took two fast steps back and fetched up hard against the wall.

"She's bitten me thumb off, the bitch!" Eyes watering in agony, Mr. Howard swayed to and fro, cradling his wounded hand against his chest. Fury flooded his face and he lunged toward her, free hand drawn back, but Bonnet seized him by the wrist and pulled him aside.

"Now then, sir," he said. "I cannot allow ye to damage her, sure. She's not yours yet, is she?"

"I don't care if she's mine or not," Howard cried, face suffused with blood. "I'll beat her to death!"

"Oh, no, surely ye don't mean that, Mr. Howard," Bonnet said, his voice jovially soothing. "A cruel waste that would be. Leave her to me, will ye, then?" Not waiting for an answer, he pulled Brianna after him, dragging her stumbling across the room, and thrust her toward the silent factotum, who had waited motionless by the door through the conversation.

"Take her out, Manny, and teach her her manners, will ye? And gag her before ye bring her back."

Emmanuel didn't smile, but a faint light seemed to burn in the black depths of his pupilless eyes. His fingers dug between the bones of her wrist and she gasped with pain, jerking in a vain attempt to free herself. With a single quick movement, the Ibo whirled her round and twisted up her arm behind her back, bending her half forward. Sharp pain shot up her arm as she felt her shoulder tendons begin to part. He pulled harder and a dark wave passed over her vision. Through it, she heard Bonnet's voice calling out behind them as Emmanuel propelled her through the door.

"Not in the face, mind, Manny, and no permanent marks."

Howard's voice had quite lost its choked note of fury. It was still choked, but with something more like awe.

"My God," he said. "Oh, my God."

"A charmin' sight, is it not?" Bonnet agreed cordially.

"Charming," Howard echoed. "Oh—the most charming thing I believe I have ever seen. Such a shade! Might I—" The hunger in his voice was evident, and Brianna felt the vibration of his footstep on the carpet, a split second before his hands clamped tight on her buttocks. She screamed behind the gag, but she was bent hard across the table, with the edge cutting into her diaphragm, and the sound came out as no more than a grunt. Howard laughed joyfully, and let go.

"Oh, look," he said, sounding enchanted. "Look, do you see? The most perfect print of my hands—so white on the crimson . . . she is so *hot* . . . oh, it's fading. Let me just—"

She clenched her legs tight together and stiffened as he fondled her naked privates, but then his touch was gone, and Bonnet had taken his hand off her neck, and was pulling his customer away from her.

"Ah, now, that's enough, sir. After all, she's not your property—not yet." Bonnet's tone was jovial, but firm. Howard's response was immediately to offer a sum that made her gasp behind the gag, but Bonnet only laughed.

"That's generous, sir, so it is, but 'twouldn't be fair on my other customers, would it, to be takin' your offer without letting them make their own? No, sir, I do appreciate it, but I mean to auction this one; I'm afraid ye'll needs be waiting on the day."

Howard was disposed to protest, to offer more—he was most urgently in earnest, he protested that he could not wait, was ravished by desire, a great deal too warm to abide delay . . . but Bonnet only demurred, and in a few moments had ushered him out of the room. Brianna heard his voice protesting, dying away as Emmanuel removed him.

She had stood up as soon as Bonnet took his hand off her neck, wriggling madly to shake her skirts down. Emmanuel had tied her hands behind her back, as well as gagging her. If he hadn't, she would have tried to kill Stephen Bonnet with her bare hands.

This thought must have been visible on her face, for Bonnet glanced at her, looked again, and laughed.

"Ye did amazing well, darlin'," he said, and leaning over, negligently pulled the gag down from her mouth. "That man will empty his purse for the chance to get his hands on your arse again."

"You God damn . . . you—" She shook with rage, and with the futility of finding any epithet that came close to being strong enough. "I will fucking *kill* you!"

He laughed again.

"Oh, now, sweetheart. For a sore arse? Consider it a repayment—in part—for my left ball." He chucked her under the chin, and went toward the table where the tray with the decanters stood. "Ye've earned a drink. Brandy or porter?"

She ignored the offer, trying to keep her rage in check. Her cheeks flamed with furious blood, and so did her outraged bottom.

"What do you mean, 'auction'?" she demanded.

"I should think that clear enough, sweetheart. Ye've heard the word, sure." Bonnet gave her a glance of mild amusement, and pouring himself a tot of brandy, drank it off in two swallows. "Hah." He exhaled, blinking, and shook his head.

"Hoo. I've two more customers in the market for someone like you, darlin'. They'll be here tomorrow or next day to be having a look. Then I'll ask for bids, and ye'll be off to the Indies by Friday, I expect."

He spoke casually, without the slightest hint of jeering. That, more than anything, made her insides waver. She was a matter of business, a piece of merchandise. To him, and to his goddamned bloody customers, too—Mr. Howard had made that clear. It didn't matter what she said; they weren't at all interested in who she was or what she might want.

Bonnet was watching her face, his pale green eyes assessing. *He* was interested, she realized, and her insides curled up into a knot.

"What did ye use on her, Manny?" he asked.

"A wooden spoon," the manservant said indifferently. "You said no marks."

Bonnet nodded, thoughtful.

"Nothing permanent, I said," he corrected. "We'll leave her as she is for Mr. Ricasoli, I think, but Mr. Houvener . . . well, we'll wait and see."

Emmanuel merely nodded, but his eyes rested on Brianna with sudden interest. Her stomach everted itself neatly and she vomited, absolutely ruining the fine silk dress.

The sound of high-pitched whinnying reached her; wild horses, rioting down the beach. If this were a romance novel, she thought grimly, she'd make a rope from the bedclothes, let herself down from the window, find the horse herd, and, by exercising her mystical skills with horses, persuade one of them to carry her to safety.

As it was, there were no bedclothes—only a ratty mattress made of ticking stuffed with sea grass—and as for getting within a mile of wild horses . . . She would have given a lot for Gideon, and felt tears prickle at thought of him.

"Oh, now you *are* losing your mind," she said aloud, wiping her eyes. "Crying over a horse." Especially *that* horse. That was so much better than thinking of Roger, though—or Jem. No, she absolutely could *not* think about Jemmy, nor the possibility of his growing up without her, without knowing why she had abandoned him. Or the new one . . . and what life might be like for the child of a slave.

But she *was* thinking of them, and the thought was enough to overcome her momentary despair.

All right, then. She was getting out of here. Preferably before Mr. Ricasoli and Mr. Houvener, whoever they were, turned up. For the thousandth time, she moved restlessly around the room, forcing herself to move slowly, look at what was there.

Damn little, and what there was, stoutly built, was the discouraging answer. She'd been given food, water for washing, a linen towel, and a hairbrush with which to tidy herself. She picked it up, assessing its potential as a weapon, then threw it down again.

The chimney stack rose through this room, but there was no open hearth. She thumped the bricks experimentally, and pried at the mortar with the end of the spoon they'd given her to eat with. She found one place where the mortar was cracked enough to pry, but a quarter of an hour's trying managed to dislodge only a few inches of mortar; the brick itself stayed firmly in place. Given a month or so, that might be worth a try—though the chances of someone her size managing to squeeze up an eighteenth-century flue . . .

It was getting up to rain; she heard the excited rattle of the palmetto leaves as the wind came through, sharp with the smell of rain. It was not quite sunset, but the clouds had darkened the sky so the room seemed dim. She had no candle; no one expected her to read or sew.

She threw her weight against the bars of the window for the dozenth time, and for the dozenth time found them solidly set and unyielding. Again, in a month, she might contrive to sharpen the spoon's end by grinding it against the chimney bricks, then use it as a chisel to chip away enough of the frame to dislodge one or two bars. But she didn't have a month.

They'd taken away the fouled dress, and left her in shift and stays. Well, that was something. She pulled off the stays, and by picking at the ends of the stitching, extracted the busk—a flat, twelve-inch strip of ivory that ran from sternum to navel. A better weapon than a hairbrush, she thought. She took it over to the chimney, and began to rasp the end against the brick, sharpening its point.

Could she stab someone with it? *Oh, yes,* she thought fiercely. *And please let it be Emmanuel.*

108

Damn Tall

Roger waited in the cover of the thick bayberry bushes near the shore; a little way beyond, Ian and Jamie lay likewise in wait.

The second ship had arrived in the morning, coming to anchor a fastidious distance beyond the slaver. Sloshing nets over the side of Roarke's ship in the guise of fishermen, they had been able to watch as first the captain of the slaver went ashore, and then, an hour later, a boat from the second ship was lowered and rowed ashore, with two men—and a small chest—in it.

"A gentleman," Claire had reported, scanning them through the telescope. "Wig, nicely dressed. The other man's a servant of some kind—is the gentleman one of Bonnet's customers, do you think?"

"I do," Jamie had said, watching the boat pull to the shore. "Take us a bit to the north, if ye please, Mr. Roarke; we'll go ashore."

The three of them had landed half a mile from the beach and worked their way down through the wood, then took up their positions in the shrubbery and settled down to wait. The sun was hot, but so close to the shore, there was a fresh breeze, and it was not uncomfortable in the shade, bar the insects. For the hundredth time, Roger brushed away something crawling on his neck.

The waiting was making him jumpy. His skin itched with salt, and the scent of the tidal forest, with its peculiar mix of aromatic pine and distant seaweed, the crunch of shell and needle beneath his feet, brought back to him in vivid detail the day he had killed Lillington.

He had gone then—as now—with the intent of killing Stephen Bonnet. But the elusive pirate had been warned, and an ambush laid. It had been by the will of God—and the skill of Jamie Fraser—that he hadn't left his own carcass in a similar forest, bones scattered by wild pigs, bleaching among the gleam of dry needles and the white of empty shells.

His throat was tight again, but he couldn't shout or sing to loosen it.

He should pray, he thought, but could not. Even the constant litany that had echoed through his heart since the night he had learned she was gone—*Lord, that she might be safe*—even that small petition had somehow dried up. His present thought—*Lord, that I might kill him*—he couldn't voice that, even to himself.

The deliberate intent and desire to murder—surely he couldn't expect such a prayer to be heard.

For a moment, he envied Jamie and Ian their faith in gods of wrath and vengeance. While Roarke and Moses had brought the fishing boat in, he had heard Jamie murmur to Claire and take her hands in his. And heard her then bless him in the Gaelic, with the invocation to Michael of the red domain, the blessing of a warrior on his way to battle.

Ian had merely sat, cross-legged and silent, watching the shore draw nearer, his face remote. If he prayed, there was no telling to whom. When they landed, though, he had paused on the bank of one of the myriad inlets, and scooping up mud in his fingers, had carefully painted his face, drawing a line from forehead to chin, then four parallel streaks across his left cheek, a thick dark circle around his right eye. It was remarkably unsettling.

Quite obviously, neither of them had the slightest qualms about the business, nor the least hesitation in asking God to aid their efforts. He envied them.

And sat in stubborn silence, the gates of heaven closed against him, his hand on the hilt of his knife and a loaded pistol in his belt, planning murder.

A little past noon, the burly captain of the slaver came back, footsteps crunching indifferently on the layer of dried pine needles. They let him pass, waiting.

Late in the afternoon, it began to rain.

She had dozed off again, from sheer boredom. It began to rain; the sound roused her briefly, then drove her more deeply into slumber, drops pattering softly on the palmetto thatch above. She woke abruptly when one of the drops fell cold on her face, followed quickly by a few of its fellows.

She jerked upright, blinking with momentary disorientation. She rubbed a hand over her face and looked up; there was a small wet patch on the plaster ceiling, surrounded by a much larger stain from previous leaks, and drops were forming in its center like magic, each perfect bead falling one after another after another to splat on the mattress ticking.

She got up to push the bed out from under the leak, and then stopped. Slowly she straightened up, and put up a hand to the wet patch. The ceiling was a normal one for the time, less than seven feet; she could reach it easily.

"She damn tall," she said aloud. "Damn right she is."

She put her hand flat on the wet patch and pushed as hard as she could. The wet plaster gave way at once, and so did the rotten laths behind it. She jerked back her hand, scratching her arm on the jagged edges of lath, and a small cascade of dirty water, centipedes, mouse droppings, and fragments of palmetto leaf poured in through the hole she'd made.

She wiped her hand on her shift, reached up, seized the edge of the hole, and pulled, ripping down chunks of lath and plaster, until she'd made a hole that would accommodate her head and shoulders.

"Okay," she whispered to the baby, or herself. She glanced around the room, put on her stays over her shift, then tucked the sharpened busk down the front.

Then, standing on the bed, she took a deep breath, shoved her steepled hands upward as though about to dive, and grabbed for anything solid enough to provide leverage. Little by little, she hauled herself, sweating and grunting, up into the steaming thatch of sharp-edged leaves, teeth gritted and eyes closed against the dirt and dead insects.

Her head thrust into moist open air and she gasped for breath. She had an elbow hooked over a beam and, using that for leverage, pulled farther up. Her legs kicked vainly in empty air, trying to propel her upward, and she felt the wrench of shoulder muscles, but sheer desperation propelled her upward—that, and the nightmare vision of Emmanuel coming into the room and seeing the bottom half of her hanging out of the ceiling.

With a rending shower of leaves, she hauled herself out, to lie flat on the rain-wet thatch of the roof. The rain was still coming down heavily, and she was soaked in moments. A little way away, she saw some sort of structure sticking up amid the palmetto leaves of the thatch, and wriggled her way cautiously toward it, constantly fearful lest the roof give way beneath her weight, probing with hands and elbows for the firmness of the roof beams below the thatched leaves.

The structure proved to be a small platform, firmly set on the beams, with a railing on one side. She scrambled onto this and crouched, panting. It was still raining onshore, but out to sea, the sky was mostly clear, and the setting sun behind her spilled a burnt, bloody orange over sky and water through black streaks of shattered cloud. It looked like the end of the world, she thought, her ribs heaving against the lacing of her stays.

From the vantage point of the roof, she could see over the scrub forest; the slice of beach she had glimpsed from her window was clearly visible—and beyond it, two ships, lying close offshore.

Two boats were pulled up on shore, though well separated from each other—probably one from each ship, she thought. One of the ships must be the slaver, the other likely Howard's. A wash of humiliated rage ran over her—she was surprised that the rain didn't steam off her skin. There was no time to dwell on that, though.

Voices came faintly through the patter of rain, and she ducked down, then realized that no one was likely to look up and see her. Raising her head to peer through the railing, she saw figures come out of the trees onto the beach—a single file of chained men, with two or three guards.

"Josh!" She strained her eyes to see, but in the eerie twilight, the figures were no more than silhouettes. She thought she made out the tall, slender figures of the two Fulani men—perhaps the shorter one behind them was Josh, but she couldn't tell.

Her fingers curled tight around the railing, impotent. She couldn't help, she knew it, but to be obliged simply to watch . . . As she watched, a thin scream came from the beach, and a smaller figure ran out of the wood, skirts flying. The guards turned, startled; one of them seized Phaedre—it had to be her; Brianna could hear her screaming "Josh! Josh!", the sound of it harsh as the cry of a distant gull.

She was struggling with the guard—some of the chained men turned abruptly, lunging at the other. A struggling knot of men fell to the sand. Someone was running toward them from the boat, something in his hand . . .

The vibration in her feet jerked her attention from the scene on the beach.

"Crap!" she said involuntarily. Emmanuel's head poked up over the edge of the roof, staring in disbelief. Then his face contorted, and he heaved himself up—there must be a ladder attached to the side of the house, she thought, well, of course there would be, you wouldn't have a lookout platform and no way to get up to it. . . .

While her mind was busying itself with *that* nonsense, her body was taking more concrete steps. She had drawn the sharpened busk and was crouched against the platform, hand low as Ian had taught her.

Emmanuel made a derisive face at the thing in her hand and grabbed at her.

They could hear the gentleman coming well before they saw him. He was singing softly to himself, a French air of some kind. He was alone; the servant must have gone back to the ship while they were making their way through the woods.

Roger got softly to his feet, crouched behind his chosen bush. His limbs were stiff, and he stretched inconspicuously.

As the gentleman drew even with him, Jamie stepped out into the path in front of him. The man—a small, foppish-looking sort—uttered a girlish shriek of alarm. Before he could flee, though, Jamie had stepped forward and grasped his arm, smiling pleasantly.

"Your servant, sir," he said courteously. "Have ye been calling upon Mr. Bonnet, by chance?"

The man blinked at him, confused.

"Bonnet? Why, why . . . yes."

Roger felt a tightness in his chest ease suddenly. *Thank God.* They'd found the right place.

"Who are you, sir?" the small man was demanding, trying to draw his forearm out of Jamie's grip, to no avail.

There was no need to keep hidden now; Roger and Ian stepped out of the bushes, and the gentleman gasped at sight of Ian in his war paint, then glanced wildly back and forth between Jamie and Roger.

Evidently settling on Roger as the most civilized-looking person present, the gentleman appealed to him.

"I beg you, sir—who are you, and what do you want?"

"We are in search of an abducted young woman," Roger said. "A very tall young woman with red hair. Have you—" Before he could finish, he saw the man's eyes dilate with panic. Jamie saw it, too, and twisted the man's wrist, sending him to his knees, mouth awry with pain.

"I think, sir," Jamie said, with impeccable courtesy, holding tight, "we must oblige you to tell us what ye know."

She couldn't let him get hold of her. That was her only conscious thought. He grabbed at her weaponless arm and she yanked free, skin slippery with rain, and struck at him in the same motion. The point of the busk skidded up his arm, leaving a reddening furrow, but he ignored this and lunged at her. She fell backward over the railing, landing awkwardly on her hands and knees in the leaves, but he hadn't got her; he'd fallen on his own knees on the platform, with a thud that shook the whole roof.

She scrabbled madly to the edge of the roof, hands and knees poking randomly through the thatch, and threw her legs over the edge into space, kicking frantically for the rungs of the ladder.

He was after her, had her wrist in a grip like an eel's bite, was hauling her back onto the roof. She drew back her free hand and lashed him hard across the face with the busk. He roared and his grip loosened; she wrenched free and dropped.

She hit the sand flat on her back with a bone-shaking *thump!* and lay paralyzed, unable to breathe, the rain pelting down on her face. A hoot of triumph came from the roof, and then a growl of exasperated dismay. He thought he'd killed her.

Great, she thought muzzily. *Keep thinking that.* The shock of impact was beginning to wear off, her diaphragm lurched into motion, and glorious air rushed into her lungs. Could she move?

She didn't know, and didn't dare to try. Through rain-clotted lashes, she saw Emmanuel's bulk ease over the edge of the roof, foot groping for the crude ladder rungs she could now see, nailed to the wall.

She'd lost the busk when she fell, but saw it gleaming dully, a foot from her head. With Emmanuel's back momentarily turned, she whipped her hand up and grabbed it, then lay still, playing possum.

They had nearly reached the house when sounds from the nearby forest stopped them. Roger froze, then ducked off the path. Jamie and Ian had already melted into the wood. The sounds weren't coming from the path, though, but from somewhere off to the left—voices, men's voices, shouting orders, and the shuffling of feet, the clink of chains.

A thrill of panic shot through him. Were they taking her away? He was already soaked with rain, but felt the bloom of cold sweat over his body, colder than the rain.

Howard, the man they'd apprehended in the wood, had assured them Brianna was safe in the house, but what would he know? He listened, straining his ears for the sound of a woman's voice, and heard it, a high, thin scream.

He jerked toward it, only to find Jamie beside him, gripping his arm.

"That's not Brianna," his father-in-law said urgently. "Ian will go. You and I—for the house!"

There was no time for argument. The sounds of violence on the beach came faintly—shouts and cries—but Jamie was right, that voice wasn't Brianna's. Ian was running toward the beach, making no effort now to be silent.

An instant's hesitation, instinct urging him to go after Ian, then Roger was on the path, following Jamie toward the house at the run.

Emmanuel bent over her; she felt his bulk and lunged upward like a striking snake, sharpened busk like a fang. She'd aimed for his head, hoping for eye or throat, but counting at least on his jerking reflexively back, putting him at a disadvantage.

He jerked, all right, up and away, but was much faster than she'd thought. She struck with all her force, and the sharpened busk drove under his arm with a rubbery shock. He froze for a moment, mouth open in incredulity, looking at the ivory rod that stuck out of his armpit. Then he wrenched it out, and lunged for her with an outraged bellow.

She was already on her feet, though, and running for the woods. From somewhere ahead, she heard more yelling—and a bloodcurdling scream. Another, and then more, these coming from the front of the house.

Dazed and terrified, she kept running, her mind only slowly grasping that some of the screams had words.

"Casteal DHUUUUUUUIN!"

Da, she thought, in absolute astonishment, then tripped over a branch on the ground and fell arse over teakettle, landing in a disheveled heap.

She struggled to her feet, thinking absurdly, *This* can't *be good for the baby,* and groping for another weapon.

Her fingers were trembling, wouldn't work. She scrabbled the ground, vainly. Then Emmanuel popped up beside her like the Demon King, grabbing her arm with a gloating, *"HA!"*

The shock made her sway, her vision going gray at the edges. She could still hear bloodcurdling screams on the distant beach, but no more yelling at the house. Emmanuel was saying something, full of satisfaction and threat, but she wasn't listening.

There seemed to be something wrong with his face; it went in and out of focus, and she blinked hard, shaking her head to clear her sight. It wasn't her eyes, though—it was him. His face melted slowly from bare-toothed menace to a look of faint astonishment. He frowned, lips pursing so she saw the pink lining of his mouth, and blinked two or three times. Then he made a small choked noise, put a hand to his chest, and dropped to his knees, still gripping her arm.

He fell over, and she landed on top of him. She pulled away—his fingers came away easily, all their strength suddenly gone—and stumbled to her feet, panting and shaking.

Emmanuel was lying on his back, legs bent under him at what would have been an excruciating angle, had he been alive. She gulped for air, trembling, afraid to believe it. But he *was* dead; there was no mistaking the look of it.

Her breath was coming better now, and she began to be conscious of the cuts and bruises on her bare feet. She still felt stunned, unable to decide what to do next.

The decision was made for her in the next instant, as Stephen Bonnet came dashing toward her through the wood.

She jerked to instant alertness, and spun on her heel to flee. She made it no more than six paces before he had an arm about her throat, dragging her off her feet.

"Hush, now, darlin'," he said in her ear, sounding breathless. He was hot, and his stubble rasped her cheek. "I mean ye no harm. I'll leave ye safe on the shore. But ye're the only thing I've got right now will keep your men from killin' me."

He ignored the body of Emmanuel entirely. The heavy forearm left her throat and he grabbed her arm, trying to drag her in the direction away from the beach—evidently, he meant to make for the hidden inlet on the opposite side of the island, where they had landed the day before. "Move, darlin'. Now."

"Let go!" She dug her feet in hard, yanking on her trapped arm. "I'm not going anywhere with you. HELP!" she shrieked as loudly as she could. "HELP! ROGER!"

He looked startled, and raised his free arm to wipe the streaming rain out of his eyes. There was something in his hand; the last of the light gleamed orange on glass. Holy Lord, he'd brought his testicle.

"Bree! Brianna! Where are you?" Roger's voice, frantic, and a jolt of adrenaline shot through her at the sound, giving her the strength to jerk her arm from Bonnet's grasp.

"Here! Here I am! Roger!" she shouted at the top of her voice.

Bonnet glanced over his shoulder; the bushes were shaking, two men at least coming through them. He wasted no time, but darted into the forest, bending low to avoid a branch, and was gone.

In the next instant, Roger crashed out of the brush and seized her, crushing her against him.

"You're all right? Has he hurt you?" He'd dropped his knife, and held her by the arms, eyes trying to look everywhere at once—her face, her body, into her eyes. . . .

"I'm fine," she said, feeling dizzy. "Roger, I'm—"

"Where has he gone?" It was her father, soaking wet and grim as death, dirk in his hand.

"That—" She turned to point, but he was already gone, running wolflike. She saw the marks of Bonnet's passage now, the scuffed footmarks clear in the muddy sand. Before she could turn round again, Roger was after him.

"Wait!" she shrieked, but no answer came save the rapidly receding rustle of brush as heavy bodies flung themselves heedlessly through.

She stood still for a moment, head hanging as she breathed. The rain was pooling in the sockets of Emmanuel's open eyes; the orange light glowed in them, making them look like the eyes of a Japanese movie monster.

That random thought passed across her mind, then vanished, leaving her blank and numb. She wasn't sure what to do at this point. There were no sounds from the beach anymore; the noises of Bonnet's flight had long since faded.

The rain was still falling, but the last of the sun shone through the wood, the long rays nearly horizontal, filling the space between the shadows with an odd, shifting light that seemed to waver as she watched, as though the world around her were about to disappear.

In the midst of it, dreamlike, she saw the women appear, the Fulani twins. They turned the identical faces of fawns to her, huge eyes black with fear, and ran into the wood. She called out to them, but they disappeared. Feeling unutterably tired, she trudged after them.

She didn't find them. Nor was there a sign of anyone else. The light began to die, and she turned back, limping, toward the house. She ached everywhere, and began to suffer from the illusion that there was no one left in the world but her. Nothing but the burning light, fading to ashes moment by moment.

Then she remembered the baby in her womb, and felt better. No matter what, she wasn't alone. Nonetheless, she gave a wide berth to the place where she thought Emmanuel's body lay. She had meant to circle back toward the house, but went too far. As she turned to go back, she caught a glimpse of them, standing together in the shelter of the trees on the other side of a stream.

The wild horses, tranquil as the trees around them, flanks gleaming bay and chestnut and black with the wet. They raised their heads, scenting her, but didn't run, only stood regarding her with big, gentle eyes.

The rain had stopped when she reached the house. Ian sat on the stoop, wringing water out of his long hair.

"You have mud on your face, Ian," she said, sinking down beside him.

"Oh, have I?" he said, giving her a half-smile. "How is it, then, coz?"

"Oh. I'm . . . I think I'm fine. What—?" She gestured at his shirt, stained with watery blood. Something seemed to have hit him in the face; besides the smudges of mud, his nose was puffed, there was a swelling just above his brow, and his clothes were torn, as well as wet.

He drew a deep, deep breath and sighed, as though he were as tired as she was.

"I got back the wee black lass," he said. "Phaedre."

That pierced the dreamlike fugue that filled her mind, but only a little.

"Phaedre," she said, the name feeling like that of someone she had once known, long ago. "Is she all right? Where—"

"In there." Ian nodded back toward the house, and she became aware that what she had thought the sound of the sea was in fact someone weeping, the small sobs of someone who has already wept herself to exhaustion, but cannot stop.

"Nay, leave her to herself, coz." Ian's hand on her arm stopped her from rising. "Ye canna help."

"But—"

He stopped her, reaching into his shirt. From around his neck, he took a battered wooden rosary, and handed it to her.

"She'll maybe want this—later. I picked it up from the sand, after the ship . . . left."

For the first time since her escape, the nausea was back, a sense of vertigo that threatened to pull her down into blackness.

"Josh," she whispered. Ian nodded silently, though it hadn't been a question.

"I'm sorry, coz," he said very softly.

It was nearly dark when Roger appeared at the edge of the wood. She hadn't been worrying, only because she was in a state of shock too deep even to think of what was happening. At sight of him, though, she was on her feet and flying toward him, all the fears she had suppressed erupting at last into tears, running down her face like the rain.

"Da," she said, choking and sniffling into his wet shirt. "He's—is he—"

"He's all right. Bree—can ye come with me? Are ye strong enough—just for a bit?"

Gulping and wiping her nose on the soggy arm of her shift, she nodded, and leaning on his arm, limped into the darkness under the trees.

Bonnet was lying against a tree, head lolling to one side. There was blood on his face, running down onto his shirt. She felt no sense of victory at sight of him, only an infinitely weary distaste.

Her father was standing silently under the same tree. When he saw her, he stepped forward and folded her wordlessly into his arms. She closed her eyes for one blissful moment, wanting nothing more than to abandon everything, let him pick her up like a child and carry her home. But they had brought her here for a reason; with immense effort, she lifted her head and looked at Bonnet.

Did they want congratulations? she wondered fuzzily. But then she remembered what Roger had told her, describing her father leading her mother through the scene of butchery, making her look, so that she would know her tormentors were dead.

"Okay," she said, swaying a little. "All right, I mean. I—I see. He's dead."

"Well . . . no. Actually, he isn't." Roger's voice held an odd note of strain, and he coughed, with a look that shot daggers at her father.

"D'ye want him dead, lass?" Her father touched her shoulder, gently. "It is your right."

"Do I—" She looked wildly from one to the other of the grave, shadowed faces, then at Bonnet, realizing for the first time that blood *was* running down his face. Dead men, as her mother had often explained, don't bleed.

They had found Bonnet, Jamie said, run him to earth like a fox, and set about him. It had been an ugly fight, close-to, with knives, as their pistols were useless in the wet. Knowing that he fought for his life, Bonnet had struck viciously—there was a red-stained gash in the shoulder of Jamie's coat, a scratch high on Roger's throat, where a knife blade had passed within a fraction of slashing his jugular. But Bonnet had fought to escape, and not to kill— retreating into a space between trees where only one could come at him, he had grappled with Jamie, thrown him off, then bolted.

Roger had given chase, and boiling with adrenaline, had thrown himself at Bonnet bodily, knocking the pirate headfirst into the tree he now lay against.

"So there he lies," Jamie said, giving Bonnet a bleak eye. "I had hoped he'd broken his neck, but no such thing, alas."

"But he is unconscious," Roger said, and swallowed.

She understood, and in her present mood, this particular male quirk of honor seemed reasonable. To kill a man in fair fight—or even an unfair fight—was one thing; to cut his throat while he lay unconscious at your feet was another.

But she hadn't understood at all. Her father wiped his dirk on his breeches and handed it to her, hilt first.

"What . . . me?" She was too shocked even to feel astonishment. The knife was heavy in her hand.

"If ye wish it," her father said, with grave courtesy. "If not, Roger Mac or I will do it. But it is your choice, *a nighean*."

Now she understood Roger's look—they had been arguing about it, before he had come to fetch her. And she understood exactly why her father offered her the choice. Whether it was vengeance or forgiveness, she held the man's life in her hand. She took a deep breath, the awareness that it would not be vengeance coming over her with something like relief.

"Brianna," Roger said softly, touching her arm. "Say the word if ye'll have him dead; I'll do it."

She nodded, and took a deep breath. She could hear the savage longing in his voice—he did. She could hear the choked sound of his voice in memory, too, when he had told her of killing Boble—when he woke from dreams of it, drenched in sweat.

She glanced at her father's face, nearly drowned in shadow. Her mother had said only a little of the violent dreams that haunted him since Culloden—but that little was enough. She could hardly ask her father to do this—to spare Roger what he suffered himself.

Jamie raised his head, feeling her eyes on him, and met her gaze, straight on. Jamie Fraser had never turned from a fight he saw as his—but this was not his fight, and he knew it. She had a sudden flash of awareness; it wasn't Roger's fight, either, though he would take the weight of it from her shoulders, and gladly.

"If you—if *we*—if we don't kill him here and now—" Her chest was tight, and she stopped for breath. "What will we do with him?"

"Take him to Wilmington," her father said matter-of-factly. "The Committee of Safety there is strong, and they know him for a pirate; they'll deal with him by law—or what passes for it now."

They'd hang him; he would be just as dead—but his blood wouldn't be on Roger's hands, or in his heart.

The light was gone. Bonnet was no more than a lumpen shape, dark against the sandy ground. He might die of his wounds, she thought, and dimly hoped so—it would save trouble. But if they took him to her mother, Claire would be compelled to try to save him. *She* never turned from a fight that was hers, either, Brianna thought wryly, and was surprised to feel a small lightening of spirit at the thought.

"Let him live to be hanged, then," she said quietly, and touched Roger's arm. "Not for his sake. For yours and mine. For your baby."

For an instant, she was sorry that she'd told him now, in the night-dark wood. She would so much have liked to see his face.

109

All the News That's
Fit to Print

FROM *L'OIGNON–INTELLIGENCER,*
SEPTEMBER 25, 1775

A ROYAL PROCLAMATION—

A Proclamation was issued in London upon the 23rd of August, in which His Majesty George III proclaims the American Colonies to be "in a State of open and avowed Rebellion."

"NOTHING BUT OUR OWN EXERTIONS MAY DEFEAT THE MINISTERIAL SENTENCE OF DEATH OR ABJECT SUBMISSION"—The Continental Congress in Philadelphia has now rejected the Objectionable Proposals put forth by Lord North, intended to promote the Object of Reconciliation. The Delegates to this Congress state unequivocally the Right of the American Colonies to raise Appropriations and to have a say in the Disbursement of Same. The Statement of the Delegates reads in Part: "As the British Ministry has pursued its Ends and prosecuted Hostilities with great Armaments and Cruelty, can the World be deceived into an Opinion that we are Unreasonable, or can it hesitate to believe with us that Nothing but our own Exertions may defeat the Ministerial Sentence of Death or Abject Submission?"

A FALCON STOOPS BUT IS DEPRIVED OF HER PREY—Upon the 9th of August, HMS Falcon, *commanded* by Captain John Linzee, gave Chase to two American Schooners, returning from the West Indies to Salem, Massachusetts. One Schooner was captured by Captain Linzee, who then pursued the other into Gloucester Harbor. Troops upon the Shore fired upon the Falcon, which did return this Fire, but was then forced to withdraw, losing both Schooners, two Barges, and Thirty-Five Men.

A NOTORIOUS PIRATE CONDEM'D—One Stephen Bonnet, known as a Pirate and Infamous Smuggler, was tryed·before the Wilmington Committee of Safety, and upon Testimony of his Crimes having been presented by a Number of Persons, was convicted of them and sentenced to Death by Drowning.

AN ALARM is raised regarding prowling Bands of Negroes, who have despoiled a number of Farms near Wilmington and Brunswick. Unarmed save for Clubs, the Ruffians have stolen Livestock, Food, and four Hogsheads of Rum.

CONGRESS CONCEIVES A PLAN FOR CURRENCY REDEMPTION—Two Million Spanish Dollars in Bills of Credit now issue forth from the Presses, with One Million Dollars more authorized by Congress, which now announces a Plan for the Redemption of this Currency, viz., that each Colony must assume Responsibility for its Portion of the Debt and must redeem the Same in four Installments, these to be paid upon the last Day of November in the Years 1779, 1780, 1781, and 1782. . . .

110

The Smell of Light

October 2, 1775

It was not thinkable to return Phaedre to River Run, even though she technically remained the property of Duncan Cameron. We had discussed the matter at some length, and finally decided not to tell Jocasta that her slave had been recovered, though we did send brief word with Ian, when he went to collect Jemmy, telling of Brianna's safe return and regretting the loss of Joshua—omitting a good bit of detail regarding the whole affair.

"Should we tell them about Neil Forbes?" I'd asked, but Jamie had shaken his head.

"Forbes willna trouble any member of my family again," he said definitely. "And to tell my aunt or Duncan about it . . . I think Duncan has sufficient trouble on his hands; he'd feel obliged to take issue wi' Forbes, and that's a stramash he doesna need to start just now. As for my aunt . . ." He didn't complete the statement, but the bleakness of his countenance spoke well enough. The MacKenzies of Leoch were a vengeful lot, and neither he nor I would put it past Jocasta to invite Neil Forbes to dinner and poison him.

"Always assuming that Mr. Forbes is accepting dinner invitations these days," I joked uneasily. "Do you know what Ian did with the . . . er . . ."

"He said he was going to feed it to his dog," Jamie replied thoughtfully. "But I dinna ken was he serious or not."

Phaedre had been a good deal shocked, both by her experiences and by the loss of Josh, and Brianna insisted that we bring her back to the Ridge with us to recover, until we could find a reasonable place for her.

"We have to get Aunt Jocasta to free her," Bree had argued.

"I think that willna be difficult," Jamie had assured her with a certain grimness. "Not knowing what we know. But wait a bit, until we find a place for the lass—then I'll see to it."

As it was, that particular matter took care of itself with stunning abruptness.

I opened the door to a knock one afternoon in October, to find three weary horses and a pack mule in the dooryard, and Jocasta, Duncan, and the black butler Ulysses standing on the stoop.

The sight of them was so utterly incongruous that I merely stood there gaping at them, until Jocasta said acerbically, "Weel, lass, d'ye mean us to stand here until we're melted away like sugar in a dish o' tea?"

It was in fact raining quite hard, and I stepped back so quickly to let them in that I trod on Adso's paw. He uttered a piercing yowl, which brought Jamie out of his study, Mrs. Bug and Amy from the kitchen—and Phaedre out of the surgery, where she had been grinding herbs for me.

"Phaedre!" Duncan's jaw dropped, and he took two steps toward her. He stopped abruptly, just before taking her into his arms, but his face suffused with joy.

"Phaedre?" said Jocasta, sounding utterly astounded. Her face had gone quite blank with shock.

Ulysses said nothing, but the look on *his* face was one of unalloyed horror. Within a second, it was gone, replaced by his usual austere expression of dignity, but I'd seen it—and kept a narrow eye on him during the ensuing confusion of exclamations and embarrassments.

Finally, I got them all out of the front hall. Jocasta suffered a diplomatic headache—though seeing her drawn face, I thought it wasn't entirely feigned—and was escorted upstairs by Amy, who put her to bed with a cold compress. Mrs. Bug went back to the kitchen, excitedly revising the supper menu. Phaedre, looking frightened, disappeared, doubtless to take refuge in Brianna's cabin and tell her all about the unexpected arrival—which meant there would be another three for supper.

Ulysses went to deal with the horses, leaving Duncan at last alone to explain matters to Jamie in the study.

"We are emigrating to Canada," he said, closing his eyes and inhaling the aroma of the glass of whisky in his hand as though it were smelling salts. He looked like he needed them; he was gaunt, and his face was nearly as gray as his hair.

"Canada?" Jamie said, as surprised as I was. "For God's sake, Duncan, what have ye been doing?"

Duncan smiled wearily, opening his eyes.

"More what I didna do, *Mac Dubh*," he said. Brianna had told us about the disappearance of the secret hoard of gold, and had mentioned something about Duncan's dealings with Lord Dunsmore in Virginia, but had been vague about it—understandably so, as she had been kidnapped a few hours afterward, and had no details.

"I should never ha' believed matters could come to such a pass—nor sae quickly," he said, shaking his head. Loyalists had gone suddenly from being a majority in the piedmont to being a threatened and frightened minority. Some folk had been literally chased from their homes, to take refuge skulking in swamps and woods; others had been beaten and badly injured.

"Even Farquard Campbell," Duncan said, and rubbed a hand tiredly over his face. "The Committee of Safety called him before them, on charges of being loyal to the Crown, and threatened to confiscate his plantation. He put up a great deal of money, pledged as surety for his good behavior, and they let him go—but it was a near thing."

Near enough to have frightened Duncan badly. The debacle of the promised guns and powder had deprived him of any influence with the local Loyalists and left him completely isolated, vulnerable to the next wave of hostilities—which any fool could see would not be long in coming.

He had therefore moved swiftly to sell River Run at a decent price, before it was seized. He had kept one or two warehouses on the river and a few other assets, but had disposed of the plantation, slaves, and livestock, and proposed to remove at once with his wife to Canada, as many other Loyalists were doing.

"Hamish MacKenzie is there, ken," he explained. "He and some others from Leoch settled in Nova Scotia, when they left Scotland in the wake of Culloden. He's Jocasta's nephew, and we've money enough—" He glanced vaguely toward the hall, where Ulysses had dumped the saddlebags. "He'll help us to find a place."

He smiled crookedly.

"And if things shouldna turn out well . . . they do say the fishing's good."

Jamie smiled at the feeble joke, and poured him more whisky, but he shook his head when he came to join me in the surgery, before dinner.

"They mean to travel overland to Virginia, and with luck take ship there for Nova Scotia. They can perhaps get out of Newport News; it's a small port, and the British blockade isna tight there— or so Duncan hopes."

"Oh, dear." It would be a grueling journey—and Jocasta was not a young woman. And the state of her eye . . . I was not fond of Jocasta, in light of what we had learned about her recently, but to think of her ripped from her home, forced to emigrate while suffering excruciating pain—well, it caused one to think there might be such a thing as divine retribution, after all.

I lowered my voice, looking over my shoulder to be sure Duncan had in fact gone upstairs. "What about Ulysses? And Phaedre?"

Jamie's lips pressed tight.

"Ah. Well, as to the lass—I asked Duncan to sell her to me. I shall set her free as quickly as I can; perhaps send her to Fergus, in New Bern. He agreed at once, and wrote out a bill of sale on the spot." He nodded toward his office. "As for Ulysses . . ." His face was grim. "I think that matter will adjust itself, Sassenach."

Mrs. Bug came bustling down the hall to announce that the supper was served, and I had no chance to ask him what he meant by that remark.

I squeezed out the poultice of witch hazel and Carolina allspice, and laid it gently over Jocasta's eyes. I'd already given her willow-bark tea for the pain, and the poultice would do nothing for the underlying glaucoma—but it would be soothing, at least, and it was a relief to both patient and physician to be able to offer something, even though that might be the merest palliative.

"Will ye have a keek in my saddlebags, lass?" she asked, stretching a little to ease herself on the bed. "There's a bittie parcel in there of an herb ye might find of interest."

I found it immediately—by smell.

"Where on earth did you get that?" I asked, halfway amused.

"Farquard Campbell," she replied matter-of-factly. "When ye told me what the difficulty was with my eyes, I asked Fentiman if he kent anything that might be of help, and he told me that he'd heard somewhere that hemp might be of use. Farquard Campbell has a field of it under cultivation, so I thought I might as well try it. It does seem to help. Would ye put it in my hand, please, niece?"

Fascinated, I put the parcel of hemp and the little stack of papers down on the table beside her, and guided her hand to it. Rolling carefully onto her side to prevent the poultice falling off, she took a good pinch of aromatic herb, sprinkled it down the center of the paper, and rolled as tidy a joint as I had ever seen in Boston.

Without comment, I held the candle flame for her to light it, and she eased herself back on the pillow, nostrils flaring as she took a deep lungful of smoke.

She smoked in silence for some time, and I busied myself in putting things away, not wanting to leave her lest she fall asleep and set the bed on fire—she was clearly exhausted, and relaxing further by the moment.

The pungent, heady smell of the smoke brought back instant, though fragmentary memories. Several of the younger medical students had smoked it on weekends, and would come to the hospital with the scent of it in their clothes. Some of the people brought into the emergency room had reeked of it. Now and then, I'd smelled the faintest hint of it on Brianna—but never inquired.

I hadn't ever tried it, myself, but now found the smell of the fragrant smoke rather soothing. Rather *too* soothing, and I went and sat down by the window, open a crack to admit fresh air.

It had been raining off and on all day, and the air was sharp with ozone and tree resins, welcomely cold against my face.

"Ye know, don't you?" Jocasta's voice came softly from behind me. I looked round; she hadn't moved, but lay like a tomb figure on the bed, straight as a die. The poultice bandage over her eyes made her look like the image of Justice—ironic, that, I thought.

"I know," I said, matching her own calm tone. "Not very fair to Duncan, was it?"

"No." The word drifted out with the smoke, almost soundless. She lifted the cigarette lazily and drew air through it, making the end glow red. I kept a narrow eye, but she seemed to have a feel for the ash, tapping it now and then into the saucer base of the candlestick.

"He knows, too," she said, almost casually. "About Phaedre. I told him, finally, to stop him searching for her. I am sure he knows about Ulysses, too—but he doesna speak of it."

She reached out, unerring, and tapped the ash neatly from the joint.

"I told him I wouldna blame him if he left me, ken." Her voice was very soft, nearly without emotion. "He wept, but then he stopped, and said to me that he had said, 'For better or for worse'—and so had I, had I not? I said I had, and he said, 'Well, then.' And here we are." She shrugged a little, settling herself more comfortably, and fell silent, smoking.

I turned my face again to the window and leaned my forehead against the frame. Below, I saw a sudden spill of light as the door opened, and a dark figure came quickly out. The door closed, and I lost sight of him in the darkness for an instant; then my eyes adapted and I saw him again, just before he vanished on the path to the barn.

"He's gone, isn't he?" Startled, I turned round to look at her, realizing that she must have heard the closing of the door below.

"Ulysses? Yes, I think so."

She was still for quite a while, the cigarette burning unregarded in her hand. Just before I thought I must rise and take it from her, she lifted it again to her lips.

"His true name was Joseph," she said softly, releasing the smoke. Wisps of it swirled slowly in a cloud around her head. "So appropriate, I always thought—for he was sold into slavery by his own people."

"Have you ever seen his face?" I asked suddenly. She shook her head, and ground out the last of the cigarette.

"Nay, but I kent him always," she said very softly. "He smelled of light."

Jamie Fraser sat patiently in the darkness of his barn. It was a small one, with stallage for only half a dozen animals, but soundly built. Rain beat solidly on the roof, and wind whined like a *ban-sidhe* round the corners, but not a drip came through the shingled roof, and the air inside was warm with the heat of somnolent beasts. Even Gideon was a-nod over his manger, half-chewed hay hanging from the corner of his mouth.

It was past midnight now, and he had been waiting for more than two hours, the pistol loaded and primed, resting on his knee.

There it was; above the rain, he heard the soft grunt of someone pushing at the door, and the rumble as it slid open, admitting a breath of cold rain to mingle with the warmer scents of hay and manure.

He sat still, not moving.

He could see a tall form pause against the lighter black of the rain-drenched night, waiting for his eyes to adapt to the dark within, then throw his weight against the heavy door to open it enough to slip inside.

The man had brought a dark-lantern, not trusting that he could find the necessary bits of harness and apply them in the dark. He drew back the slide and turned the lantern slowly, letting the shaft of light travel over the stalls, one by one. The three horses Jocasta had brought were here, but done in. Jamie heard the man click his tongue softly in consideration, turning the light back and forth between the mare, Jerusha, and Gideon.

Making up his mind, Ulysses set the lantern on the floor, and made to pull the pin fastening the door to Gideon's stall.

"It would serve ye right, and I let ye take him," Jamie said conversationally.

The butler let out a sharp yelp and whirled round, glaring, his fists clenched. He couldn't see Jamie in the dark, but the evidence of his ears caught up with him a second later, and he breathed deeply and lowered his fists, realizing who it was.

"Mr. Fraser," he said. His eyes were live in the lantern light, and watchful. "You took me by surprise."

"Well, I did intend to," Jamie replied equably. "Ye mean to be off, I suppose."

He could see thoughts flit through the butler's eyes, quick as dragonflies, wondering, calculating. But Ulysses was no fool, and came to the correct conclusion.

"The girl's told you, then," he said, quite calmly. "Shall you kill me—for your aunt's honor?" Had that last been said with any trace of a sneer, Jamie might have killed him indeed—he'd been of two minds on the matter while he waited. But it was said simply, and Jamie's finger eased on the trigger.

"If I were a younger man, I would," he said, matching Ulysses's tone. *And if I did not have a wife and daughter who once called a black man friend.*

"As it is," he went on, lowering the pistol, "I try not to kill these days unless I must." *Or until I must.* "Do ye offer me denial? For I think there can be nay defense."

The butler shook his head slightly. The light gleamed on his skin, dark, with a reddish undertone that made him look as though carved from aged cinnabar.

"I loved her," he said softly, and spread his hands. "Kill me." He was dressed for traveling, in cloak and hat, with a pouch and canteen hung at his belt, but no knife. Slaves, even trusted ones, dared not go armed.

Curiosity warred with distaste, and—as usual in such warfare—curiosity won.

"Phaedre said ye lay with my aunt, even before her husband died. Is that true?"

"It is," Ulysses said softly, his expression unreadable. "I do not justify it. I cannot. But I loved her, and if I must die for that . . ."

Jamie believed the man; his sincerity was evident in voice and gesture. And knowing his aunt as he did, he was less inclined to blame Ulysses than the world at large would be. At the same time, he was not letting down his guard; Ulysses was good-size, and quick. And a man who thought he had nothing to lose was very dangerous indeed.

"Where did ye mean to go?" he asked with a nod toward the horses.

"Virginia," the black man replied with a barely perceptible hesitation. "Lord Dunsmore has offered freedom to any slave who will join his army."

He hadn't meant to ask, though it was a question that had raised itself in his mind from the moment he heard Phaedre's story. With this opening, though, he could not resist.

"Why did she not free you?" he asked. "After Hector Cameron died?"

"She did" was the surprising answer. The butler touched the breast of his coat. "She wrote the papers of manumission nearly twenty years ago—she said she could not bear to think that I came to her bed only because I must. But a request for manumission must be approved by the Assembly, you know. And if I had been openly freed, I could not have stayed to serve her as I did." That was true enough; a freed slave was compelled to leave the colony within ten days or risk being enslaved again, by anyone who chose to take him; the vision of large gangs of free Negroes roaming the countryside was one that made the Council and Assembly shit themselves with fear.

The butler looked down for a moment, eyes hooded against the light.

"I could choose Jo—or freedom. I chose her."

"Aye, verra romantic," Jamie said with extreme dryness— though in fact, he was not unaffected by the statement. Jocasta MacKenzie had married for duty, and duty again—and he thought she had had little happiness in any of her marriages until finding some measure of contentment with Duncan. He was shocked at her choice, disapproving of her adultery, and very angry indeed at her deception of Duncan, but some part of him—the MacKenzie part, doubtless—could not but admire her boldness in taking happiness where she could.

He sighed deeply. The rain was easing now; the thundering on the roof had dwindled to a soft pattering.

"Well, then. I have one question more."

Ulysses inclined his head gravely, in a gesture Jamie had seen a thousand times. *At your service, sir,* it said—and *that* was done with more irony than there was in anything the man had said.

"Where is the gold?"

Ulysses's head jerked up, eyes wide with startlement. For the first time, Jamie felt a shred of doubt.

"You think *I* took it?" the butler said incredulously. But then his mouth twisted to one side. "I suppose you would, after all." He rubbed a hand under his nose, looking worried and unhappy—as well he might, Jamie reflected.

They stood regarding each other in silence for some time, at an impasse. Jamie did not have the feeling that the other was attempting to deceive him—and God knew the man was good at *that*, he thought cynically.

At last, Ulysses heaved his wide shoulders, and let them drop in helplessness.

"I cannot prove that I did not," he said. "I can offer nothing save my word of honor—and I am not entitled to have such a thing." For the first time, bitterness rang in his voice.

Jamie suddenly felt very tired. The horses and mules had long since gone back to their drowse, and he wanted nothing so much as his own bed, and his wife beside him. He also wanted Ulysses to be gone, long before Duncan discovered his perfidy. And while Ulysses was patently the most obvious person to have taken the gold, the fact remained that he could have taken it anytime in the last twenty years, with a good deal less danger. Why now?

"Will ye swear on my aunt's head?" he asked abruptly. Ulysses's eyes were sharp, shining in the lantern light, but steady.

"Yes," he said at last, quietly. "I do so swear."

Jamie was about to dismiss him, when one last thought occurred to him.

"Do you have children?" he asked.

Indecision crossed the chiseled face; surprise and wariness, mingled with something else.

"None I would claim," he said at last, and Jamie saw what it was—scorn, mixed with shame. His jaw tensed, and his chin rose slightly. "Why do you ask me that?"

Jamie met his gaze for a moment, thinking of Brianna growing heavy with child.

"Because," he said at last, "it is only the hope of betterment for my children, and theirs, that gives me the courage to do what must be done here." Ulysses's face had gone blank; it gleamed black and impassive in the light.

"If you have no stake in the future, you have no reason to suffer for it. Such children as you may have—"

"They are slaves, born of slave women. What can they be, to me?" Ulysses's hands were clenched, pressed against his thighs.

"Then go," Jamie said softly, and stood aside, gesturing toward the door with the barrel of his pistol. "Die free, at least."

111

January Twenty-first

Januray 21 was the coldest day of the year. Snow had fallen a few days before, but now the air was like cut crystal, the dawn sky so pale it looked white, and the packed snow chirped like crickets under our boots. Snow, snow-shrouded trees, the icicles that hung from the eaves of the house—the whole world seemed blue with cold. All of the stock had been put up the night before in stable or barn, with the exception of the white sow, who appeared to be hibernating under the house.

I peered dubiously at the small, melted hole in the crust of snow that marked the sow's entrance; long, stertorous snores were audible inside, and a faint warmth emanated from the hole.

"Come along, *mo nighean.* Yon creature wouldna notice if the house fell down atop her." Jamie had come down from feeding the animals in the stable, and was hovering impatiently behind me, chafing his hands in the big blue mittens Bree had knitted for him.

"What, not even if it was on fire?" I said, thinking of Lamb's "Essay on Roast Pork." But I turned obligingly to follow him down the trampled path past the side of the house, then slowly, slipping on the icy patches, across the wide clearing toward Bree and Roger's cabin.

"Ye're sure the hearth fire's out?" Jamie asked, for the third time. His breath wreathed round his head like a veil as he looked over his shoulder at me. He had lost his woolen cap hunting, and instead had a woolly white muffler wrapped around his ears and tied on top of his head, the long ends flopping, which made him look absurdly like an enormous rabbit.

"It is," I assured him, suppressing an urge to laugh at sight of him. His long nose was pink with cold, and twitched suspiciously, and I buried my face in my own muffler, making small snorting noises that emerged as puffs of white, like a steam engine.

"And the bedroom candle? The wee lamp in your surgery?"

"Yes," I assured him, emerging from the depths of the muffler. My eyes were watering and I would have liked to wipe them, but I had a huge bundle in one arm and a covered basket hung on the other. This contained Adso, who had been forcibly removed from the house, and wasn't pleased about it; small growls emerged from the basket, and it swayed and thumped against my leg.

"And the rush dip in the pantry, and the candle in the wall sconce in the hall, and the brazier in your office, and the fish-oil lantern you use in the stables. I went over the whole house with a nit comb. Not a spark anywhere."

"Well enough, then," he said—but couldn't help an uneasy glance backward at the house. I looked, too; it looked cold and forlorn, the white of its boards rather grimy against the pristine snow.

"It won't be an accident," I said. "Not unless the white sow is playing with matches in her den."

That made him smile, in spite of the circumstances. Frankly, at the moment, the circumstances struck me as slightly absurd; the whole world seemed deserted, frozen solid and immobile under a winter sky. Nothing seemed less likely than that cataclysm could descend to destroy the house by fire. Still . . . better safe than sorry. And as Jamie had remarked more than once during the years since Roger and Bree had brought word of that sinister newspaper clipping, "If ye ken the house is meant to burn down on a certain day, why would ye be standing in it?"

So we weren't standing in it. Mrs. Bug had been told to stay at home, and Amy McCallum and her two little boys were already at Brianna's cabin—puzzled, but obliging. If Himself said that no one was to set foot in the house until dawn tomorrow . . . well, then, there was nothing more to be said, was there?

Ian had been up since before dawn, chopping kindling and hauling in firewood from the shed; everyone would be snug and warm.

Jamie himself had been up all night, tending stock, dispersing his armory—there was not a grain of gunpowder anywhere in the house, either—and prowling restlessly upstairs and down, alert to every cracking ember on a hearth, every burning candle flame, any faint noise without that might portend the approach of an enemy. The only thing he hadn't done was to sit on the roof with a wet sack, keeping a suspicious eye out for lightning—and that, only because it had been a cloudless night, the stars immense and bright overhead, burning in the frozen void.

I hadn't slept a great deal, either, disturbed equally by Jamie's prowling and by vivid dreams of conflagration.

The only conflagration visible, though, was the one sending a welcome shower of smoke and sparks from Brianna's chimney, and we opened the door to the grateful warmth of a roaring hearth and a number of bodies.

Aidan and Orrie, roused in the dark and dragged through the cold, had promptly crawled into Jemmy's trundle, and the three little boys were sound asleep, curled up like hedgehogs beneath their quilt. Amy was helping Bree with the breakfast; savory smells of porridge and bacon rose from the hearth.

"Is all well, ma'am?" Amy hurried over to take the big bundle I had brought—this contained my medical chest, the more scarce and valuable herbs from my surgery—and the sealed jar with the latest shipment of white phosphorus that Lord John had sent as a farewell present to Brianna.

"It is," I assured her, setting Adso's basket on the floor. I yawned, and eyed the bed wistfully, but set about to stow my chest in the lean-to pantry, where the children wouldn't get into it. I put the phosphorus on the highest shelf, well back from the edge, and moved a large cheese in front of it, just in case.

Jamie had divested himself of cloak and rabbit ears, and handing Roger the fowling piece, shot pouch, and powder horn he'd carried, was stamping snow from his boots. I saw him glance round the cabin, counting heads, then, at last, draw a small breath, nodding to himself. All safe, so far.

The morning passed peacefully. Breakfast eaten and cleared away, Amy, Bree, and I settled down by the fire with an enormous heap of mending. Adso, tail still twitching with indignation, had taken up a place on a high shelf, from whence he glared at Rollo, who had taken over the trundle bed when the boys got out of it.

Aidan and Jemmy, each now the proud possessor of *two* vrooms, drove them over hearthstones, under the bed, and through our feet, but for the most part, refrained from punching each other or stepping on Orrie, who was sitting placidly under the table gnawing on a piece of toast. Jamie, Roger, and Ian took turns going outside to pace back and forth and stare at the Big House, deserted in the shelter of the snow-dusted spruce.

As Roger came back from one of these expeditions, Brianna looked up suddenly from the sock she was darning.

"What?" he said, seeing her face.

"Oh." She had paused, needle halfway through the sock, and now looked down, completing her stitch. "Nothing. Just a—just a thought."

The tone of her voice made Jamie, who had been frowning his way through a battered copy of *Evelina*, look up.

"What sort of thought was that, *a nighean*?" he asked, his radar quite as good as Roger's.

"Er . . . well." She bit her lower lip, but then blurted, "What if it's *this* house?"

That froze everyone except the little boys, who continued crawling industriously around the room and over bed and table, screeching and vrooming.

"It could be, couldn't it?" Bree looked round, from rooftree to hearth. "All the—the prophecy said"—with an awkward nod toward Amy McCallum—"was *the home of James Fraser* would burn. But this was your home, to start with. And it's not like there's a street address. It just said, *On Fraser's Ridge.*"

Everyone stared at her, and she flushed deeply, dropping her eyes to the sock.

"I mean . . . it's not like they—er, prophecies—like they're always accurate, is it? They might have got the details wrong."

Amy nodded seriously; evidently, vagueness in the matter of detail was an accepted characteristic of prophecies.

Roger cleared his throat explosively; Jamie and Ian exchanged glances, then looked at the fire, leaping on the hearth and the towering stack of bone-dry firewood next to it, the overflowing kindling basket . . . Everyone's eyes turned expectantly to Jamie, whose face was a study in conflicting emotions.

"I suppose," he said slowly, "we could remove to Arch's place."

I began to count on my fingers: "You, me, Roger, Bree, Ian, Amy, Aidan, Orrie, Jemmy—plus Mr. and Mrs. Bug—is eleven people. In a one-room cabin that measures eight feet by ten?" I closed my fists and stared at him. "No one would have to set the place on fire; half of us would be sitting in the hearth already, well alight."

"Mmphm. Well, then . . . the Christie place is empty."

Amy's eyes went round with horror, and everyone looked automatically away from everyone else. Jamie took a deep breath and let it out, audibly.

"Perhaps we'll just be . . . very careful," I suggested. Everyone exhaled slightly, and we resumed our occupations, though without our former sense of snug safety.

Dinner passed without incident, but in midafternoon, a knock came on the door. Amy screamed, and Brianna dropped the shirt she was mending into the fire. Ian leaped to his feet and jerked the door open, and Rollo, jerked out of a doze, charged past him, roaring.

Jamie and Roger struck the doorway—and each other—simultaneously, stuck for an instant, and fell through. All the little boys shrieked and ran to their respective mothers, who were frantically beating at the smoldering shirt as though it were a live snake.

I had leaped to my feet, but was pressed against the wall, unable to get past Bree and Amy. Adso, startled by the racket and by my popping up beside him, hissed and took a swipe at me, narrowly missing my eye.

A number of oaths in a mixture of languages were coming from the dooryard, accompanied by a series of sharp barks from Rollo. Everyone sounded thoroughly annoyed, but there were no sounds of conflict. I edged my way delicately past the knot of mothers and sons, and peered out.

Major MacDonald, wet to the eyebrows and covered in clumps of snow and dirty slush, was gesticulating with some energy at Jamie, while Ian rebuked Rollo, and Roger—from the look on his face—was trying very hard not to burst out laughing.

Jamie, compelled by his own sense of propriety, but eyeing the Major with deep suspicion, invited him in. The inside of the cabin smelled of burned fabric, but at least the riot had calmed down, and the Major greeted us all with a fair assumption of cordiality. There was a lot of fuss, getting him stripped of his soaking-wet clothes, dried off, and—for lack of any better alternative—temporarily swathed in Roger's spare shirt and breeches, in which he appeared to be drowning, as he was a good six inches shorter than Roger.

Food and whisky having been ceremonially offered and accepted, the household fixed the Major with a collective eye and waited to hear what had brought him to the mountains in the dead of winter.

Jamie exchanged a brief glance with me, indicating that he could hazard a guess. So could I.

"I have come, sir," MacDonald said formally, hitching up the shirt to keep it from sliding off his shoulder, "to offer ye command of a company of militia, under the orders of General Hugh MacDonald. The General's troops are gathering, even as we speak, and will undertake their march to Wilmington at the end of the month."

I felt a deep qualm of apprehension at that. I was accustomed to MacDonald's chronic optimism and tendency to overstatement, but there was nothing of exaggeration in this statement. Did that mean that the help Governor Martin had requested, the troops from Ireland, would be landing soon, to meet General MacDonald's troops at the coast?

"The General's troops," Jamie said, poking up the fire. He and MacDonald had taken over the fireside, with Roger and Ian ranged on either side of them, like firedogs. Bree, Amy, and I repaired to the bed, where we perched like a row of roosting hens, watching the conversation with a mingling of interest and alarm, while the little boys retired under the table.

"How many men does he have, would ye say, Donald?"

I saw MacDonald hesitate, torn between truth and desire. He coughed, though, and said matter-of-factly, "He had a few more than a thousand when I left him. Ye ken weel, though—once we begin to move, others will come to join us. Many others. The more particularly," he added pointedly, "if such gentlemen as yourself are in command."

Jamie didn't reply to that at once. Meditatively, he shoved a burning wood fragment back into the fire with his foot.

"Powder and shot?" he asked. "Arms?"

"Aye, well; we'd a bit of a disappointment there." MacDonald took a sip of his whisky. "Duncan Innes had promised us a great deal in that way—but in the end, he was obliged to renege upon his promise." The Major's lips pressed tight, and I thought from the expression on his face that perhaps Duncan had not been overreacting in his decision to move to Canada.

"Still," MacDonald continued more cheerfully, "we are not destitute in that regard. And those gallant gentlemen who have flocked to our cause—and who *will* come to join us—bring with them both their own weapons and their courage. You, of all people, must appreciate the force of the Hieland charge!"

Jamie looked up at that, and regarded MacDonald for a long moment before replying.

"Aye, well. Ye were behind the cannon at Culloden, Donald. I was in front of them. With a sword in my hand." He took up his own glass and drained it, then got up and moved to pour another, leaving MacDonald to recover his countenance.

"*Touché*, Major," Brianna murmured under her breath. I didn't think Jamie had ever before referred to the fact that the Major had fought with the government forces during the Rising—but I wasn't surprised that he hadn't forgotten.

With a brief nod to the company, Jamie stepped outside—ostensibly to visit the privy, more likely to check on the well-being of the house. Still more likely to give MacDonald a little breathing room.

Roger, with the courtesy of a host—and the suppressed keenness of a historian—was asking MacDonald questions regarding the General and his activities. Ian, impassive and watchful, sat by his feet, one hand toying with Rollo's ruff.

"The General's rather elderly for such a campaign, surely?" Roger took another stick of wood and pushed it into the fire. "Especially a winter campaign."

"He has the odd wee spell of catarrh," MacDonald admitted, offhand. "But who doesna, in this climate? And Donald McLeod, his lieutenant, is a man of vigor. I assure ye, sir, should the General be at any point indisposed, Colonel McLeod is more than capable of leading the troops to victory!"

He went on at some length about the virtues—both personal and military—of Donald McLeod. I ceased listening, my attention distracted by a stealthy movement on the shelf above his head. Adso.

MacDonald's red coat was spread over the back of a chair to dry, steaming in the heat. His wig, damp and disheveled from Rollo's attack, hung on the cloak peg above it. I got up hastily and possessed myself of the wig, receiving a look of puzzlement from the Major, and one of green-eyed hostility from Adso, who plainly considered it low of me to hog this desirable prey for myself.

"Er . . . I'll just . . . um . . . put it somewhere safe, shall I?" Clutching the damp mass of horsehair to my bosom, I sidled outside and round to the pantry, where I tucked the wig safely away behind the cheese with the phosphorus.

Coming out, I met Jamie, red-nosed with cold, coming back from a reconnaissance of the Big House.

"All's well," he assured me. He glanced up at the chimney above us, spuming clouds of thick gray smoke. "Ye dinna suppose the lass might be right, do ye?" He sounded as though he were joking, but he wasn't.

"God knows. *How* long 'til tomorrow's dawn?" The shadows were already falling long, violet and chill across the snow.

"Too long." He had violet shadows in his face, too, from one sleepless night; this would be another. He hugged me against himself for a moment, though, warm in spite of the fact that he wore nothing over his shirt but the rough jacket in which he did chores.

"Ye dinna suppose MacDonald will come back and fire the house, if I refuse him, do ye?" he asked, releasing me with a fair attempt at a smile.

"What do you mean '*if*'?" I demanded, but he was already on his way back in.

MacDonald stood up in respect when Jamie came in, waiting until he was seated again before taking his own stool.

"Have ye had a moment, then, to think on my offer, Mr. Fraser?" he asked formally. "Your presence would be of the greatest value—and valued greatly by General MacDonald and the Governor, as well as myself."

Jamie sat silent for a moment, looking into the fire.

"It grieves me, Donald, that we should find ourselves so opposed," he said at last, looking up. "Ye canna be in ignorance, though, of my position in this matter. I have declared myself."

MacDonald nodded, lips tightening a little.

"I ken what ye've done. But it is not too late for remedy. Ye've done nothing yet that is irrevocable—and a man may surely admit mistake."

Jamie's mouth twitched a little.

"Oh, aye, Donald. Might you admit your own mistake, then, and join the cause of liberty?"

MacDonald drew himself up.

"It may please ye to tease, Mr. Fraser," he said, obviously keeping a grip on his temper, "but my offer is made in earnest."

"I know that, Major. My apologies for undue levity. And also for the fact that I must make ye a poor reward of your efforts, coming so far in bitter weather."

"Ye refuse, then?" Red smudges burned on MacDonald's cheeks, and his pale blue eyes had gone the color of the winter sky. "Ye will abandon your kin, your ain folk? Ye would betray your blood, as well as your oath?"

Jamie had opened his mouth to reply, but stopped at this. I could feel something going on inside him. Shock, at this blunt—and very accurate—accusation? Hesitation? He had never discussed the situation in those terms, but he must have grasped them. Most of the Highlanders in the colony either had joined the Loyalist side already—like Duncan and Jocasta—or likely would.

His declaration had cut him off from a great many friends—and might well cut him off from the remnants of his family in the New World, as well. Now MacDonald was holding out the apple of temptation, the call of clan and blood.

But he had had years to think of it, to ready himself.

"I have said what I must, Donald," he said quietly. "I have pledged myself and my house to what I believe is right. I cannot do otherwise."

MacDonald sat for a moment, looking at him narrowly. Then, without a word, he stood and pulled Roger's shirt off over his head. His torso was pale and lean, but with a slight middle-aged softness round the waist, and bore several white scars, the marks of bullet wounds and sabre cuts.

"You don't mean to go, surely, Major? It's freezing out, and nearly dark!" I came to stand by Jamie, and Roger and Bree rose, too, adding their protestations to mine. MacDonald, though, was obdurate, merely shaking his head as he pulled on his own damp clothing, fastening his coat with difficulty, as the buttonholes were stiff with damp.

"I will not take hospitality from the hand of a traitor, mum," he said very quietly, and bowed to me. He straightened then, and met Jamie's eye, man to man.

"We shall not meet again as friends, Mr. Fraser," he said. "I regret it."

"Then let us hope we do not meet again at all, Major," Jamie said. "I too regret it."

MacDonald bowed again, to the rest of the company, and clapped his hat on his head. His expression changed as he did so and felt the damp coldness of it on his bare head.

"Oh, your wig! Just a moment, Major—I'll fetch it." I rushed out and round to the pantry—just in time to hear a crash as something fell inside. I jerked open the door, left ajar from my last visit, and Adso streaked past me, the Major's wig in his mouth. Inside, the lean-to was in brilliant blue flames.

I had initially wondered how I would keep awake all night. In the event, it wasn't difficult at all. In the aftermath of the blaze, I wasn't sure I'd ever sleep again.

It could have been much worse; Major MacDonald, in spite of now being a sworn enemy, had come nobly to our aid, rushing out and flinging his still-wet cloak over the blaze, thus preventing the total destruction of the pantry—and, doubtless, the cabin. The cloak had not put out the fire entirely, though, and quenching the flames that sprang up here and there had entailed a great deal of excitement and rushing about, in the course of which Orrie McCallum was misplaced, toddled off, and fell into the ground-hog kiln, where he was found—many frantic minutes later—by Rollo.

He was fished out undamaged, but the hullabaloo caused Brianna to have what she thought was premature labor. Fortunately, this proved to be merely a bad case of hiccups, caused by the combination of nervous strain and eating excessive quantities of sauerkraut and dried-apple pie, for which she had conceived a recent craving.

"Flammable, she said." Jamie looked at the charred remains of the pantry floor, then at Brianna, who had, in spite of my recommendation that she lie down, come out to see what could be salvaged from the smoking remains. He shook his head. "It's a miracle that ye've not burnt the place to ashes long since, lass."

She emitted a smothered "hic!" and glowered at him, one hand on her bulging stomach.

"*Me?* You'd better not be try—hic!—ing to make out that this is *my*—hic!—fault. Did *I* put the Major's—hic!—wig next to the—"

"BOO!" Roger bellowed, darting a hand at her face.

She shrieked, and hit him. Jemmy and Aidan, running out to see what the commotion was about, started dancing round her, ecstatically shouting, "Boo! Boo!" like a gang of miniature lunatic ghosts.

Bree, her eyes gleaming dangerously, bent and scooped up a handful of snow. In an instant, she had molded it into a ball, which she flung at her husband's head with deadly accuracy. It struck him right between the eyes, exploding in a shower that left white granules clinging to his eyebrows and melting globs of snow running down his cheeks.

"What?" he said incredulously. "What's that for? I was only trying to—hey!" He ducked the next one, only to be pelted round the knees and waist by handsful of snow lobbed at short range by Jemmy and Aidan, quite berserk by now.

Modestly accepting thanks for his action earlier, the Major had been persuaded—not least by the fact that it was now full dark and beginning to snow again—to accept the hospitality of the cabin, with the understanding that it was Roger, not Jamie, who was offering it. Watching his hosts whooping and hiccing as they plastered one another with snow, he looked as though he might be having second thoughts about being so fine as to refuse to dine with a traitor, but he rather stiffly bowed in response when Jamie and I bade him farewell, then trudged into the cabin, the muddy shreds that Adso had left of his wig clasped in his hand.

It seemed extremely—and most gratefully—quiet as we made our way through the falling snow toward our own house, alone. The sky had gone a pinkish lavender, and the flakes floated down around us, supernatural in their silence.

The house loomed before us, its quiet bulk somehow welcoming, in spite of the darkened windows. Snow was swirling across the porch in little eddies, piling in drifts on the sills.

"I suppose it would be harder for a fire to start if it's snowing—wouldn't you think?"

Jamie bent to unlock the front door.

"I dinna much mind if the place bursts into flame by spontaneous combustion, Sassenach, provided I have my supper first."

"A cold supper, were you thinking?" I asked dubiously.

"I was not," he said firmly. "I mean to light a roaring fire in the kitchen hearth, fry up a dozen eggs in butter, and eat them all, then lay ye down on the hearth rug and roger ye 'til you—is that all right?" he inquired, noticing my look.

"'Til I what?" I asked, fascinated by his description of the evening's program.

"'Til ye burst into flame and take me with ye, I suppose," he said, and stooping, swooped me up into his arms and carried me across the darkened threshold.

112

Oathbreaker

February 2, 1776

He called them all together, and they came. The Jacobites of Ardsmuir, the fishermen from Thurso, the outcasts and opportunists who had come to settle on the Ridge over the last six years. He had called for the men, and most came alone, making their way through the dripping woods, slipping on mossy rocks and muddy trails. Some of the wives came, as well, though, curious, wary, though they hung modestly back and allowed Claire to shepherd them into the house one by one.

The men stood in the dooryard, and he regretted that; the memory of the last time they had gathered here was much too fresh in everyone's mind. But there was no choice about it; there were too

many to fit in the house. And it was broad day, now, not night—
though he saw more than one man turn his head sharply to glance
at the chestnut trees, as though he saw the ghost of Thomas
Christie there, poised once more to walk through the crowd.

He crossed himself, and said a hasty prayer, as he always did
when he thought of Tom Christie, then stepped out on the porch.
They had been talking together—awkwardly, but with a fair assumption of ease—but the talk died abruptly when he appeared.

"I have received word summoning me to Wilmington," he said
to them without preamble. "I go to join the militias there, and I
will take with me such men as will come willingly."

They gaped at him like sheep disturbed at grazing. He had a
moment's unsettling impulse to laugh, but it passed at once.

"We will go as militia, but I do not command your service."
Privately, he doubted that he *could* command more than a handful
of them now, but as well to put a good face on it.

Most were still blinking at him, but one or two had got a grip
on themselves.

"You declare yourself a rebel, *Mac Dubh*?" That was Murdo,
bless him. Loyal as a dog, but slow of thought. He needed things
to be put in the simplest of terms, but once grasped, he would deal
with them tenaciously.

"Aye, Murdo, I do. I am a rebel. So will any man be who
marches with me."

That caused a fair degree of murmuring, glances of doubt. Here
and there in the crowd, he heard the word "oath," and steeled himself for the obvious question.

He was taken aback by the man who asked it, though. Arch
Bug drew himself up, tall and stern.

"Ye swore an oath to the King, *Seaumais mac Brian,*" he said,
his voice unexpectedly sharp. "So did we all."

There was a murmur of agreement at this, and faces turned to
him, frowning, uneasy. He took a deep breath, and felt his stomach
knot. Even now, knowing what he knew, and knowing too the im-
morality of a forced oath, to break his sworn word openly made
him feel that he had stepped on a step that wasn't there.

"So did we all," he agreed. "But it was an oath forced upon us
as captives, not one given as men of honor."

This was patently true; still, it was an oath, and Highlanders
did not take any oath lightly. *May I die and be buried far from my*

kin . . . Oath or no, he thought grimly, that fate would likely be theirs.

"But an oath nonetheless, sir," said Hiram Crombie, lips drawn tight. "We have sworn before God. Do you ask us to put aside such a thing?" Several of the Presbyterians murmured acquiescence, drawing closer to Crombie in show of support.

He took another deep breath, feeling his belly tighten.

"I ask nothing." And knowing full well what he did, despising himself in a way for doing it—he fell back upon the ancient weapons of rhetoric and idealism.

"I said that the oath of loyalty to the King was an oath extorted, not given. Such an oath is without power, for no man swears freely, save he is free himself."

No one shouted disagreement, so he went on, voice pitched to carry, but not shouting.

"Ye'll ken the Declaration of Arbroath, will ye? Four hundred years since, it was our sires, our grandsires, who put their hands to these words: . . . *for as long as but a hundred of us remain alive, never will we on any conditions be brought under English rule.*" He stopped to steady his voice, then went on. *"It is in truth not for glory, nor riches, nor honours that we are fighting, but for freedom—for that alone, which no honest man gives up but with life itself."*

He stopped dead then. Not for its effect on the men to whom he spoke, but because of the words themselves—for in speaking them, he had found himself unexpectedly face to face with his own conscience.

To this point, he had been dubious about the justifications of the revolution, and more so of its ends; he had been compelled to the rebel stand because of what Claire, Brianna, and Roger Mac had told him. But in the speaking of the ancient words, he found the conviction he thought he pretended—and was stricken by the thought that he did indeed go to fight for something more than the welfare of his own people.

And ye'll end up just as dead in the end, he thought, resigned. *I dinna expect it hurts less, to ken it's for good cause—but maybe so.*

"I shall leave in a week," he said quietly, and left them staring after him.

He had expected his Ardsmuir men to come: the three Lindsay brothers, Hugh Abernathy, Padraic MacNeill, and the rest. Not expected, but gladly welcomed, were Robin McGillivray and his son, Manfred.

Ute McGillivray had forgiven him, he saw, with a certain sense of amusement. Besides Robin and Freddie, fifteen men from near Salem had come, all relatives of the redoubtable *frau*.

A great surprise, though, was Hiram Crombie, who alone of the fisher-folk had decided to join him.

"I have prayed on the matter," Hiram informed him, managing to look more piously sour than usual, "and I believe ye're right about the oath. I expect ye'll have us all hangit and burned oot of our homes—but I'll come, nonetheless."

The rest—with great mutterings and agitated debate—had not. He didn't blame them. Having survived the aftermath of Culloden, the perilous voyage to the colonies, and the hardship of exile, the very last thing a sensible person could wish was to take up arms against the King.

The greatest surprise, though, awaited him as his small company rode out of Cooperville and turned into the road that led south.

A company of men, some forty strong, was waiting at the crossroad. He drew near warily, and a single man spurred out of the crowd and drew up with him—Richard Brown, pale-faced and grim.

"I hear you go to Wilmington," Brown said without preamble. "If so be as it's agreeable, my men and I will ride with you." He coughed, and added, "Under your command, to be sure."

Behind him, he heard a small "hmph!" from Claire, and suppressed a smile. He was quite aware of the phalanx of narrowed eyes at his back. He caught Roger Mac's eye, and his son-in-law gave a small nod. War made strange bedfellows; Roger Mac knew that as well as he did—and for himself, he had fought with worse than Brown, during the Rising.

"Be welcome, then," he said, and bowed from his saddle. "You and your men."

We met another militia company near a place called Moore's Creek, and camped with them under the longleaf pines. There had been a bad ice storm the day before, and the ground was thick with fallen branches, some as large around as my waist. It made the going more difficult, but had its advantages, so far as making campfires went.

I was throwing a hastily assembled bucket of ingredients into the kettle for stew—scraps of ham, with bones, beans, rice, onions, carrots, crumbled stale biscuit—and listening to the other militia commander, Robert Borthy, who was telling Jamie—with considerable levity—about the state of the Emigrant Highland Regiment, as our opponents were formally known.

"There can't be more than five or six hundred, all told," he was saying with amused derision. "Old MacDonald and his aides have been tryin' to scoop 'em up from the countryside for months, and I gather the effort has been akin to scoopin' water with a sieve."

On one occasion, Alexander McLean, one of the general's aides, had set up a rendezvous point, calling upon all the Highlanders and Scotch–Irish in the neighborhood to assemble—cannily providing a hogshead of liquor as inducement. Some five hundred men had in fact shown up—but as soon as the liquor was drunk, they had melted away again, leaving McLean alone, and completely lost.

"The poor man wandered about for nearly two days, lookin' for the road, before someone took pity on him and led him back to civilization." Borthy, a hearty backwoods soul with a thick brown beard, grinned widely at the tale, and accepted a cup of ale with due thanks before going on.

"God knows where the rest of 'em are now. I hear tell that what troops Old MacDonald has are mostly brand-new emigrants—the Governor made 'em swear to take up arms to defend the colony before he'd grant them land. Most of them poor sods are fresh off the boat from Scotland—they don't know north from south, let alone just where they are."

"Oh, I ken where they are, even if they don't." Ian came into the firelight, grubby but cheerful. He had been riding dispatches back and forth among the various militia companies converging on Wilmington, and his statement caused a rush of general interest.

"Where?" Richard Brown leaned forward into the firelight, narrow face keen and foxy.

"They're comin' down Negro Head Point Road, marching like a proper regiment," Ian said, sinking onto a hastily offered log with a small groan. "Is there anything hot to drink, Auntie? I'm frozen and parched, both."

There was a nasty sort of dark liquid, called "coffee" for courtesy's sake, and made from boiling burned acorns. I rather dubiously poured him a cup, but he consumed it with every evidence of enjoyment, meanwhile recounting the results of his expeditions.

"They meant to circle round to the west, but Colonel Howe's men got there first, and cut them off. So then they went across, meaning to take the ford—but Colonel Moore put his men to the quick-step and marched all night to forestall them."

"They made no move to engage either Howe or Moore?" Jamie asked, frowning. Ian shook his head, and gulped the rest of his acorn coffee.

"Wouldna come close. Colonel Moore says they dinna mean to engage until they reach Wilmington—they're expecting reinforcement there."

I exchanged a glance with Jamie. The expected reinforcement was presumably the British regular troops, promised by General Gage. But a rider from Brunswick we had met the day before had told us that no ships had arrived when *he* left the coast, four days before. If there was reinforcement awaiting them, it would have to come from the local Loyalists—and from the various rumors and reports we'd heard so far, the local Loyalists were a weak reed on which to lean.

"Well, so. They're cut off on either side, aye? Straight down the road is where they're headed—they might reach the bridge late tomorrow."

"How far is it, Ian?" Jamie asked, squinting through the vista of longleaf pines. The trees were very tall, and the grassland under them wide open—very reasonable for riding.

"Maybe half a day on horseback."

"Aye, then." Jamie relaxed a little, and reached for his own cup of the vile brew. "We've time to sleep first, then."

We reached the bridge at Moore's Creek by midday the next day, and joined the company commanded by Richard Caswell, who greeted Jamie with pleasure.

The Highland regiment was nowhere in sight—but dispatch

riders arrived regularly, reporting their steady movement down Negro Head Point Road—a wide wagon thoroughfare that led directly to the solid plank bridge that crossed the Widow Moore's Creek.

Jamie, Caswell, and several of the other commanders were walking up and down the bank, pointing at the bridge and up and down the shore. The creek ran through a stretch of treacherous, swampy ground, with cypress trees stretching up from water and mud. The creek itself deepened as it narrowed, though—a plumb line that some curious soul dropped into the water off the bridge said it was fifteen feet deep at that point—and the bridge was the only feasible place for an army of any size to cross.

Which did a great deal to explain Jamie's silence over supper. He had helped to throw up a small earthwork on the far side of the creek, and his hands were smeared with dirt—and grease.

"They've cannon," he said quietly, seeing me eye the smudges on his hands. He wiped them absently on his breeks, much the worse for wear. "Two small guns from the town—but cannon, nonetheless." He looked toward the bridge, and grimaced slightly.

I knew what he was thinking—and why.

Ye were behind the cannon at Culloden, Donald, he had said to the Major. *I was in front of them. With a sword in my hand.* Swords were the Highlanders' natural weapons—and for most, likely their only weapons. From all we had heard, General MacDonald had managed to assemble only a small quantity of muskets and powder; most of his troops were armed with broadswords and targes. And they were marching straight into ambush.

"Oh, Christ," Jamie said, so softly I could barely hear him. "The poor wee fools. The poor gallant wee fools."

Matters became still worse—or much better, depending on your viewpoint—as dusk fell. The temperature had risen since the ice storm, but the ground was sodden; moisture rose from it during the day, but then as night came on, condensed into a fog so thick that even the campfires were barely visible, each one glowing like a sullen coal in the mist.

Excitement was passing through the militia like a mosquito-borne fever, as the new conditions gave rise to new plans.

"Now," Ian said softly, appearing like a ghost out of the fog beside Jamie. "Caswell's ready."

Such supplies as we had were already packed; carrying guns, powder, and food, eight hundred men, together with an uncounted quantity of camp-followers like myself, stole quietly through the mist toward the bridge, leaving the campfires burning behind us.

I wasn't sure exactly where MacDonald's troops were just now—they might be still on the wagon road, or might have cautiously detoured, coming down to the edge of the swamp to reconnoiter. Good luck to them in *that* case, I thought. My own insides were tight with tension as I stepped carefully across the bridge; it was silly to tiptoe, but I felt a reluctance to put my feet down firmly—the fog and silence compelled a sense of secrecy and furtiveness.

I stubbed a toe against an uneven plank and lurched forward, but Roger, walking beside me, caught me by the arm and set me upright. I squeezed his arm, and he smiled a little, his face barely visible through the mist, though he was no more than a foot away.

He knew quite as well as Jamie and the rest did what was coming. Nonetheless, I sensed a strong excitement in him, mingled with dread. It was, after all, to be his first battle.

On the other side, we dispersed to make fresh camps on the hill above the circular earthwork the men had thrown up a hundred yards from the creek. I passed close enough to the guns to see their elongated snouts, poking inquisitively through the mist: Mother Covington and her daughter, the men called the two cannon—I wondered idly which was which, and who the original Mother Covington might have been. A redoubtable lady, I assumed—or possibly the proprietor of the local brothel.

Firewood was easy to find; the ice storm had extended to the pines near the creek, too. It was, however, bloody damp, and damned if I was going to spend an hour on my knees with a tinderbox. Luckily, no one could see *what* I was doing in this pea-soup fog, and I stealthily removed a small tin of Brianna's matches from my pocket.

As I was blowing on the kindling, I heard a series of odd, rending screeches from the direction of the bridge, and knelt upright, staring down the hill. I couldn't see anything, of course, but real-

zed almost at once that it was the sound of nails giving way as
planks were pried up—they were dismantling the bridge.

It seemed a long time before Jamie came to find me. He re-
used food, but sat against a tree and beckoned to me. I sat down
between his knees and leaned back against him, grateful for his
warmth; the night was cold, with a damp that crept into every
crevice and chilled the marrow.

"Surely they'll see that the bridge is out?" I said, after a long si-
ence filled with the myriad noises of the men working below.

"Not if the fog lasts 'til morning—and it will." Jamie sounded
esigned, but he seemed more peaceful than he had earlier. We sat
quietly together for some time, watching the play of flames on the
og—an eerie sight, as the fire seemed to shimmer and merge
with the mist, the flames stretching strangely up and up, disappearing into the swirl of white.

"D'ye believe in ghosts, Sassenach?" Jamie asked suddenly.

"Er . . . well, not to put too fine a point on it, yes," I said. He
knew I did, because I'd told him about my meeting with the Indian
whose face was painted black. I knew he did, too—he was a
Highlander. "Why, have you seen one?"

He shook his head, wrapping his arms more securely around
me.

"Not to say 'seen,'" he said, sounding thoughtful. "But I will
be damned if he's no there."

"Who?" I said, rather startled at this.

"Murtagh," he said, surprising me further. He shifted more
comfortably, resettling me against him. "Ever since the fog came
n, I've had the most peculiar sense of him, just by me."

"Really?" This was fascinating, but made me thoroughly uneasy. Murtagh, Jamie's godfather, had died at Culloden, and—so
ar as I knew—hadn't been going about manifesting himself
since. I didn't doubt his presence; Murtagh's had been an ex-
remely strong—if dour—personality, and if Jamie said he was
here, he very likely was. What made me uneasy was the contemplation of just *why* he might be there.

I concentrated for a time, but got no sense of the tough little
Scotsman myself. Evidently, he was only interested in Jamie. *That*
rightened me.

While the conclusion of the morrow's battle was a foregone
one, a battle was a battle, and men might be killed on the winning

side, as well. Murtagh had been Jamie's godfather, and took hi
duty to Jamie seriously. I sincerely hoped he hadn't had word tha
Jamie was about to be killed, and shown up to conduct him to
heaven—visions on the eve of battle were a fairly common occurrence in Highland lore, but Jamie did say he hadn't *seen* Murtagh
That was something, I supposed.

"He, um, hasn't *said* anything to you, has he?"

Jamie shook his head, seeming unfazed by this ghostly visitation.

"Nay, he's just . . . there." He seemed, in fact, to find thi:
"thereness" a comfort, and so I didn't voice my own doubts and
fears. I had them, nonetheless, and spent the rest of the short nigh
pressed close against my husband, as though daring Murtagh or
anyone else to take him from me.

113

The Ghosts of Culloden

C ome dawn, Roger stood behind the low earthwork by hi:
father-in-law, musket in hand, straining his eyes to peer
into the mist. The sounds of an army came to him clearly
sound carried through fog. The measured tramp of feet, though
they were not marching in any sort of unison. The clank of meta
and rustle of cloth. Voices—the shouts of officers, he thought, be
ginning to rally their troops.

They would by now have found the deserted campfires; they'c
know that the enemy now lay across the creek.

The smell of tallow was strong in the air; Alexande:
Lillington's men had greased the support timbers, after the plank
had been removed. He'd been grasping his gun for hours, i

eemed, and yet the metal was still cold in his hand—his fingers were stiff.

"D'ye hear the shouting?" Jamie nodded toward the mist that id the far bank. The wind had changed; no more than disconnected Gaelic phrases came from beyond the ghostly cypress unks, and I made no sense of them. Jamie did.

"Whoever's leading them—I think it's McLeod, by the voice—e means to charge the creek," he said.

"But that's suicide!" Roger blurted. "Surely they know—surely omeone's seen the bridge?"

"They are Highlanders," Jamie said, still softly, eyes on the amrod he pulled from its rest. "They will follow the man to whom they vow loyalty, even though he leads them to their eath."

Ian was nearby; he glanced quickly toward Roger, then over is shoulder, where Kenny and Murdo Lindsay stood with Ronnie inclair and the McGillivrays. They stood in a casual knot, but very hand touched a musket or rifle, and their eyes darted toward amie every few seconds.

They had joined Colonel Lillington's men on this side of the reek; Lillington was passing to and fro through the men, eyes arting back and forth, assessing readiness.

Lillington stopped abruptly at sight of Jamie, and Roger felt a ervous qualm in the pit of his stomach. Randall Lillington had een a second cousin of the Colonel's.

Alexander Lillington wasn't a man to hide his thoughts; it had uite evidently dawned on him that his own men were forty feet way and that Jamie's men stood between him and them. His eyes arted toward the mist, where Donald McLeod's bellowing was be-ng answered by increasing roars from the Highlanders with him, en back at Jamie.

"What does he say?" Lillington demanded, rising on his toes nd frowning toward the far bank, as though concentration might ield him meaning.

"He says to them that courage will carry the day." Jamie glanced oward the crest of the rise behind them. Mother Covington's long lack snout was just visible through the mist. *"Would that it could,"* e added quietly in Gaelic.

Alexander Lillington reached out suddenly and grabbed Jamie's rist.

"And you, sir?" he said, suspicion open in eyes and voice. "A₁ you not a Highlander, as well?"

Lillington's other hand was on the pistol in his belt. Roger fe the casual talk among the men behind him stop, and glanced bac All Jamie's men were watching, with expressions of great intere but no particular alarm. Evidently, they felt Jamie could deal wi Lillington by himself.

"I ask you, sir—to whom is your loyalty?"

"Where do I stand, sir?" Jamie said with elaborate politenes "On this side of the creek, or on that?"

A few men grinned at that, but forbore to laugh; the questic of loyalty was a raw one still, and no man would risk it unnece sarily.

Lillington's grip on his wrist relaxed, but did not yet let g‹ though he acknowledged Jamie's statement with a nod.

"Well enough. But how are we to know that you do not mea to turn and fall upon us in battle? For you *are* a Highlander, a₁ you not? And your men?"

"I am a Highlander," Jamie said bleakly. He glanced onc more at the far bank, where occasional glimpses of tartan showe through the mist, and then back. The shouting echoed from th fog. "And I am the sire of Americans." He pulled his wrist fro₁ Lillington's grasp.

"And I give ye leave, sir," he continued evenly, lifting his rif and standing it on its butt, "to stand behind me and thrust yo₁ sword through my heart if I fire amiss."

With that, he turned his back on Lillington and loaded his gu₁ ramming ball, powder, and patch with great precision.

A voice bellowed from the fog, and a hundred oth‹ throats took up the cry in Gaelic. *"KING GEORGE AN BROADSWORDS!"*

The last Highland charge had begun.

They burst out of the mist a hundred feet from the bridg howling, and his heart jumped in his chest. For an instant—an i₁ stant only—he felt he ran with them, and the wind of it snapped ₁ his shirt, cold on his body.

But he stood stock-still, Murtagh beside him, looking cynical‹

on. Roger Mac coughed, and Jamie raised the rifle to his shoulder, waiting.

"Fire!" The volley struck them just before they reached the gutted bridge; half a dozen fell in the road, but the others came on. Then the cannon fired from the hill above, one and then the other, and the concussion of their discharge was like a shove against his back.

He had fired with the volley, aiming above their heads. Now swung the rifle down and pulled the ramrod. There was screaming on both sides, the shriek of wounded and the stronger bellowing of battle.

"A righ! A righ!" The King! The King!

McLeod was at the bridge; he'd been hit, there was blood on his coat, but he brandished sword and targe, and ran onto the bridge, stabbing his sword into the wood to anchor himself.

The cannon spoke again, but were aimed too high; most of the Highlanders had crowded down to the banks of the creek—some were in the water, clinging to the bridge supports, inching across. More were on the timbers, slipping, using their swords like McLeod to keep their balance.

"Fire!" and he fired, powder smoke blending with the fog. The cannon had the range, they spoke one-two, and he felt the blast push against him, felt as though the shot had torn through him. Most of those on the bridge were in the water now, more threw themselves flat upon the timbers, trying to wriggle their way across, only to be picked off by the muskets, every man firing at will from the redoubt.

He loaded, and fired.

There he is, said a voice, dispassionate; he had no notion was it his, or Murtagh's.

McLeod was dead, his body floating in the creek for an instant before the weight of the black water pulled him down. Many men were struggling in that water—the creek was deep here, and mortal cold. Few Highlanders could swim.

He glimpsed Allan MacDonald, Flora's husband, pale and staring in the crowd on the shore.

Major Donald MacDonald floundered, rising halfway in the water. His wig was gone and his head showed bare and wounded, blood running from his scalp down over his face. His teeth were bared, clenched in agony or ferocity, there was no telling which.

Another shot struck him and he fell with a splash—but rose again slow, slow, and then pitched forward into water too deep to stand but rose yet again, splashing frantically, spraying blood from his shattered mouth in the effort to breathe.

Let it be you, then, lad, said the dispassionate voice. He raised his rifle and shot MacDonald cleanly through the throat. He fell backward and sank at once.

It was over in minutes, the fog thick with powder smoke, the black creek choked with the dying and dead.

"King George and broadswords, eh?" said Caswell, bleakly surveying the damage. "Broadswords against cannon. Poor buggers."

On the other side, all was confusion. Those who had not fallen at the bridge were in flight. Already, men on this side of the creek were carrying the timbers down to repair the bridge. Those who were running wouldn't get far.

He should go, too, summon his men to help in pursuit. But he stood as though turned to stone, the cold wind singing in his ears.

Jack Randall stood still. His sword was in his hand, but he made no effort to raise it. Only stood there, that odd smile on his lips, dark eyes burning in Jamie's own.

If he had been able to break that gaze . . . but he couldn't, and so caught the blur of movement behind Randall. Murtagh, running, bounding tussocks like a sheep. And the glint of his godfather's blade—had he seen that, or only imagined it? No matter, he'd known without doubt from the cock of Murtagh's arm, and seen before it happened the murderous strike come upward toward the Captain's red-clad back.

But Randall spun, warned maybe by some change in his eyes, the sob of Murtagh's breath—or only by a soldier's instinct. Too late to avoid the thrust, but soon enough that the dirk missed its fatal aim into the kidney. Randall had grunted with the blow— Christ, he could hear it—and jerked aside staggering, but turning as he fell, grasping Murtagh's wrist, dragging him down in a shower of spray from the wet gorse they fell through.

They had rolled away into a hollow, locked together, strug-gling, and he had flung himself through the clinging plants in pursuit, some weapon—what, what had he held?—in his fist.

But the feel of it faded against his skin; he felt the weight of the thing in his hand, but there was no shape of hilt or trigger to re-mind him, and it was gone again.

Leaving him with that one image: Murtagh. Murtagh, teeth clenched and bared as he struck. Murtagh, running, coming to save him.

He became slowly aware again of where he was. There was a hand on his arm—Roger Mac, white-faced, but steady.

"I am going to see to them," Roger Mac said, with a brief nod toward the creek. "You're all right, yourself?"

"Aye, of course," he said, though with the feeling he so often had in waking from a dream—as though he were not in fact quite real.

Roger Mac nodded and turned to walk away. Then suddenly turned back, and laying his hand once more on Jamie's arm, said very quietly, *"Ego te absolvo."* Then turned again and went res-olutely to tend the dying and bless the dead.

PART

TWELVE

Time Will Not Be Ours Forever

114

Amanda

FROM *L'OIGNON–INTELLIGENCER*,
MAY 15, 1776

INDEPENDENCE!!

In the Wake of the famous Victory at Moore's Creek Bridge, the Fourth Provincial Congress of North Carolina has voted to adopt the Halifax Resolves. These Resolutions authorize Delegates to the Continental Congress to concur with the other Delegates of the other Colonies in declaring Independency and forming foreign Alliances, reserving to this Colony the sole and exclusive Right of forming a Constitution and Laws for this Colony, and by Passage of the Halifax Resolves, North Carolina thus becomes the first Colony officially to indorse Independency.

THE FIRST SHIP of a Fleet commanded by Sir Peter Parker has arrived at the Mouth of the Cape Fear River, upon the eighteenth of April. The Fleet consists of nine Ships in total, and is bringing British Troops to pacify and unite the Colony, by the Word of Governor Josiah Martin.

STOLEN: Goods amounting to twenty-six Pounds, ten Shillings and Fourpence in Total, abstracted from the Warehouse of Mr. Neil Forbes on Water Street. Thieves broke a Hole in the Back of the Warehouse during the Night of May twelfth, and carried the Goods away by

*means of a Wagon. Two Men, one White, one Black, were
seen driving a Wagon away with a Team of bay Mules. Any
Word pertaining to this atrocious Crime will be generously
Rewarded. Apply to W. Jones, in care of the Gull and
Oyster on the Market Square.*

*BORN, to Captain Roger MacKenzie of Fraser's Ridge
and his lady, a girl, on the twenty-first of April. Child and
Mother are reported in good Health, the Child's name
given as Amanda Claire Hope MacKenzie.*

Roger had never felt so terrified as he did when his newborn
daughter was placed in his arms for the first time. Minutes old,
skin tender and perfect as an orchid's, she was so delicate he
feared he would leave fingerprints on her—but so alluring that
he had to touch her, drawing the back of his knuckle gently, so
gently, down the perfect curve of her fat little cheek, stroking
the black cobweb silk of her hair with an unbelieving forefinger.

"She looks like you." Brianna, sweaty, disheveled, deflated—
and so beautiful he could scarcely bear to look at her—lay back
against the pillows with a grin that came and went like the
Cheshire Cat's—never entirely absent, even though it faded now
and then from tiredness.

"Does she?" He studied the tiny face with complete absorption. Not for any sign of himself—only because he couldn't take
his eyes off her.

He had come to know her intimately, through the months of
being roused suddenly by pokes and kicks, of watching the liquid
heave of Brianna's belly, of feeling the little one swell and retreat
under his hands as he lay behind his wife, cupping her stomach
and making jokes.

But he'd known her as Little Otto, the private name they'd
used for the unborn child. Otto had had a distinct personality—
and for a moment, he felt a ridiculous pang of loss, realizing that
Otto was gone. This tiny, exquisite being was someone entirely
new.

"Is she Marjorie, do you think?" Bree was lifting her head,
peering at the blanket-wrapped bundle. They'd discussed names
for months, making lists, arguing, making fun of each other's

hoices, choosing ridiculous things like Montgomery or
Agatha. At last, tentatively, they'd decided that if it was a boy,
he name might be Michael; if a girl, Marjorie, after Roger's
mother.

His daughter opened her eyes quite suddenly and looked at
him. Her eyes were slanted; he wondered if they would stay that
way, like her mother's. A sort of soft, middle blue, like the sky in
mid-morning—nothing remarkable, at a glance, but when you
looked straight into it . . . vast, illimitable.

"No," he said softly, staring into those eyes. Could she see him
yet? he wondered.

"No," he said again. "Her name's Amanda."

I hadn't said anything to begin with. It was a common thing in
newborns—especially babies born a bit early, as Amanda had
been—nothing to worry about.

The ductus arteriosus is a small blood vessel that in the fetus
joins the aorta to the pulmonary artery. Babies have lungs, of
course, but prior to birth don't use them; all their oxygen comes
from the placenta, via the umbilical cord. Ergo, no need for blood
to be circulated to the lungs, save to nourish the developing tissue—and so the ductus arteriosus bypasses the pulmonary circulation.

At birth, though, the baby takes its first breath, and oxygen
sensors in this small vessel cause it to contract—and close permanently. With the ductus arteriosus closed, blood heads out from
the heart to the lungs, picks up oxygen, and comes back to be
pumped out to the rest of the body. A neat and elegant system—
save that it doesn't always work properly.

The ductus arteriosus doesn't always close. If it doesn't, blood
still does go to the lungs, of course—but the bypass is still there.
Too much blood goes to the lungs, in some cases, and floods
them. The lungs swell, become congested, and with diverted
blood flow to the body, there are problems with oxygenation—
which can become acute.

I moved my stethoscope over the tiny chest, ear pressed to it, listening intently. It was my best stethoscope, a model from the nineteenth century called a Pinard—a bell with a flattened disc at one

end, to which I pressed my ear. I had one carved of wood; this one
was made of pewter; Brianna had sand-cast it for me.

In fact, though, the murmur was so distinct that I felt as though
I barely needed a stethoscope. Not a click or a misplaced beat, no
a too-long pause or a leaky swish—there were any number of un
usual sounds a heart could make, and auscultation was the firs
step of diagnosis. Atrial defects, ventral defects, malformed
valves—all have specific murmurs, some occurring between
beats, some blending with the heart sounds.

When the ductus arteriosus fails to close, it's said to be
"patent"—open. A patent ductus arteriosus makes a continuou
shushing murmur, soft, but audible with a little concentration, par
ticularly in the supraclavicular and cervical regions.

For the hundredth time in two days, I bent close, ear pressed to
the Pinard as I moved it over Amanda's neck and chest, hoping
against hope that the sound would have disappeared.

It hadn't.

"Turn your head, lovey, yes, that's right. . . ." I breathed, deli
cately turning her head away from me, Pinard pressed to the side
of her neck. It was hard to get the stethoscope close to her fat lit
tle neck . . . there. The murmur increased. Amanda made a little
breathy noise that sounded like a giggle. I brought her head back
the other way—the sound decreased.

"Oh, bloody hell," I said softly, so as not to scare her. I pu
down the Pinard and picked her up, cradling her against my shoulder. We were alone; Brianna had gone up to my room for a nap
and everyone else was out.

I carried her to the surgery window and looked out; it was a
beautiful day in the mountain spring. The wrens were nesting under the eaves again; I could hear them above me, rustling round
with sticks, conversing in small, clear chirps.

"Bird," I said, my lips close to her tiny seashell of an ear
"Noisy bird." She squirmed lazily, and farted in reply.

"Right," I said, smiling despite myself. I held her out a little, so
I could look into her face—lovely, perfect—but not as fat as it had
been when she was born a week before.

It was perfectly normal for babies to lose a little weight at first.
I told myself. It was.

A patent ductus arteriosus may have no symptoms, beyond
that odd, continuous murmur. But it may. A bad one deprives the

child of needed oxygen; the main symptoms are pulmonary—wheezing; rapid, shallow breathing; bad color—and failure to thrive, because of the energy burned up in the effort to get enough oxygen.

"Just let Grannie have a little listen again," I said, laying her down on the quilt I'd spread over the surgery table. She gurgled and kicked as I picked up the Pinard and placed it on her chest again, moving it over neck, shoulder, arm . . .

"Oh, Jesus," I whispered, closing my eyes. "Don't let it be bad." But the sound of the murmur seemed to grow louder, drowning my prayers.

I opened my eyes to see Brianna, standing in the doorway.

"I knew there was *something* wrong," she said steadily, wiping Mandy's bottom with a damp rag before rediapering her. "She doesn't nurse like Jemmy did. She acts hungry, but she'll only nurse for a few minutes before she falls asleep. Then she wakes up and fusses again a few minutes later."

She sat down and offered Mandy a breast, as though in illustration of the difficulty. Sure enough, the baby latched on with every evidence of starvation. As she nursed, I picked up one of the tiny fists, unfolding her fingers. The minute nails were faintly tinged with blue.

"So," Brianna said calmly, "what happens now?"

"I don't know." This was the usual answer in most cases, truth be told—but it was always unsatisfactory, and clearly not less so now. "Sometimes there are no symptoms, or only very minor ones," I said, trying for amendment. "If the opening is very large, and you have pulmonary symptoms—and we have—then . . . she *might* be all right, only not thriving—not growing properly, because of the feeding difficulties. Or"—I took a deep breath, steeling myself—"she could develop heart failure. Or pulmonary hypertension—that's a very high blood pressure in the lungs—"

"I know what it is," Bree said, her voice tight. "Or?"

"Or infective endocarditis. Or—not."

"Will she die?" she asked bluntly, looking up at me. Her jaw was set, but I saw the way she held Amanda closer, waiting for an answer. I could give her nothing but the truth.

"Probably." The word hung in the air between us, hideous.

"I can't say for sure, but—"

"Probably," Brianna echoed, and I nodded, turning away, un able to look at her face. Without such modern assistances as a echocardiogram, I of course couldn't judge the extent of the prob lem. But I had not only the evidence of my eyes and ears, but wha I had felt passing from her skin to mine—that sense of not-right ness, that eerie conviction that comes now and then.

"Can you fix it?" I heard the tremor in Brianna's voice, and went at once to put my arms around her. Her head was bent over Amanda, and I saw the tears fall, one, then another, darkening the wispy curls on top of the baby's head.

"No," I whispered, holding them both. Despair washed over me, but I tightened my hold, as though I could keep time and blood both at bay. "No, I can't."

"Well, there's no choice, is there?" Roger felt preternatu rally calm, recognizing it as the artificial calm produced by shock but wishing to cling to it as long as possible. "You've got to go."

Brianna leveled a look at him, but didn't reply. Her hand roamed over the baby, sleeping in her lap, smoothing the woolly blanket over and over again.

Claire had explained it all to him, more than once, patiently seeing that he could not take it in. He still did not believe it—bu the sight of those tiny fingernails, turning blue as Amanda strove to suck, had sunk into him like an owl's talons.

It was, she had said, a simple operation—in a modern operat ing room.

"You can't . . . ?" he'd asked, with a vague motion toward her surgery. "With the ether?"

She'd closed her eyes and shaken her head, looking nearly as ill as he felt.

"No. I can do very simple things—hernias, appendixes, ton sils—and even those are a risk. But something so invasive, on such a tiny body . . . no," she repeated, and he saw resignation in her face when she met his eyes. "No. If she's to live—you have to take her back."

And so they had begun to discuss the unthinkable. Because

there *were* choices—and decisions to be made. But the unalterable basic fact was clear. Amanda must go through the stones—if she could.

Jamie Fraser took his father's ruby ring, and held it over the face of his granddaughter. Amanda's eyes fixed on it at once, and she stuck out her tongue with interest. He smiled, despite the heaviness of his heart, and lowered the ring for her to grab at.

"She likes that well enough," he said, skillfully removing it from her grip before she could get it into her mouth. "Let's try the other."

The other was Claire's amulet—the tiny, battered leather pouch given to her by an Indian wisewoman years before. It contained assorted bits and bobs, herbs, he thought, and feathers, perhaps the tiny bones of a bat. But in among them was a lump of stone—nothing much to look at, but a true gemstone, a raw sapphire.

Amanda turned her head at once, more interested in the pouch than she had been in the shiny ring. She made cooing noises and batted wildly with both hands, trying to reach it.

Brianna took a deep, half-strangled breath.

"Maybe," she said, in the voice of one who fears as much as hopes. "But we can't tell for sure. What if I—take her, and I go through, but she can't?"

They all looked at one another in silence, envisioning the possibility.

"You'd come back," Roger said gruffly, and put a hand on Bree's shoulder. "You'd come right back."

The tension in her body eased a little at his touch. "I'd try," she said, and attempted a smile.

Jamie cleared his throat.

"Is wee Jem about?"

Of course he was; he never went far from home or Brianna these days, seeming to sense that something was wrong. He was retrieved from Jamie's study, where he had been spelling out words in—

"Jesus Christ on a piece of toast!" his grandmother blurted, snatching the book from him. "Jamie! How *could* you?"

Jamie felt a deep blush rise over him. How could he, indeed? He'd taken the battered copy of *Fanny Hill* in trade, part of a parcel of used books bought from a tinker. He hadn't looked at the books before buying them, and when he did come to look them over . . . Well, it was quite against his instincts to throw away a book—any book.

"What's P-H-A-L-L-U-S?" Jemmy was asking his father.

"Another word for prick," Roger said briefly. "Don't bloody use it. Listen—can ye hear anything, when ye listen to that stone?" He indicated Jamie's ring lying on the table. Jem's face lighted at sight of it.

"Sure," he said.

"What, from there?" Brianna said, incredulous. Jem looked around the circle of parents and grandparents, surprised at their interest. "Sure," he repeated. "It sings."

"Do ye think wee Mandy can hear it sing, too?" Jamie asked carefully. His heart was beating heavily, afraid to know, either way.

Jemmy picked up the ring and leaned over Mandy's basket, holding it directly over her face. She kicked energetically and made noises—but whether because of the ring, or merely at the sight of her brother . . .

"She can hear it," Jem said, smiling into his sister's face.

"How do you know?" Claire asked, curious. Jem looked up at her, surprised.

"She says so."

Nothing was settled. At the same time, everything was settled. I was in no doubt as to what my ears and my fingers told me—Amanda's condition was slowly worsening. Very slowly—it might take a year, two years, before serious damage began to show—but it was coming.

Jem might be right; he might not be. But we had to proceed on the assumption that he was.

There were arguments, discussions—tears. Not yet any decision as to who should attempt the journey through the stones. Brianna and Amanda must go; that was certain. But ought Roger to go with them? Or Jemmy?

"I will not let you go without me," Roger said through his teeth.

"I don't *want* to go without you!" Bree cried, looking exasperated. "But how can we leave Jemmy here, without us? And how can we make him go? A baby—we think that can work, because of the legends, but Jem—how will he make it? We can't let him risk being killed!"

I looked at the stones on the table—Jamie's ring, my pouch with the sapphire.

"I think," I said carefully, "that we need to find two more stones. Just in case."

And so, in late June, we came down from the mountain, into turmoil.

115

Nosepicker

July 4, 1776

I t was close and hot in the inn room, but I couldn't go out; little Amanda had finally fussed herself to sleep—she had a rash on her bottom, poor thing—and was curled in her basket, tiny thumb in her mouth and a frown on her face.

I unfolded the gauze mosquito netting and draped it carefully over the basket, then opened the window. The air outside was hot, too, but fresh, and moving. I pulled off my cap—without it, Mandy was fond of clutching my hair in both her hands and yanking; she had an amazing amount of strength, for a child with a heart defect. For the millionth time, I wondered whether I could have been wrong.

But I wasn't. She was asleep now, with the delicate rose bloom of a healthy baby on her cheeks; awake and kicking, that soft flush faded, and an equally beautiful but unearthly blue tinge showed now and then in her lips, in the beds of her tiny nails. She was still lively—but tiny. Bree and Roger were both large people; Jemmy had put on weight like a small hippopotamus through his first several years of life. Mandy weighed scarcely more than she had at birth.

No, I wasn't wrong. I moved her basket to the table, where the warm breeze could play over her, and sat down beside it, laying my fingers gently on her chest.

I could feel it. Just as I had in the beginning, but stronger now that I knew what it was. If I had had a proper operating suite, the blood transfusions, the calibrated and carefully administered anesthesia, the oxygen mask, the swift, trained nurses . . . No surgery on the heart is a minor thing, and surgery on an infant is always a great risk—but I could have done it. Could feel in the tips of my fingers exactly what needed to be done, could see in the back of my eyes the heart, smaller than my fist, the slippery, pumping, rubbery muscle and the blood washing through the ductus arteriosus, a small vessel, no bigger than an eighth of an inch in circumference. A small nick in the axillary vessel, a quick ligation of the ductus itself with a number-8 silk ligature. Done.

I knew. But knowledge is not, alas, always power. Nor is desire. It wouldn't be me who would save this precious granddaughter.

Would anyone? I wondered, giving way momentarily to the dark thoughts I fought to keep at bay when anyone else was near. Jemmy might not be right. Any baby might grab at a brightly colored shiny thing like a ruby ring—but then I remembered her cooing, batting at my decrepit leather amulet pouch with the raw sapphire inside.

Perhaps. I didn't want to think about the dangers of the passage—or the certainty of permanent separation, no matter whether the journey through the stones was successful or not.

There were noises outside; I looked toward the harbor, and saw the masts of a large ship, far out to sea. Another, still farther out. My heart skipped a beat.

They were oceangoing ships, not the little packet boats and fishing smacks that sailed up and down the coast. Could they be part of the fleet, sent in answer to Governor Martin's plea for help to suppress, subdue, and reclaim the colony? The first ship of that fleet had arrived at Cape Fear in late April—but the troops it carried had been lying low, waiting for the rest.

I watched for some time, but the ships didn't come in closer. Perhaps they were hanging off, waiting for the rest of the fleet? Perhaps they weren't British ships at all, but Americans, escaping the British blockade of New England by sailing south.

I was distracted from my thoughts by the clumping of male feet on the stairs, accompanied by snorts and that peculiarly Scottish sort of giggling usually depicted in print—but by no means adequately—as "Heuch, heuch, heuch!"

It was clearly Jamie and Ian, though I couldn't understand what was giving rise to so much hilarity, since when last seen they had been bound for the docks, charged with dispatching a shipment of tobacco leaves, obtaining pepper, salt, sugar, cinnamon—if findable—and pins—somewhat rarer than cinnamon—for Mrs. Bug, and procuring a large fish of some edible sort for our supper.

They'd got the fish, at least: a large king mackerel. Jamie was carrying it by the tail, whatever it had been wrapped in having evidently been lost in some accident. His queue had come undone, so that long red strands frayed out over the shoulder of his coat, which in turn had a sleeve half wrenched off, a fold of white shirt protruding through the torn seam. He was covered with dust, as was the fish, and while the latter's eyes both bulged accusingly, one of his own was swollen nearly shut.

"Oh, God," I said, burying my face in one hand. I looked up at him through splayed fingers. "Don't tell me. Neil Forbes?"

"Ach, no," he said, dropping the fish with a splat on the table in front of me. "A wee difference of opinion wi' the Wilmington Chowder and Marching Society."

"A difference of opinion," I repeated.

"Aye, they thought they'd throw us in the harbor, and we thought they wouldn't." He slung a chair round with his boot and sat down on it backward, arms crossed on its back. He looked indecently cheerful, face flushed with sun and laughter.

"I don't want to know," I said, though of course I did. I glanced at Ian, who was still sniggering quietly to himself, and observed that while he was slightly less battered than Jamie, he had one forefinger lodged in his nose up to the knuckle.

"Have you got a bloody nose, Ian?"

He shook his head, still giggling. "No, Auntie. Some o' the Society do, though."

"Well, why have you got your finger up your nose, then? Have you picked up a tick or something?"

"No, he's keepin' his brains from falling out," Jamie said, and went off into another fit. I glanced at the basket, but Mandy slept peacefully on, quite used to racket.

"Well, maybe you'd best stick both your own fingers up your nose, then," I suggested. "Keep you out of trouble for a moment or two, at least." I tilted up Jamie's chin to get a better look at the eye. "You hit someone with that fish, didn't you?"

The giggling had died down to a subterranean vibration between them, but threatened at this to break out anew.

"Gilbert Butler," Jamie said with a masterful effort at self-control. "Smack across the face. Sent him straight across the quay and into the water."

Ian's shoulders shook with remembered ecstasy.

"Bride, what a splash! Oh, it was a braw fight, Auntie! I thought I'd broke my hand on a fellow's jaw, but it's all right now the deadness has worn off. Just a bit numb and tingly." He wiggled the free fingers of his hand at me in illustration, wincing only slightly as he did so.

"Do take your finger out of your nose, Ian," I said, anxiety over their condition fading into annoyance at how they'd got that way. "You look like a half-wit."

For some reason, they both found that hysterically funny and laughed like loons. Ian did, however, eventually withdraw the finger, with an expression of wary cautiousness, as though he truly expected his brains to follow in its wake. Nothing did emerge, though, not even the ordinary bits of unsavory excreta one might expect from such a maneuver.

Ian looked puzzled, then mildly alarmed. He sniffed, prodding experimentally at his nose, then stuck the finger back into his nostril, rooting vigorously.

Jamie went on grinning, but his amusement began to fade as Ian's explorations became more frantic.

"What? Ye've not lost it, have ye, lad?"

Ian shook his head, frowning.

"Nay, I feel it. It's . . ." He stopped, giving Jamie a panic-stricken look over the embedded finger. "It's stuck, Uncle Jamie! I canna get it out!"

Jamie was on his feet at once. He pulled the finger from its resting-place with a moist, sucking noise, then tilted back Ian's head, peering urgently up his nose with his one good eye.

"Bring a light, Sassenach, will ye?"

There was a candlestick on the table, but I knew from experience that the only likely effect of using a candle to look up someone's nose was to set their nose hairs on fire. Instead, I bent and pulled my medical kit out from under the settle where I had stowed it.

"I'll get it," I said, with the confidence of one who has removed everything from cherry pits to live insects from the nasal cavities of small children. I drew out my longest pair of thin forceps, and clicked the slender blades together in token of assurance. "Whatever it is. Just keep quite still, Ian."

The whites of Ian's eyes showed briefly in alarm as he looked at the shining metal of the forceps, and he looked pleadingly at Jamie.

"Wait. I've a better idea." Jamie laid a quelling hand on my arm for an instant, then disappeared out the door. He thundered downstairs, and I heard a sudden burst of laughter from below, as the door to the taproom opened. The sound was as suddenly cut off as the door closed, like the valve on a faucet.

"Are you all right, Ian?" There was a smear of red on his upper lip; his nose *was* beginning to bleed, aggravated by his jabbings and pokings.

"Well, I do hope so, Auntie." His original jubilation was beginning to be replaced by a certain expression of worry. "Ye dinna think I can have pushed it into my brain, do ye?"

"I think it very unlikely. What on earth—"

But the door below had opened and closed again, spilling another brief spurt of talk and laughter into the stairwell. Jamie took the stairs two at a time and popped back into the room, smelling of hot bread and ale, and holding a small, battered snuffbox in his hand.

Ian seized on this with gratitude and, sprinkling a quick pinch of black, dusty grains on the back of his hand, hastily inhaled it.

For an instant, all three of us held breathless—and then it came, a sneeze of gargantuan proportions that rocked Ian's body back on its stool, even as his head flew forward—and a small, hard object struck the table with a *ping!* and bounced off into the hearth.

Ian went on sneezing, in a fusillade of hapless snorts and explosions, but Jamie and I were both on our knees, scrabbling in the ashes, heedless of filth.

"I've got it! I think," I added, sitting back on my heels and peering at the handful of ashes I held, in the midst of which was a small, round, dust-covered object.

"Aye, that's it." Jamie seized my neglected forceps from the table, plucked the object delicately from my hand, and dropped it into my glass of water. A delicate plume of ash and soot floated up through the water to form a dusty gray film on the surface. Below, the object glittered up at us, serene and glowing, its beauty at last revealed. A faceted clear stone, the color of golden sherry, half the size of my thumbnail.

"Chrysoberyl," Jamie said softly, a hand on my back. He looked at Mandy's basket, the silky black curls lifting gently in the breeze. "D'ye think it will serve?"

Ian, still wheezing and watery-eyed, and with a red-stained handkerchief pressed to his much-abused proboscis, came to look over my other shoulder.

"Half-wit, is it?" he said in tones of deep satisfaction. "Ha!"

"Wherever did you get that? Or rather," I corrected myself, "who did you steal it from?"

"Neil Forbes." Jamie picked the gem up, turning it gently over in his fingers. "There were a good deal more o' the Chowder Society than there were of us, so we ran down the street and round the corner, down between the warehouses there."

"I kent Forbes's place, aye, because I'd been there before," Ian put in. One of Mandy's feet was sticking up out of the basket; he touched the sole of it with a fingertip, and smiled to see her toes extend in reflex. "There was a great hole in the back where someone had broken down the wall, just covered over with a sheet of canvas, nailed over it, like. So we pulled it loose and ducked inside."

Where they had found themselves standing next to the small enclosed space Forbes used for an office—and for the moment, deserted.

"It was sitting in a bittie wee box on the desk," Ian said, coming to look proprietorially at the chrysoberyl. "Just sitting there! I'd just picked it up to look at, when we hear the watchman coming. So—" He shrugged and smiled at me, happiness momentarily transforming his homely features.

"And you think the watchman won't tell him you were there?" I asked skeptically. The two of them could scarcely be more conspicuous.

"Oh, I imagine he will." Jamie bent over Mandy's basket, holding the chrysoberyl between thumb and forefinger. "Look what Grandda and Uncle Ian have brought ye, *a muirninn,*" he said softly.

"We decided that it was a small enough ransom to pay for what he did to Brianna," Ian said, sobering somewhat. "I expect Mr. Forbes may feel it reasonable, too. And if not—" He smiled again, though not with happiness, and put his hand to his knife. "He's got another ear, after all."

Very slowly, a tiny fist rose through the netting, fingers flexing as they grasped at the stone.

"Is she still asleep?" I whispered. Jamie nodded, and gently withdrew the stone.

On the far side of the table, the fish stared austerely at the ceiling, ignoring everything.

116

The Ninth Earl of Ellesmere

July 9, 1776

"The water won't be cold."

She'd spoken automatically, without thinking.

"I shouldn't think that will matter much." A nerve jumped in Roger's cheek, and he turned away abruptly. She reached out, touching him delicately, as though he were a bomb that might explode if jarred. He glanced at her, hesitated, then took the hand she offered him, with a small, crooked smile.

"Sorry," he said.

"I'm sorry, too," she said softly. They stood close together, fingers knotted, watching the tide recede across the narrow beach, a fraction of an inch uncovered with each lap of the tiny waves.

The flats were gray and bleak in the evening light, pebble-strewn and rust-stained from the peaty waters of the river. With the tide going out, the harbor water was brown and feculent, the stain reaching past the ships at anchor, nearly to the open sea. When it turned, the clear gray water of the ocean would flow in, sweeping up the Cape Fear, obliterating the mudflats and everything on them.

"Over there," she said, still softly, though there was no one near enough to hear them. She tilted her head, indicating a group of weathered mooring posts driven deep into the mud. A skiff was tied to one; two of the pirettas, the four-oared "dragonflies" that plied the harbor, to another.

"You're sure?" He shifted his weight, glancing up and down the shore.

The narrow beach fell away into cold pebbles, exposed and gleaming with the leaving of the tide. Small crabs skittered hastily among them, not to waste a moment's gleaning.

"I'm sure. People in the Blue Boar were talking about it. A traveler asked where, and Mrs. Smoots said it was the old mooring posts, near the warehouses." A torn flounder lay dead among the rocks, white flesh washed clean and bloodless. The small busy claws picked and shredded, tiny maws gaped and gulped, pinching at morsels. She felt her gorge rise at the sight, and swallowed hard. It wouldn't matter what came after; she knew that. But still . . .

Roger nodded absently. His eyes narrowed against the harbor wind, calculating distances.

"There'll be quite a crowd, I expect."

There already was one; the turn of the tide wouldn't be for an hour or more, but people were drifting down to the harbor in twos and threes and fours, standing in the lee of the chandlery to smoke their pipes, sitting on the barrels of salt fish to talk and gesture. Mrs. Smoots had been right; several were pointing out the mooring posts to their less knowledgeable companions.

Roger shook his head.

"It'll have to be from that side; the best view is from there." He nodded across the inner arc of the harbor toward the three ships that rocked at the main quay. "From one of the ships? What do you think?"

Brianna fumbled in the pocket tied at her waist, and pulled out her small brass telescope. She frowned in concentration, lips pursed as she surveyed the ships—a fishing ketch, Mr. Chester's brig, and a larger ship, part of the British fleet, that had come in in the early afternoon.

"Whoa, Nellie," she murmured, arresting the sweep of her gaze as the pale blotch of a head filled the lens. "Is that who I think . . . hot dog, it is!" A tiny flame of delight flared in her bosom, warming her.

"Is who?" Roger squinted, straining to see unaided.

"It's John! Lord John!"

"Lord John Grey? You're sure?"

"Yes! On the brig—he must have come down from Virginia.

Woops, he's gone now—but he's there, I saw him!" She turned to Roger, excited, folding her telescope as she gripped him by the arm.

"Come on! Let's go and find him. He'll help."

Roger followed, though with considerably less enthusiasm.

"You're going to tell him? Do you think that's wise?"

"No, but it doesn't matter. He knows me."

Roger looked sharply at her, but the dark look on his face thawed into a reluctant smile.

"You mean he knows better than to try stopping you doing whatever you've made up your bloody-minded mind to do?"

She smiled back at him, thanking him with her eyes. He didn't like it—in fact, he hated it, and she didn't blame him—but he wouldn't try to stop her, either. He knew her, too.

"Yes. Come on, before he disappears!"

It was a slow slog round the curve of the harbor, pushing through the knots of gathering sightseers. Outside The Breakers, the crowd grew abruptly thicker. A cluster of red-coated soldiers stood and sat in disarray on the pavement, seabags and chests scattered round them, their number too great to fit inside the tavern. Ale pots and pints of cider were being passed from hand to hand from the interior of the public house, slopping freely on the heads of those over whom they passed.

A sergeant, harrassed but competent, was leaning against the timbered wall of the inn, riffling through a sheaf of papers, issuing orders and eating a meat pie, simultaneously. Brianna wrinkled her nose as they stepped carefully through the obstacle course of scattered men and luggage; a reek of seasickness and unclean flesh rose from the serried ranks.

A few onlookers muttered under their breath at sight of the soldiers; several more cheered and waved as they passed, to receive genial shouts in return. Newly liberated from the bowels of the *Scorpion,* the soldiers were too thrilled with their freedom and the taste of fresh food and drink to care who did or said anything whatever.

Roger stepped in front of her, thrusting a way through the crowd with shoulders and elbows. Appreciative shouts and whistles rose from the soldiers as they saw her, but she kept her head down, eyes fixed on Roger's feet as he shoved ahead.

She heaved a sigh of relief as they emerged from the press at the head of the quay. The soldiers' equipment was being unloaded from the *Scorpion* at the far side of the dock, but there was little foot traffic near the brig. She paused, looking to and fro for a glimpse of Lord John's distinctive fair head.

"There he is!" Roger tugged at her arm, and she swung in the direction he was pointing, only to collide heavily with him as he stepped abruptly back.

"What—" she began crossly, but then stopped, feeling as though she had been punched in the chest.

"Who in God's holy name is *that*?" Roger spoke softly, echoing her thoughts.

Lord John Grey stood near the far end of the quay, in animated conversation with one of the red-coated soldiers. An officer; gold braid gleamed on his shoulder and he carried a laced tricorne beneath one arm. It wasn't the man's uniform that caught her attention, though.

"Jesus H. Roosevelt Christ," she whispered, feeling numb around the lips.

He was tall—very tall—with a breadth of shoulder and a stretch of white-stockinged calf that were attracting admiring glances from a cluster of oyster girls. It was something more than height or build that made gooseflesh ripple down the length of her spine, though; it was the fact of his carriage, his outline, a cock of the head and an air of physical self-confidence that drew eyes like a magnet.

"It's Da," she said, knowing even as she spoke that this was ridiculous. Even had Jamie Fraser for some unimaginable reason chosen to disguise himself in a soldier's uniform and come down to the docks, this man was different. As he turned to look at something across the harbor, she saw that he *was* different—lean, like her father, and muscular, but still with the slenderness of boyishness. Graceful—like Jamie—but with the slight hesitancy of teenaged awkwardness not long past.

He turned further, backlit by the glow of light off the water, and she felt her knees go weak. A long, straight nose, rising to a high forehead . . . the sudden curve of a broad Viking cheekbone . . . Roger gripped her tightly by the arm, but his attention was as riveted on the young man as hers was.

"I . . . will . . . be . . . damned," he said.

She gulped air, trying to get enough breath.

"You and me both. *And* him."

"Him?"

"Him, him, *and* him!" Lord John, the mysterious young soldier—and most of all, her father. "Come on." She pulled free and strode down the quay, feeling oddly disembodied, as though she watched herself from a distance.

It was like watching herself come toward a fun-house mirror, seeing herself—her face, her height, her gestures—suddenly transposed inside a red coat and doeskin breeches. His hair was dark, chestnut-brown, not red, but it was thick like hers, with the same slight wave to it, the same cowlick that lifted it off his brow.

Lord John turned his head slightly, and caught sight of her. His eyes bulged and a look of absolute horror blanched his features. He made a feeble flapping motion with one hand, trying to stop her coming nearer, but he might as well have tried to stop the Cornish Express.

"Hello there!" she said brightly. "Fancy meeting *you* here, Lord John!"

Lord John made a faint quacking noise, like a stepped-on duck, but she wasn't paying attention. The young man turned to face her, smiling cordially.

Holy God, he had her father's eyes, too. Dark-lashed, and so young the skin near them was fresh and clear, completely unlined—but the same slanted blue Fraser cat eyes. Just like hers.

Her heart was hammering so hard in her chest she was sure they could hear it. The young man seemed to find nothing amiss, though; he bowed to her, smiling, but very correct.

"Your servant, ma'am," he said. He glanced at Lord John, plainly expecting an introduction.

Lord John pulled himself together with an obvious effort, and made her a leg.

"My dear. How . . . delightful to encounter you again. I had no idea. . . ."

Yeah, I bet you didn't, she thought, but went on smiling pleasantly. She could feel Roger beside her, nodding and saying something in response to his Lordship's greeting, trying his best not to stare.

"My son," Lord John was saying. "William, Lord Ellesmere." He eyed her narrowly, as though daring her to say anything. "Might I present Mr. Roger MacKenzie, William? And his wife."

"Sir. Mrs. MacKenzie." The young man took her hand before she realized what he meant to do, and bowed low over it, planting a small formal kiss upon her knuckles.

She nearly gasped at the unexpected touch of his breath on her skin, but instead gripped his hand, much harder than she'd meant to. He looked momentarily disconcerted, but extricated himself with reasonable grace. He was much younger than she'd thought at first glance; it was the uniform and the air of self-possession that made him seem older. He was looking at her with a slight frown on his clear-cut features, as though trying to place her.

"I think . . ." he began, hesitant. "Have we met, Mrs. MacKenzie?"

"No," she said, astonished to hear her voice emerge sounding normal. "No, I'm afraid not. I would have remembered." She darted a daggerlike glance at Lord John, who had gone slightly green around the gills.

Lord John had been a soldier, too, though. He pulled himself together with a visible effort, putting a hand on William's arm.

"You'd best go and see to your men, William," he said. "Shall we dine together later?"

"I am engaged to the Colonel for supper, Father," William said. "But I am sure he would not object, were you to join us. It may be quite late, though," he added. "I understand there is to be an execution in the morning, and my troops are asked to be at the ready, in case of disturbance in the town. It will take some time to settle and organize everything."

"Disturbance." Lord John was eyeing her over William's shoulder. "Is a disturbance expected, then?"

William shrugged.

"I cannot say, Papa. Apparently it is not a political matter, though, but only a pirate. I shouldn't think there would be any trouble."

"These days everything is a political matter, Willie," his father said, rather sharply. "Never forget that. And it's always wiser to expect trouble than to meet it unprepared."

The young man flushed slightly, but kept his countenance.

"Quite," he said in clipped tones. "I am sure you have a familiarity with the local conditions which I lack. I am obliged to you for your advice, Father." He relaxed slightly, and turned to bow to Brianna.

"Pleased to have your acquaintance, Mrs. MacKenzie. Your servant, sir." He nodded to Roger, turned, and strode off down the quay, adjusting his tricorne to the proper angle of authority.

Brianna inhaled deeply, hoping that by the time she let her breath out, she would have words to go with it. Lord John beat her to it.

"Yes," he said simply. "Of course he is."

Amid the logjam of thoughts, reactions, and emotions that clogged her brain, she seized on the one that seemed momentarily most important.

"Does my mother know?"

"Does Jamie know?" Roger asked at the same instant. She looked at him in surprise, and he raised one eyebrow at her. Yes, a man could certainly father a child without realizing it. He had.

Lord John sighed. With William's departure, he had relaxed somewhat, and the natural color was coming back to his face. He had been a soldier long enough to recognize the inevitable when he saw it.

"They both know, yes."

"How old is he?" Roger asked abruptly. Lord John shot him a sharp glance.

"Eighteen. And to save your counting backward, it was 1758. In a place called Helwater, in the Lake District."

Brianna took another breath, finding this one came a little easier.

"Okay. So it—he—it was before my mother . . . came back."

"Yes. From France, supposedly. Where, I gather, you were born and raised." He gave her a gimlet look; he knew she spoke no more than bastard French.

She could feel the blood rushing to her face.

"This is no time for secrets," she said. "If you want to know about my mother and me, I'll tell you—but *you're* going to tell me about *him.*" She jerked her head angrily backward, toward the tavern. "About my brother!"

Lord John pursed his lips, regarding her through narrowed eyes as he thought. Finally he nodded.

"I see no help for it. One thing, though—are your parents here, in Wilmington?"

"Yes. In fact . . ." She looked upward, trying to make out the position of the sun through the thin coastal haze. It hung just above the horizon, a disc of burning gold. "We were going to meet them for supper."

"Here?"

"Yes."

Lord John swung round to Roger.

"Mr. MacKenzie. You will very much oblige me, sir, if you will go at once to find your father-in-law, and apprise him of the presence of the ninth Earl of Ellesmere. Tell him that I trust his good judgment will dictate an immediate removal from Wilmington upon receipt of this news."

Roger stared at him for a moment, brows quirked in interest.

"The Earl of Ellesmere? How the hell did he manage that?"

Lord John had recovered all his natural color, and a bit more. He was distinctly pink in the face.

"Never mind! Will you go? Jamie must leave the town, at once, before they meet by inadvertence—or before someone sees the two of them separately and begins to speculate aloud."

"I doubt Jamie will leave," Roger said, looking at Lord John with a certain degree of speculation himself. "Not before tomorrow, in any case."

"Why not?" Lord John demanded, looking from one to the other. "Why are you all here in the first place? It isn't the exe—oh, good Lord, don't tell me." He clapped a hand to his face, and dragged it slowly down, glaring through his fingers with the expression of a man tried beyond bearing.

Brianna bit her lower lip. When she spotted Lord John, she had been not only pleased but relieved of a small bit of her burden of worry, counting on him to help in her plan. With this new complication, though, she felt torn in two, unable to cope with either situation, or even to think about them coherently. She looked over at Roger, seeking advice.

He met her eyes in one of those long, unspoken marital exchanges. Then he nodded, making the decision for her.

"I'll go find Jamie. You have a bit of a chat with his Lordship, eh?"

He bent and kissed her, hard, then turned and strode away down the dock, walking in a way that made people draw unconsciously aside, avoiding the touch of his garments.

Lord John had closed his eyes, and appeared to be praying—

presumably for strength. She gripped him by the arm and his eyes sprang open, startled as though he had been bitten by a horse.

"Is it as striking as I think?" she said. "Him and me?" The word felt funny on her tongue. *Him.*

Lord John looked at her, fair brow furrowed in troubled concentration as he searched her face, feature by feature.

"I think so," he said slowly. "To me, certainly. To a casual observer, perhaps much less so. There is the difference of coloring, to be sure, and of sex; his uniform . . . but, my dear, you know that your own appearance is so striking—" So freakish, he meant. She sighed, taking his meaning.

"People stare at me anyway," she finished for him. She pulled down the brim of her hat, drawing it far enough forward to hide not only hair but face, as well, and glowered at him from its shadow. "Then we'd better go where no one who knows him will see me, hadn't we?"

The quay and the market streets were thronged. Every public house in town—and not a few private ones—would soon be full of quartered soldiers. Her father and Jem were with Alexander Lillington, her mother and Mandy at Dr. Fentiman's, both places centers of business and gossip, and she had declared that she possessed no intention of going near either parent in any case— not until she knew all there was to know. Lord John thought that might be rather more than he was himself prepared to tell her, but this was not a time for quibbles.

Still, the exigencies of privacy left them a choice of graveyard or the deserted racetrack, and Brianna said—a marked edge in her voice—that under the circumstances, she wanted no heavy-handed reminders of mortality.

"These mortal circumstances," he said carefully, leading her around a large puddle. "You refer to tomorrow's execution? It *is* Stephen Bonnet, I collect?"

"Yes," she said, distracted. "That can wait, though. You aren't engaged for supper, are you?"

"No. But—"

"William," she said, eyes on her shoes as they paced slowly round the sandy oval. "William, ninth Earl of Ellesmere, you said?"

"William Clarence Henry George," Lord John agreed. "Viscount Ashness, Master of Helwater, Baron Derwent, and, yes, ninth Earl of Ellesmere."

She pursed her lips.

"Which would sort of indicate that the world at large thinks his father is somebody else. Not Jamie Fraser, I mean."

"*Was* somebody else," he corrected. "One Ludovic, eighth Earl of Ellesmere, to be precise. I understand that the eighth earl unfortunately died on the day his . . . er . . . his heir was born."

"Died of what? Shock?" She was clearly in a dangerous mood; he was interested to note both her father's manner of controlled ferocity and her mother's sharp tongue at work—the combination was both fascinating and alarming. He hadn't any intention of allowing her to run this interview on her own terms, though.

"Gunshot," he said with affected cheerfulness. "Your father shot him."

She made a small choking noise and stopped dead.

"That is not, by the way, common knowledge," he said, affecting not to notice her reaction. "The coroner's court returned a verdict of death by misadventure—which was not incorrect, I believe."

"Not incorrect," she murmured, sounding a trifle dazed. "I guess being shot is pretty misadventurous, all right."

"Of course there was talk," he said, offhanded, taking her arm and urging her forward again. "But the only witness, aside from William's grandparents, was an Irish coachman, who was rather quickly pensioned off to County Sligo, following the incident. The child's mother having also died that day, gossip was inclined to consider his lordship's death as—"

"His mother's dead, too?" She didn't stop this time, but turned to give him a penetrating glance from those deep blue eyes. Lord John had had sufficient practice in withstanding Fraser cat looks, though, and was not discomposed.

"Her name was Geneva Dunsany. She died shortly after William's birth—of an entirely natural hemorrhage," he assured her.

"Entirely natural," she muttered, half under her breath. She shot him another look. "This Geneva—she was married to the earl? When she and Da . . ." The words seemed to stick in her throat; he could see doubt and repugnance struggling with her memories of William's undeniable face—and her knowledge of her father's character.

"He has not told me, and I would in no circumstance ask him," he said firmly. She gave him another of those looks, which he returned with interest. "Whatever the nature of Jamie's relations with Geneva Dunsany, I cannot conceive of his committing an act of such dishonor as to deceive another man in his marriage."

She relaxed fractionally, though her grip on his arm remained.

"Neither can I," she said, rather grudgingly. "But—" Her lips compressed, relaxed. "Was he in love with her, do you think?" she blurted.

What startled him was not the question, but the realization that it had never once occurred to him to ask it—certainly not of Jamie, but not even of himself. Why not? he wondered. He had no right to jealousy, and if he was fool enough to suffer it, it would have been considerably *ex post facto* in the case of Geneva Dunsany; he had had no inkling of William's origins until several years after the girl's death.

"I have no idea," he said shortly.

Brianna's fingers drummed restlessly on his arm; she would have pulled free, but he put a hand on hers to still her.

"Damn," she muttered, but ceased fidgeting, and walked on, matching the length of his shorter stride. Weeds had sprung up in the oval, were sprouting through the sand of the track. She kicked at a clump of wild rye grass, sending a spray of dry seeds flying.

"If they were in love, why didn't he marry her?" she asked at last.

He laughed, in sheer incredulity at the notion.

"Marry her! My dear girl, he was the family groom!"

A look of puzzlement flashed in her eye—he would have sworn that if she had spoken, the word would have been *"So?"*

"Where in the name of God were you raised?" he demanded, stopping dead.

He could see things moving in her eyes; she had Jamie's trick of keeping her face a mask, but her mother's transparency still shone from within. He saw the decision in her eyes, a moment before the slow smile touched her lips.

"Boston," she said. "I'm an American. But you knew I was a barbarian already, didn't you?"

He grunted in response.

"That does go some distance toward explaining your remarkably republican attitudes," he replied very dryly. "Though I would strongly suggest that you disguise these dangerous sentiments, for the sake of your family. Your father is in sufficient trouble on his own account. However, you may accept my assurance that it would not be possible for the daughter of a baronet to marry a groom, no matter how exigent the nature of their emotions."

Her turn to grunt at that; a highly expressive, if totally unfeminine sound. He sighed, and took her hand again, tucking it in the curve of his elbow for safekeeping.

"He was a paroled prisoner, too—a Jacobite, a traitor. Believe me, marriage would not have occurred to either of them."

The damp air was misting on her skin, clinging to the down hairs on her cheeks.

"But that was in another country," she quoted softly. *"And besides, the wench is dead."*

"Very true," he said quietly.

They scuffed silently through the damp sand for a few moments, each alone in thought. At last Brianna heaved a sigh, deep enough that he felt as well as heard it.

"Well, she's dead, anyway, and the earl—do you know *why* Da killed him? Did he tell you that?"

"Your father has never spoken of the matter—of Geneva, of the earl, or even directly of William's parentage—to me." He spoke precisely, eyes fixed on a pair of gulls probing the sand near a clump of saw grass. "But I know, yes."

He glanced at her.

"William is *my* son, after all. In the sense of common usage, at least." In a great deal more than that, but that was not a matter he chose to discuss with Jamie's daughter.

Her eyebrows rose.

"Yes. How did that happen?"

"As I told you, both of William's parents—his putative parents—died on the day of his birth. His father—the earl, I mean—had no close kin, so the boy was left to the guardianship of his grandfather, Lord Dunsany. Geneva's sister, Isobel, became William's mother in all but fact. And I—" He shrugged, nonchalant. "I married Isobel. I became William's guardian, with Dunsany's consent, and he has regarded me as his stepfather since he was six years old—he is my son."

"You? You *married*?" She was goggling down at him, with an air of incredulity that he found offensive.

"You have the most peculiar notions concerning marriage," he said crossly. "It was an eminently suitable match."

One red eyebrow went up in a gesture that was Jamie to the life.

"Did your wife think so?" she asked, in an uncanny echo of her mother's voice, asking the same question. When her mother had asked it, he had been nonplussed. This time, he was prepared.

"That," he said tersely, "was in another country. And Isobel . . ." As he had hoped, that silenced her.

A fire was burning at the far end of the sandy oval, where travelers had made a rough camp. People come downriver to see the execution, he wondered? Men seeking to enlist in the rebel militias? A figure moved, dimly seen through the haze of smoke, and he turned, leading Brianna back along the way they had come. This conversation was sufficiently awkward, without the risk of interruption.

"You asked about Ellesmere," he said, taking control of the conversation once more. "The story given to the coroner's court by Lord Dunsany was that Ellesmere had been showing him a new pistol, which discharged by accident. It was the sort of story that is told in order to be disbelieved—giving the impression that in reality the earl had shot himself, doubtless from grief at the death of his wife, but that the Dunsanys wished to avoid the stigma of suicide, for the sake of the child. The coroner naturally perceived both the falsity of the story and the wisdom of allowing it to stand."

"That's not what I asked," she said, a noticeable edge in her voice. "I asked why my father shot him."

He sighed. She could have found gainful employment with the Spanish Inquisition, he thought ruefully; no chance of escape or evasion.

"I understand that his Lordship, apprehending that the newborn infant was in fact not of his blood, intended to expunge the stain upon his honor by dropping the child out of the window, onto the slates in the courtyard thirty feet below," he said bluntly.

Her face had paled perceptibly.

"How did he find out?" she demanded. "And if Da was a

groom, why was he there? Did the earl know he was—responsible?" She shuddered, plainly envisioning a scene in which Jamie was summoned to the earl's presence, to witness the death of his illegitimate offspring before facing a similar fate himself. John had no difficulty in discerning her imagination; he had envisioned such a scene himself, more than once.

"An acute choice of words," he replied dryly. "Jamie Fraser is 'responsible' for more than any man I know. As to the rest, I have no idea. I know the essentials of what happened, because Isobel knew; her mother was present and presumably told her only the briefest outline of the incident."

"Huh." She kicked a small stone, deliberately. It skittered across the packed sand in front of her, ending a few feet away. "And you never asked Da about it?"

The stone lay in his line of march; he kicked it neatly as he walked, rolling it back into her path.

"I have never spoken to your father regarding Geneva, Ellesmere, or William himself—save to inform him of my marriage to Isobel and to assure him that I would fulfill my responsibilities as William's guardian to the best of my ability."

She set her foot on the stone, driving it into the soft sand, and stopped.

"You never said *anything* to him? What did he say to you?" she demanded.

"Nothing." He returned her stare.

"Why did you marry Isobel?"

He sighed, but there was no point in evasion.

"In order to take care of William."

The thick red brows nearly touched her hairline.

"So you got married, in spite of—I mean, you turned your whole life upside down, just to take care of Jamie Fraser's illegitimate son? And neither one of you ever *talked* about it?"

"No," he said, baffled. "Of course not."

Slowly, the brows came down again, and she shook her head.

"Men," she said cryptically. She glanced back toward the town. The air was calm, and a haze from the chimneys of Wilmington lay heavy above the trees. No roofs showed; it might have been a dragon that lay sleeping on the shore, for all that could be seen. The low, rumbling noise was not a reptilian snore, though; a small but constant stream of people had been passing by the track, headed for the town, and the reverberations of an increasing crowd were clearly audible, whenever the wind was right.

"It's nearly dark. I have to go back." She turned toward the lane that led into town, and he followed, relieved for the moment, but under no illusion that the inquisition was over.

She had only one more question, though.

"When are you going to tell him?" she asked, turning to look at him as she reached the edge of the trees.

"Tell who what?" he replied, startled.

"Him." She frowned at him, irritated. "William. My brother." The irritation faded as she tasted the word. She was still pale, but a sort of excitement had begun to glow beneath her skin. Lord John felt as though he had eaten something that violently disagreed with him. A cold sweat broke out along his jaw, and his guts clenched into fistlike knots. His knees turned to water.

"Are you quite mad?" He grasped at her arm, as much to keep from stumbling as to prevent her going off.

"I gather he doesn't know who his father really is," she said with a bit of asperity. "Given that you and Da never talked to each other about it, you probably didn't see any point talking to *him,* either. But he's grown up now—he has a right to know, surely."

Lord John closed his eyes with a low moan.

"Are you all right?" she asked. He felt her bending close to inspect him. "You don't look very good."

"Sit." He sat himself, back to a tree, and pulled her down beside him on the ground. He breathed deeply, keeping his eyes closed while his mind raced. Surely she was joking? Surely not, his cynically observant self assured him. She had a marked sense of humor, but it wasn't in evidence at the moment.

She couldn't. He couldn't let her. It was inconceivable that she—but how could he stop her? If she wouldn't listen to him, perhaps Jamie or her mother . . .

A hand touched his shoulder.

"I'm sorry," she said softly. "I didn't stop to think."

Relief filled him. He felt his bowels begin to uncramp, and opened his eyes to see her gazing at him with a peculiar sort of limpid sympathy that he didn't understand at all. His bowels promptly convulsed again, making him fear that he was about to suffer an embarrassing attack of flatulence on the spot.

His bowels had read her better than he had.

"I should have thought," she reproached herself. "I should have known how you'd feel about it. You said it yourself—he's *your* son. You've raised him all this time, I can see how much you love him. It must make you feel terrible to think of William finding out about Da and maybe blaming you for not telling him sooner." Her hand was massaging his collarbone in what he assumed was meant to be a soothing gesture. If that was her intent, the movement had singularly failed.

"But—" he began, but she had taken his hand in both hers and was squeezing it earnestly, her blue eyes shimmering with tears.

"He won't," she assured him. "William would never stop loving you. Believe me. It was the same for me—when I found out about Da. I didn't want to believe it at first; I *had* a father, and I loved him, and I didn't want another one. But then I met Da, and it was—he was . . . who he is—" She shrugged slightly, and lifted one hand to wipe her eyes on the lace at her wrist.

"But I haven't forgotten my other father," she said very softly. "I never will. Never."

Touched despite the general seriousness of the situation, Lord John cleared his throat.

"Yes. Well. I am sure your sentiments do you great credit, my dear. And while I hope that I likewise enjoy William's affectionate regard at present and will continue to do so in future, that is really not the point I was endeavoring to make."

"It's not?" She looked up, wide-eyed, tears clumping her lashes into dark spikes. She was really a lovely young woman, and he felt a small twinge of tenderness.

"No," he said, quite gently under the circumstances. "Look, my love. I told you who William is—or who he thinks he is."

"Viscount Whatnot, you mean?"

He sighed deeply.

"Quite. The five people who know of his true parentage have expended considerable effort for the last eighteeen years, to the end that no one—William included—should ever have cause to doubt that he *is* the ninth Earl of Ellesmere."

She looked down at that, her thick brows knitted, lips compressed. Christ, he hoped that her husband had succeeded in locating Jamie Fraser in time. Jamie Fraser was the only person who had a hope of being more effectually stubborn than his daughter.

"You don't understand," she said finally. She looked up, and he saw that she had come to some decision.

"We're leaving," she said abruptly. "Roger and I and the—the children."

"Oh?" he said cautiously. This might be good news—on several counts. "Where do you propose to go? Will you remove to England? Or Scotland? If England or Canada, I have several social connexions who might be of—"

"No. Not there. Not anywhere you have 'connexions.'" She smiled painfully at him, then swallowed before continuing.

"But you see—we'll be gone. For—for good. I won't—I don' think I'll ever see you again." That realization had just dawned on her; he saw it on her face, and despite the strength of the pang it gave him, he was deeply moved by her obvious distress at the thought.

"I will miss you very much, Brianna," he said gently. He had been a soldier most of his life, and then a diplomat. He had learned to live with separation and absence, with the occasional death of friends left behind. But the notion of never seeing this odd girl again caused him a most unexpected degree of grief. Almost, he thought with surprise, as though she were his own daughter.

But he had a son, as well, and her next words snapped him back to full alertness.

"So you see," she said, leaning toward him with an intentness that he would otherwise have found charming, "I have to talk to William, and tell him. We'll never have another chance." Then her face changed, and she put a hand to her bosom.

"I have to go," she said abruptly. "Mandy—Amanda, my daughter—she needs to be fed."

And with that, she was up and gone, scudding across the sand of the racetrack like a storm cloud, leaving the threat of destruction and upheaval in her wake.

117

Surely Justice and Mercy Shall Follow Me

July 10, 1776

The tide turned from the ebb just before five o'clock in the morning. The sky was fully light, a clear pale color without clouds, and the mudflats beyond the quay stretched gray and shining, their smoothness marred here and there by weed and stubborn sea grass, sprouting from the mud like clumps of hair.

Everyone rose with the dawn; there were plenty of people on the quay to see the small procession go out, two officers from the Wilmington Committee of Safety, a representative from the Merchants Association, a minister carrying a Bible, and the prisoner, a tall, wide-shouldered figure, walking bare-headed across the stinking mud. Behind them all came a slave, carrying the ropes.

"I don't want to watch this," Brianna said under her breath. She was very pale, her arms folded over her middle as though she had a stomachache.

"Let's go, then." Roger took her arm, but she pulled back.

"No. I have to."

She dropped her arms and stood straight, watching. People around them were jostling for a better view, jeering and catcalling so loudly that whatever was said out there was inaudible. It didn't take long. The slave, a big man, grabbed the mooring post and shook it, testing for steadfastness. Then stood back, while the two officers backed Stephen Bonnet up to the stake and wrapped his body with rope from chest to knees. The bastard wasn't going anywhere.

Roger thought he should be searching his heart for compassion, praying for the man. He couldn't. Tried to ask forgiveness and couldn't do that, either. Something like a ball of worms churned in his belly. He felt as though he were himself tied to a stake, waiting to drown.

The black-coated minister leaned close, his hair whipping in the early morning breeze, mouth moving. Roger didn't think that Bonnet made any reply, but couldn't tell for sure. After a few moments, the men doffed their hats, stood while the minister prayed, then put them on again and headed back toward shore, their boots squelching, ankle-deep in the sandy mud.

The moment the officials had disappeared, a stream of people poured out onto the mud: sightseers, hopping children—and a man with a notebook and pencil, who Roger recognized as Amos Crupp, the current proprietor of the *Wilmington Gazette*.

"Well, that'll be a scoop, won't it?" Roger muttered. No matter what Bonnet actually said—or didn't—there would undoubtedly be a broadsheet hawked through the streets tomorrow, containing either a lurid confession or mawkish reports of remorse—perhaps both.

"Okay, I *really* can't watch this." Abruptly, Brianna turned, taking his arm.

She made it past the row of warehouses before turning abruptly to him, burying her face in his chest and bursting into tears.

"Ssh. It's okay—it's going to be all right." He patted her, tried to infuse some conviction into the words, but his own throat had a lump in it the size of a lemon. He finally took her by the shoulders and held her away from him, so that he could look into her eyes.

"Ye don't have to do it," he said.

She stopped crying and sniffed, wiping her nose on her sleeve like Jemmy—but wouldn't meet his eyes.

"It's—I'm okay It's not even *him*. It's just—just everything. M-Mandy"—her voice wavered on the word—"and meeting my brother—Oh, Roger, if I can't tell him, he'll never know, and I'll never see him or Lord John again. Or Mama—" Fresh tears overwhelmed her, welling up in her eyes, but she gulped and swallowed, forcing them back.

"It's not him," she said in a choked, exhausted voice.

"Maybe it's not," he said softly. "But ye still don't have to do it." His stomach still churned, and his hands felt shaky, but resolution filled him.

"I should have killed him on Ocracoke," she said, closing her eyes and brushing back strands of loosened hair. The sun was higher now, and bright. "I was a coward. I th-thought it would be easier to let—let the law do it." She opened her eyes, and now did meet his gaze, her eyes reddened but clear. "I can't let it happen this way, even if I hadn't given my word."

Roger understood that; he felt the terror of the tide coming in, that inexorable creep of water, rising in his bones. It would be nearly nine hours before the water reached Bonnet's chin; he was a tall man.

"I'll do it," he said very firmly.

She made a small attempt at a smile, but abandoned it.

"No," she said. "You won't." She looked—and sounded—absolutely drained; neither of them had slept much the night before. But she also sounded determined, and he recognized Jamie Fraser's stubborn blood.

Well, what the hell—he had some of that blood, too.

"I told ye," he said. "What your father said, that time. *'It is myself who kills for her.'* If it has to be done"—and he was obliged to agree with her; he couldn't stand it, either—"then I'll do it."

She was getting a grip on herself. She wiped her face with a fold of her skirt, and took a deep breath before meeting his eyes again. Hers were deep and vivid blue, much darker than the sky.

"You told me. And you told me why he said that, too—what he said to Arch Bug: *'There is a vow upon her.'* She's a doctor; she doesn't kill people."

The hell she doesn't, Roger thought, but better judgment prevented his saying so. Before he could think of something more tactful, she went on, placing her hands flat on his chest.

"You have one, too," she said. That stopped him cold.

"No, I haven't."

"Oh, yes, you do." She was quietly emphatic. "Maybe it isn't official yet—but it doesn't need to be. Maybe it doesn't even have words, the vow that you took—but you did it, and I know it."

He couldn't deny it, and was moved that she *did* know it.

"Aye, well . . ." He put his hands over hers, clasping her long, strong fingers. "And I made one to you, too, when I told ye. I said I would never put God before my—my love for you." Love. He couldn't believe that he was discussing such a thing in terms of love. And yet, he had the queerest feeling that that was exactly how she saw it.

"I don't have that sort of vow," she said firmly, and pulled her hands out of his. "And I gave my word."

She had gone with Jamie after dark the night before, to the place where the pirate was being held. Roger had no idea what sort of bribery or force of personality had been employed, but they had been admitted. Jamie had brought her back to their room very late, white-faced, with a sheaf of papers that she handed over to her father. Affidavits, she said; sworn statements of Stephen Bonnet's business dealings with various merchants up and down the coast.

Roger had given Jamie a murderous look, and got the same back, with interest. *This is war,* Fraser's narrowed eyes had said. *And I will use any weapon I can.* But all he had said was, "Good night, then, *a nighean,*" and touched her hair with tenderness before departing.

Brianna had sat down with Mandy and nursed her, eyes closed, refusing to speak. After a time, her face eased from its white, strained lines, and she burped the baby and laid her sleeping in her basket. Then she came to bed, and made love to him with a silent fierceness that surprised him. But not as much as she surprised him now.

"And there's one other thing," she said, sober and slightly sad. "I'm the only person in the world for whom this isn't murder."

With that, she turned and walked away fast, toward the inn where Mandy waited to be fed. Out on the mudflats, he could still hear the sound of excited voices, raucous as gulls.

At two o'clock in the afternoon, Roger helped his wife into a small rowboat, tied to the quay near the row of warehouses. The tide had been coming in all day; the water was more than five feet deep. Out in the midst of the shining gray stood the cluster of mooring posts—and the small dark head of the pirate.

Brianna was remote as a pagan statue, her face expressionless.

She lifted her skirts to step into the boat, and sat down, the weight in her pocket clunking against the wooden slat as she did so.

Roger took up the oars and rowed, heading toward the posts. They would arouse no particular interest; boats had been going out ever since noon, carrying sightseers who wished to look upon the condemned man's face, shout taunts, or clip a strand of his hair for a souvenir.

He couldn't see where he was going; Brianna directed him left or right with a silent tilt of her head. She could see; she sat straight and tall, her right hand hidden in her skirt.

Then she lifted her left hand suddenly, and Roger lay on the oars, digging with one to slew the tiny craft around.

Bonnet's lips were cracked, his face chapped and crusted with salt, his lids so reddened that he could barely open his eyes. But his head lifted as they drew near, and Roger saw a man ravished, helpless and dreading a coming embrace—so much that he half welcomes its seductive touch, yielding his flesh to cold fingers and the overwhelming kiss that steals his breath.

"Ye've left it late enough, darlin'," he said to Brianna, and the cracked lips parted in a grin that split them and left blood on his teeth. "I knew ye'd come, though."

Roger paddled with one oar, working the boat close, then closer. He was looking over his shoulder when Brianna drew the gilt-handled pistol from her pocket, and put the barrel to Stephen Bonnet's ear.

"Go with God, Stephen," she said clearly, in Gaelic, and pulled the trigger. Then she dropped the gun into the water and turned round to face her husband.

"Take us home," she said.

118

Regret

L ord John stepped into his room at the inn, and was surprised—astonished, in fact—to discover that he had a visitor.

"John." Jamie Fraser turned from the window, and gave him a
small smile.

"Jamie." He returned it, trying to control the sudden sense of
elation he felt. He had used Jamie Fraser's Christian name perhaps three times in the last twenty-five years; the intimacy of it
was exhilarating, but he mustn't let it show.

"Will I order us refreshment?" he asked politely. Jamie had not
moved from the window; he glanced out, then back at John and
shook his head, still smiling faintly.

"I thank ye, no. We are enemies, are we not?"

"We find ourselves regrettably upon opposing sides of what I
trust will be a short-lived conflict," Lord John corrected.

Fraser looked down at him, with an odd, regretful sort of expression.

"Not short," he said. "But regrettable, aye."

"Indeed." Lord John cleared his throat, and moved to the window, careful not to brush against his visitor. He looked out, and
saw the likely reason for Fraser's visit.

"Ah," he said, seeing Brianna Fraser MacKenzie on the
wooden sidewalk below. "Oh!" he said, in a different tone. For
William Clarence Henry George Ransom, ninth Earl of
Ellesmere, had just come out of the inn and bowed to her.

"Sweet Jesus," he said, apprehension making his scalp prickle.
"Will she tell him?"

Fraser shook his head, his eyes on the two young people below.

"She will not," he said quietly. "She gave me her word."

Relief coursed through his veins like water.

"Thank you," he said. Fraser shrugged slightly, dismissing it. It was, after all, what he desired, as well—or so Lord John assumed.

The two of them were talking together—William said something and Brianna laughed, throwing back her hair. Jamie watched in fascination. Dear God, they were alike! The small tricks of expression, of posture, of gesture . . . It must be apparent to the most casual observer. In fact, he saw a couple pass them and the woman smile, pleased at the sight of the handsome matched pair.

"She will not tell him," Lord John repeated, somewhat dismayed by the sight. "But she displays herself to him. Will he not—but no. I don't suppose he will."

"I hope not," Jamie said, eyes still fixed on them. "But if he does—he still will not *know*. And she insisted she must see him once more—that was the price of her silence."

John nodded, silent. Brianna's husband was coming now, their little boy held by one hand, his hair as vivid as his mother's in the bright summer sun. He held a baby in the crook of his arm— Brianna took it from him, turning back the blanket to display the child to William, who inspected it with every indication of politeness.

He realized suddenly that every fragment of Fraser's being was focused on the scene outside. Of course; he had not seen Willie since the boy was twelve. And to see the two together—his daughter and the son he could never speak to or acknowledge. He would have touched Fraser, put a hand on his arm in sympathy, but knowing the probable effect of his touch, forbore to do it.

"I have come," Fraser said suddenly, "to ask a favor of you."

"I am your servant, sir," Lord John said, terribly pleased, but taking refuge in formality.

"Not for myself," Fraser said with a glance at him. "For Brianna."

"My pleasure will be the greater," John assured him. "I am exceeding fond of your daughter, her temperamental resemblances to her sire notwithstanding."

The corner of Fraser's mouth lifted, and he returned his gaze to the scene below.

"Indeed," he said. "Well, then. I canna tell ye why I require this—but I need a jewel."

"A jewel?" Lord John's voice sounded blank, even to his own ears. "What sort of jewel?"

"Any sort." Fraser shrugged, impatient. "It doesna matter—so long as it should be some precious gem. I once gave ye such a stone—" His mouth twitched at that; he had handed over the stone, a sapphire, under duress, as a prisoner of the Crown. "Though I dinna suppose ye'd have that by ye, still."

In point of fact, he did. That particular sapphire had traveled with him for the last twenty-five years, and was at this moment in the pocket of his waistcoat.

He glanced at his left hand, which bore a broad gold band, set with a brilliant, faceted sapphire. Hector's ring. Given to him by his first lover at the age of sixteen. Hector had died at Culloden—the day after John had met James Fraser, in the dark of a Scottish mountain pass.

Without hesitation, but with some difficulty—the ring had been worn a long time, and had sunk a little way into the flesh of his finger—he twisted it off and dropped it into Jamie's hand.

Fraser's brows rose in astonishment.

"This? Are ye sur—"

"Take it." He reached out then, and closed Jamie's fingers around it with his own. The contact was fleeting, but his hand tingled, and he closed his own fist, hoping to keep the sensation.

"Thank you," Jamie said again, quietly.

"It is—my very great pleasure." The party below was breaking up—Brianna was taking her leave, the baby held in her arms, her husband and son already halfway down the walk. William bowed, hat off, the shape of his chestnut head so perfectly echoing that of the red—

Suddenly, Lord John could not bear to see them part. He wished to keep that, too—the sight of them together. He closed his eyes and stood, hands on the sill, feeling the movement of the breeze past his face. Something touched his shoulder, very briefly, and he felt a sense of movement in the air beside him.

When he opened his eyes again, all three of them were gone.

119

Loth to Depart

September 1776

Roger was laying the last of the water pipes when Aidan and Jemmy popped up beside him, sudden as a pair of jack-in-the-boxes.

"Daddy, Daddy, Bobby's here!"

"What, Bobby Higgins?" Roger straightened up, feeling his back muscles protest, and looked toward the Big House, but saw no sign of a horse. "Where is he?"

"He went up to the graveyard," Aidan said, looking important. "D'ye think he's gone to look for the ghost?"

"I doubt it," Roger said calmly. "What ghost?"

"Malva Christie's," Aidan said promptly. "She walks. Everybody says so." He spoke bravely, but wrapped his arms about himself. Jemmy, who plainly hadn't heard that bit of news before, looked wide-eyed.

"Why does she walk? Where's she going?"

"Because she was murrrrderrred, silly," Aidan said. "Folk what are murdered always walk. They're lookin' for the one who killed them."

"Nonsense," Roger said firmly, seeing the uneasy look on Jemmy's face. Jem had known Malva Christie was dead, of course; he'd gone to her funeral, along with all the other children on the Ridge. But he and Brianna had simply told the boy that Malva had died, not that she had been murdered.

Well, Roger thought grimly, little hope of keeping something like that secret. He hoped Jem wouldn't have nightmares.

"Malva's not walking about looking for anyone," he said, with as much conviction as he could infuse into his voice. "Her soul is in heaven with Jesus, where she's happy and peaceful—and her body . . . well, when people die, they don't need their bodies anymore, and so we bury them, and there they stay, all tidy in their graves, until the Last Day."

Aidan looked patently unconvinced by this.

"Joey McLaughlin saw her, two weeks ago Friday," he said, bobbing up and down on his toes. "A-flittin' through the wood, he said, all dressed in black—and howlin' most mournful!"

Jemmy was beginning to look truly upset. Roger laid down the spade, and picked Jem up in his arms.

"I expect Joey McLaughlin was a bit the worse for a dram too much," he said. Both boys were entirely familiar with the concept of drunkenness. "If it was flitting through the wood howling, it was most likely Rollo he saw. Come on, though, we'll go find Bobby, and ye'll see Malva's grave for yourselves."

He put out a hand to Aidan, who took it happily and chattered like a magpie all the way up the hill.

And what was Aidan going to do, when he left? he wondered. The idea of leaving, at first so abrupt as to seem completely unreal, unthinkable, had been filtering into his consciousness, day by day. As he worked at the chores, dug the trenches for Brianna's water pipes, carried hay, chopped wood, he would try to think: "Not much longer." And yet it seemed impossible that one day he would not be on the Ridge, would not push open the door to the cabin and find Brianna involved in some fiendish experiment on the kitchen table, Jem and Aidan madly vrooming around her feet.

The feeling of unreality was even more pronounced when he preached of a Sunday or went round as minister—if yet without portfolio—to visit the sick or counsel the troubled. Looking into all those faces—attentive, excited, bored, dour, or preoccupied—he simply couldn't believe that he meant to go, callously to abandon them all. How would he tell them? he wondered, with a sort of anguish at the thought. Especially the ones he felt most responsible for—Aidan and his mother.

He'd prayed about it, looking for strength, for guidance.

And yet . . . and yet the vision of Amanda's tiny blue fingernails, the faint wheeze of her breathing, never left him. And the looming stones by the creek on Ocracoke seemed to grow nearer, more solid, day by day.

Bobby Higgins was indeed in the graveyard, his horse tethered under the pines. He was sitting by Malva's grave, head bowed in contemplation, though he looked up at once when Roger and the boys appeared. He looked pale and somber, but scrambled to his feet and shook Roger's hand.

"I'm glad to see ye back, Bobby. Here, you lot go and play, aye?" He set Jemmy down, and was pleased to see that after one suspicious glance at Malva's grave—adorned with a wilted bunch of wildflowers—Jemmy went off quite happily with Aidan to hunt for squirrels and chipmunks in the wood.

"I—er—wasn't expecting to see you again," he added a little awkwardly. Bobby looked down, slowly dusting pine needles from his breeches.

"Well, zur . . . the fact of the matter is, I've come to stay. If so be as that's agreeable," he added hastily.

"To stay? But—of course it's fine," Roger said, recovering from his surprise. "Have you—that is—you've not had a falling-out with his Lordship, I hope?"

Bobby looked astonished at the thought, and shook his head decidedly.

"Oh, no, zur! His Lordship's been proper kind to me, ever since he took me on." He hesitated, biting his lower lip. "It's only—well, ye see, zur, there's a deal of folk what come to stay with his Lordship these days. Politicals, and—and army folk."

Despite himself, he touched the brand on his cheek, which had faded now to a pinkish scar but was still apparent—and always would be. Roger understood.

"You weren't comfortable there any longer, I suppose?"

"That's it, zur." Bobby gave him a grateful look. "Time was, 'twas just his Lordship and me and Manoke the cook. Sometimes a guest would come for dinner or to stay a few days, but 'twas all easy and what ye might call simple. When I went for to run messages or errands for his Lordship, folk would stare, but only for the first time or two; after that, they'd be used to this"—he touched his face again—"and it was all right. But now . . ." He trailed off unhappily, leaving Roger to imagine the probable response of British army officers, starched, polished, and either openly disapproving of this blot on the service—or painfully polite.

"His Lordship saw the difficulty; he's good that way. And he said as how he would miss me, but if I chose to seek my fortune elsewhere, he would give me ten pounds and his best wishes."

Roger whistled respectfully. Ten pounds was a very respectable sum. Not a fortune, but quite enough to set Bobby on his road.

"Very nice," he said. "Did he know ye meant to come here?"

Bobby shook his head.

"I wasn't sure myself," he admitted. "Once, I should—" He cut himself off abruptly, with a glance at Malva's grave, then turned back to Roger, clearing his throat.

"I thought I best talk to Mr. Fraser, before I was to make up my mind. Could be there's naught for me here any longer, either." This was phrased as a statement, but the question was clear. Everyone on the Ridge knew Bobby and accepted him; that wasn't the difficulty. But with Lizzie married and Malva gone . . . Bobby wanted a wife.

"Oh . . . I think ye might find yourself welcome," Roger said with a thoughtful look at Aidan, hanging upside down by his knees from a tree branch, while Jemmy pegged pinecones at him. A most peculiar feeling went through him—something between gratitude and jealousy—but he pushed the latter feeling firmly down.

"Aidan!" he shouted. "Jem! Time to go!" And turned casually back to Bobby, saying, "I think ye'll maybe not have met Aidan's mother, Amy McCallum—a young widow, aye, with a house and a bit of land. She's come to work at the Big House; if ye'll come sit down to supper there . . ."

"I've thought of it now and then," Jamie admitted. "Wondered, ye ken? What if I could? How would it be?"

He glanced at Brianna, smiling, but a little helpless, and shrugged.

"What d'ye think, lass? What should I do there? How would it be?"

"Well, it—" she began, and stopped, trying to envision him in that world—behind the wheel of a car? Going to an office, in a three-piece suit? That idea was so ludicrous, she laughed. Or sitting in a darkened theater, watching Godzilla films with Jem and Roger?

"What's Jamie spelled backward?" she asked.

"Eimaj, I suppose," he replied, bewildered. "Why?"

"I think you'd do fine," she said, smiling. "Never mind.

You'd—well, I suppose you could . . . publish newspapers. The printing presses are bigger and faster, and it takes a lot more people to gather the news, but otherwise—I don't think it's so different then from what it is now. You know how to do that."

He nodded, a crease of concentration forming between the thick brows that were so like hers.

"I suppose so," he said a little dubiously. "Could I be a farmer, d'ye think? Surely folk still eat; someone must feed them."

"You could." She looked round, taking fresh note of all the homely details of the place: the chickens scratching peaceably in the dirt; the soft, weathered boards of the stable; the thrown-up dirt near the foundation of the house where the white pig had burrowed in. "There are people then who still farm just this way; small places, way up in the mountains. It's a hard life—" She saw him smile, and laughed in return. "All right, it's not any harder than it is now—but it's a lot easier in the cities."

She paused, thinking.

"You wouldn't have to fight," she said finally.

He seemed surprised at that.

"No? But ye did say there are wars."

"There certainly are," she said, needles of ice piercing her belly, as the images pierced her mind: fields of poppies, fields of white crosses—a man on fire, a naked child running with burned skin, the contorted face of a man in the instant before the bullet entered his brain. "But—but then it's only the young men who fight. And not all of them; only some."

"Mmphm." He thought for a bit, his brow furrowed, then looked up searching her face.

"This world of yours, this America," he said finally, matter-of-factly. "The freedom that ye go to. There will be a fearful price to be paid. Will it be worth it, do ye think?"

It was her turn then to be silent and think. At last she put her hand on his arm—solid, warm, steady as iron.

"Almost nothing would be worth losing you," she whispered. "But maybe that comes close."

As the world turns toward winter and the nights grow long, people begin to wake in the dark. Lying in bed too long cramps the limbs, and dreams dreamt too long turn inward on themselves, grotesque as a Mandarin's fingernails. By and large, the human body isn't adapted for more than seven or eight hours' sleep—but what happens when the nights are longer than that?

What happens is the second sleep. You fall asleep from tiredness, soon after dark—but then wake again, rising toward the surface of your dreams like a trout coming up to feed. And should your sleeping partner also wake then—and people who have slept together for a good many years know at once when each other wakes—you have a small, private place to share, deep in the night. A place in which to rise, to stretch, to bring a juicy apple back to bed, to share slice by slice, fingers brushing lips. To have the luxury of conversation, uninterrupted by the business of the day. To make love slowly in the light of an autumn moon.

And then, to lie close, and let a lover's dreams caress your skin as you begin to sink once more beneath the waves of consciousness, blissful in the knowledge that dawn is far off—that's second sleep.

I came very slowly to the surface of my first sleep, to find that the highly erotic dream I had been having had some basis in reality.

"I'd never thought myself the sort who'd molest a corpse, Sassenach." Jamie's voice tickled the tender flesh below my ear, murmuring. "But I will say the notion has more appeal than I'd thought."

I wasn't sufficiently coherent as to respond to this, but thrust my hips back toward him in a fashion that he seemed to find as eloquent an invitation as one written in calligraphy on parchment. He took a deep breath, a firm grip on my buttocks, and brought me to an awakening that could be called rude in several senses of the word.

I squirmed like a worm impaled on a fish-hook, making small urgent noises that he interpreted correctly, rolling me onto my face and proceeding to leave me in no doubt that I was not merely alive and awake, but functioning.

I emerged at length from a nest of flattened pillows, damp, gasping, quivering in every engorged and slippery nerve-ending, and thoroughly awake.

"What brought that on?" I inquired. He hadn't pulled away; we lay still joined, washed in the light of a big golden half-moon, riding low in the sky above the chestnut trees. He made a small sound, partly amusement, partly dismay.

"I canna look at ye asleep without wanting to wake ye, Sassenach." His hand cupped my breast, gently now. "I suppose I find myself lonely without ye."

There was an odd note in his voice, and I turned my head toward him, but couldn't see him in the dark behind me. Instead, I put back a hand and touched the leg still wrapped halfway over mine. Even relaxed, it was hard, the long groove of the muscle graceful under my fingers.

"I'm here," I said, and his arm tightened suddenly round me.

I heard the breath catch in his throat, and my hand tightened on his thigh.

"What is it?" I said.

He drew breath, but didn't answer at once. I felt him draw back a little, and fumble under the pillow. Then his hand came round me again, but this time seeking the hand that lay on his leg. His fingers curled into mine, and I felt a small, hard, roundish object thrust into my hand.

I heard him swallow.

The stone, whatever it was, seemed slightly warm to the touch. I ran a thumb slowly over it; a raw stone of some kind, but big, the size of one of my finger-joints.

"Jamie . . ." I said, feeling my throat close.

"I love you," he said, so softly that I barely heard him, close as we were.

I lay still for a moment, feeling the stone grow warmer in the palm of my hand. Surely it was imagination that made it seem to throb in time with my heart. Where on earth had he gotten it?

Then I moved—not suddenly, but with deliberation, my body sliding slowly free of his. I rose, feeling light-headed, and crossed the room. Pushed open the window to feel the sharp touch of the autumn wind on my naked bed-warm skin, and drawing back my arm, hurled the tiny object into the night.

Then I came back to bed, saw his hair a dark mass on the pillow, and the shine of his eyes in the moonlight.

"I love you," I whispered, and slid under the sheet beside him, putting my arms around him, hugging him close, warmer than the stone—so much warmer—and his heart beat with mine.

"I'm none so brave as I was before, ken?" he said very softly. "Not brave enough to live without ye anymore."

But brave enough to try.

I drew his head down to me, stroking the tumble of his hair, coarse and smooth at once, live beneath my fingers.

"Lay your head, man," I said softly. "It's a long time 'ti dawn."

120

If Only for Myself

The sky was a flat, leaden color, threatening rain, and the wind gusted through the palmettos, rattling the leaves like sabers. Down in the depths of the tidal forest, the four stones loomed beside the creek.

"I am the wife of the laird of Balnain," Brianna whispered, next to me. "The faeries have stolen me over again." She was white to the lips, Amanda clutched close to her breast.

We had made our farewells—we had been saying farewell, I thought, since the day I pressed the stethoscope to Mandy's heart. But Brianna turned and flung herself—baby and all—at Jamie, who pressed her so tight against his heart, I thought one of them must break.

Then she was flying at me, a cloud of cloak and loosened hair, and her face was cold against mine, her tears and mine mingling on my skin.

"I love you, Mama! I love you!" she said in desperation, then turned and, without looking back, began to walk the pattern

Donner had described, quietly chanting under her breath. A circle right, between two stones, a circle left, and back through the center—and then to the left of the largest stone.

I had been expecting it; when she began to walk the pattern, I had run away from the stones, stopping at what I thought a safe distance. It wasn't. The sound of them—a roar, this time, instead of a shriek—thundered through me, stopping my breath and nearly my heart. Pain froze in a band round my chest and I dropped to my knees, swaying and helpless.

They were gone. I could see Jamie and Roger running to check—terrified of finding bodies, at once desolate and elated to find none. I couldn't see well—my vision swam, flickering in and out—but didn't need to. I knew they were gone, from the hole in my heart.

"Two down," Roger whispered. His voice was no more than a faint rasp, and he cleared his throat, hard. "Jeremiah." He looked down at Jem, who blinked and sniffed, and drew himself up tall at the sound of his formal name.

"Ye ken what we're about now, aye?" Jemmy nodded, though he flicked a scared glance toward the towering stone where his mother and his baby sister had just vanished. He swallowed hard, and wiped the tears off his cheeks.

"Well, then." Roger reached out a hand and rested it gently on Jemmy's head. "Know this, *mo mac*—I shall love ye all my life, and never forget ye. But this is a terrible thing we're doing, and ye need not come with me. Ye can stay with your grandda and grannie Claire; it will be all right."

"Won't I—won't I see Mama again?" Jemmy's eyes were huge, and he couldn't keep from looking at the stone.

"I don't know," Roger said, and I could see the tears he was fighting himself, and hear them in his thickened voice. He didn't know whether he would ever see Brianna again himself, or baby Mandy. "Probably . . . probably not."

Jamie looked down at Jem, who was clinging to his hand, looking back and forth between father and grandfather, confusion, fright, and longing in his face.

"If one day, *a bhailach*," Jamie said conversationally, "ye should meet a verra large mouse named Michael—ye'll tell him your grandsire sends his regards." He opened his hand, then, letting go, and nodded toward Roger.

Jem stood staring for a moment, then dug in his feet and sprinted toward Roger, sand spurting from under his shoes. He leaped into his father's arms, clutching him around the neck, and with a final glance backward, Roger turned and stepped behind the stone, and the inside of my head exploded in fire.

Unimaginable time later, I came slowly back, coming down from the clouds in fragments, like hailstones. And found myself lying with my head in Jamie's lap. And heard him saying softly, to himself or to me, "For your sake, I will continue—though for mine alone . . . I would not."

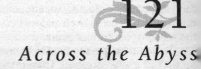

121

Across the Abyss

Three nights later, I woke from a restless sleep in an inn in Wilmington, my throat parched as the salt bacon I had eaten in the dinner stew. Sitting up to find water, I found that I was alone—the moonlight through the window shone white on the vacant pillow beside me.

I found Jamie outside, behind the inn, his nightshirt a pale blotch in the darkness of the innyard. He was sitting on the ground with his back against a chopping block, arms wrapped about his knees.

He didn't speak as I came toward him, but turned his head, body shifting in a silent welcome. I sat down on the chopping block behind him, and he leaned his head back against my thigh, with a long, deep sigh.

"Couldn't sleep?" I touched him gently, smoothing back the hair from his face. He slept with it unbound, and it fell thick and wild about his shoulders, tangled from bed.

"Nay, I slept," he said quietly. His eyes were open, looking up at the great gold moon, three-quarters full over the aspens near the inn. "I had a dream."

"A nightmare?" He had them seldom anymore, but they did come sometimes: the bloody memories of Culloden, of futile death and slaughter; prison dreams of hunger and confinement—and sometimes, very rarely, Jack Randall returned to him in sleep, with loving cruelty. Such dreams would always drive him from his bed to walk to and fro for hours, until exhaustion cleansed him of their visions. But he had not dreamed that way since Moore's Creek Bridge.

"No," he said, sounding half-surprised. "Not at all. I dreamed of her—of our lassie—and the bairns."

My heart gave an odd little hop, the consequence of startlement and what might almost have been envy.

"You dreamed about Brianna and the children? What happened?"

He smiled, face tranquil and abstracted in the moonlight, as though he still saw some part of the dream before him.

"It is all right," he said. "They are safe. I saw them in a town—it seemed like Inverness, but it was different, somehow. They walked up the step of a house—Roger Mac was with them," he added, offhand. "They knocked at the door, and a wee brown-haired woman opened to them. She laughed wi' joy to see them, and brought them in, and they went down a hallway, wi' strange things like bowls hanging from the ceiling.

"Then they were in a room, wi' sofas and chairs, and the room had great windows all down one wall, from the floor to the ceiling, and the afternoon sun was streaming in, setting Brianna's hair to fire, and makin' wee Mandy cry when it got in her eyes."

"Did . . . did any of them call the brown-haired woman by name?" I asked, my heart beating in a queer, fast way.

He frowned, moonlight making a cross of light over nose and brows.

"Aye, they did," he said. "I canna just—oh, aye; Roger Mac called her Fiona."

"Did he?" I said. My hands rested on his shoulder, and my mouth was a hundred times drier than it had been when I woke up. The night was chilly, but not enough to account for the temperature of my hands.

I had told Jamie any amount of things about my own time over the years of our marriage. About trains and planes and automobiles and wars and indoor plumbing. But I was nearly sure that I had never told him what the study looked like in the manse where Roger had grown up with his adoptive father.

The room with the window wall, made to accommodate the Reverend's painting hobby. The manse with its long hallway furnished with old-fashioned light fixtures, shaped like hanging bowls. And I knew I had never told him about the Reverend's last housekeeper, a girl with dark, curly hair, called Fiona.

"Were they happy?" I asked at last, very quietly.

"Aye. Brianna and the lad—they had some shadows to their faces, but I could see they were glad nonetheless. They all sat down to eat—Brianna and her lad close together, leaning on each other—and wee Jem stuffed his face wi' cakes and cream." He smiled at the picture, teeth a brief gleam in the darkness.

"Oh—at the last, just before I woke . . . wee Jem was messin' about, picking things up and putting them down as he does. There was a . . . thing . . on the table. I couldna say what it was; I've never seen the like."

He held his hands about six inches apart, frowning at them. "It was maybe this wide, and just a bit longer—something like a box, maybe, only sort of . . . humped."

"Humped?" I said, puzzled as to what this could be.

"Aye, and it had a thing on top like a wee club, only wi' a knob to each end, and the club was tied to the box wi' a sort of black cord, curled up on itself like a piggie's tail. Jem saw it, and he reached out his hand, and said, 'I want to talk to Grandda.' And then I woke."

He leaned his head back farther, so as to look up into my face.

"Would ye ken what a thing like that might be, Sassenach? It was like nothing I've ever seen."

The autumn wind came rustling down from the hill, dry leaves hurrying in its wake, quick and light as the footsteps of a ghost, and I felt the hair rise on nape and forearms.

"Yes, I know," I said. "I've told you about them, I know." I didn't think, though, that I had ever described one to him, in more than general terms. I cleared my throat.

"It's called a telephone."

122

The Guardian

It was November; there were no flowers. But the holly bushes gleamed dark green, and the berries had begun to ripen. I cut a small bunch, careful of the prickles, added a tender branch of spruce for fragrance, and climbed the steep trail to the tiny graveyard.

I went every week, to leave some small token on Malva's grave, and say a prayer. She and her child had not been buried with a cairn—her father hadn't wanted such a pagan custom—but people came and left pebbles there by way of remembrance. It gave me some small comfort to see them; there were others who remembered her.

I stopped abruptly at the head of the trail; someone was kneeling by her grave—a young man. I caught the murmur of his voice, low and conversational, and would have turned about to go, save that he raised his head, and the wind caught his hair, short and tufted, like an owl's feathers. Allan Christie.

He saw me, too, and stiffened. There was nothing to do but go and speak to him, though, and so I went.

"Mr. Christie," I said, the words feeling strange in my mouth. That was what I had called his father. "I'm sorry for your loss."

He stared up at me blankly; then some sort of awareness seemed to stir in his eyes. Gray eyes, rimmed with black lashes, so much like those of his father and sister. Bloodshot with weeping and lack of sleep, judging from the shocking smudges under them.

"Aye," he said. "My loss. Aye."

I stepped around him to lay down my evergreen bouquet, and with a small spurt of alarm, saw that there was a pistol on the ground beside him, cocked and primed.

"Where have you been?" I said as casually as possible, under the circumstances. "We've missed you."

He shrugged, as though it really didn't matter where he'd been—perhaps it didn't. He wasn't looking at me anymore, but at the stone we'd placed at the head of her grave.

"Places," he said vaguely. "But I had to come back." He turned away a little, plainly indicating that he wanted me to leave. Instead, I pulled up my skirts and knelt gingerly beside him. I didn't *think* he'd blow his brains out in front of me. I had no idea what to do, other than to try to make him talk to me and hope that someone else would come along.

"We're glad to have you home," I said, trying for an easy, conversational note.

"Aye," he said vaguely. And again, his eyes going to the headstone, "I had to come back." His hand wandered toward the pistol, and I seized it, startling him.

"I know you loved your sister very much," I said. "It—it was a terrible shock to you, I know." What, what did one say? There were things one might say to a person contemplating suicide, I knew, but what?

"Your life has value." I'd said that to Tom Christie, who had only replied, *"If it did not, this would not matter."* But how should I convince his son of that?

"Your father loved you both," I said, wondering as I said it whether he knew what his father had done. His fingers were very cold, and I wrapped both my hands round his, trying to offer him a little warmth, hoping that the human contact would help.

"Not as I loved her," he said softly, not looking at me. "I loved her all her life, from the time she was born and they gave her me to hold. There was nay other, for either of us. Faither was gone to prison, and then my mither—ah, Mither." His lips pulled back, as though to laugh, but there was no sound.

"I know about your mother," I said. "Your father told me."

"Did he?" His head jerked up to look at me, eyes clear and hard. "Did he tell ye they took me and Malva to her execution?"

"I—no. I don't think he knew, did he?" My stomach clenched.

"He did. I told him, later, when he sent for us, brought us here. He said that was good, we'd seen with our own eyes the ends of wickedness. He bade me remember the lesson—and so I did," he added more quietly.

"How—how old were you?" I asked, horrified.

"Ten. Malva was nay more than two; she'd no idea what was happening. She cried out for her Mam when they brought Mither out to the hangsman, and kicked and screamed, reaching out for her."

He swallowed, and turned his head away.

"I tried to take her, to push her head into my bosom, so she shouldna see—but they wouldna let me have her. They held her wee head and made her watch, and Auntie Darla saying in her ear that this was what happened to witches, and pinching her legs 'til she shrieked. We lived with Auntie Darla for six years after that," he said, his face remote.

"She wasna best pleased about it, but she said she kent her Christian duty. The auld besom barely fed us, and 'twas me took care of Malva."

He was silent for a bit, and so was I, thinking the best—the only—thing I could offer him now was the chance to speak. He pulled his hand from mine, leaned over, and touched the gravestone. It was no more than a lump of granite, but someone had gone to the trouble to carve her name on it—only the one word, MALVA, in crude block letters. It reminded me of the memorials that dotted Culloden, the clanstones, each with a single name.

"She was perfect," he whispered. His finger traced its way over the stone, delicate, as though he touched her flesh. "So perfect. Her wee privates looked like a flower's bud, and her skin sae fresh and soft. . . ."

A sense of coldness grew in the pit of my stomach. Did he mean . . . yes, of course he did. A sense of inevitable despair began to grow within me.

"She was mine," he said, and looking up to see my eye upon him, repeated it more loudly. "She was mine!"

He looked down, then, at the grave, and his mouth turned in upon itself, in grief and anger.

"The auld man never knew—never guessed what we were to each other."

Didn't he? I thought. Tom Christie might have confessed to the crime to save one he loved—but he loved more than one. Having lost a daughter—or rather, a niece—would he not do all he could to save the son who was the last remnant of his blood?

"You killed her," I said quietly. I was in no doubt, and he showed no surprise.

"He would ha' sold her away, given her to some clod of a farmer." Allan's fist clenched on his thigh. "I thought of that, as she grew older, and sometimes when I would lie with her, I couldna bear the thought, and would slap her face, only from the rage of thinking of it."

He drew a deep, ragged breath.

"It wasna her fault, none of it. But I thought it was. And then I caught her wi' that soldier, and again, wi' filthy wee Henderson. I beat her for it, but she cried out that she couldna help it—she was with child."

"Yours?"

He nodded, slowly.

"I never thought of it. I should, of course. But I never did. She was always wee Malva, see, a bittie wee lass. I saw her breasts swell, aye, and the hair come out to mar her sweet flesh—but I just never thought . . ."

He shook his head, unable to deal with the thought, even now.

"She said she must marry—and there must be reason for her husband to think the child his, whoever she wed. If she couldna make the soldier wed her, then it must be another. So she took as many lovers as she might, quickly.

"I put a stop to that, though," he assured me, a faintly nauseating tone of self-righteousness in his voice. "I told her I wouldna have it—I would think of another way."

"And so you put her up to saying the child was Jamie's." My horror at the story and my anger at what he had done to us was subsumed by a flood of sorrow. *Oh, Malva,* I thought in despair. *Oh, my darling Malva. Why didn't you tell me?* But of course she wouldn't have told me. Her only confidant was Allan.

He nodded, and reached out to touch the stone again. A gust of wind quivered through the holly, stirring the stiff leaves.

"It would explain the bairn, see, but she wouldna have to wed anyone. I thought—Himself would give her money to go away, and I would go with her. We could go to Canada, perhaps, or to the Indies." His voice sounded dreamy, as though he envisioned some idyllic life, where no one knew.

"But why did you kill her?" I burst out. "What made you *do* that?" The sorrow and the senselessness were overwhelming; I clenched my hands in my apron, not to batter him.

"I had to," he said heavily. "She said she couldna go through with it." He blinked, looking down, and I saw that his eyes were heavy with tears.

"She said—she loved you," he said, low-voiced and thick. "She couldna hurt ye so. She meant to tell the truth. No matter what I said to her, she just kept saying that—she loved ye, and she'd tell."

He closed his eyes, shoulders slumping. Two tears ran down his cheeks.

"Why, hinny?" he cried, crossing his arms over his belly in a spasm of grief. "Why did ye make me do it? Ye shouldna have loved anyone but me."

He sobbed then, like a child, and curled into himself, weeping. I was weeping, too, for the loss and the pointlessness, for the utter, terrible *waste* of it all. But I reached out and took the gun from the ground. Hands shaking, I dumped out the priming pan, and shook the ball from the barrel, then put the pistol in the pocket of my apron.

"Leave," I said, my voice half-choked. "Go away again, Allan. There are too many people dead."

He was too grief-stricken to hear me; I shook him by the shoulder and said it again, more strongly.

"You can't kill yourself. I forbid it, do you hear?"

"And who are you to say?" he cried, turning on me. His face was contorted with anguish. "I cannot live, I cannot!"

But Tom Christie had given up his life for his son, as well as for me; I couldn't let that sacrifice go for naught.

"You must," I said, and stood up, feeling light-headed, unsure whether my knees would hold me. "Do you hear me? You must!"

He looked up, eyes burning through the tears, but didn't speak. There was a keening whine like the hum of a mosquito, and a soft, sudden thump. He didn't change expression, but his eyes slowly died. He stayed on his knees for a moment, but bowed then forward, like a flower nodding on its stem, so I saw the arrow protruding from the center of his back. He coughed, once, sputtering blood, and fell sideways, curled on his sister's grave. His legs jerked spasmodically, grotesquely froglike. Then he lay still.

I stood stupidly staring at him for some immeasurable span of time, becoming only gradually aware that Ian had walked out of the wood and stood beside me, bow over his shoulder. Rollo nosed curiously at the body, whining.

"He's right, Auntie," Ian said quietly. "He can't."

123

Return of the Native

O ld Grannie Abernathy looked at least a hundred and two. She admitted—under pressure—to ninety-one. She was nearly blind and nearly deaf, curled up like a pretzel from osteoporosis, and with skin gone so fragile that the merest scrape tore it like paper.

"I'm nay more than a bag o' bones," she said every time I saw her, shaking a head that trembled with palsy. "But at least I've still got maist o' my teeth!"

For a wonder, she had; I thought that was the only reason she had made it this far—unlike many people half her age, she wasn't reduced to living on porridge, but could still stomach meat and greens. Perhaps it was improved nutrition that kept her going— perhaps it was mere stubbornness. Her married name was Abernathy, but she had, she confided, been born a Fraser.

Smiling at the thought, I finished wrapping the bandage about her sticklike shin. Her legs and feet had almost no flesh upon them, and felt hard and cold as wood. She'd knocked her shin against the leg of the table and taken off a strip of skin the width of a finger; such a minor injury that a younger person would think nothing of it—but her family worried over her, and had sent for me.

"It will be slow healing, but if you keep it clean—for God's sake, do *not* let her put hog fat on it!—I think it will be all right." The younger Mrs. Abernathy, known as Young Grannie—herself about seventy—gave me a sharp eye at that; like her mother-in-law, she put a good deal of faith in hog fat and turpentine as cure-alls, but nodded grudgingly. Her daughter, whose high-flown name of Arabella had been shortened to the cozier Grannie Belly, grinned at me behind Young Grannie's back. She had been less fortunate in the way of teeth—her smile showed significant gaps—but was cheerful and good-natured.

"Willie B.," she instructed a teenaged grandson, "just be steppin' doon to the root cellar, and bringing up a wee sack of turnips for Herself."

I made the usual protestations, but all parties concerned were comfortably aware of the proper protocol in such matters, and within a few minutes, I was on my way home, the richer by five pounds of turnips.

They were welcome. I had forced myself to go back to my garden in the spring after Malva's death—I had to; sentiment was all very well, but we had to eat. The subsequent disturbances of life and my prolonged absences, though, had resulted in dreadful neglect of the autumn crop. Despite Mrs. Bug's best efforts, the turnips had all succumbed to thrips and black rot.

Our supplies in general were sadly depleted. With Jamie and Ian gone so frequently, not there to harvest or hunt, and without Bree and Roger, the grain crops had been half of their usual yield, and only a pitiful single haunch of venison hung in the smoking shed. We needed nearly all the grain for our own use; there was none to trade or sell, and only a scant few bags of barleycorn sat under canvas near the malting shed—where they were likely to rot, I thought grimly, as no one had had time to see to the malting of a fresh batch before the cold weather set in.

Mrs. Bug was slowly rebuilding her flock of chickens, after a disastrous attack by a fox that got into the henhouse—but it was slow going, and we got only the occasional egg for breakfast, grudgingly spared.

On the other hand, I reflected more cheerfully, we *did* have ham. Lots of ham. Likewise, immense quantities of bacon, head-cheese, pork chops, tenderloin . . . to say nothing of suet and rendered fat.

The thought led me back to hog fat, and to the crowded, overflowingly familiar coziness of the Abernathys' cluster of cabins—and by contrast, to thought of the dreadful emptiness at the Big House.

In a place with so many people, how could the loss of only four be so important? I had to stop and lean against a tree, let the sorrow wash through me, making no attempt to stop it. I'd learned. *"Ye canna hold a ghost at bay,"* Jamie had told me. *"Let them in."*

I let them in—I could never keep them out. And took what small comfort I could in hoping—no, I didn't hope, I told myself fiercely, I *knew*—that they were not ghosts in fact. Not dead, but only . . . elsewhere.

After a few moments, the overwhelming grief began to recede, going slowly as the ebbing tide. Sometimes it uncovered treasure: small forgotten images of Jemmy's face, smeared with honey, Brianna's laughter, Roger's hands, deft with a knife, carving one of the little cars—the house was still littered with them—then leaning to spear a muffin from a passing plate. And if to look at these caused fresh pain, at least I had them, and could keep them in my heart, knowing that in the fullness of time, they would bring consolation.

I breathed, and felt the tightness in my chest and throat ease. Amanda was not the only one who might benefit from modern surgery, I thought. I couldn't tell what might be done for Roger's vocal cords, but maybe . . . and yet, his voice now was good. Full and resonant, if rough. Perhaps he would choose to keep it as it was—he'd fought for it, and earned it.

The tree I leaned against was a pine; the needles swayed softly above me, then settled, as though in agreement. I had to go; it was late in the day and the air was growing colder.

Wiping my eyes, I settled the hood of my cloak and went on. It was a long walk from the Abernathys'—I should really have ridden Clarence, but he'd come up lame the day before, and I'd let him rest. I'd have to hurry, though, if I was to reach home before dark.

I cast a wary eye upward, judging the clouds, which had that soft, uniform gray of coming snow. The air was cold and thick with moisture; when the temperature dropped at nightfall, snow would fall.

The sky was still light, but only just, as I came down past the springhouse and into the backyard. Light enough to tell me that something was wrong, though—the back door stood open.

That set off alarm bells, and I turned to run back into the woods. I turned, and ran smack into a man who had come out of the trees behind me.

"Who the hell are you?" I demanded, stepping hastily back.

"Don't worry about that, Mrs.," he said, and grabbing me by the arm, yelled toward the house, "Hey, Donner! I got her!"

Whatever Wendigo Donner been doing for the last year, it hadn't been profitable, by the looks of him. Never a natty dresser at the best of times, he was now so ragged that his coat was literally falling apart, and a slice of stringy buttock showed through a rent in his breeches. His mane of hair was greasy and matted, and he stank.

"Where are they?" he demanded hoarsely.

"Where are what?" I swung round to face his companion, who seemed in slightly better condition. "And where are my housemaid and her sons?" We were standing in the kitchen, and the hearth fire was out; Mrs. Bug hadn't come that morning, and wherever Amy and the boys were, they'd been gone for some time.

"Dunno." The man shrugged, indifferent. "Wasn't nobody to home when we came."

"Where are the jewels?" Donner grabbed at my arm, jerking me round to face him. His eyes were sunk in his head, and his grip was hot; he was burning with fever.

"I haven't got any," I said shortly. "You're ill. You should—"

"You do! I know you do! Everybody knows!"

That gave me momentary pause. Gossip being what it was, everybody likely *thought* they knew that Jamie had a small cache of jewels. Small wonder if word of this hypothetical treasure had reached Donner—and little likelihood that I could convince him otherwise. I had no choice but to try, though.

"They're gone," I said simply.

Something flickered in his eyes at that.

"How?" he said.

I raised an eyebrow in the direction of his accomplice. Did he want the man to know?

"Go find Richie and Jed," Donner said briefly to the thug, who shrugged and went out. Richie and Jed? How on earth many people had he brought? Past the first shock of seeing him, I now became aware that there were thumping feet upstairs, and the sound of cupboard doors being banged impatiently down the hall.

"My surgery! Get them out of there!" I dove for the door to the hallway, intending to perform this office myself, but Donner grabbed at my cloak to stop me.

I was bloody tired of being manhandled, and I wasn't afraid of this miserable excuse for a human being.

"Let go!" I snapped, and kicked him briskly in the kneecap to emphasize the point. He yelped, but let go; I could hear him cursing behind me as I rushed through the door and down the hall.

Papers and books had been flung out into the hallway from Jamie's office, and a puddle of ink had been poured over them. The explanation of the ink was apparent when I saw the thug rifling my surgery—he had a big blot of ink on the front of his shirt, where he had apparently sequestered the stolen pewter inkwell.

"What are you *doing*, you nitwit?" I said. The thug, a boy of sixteen or so, blinked at me, mouth open. He had one of Mr. Blogweather's perfect glass globes in his hand; at this, he grinned maliciously and let it drop to the floor, where it shattered into a spray of fragments. One of the flying shards lanced through his cheek, slicing it open; he didn't feel it, until the blood began to well. Then he put a hand to the wound, frowning in puzzlement, and bellowed in fright at the blood on his hand.

"Crap," said Donner, behind me. He put his arms around me, and dragged me after him back to the kitchen.

"Look," he said urgently, releasing me. "All I want is two. You can keep the rest. I gotta have one to pay these guys, and one to—to travel with."

"But it's true," I insisted, knowing that he wouldn't believe me. "We haven't got any. My daughter and her family—they've gone. Gone back. They used all we had. There aren't any more."

He stared at me, disbelief plain in his burning eyes.

"Yes, there are," he said positively. "There have to be. I gotta get out of here!"

"Why?"

"Never you mind. I gotta go, and quick." He swallowed, eyes darting around the kitchen, as though the gems might be sitting casually on the sideboard. "Where are they?"

A hideous crash from the surgery, followed by an outbreak of shouted curses, prevented any reply I might have made. I moved by reflex toward the door, but Donner moved in front of me.

I was infuriated at this invasion, and beginning to be alarmed. While I'd never seen any indication of violence from Donner, I wasn't so sure about the men he'd brought with him. They *might* eventually give up and leave, when it became apparent that there were in fact no gems on the premises—or they might try to beat the location of said gems out of me.

I pulled my cloak more tightly around myself and sat down on a bench, trying to think calmly.

"Look," I said to Donner. "You've taken the house apart—" A crash from upstairs shook the house, and I jumped. My God, it sounded as though they'd tipped over the wardrobe. "You've taken the house apart," I repeated, through gritted teeth, "and you haven't found anything. Wouldn't I give them to you, if I had any, to save you wrecking the place?"

"No, I don't reckon you would. I wouldn't, if I was you." He rubbed a hand across his mouth. "*You* know what's going on—the war and all." He shook his head in confusion. "I didn't know it would be this way. Swear to God, half the people I meet don't know which way is up anymore. I thought it'd be like, you know, redcoats and all, and you just keep away from anybody in a uniform, keep away from the battles, and it'd be fine. But I haven't seen a redcoat *anywhere*, and people—you know, just plain old *people*—they're shooting each other and running around burning up each other's houses. . . ."

He closed his eyes for a minute. His cheeks went from red one moment to white the next; I could see he was very ill. I could hear him, too; the breath rattled wetly in his chest, and he wheezed faintly. If he fainted, how would I get rid of his companions?

"Anyway," he said, opening his eyes. "I'm going. Going back. I don't care what things are like then; it's a hell of a lot better'n here."

"What about the Indians?" I inquired, with no more than a touch of sarcasm. "Leaving them to their own devices, are you?"

"Yeah," he said, missing the sarcasm. "Tell you the truth, I'm not so keen on Indians anymore, either." He rubbed absently at his upper chest, and I saw a large, puckered scar through a rent in his shirt.

"Man," he said, longing clear in his voice, "what I wouldn't give for a cold Bud and a baseball game on TV." Then his wandering attention snapped back to me. "So," he said in a halfway reasonable tone, "I need those diamonds. Or whatever. Hand 'em over and we'll leave."

I had been turning over various schemes for getting rid of them, to no particular avail, and was getting more uneasy by the moment. We had very little worth stealing, and from the looks of the rifled sideboard, they'd already got what there was—including, I realized, with a fresh stab of alarm, the pistols and powder. Before too much longer, they'd grow impatient.

Someone might come—Amy and the boys were likely at Brianna's cabin, which they were in process of moving into; they could come back at any moment. Someone could come looking for Jamie or myself—though the chances of that receded by the moment, with the dying light. Even if someone did, though, the effect was likely to be disastrous.

Then I heard voices on the front porch, and the stamping of feet, and leapt to my own feet, my heart in my mouth.

"Would you quit doin' that?" Donner said irritably. "You're the jumpiest twat I ever saw."

I ignored him, having recognized one of the voices. Sure enough, in the next moment, two of the thugs, brandishing pistols, shoved Jamie into the kitchen.

He was wary and disheveled, but his eyes went immediately to me, running up and down my body to assure himself that I was all right.

"I'm fine," I said briefly. "These idiots think we have gemstones, and they want them."

"So they said." He straightened himself, shrugging to settle the coat on his shoulders, and glanced at the cupboards, hanging open, and the despoiled sideboard. Even the pie hutch had been overturned, and the remains of a raisin pie lay squashed on the floor, marked with a large heelprint. "I gather they've looked."

"Look, mate," said one of the thugs, reasonably, "all we want's the swag. Just tell us where it is, and we go, no 'arm done, eh?"

Jamie rubbed the bridge of his nose, eyeing the man who'd spoken.

"I imagine my wife has told ye that we have no gems?"

"Well, she would, wouldn't she?" the thug said tolerantly. "Women, you know." He seemed to feel that now Jamie had showed up, they could get on with things in a more businesslike fashion, man-to-man.

Jamie sighed and sat down.

"Why d'ye think I've got any?" he inquired, rather mildly. "I have had, I admit—but no longer. They've been sold."

"Where's the money, then?" The second thug was obviously quite willing to settle for that, no matter what Donner thought.

"Spent," Jamie said briefly. "I'm a colonel of militia—surely ye ken that much? It's an expensive business, provisioning a militia company. Food, guns, powder, shoes—it adds up, aye? Why, the cost in shoe leather alone—and then, to say nothing of shoon for the horses! Wagons, too; ye wouldna believe the scandalous cost of wagons. . . ."

One of the thugs was frowning, but half-nodding, following this reasonable exegesis. Donner and his other companion were noticeably agitated, though.

"Shut up about the damn wagons," Donner said rudely, and bending, he snatched up one of Mrs. Bug's butcher knives from the floor. "Now, look," he said, scowling and trying to look menacing. "I've *had* it with the stalling around. You tell me where they are, or—or I'll—I'll cut her! Yeah, I'll cut her throat. Swear I will." With this, he clutched me by the shoulder and put the knife to my throat.

It had become clear to me some little time ago that Jamie *was* stalling for time, which meant that he expected something to happen. Which in turn meant he was expecting someone to come. That was reassuring, but I did think the apparent nonchalance of his demeanor in the face of my theoretically impending demise was perhaps carrying things a trifle too far.

"Oh," he said, scratching at the side of his neck. "Well, I wouldna do that, if I were you. She's the one who kens where the gems are, aye?"

"I *what*?" I cried indignantly.

"She is?" One of the other thugs brightened at that.

"Oh, aye," Jamie assured him. "Last time I went out wi' the militia, she hid them. Wouldna tell me where she'd put them."

"Wait—I thought you said you sold 'em and spent the money," Donner said, plainly confused.

"I was lying," Jamie explained, patient.

"Oh."

"But if ye're going to kill my wife, well, then, of course that alters the case."

"Oh," said Donner, looking somewhat happier. "Yeah. Exactly!"

"I believe we havena been introduced, sir," Jamie said politely, extending a hand. "I am James Fraser. And you are . . . ?"

Donner hesitated for a minute, unsure what to do with the knife in his right hand, but then shifted it awkwardly to his left and leaned forward to shake Jamie's hand briefly.

"Wendigo Donner," he said. "Okay, now we're getting somewhere."

I made a rude noise, but it was drowned by a series of crashes and the sound of breaking glass from the surgery. The lout in there must be clearing the shelves wholesale, flinging bottles and jars on the floor. I grasped Donner's hand and pulled the knife away from my throat, then sprang to my feet, in much the same state of insane fury in which I had once torched a field full of grasshoppers.

This time, it was Jamie who seized me around the middle as I darted toward the door, swinging me half off my feet.

"Let go! I'll frigging *kill* him!" I said, kicking madly.

"Well, wait just a bit about that, Sassenach," he said, low-voiced, and lugged me back to the table, where he sat down with his arms wrapped around me, holding me firmly pinned on his lap. Further sounds of depredation came down the hall—the splintering of wood and crunch of glass under a bootheel. Evidently, the young lout had given up searching for anything and was simply destroying for the fun of it.

I took a deep breath, preparatory to emitting a scream of frustration, but stopped.

"Jeez," Donner said, wrinkling his nose. "What's that smell? Somebody cut one?" He looked accusingly at me, but I paid no attention. It was ether, heavy and sickly sweet.

Jamie stiffened slightly. He knew what it was, too, and essentially what it did.

Then he took a deep breath and carefully moved me off his lap, setting me on the bench beside him. I saw his eyes go to the knife sagging in Donner's hand, and heard what his keener ears had already picked up. Someone was coming.

He moved a little forward, getting his feet under him to spring, and flicked his eyes toward the cold hearth, where a heavy Dutch oven was sitting in the ashes. I nodded, very briefly, and as the back door opened, made a lunge across the kitchen.

Donner, with unexpected swiftness, stuck out a leg and tripped me. I fell headlong and slid, fetching up against the settle with a head-ringing thump. I groaned and lay still for a few moments, eyes closed, feeling all at once that I was much too old for this sort of carry-on. I opened my eyes reluctantly, and very stiffly got to my feet, to find the kitchen now full of people.

Donner's original sidekick had returned with two others, presumably Richie and Jed, and with them, the Bugs, Murdina looking alarmed, and Arch, coldly furious.

"*A leannan!*" Mrs. Bug cried, rushing toward me. "Are ye hurt, then?"

"No, no," I said, still rather dazed. "Just let me . . . sit down for a moment." I looked at Donner, but he no longer held his knife. He had been frowning at the floor—evidently he had dropped it when he tripped me—but his head jerked up at sight of the newcomers.

"What? Did you find anything?" he asked eagerly, for both Richie and Jed were beaming with self-importance.

"Sure did," one of them assured him. "Looka here!" He was holding Mrs. Bug's workbag, and at this, he upended it and shook the contents out onto the table, where a mass of woolly knitting landed with a massive *thunk!* Eager hands pawed the wool away, revealing an eight-inch-long ingot of gold, the metal shaved away at one end, and stamped in the center with the royal French fleur-de-lis.

Stunned silence followed the appearance of this apparition. Even Jamie looked completely nonplussed.

Mrs. Bug had been pale when they came in; now she had gone the color of chalk, and her lips had disappeared. Arch's eyes went straight to Jamie's, dark and defiant.

The only person unimpressed by sight of the glowing metal was Donner.

"Well, neato-mosquito," he said. "What about the jewels? Keep your eye on the goal here, people!"

His accomplices, however, had lost interest in theoretical jewels, with solid gold actually in hand, and were simultaneously discussing the possibility of more and squabbling over who should have custody of the present ingot.

My own head was spinning: from the blow, from the sudden appearance of the ingot and its revelations regarding the Bugs—and particularly from the fumes of ether, which were getting notably stronger. No one in the kitchen had noticed, but all sound from the surgery had ceased; the young lout in there had undoubtedly passed out.

The bottle of ether had been nearly full; enough to anesthetize a dozen elephants, I thought dizzily—or a houseful of people. Already, I could see Donner struggling to keep his head upright. A few minutes more, and all the thugs would likely have subsided into a state of innocuous desuetude—but so would we.

Ether is heavier than air; the stuff would sink to the floor, where it would gradually rise in a pool around our knees. I stood up, taking a quick breath from the presumably purer air higher up. I had to get the window open.

Jamie and Arch were speaking Gaelic to each other, much too fast for me to follow, even had my head been in normal working order. Donner was frowning at them, mouth open as though he meant to tell them to stop but couldn't quite find the words.

I fumbled with the catch of the inside shutters, having to concentrate very hard in order to make my fingers work. Finally, the latch flipped free and I swung the shutter open—revealing the leering face of an unfamiliar Indian in the twilight outside the window.

I shrieked and staggered back. Next thing, the back door sprang open and a squat bearded figure rushed in, bellowing in some incomprehensible tongue, followed by Ian, who was followed by yet another strange Indian, screaming and laying about himself with something—tomahawk? club? I couldn't get my eyes to focus well enough to tell.

All was pandemonium, seen through glazed eyes. I clutched the windowsill to keep from sinking to the floor, but couldn't summon the presence of mind to open the damn window. Everyone was struggling and fighting, but the inhabitants of the kitchen were doing it in slow motion, yelling and staggering like drunks. As I watched, my mouth hanging unbecomingly open, Jamie painstakingly drew Donner's knife out from under his buttocks, brought it up in a slow, graceful arc, and buried it under Donner's breastbone.

Something flew past my ear and crashed through the window, destroying what was probably the only intact pane of glass left in the house.

I breathed in deep gulps of fresh air, trying to clear my head, and made frantic waving motions with my hands, shouting—or trying to shout—"Get out! Get out!"

Mrs. Bug was trying to do just that, crawling on hands and knees toward the half-open door. Arch hit the wall and slid slowly down beside her, face gone blank. Donner had fallen face forward over the table, his blood dripping nastily onto the floorboards, and another thug was lying in the extinct hearth, his skull crushed. Jamie was still upright, swaying, and the squat bearded figure was standing beside him, shaking his head and looking confused as the fumes began to affect him.

"What's going on?" I heard him ask.

The kitchen was nearly dark now, the figures swaying like fronds of kelp in some underwater forest.

I closed my eyes for a second. When I opened them again, Ian was saying, "Wait, I'll light a candle." He had one of Brianna's matches in his hand, the tin in the other.

"IAN!" I shrieked, and then he struck the match.

There was a soft *whoof!* noise, then a louder *whoomp!* as the ether in the surgery ignited, and suddenly we were standing in a pool of fire. For a fraction of a second, I felt nothing, and then a burst of searing heat. Jamie seized my arm and hurled me toward the door; I staggered out, fell into the blackberry bushes, and rolled through them, thrashing and flailing at my smoking skirts.

Panicked and still uncoordinated from the ether, I struggled with the strings of my apron, finally managing to rip loose the strings and wriggle out of it. My linen petticoats were singed, but not charred. I crouched panting in the dead weeds of the dooryard, unable to do anything for the moment but breathe. The smell of smoke was strong and pungent.

Mrs. Bug was on the back porch on her knees, jerking off her cap, which was on fire.

Men erupted through the back door, beating at their clothes and hair. Rollo was in the yard, barking hysterically, and on the other side of the house, I could hear the screams of frightened horses. Someone had got Arch Bug out—he was stretched at full length in the dead grass, most of his hair and eyebrows gone, but evidently still alive.

My legs were red and blistered, but I wasn't badly burned—thank God for layers of linen and cotton, which burn slowly, I thought groggily. Had I been wearing something modern like rayon, I should have gone up like a torch.

The thought made me look back toward the house. It was full dark by now, and all the windows on the lower floor were alight. Flame danced in the open door. The place looked like an immense jack-o'-lantern.

"Ye're Mistress Fraser, I suppose?" The squat, bearded person bent over me, speaking in a soft Scottish burr.

"Yes," I said, coming gradually to myself. "Who are you, and where's Jamie?"

"Here, Sassenach." Jamie stumbled out of the dark and sat down heavily beside me. He waved a hand at the Scotsman. "May I present Mr. Alexander Cameron, known more generally as Scotchee?"

"Your servant, ma'am," he said politely.

I was feeling gingerly at my hair. Clumps of it had been singed to crispy thread, but at least I still had some.

I felt, rather than saw, Jamie look up at the house. I followed the direction of his glance, and saw a dark figure at the window upstairs, framed in the dim glow from the burning downstairs. He shouted something in the incomprehensible tongue, and began throwing things out of the window.

"Who's *that*?" I asked, feeling more than slightly surreal.

"Oh." Jamie rubbed at his face. "That would be Goose."

"Of course it would," I said, nodding. "He'll be a cooked goose, if he stays in there." This struck me as wildly hilarious, and I doubled up in laughter.

Evidently, it wasn't quite as witty as I'd thought; no one else seemed to think it funny. Jamie stood up and shouted something at the dark figure, who waved nonchalantly and turned back into the room.

"There's a ladder in the barn," Jamie said calmly to Scotchee, and they moved off into the darkness.

The house burned fairly slowly for a while; there weren't a lot of easily flammable objects down below, bar the books and papers in Jamie's study. A tall figure belted out of the back door, shirt pulled up over his nose with one hand, the tail of his shirt held up with the other to form a bag.

Ian came to a stop beside me, dropped to his knees, gasping, and let down his shirttail, releasing a pile of small objects.

"That's all I could get, I'm afraid, Auntie." He coughed a few times, waving his hand in front of his face. "D'ye ken what happened?"

"It's not important," I said. The heat was becoming more intense, and I struggled to my knees. "Come on; we'll need to get Arch further away."

The effects of the ether had mostly worn off, but I was still conscious of a strong sense of unreality. I hadn't anything but cold well water with which to treat burns, but bathed Arch's neck and hands, which had been badly blistered. Mrs. Bug's hair had been singed, but she, like me, had been largely protected by her heavy skirts.

Neither she nor Arch said a word.

Amy McCallum came running up, face pale in the fiery glow; I told her to take the Bugs to Brianna's cabin—hers now—and for God's sake, keep the little boys safe away. She nodded and went, she and Mrs. Bug supporting Arch's tall form between them.

No one made any effort to bring out the bodies of Donner and his companions.

I could see when the fire took hold in the stairwell; there was a sudden strong glow in the upstairs windows, and shortly thereafter, I could see flames in the heart of the house.

Snow began to fall, in thick, heavy, silent flakes. Within half an hour, the ground, trees, and bushes were dusted with white. The flames glowed red and gold, and the white snow reflected a soft reddish glow; the whole clearing seemed filled with the light of the fire.

Somewhere around midnight, the roof fell in, with a crash of

glowing timbers and a tremendous shower of sparks that foun-
tained high into the night. The sight was so beautiful that everyone watching went "Oooooh!" in involuntary awe.

Jamie's arm tightened round me. We could not look away.

"What's the date today?" I asked suddenly.

He frowned for a moment, thinking, then said, "December
twenty-first."

"And we aren't dead, either. Bloody newspapers," I said.
"They never get *anything* right."

For some reason, he thought *that* was very funny indeed, and
laughed until he had to sit down on the ground.

124

Property of the King

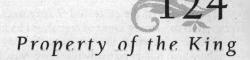

We spent the remainder of the night sleeping—or at
least horizontal—on the floor of the cabin, with the
Bugs, Goose and his brother, Light—who confused
me initially by referring to themselves as Jamie's "sons"—
Scotchee, and Ian. On their way to visit Bird's village, the
Indians—for Alexander Cameron was as much an Indian as the
others, I thought—had met Jamie and Ian, hunting, and accepted
Jamie's hospitality.

"Though it was a warmer welcome than we expected, Bear-
Killer!" Goose said, laughing.

They did not ask who Donner was, nor make any reference to
the men whose bodies burned in the funeral pyre of the house—
only asked awed questions about the ether, and shook their heads
in amazement, watching the fire.

For Jamie's part, I noticed that he did not ask why they were going to Bird's village—and concluded that he did not want to hear that some of the Cherokee had decided to support the King. He listened to the talk, but said little, spending his time fingering through the pile of objects saved from the fire. There was little of value there—a few scorched, loose pages from my casebook, some pewter spoons, a bullet mold. But when he fell asleep at last next to me, I saw that his fist was closed around something, and peering closely in the dark, made out the protruding head of the little cherrywood snake.

I woke just past dawn to find Aidan peering down at me, Adso in his arms.

"I found your wee cheetie in my bed," Aidan whispered. "D'ye want him?"

I was about to refuse, but then saw the look in Adso's eye. He was very tolerant of small children normally, but Aidan was holding him round the middle like a bag of laundry, his back legs dangling ludicrously.

"Yes," I said, my voice hoarse from smoke. "Here—I'll take him."

I sat up, but having accepted the cat, saw that most of the household was still asleep, rolled in blankets on the floor. Two notable exceptions: Jamie and Arch Bug were missing. I got up, and borrowing Amy's cloak from beside the door, went out.

The snow had stopped during the night, but there were two or three inches on the ground. I put Adso down under the eaves, where the ground was clear, and then—with a deep breath to steady myself—turned to look at the house.

Steam rose from the charred remains, which stood inkblot black and stark against the white-furred trees behind it. Only about half the house had burned completely; the west wall was still standing, as were the stone chimney stacks. The rest was a mass of charred timbers and mounded ash, already turning gray. The upper story was completely gone, and as for my surgery . . .

I turned away, hearing voices behind the house. Jamie and Arch were in the woodshed, but the door was open; I could see them inside, face to face. Jamie saw me hovering, and beckoned me in with a nod.

"Good morning, Arch," I said, peering at our erstwhile factor. "How are you?"

"I've been better, *a nighean,* thank ye kindly," he said, and coughed. His voice was little more than a harsh whisper, damaged by smoke, and there were enormous, fluid-filled blisters on both hands and face. Bar the loss of his hair and eyebrows, though, thought he was otherwise all right.

"Arch was just about to explain this to me, Sassenach." Jamie pointed a toe at the gleaming metal of the gold ingot lying in the sawdust and wood chips at his feet. "Were ye not, Arch?"

His voice was outwardly pleasant, but I heard the steel in it as clearly as Arch did. Arch Bug was no pushover, though, eyebrows or no eyebrows.

"I owe ye nay explanations of anything, *Seaumais mac Brian*," he said with equal pleasantness.

"I give ye the chance of explanation, man, not the choice." He'd dropped the pleasant tone. Jamie was smudged with soot, and scorched round the edges, but his eyebrows were intact and being put to good use. He turned to me, gesturing to the gold.

"Ye've seen it before, aye?"

"Of course." The last time I'd seen it, it had been gleaming in the lantern light, packed solid with its fellows in the bottom of a coffin in Hector Cameron's mausoleum, but the shape of the ingots and the fleur-de-lis stamp were unmistakable. "Unless Louis of France has been sending someone else vast quantities of gold, it's part of Jocasta's hoard."

"That it is not, and never was," Arch corrected me firmly.

"Aye?" Jamie cocked a thick brow at him. "To whom does it belong, then, if not to Jocasta Cameron? D'ye claim it as your own?"

"I do not." He hesitated, but the urge to speak was powerful. "It is the property of the King," he said, and his old mouth closed tight on the last word.

"What, the King of—oh," I said, realizing at long last. "*That* king."

"*Le roi, c'est mort*," Jamie said softly, as though to himself, but Arch turned fiercely to him.

"Is Scotland dead?"

Jamie drew breath, but didn't speak at once. Instead, he gestured me to a seat on the stack of chopped cordwood, and nodded at Arch to take another, before sitting down beside me.

"Scotland will die when her last son does, *a charaid*," he said, and waved a hand toward the door, taking in the mountains and ollows around us—and all the people therein. "How many are ere? How many will be? Scotland lives—but not in Italy." In Rome, he meant, where Charles Stuart eked out what remained to im of a life, drowning his disappointed dreams of a crown in drink.

Arch narrowed his eyes at this, but kept a stubborn silence.

"Ye were the third man, were ye not?" Jamie asked, disregarding this. "When the gold was brought ashore from France. Dougal MacKenzie took one-third, and Hector Cameron another. I couldna say what Dougal did with his—gave it to Charles Stuart, most likely, and may God have mercy on his soul for that. You were tacksman to Malcolm Grant; he sent ye, did he not? You took one-third of the gold on his behalf. Did ye give it to him?"

Arch nodded, slowly.

"It was given in trust," he said, and his voice cracked. He cleared his throat and spat, the mucus tinged with black. "To me, and then to the Grant—who should have given it in turn to the King's son."

"Did he?" Jamie asked, interested. "Or did he think, like Hector Cameron, that it was too late?"

It had been; the cause was already lost at that point—no gold could have made a difference. Arch's lips pressed so tightly together as almost to be invisible.

"He did what he did," he said shortly. "What he thought right. That money was spent for the welfare of the clan. But Hector Cameron was a traitor, and his wife with him."

"It was you who spoke to Jocasta in her tent," I said suddenly, realizing. "At the Gathering where you met Jamie. You'd come there to find her, hadn't you?"

Arch seemed surprised that I had spoken, but inclined his head an inch or so in acknowledgment. I wondered whether he had accepted—had sought?—a place with Jamie on account of his relationship with Jocasta.

"And that"—I poked a toe at the shaved ingot—"you found in Jocasta's house, when you went with Roger and Duncan to bring back the fisher-folk." Proof—if he had needed it—that Jocasta did indeed still have Hector's share of the French gold.

"What I am wondering, myself," Jamie said, rubbing a finger down the long, straight bridge of his nose, "is how the devil ye found the rest of it, and then got it away."

Arch's lips pursed for a moment, then reluctantly unsealed themselves.

"'Twas no great feat. I saw the salt at Hector's tomb—the way the black slaves kept awa'. If he didna rest easy, it was nay wonder—but where would the gold better be, save wi' him?" A wintry light shone in his faded eyes. "I kent Hector Cameron, a bit. He wasna the man to give up anything, only by reason of bein dead."

Arch made frequent trips to Cross Creek as factor, to buy and trade. He was not usually a guest at River Run, but had been there often enough to be familiar with the property. If anyone saw a figure near the mausoleum at night—well, everyone knew that Hector Cameron's ghost "walked," confined to one spot only by the lines of salt; no one would ever go close enough to investigate.

And so he had simply abstracted one ingot on each trip—and not on every trip—eventually removing the whole hoard, before Duncan Innes discovered the loss.

"I shouldna have kept out that first ingot, I see that," he said, ruefully nodding at it. "At the first, though, I thought we might have need of it—Murdina and I. And then, when she was obliged to kill yon Brown—"

Jamie's head jerked up, and we both stared at him. He coughed.

"The wicked creature grew well enough to poke about the cabin when she was oot; he found that"—he nodded again at the ingot—"in her workbag, where she'd hidden it. He couldna ken, of course, what it was—but he kent well enough that ragged folk such as we ought not to have such a thing." His thin mouth pressed tight again, and I remembered that he had been chief tacksman for the Grant of clan Grant—a man of worth. Once.

"He asked about it, and she wouldna tell him anything, of course. But then, when he made his way to your house, she feared he would tell what he'd seen. And so she made an end to him."

It was said calmly; after all, what else could she do? Not for the first time, I wondered just what other things the Bugs had done—or been forced to do—in the years after Culloden.

"Well, ye kept the gold out of King George's hands, at least," Jamie said, a certain note of bleakness in his voice. I thought he was thinking of the battle at Moore's Creek Bridge. If Hugh MacDonald had had that gold, with which to buy powder and arms, the victory there would not have been so easily won. Nor would the Highlanders have been slaughtered—again—charging sword in hand into the mouths of cannon.

"Arch," I said, when the silence threatened to become oppressive, "*what,* exactly, did you plan to do with it?"

He blinked at that, and looked down at the ingot.

"I . . . I meant at first only to see if it was true what I'd heard—that Hector Cameron had taken his part of the gold away with him, used it for his own ends. Then I found Hector dead, but 'twas clear from the way his wife lived that he had indeed taken it. So I wondered—was there any left?"

One hand crept up, massaging his withered throat.

"To tell ye the truth, mistress—I wished mostly to take it back from Jocasta Cameron. Having done that, though . . ." His voice died away, but then he shook himself.

"I am a man of my word, *Seaumais mac Brian.* I swore an oath to my chief—and kept it, 'til he died. I swore my oath to the King across the water"—James Stuart, he meant—"but he is dead, now, too. And then—I swore loyalty to George of England when I came upon this shore. So tell me now where my duty lies?"

"Ye swore an oath to me, too, *Archibald mac Donagh,*" Jamie said.

Arch smiled at that, a wry expression, but a smile nonetheless.

"And by reason of that oath, ye're still alive, *Seaumais mac Brian,*" he said. "I could have killed ye last night in your sleep and been well awa'."

Jamie's mouth twisted in a look that expressed considerable doubt of this statement, but he forbore to contradict.

"You are free of your oath to me," he said formally in Gaelic. "Take your life from my hand." And inclining his head toward the ingot, said, "Take that—and go."

Arch regarded him for a moment, unblinking. Then stooped, picked up the ingot, and went.

"You didn't ask him where the gold is now," I observed, watching the tall old man make his way round the cabin to rouse his wife.

"Ye think he would ha' told me?" He stood up then, and stretched himself. Then he shook himself like a dog, and went to stand in the doorway of the shed, arms braced in the door frame, looking out. It was beginning to snow again.

"I see it's not only the Frasers who are stubborn as rocks," I said, coming to stand beside him. "Scotland lives, all right." That made him laugh.

He put one arm around me, and I rested my head on his shoulder.

"Your hair smells of smoke, Sassenach," he said softly.

"Everything smells of smoke," I replied just as softly.

The burned ruins of the house were still too warm for snow to stick, but that would pass. If it went on snowing, by tomorrow the house would be obliterated, white as the rocks and trees. We, too—eventually.

I thought of Jocasta and Duncan, gone to the safety of Canada, the welcome of kinfolk. Where would the Bugs go—back to Scotland? For an instant, I longed to go, too. Away from loss and desolation. Home.

But then I remembered.

"So long as one hundred of us remain alive . . . ," I quoted.

Jamie tilted his head against mine for a moment, then raised it and turned to look down at me.

"And when ye go to a sick man's bed, Sassenach—to a wounding or a birth—how is it, then, that ye can rise from your own bed, even from mortal weariness, and go in the dark, alone? Why is it that ye willna wait, that ye dinna say no, ever? Why is it that ye willna forbear, even when ye know the case to be hopeless?"

"I can't." I kept my gaze on the ruin of the house, its ashes growing cold before my eyes. I knew what he meant, the unwelcome truth he would force me to speak—but the truth lay between us, and must be told. "I cannot . . . can *not* . . . admit . . . that there is anything to do but win."

He cupped my chin and tilted my face upward, so that I was obliged to meet his eyes. His own face was worn with tiredness, the lines cut deep by eyes and mouth, but the eyes themselves were clear, cool, and fathomless as the waters of a hidden spring.

"Nor can I," he said.

"I know."

"Ye can at least promise me the victory," he said, but his voice held the whisper of a question.

"Yes," I said, and touched his face. I sounded choked, and my vision blurred. "Yes, I can promise that. This time." No mention made of what that promise spared, of the things I could not guaruntee. Not life, not safety. Not home, nor family; not law nor legacy. Just the one thing—or maybe two.

"The victory," I said. "And that I will be with you 'til the end."

He closed his eyes for a moment. Snowflakes pelted down, melting as they struck his face, sticking for an instant, white on his lashes. Then he opened his eyes and looked at me.

"That is enough," he said softly. "I ask no more."

He reached forward then and took me in his arms, held me close for a moment, the breath of snow and ashes cold around us. Then he kissed me, released me, and I took a deep breath of cold air, harsh with the scent of burning. I brushed a floating smut off my arm.

"Well . . . good. *Bloody* good. Er . . ." I hesitated. "What do you suggest we do next?"

He stood looking at the charred ruin, eyes narrowed, then lifted his shoulders and let them fall.

"I think," he said slowly, "we shall go—" He stopped suddenly, frowning. "What in God's name . . . ?"

Something was moving at the side of the house. I blinked away the snowflakes, standing on tiptoe to see better.

"Oh, it *can't* be!" I said—but it was. With a tremendous upheaval of snow, dirt, and charred wood, the white sow thrust her way into daylight. Fully emerged, she shook her massive shoulders, then, pink snout twitching irritably, moved purposefully off toward the wood. A moment later, a smaller version likewise emerged—and another, and another . . . and eight half-grown piglets, some white, some spotted, and one as black as the timbers of the house, trotted off in a line, following their mother.

"Scotland lives," I said again, giggling uncontrollably. "Er— where did you say we were going?"

"To Scotland," he said as though this were obvious. "To fetch my printing press."

He was still looking at the house, but his eyes were fixed somewhere beyond the ashes, far beyond the present moment. An owl hooted deep in the distant wood, startled from its sleep. He stood silent for a bit, then shook off his reverie, and smiled at me, snow melting in his hair.

"And then," he said simply, "we shall come back to fight."

He took my hand and turned away from the house, toward the barn where the horses stood waiting, patient in the cold.

Epilogue I
Lallybroch

The penlight's beam moved slowly across the heavy oak rafter, paused at a suspicious hole, then passed on. The heavyset man wore a frown of scrupulous concentration, lips pursed like one momentarily expecting some unpleasant surprise.

Brianna stood beside him, looking up at the shadowed recesses of the ceiling in the entry hall, wearing a similar frown of concentration. She would not recognize woodworm or termites unless a rafter actually fell on her, she thought, but it seemed polite to behave as though she were paying attention.

In fact, only half her attention was focused on the heavyset gentleman's murmured remarks to his helot, a small young woman in an overall too big for her, with pink streaks in her hair. The other half was focused on the noises from upstairs, where the children were theoretically playing hide 'n seek among the jumble of packing boxes. Fiona had brought over her brood of three small fiends, and then craftily abandoned them, running off to do an errand of some sort, promising to return by teatime.

Brianna glanced at her wristwatch, still surprised at seeing it there. Half an hour yet to go. If they could avoid bloodshed until—

A piercing scream from upstairs made her grimace. The helot, less hardened, dropped her clipboard with a yelp.

"MAMA!" Jem, in tattling mode.

"WHAT?" she roared in answer. "I'm BUSY!"

"But Mama! Mandy *hit* me!" came an indignant report from the top of the stairs. Looking up, she could see the top of his head, the light from the window glowing on his hair.

"She did? Well—"

"With a *stick*!"

"What sort of—"

"On *purpose*!"

"Well, I don't think—"

"AND . . ."—a pause before the damning denouement—"SHE DIDN'T SAY SHE WAS SORRY!"

The builder and his helot had given up looking for woodworm in favor of following this gripping narrative, and now both of them looked at Brianna, doubtless in expectation of some Solomonic decree.

Brianna closed her eyes momentarily.

"MANDY," she bellowed. "Say you're sorry!"

"Non't!" came a high-pitched refusal from above.

"Aye, ye will!" came Jem's voice, followed by scuffling. Brianna headed for the stair, blood in her eye. Just as she set her foot on the tread, Jem uttered a piercing squeal.

"She BIT me!"

"Jeremiah MacKenzie, don't you *dare* bite her back!" she shouted. "Both of you stop it this instant!"

Jem thrust a disheveled head through the banister, hair sticking up on end. He was wearing bright blue eye shadow, and someone had applied pink lipstick in a crude mouth-shape from one ear to the other.

"She's a feisty wee baggage," he ferociously informed the fascinated spectators below. "My grandda said so."

Brianna wasn't sure whether to laugh, cry, or utter a loud shriek, but with a hasty wave at the builder and his assistant, she ran up the stairs to sort them out.

The sorting took rather more time than expected, since she discovered in the process that Fiona's three little girls, so notably quiet during the latest squabble, had been quiet because—having decorated Jem, Mandy, and themselves—they were busily engaged in painting faces on the bathroom walls with Brianna's new makeup.

Coming back down a quarter of an hour later, she discovered the builder sitting peaceably on an upturned coal scuttle, having his tea break, while the helot wandered open-mouthed about the entry hall, a half-eaten scone in one hand.

"All those kids yours?" she asked Brianna, with a sympathetic quirk of one pierced brow.

"No, thank God. Does everything look all right down here?"

"Touch o' damp," the builder said cheerfully. "Only to be expected, though, old place like this. When's it built, then, hen, d'ye know?"

"1721, thickie," the helot said, with comfortable scorn. "Did ye not see it carved in the lintel, there, where we came in?"

"Nah, then, is it?" The builder looked interested, but not enough to get up and look for himself. "Cost a fortune to put back in shape, won't it?" He nodded at the wall, where one of the oak panels showed the damage of boots and sabers, crisscrossed with slashes whose rawness had darkened with the years, but still showed clear.

"No, we won't fix that," Brianna said, a lump in her throat. "That was done right after the '45. It'll stay that way." *We keep it so,* her uncle had told her, *to remember always what the English are.*

"Oh, historic-like. Right you are, then," the builder said, nodding wisely. "Americans don't often mind about the history so much, do they? Wanting all mod cons, electric cookers, effing automatic thisses and thats. Central heating!"

"I'll settle for toilets that flush," she assured him. "That, and hot water. Speaking of which, will you have a look at the boiler? It's in a shed in the yard, and it's fifty years old if it's a day. And we'll want to replace the geyser in the upstairs bath, too."

"Oh, aye." The builder brushed crumbs from his shirt, corked his Thermos flask, and rose ponderously to his feet. "Come on, Angie, let's have a look, then."

Brianna hovered suspiciously at the foot of the stair, listening for any sounds of riot before following, but all was well above; she could hear the crash of building blocks, evidently being thrown at the walls, but no yells of outrage. She turned to follow, just in time to see the builder, who had paused to look up at the lintel.

"The '45, eh? Ever think what it'd be like?" he was saying. "If Bonnie Prince Charlie had won, I mean."

"Oh, in your dreams, Stan! He'd never a chance, bloody Eyetalian ponce."

"Naw, naw, he'd have done it, sure, was it no for the effing

Campbells. Traitors, aye? To a man. And a woman, too, I expect," he added, laughing—from which Brianna gathered that the helot's last name was very likely Campbell.

They passed on toward the shed, their argument growing more heated, but she stopped, not wanting to go after them until she had herself under control.

Oh, God, she prayed passionately, *oh, God—that they might be safe! Please, please, let them be safe.* It didn't matter how ridiculous it might be to pray for the safety of people who had been—who had to be—dead for more than two hundred years. It was the only thing she could do, and did it several times each day, whenever she thought of them. Much more often, now that they had come to Lallybroch.

She blinked back tears, and saw Roger's Mini Cooper come down the winding drive. The backseat was piled high with boxes; he was finally clearing out the last bits of rubbish from the Reverend's garage, salvaging those items that might have value to someone—a dismayingly high proportion of the contents.

"Just in time," she said, a little shaky, as he came up the walk smiling, a large box under his arm. She still found him startling with short hair. "Ten minutes more, and I'd kill somebody, for sure. Probably Fiona, for starters."

"Oh, aye?" He bent and kissed her with particular enthusiasm, indicating that he probably hadn't heard what she'd said. "I've got something."

"So I see. What—"

"Damned if I know."

The box he laid on the ancient dining table was wood, as well; a sizable casket made of maple, darkened by years, soot, and handling, but with the workmanship still apparent to her practiced eye. It was beautifully made, the joints perfectly dovetailed, with a sliding top—but the top didn't slide, having been at some point sealed with a thick bead of what looked like melted beeswax, gone black with age.

The most striking thing about it, though, was the top. Burned into the wood was a name: *Jeremiah Alexander Ian Fraser MacKenzie.*

She felt a clenching in her lower belly at the sight of it, and glanced up at Roger, who was tense with some suppressed feeling; she could feel it vibrating through him.

"What?" she whispered. "Who *is* that?"

Roger shook his head, and pulled a filthy envelope from his pocket.

"This was with it, taped to the side. It's the Reverend's handwriting, one of the little notes he'd sometimes put with something to explain its significance, just in case. But I can't say this is an explanation, exactly."

The note was brief, stating merely that the box had come from a defunct banking house in Edinburgh. Instructions had been stored with the box, stating that it was not to be opened, save by the person whose name was inscribed thereon. The original instructions had perished, but were passed on verbally by the person from whom he obtained the box.

"And who was *that*?" she asked.

"No idea. Do you have a knife?"

"Do I have a knife," she muttered, digging in the pocket of her jeans. "Do I ever *not* have a knife?"

"That was a rhetorical question," he said, kissing her hand and taking the bright red Swiss Army knife she offered him.

The beeswax cracked and split away easily; the lid of the box, though, was unwilling to yield after so many years. It took both of them—one clutching the box, the other pushing and pulling on the lid—but finally, it came free with a small squealing noise.

The ghost of a scent floated out; something indistinguishable, but plantlike in origin.

"Mama," she said involuntarily. Roger glanced at her, startled, but she gestured at him urgently to go on. He reached carefully into the box and removed its contents: a stack of letters, folded and sealed with wax, two books—and a small snake made of cherrywood, heavily polished by long handling.

She made a small, inarticulate sound and seized the top letter, pressing it so hard against her chest that the paper crackled and the wax seal split and fell away. The thick, soft paper, whose fibers showed the faint stains of what had once been flowers.

Tears were falling down her face, and Roger was saying something, but she didn't attend the words, and the children were making an uproar upstairs, the builders were still arguing outside, and the only thing in the world she could see were the faded words on the page, written in a sprawling, difficult hand.

December 31, 1776

My dear daughter,

    As you will see if ever you receive this, we are alive....

Epilogue II
The Devil Is in the Details

"What's this, then?" Amos Crupp squinted at the page laid out in the bed of the press, reading it backward with the ease of long experience.

"*It is with grief that the news is received of the deaths by fire* . . . Where'd that come from?"

"Note from a subscriber," said Sampson, his new printer's devil, shrugging as he inked the plate. "Good for a bit of filler, there, I thought; General Washington's address to the troops run short of the page."

"Hmph. I s'pose. Very old news, though," Crupp said, glancing at the date. "January?"

"Well, no," the devil admitted, heaving down on the lever that lowered the page onto the plate of inked type. The press sprang up again, the letters wet and black on the paper, and he picked the sheet off with nimble fingertips, hanging it up to dry. "'Twas December, by the notice. But I'd set the page in Baskerville twelve-point, and the slugs for November and December are missing in that font. Not room to do it in separate letters, and not worth the labor to reset the whole page."

"To be sure," said Amos, losing interest in the matter, as he perused the last paragraphs of Washington's speech. "Scarcely signifies, anyway. After all, they're all dead, aren't they?"

Read on for an exclusive and revealing interview with
the author of *A Breath of Snow and Ashes*,
Diana Gabaldon

In June 2006, we asked Diana Gabaldon if she would answer some questions regarding her researching and writing processes as well as her thoughts on Jamie and Claire Fraser. Her responses were both generous and illuminating. Here's a transcript of the interview for your enjoyment.

Part of what brings the Jamie & Claire series to such stunning life is the meticulously well-researched historical and cultural background. What is your fascination with the time period and the setting of the novels, and how do you do your research for each one?

Well, I hadn't got one—a fascination for the time period, I mean. I just wanted to write a novel (for the purposes of learning exactly how that was done), chose historical fiction as being the easiest thing for a scientist who was used to looking things up at the library, and chose the '45 as a good background on the basis of having seen a Really Ancient re-run of *Dr. Who* on public television—an episode featuring a nice young man in a kilt, from 1745.

"Well, that's fetching," I said to myself.

"You want to write a book, it doesn't really matter where you set it, so long as you pick a point and start," I further said to myself. "Fine. Scotland, eighteenth century." And there we were.

That said, once I began looking into it, it was apparent that the eighteenth century was a Highly Interesting period. It's a time—particularly the last half, which is when my books are set—during which there was enormous intellectual *and* political ferment, with consequent upheavals (wars are always good grist for a storyteller; just ask Homer), social change (fall of monarchy, rise of democracy, the beginning of the abolition of slavery—an unfortunately long-lived institution that hasn't yet been eradicated, but progress is progress—the paradoxical emergence of populism *and* an emphasis on the worth of the common individual, cool stuff like that), along with a spirit of inquiry, exploration, and discovery that ushered in the beginning of the scientific age and remapped the globe (incidentally exterminating a few native populations here and there, but nothing happens without cost, now, does it?), etc., etc., all of these processes forming the arch of an amazing historical bridge that spans the cultural distance between the Middle Ages and the modern world.

On a more prosaic level, the nice thing about the eighteenth century is that English was written in a thoroughly recognizable modern form, so that I wasn't obliged to learn Ancient French (the modern sort is quite awkward enough), Hebrew, or Greek in order to do research. By the same token, it's sufficiently near to hand, historically speaking, that a tremendous amount of primary source material is still readily available—while at the same time, the clothes and customs were sufficiently different as to allow me to exploit the notion that the past really *is* another country.

How do I do research? Well, bear in mind that I *was* a scientist (I have assorted degrees in various areas of the biological sciences, including a Ph.D. in <deep breath> Quantitative Behavioral Ecology (don't trouble about it; it's just Animal Behavior with a lot of statistics)). Which naturally means that I have a thoroughly organized, highly-thought-out, planned-to-the-last-inch research strategy involving wall-charts, hundreds of index cards, and massive binders of information . . . not.

Which means I understand the labyrinthine processes both of human knowledge and my own mind well enough to know that the most effective way of doing research (for me) is to find a loose end and pull. Then I follow the unraveling string, keeping a cautious eye out for lurking Minotaurs.

In terms of these books, the loose end I pulled belonged to a young man in a kilt.

Hence—Scotland, eighteenth century.

The series is wonderfully complex, with plots and sub-plots and an amazing array of characters. How do you plot out such a many-layered construct from beginning to end? Do you plan ahead for the series as a whole or take every book and continue at that point? And how do you then manage to keep everything and everyone straight from beginning to end?

Um . . . I don't. I don't plot them out from beginning to end, and I don't plan either separate books or the series.

I suppose I *do* (more or less) keep everyone and everything straight—we'll hope as much, anyway—but I don't do that "from beginning to end," either.

I don't use outlines and I don't work in a *straight* line. I write in disconnected bits and pieces—where I can "see" things happening—and as the process goes on and I do more research—I begin to see the linkages between the bits, and they start to coalesce into larger bits, which in turn eventually form still-larger "chunks." By the time I've achieved chunk-hood, I generally have a relatively good notion both of the historical timeline to be dealt with in this particular book, and of the focus-points on that line.

(By "focus-points," I mean those historical events that I want to use in the story, and the level of depth in which I mean to use them. Some events, for example, I'll want to "live through," with a chief character observing and being directly involved. Other events may be used peripherally—either incorporated as mechanisms of the plot, or merely "told" as having occurred prior, or having been lived through by a minor character who will conveniently summarize the occurrence for us—though always with the intent of providing a three-dimensional impression of the times.)

The chunks of text can then be stood up (mentally) against this timeline, rather like a police lineup. This gives me a rough chronology of the book (i.e., I'll know—at last—how much time is covered, and which spans of time are dealt with in detail), and with luck, this is also where I see the Shape of the book.

All of my books have a distinct underlying Shape. Once I've seen the Shape for a particular book, the writing becomes much faster and easier, because I'll know which bits are missing, and precisely *where* a new bit is going to fit. (The Shape for *Cross Stitch*, for example, is three overlapping triangles, the apices corresponding to the major dramatic climaxes in the story. The first occurs when Jamie takes Claire back to the stones to make her choice, the second, when Claire rescues Jamie from Wentworth Prison, and the third, when she ransoms his soul at the Abbey. The Shape for *A Breath of Snow and Ashes* . . . well, you know that well-known Japanese print, "The Great Wave Off Kanagawa"? It looks like that—only there are two of them.)

Anyway, I don't really keep notes, as such; I keep things "straight," because I literally do see and experience what I'm writing—I can't forget who Monsieur Forez is, anymore than I'd forget who my husband's second cousin Bill is.

It's a very organic process, though; something like growing rock crystals in your basement. Or mushrooms.

The clash between Claire's reality and the historical era she travels to is very subtly portrayed in the novel and it does make a plausible case for the co-existence of different olds in time that overlap at critical points around the world. What was your experience working with that concept? And do you believe in it yourself?

What was my experience working with that concept? Ah . . . six (so far) fairly massive novels, and a non-fiction companion volume. What else?

(Well, I *was* also asked to write up "The Gabaldon Theory of Time Travel" for the *Journal of Transfigural Mathematics* (Berlin)—and did. They published it seven or eight years ago, but I'm afraid I don't have the Volume and issue number easily to hand.)

As for belief . . . certainly I believe in the theoretical possibility of time travel—so do a number of other fairly respectable scientists. Likewise, I believe absolutely that Claire did it; you can't expect readers to believe something that the author patently *doesn't*.

Your books are so well researched – how long did it take you to research A Breath of Snow and Ashes *– and how long did it take you to write? Do you prefer researching or writing?*

If you'll pardon my saying so, most of your questions seem based on the grossly mistaken assumption that all novelists work in the same way—and that you know what that way is: i.e., plan things out in tedious detail, then, outline in hand, start in on the research, taking billions of notes, after which, you sit down and type the thing out from Chapter One to The End.

I daresay a good many writers do work like that, and more power to them if they do. It's very tidy-minded and appealing. Personally, I couldn't work like that if my life depended on it.

Anyway, to address the actual question: It takes me two to three years to finish one of these enormous books (by contrast, the shorter *Lord John* novels seem to take about six months—but then, I was under the delusion that *Private Matter* was a short story, when I wrote it), and I do the research and the writing concurrently. Both processes feed off each other in a nice circular fashion; some entertaining tidbit (such as the information that eighteenth-century French executioners were given the bodies of executed criminals as a perquisite of the job, and made a tidy profit from selling the bits, including "hanged-man's grease"—a highly desirable and expensive ointment produced from the rendered body fat of criminals; excellent for arthritis, I'm told)—discovered (usually by accident) in the research gives rise to a scene or subplot—which in turn require more details, which leads back into the (constantly ongoing) research, which provides not only the requisite detail for the problem at hand, but tons more that will instigate further scenes, characters, and ideas.

People do ask whether I have cadres of research assistants—to which the answer is no. I couldn't possibly tell an assistant what to look for, since I'm not generally sure of what I'm looking for until I've found it—and what I find along the way may turn out to be much more important than what I thought I wanted to begin with.

I call it "Hot Dogs and Beans." (Do you have hot-dogs? Bangers and mash would work as well, as a metaphor, if not.) Say that you—as chief cook of the household—have decided to make a simple supper of hot-dogs and tinned beans. So you set off for the supermarket with that in mind. But on the way back to the smoked-meats section, you see that the store is having a special sale of fresh organic chicken breasts. Oh, well, now . . . chicken curry suddenly sounds immensely more appealing than hot-dogs. So you

ick out the chicken, then go to get the mango-papaya-
pplesauce blend, spices, and V-8 juice for the sauce, the
mango chutney . . . and opposite the chutney is an appetiz-
1g array of fresh green produce, at the end of which is the
ish counter, supplied with dazzling mounds of fresh tiny
hrimp . . . well, now, a chilled shrimp salad for starter, a
ice curry with chutney—and something robust, like
strong Riesling, to wash it down. Something simple for
essert, perhaps a pineapple sorbet . . .

So, I do my own research, and end up with an excel-
ent—if unplanned—supper. You use research assistants,
ou get hot-dogs and beans.

lthough your series has a strong romance element, it's
ery much rooted in historical fact. What do you think of
he view that historical fiction is more 'truthful' than con-
entional history, in that it brings past events more vividly
o life?

\h . . . why, exactly, would "a strong romance element"
by which I assume you mean merely that the relationships
among characters are an important part of the story) imply
nything whatever regarding the historical accuracy of the
ooks?

As for the truth of history . . . well, let's put it this way; I
was a scientist. I know the difference between objective
fields of study, in which (putting aside purely philosophical
arguments as to the nature of reality) there is a consensus
regarding standards of measurement and those phenomena
hat can *be* measured—and those fields that are almost
purely subjective. History, of course, is one of the latter.

With the exception of "facts" (which upon closer examination often tend to be no such thing)—the dates of battles,
the names of monarchs, the provisions of treaties—and

the mute testimony of artifacts (concrete, but sometime baffling), history is no more (and no less) than a recorde collection of perceptions and attitudes. Which is precise what a novel is, if better structured for dramatic impact.

Look. All art rests on the same principle as doe science: the existence of patterns in chaos. Both goo science and good art depend upon the practitioner's abilit to see those patterns and explicate them. It's just that you're doing science, the chaos you're working with limited to that of the natural world. If you're an artist, yo may use *both* natural chaos, and that generated by you own humanity, experience, and imagination.

History falls somewhere in the no-man's-land betwee The chaos is *theoretically* limited to a body of actual phys ical occurrence, but in actuality, a historian's job is als to draw out the patterns of causality and predication—i essence, to perceive a pattern within an arbitrarily selected portion of a continuous process. This means, i most cases, the introduction of the historian's ow perspective, biases, and skill at interpretation. Which again, is precisely what a novelist is doing, albeit with th extra freedom engendered by imagination. We have wide limits to our chaos, is about it—and we needn't do foot notes unless we like.

Historical fiction isn't more "truthful" than histor because it shows events vividly. That's a matter of craft; can animate Thomas Paine as effectively as Jamie Frase (in fact, I did just that, when writing an Introduction to recent new edition of COMMON SENSE). It's mor "truthful" only because it says "Fiction" on the spine.

As a Sassenach from the Twentieth Century, Claire is in unique position to comment on and describe Scotland ir the eighteenth century, and later, the beginnings of America

*ould you like to comment on why you decided to use the
ne travel aspect in this way?*

'ell, it seemed an obvious advantage, once she'd made it
:ear that she *was* a time-traveler (it wasn't my idea, I assure
ou; this was a perfectly straightforward historical novel,
'a James Clavell/James Michener—until about the third
ay, which was the point when I introduced an
nglishwoman into the plot, and she refused to shut up and
.lk like an eighteenth-century person. Just kept making
mart-ass modern remarks about everything she saw—and
ook over and started telling the story herself. To which I
eplied, "Well, I'm not going to fight with *you* all the way
hrough this book. No one's ever going to see this; it doesn't
natter *what* bizarre thing I do—go ahead and be modern;
ll figure out how you got there later."). That juxtaposition
f cultural frames of reference gives me (as the author)
onderful opportunities for both historical perspective and
ontemporary social commentary—as well as allowing
laire considerable scope for her rather acerbic opinions.

*amie has tremendous sex appeal and his relationship with
'laire is both passionate and tender. Were you at all sur-
rised by your fans' reaction to these characters and their
elationship?*

Jo. Not-yet-published writers are always worriedly asking,
How do I know whether what I've written is any good?" To
vhich I reply, "Well, you do *read*, I hope. How do you know
ny book you read is good?" If you have any sense of
terary judgement at all, it's certainly possible to apply it to
our own work; the trick is just to let the manuscript "cool"
bit, so that you're able to separate the text from the emo-
onal experience of writing it.

My mother taught me to read at the age of three and I'v
been doing it ever since. So I had a fairly reasonable noti
that these were engaging characters.

Also, as the result of an argument with a (male) frier
in the literary group I was hanging round with online (n
a writers' group; just people who liked to talk abo
books) during the time I wrote *Cross Stitch*, I ended u
posting a brief scene from the book (my friend asserte
that he knew what being pregnant was like, as "my wife
had three children!" I assured him he didn't—I've ha
three children). Everyone who'd been following the argu
ment rushed off to read the piece—and came rushin
back enthusiastically, asking what sort of story this was
(Answer being, "I don't know.") and, where was th
beginning ("Haven't written that yet."), and culminatin
with, "Well, put up some more of it! These people ar
fascinating!"

It was of course great to have such positive feedbac
from the very beginning, and I'm forever grateful to all th
kind people who made such encouraging and helpf
comments to me whenever I posted a small bit of th
book—it was very reassuring to a novice novelist. So
wasn't all that surprised that other readers also liked th
story and characters—very pleased, though!

*You are obviously extremely well read and Jamie an
Claire have the sort of "great love" that equals some othe
classic literary relationships. What is it that makes thei
relationship ring true for so many people? Do they hav
any literary antecedents? Who are the great romanti
couples in literature for you?*

No, I don't think they have any literary antecedents—nc
ones that I'm consciously aware of, at least. The thin

bout "great romantic couples in literature" is that virtually
all of them are a) very young, and b) their story is limited
o the courtship phase of the relationship.

Courtship stories of course have great universal appeal;
hat's why "romance" (in the twentieth—twenty-first-
century meaning of the term, as opposed to the original
eighteenth—nineteenth century version—in which a
"romance" merely meant exciting fiction, but with no
equirement that a love story be involved; *Robinson
Crusoe* was referred to as a "Romance" at the time of its
publication, for instance, as was *Treasure Island*, a century
ater. Neither one even has major female characters!) is so
enduringly popular. But whether it's Romeo and Juliet,
Tristan und Isolde, Dante and Beatrice, or that annoying
adulterous couple in *The Bridges Of Madison County* (at
east they were middle-aged) . . . the story is limited to
heir courtship. In a standard romance, the story is simply
over, once the couple come together, whether the aftermath
s "happily ever after" or tragic parting (interestingly
enough, men tend to write romances with the tragic endings
where one or both parties end up dead, whereas female
authors almost always do the happy endings).

I do enjoy well-written romances (in either sense of the
term) myself, but wasn't really interested in writing the
usual twentieth-century variety, either happy or tragic.
There was a most interesting relationship evolving among
Claire Randall, Frank Randall, and Jamie Fraser (to say the
least), but it didn't seem to be *quite* the usual sort of love
story . . . and as I realized that their story did continue past
the "coming-together" point, it occurred to me that it
would be an interesting literary challenge to write not a
courtship story—but the story of an entire marriage.
Anyone can figure out what makes two people attractive to
each other; a bit more interesting (and a good deal rarer) to

figure out how two people maintain a good marriage ove
the course of a lifetime (even a more than usually adven
turous lifetime).

To the best of my knowledge, no one's ever done that—
save perhaps Dorothy L. Sayers, to a very limited degre
(i.e., she did have one novel post-marriage, in which th
characters' relationship continued to evolve). There ar
continuing series—mostly mystery—featuring marrie
couples, of course, but the relationship between character
doesn't usually change much, and plays relatively little rol
in the story.

The relationship among Claire, Jamie, and Fran
(because the triangle does continue to have influence
throughout) isn't the only major element of these books, o
course; we're essentially looking at the whole of the secon
half of the eighteenth century—politics, wars, morals
explorations, philosophy, art, science, man-vs.-nature, th
nature of kinship bonds and the formation of community
the Scottish diaspora, etc., etc. But a good novel (by my
standards) always rests on the quality of the characters, and
on their passion (by which I do *not* mean heavy breathing
and the exchange of bodily fluids, but rather a depth o
honest feeling, and the capacity for both commitment and
suffering—not necessarily in the context of a relationship
either).

As to why they ring true . . . they're real people. As one
enthusiastic reader noted, "What I especially like is that
people go to the bathroom in your books!" I assume she
didn't mean this quite *literally* . . . but the point is that
while Jamie's and Claire's relationship may be on occasion
molten lava and the like, they remain thoroughly human,
and both they and their relationship are painted with attention to the mundane—if picturesque—details of daily life
(as when Jamie explains to Claire that he's been instructing

his very young nephew in, "The fine art of not pissing on your feet." Or remarks in the aftermath of a night of alcoholic passion that he smells like a dead boar).

Jamie is a wonderful character - part dashing romantic hero, part complex, three-dimensional ever-evolving personality. Is he based on a historical figure? And if so, how did you stumble upon him?

No, he isn't based on a historical character. And while my husband does have red hair and *is* six-foot-four, Jamie Fraser isn't based on him, either (it's just that I like tall redheads with a clever sense of humor). He's his own man; always has been.

How similar would you say you were to Claire? Are your personalities similar? Given the chance, would you ever leave your twenty-first century life behind and travel back in time? Is this, in a sense, what you're doing with your writing?

<mild snort> People ask that one all the time—to the point where I reply, "15.8%" to the "how similar are you . . . ?" question. I suppose they assume that since the first book is written in first person, as are substantial chunks of the rest, there must be a strong autobiographical component— whereas in fact, it's merely that I found first person narration the easiest viewpoint to handle, and saw no reason to make things difficult for myself at that point.

As to similarities in personality, etc . . . let me put it this way. There's a local readers' group who take me out to a lovely formal tea every spring, both to visit, and in hopes of picking my brain as to what I'm writing at present. On one of these occasions, the members got started on Black

Jack Randall. "Oh, I just *loathe* that man!" one woman said. "I despise him—he's such scum!" Similar opinions were heartily expressed by all and sundry round the table. Whilst I sat quietly sipping my Earl Grey and thinking. "You have no idea at all that you're *talking* to Black Jack Randall, do you?"

Would I travel back in time, given the chance? Not unless I were assured of a safe return. Which, fortunately, is usually the case when I write.

A few years ago, Salon.com mentioned that you reversed the gender roles with this series, particularly in Cross Stitch*, where Claire takes the role of the older, more experienced mysterious stranger, while Jamie becomes more of a romantic "heroine" - although, as the writer of the article points out, he's certainly no wimp. What are your thoughts on this idea?*

Well, as I say, I wasn't setting out to write a romance, but I do read them. And when I was in the early stages of work on *Cross Stitch*, I happened—purely by accident—to read three such novels in a row, in every single one of which a young virgin was raped by some beastly villain, but nonetheless managed to end up married to a much older/wiser hero (this was some eighteen years ago; rape was still a *sine qua non* of romance novels, which it isn't any longer, thank goodness). "Oh, come *on*," I recall saying. "Enough with the virginal eighteen-year-olds. And why does *she* have to get raped all the time. Let George do it, why not."

I didn't intend anyone to *see* the book, let alone try to have it published, so I really wasn't concerned with how anyone might respond to anything in it. I had no one to please save myself; I could put in anything I liked. And as ou so kindly note above, I do read a lot—I like lots of different things. So I did any number of things in *Cross Stitch*, purely as a matter of whim. Jamie's being the younger virgin was just one of those things.

(I might note that the nice Salon.com reviewer (a gentleman named McNett) also observed that while Jamie had certain "eighteenth-century issues" with having his butt saved by the heroine now and then, he was on the whole inclined to appreciate the courtesy.)

Outlander - which is the American title for Cross Stitch - *refers very obviously to Claire. She is the "outsider" or "foreigner". But it strikes me that Jamie also has qualities of the outsider within him - what do you think?*

I imagine any good protagonist has that. Conflict is the essential element of a good story; thus the central character is always going to be in conflict with *something*— preferably with lots of things. That being so, many (if not all) "heroes" (in the classic, Joseph Campbell sense of the term) are indeed outsiders in one way or another. Social isolation not only creates conflict, but focuses attention on the hero and allows the author to point up his qualities— whether good or bad.

In this particular instance, Jamie's conflicts with the English army, Black Jack Randall, and various branches of his family not only isolate him and emphasize his heroic qualities (as Claire notes approvingly in a later book, "You're apparently very hard to kill. I find that comforting."), but also makes his relationship with Claire that much more central and interesting, as she is virtually the sole person upon whom he can utterly depend—as he is, for her.

What's in store in the future for Jamie and Claire? And what's next for you as a writer?

What's in store for Jamie and Claire? If I knew, I wouldn' tell you.

As for me . . . well, there *is* at least one more book in Jamie and Claire's story; perhaps two. (I have to get all the way through the American Revolution, and as I told my husband, "It took me three books to deal adequately with the Jacobite Rising, and that was a war that lasted six months, with three battles.")

Besides that, I have two further novels about Lord John Grey under contract (I should finish the next of these— *Lord John and the Brotherhood of the Blade*—this fall), and have just completed a collection of short fiction about Lord John. Three novellas—"Lord John and the Hellfire Club," "Lord John and the Succubus," and "Lord John and the Haunted Soldier"—will be published under the overall volume title, *Lord John and the Hand of Devils.* This collected volume will be published in Germany in August (as *Lord John Und Der Hand Des Teufels*)—but since the events in "Haunted Soldier" occur *after* the events in *Brotherhood Of The Blade*, I believe the US/UK/Australia/ New Zealand publishers all would like to publish *Blade* first, with *Devils* to follow.

And then, I do have a contract for two contemporary mysteries (set in Arizona), the first of which—*Red Ant's Head*—is about half-completed. I'm hoping to finish this one by sometime early next year, but no guarantees.

Hope you'll enjoy them all, as they come!

June 2006